GHOST ARCHIPELAGO

FARWANDER

OSPREY
GAMES

FROSTGRAVE
GHOST ARCHIPELAGO

FARWANDER

BEN COUNTER

OSPREY GAMES
Bloomsbury Publishing Plc
PO Box 883, Oxford, OX1 9PL, UK
1385 Broadway, 5th Floor, New York, NY 10018, USA
E-mail: info@ospreygames.co.uk
www.ospreygames.co.uk

OSPREY GAMES is a trademark of Osprey Publishing Ltd
First published in Great Britain in 2018

A catalogue record for this book is available from the British Library.

ISBN:
PB 9781472832726
eBook 9781472832733
ePDF 9781472832740
XML 9781472832757

18 19 20 21 22 10 9 8 7 6 5 4 3 2 1

Originated by PDQ Digital Media Solutions, Bungay, UK
Printed and bound in Great Britain by
CPI (Group) UK Ltd, Croydon CR0 4YY

Osprey Games supports the Woodland Trust, the UK's leading woodland
conservation charity. Between 2014 and 2018 our donations are being
spent on their Centenary Woods project in the UK.

To find out more about our authors and books visit **www.
ospreypublishing.com**. Here you will find extracts, author interviews,
details of forthcoming events and the option to sign up for our newsletter.

CHAPTER 1

'I'm sure,' said Farwander, 'we can come to an agreement.'

By way of reply, Big Marga put the tenderising hammer back onto the table and selected a pair of black iron pincers instead.

'After all,' continued Farwander with what he hoped was a winning smile, 'what is money, at the end of the day?'

'The only thing that matters,' replied Big Marga as she gave the pincers a couple of test snips. 'That's what you nobs are built on, ain't it? Money? Great big piles of money?'

'I'm afraid, dear Miss Marga, that is something of a...'

'Just tek 'is cods off,' said one of Marga's underlings, of whom three were present in the room. Although the place was large – it had once been a splendid mansion on the outskirts of Last Fathom – the trio of leg-breakers, and the substantial bulk of Big Marga herself, seemed to take up all available room. Marga's trade was as a butcher and all four wore leather aprons and white shirts, their sleeves stained brown with old blood. Their knuckles were covered in scars and the whole crew didn't have a discernible neck between them.

'Now that's the first good idea I heard all day,' said Marga, flashing a set of gappy teeth. 'You gives what you owes me, in return for me leavin' your family jewels where they are.'

'Now regrettably, as we have already ascertained, there is no money.' Farwander gave up on the smile. There had, it was true, been some maidens who had fallen for it, but he doubted Big Marga went for his type.

'Don't talk giblets. You're a nob. You got money comin' out of yer stuffing-hole.'

'Don't let the name and the airs fool you, Madame,' replied Farwander. 'The venn Farwanders have not had a pitcher to make water in for three generations.'

'So what 'appened to what I loaned you?' Big Marga leaned in close and brandished the pincers in his face. Marga was a powerful woman and it would be barely any effort at all for her to remove Farwander's nose with them.

'I was robbed,' replied Farwander.

'So was I. By you.'

'Yes, it weaves quite the tapestry of sorrow. The fact remains, Lady Marga, that I am just as much the victim as you are. Should you wish the return of your capital you should enquire at the home of an apothecary named...'

'What we hangin' around 'ere for?' asked another of Marga's meat piles. 'He doesn't 'ave it. Write it off like, and send 'im back out missin' somethin' so's everyone else knows not to cross us.'

'They knows that already!' snapped Big Marga. 'All of Last bloody Fathom knows you don't owe Big Marga nothin' you can't pay! It's idiots like this as never learn!'

Farwander used the conversation between Marga and her minions to get a better appreciation of his surroundings.

The decaying mansion was one the underworld of Last Fathom used as neutral ground to make deals or agree pacts between the various crews. Farwander was currently tied to a chair in the mansion's grand entrance hall. A double staircase ran around both sides of the room to a landing that had since half-collapsed with damp and neglect. Pale spaces on the wood-panelled walls showed where paintings had long since been looted and the only furnishings were a few mouldering heaps of splinters. The main doors had long since departed their frame but the way out that way was blocked by the three butchers. The back way went through the remains of the servants' quarters and kitchen.

It was not very promising. Then again, neither were the prospects afforded by staying tied to the chair.

It was not an easy decision to make, since it would probably lead to his death. But it was the only option Farwander could take, as all the other choices were worse. So he made it.

Farwander had learned over the years that a man should never go anywhere without at least three sharp implements. He could be disarmed of one, and the second could be found if he was searched, both of which had happened as soon as Marga's butchers had dragged him off the streets of Last Fathom for transport to this dismal place. The third, however, was a tiny blade no bigger than his thumbnail that he kept concealed in the ruffled cuff of his shirt. The trappings of a would-be nobleman meant he could wear such an impractical garment without it seeming suspicious. In truth it was purely practical, since the cuff gave him a place to hide things, like the blade he was now using to saw through the ropes holding his arms to the back of the chair.

'Shut up the lot of you,' snarled Big Marga at her butchers. 'It's my crew, I'll cut off whatever I want!'

The ropes came loose and Farwander jumped from the chair.

Farwander was quick enough to get a few steps' head start on Big Marga's crew. They bunched together to block his way to the main entrance, so Farwander bolted in the other direction.

Marga made a furious and frustrated noise, and loomed towards him like a rosy-cheeked tidal wave.

Farwander ducked under a swingeing haymaker from Big Marga and headed for the grand staircase behind her. The damp, rotted steps sagged beneath his feet as he leapt up the staircase three steps at a time.

'You cheeky bugger!' yelled Big Marga after him as the crew gave chase. Farwander reached the landing as they thundered up the stairs behind him.

Most of the landing had fallen away. Enough remained to give Farwander a way into the east wing of the mansion, through a door promising only darkness and rot. It was better than anything that lay behind him, though. He slipped and wrenched his ankle as he turned, and had to scrabble on all fours towards the doorway as Marga reached the landing behind him.

'I'll 'ave your guts, you sod!' she yelled. 'I'll pull 'em out through your...'

Big Marga was indeed a big woman. It was her tremendous strength that had not only made her an excellent butcher, able to cleave through a carcass with a single blow, but had dealt with all of Last Fathom's leg-breakers and extortionists who assumed that a woman would be easy to intimidate. She had crushed them all, figuratively and literally, and made herself one of the port's most feared individuals. Once she got her trunklike arms around a soul, she would crush the life out of him. She had won underworld wars with a meaty hand around an enemy's throat, or by pinning a foe down with her substantial bulk until he stopped wriggling beneath her pounding fists. She was a brutal, towering, shaven bear of a woman.

Farwander, though not a small man, was much smaller than her. As a result, the rotten landing had supported him. It did not give the same courtesy to Big Marga.

The landing collapsed, throwing Marga and her crew back down into the entrance hall in a crash of splintering wood and curses. Farwander plunged into the gloom of the east wing and had to fight to keep his footing on the slimy floorboards. He could hear Marga raging incoherently behind him as he tore through curtains of damp spiderwebs and struggled to find a way out.

One long-boarded up window showed a crack of light where a board had fallen away. Farwander grabbed at the remaining boards. Damp mossy wood came out in clumps. Three boards went and the hole was big enough to climb through. Farwander did so, ignoring the tearing sounds from his fine breeches catching on a nail.

It was a considerable drop down to the tangle of overgrown trash and debris piled up against the back of the mansion. Farwander let go and tumbled into the mess, putting out a hand to protect himself and feeling it plunging into mud and slime. He fought to extricate himself and his panic rose to the sound of Marga's crew rampaging out through the mansion's front door.

Even in such straits, a ridiculous, petulant voice at the back of his mind bemoaned his current situation's lack of dignity.

There weren't many places he could run where Big Marga wouldn't find him. The whole of Last Fathom knew her name, and knew that when she sent the word out to bring in a particular soul, that soul was dead. But apart from Last Fathom, there wasn't anywhere else. The swamplands surrounding the port would be as likely to kill him as Marga herself. Farwander had no money, no friends and no way of leaving the city before some cutthroat on horseback rode him down on the path. So it was down into the tangle of Last Fathom that Farwander ran, reasoning that only in the press of people could he hope to find somewhere to hide.

CHAPTER 2

Last Fathom was built on a suspect foundation of duckboards and sunken piles, placed over the swamps surrounding a natural harbour. It was the harbour that had given the place a reason to exist and the town had been established in spite of the fact that the land was inimical to habitation in every other way. Clusters of buildings clung precariously at the crossroads of wooden walkways. The few pieces of solid ground were given over to stone watchtowers looking out over the ocean, or to temples and shrines that flourished here in spite of the impiety of the typical Last Fathomite. This was a town where one took everything one could get, and if that meant buying a little extra good luck from the appropriate god, then so be it.

The harbour itself was rarely without a flotilla of trading ships and the smaller craft that served and piloted them. Last Fathom was the safest harbour for weeks of sailing in any direction. The goods and money that moved through the port were the ground in which the town's underworld had taken root, and just about everyone in Last Fathom was tied into exploiting the opportunities that arose with every new ship on the horizon. From the urchins in the streets to the Wind and Storm Wardens in their grand lodges on the quayside, everyone in this town was grafting off their own piece somewhere along the line.

Farwander pondered this as he made his way through the grimy market streets of the Hangman's Cross. Men were no longer strung up from the spindly trees that rose between the ramshackle buildings, but a couple of the old gibbets remained and the name had stuck. Market stalls sold everything here, half of it to serve the crews of visiting ships, half of them offloading stolen or jettisoned goods spirited away from the harbour in the middle of the night.

'Fresh from the archipelago!' cried a hawker, whose stall was full of peculiar trinkets of stone, bronze and carved bone. 'Not gonna come around again for hundreds of years! This is history, ladies and gents! You, Madame, get yourself something beautiful! When the mists roll in again, this'll be worth thousands!'

Farwander ducked into a doorway and watched the hawker for a while. He had heard the rumours of the island chain returning, and of the rush to plunder it for whatever secrets and treasures it held before it vanished again into the mists, or beneath the waves, and into realms of memory. It all sounded as fanciful as a fairytale, and about as distant from Farwander's own existence as possible.

His train of thought was broken by the sight of an immense shaven-headed man, like a golem carved from pink meat, moving through the crowds. Even without the apron and bloodstains, Farwander would have instantly pegged the man as one of Big Marga's. He was going from stall to stall questioning the hawkers, and Farwander knew full well he would be asking if any of them had seen a slender chap with oil-black hair on the scummier side of dashing, who looked like he had been beaten up and threatened with dismemberment less than an hour before.

It hadn't taken them long, thought Farwander bitterly. Big Marga had sent the whole of Last Fathom after him.

Farwander quickened his step and headed down a row of pungent stalls selling fish. Every eye seemed turned on him. His hands seemed to itch – he needed a weapon, he needed an edge, anything to give him an advantage. A squat fishmonger watched him pass, cleaver in hand, and Farwander was certain the man's piggy eyes were trying to decide if the hassled, hurrying man was the same one whose organs of generation would earn a pouch full of gold from Big Marga.

'You going somewhere?'

Farwander halted as a stranger stepped in front of him. It was a grizzled fellow of indeterminate age, with scraggly grey hair clinging to his scarred scalp and chin. He wore a long embroidered coat and smelled of low tide.

'Nowhere, thanks,' said Farwander.

The sea dog stepped to the side, blocking him off. 'You look like a man with a lot on his mind.'

'I'm fine, good sir, if I could just...'

'Need something to take the teeth out of it all? I got some grog like nothing you ever drank. Got Witherbloom seeds, ground Bloodvine pods, best in the town. Pure stuff, matey, best prices.'

'No, thank you.' Farwander pushed past the sea dog and headed for an archway leading out of Hangman's Cross in the direction of the ocean.

'Suit yourself,' said the sea dog with a gap-toothed grin. 'Oi!' he yelled. 'I've found 'im!'

The stranger's cry was echoed by raised voices back in the market, and Farwander gave up trying to look like anything but a fugitive. He sprinted through the archway and the rickety wooden buildings of Last Fathom raced past. Now he was out of the market he felt witheringly exposed, with hiding places receding from him and his every move open to anyone who happened to be glancing down the street.

Farwander pounded the duckboards in the direction of the docks. The masts and rigging of docked ships loomed between the tottering tenement blocks and taverns. His mind raced as he weighed up potential bolt-holes – taverns, flophouses, alleyways. None of them were close or inviting enough.

He shoved people and knocked them aside as every lumbering pedestrian in the town seemed to emerge from their homes at once to get in his way. Behind him a rising commotion grew closer as more would-be bounty hunters joined in the chase.

Farwander was fit enough, but his lungs were already burning as he passed the Temple Of The Seven Riders and the raucous drinking holes of Grey Saints' Square. He glanced behind him and could pick out a few tough-looking pursuers negotiating the unsteady streets of Last Fathom behind him. One was the butcher he had seen canvassing the market stalls in Hangman's Cross, along with a second butcher who was brandishing a gleaming steel hook. Three or four more looked like they had just been caught up in the chase, typical weasely grifters who made up the bulk of Last Fathom's lowest strata and would do anything for the promise of money.

A drunken tar reeled out of a tavern doorway ahead of Farwander. It was a portly man in a long frock coat and three-cornered hat, bellowing a tuneless song through a bushy black beard. He had a basked-hilted cutlass in a scabbard hanging loosely from his belt. Farwander grabbed the sword's grip and swiped it from the man's scabbard as he passed, ignoring the drunkard's bellow of surprise.

At least he had a sword now. Still, the thought was little comfort as Farwander emerged onto the quayside of Last Fathom's docks.

If he had tried to head into the swamps and forests, Farwander would have been ridden down by the riders Big Marga would be sure to have sent after him. That left only one way out of the town for Farwander. It was on the deck of one of the ships now moored at the docks.

Ships from all over the surrounding lands came through Last Fathom, from the stern magocracies of the north to the scattered island principalities in the southern oceans. Flags of every colour flew from the masts of a dozen ships. One was a lurching blackened hulk, barely seaworthy, with fifty men unloading boxes and bundles from its cavernous hull. Another was as sleek as a dart with several ballistae mounted on its deck and fearsome eagle's head carved into its prow. Several smaller pilot ships wheeled around the harbour in a complex dance, guiding larger ships in and out of the port.

Farwander ran to the edge of the quay, where dozens of dockers and labourers glared at the sweating sword-brandishing fugitive. The ship moored directly ahead of him was a trader that had seen better days, with several men engaged in loading supplies. It wouldn't leave for a good while yet. That was no use to him, not unless he wanted the distinction of dying on a ship instead of the land.

'Give it up, Farwander,' said the butcher with the hook. He and the other pursuers were fanning out around Farwander, cutting off his avenues of escape. The other butcher had produced a wooden mallet of the kind used to stun animals for slaughter.

'Surely, gentlemen,' said Farwander, 'we can come to some arrangement?'

'Ye gods, not this again,' said Mallet. 'He always does this. Just kill him.'

Hook lunged at Farwander, aiming to drive the point of his weapon into Farwander's throat. Farwander ducked back a half-step, out of the arc of the hook to leave the man's side exposed to him. Farwander slashed up at the butcher's arm with the cutlass. The cutlass blade was ill-kept, spotted with rust and unconscionably blunt, but it was enough to rip a long red gash along the underside of Hook's bicep.

Hook yelled and scrambled back a step, clutching his arm to his chest.

'Poor form,' said Farwander. 'Where is your guard? Where is your counter? Are you killing me or chopping wood?' He dropped into a high guard, the cutlass blade glowing dully in the reflected sun.

'Who wants him?' said Mallet. He glanced at the street toughs who had joined in the chase. One was a skinny chinless wretch with a dagger in his hand. The wretch shook his head in reply.

'Not me,' said a second, a woman with the leather coat and dagger belt of a mercenary. 'Knock him out and I'll finish him. We'll share the purse.'

Farwander swept the blade in a couple of impressive-looking cuts and put up his guard again. His most well-honed skill was looking like an impressive swordsman regardless of the odds against him. Behind the flourish of his blade his heart hammered and his mouth was dry. He suddenly felt exhausted, as if the previous moments of exertion had all caught up with him at once. The sword felt like a bar of lead in his hand.

'No one?' said Mallet disdainfully. 'Bunch of rabbit-hearts. I'll have your head, pretty boy!'

'Pretty?' said Farwander, hoping the fear and exhaustion wasn't showing in his voice. 'Been a long time since anyone called me that. You'll excuse me if I don't return the compliment.'

Mallet came at Farwander faster than he had anticipated. Farwander threw himself onto his back to avoid the horizontal swing of the mallet's head, which passed close enough to his nose for him to smell the blood caked on it. Farwander swivelled on his back and rolled onto his feet again, stabbing with the cutlass point at Mallet's thigh. The blunt tip didn't punch through the butcher's leather apron and Mallet cracked a vicious backhand against the side of Farwander's head.

Farwander, forced to fall back on childhood instincts, booted Mallet in the groin. Mallet doubled over with a grunt and Farwander smacked the hilt of the cutlass against the back of his skull.

The wretch with the dagger was beside him, aiming a stab at Farwander's guts. Farwander aimed a cut down at his shoulder and felt the blade jarring against the wretch's collarbone. The wretch fell away, crying out, clamping a hand to his wounded shoulder.

Farwander backed rapidly down the quay, trying to keep the assailants from surrounding him. He recognised the curious dynamic of many men fighting against one, but with none of the many willing to risk injury by being the first to attack. Two of their number were wounded and neither the butchers nor the assorted cutthroats wanted to be next. Farwander's swordplay had bought him a few more moments of life, although he had no idea of what he was going to do with them.

'Hey!' came a voice from behind him and above. 'We got room for one more!'

Farwander risked a glance over his shoulder. He had passed the trading ship and reached another that was just pulling away from the quay as the dockhands unlooped the ropes holding it fast. Its topsails were unfurled and the wind had filled them, propelling it slowly out into the harbour. The voice had come from a bearded crewman barely visible over the deck rail.

It was a largely unremarkable trader, but it looked in decent shape and the crew on the deck had the air of basic competence.

Towards the stern hung one of the ropes the dockers had just cast off. It was being reeled in rapidly by another crewman on the ship's deck. Farwander turned and ran, presenting his back to his attackers, sure a dagger would be planted between his shoulder blades before he could make a step.

The ship picked up speed and seemed to race towards him.

Farwander planted a foot on the edge of the quay and launched himself across the gap between dry land and the hull of the ship. He grabbed at the rope and caught it, feeling it burn his palms as he held on and banged into the hull.

A furious grunt below him told him he hadn't been the only one to jump. Mallet had made the leap, too, having dropped his weapon and recovered from the stunning blow to the back of his head. Blood was running from one of his ears and his face was creased up with anger. Farwander lifted a foot and stamped down as hard as he could into the centre of Mallet's face.

He was sure he could hear the crunch as the butcher's nose broke. He definitely heard the splash as Mallet, stunned again, plunged into the suspect waters of Last Fathom's harbour.

Farwander clambered up the rope, finally dragging himself over the rail and flopping onto the deck like a landed fish. The ship's crew regarded him with mild surprise, then went back to the business of getting the ship's voyage underway.

The crewman who had shouted to him stood over him with a smile on his pockmarked face. He was skinny and salt-burned, the kind of man who had spent his whole adult life hauling cargo and pulling ropes at sea. 'We was runnin' a little light on hands,' he said. 'Looks like we done each other a favour, eh?'

The crewman's accent was thick and jovial. It occurred to Farwander that he didn't know where the ship was from – its flag was red with a blue pig's head, and he didn't recognise it.

'You... you could say that,' said Farwander, pulling himself to his feet. 'If you are in need of a general-purpose ne'er-do-well I'd say you're in luck.'

'Can you cook?'

'Regrettably, Sir, I cannot.'

'Then you best be one for learnin',' said the crewman. 'This here's the *Salted Swine*. She's no better than the next tub but she floats aright, which I'd say is the best you could hope for in your position. We need hands in the galley and on the rigging when needs be. Grub's foul and the grog's worse, you gets a quarter-share and that's only if we makes anything. Welcome aboard.'

'Pleased to make your acquaintance. Farwander.' He held out a hand, which the crewman took. Farwander became very aware the hand he was shaking was missing some fingers.

'Flench,' came the reply.

A cry came from the wheel in some truncated sailor's cant Farwander didn't know. Crewman were suddenly scurrying all across the deck, up masts and rigging, brandishing hooked poles to unfurl sails or hauling on some of the hundreds of ropes with which the *Salted Swine* was festooned.

'Wait!' called Farwander as Flench headed towards the bow. 'Where are we going?'

'The Ghosts!' came the reply, and then Flench was lost in the confusion of rigging and trim as the *Salted Swine* pulled away from Last Fathom.

CHAPTER 3

Two weeks out, the world seemed to have shrunk. It was composed, not of scattered cities and distant lands, but of a single circle of ocean that stretched from one horizon to the other, and the rickety wooden island of the *Salted Swine*.

The narrow confines of his world were the most overwhelming impression Farwander had of ocean travel. There was the constant cycle of work to keep the ship heading in roughly the right direction, the blank, dreamless sleep of exhaustion and the rapid abandonment of basic hygiene – these had made their impression on him, too, as ways of life emblematic of the sea. But what really struck him was the way the rest of the world might have just dropped off the horizon and plunged into oblivion, for all he knew being restricted to the creaking box of the *Salted Swine*.

The only mitigating action was to take his rare moments of spare time and spend them on the deck in the open, where the scale of the sky was the sole reminder that there was still a bigger world out there. And this night, he had company on there, and not just the ever-present gaggle of the ship's crew. This night, Dascia the Warden took to the deck.

It was a strange, hypnotic thing to watch her perched on the prow of the ship, the wind whipping her long dark blue fabric trails around her, her long sorrowful face tinged by the sunset. The first time he had seen the Storm Warden walk onto deck, Farwander had told himself not to stare. He knew of the work of the Wardens, of course, but he had seen only the low-rent hedge wizards who worked out of the dockside lodges and were as much grifters and chancers as everyone else in Last Fathom. Dascia was something else.

For one, she was from a city far from Last Fathom, and wore her black hair bound up in a tight turban of blue silk and silver beads. Her many layers of blue and turquoise robes fluttered around her even when the air was still. Her eyes were bright flecks set deep in a face so pale it was tinged grey-blue like the moon.

Farwander watched as Dascia took a handful of bones from a pouch on her waist and cast them into the sea before the ship. She cried out in words of a language Farwander didn't know, as if pleading with a distant loved one to return, and her words were snatched from her mouth by the sudden wind that blustered across the deck. Farwander felt his neck prickle with static electricity, echoed by the flashes of blue-white lightning in the distant clouds that had gathered around the darkening horizon.

'Get your carcasses aloft!' came the cry from the bosun, a brawny barrel-shaped man with knuckles covered in scars. 'Wind's coming in! Secure the decks and batten all!'

The crew were clambering and hauling to get the main sails ready and point the ship in the perfect direction.

Normally the growing storm would be something to be avoided, or ridden out with main sails struck. But this was *their* storm, one they had conjured up for the purpose. Farwander could feel the excitement in the crew. As much as they had anticipated this, it was still dangerous. The storm did not always play nice.

Dascia spread her arms, like a dancer accepting applause, and from the space her arms encircled crackled blue fingers of electricity. A flock of birds suddenly appeared from the corona of power, lightning arcing off their black feathers as they rushed from Dascia's embrace into the darkening sky. The storm flock wheeled above the ship, spiralling upwards.

Farwander couldn't stop watching. He had given up any pretence not to stare, now.

'Cap'n wants a storm, not a hurricane!' called Flench from amidships, where he was hauling the rope that unfurled the topsail. 'You'll be dismastin' us, Dascia!'

Dascia turned to glare at Flench. 'The storm does as the storm is,' she said. 'It cannot be controlled, only beckoned.'

'You're beckoning it pretty strong!' replied Flench. The wind was whipping across the deck now, forcing men to tie down loose ropes and stow anything that could be picked up by the growing gale.

'As I was asked,' replied Dascia.

The captain of the *Salted Swine*, a girthy and solid-faced woman named Stennby, had watched proceedings from her position near the ship's wheel. With a flourish of a hand she gave the order for the crew to withdraw and ride out the winds. Already the sails were filling to a full billow and the ship was picking up pace. The ocean lashed past and the ship's prow knifed through the waves. Behind them the storm grew darker and stronger, and the ship was riding ahead of it like an animal fleeing a predator.

Farwander held onto the deck rail as the ship began to rise and fall and he made his way towards the hatch amidships.

'How do you do it?' he asked Dascia as she passed. Unlike everyone else Dascia seemed to have perfect footing on the deck even with the wind and the pitching of the ship.

'The storm must be beckoned down,' she replied simply, as if what she did was no more remarkable than tilling a field or shaping a horseshoe. 'It is like a sulking child. It must be cajoled and begged, and sometimes threatened. But once it is roused, it cannot be quietened again until it is exhausted.'

'I always thought the Wardens were charlatans,' said Farwander as he and Dascia ducked below decks, into the sweaty, creaking warmth within the hull.

'You knew the wrong Wardens,' replied Dascia. The crew parted for her with a respect they never showed each other, and she headed for her quarters in the stern. They were alongside the captain's cabin, and from what Farwander had seen, Dascia had the most comfortable berth on the ship.

'So you made her acquaintance at last,' said Flench with a grin from the hammock he had commandeered. Farwander leaned against the joist beside him. 'Not your usual.'

'Indeed not,' said Farwander.

'She's bloody expensive,' continued Flench. 'Worth it, though. Without her we'd never reach the Ghosts.'

'And are the islands worth it?' asked Farwander.

'Cap'n thinks so. So do the souls who risked money on us. Now I'm not sayin' there's a hold full of treasure around every rock over there, nor that the natives plate their bedpans with gold. But there were plenty of folk came back rich two hundred years ago last time the Ghost Archipelago appeared. Some with gold, some with more. They say the Heritors are coming back out of the woodwork.'

'Never really believed in those stories,' said Farwander.

'You never believed a sallow girl could call down a storm,' said Flench, 'but here we are. Turns out there are a lot of ladies and gents who were born to the line of those what explored the Ghosts last time, or at least say they were. They're buying up fleets to head back there and find the same thing their granddaddies did.'

'The Pool?'

'The Pool.' Flench shrugged. 'But I suppose you don't believe in that neither.'

'As of a few minutes ago, my friend, my previous beliefs mean nothing. When one suddenly finds oneself on a voyage to a place that did not exist until a few months ago, with a sorcerer on board and no idea of where he is going to end up, one learns quickly to keep an open mind.'

'Well sounds like you'll need it. Real or not, all the Heritors are headed for the Ghosts. Duke Bartholemew Hexis set out from Rilesport just before we did. He has a hundred men with him. Word is, Agnar the Knife and Lady Temnos are at sail, too.'

'That's... that's jolly interesting,' said Farwander. 'I take it our Captain is not among such exalted company?'

'We'd have a damn sounder tub if Cap'n Stennby was a Heritor,' said Flench with a chuckle. 'No, but she's one of many thinkin' they can make money out of the Heritors all rushin' to the Ghosts to find... well, to find whatever it is they're lookin' for, native gold or otherwise. All those crews'll need supplies, sword arms, all that if they're going to explore the interior. Doesn't matter if a man can lift a bull over his head or regrow a lost arm, he still has to feed his crew and he still has to pay to do it.'

'And you?' asked Farwander.

'Me? I'll do whatever needs doin'. Not like I had anything back in Rileport to keep me there. I'm curious about you, though. You didn't seem to have much of a plan back at Last Fathom 'cept for saving the skin on your rump. What'll you do when we reach the archipelago?'

'I have my skills,' said Farwander. 'I'm not quite as useless as I seem.'

'Be bloody impressive if you were,' said Flench. He turned over in his hammock and immediately began snoring, in spite of the fact that the ship was pitching up and down to the roar of the waves and the thunder of the following storm.

The rest of the crew were resting as best they could, wedged into every available space below decks as the *Salted Swine* raced ahead of the storm. Every one wore the garb of a different city or land, united for the moment in the fragility of men made vulnerable by the capriciousness of the sea.

And in that moment, Farwander had never felt so far from home, or so completely at the mercy of powers beyond his control. He squeezed himself into the space beneath the hammock, and with his stomach churning and his ears full of the ocean's anger, he tried and failed to sleep.

* * *

The first sight of the Ghost Archipelago held such dread and promise in the scattered flecks of land, that it seemed impossible they were just stone and earth. Even as a strip of distant peaks, wreathed in the mists that had hidden them from the world for two centuries, the sight of them was all but overwhelming.

They were real.

For three weeks at sea, Farwander had pushed the fear into the back of his mind that the *Salted Swine* was sailing to a nonexistent place and the crew would meet their end in the middle of an endless, landless sea. He had become a decent galley cook and a barely competent deckhand in that time, but he was still marked out by the fact that he hadn't deliberately joined this voyage to reach the Ghost Archipelago and did not see the same fortunes in its jungles and caverns as the rest of the crew. Now the sight of something real on the horizon was a tremendous relief.

Flench and Captain Stennby joined Farwander near the prow. 'Let us not celebrate overmuch,' said Stennby, as ever unsmiling beneath her grand feathered hat. 'What do you see, Mr Flench?'

Flench took out a spyglass and extended it. He held it up to his eye and grimaced as he peered through it for a long minute.

'Cape Cadaver dead ahead,' he said eventually. 'Flying the flags of the *Quartered Man*. Dascia led us true.'

'Very good, Mr Flench. Have the landing boats made ready.'

'Aye, Cap'n,' said Flench, and turned to start yelling orders at the crew.

Farwander realised Captain Stennby had turned her narrow eyes on him. 'You,' she said. 'Farwander.'

'Yes, Captain?' It was the first time the captain had ever spoken to Farwander, or seemed to notice him.

'You were promised a quarter-share, is that correct?'

'It is.'

'But you will not collect it.'

'I don't understand.'

'You will not be on the *Salted Swine* when she returns to Rileport. You will leave us at Cape Cadaver, I would wager. In any case, you will not finish our voyage with us, and so there will be no purse for you to take a share of. I know the look of one who is on for the duration, sir, and you do not have it. You will seek your fortune on your own.'

'I admit, Captain, I do feel the itch. A rogue, one might call me. A survivor. A jack of many trades. I'm not much use when it comes to loading cargo and pulling ropes on a trader. If the Ghost Archipelago is such a treasure hunter's paradise as they say, a man such as me has no choice but to take from it what he can.'

'I see.' It was impossible to read an expression from Stennby's wind-burned face. 'I run a ship with a firm hand, but a fair one. You might not have been on our ship's complement when we left Rileport but you worked your share and I would not have you do that for nothing. It will not be the equal of a share if our endeavours are successful, but then you will only have worked half the voyage. I shall see the quartermaster settle up with you when we dock.'

'If I may,' said Farwander, 'I find surprisingly little use for money. Would it please you to be paid in kind?'

'I suppose. What do you want?'

'A decent sword.' Farwander drew the cutlass he wore, the same one he had taken from the drunkard at Last Fathom. 'Look at this dull disgrace. I would not dishonour a man by running him through with this. I used it to cut meat in the galley and it was barely up to the task. I need a good blade in my hand, Captain. Anything the Ghost Archipelago has for me, I can deal with it as long as I have a sword worth the name.'

'Very well. That can be arranged.' Stennby turned to one of the crew, a rope-muscled salt with a missing ear. 'You! My sword! Not the dress, the dueller.'

The tar nodded and scurried off towards the captain's quarters at the rear of the ship.

'What do you think lies out there?' asked Farwander, looking back towards the island of the Ghost Archipelago.

'Opportunities for gainful employment at well above the usual rates,' replied Captain Stennby. 'And the chance to purchase goods with the monies so gained for transport back to the mainland for sale at greatly inflated sums. Otherwise, I would not have risked my ship and my reputation coming here. But that is not what I imagine you meant, Mr Farwander.'

'Do you think the Crystal Pool is there to be found?'

'The Heritors got their power from somewhere.'

'Lots of them will die trying to find it.'

'Not before paying me to make their deaths possible. And people are a determined lot, especially a Heritor. If it's there, if it's worth what they say, someone will find it. Thus is the nature of humankind. It was what took us across the oceans in the first place! It is what brought the Heritors' ancestors to these islands.'

'Perhaps I do not have quite the same faith in people as you do, Captain,' said Farwander distantly.

The one-eared tar returned with Stennby's sword. Farwander saw it was a long, straight blade, with a finger guard over the crossbar and a polished sphere of jet set into the pommel. Stennby took the sword and handed it to Farwander. 'I find a cutlass far more forgiving on the deck of a ship,' said the captain. 'As pretty as this is, it does me little good. I have not the refinement for such a weapon. This is all riposte and thrust when I would far rather cut a fellow's arm off and be done with it.'

Farwander slid the blade from the scabbard. It was good steel. Very good. The balance was excellent, too. 'This is worth rather more than a quarter-share,' he said.

'Not to me. And I would be no friend to my crew if I were to permit you to wander the Ghost Archipelago with that bread knife you were carrying.'

Farwander gave the sword a couple of practice swings. It was similar to the kind he had trained with, with a four foot blade and keen double edge. It could be wielded with one hand for quick stabs and slashes to an unarmoured opponent, two hands to thrust into armour.

'My thanks,' he said simply.

The timbers of the ship's crane creaked as the landing boat was swung out over the side, ready to be lowered. Flench stood ready at the capstan to lower it. 'No sense in your remaining on board,' said Stennby. 'Come ashore with me if you will, Mr Farwander. It is time for you to begin your real journey.'

Farwander couldn't be sure what Cape Cadaver was. It certainly wasn't a town. It might have been a harbour, although the flotilla of ships that made up the place took up almost the whole bay. The pioneers who landed here had bypassed the whole process of building a place to live and had made one by lashing together their ships into a single creaking, undulating wooden sprawl, some with the masts still standing, all of them with a bewildering forest of flags flying in every colour. Newer ships were moored on wood piles sunk into the shallow bay's water, or were just tied on to the edge of the flotilla as it grew.

The first ship to moor in the harbour was the *Quartered Man*, or so Farwander had heard it from Flench. The flag, with its dark blue and purple field behind the image of a man divided into four, hung to indicate the berths solid enough for a ship to moor at. Farwander couldn't make out anything that might have been the *Quartered Man* among the riot of ships of every size and style of construction. Captain Stennby seemed to know her way around and headed off on her own business, and the rest of the crew had dived into the various drinking establishments and gambling pits that made up the lifeblood of Cape Cadaver. Farwander was suddenly alone, paradoxically given the fleshpot the harbour had become.

There was music coming from somewhere, oozing through the close and humid air. As dusk gathered, thousands of lanterns were hung and Cape Cadaver seemed assailed by a swarm of fireflies. Farwander's first glimpses of the Ghost Archipelago's inhabitants were of the clashing clothing, arms and skin tones of the many nations who had come there to seek their fortune, all united here by the precariousness of their grip on the island chain. Pastel silks rubbed shoulders with cracked leather and hide. A turbaned merchant dripping with jewels walked with a bodyguard of tattooed nomads with sharpened teeth. Slender, sharp-eyed traders in wide conical hats drank grog with the kind of hefty bearded pirate who would have fancied himself a lord of Last Fathom.

It was a bewildering, overwhelming place. Every turn of the wind brought a new and powerful smell – spices, spilt rum, sweat, decaying seaweed, boiling stew. Every ship seemed to have its own minstrel playing some exotic instrument or keening out a shanty in another language. Farwander quite liked it. As precarious as it felt, it wasn't Last Fathom.

CHAPTER 4

Farwander found the place he was looking for after a good few hours negotiating the flotilla. It was marked by the flag showing a bird of prey impaled with an arrow. The flag hung from the middle mast of a ship made accessible by planks nailed to its deck rails to form bridges with its neighbours. The sound of raised voices, laughter and clanking tankards came from the rickety structure built onto its deck. One of the first tasks for the settlers of Cape Cadaver had been to establish a place to drink, and this was one of the results.

Farwander walked in through the door and was hit by the blood-warm fug of sweat and booze. The drinking hole was packed. A pair of old tars seemed engaged in a competition to see who could play his accordion the fastest and a portly exhausted-looking man in an apron was struggling to keep the dozens of patrons supplied with tankards of grog. Farwander shouldered his way through the throng to reach the man.

'You know a Leveret?' he asked the proprietor.

'That depends,' came the reply.

Farwander handed the proprietor a handful of coins, which represented almost all the wealth he possessed. He had carried them in his pocket since Last Fathom. 'I'll take a half,' he said.

The proprietor thrust a mug into Farwander's hand and turned to the back of the room. 'Pavine!' he yelled 'One for you!'

Farwander headed in the indicated direction to find a woman sitting along at a small table in a cramped corner. Her face was slim and sharp, framed by draggles of stringy blonde hair. She wore the remnants of an officer's uniform from a navy Farwander did not recognise. Most notably, she was surrounded by a complex and pervasive odour of her own, one which must have been built up over years of cultivation.

Farwander put his mug on the table and sat opposite the woman. 'I heard you were hiring.'

Leveret Pavine scrutinised Farwander without shame. 'Who'd you hear that from?' she asked, in a suspicious and scratchy voice.

'I asked around,' replied Farwander. 'A man on the *Swiftwind's Herald* tried to sell me a monkey as soon as I landed. He said I'd find an agent named Leveret under the sign of the Raptor Turned Prey. Said there was work.'

'Yeah, well, not for everyone. Did you buy the monkey?'

'I did not.'

'Just as well. Thieving little buggers. So what's to get a girl's attention on you that the rest of these salty bastards don't have?'

'Do you know the Agridulce School?'

'No.'

'Exactly. Not many do. The art of the Bittersweet

Blade.' Farwander showed her Captain Stennby's sword. 'There are only four men who have studied it alive today. One of them is eighty years old, another is half mad from syphilis and the third lost an arm. The last one is me. I learned it from the one without an arm, although he had two when I knew him.'

'So you can swordfight.'

'Madame, what I do is art.'

'Every man in this room can swordfight,' said Leveret. 'And they don't have to prance around like a knob-end first.'

'But you don't work for one of these men. I understand you are an agent working on behalf of a far more exalted personage than anyone who would drink rat squeezings like this.' He raised his mug to Leveret and took a sip. It was rough and strong, as he had expected.

'The Lady don't need more fighting men,' said Leveret. 'She brought half an army with her. Bring me a fellow what can guide us through the jungle or tell which fruit'll turn your guts inside out, or can patch a belly wound gone bad. Give me a Warden what knows a northerly wind from a kick in the arse. Don't give me another warm body with a sword, I got too many of those as it is.'

'Think of me as a fashion accessory,' said Farwander with his most winning smile. 'The Lady – Lady Temnos, I take it? - she has to impress as well as overcome. She needs the airs and presence of a Heritor. What lady of ambition goes without a personal champion and instructor? The strength of a Heritor is multiplied tenfold with the addition of sound martial techniques.'

'Lady Temnos could pull your arms and legs off,' said Leveret, 'with not a bead of sweat on her pretty forehead. She don't need technique.'

'I assure you, a man like me is essential to your expedition. What can I say to convince you?'

Leveret scowled at him. 'You better not be trying it on.'

'Madame, I would never do such a thing,' said Farwander, and for once he meant it.

'I got to bring in enough skilled men to set off in three days,' said Leveret. 'I can't be wasting my time with a simpering bloody ornament like you.'

Behind Farwander, in the centre of the room, an enormous bearded walrus of a man leapt up from his seat, scattering empty mugs onto the floor. He glared down at the shaft of metal extending from his shoulder. 'Oi!' he yelled. 'Which of you sods did that?'

It was a crossbow bolt. The whistle and twang of the shot had been masked by the background noise of dozens of drinking sailors, but the end result had not.

Farwander had the sudden, complete certainty that the bolt had not been meant for the huge sailor. He had leaned over the dice game he and his friends were playing, and had interposed himself between the doorway and Leveret's table. The bolt had been meant for her.

The accordion players faltered as a newcomer to the establishment stood in the doorway, his face obscured by a black three-cornered hat and the rest of him hidden in a long dark leather coat. He slipped a second bolt into the crossbow in his hand. Before the wounded sailor could move again, the bolt flicked across the room and straight through his throat.

'Right!' shouted another sailor, this one rangy and tall with a face scarred into a permanent sneer. 'I don't know who he was but you don't interrupt a man's grog by killin' 'im!' The sailor drew a dagger to a rousing cheer of assent.

Farwander had the presence of mind to draw his sword from it scabbard, as the whole place erupted into chaos.

The newcomer dived in through the door, followed by half a dozen more. Even more assailants burst in through a rear entrance. Someone threw a chair and a table overturned. The drinking hole devolved in a second into a mass of fists, knives and stamping feet. Glass broke and an accordion screamed as it was crushed underfoot.

Farwander grabbed Leveret by the collar of her officer's jacket and hauled her up out of her chair, dragging her behind him as he searched for a way out. Both ways in were blocked by the men assaulting the place – they all, he saw now, seemed dressed to obscure their true selves, in cloaks and long coats, black scarves and hats pulled low. Most had crossbows, others drew swords and daggers. Bolts whistled across the room, thunking into the walls.

One of the attackers had barged his way across the room, heading straight for Farwander and Leveret. Beneath the brim of his hat, Farwander caught a glimpse of livid, blistered flesh. The man had a dagger in his hand and roared in fury as he charged.

Farwander's blade was too long to be brought to bear in the moment. So he let the man come at him, pivoting on his back foot and letting the momentum take the assailant past him and into the wall behind.

The attacker slammed into the wall with a splintering of wood. Leveret grabbed a chair off the floor and, before the attacker could get his senses back, swung the chair at his head.

Leveret was stronger than she looked. Either that, or the shack on the ship's deck was even more rickety than it first appeared. The impact drove the attacker right through the wall and out onto the deck. The moist, hazy fug of the drinking hole billowed out into the night air.

Farwander leapt through the hole suddenly torn in the side of the shack. Leveret followed him. The attacker jumped to his feet on the deck, throwing his hat and coat aside.

Farwander immediately realised why the attackers had tried to cover up. Every inch of the man's body was covered in scar tissue, raised in lines and welts to echo the coils of an octopus. The coils covered his face and shaven scalp, too, so it was hard to make out the facial features among the scars. He bared his teeth and leapt at Farwander, dagger still in his hand.

'Drown in the Deeps!' he hissed as he drove the dagger towards Farwander's neck.

Farwander let the dagger pass just by his throat, nicking the skin with its jagged edge. He drove a knee up into the scarred man's midriff, used the moment that bought him to duck back a step, and brought his sword around in a chest-high slash. He felt the blade bite into skin and muscle, withdrew it, and thrust it into the enemy's exposed abdomen.

The man yelped as the blade punched into his gut. Farwander aimed a boot at his chest and kicked hard. He slid off the blade and toppled over the deck rail, pitching headlong into the murky waters between the ships.

'You know these rapscallions?' said Farwander, catching his breath.

'Brotherhood of Scaraveyla,' replied Leveret, who had emerged behind him onto the deck.

'The what of the who?'

'There's dozens of them,' scowled Leveret. 'Bloody move!'

The Brotherhood, whoever they were, had realised Leveret and Farwander were no longer in the drinking hole. They were spilling back out onto the deck, yelling orders to hunt 'the woman' down. Leveret jumped over the gap into which the last attacker had plunged, landing on the deck of the next ship along. Farwander followed her, rounding a corner to put something solid between him and the Brotherhood in pursuit. A trio of crossbow bolts thumped into the wood behind him.

'You know them?' he said as they ran.

'Not bloody likely,' replied Leveret.

'They know you.'

'Lucky them.'

They vaulted onto the next ship, a fast, slender vessel now trapped between a pair of ungainly neighbours. A party of four Brotherhood toughs, no longer bothering to hide their identities, had moved around to cut them off from the other side.

'How many of these carbuncles are there?' said Farwander, arresting his sprint as the Brotherhood jumped onto the deck of the slender ship.

'The sod should I know?' replied Leveret tetchily.

'Tell the Temnos wench the kraken will take her!' growled the closest, who had thrown off his shirt to show off his ropily muscled, tentacle-scarred body. 'After I hang your head from the yard-arm!'

'How'm I gonna tell her anything if you just cut me head off?' retorted Leveret. 'You bloody idiots.'

By way of reply, the Brother of Scaraveyla brandished his cutlass and ran at Leveret with a roar. Suddenly a dagger was in Leveret's hand, then just as quickly it was out of it, spinning towards the Brother in a well-practised throw.

Leveret missed, but she missed low. The dagger speared into the meat of the Brother's thigh. He pitched face-first onto the deck and Leveret was on him, aiming a sharp-toed kick right into his temple. She pulled the dagger back out of his thigh and plunged it into his back between the shoulder blades.

Two more were following their dying comrade. Farwander glanced up at the rigging – the ship still had the sails furled on the sloping yard of its middle mast. Rapidly running through the knowledge of rigging he had gleaned on his voyage over, he slashed at one of the ropes running parallel to the mast. The keen edge sliced through the rope and the loose sail billowed down onto the deck, settling on top of the two charging men.

That left one more Brother of Scaraveyla, but this one was easily big enough to count for two. His skin was carved and blistered up so it looked like his massive arms were wrapped in octopus tentacles. Steel rings were set into his flesh, as if ropes could be tied to them so he could be restrained. His face was a knot of snarling scar tissue. He carried a two-handed axe.

'Evening,' said Farwander. 'Lovely night for it.'

The huge Brother swung his axe in an enormous arc. Farwander had misjudged the giant man's reach and had to jump backwards to keep his head on his shoulders. Farwander tried to parry the Brother's backswing but the impact almost jarred the sword out of his hand. He switched to a two-handed grip, danced around the giant's clumsy downward stroke and aimed a thrust into the unprotected flank, putting his whole bodyweight behind the blow.

Layers of scar tissue and iron stopped the blow from driving all the way home. Anyone else would have been run through. It was a debilitating blow but one that a truly crazed individual might survive long enough to do some serious damage. Farwander's options were rushing through his mind when the giant spun away from him, tearing the sword out of his hands. The blade was still lodged in the scarred man's side and he slouched against the deck rail, grunting in pain.

The two men under the fallen sail had fought their way out. One of them turned to see Leveret bearing down on him, with her face creased up with anger.

'Suck on this, yer ronyon!' she growled as she grabbed the back of the enemy's head, dragged him towards her and plunged her dagger into the back of his neck.

The second man was going to impale Leveret with the sword he had managed to extricate from the sailcloth. Farwander was unarmed and had a couple of heartbeats to act. The only object nearby was a lantern hanging from the middle mast. He grabbed the lantern and ran at the sword-bearing man, swinging his improvised weapon like a club.

The glass and flimsy iron of the lantern exploded in a burst of fragmented fire. The Brother screamed and fell backwards as flame ran across his mutilated skin. Leveret looked up at the spectacle in surprise as she fought to pull her dagger from the back of the other enemy's skull.

Farwander's training had emphasised the flow and dance of swordplay, a sequence of flawlessly linked thrusts, cuts and parries that left no room for an opponent to strike. But sometimes, the circumstances were not right for the beautiful ballet of the blade. Sometimes a chap just had to aim a boot into his opponent's groin, which was what Farwander did in that moment, as hard as he could.

His foot impacted with a satisfying crunch. The burning Brother howled and doubled over. It was probably something of a relief when Leveret pounced on him, flipped him over and stabbed her dagger down into his chest.

The huge Brother was struggling to his feet, still with Farwander's sword sticking out between his ribs. 'Grab a leg,' said Farwander.

He and Leveret each took hold of one of the huge man's legs. Farwander grasped the hilt of the sword and together, they tipped him over the edge of the ship. He landed with a fearsome splash, leaving his huge axe and a liberal smearing of blood on the deck.

Farwander and Leveret could only stand there and gasp down breaths for a long moment. Leveret leaned against the deck rail and wiped the blood off her dagger. Farwander took a rag from his pocket and cleaned off his sword as best he could.

Somewhere behind them, the fighting in the Raptor Turned Prey was continuing. Raised voices and clashing metal rang through the night. The Brotherhood had picked the wrong place to stage their attack – the drunken salts were fighting back, revelling in a decent excuse to crack skulls and shed blood. Farwander and Leveret still had to keep moving, but the immediate pursuit was gone.

Leveret hid her dagger back somewhere in her naval coat. She wiped sweat and spots off blood off her face with the back of a grimy hand.

'Alright,' she said. 'You're in.'

CHAPTER 5

Even from this distance, the temple looked like an evil place. It was built into tumbledown ruins on a hillside overlooking Cape Cadaver, as if looking balefully down to observe everything that went on in the harbour. It was no accident it was not built on the deck of one of Cape Cadaver's ships, as the shrines of other sailors' gods had been. No one would permit the structure to be raised on his ship, because no one would admit to worshipping this particular god.

It had once been the ruin of a tower built by whoever had lived on this island long before the Ghost Archipelago had last emerged from the mists, but it had since been repurposed for a far less benign task than keeping watch. The massive stones had been shored up with timbers and wooden walls used to complete the temple's shape. Rags of sharkskin hung from the eaves. The splintered figureheads and tattered flags of foundered ships were nailed to the walls, or arranged around the temple like severed heads around a madman's fortress. Even the jungle that clung to the hillside seemed to recoil from the place, leaving the bleached skeleton of stone and new infection of black wood open to the humid air.

'They built it as soon as the first ships landed,' said Leveret. She had pointed out the hillside temple as she and Farwander made their way along the shoreline path away from Cape Cadaver, towards the other side of the headland forming the harbour's eastern side. 'Plenty of rough seas, plenty of men lost. The ones what made it to the Archipelago decided they needed somewhere to leave offerings for the Shipwreck Queen. Better safe than sorry.'

'So that's Scaraveyla,' said Farwander. 'The Kraken Queen.'

'Yep. She'll drown you for the hell of it and sink your ship beneath you for lookin' at her wrong. If you believes all that, of course.'

'The Brotherhood evidently do.'

'Yeah, well, they're something else. The temple's for folks like me and you what want to hedge our bets and leave a few coins to her. The Brotherhood of Scaraveyla are survivors, they say. Survivors and marooned men what went mad. Now there's nothing in their minds 'cept the Kraken Queen and bringing everyone else down into the depths with them.'

'Then what do they want with you and Lady Temnos?'

'Gods know,' said Leveret. 'Not that I'm ungrateful you stopped them from gettin' it.'

'Glad I could help.'

'Course you are.' Leveret grinned at him, showing off the gaps in her yellowish teeth. 'It got you into the Lady's mob. But saving my worthless arse is saving it, and Leveret Pavine pays people what she owes. So you're in. I can't speak for the Lady though. If she doesn't take a liking to you, you're back on your ear.'

Farwander had not seen the jungle of the Ghost Archipelago in the sunlight until now. It was a dense, choking blanket draped over the island, exuding the muggy, wet warmth that enveloped the whole Archipelago. It was such an extraordinarily vivid green it seemed like he was seeing the colour for the first time. Ravines and tunnels wound through the jungle, leading from the shoreline deep into the interior, and Farwander could only imagine how easy it would be to get lost in there. Every now and again a bird would flit from the canopy in a bright flash of plumage to rise on the warm air. From the jungle's depths issued a constant stream of background noise – squawking, hooting, barking, shrieking, the sounds of the inhabitants of the dark green world inside.

'You a long way from Last Fathom,' said Leveret, as if reading his thoughts. 'The Ghosts treat everyone the same. Whatever you had back there, you ain't got it here.'

'If you seek to discourage me, madam, I fear you are ill-advised. I had nothing in Last Fathom, so I have nothing to lose.'

'But what about them airs?' said Leveret, glaring at him and encompassing Farwander with a wave of the hand. 'Them ruffs? All them words? Posh sword and all? You can't tell me you got no money. You'd better not be one of them that pretends he's got a high-born name when he was whelped in the mud. Not much I can do with that sort of liar.'

'No, the name and the manners are real,' replied Farwander. 'The name of the venn Farwanders used to mean something. We started out as generals for hire as I understand it, then some enterprising ancestor asked for his payment in land instead of gold and suddenly we're the landed gentry. There was money, too. They were prudent men. They built estates, married right, all the usual business.'

'So what happened?'

'My great-uncle,' said Farwander. 'I never met him, mind you, this was all before I was born. Prince Asclepius of Dovann was trying to usurp the throne from his father, so...'

'Prince who?' interrupted Leveret.

'Doesn't matter. There's always some prince or duke or under-earl trying to sit on one throne or another. Anyhow, he needed an army. So my great-uncle Sarven offered his services as a general in return for a goodly chunk of the kingdom the prince was hoping to seize. Standard procedure, you might say, it's how the Farwanders built their fortune. The king of Dovann was encamped while prosecuting some tedious campaign and my great-uncle marched on him with an army three times the size to ambush them and take the king. Simplicity itself.'

'I'm guessing this don't turn out to be simple after all.'

'Indeed, you are a most perceptive woman. Sarven failed to account for the large swamp between him and the king's encampment. Armoured men and heavy cavalry are jolly useful in a battle but one thing they cannot do is swim. Three thousand men went in, two hundred and thirty-five came out. The swamp ate the rest, including my great-uncle and more importantly the pay chest full of

Prince Asclepius' gold. You will have inferred by now that my great-uncle Sarven was an idiot.'

'Well, they do say every family squirts out a slackjaw every now and again,' said Leveret with a shrug.

'And so it was that the venn Farwanders fell from grace, just in time for me to exist.'

'Sad story,' agreed Leveret, 'but I've heard worse. We're here.'

The two rounded the headland, revealing the stretch of shoreline running eastwards from Cape Cadaver. Farwander realised the Cape wasn't the only place one could moor a ship on the island, because off the coast was moored a quite splendid ship the likes of which he had never seen, and barely imagined, before.

For a moment Farwander's mind tried to dismiss the sight of the gargantuan ship as a trick of light and distance. But then he counted the masts, nine of them, and the lines of four decks above the surface. Gilded stars studded the sides of the huge ship and several fortified sections rose from her deck, each with battlements like a miniature castle and siege weapons bristling. A seagoing fortress, thought Farwander, crewed by the population of a whole town.

A pair of smaller ships were moored nearby, looking like petty rowboats next to the enormous flagship. They were of fine and elegant design with low, sweeping lines, built to sail as swift and straight as arrows. They were unlike the ships that normally docked at Last Fathom and Farwander knew their purpose right away – outriders to range ahead of the flagship, scout ahead and ensure the path was safe

'The Lady's ship,' said Leveret matter of factly. 'The *Legacy*. Prettiest thing ever to come out of Rilesport 'cept me.' She gave Farwander a black-toothed smile.

'Lady Temnos must have brought half of Rilesport with her for a crew,' said Farwander, unable to keep from sounding impressed.

'And Corrinhelm and Tessmere too,' said Leveret. 'Most anyone what can pull a rope and don't mind dyin' for the promise of gold. Got five hundred men on the *Legacy* alone. 'Course that's not nearly as many as your granddad got drowned.'

'Great-uncle,' said Farwander.

Just down the shore was a small encampment of bivouacs and bonfires, with a few crewmen wearing the bright sashes of the Rilesport free merchant fleet worn over piecemeal leather armour. One of them saw Leveret and Farwander and waved. Leveret returned the gesture, and the crewmen dragged a rowboat towards the edge of the water.

'Just so's you know, ladies don't do no rowing,' said Leveret as she led the way down to the camp.

'And what about you?' said Farwander.

'All right, I'll give you that one. You're still rowing, though.'

The crewman walked up to Leveret. 'Heard there was some blood flowing last night,' he said. He was a tough-looking type but with an air of dim affability. He regarded Leveret with the respect of equality that Farwander knew must be earned.

'Most of it thanks to this one,' said Leveret, jerking a thumb at Farwander. 'He's got a sword that's ever so fancy.'

'So he has,' replied the crewman, looking down at the hilt of Farwander's blade. 'But does he know what to do with it?'

'Grieff'll see you good as long as the grog's not in 'im,' said Leveret by way of introduction. 'Grieff, this streak of bladderwrack calls 'imself Farwander. Gonna teach the Lady how to swordfight.'

'Best of luck to you, Farwander,' said Grieff, clutching Farwander's hand in a tight grip. 'Itchin' to know how that turns out.'

Farwander expected the *Legacy* to revert to a sensible size as he rowed across to the mooring, but as he got closer she loomed even huger until she seemed an island of the Ghost Archipelago in her own right. Leveret pointed out the two smaller ships of Lady Temnos' fleet – the *Lightning Child* under Captain Al'Harhi, and the *Wave Demon*. Farwander glimpsed their crews in their bright sashes, and occasionally the outlandish figure of a Warden on the deck.

The boat reached the *Legacy*, and the hull was like a solid cliff face rising up impossibly high. The crew let down ladders for Farwander and Leveret to clamber up to a hatch on the second deck. The inside could have been an unusually neat tenement block, divided into barracks and storerooms for hundreds of men. Racks of weapons hung at every hatch, along with massive mounted weapons like oversized crossbows that could be swung out of the hatches and loaded with javelin-sized bolts. The crew nodded salutes to Leveret as she led the way through the confusing interior, past map rooms, galleys and surgeons' quarters.

'All right, it shouldn't be complicated but just so's we're clear,' said Leveret, 'don't talk out of turn and don't act like you're her equal. Poncy name or not, she's a Heritor which you ain't. I'm the one that brought you here so if you offend her ladyship it comes back to me, and if that happens I'll string you up from the yard by your knackers.'

'Understood,' replied Farwander.

They approached a grand set of double doors that could have come from a mansion's ballroom, carved with dolphins leaping from swirling waves. Leveret banged a fist three times on the doors and pushed them open, indicating Farwander should enter without her.

Inside was a grand chamber that had no place on a ship. The high ceiling was covered in frescoes of a sunny sky with all manner of exotic beasts flying around a central sun. Ceiling-high windows looked out from the stern of the ship, giving a splendid view of the vibrant blue sea. The strains of delicate music reached Farwander's ears, emanating from the harp being played by a maiden in a green dress. She sat on a stool playing the gilded instrument from a small raised stage at one side of the hall.

Her work was being appreciated by the room's other occupant, a second woman with luxuriant dark hair piled high on her head and festooned with jewels. Her dress, voluminous and pale blue, could have graced a king's court.

Farwander took a pace forward but the gowned woman raised a hand and stopped him with a gesture. Even with her back to him, Farwander could feel the power of her presence. He had encountered just about every type of person there was, including plenty of cultured and high-born women, but even he felt his heart speeding up as if he was gazing into an abyss seething with the unknown and unpredictable.

Farwander waited until the harpist ended her song with a flourish. The listener gave her a nod, and the harpist took her leave, sweeping out past Farwander without a glance at him.

Farwander stood there for a long moment, uncertain if he should speak first. Then he remembered Leveret's warning, and did not.

The lady turned. She was handsome – not pretty, but powerful, with a strong-featured face that stood out in spite of the lavishness of her clothing and jewellery. Diamonds glittered around her throat and Farwander saw, for the first time, the slender sword that managed to look perfectly normal scabbarded at the cinched waist of her ballgown.

'What is your name?' asked Lady Temnos.

'Aldebrecht Beros Quovanticos venn Farwander,' he replied.

Lady Temnos' eyebrow flickered in faint surprise. 'Very impressive.'

'I am not in the habit of using the whole appellation, my lady.'

'Probably wise. I understand my agent recommended you for my expedition.'

'That is correct. Miss Pavine said you may have use of one such as I.'

'Then what use are you, Mister Farwander?'

CHAPTER 5

Farwander swallowed, suddenly intensely aware of his lack of standing compared to the noble-born Heritor standing in front of him. He had never had a problem extolling his own virtues – but now, it seemed the most difficult thing in the world just to speak.

'I am an expert in swordplay and its instruction,' he said through a dry mouth. 'Miss Pavine has seen the evidence of this. I am the final master of the Art of the Bittersweet Blade. The form is extinct save in me and those to whom I teach it.'

'And are you going to teach it to me?' said Lady Temnos. It was impossible to tell whether she was impressed or not.

'If it pleases your ladyship,' replied Farwander.

Lady Temnos drew her sword. It was a beautiful weapon, highly ornamented, with red and blue lacquer inlaid in its gilded basket hilt. 'Then shall we begin?'

Farwander could think of no reply save to draw his own sword. To anyone else, he would have delivered a lecture on how the sword form must first be studied in word and illustration, long before the student put his hand on the hilt of a sword. But he felt by a very strong instinct that it would not be wise to do so here.

Lady Temnos circled him slowly with the point of her blade hovering in the direction of Farwander's chest. She moved with a smooth grace, the hem of her gown sweeping the polished board of the floor.

'What are your thoughts, master of the Bittersweet Blade?' asked Lady Temnos as Farwander circled her in turn, keeping a nervous distance between them.

'Your form is excellent,' he said. 'I see a practiced poise in you. But your sword is a duelling weapon, your ladyship, for fights where there are rules and decorum. On the seas, in mortal battle, it will fail you. Only the best steel will not shatter or bend when met by even the crudest-forged blade of a heavier sword.'

'Such as yours?' asked Lady Temnos.

'I arm myself for both the flourish and the kill, my lady.'

'Then demonstrate.'

Lady Temnos moved much, much faster than Farwander had expected. She covered the distance between them in a heartbeat and it was only the ingrained reflexes of the sparring circle that brought the tip of Farwander's blade in a sharp half-circle to bat the point of her sword aside. She followed up with two sharp thrusts he ducked aside from, before aiming a cut from his own blade down at her shoulder. He would have stopped the blow a fingertip before it hit, but Lady Temnos brought her hand up and caught his sword with the hilt of her own.

She was stronger that she looked, as well as faster. A lot stronger. Most other fighters would have had the duelling blade jarred out of their hand. Instead Lady Temnos spun out of Farwander's armspan and slashed low. Farwander had to jump back in an ungainly hop.

There was a faint smile on Lady Temnos' face. She hadn't broken a sweat and her breath was steady. 'Are you going easy on me, Master Farwander?'

'I am,' said Farwander, reasoning it was unwise to lie to this woman. 'Until I know the full depth of your skill.'

'Pray cease. Fight me as you would fight any deadly foe.'

'Very well.'

Farwander lunged in, feinting high, then turned the blow low so Lady Temnos had to throw her blade in the way. The impact was stronger this time, and at a cruel angle. Her hand was thrown back, leaving her torso open. She spun to the side, thwarting his horizontal slash, but he pressed in and shoved her back with a boot to the gut.

Lady Temnos gasped, and indignation flushed across her face at such an ungentlemanly blow. It had opened up the distance Farwander needed. He put his shoulder behind his sword and thrust at her unprotected torso.

He halted the blade just before it punched through the bodice of her gown.

'That is the murder-blow,' he said. 'Through the ribs and into the heart. You have a pretty blade, my lady, and a prettier means of employing it. But it is not the way to survive a struggle to the death.'

By way of reply, Lady Temnos grabbed Farwander around the top of his sword-arm. Her grip was stronger than any he had ever felt. With a wrenching pain he was lifted off the floor and hurled across the room.

Farwander sailed clean across the room and slammed into the wall. Hs head rang off the wood panelling and white lights burst in front of his eyes. When his senses returned he was sprawled on the floor, surrounded by splintered panelling and with a hammer striking at the inside of his skull. The pain in his arm caught up with him and he could do nothing but gasp down breaths like a landed fish.

Lady Temnos slid her sword back into its scabbard. 'I need people who can fight,' she said. 'And men who can convey the majesty of the Temnos name. But above all, I need men and women who understand their limitations. Your swordsmanship is excellent and is indeed far beyond mine. But if you come to fight a Heritor, Master Farwander, you will die. No matter how fine your bladework, how dashing your smile, how honeyed your words, you will die. You come to me as a teacher, but that is my lesson to you.'

Farwander got painfully to his feet. Every muscle and bone seemed bruised at once. He noticed Lady Temnos wiping her hand across her face, and glimpsed a flash of crimson. She was bleeding from the nose. Her burst of strength had not been without its price.

'Unless you are in the habit of murdering your own men,' said Farwander, 'I take it you are warning me about another Heritor?'

Lady Temnos regarded the blood smeared on her knuckles. She gave him an unguarded look, suddenly vulnerable, before the veneer of the invincible lady returned. 'Have you heard the name of Lord Hekatar?' she said.

'I have not.' Farwander picked his sword up off the floor and scabbarded it.

'But you know of the Cult of Scaraveyla.'

'I have had the misfortune of their company. Miss Pavine and I encountered them in Cape Cadaver.'

'Then you know they have an interest in my expedition. They are testing my defences and my resolve. The word upon the waves is that Lord Hekatar has united them under his command. He is a Heritor from the mountain kingdoms of Zharn, far to the west of our lands. Some say his ancestor Silvanta Hex drank of the Crystal Pool beside Arcturaval Temnos, who founded my own line. But they do not say it in my earshot.'

'Do you know what this Hekatar wants with you, my lady?'

'He is after the same prize as I,' replied Lady Temnos.

'May I ask what that is?'

'The fewer who know that, Master Farwander, the better.' She looked him up and down as if seeing him for the first time. 'Are you hurt?'

'Nothing I cannot walk off, my lady.'

'Good. Pavine will assign you to a ship. If the Brotherhood of Scaraveyla are making their move against us, we must set sail sooner than I intended.'

'What will my duties be?' asked Farwander.

'Teach me the way of the Bittersweet Blade,' replied Lady Temnos. 'Is that not why you are here?'

'Very well, my lady,' said Farwander. The aching in his ribs was catching up to him, and it hurt him to give her the small bow that was required.

'Then go,' said Lady Temnos. 'I am minded towards music until we depart.'

CHAPTER 6

Leveret put Farwander on the *Wave Demon*. Captain Hakespure helmed her, along with a crew he had taken on missions of subterfuge and smuggling for just about every kingdom with a coastline. Over the years Hakespure had lost his best men to combat, accident, disease and desertion, and Farwander was the kind of fighting man he needed to shore up his ship's capacity to survive any misadventure.

The ship was shaped like a slender knife that cut through the waves, driven by her trio of triangular sails. The ballista on her prow was mounted over a figurehead shaped like a grinning devil, its teeth bared against the salt spray. Her hull was painted with stormy clouds, and the winged dark figures that wheeled through them. When Lady Temnos' fleet set off from the environs of Cape Cadaver, the *Wave Demon* was in the vanguard, slicing ahead of a light wind away from the island and into the misty stretches of ocean between the islands.

Captain Hakespure leaned against the stern deck rail, watching the masts of the rest of the fleet scattered across the horizon behind them. 'You know where we're going, Farwander?' he asked.

'Only that it's somewhere else in the Ghosts,' replied

Farwander. He had the same duties as the rest of the *Wave Demon*'s small complement of fighting men – nothing so strenuous as climbing the rigging or hauling the wheel, in return for being the first in the way of injury and death when swords were drawn. He had the leisure to spend time on deck with the captain, who was a man he had instantly decided to like.

'Penitent's Landing,' said the captain. He was an older man than usually served aboard, which meant he was good at his job because the sea had not managed to claim his life or too many limbs over the decades. He had grey hair tied back under a bicorne hat and wore the fanciful well-worn velvets and brocade of a man whose image was well beyond his means. 'Word is, the first Heritors found and mapped it, excepting the interior. There's a volcano residing in its midmost parts and there it is your treasure will be found a-languishing.'

'A volcano?'

'Aye, lad, fountain of the earth's liquid fury! Quite a thing to behold, they say, when it's in its awakening. And still awake it is, or was when last mortal eyes espied it.'

'What does Lady Temnos want there?'

Hakespure smiled at that. His well-worn face creased easily around the eyes and mouth. 'Now that's approximating to the question, isn't it? There are plenty of words upon the spray about that very matter's particularities. Just what her ladyship's after depends on what you happen to be believing.'

'And what do you believe?'

'Land ho!' came a cry from the crow's nest on the

middle mast. Hakespure took out his spyglass, an item as well-used as he was, and peered in the direction of the lookout's outstretched arm. Farwander could just make out a grimy smudge through the gauzy mists hanging around the horizon to port.

'It's Dead Lizard Point,' said the ship's navigator, a burly and blunt woman named Gavel. She had a couple of rolls of parchment under her arm, covered in inky scratches. Like most of the ship's crew she wore a piecemeal of clothing from the various ports and kingdoms the ship had visited, buckled together with segments of battered leather armour. 'We're further west than I anticipated.'

'Will that be becoming a problem, Miss Gavel?' asked the captain.

"Course it's not a bloody problem, you salty old trout,' she replied. 'We're on course. Just need to swing a few minutes eastwards. You think I don't know one end of my compasses from another?'

'Instruct the wheel, Miss Gavel,' said Hakespure.

'Thinks it's a problem, the bilious eel,' muttered Gavel as she headed to the helm where two muscular crew handled the ship's wheel. 'Thinks I got no more sense than seaweed.'

'That woman,' said Hakespure to himself as Gavel started berating the men at the wheel. 'Gods, but I love her.'

The ship's rigging jangled as the *Wave Demon* turned a few degrees. Farwander felt the wind through his hair – it had a damp chill to it, as the ship headed towards waters more deeply wreathed in the mists ahead of them. One minute the archipelago's islands were bathed in tropical sun, the next they were isolated by walls of dense sea mist. The weather itself here was unnatural, like everything else – the vivid greens of the jungle, the baffling power games of the Heritors, the madmen who worshipped its shipwrecking goddess.

'What's in the volcano?' asked Farwander.

'The who the what now? Ah, yes, the volcano. Mount Golca is how she's appellated. Like I was intimating, there's plenty of treasures folks say are incumbent within, but there's one that I find most veridical of them all.'

'And that is?' Farwander had learned within the first moments of their acquaintance to show patience when talking to the old captain.

'A vessel,' said Hakespure. 'An urn. A pitcher, if you will. Amphora, maybe. And within this vessel are waters drawn from the Crystal Pool. Mystically maintained from the fate of evaporation, they are, and within them is all the thaumaturgical wonder of the pool itself. With its possession, one could recreate the magic of the Crystal Pool. Lord Arcturaval set it there, or wrote down its location, and bequeathified its location to his family line. Lady Temnos wants to patriate it in her own domicile, and with a Crystal Pool of her very own become the most powerful soul in this world or any other.' He turned to Farwander with a waggle of the eyebrow. 'Now that's worth hiring even a barnacled haddock like myself, wouldn't you concur?'

'Worth dying for,' agreed Farwander. 'Definitely worth watching other people die for. And Hekatar's after it as well?'

'Mayhap he is,' said Hakespure. 'Perchance he's just on the assumption Lady Temnos must be after something worthwhile, and wants to weaken her before ambuscading her prize right from under her ladylike rump.'

Dead Lizard Point slid past over the horizon and the mists closed in. The crew struck the fore and aft sails as the fleet slowed down to pick its way through the gloom, and Lady Temnos' expedition plunged deeper into the heart of the Ghost Archipelago.

* * *

They put in at a tiny uninhabited island with a freshwater spring, so parties of men could land and draw off caskets of drinking water. It was the fifth day, making slow progress through the mist-shrouded maze of the Archipelago. Gavel had worked from charts older than most of the crew's family names, sketching additions and changes as she went, while every eye on the ship peered into the mists for a sandbank or rocky shoal just under the surface. The crew's job was one of the most important in the fleet – If the way ahead was dangerous, the *Legacy's* only warning would be the flags of the *Wave Demon* flashing red and black.

Flag signs from the *Legacy* had commanded that Farwander report to Lady Temnos while the fleet was temporarily at anchor. A launch had taken him across to the immense ship, where Lady Temnos' flag-captain had waved him down to a chamber concealed deep in the heart of the ship.

Lady Temnos was waiting for him. She had dispensed with the ballgown but looked no less splendid in a tight bodice of emerald green and dark leather britches. Her hair was tied back, her face more open.

'My lady, said Farwander with a bow. 'I see you have taken a more suitable weapon.'

'Less fitting to my station,' replied Lady Temnos. 'But practicalities must force our hand when at sea.' She drew the sword she now wore – a blade a little shorter than Farwander's own but of clearly superior make, with ripples through the steel indicating dozens or hundreds of foldings and a crossbar edged in gold. 'Shall we?' she asked.

'Very well. Your first lesson, my lady, shall be on the very nature of the Bittersweet Blade. The philosophy behind it. It was many weeks before my mentor permitted me to touch a blade, though I expect you to be a rather more attentive pupil than I. The first skill I had to master was patience, and a harder lesson I have never learned. But for our purposes, it should suffice to speak to you of what we mean to achieve with this sword form.'

Farwander's words flowed smoothly, for which he was grateful. He was tongue-tied while in Lady Temnos' presence on every subject save swordplay, in which he was so well-versed he could simply reel out the words with which he had been lectured many times.

'We wish to defeat our enemies and protect our lives,' replied Lady Temnos.

'Quite so, my lady. But that is not so easily comprehended a task as it might seem. Take, for example, the murder-stroke. This is an ugly thing, is it not? It means the mutilation of flesh and bone. Injury and death. A man might void his guts, or his bowels, upon receiving it, he might cry out and whimper like a child. It is no little thing to speak to a lady of such matters, but that is what we are discussing. Death, and the means of inflicting it.'

Lady Temnos, thankfully, did not flinch at the mention of swordplay's uglier side. If she had, there would have been little Farwander could hope to teach her.

'So,' he continued, 'this art begins not with the guard or the posture, as most schools would have it. It starts with the kill. Remain still for a moment.'

Lady Temnos stood unmoving as Farwander stood close to her and drew his sword. He held the blade up close to the side of her right temple. 'A fracture to the skull,' he said. 'Bleeding in the brain. Unconsciousness, from which one never wakes.' He moved the blade down to just beneath her jawbone. 'A cut to the jugular, here, or the artery, here. Or the fracture of the cartilaginous material in the throat, or severing of the windpipe. Exsanguination or asphyxiation.' Next, the blade wavered close to the angle of the jaw just beneath the ear. 'Fracture of the jawbone and driving of the bone into the brain.'

Lady Temnos, again, did not move or flinch. She understood matters of death, then. It might have come from experience in her life. Others were simply born with that understanding. Some could never gain it, no matter how much they were instructed or immersed in death. Thankfully, Lady Temnos was clearly not one of them.

He held the flat of the blade against her arm. 'Deep cut to the artery in the upper arm,' he said. 'Exsanguination and...'

'Not I,' said Lady Temnos. 'I am a Heritor. Unless death is instantaneous, it does not come to us.'

'But it will come to your enemies,' continued Farwander. 'And even if a wound is not lethal, if it causes so much as a second's incapacitation, it can be parlayed into a wound that most certainly is. I say this not to counter your statement and maintain my status as teacher over my pupil. It is because I have seen it, my lady.'

'I am well aware, Master Farwander, that I have asked you to teach me how to kill. This needs no explanation.'

'Could you kill Hekatar, if you were to face him? Here, as you face me?'

Lady Temnos' expression shifted, and for a moment, Farwander saw a weakness in her, her true self hidden behind the raw power and presence of a Heritor. 'I do not know,' she said.

'Then I will show you. Lesson one!' He stepped back from her and cut a flourish in the air with his sword. 'A thrust to the heart is a picturesque way to kill a man. But the heart is protected by the ribcage, and by whatever armour your enemy chooses to clad about himself. A heart-strike will kill, yes – it will kill you, as your blade misses, or strikes a breastplate of steel, and you are left open to his vengeance. A cut to the neck that decapitates is a heroic and savage victory, but it is one every man who holds a sword will fear and guard against. Any blow that incapacitates and kills will suffice, be it the ugliest pommel-bash or foot to the groin. The Bittersweet Blade is an art of beauty, precisely because it makes possible this final ugliness.

'Lesson two! No man dies instantly. He can have his head struck off, his heart torn out, his belly slit, and still he will have motion in his limbs for far longer than required to kill you in return. The Bittersweet Blade is about the infliction of death. It is not achieved until that death has occurred. Grace in conduct and movement, ruthlessness in execution. Finish the kill.

'That said, there are three hundred murder-blows the art teaches. You need not know them all, just those that will be most visible to you in the heat of combat. I have mentioned a few, but there are others. The bloodletting of the thigh, the knee or boot heel to the small of the back, the pommel to the rear of the skull, the...'

'Wait,' said Lady Temnos, holding up a hand.

A few seconds later, Farwander heard it too – commotion on the decks above, raised voices and the pounding of feet. Lady Temnos, still with her sword in hand, ran out of the sparring room and halted one of the crewmen running past with a glare.

'Beast in the water,' said the crewman. 'Captain's called all hands to fend her off.'

Farwander followed Lady Temnos as she ran for the stairs leading to the top deck. He emerged into the misty air to see dozens of marines and sailors wielding cutlasses and boarding pikes, crowding against the port side of the ship.

'Watch yourselves! There she breaches!' cried a voice, and a roar of sucking, churning water was followed by a wave of stench like a whole fish market left in a week of sun. Men scattered as an enormous tentacle, scarred and pitted, loomed over the deck rail. In a shower of brine it slammed down against the deck with a splintering of wood and a cacophony of alarm.

The creature to which the tentacle belonged was truly immense, to menace a ship the size of the *Legacy*. The tentacle withdrew and its spiny scales ripped deep gouges in the deck. It took men with it, leaving pools of blood and seawater behind.

The whole ship lurched under the weight of the assault. Farwander grabbed the nearby mast to steady himself. Ropes snapped and wood splintered.

'Break out the crossbows!' yelled Lady Temnos. 'Man the port ballistae!'

Farwander had listened to tales of such beasts that lurked in the lightless depths of exotic oceans. He had heard drunken men claiming to have seen them, or to know of someone who had been dragged into the sea by such a monstrosity. But this was the first time he had ever seen one – or smelled one – in the flesh. As two more tentacles unfurled above the deck rail, casting a shadow across the width of the ship, he could only marvel at the scale of it. He had thought the *Legacy* herself would be the most remarkable sight he would see in the Ghost Archipelago. Now he realised he had only begun to glimpse what this region had waiting for him.

One tentacle wrapped around a mid-mast. The mast bowed and creaked, and a crewman shaken loose from the rigging thumped wetly onto the deck beside Farwander. The second tentacle lurched out over the deck, sweeping just below head height. Farwander had to duck to keep his head being taken off by the mass of gristle and scale that swung like a yacht's boom across the ship.

The tentacle withdrew, coiling up and then reaching down with the tip as if probing for a morsel to scoop up. It reached towards Farwander, who with more of an instinct than a plan slashed at it with his sword. The keen blade sliced through briny muscle and cut off the tip of the tentacle, releasing a flood of dark grey foulness that spilled onto the deck planks around him.

The tentacle recoiled and Farwander ran for the stern of the ship, further from the kraken's assault. Other crewmen were trying to lever the first tentacle off the mast with boarding pikes and axes. Lady Temnos was up by the wheel on the quarterdeck, ordering men to take up position with crossbows ready to fire. Also at the back of the ship was a figure Farwander recognised as the expedition's Warden, Karanas, a red-haired and bearded man in a garment of grimy dark green with powerfully muscled forearms.

'Do they come in close to ships at anchor like this?' asked Farwander as the ship rocked again.

Karanas glared at him. 'What does it matter, laddie? This one has.'

'But is it normal?'

'Who can know the mind of the beastie? Hungry or wounded, perhaps, to seek prey on the surface.' Karanas turned towards the sea and raised his arms. From the ocean rose a trio of tide-smoothed rocks, answering the call of the Earth Warden. With a snarl and a grunt, Karanas clenched his fists and the rocks spun across the deck, slamming wetly into another tentacle trying to find purchase on the deck.

'We need to launch a boat,' said Farwander.

'You taking leave of your senses, ye fairdegook? This'n will swallow ye down!'

'Lady Temnos!' shouted Farwander. 'I need six men, good rowers, and send the launch down.'

The kraken lurched higher this time, the hulk of its body slamming into the side and shuddering the masts. A few men fired crossbows down at its body.

'Go!' shouted Lady Temnos. 'You men, make yourselves useful! Launch the boat and be quick!'

Farwander and a gaggle of crewmen swung one of the ship's launches over the side of the deck that was not being menaced by the kraken. He jumped into the boat and it juddered its way down to the churning water, gripping the side of the boat as the ropes swung it out and battered it against the hull again. The boat all but fell the last deck or so, hitting the water with a splash.

Farwander looked over the faces of the men Lady Temnos had sent with him. They looked steady enough, though none too happy about suddenly finding themselves outside the relative safety of the *Legacy*.

'Get us to the island,' said Farwander.

One of the crewmen, a heavily weathered man with a brutal scar over one of his eyes, glared at him. 'You thinkin' to run?'

'No, I'm thinking to save the bloody ship. It's not a coincidence this thing found us here. Someone sent it. Get us to the island.'

The men rowed through the foaming sea for the small uninhabited island where the expedition had taken on fresh water. The boat rounded the stern and Farwander saw the full mass of the kraken for the first time. He was almost unable to haul on his own oar – it was a battle to do anything but gawp at the creature.

It was something like an octopus of astonishing size, its hide grizzled and scarred in a way that signified immense age. It had tentacles seemingly without number, loops of them breaking the surface of the sea or groping at the side of the *Legacy*. An immense, milky eye, with an hourglass-shaped pupil, stared from one side of the beast's corrupted mass.

'Thank the gods it's got a bigger meal in front of it,' said the scar-faced crewman. 'We'd make a dainty morsel.'

'Speak for yourself,' said another man, this one portly and blustering. 'I'd intend to give the beggar indigestion.'

The kraken lurched up further out of the ocean. It revealed the pinkish mass of its maw, a huge sucking cavity ringed with sabre-length teeth. A volley of crossbow bolts rained down at it, aiming for the mouth and eyes. Though the sea foamed foully around it with the kraken's blood, it was impossible to tell if the crossbow fire was doing anything to discourage it. In places the hull of the *Legacy* had been laid open, leaving the inner decks open to the air and sea where the tentacles had ripped away at the wood.

The boat made decent speed towards the island. It was little more than a large outcrop of rock in the ocean, with a raised section in the middle supporting a hardy spray of trees. As soon as rocks scraped against the bottom of the boat, Farwander vaulted the side and forged through the chest-deep water on uncertain footing.

The small party reached dry land, eager to get out of the water even though the kraken was some distance from them.

'What we here for?' asked Scar-face.

As if in reply, an arrow speared from between the island's trees and impaled one of the crew through the thigh. The man yelped and fell back into the water. Another man grabbed him under the arms and hauled him towards the uneven shore.

'Right, you buggers!' yelled Scar-face, waving a billhook. 'I'll shove this up yer fundament, so I will!'

The crewmen of the *Legacy* were an ordered and disciplined lot, at least by the standard of the sailors common to Last Fathom, but when Lady Temnos was not there to give them orders they were quick to anger and fight. They leapt out of the ocean with weapons drawn, rushing to get to grips with an unseen enemy. Farwander went in their wake as another of them fell, this time with an arrow through the biceps.

He saw movement through the trees. Men were waiting for them. The island was not as uninhabited as it seemed – but their enemy here had not taken the easy prey, the parties who came to the island for water. Instead they had stayed concealed until now, when they could hit the whole fleet the hardest.

Scar-face dived into the small, seablown forest. The sound of steel on steel came from between the trees. Farwander followed, catching sight of a face – scarred, mutilated – scowling at him down the length of an arrow.

Farwander dived painfully to the rocky ground and rolled as the arrow whistled over him. He came up running and dived right at the enemy, bringing his sword down over his head.

The forest parted before him. He was suddenly face to face with the too-familiar sight of a Brother of Scaraveyla, stripped to the waist to display the tentacled scars covering his body. The cultist had dropped his bow and was drawing a long-bladed dagger.

Farwander lunged at the man, an uneducated, crude blow but one warranted by the sudden closeness and fury of the encounter. The cultist slapped the blade aside, incurring a deep and ugly wound along the forearm as he did so, coming at Farwander with his dagger held point-down to stab into his upper chest.

Farwander was ready. The obvious kill rarely worked. He used the cultist's eagerness to close to his advantage, and snapped his forehead into the cultist's face. He felt the gristle of the nose crunching and for a moment the cultist was rendered reeling and insensible by the blow to the nose. White sparks burst in front of Farwander's eyes with the impact but he still followed up, driving the blade upwards under the cultist's jaw.

The point speared up through the top of the cultist's throat and up again through his palette. Farwander's sword pierced the base of the cultist's brain and he died on the spot, his limbs falling limp as if he were a marionette with the strings cut. Farwander lowered the blade and let the body slip off it, and he glanced around to take stock of his situation.

Half a dozen cultists were battling the crewmen from the *Legacy*, the fight close and bloody among the trees. Farwander slashed at a cultist who came at him, felt the bite of his sword into muscle and let the man barrel past him into the other crewmen. He forged through the trees, emerging on the other side of the small stand to see the far shore of the island.

There, sitting half-immersed in the freshwater stream that the Legacy's crew had collected water from earlier, was his quarry. It was another cultist, but it was not one of the madmen the cult despatched solely to kill.

This one had several extra arms sewn onto his bare torso. Each arm clutched blindly in imitation of the groping limbs of an octopus. The cultist's flesh, scarified with the suckered coils of the Kraken Queen, glistened with blood from the many shallow cuts he had opened up to turn the water around him a slick pink. He sat in an attitude of meditation, with what could be understood of his scarred face being locked in an expression of great effort and concentration.

Farwander was looking at a Warden, but not like the ones in Lady Temnos' fleet or on board the *Salted Swine*. It was a worker of Scaraveyla's magic, the same magic that had drawn the kraken to this tiny island and set it upon the fleet.

It was no coincidence the beast had gone straight for the *Legacy*. Something had summoned it from the deeps using magic like that of the Wardens. Add in the Brotherhood's interest in Lady Temnos' quest, and it had seemed inevitable they would be found nearby.

The cultist turned to face Farwander. His extra limbs unfurled around him like the fronds of an anemone. The cultist smiled, showing teeth filed to points like those of a shark. 'Have you come for the dark and quiet?' he said calmly. 'To sink into the Oblivion Deeps?'

Farwander's answer was a long horizontal slash right at the cultist warden's shoulder. The warden put up a couple of his extra hands and Farwander's sword sliced through two of them. The severed hands splashed into the waters of the spring. Three more hands reached at Farwander, grabbing him by his left arm and shoulder, reeling him in closer to the Warden.

Farwander had fought men of every size and shape, but never one with more than two arms. He fought to wrest his blade free from the hands grabbing at his sword arm. The cultist grinned, his face inches from his, and placed one of his original hands on Farwander's forehead.

Farwander felt a tightness in his chest. He coughed and tasted acrid salt water in his mouth.

'Breathe deep of her brine,' hissed the cult warden. Farwander fought to get free even as his lungs screamed out for air and he felt them filling up with seawater.

It was magic. A Warden's trick. Farwander knew everything about bladework, but nothing about defeating an opponent who could alter the rules of reality around him.

Panicking, he kicked out at the front of the cultist's knee. It was an old, ingrained reaction, as drilled into him by an old instructor. Amateurs forget to focus on their footwork and left their legs open to attack. A good hit to the knee, meanwhile, would end a fight instantly. Farwander's fear gave him strength and the cultist's knee buckled. The warden dropped onto his ruined knee, dragging Farwander down with him, into the foaming pink stream.

The grip on Farwander relaxed momentarily. He ripped his sword arm free and lashed out with a crude slash, down at the flailing cultist.

The blade hit one of the cultist's original arms. With the judder of shattering bone, the blow took the arm clean off. The cultist cried out and lost his grip entirely. Farwander groped at the edge of the stream and his hand closed on a large rough stone. He brought it around in an arc that smacked the stone into the side of the cultist's skull. The cultist slumped against the bank of the stream with blood pumping from the stump of his severed arm.

Farwander's stomach and chest convulsed. With a heave, he threw up a stream of bilious seawater from his lungs, coughing and spluttering as it poured out of him. He felt hands grabbing him to steady him as the crewmen rushed from the trees to help him, before his vision turned white at the edges.

Then, his body still racked with spasms, he didn't think anything at all.

* * *

'You nearly drowned,' said the voice. It was dry and scratchy, like straw ready for burning.

Farwander forced his eyes open. His throat was raw but at least he could draw breath.

He was looking up at the surgeon on the *Legacy*, a skeletal and desiccated soul who called himself Doctor Trass. Trass' surgery was a small cabin near the prow, with two large trestle tables and an ominous array of saws and blades hanging on the walls. Trass wore a long leather apron uncomfortably reminiscent of Big Marga's crew of butchers back in Last Fathom. His small round spectacles were clamped to his nose by wire and his mouth was hidden behind distinguished grey whiskers.

'I've seen plenty of near-drownings,' continued Trass, 'but never in a man who never went into the water.'

'What of the Warden?' rasped Farwander. His throat felt like someone had packed it with gravel.

'Alive,' replied Trass. 'Some of my best work, I must say, not that I'm happy to see it go to waste on a soul such as that.'

'And the beast?'

'Slunk back beneath the waves,' replied the surgeon. 'Not for me to say if it was a maw full of crossbow bolts or your knocking out the Warden that's to thank for that. The *Legacy* has lost some of her looks but she's still seaworthy.'

'How many men did we lose?'

'Twelve,' replied Trass simply.

Farwander sat up. He ached all over, but he didn't feel any serious injuries. He was still wearing the clothes in which he had ventured onto the island – they had once been fine, at least by Last Fathom's standards, but now they were grey and ragged. 'Where is he?'

'Awaiting her ladyship's pleasure in the brig.'

'Is he guarded?'

'Of course he is. It was a demon's own work to keep the men from stringing him up. Her Ladyship had to threaten a round of whippings to see him safe into the brig.'

'I need to talk to him.'

'Same thing her ladyship said. If you hurry, you might get there before she throttles the beggar.'

Farwander stretched experimentally. His spine creaked and cracked and his ribs complained as he tried a deep breath. 'Are you sure I shouldn't... I don't know... rest?'

Trass shrugged. 'Probably. Would that stop you taking your leave from my surgery?'

'Probably not.'

'Then off you go. Be quick about it, I may have need of the bed.'

* * *

The cultist was held in a cell down by the bilge, in a block of cells fronted by bars. A ship the size of the *Legacy* could never be completely watertight and seawater dribbled in through the hull to gather here, at the level of the keel, forming a grey layer of standing water that bred stench and chill. It served both to remind the prisoners of the lowliness of their situation, and to inform them bluntly that if the ship took on water in haste, they would be the first to drown.

Lady Temnos was already there, perched on a stool to save her from the rank bilgewater. Three sturdy crewmen were down there with her, in case the prisoner somehow gained the power to meld through the bars of his cell – although, Farwander reflected, for all he knew the magic-wielding cultist could do exactly that.

Lady Temnos beckoned Farwander over as he made his way down the tight stairway into the brig. 'He hasn't spoken,' she said quietly. 'So far I have employed only words. I intended to keep this ladylike for as long as possible.'

'Very laudable,' said Farwander.

'And not very effective. I understand it was you who brought this flotsam in?'

'I was not alone. But for the men who went with me, I would not have left that island, much less with a captive.'

'Humility ill suits you, Master Farwander.'

Farwander couldn't tell if she was joking. He looked into the cell beside her. At the back of the cell, sitting in the filmy grey bilgewater, was the cultist Warden. He was a sorry sight. He was not a small man, but huddled in the corner of the cell he seemed ready to shrivel up and vanish. He still had three arms and the stumps of several more sewn onto his heavily scarred torso. The stump of the real arm Farwander had severed was bound up with bandages already stained brown-black with blood. One side of his face was swollen and red from Farwander's crude but effective attack with the rock. It seemed his additional arms no longer had the power to move independently, for they hung limp and dead. From the smell, they had just started to decay.

The Warden's scars were deeper and more built up than on any Brother of Scaraveyla Farwander had seen. They must have been the result of repeated, agonising scarifications, creating intricate, tight ridges of scar tissue picking out the coils and suckers of the kraken. The face he had originally possessed was lost in those coils, as if the kraken had almost finished devouring him.

'You,' said the cultist. His voice was a painful croak. 'You owe me several arms.'

'You owe me several crew,' replied Farwander.

The cultist smiled, flashing his stained shark's teeth. 'You have plenty more of those.'

Farwander was aware of Lady Temnos suddenly being very attentive. She hadn't got the cultist to speak, but he spoke to Farwander unbidden. It was on the cultist's terms, but it was still more than silence.

'So let's start with the basics,' said Farwander. 'What are you?'

'The living will of the Kraken Queen.'

Farwander raised an eyebrow. 'A little cryptic, but it's something. You're a Warden. A magic worker.'

'No, dryfoot. I am not like the Wardens you know. They eke out the grudging favour of the elements and believe they are like gods. I am the conduit through which the Kraken Queen creates the end of your world.'

'So you're a prophet of Scaraveyla?'

The cultist spat into the water. 'Speak not her name.'

'Very well. You're a prophet of the salty Bitch-Queen?'

The cultist sprang to his feet and his remaining hand grabbed one of the bars of the door. 'A prophet? No. A weapon? Yes. But the prophet would suck your mind out through your nose, you mewling whelp!'

'Maybe I should meet him, and see if he's good for it.'

'You will. You all will.'

'Should I tell him you said hello?'

'Tell him you pledge yourself to the Kraken Queen, and maybe he will make it quick.'

'And to whom should I address this plea?'

'Hekatar!' shouted the cultist. There was brine and rotting seaweed on his breath.

'And why does he want Lady Temnos' fleet destroyed?'

The cultist's breath hitched and he backed away from the bars. 'He keeps his secrets. They are not mine to speak. I am a tool in his hand.'

'That you certainly are,' said Farwander. 'And it was Hekatar who ordered you to call forth the kraken that attacked us.'

'To test your resolve, dryfoot. You still sail, but you fear us. My work is done. I have done my duty to my Queen and my prophet.'

'That would explain why I hear no brothers rushing to save you. No slapping of tentacles against the hull. Lord Hekatar has made his use of you and left you to rot here. Scaraveyla is done with you. They have discarded their tool.'

'Until I swim in the Oblivion Deeps. Until I see your corpses float down there, bloated and foul for the crabs to eat. I will join her in the Deeps forever. You will just be dead.'

Farwander nodded. 'Very eloquent. You learned it all by rote I take? How long before you could recite it all perfectly? I expect you even believed it in the end.'

The cultist scowled and slid down against the back wall until he was sitting in the water. 'It would make you feel victorious to keelhaul me,' he said sullenly. 'Cherish it. It is the last triumph you will ever feel.'

For a while Farwander was silent, and just left the cultist there to stew in the filthy bilgewater. Lady Temnos did not move. She knew as well as Farwander did they had to get more out of this maniac before they could call the losses to the kraken anything but in vain.

Eventually, Farwander kneeled in front of the cell. 'Or you could make me understand,' he said.

The cultist had the light of the fanatic in his eyes – he was not just mad, he was a believer. In Farwander's experience, there was nothing a fanatic loved more than explaining why he was right.

'You cannot understand,' said the cultist. 'You have never clung to a piece of driftwood for five days, and waited for death to take you. You have not seen the things she shows you. And when that hand reaches down, and tells you that you will survive, and be transformed...' The cultist looked up with the thousand-league stare Farwander knew from prisoners and the insane. 'That, you can never understand.'

'We'll see about that,' said Farwander. 'Start by telling me your name.'

'I left my name behind with my ship and my crew. There was a man once who answered to it, but he is drowned. Scaraveyla will give me a name when I have earned one.'

'You said she showed you things. What did you see?'

The cultist took in a deep breath and leaned back against the cell wall, like a storyteller about to embark upon a grand tale. 'Imagine... imagine a thousand thousand souls. All men and women, all of them with dreams, loved ones, pasts and futures, all of that encompassed in one anguished face when it all ended. All those drowners, all crying out in sorrow for what they have lost. And you can see them all at once, as if they were the grains of sand on a beach but you can make out every single one in all its details.

'Now, among all those poor dead fools, there is just one who rises out of them. He is carried aloft by the currents rising up from the very deepest trenches of the ocean floor. Because alone among them, he is the one who can offer proper gratitude to the one who saved him. A single grain of sand on that beach, chosen out of all of them. Now, imagine that one lone soul... is you.'

Farwander knew better than to interrupt. The cultist had waited years to give his sermon and he wasn't going to rob him of that chance now.

'And then that vanishes, and you see something else. You see where those other drowners are going. The Oblivion Deeps. The silt drifts down over layers of the dead. The creatures of the ocean bed make their lairs in the broken hulls of sunken ships, and become huge and hungry. All the life down there finds its root in the bloated flesh of those that drown and sink. To them, it's hell.

'But to you, who was chosen, it is beautiful, because you can see what it really is. All that death gives rise to life, and that life lives on in us. And you see Scaraveyla watching over it all, not the demon or the tyrant the drowners see, but our queen, our mother. They see her monstrous. We see her beautiful.' The cultist's face took on a dreamy cast like a man drugged into a stupor.

'And did she show the same thing to Hekatar?' said Farwander, eager not to lose the cultist to his delirious memories.

'No, the prophet was never wrecked,' replied the cultist. 'The Kraken Queen chose him. He sent so many souls into the Oblivion Deeps that she heard his name on their lips, and she sent all the beasts of the sea to find him. They found him by following the trail he left. Men he took alive he cut to pieces and threw to the sharks. His wake was a red streak bobbing with human chum. The tentacled beasts followed it and came to his ship, and his crew quaked at the sight of them. But not Hekatar. He knew they were there to pay their respects, because he was a terror of the seas just like them.'

'And then?' Farwander was loath to interrupt, but if the cultist went off on a tangent he might never be brought back.

'Scaraveyla called her down to him and he dived into the ocean. He swam to the Oblivion Deeps and spoke to her face to face. Men who saw her went mad, but not Hekatar. She told him he was her prophet, for he was a man who was like unto a kraken himself. When he rose up from the Oblivion Deeps he was her herald on the surface, a giant of a man with the strength of a hundred. She gifted him a fleet and an entourage of ocean beasts to move as her hand across the waters. All those she had saved could sense him like the taste of blood in the water and in a great shoal we went to him. And now, we sail.'

'What does Hekatar want with Lady Temnos?'

The cultist smiled again, revealing those teeth filed to predatory points. 'To drown her,' said the cultist. 'To drown you all.'

Farwander followed Lady Temnos back to the upper decks. It was relief to leave the reek of the bilge behind.

'This Hekatar calls himself a prophet,' said Lady Temnos. 'I prefer enemies who at least believe they are human.'

'Is a Heritor so different from a prophet?' asked Farwander, and Lady Temnos' glare instantly caused him to regret it.

'I do not claim a god speaks to me,' she retorted. 'What I do, I do for myself. In this I am honest. No deity puppets me to some destiny.'

'Glad to hear it, but as loyal as your crew are to you, my lady, they are not fanatics. If that wretch is any evidence, the Brotherhood will walk to their deaths for Lord Hekatar if they believe he is the vessel of their god. And they are working with more than faith alone. He called forth the kraken. They at least have the arts of the Wardens at their disposal.'

'I am not ignorant of any of this, Master Farwander.'

'My apologies. I fear the Brotherhood of Scaraveyla, my lady. I do not admit that lightly, but they scare me. My forthrightness is driven by my concern for the safety of this fleet.'

'You have the luxury of fear. I do not. The fleet must weigh anchor the moment our hull is shored up. The Brotherhood know where we are and I would stay ahead of them. Return to the *Wave Demon* and tell Captain Hakespure he will need to pick up the pace. Reckless speed is less perilous to us now than falling behind.'

'Those are your orders?'

'They are.'

'Then before I leave, may I ask what you intend to do with the prisoner?'

'It is best as few know as possible. Rumours spread.'

'I understand.'

'Then get to your duties, Master Farwander.'

CHAPTER 7

The Ghost Archipelago changed. Lush jungle islands were replaced by barren outposts covered in death. Then those, too, faded away into the mists and the islands formed soaring mesas of sheer cliffs, topped with unattainable jungle like a verdant crown. Arches too elegant to have been carved by the waves rose and fell beneath the surface. Treacherous banks of coral and rock formed labyrinths that forced the *Wave Demon* to pick its way ahead, dropping markers to lead the fleet around the deadliest waters.

'I was cogitating on the men we've lost,' said Captain Hakespure one night, as he walked the deck and Farwander was helping keep watch. The mists had rolled back and the unfamiliar stars were sprayed across a clear sky.

'I didn't think we'd start losing them so soon,' said Farwander.

Hakespure sucked on his teeth in a way that indicated he was deep in thought. 'Them that's dead is one thing. They can be sepulchred in the deeps and words said for them, and those that are left behind make haste with the rest of their living. But those that live, they're what the Brotherhood feeds on.'

'You think we'll see them again on the Brotherhood's side?'

'Oh, I fear it, aye.' Hakespure nodded grimly. 'Men unremember what they are on the waves. Think on one stranded in a ship's boat. He's got vittles and water for a few days. Then they run out. He becomes demented from the seawater and the despairing. Perhaps he eats his brother. Don't be shocked, it's occurring, and more often than you'd allow. Afore long, he's scrambled as an albatross. Mad as a flying fish. Perhaps a kind soul finds him, brings him aboard, deposits him at a port a drivelling beggar. Sometimes it's the Brotherhood that finds him. And that poor soul becomes something terrible in their pincers, he does.'

'You seem to know a lot about it,' said Farwander.

'Well, I hears things. I've been on these here oceans a long old year, young'un, probably longer than you've been alive. I'm quite as old as I look, you know.'

Farwander couldn't help raising an eyebrow at that, since Hakespure looked like something dredged up from the seabed after a few centuries marinating in the brine. 'I'd never heard of Scaraveyla or any of this, until I arrived at the Ghosts.'

'Oh, she has different namings. Sometimes it's a man who is the storm, sometimes a great fish that'll swallow you down. Sometimes a monstrosity what's all coils and heads and such forth. Us sailors give it different names but it's much the same thing. Always a dark thing under the waves that rises up, and destroys, and promises the aeons to them what survive and obey it. She's real, this Scaraveyla. As real as the men as are plucked up off shipwrecks to join her.

Always knew I'd find her, you know. They say every old sailor does in the end.'

'"They" seem to say a lot of things,' said Farwander.

'That they do,' agreed Hakespure. 'But between yourself and mine, I don't think I'm coming back from this voyaging. Feels like the Shipwreck Queen, or whatever form she's taking, has been after me for as long as I've been on the waves.'

A long moment passed. The lookout clambered down from the crow's nest as the watch changed.

'The Brotherhood are all madmen,' said Farwander. 'I spoke with one. He was completely insane. Whoever he was once, he was changed.'

'Aren't we all madmen?' Hakespure smiled up at the sky. 'We're on a leaky tub in an ocean that doesn't exist for the better part of all time, looking for a gewgaw in a volcano. A man that writes a book, he could put that as what madness means and no one would call him wrong.'

'It's not dying out here that really frightens me,' said Farwander, looking down at the dark water sluicing past the ship's hull. 'I've been in plenty of places that told me I was going to die. I'd almost say I was used to it. But that wretch down there in the brig... he was a man, like me. He might have been anyone. Maybe kinder, smarter, better than I could ever be. Then fate decided to cut him down and drive him mad, and he became something awful.'

'You're scared that if you get marooned or adrifted,' said Hakespure, 'you could be him.'

'Boat ahoy!' Came a cry from the crow's nest. The new watchman had hardly had time to settle down into the rickety platform before he had jumped to his feet and pointed towards the port bow. Hakespure hurried to the prow, where sure enough past the horned figurehead could be seen a sliver of deeper darkness against the black waters, surrounded by flurries of foam that picked out the faint starlight.

''Tis just a canoe,' said Hakespure. 'Nothing to afear us. Bring me a lantern!'

One of the crew found a lit lantern and the captain flashed a signal to the approaching boat. It lit its own light, a burning torch held high, and as it got closer Farwander could make out the strong, blocky faces of a dozen sturdy men rowing the canoe. They were well muscled as only men who spend their life in such labour could be. Their skin was covered in black tattoos that turned large portions of their skin into abstract patterns. The man holding the torch was different – a skinny tar of a man in what had once been a simple shirt and breeches, but were long since ragged and grey. The man himself was ragged and grey as well, with an unshaven and weatherworn face.

'Hello there!' cried the man as the canoe drew alongside the *Wave Demon*. 'A surprise to see a familiar face this far out!' He pointed to one of the other men, who was standing proud of his fellow rowers. It was a giant of a fellow with more skin tattooed than not. 'Kwaylo here says to warn you!'

'Warn us of what?' demanded the captain. 'And who you be?'

'Which one you want first?'

'The second.'

'Right, well, the name's Boggins. Got myself lost on a prospecting voyage, didn't I? And these lads here picked me up and gave me employment speaking the language.'

'So them're tribal types,' said Hakespure to Farwander. 'Heard tell there were folks that domiciled on these islands already. '

'What have they been doing the last two hundred years?' asked Farwander. It was the first he had heard of the natives of the Ghost Archipelago, but then again every day brought some new startling tidbit about the formerly vanished islands.

'Expect they'd be inquiring the same of us,' replied the captain. He shouted back down to the boat. 'So what of the warning?'

The tribe's leader spoke a few rapid words to Boggins, who addressed Hakespure apologetically. 'The chief here says that even idiots who sail round his islands looking for treasure should be given forewarning of dangers hereabouts. His words, sir, not mine. I have to tell you exact, they're very particular about that.'

'I'm understanding of you, my fellow, don't be dreadful of that. So what is it that imperils us so?'

'He says the sea's gone dark to the east and north of here,' replied Boggins, relaying the words of the chief. 'Boats he sent out there have not returned. There's been no word from the islands there for more than a tenday. His people are drawing back to the forts in the hills until it passes. Word is there are ships spotted nearby, but none they recognise. Not privateers or traders like yourselves.'

'Thank his chieftainship for the warning. But I do not command this fleet, and she that does won't be turning back.'

'Then he will pray for you, even if you don't deserve it,' replied Boggins. 'He asks where you're heading.'

'Penitent's Landing!' said Hakespure. 'Environs of Mount Golca.'

'Oh, aye,' said Boggins. 'They know of it. They say there's a dragon that lives there.'

'Golca's a volcano,' said Farwander. 'Dragons and volcanoes both breathe fire.'

'Oh, so these folks are savages who think any strange thing is some monster or other?' retorted Boggins, who had far sharper hearing that Farwander had assumed. 'They know what a sodding volcano is. If they say there's a bloody great dragon there, then there is. These folks are cleverer than you or me when it comes to these islands. Heed them, sirs, or the chief here will be proven right that you're all gold-grubbing morons.' The chief spoke to Boggins for a moment, before Boggins addressed the captain again. 'He says he's got a map here to trade you.'

'A map?' said Hakespure. 'Mighty convenient.'

'When he learned us lot were back, he ordered his trackers and sailors draw up maps of the islands. He knew you'd pay through the eyes for 'em. Like I said, they're clever. Got one of the island of Mount Golca and the waters around it, if you've got the price.'

'I have a chest of gold my lady has authorised for trade,' replied Hakespure. 'She would be willing to part with it for such knowledge.'

Boggins laughed. 'These lads don't need gold. They got gold coming out of their never-minds.'

'We have two dozen crossbows,' called down Farwander.

Boggins consulted with the chief for a few moments. 'Aye,' he said at length, 'he'll take that.'

The trade took less than an hour to complete. The ship's complement of crossbows was lowered down and, after passing inspection from the chief via a few test fires, was accepted in return for a tightly bound roll of cured hide.

Navigator Gavel had by now emerged to see what the commotion was and she regarded the map with some hostility. 'What the blazes is this?' she demanded.

'The waters enveloping the environs of Mount Golca,' said Hakespure grandly.

Gavel unfurled the map as the native canoe cast off and its men began the rhythmic chant that kept their oars in time. Gavel shone the captain's lantern on the roll of hide. The map was an intricate labyrinth of inked lines and pictographs, surrounding the image of a smoking mountain.

'That'll be the volcano,' said Hakespure.

'Of course it bloody is, I'm not blind. Credit me with the sense of a lobster, would you?' Gavel cast a suspicious eye over the map. 'The western coast looks the same as what I've got. The old charts never mapped the rest of it, though.'

'Those look like warnings,' said Farwander, indicating pictographs clustered around the island's interior.

'What, all them skulls, you mean? Yes, I think you might just have had a stroke of genius there Master Farwander, have a biscuit.' She turned her critical attention back to the map. 'There's a bay on the north side. Better than trying to land on the rocks to the west. And if these here are shoals it'll do us well to keep wide of them lest the *Legacy* scrapes her big old rump on them.'

'Then providence has engrafted us with a great boon!' said Hakespure. 'A deal well made, I would proclaim!'

'Aye, don't go preening yer knickers just yet, we've got a ways to go. Right, I'll take this downside and mark 'er up. See if it matches what the last explorers mapped. 'Till then try not to hit any whales, you manxsome crab.'

Gavel stomped off back to her map room lair amidships. Hakespure watched her go admiringly. 'May just get to Mount Golca enlivened after all,' he said.

'The chief's warning sounded fairly dire,' said Farwander. 'It sounded like they know these waters. Better than us newcomers, anyway.'

'And it shall be passed on as necessitated,' said Hakespure. 'But would you wager Lady Temnos will turn her petticoats about at such a warning? We forge on, Master Farwander!'

Orders went up to get the ship on the move again. The dawn was just filtering through the misty horizon, revealing nothing for the moment but more sea.

* * *

The first sight they had of the island was the smoke. It resolved into a dark column against the veil of mists that had rolled in the day before. It reached up as high as the scattered clouds overhead, like a vast grey-black arm trying to reach through the blue of the sky. An hour later and the first ripples of land accompanied it on the horizon, clustered around the asymmetrical cone of the volcano.

The *Lightning Child* was sailing alongside the *Wave Demon* as the two ranged ahead of the flagship. Captain

Al'Harhi put up flags of alert just as the shouts came down from the *Wave Demon*'s nest that land had been sighted.

Farwander had been trying to sleep without much success when a commotion came over the ship. Every sailor rushed to the deck to see their destination. He realised in that moment just how few of them must have believed they would ever see it. The island was a myth even in the greater legend that was the Ghost Archipelago. As they peered through the morning glare to see the lopsided slopes and their grey billows of ash, the treasure that was their objective transitioned from an unlikely idea to something real. Something they could see, maybe even grasp.

Whatever that treasure actually is, thought Farwander, as he joined the crew at the prow rail.

'Looks like she's about to blow,' said one of the crew beside him. It was a man with a single large loop of gold through one ear, enough to pay for his funeral should he die during the voyage. 'Best get in and out.'

'Nah, look at all that green,' said another crewman. This one had the tip of his nose missing. 'That jungle ain't been erupted on for a long old time.'

'That just means she's been belching,' countered Gold-Ear. 'It's the ash what makes stuff grow. It's fertile, innit?'

'Yeah, like your sister,' said Noseless.

'Right, you buggers!' said Navigator Gavel, wading into the crowd of crewmen like an iceberg. 'Map says there's reefs dead ahead. Halve the sails and take us hard northward afore she scrapes her gusset!'

'How easy will it be to get to shore?' asked Farwander as Gavel stood arms folded at the rail beside him.

'Nothin' I can't handle now we've got a legible map and a half-decent sea,' replied Gavel. 'That's if His Haddockship listens to a blamed word I say.'

'Ever think you'd see Penitent's Landing for real?'

Gavel took a deep, thoughtful breath. 'Can't say that I did. Not like I was assuming we'd die out here or nothing. More like... I thought we'd sail around a few godsforsaken rocks, find nothing and head back, wiser and poorer, ready to do it all again.' She gestured towards Penitent's Landing, which was rising from the horizon as they closed. 'Didn't think we'd actually find this, like what we were looking for. Almost seems too easy.'

'You think it's been easy?' asked Farwander, thinking of the kraken lurching up from the ocean and clamping onto the *Legacy*.

'The voyage? No, you insolent squid, I don't. It's just anyone what's spent her time at sea knows not to assume everything's going to be right there where she expects it.'

'Not a comforting thing to hear from a navigator.'

'Well, aren't you in a feisty old mood, Master Farwander? I'll have you know, 'til this morn I've never once read a map drawn by someone who knew a halibut from a horizon. All "Here be dragons" and "Beware of cannibals", and a lot of drawing of whales and suchlike. Most of the time it's a miracle if they've got North in the right place.' She held up the native map. 'Now this, it's done right. Not perfect, I'll wager, and still too many little pictures. But I'll be keelhauled if it doesn't show this island where it actually is. It's enough to make a girl suspicious, is all I'm saying.'

Gavel retreated to the aft deck to berate the captain for something or other and Farwander watched the island revealed, rock by rock and tree by tree. It was easy to see how such a place could become the seat of myth. There was something about the fearsome cliffs and vibrant green of the crowning volcanic peak and the stream of grey smoke that made it look like it had been painted instead of forming naturally – a product of a portentous imagination rather than the ocean.

The *Wave Demon* and *Lightning Child* both made the turn northwards, aiming to skirt around the island and close in on its sheltered northern shore. Farwander could see Captain Al'Harhi, a dashing man with a fearsomely black beard and moustache, brandishing a curved sword as he gave the orders to his men. Both ships furled some sails to slow them down so the flagship could catch up and follow their lead.

'Now that island,' said Hakespure, taking his place beside Farwander, 'is what they call a portside girl. Looks pretty enough now but it might not be the same story when ye gets up close.'

Farwander raised an eyebrow in surprise. 'Miss Gavel hear you say that?'

'She's the one that taught it me,' chuckled Hakespure. 'Can tell this island's a dark place, as pretty as she is. I'm perceiving it in these old bones. Known it from the moment we left Cape Cadaver.'

'Then why did you follow Lady Temnos here?'

'I'm a sailor, lad. I sails. Not much else I could do when there's somewhere to be getting to and a boat needs a man captaining it, is there? Not like I can be aseated on the shore and dream of the ocean when she's right there to be plied upon.'

Farwander thought Hakespure could comfortably do exactly that, but didn't pursue the issue. 'What do you think we'll find?'

'Whoever was there first,' replied Hakespure. 'We met the native types already. Who's to say there aren't thousands of them, only a mite less friendly? Look at how winsome an isle she be. We're not the first to see her and decide she needs a good wanderin' upon, mark me well.'

'It might not be the natives we need to worry about,' said Farwander. 'We're not the only ones on these seas.'

'Aye, very true,' agreed Hakespure. 'So, Master Farwander, are you envisioning having the honorific of landing first?'

'I hadn't thought about it.'

'Lady Temnos will surely be on the first boat, lad, and she'll want you with her. She's taken an affection for you, so I hear.'

Farwander stood back from the rail, genuinely alarmed. 'From who?'

Hakespure was about to reply when the bell clanged from the crow's nest. The lookout leaned down and yelled at the top of his lungs.

'Ship ahoy! And it's not ours!'

CHAPTER 8

Farwander could see now the black masts to the south of the fleet's position, at least three or four vessels definitely not from Lady Temnos' fleet. They flew no flag and their sails seemed ragged and torn, patchworked from different colours. They were too far away to make an accurate guess at their numbers, but Farwander was certain it was a substantial fleet that had elected to give battle in the waters around Penitent's Landing.

Though the *Wave Demon* had restocked its crossbows, it was still a thinly stretched complement of arms and men that gathered on the deck. They were waiting for an inspirational speech from their captain, which Farwander realised was unlikely to be a skill prominent in Hakespure's repertoire. Before Hakespure could start burbling whatever came to his mind, Farwander stepped up onto the aft deck to address them.

'Which men among you have fought on land?' Farwander said to the gathered crew of the *Wave Demon*. 'As soldiers?' A few hands went up. 'Then let the rest look to you. You other men, follow their lead. Stay close, do not let yourself be surrounded. It is better to protect your back than to kill the enemy in front of you. Do not be proud. Stay alive first.

'If you are afraid, stay afraid. It will keep you safe. If you are brave, stay brave. It will help the men around you and strike fear into the foe. Above all, you are one. An individual will die. The whole group of us will survive. And if you get the chance, stab for the gut.'

The crew didn't seem overly inspired, but Farwander considered it a reasonable effort considering he had come up with it on the fly. Captain Hakespure seemed content with the performance.

The *Lightning Child* had a larger complement of fighting men, all marines in Captain Al'Harhi's personal employ as fearsome and flamboyant as he was. Al'Harhi was speaking to them now in a language Farwander did not know, but with an unmistakable confidence and strident tone that Farwander wished he could match.

A string of signal flags were quickly hoisted between the masts of the *Wave Demon* to warn the *Legacy* she had company on the sea. Farwander, meanwhile, observed his own ship's fighting men. They were a ragged band of tars, tough and reliable on the ocean, and they would fancy themselves in a fight – but Hakespure was not a mercenary general who taught discipline and skill to his men. Individually, they were rough and vicious. En masse, they were an eminently breakable rabble. Noseless and Gold-Ear were among the more experienced among them, along with Navigator Gavel who had emerged from her map room carrying a massive club of well-used and polished wood.

It was not much of an army.

From the opposing fleet flew a battery of black-fletched shapes that fell short of the *Wave Demon* by some distance in a flurry of foam. 'Ranging shots!' called Farwander. 'They're trying to find their bow range!'

'Your recommendings, Master Farwander?' asked Hakespure.

'We have three choices, as I see it. We close, we flee, or we stand,' said Farwander. 'If we close we'll cut down their bowshots but we could find ourselves surrounded by two or more ships. If we flee, we'll stay out of range but the *Legacy* will be defenceless. Staying is least tempting, captain. We'd just be waiting for them to make their own plan against us.'

The *Lightning Child* was unfurling her sails and turning her prow towards the opposing fleet. 'Looks like Al'Harhi has made his decision,' said Hakespure.

'Then we close,' said Farwander.

'Full ahead! Show them our prow!' ordered Hakespure. By the time the *Lightning Child* passed them the *Wave Demon* was up to speed, and the opposing ships were growing in detail as they closed.

The enemy ships looked barely seaworthy. They were hulks of black-rotted wood with sections of their hulls missing, revealing beams like broken ribs. Their sides were streaming with seaweed and barnacles. They looked like wrecks dredged up from the deeps and given motion by some magic or miracle. They seemed not to be seaborne vessels at all, but the ghosts of long-lost wrecks, like a drunken sailor's fanciful tale made real. Even their sails were too torn and full of holes to bear them ahead on a wind, but still they were approaching rapidly enough to send the water foaming up beneath their prows.

CHAPTER 8

Farwander could see three such ships close enough to make out any detail, and from the nearest another ranging volley of bowfire spattered into the sea. It was closer but ill-aimed.

Farwander's heart was thrumming in his chest. As apprehensive as he was, there was something other than panic in his heart. It wasn't excitement, because he had seen enough bloodshed to learn not to relish its approach. It was the feeling that he was back in a world he understood. The Ghost Archipelago was full of unknowns to him, from the mysterious islands themselves to the prize Lady Temnos was after. But now, staring down an enemy with a good sword in his hand, he at least felt he understood what he was doing.

Another volley swept in from the nearest hulk. Dozens of quarrels thumped into the hull and masts as the *Wave Demon*'s men ducked behind the deck rail and masts for cover.

'Steady, boys!' shouted Captain Hakespure.

'Steady yourself,' retorted Gavel. 'I'll bet gold to cats' eggs you foul yourself afore we're done.'

The ships were close enough now for Farwander to see the enemy crew. Scores of them crowded the deck of each hulk. Their skin was blistered crimson with scars. Their officers wore cloaks of scaled skin cut from some sea-beast and carried barbed scourges. Farwander's bile rose as he recognised the cultists of the Brotherhood of Scaraveyla.

Before now, he could at least have imagined they were a small band of fanatics, dangerous and mad but few in number. He could not take solace in that idea any longer.

Hundreds of the Brotherhood were crammed onto the hulks. There must have been thousands in the whole fleet. They were an army and a navy such as a small kingdom could field.

On the sails above them were embroidered crude emblems of the kraken. Each ship was a floating temple to the Shipwreck Queen, and Farwander had the absurd idea they were indeed shipwrecks sent up from the sea bed by Scaraveyla herself.

But the strangest thing was in the waters around each hulk. The sea churned not just with the rushing of the ship, but with dark, pulsing masses glimpsed through the tears in the hull. Farwander could make out the gnarled coils of a massive creature trapped there. The water foamed pink from the open wounds in its flesh.

No wonder the ships did not look seaworthy. They weren't – at least, they were incapable of staying afloat on their own. The Brotherhood's Wardens had called up beasts of the ocean and trapped them in the hulls of wrecked ships to keep them aloft and give them the motive force their sails alone could not. Farwander's guts lurched as one immense eye rolled towards him, filmy and smeared with cataracts.

The next volley of crossbow bolts was answered from the *Wave Demon*'s crew. Cultists cried out as a few bolts found their mark. One toppled over the rail of the hulk and vanished amid the blood-streaked foam. Strangled voices reached Farwander's ears, and he knew the Brotherhood were chanting the praises of the Kraken Queen even as their first blood was shed.

Farwander crouched by the deck rail, watching as the enemy hulk pulled hard to starboard to present its side to the *Wave Demon*. The cultists threw grappling hooks across the closing gulf between the ships. One hook lodged on the rail beside Farwander and he sliced through the rope with Captain Stennby's sword. A dozen more found purchase on the hull or in the rigging, and the cultists on the hulk's deck heaved on the ropes to close the gap further.

One of the cultists, a burly man with a cloak of tentacles whipping around his shoulders, jumped up onto the hulk's quarterdeck with the end of a rope in his hand. The other end was a grapple tangled in the *Wave Demon*'s rigging. He brandished a monstrous scourge of leather strips and jagged metal barbs. His face was split in two by a grotesquely widened mouth, forming a grinning maw of filed teeth like that of a shark. With a bellow, he leapt off the quarterdeck and swung across to land on the mid-deck of the *Wave Demon*.

More cultists followed their champion across the gulf between the ships. Some fell as grapples came loose or crossbow fire punched through their bodies as they swung. Others made the leap to the *Wave Demon* successfully. One thudded into the deck rail a short way along from Farwander and tried to clamber over it onto the deck. Farwander ran at him, lancing the cultist just below the solar plexus with a sword-thrust. The man fell off his sword into the churning sea, but as Farwander turned to take stock of the situation the whole *Wave Demon* was suddenly full of yelling, battling men.

It was a screaming, swirling maelstrom without battle lines, without objective except for each man to survive and kill the enemy nearest to him. Farwander parried a cutlass that swung at him out of nowhere and booted the charging cultist in the chest, opening up enough space to cut him down with a slash across the belly. The cultist screamed and fell back into the throng, and it was impossible to tell if Farwander had put him down for good.

The champion cultist was roaring as he lashed around him with the scourge, ripping red lines through the flesh of cultist and crewman alike. More cultists made the leap across and the *Wave Demon*'s crew were rapidly becoming in danger of being overrun.

'Draw up at the quarterdeck!' yelled Farwander. 'Form up!'

Noseless and Gold-Ear did their best to rally men around them, but the fighting was too fragmented and vicious to allow for a coherent plan. Men fought in twos and threes, or were cornered alone and dragged down. Gavel swung her club around her in furious arcs, not caring what she hit, opening a semicircle of fractured skulls and broken limbs in front of her. Hakespure was trying to make it across the deck towards her but every step had to forge through a pressing mass of battling flesh.

The worst aspect of it was the fact that the battle was on the deck of the *Wave Demon*. The cultists had attacked with such speed and fury that the *Wave Demon*'s crew had been given no chance to take the battle to the cultists and board them first. The cultists were fighting for victory, the crewmen for survival. They had already lost half the battle and it was the *Wave Demon,* not the cultist hulk, that was facing its end.

Farwander skewered one cultist through the throat and barged another overboard. He spun, parried more through instinct than foreknowledge of an incoming blow, and rammed his sword's jet pommel into the temple of a cultist trying to disembowel him with a hooked dagger. The objectives he had tried to keep in mind were gone now and he fought just to keep himself alive and in possession of his senses.

A roar went up from the prow of the boat. Farwander risked a glance that way and saw the *Lightning Child* slewing around, Al'Harhi's fighting men in the rigging ready to swing across to join the fight. Al'Harhi himself was among them, bronze scimitar in hand. A cheer went up from the *Wave Demon*'s crew as the *Lightning Child* closed the distance and a dozen men made the leap onto the deck. Farwander let his own heart leap to see new allies join the fight.

Al'Harhi landed on the prow and was immediately surrounded by three cultists. By the time Farwander reached him one was dead, cleaved down through the shoulder to the mid-chest by a scimitar's stroke. Farwander cut down at the legs of another cultist, who sprawled to the deck before Farwander finished him with a stab through the back of the neck.

Al'Harhi was duelling with the last cultist, and this one was trained, a muscular and quick individual with a short sword in one hand and a dagger in the other. Al'Harhi parried the blade and spun out of the way of the dagger as another cultist clambered over the prow behind him, a bloodstained billhook in hand.

Farwander dived at the cultist newcomer and slashed at his weapon hand. The cultist dropped the billhook and Farwander rammed a desperate knee into the side of his head. The cultist tumbled away, cracking his skull against the *Wave Demon*'s figurehead before vanishing beneath the waves.

With a yell of triumph, Al'Harhi sliced the head clean off the cultist facing him. 'Well met,' he said in the seconds he had bought himself.

'Well met, Captain,' said Farwander, out of breath. 'You find us not at our best.'

'I see you cannot keep your deck tidy,' replied Al'Harhi. 'Let us clear away this flotsam!'

'Cut us loose!' yelled Farwander to the *Wave Demon*'s crew. Emboldened, the crew began slashing at the lines holding the *Wave Demon* and the hulk together. Farwander led the way, the fine steel of Captain Stennby's blade slicing through the ropes. Al'Harhi's men were well-disciplined, swift and deadly, and the cultists there thrown back to the side of the deck. Navigator Gavel was in the midst of Al'Harhi's men, bludgeoning wildly into the cultists who tried to scramble up onto the quarterdeck.

They might win. They might fend off the assault and emerge from the battle bloodied but victorious. There was hope, in that moment, that they had survived.

That was what sparked the doubt in Farwander's chest. It was too good to be true that they had weathered whatever storm the Brotherhood of Scaraveyla had brewed up for them. He cursed himself for congratulating himself so early. He cut through another line and ran to the prow of the ship, scanning the horizon for the rest of the enemy fleet.

He saw the Brotherhood's battle plan in action. Their first hulks were sent forward to break up and entangle Lady Temnos' outrider ships. These hulks were disposable pawns thrown forward with abandon, crewed by men who would not be missed, with their role not to destroy the enemy but to open up the way to the *Legacy*. The Brotherhood's goal was a chaotic battle without lines or strategy, where the defensive posturing of Lady Temnos' fleet fell apart under the Brotherhood's reckless spending of their own lives.

The *Legacy* would be laid open for the killing blow. And in that moment Farwander had his first glimpse of the weapon the Brotherhood were going to use to kill it.

Beyond the creaking mass of the hulk with which the *Wave Demon* was engaged, a huge dark mass came into view, surrounded by waters churning pink with blood. It was not a ship at all but an awful abomination, the seagoing echo of a mad surgeon's experiments, as unnatural and stomach-churning as the cultist Warden with his grafted limbs.

Farwander tried to look away and focus on the fighting around him, but he couldn't. The sight approaching was so appalling that his eyes refused to let anything else compete with it for space in his mind.

The shattered carcass of an enormous wrecked ship loomed through the ocean, a lopsided hulk of such size it looked more like a mobile island than anything that had ever been laid out in a shipyard. It was a shapeless horror of splintered wood hung with skeletons and fresher corpses, a seagoing trophy rack with tattered banners showing the emblem of the kraken. Its asymmetry and tormented state were such that the fact it floated at all was a crime against all nature.

Hundreds of Scaraveyla's cultists crammed the decks, which were covered in makeshift shacks and buildings giving the appearance of the seagoing shanty town. Amidships was a tottering wooden tower with an enormous white-painted emblem of a giant squid trailing long ragged streamers of sailcloth in imitation of tentacles. Beneath the wooden emblem were nailed the prows of scores of ships, displayed like the scalps of defeated enemies. Farwander saw the echoes of Scaraveyla's temple back at Cape Cadaver. The ship was a floating cathedral to the Shipwreck Goddess, an altar to the Kraken Queen.

The Brotherhood's flagship brought the smell of death with it on the salt breeze. Bloated corpses and the rot of low tide, the stench of a whaler's deck covered in butchered meat, the head-spinning reek of all the ocean's dead bubbled up to the surface.

The corpse-festooned, jagged prow of the hulk was aimed right at the *Wave Demon*.

'Hakespure!' yelled Farwander, tearing his eyes off the sight at last. 'Al'Harhi! That damned thing will split us in two!'

'Gods on high,' said Al'Harhi as he saw the approaching monstrosity. 'What is this foulness? We cannot stand before such a thing.'

'Agreed,' said Farwander. 'We have to get these grapples cut off and get out of its way. Abandon ship if we can't. It'll keelhaul this whole ship.'

Hakespure limped towards the prow, a dagger in his hand well blooded with fighting the invading cultists. 'And you would have me jettison myself?' he demanded. 'They'll not take my ship while I yet live! I'll not be in abandonment of her, Master Farwander!'

'Then you'll die!' shouted back Farwander.

'Then die I shall,' replied Hakespure.

Farwander turned back to Al'Harhi. 'Abandon the *Wave Demon*! Get your ship cut free!'

'And you?' said Al'Harhi.

'I'll think of something.'

The few remaining cultists on the *Wave Demon* cheered when they saw Scaraveyla's flagship bearing down at them. Their scourge-wielding champion, who had somehow survived this long, jumped up into the rigging so all could see him. 'Behold!' he yelled. 'The *Prophet's Wrath* falls upon the unbelievers! The Oblivion Deeps are calling! The Kraken Queen can taste your final breaths!'

The cultists still on their own ship were drawing deep cuts down their torsos with daggers and cutlasses, and their fresh blood gleamed in the sun. As if in reply, a tremendous deep groaning sounded from beneath the waves, so loud and low it shuddered the deck beneath Farwander's feet.

The source was the mass of bloody foaming surf around the hulls of the *Prophet's Wrath*. There, through the tears in the shattered hulls, Farwander could glimpse the immense shape of the creature trapped within the enormous ship. It was a whale, held in place by rusted chains, and the sounds were the moans of its anguish. On the decks of the *Prophet's Wrath* were the cult's own Wardens, like the one Farwander had captured, chanting and throwing offerings of bones and gold coins into the sea as they worked the magic that drove the whale onwards.

There was no way to stop it. The *Prophet's Wrath* picked up speed and every one of the corpses on its prow came into view as it closed. Among the dead were bones picked clean by seagulls, alongside fresh bodies of shipwrecked sailors and Archipelago natives alike. As well as a cathedral, a fortress, and a weapon of war, the *Prophet's Wrath* was a seagoing graveyard, and among its trophies were the scarred corpses of weak or disobedient cultists whose punishment was to serve as decoration on her prow.

Farwander sheathed his sword – the fighting was done. Now there was only dying left.

With an awful crunch and scream of tearing wood, the prow of the *Prophet's Wrath* slammed into the side of the cultist hulk. It tore right through the ship, the tumult and destruction accompanied by the thrashing of the giant whale inside the hull. The hulk was shredded and crushed by the jagged mass of the *Prophet's Wrath*, and its loss meant nothing to the cultists on its decks, because the smaller ship had served its purpose in pinning the prey in place for the kill.

The *Prophet's Wrath* had lost no speed as it chewed through the lesser cultist ship. Then with an awful booming and shattering of wood, it impacted against the *Wave Demon* as the Brotherhood screamed in triumph.

The deck splintered and tilted beneath Farwander's feet. He ran for the edge of the deck, but unlike most of the crew he was not trying to get away from the destruction and towards the long drop into the sea. Instead he headed towards the only stable object anywhere near – the *Prophet's Wrath* itself. He reached the collapsing edge of the *Wave Demon's* deck and jumped, throwing everything into a blind, flailing leap across the churning gulf of shattered wreckage.

The black, bloodstained wood rushed past him. He felt the spikes on the prow tearing through him. He threw out a hand and felt it close on something solid. His body thumped into the wood and he clung on as the *Wave Demon* came apart around him. He saw the cult champion, still hanging to the rigging, vanishing as the ship split in two and each half plunged into the sea. The masts snapped and the keel was thrown up out of the water, revealing the barnacles clinging to the wood. He saw bodies fall into the waters, cultists and crewman alike, and disappear.

The death of the *Wave Demon* was an act of violence such as Farwander had never seen. Her innards were ripped open, with the guts of the inner decks bursting outwards as the ship collapsed. Sailcloth and shredded hammocks tore like skin. The detritus of weeks at sea vomited forth in a flood of broken flotsam. The bodies mixed up in it all were just more debris, jettisoned from the *Wave Demon's* corpse in a final awful spasm of death.

Al'Harhi's men hadn't been given nearly enough time to cut the *Lightning Child* free. She was still trying to manoeuvre free of the *Wave Demon's* remains when the *Prophet's Wrath* caught up with her.

The *Lightning Child* was missed by the prow of the *Prophet's Wrath*, but she did not escape. The side of the hulk slammed into the *Lightning Child* and Al'Harhi's ship was ground against the jagged hull like grain against a millstone. Her hull was shredded away, laying the ship open to the ocean, and she tilted down onto her port side as the wake of the *Prophet's Wrath* swamped her and swung her around. The last Farwander saw of the *Lightning Child*, her masts were level with the ocean and men were scrambling across her uppermost side or sliding down into the foaming water.

Farwander took breathless stock of his situation. He had grabbed one of the wooden spikes covering the hull of the *Prophet's Wrath*. All around him were bodies impaled on other spikes – some of them old and mummified by the salt spray, others new and horribly fresh, their eyes still staring from their bloodstained faces locked in the expressions of death. Some of them bore the scars of the Brotherhood of Scaraveyla. Others were sailors and explorers from the many cultures that had come to the Ghost Archipelago to seek their fortunes, and had instead found a horrible end as sacrifices to the Kraken Queen.

The absurd thought entered Farwander's head that aside from breathing, he was identical to the fresher bodies, just one step removed from being a trophy displayed to glorify Scaraveyla's name.

He glanced behind him, to see that the *Legacy* was turning to flee from the *Prophet's Wrath* – and for all the *Legacy's* tremendous size, Farwander did not fancy its chances against the floating cathedral of Scaraveyla. Through the spray and bedlam of the *Wave Demon's* death, Farwander could see nothing good for Lady Temnos' ship as the Brotherhood fleet gave chase.

Farwander looked upwards, through the forest of impaled corpses. A few cultists had gathered on the prow to watch the fallen crewmen thrashing in the debris-choked waters below. None of them had yet seen Farwander, though he was intensely aware that if any of them did he had no way to hide.

'Begone!' bellowed a thunderous voice.

The cultists scattered like scolded dogs. In their place appeared on the prow a horror as complete as the *Prophet's Wrath* itself. Farwander's breath froze in his throat as the huge cloaked figure came into view.

It was easily eight feet tall, more by far than just a man. Its broad frame was covered by a cloak of tattered black leather, crowned around the neck and shoulders by a mass of black iron spikes, entwined like thorny bracken. The figure was armoured in dark iron with the relief of a muscular and brutal form picked out in silver. The armour's visor covered the upper half of the face with a mask in the shape of a kraken, with the coils reaching down over the figure's cheekbones. The face was like tanned and rugged leather, layered over with dark grey tattoos of tightly coiled tentacles. The teeth, when the figure grimaced, were sharp steel needles in double rows like shark's teeth.

In the figure's hand was the anchor of a sunken ship, still encrusted with barnacles and wisps of dried seaweed, wielded like a weapon that weighed no more than a dagger.

Lord Hekatar, the Prophet of Scaraveyla, glared down at Farwander, and behind the mask the Heritor's eyes narrowed in disdain. Hekatar pointed down at Farwander with a gauntleted hand.

'One yet denies the pull of the Oblivion Deeps,' said that terrible voice, deeper than the agonised moans of the whale trapped in the hull of the *Prophet's Wrath*. 'This filth must be cleaned away.'

Farwander was frozen. The sight of Lord Hekatar was overwhelming. It filled his mind so completely there was not enough room for any other thought. The *Prophet's Wrath* had demanded his attention, but the prophet himself demanded awe. No wonder, he thought in that moment, this creature had gathered these thousands of madmen around him and turned this crazed survivor-cult into a navy that had put Lady Temnos to flight. This was a man born to power, one whose presence made it impossible for him to be anything other than a leader, a warlord, a titan at the head of a conquering horde.

Farwander could not tell if it was some desperate force of will that forced his hands to open. Perhaps it was fatigue. Perhaps it was a primal need to get away from Lord Hekatar, bypassing the conscious mind completely. Either way, Farwander realised he was not clinging to the hull spike any more. Instead, the image of Lord Hekatar was racing away from him as the pitted and bloodstained hull of the *Prophet's Wrath* hurtled by.

Farwander had let go. Better to feel the merciless grip of the ocean than to remain there under Hekatar's scrutiny a moment longer. It was a strange relief that washed over Farwander as the sight of Hekatar receded as he fell.

Hekatar raised his anchor as if in anger, and the churning ocean slammed into Farwander's back. Hands of sodden, splintered wood grabbed him and dragged him down. His eyes and lungs filled with blackness. The awful drone of the captive whale sang him down into nothingness, and he thought in the void he could glimpse the endless abyss of the Oblivion Deeps.

CHAPTER 9

It was a place beyond reality, not just a region of the lightless ocean but somewhere that connected to everywhere and every mind. It bound the world and its inhabitants together. Everyone went there in the end, but only those who had suffered and bled into the unforgiving brine could fall into its vaults on their own terms.

Immense sea beasts, larger by magnitudes than any that could be summoned to the surface, moved through the deeps. Gargantuan, age-scarred bodies moved through the darkness. The gelid bodies of ancient kraken were followed by leagues-long trails of venomous tentacles. Sinuous draconic shapes wound with no end. The deeps were full of yawning, fanged maws that could swallow a warfleet whole. Stranger things still writhed through the silt of the ocean bed, blind and hungry.

A thousand souls, sunk through the Oblivion Deeps. They thrashed in anguish, but they were silent for they had no breath in their lungs to cry out. From their throats flowed only salt water. Others, covered in the scars of Scaraveyla's cult, swam down eagerly, their faces bright with religious ecstasy as they fought to reach the lowest depths first. The priests and champions among them led the shoals of cultists further down, and their prayers echoed among the distant thunder of whalesong.

And down even further than that, past the regions haunted by oceanic monsters and the craggy peaks of undersea mountains, were the very furthest reaches of the Oblivion Deeps. There, the sea bed was hidden beneath a carpet of ruin. Thousands of shipwrecks lay there in a forest of broken masts and splintered figureheads, piled up like corpses in a mass grave. Torn flags waved in the undersea currents. Bleached bones stared up from sundered hulls. Coral had encrusted many of them so it was impossible to tell where one ship ended and the other began, as the relentless hunger of the sea devoured them all.

All the jetsam of the oceans gathered there to lie in the lightless cold. Treasures lost at sea lay forgotten in the murk. The hoards of gold coins and handfuls of gemstones would never glitter again, for they were as far from the light as it was possible to be. They lay among the bones of those who had followed them into the waters, alongside the daggers and cutlasses that had not been enough to save them. The wealth of nations lay there, locked away at the bottom of the sea.

The owner of all that wealth, the richest being in the world, watched over this sunken realm. On a throne of sunken ships sat Scaraveyla, the Kraken Queen, the Shipwreck Goddess. From some angles, to some minds, she was a tentacled monstrosity of impossible size with awful intelligence burning in its red eyes. From others she was a proud and haughty queen with skin the ivory of brine-sodden flesh and black hair flowing like a field of seaweed. Her body was festooned with tarnished gold harvested from hundreds of sunken pirate wrecks. And sometimes she was not one being at all but a whirling mass of captive souls torn screaming from those she drowned, keening out an unending chorus of misery.

Around her gathered the drowned men of her church, the cultists who had survived her wrath and given their lives to her, ranked up in choirs to sing to her undying glory. These were the men and women who would crew her risen fleets when the graveyard of ships was resurrected and covered the ocean from one horizon to another. This was her blessed Brotherhood. These were the rulers of the world to come, when Scaraveyla took her rightful dominion of the surface as well as the depths.

And when that happened, when the Kraken Queen had reaped her due from the fools who sought to sail her ocean, all the world would come to look like the Oblivion Deeps.

* * *

'I should've bloody known you'd survive,' said a familiar voice. 'I told you, 'e's like a bloody weevil, 'e is.'

Farwander forced his salt-encrusted eye open. Even with nostrils full of brine he was aware of Leveret Pavine's distinctive aroma. Sure enough she was sitting above him in the rowboat, pulling on the oars along with the crewman Farwander recognised as her friend Grieff. There was no one else in the boat, which Farwander realised now had taken on the half a foot of water he was now lying in.

'Well, I know I'm not dead,' croaked Farwander, 'because you wouldn't be the first thing I would see in heaven.'

'Lucky we spotted you,' said Grieff. 'You were holding on to the *Wave Demon*'s figurehead. I wanted to leave you for dead but she said bring you in.'

They weren't the most flattering words, but Farwander kept that thought to himself. 'What happened to the *Legacy*?' he asked instead. 'Where is Lady Temnos?'

'Word is she gave the order to go for the island and beach her,' said Leveret. 'Get everyone onto land and take their chances there. Sad to see the old girl go, but which one of us thought she'd really be making it back to Rileport, eh? And Lady Temnos, well, she's a Heritor, I doubt she'll go down to anything petty as a sea battle. Think most of her crew made for shore so that's where we're headed. That big old hulk that sunk you and the *Lightning Child*, I never seen anything like it on or off the sea.'

'It's called the *Prophet's Wrath*,' said Farwander. 'Hekatar was on board.'

'You seen 'im?' asked Leveret, with a faint trace of admiration in her voice.

'I did.'

'Well scourge my backside, what a bloody honour.'

Farwander pulled himself up to sitting. He saw the boat was close to the island, with the smouldering cone of Mount Golca dominating the horizon. Some more rowboats were taking gaggles of survivors towards the coast. Here and there were patches of flotsam and wreckage from the battle, carried on the currents. A barrel, a tangled hammock, chunks of splintered wood.

'Oi!' came a yell from one of the other boats. Farwander peered across the ocean's glare and saw the matronly form of Navigator Gavel commanding a boat. She had the rolled-up map in her hand. 'Follow me or you'll split your rump on the coral!'

'She's got a map,' said Farwander, taken aback that Gavel had even made it off the *Wave Demon* alive. Then again, he reflected, she struck him as a lot more formidable than he was, and he had made it, too. 'Do as she says.'

It was already late in the day. The sun had turned orange by the time Leveret's boat made it to the beach, which Farwander recognised as one of the many bays along the northern part of the island's shore. They were not the first to land – already the survivors had started setting up simple shelters of branches and leaves on the beaches or just inside the treeline. Leveret beached the boat and Farwander and Grieff dragged it up clear of the tide line.

Farwander had thought his first steps onto Penitent's Landing would be more auspicious than this. Still, the island's grandeur could not be completely masked by the grimness of the circumstances. Inland, the dense carpet of the jungle formed a rarely broken canopy that only yielded to the slopes of the volcano. Gavel had led them well, for while much of the island was surrounded by unwelcoming cliffs, this stretch of the northern shore had less intimidating sandy beaches that had allowed the boats of the fleet's survivors to reach safety without a treacherous climb.

In other circumstances, the tropical beach would have been a welcome sight. Beautiful, even. As it was, Farwander could only view it as being one step better than the open water.

'I don't see any wounded,' said Farwander as the trio trudged up the beach.

'Don't get 'em after that kind of hiding,' said Leveret. 'You either go into the brine able-bodied or you die. Ain't many wounded can have made the swim.'

It was a gruesome thought. The sea did not show mercy when a man went into it with a broken leg or arm, or knocked senseless. The sea didn't care.

Farwander thought of the faces of the many crew he had come across and wondered which ones were still alive. Bizarrely, he thought of the harpist who had played for Lady Temnos the first time he had met her. Was that young maiden still alive? He could not see her face among the bedraggled survivors. He cast the thought from his mind.

Karanas, Lady Temnos' Earth Warden, was a short way up the beach. As he weaved patterns in the air with his hands, loose rocks were gathering to form a wall beside him, forming a break against the prevailing wind and shielding the light of a firepit from enemy eyes. Crew from the *Legacy* were with him, gathering bundles of firewood.

'Master Farwander,' said Karanas as Farwander approached. 'Many men consigned to the deeps today, laddie, yet we are not among them. Quite the hand fate has dealt us.'

'She's certainly keeping things interesting,' replied Farwander. 'Do you know if Lady Temnos made it?'

'That she did,' said Karanas. 'The *Legacy*, alas, did not. She rode onto the coral and broke her back. She sank quickly, but by then most of the men had abandoned her. Her ladyship is ashore, gathering her remaining strength. Perhaps more shall make it to land during the night, perhaps we have all who survive. We shall know in the morning.'

The earth and rocks beside Karanas were now formed into a sturdy sheltering wall. One soldier was already returning from the jungle with a brightly-plumed bird he had shot down with his crossbow, ready to cook for the night.

'Then I take it we're still making for the volcano?' asked Farwander.

Karanas looked at Farwander as if he had just asked if they were to continue breathing. 'Well, we're here now, laddie. Not much point in anything if we just stand here and look at the damned thing.'

Farwander sat down beside the fire as one of the crewmen started trying to light it with a flint. 'So,' he said, 'what do you think is up there?'

'The treasure her ladyship seeks, you mean?' Karanas gathered his plaid kilts around him and sat beside Farwander. The shadows were growing long, and soon it would be night. 'Well, that's quite the tale. It goes no further than us two, now, understand. But ye know of Arcturaval Temnos, he who drank from the Crystal Pool and who founded Lady Temnos' line?'

'I've heard the name.'

'Ah, well, ye ken what happened to him?'

Farwander shrugged. 'Came back to Rileport and eventually died, I assumed.'

'Now that's where you're wrong.' Karanas leaned close and dropped his voice, as if sharing the details of a daring conspiracy. 'He never left this island.'

Farwander raised an eyebrow. 'His body's here?'

'Now, I didnae say he was dead. 'Tis a sorry tale, and one that hasnae ended yet. You see, he drank from the pool but was betrayed by his fellow explorers. They put a dirk in his back and left him fer dead. They weren't the sharpest of swords, for they forgot that having just drunk from the pool, old Arcturaval was a difficult soul to kill. Still, he knew if he just lay there bleeding he'd die eventually.

'Now the pool had given him all kinds of magical powers we dinnae remember now. Folks say they first Heritors could fly, shoot fire from their eyes, all manner of tall tales. But what's true is that Arcturaval had the power to send a body into a place beyond death. He used his newfound magic to put himself into a sleep where he wouldnae age or decay. Beyond the years and all disease he was, until the Ghost Archipelago emerged from the mists again. All that time he's been healing the wounds they betrayers dealt him. Now Lady Temnos is here to wake him from his repose, rescue him and return him to her homeland to reign as a king.'

'I see,' said Farwander. 'And if Arcturaval has been sleeping here for two hundred years, then how did he manage to found an entire noble line? The mechanics of reproduction would seem to make it unlikely.'

'They say he impregnated a sturdy-hipped lass afore he entered his slumber,' replied Karanas. 'Either that or it's all magic, depending on who ye ask.'

'And where did you hear all this?'

''Tis the word upon the waves, laddie.'

The fire was lit and Farwander poked the kindling with a sodden toe. At least he would have a chance to dry off by the fire. 'Everyone thinks they know what's in that volcano,' he said, 'which means that no one really does. Perhaps even Lady Temnos doesn't know. Could be everyone has convinced themselves that whatever the legends of Mount Golca, the fact there's so many of them means there must be something there, even if they can't be sure what it actually is.'

'Ye dinnae reckon it's Arcturaval?'

Farwander shrugged. 'It's as likely as anything else, I suppose. I'd imagine most of the crew picture a hoard of gold and gemstones and so on. People do like to keep things simple.'

'Perhaps. Still worth finding, whatever the treasure may be.'

'Worth a few hundred men sent to the Oblivion Deeps?'

Karanas scowled. 'Dinnae tell me ye believe in that drivel,' he said. 'That's the Kraken Queen's nonsense.'

Along the shore, the faint glimmers of firelight shone between the trees, and against the last rays of the sun Farwander saw the tall masts of the *Legacy* beached some way eastwards. All that remained of Lady Temnos' fleet were now cowering on the strip of beach in shelters scraped into the sand. It wasn't much to speak of, given the size of the expedition that had left Cape Cadaver. But, thought Farwander, it would have to do.

The first night on Penitent's Landing commenced in sodden despair, and little hope the morning would be better.

* * *

Lady Temnos let word out that she desired certain principals among the expedition to attend upon her for a short hike into the jungle, along a bright clear stream that ran through the exposed roots of the jungle trees. Even with her fleet destroyed and her flagship aground, there was never any suggestion she was no longer in charge. She was a Heritor, after all, and the rest were just lesser men and women.

One of the names commanded to attend was Farwander, which was something of a surprise to the man himself since he doubted her ladyship was interested in any more swordplay lessons. Karanas was another, of course, so with the dawn the two set off to attend on the lady.

As Farwander trudged along the shore, he caught the smell of an agreeably spiced stew and could not help but feel his attention drawn to the encampment of sailors and soldiers gathered around a large cauldron.

'Of all the things to save,' said Farwander as he passed them, 'you gave a space in the boat to the pot.'

'Course I bloody did,' retorted Navigator Gavel, who Farwander now saw had taken her place as the central figure of this encampment. 'There was few enough men alive to fill the boat as it was. And I'm not eating nothing raw in this dump-hole, so I saved the cookpot. Turns out

I'm the only one that did because I'm the only one for a thousand leagues around that don't have his bollocks for his brains. Aye me, you're worse than my man.'

'Madame, are you still in possession of that map?'

'No, I wiped my arse on it,' said Gavel with a roll of the eyes. 'Of course I've still got it, you moron.'

'Then might I request you join me?' asked Farwander. 'I think her ladyship might well wish to see it.'

Gavel looked disparagingly at the other men who were eagerly spooning out helpings of stew for themselves. 'You divots not going to kill yourselves while I'm gone?' she asked. A few shakes of the head served as a reply. 'Aye, well, if it helps us get off this beach,' she said. 'Some dirty great sea beast'll snatch us all up otherwise.'

Karanas had already forged on into the jungle, so Farwander and Gavel made their way together into the treeline and along the shore of the trickling stream. The jungle rapidly grew in scale until the flying roots reached up over their heads like the beams of half-built houses. The green of the canopy was far, far overhead, as if it was a sky composed of leaves. Dense sprays of green clung to the tree trunks further down, hungry for the beams of sunlight that fell through the gaps in the canopy. Underfoot the ground was spongy, the rich, dark mulch of decayed leaves from which grew new saplings and clumps of huge-leafed plants.

Life was everywhere. The air was thick with it. Buzzing insects clung to every bend in the stream and every pool of still water. Clouds of birds alighted from the higher branches, and every few moments something screeched or hooted in the middle distance. The air was so humid that beads of water clung to Farwander's face even before the morning heat brought out the sweat.

'We lost a lot of men,' said Farwander as they walked, 'and we all lost a lot of friends. But I know you and Captain Hakespure were close.'

'Close? Is that how you put it?' replied Gavel. 'You're a purse-mouthed prude, you are. He was my man.'

'Well, I didn't want to put it indelicately.'

'He never put anything delicately in his life. Nor did I. It's why I put up with the salty old porpoise. Did you see him go?'

'No, Madame, I did not.'

'Nor I. Hope it was quick.'

They proceeded in a nervy silence. Farwander was rarely lost for words but he couldn't think of anything that might console her without sounding false or forced, so he kept quiet. Gavel did the same. Farwander looked through the endless reaches of the forest around him, just to keep from having to acknowledge the mystifyingly bereaved woman beside him. He saw not just tree trunks, but the telltale rough square shapes of rocks that must have been carved and piled up by intelligent hands, before collapsing with age and the disruptive growth of the forest.

Here stood half of an arch, colonised by mosses and saplings. There was a stretch of wall with the remnants of a right angle before it was usurped by a mass of immense roots. A fallen tree had plunged right through a larger ruin an age ago, leaving stumps of broken pillars and heaps of rubble.

'We're not the first people here,' said Farwander. 'And neither were the first Heritors.'

'Well, someone had to make all the stuff on this map,' said Gavel. She had the roll of hide in a tubular map case strapped over her shoulder. 'Been looking at it. The native folk scouted it out but they didn't like what they found. Half of it's covered in skulls that say to stay away. There's ruins here and there, more further inland. I got no idea of who built 'em but it's not the natives we met. It was someone who's been gone for a long time, I'd wager. Nasty folk too, or at least that's what the natives think.'

'Anything on the map about what's in the volcano?'

Gavel shrugged. 'Big skull and a bunch of snakes,' she said. 'Don't think they meant it literally though. Something dangerous, that's for sure. Course everyone's supposing it's there to protect something worth haring across the sea for, and who am I to say they're wrong?'

'Do you think it's Arcturaval Temnos?'

Gavel snorted a laugh. 'You were talking to Karanas,' she said. 'I thought he must be drinking the brine to think that. My guess is, whoever used to live on this island kept all their valuables up there on the mountain to keep 'em safe. Gold and whatnot, I suppose. Could be it's still there.'

'A native treasury,' said Farwander. 'That would seem more plausible than the alternatives I've heard.'

'Oh, aye? And what do you think it is?'

'What I think,' replied Farwander, 'is that if Lady Temnos believes it's worth the risk, then so do I.'

Gavel smiled at that. 'You bloody liar.'

Lady Temnos had set up her own camp in a square of ruins where partially standing walls provided ample shelter from the elements, and even from the likelihood of rain with a roof of woven leaves her crew had set up overhead. It was even defensible, with rocks piled up to form cover and murder-holes opened in the walls for crossbows. A few planks of wood had been set up into a table at which Lady Temnos sat, surrounded by the surviving leaders of her expedition. Karanas and Leveret were there, along with a few officers Farwander didn't recognise.

'Master Farwander, I am glad to see you yet live.' Lady Temnos spoke without apparent emotion. She turned her gaze to Gavel. 'And you are?'

'Chrysanthemum Gavel, your ladyship. Representing Captain Gerontius Hakespure, who perished.'

'He will be missed.'

'Aye, he will. Thank you, my lady.'

'We have a map,' said Farwander, 'of Penitent's Landing. Penned by natives. It proved useful in navigating here. It may still be so.'

'We would see it,' said Lady Temnos.

The map was duly rolled out on the makeshift table. The gathered officers stared at it for a good long while, trying to decipher its pictograms. Mount Golca was indeed surmounted by a large and angry skull with unpromisingly red eyes, and snakes were depicted coiling around its base. Several sketches of ruins were surrounded with similarly dire images of warning. The river they had walked along was also shown, and their current location was roughly between two structures the natives had thought were interesting enough to give undecipherable pictographic names.

'These swamps would give us trouble,' said Lady Temnos, indicating the region directly between the northern coast and Mount Golca. 'We shall have to go around. If the Brotherhood fleet intends to make a landing it will be here.' She pointed at a bay on the western coast of the island. 'So we should give that a wide berth too.'

Farwander pointed out a tower that, from its stylised image, reached above the jungle canopy. 'If we use this as a landmark we can stay on course. If we keep it to our east we'll reach this river and follow it back to its source on the mountain.' The river was a much more impressive one than the stream they had followed, a wide strip of blue that bisected the eastern half of Penitent's Landing.

'And who, sir, are you?' asked one of the officers, a strapping gentleman with a lavish handlebar moustache and a mirror-bright breastplate with the image of duelling unicorns.

'Master Farwander acquitted himself well in the battle, Captain Vormish,' said Lady Temnos. 'I requested his attendance.'

'Ah, you are the swordplay instructor,' said Vormish, with an unimpressed raise of the eyebrow.

'I am,' replied Farwander, intensely aware of how unnecessary such a thing as a swordplay tutor was in the jungle.

'I advocate swinging southwards,' said Lady Temnos, indicating a path well away from Farwander's suggestion. 'The natives thought the environs to the east and north of here were dangerous and I have no reason to doubt them. The volcano itself shall form all the point of navigation we require.' She looked among the faces of her officers. 'Gather your men. Do not try to march them as one, even drilled fighting men would not maintain order in this terrain. Take as many as you yourselves can command. Get them to this ridge.' Here she ran a finger along a feature on the map picked out with the images of gambolling monkeys. It looked, at least, less hostile than the various other deathtraps and natives had scribbled warnings about. 'There we shall regroup and move on. We must do this now, gentlemen, for the Brotherhood still wants our blood and they know full well we are on this island. We keep moving or they will ride us down. Go.'

The expedition's leaders had all the orders they needed. They headed off to the encampments by the shore. Farwander watched them go and wondered if they felt as bedraggled and defeated as he did, and were just puffing out their chests and acting as they thought their mistress required. Farwander knew how to present a bold face to the world, but he didn't have quite that much bluster in him that morning.

'I would have you stay with me, Master Farwander,' said Lady Temnos. 'What knowledge have you of pathfinding in such an environment?'

'Regrettably none, my lady.'

'I done a bit,' offered Leveret, who had watched proceedings while messily eating a peach-like fruit from one of the trees. 'You want to be at the head, ladyship. Them that's hunting us'll pick off the stragglers behind.'

'Like animals,' said Lady Temnos.

'Aye, like animals.' Leveret looked slyly at Farwander. 'Hope he can keep up. What d'you need him with you for anyway, ladyship?'

'I still have sword forms to learn,' replied Lady Temnos.

Farwander put a hand to the pommel of his sword. The weapon had somehow stayed with him, even after he had been thrown into the drink and been fished out by Leveret. It was, he realised, rather more valuable to Lady Temnos than he was.

* * *

The expedition moved in groups of a dozen or so men, trudging through the mulchy ground, hacking their way through with cutlasses and bills where the vegetation tangled in too close or wading hip-deep in sludge when the ground proved sodden and hungry. The glowering shape of Mount Golca did not seem to move no matter how far they forged through the jungle, and as gloom drew in the word was spread to make camp and post sentries. Already, by then, the hundreds of survivors had become strung out for miles through the clinging forest of Penitent's Landing.

The sun was dipping behind the canopy's edge as Farwander crested a low ridge and saw Lady Temnos a short way ahead, surveying the unpromising stretch of forest ahead.

'We'd better get camp soon or it'll be black as a sluggard's tooth,' said Leveret. She was hardier than she looked and had kept pace with Lady Temnos' small party alongside Farwander.

'We made good speed,' said Farwander.

'Aye, well, we'll see if we can keep that up tomorrow,' said Leveret. 'Soon as folks get tired and hungry it'll grind down real slow. That's when we'll start leaving men behind and never find 'em again.'

'Well we won't be wantin' for eatin' tonight,' said Grieff, who came lumbering through the undergrowth towards them. Grieff seemed to hover permanently around Leveret, as if he were a fly that had mistaken her for spoiled meat. 'What d'you think squawked this one out?'

Grieff was carrying an egg almost the size of a man's torso. The man's burly arms struggled to encompass it.

'Where the hell's arse did you get that?' asked Leveret.

'There's a clutch of them down the ridge,' said Grieff with a triumphant smile. 'Enough for a hundred men, I swear. Fancy boiled or scrambled?'

'Put it back you imbecile,' snapped Leveret. 'You got no idea what made it.'

Grieff shrugged. 'What's the worst it could be? Bloody big chicken's still just a chicken.'

'Mr Grieff,' said Lady Temnos, trudging up the slope. 'Is there some impediment?'

Her answer came not from Grieff, but from the jungle up ahead. It was a long, low braying sound, quite unlike any sound Farwander had heard an animal make in his time. It was echoed a moment later by dozens more, lowing and roaring from a wide frontage ahead of them. The whole party of the crewmen halted and tried to peer through the darkening forest to see the source of the noise.

'Did you see anywhere nearby that can be defended?' asked Farwander, hoping his nerves did not come through in his voice.

'Not unless you can climb trees,' replied Leveret.

The sound came again, louder and closer, and this time Farwander could make out the splintering of saplings underhoof. The ground thrummed with a low, powerful vibration just beyond hearing.

'Run!' came a cry from up ahead. Some of the crewmen ranged in front of the party, scouting for dangers, and one such man had evidently found what he was looking for. He emerged from the trees at a run and Farwander saw it was one of the *Legacy's* surviving crewmen, though from the look on his face he didn't think he'd be surviving much longer.

A mass of dark, thundering flesh erupted from the jungle behind him. Suddenly the jungle was disgorging dozens of creatures, each easily twice the height of a sturdy man, loping on hind legs and smashing branches aside as they charged. They were lizardlike in appearance, with patterned scales and bony crests around their massive skulls, and each sported an enormous mouth crammed with fangs. Their size was counterweighed by the thick, muscular tails that swayed behind them as they ran.

The fleeing crewman vanished beneath their clawed feet before anyone else could move.

'Flee!' yelled Lady Temnos. 'Find high ground!'

There was no order in the crew as they fled the stampede. The saurians spread out so there was no safe direction. Leveret, Farwander and Lady Temnos broke to the left of the stampede, down the reverse slope of the ridge. Farwander felt branches scratching at him as he sprinted. Leveret swore and spat as she tripped and pitched face-down in the mulch – Lady Temnos grabbed her arm and hauled her to her feet.

A saurian, the fastest among the herd, crested the ridge and leaped down at them. Farwander threw himself to the side as it thudded to the ground, throwing clods of cold mulch everywhere. Up close it was more appalling still, its scaled hide covered in old scars and war wounds, its mad rolling eyes set into a bestial face composed of a huge hungry snarl. It smelled appalling, like old ordure and rotting meat. Everything about it suggested a predator that ran with a pack to bring down larger prey, but that was more than capable of fighting alone if the need arose.

Its gigantic wedge-shaped head loomed down at Farwander. He drew his sword and went for its eye, the thrust going wide and glancing off the beast's brow ridge. The saurian snapped down at him, almost taking his sword arm off.

Crewman Grieff, still clutching the enormous egg, tumbled down the slope and sprawled down in the mulch. The saurian rounded on him, emitting a terrifying growl that felt like the shaking of the earth. Grieff scrabbled away from it, holding up the egg like a shield.

Farwander saw his opening, and struck. The steel was good enough, the edge fine enough, to take the blade through the saurian's dense scales and leather-tough muscles. His shoulder-high slash went through the back of the saurian's thigh, glancing off the thigh bone inside.

It was an educated guess, but a guess nonetheless, that the saurian had a tendon in the back of the leg that it could sore do without. One of the debilitating blows he had learned early on in his swordfighting instruction was a cut to the hamstring, which would sever the tendon and render the leg completely useless. On a man-sized opponent this was a virtual kill, since a man in pain unable to get off the ground was unable to defend himself.

It turned out that on an enormous carnivorous lizard, the effect was rather less final. The saurian did indeed thump to the ground as its leg collapsed under it, and it let out a roaring howl of pain. But while a man would be limited to waving his blade around ineffectively, the saurian was capable of biting everything around it with its enormous set of clamping, fanged jaws. It lunged at Farwander and would have bisected him at the waist if he had not scrabbled backwards like a fleeing insect.

Lady Temnos skirted behind the stricken saurian as its attention was on Farwander. She dropped her sword on the ground and Farwander thought it was through fear or shock, until she ran right at the beast with her fist drawn back.

With deep, meaty thwack, Lady Temnos' fist slammed into the side of the saurian's skull. The beast's head snapped to the side in a shower of shattered fangs. It flopped unconscious to the ground, exhaling an exhausted rumble.

'You had to grab the sodding egg!' snarled Leveret, who had drawn her dagger to defend herself in spite of the fact that the weapon was rather smaller than one of the beast's teeth.

'I was hungry!' complained Grieff from the ground.

The other saurians were still thundering through the jungle. Cries of alarm and warning were coming from everywhere. None of the other crew were anywhere near.

'We can't stay here,' said Lady Temnos. She pointed to the jungle beyond Farwander. 'The ruins, there. Get to cover.'

'My lady,' said Farwander as he hurried alongside her towards the tumbled walls and pillars she had indicated. 'You're hurt.'

Lady Temnos put a hand to the side of her neck. It came away bloody. A trickle of red was flowing from her left ear. 'It is nothing,' she said. 'Just the blood burn.'

Hungry eyes and hungrier jaws were roving through the jungle around them, closing in from everywhere. The saurian Lady Temnos had dispatched was not the largest of them, and some already had flesh blood smeared around their jaws. Grieff and Leveret followed into the ruins, which had once formed a large rectangular building of several floors now compacted and overgrown into a mass of mossy stone and roots.

Farwander saw the remnants of a large archway which still gave access to the building's interior. It looked far too narrow to admit a saurian all the way through. He led the way through as the hungry growling grew closer.

'Never has such a hole seemed so hospitable,' he said as he made his way inside. There was still enough room to stand and the jungle had not quite forced its way within. The chamber had once been deeply carved with ornate, spiralling designs and held up by sturdy pillars. The floor was still covered by tiles that retained a glimmer of colour even as the fading daylight struggled to make it through the entrance.

'Where was this?' asked Lady Temnos. 'Who built it?'

'Someone we should probably be glad isn't home,' replied Farwander. 'This place used to be huge. I doubt they would have been terribly impressed by us when they were at their height.'

'Whoever it was,' said Leveret, examining the carvings winding around one of the pillars, 'they were big on snakes.'

A terrific rumble of stampeding hooves approached, like the roll of a thunderstorm breaking overhead. A moment later a wall of scaly flesh slammed into the archway, scattering fallen rubble into the chamber. A chunk of the ceiling fell in and the light was suddenly cut off. In the gloom., Farwander could make out snapping teeth and the glint of a furious eye.

'Go! Go!' he said unnecessarily.

Grieff stumbled and almost fell flat on his face as the party ran deeper into the ruin. At least, Farwander noted, he had relinquished his egg. More rock fell and the light was cut off completely.

'Tell me someone has light,' said Grieff.

Farwander was aware that Leveret was nearby from her distinctive aroma. It was she who struck a flint, and after a few mutteringly frustrating tries finally got the corner of a rag lit. By the flickering flame, Farwander could confirm her opinion of the ruin's builders. The coils of a huge python covered the wall behind Leveret, and every decoration and motif seemed to echo the curve of a serpentine body or the spike of a venomous fang.

'Look for something we can make a torch out of,' said Leveret.

'Well, we're not going back,' mused Farwander, glancing back at the now-vanished archway, which had been replaced with a drift of fallen rubble. 'We need to find another way out.'

'What if there ain't one?' asked Grieff.

'Then we'll die,' replied Farwander. 'That's not going to stop me looking for one, though.'

Lady Temnos found an age-withered bone on the floor and Leveret wrapped a strip of fabric around it to form a crude torch. By its light the temple's decoration jumped out vividly. The floor was tiled in once-rich reds and ochres. The serpentine patterning on the walls was green and yellow. The chamber led deeper into the ruin, where pillars and archways divided the interior into sub-chambers. A large bronze bowl stood in the centre of the chamber, with the tiling radiating off from it to mark it as the focus of the place. Leveret leaned over the bowl, hoping to light a fire there so she didn't have to rely on the torch.

'It's full of bones,' she said. 'They're burned.'

'In the catalogue of potential omens,' said Farwander, 'that does not seem like a good one.'

'Yeah, well, I think this place had a big old skull over it on the map,' said Leveret. 'Probably shouldn't expect it to be welcomin'.'

'This was a place of sacrifice,' said Lady Temnos, examining the wall carvings. 'Offerings were brought here under the eyes of their gods.'

'Whose gods?' asked Grieff.

'Now that,' said Lady Temnos, 'is the question.'

'Bloody hells alive,' swore Leveret. She was holding the torch at one of the archways, using its flame to look beyond.

The others ran to the archway, and they saw what she saw in the chamber beyond.

The god of this temple was a huge and muscular being whose immense squatting body took up fully half the high-ceilinged temple chamber beyond. It had three heads, each of a snake – one hooded like a cobra, one with exaggerated venomous fangs, and one rendered as a grinning lizard skull. On the floor in front of it, between its massive flabby claws, was a waist-high block of stone stained black.

In front of the deity's statue were two dozen smaller stone blocks. Streaks of rust showed where iron fittings had once been driven into the blocks. Sorry heaps of bones lay scattered around each.

Farwander walked gingerly into the chamber. The statue's six eyes seemed to follow him. He looked down at the nearest pile of bones, identifying a ribcage and spine, and the arm bones stretched out as if still in supplication.

There were, however, no legs to the skeleton. And there were far, far too many vertebrae.

'What were they?' asked Lady Temnos beside him.

'Men from the waist up,' said Farwander. 'Snakes from the waist down. Have you ever heard of such things?'

'Rumours,' said Lady Temnos. 'My forefather Arcturaval said he had seen them, but not up close. Natives of the Archipelago, he wrote, though not like the human natives at all. They had a cruel and evil reputation. He wrote that he had questioned his sanity towards the end of his voyage and wondered if the serpent folk were the visions of a fevered mind. Now I think he may have been more in possession of his faculties than he realised.'

'It's a temple,' said Grieff. 'Right?'

'Yes, Grieff, it's a temple,' said Leveret scornfully. She was examining the statue and altar more closely by torchlight. 'Well done, have a ship's biscuit.'

'Look, I'm sorry about the egg, all right?' said Grieff. 'I didn't know there was a lot of bloody great lizards around the corner.'

'One of many things you don't know, Grieff,' retorted Leveret. 'Like how to think.'

'Is there any way out?' asked Farwander. There were no obvious exits but the snake carvings covering the walls, or the statue itself, could easily have concealed a hidden exit. 'As stimulating as this conversation is, I'd rather it not be the last one I hear.'

'This was more than just a place of worship,' Lady Temnos said, looking up into the faces of the serpent people's god. 'They were chained up to die here.'

'As a punishment?' asked Farwander.

'Or as a test. And these were the ones that failed.'

'So how do we get out?' asked Grieff plaintively. He was examining the area around the sides of the statue, and failing to find any doorways that might get the party out of the temple chamber.

'You remember this is their turf,' said Leveret. She had propped her makeshift torch against the altar stone and had her dagger in one hand, hovering over the palm of the other. Farwander realised what had stained the altar black, just as Leveret pulled the edge of the blade along her palm. 'You got to do what they do.'

'What the hells are you doing?' said Grieff.

'Same thing was done in this chamber,' said Leveret. 'Listen, you find an altar to a god what's demandin' an offering, you give it. Ain't a sailor afloat would leave a collection plate empty lest he gets on the nerves of the wrong god, except you maybe because you're an idiot.' She winced as the blade cut her palm.

Farwander regarded her sacrificial offering with alarm. 'Miss Pavine, are you sure that's...'

Leveret's blood dripped onto the altar, as thousands of throats' worth of blood had done in ages past.

The ground shook in response. From somewhere deeper in the building came a grinding of stone on stone. The central portion of the floor shuddered violently and dropped suddenly, throwing Farwander off his feet. The whole floor section sank into the ground beneath it, forming a shaft of cut stone with Farwander, Grieff and Lady Temnos at the bottom.

'Sorcery,' growled Lady Temnos as she looked for something hold on to. 'This place is not so dead as it seemed!'

'Leveret, what did you do?' shouted Grieff.

Leveret's face appeared at the top, getting rapidly smaller as the floor descended.

'Not my fault,' she replied. 'I didn't know it'd do that!'

'Why would anyone build this?' lamented Grieff. 'Why?'

'Where are you lot going?' demanded Leveret.

'Find another way!' called Farwander up to Leveret. 'Meet us outside!'

'Yeah, 'cause it's that easy,' replied Leveret, before her voice was drowned out by the grinding of whatever mechanisms were lowering the floor section.

The floor descended into another chamber far below the first. The air was choking with age. Farwander put a hand to his mouth and tried to breathe through the staleness and dust. The light from Leveret's torch above failed to reach down this far and everything was dark, but Farwander had a sense of great size as the noise of machinery echoed around him.

With a scrape of stone, the floor settled and the descent stopped. Farwander tried to peer into the darkness but he could make nothing out.

'Stay close,' warned Lady Temnos. 'We don't know what's down here.'

'A bloody awful place to die, that's what,' coughed Grieff. 'Leveret! Leveret, where are you, girl? Got a... I dunno, a rope or something?'

If Leveret replied, she was too far above to be heard.

'How did she do that?' continued Grieff. 'With the blood. Was it magic?'

'Yes, it was magic,' said Farwander. 'Not sure that should be so surprising.'

'Just didn't think Leveret could pull it off, that's all.'

Farwander held his sword out in front of him and took a few wary steps. The ground was loose and crunching under his feet. 'I think Leveret passed the test,' he said. 'This is the next one.'

'A test of what?' asked Grieff. 'How to see in the dark?'

'Maybe the serpent folk could,' said Farwander.

'Well what are we supposed to do?'

'You could try a vow of silence,' Farwander muttered as he took another careful step.

A whoosh of hot air hit him in the face. Deep red flared in front of him, then a ripple of orange. He jumped backwards as fire swept through the chamber, suddenly illuminating the vast space in the deep ruddy tones of flame.

The whole floor was covered in flammable coals, the loose surface Farwander had felt underfoot. A source of ignition had set fire to it, and in seconds that fire had spread around the whole chamber leaving only the square of flooring that had descended from above. That area formed an island of safety against the back wall, with the heat from the burning coals battering at the three people sheltering there.

The chamber's high, curved ceiling was covered in spiderwebs, and in places chunks of it had fallen in where tree roots and the weight of ages had loosened the stones. It was supported by stone ribs carved to resemble serpents. At the opposite end of the chamber from Farwander's position was an archway in the shape of an enormous snake's mouth, the glass panels inset for its eyes winking redly in the firelight. The only way to the archway was across the burning coals, which continued down the tunnel of the stone snake's throat.

'It's a test of resolve,' said Lady Temnos. 'The last one was a test of sacrifice. To move on we must endure the fire.'

'Well that's wonderful,' said Grieff. 'Your bloody ladyship led us straight into another new way for us to die.'

'We took shelter here,' replied Lady Temnos levelly. 'There was no way to...'

'You brought us to this bloody island!' shouted Grieff. 'You could've turned back! The natives said the Brotherhood were out there! They sent a kraken after us! But you went on anyway, because what does it matter how many men have to die for whatever the hells it is you're after up there?'

Lady Temnos moved much, much faster than Grieff could react. Her hand was suddenly around his throat and she hauled him off his feet, slamming him hard into the wall behind him. His eyes bulged out as the grip tightened around his neck. Lady Temnos' strength was massive and Farwander could tell she was only exhibiting a fraction of it. She could have popped Grieff's head clean off his shoulders, and they all knew it.

'You are here for a cut of the riches we will find,' she said calmly. 'You claim your share, you suffer the dangers. No one has ever told you any different.'

'Keep it,' spluttered Grieff. 'Keep it all.'

Lady Temnos threw Grieff to the floor. He clutched at his throat, wheezing out desperate breaths.

'You were eager enough for my leadership when you wanted to go home rich,' continued Lady Temnos.

Farwander put a hand to the chamber's back wall. He had heard something there, among the rush and crackle of the fire. He felt it now, a vibration through the stone.

'And what good has it done us?' gasped Grieff from the floor. 'Half of us are down in the brine. The other half are gods know where. And we have to starve down here or burn alive.'

'If I care so little for your lives,' replied Lady Temnos, 'perhaps I should be done with you now? I would be free of your complaining. Maybe I should use you as a stepping stone across this fire. Or perhaps you will make yourself of some use and find a solution instead of cursing the one who gave you the chance to make something of yourself.'

Farwander put an ear to the stone of the back wall. The sound was difficult to pick out, but he could hear it among the growl and crackle of the fire. He took a step back and aimed a firm kick at the wall. Mortar trickled and a stone loosened a little. He took a short run up this time and drove his foot against the wall again. It was with satisfaction that he felt the stone shift.

'What are you doing?' asked Lady Temnos.

The third kick brought the section of the wall in. A mist of water sprayed from the opening. 'It's an underground river,' said Farwander. 'It's what powered the mechanism that brought us down here. There's a waterwheel back there somewhere, connected to all this.'

Water was gathering on the section of the flooring. Where it spread to the edge of the coals it hissed and spat as the fire was extinguished. The smoke and steam made it even harder to breathe, but Farwander kept his head low and poked at the doused coals with the toe of his shoe. They were hot, but bearable. He made his way slowly across the coals as the water continued to pour in, with Lady Temnos and a sour-faced Grieff behind him. After a few minutes the snake-jaw archway loomed over them and they made their way down its dark stone throat.

'Well, we passed that test, too,' said Lady Temnos as they advanced into the darkness. With the fires mostly doused, the light was gone, too. 'Not in the way the serpent people intended, though.'

'It makes me wonder if there will be another one,' he said. 'Or if we're about to come on the reward for passing. I'm not sure which one I relish least.'

The warm coals ended and Farwander felt cold stone under his feet. The air here was fouler and damper, and he wondered if he should be grateful it was so difficult to see. Then, he caught a glimmer of light.

'Sunlight up ahead,' he said. 'If there's a way out it'll be there.'

'Thank the gods,' said Grieff.

'We are not out yet,' said Lady Temnos.

Grieff fell silent again. Farwander was aware of loose trash and yielding surfaces underfoot. The smell was of something decaying, mostly vegetation that had blown in through the gaps in the ceiling ahead but also something deeper and meatier, something that had not withered away to dust like everything elsewhere in the temple but was still fresh enough to lend an acridity to the air.

'Don't move,' said Lady Temnos. Farwander froze, and a moment later heard what she had – something shifting nearby, skin on stone, the heave of massive flesh drawing breath.

'Ye fates, what is that?' asked Grieff.

'Quiet!' snapped Lady Temnos.

Farwander had his sword drawn, holding it in front of him like a cat's whisker reaching out for contact. He slipped on a slimy patch and stumbled, narrowly avoiding turning his ankle on the uneven floor. 'Close, in,' he said, forcing his voice to stay calm. 'Don't get split up.'

Something fell and scattered across the ground, and Farwander was somehow completely certain it was a heap of bones. The slither of scales on stone turned into an urgent rush and muscles creaked.

Grieff screamed.

It wasn't just a yelp of fear. It was primal and brutal, wrenched up from the depths of his lungs.

The sound of tearing flesh told Farwander that whatever was in there with them, it intended to feed, and it had started with Grieff.

A mass of scaled muscle slammed into Farwander's shoulder and threw him into a heap of rotting spoil. Bones crunched under the impact. Thankfully, just like during the sea battle, he kept hold of Captain Stennby's sword and lashed out with it. He felt the blade bite into something glancingly, and heard a vicious hiss fill the chamber in answer.

'Lady Temnos!' shouted Farwander. 'Where are you? Speak to me!'

The answer came not from Lady Temnos but from Grieff again, who let out an awful gurgling howl cut short by a wet, gristly crunch of ravenous jaws.

Farwander could tell from the sound of the creature's body on the floor, from the change in the air, that it was rearing up above him. Duellist's instinct, perhaps, or luck, or the intervention of those gods who saw fit to look down at Penitent's Landing in that moment. Whatever it was, he met the creature with a full lunge from a crouch, putting his shoulder behind the thrust up and away.

The point met flesh and sliced deep into it. The edge ground against bone. Farwander gave the blade a brutal twist, something he would hesitate to do on a human opponent, and he could hear the ripping of sinews. A spittle-laced hiss sprayed down at him and he knew he had hurt it. He pulled the blade out with an effort and slashed at the same height, biting deep again.

This time he was met by a spray of blood, and he could not deny the savage joy it gave him.

From deeper in the chamber he could hear the sound of shifting stone. The flicker of sunlight widened and picked out scarred, jagged scales and the flicker of a narrow yellow eye.

Lady Temnos growled with effort and took the entire weight of a huge boulder on her shoulders. She was silhouetted against the light from outside, a slender frame hefting a gargantuan weight in a way that made it seem her body had to snap under the force. But she shifted the stone on her shoulders and heaved it to one side, and it crashed to the forest floor.

From the sunlight suddenly bleeding in Farwander could finally see his surroundings. This part of the temple was a natural cave with the floor levelled out a little and the walls crudely expanded. Heaps of leaf spoil and prey carcasses were piled up around the sides of the cave, with skeletons picked clean along with newer kills waiting to be eaten. A juvenile elephant lay with an antelope corpse on top of it. What looked like a badly mangled buffalo was buried in leaf trash.

Rearing up above Farwander, furious at the invasion of its lair, was a snake of immense size. The top of its skull was at a level twice Farwander's height, and its body length was coiled around the rest of the cave. Its scales were dull and gnarled with age but still showed the mottled green-brown and black of a python. Its yellow eyes were fixed on him and from its gore-spattered jaws hung one of Grieff's arms.

Farwander had impaled it through the neck, and cut a deep slash just below that. It had not been enough to kill it, but he had definitely got its attention.

Farwander rolled away through the rotting spoil as the snake struck. It moved faster than anything that size should have been able to, and its nose thumped into the wall behind where Farwander had been kneeling. Farwander sprinted for the exit Lady Temnos had opened up, and up ahead he saw her stumble as if hit with a sudden dizziness.

The thick trunk of the snake's body whipped from the shadows at Farwander. He vaulted the tail and ran headlong the rest of the way, followed by the snake's angry hisses. He burst out into the forest and was shocked to see night had fallen – the cave had been illuminated not by sunlight at all, but by the light of the full moon breaking through the jungle canopy.

Farwander paused to grab Lady Temnos and put his shoulder under her arm, propping her up. Too late he felt the rush of air as the snake erupted from the cave behind him. He threw himself face-down, taking Lady Temnos with him, as the snake's bloody jaws snapped wetly shut above him.

Farwander jumped to his feet and fended off the snake as best he could, banking on its wariness of him from its previous wounds to keep it backing off from his blade. The snake hissed and spat as its whole body slithered out of the cave, and it kept its yellow eyes fixed on him as it encircled him. Before Farwander knew it, the snake had completely surrounded him with its body, so he was penned in by a waist-high wall of flesh.

The snake constricted its coil, drawing in its body around Farwander. The ring of slithering muscle didn't give him enough room to take a pace in any direction. He crouched, ready to jump, but the snake snapped down at him and only a desperate slash, that rang off one of its gory fangs, turned its head aside.

Somehow, Lady Temnos was on the rocks above the cave entrance. She was behind the snake's head, unseen. Blood was wet on her face. She wrapped her arms around a rock almost as big as she was and wrenched it out of place, in a shower of dirt and moss. She took the weight on her back leg and heaved the boulder down off her perch.

The rock slammed into the top of the snake's skull. Its head was driven down into the dirt at Farwander's feet. Its yellow eyes bulged and bone cracked. The stone was embedded in its fractured skull and something tore in its mouth, for blood spurted from between its jaws.

Farwander did not pause to draw breath. He grabbed the snake's brow ridge for purchase and drove his sword into its eye. The blade passed through the tissue of its eye and deep into its skull, piercing its diminutive lizard brain.

The snake hissed and thrashed for a good few minutes afterwards. Farwander held on, twisting and stabbing the sword to open up an even more gruesome wound. By the time the giant snake stopped thrashing, his sword arm was soaked red to the elbow.

Farwander grunted as he pulled his sword out. 'My lady!' he called out. He could not see her above the cave entrance.

He scrambled up the rocks to find her crouched there, gasping from the exertion. Her hair was wet with blood and sweat. Farwander squatted beside her and put a hand on her arm. It was hot, as if she was in the grip of a fever.

'The blood burn. The price a Heritor pays.'

Farwander tilted her face upwards. A rivulet of blood trickled from the corner of her eye. More was smeared around her mouth and ear. It had started to clot in her hair. 'The price?'

Lady Temnos brushed Farwander's hand away. 'Power does not come from nowhere,' she said. 'Like everything, it has to be paid for. When we use the strength our bloodline gives us, it takes its toll on our bodies. We must pay for our power in pain, Mr Farwander. That is why I do not use it lightly.'

'And here was I thinking you were indestructible.'

'It is nothing.'

'It is not nothing,' said Farwander. 'What if you pushed your powers too hard?'

'It would be far preferable to not pushing hard enough.' Lady Temnos' face hardened. 'I am not some weak creature to be fawned over and preserved, Master Farwander. By now you should know I am not the weakling men assume me to be.'

'From what I have just seen you do, my lady, weakness is the last attribute I would associate with you. But whatever you brought me into the expedition for, on this island part of my duty is to protect you on the rare occasion you need it. So I see you driving yourself to the point of death, and I fear for you.'

Lady Temnos got shakily to her feet. 'Your concern is noted,' she said. She looked down at the corpse of the enormous snake. 'Is it dead?'

'Nothing has ever been deader, my lady.'

Lady Temnos and Farwander descended from the rocks. The snake's blood had seeped into the rich earth and already columns of ants were beginning to traverse its huge sinuous body.

'I have seen your strength,' said Farwander. 'Is there any other ability of yours it would benefit me to know about?'

'Regenerative properties,' replied Lady Temnos. 'I have never been ill a day in my life. In athletic prowess I eclipse any man. I heal the damage from the blood burn quickly enough, but not instantly. All Heritors are different, depending on bloodline and chance. My mother could hypnotise a man with a glance, but sadly that has skipped a generation. My particular gifts concern the strength and health of my body.'

'Could the blood burn kill you?'

'I can drive myself to unconsciousness, certainly. As for any further, I cannot say.'

Farwander crested a low rise in an attempt to get better stock of his surroundings. They had travelled some way through the temple of the serpent people. He could not see any other expedition members nearby, but on the positive side, he could see no more oversized lizard predators either.

'Farwander, you lucky swinedog!' shouted a shrill, crotchety voice. Leveret emerged from between the trees, from a direction where Farwander could also hear the rushing of a stream. 'I thought you buggers were dead.'

'Not for want of trying,' replied Farwander.

As Leveret got closer Farwander could see she was soaking wet. 'River broke through the wall. Followed it outside, to here. Months at sea, almost sunk by a sodding kraken, and it's on land that I nearly drown.' Somehow, her soaking had not diminished her odour.

'Good to see you safe,' said Farwander.

'Aye, well, where's Grieff and her ladyship?'

'Lady Temnos is with me. Grieff is dead.'

Leveret paused at that, and resignation passed across her face. 'Yeah, well, it was a matter of time I suppose. How did it happen?'

Farwander considered briefly whether he should lie to her. 'He was eaten,' he said. 'A snake. It was quick.'

Leveret walked briskly past him. 'Where to next?'

'Lady Temnos will decide. Probably stick to the plan and hope we meet up with others on the way.'

'Bit of a bloody shambles, isn't it?'

'I would agree to the sentiment, if not the words.'

Lady Temnos did not comment on the unlikeliness of Leveret's survival, nor on the loss of Grieff. She led them, as Farwander had suspected, on the route she had agreed with her captains, as best she could tell from the location of Mount Golca edged blue by the moonlight. The jungle thinned out a little here, with hundreds of younger saplings finding purchase in the open areas between the ancient trees.

Lady Temnos suggested a low hill covered in juvenile trees as a place to camp for what remained of the night. All three were exhausted and hungry, and there seemed little point in keeping the pace fast when they weren't sure when or where they would meet up with anyone else from the expedition. A small, smoky fire was established and Leveret showed a talent for sleeping at a moment's notice, as she was snoring as soon as her head hit the dirt.

'This island is not as uninhabited as we might have hoped,' said Farwander as he and Lady Temnos sat and waited for their tiredness to claim them. Leveret's snoring was not helping them in that regard. 'Even if the serpent people have died out on this island, they still found their way to make our lives interesting.'

'There is much we do not know about the Ghost Archipelago,' said Lady Temnos. 'Far more than we do know.'

'Did Arcturaval have any thoughts on the matter?'

'He said Penitent's Landing was dangerous,' said Lady Temnos. 'The journey here, the island, the journey back. Everything. I have read his journals from the voyage but they were... inconsistent.'

'It sounds like he had a demon's own time of it.'

'The first to drink from the Crystal Pool were supposed to be like gods among men,' said Lady Temnos. 'I think many would be dismayed to read how human they were. Arcturaval left a lot of himself on Penitent's Landing, for all the power he brought back. Truth be told, Master Farwander, I do not know if he came to Penitent's Landing before or after he drank from the Pool. His writings made little virtue of describing the passage of time.'

'But he described something on this island that you want to rediscover.'

Lady Temnos smiled. 'He did, and I intend to find it. It is to discourage others from seeking it on their own that I keep its nature to myself.'

Farwander held his hands up like a man proclaiming innocence. 'My lady, I would not dream of trying to acquire the treasure of Mount Golca for myself.'

'That is just as well, Master Farwander, for you would perish in the attempt.'

'I cannot but help think Arcturaval could had left us more definitive clues about what we were going to find here. Deadly serpentine ruins would have been a useful warning to have.'

'I do not believe he anticipated anyone would follow him out here,' said Lady Temnos.

'So the treasure is not something he left here to be recovered?'

'I will not be drawn on the question,' said Lady Temnos, with a tone of finality Farwander thought it wise to heed.

'A shame about Grieff,' he said. 'We have lost too many men already.'

'Men will die,' said Lady Temnos. 'We will not last long without acknowledging that.'

'Leveret took it hard.' He looked down at the sleeping woman, who had instantly fallen into a deep stentorious slumber. 'She tried to hide it but even she couldn't completely.'

'We've all lost crewmates.'

'He was more,' said Farwander. Lady Temnos raised an eyebrow in surprise. 'It wasn't hard to tell,' he continued. 'I appreciate such things might not be obvious from your position on high, but for us lowly folks it was pretty clear.'

'I expected Miss Pavine to be of better judgement,' said Lady Temnos, digesting this information. 'Grieff was a fool.'

'I won't argue with you on that point. But he was not completely wrong.'

'I beg your pardon?'

'There have been a thousand times, my lady, when you could have turned back, but rather fewer reasons to carry on. When we learned the Brotherhood were intent on stopping the expedition, you could have sailed back to Rileport. When we captured that hapless fool of a Warden we knew they could send the beasts of the sea at us, but you did not turn back. And when Lord Hekatar broke our fleet, you could have focused on escaping this island and getting back to civilisation instead of forging on for the mountain. But you did not. Men will follow a Heritor, it is true, but that does not mean the Heritor is always right in leading them. As you say, a lot of men have died. There will be more to come before all this is over. Lady Temnos, what have you bought with their lives?'

'Do you forget your place, Master Farwander?'

'My place does not mean a great deal from where I am sitting. It is the place of a man whose priority is surviving, but whose only guide in this dark place seems intent on finding a nameless treasure in the heart of a volcano in spite of how many madmen and beasts are equally intent on killing us all.'

'Do you think to abandon me?' demanded Lady Temnos.

'No, my lady. You are the only uniting force among those of us who survive. But I fear you will use the authority of a Heritor to continue with your treasure hunt and care nothing for whether any of us make it off this island alive.'

'Then what would you have me do? Would you have me turn back, Master Farwander? Would you have Lady Jessicara Temnos return to her home in rags, with nothing to show?'

'Heavens forbid you should be brought down to our level, my lady.'

Lady Temnos was on her feet, fists bunched. 'You dare! How can you lecture me when you know nothing of the demands on a Heritor? You have never lived a life where anything short of greatness is a failure. You have never seen the eyes on you waiting for you to show the weakness of a normal human, so they can swoop in and usurp everything you own. I will return to my home in triumph or I will not return. You can slink back to Last Fathom and blend in with the scum again if that makes you happy. I do not have that luxury.'

'Or you could abandon the same conceit as Hekatar,' replied Farwander, 'and stop pretending you are a god among us mortals.'

'I am not like him!' shouted Lady Temnos. 'I am no madman!' She forced her voice down, fighting with the effort of keeping her temper. 'You have no idea what it is like to be robbed of the freedom to fail. You can walk away from anything with a smile and a cutting word. Your name means nothing. If I turn back, every smirking wretch will spit upon the name of House Temnos.' She sat down again, and a drop of blood ran from her nose. The blood burn had been ignited inside her, and she had commanded it to calm down. 'Walk away if you will,' she said. 'Do not presume to understand.'

Leveret turned over and squinted at them through the dying firelight. 'Are you two done?' she croaked, and instantly fell back to sleep.

CHAPTER 10

A band of survivors had found a ruin that the jungle had stripped of its roof, and within its half-tumbled walls set up a temporary defensive structure where they could wait until they could decide what to do. They had piled up branches and fallen trunks to cover the breaches in the walls and dug pits for the bodies of those whose injuries would soon claim them. It was a bleak, exposed scrape of a place, but for the moment it counted as their fortress.

It was also located on the route south-east around the inaccessible lower slopes of Mount Golca, so Lady Temnos spotted it as her small, exhausted party made their way through the jungle. Some enterprising soul had hung a ship's flag he had rescued for some reason from the sea battle, and its bright red and blue colours had caught her eye through the trees.

Farwander followed Lady Temnos as she approached the encampment. They had spoken barely a word since the night before. Leveret trudged sullenly alongside them, somehow grumpier than normal with her sleep having been interrupted.

Captain Vormish's grandly moustachioed face appeared at the top of the wall. 'It gladdens my heart that you yet live, my lady!' he boomed.

Farwander had no great love for Vormish but it was still a relief to see him. A few other dirty, tired faces joined Vormish at the wall to see if Lady Temnos really had survived the jungle to join them.

'How many are with you?' asked Lady Temnos.

'Just under two hundred,' said Vormish. 'But we are dwindling by the hour.'

'How so?'

'Enter, my lady, and I will explain.'

Inside the ruins the crew had made camp as best they could, with several fire pits dug and shelters set up against the sturdiest walls. The Earth Warden Karanas was repairing one of the fallen wall sections, using gestures to command the rocks to roll back into place. Several wounded lay in the centre of the camp, covered in tattered jackets that served as blankets.

'Those wounded are new,' said Farwander. 'They weren't carried here.'

'What has happened, Captain Vormish?' demanded Lady Temnos.

'The Brotherhood are making their move,' said Vormish. 'They have sent an abomination after us.'

'We are far from the sea,' said Farwander. 'How have they managed that?'

'It is not a kraken, and it is not a natural creature,' explained Vormish. 'Foul magic has made it. I have sent men out to gather food and firewood, but it has preyed upon them. I must either send men to their deaths, huddle here and starve, or lead my whole command into the jaws of the beast.'

'Well, Captain, you need bear that burden no longer,' said Lady Temnos. 'The command is mine now.'

'Of course, my lady.'

As before, there was no question that Lady Temnos was now in charge. Farwander imagined Vormish would be loath to give up even the command of such an uninspiring place as this, to anyone except a Heritor. Perhaps, he thought, the very authority that came with the status of a Heritor was Lady Temnos' greatest power, far eclipsing her enhanced physical abilities. It was not the strength of her body, after all, that had caused hundreds of men to follow her across the ocean to Penitent's Landing.

'So what do we do about this thing?' asked Leveret. Alone among the crew, Farwander had learned, Leveret seemed to have the liberty to speak to Lady Temnos as bluntly as she wished.

'We kill it,' replied Lady Temnos.

* * *

The dying man recalled the darkness given form, coalescing into a mass of tentacles and teeth and surging out of the jungle. In the fever of his injuries, he recalled the cautionary tales taught to him by his father, who described nameless horrors lurking in the woods to devour disobedient children. He spoke of it all to Farwander, before falling back into a sleep from which he never woke.

A survivor showed the three brutally deep claw marks on his torso with a mixture of dread and pride. He described the perpetrator as a whole herd of saurians, like the ones that had stormed the expedition a little over a day previously, but of far greater speed and cunning. The man's wounds were starting to fester and he was showing the first twitches of fever, so it could not be certain if his words were from memory or delirium.

Another survivor only saw it from a distance. He recalled its head brushing the jungle canopy, accompanied by a mass of searching tendrils, and he whispered it was an abomination dredged up from the Oblivion Deeps to hunt those the Kraken Queen believed should be lying drowned in her domain of wreckage and death. In his fear he had come to believe completely in the tales of Scaraveyla and her undersea realm, and Farwander had forced himself not to question the man further to see if his visions matched Farwander's own.

'Not much to go on,' said Farwander as he ate for the first time in what felt like an age. It wasn't much, just a few strips of meat from a scrawny bird cooked over the fire in front of him, and his stomach so yearned for more it almost felt like he should have stayed hungry.

''Tis no' a natural beastie, that's fer sure,' said Karanas, who had joined Farwander in the scanty feast. 'These lizards I've seen afore on the islands, and heard of worse. But the thing that killed those laddies isn't born of these shores. I can feel the ground's disgust at it. Penitent's Landing isnae too keen on us, but it hates that thing more.'

'Could the Brotherhood be controlling it?' asked Farwander.

'I cannae say fer sure what they can do. They sent the kraken after the *Legacy*. They bind sea beasties to their fleet. I dare say they could command this predator, too.'

'Then could they have made it?'

Karanas let out a low whistle. 'I hope not, laddie. I hope not.'

The day had been long and grim so far. Scavengers had dared not venture far from the ruins and the forest had already been plucked bare of anything edible. Some able crossbowmen had returned with braces of colourful birds, but it hadn't been nearly enough to satisfy the crew. Captain Vormish walked across the sorry camp and somehow his breastplate retained enough polish to reflect the noonday sun that dappled down through the canopy.

'So, Master Farwander,' said Vormish, 'I take it the Warden here has apprised you of our situation?'

'He has, Captain.'

'And your take on it?'

'I agree with Lady Temnos. The only solution is to kill it. And soon, for the Brotherhood's desire is to keep us here.'

'And you have a plan to do so?'

'I need your best hunters and shooters,' said Farwander. 'Strong and able-bodied men, as many as you can spare without leaving the wounded unguarded. And Karanas here.'

Vormish did not look impressed. 'And your plan?'

'Hunt it down, of course. This is not the time to over-think things.'

'You think it will be so simple? I have ridden after every form of prey that exists back across the sea, sir, and I can assure you this quarry will not roll over and die for you, as you seem to hope.'

'I'm not hoping for anything,' said Farwander. 'Captain Vormish, my plan is not foolproof or even likely to succeed, but it is better than any of the alternatives. Walk out with us or stay here, but if you're as good a hunter as you say we can hardly do without you. The men won't run if they know you're watching. The sun is at its highest and the visibility will never be better. Ready?'

Vormish looked taken aback at first, for he was not a man used to acting on the plans of another. But his eye flickered to the bodies lined up under makeshift covering, waiting for a party of men to bury them outside the walls of the ruins. He gripped the pommel of his sword and puffed out his chest, so his breastplate glimmered even brighter. 'Ready I am, sir,' he said.

* * *

The jungle closed in, dense and sweltering. Farwander ran his grimy sleeve over his face, but the salt of his sweat still stung his eyes. The ground was sodden and just walking was exhausting.

This far into the jungle, life mixed with death. Everything stank of rot. The ground rose and fell into sharp gullies, in which gathered countless seasons' worth of decaying plant matter. Thick blankets of flies rose from animal corpses as the hunting party disturbed them, and obscenely huge foul-smelling flowers clustered around the most foetid patches of bog.

In other circumstances, such a region of jungle would have been avoided by the crew. It was easy to get lost, to become nauseated by the diseased air, or simply to sink into the marshy ground. But the beast's trail had led here, into the densest foulness of the jungle.

If it was indeed not a natural inhabitant of Penitent's Landing, the beast had chosen this region to be its lair, or else had been directed to haunt this place by the Brotherhood's Wardens where it was within easy striking distance of the expedition. It was a logical place for it to inhabit. The very ground and air were steeped in death here, as if death had come to be wrapped around the beast's environs like a cloak.

The party paused at a deep cleft in the ground where some ancient upheaval had lifted the jungle floor and left a gully choked with mulch. The visibility was low as mists rolled in, pouring down off the slopes of Mount Golca and turning the air as damp as the midst of a rainstorm. Karanas crouched near the foot of a huge black tree wound with creepers.

''Tis big, whatever it is,' said the Earth Warden. Though Captain Vormish had selected a strapping youth named Gertrum as the expedition's best hunter, it was Karanas who was their best tracker. He could hear the whispers from the earth itself. 'Aye, the ground here weeps in pain of it. See here? Three toes, each with a claw. Vicious swine, so it is. But then we knew that.'

Farwander looked down at the footprint the beast had left in the black earth. It was indeed huge, something like that of an immense bird but far more weighty and muscular, with claws that had sunk deep into the ground.

'Is it close?'

'It's fast,' replied Karanas. 'That means wherever it is, laddie, it's close.'

'If we stray much further we may not make it back,' said Vormish. In spite of the heat and the gruelling pace the hunters had kept up, he still wore his breastplate, though it was no longer brightly polished and his moustache had begun to wilt.

'I'll lead us back,' said Karanas.

'And if you are the first one the beast takes?'

'Then you're up ordure creek,' replied Karanas.

'Hear that?' said Gertrum, head inclined and brow furrowed. He was tall, muscular and handsome, though simple-spoken and with nothing of a leader about him. Farwander guessed he had grown up as a forester, hunting game or shooting down birds that troubled his family farm. 'Water.'

'We're nearer the river than I thought,' said Karanas. 'Good ear, lad.'

The party advanced until Farwander could hear the water, too. A sluggish river cut through the jungle, at the base of a deep ravine it had carved through the ground. Exposed tree roots were polished ivory by the passage of water and pockets of foulness gathered in stagnant pools where the river's path had become choked with debris and rot. An enormous tree leaned over the river, dangling streamers of moss over the water.

'Here,' said Farwander.

'Aye, said Karanas, 'as good as anywhere else.' He turned to Gertrum. 'Go find us a kill, lad, Make it a good one.'

Gertrum nodded, beckoned two more crossbowmen over and headed off into the mists, with a certainty that suggested he had a natural affinity for tracking down prey.

'If it catches us here, it's over,' said Karanas. 'No walls here to run to.'

'The river might give us a chance,' said Farwander. 'At least, if it can't swim.'

'Pretty big "if" there. Leaving a lot to chance.'

'But you'll see it coming.'

'If the earth speaks to me here, aye. 'Tis a surly and hateful place, this. The earth may stay silent just to spite us.'

'You know, Karanas, you're not one for filling a fellow with confidence.'

Karanas shrugged. 'Wasnae aware that was my job.'

'Might as well make it marginally more difficult for us to die,' said Vormish to the men. 'Set up a picket. A man at each corner. Make what shelter you can and find some dry wood. Come, come, no need to look so morose about it! Think about the delightful adventure we're all on!'

Vormish had a rare talent for making men do what they felt far too miserable and tired to do, which Farwander had to concede was an impressively useful skill. Soon watches were set up so the men could rest without letting their guard down. A fire proved more difficult, with a miserable smoky smouldering all the men could coax from the damp wood they gathered.

Night drew in. The sun had difficulty enough reaching through the dense canopy here, but the shadowy green became almost impenetrably dark after dusk. Farwander could grab only a couple of uncomfortable hours of sleep. He was convinced he would wake with some slimy thing crawling across him, or would open his eyes to find that every other member of the hunting party was dead and he was alone in a clutch of corpses.

He dreamed of tentacles and teeth half-glimpsed through the black ocean, immense coiling shapes churning in darkness. He gasped down a desperate breath and for an awful moment he was convinced he was deep beneath the surface of the sea, choking on a lungful of brine.

He opened his eyes to the pre-dawn grey. Three figures were silhouetted against the filmy light just bleeding through the canopy – Gertrum and his companions. Gertrum had a large deer slung over his shoulders, carried like an ox carries a yoke. Farwander could see the bolt protruding from the deer's neck. It had been a hell of a shot, he thought.

'Get up,' said Captain Vormish, prodding Farwander with the point of his boot. As far as Farwander could tell, Vormish hadn't slept at all. 'This is your plan. Time to see it through.'

Vormish had already given the hunters their directions. Farwander had little to do but wait with Karanas where the Earth Warden set cross-legged on a spit of exposed rock, listening.

'It's here,' said Karanas eventually, as the morning sun struggled to break through the trees.

Farwander waved the signal to Gertrum, who hefted the weight of the slain deer and clambered along the length of the tree trunk overhanging the river. He tied a rope to the deer's back legs, and the other to a branch of the tree. He took out his skinning knife and deftly cut the deer's throat.

Gertrum dropped the deer, which bounced and dangled from the rope. Its open throat let a trickle of blood fall into the river, where its drops dispersed pinkly in the waters.

Farwander crouched and watched for a long moment, and realised he was holding his breath. He looked around at Karanas.

'Aye,' said the Warden. It was all he needed to say.

Farwander heard the impact moments later. A deep, weighty thud into the damp earth. It was followed by another, then another, growing louder each time.

Footsteps.

Even though the men knew to be silent, Farwander could still make out the intakes of breath as it came into sight. It was a shape among the trees, darkness upon darkness, far larger than the herd creatures that had stampeded through the expedition. Its shape was indistinct but Farwander had a sense of its huge head and oversized jaws, and the length of its body with a massive tail balancing the weight of its skull. With each thump of its footfall it resolved into a more definite shape, and it just kept getting worse.

But there was something else. A wrongness about its silhouette, a distortion around it that told Farwander this was not just a larger version of the saurians he had already seen.

The thing paused and Farwander could hear its breath. It was sniffing. It could smell the blood of Gertrum's kill.

Then it crunched through the nearest layer of trees, and Farwander saw what it really was.

It had been a gigantic saurian predator, built purely to kill. Its immense jaws and rows of ivory teeth, and the massively powerful legs with their three murderous claws, could not have been for anything else but killing and dismembering its prey. But that was not what made it truly terrible.

Its forelimbs were gone, and in its place were two long, thick tentacles like those of a giant and ancient octopus. More tentacles sprouted from its spine. Its body was covered in scars where its flesh had been pared apart and sewn crudely back together, and its scaled and leathery skin was branded with the symbols of an arcane language Farwander was glad he didn't know. It let out a long, low rumble from its enormous lungs, and it brought with it the stench of the ocean's rot, all the death left behind by the neap tide, all the malice and lethality of Scaraveyla's realm bound into this land-walking creature.

On the tree trunk, Gertrum froze. Karanas stood carefully and stepped out of the creature's line of sight, behind the tree. Farwander crouched down and wished the ground would open up so he could have a way to get free of the monster's raw, harrowing presence.

But that would do no good. It would hunt him down, as it had so many men of the expedition already.

The saurian horror walked up to the river bank and lowered its head towards the hanging deer. Farwander could see the deep creases and scars of great age around its small yellow eyes. It took a step into the river and the water foamed up around its leg.

Hunger was winning. The saurian stepped into the river and waded towards the deer. It crouched down, ready to leap up at the morsel.

'Now!' yelled Farwander.

The men gathered by Captain Vormish had been sturdy and strong, but even for them the work had been taxing. They had hacked almost the whole way through the trunk of the overhanging tree, while shoring up the growing cut with wedges of wood. It had threatened to fall many times during the night, and it wasn't certain it would even hold Gertrum's weight.

Now those men hauled on the ropes they had tied to the wedges, and tore them out. With a splintering and screaming of breaking wood, the overhanging trunk fell into the river, just as the saurian's jaws yawned up to close on the deer.

The tree crashed down on the saurian, hitting it where its muscular neck joined its torso. With a bellow it was forced down into the waters, which foamed up around it. Gertrum leaped clear and hit the bank chest-first, scrabbling to keep from slipping back down into the saurian's reach.

The men ran to the bank, crossbows in hand. In moments a hail of bolts was raining down at the creature. Most bounced off but some found a weak spot and blood spurted from new wounds.

The saurian lashed up with one of its grafted tentacles and snatched a man off the riverbank, hurling him downriver. It reared up, lifting the immense weight of the fallen tree and threatening to shrug it free.

CHAPTER 10

'Away and be broken, ye beastie!' yelled Karanas. With a straining of his sinews, his magic lifted the rock he had been sitting on from the ground. Moss and mulch rained down as the rock hovered in the air, and was cast at the saurian. Trapped beneath the tree, it was unable to lurch out of the way, and the rock crunched into the side of its skull.

'The bolts are no good!' shouted Farwander. 'Get in and finish it!'

He could not fully believe he had given such an insane order. And yet there he was, running full pelt towards the monstrosity even as every sinew in him demanded he turn back and run the other way. The smell of oceanic rot was almost overpowering as Farwander reached the bank with his sword drawn.

The saurian lashed out at him with a tentacle. Farwander rolled out of the way. One of the smaller ones on the creature's back snaked out as he slithered down the river bank, but he slashed at it and the good steel of his blade sliced it clean off.

The saurian roared. The deafening sound was not as bad as the rotting meat on its breath. Farwander waded into the thigh-deep water and stabbed up at its exposed throat.

The other men were doing the same around him. Vormish led them, brandishing his cutlass like a beacon for them to follow. The saurian thrashed again to throw the weight of the tree off it but a crossbow quarrel appeared in its eye, and Farwander didn't have to look up to the far bank to know Gertrum had made the shot.

The saurian's head swung low as the shock of its ruined eye hit it. Farwander lunged again and the blade sunk deep into the flesh of its throat.

It was ugly butcher's work, and it took an appallingly long time. With every wound the beast weakened, and more men were able to get at it with their cutlasses and knives. The water foamed pink with its blood. Its grafted tentacles thrashed out at them, but its strength failed and the men it struck staggered back up out of the water.

Farwander's fine blade was put to work as a butchery knife, sawing through meat and sinew. He opened up a vein in its neck and its noxious blood spilled down over him. Vormish climbed onto its back and hacked at the rear of its skull, trying to cut through its spine.

Finally, thankfully, after a long and punishing labour, it was dead.

Farwander climbed back up the slope from the swamp of mud and gore the river had become. He was covered in it. Vormish was similarly filthy and his breastplate looked like it would never shine again.

'I did not think it would work, Master Farwander,' said Vormish. 'I must speak the truth on that.'

'Then why did you follow me?'

'A plan doomed to fail is better than no plan. Even to fail here would be better than to wait in that ruin to die. A lesson hard to learn, yes sir! But one a man must if he is to lead fighting men.' Vormish gestured at the mass of torn flesh that had once been the predator. 'No natural beast.'

'It is not,' agreed Farwander. 'The Brotherhood made it. They put the mark of Scaraveyla upon it.'

Karanas clambered down the bank to get a closer look at the creature. He examined the places where the tentacles joined its saurian hide. They had been stitched onto the saurian's torso in a manner that reminded Farwander of an exceptionally crudely done work of taxidermy.

'Bloody bad work, this,' said Karanas. 'But these tentacles moved. The flesh is grown together. It should all be dead, but it's not. Aye, this is the work of their Kraken Wardens. Not just butchery but magic, too.'

'I've seen what Wardens can do,' said Farwander, 'but I didn't even know magic like this existed. Why would anyone seek it out? Why would they even try to see if they could do something like this?'

'Because nature to one such as I is an ally to be respected and begged for help,' said Karanas. 'And given her right honours in return. But to others, it's a wild animal to be turned into a wee pet. Whoever done this, they hate the world that made the creatures they bound together. They see the world and they want to change it, not just because it's useful to them, but because they can. They want to rise above it and prove themselves superior. The man that did this, he thinks he's a god.'

'That sounds like Hekatar, sure enough,' said Farwander.

'Aye, and whatever the reasoning for it, the Wardens that made this beastie did it on land,' replied Karanas. 'They found themselves the biggest, meanest lizard they could and made this out of it. Had to have landed first, to do it, and in force.'

'Then the Brotherhood are ahead of us,' said Vormish. 'They know we are here and have the means to send such horrors against us.'

'This has become their ground,' said Farwander.

'And this has become a war,' added Vormish, with a smile glimmering beneath his moustache. 'And war, Master Farwander, I know.'

CHAPTER 11

He dreamed, when they next found luxury to sleep, of the Oblivion Deeps again.

It felt familiar now, like a bad memory from his childhood. This time he was one of the souls sinking into the Deeps, newly drowned and ignorant of the fate waiting beneath it. He was one of the grains of sand the cultist Warden had told him of, one of the thousands who had failed to gain the favour of Scaraveyla.

He felt the brine burning his lungs as he breathed it in. His body was racked with the anguish of his last moments as the sea had taken him. Coldness and fear enveloped him. His chest was an angry knot of pain.

He was plucked from the wayward currents, the way that a shark plucked a bleeding fish that had fallen behind its shoal, and brought down through the lightless fathoms to the Shipwreck Throne. He was chosen, but not like the favoured of Scaraveyla – it was more like the way a predator chose a prey from the herd, seeking out the weakest and sickest, the one who could not fend for himself.

He was something weak enough to be toyed with, to be singled out and made to suffer.

There hundreds of fathoms below sat Scaraveyla, surrounded by a legion of her cultists. Farwander could not decide on her form, for it shifted constantly. Here she was a bloated monstrosity of scales and suckers, there an elegant queen with dark eyes. Now her body was an inchoate mass of churning blackness, then the insubstantial ghosts of a million drowned mariners. The madness would have made him black out, were he not forced into wakefulness by the constant screaming of his lungs.

'So,' said Scaraveyla, 'who is this?'

It was only in a dream that such a voice could exist. It was not sound, just pure meaning that overwhelmed Farwander's senses. It was not the voice of a woman or a monster. It just was.

Farwander tried to formulate a pithy reply so he could at least respond to her in the manner he had always done to those who confronted him, but there was no air in his throat, only seawater. He spluttered and heaved uselessly, and on her many faces Scaraveyla wore an expression of faintly amused curiosity.

'This is the one who wanders the surface,' said Scaraveyla. 'My ocean. My realm. And he crawls upon it like an idiot infant. Why?'

The chill of the ocean gripped him and crushed. Farwander felt bones cracking. Pain flared everywhere on his body at once. He thrashed and tried to cry out, but the water in his lungs made no sound. The Kraken Queen knew he could not answer. She just wanted to feel him suffer.

The monsters of the deep drifted past, turning their many eyes towards the spectacle of Scaraveyla tormenting a chosen soul. It was a rare entertainment, to see her dismember a newcomer to the Oblivion Deeps. The choirs of the Brotherhood watched from the foot of Scaraveyla's throne, transfixed by the beauty only they could perceive radiating off their queen.

'You are looking for something. Why else would a dry-footed fool trespass on the Kraken Queen's ocean? Something you desire more than life itself, to risk that life within my coils. What is it? What do you want?'

Her tentacles were around him, constricting and crushing. Her bony squid's beak snapped inside her immense mass of swarming tendrils. Her perfect, chill beauty iced over with satisfaction to feel him struggle and thrash.

'What are you searching for? What is the treasure of Mount Golca?'

Finally, the air bubbled up from the base of Farwander's lungs, and he had a voice. He screamed out the answer, for he was no longer in control of his own body.

He told her everything.

And the Kraken Queen laughed.

The expedition picked up wanderers and stragglers here and there. A company of marines, survivors from the *Lightning Child*, had banded together and forged through the jungle to rejoin with Lady Temnos at the ruins. They were splendidly outfitted in bronze armour and scarlet plumes, and had been recruited by Captain Al'Harhi from the men who guarded the walls of the city-state of Havenmoor. Navigator Gavel had led a band of stragglers through the swampy ground and linked up with the main body of men once Lady Temnos had led them out of the ruins and towards the more accessible slopes of Mount Golca.

They had fewer than three hundred souls left. The rest were dead, or scattered in small groups across Penitent's Landing with no ready way of linking up. Some, though no one spoke of them, must have been salvaged from the sea barely alive by the Brotherhood of Scaraveyla, and been converted through madness and torment into new devotees of the Kraken Queen. It was not much to say for the fleet that had left Cape Cadaver.

As the expedition trudged around the forbidding south slopes of the mountain and swung northwards to reach its eastern face, they saw more and more of the markings Farwander recognised from the native map. Skulls were nailed to the boughs of trees and here and there were old structures of wood, made of stripped branches lashed together in simple frameworks, which Farwander was certain were made for suspending the corpses of the sacrificed.

The jungle floor was broken by stumps of fallen columns and traces of building walls. They passed through a village almost entirely swallowed by moss and root, with a wide-mouthed well at the bottom of which could be glimpsed the mouldering bones and white teeth of ancient skeletons. The bones were human, not serpentine, so there were at least two peoples once on Penitent's Landing.

But that had been long ago. The birds shrieked through the treetops and the fauna crept warily at the edge of the scouts' vision, but anything sentient or civilised had died off. The island was selective about who was permitted to survive on its back.

Once, there had been temples and settlements here, teeming with people. And Penitent's Landing had killed them.

* * *

'Hold up,' said Leveret, and Farwander stopped trudging through the dense undergrowth and pressed against the bole of a tree. He and Leveret were ranging ahead of the expedition, which had been organised by Vormish into columns to roughly approximate an army on the march. The best hunters and a few other souls trusted by Lady Temnos were sent to pathfind, survey obstacles to the march and hunt for enemies up ahead. The jungle here had closed in, not noxious and hungry like the swampy ground but lush and dense, with patches of thorns or stinging leaves to keep things interesting.

The wall of green broke up ahead. Through the rustling of the leaves and the hooting of the birds, Farwander could hear the rush of water. He slithered a little further through the undergrowth until he could see a pair of structures up ahead.

They were statues. Each was of a human, he guessed, albeit rendered in a stylised and square-lined way. They squatted to either side of a stone bridge that spanned a gorge running through the jungle like a deep and unhealed wound. The bridge looked solid, built of massive stone presumably quarried from the slope of Mount Golca that swept skywards beyond the river. It was wide enough for ten men to march side by side. A pair of matching figures marked the other side of the span, where the jungle again took over in a dense green curtain.

'We have to cross that,' said Leveret.

'At least it hasn't fallen into the river,' said Farwander. 'Everything else on this island seems to have collapsed a few hundred years ago.'

'Wasn't on the bloody map,' grumbled Leveret.

'Wait.' Farwander pointed to the far side of the bridge. 'There's something there.'

From the treeline emerged a figure, blending at first with the shadows between the tree trunks but emerging into the light. It was shirtless and carrying a bow with an arrow nocked. Farwander could make out the shaven head and luridly scarred skin, still red and weeping from the recent wounds that covered the man's arms and torso.

'Brotherhood,' hissed Farwander.

'Well that's just spiffing,' said Leveret.

More cultists emerged from the forest to take up positions on the far side of the bridge, scanning the forest down the length of an arrow. A phalanx of larger cultists, senior brothers with their flesh gnarled with aged scars, marched out and stood just on the span of the bridge. They surrounded a priest in purple and black robes, who trailed long streamers from his shoulders in imitation of a squid's tentacles. His face was hidden behind a wooden mask painted purple, with large black eyes like those of something that lived beneath the mud.

'Lady Temnos!' cried the priest stridently. A flight of birds took up in panic at the sound. 'The Prophet of the

Kraken Queen would speak with you! Your men are exhausted and diseased. Their brethren sink bloated into Scaraveyla's realm.' The priest walked further onto the bridge, gesturing extravagantly. 'You will die on this island. It is no great shame to seek deliverance from your fate, and it will be granted. The Prophet will parley with you, as a mark of respect to a fellow Heritor. I beg you to accept his generosity, my lady. It is rare, and will not be repeated.'

The herald of Scaraveyla retreated back into the cover of the forest, leaving the cultist archers there to watch the far side.

'Well he was a knobhead,' said Leveret.

'Quite so,' said Farwander. 'Vormish was right. The cult's ahead of us. They're going for Mount Golca and they're going to hold this bridge to keep us from making a race of it.'

'What's all the parley about then?'

'A chance to draw out Lady Temnos and kill her, I expect.'

Leveret sniffed. 'Yeah, but she's still gonna go out there.'

'Yes, I rather suspect she is. You'd better head back and get word to the rest. We don't need Vormish blundering into this lot.'

'What will you do?'

'See if the knobhead has anything else to say for himself.'

'Right you are.' Leveret scrabbled back into the cover of the denser jungle, leaving Farwander to keep watch and wonder what the expedition was supposed to do now.

* * *

'I am no fool,' said Lady Temnos. 'Hekatar means to see me dead. This is an attempt to make that happen.'

'It's a rather crude attempt,' said Vormish. 'If I might say so.'

'So,' said Karanas, 'who's going with ye?'

The impromptu meeting of the expedition's surviving leaders took place in a hollow formed by a fallen tree, the enormous girth of which had ripped up a crater in the jungle floor where its roots had been torn out. They were sheltered from earshot of the rest of the expedition and any Brotherhood spies who might be lurking in the trees. Farwander had made his way back there to report that the priest of Scaraveyla had not emerged again to spout pomposity into the jungle.

One of Lady Temnos' Heritor powers appeared to be remaining dignified in appearance in spite of a trek through the jungle, and she looked presentable in her light leather armour and duellist's shoulder guard, her hair tied back and her sword at her side. Even Vormish's breastplate had lost its shine.

'I will take Master Farwander,' said Lady Temnos.

'Me?' said Farwander, unguardedly.

'A Heritor must present herself with the poise of a ruler and a warrior,' replied Lady Temnos. 'Is that not one of the arguments you made in favour of my bringing you on this expedition? You are the closest thing we have to a bona fide aristocrat, at least still among the living. I will need to you project the correct image.'

'Hekatar will try to kill you,' said Farwander.

'Then I shall have your Bittersweet Blade to defend me,' replied Lady Temnos simply. 'Besides, I cannot risk our Earth Warden.'

Karanas shrugged. 'Sorry, laddie. Wish I could be there at yer side, I really do.'

'Vormish,' said Lady Temnos, 'draw up the men ready to retreat back the way we came if anything happens to me. It may be you can find a defensive position there.'

'I see,' said Vormish, making an effort to appear unmoved and stoic. 'Anything else?'

'Keep as many alive as you can,' said Lady Temnos, 'but not at the expense of falling into the Brotherhood's hands. Scaraveyla has taken too many of our living already.'

'It shall be done, my lady.'

Lady Temnos turned back to Farwander. 'We should make haste. I doubt the Prophet of Scaraveyla is used to being kept waiting.'

'One moment,' said Farwander. Lady Temnos paused midway through walking out of the hollow, and gave him a look that suggested she was unused to being told to halt by anyone.

'What are you going to do?' he said.

'Talk to him,' replied Lady Temnos, and walked away. Farwander, unable to think of any other course of action, followed her.

* * *

The Priest of Scaraveyla came out to meet them, still covered by the cultist bowmen and flanked by two enormous cultist hulks. The warriors' muscles strained to burst from their tentacle-scarred skin, and each carried a vicious scourge entwined with steel shards.

Lady Temnos walked briskly onto the bridge with Farwander beside her. He could not help but glance over the edge of the bridge's wall. The gorge beneath must have been a hundred feet deep. The water below foamed and rushed over a rapid of rocks and fallen trees.

'I can't help but feel outnumbered,' said Farwander, his eyes flickering between the bowmen and the massive warriors guarding the priest.

'I wonder, Master Farwander, if you ever speak but in jest,' said Lady Temnos. 'I suggest it would be prudent to let me do the talking.'

'Normally that's something I say to other people,' replied Farwander, 'but for once I think I'd be better as the silent presence at this particular negotiation.'

'Lady Temnos!' said the priest, his arms wide as if greeting an old family member. 'With what joy I regard your countenance! Truly the Kraken Queen smiles on us all.'

Farwander couldn't imagine Scaraveyla smiling at anyone. He was sure Lady Temnos shuddered at the priest's tone.

'I am here for Hekatar,' said Lady Temnos. 'Not for you.'

'But of course,' said the priest. 'I am but his herald, he who goes before so the world might know to kneel.' He stepped aside, as did the warriors protecting him. From the jungle walked Lord Hekatar.

The image of the Prophet of Scaraveyla was burned into Farwander's memory, but still his mind reeled as if he saw him for the first time. Hekatar wore his black iron armour in spite of the sweltering damp of the jungle and most of his face was hidden behind the kraken visor of his helm. The leather cloak sighed against the undergrowth as he walked. Hekatar's weapon, the shipwreck anchor, was strapped to his back. It would have needed several men to lift it, but Farwander knew by some instinct that Hekatar could wield it as deftly as a razor.

Farwander felt like his eyes were being driven back into his head by the raw presence of the Prophet of Scaraveyla, but he could not look away. Hekatar demanded the attention of everyone around him, whether it was through devotion, hate, or simple fear.

Hekatar walked to the middle of the bridge. Lady Temnos hesitated for just a moment, then walked onto the bridge herself, stopping shortly before Hekatar. Farwander realised he was staying half a step behind her, just so there was someone between himself and the prophet.

'Lady Temnos,' intoned Hekatar, in a voice like a crashing wave. 'I will not demand you kneel.'

'That is just as well,' said Lady Temnos. 'You would have been disappointed.'

'You need not die upon this island.' Hekatar held out a gauntleted hand. 'I do not seek your death.'

'No,' replied Lady Temnos coldly. 'You want the treasure of Mount Golca.'

'And I will take it. You are not the greatest obstacle before me. This jungle, the mountain, the voyage to this place, they are all greater barriers to me than you and your men. I will overcome them all. I will crush them, if they remain in my path. If they remove themselves from my path, they will be unharmed.'

'So you will let me go.'

'I will give you leave to return to your ships, and leave this island.'

'The ships you sank.'

'I have no care for how you depart. My mercy ends upon this bridge. I give you an alternative to inevitable extermination at my hands. Turn around and leave Mount Golca, and do not come back, and you will survive. That is all I will give you.'

'You sent a beast to devour us,' said Lady Temnos. Her voice was forcedly level, as if she was demanding she show no anger or disgust towards Hekatar. 'Taking our leave from here is less appealing knowing your priests may be concocting more such things to be set upon us.'

'Then when you depart, you would be advised to make haste, for once turned loose the spawn of Scaraveyla will not stop until they are sated or dead.'

'I see,' said Lady Temnos. 'Are you finished?'

Only silence responded to her. Hekatar wore no expression on what little could be seen of his face.

'Then I fear neither of us will get what we want,' continued Lady Temnos. 'I did not come to this bridge so I could agree not to cross it. I am here for what lies in the mountain, and I will return with it or die.'

'Then why did you come here?' said Hekatar.

'To stand before you,' replied Lady Temnos. 'To be within a sword-thrust of my enemy.'

'As I thought,' said Hekatar. 'Then begin.'

Farwander knew Lady Temnos was strong, but he had not expected her speed. Her sword was in her hand and she was darting at Hekatar, the point of her blade aimed up at his throat.

Farwander had trained a part of his mind to dissect the motion and sequence of a swordfight. He automatically evaluated the moves and responses of each combatant, even while the rest of his mind was reeling with shock and panic.

Lady Temnos had forgotten in that moment everything Farwander had tried to teach her. The obvious kill-stroke might have caught out an unaware or untested swordsman, who would have been unable to counter her furious speed. But Hekatar was a Heritor too, and he wore the presence of a man who knew death so well that it could never come at him by surprise.

Hekatar stepped aside and Lady Temnos' sword drew sparks from a thorned iron shoulder pad. He reached over his shoulder and tore the anchor from its scabbard. He didn't even swing it at her – he just slammed the back of his gauntlet into her, catching her square in the chest and throwing her against the wall that kept her from plunging over the edge of the bridge.

With space opened up between Lady Temnos and Hekatar, the cultist archers had their target. Half a dozen arrows were loosed. Most pinged against the stonework as Lady Temnos rolled with the impact back to her feet. She held her left arm in front of her torso and two arrows speared into it. A normal mortal's arm bones would have been broken, or the pain would have incapacitated them, but Lady Temnos just sneered as if the arrows were no more than a distraction.

Farwander forced himself to look past the immense armoured form of Lord Hekatar. The two cultist warriors were rushing the bridge. The closest one had his scourge whirling over his head, ready to flay Lady Temnos' flesh from her bones. Farwander sprinted past Hekatar, relying on his relative insignificance to keep him safe from the swinging anchor, and made a course to head off the warrior.

The man was not far short of Hekatar's height. His bare chest was wrapped around with tentacle scars and his lower half was clad in sheets of sharkskin. His head was shaven save for the locks of hair that ran down the middle of his scalp. He did not expect Farwander and took a moment to turn on him, by which time Farwander was close enough to bring him within the arc of his sword.

Captain Stennby's blade sliced clean through the sharkskin and into muscle. Farwander felt the edge slide along the bone of the cultist's shin as it bit through the meat of the calf. The cultist grunted and dropped to one knee, and for a moment Farwander and his enemy seemed of equal statue.

The cultist whipped the scourge around at Farwander. The sword was ill suited for parrying such a weapon but it was all Farwander had. He took the impact on the blade and the strips of leather whipped around the sword. A couple got through and lashed his sword arm and side with its metal barbs.

He would worry about the pain later.

With his sword temporarily entangled, Farwander was not above using whatever means of delivering damage and incapacitation he could think of. The school of the Bittersweet Blade taught that any means of attaining victory was justifiable if that victory was itself just. Thus it was that Farwander stamped down on the cultist's knee. Farwander's heel impacted with the crunch of the kneecap being driven out of position.

The warrior bellowed and fell against the bridge wall. Farwander followed up with a thumb in the eye that was now at the level of his chest. The cultist roared and limped away backwards, swiping with a meaty paw at Farwander as he tried to open the distance up again. Farwander ducked the blow and pulled hard on his sword, which slipped out of the coils of the warrior's scourge. Farwander used every step of the space between them, putting his shoulder and full weight behind a thrust that punched straight through the flailing scourge and into the warrior's stomach.

Hulking meat golem or no, there was not a man alive who could take a blade to the gut and continue. Farwander made sure by forcing the edge of the blade out through the side of the warrior's torso, trusting in Stennby's fine steel to slice through intestine and abdominal muscle.

The warrior would live for a while after he slumped to the stone of the bridge. He might even make it off the bridge, with help, and perhaps live for a few days. But the foulness in his gut would seep into his blood and his insides would become poisoned, he would suffer terrible fevers and pain, and he would die. More importantly in that moment, he would never fight again.

The Bittersweet Blade was about victory. Anything was justified in that.

The fight had taken a few seconds. The second warrior was up to him now, this time heading straight for him and ready to smash through his guard with an overhead blow of the scourge. Farwander was suddenly very certain he was going to die.

A pair of fletched bolts appeared in the warrior's neck and chest. The one in his neck he felt. He paused in his charge and clutched at the crossbow bolt protruding from the side of his throat. Another trio of bolts smacked into his ample flesh and he fell against the wall of the bridge with his thigh and right arm pierced.

From the jungle behind him were charging the men of Lady Temnos' expedition. Vormish led the marines from the *Lightning Child*, accompanied by the hunters and marksmen who had participated in the kill of the Brotherhood's beast. Farwander guessed it was Gertrum who had fired one of the shots that found their mark, probably the one in the warrior's throat.

The warrior tore the bolt out of his neck. The bolt's head took a good chunk of his neck with it. Blood sluiced down his chest. He would die, too, and rather more quickly than the one Farwander had felled.

Farwander did not allow himself the luxury of exulting in his unexpected survival. Cultist archers were running to take up better positions and from the jungle came the howling and screeching of fanatical voices raised high in the praises of Scaraveyla. Neither side had trusted their leaders to keep matters to words alone. They had both been poised to fight, and now the Heritors had given them permission.

'Now is your hour!' yelled Captain Vormish as he charged at the head of the marines. 'Your Lady calls and thus we answer!'

'Dive!' screamed the Priest of Scaraveyla, borne forward on a tide of charging cultists. 'Dive into the Oblivion Deeps! Drown them in their blood!'

Lady Temnos was on her feet. Hekatar loomed above her with his anchor raised to bring it down on her. Lady Temnos jumped off the bridge wall right at him and slammed a fist into his faceplate.

Hekatar roared and stumbled across the bridge, steadying himself against the wall near Farwander. He glanced in Farwander's direction, and Farwander could see his eye through a crack in his faceplate. It was black, and set deep in a pit of scar tissue.

'You,' said Hekatar. 'I know you.'

Farwander could taste the brine in the back of his throat. He was back clinging to the hull of the Brotherhood's flagship, with Hekatar looking down at him, certain he would die.

A band of the *Lightning Child* marines barged into the space between Farwander and the Prophet of Scaraveyla. Two had bill hooks and thrust them at Hekatar like spears, and the other carried a cutlass.

Hekatar's anchor swung in a wide arc that speared one marine through the chest and slammed into the second. Both men were hurled off the edge of the bridge and tumbled into the ravine beneath. Hekatar's backstroke almost took the head off the third marine and shattered the haft of his bill. The marine dodged back and Farwander went with him as Hekatar hefted the weight of the huge anchor again.

'Wait!' Shouted Farwander at Hekatar. 'What is the treasure of Mount Golca?'

Hekatar paused, and a confusion flickered in his one visible eye.

The few seconds that bought gave Farwander the chance to get out of the front line before the cultists and the marines swarmed around him, and the sound of clashing steel fell like thunder. He pushed through the throng to where he had last seen Lady Temnos, and found her cutting down a Brotherhood cultist whose decision to charge straight at her with a dagger in each hand was the last mistake he ever made.

Lady Temnos had recovered some of her senses and her form was better, drawing attackers into her guard, cutting off their attacks and slicing through them with her inhuman strength. Farwander wished, absurdly, he could just stand there and watch her fight.

'We have to get off this bridge!' said Farwander to Lady Temnos.

She glanced at him as if he had interrupted her rudely. He saw her nose was bleeding, and another trickle of blood had run out of her right ear. 'We fight!' she snarled in reply.

'They're here for you!' shouted Farwander in reply. An arrow clattered off the stonework beside him and he was intensely aware of how easy it would be to die in that very moment. 'All of this is to kill you!'

'Then we will make them work for it!' Lady Temnos punctuated her words with sword-thrusts, each one slicing deep into the wall of flesh that tried to crush her against the bridge wall.

Farwander waded in beside her, knowing there was little room for proper swordplay in this press. It was about strength, relentlessness, awareness and courage, not skill. Leering, scarred faces rushed at him and he cut them down. Cutlasses fought to bear down at him through the throng of bodies. Arrows from both sides hit men from both sides.

He stabbed one cultist in the gut, grunted as he pulled the blade out and slashed another across the chest. The fine steel severed a hand, a shin, an arm. He kicked one man in the groin and grabbed another by the scruff of the neck, hurling him over the side of the bridge.

He fought well, he knew that. He could take pride in the blood he shed to protect Lady Temnos, who had brought him to this bridge to keep her safe. But he would die here, doing this.

'Rocks and dirt of Penitent's Landing!' cried Warden Karanas from the end of the bridge. 'I feel yer disgust! I feel yer hate! Through me, give it form! Through these hands, cast the parasites out!'

Farwander saw Karanas lifted above the battle by the force of the power he could feel thick and crackling in the air. Karanas was surrounded by an orbiting halo of rocks and his red hair waved around his head, held on end by the flood of power.

Farwander realised he had never before seen a Warden at the peak of their power. Dascia on the *Salted Swine* had called down the storm, and he had been in awe. But when he felt the rumble of the island's own rage through his feet, he knew Karanas was creating a work of far greater scale.

'My lady,' said Farwander, grabbing Lady Temnos' shoulder. 'Fall back. He's going to collapse the bridge.'

Captain Vormish could feel it too. He shouted for the marines and expedition crewmen to fall back, and the marines did so in good enough order to fend off the cultists with a bristling bank of spears and bill hooks. The cultists surged in their wake, rushing around the advancing Hekatar to claim more and more of the bridge with every step.

When they reached the far side they would swarm into the jungle and every single member of Lady Temnos' expedition would be chased down and killed.

A block of stone rose from the bridge wall. Another slab lifted out from the surface of the bridge and Farwander glimpsed the corpse-choked waters of the foaming river below.

'All yer hate,' said Karanas, 'all yer rage, it cannot compare to the hatred this island feels for ye. For yer Brotherhood. For the Kraken Queen!'

The bridge fell out beneath Farwander's feet. He fell onto his front, hitting stone chest-first, and his legs kicked out over nothing. Lady Temnos grabbed his arm and dragged him onto the bridge as the middle of it collapsed.

Blocks of stone fell into the river. Dozens of men followed. Cultists flailed and shrieked as they fell. Farwander's stomach cramped at the wet thuds of their bodies hitting the rocks, and then the growing pile of the dead, far below.

Farwander clambered onto the crumbling stump of the bridge. He saw some of the marines had been caught in the collapse but the great majority of the fallen were Brotherhood cultists. He looked back to the far side of the bridge and saw Hekatar on the edge of the collapse, blood-slicked anchor in hand, stepping away from the edge. The priest of Scaraveyla was wailing like a hysterical mourner even as more cultists were pushed over the edge by the advance of their unmanageable throng. A few arrows streaked across the ravine from the Brotherhood's archers, but most were concerned primarily with retreating into the jungle and avoiding the scrum pushing back from what remained of the bridge.

Farwander followed Lady Temnos off the bridge. His throat was suddenly raw and his body aching. It was a feeling he knew well, for his body had finished priming itself for the fight and given itself leave to feel the pain of the pulled muscles and bruises of the battle. That pain and exhaustion hit all at once and it was with sloping shoulders and a limping gait that he reached the edge of the jungle, where Warden Karanas was only now descending back down to the ground.

Hekatar was gone now, withdrawn into the jungle. The most maddened of the cultists remained on the bridge, screaming and howling at the expedition members. More screams reached up from the ravine as those who had survived the fall succumbed to their injuries.

'Buggering hells,' said Leveret as Farwander passed her. She had watched the eruption of violence from the treeline where they had first spotted the priest of Scaraveyla. 'Who won?'

Farwander did not answer her. For the first time, the enclosing dark green of the jungle felt safer than the open.

CHAPTER 12

''Twas the island,' said Karanas. Farwander had stuck close to him as they ranged along the edge of the ravine, partly to watch over the Earth Warden in case of more unexpected displays of power, and partly because he just wanted to know what in the many hells had happened at the bridge.

'The island?' asked Farwander dumbly.

'Aye. The island.' Karanas had spoken little in the day or so since he had collapsed the bridge before the slopes of Mount Golca. Farwander wondered if Karanas had not been ready for the level of power he had channelled through himself, and was in a sort of shock.

'What do you mean?'

'She spoke to me,' replied Karanas.

The two of them were scouting upstream. Several parties had been despatched to search the nearby jungle for a way across the river, or an alternative route to the eastern slopes of the mountain. The rest of the expedition were camped near the ruined bridge to rest and tend to their wounded as Lady Temnos consulted with the surviving leaders about what to do next. That Karanas was not with her suggested she, too, was wary of what the Warden might do.

'I felt her hatred,' continued Karanas as he used a ship's bill knife to hack through the dense vines and branches ahead of him. 'I've known it since I set foot on Penitent's Landing, but I knew it fer sure when they sent that beastie after us. She hates them, this island.'

'The Brotherhood?'

'Aye, lad. They're everything the island hates. Taking what's there and... corrupting it. Corrupting the ground they walk on. When I work my magic, I speak to the earth, and if I listen, I can hear it talk back. The island's shouting to me now. When I asked her what she wanted, she replied with the power you saw at the bridge.'

'It scared us,' said Farwander. It was the first time he had voiced the thought out loud, but he had seen the same reaction in the faces of everyone who had witnessed it first hand.

'Aye, lad, well, you didnae have to feel it.'

Karanas hacked at the jungle again and a tangle of vegetation fell away. The ravine was revealed beyond it, and a slope of collapsed dirt and rocks that choked the river into a stretch of shallow foaming. Fallen trees lay upended with sprays of roots in the air and their trunks rotting in the water. The river had widened and eaten away the loose fallen earth where a landslide long ago had created the shallows.

'Here,' said Karanas. 'We can ford it here.'

Farwander realised he was right. It would not be easy, but a group of men could cross the river here where the rocks, dirt and trees trunks had widened and lowered it. The ravine made that impossible in both directions. But here, it could be done. Karanas scrabbled down the slope and began to cross the river, stepping from one rock to the next. Farwander felt the air thickening and a couple of rocks rolled out of the water and into position around Karanas, shoring up the footing around him and forming a more solid path across.

'Tell her Ladyship, lad,' said Karanas. 'Get the men here and get them across afore the Brotherhood finds this place, too.'

As Farwander made his way back towards Lady Temnos' encampment, he could not help the thoughts that gathered at the forefront of his mind. He had always worked on the fly, coming up with a plan or a way out as circumstances allowed. He was doing it now, instinctively.

The island itself hated the Brotherhood of Scaraveyla. It was a bizarre concept, but it made as much sense as anything else that had happened on Penitent's Landing and if anyone could read the will of the land it was an Earth Warden. Gradually a plan was crystallising amid his thoughts, embryonic but tantalising.

Maybe he could do it. Maybe he could get off this island alive.

Maybe he would win.

* * *

The gates of Mount Golca told them they were not the first to hope to ascend it.

The ancestors of the Heritors had been there before, of course, including Lord Arcturaval Temnos, when they had climbed to discover the secret at its summit. But even then, last time the Ghost Archipelago had emerged from the mists, they had been interlopers in a well-established realm.

A pair of immense gates were carved into the rock of the lower slopes, crowned with an archway formed by two snakes rearing up from the living rock. The gates were deeply carved with images of warfare and sacrifice, fully five times the height of a man, and stood open a crack leading to the utter blackness inside. The slopes above were studded with structures – lookouts for observing the approaches to the mountain, turrets and defensive towers, mountings for siege weapons and lofty eyries up towards the volcano's smoky crater. Here and there chimneys had been opened up to draw off the toxic smoke, and they exuded grey plumes from the mouths of striking serpents or howling skulls. The structures, some fallen into ruins, suggested the whole mountain was riddled with tunnels and chambers like an insect's hive.

Farwander recognised the lines of the serpent people's architecture from the temple ruin, but here it was much more massive and seemed largely intact. What struck Farwander, as he emerged from the treeline to stand before the gates, was just how far the serpent people had gone to create an intimidating entrance to the mountain realm. That left, of course, the mystery of who they were trying to impress.

'You reckon the Brotherhood got in first?' asked Leveret as she trudged out of the jungle beside Farwander. The rest of the expedition were strung out behind them, having forded the river over the course of the day. The Brotherhood had not shown their mutilated faces, but that didn't mean they weren't nearby.

'Probably,' replied Farwander. 'I'd wager Hekatar has sent in some disposable idiots to see if any of them come back.'

'Thought we'd just be climbing it,' said Leveret. 'Not sure if I like the idea of going inside more or less.'

'Should be easier on the knees,' said Farwander with a shrug.

Lady Temnos stepped out of the jungle to regard the gates. She was flanked by a band of marines, who had naturally gravitated to her to serve as an honour guard without any order being given.

'Your thoughts, Master Farwander, Mistress Pavine?'

'It was hardly a sugary feast the last such ruin we entered,' said Farwander. 'But it's an option. There may be a way to the top from the inside. It's as promising as climbing the outside, I'd say.'

'Whatever we do, we better do it quick,' said Leveret. 'Brotherhood's been ahead of us this whole time. If they're not now, it won't be for long.'

'Vormish will take the fittest men and climb,' said Lady Temnos. 'A smaller force will seek a way up from the inside.'

'And who will these disposable idiots be?' asked Farwander with a sigh.

Lady Temnos gave him an unimpressed look. 'As you said, the last time we entered such a place it was less than welcoming. But you survived it. Choose those who will go with you.'

'Yes, my lady.' Farwander had known as soon as he had seen them that he would be walking through those serpent-guarded gates. It seemed a fate as inevitable as Leveret's odour. 'And where will you go?'

'Up the side of the mountain,' said Lady Temnos, gesturing at the smouldering peak high above. 'The strain of the climb holds no fear for me. If there is no way in at the top, Warden Karanas or I shall make one.'

'You're gonna want me, right?' said Leveret.

'I have no wish to put you in danger,' replied Farwander. 'But I would rather have men and women with brains between...'

'Shut it,' snapped Leveret. 'You've got me.'

It did not take long for Farwander to select a miniature expedition of his own. Lady Temnos was not willing to spare many souls from the ascent, because of the likelihood of encountering the Brotherhood on their own way up. Farwander took Leveret with him, and the hunter Gertrum whose instincts were as sharp as his aim. Three of the *Lightning Child* marines, named Riqa, Al'Ham and Quan, asked to join him after learning he had been there when Captain Al'Harhi had died.

'I'm not hoiking this old carcass up the side of a bloody mountain,' Navigator Gavel had opined, 'no matter what her Silky Seaweedship says.' So she joined Farwander too, and brought with her a small and obedient cabin lad named Scrafe whom she had pressed into carrying her cookpot and various implements.

So it was that the seven of them followed Farwander through the serpent gates and into Mount Golca.

* * *

'I still reckon,' said Gavel, 'it's just your common or garden heap of gold and gems and suchlike.'

The small party was moving through the lofty, crudely hewn passageways adjoining the hall beyond the gateway. The interior of the mountain had been carved out to impress with scale, not intricacy. The marines were taking turns carrying a torch to light their way in the pitch blackness and its light struggled to reach the ceiling.

'Don't seem hardly worth it,' said Leveret. 'I mean, gold and shinies are worth it, sort of, true, but I'd feel robbed if it weren't something a bit more... I dunno, mythical.'

'Well, that's what you'd think,' said Gavel, 'if you had the mind of a whelk. If it's some magical gewgaw, what good will it do? Pretty to look at, maybe do a few parlour tricks, but nothing a well-fed army can't and there's plenty enough of those in the world. And if it is a map to the Crystal Pool, who's to say the Ghosts won't just fade back into the mist tomorrow and leave you with a map to sod all? But a goodly heap of shininess, now that you can build a kingdom on.'

'I suppose,' said Leveret. 'Hadn't thought about it.'

'Easier to split, too,' said Gavel. 'Not sure how happy I'd be to have one-two-hundredth of a map to somewhere I'll never go.'

'What's this?' asked the marine Riqa, who was holding the torch just up ahead. Its light had caught on a carved frieze just above head height, painted in age-faded reds and yellows.

'These serpent chaps loved to draw themselves everywhere,' said Farwander, who had been listening to Gavel and Leveret with interest. 'I think they had a high opinion of their kind.'

'What does it mean?' asked Scrafe. He was a scrawny lad of uncertain age wearing the tatters of an old naval uniform a few sizes too big for him that looked like he had taken it off a corpse. His apparent size was further decreased by his stoop under the weight of Gavel's cookpot. All manner of cooking implements and boxes and bundles of ingredients hung from his unimpressive frame. He had a thin, lank face, but his eyes were still bright.

Farwander peered up at the sculpture. It would have been easy to ignore, but something about the very act of carving their history into Mount Golca told Farwander it was important to the serpent people, at least. The symbol of Mount Golca itself took up much of the carved panel, with red plumes of fire and smoke issuing from its crater. On a pyramid before the mountain stood a stylised snakeman wearing lizardlike skulls as shoulder guards. The steps of the pyramid were covered in body parts – limbs, torsos, heads, all cast there by serpent priests butchering the humans being herded there for sacrifice.

In spite of the stylised renderings of the scene, with its block figures and unnatural poses, the sight of it turned Farwander's stomach. 'It's one of their leaders,' he said, with a foul taste growing in the back of his throat.

'The one as built this place?' said Scrafe.

'Maybe.'

'Well 'e's gone now,' said Gavel. 'So don't pay it no mind.'

Farwander knew someone didn't need to be still alive to be dangerous. Whoever had designed the trials in the serpent temple had killed Grieff and almost done the same to himself and Lady Temnos, and that particular serpent person architect had been dead for who knows how long. But he did not give voice to the thought yet. Mount Golca was threatening enough as it was.

'The tunnel opens up ahead,' said Gertrum. He had sharper eyes than anyone Farwander had ever met and could see in almost complete darkness, it seemed. Riqa brought the torch towards him and revealed a series of archways cut into the side of the passageway that led to a much larger space beyond. A faint ruddy light caught the edge of the furthest archway, and it wasn't from the torch.

The passageways had been cold compared to the jungle heat outside. All the warmth had bled into the cold stone. But now Farwander could feel a heat on the faint currents of air within the mountain that had not been there before.

Farwander stepped past Gertrum over the threshold, and saw the city.

Mount Golca naturally had a hollow heart, he saw that now. In a past age the passage of lava had formed a shaft running most of the height of the mountain, before the molten rock had changed to a new channel and left the shaft empty. And it was into that shaft the serpent people had built their city.

Farwander had assumed the serpent people had a sizeable settlement somewhere on Penitent's Landing, but that it was either swallowed by the jungle far away from anywhere the expedition had trodden, or had been razed to the ground in some catastrophe. Now he saw they had built it here, in the mountain. The shaft was ringed with wide ledges that fronted onto buildings cut into the rock, from the thousands of windows of homes and businesses to the grand steps of temples and expanses of parade and duelling grounds. The dull vermilion light came from a cascade of lava that poured down one section of the shaft, like a waterfall of liquid fire, to plunge into a lake of it below Farwander's level in the roots of the mountain.

He could make out a temple with an enormous serpent's mouth forming the gate, with channels cut around it for water to pour through from a source higher up. The water fed what had once been a garden planted on one of the ledges, but which had long since died to a tangle of blackened wood. The biggest structure was half a pyramid built into the wall of the shaft, like the stepped sacrificial structure from the sculpture. A wide plaza surrounded it, covered in statues. Staircases looped in and out of the shaft wall, giving access to the various levels, and bridges criss-crossed the space, some of them combining in larger platforms where particularly prestigious structures were built.

For a long while Farwander could only stare at it. He could not imagine what it had taken to build the place, or how long the serpent people had laboured to construct their capital. What must it have looked like when it was inhabited? Did only the serpent people live there, or did their human slaves – he was sure now the island had been populated by thousands of them if only to provide sacrifices

– make up the majority of the population? Was it once hung with lights, or did the serpent people not need light to see by?

How many bones had scorched away to nothing in the pool of lava churning below?

'Well, well,' said Leveret, joining Farwander at the threshold of the city. 'This is where those scaly gits lived.'

'Used to, maybe,' added Gavel. 'Where did they go?'

Riqa knelt at the edge of the walkway running around the inside of the shaft, and held his torch over the edge. Its light was dwarfed by the scale of the space inside the mountain, and it reached only a few feet before it was swamped by the blackness that was only broken by the lava pool far below.

Then, in a flurry of movement too fast to follow, Riqa was gone.

The sound was the clacking of nails on stone, and a strangled yelp from Riqa's throat. Then the clatter of his armour against the edge of the walkway, and silence.

Farwander did not know him, any more than he knew the other men of the *Lightning Child*. But still he felt the sting of the man being taken by the darkness, so swiftly he must have had no time even to think.

That was all it took. One moment of malice from the shadows of Mount Golca, and a man was gone.

'Tar my giblets, what was that?' gasped Navigator Gavel. She pulled out the cleaver that served as cooking utensil and weapon.

'Oi!' shouted Leveret back to the remaining marines. 'Give us some light!'

'Where is Riqa?' replied Al'Ham.

'Gone,' replied Leveret. 'And we're gone too if we can't bloody see!'

Quan ran through the archway. He was armed with a bill, with its machete-like blade mounted on a long haft to fend off boarders and hack at rigging. 'When the night takes a brother,' he shouted into the void, 'we cut the sunlight from it! Come forth, O foul, and be illuminated!'

The next attack came not from below the edge of the walkway, but from above. Farwander caught its movement and drew his sword instinctively as it fell from the level above. It was pale flesh and wriggling limbs, and Quan was too slow to react before it was on him.

In the ruddy light of the lava, Farwander could barely make out the struggle. Quan tried to force his bill hook from the pallid coils but the scaly form was wrapped around him. He let the weapon go and drew a knife from his belt, and Farwander heard the too-familiar sound of steel puncturing flesh.

Leveret ran forward with her dagger out. Farwander heard the fight and knew he could do nothing in the dark with his longer blade. He turned around, scanning the carved rock above him for more movement, and he saw it – pallid flesh tinted pink by the glow of the lava, the suggestion of huge wet eyes and ropes of glistening drool.

The shape slithered along the rock ceiling above him. Farwander slashed up at it, felt the tip of his sword connect, and heard a vicious hiss as it withdrew. Warm globs of spittle spattered on his face and he could not help but wipe the worst of it off his face with his sleeve.

'Back!' shouted Gavel. 'Get back! Don't let them get around you!'

The thing attacking Quan let out a terrible babbling shriek and Farwander heard tearing flesh. He saw Al'Ham watching the way behind them, back towards the city, as he tried to strike a flint to light the torch in his hand. He looked up in alarm and gave up, drawing his cutlass instead. 'They're behind us!' he shouted.

Farwander's mind whirled. He could hear them, whatever they were, hissing and scraping along the stone in the darkness. He remembered an entrance into the side of the shaft wall a short sprint around the walkway and made for it, holding his sword in front of him like a blind man's stick.

'Follow me!' he shouted, feeling suddenly helpless as the commotion continued from the edge. 'Stick together! Stick tight!'

Gavel was beside him, waving her cleaver around as if trying to bisect a fly. 'What in the soggy hells are they?'

Farwander didn't want to speculate on the answer. He found the archway and ran through it, banging his shins on an unexpected lip of stone and stumbling in the almost total darkness.

A crossbow bolt whistled past his ear and hit something yielding in the room ahead of him.

'Got it,' said Gertrum as he ran past Farwander. It was impossible to see what he had got. Farwander just put his faith in the hunter's instincts and followed the sound of Gertrum's footsteps.

It seemed like they plunged through so many doorways and rooms that it would be impossible to find the way back out. Farwander was only vaguely aware of the shapes of the doors and walls around him, more by instinct than by sight. He wasn't even sure which of the small party were following Gertrum through the city of the serpent men.

Eventually, after a time and distance Farwander could not guess at, Gertrum paused up ahead. Farwander crouched down beside the hunter, trying to catch his breath. Light flickered as Gertrum struck a flint, and then Farwander's eyes were forced shut by the sudden light from a torch in Gertrum's hand.

They had made it to the entrance hall to an elaborate building that reached further into the wall of the shaft. Its elaborate, heavily painted carvings suggested the coils and fangs of snakes, but without definite form in their swirls and angles as if the sculptor feared to depict an actual serpent. Farwander guessed the place was religious, as the large pillared hall beyond had the high vaulted ceiling and side chapels he associated with a place of worship.

'Speak to me,' he called back into the darkness. 'Tell me you're alive.'

'Yeah, I'm alive,' said Leveret. She and Quan were carrying a creature between them, and in the torchlight Farwander could see its fresh blood glistening on pale scales.

Gavel was just behind them. She was a hefty woman, not built for hurrying. 'Scrafe!' she gasped between breaths. 'Where are you, boy? You been et?'

Scrafe appeared jogging behind her, eyes wide with panic and sweat glistening on him. Finally, Al'Ham brought up the rear, watching behind him with his cutlass in hand.

No Riqa. If he hadn't been dead the moment the things struck, he was definitely lost now.

'Are they following?' asked Farwander.

'No,' replied Gertrum. 'We scared them off.'

'What now?' asked Leveret.

'Hold up here,' said Gertrum. 'Looks like we can barricade it safe enough. Rest, eat, push on.' Then, as if realising he wasn't nominally in charge, he turned to Farwander. 'If that's...'

'Good call,' said Farwander. 'Al'Ham, bar the door.'

They had found themselves a in temple, where the faithful prayed to an altar built of gigantic saurian bones. Farwander lit a torch and checked each of the shrines that branched off from the large, gloomy nave. One held a statue of a serpent man in armour, brandishing a sword made from a split baton of wood with blades of sharp stone along its length. Another held a waist-high pyramid of human skulls, with hundreds of rusted manacles hanging from the walls.

Though he had seen very little of the serpent person culture, Farwander had decided he didn't like it.

Behind the altar was a set of painted friezes of the kind the serpent people evidently favoured for recording their history. Many of the events were obscure or unintelligible, mostly wars with indistinct serpentine armies marching or series of chieftains and generals with their honorifics painted in an unfamiliar pictographic language. But at the top, given the greatest prominence, were panels from the life of the serpent person prophet, with the lizard skulls worn as shoulder guards and sacrifices butchered everywhere he slithered.

This prophet was shown preaching to gatherings of chieftains and soothsayers, presiding over mass sacrifices and blessing the weapons of the serpent people's armies. Human slave craftsmen were put to work creating wooden images of a dark, bat-winged presence, which were then erected all over Penitent's Landing. Some such images of the prophet's god were taller than the jungle canopy. Farwander wondered why the expedition had not come across any of them.

He caught the smell of cooking meat. Gavel had already set up her pot over a makeshift fire and was thickening a stew with handfuls of grain. It had been a long day even before Farwander had led his ropey crew into Mount Golca. Now they were tired and dismayed. A decent feed was exactly what they needed.

'Look at this ugly swine,' said Leveret as Farwander returned to join the band. She and Quan had dumped the creature on the floor of the chapel and Farwander saw it properly for the first time.

It was a serpent person, though there the similarity ended between this sorry creature and the warriors and priests depicted in the temple. The creature Leveret and Quan had killed was pallid and emaciated, with scales from white to pale pink along the belly. Its serpentine lower half was skinny enough for the shape of the ribs to show through to the tip of the tail. Its humanoid upper half was covered in old scars criss-crossing its corded muscle and bone. Leveret had stabbed it a dozen times in the chest.

Its face had a wide, fanged mouth and no nose. Sensor pits gaped on either side of its jaw. Its eyes were huge and dark, much larger than the statues and paintings of its kin. Farwander could see his face reflected in those eyes from the light from Gavel's fire.

'Seen things like this living in caves,' said Gertrum, regarding the creature. 'Grow up with no light. No colour to them, eyes like this to see in the dark. They have to turn scavenger, else prey on each other.'

'They're the serpent people that got left behind,' said Farwander. 'When the city fell, these were abandoned here, or chose to stay. Then the darkness turned them into... this.'

'So where did the other ones go?' Leveret chewed on a chunk of meat from Gavel's pot. 'Should be thousands of 'em in this hole.'

'Does it matter?' asked Quan. 'They are not here now. Praise whatever god removed them from our path and move on.'

'I'd rather know what manner of dung-hole I've ended up in,' said Leveret. ''Specially if there's something here that killed the last lot.'

'Pray we will not tarry here long enough to find it,' said Al'Ham, taking a seat beside his fellow marine.

'Pray to who?' asked Leveret, with the ghost of a mischievous smile.

''Ere we go,' said Gavel quietly.

'General Reslan,' said Al'Ham. 'Patron of all those who fight and die for money.'

'We left a third of our last year's pay at his temple in Rilesport,' added Quan.

'Value for money, was it?' said Leveret.

'We still live,' replied Quan. 'I'd say that was a good deal. And it has worked before, too. The General has watched over me plenty of times when otherwise I should have died.'

'It was his blessing alone that took us through Whitebone Marsh,' said Quan, nodding gravely. 'Aye, three companies went in. Us of the *Lightning Child*, Lackwit's Marauders and the Company of Cranes. Naught but twenty men came out. More died from the disease than from the battle.'

'I lay for three days beneath a heap of the dead after our flank collapsed,' said Al'Ham.

Quan grunted. 'Luxury,' he said.

'Reminds me of when my Hakespure and me were running the South-Eastern Straits,' said Gavel, 'running a cargo of cloth, spices and cheese. Ran our keel into a reef. Ship went down with almost all our hands. Got stuck there for three weeks, was half mad with the brine by the end of it. My Hakespure, he said "Chrysanthemum, my dear, you need to die for a cause what's worth it. Don't go breathin' yer last for a boatload of cheese." And I said, you're right, you pickled old albatross, so I went and lived.'

'That's nothin,' said Leveret. 'I got faced down by five of these lads in Harrowcliffe one time. They thought I'd ripped 'em off over a box of blackroot.'

'And had you?' asked Gavel.

'Never you mind,' snapped Leveret. 'That's not the point. Anyway, they all said they were going to cut a piece of me off and put me back together again all upside-down and wrong way round. So I lets 'em talk it up a bit while thinking, "well this is it Leveret, you're going to die." Then some idiot with bladders for brains runs his cart out of control and the whole bloody thing crashes into the alleyway and then it's all screaming and shouting and stabbing at everything. No idea how I got out. Lost the tip of me big toe in that one.'

'I never had an adventure,' said Scrafe.

'You're on one now,' said Gavel, cuffing him round the back of the head. 'Be grateful.'

'Don't tell me you haven't done your share of derring-do,' said Leveret, looking at Gertrum. 'Big strong lad like you.'

Gertrum paused mid-mouthful, unsure of how to react to Leveret's attentions. 'Where I come from,' he said, 'you hunt or you die. If you can't kill and skin a catch by eleven years old you're put out to starve.' He thought for a moment, remembering. 'Almost lost a leg to a twelve-point buck. Another time my party got caught in a blizzard for half a season, saw men eating each other. Next year I walked over the Slave Collar Mountains to find a hunting ground that wasn't there.' He shrugged. 'The usual.'

Farwander realised everyone was now looking at him. He felt himself deflating.

'So, Master Farwander,' said Gavel, 'you must have been in and out of a few maiden's windows. Fought a few duels. Talked your way out of a few mortal scrapes.'

'All very true,' said Farwander, 'although there haven't been as many maiden's windows as I'd have wanted. And duels – well, yes, I did have to fight a chap who was convinced I had impregnated his daughter, although I'm fairly sure he was mistaken. I cut him in the bicep deep enough for his arm to be amputated. A very nasty business, and the impregnated daughter in question never spoke to me again.'

'And that silver tongue of yours?' asked Leveret with a smile.

'Got me onto Lady Temnos' fleet,' said Farwander. 'I'd say that's the most dramatic thing I've ever talked my way into or out of.'

Thankfully, that seemed to satisfy them. Farwander had little desire to recount his various escapades. He was sure they would have had a good laugh at his run-in with Big Marga's butchers, or any of the other scum and criminals of Last Fathom and beyond. It was true he had been to many places and done all sorts of things when he'd got there, but he did not have the drive to recount them all. He might have, once, when giddy with strong wine other people had bought for him in a dingy drinking hole, and there were plenty of idiots to impress. Not now.

So many had died on their way to Penitent's Landing, all of them without knowing why they were dying, that it didn't feel right to boast of the times he had survived. He thought of Riqa, dragged into the darkness, and of the men who had tumbled into the river ravine. He thought of Captain Al'Harhi, disappearing in the chaos of foaming brine and splintering wood. Somehow, Farwander was still alive. It made sense for Lady Temnos to survive, of course. She was a Heritor – not only stronger and tougher than any other mortal, but blessed by fate to hold a grand part in whatever events were to play out in the Ghost Archipelago.

Even Leveret had something of the indestructible vermin about her, as if whatever happened she would crawl out from under a rock unscathed save for another layer of filth. But why should Farwander live? What did he have that the gods wanted to continue existing?

He took another mouthful of Gavel's stew. The meat's suspicious origins were masked by good handfuls of spices. He was again aware of how tired he was, as if he had not stopped struggling since the moment he had jumped off the dock at Last Fathom.

The ragged band of explorers got what rest they could. Farwander could not sleep for a long time. His mind raced. Above all, it forced his eyes back to the frieze, where the prophet of the serpent people's black-winged god held court over his devotee.

Something was slotting into place in the back of his mind. He was afraid to grasp it, in case it slithered away like a devolved serpent person and he lost it completely. It was close, though. He would have it soon. If, for some reason, he continued to survive.

Farwander did not sleep well, but when he did, he was back underwater.

This time he was forgotten. He was an interloper here, not cast down after drowning but venturing here like a thief or a spy. Though he did not will it, he was swimming downwards, deeper and deeper, through the layers of cold and pressure.

Titanic whales drifted past, and he could feel their fear, for they knew one day they would be imprisoned in an unseaworthy hulk and driven to war. He could feel the krakens' hunger as they prowled below, eager to wrap their coils around anything that strayed too far to their dense, chill level of the ocean.

He sank further and further down, gasping out his breath in a string of bubbles. Around him drifted the bodies of the dead at the bridge, as if the rushing waters of the river had unexpectedly delivered them all the way down into the Oblivion Deeps. He saw the life winking out of corpses' eyes. They wore the armour of the marines from the *Lightning Child*, the piecemeal naval uniforms of buccaneers, the threadbare breeches and rags of lifelong tars.

Scaraveyla's realm rolled out beneath him, emerging from the silt and detritus of the ocean floor. Farwander recognised the tapering prow of the *Wave Demon*, and the rest of the ship nearby, sunken in two pieces after being sliced in half by the *Prophet's Wrath*. The mangled remains of the *Lightning Child* were barely recognisable as a ship, for the hull of Hekatar's flagship had ground her to splinters.

A thousand dead men bloated in the silt, feasted on by crabs and nibbling fish, with worms writhing through their flesh. They were in the process of ceasing to be men at all, and joining the layer of pale deposit that washed around the shattered hulls.

Farwander could not see Scaraveyla, for she was far away, but he could feel her watching him with glee. From her shipwreck throne she was laughing to see him tumbling, helpless, unable to kick his legs or draw breath. He realised he could not swim any more but was in the grip of the ocean, his body now as lifeless and unresponsive as a dead man's.

The Kraken Queen was still chuckling at his plight as Farwander settled into the salty mere of corpses. Their soft flesh parted beneath him and the bodies welcomed him in as one of their own. Yielding, puffy skin split beneath him and the water pinked as their organs dissolved. He thrashed uselessly in his panic, and the ocean turned as dark as ink.

CHAPTER 13

'Get up,' said Gertrum, shaking Farwander by the shoulder. 'They're at the door.'

Farwander forced the images of Scaraveyla's realm out of his mind. He remembered where he was – the temple in the city within Mount Golca, deep in the haunted dark.

The serpent people were scrabbling at the door the marines had barred. The rest of the crew were smothering the fire and readying their weapons. Al'Ham was already carrying a lit torch ready to move on into the darkness.

'There's another way out past the altar,' said Gertrum. 'Hidden passageway.'

Farwander did not have the luxury of waking up by stages. He made himself jump to his feet, ready to move.

Leveret had found the exit beneath the frieze depicting the serpent man prophet. A hidden catch at the base of the painting made a section of the wall swing out, revealing a dusty and cobwebbed passageway. Farwander followed Al'Ham and Gertrum through, crouching to fit through the narrow confines.

'Why did they need a secret passageway?' asked Quan.

'Smoke and mirror stuff,' said Leveret. 'Make a big bang, priest appears like by magic, suddenly everybody believes in your god.'

'Or to get away if the flock turned on the shepherd,' said Al'Ham. 'Holy men of our land must take care not to claim they are greater than the gods they serve, or should be richer than the people they lead. Otherwise they are apt to be impaled over the temple doors.'

'Charming,' said Farwander.

'It works,' replied Al'Ham.

The passageway opened up into a tangle of passageways and buildings chiselled into the rock of Mount Golca. Farwander could not tell if they were homes, slave quarters, shopfronts, or had some purpose a two-legged soul could never divine. Statues were everywhere, all of them of serpent people differentiated by the arms and armour they wore and the implements of priesthood or state they carried. Going by their art, every serpent person went about festooned with chains and armour plates, and carried handfuls of sceptres, orbs, staves and ceremonial swords.

Farwander was beginning to get a feel for the serpent people's sense of their own importance. It did not endear them to him any further.

After what seemed like hours, although it was impossible to tell, their path looped back to the main shaft of the city and the cascading lava glowed dully up ahead. Farwander emerged onto a wide plaza that ringed half the circumference of the shaft, with a slender bridge crossing the space and supporting a temple-like building in the centre. The heat of the lava beat against his face.

He stepped carefully to the edge of the plaza and leaned over the edge, holding his torch to see. The levels of walkways and bridges below swarmed with pale, glistening bodies, as if they were covered in huge maggots.

'There are hundreds of them,' he said. 'They've got our scent.'

'No stopping from now on, then,' said Leveret, watching alongside him. 'Not letting these buggers catch up with us.'

'What if there's no way up at the top?' asked Scrafe, tremulously.

'Then we die, don't we?' scolded Gavel. 'Not going to stop us getting up there, though, is it? Because if we stay here we die, whatever's at the top.'

'Sh!' Gertrum held up a hand to hush the rest of the company. Gavel looked about to retort angrily, but swallowed her words, because she heard it too.

Steel on steel. The sounds of battle, somewhere above them.

'They're fighting the Brotherhood,' said Leveret quietly.

'If we can hear them, there's a way out,' added Gertrum.

'And a way in,' said Farwander. He looked across the yawning chasm, past the sluggish ribbon of falling lava. A couple of levels above was the grand pyramidal structure he had seen earlier, the one that echoed the sacrificial structure he had seen in the depictions of the prophet. 'I think we can get up there,' he said, picking out shapes in the gloom. 'If we cross here and make it to the pyramid, it looks like it connects to the structures at the top. We'll climb if we have to.'

'Speak for yourself,' said Gavel, darkly.

It was difficult to make out anything at the top of the shaft. The lava streamed through an aperture in the rock around which were carved structures that looked like they had been breached and partially destroyed by the lava's intrusion. The ornateness of the sculpture suggested something important or valuable up there, perhaps even the treasure the volcano guarded, but whether it was still intact was another matter entirely.

'Feel free to stay behind, Miss Gavel,' said Farwander, and led the way across the bridge.

The suspended structure was a lavish house, like an official residence for some serpent man dignitary, with a huge stone bed and rooms hung with manacles that had to be slave quarters. It was abandoned and ransacked, and parts of it were scorched as if it had been put to the torch.

The far end of the bridge was staked out with iron spikes. Though they had corroded with age, they still held the remnants of skulls.

'Not human,' said Gertrum, examining the skulls. 'Serpent men.'

'Not slave sacrifices, then,' said Farwander. 'Criminals. Or heretics.'

A stone staircase wound up the wall towards the pyramid above. Every step was marked with another stake, most of them with skulls still impaled on them. A collection of skull fragments and loose jawbones had gathered at the base of the stairs where they had fallen from above. It was not particularly welcoming, reflected Farwander, but it was better than remaining where they were to wait for the city's devolved inhabitants.

He heard the clashes from above again. This time he could make out voices raised in pain and anger. He could not pick out individual voices, or tell whether he was listening to the madmen of the Brotherhood or the expedition members who had ascended Mount Golca. The only thing he could be sure of was that people were dying.

He reached the top of the staircase and the pyramid loomed above him. Its steps were formed from immense sandstone blocks that must have been transported from outside the mountain. A central stairway led to the top, and everywhere there were heaps of bones and skulls piled up like drifts of fallen leaves. The sculptures on every surface depicted stylised sacrifices, with hearts cut out and heads sawn off by serpent man priests.

Farwander was at the corrupted heart of the serpent people's city. He could feel the weight of the malice here, the evil and suffering that suffused the bloodsoaked stones. And he could feel the answers, waiting to be uncovered.

Al'Ham and Quan spread out, checking the dark corners for enemies. Unless the dead could walk, which was not out of the question here, there was no immediate threat lurking around the pyramid. The rest of the company watched warily behind them as the slithering and snapping of the devolved serpent people echoed up from the chasm.

'Gods, they just get more cheerful, don't they?' said Leveret, regarding the bone-covered pyramid with distaste. 'Whoever these sods were, they weren't ones for making a welcoming impression.'

'We can get to the sculptures above,' said Gertrum, peering upwards. 'Climb to the top from there.'

'Who's climbing?' retorted Gavel, who was leaning on Scrafe as she got her breath back from climbing the stairs. 'It's so I didn't have to climb anything I walked into this blamed mountain.'

Gertrum clambered onto the first storey, scattering mouldering bones.

'Sod that,' said Gavel, heading for the staircase leading up the centre of the pyramid's face.

The first step held. So did the next half dozen. But when Gavel reached the eighth step, it sunk into the pyramid with a clunk and the whole pyramid shuddered. Fragments of mortar and bone clattered down onto the plaza surrounding it. Gavel yelped and fell backwards, grabbing the block beside her for stability. Below her, Scrafe slipped and fell to the floor.

'Well, bugger,' said Leveret, as the whole pyramid split down the middle and began to fold into itself, forming a vertical chasm leading deep into the side of the volcano.

The ledge beneath Farwander's feet tilted and split. Chunks of it fell into the chasm, tumbling towards the pool of lava far, far below them. Farwander ran for the shifting pyramid even as iron glinted in the dull red light and articulated blades folded out from the darkness.

It was a machine, he realised, for sacrifices. An automated monstrosity for turning the living into diced and mutilated tributes to the gods of the serpent people. Gertrum was holding on and climbing as bladed wheels taller than a ship's mast unfurled from the pyramid and carved right past him.

Gavel sprinted from a blade that swung like a pendulum towards her. As the ledge collapsed, Farwander and Leveret had to run into the arc of those blades, with every second a new one emerging to dismember them.

Al'Ham was not fast enough to avoid the pendulum blades that swung between the huge wheels. He ran under one, ducking out of its swing, but the next hit him at shoulder height and sliced his torso in two lengthways. Farwander looked away before the marine's body came apart.

There was no choice but to run into the same storm of swinging blades that had killed Al'Ham. If he stayed where he was, Farwander would die. Leveret was beside him and she was light enough on her feet to scamper past the bladed pendulums. Farwander followed her, rolling out of the way of a blade that swung at him out of the darkness. Leveret grabbed him by the arm and dragged him out of the path of the bladed wheel as it pivoted inwards to chew up anyone trying to evade it.

Above him, Farwander could just see the workings of the huge machine. It was lit by the dying flame of Al'Ham's discarded torch. Chains and ropes attached to swinging weights powered the machine, keeping it in constant motion as if the builders expected an unending stream of hapless sacrifices to be herded into its maw.

Farwander drew his sword, Captain Stennby's beautiful sword that had proven itself over and over again in his hand. He owed his life to that steel, when a lesser weapon would have let him down. He reached back, gripping it like a javelin, and hurled it at the machinery.

The blade jammed in a length of chain and the fine steel of the blade bent between the teeth of a pair of cogs. With a scream, something unseated in the machinery and lengths of broken iron fell between the blades. One of the pendulum blades came free and smashed through the surface, taking several massive chunks of sandstone with it. The awful sound of destruction hammered against Farwander's head and he could barely see through the overwhelming of his senses.

Farwander staggered out of the reach of the blades that still swung. The shattered workings created a path through the deathtraps through which he could escape the collapse still happening behind him. Leveret had her hands clamped to her ears as she ran and Gavel was almost caught up with them. He couldn't see Gertrum or Quan.

Gavel was shouting something, Farwander had to concentrate to make out the words.

'Where's the boy?' she was yelling.

Farwander tried to shake the ringing out of his head. He stumbled further into the unfolded pyramid and blinked in the sudden light from a torch.

It was Scrafe, who had somehow contrived to survive this far and was striking a flint to light another torch. In the darkness, the dusty, cobwebbed interior of the pyramid was revealed. Farwander wondered how many slaves had suffered to build it all, how many human or serpent person draftsmen had laboured to make it possible.

The interior formed a passageway littered with hewn and broken bones, leading to an inner chamber. Farwander noted with distaste that as his hearing returned, the bones crunched underfoot as he walked towards Scrafe and the inner chamber.

'I saw the soldier die,' said Scrafe, his face pale and glistening with sweat.

'He's gone but we are not,' said Farwander. 'Cling to that and mourn him when we are safe.'

'What about the other one?'

'I do not know,' said Farwander, feeling suddenly useless against the ancient malice of the serpent people. Quan might be dead or alive, he had no idea.

Ahead was another corpse, this one proudly displayed, unlike the numberless bodies cut to pieces by the sacrificial machine. Farwander could not help but walk up to it as he recognised the shape of a large warlike serpent person, and the twin skull shoulder guards.

It was the prophet whose deeds were commemorated throughout the city. Farwander knew his bone armour and the implements of his priesthood. The skulls of his own sacrificial victims were still hung around his neck, their craniums clubbed or hacked open.

The corpse was desiccated and long dead. Going by the cords around its neck, the prophet had been strangled where it now sat on a mocking throne of sandstone blocks. Around it were the defaced statues of its bat-winged god, with any features gouged out of the wood.

'Ugly git,' said Leveret as she regarded the prophet's corpse.

'He was sacrificed in the end, too,' mused Farwander. 'And his god's image cast down.' He tilted the corpse's dry, grimacing head to the side, regarding the empty eye sockets and bared, age-browned fangs. 'A false prophet.'

'Unless you're plannin' to get married to it,' said Leveret, 'we should probably keep on going up. If those wriggly sods downstairs didn't know where we are, they do now. Looks like we can still climb all this.'

'Right, you heard her,' said Gavel to Scrafe. 'Get your backside up there.'

Farwander forced himself to forget, for the time being, the men who had just died in front of him or been swallowed by the darkness like Riqa before them. The inside of the pyramid was constructed of the same huge sandstone blocks that made for a solid if tiring climb. By the time he reached the top of the pyramid, the sounds of battle were filtering down from above once more, and Farwander was sure he could differentiate now between the yelled orders of the marines and crewmen, and the howls of the Brotherhood's cultists.

The heat from the falling stream of lava was punishing now, as Farwander found a handhold on the carvings around the pinnacle of the shaft. He could see now a ring of windows leading into a circular chamber at the very top, the way out of the serpent people's city and into whatever lay at the top of Mount Golca. Climbing there wasn't the safest or most efficient way to get there, but he didn't fancy his chances of finding another way before the city's feral inhabitants caught up with him. He grabbed a handhold, hooked his foot into the open eye socket of a carved serpent, and began the climb.

Voices echoed down from above. He spotted a face looking down from one of the upper windows, but it ducked back before he could make out any details through the haze coming off the stream of lava.

'Who the arse was that?' exclaimed Leveret somewhere below.

A crossbow bolt whistled across the shaft and thunked into flesh. With a strangled cry, a body fell from the chamber above. Farwander had an impression of pale, scarred flesh as it plunged past – a Brotherhood cultist, with a bolt clean through his neck.

Farwander peered past the flow of lava to see Gertrum clinging to the carvings opposite, reloading his crossbow one-handed.

Farwander smiled with relief. 'Gertrum! Glad you're...'

A Brotherhood cultist screamed and leapt from the window directly above Farwander, swinging down on a length of chain. Farwander swung out by one hand to avoid the cultist's foot as it kicked right at his head. The cultist slammed into the wall and drew a dagger with his free hand, the other still clinging to the chain.

Farwander realised in that moment two very pertinent facts – the Brotherhood had made it inside the volcano, and he was clinging to a wall and unarmed. The cultist stabbed at him with the dagger and Farwander instinctively grabbed at the man's wrist, the fingers of his other hand turning white as they supported his whole weight on the carvings.

The cultist kicked again and Farwander took a blow to the ribs. He smacked the cultist's hand into the stone but he didn't loose his grip on his dagger. Farwander kept one foothold and kicked back, flailing uselessly at the cultist's legs.

The cultist's face was a scarred horror pierced through with shards of needle-like metal. His lips were pinned shut and his eyes were set into scorched black-red pits. Whoever this man had once been, the worship of Scaraveyla had erased everything human about him.

Farwander let go of the wall and reached for the chain above him. He grabbed it and hugged the cultist in tight, still controlling the wrist of the hand that held the dagger. He twisted the cultist's arm behind him and felt a joint wrenching. The dagger flashed as it fell out of the cultist's hand and spiralled down into the darkness of the shaft.

Farwander had a free hand now. He groped at the cultist's face and his fingers closed around one of the shards of metal impaled in the man's face. He twisted and pulled and the shard came free.

Farwander stabbed the shard back at the cultist, aiming for his throat. The point pierced skin and blunted against bone. The cultist yelled and clutched at his neck, momentarily forgetting to hang on to the chain. He lost his grip entirely and fell, kicking out frantically at nothing as he plunged.

Farwander grabbed the chain with both hands and used it to climb the rest of the way to the window, hauling himself belly-first into the chamber at the top of the serpent people's city. Gertrum was already there, snapping off another crossbow shot at a cultist in a different window who fell with a bolt sticking out of his belly.

Farwander took stock of his surroundings. The circular chamber ran around the pinnacle of the shaft, with several stairways leading up out of it. From each archway came the sounds of battle more immediate than before, and Farwander knew the way to the volcano's summit lay through one of them.

Arranged around the circular room were eight coffin-sized vessels of stone, each with a lid carved deeply with the pictographic language of the serpent people. Farwander realised with a lurch that if Mount Golca held any great treasure at all, it lay within those coffins.

Bodies, he wondered? The corpses of the kings of the serpent empire, or of those explorers who came to Penitent's Landing two centuries before and never made it back? A trove of priceless burial goods, or a store of some knowledge with a value beyond gold? Perhaps each was full of waters drawn from the Crystal Pool. Perhaps they contained no more than dust and cobwebs.

Farwander turned his attention to the painted walls. Like so much of the rest of the city, they recorded the history of the inhabitants of the fallen serpent empire. This time, however, they showed destruction. Tidal waves drowned whole swathes of jungle. Pyramids and columned temples were collapsed by earthquake and landslide. A lava flow from the side of Mount Golca drowned an army of serpent warriors and slave soldiers, and left charred skeletons behind.

The idols of the bat-winged god were torn down. The prophet was seen only as he was hauled towards the open pyramidal structure in the city, held by chains of gold and dragged by a host of serpent warriors.

'A false prophet,' repeated Farwander.

'So,' said Leveret behind him, dusting off her hands after the climb and regarding the sarcophagi. 'We gonna... you know? Open them?'

Farwander ran to the window behind him and looked back down towards the pyramid. There he saw Navigator Gavel and Scrafe standing at the top, the albino serpent people slithering up over its base.

'Gavel!' shouted Farwander. 'They're closing in! The way to the summit is up here!'

'Sorry, Master Farwander,' called Gavel in response. 'I'm not making that. This saggy old jellyfish isn't made for climbing. Best I fend for myself down 'ere.'

Farwander grabbed the chain the cultist had used, but it was far too short to reach down to Gavel's position. 'I can't leave you,' he said.

'Don't you worry,' said Gavel. 'Hasn't really been the same without my Hakespure. It all stopped being fun when 'e went into the ocean. 'Sides, I got Scrafe here to look after me.'

Scrafe saluted Farwander from his position beside her. He had a dagger in his hand, and looked as certain as Farwander had ever seen him.

'So, Farwander,' said Leveret from the chamber behind him. 'What we doing?'

Farwander looked back at her, and at the sarcophagi waiting to be prised open. Gertrum was waiting beside one expectantly.

'Hope it's worth it,' said Farwander. 'Whatever it is.'

And he headed for the nearest archway, where he could feel the smoky breeze from the volcano's crater.

CHAPTER 14

He had known it, he realised now, from the first moment he had seen the immense hulk of the *Prophet's Wrath*, and heard the terrible song of its trapped whale. He had known all he needed to from the moment he heard of Lord Hekatar, the Prophet of Scaraveyla, and the army of madmen who fought and died at his command.

By the time he had come face to face with Hekatar, he had been certain. It was only when he had witnessed the prophet battling Lady Temnos at the bridge that it had all started coming together at the forefront of his mind. Warden Karanas' words, and the fate of the serpent people's prophet, had only confirmed what he had been denying to himself.

Farwander mused on this as he ran up the tightly winding stairs towards the source of the hot, ashen air. Penitent's Landing made an awful sort of sense, as if every bizarre and dangerous trial had been a new argument in favour of an underlying logic he could no longer ignore.

He reached the top of the stairs and winced in the sudden sunlight – even through the thick gauze of volcanic smoke, the light was far greater than the city's darkness to which his eyes had become accustomed. The sound of battle hammered against him and he fought to open his eyes and see where he was.

He was in the crater. The air scorched around him and he was emerging from one of dozens of smoking fumaroles in the bowl of loose volcanic rock. In some past age an eruption had blasted the peak off the mountain leaving this rough bowl-shaped depression at the top of Mount Golca, riddled with caves and tunnel entrances. It was from several of these that the smoke issued, combining into the pall that hung over the mountain. The heat pulsed up from beneath, and Farwander could imagine the pulsing red mass of molten rock beneath his feet.

On the lip of the crater, above Farwander, were the men of the expedition. Crossbowmen were lined up on the ridge firing volley after volley down into the enemy Farwander could not yet see. He estimated about fifty men still held the ridge. The sound of raised voices reached a crescendo, met by a voice Farwander recognised as Captain Vormish.

'Hold, my boys! Hold, my brothers! Bleed them white on this rock!' Vormish brandished his sword like a beacon for the men to rally around, and with a roar the enemy charged up the slope onto the ridge.

The Brotherhood had men to spare, it seemed. It had enough cultists still living to throw them against the expedition's tenuous foothold on the volcanic peak. They burst into view on the ridge as they charged into a raking hail of crossbow fire, then into the daggers and swords of the defenders. Farwander's stomach turned at the sound of screams and dying gurgles, at the ripping of steel through muscle and skin. Men from both sides tumbled down the slope, some catching fire as they rolled over a fumarole venting the raw heat of the lava inside the volcano. One, a dead cultist, rolled past Farwander as he made his uncertain way up the slope. It was a low-level cultist, with much of his skin still unscarred. He dropped his weapon, a rusted cutlass, nearby, and Farwander picked it up so at least he had a weapon in his hand.

After Captain Stennby's blade, the cutlass was a crude and ugly weapon. It was good for cutting rope and splitting coconuts, not for relying on in the slash and parry of battle. It was better than nothing, but that was all Farwander could say about it.

A wounded crewman clattered down the slope beside Farwander. It was one of the *Lightning Child* marines, cut deeply across the abdomen in a wound he would not survive. Farwander forced himself not to look into the man's eyes as he struggled to keep his footing on the loose pumice.

The crewmen on the ridge were struggling face to face with the cultists now, with Vormish himself despatching one with a thrust to the throat before kicking a second back off the ridge.

A couple of cultists burst through the expedition lines and slithered a short way down into the crater. Farwander realised they were fixed on him now, perhaps recognising the same swordsman who had stood beside Lady Temnos at the bridge. One screamed and ran at Farwander, uncoordinated and stumbling on the steep slope downwards. Farwander knocked the cultist's broad hacking blade aside with the cutlass and brought the pommel down on the back of his head before swinging the blade under him and slashing up into the cultist's torso. The cultist rolled away with a spluttering cry as the second leaped at Farwander, both hands behind his head to bring his own sword down on Farwander's skull.

Even on the loose footing, it was easy enough to pivot out of the way of the clumsy blow. The cultist was completely exposed with his back to Farwander now. Farwander cut down into the cultist's upper back with a blow that crunched through his spine and rendered him totally incapacitated before he fell face-first onto the ground.

It was ugly, brutal killing work. Farwander felt his bile rise with it. No one else needed to die on this island. No one had needed to die in the first place.

'Master Farwander, you live!' exclaimed Captain Vormish as Farwander reached the ridge. 'I had thought the mountain had swallowed you.' He clapped Farwander on the shoulder as if they were old comrades. Vormish had fought hard and his breastplate was dented and spattered with grime and blood. 'What have you found? Is our treasure within?'

'Where is Lady Temnos?' asked Farwander.

'Behold,' said Vormish, pointing down the mountain slope below him.

On the mountain slope immediately below the ridge, small knots of crewmen and marines were fighting the remains of the wave of cultists that had charged the ridge. Bodies lay everywhere, and Farwander could read the expedition's retreat to the crater ridge in the places where the corpses lay thickest.

The Brotherhood had yet to commit the majority of their cultists, of whom hundreds had made the trek up the mountain to take cover among the boulders and sub-peaks clustered below the summit. They waited in a great chanting mass, ready for the order to stream up the slope and engage. Priests chanted prayers and the cultists screamed their replies.

Warden Karanas hurled rocks down at the cultists and with every one another body was crushed and broken, but there were so many cultists and so few crewmen.

In the middle of it all, surrounded by the bodies of a dozen dead cultists, was Lady Temnos. The Brotherhood sent a constant stream of cultists at her, as if it was unable to keep the most death-hungry of them from rushing at the expedition's most valuable target. She was armed with a sword in each hand and moved with arcane swiftness, every blow accompanied with the crunch of shattering bones. Even from a distance, Farwander could make out the blood on her face trickling from her nose and ears. The blood burn was punishing her, even as she butchered every enemy that came within a sword-stroke of her.

'You need to get off this ridge,' said Farwander.

'This is all we have,' replied Vormish.

'Not for much longer. Either you die here, or you let the mountain do the fighting.'

'What are you blathering about? What addle-pated man is this I speak to?'

'Just get them off the peak,' said Farwander. ' Down the other side. Clear of the crater.'

Farwander didn't wait for Vormish to respond. He might listen, he might not. Probably not, but ultimately, it did not matter. He ran down the slope through the knots of fighting men, towards the corpse-strewn slope where Lady Temnos held her own. He spotted the priests and champions of the Brotherhood waiting for the battle's final act, knowing the expedition could put on a show of fighting well but no more.

What goal did they think they had at the mountain's peak? A treasure so vast their church could buy its own nation and join the powers of the world? Some magical boon so great it would raise Scaraveyla from the Oblivion Deeps to turn the surface into her kingdom? The way to the Crystal Pool, so their prophet could live forever and become more powerful than any Heritor?

In their madness, did they really care?

'My lady!' shouted Farwander as he reached Lady Temnos' position. A lull in the fighting gave Lady Temnos the opportunity to look around at Farwander's voice. Her face was spattered with blood, some of it from the cultists she had despatched with her swords, some from the vessels ruptured by the Blood Burn. For a moment fury flashed in her eyes and she saw in Farwander just another enemy to be despatched, before reason took a hold of her and she recognised him.

'Of course Master Farwander lives,' she said. 'A mere volcano cannot crush this bug.' He couldn't tell if it was a smile on her face, or disdain.

'This battle is lost,' said Farwander. 'But not everything.'

'We have our pride to defend,' replied Lady Temnos. 'That is worth dying for, even on this godsforsaken rock.'

'No, my lady. I mean we can beat them, but not like this.'

'Explain.'

Farwander looked past her, down the slope of Mount Golca to where the Brotherhood of Scaraveyla was massing among the serpentine ruins. 'He has to make it to the crater.'

Lady Temnos followed his gaze. There, among the gathered throng of cultists, could just be glimpsed the thorny armour and black iron mask of the Prophet of Scaraveyla. The shape of his anchor stood out among the jostling cultists. He was watching, waiting for the battle's final stages when he could stride through the corpses and claim victory.

'He will,' said Lady Temnos.

'Just him. In person. Karanas was right, this island hates the Brotherhood, but it's more than that. It hates Lord Hekatar. It killed one like him before and it will do it again, we just have to give it the chance.'

'He will take the treasure.'

'There is no treasure, my lady. Nothing we'll leave this island with, anyway.' Farwander walked up to her and put a hand on her shoulder. 'And my lady, even if all I speak is nonsense, would you rather die under a heap of these idiots, or face to face with him?'

Lady Temnos nodded, looking suddenly exhausted and out of breath. 'We can end it like that?'

'Do you think he could resist it?'

She smiled bitterly at that. 'No, Master Farwander. No, he could not.'

She turned away from him and climbed to the top of the tumbled ruin of a watchtower. A few bowshots from the Brotherhood whistled past her, but she ignored them.

She was a Heritor of the Crystal Pool. It was not for a stray arrow to bring her low. She held her sword high and glared down at the Brotherhood.

'Hekatar!' she yelled. Her voice carried down the mountain slopes as loud as a peal of thunder. 'Kneel in fear below me! Or stand before me and die!'

The priests cried out their orders. The massing cultists drew back and the sporadic bowfire fell silent. The cultist lines parted and Lord Hekatar strode through them. The cultists threw themselves face-down on the pumice slope before him and the priests howled wordless hymns of praise.

Farwander glanced back up towards the ridge around the crater. Vormish was drawing his men back, skirting around the crater to retreat down a reverse slope. Both sides had felt the battle turn. This was the way it had to end – the two Heritors locked in combat, with the conquering Hekatar crushing the valiant Lady Temnos and seizing his prize.

Farwander moved behind an outcropping of collapsed wall to keep from drawing Hekatar's attention. He was not a part of this battle's conclusion. Not yet.

'Lady Temnos,' intoned Lord Hekatar. 'I cannot fault your bravery or your strength. It is for this that I grant you such a death. Those you leave behind shall speak of your valour. Your people will sing of this death.'

'My people will sing of the moment I sail back home and throw your head from the prow of my ship,' replied Lady Temnos.

Lord Hekatar let out a low chuckle. 'Your blade is blunted on half my army. Your strength ebbs. You have but little blood left to burn. None will think any the less of you if you submit and accept your death from me now, in one painless stroke.'

'No, Lord Hekatar. If you want my death in your legend, you will have to bleed to get it.'

'As I hoped,' said Hekatar, and drew the anchor from his back.

The last time they had fought, they had been hemmed in by the confines of the bridge and the battling throng around them. Now there was nothing to obstruct them.

Hekatar struck first, as Farwander had known he would. He brought the anchor down in an overhand strike that fell like a meteor and drove a new crater in the mountain slope. Lady Temnos jumped back through the shower of pulverised rock and lunged back with a sword-thrust the prophet batted aside with a gauntleted hand. She punched him square in his visored face and he took a step back with an angry grunt, before ramming the end of the anchor into her stomach and throwing her clean off her feet.

Lady Temnos tumbled end over end up the slope. She rolled to her feet, breathing heavily, a new trickle of blood running from her ear down her neck.

'I cannot promise I shall leave of you a beautiful corpse,' said Hekatar, advancing on her.

'I promise you that I shall not,' replied Lady Temnos.

She struck first this time. Her low cut almost caught him in the midriff but he brought the haft of the anchor up to block it. She drove the pommel of her sword up into his chin and followed up with a kick to the midriff that drove him back a pace. She slashed at his throat and caught him in the shoulder.

The blade found a gap in his armour beneath the ornate shoulder guard. Hekatar yelled and a spray of crimson turned the grey volcanic slope black beneath him. Lady Temnos cuffed him around the side of the head with a backhand fuelled by her Heritor's strength and he dropped to one knee, the tentacles of his kraken visor split and dented.

Hekatar's free hand caught Lady Temnos around the throat. His gauntlet closed around her neck and she kicked frantically, because in spite of all her superhuman strength, she still needed to breathe.

'No, I shall leave no beautiful corpse,' he said as he rose again to his feet and lifted Lady Temnos off the ground. 'I shall throw you to the dogs of my cult. Every one of them shall have their scrap of Lady Temnos. But not before I have taken your skin, pretty one, to fly like a banner from the prow of my ship. My drummers will beat time with your bones. I shall drink from your skull. And when pirate captains wish to quell a mutinous crew, they will tell them of the fate that befell Lady Temnos.'

Her face was turning red. She clawed at his gauntlet but she could find no purchase. Her sword had dropped from her hand and her eyes rolled back blankly.

Farwander ran out from the cover of the ruined wall. Lord Hekatar had not noticed him, so fixated was the prophet on Lady Temnos. Farwander sprinted up behind Hekatar and snatched Lady Temnos' sword off the ground. It was not quite the equal of Captain Stennby's, perhaps, but it was good enough.

Farwander could only see one weak point in Hekatar's armour. Where the armour of the thigh and lower leg joined, there was a gap revealing the leather webbing underneath. Farwander drove the point of the sword into the back of Hekatar's knee, and felt it sink in halfway to the hilt.

Hekatar roared and spun around, dropping Lady Temnos. Farwander wrenched the blade out and stumbled back, landing on his backside on the loose rocks of the slope. Hekatar raised the anchor above him, and Farwander knew he would not be able to avoid it. The brine-pitted steel would tear straight through him and leave not even enough to be identified as a man.

The sword was useless now in Farwander's hands. The Bittersweet Blade had not taught him anything about defeating a Heritor. So he flung it instead to someone who would use it – Lady Temnos, lying on the slope with her senses returning to her.

Lady Temnos snatched the sword out of the air and sprang to her feet, leaping at Lord Hekatar and slashing at his head. Hekatar sensed the blow coming and turned away from Farwander in time to parry it with his anchor. Lady Temnos struck again and again, too fast to follow. Sparks rang off Hekatar's armour and the report of steel on steel rang across the mountain.

But Hekatar was stronger, and while Lady Temnos was faster at her best, exhaustion and blood burn had slowed her down. Hekatar took each blow on his armour, and for all his steel plates were buckled and scored Lady Temnos' sword could not break through to the prophet's flesh.

Lord Hekatar saw his opening. Lady Temnos struck wildly at his neck but he ducked it and rammed a fist up into her stomach. She doubled over, incapacitated for the moment, and he swung at her full force with his anchor. It slammed into her and threw her up the slope, sprawling through the stones, to the ridge around the crater.

This time she did not spring back to her feet. She coughed and tried to stand, faltering. Farwander followed Hekatar warily up the slope as the prophet stalked towards Lady Temnos. Everything was suddenly silent, with the ringing of steel and the clash of battle replaced only with the faint rumble and vibration of the volcano underfoot.

Lady Temnos clambered over the ridge and slid down into the crater, out of sight. Hekatar stood on the ridge looking down at her.

'There is nowhere left to flee,' he said. 'That taste in your mouth, that weight upon your shoulders, that you have never felt before – that is the feeling of defeat.'

Hekatar stepped down the ridge into the crater. Farwander reached the ridge behind him and looked down at Lady Temnos struggling to stay on her feet. She was covered in blood now. It was matted in her hair and streaming down her face. Only her furious, defiant eyes stood out from it.

Hekatar walked warily towards Lady Temnos as if expecting her to leap at him any moment, but Farwander could see she was beaten. She was propping herself up with the sword now, which in any case was bent and blunted by the fruitless assault against the Prophet of Scaraveyla.

'Let your last moments be honourable ones,' continued Lord Hekatar. 'From this world, you can take nothing more.'

Lady Temnos' reply was masked by the thunderous rumble from beneath the crater. Farwander was sure, however, that it was very rude.

The whole peak shuddered. Loose rocks sluiced down the mountainside. Farwander could barely keep his footing on the crater ridge. Lady Temnos fell and Hekatar stumbled to one knee.

The ground was collapsing in the crater, revealing the raw flow of lava beneath. Molten rock bubbled up, accompanied by blasts of ember-heavy smoke from the belching fumaroles. The air thickened and darkened as ash and smoke was thrown up into the air. Farwander felt a terrific heat, as if a wall of it was suddenly leaning against him, trying to force him back.

Penitent's Landing was speaking its piece at last. Mount Golca was the instrument of its will. The crater was its mouth, opening wide to give it voice. In spite of the immense danger yawning open in front of him, Farwander felt his heart swell. The island had finally got the chance to vent all its hatred, all the same disgust he felt at the Brotherhood and their wanton corrupting of everything around them. He wanted to echo the island's wordless cry of rage.

Men were yelling somewhere. The priests' voices were raised in alarm, ordering the retreat. Perhaps Vormish's voice was among them as he marshalled what remained of the expedition down the mountain.

One of the corpses of the men killed in the fight at the ridge rolled into a hole opening up in the crater. It vanished into the lava in a burst of flame.

Farwander put thoughts of exultation from his mind. He had moments to make his choice about which path to take now. A sprint down the mountain, away from the destruction, was tempting. Gravity would be on his side, after all. It was his best chance of surviving. But then, what kind of a man would that be who survived?

He cursed himself a thousand times as he ran down into the collapsing crater. He was a fool, he told himself. His idiocy was finally going to kill him. But he knew in that moment, with the mountain shuddering and roaring around him, that this was the only choice he could make.

The heat was furious and he was sure it would scour his skin from him. He breathed in ash and embers, and his lungs screamed.

Lady Temnos was struggling up out of the crater, but she would not make it. Farwander could see that now. Her leg kept folding under her and he guessed it was broken. The sword made a poor crutch in the loose rocks of the crater and the ground was collapsing around her. She would not outpace the bubbling lava beginning to fill the crater like water filled a bowl.

Farwander reached her and grabbed her arm. She said nothing as she leaned her weight against him. She let go the sword and it slipped through a growing crack in the ground, swallowed by the lava. Farwander grimaced as he powered up the slope, legs complaining with the extra weight, hair and eyebrows singeing.

Everything was fire and heat. The ground shook again and a portion of the ridge plunged into a cavity that rapidly filled with lava. The heat from it hit Farwander so hard he fell and had to pick himself back up again from the scorching ground.

Lady Temnos put the last of her energy into helping him in return. It was as one broken, stooped person that they reached the ridge and all but fell over it.

Farwander found himself looking back down into the crater. The whole top of the mountain was collapsing into the hollow peak, replaced with a great upwelling of molten rock. In the middle of it all was Lord Hekatar.

The Prophet of Scaraveyla was up to his knees in lava. He still lived, and was trying to trudge through the liquid fire towards safety. Farwander would have liked to watch him die, but he did not have that luxury now. He turned back to Lady Temnos, who was trying to get back to her feet. He propped her up again and half-ran, half-slid down the slope away from the crater, past the scattered corpses of the battle's dead.

Watchtowers and shrines fell or were swallowed by outburstings of lava. Chunks of the slope further down were collapsing and streams of lava emerged like blood from fresh wounds.

The main body of cultists had been caught completely unawares by the mountain's sudden quaking and they were in utter disarray. Without Hekatar there to lead them, they stampeded with no sense or plan. Cultists were trampled underfoot as they fled. A priest shrieked as his robes caught flame. Farwander could only guess at how many would make it off the mountain to relative safety, and he did not rate that number very high.

The sky turned as dark as night with the billowings of ashen smoke. The volcano's shadow spread like a black stain across the jungles of Penitent's Landing far below. Even the ocean shuddered in sympathy with the rumblings of the mountain, for the dark blue of the sea was streaked with the white of churning breakers.

Everything was a flaming, deafening chaos. All Farwander could do was keep running and hope he did not fall into a sudden crevasse of surging lava.

A vast plume of molten rock was thrown up from the crater, like a flaming orange tongue lapping towards the smoky sky. A sound like thunder, impossibly close, hammered against Farwander's skull.

In spite of the deafening boom, Farwander was sure he could hear Lord Hekatar yelling in defiance as the top of Mount Golca erupted.

CHAPTER 15

The rain was black. It was so heavy with ash and smoke dust that it fell in oily clods, pattering against the sparse vegetation that clung to the lower slopes. The heat from the mountain radiated from above, turning the downpour into a lukewarm, clammy drizzle.

Below, the jungle shuddered and darkened. Dark rivulets ran down the huge waxy leaves of the canopy, giving Penitent's Landing a diseased look like a weeping wound. The sound of fat raindrops on the canopy merged into a faint background hiss.

Farwander sheltered from the downpour. Being cold, wet and even more filthy was not at the top of his list of priorities. He had found what remained of an archway in the shape of two entwined snakes. It framed an entrance into Mount Golca, but Farwander's priorities also did not include returning to the haunted interior of the serpent people's mountain so he just used it for the protection it afforded from the elements.

The mountain had stopped shaking at full violence an hour or so before. The upper fifth or so of it was gone, collapsed into the hollow shaft of the city or blasted into the air by bursts of incandescent lava. The lava flow ran down the far side of the mountain, and some of the smoke now billowing over Penitent's Landing was from the jungle incinerated by the molten flow.

Farwander had kept ahead of the worst devastation in a fevered, punishing flight downhill, during which he had become separated from Lady Temnos. Her powers of regeneration had kicked in and returned her strength as they fled, and she had soon outpaced him. He had little doubt that Lady Temnos had found her way to safety. Even battered and weakened by her encounter with Hekatar, she was still far tougher than Farwander.

In the time since then, he had spotted a few knots of men making their way back down to the jungle. They had been groups of the expedition's crewmen primarily. A few bands of cultists had made the descent, shocked and made sullen by the loss of their goddess' prophet. Thankfully all had passed by Farwander's shelter without trying to share it. He was not in the mood for company.

Eventually the ashen rain eased off, and the smoky clouds parted enough to let a little sunlight down onto the island. Some parts of it were almost beautiful as the sharp, deep green of the jungle emerged among the gloom.

Farwander stepped out from the archway. The sky above was multicoloured like a collection of overlapping bruises, with a pale ravine through the middle allowing the sun to shine through. Farwander couldn't yet tell what time of day it was. Since he had entered Mount Golca, time had ceased to mean a great deal.

Farwander picked his way down the loose slope. The ashy rain was drying around him, letting out a rich, deep smell of burned wood and smoke. The lower slope here was scattered with plants that could not thrive beneath the smothering jungle canopy. Instead they found their sustenance in the fertile volcanic ash, with hardy roots that wound between the rocks. They had evolved to survive on this volcano's unique cocktail of minerals. They were less spectacular than the soaring trees below but they were miraculous in their own right, because there was nowhere they could survive other than the lower slopes of Mount Golca.

Some bore oddly shaped spore pods, ripe to burst and scatter seeds across the slope. Others were just scrubby handfuls of thorny branches. Farwander ignored them, crouching down to look for flowers blooming in this unpromising soil.

He spotted one, nestling at the base of another plant. It was so tiny he would have missed it if he had not known what to look for. The flower's petals were a deep blue, like the ocean at dusk. An unusual colour.

Farwander picked the tiny bloom and placed it carefully in the pouch he had tied to his belt. He scrabbled through the rocks of the slope for a while longer, finding more dark blue flowers and pocketing them.

He spent a couple of hours on his hands and knees, working his fingers raw. The flowers were cunningly hidden but he outsmarted them and soon his pouch was half filled with them. He moved down the slope towards a stand of hardy trees that had somehow found somewhere to sink their roots into the side of the mountain, forming a miniature forest far above its parent jungle. Farwander skirted around it – the flowers would not thrive there.

He heard a sound from the trees, something that did not belong there. A cough, a cry. Someone stricken and in pain. Farwander drew his dagger, the only weapon he had now, picked up from where it had been dropped by a fleeing crewman in the delirious flight from Mount Golca's eruption.

Farwander approached the trees warily. Now he saw one of them had been ripped out of the slope and lay with its roots exposed. Something huge had slammed into the copse, leaving a furrow in the slope and a gap in the trees. It was like the mark left by the impact of a meteor or a siege weapon.

Farwander peered into the copse as if into the entrance to a tunnel. Glowing embers still clung to the scarred trees, and to the scar in the ground left over from a fiery impact. He could hear laboured breathing from the dark interior of the copse, huge and deep like that of a wounded animal.

'You,' said a grinding, choked voice. 'A thousand men die on this mountain, and yet you do not.'

Farwander could see something moving in the gloom. A human figure, huge and armoured, surrounded by a haze of smoke. He could smell cooked and spoiled flesh.

'Like vermin,' said the voice again. 'Like that final vermin that will not die. The last rat on the ship.'

The figure struggled to one knee, and Farwander recognised what remained of Lord Hekatar.

The eruption of the crater had thrown the Prophet of Scaraveyla clear of the mountain peak. He had come to rest here, his fall arrested by the trees. And he was still alive.

Hekatar's armour had been blasted off him, or melted into his skin. Plates of it clung to his flesh, which was blistered and scorched so the scars of Scaraveyla's coils were almost lost among the burns. His visor was half bent away, revealing the solid, brutal features of a face also rendered almost inhuman by the burns. The tatters of his cloak dragged behind him. Where the prophet's skin had split, raw and bloody muscle was revealed oozing and wet. The worst burns were around his lower legs, which had been immersed in lava. They were blackened and useless, like lengths of charcoaled wood. His least damaged hand still clutched the haft of his anchor.

'Are you talking about me,' said Farwander, 'or yourself?'

Hekatar coughed, and spat out a wad of gory spittle. 'You live by no more than random chance,' growled Hekatar. His throat was as burned as the rest of him and every syllable came with the rasping, gurgling signature of pain. 'Just some gods-cursed fate. I had her dead. I had you all dead. Then the mountain erupted.'

'Chance?' said Farwander. 'My lord, it was not chance. I had thought you would at least have the sense to recognise that when it happened.'

Hekatar lurched forward. He dragged his anchor behind him, though his blistered muscles no longer had the strength to heft it off the ground. 'Are insults all you can throw, swordsman?'

'You still haven't worked it out,' said Farwander. Though Hekatar was still huge and terrible, his every move was agonising. The prophet was sluggish and unbalanced. Farwander could have just cuffed him around the head and retreated before Hekatar could react, and bullied him like a child tormenting a dog.

Farwander walked into the copse. The stench of burned flesh was eye-wateringly strong. 'It was the mask that first gave me the idea,' said Farwander. 'The ridiculous tentacled thing on your face. And the cloak. The first time I saw you on your ship, I knew what you were. And the name! "Hekatar". My lord, you fell prey to the trap of simply trying too hard.'

Hekatar tried to surge forward and leap on Farwander like a striking snake. But he could barely move, and with a growl of pain he stumbled forward to land flat on his face. He propped himself up again on the anchor, letting out a spluttering roar of frustration.

'Maybe there is a Scaraveyla,' continued Farwander. 'The poor idiots of your cult certainly think so. But you're no prophet. You're a Heritor, that much is true. But all this "herald of the Kraken Queen" business was just to get a few thousand fanatical morons on your side. Scaraveyla doesn't care about you and you don't care about her, you just needed a fleet and some disposable fools to hunt down the treasure of Mount Golca. So you created this... this fairytale ogre to impress them. The mask, the armour, the name, that anchor. It's a show. It's a good one, but it's not perfect.'

Hekatar swung his anchor at Farwander. The pitted steel crunched through the trees, for Hekatar still had the strength of a Heritor in his mutilated body. Farwander stepped out of the weapon's arc easily and Hekatar fell on his face again.

'I am the son of the Shipwreck Queen!' roared Hekatar. 'I am the Prophet of the Oblivion Deeps!'

'There was someone who said something very similar on this island, once,' said Farwander. 'One of the serpent men. He claimed he was the prophet of some dark god of sacrifice. But Penitent's Landing objected, and destroyed the serpent people. They sacrificed the false prophet to appease it, but it was too late. That is why the island hates you, my Lord. It despises nothing more than a false prophet.'

Hekatar tried to pull himself to his feet against the trunk of a tree. 'Were you put on this island to mock me, vermin? I shall take you off it for the same reason!'

'I'm actually on this island for these,' replied Farwander airily. He took out one of the blooms from the pouch on his belt, holding it up for the false Prophet of Scaraveyla to see.

'Flowers,' growled Hekatar. 'You're picking flowers.'

'Not just flowers,' said Farwander, in a tone very much like the ones his sword instructors would use when explaining to him the principles of the Bittersweet Blade. 'The blooms of the Penitent's Grace. They grow only in one place in all the world, here, on the lower slopes of Mount Golca. As described by Lord Arcturaval Temnos when he visited Penitent's Landing two hundred years ago, along with the plant's miraculous properties. If there really is a treasure of Mount Golca, this is it.'

Farwander walked closer to Lord Hekatar now. It was a strange exhilaration he felt, knowing he was in the presence of a force of destruction that was now incapable of hurting him. One of Hekatar's eyes was covered by the melted visor that had fused with the bones of his face – the other one, set deep in weeping scar tissue, glared at him with a fury made more intense by the fact it could not be turned into violence.

'What did you think was at the peak?' asked Farwander. 'Everyone has a different story about it. What was yours?'

Hekatar's reply was limited to an angry, ragged breathing.

'Or did you have no idea at all?' said Farwander. 'You just heard there was something worth finding, so you set sail for the same place. Maybe your cult would have abandoned you if you hadn't given them a goal at the end of your voyage. You had to give them something to do, and a trophy to take back to the mainland. Well, whatever the treasure is, it's gone now. The eruption wiped out anything the serpent people had stashed there. '

Hekatar shot out a hand and grabbed Farwander by the ankle. His grip was still steel-tight. Hekatar growled and brought the anchor behind him, winding up for a huge, final overhand strike with the last of his Heritor's strength, to impale Farwander through the skull and pin him to the slope of Mount Golca forever.

Farwander grabbed one of the bent tentacles of Hekatar's kraken mask. He wrenched the prophet's head back, and rammed the point of his dagger into the underside of the prophet's jaw.

A Heritor could survive wounds that would fell a normal man – the fact Hekatar was alive now was testament to that. But for all his superhuman power, he still could not live without a functioning brain. The dagger punched up through the lower jaw and the palate, and up into Hekatar's brain stem.

Of all the murder-blows Farwander had learned, this was the most immediate and effective. Even a sword-thrust to the heart would not render a foe as instantly and completely dead as the obliteration of this place, nestled beneath the lobes of the brain, justifiably well-protected by the bones of the skull. One of the only ways to get to it was through the underside of the jaw. It was rare indeed that an opponent would present it as a target, but equally, it was rare that an opponent would have just been weakened by exposure to an erupting volcano.

Farwander twisted the dagger, because no one had ever been ill served by confirming the kill. He felt the gristle and crunch of bone and sinew parting. Hekatar's good eye rolled back in his head and the anchor dropped from his nerveless fingers.

Farwander put a foot against Hekatar's collarbone and forced the dagger back out. Hekatar slumped to the ground, dead before the blade had been withdrawn.

It was an unspectacular, rather pathetic death for the false Prophet of Scaraveyla, which seemed to Farwander to be completely appropriate.

He left Hekatar there to rot, and continued picking flowers.

Up here, the stink of Last Fathom didn't quite reach. But for the paucity of fertile land, this area upland of the port would have been hugely desirable, a playground for the wealthy who had parlayed their piratical spoils or the fruits of a lucky deal into a farm or estate. As it was, the scattered farms and hamlets were mostly unoccupied, and the region's only real benefit was a view of Last Fathom and the ocean beyond that made the place look almost picturesque.

It was a most peculiar feeling to see the house again. It was not just the time since he had been here last, or even the distance he had covered in the meantime. It was the promises he had made when he left, and the sheer unlikelihood of his ever being able to keep them. Of all the people to have made a grand claim, and then actually returned to fulfil it, it seemed the least likely one possible was Aldebrecht Beros Quovanticos venn Farwander.

Farwander swung down off the horse he had hired in Last Fathom. It was a ragged old nag, but it had got him up here to the place he had grown up. As he led the horse to the stables adjoining the farmhouse, he was struck by a sudden and immediate fear that the house was empty. It would be a dead, silent place covered in the thin layer of dust that had gathered since he had left to fulfil his promise.

The water trough was full. As the horse drank, Farwander realised that meant someone was home.

He pushed open the door to the farmhouse. The kitchen was the shadowy place he remembered, full of the old smells – herbs, flour, firewood. The kettle had gone cold on the stove. The layout of the house was etched into his memory – the front room and pantry, with the bedrooms and spinning loft on the upper floor.

Farwander sat down at one of the chairs at the kitchen table. He suddenly felt the weight of the distance between him and Penitent's Landing, all the ocean miles he had covered there and back. It had been on a native canoe that he had made it back from the island. The inhabitants of the nearby island had ventured close to witness the eruption of Mount Golca and plead with the mountain not to belch out smooch smoke it darkened the skies over their own islands, too. They had picked up handfuls of survivors from the expedition, among them Farwander. He had taken half a dozen ships to make the short hops across a mercifully calm sea back to Cape Cadaver.

There had been no kraken this time. There was no one to summon them up from the Oblivion Deeps.

By the time Farwander had left the Ghost Archipelago, he had begun to hear tales of other bands of survivors from the expedition making it back to safety. They brought with them stories of lost serpent people kingdoms, volcanic disasters, and the scourge that was the cult of Scaraveyla. The last rumour he heard, from a docker as he boarded a trader returning to Last Fathom, was that Lady Temnos was a few days out of Cape Cadaver and intended to raise another force for another expedition.

Farwander heard someone moving around upstairs. He was not afraid. It was such a familiar sound it was easy to imagine he had never left, and that everything since he had last left this house was a flight of his imagination. But the aches in his bones and the new scars on his body were proof it really had all happened.

A woman in the later reaches of middle age shuffled into the room. She wore a dusty housedress and had her grey-streaked hair tied up in a simple bun. She took the kettle and filled it from a basin, then took a tinder and began striking it over the firewood in the stove.

'Mother,' said Farwander.

She put her hand to her chest and almost dropped the kettle. 'Alder!' she exclaimed. 'Oh, Aldebrecht, you almost stopped my heart!'

'I'm sorry,' said Farwander. 'I didn't know if anyone was...'

She was across the room and throwing her arms around him before he could finish. He held the familiar warmth of his mother close for a long time, and when she drew away her cheeks were wet with tears. She had been a beautiful woman, and it had still not left her. Farwander had got his looks from her side of the family.

Farwander swallowed. The words had to be said, but he was afraid of them. 'Is she..?'

'She's alive,' said his mother, and Farwander sank back into the kitchen chair.

'I thought... I was sure she would...'

'I'll put the kettle on,' said his mother, returning to the stove to potter. 'So, Aldebrecht, a mother must know. Where have you been?'

Farwander let out a long breath. What a question, he thought. 'Well, at first I stayed close to home. I found an apothecary who claimed he had a cure from a Vine Warden who could grow a particular exotic root to order.'

'And he required payment up front, I take it?'

'Don't look at me like that, mother. Of course I know it was a scam now. But we were desperate. You'd have done the same thing, don't tell me you wouldn't.'

'I'm telling you nothing,' replied his mother, in a way that told him a great deal.

'So I borrowed some money and this apothecary took it, of course. Felt rather stupid, yes, I admit. Not as stupid as when the people I'd borrowed from wanted their money back, though. Lady by the name of Big Marga. Had quite the narrow escape from her tender embrace.'

'Well the narrower the escape the better with you.'

'Very true. But at that point I had no money and no magical nonexistent healing root. And Last Fathom wasn't so welcoming for me any more.'

As the water boiled, his mother sat beside him at the table. 'Where did you go?' she asked.

'The Ghost Archipelago.'

She made an impressed little noise. 'I thought that was a rumour. Lot of islands appearing out of nowhere, men risking everything to plunder them for treasure. All sorts of nonsense stories come out of the town.'

'No, the Ghosts are real. Don't know if I'd recommend it, though.'

'So why on earth would you go somewhere like that?'

'It wasn't entirely voluntary at first,' said Farwander. 'But then I heard someone mention the name Temnos.'

'Oh?'

'Lord Arcturaval Temnos. I remembered his name from one of the books you found us. He went to one of the islands, Penitent's Landing, and when he returned he wrote of what he found there. Plants and animals, all manner of strange things. One of them was a flower that only grew on the slopes of the volcano on the island he visited on his way to the Crystal Pool. He called it the Penitent's Grace. It cured a lot of things.'

'A flower?'

Farwander put the pouch on the table and took out a pinch of dried, dark blue petals. 'Dried and boiled in water to make an infusion, and administered to the sufferer one draught every dawn.'

'Hmm. I should have known it was tea that would solve all this. Speaking of which.' The kettle whistled and Farwander's mother, Erszebet Hepshebah venn Farwander, pottered around the stove pouring them each a cup of the strong, herby tea she had kept in the cupboard since he could remember.

They didn't speak until the tea was done and cool enough to drink. Farwander took a sip, and felt some of that weight drop off him. 'I've missed this,' he said. 'Not a drop of tea on any ship I sailed on.'

'No tea?' said his mother, creasing her brow. 'What savages.'

'You have no idea.'

She looked at the pinch of flowers, picked up a bloom, and sniffed it carefully. 'So. Can it cure the Blackspine?'

Farwander took another long swallow of tea. 'It worked on the one patient Arcturaval tried it on. He didn't bring enough back to do more than that.'

'And did you?'

'Mother, I picked that mountain bald. My fingers bled by the end of it.'

'Good boy.'

There was silence for a while, until Farwander had finished his cup of tea. 'How is she?'

'Come.'

His mother led him upstairs, to one of the bedrooms. In the bed, lying just as he had left her, was his sister.

Berenice Ismene venn Farwander was pale and thin, for the illness had dragged all the life and substance out of her. Her eyes were dark and sunken. The wildflowers by her bed were fresh, and Farwander knew his mother had replaced them every morning with new ones picked from the house's grounds.

Beneath Berenice's nightclothes, Farwander knew, was a strip of darkened and bruised skin down the middle of her back, the telltale sign of the disease that withered away and took its victims with no hope of cure. No hope, that was, until Lord Arcturaval Temnos had made a note in his natural history of the Ghost Archipelago two hundred years ago.

'I promised you,' said Farwander to his sleeping sister. 'I came back. I'll save you.' He turned to his mother, who had dried her tears away and finally looked as sensible and solid as she had ever been. 'It's supposed to be at dawn, but...'

'I'll make up a draught,' she said, and headed back down to the kitchen.

With the best will in the world, Farwander wasn't going to refound the venn Farwander line. It was not within his capacity to build a respectable and successful family, a stable dynasty that could redress the legacy of his great-uncle Sarven and make the family mean something again. Aldebrecht couldn't do it – it would be a miracle if he could find a woman to stand him long enough to sire an heir, let alone start a bloodline.

But Berenice was kind and clever. She was loving enough to raise fine children but sharp enough to ensure they had the right father. If Farwander had his mother's looks, Berenice had both her looks and her sense. It should have been him struck down by the Blackspine.

His mother had thought so, too. She would never have said it, and losing her son would have devastated her. But losing the future of her family would be an extra grief, and so Farwander had promised he would save his sister and spare his mother the anguish of seeing her family line wither away.

Farwander sat by Berenice's bed and began to tell her of his flight from Last Fathom, Big Marga and the *Salted Swine*. The whole journey spilled out, though he skirted around the most gruesome moments of violence and painted a few of his crewmates in a more positive light. The Ghost Archipelago was a dark and terrible place, but it was also heartbreakingly beautiful, and he knew Berenice would have loved to see it.

Perhaps she still would.

His mother entered the room with a steaming mug. It filled the room with a strong, dark smell that brought back the rich mulch of the jungle floor and the wet bark of its trees.

'She wakes now and again,' she said as she held the mug to Berenice's lips. 'She asks if you have returned. Sometimes she has bad dreams, poor thing.'

Berenice swallowed and coughed slightly. Her mother waited for a moment before feeding her some more.

'I heard of another ship coming in from the Ghosts,' said Farwander's mother. 'Laden with gold, they say. Some woman made it from nothing, came back rich. She's taking a whole mess of men back to the Ghosts with her to do it again. Name of Lady Pavine.'

Farwander smiled. 'I imagine Lady Pavine is exaggerating the scale of her new-found riches. But it's good to know she made it out with something.'

'You knew her?'

'I ran across her, yes.'

'You could have come back with a wife at least, Alder.'

'Believe me, Lady Pavine would not be the kind of matriarch the venn Farwanders need.'

This time Berenice drank the infusion down, murmured something Farwander did not hear, and laid her head down again.

'Will you go back?' said his mother.

Farwander was caught unawares by the question. 'Why would I go back?'

'Last Fathom was never much of a playground for you, Aldebrecht. If Berenice gets better, I doubt we'll stay. And where would we take you that you can't get yourself in trouble? It sounds like the Ghost Archipelago is somewhere those tendencies that make me tear my hair out are just what you need to get by. And if your sister is going to reverse our fortunes, we could do with a shipload of treasure to help get things started. Not that I want you to go, Alder, but if you're not going to give me a clutch of grandchildren you might as well do something useful with yourself and make us rich.' She said the words with an impish smile that told him she was exaggerating her feelings, but not by much.

Berenice's bedroom window looked down towards Last Fathom, and beyond it the sea glittered. Farwander imagined how it might, given a few days away from the grimness of surviving at sea, be an inviting sight – the ocean, endless and bright, with the seductive mysteries of the Ghost Archipelago waiting beyond.

'Give it a couple of weeks,' he said, 'and I'll have forgotten all the dangers.'

'And you'll want to go back.'

Farwander thought of the sarcophagi at the pinnacle of Mount Golca, and the riches Leveret had found there and managed to bring back. Gold? Silver? Gem-studded grave goods looted from the skeletons of serpent warriors? And she hadn't even known what she was looking for. Gods knew what else there was to find out there.

'Probably,' he said, and his fingers suddenly itched to hold a sword.

THE BEAST PIT

By
Joseph A. McCullough

Thank you for reading *Ghost Archipelago: Farwander* by Ben Counter. The setting for this novel comes from a tabletop wargame I designed called *Frostgrave: Ghost Archipelago*. In this game, each player takes on the role of a Heritor, recruits a Warden, and assembles a band of hardy adventurers to go explore the Lost Isles, looking for treasure and, of course, the Crystal Pool. The game is designed to be fast, friendly and fun, so if you have ever considered jumping into the wonderful hobby of tabletop miniature wargaming, check it out. For those already playing the game, I present this exclusive scenario, loosely based on one of the more intense scenes in *Farwander*.

* * *

After hours tramping through the thick jungle, the foliage begins to open up, and you see a small clearing. In the midst of the clearing is a large pit, covered with a crude collection of branches and leaves. Only a creature that was nearly blind could miss such a trap. Then again, considering the size of the hole, perhaps the pit was created to catch a creature so large that could barely see the ground. As you get closer, you see light glinting off several objects near the pit. If you didn't know better, you'd swear there was gold just lying about…

SET-UP

Place a covered pit in the exact centre of the table. This can just be a circle of leaves or small branches. The pit should form a crude circle approximately 8" in diameter. Place the central treasure in the exact centre of the pit. Place four additional treasures on the table so that they form an 'X' around the central treasure. Each of these treasure should be 8" from the central treasure on a line to one of the four corners of the table.

The rest of the table should be loosely filled with rocks, patches of foliage, and perhaps an overgrown ruin of some sort.

SPECIAL RULES

At the end of the second turn, place a mutilated monarch (see below) at the centre point of one randomly determined table edge. This creature follows the rules for uncontrolled creatures, except that if it is called upon to make a random move, it will instead move towards the closest treasure token, regardless of whether or not it is in line of sight.

Any time the mutilated monarch moves onto any portion of the pit, roll a die. On a 12+, the pit covering collapses and the monarch (and any other figure standing on the pit top) tumble into it. All figures, including the mutilated monarch, should immediately roll a die and take that many points of damage (do not subtract armour from this roll). Once in the pit, the mutilated monarch will be unable to escape for the rest of the game. Crew figures can climb out as normal (treat the pit as 4" deep). If the mutilated monarch is in the pit, any figure standing on the edge may attack it. Regardless of the outcome of the fight, however, this figure is not considered to be in combat and may move away at any time.

The pit will not collapse under the weight of crewmen, no matter how many are standing on the pit.

TREASURE AND EXPERIENCE

Treasure is rolled for as normal after this scenario. Experience is gained as normal with the following additions:

- +20 Experience points if the Heritor is on the table when the mutilated monarch falls into the pit.
- +30 Experience points if the Heritor is on the table when the mutilated monarch is killed.

THE MUTILATED MONARCH

This poor saurian was captured and mutilated by dark magic. Its forelimbs have been replaced with large tentacles, and a large number of smaller tentacles have also been grafted onto its torso. It is a wretched and tormented creature, driven to madness by its constant pain.

Because of all of the tentacles on its body, it is especially hard to escape combat with the mutilated monarch. In order to push back the mutilated monarch, or to step back from combat, a figure must actually cause damage in a fight – simply winning the fight is not enough.

Monarch						
M	F	S	A	W	H	Notes
6	+8	+0	12	+5	28	Saurian, Large, Powerful (treat as using Two-Handed Weapon), Tentacles

AUTHOR BIO

Ben Counter is a veteran of game-related science fiction and fantasy with a love of action scenes, black humour and anything with tentacles.

He lives on the south coast of the UK and, at odds with tradition, has no cats, He is a miniature painting fanatic and avid tabletop games. He is almost certainly nerdier than you.

Schubert, Friedr

Reise durch das nö und Lappland

Im Jahre 1817

Schubert, Friedrich Wilhelm von

Reise durch das nördliche Schweden und Lappland

Im Jahre 1817

Inktank publishing, 2018

www.inktank-publishing.com

ISBN/EAN: 9783747704172

Reise

durch das

nördliche Schweden und Lappland,

oder

durch Gestrikland, Helsingland, Medelpad, Angermanland,
Westerbotten, Lappland, Jemteland und Herjeådalen,

im Jahre 1817,

von

Friedrich Wilhelm von Schubert,

der Theologie Doctor und Professor an der Königl. Preuß. Universität zu Greifswald,
designirtem Königl. Superintendenten und Pastor zu Altenkirchen auf der Insel Rügen.

Mit einem Kupfer.

Leipzig, 1823,
J. C. Hinrichssche Buchhandlung.

Inhalt

der

Reise durch Nordschweden und Lappland.

Kapitel 27.

Sechszehntes Kapitel.

Reise von Upsala nach Gefle.

Osterby. Eisengruben Dannemora. Löfftad. Elfkarlebn. Wasserfälle des Dalelf. Der Lachsfang. Die
letzten Eichen gegen Norden. Eintritt in Norrland.
Stadt Gefle: Kirche, Hafen, Handel, Rathhaus,
Schulen, Fluß Gefle. Das Län Gefleborg.

Am 6. Junius. Von Upsala nach Uggelsta 1½ Meilen;
von Uggelsta nach Andersby 2½ Meilen; von Andersby
nach Osterby ½ Meilen. — Zusammen 4½ Meilen.

Um 12 Uhr verließ ich die Stadt Upsala, und langte bald, neben
mehreren alten Grabhügeln, die überhaupt in Upland zahlreich
sind, zur Kirche Gambla (Alt) Upsala. Die Kirche ist einfach
und freundlich, sie hat eine Orgel und im Chor einen Runenstein mit Kreuz; ein zweiter Runenstein, der aber sehr beschä-
digt ist, in der Mitte mit einer schiffsähnlichen Figur, liegt neben
der inneren Kirchthüre. Ein hölzernes Bild Thor's wird gezeigt, aber es ist schwerlich heidnischen Ursprungs. Eine eiserne
Streitart, Stücke von Schwerdtern, Urnen ꝛc., die vor kurzem
beim Bau des Armenhauses gefunden wurden, zeugen von hohem
Alter. Was sonst Alt-Upsala aus grauer Vorzeit besaß, ist
längst nach Neu-Upsala verpflanzt worden; auch die Gebeine König Erich des Heiligen ruhten hier. Im Thurme, der,
wie oben bemerkt, einst Theil des Odinstempels gewesen seyn
soll, finden sich alte Oeffnungen, deren einige jetzt als Fenster

II.   A

benutzt werden. Auf dem Kirchhofe stieß man vor einigen Jahren auf eine alte Mauer, die den Tempel Odins angehört haben
mag. Der Kirche gegenüber liegt das freundliche Pfarrhaus,
vor welchem eine kleine Wiese mit Gebüsch einen lieblichen Vor-
grund bildet; hier soll sich einst der Hain Odins erhoben haben.
In der Nähe der Kirche findet man ferner das Gemeinde- und
das Schulhaus. Die Schule, deren Lehrer ein ordinirter Geistlicher ist, ward durch ein Vermächtniß des Obersten Erik
Ahlberg, dessen Bild die Kirche schmückt, gestiftet. Erik
Ahlberg hatte als gemeiner Soldat, eines Liebesabentheuers
mit einem Fräulein wegen, das Vaterland verlassen müssen, und
war in Französische Dienste getreten, in welchen er zur Würde
eines Obersten sich emporschwang. Bruderkinder Ahlbergs
leben noch im Kirchspiel. Im Gemeindehause (sockenstuga)
wird Kirchspielsstand gehalten; ein Theil des Hauses dient zur
Wohnung der gebrechlichsten und verlassensten Armen, die aber
nur mit Mühe hatten bewogen werden können, ihre neue Wohnung zu beziehen, weil dieselbe von der Anhöhe, auf welcher
einst das heidnische Disating (vergl. Kap. 15.) gehalten wurde,
nahe begränzt wird. Die kranken Armen haben ihr eigenes
Zimmer. Das Haus, erst seit 1816 gebauet, war noch nicht
vollendet. Ich bestieg die Tingshög, die eine schöne Aussicht
über Alt- und Neu-Upsala und die Umgegend gewährt. Der
Fuß der Anhöhe hat durch Abstechen für Wegebesserung verloren, bis Gustav III. das ältere Gesetz gegen Zerstörung von Al-
terthümern erneuerte. Der Gerichtshöhe gegenüber steigen die
drei Königshöhen (kungshögar), cylinderförmige Grabhöhen,
mit weiter Aussicht, empor.

Neben niedrigen Felsen, durch eine fruchtbare, aber baum-
lose Gegend, Bauern- und Soldatenhöfen vorüber, erreichte ich
Uggelsta, wo ein Lieutenant den Gästgifvaregård gepachtet hat.
Daneben wohnt der bescheidene Hällkarl. Während ich hier des
Pferdes wartete, unterhielt ich mich mit der freundlichen Haus-
frau, die ihr vor wenig Monaten gebornes liebliches Kind auf

den Armen trug. Ueberhaupt wohnt in diesem Theile von Upland ein biederer Schlag von Menschen, wie man es schon an
den herzlichen Grüßen inne wird.

Der Weg von Uggelsta nach Andersby führt, der
hochgelegenen Kirche Lena vorüber, durch das Gräflich-Brahe-
sche große Eisenhüttenwerk Wattholma. Alleen durchschneiden
das Dorf und Wiesen breiten sich vor den Häusern aus. Hinter
Wattholma wird die Gegend waldiger und schöner. Man
fährt neben dem Gräflich-Braheschen Schloß Salstad, auch vielen hübschen Dörfern und Höhen hin; vor Knifstad erblickt
man einen schönen Waldsee und erreicht bald durch Wald und
über Höhen den netten Gästgifvaregård Andersby.

Von Andersby bis Österby hat man einen lieblichen Weg
durch Granwald neben Wiesen, dem hübschen Dannemora-
See, den die Gruben und die Kirche umgeben, und den zierlichen Wohnungen der Grubenarbeiter. Es war Abend, als ich
in Österby anlangte, wo mich der biedere Besitzer, Brukspa-
patron Tham, mit vieler Herzlichkeit empfing. Nach dem
Abendessen wurde der Hochofen, dessen Feuer gar herrlich in die Dämmerung leuchtete, in Augenschein genommen.
Nachdem das Erz geröstet und gepocht worden, wird es im
Hochofen ausgeschmolzen. Die Schlacken, welche man früher
wegwarf, werden jetzt, nach der Erfindung des vor nicht langer
Zeit in Söderfors verstorbenen Arbeiters Grönquist, zu Ei-
sensteinen bereitet, die die Stelle guter Mauersteine vertreten;
man bereitet die Eisensteine, indem man die Schlacken in einem
schönen Feuerstrom aus dem Ofen in Formen fließen läßt.
Österby schmiedet jährlich etwa 3000 Schiffspfund Stangeneisen
und Stahl aus und beschäftiget 500 Familien. Nur ein Theil
der Arbeiter wohnt am Orte; diese arbeiten von 6 Uhr Morgens
bis 7, die entfernter wohnenden nur bis 6 Uhr Abends.

Am nächsten Morgen besah ich das Bruk. Es liegt gar
freundlich zwischen Wiesen, Seen, Wald und Kornfeldern, wird
von Alleen durchschnitten und hat ganz das Ansehen einer kleinen

A 2

Stadt. Das Bruk hat eine eigene Kirche und Schule, welcher letzteren ein Geistlicher vorsteht; die Kirche, Seitengebäude des Schlosses, schmücken einige schöne Gemälde. Den Wohnungen der Bruksarbeiter sieht man den Wohlstand der Bewohner an: jeder Arbeiter hat, außer einem Tagelohn von 5 Schillingen Riksgäld, ein kleines Ackerstück, Weide für 2 Kühe und 5 bis 7 Schaafe, Korn und Heringe, überdieß etwas Gewisses an Korn für die Frau und für jedes Kind unter 15 Jahren. Der Bruksarzt heilt unentgeltlich, doch ist nur bei Unglücksfällen die Arznei frei.

Das schöne, vor etwa 50 Jahren neuerbaute, Schloß, welches Herr Tham bewohnt, wird vorne von Wiesen, durch welche sich Wege schlängeln, hinten von einem freundlichen Park umgeben. Den Park begränzt ein See, im See liegt eine Insel, auf welcher im Gebüsch hübsche Spaziergänge angelegt sind, sie ist durch Brücken mit dem Park verbunden. Im Schloß findet man eine große Sammlung von Ölgemälden und Kupferstichen. Herr Tham, ein denkender Landwirth, hat mancherlei nützliche neue Einrichtungen in der Ackerwirthschaft getroffen.

Von Österby machte ich in Begleitung des Herrn Tham und des Landmessers Ribbarbjelke eine Excursion nach den nur eine Achtel Meile entfernten Gruben von Dannemora. Der Weg führt durch Wald, aber des Waldes wird, der vielen Hütten wegen, in diesem Theil von Upland immer weniger, so daß die Hütten schwerlich noch lange werden bestehen können, wenn nicht ansehnliche neue Anpflanzungen entstehen. In Dannemora wohnt der Geschworne Beronius, einer der vorzüglichsten mechanischen Köpfe Schwedens. Er hat mehrere wichtige neue Erfindungen gemacht und ältere verbessert.

Die unerschöpflichen Eisengruben von Dannemora sind, die zum Theil noch reichhaltigeren Lappischen ausgenommen, die reichsten in ganz Schweden, denn ihr Gehalt ist 15 bis 70 Prozent. Das treffliche Eisen von Dannemora läßt sich leichter als anderes Schwedisches Eisen verarbeiten. Die Gruben laufen zum Theil unter dem Dannemora-See fort, der durch andrängendes Wasser die Arbeit schwieriger und kostbarer, ja einige Gruben völlig unbrauchbar macht. Nur eine der jetzt bearbeiteten Gruben ist so dunkel, daß man beim Schein der Lampe arbeitet; in die übrigen fällt das Tageslicht, daher sie auch nicht feucht sind, und weder einfahrende Arbeiter noch Fremde sich der Grubenkittel bedienen. Man fährt in Tonnen, oder steigt, in 10 Minuten, auf Leitern hinab. Man überschauet die Gruben auch sehr gut von oben, aber ihr Anblick ist nicht schön. Hart am Rande der einen Grube findet man einen kleinen See. In der Tiefe der Gruben liegt Eis, welches bisher nicht schmolz, wiewohl Wasser hinzuströmt; doch hoffte man mittelst verstärkter Wasserströmung es zum Schmelzen zu bringen. Die schon oft beschriebene innere Einrichtung der Gruben übergehe ich mit Stillschweigen, da ich sie nicht durch eigene Ansicht kennen lernte. Das gewonnene Eisen wird in Österby, Löfstad, Söderfors und vielen andern Hütten in und außer Upland verarbeitet; in Dannemora giebt es keine Schmelzhütte. Die Gruben gehören einer Interessentschaft.

Der Ort Dannemora ist kleiner und unregelmäßiger gebaut als Österby, auch ohne Gasthof, daher die Fremden in dem wohleingerichteten Gasthofe zu Österby übernachten. Wie in Österby, wohnt auch in Dannemora ein Grubenarzt.

Von Dannemora fuhr ich nach Österby zurück, sagte meinen lieben Wirthen ein dankbares Lebewohl, und setzte dann die Reise auf dem kürzesten Wege über Löfstad und Elfkarleby nach Gefle fort. Ein zweiter, aber weiterer, Weg führt über das reizende Söderfors, seit 1748 Eigenthum der Grill'schen Familie, 7 Meilen von Upsala und 5¼ Meile von Gefle entfernt. Söderfors verdankt sein Entstehen seiner Schiffsankerschmiede, welche 1675 der Bergmeister in Upland und Norrland, Clás Depken, der unter dem Namen Ankarström in den Adelstand erhoben wurde, anlegte, nachdem bis dahin die

Anker aus dem Auslande bezogen, oder durch Maschinen, ohne Wasserhämmer, geschmiedet worden waren. Seit 1699 bildet Söderfors ein eigenes Pastorat. Söderfors, auf einer Insel des Dalelf, hat einen schönen Park und ein naturhistorisches Museum. Letzteres gründete seit 1783 der Besitzer von Söderfors, Adolph Grill. Das Museum, welches nach Adolph Grill's und seiner Gattin Tode eben verkauft werden sollte, ist besonders reich an Vogelarten, zumal Schwedischen, die man fast vollständig findet, und Schnecken; auch ist eine kostbare naturhistorische Bibliothek mit dem Museum verbunden.

———

Am 7. Jun. Von Österby nach Bro ¾ Meile; von Bro nach Hakansbo 1¼ Meile; von Hakansbo nach Stårplinge 1¼ Meilen; von Stårplinge nach Elfkarleby 3 Meilen. — Zusammen 6¼ Meilen.

Von Österby bis Bro hat man Wald und Wiesen, und fährt neben freundlichen Wohnungen der Arbeiter hin. Schlagbäume findet man hier überall in Menge, denn Upland, diese trefflich bebaute Provinz, ist, wie Ångermanland, das rechte Land der Schlagbäume. Jedes Häuschen, jedes für sich bestehende Aeckerchen, jeder Waldtheil, hat seine zwei Hecken, die meist so eingerichtet sind, daß sie von selbst, mittelst großer Hebebäume, sich schließen. In Bro gesellte sich zu mir ein Helsinger, den Herr Tham hatte kommen lassen, um das Säen des Flachses und das Weben nach Norrländischer Weise in Österby zu lehren. Dies war der erste Helsingländer, den ich sah; in seinem Wesen sprach sich ganz der Sinn für Freiheit und Eigenthum und die heiße Liebe zur Heimath, die selbst das Gute in der Fremde wenig achtet, neben der dem Schwedischen Volke überhaupt eigenthümlichen vertrauten Bekanntschaft mit der heiligen Schrift und Anhänglichkeit an König, Vaterland und Gesetz, aus welches alles ich bald als den Charakter der Bewohner Helsinglands kennen lernen sollte.

Mein Helsingländer fuhr mit dem Gästgifvare voran. Kaum war ich eine Viertelmeile gefahren, als das Sielenzeug riß, so daß das Weiterfahren unmöglich wurde; flugs schwang sich mein Skjutsbonde, die Frau des Gästgifvare, auf das Pferd und ritt heim, zu bessern. Mittlerweile lagerte ich mich am Wege: vor mir dufteten Veilchen, die man hauptsächlich im nördlichen Schweden wildwachsend findet, rings um üppige Wiesen; auf dieser lieblichen Stelle schrieb ich in mein Tagebuch und hielt dann ein kleines Mahl, bis die Führerin mit Pferd und Sielenzeug zurückkam. Dann ging es weiter am Rande lieblicher Wiesen, nach dem großen de Geerschen Eisenhüttenwerk Löfstad. Löfstad hat, wie Österby, das Ansehen einer kleinen Stadt, mit regelmäßigen Straßen, welche hohe Laubbäume beschatten, aber eine minder schöne Lage. Seit im Jahr 1719 die Russen den Ort zerstörten, ist er neu aufgebauet worden. Die schöne Brukskirche, im Innern durch eine Orgel von ansehnlicher Größe geschmückt, wird von Bäumen und Gartenbeeten umgeben. Der Begräbnißplatz des Bruks liegt eine halbe Meile entfernt, neben der Mutterkirche gleiches Namens. Das Bruk hat seinen eigenen Arzt und soll an 1000 Menschen beschäftigen. Ein stattlicher Gasthof ist vorhanden. Das einfache, massive herrschaftliche Wohnhaus wird von ansehnlichen Nebengebäuden, auch einer Reitbahn, und einem zwar nicht großen, aber schönen Garten, in dessen Treibhäusern der Wein an Wänden, wie auf Lohe unter Fenstern, gezogen wird, umgeben; ein kleiner Park wurde eben angelegt; aus den Zimmern, welche Gemälde schmücken, überblickt man die liebliche Umgegend. Nebengebäude enthalten eine Bibliothek von etwa 6000 Bänden aus allen Wissenschaften, viele Kupferstiche, eine Mineraliensammlung, in welcher mich der durchaus vollständige Abdruck eines kleinen Fisches auf Schiefer vorzugsweise interessirte, einen physikalischen Apparat und eine Gewehr und Antiquitätenkammer.

Von Löfstad bis Skärplinge hat man noch eine volle Meile durch Wald, neben Wiesen, fruchtbaren Feldern und einigen Dörfern; die Gegend ist völlig eben. Man fährt der Mutterkirche Löfstad vorüber. Skärplinge hat einen guten und geräumigen Gasthof.

Die Poststraße von Skärplinge, von wo links eine Straße über Räcknö nach Söderfors abführt, nach Elf-karleby, beträgt 3 Meilen; mein Skjutsbonde wählte aber beim Fischerdorfe Loiten einen Richtweg, der um eine halbe Meile kürzer war. Oft zeigen sich die bewaldeten Busen der Ostsee. Nach etwa 1 Meile erreicht man das große de Geer-sche Eisenbruk Carlsholm, welches zwischen Wiesen und Wald eine recht anmuthige Lage hat. Ueberhaupt hat man auf der letzten Hälfte des Weges Nadel- und Birkenwald, der nur durch das Bruk Carlsholm unterbrochen wird. Jetzt aber er-schallt aus der Ferne ein dumpfes Getöse, man kommt näher, glaubt Donnerschläge zu vernehmen, die von den Felsen zurück-geworfen werden, plötzlich öffnet sich der Wald, der majestätische Dalelf mit seinen Wasserfällen wird sichtbar, man fährt herab an das Ufer und über eine lange Brücke, die mitten über die fürchterlichen Katarakten wegführt. Sie ist von Holz und ruht auf zwei steinernen Pfeilern. Der Bau begann im Jahr 1814 und wurde 1816 durch Dalekarlier, aus deren Heimath der Dalelf herabkommt, vollendet; zugleich ward das Bette des Flusses, hier an seiner Mündung in die Ostsee, gereiniget. — Schon war es 10 Uhr Abends, als ich anlangte; bis nach 11 Uhr stand ich, bewundernd, vor der großen Naturscene da; denn es war hell genug, um alles Einzelne genau zu unterscheiden. Die Wasserfälle sind unzählich, der größern sind drei. Nachdem der sehr breite Strom bisher sanft zwischen Waldufern geflossen, stürzt er plötzlich in eine Tiefe von etwa 20 Ellen herab. Dann theilt er sich in drei Arme, welche zwei bewaldete Inseln ein-schließen. Jeder dieser Aerme bildet einen Fall, den schönsten bildet der erste Arm unweit einer Wassermühle, neben welcher der beste Standpunkt zum Ueberschauen ist. Gleich Wolken-säulen steigt die in Staub aufgelöste Wassermasse gen Himmel empor, eben so die Wassermasse des fast gleich bedeutenden Falles des zweiten Armes. Der geringste ist der Fall des dritten Arms. Dann vereinigen sich die drei Arme und fließen einige 100 Ellen lang der Brücke zu, indem sie bis hinter der Brücke ununterbrochen kleine Wasserfälle bilden. Will man die einzelnen Fälle betrachten, so gehe man von der Sägemühle, längs des hohen Ufers, am Zaun bis zur Brücke fort, und man genießt das ganze erhabene Schauspiel. Die Wassermasse ist größer als die des Rheinfalls bei Schafhausen und die der Katarakten bei Trollhätta; letztere aber sind höher. Bald hinter dem ersten großen Fall trifft man die erste Lachsfischerei, worauf hernach mehrere folgen. Der Lachs wird in den Flüssen auf verschiedene Weise gefangen, gewöhnlich in Steinkisten mit verzäunten Oeffnungen; der Lachs, der hier nicht durchkommen kann, sucht sich durch ein geflochtenes danebenstehendes Gefäß einen Ausgang zu bahnen, verwickelt sich unter diesen Versuchen und wird gefangen. Am reichsten ist der Fang bei Wasserfällen. Der Lachs von Elfkarleby ist berühmt; er wird frisch und geräuchert verkauft; dieses Jahr frisch das Pfund zu 15, geräuchert zu 28 Schill. Riksgälds. — Bei der Brücke wird ein geringes Brückengeld entrichtet. Eine Viertelstunde hinter der Brücke erreicht man den hübschen Gästgifvaregärd, wo ich mir gebratenen Lachs und Ziegenkäse trefflich schmecken ließ und recht gut übernachtete. Der Ziegenkäse ist sehr fett; er wird aus reiner Ziegenmilch bereitet. Auch Schaafe hält man in diesen Gegenden, sie sind aber, wie alle Schwedischen Schaafe, klein und werden nicht gemolken. Nach einem schönen Tage wurde es jetzt plötzlich und heftig kalt. Dunkel wird es um diese Jahreszeit in dieser Höhe nicht mehr; es dämmert nur und ist noch immer so hell, daß man schreiben kann.

Abwärts im Dalelf trifft man auf einer Insel das große und schön gelegene Hüttenwerk Elfkarlebn.

Am 8. Jun. Von Elfkarleby nach Gefle 2⅓ Meile.

Erst um 8⅓ Uhr fuhr ich aus, und hatte daher nicht wenig von der Hitze des Tages zu leiden. Man fährt viel durch Wald, doch zeigen sich hier und da die schönen Ufer des Dalelf und einzelne Seen; beim Eisenbruk Harnäs erblickt man das offene Meer. Hier stehen, den geographischen Handbüchern nach, die letzten Eichen gegen Norden, aber wenn gleich Forsbacka, westlich von Gefle, ein schönes Gut des vormaligen Landshöfding von Dalekarlien, Baron Nordin, und ein Vergnügungsort der Bewohner von Gefle, wo auch Eichen fortkommen, fast in gleicher Höhe wie Harnäs liegt, so gedeihen doch die Eichen auch noch auf den Inseln des Flusses Testebo, der oberhalb Gefle fließt und sich bei Gefle ins Meer ergießt. In Harnäs scheidet ein Fluß Upland von Gestrikland. Gefleborg's Län, welches Gestrikland und Helsingland umfaßt (171½ □M., im J. 1819 mit 91,010 Seelen) beginnt, und mit ihm das herrliche Norrland, dieses Paradies von Schweden, das die schönsten Gegenden und die kernhaftesten und wohlhabendsten Einwohner des Reichs enthält. Ein kräftiger, hoher Wuchs, Seelenkraft, unerschütterliche Liebe zur Religion und zum Vaterlande, Reinlichkeit, Tüchtigkeit und Dauerhaftigkeit in Wohnungen und Arbeiten, sind das Eigenthümliche dieser Menschen.

Norrland begreift die Provinzen Gestrikland, Helsingland, Medelpad, Ångermanland, Westerbotten und Norrbotten, im Osten und Norden, und Dalekarlien, Herjeådalen und Jemteland im Westen. Am wenigsten schön sind Gestrikland und Herjeådalen nebst Theilen von Wester- und Norrbotten; in den übrigen Provinzen reiset man wie in einem großen Garten. Die Fruchtbarkeit der meisten dieser Provinzen ist da, wo sie angebaut sind, groß, in den nördlicheren kommt aber öfters das Korn nicht zur Reife. Die Viehzucht ist in Norrland ansehnlich, und ist ganz die Schweizerische Sennenwirthschaft üblich. In den Küstenländern ist die Fischerei nicht unbedeutend. —

Der Weg von Harnäs nach Gefle hat wenig Interessantes. Um 11¾ Uhr langte ich in Gefle an. Es war Sonntag; ein Paar Stunden nach meiner Ankunft begann der Nachmittagsgottesdienst, den ich besuchte. Die Versammlung war minder zahlreich; denn viele Bürgerfamilien waren auf den Strömlingsfang gezogen, der sie mehrere Wochen im Sommer an den nördlichen Küsten des Bothnischen Meerbusens beschäftigt, wo sie dann in Hütten wohnen und an Sonntagen ihren gemeinsamen Gottesdienst halten. Dieser Strömlingsfang ist ein Hauptnahrungszweig aller Küstenstädte des östlichen Schwedens, zumal in Norrland; nicht minder vieler Landbewohner. — In der Kirche herrschte große Stille und Andacht. Die vom Prediger gesprochenen Gebete und biblischen Worte wurden, wie es in allen Schwedischen Kirchen üblich ist, von der Gemeinde leise nachgesprochen; der Gottesdienst währte 1½ Stunde. Hier fand ich zuerst die nur noch an wenigen Orten bestehende Sitte, daß zwei Kirchenwächter mit langen Stäben in der Kirche umhergingen, um Unordnungen in der Stille zu heben, die Schlafenden oder Sprechenden sanft zurecht zu weisen u. dergl. m., doch bemerkte ich nicht, daß sich etwas ereignete, wo sie ihres Amtes pflegen konnten. Die Kirche ist geräumig und schön und hat vor kurzem eine neue große Orgel erhalten, die Ström in Stockholm bauete und die an 12,000 Bankthaler kostete, welche Summe theils durch freiwillige Gaben der Einwohner, theils durch Anleihen der Kirchencasse aufgebracht ward. Den Altar schmücken Vergoldungen und ein Altarblatt in Holz en basrelief, in drei über einander stehenden Bildern darstellend die Einsetzung des heiligen Abendmahls, die Kreuzigung und die Himmelfahrt Christi. Um die Kirche herum ist ein hübscher freier Platz. Außer dieser Stadtkirche hat Gefle noch eine kleine Hospitalkirche. Der Begräbnißplatz liegt außerhalb der Stadt.

Der übrige Theil des Tages verging mit Besuchen und Besichtigungen; auf letzteren begleitete mich D. Lundström, Pastor der Stadt (denn Gefle bildet ein Pastorat). Auf einer schönen, mit Bäumen umpflanzten Wieseninsel in dem die Stadt durchströmenden Fluß Gefle, — die zur Pfarre gehört und ein freundliches Lusthaus trägt — sah ich dem Lachsfange zu: der Lachs wird umschlossen, mit einem Haken herausgerissen und mit Schlägen vor den Kopf getödtet. Man bereitet in Gefle den Lachs schon ganz auf Norrländische Weise, d. h. theils, wie auch an andern Orten, stark gesalzen, eingekocht, gebraten, geräuchert, theils und am häufigsten, und diese Bereitungsart ist Norrland eigenthümlich (wenn gleich sie auch in Schottland üblich seyn soll), zu Graflax. Um Graflax zu bereiten, schneidet man frischen rohen Lachs in Stücken, bestreuet diese mit ein wenig Salz, auch wohl etwas Zucker, und läßt sie so eine kürzere oder längere Zeit, am besten 2 bis 3 Tage bedeckt liegen. So hält der Lachs sich ziemlich lange, am längsten, wenn er, wie an einigen Orten geschieht, zweimal gesalzen wird. Mit Oel und Essig, auch Zucker, gegessen, ist der Graflax eine sehr wohlschmeckende Speise, wohlschmeckender als gekochter oder geräucherter Lachs. Eine nothwendige Bedingung ist aber, daß die Bereitung möglichst bald nach dem Fange geschehe. Schon eine Viertelstunde nach dem Fange ist der Graflax genießbar; doch schmeckt er besser, wenn er einige Stunden oder einen Tag im Salze gelegen hat. — Von diesem Graflax ist der auf gewöhnliche Weise stärker eingesalzene Lachs verschieden. Dieser hält sich mehrere Jahre, dagegen der geräucherte bald hart und unbrauchbar wird; daher das Räuchern des Lachses nur an wenigen Orten Norrlands, wo der Lachsfang einen so bedeutenden Nahrungszweig bildet, üblich ist. Man kocht auch den Lachs mit Mehl und Grütze zu einem Brey.

Gefle treibt nach Stockholm und Götheborg den meisten ausländischen Handel in ganz Schweden. Im Jahr 1815 zählte es 83 eigne Schiffe. Der Handel überhaupt ist hier bedeutender als in Norrköping, und um so vortheilhafter, da die Ausfuhr, die, einen großen Theil nach, in Eisen, Theer, Balken und Brettern bestehe, die Einfuhr um ein sehr beträcht-

liches übersteigt; denn theils bedarf das sparsam bebaute Norrland bei der frugalen Lebensweise seiner Bewohner wenig, theils
wird vieles über Stockholm eingeführt. Die Finnen kommen
ziemlich zahlreich nach Gefle. Größere und kleinere Kaufleute
sind an 80, deren meiste ausländischen Handel treiben. Zur
Vertiefung des Hafens, dessen Einlauf eine Schanze auf einer
kleinen Insel beschützt, wird ein durch Pferde gezogener Polheim-
scher Bagger angewandt. — Gefle hat ferner berühmte Ta-
baksfabriken, die in Hinsicht des Rauchtabaks das sind, was rücksichtlich des Schnupftabaks die Fabriken von Norrköping; auch
eine Zucker- und eine Segeltuchfabrik bestehen. Im Jahr 1815
zählte Gefle 6595 Einwohner.

Gefle ist ferner der Sitz des Landshöfdings über Gefleborgs Län, der auf dem hoch und reizend gelegenen Schlosse im
Fluß Gefle residirt. Hier hielt Gustav III. zu Anfange des
Jahres 1792 einen Reichstag. Aus dem Schlosse genießt man
schöne und weite Meer- und Landaussichten. Dem Schlosse gegenüber liegen die Gebäude für die Kanzlei und das Comptoir
(Renterey) des Landshöfding. Wie gewöhnlich in den Resi-
denzstädten der Landshöfdinge, so findet man auch in Gefle eine
Buchdruckerey, in welcher ein Wochenblatt erscheint. Seit kurzem ist auch eine Buchhandlung errichtet worden; eine Leihbibliothek besteht.

Das Rathhaus am großen Markt ist eines der schönsten
im Reich. In einigen Zimmern desselben hält der für Wohl-
thätigkeit und gesellschaftliche Vergnügungen vom vorigen Landshöfding, Grafen Cronstedt, gestiftete, aus Männern und Frauen
bestehende Orden Idka dygden (übe die Tugend) im Winter
Bälle. Der Orden hat mehrere Grade und zählt bereits an
600 Mitglieder. Den geselligen Vereinen gehen öfters Aufnah-
men voran. Der Orden pro amico ist erloschen. Ein Dilet-
tantentheater ist neuerdings gestiftet worden. Die Stadt hat
meist breite und regelmäßige Gassen, deren Häuser jedoch größtentheils von Holz sind. Eine schöne Promenade, Brobänkar ge-

nannt, ist längs des Hafens angelegt worden: aus Ballast entstanden, bildet sie jetzt eine große Wiese mit dreifacher Baum-
reihe, zu welcher noch eine vierte hinzukommen sollte; daneben
liegen Dreimaster und kleinere Schiffe, weiterhin die vielen Materialbuden.

Gefle besitzt mehrere Schulen. Das Gymnasium und die
Trivialschule sind in einem neuen steinernen Gebäude vereiniget.
Das Gymnasium nimmt den obern, die Trivialschule den untern
Stock ein; jenes zählt 4 Klassen und 40 Schüler, diese 5 Klassen und 180 Schüler. Ich wohnte hier am Montag Morgen
den Gebeten bei, womit der Unterricht täglich eröffnet und geschlossen wird; alle Klassen sind zugegen. Das Gymnasium besitzt einen physikalischen Apparat, naturgeschichtliche, Globen- und
Karten-Sammlungen und eine beträchtliche Bibliothek, die schon
1907 Bände stark war, als sie vor kurzem Kanzleirath Schön-
berg noch mit einigen tausend Bänden aus allen Wissenschaften
vermehrte. Das Gymnasium hat einen hübschen Saal für
Schulfeierlichkeiten, wo auch schon öffentliche Concerte gehalten
wurden.

Die Elementarschule der Stadt ist eine höhere Bür-
gerschule, die der Commerzienrath Pehr Brandström im Jahre
1795 durch ein Kapital von 10,000 Rthlrn. stiftete und für
welche der Stifter eine eigene Schulordnung vorschlug, die der
König 1796 bestätigte. Die Verwaltung führt eine Direction, die
aus dem Stifter, seit 1808 dem Schwiegersohn desselben, Herrn
Ennes, dem Landshöfding, dem Pastor, dem Bürgermeister,
1 Rathsverwandten (rådman), 1 Kaufmann und 1 Handwerker
besteht und den Inspector und die Lehrer der Schule ernennt.
Die Lehrer sind Literaten, sie stehen den Collegen an den Trivialschulen gleich und sind berechtigt, ihre Dienstjahre bei An-
suchung um Pfarren doppelt zu zählen, und nach einer gewissen
Zahl solcher Dienstjahre um Pfarrstellen unmittelbar beim Könige nachsuchen. Die Unterrichtsgegenstände sind Religion, Schreiben und Rechnen nebst Italienischer Buchführung und besonderer

Anleitung zum Briefschreiben, neuere Sprachen, Staats- und Privat-Haushaltung, vaterländische Geschichte, Geschichte des Handels und Geographie. Die Zahl der Schüler ist auf 24 festgesetzt, bei deren Auswahl auf Stand und Geburt nicht geachtet wird. 12 derselben bezahlen ein mäßiges Schulgeld. Kenntniß der Hauptpunkte des Christenthums, deutliches Schreiben, einige Fertigkeit im Rechnen ist Bedingung der Aufnahme. Keiner bleibt länger als 5 Jahre in der Schule. Wer bei Anfang eines neuen Termins ohne triftige Gründe länger als 5 Tage versäumt, wird für diesen Termin von der Schule ausgeschlossen. Die beiden jährlichen Unterrichtstermine sind vom 16. Jan. bis 16. Jul. und vom 16. Aug. bis 16. Dec.; halbjährlich wird ein Examen gehalten. Das Schulhaus, ein großes massives Gebäude, ward vom Stifter geschenkt; es enthält auch Wohnungen für Lehrer und einige Schüler. Die Schule, welche auch eine kleine Bibliothek besitzt, ward am 16. Januar 1797 eröffnet, und hat seitdem mehrere Legate erhalten, durch welche der Gehalt der Lehrer allmälig erhöht werden konnte. Herr Ennes, ein wohlhabender Kaufmann, hat sich während seiner Theilnahme an der Direction große Verdienste um die Anstalt erworben, er opfert viel für die Schule auf, so wie er überhaupt von seinem großen Vermögen auf eine edle und wohlthätige Weise Gebrauch macht; auch bei andern öffentlichen Anstalten ist er thätig. Zur Elementarschule kommt jetzt, mittelst der ausgesetzten Kapitalien, eine Armenschule hinzu. — Noch eine andere Armenschule, eine Industrieschule für arme Mädchen und eine Waisenschule bestehen. In allen Armenschulen erhalten die Kinder auch Mittagsessen. Eine ehemalige Kaserne dient als Armenhaus; daneben besteht ein freiwilliges Arbeitshaus. Für dürftige Militairpflichtige der Stadt ward vor kurzem ein besonderer Fond gestiftet; arme und gebrechliche Seeleute unterstützt das Seemannshaus (Sjömannshus); für die Pauvres honteux sorgen die Musikliebhaber und die Wittwenanstalt. Ueberdieß ertheilt die öffentliche Armenpflege an die Armen der Stadt monatliche Unterstützungen, wie Beihülfen in der Noth, reiche Rumfordsche Suppe, auch Kleidung, versieht die Kranken mit Arzenei und unterstützt beim Begräbniß. Mit dem Hospital für Irren und alte Leute ist das Länslazareth verbunden.

Gefle ist die älteste Stadt in Norrland. Ihre Polhöhe beträgt 59° 43' 30". Der breite und reißende Gefleftrom theilt sie in zwei Hälften und bildet mitten in der Stadt kleine Wasserfälle. An den Ufern sind Gärten angelegt, wie überhaupt die vielen Gärten und Wiesen der Stadt ein sehr freundliches Ansehen geben. In das Lob, welches schon häufig Fremde der Artigkeit und Gastfreiheit der Einwohner ertheilen, muß auch ich von ganzem Herzen einstimmen; insbesondere habe ich die Güte zu rühmen, durch welche mich der biedre Landshöfding, Graf Sparre, und dessen liebenswürdige Gattin so sehr verpflichteten.

Vor kurzem hatte sich auch für Gefleborgs Län eine Landhaushaltungsgesellschaft gebildet, deren Statuten eben dem Könige zur Bestätigung vorgelegt worden waren. Der Sitz der Gesellschaft sollte Gefle seyn. In Nord-Helsingland ward bereits 1811 eine sogenannte Landmanns-Gesellschaft errichtet, die vier Mal jährlich Zusammenkünfte hält, auch Schriften herausgiebt und die Beförderung ländlicher Nahrungen und überhaupt bürgerlicher Tugenden sich als Zweck vorgesetzt hat. Der Ackerbau in Gefleborgs Län ist großer Verbesserungen fähig; denn bisher wird wenig Korn gebaut, es könnte aber viel mehr gebaut werden. An mehreren Orten ißt man Gerstenbrot. Bollnäs in Helsingland ist das einzige Pastorat im Län, welches hinreichend Korn baut, alle übrige müssen kaufen. Kartoffeln werden viel gebaut. Die Viehzucht ist schon in Gestrikland sehr bedeutend, noch bedeutender in Helsingland. Nord-Gestrikland ist rücksichtlich der Vegetation Süd-Wermeland und Süd-Finnland gleich. Der Fang wilder Vögel ist in Helsingland bedeutender als in Gestrikland. Die eigentliche Norrländische Vegetation beginnt in Helsingland. Der Sommer ist dort sehr kurz, aber heiß. Alles reift schnell, daher die Landarbeiten sich nirgends mehr drängen, als in Norrland. Man erndtet von 2 Uhr Morgens bis 11 Uhr Mittags, von 11 bis 1 sind Ruhestunden, worauf bis 9 oder 10 Uhr Abends die Erndtearbeit fortgesetzt wird. Man erndtet gern frühe und spät, weil sich dann das Korn am besten schneiden läßt. — Nur ein adeliges Gut giebt es in Gefleborgs Län, nämlich Wi in Gestrikland.

Zur Stadtpfarre Gefle gehört auch die Landpfarre Wahlbo. Hier, im Dorfe Öfverhärde, ereignete sich im Jahr 1735 ein merkwürdiger Vorfall, der auch durch den Druck bekannt gemacht worden ist. Ein Bauer, Jons Larsson, schoß, indem er mit einer Jagdflinte zwei Brachvögel erlegte, sich die beiden Schrauben in den Kopf; die Schrauben konnten, Gefahr halber, nicht herausgenommen werden, dennoch blieb Jons Larsson gesund und lebte noch volle 21 Jahre.

Siebzehntes Kapitel.

Gestrikland und Helsingland.

Jährliche Steuerregulirung. — Die großen und bequemen Wohnungen der Norrländer. — Tracht und Charakter der Gestrikländer. — Norrlands Sennenwirthschaft. — Häßjor (Gerüste zum Trocknen der Garben). — Dreschwagen. — Eintritt in Helsingland. — Die rüstigen Helsinger. — Reizende Thäler. — Das Helsinge-Regiment. — Gustav I. 1521 in Helsingland. — Stadt Söderhamn. — Stadt Hudikswall. — Dickmilch. — Kirche Gnarp. — Gastfreiheit. — Kirchspiellappen. — Der Gränzwald. — Eintritt in Medelpad.

Am 9. Jun. Von Gefle nach Tröbje 1½ Meile; von Tröbje nach Berg 1½ Meile; von Berg nach Strätjära 3 Meilen. Zusammen 6½ Meilen.

II.   B

Nach 10 Uhr Vormittags fuhr ich ab. Durch eine Reihe schöner Gärten erreicht man bald Mynäs. Hier war eben eine Taxerings-Committee mit Festsetzung der Steuern für das folgende Jahr beschäftiget. Es giebt nämlich in Schweden außer den ordentlichen festen Steuern auch außerordentliche, wandelbare und freiwillige Steuern, die von sämmtlichen Ständen auf dem Reichstage, so fern es die Bedürfnisse des Staats erfordern, unter dem Namen einer allgemeinen Bewilligung (allmänna bevillning), übernommen werden, aber nur bis zum nächsten Reichstage fortdauern, wo sie dann aufhören, oder, aufs neue, nach einer neuen Feststellung ihrer Höhe, übernommen werden. Zu dieser Bewilligung gehören verschiedene Arten von Steuern. Die Vertheilung dieser Steuern über die einzelnen Steuerpflichtigen überläßt der Staat den Steuerpflichtigen selbst, und wird hier auf folgende Weise verfahren: Nachdem zuvörderst ein Verzeichniß der Steuerpflichtigen errichtet (mantalsskrifning), auf einem Kirchspielsstande verlesen und durch die Unterschrift des Pastors und zweier Gemeindeglieder für die betreffende Gemeinde bestätigt oder berichtigt worden, tritt in jedem Kirchspiel eine Vorbereitungs-Committee (beredningscommittée) zusammen; doch können sich auch mehrere Kirchspiele zu Einer solchen Committee vereinigen; die Committee besteht aus dem Pastor, als ständigem Mitglied ohne Wahl, und mindestens 5, höchstens 6, oder, wenn mehrere Kirchspiele sich zu Einer Committee vereinigten, 7 auf einem Kirchspiele erwählten Mitgliedern; die eine Hälfte derselben muß dem Adel oder den Standespersonen, die andere dem Bauerstande angehören, kein Erwählter darf weigern; der Präses der Committee wird von der Committee aus ihrer Mitte erwählt; jedes Mitglied dieser und der beiden andern unten zu nennenden Committeen wird das erste Mal, wo es das Geschäft verrichtet, vereidet. Die Vorbereitungs-Committee prüft die Angaben der Einzelnen, taxirt den Werth der liegenden Gründe und schlägt den Steueransatz vor. Ein

Kron-Einhebungs-Beamter, der Háradsschreiber, ist zugegen und führt das Protokoll. Ist das Geschäft der Vorbereitungs-Committee geendet, so hebt das der Tarirungs- (taxerings) Committee an. Diese umfaßt die Bezirke mehrerer Vorbereitungs-Committeen, und hat jeder Landshöfding zu bestimmen, wie viele Tarirungs-Committeen in seinem Län sich bilden sollen. Die Mitglieder der Tarirungs-Committee (2 Adelige, 2 Geistliche, 3 Bauern und 2 Standespersonen) werden von den Vorbereitungs-Committeen, die zu ihrem Bezirk gehören, mittelst geschlossener Zettel erwählt; der Landshöfding führt den Vorsitz. Die Tarirungs-Committee prüft die Vorschläge der Vorbereitungs-Committeen und setzt die Steuern der Einzelnen fest; etwa erforderlicher Auskunft wegen ist, außer dem Háradsschreiber, auch der Kronvoigt, welcher das Protokoll führt, zugegen. In den Städten sitzen in den Committeen auch Bürger, in den Universitätsstädten auch Professoren, dagegen in den besondern Tarirungs-Committeen der Universität auch Standespersonen unter städtischer Jurisdiction. — Schließlich schlägt jede Tarirungs-Committee des Läns aus ihrer Mitte Mitglieder einer zu bildenden allgemeinen Prüfungs- (pröfnings)-Committee vor, aus jedem Stande und Klasse Einen. Der Landshöfding wählt aus den Vorgeschlagenen, wo möglich, so, daß aus jeder Tarirungs-Committee Einer Mitglied der Prüfungs-Committee wird; doch ist die Zahl der Mitglieder auf 15 festgesetzt (3 Adelige, 3 Geistliche, 3 Bürger, 3 Standespersonen und 3 Bauern). Bei der Prüfungs-Committee kann über das Verfahren der Tarirungs-Committeen Beschwerde geführt werden. Der Zusammentritt der Prüfungs-Committee erfolgt zwei Monate nach beendigten Sitzungen der Tarirungs-Committeen. Die Prüfungs-Committee fällt die letzte Entscheidung, indem sie die Steuerlisten für sämmtliche Kirchspiele des Läns unabänderlich feststellt, worauf nun die Einhebungstage anberaumt werden.

Solche Steuerregulirung findet alljährlich Statt, so lange die Bewilligung gilt, weil sich ja seit dem verflossenen Jahre

B 2

die Vermögensumstände des Einen oder Andern verändert haben könnten. — Die Committee, welche ich in Nynäs versammelt fand, war eine Taxirungs-Committee. Ich wohnte eine kurze Zeit ihren Berathungen bei, die ganz dem Geiste eines freien, edlen Volks angemessen waren. So besteuert sich die Nation selbst, die Auflagen werden den individuellen Verhältnissen angepaßt, und jeder (denn es gilt hier keine Exemtion) giebt mit Willigkeit nach Vermögen einen Beitrag zur Aufrechthaltung des Ganzen. Auch Geistliche waren zugegen, nicht blos als Vertreter der Geringeren und Minderbegüterten, als Förderer der Milde und Billigkeit, sondern als die rechten Väter ihrer Gemeinden, denen die wirkliche Lage der Gemeindeglieder am genauesten bekannt seyn soll, und bei den bestehenden kirchlichen Einrichtungen, namentlich der des Hausverhörs ꝛc. auch bekannt seyn kann.

Unweit Nynäs fährt man einen Hügel hinan, wo man, bei Sätra, den schönsten Ueberblick über die Stadt Gefle hat, die hier eine Ausdehnung zeigt, welche eine viel größere Zahl von Häusern und Einwohnern vermuthen läßt, als wirklich vorhanden sind. Schon bei Sätra trifft man eine Menge auf den Wiesen zerstreuter Heuscheuern und das Wohnhaus umgebende zahlreiche kleine landwirthschaftliche Gebäude; und mit dem Eintritt in Helsingland wächset noch die Zahl dieser, wie jener. Eine dem Schwedischen und Norwegischen Norrland (nördlichen Schweden und Norwegen) eigenthümliche Sitte, von welcher ich weiterhin näher reden werde. Die Wohnhäuser haben gewöhnlich vorne bedeckte Bretterlauben, aus welchen man in das eigentliche Haus tritt. Die Kleidung der Bauern ist reinlich, tüchtig und vollständig; sie tragen kurze Beinkleider, bunte wollene Strümpfe, Schuhe mit großen runden Schnallen, Hüte mit bunten Schnüren. Alles verräth am Gestrikländer Wohlstand und Kraft. Ungefälliges Wesen habe ich keinesweges so allgemein gefunden, daß ich es, gleich anderen Reisenden, Character des Gestrikländers

nennen könnte. Von Sätra bis Tröbje ist meist Wald, eben
so zwischen Tröbje und Berg, wo man aber auch viele niedrige Wiesen sieht. Auf letzterer Station fährt man zwei Mal
einer Reihe von Sennhütten, zu beiden Seiten des Weges,
vorbei, andere liegen am Meere, welches hier den schönen
Hamrängesjärd bildet, und schließen sich an die Fischerhütten an,
die zur Zeit des Strömlingsfanges benutzt werden. Die Sennenwirthschaft hebt in Gestrikland an und geht durch ganz Norrland fort. Neben den Sennhütten bleiben die Kuh- und Zie-
genheerden, den Sommer über, Tag und Nacht im Freien; in
den Hütten wird Butter, fetter Käse und mesost (Käse aus Molken) bereitet. Um Johannis pflegen die Heerden auf drei Wochen nach Hause oder nach andern Sennhütten zu ziehen, damit
inzwischen wieder Gras wachse, kehren dann zurück und bleiben,
bis sie um Michaelis ganz heimziehen; jeder Hof schickt ein 10
bis 30jähriges Mädchen mit. Am Sonntage, bevor diese Mädchen zu den Sennhütten gehen, genießen sie das heilige Abendmahl; nach den Sennhütten nehmen sie ihre Gesang- und Gebetbücher mit, selten eine Bibel (denn jeder Hof besitzt gewöhnlich nur Eine Bibel), halten ihre Morgen- und Abendgebete
und am Sonntag ihre Hausandacht.

Neben dem Gästgifvaregärd Berg liegt die Kirche Hamränge.
Zwischen Berg und Strätjära fährt man dem schön gelegenen
Bruk Wifors vorüber. Hinter Wifors führt ein Weg rechts
nach dem, am Meer, an der Gränze von Helsingland, gelegenen
ansehnlichen Eisenbruk Axmar; links führt die große Nordische
Straße wohl eine Meile lang durch Gran- und Fichtenwald;
ein hübsches Köhlerhaus ist die einzige Menschenwohnung, die
die Einsamkeit unterbricht; dann geht es wieder im Walde fort,
bis zum Dorfe Tönnebro, wo der See gleiches Namens die
Gränze macht. In Tönnebro, auf der Hälfte des Weges, hält
man des langen Hälls wegen, eine Viertelstunde an. Tönnebro
liegt schon in Helsingland. Bis eine Viertelmeile vor Strätjära
fährt man im dichten Walde fort. Hier sind oft Schneepflüge,

auch Haufen Brennholz, welches des leichtern Transports wegen schon im Walde klein gehauen wird, aufgestellt. Beim Austritt aus dem Walde erblickt man eine Kette blauer Berge. Die Zahl der Höfe mehrt sich, die Wohnhäuser umgiebt nach Norrländischer Weise eine Menge hölzerner Gebäude, denn zu jedem landwirthschaftlichen Gebrauch ist ein besonderes kleines Gebäude errichtet; es giebt mehrere Vorrathshäuser, Kornbuden ꝛc.; selbst das Wohnhaus besteht aus mehreren Gebäuden, als Wohngebäude, Fremdenhaus ꝛc. So hat denn ein Norrländischer Hof fast das Ansehen eines kleinen Dorfes. Neben den Scheunen oder noch häufiger auf den Feldern findet man sogenannte Hässjor (Treckengerüste), einfache oder doppelte: die einfachen bildet eine dicke, 14 bis 15 Ellen lange, aufrechtstehende Stange mit viereckigen Löchern, in welche man 8 bis 10 Ellen lange Querstangen einsteckt; die Hauptstange wird unten durch 4 stützende Seitenstangen, oben durch ein bretternes Wetterdach, welches zugleich die obern Garben gegen den Regen sichert, gehalten; in die Räume zwischen den Stangen werden die Garben am liebsten noch am selbigen Tage, an welchem das Korn gemähet wurde, eingeschoben; in dieser Enge sind sie vor dem Durchnäßen geschützt und trocknen zugleich schneller und völliger, als wenn sie auf dem Felde in Haufen gesetzt worden wären. Das ganze Gerüste ist stark in der Erde befestigt. Die doppelten Hässjor bilden zwei einfache, die neben einander stehen und durch breite Querhölzer verbunden sind. Die Hässjor errichtet man gerne gegen Nordost und Nordwest, weil diese Winde in Norrland am meisten trocknen. Ist das gemähte Korn sehr naß, so wird die Garbe loser gebunden und minder fest eingeschoben. Man hat zwar an manchen Orten auch Darrhäuser (rior), doch werden diese häufiger zum Trocknen der ausgedroschenen Körner angewandt, da sie dem Stroh leicht einen räucherigen Geschmack mittheilen, der dem Vieh zuwider ist. Unter den Hässjor hat man häufig hölzerne Dreschtennen, die 60 bis 100 Ellen lang sind; hier drischt man mittelst eines von einem oder zwei Pferden getriebenen eisernen Dreschwagens. Am Ende der Tenne liegt eine sich ein wenig senkende hölzerne Brücke, wo die Pferde mit dem Wagen stehen bleiben können, so daß der Dreschprozeß bis an das äußerste Ende der Tenne fortgesetzt wird. Zur Erhaltung der nöthigen Reinlichkeit ist unter dem Schwanze des Pferdes ein Beutel festgebunden. Das ausgedroschene Korn wird mittelst eines Brettes zur Seite geschoben, und nachdem es sich gehäuft hat, durch einen hinten angespannten Schneepflug von der Tenne weggenommen; das Stroh wird mit einer Egge weggezogen. Ist es bei feuchter Witterung schwer, die Körner von der Aehre zu sondern, so wendet man die Garben, die überdieß sehr eben liegen müssen, zwei Mal. Das Dreschen mittelst Dreschwagen geht sehr geschwinde von Statten, man drischt auf diese Weise binnen 1 Monat, was durch Dreschflegel nur in 8 bis 10 Monaten gedroschen werden kann.

Von Gefle an findet man auf jedem Gästgifvaregård 4 Hüllpferde, die, da auf dieser Straße nicht viel gereiset wird, stets gleich zu bekommen sind; man kann daher, wenn man nicht mehr als 1 oder 2 Pferde gebraucht, des Vorboten überhoben seyn. Die Stelle des Hållkarl vertritt in diesen Provinzen gewöhnlich der Gästgifvare selbst. Die Pferde sind groß, stark und sehr rasch. Je höher gegen Norden, desto schneller reiset man. Aber man hat seine liebe Noth mit dem Abspringen der Fuhrleute bei Hügeln, um die Last zu erleichtern. Ehe man es sich versieht, sind sie vom Wagen herab und laufen neben demselben, oft keuchend, einher, indem sie, damit der Reisende nicht aufgehalten werde, die Pferde antreiben; dennoch kann es nicht fehlen, daß auf solche Weise Aufenthalt entsteht; schon aus Schonung des Fuhrmanns fährt man langsamer, und ist überdieß in unaufhörlicher Angst, daß derselbe bei seinem gefährlichen Lauf Schaden nehme.

In Strätjära, dem ersten Helsingischen Gästgifvaregård, übernachtete ich. Das Brot, welches ich hier genoß, war aus Roggen und Gerste gemischt; es schmeckte ein wenig süß, aber ganz angenehm. Uebrigens zeugte in Strätjära alles von der Reinlichkeit und Tüchtigkeit der Helsingländer. Männer und Frauen sind groß von Wuchs, kräftig von Körperbau, voll Muth und Selbstgefühl, voll Liebe für Freiheit, Gesetz und Vaterland, gastfrei, dienstfertig ohne Eigennutz, sanft und wohlwollend, still und ernst; selbst in Gasthöfen, wo viele Menschen versammelt sind, geht es in manchen Gegenden Helsinglands so still und bescheiden zu, als wäre eine Gesellschaft von Honoratioren in einem Privatzirkel versammelt. Wirklich ist aber auch der geringe Helsingländer, wie überhaupt der Norrländer, sehr gebildet: in christlicher Erkenntniß, im Lesen, Schreiben und Rechnen ist er wohlbewandert, kennt das Wesentlichste der Verfassung des Vaterlandes, wie die besondern Verhältnisse seiner Provinz. Vor den übrigen Norrländern hat er großes mechanisches Genie voraus, und mehrere Helsingsche Bauern haben treffliche landwirthschaftliche Maschinen erfunden. Flachsbau und Bereitung grober Leinewand (Nord-Helsingland fertigt jährlich 500,000 Ellen) bilden einen ansehnlichen Nahrungszweig; in den Häusern der Geringeren wie der Vornehmern, findet man Weberstühle. In einigen Thälern wird viel Korn gebauet, doch producirt die Provinz selten so viel, als sie bedarf. Bedeutend ist der Handel mit Vogelwildprett: Auer-, Birk-, Hasel-, Repp- und Schneehühnern, zumal im nördlichen Helsingland. Mit diesen und andern Producten des Landes treiben Bauern und Bauerknechte Handel, indem sie selbige selbst verfahren, und allerlei fremde, doch meistens nothwendige Waaren zum eignen Gebrauch und zum Verkauf mit zurückbringen. Die Entfernung der Städte mag diesen Landhandel, wenigstens in mehreren Gemeinden, unentbehrlich machen; aber daß er in moralischer Hinsicht verderblich wirkt, nicht selten Armuth erzeugt, und Krankheiten unter das Volk bringt, die man früher nicht kannte, ist unleugbar.

An Beerenarten ist in Helsingland Ueberfluß: zuerst, 14 Tage nach Johannis, reifen die Heidelbeere (blåbär), und die Multbeere (hjortron, rubus chamaemorus), letztere wächset besonders auf Schwendeland; dann folgt die liebliche Feldbeere (Ackerbeere, åkerbär, rubus arcticus), die man aber erst in Ångermanland findet, am meisten auf Wiesen, die vorher Aecker waren, nicht im Walde; um den Anfang des Septembers reift die Preisselbeere (lingon, vaccinium vitis idea).

Hauptnahrungszweig der Helsingländer ist die Viehzucht: sie wird meist als Sennenwirthschaft getrieben, theils auf Bergen, theils in Wald- und Wiesenebenen. Die Sennhütten, 1 bis 3 Meilen vom Wohnhofe entfernt, nennt man Fábodar (Viehbuden), oder blos Bodar, im östlichen Helsingland auch Bolanden, welches Wort eigentlich Außenhöfe mit Acker bezeichnet. Solche Außenhöfe (vergl. Kap. 28) sind mit sehr vielen Helsingischen Bauerhöfen verbunden. Der Helsingische Bauer (Edelhöfe giebt es gar nicht im Lande) hat, wo nicht schon die Zerstückelung der Ländereien zum Besten der einzelnen Familienglieder begonnen hat, großen Landbesitz. Diesen hat er theils an Torpare (Dienstbauern) und Backstugubaer (Kathenleute), die für ihr Acker- und Wiesen- oder Gartenland gewisse Dienste leisten, ausgethan, theils bewirthschaftet er ihn selbst, von zwei Höfen aus, die er zu verschiedenen Zeiten des Jahres bewohnt, dem Haupthofe und dem von diesem oft mehrere Meilen entfernten Außenhofe (bolanden). Beide Höfe sind wohlgebaut, doch der Haupthof am vorzüglichsten, hier findet man nicht selten Wohnungen von zwei Stockwerken und 8 bis 10, mit Kaminen, statt der Oefen, versehenen Zimmern (s. Kap. 28), und überdieß eine Menge besonderer Wirhschaftsgebäude; die Vorrathshäuser ruhen auf hohen Pfählen; alle Gebäude sind mit Birkenrinde und darüber Bretter, gedeckt. In den Zimmern, wie neben den Häusern im Freien, sind zuweilen Kästchen mit Sämereien ausgestellt.

Helsingland besteht aus Bergrücken von mittlerer Höhe und Thälern, in welchen die, durch die zahlreichen Nebengebäude, oft an Umfang kleinen Städten gleichenden Dörfer liegen. Das Land ist reich an Seen, auch durchströmt es ein ansehnlicher

Fluß, der Ljusna-Elf. Das Hauptkorn ist Gerste, doch bauet man auch Roggen, Hafer und Erbsen; zur Roggenaussaat verwendet man in ganz Norrland, wie auch in südlicher gelegenen Provinzen, gern den Finnischen oder sogenannten Wasa-Roggen. Kartoffeln werden viel gebauet. Was der Landmann an Holz-, Eisen- und Lederwaaren bedarf, verfertigt er selbst. An den Küsten ist der Fischfang sehr einträglich, besonders der Strömlingsfang. Einen Theil von Nordhelsingland ausgenommen, herrscht im übrigen Lande meist Wohlstand, den auch die nette selbstgefertigte Kleidung verräth. Die Männer tragen die Haare verschnitten, mit herabrollenden Locken. In neuerer Zeit hat indeß der Luxus sehr zugenommen und eben so wohl die einfache Lebensweise als den Wohlstand vermindert.

——

Am 10. Jun. Von Strätjära nach Mo-Myskje 1¼ Meile; von Mo-Myskje nach Kungsgården 1¼ Meile; von Kungsgården nach Bro 2⅔ Meile; von Bro nach Iggesund 1¼ Meile; von Iggesund nach Sanna 1⅔ Meilen. — Zusammen 8⅓ Meilen.

Nachdem ich mich an trefflichem Kaffee gelabt, der in Helsingland durch die vorzügliche Sahne besonders wohlschmeckend ist, fuhr ich aus. Der schöne Morgen, die reizende Gegend, die Biederkeit der Menschen, alles setzte mich in die heiterste Stimmung. Mein Skjutsbonde war ein frommer und fröhlicher Jüngling, der durch liebliche Weisen den Weg verkürzte. Weite Wald- und Wiesenthäler, mit kleinen Heuscheunen, in welchen man das Heu aufbewahrt, bis Wege und Raum das Heimfahren verstatten, bedeckt, oder mit Dörfern ausgefüllt, scheiden die bewaldeten Bergrücken, über welche man fährt und wo Veilchen, Heidelbeeren u. s. w. am Wege blühen. Auf einer Brücke fährt man über den breiten Ljusna-Elf, der zwischen Feld- und Wiesenufern fließt und oberhalb und unter der Brücke Wasserfälle bildet, und erreicht bald Mo-Myskje, welches zwischen seinen Waldbergen recht malerisch da liegt. In einiger Entfernung links von Mo-Myskje trifft man die ansehnliche Linnenfabrik Flor, wo auch Dammasttischzeug verfertiget wird.

In Mo-Myskje erschallte aus einem Bauerhofe militairische Musik. Das Helsinge-Regiment, welches Helsingland gemeinschaftlich mit Gestrikland unterhält, hatte eben sein jährliches Möte und campirte außerhalb des Dorfs. Ich fuhr hinaus ins Lager. Ein großes hölzernes Gebäude mit Wirthschaftshäusern und Ställen umher war für die Officiere aufgeführt; für die Soldaten Lauben oder Kegelhütten aus Stangen, mit Birkenrinde und Granreisern bekleidet, errichtet. Nur ein Theil des Regiments war bisher angelangt, und wohnten daher die Officiere noch im Dorfe. Aus dem Lager fuhr ich in den Wald zurück, und dann auf Bergrücken neben den lieblichsten Seitenthälern, welche Heuscheunen und Dörfer ausfüllten, neben der hübschen Kirche Söderala hin nach dem Gästgifvaregård Kungsgården. Nicht selten liegen in den weiten Helsingischen Thälern mehrere Dörfer beisammen, so daß sie das ganze Thal bedecken; oft sind es Waldthäler mit Wiesen und einzelnen romantisch gelegenen Höfen. Von den Bergen hat man die freundlichsten Uebersichten über die reizenden Thäler. Diese stets wechselnden Berge und Thäler, hier und da mit lieblichen Seen und Flüssen, geben der Landschaft einen ganz Schweizerischen Charakter, doch sind die Bergrücken wenig hoch. In dieser Hinsicht erinnert Angermannland noch mehr an jenes vielgepriesene Alpenland. Einige Schritte von Kungsgården, auf einem Hügel, von welchem man auf ein schönes Thal hinabblickt, hat die (jetzt erloschene) Gesellschaft pro amico in Gefle einen Stein errichten lassen, zum Gedächtniß der Zeit, wo hier Gustav Wasa die Helsinger zur Rettung des Vaterlandes aufforderte: Die Inschrift lautet folgendermaßen:

„Här upmuntrede Gustaf I. år 1521, samlade Helsingar til rikets räddning. Frihetshjalter til åra, under ättlingens Gustaf III. regering, restes stenen, år 1773 af Sällskapet pro amico."

d. i. „Hier ermunterte Gustav I., im Jahr 1521, die versammelten Helsinger zur Rettung des Reichs. Dem Helden der Freiheit zu Ehren wurde unter seines Nachkommen Gustavs III. Regierung dieser Stein im Jahr 1773 errichtet von der Gesellschaft pro amico."

Neben Kungsgården liegt die Kirche Norrala; auf dem Kirchhofe, ist, nach dem Bericht Adams von Bremen, das Grab des heiligen Stephanus (St. Staffan), des ersten christlichen Lehrers in Helsingland um 1064.

Zwischen Mo-Myskje und Kungsgården hat man bei der Kirche Söderala etwa eine halbe Meile zu dem einen der beiden Helsingischen Städtchen, Söderhamn. Sie liegt zwischen zwei Bergen an einer Meeresbucht, hatte im Jahr 1815 nur 1397 Einwohner, treibt aber ziemlich viel Handel und ist recht wohlhabend. Im Sommer wohnt man viel auf kleinen Landhäusern am Meer, wo man die Schiffe einlaufen sieht. Im Winter herrscht viel geselliges Leben; zwei Mal wöchentlich hat man musikalische Zusammenkünfte, außerdem giebt es Klubbs für die Männer und Klubbs für die Frauen; zu letzteren werden auch wohl junge Mädchen und junge Männer zugezogen, es wird musicirt und getanzt. Alle diese Zusammenkünfte finden in Privathäusern Statt. Gegen Fremde ist man sehr gastfrei; oft ladet man sie ein, so bald man nur ihre Anwesenheit im Ort erfährt, ohne vorher ihre Bekanntschaft gemacht zu haben. — Vor einigen Jahren erhielten Söderhamn und Hudikswall Stapelgerechtigkeit; seitdem ist der ausländische Handel ziemlich bedeutend. In Söderhamn wohnt auch ein Instrumentenmacher.

Von Kungsgården nach Bro hat man die schönsten Waldwiesen, Thäler mit Dörfern angefüllt, Seen, Bäche, oder vielmehr kleine Flüsse, die längs des Weges rinnen oder über welche man fährt, und die zum Theil hübsche Wasserfälle bil-ten. Man fährt meist auf sanften Höhen hin; links im Innern des Landes, erblickt man in weiter Ferne eine hohe Bergkette. Der Wald besteht noch immer aus Birken, Gränen und Fichten; letztere sind vorherrschend. Dreiviertel Meilen von Kungsgärden kommt man einer Reihe von Sennhütten vorbei, die zu dem ½ Meile entfernten Dorfe Ale gehören; jeder Bauernhof hat sein, durch Zäune abgestecktes Eigenthum, nämlich ein Häuschen, mit Zimmern, Schlafkammern für die Senninnen, und einen Eiskeller zur Aufbewahrung der Butter ꝛc., alles ist aufs bequemste eingerichtet, selbst Schlaguhren findet man, auch Ställe, in welche das Vieh am Abend getrieben wird; beim Melken Morgens und Abends bedient man sich. ziemlich großer Schemel mit 4 Füßen, größer als die in den Sennhütten der Schweiz; auch hat man Holzschuppen, Heuscheunen u. dgl. m. — Auf der Hälfte der Station findet man zwei Wirthshäuser mit Nebengebäuden, als Ruhestellen. Dann fährt man durch Wald neben Wiesen und Thälern nach dem Gästgifvaregård Bro, welchem zunächst man die Kirche Enånger in freundlicher Lage erblickt.

Von Bro nach Igggesund hat man die üppigsten Thäler, hier und da mit Waldfelsen. Zwei Mal fährt man neben Meerbusen hin, die mit ihren Waldufern und Inseln still und freundlich da liegen; viele stirle Hügel (backar *) hat man zu überfahren. So erreicht man unweit Njutånger's Kirche das Bruk und das Häll Iggesund. Iggesund liegt sehr malerisch an einem reißenden Strom, der die Gewässer der großen Seen Dellen dem Meere zuführt. Man fährt über eine Brücke, wo der Strom mehrere schöne Fälle bildet und sich im Hintergrunde nahe liebliche Waldberge zeigen. Oberhalb Iggesund theilt sich der Strom in zwei Arme; hier liegt die Papiermühle Östanå; die zweite, welche Helsingland besitzt, ist bei Mo.

---

*) Backe nennt man einen Hügel, der jäh und hoch, doch nicht hoch genug ist, um den Namen eines Berges zu verdienen.

Zwischen Iggesund und Sanna fährt man über Waldberge in ein liebliches Bergthal hinab, wo Wiesen, Aecker und
Häuser neben einander fortlaufen; hier liegt unter einer Polhöhe
von 61° 44′ 8″, das zweite Helsingische Städtchen, und zwar
das größere, (denn es enthielt im Jahr 1815. 1609 Einwohner), — Hudikswall, an dessen Thoren man vorüber fährt.
Hudikswall ist ein freundlicher Ort, an einer Meeresbucht, Hudiks-
wallsfjärden, mit vortrefflichem Hafen; er treibt ansehnlichen
Handel mit Landesprodukten, insbesondere Holzwaaren, Leinewand
und Vögeln. Im Sommer hält sich ein großer Theil der Einwohner zum Strömlingsfang in den Schären auf, hier haben sie
4 Kapellen, in welchen die Geistlichkeit der Stadt 5 Mal im
Sommer Gottesdienst hält; an den übrigen Sonntagen liest ein
Fischer, dem dieses Geschäft übertragen ist, aus einer Postille
vor. Wie in Söderhamn, so herrscht auch in Hudikswall viel
Sinn für Musik. Der Zolleinnehmer Finerus hat eine musikalische Gesellschaft gestiftet, welche sich wöchentlich ein Mal versammelt; man kommt in Privathäusern zusammen und bleibt
zu einem frugalen Abendessen *). In Hudikswall befindet sich
eine Trivialschule, deren Rector eine Lesegesellschaft eingerichtet
hat, die wissenschaftliche Bücher und Romane enthält und durch
Beiträge der Pastoren und der Lesenden besteht. Die Straßen
sind breit und gerade.

Unweit Hudikswall erreicht man den Gästgifvaregärd Sanna, wo ich, da es schon spät geworden war, übernachtete. Hier
vermißte ich zuerst in Helsingland Reinlichkeit und gute Bewirthung. Freilich gehört Sanna zu den kleineren Gasthöfen, wie
man dergleichen zuweilen auf dem Lande findet, wo der Fremde
mit einigen Lebensmitteln, mit Betttüchern und Fenstervorhängen
versehen seyn muß. Auch letztere dürfen nicht fehlen, wenn
man im Sommer in Nordschweden reiset; denn um diese Jahrs-

---

*) Auch die Krönung Karls XIV. Johann ward am 11. Mai
1818 in Hudikswall unter andern mit einem Liebhaberconcerte gefeiert.

zeit wird es dort in den Nächten nicht dunkel, und, wer daran nicht gewohnt ist, hat schwer, in einem weder mit Fensterladen noch Vorhängen versehenen Zimmer zu schlafen. Zwar mangelt es auch in den kleinen Gasthöfen an Wäsche nicht ganz, aber man hat oft nur so wenige Laken und Vorhänge, daß, wenn gewaschen wird, wenigstens die Fenster ohne Vorhänge bleiben.

Am 11. Jun. Von Sanna nach Mälsta 1 Meile; von Mälsta nach Bringsta 1½ Meilen; von Bringsta nach Gryssie 1¼ Meile; von Gryssie nach Maj 2 Meilen. — Zusammen 6½ Meilen.

Zwischen Sanna und Mälsta ist der Weg ziemlich bergig, zu Anfang und am Ende führt er durch schöne Thäler, die mit Laubgebüsch umgeben und mit Dörfern ausgefüllt sind; Acker sieht man wenig, hier und da stößt man auf läutende Heerden, denn noch war das Vieh nicht zu den Sennhütten gezogen; auch viele Schaafe werden gehalten; die Mitte der Station ist Laub= und Nadelwald. Ich begegnete vielen Einspännern der Bauern, die nach Hudikswall fuhren, um dort das durch die königliche allgemeine Magazindirection in Stockholm für sie eingesandte Saatkorn in Empfang zu nehmen; das Fahren mit Einspännern ist in Norrland allgemein.

Auch das zweite Häll von Mälsta nach Bringsta ist schön. Auch hier giebt es volkreiche Thäler, deren jedes, wie überhaupt die Thäler Helsinglands, sich durch Mannigfaltigkeit und Eigenthümlichkeit seiner Wege auszeichnet. Der größere Theil des Weges ist gemischter Wald, wo zuweilen ein reißender Waldbach schon aus der Ferne erschallt; die letzte halbe Meile nehmen ein Bergrücken und drei ·herrliche Thäler ein, in deren letzterm die Kirche Harmångar und der Gästgifvaregård Bringsta liegen. In Bringsta hielt ich ein treffliches Mittagsmahl, ganz in ächt Norrländischen Producten bestehend, Grassar, welchen Orre (Birkhuhn) mit Lingon und Tättmjölk, d. i. Fettkrautsmilch. Die letztere hat gar keine Molken, ist ganz weiß, schlüpfrig, zusammenhängend und dick wie Syrup; sie schmeckt mit und ohne Zucker sehr angenehm, an sich ist sie säuerlich, wird aber durch Zumischung von Sahne und Milch süßer; sie sättigt sehr, ist nahrhafter als süße Milch, hält sich länger und kann eine längere Zeit hindurch ununterbrochener, als diese, ohne Widerwillen zu erregen, genossen werden. Die Dichtmilch, wie man sie nennen könnte, der Sache und dem Schwedischen Namen nach, wird auf folgende Weise bereitet: man legt Fettkraut (Pinguecula, oder Drosera) in süße Milch und läßt es darin 4 oder 5 Tage liegen, bis die Milch geronnen ist. Hat man einen Trog nur mit einigen Löffeln voll Dichtmilch bestrichen, so wird dadurch die eingegossene frische Milch nach 2 Tagen zu Tåttmjölk; ein mit Dichtmilch ausgestrichener Trog kann, wenn er vor Staub gesichert wird, selbst im Winter auf diese Weise benutzt werden. Am liebsten verwendet man zu Dichtmilch die Milch der Ziegen.

Die sieben Viertel Meilen von Bringsta nach Gryssja sind höchst anmuthig, nur in der Mitte hat man Laub- und Nadelwald, auf der übrigen Station des Weges weite Thäler, mit Dörfern bedeckt, die von Wiesen und Kornfeldern umgeben werden; rings um Birken und Erlengebüsch, Bäche rieseln am Wege. In dem schönen Thale von Jättendal, welches an der östlichen Seite ein lieblicher See umfließt, ragt, wie es einem Gotteshause gebührt, über die vielen schönen Häuser des Thals Jättendal's prächtige steinerne Kirche empor. Wie ganz anders ist es doch in mehreren Theilen von Deutschland und an einigen wenigen Orten Schonens, besonders in den Bruk, wo die Kirchen oft klein und schmutzig da stehen, oder doch den Menschenwohnungen völlig gleich gemacht sind, der kleinen niedrigen Kirchen des armen, aber gottesfürchtigen Islands nicht zu gedenken *).

_____

E. Henderson Tagebuch eines Aufenthalts in Island in den Jahren 1814 und 1815, übersetzt von Franceson. 2 Bände. Berlin, 1820. 1821.

Noch schöner ist das sich in mehrere Theile sondernde Thal, wo Gnarps Kirche und Pfarrhof liegen und der Gnarpfluß zwischen hohen Wiesenufern sich hindurchschlängelt. In Gnarp sandte ich meinen Skjutsbonde auf den Pfarrhof und ließ um Erlaubniß bitten, das Innere der Kirche zu sehen. Sofort kam die Pröbstin Löman mit dem Kirchenschlüssel, und entschuldigte, daß sie selbst komme, da ihr Mann verreist und auch das Dienstmädchen nicht zu Hause sey. Ich ließ mir gern die liebenswürdige Führerin gefallen. Eine herrliche Aussicht empfängt den Wanderer auf dem Kirchhofe, zu welchem eiserne Gitterthüren führen. Die Kirche, vor etwa 20 Jahren neu gebauet, ist ein großes steinernes Gebäude. Das Innere derselben ist einfach, aber schön; die Kanzel ist vergoldet und mit passenden Sinnbildern geschmückt, eben so der Altar. In den Kirchstühlen fand ich viele Gesangbücher; denn jeder Hof hat gewöhnlich mehrere Exemplare des Gesangbuches, davon eines immer in der Kirche bleibt. Auch das Pfarrhaus ist groß und schön, wie überhaupt die Kirchen und Pfarrhäuser Helsinglands. Die Pfarren sind meistens nicht sehr einträglich. Die Lage des Pfarrhofs ist sehr schön; ein freundliches Gärtchen umgiebt das Wohnhaus. Nachdem ich die Kirche besehen, bat die Pröbstin auf eine so herzliche Weise, in den Pfarrhof einzutreten, daß ich, aller Eile ungeachtet, nicht widerstehen konnte. Ich trat ein, kostete das treffliche Öl (Starkbier), welches mir vorgesetzt wurde, unterhielt mich recht angenehm, und sagte dann den guten Leuten, bei denen ich gern länger geblieben wäre, hätte es die Zeit erlaubt, ein herzliches Lebewohl, nachdem ich hatte versprechen müssen, auf der Rückreise, wenn ich des Weges käme, wieder einzusprechen. Ein Südländer hat keinen Begriff von der Gastfreiheit, die hier im Norden herrscht; überall ist man willkommen und freundlich empfangen, und man kränkt, wenn man von dem mit so großer Herzlichkeit Dargebrachten keinen Gebrauch macht. Auch der ganz Fremde bedarf in diesen Gegenden keiner Adressen. Spricht man vor, zumal gegen Abend, so versteht es sich so

II.   C sehr von selbst, daß man die Nacht bleibt, daß man gar nicht einmal dazu eingeladen wird. Ehe man diese Sitte kennt, befindet man sich freilich in einiger Verlegenheit; mir ist es zuweilen so ergangen: erst als ich Miene machte, weiter zu reisen, wurde ich gebeten zu bleiben, und als ich nun einwilligte, und das Nöthige beim Wagen beordern wollte, hatte man schon ausgespannt, und noch ehe man gebeten zu übernachten, die Sachen aufs Logierzimmer gestellt. Es war mir um so unangenehmer, den Propst Löman nicht persönlich kennen gelernt zu haben, da ich hernach so viel Gutes von diesem braven und thätigen Manne vernahm und mein Rückweg nicht über Gnarp führte.

Unweit Gnarp erreicht man den Gästgifvaregård Gryttje.

Auch das kleine Pastorat Gnarp hat seinen Kirchspielslappen, der mit seiner Familie eine Achtel-Meile von der Kirche wohnt. Solche Lappen giebt es in den meisten Helsingischen Kirchspielen; sie verrichten das Abledern des Viehes, flechten Körbe u. dgl. m. Im höhern Norrland bedient man sich solcher Lappen als Hirten. Diese Lappen sind die ärmsten unter ihrem Volk und gewöhnlich der Schwedischen Sprache mächtig. Wiewohl sie für ihre Verrichtungen bezahlt werden, pflegen sie doch in den Kirchspielen zu betteln.

Von Gryttje aus fährt man eine kleine Strecke im schönen Thale fort, und gelangt dann in den Gränzwald Ireskog, welcher Helsingland von Medelpad scheidet. Fast 2 Meilen fährt man im dichten Walde, der aus Birken, Granen und Fichten besteht; letztere sind vorherrschend; am Wege rieseln oft Bäche. Nachdem man 1 Meile gefahren, befindet man sich auf einer Steile, wo der Wald gelichtet ist; hier stehen mehrere Sennhütten, einige Torparewohnungen und ein Paar Häuserchen mit einem Zimmer und einer Kammer, die zur Zeit der Heuernte von den Mähern bewohnt werden. Die Sennhütten waren recht freundlich eingerichtet mit Wohnzimmer, Käsekammer und Ställen. Noch standen die Hütten leer, aber nach ein Paar Tagen

sollte das Vieh hergetrieben werden. Jedes Dorf hat zwei Fä-
bodstellen, mit deren Benutzung es abwechselt; in der Zwischen-
zeit ziehen die Heerden auf 8 Tage bis 3 Wochen heim, damit
dann die Milch zu Hause benutzt werden könne. Die Sennenmädchen bereiten Butter und Käse; alle 14 Tage kommen die
Männer aus den Höfen, das Bereitete heimzuführen. — Jene
Sammlung von Sennhütten, Wohnhäusern ꝛc. heißt Ärskogskrogen, wiewohl kein Krug vorhanden ist. Eine Achtel-Meile
hinter Ärskogskrogen beginnt Medelpad; ein über einem Steinhaufen aufgerichteter Stein bezeichnet die Gränze, welche im Jahr
1769 unter der Verwaltung des thätigen Landshöfding Örn-
stölb genau bestimmt wurde. Man ist nun wieder im Walde
Ärskog, den Boden bedeckt jetzt aber ein wahres Steinmeer, aus
welchem auch Felsen sich emporthürmen; erst vor Maj verschwinden, mit dem Walde diese Steinmassen. In der Ferne erscheinen jetzt hohe Bergkuppen; man fährt herab in das reizende
Thal, welches der Majfluß durchströmt, und über diesen Fluß
zum gleichnamigen Dorf und Gästgifvaregård. Es war um die
eilfte Stunde, als ich im Maj anlangte, aber noch stand die
Sonne am Horizont. Nachdem ich mich durch ein tüchtiges
Mahl gestärkt, schrieb ich bis Mitternacht ohne Licht,
und schlief dann trefflich, unter einem sauber an der untern Seite
mit Leinewand gefütterten, Schaaffell (Schaaffelle als Bettdecken
findet man nun häufig), in dem durch dichte Vorhänge vor dem
Eindringen des Tageslichtes geschützten Bette. Abend und
Morgen waren kalt, aber das Kaminfeuer verbreitete eine
behagliche Wärme.

Noch immer sind die Wohnungen der Bauern sehr geräumig; doch ist das Wohnzimmer nur oft zugleich Küche, ohne daß
dadurch der Reinlichkeit Eintrag geschiehe; die Fugen in den
Wänden, sind, wie häufig in Norrland, insbesondere den obern
Provinzen, mit Moos ausgefüllt, wodurch die Kälte gar sehr abgehalten wird. Die Zahl der Nebengebäude ist auf den Höfen
schon geringer als in Helsingland; Häßjor zum Trocknen des

C 2

Korns findet man neben jedem Hofe. Die Menschen sind schlanker von Statur, hübscher, geistvoller und interessanter, zumal die Weiber; aber an den Küsten ist die Einfachheit und Reinheit der Sitten gewichen, während sie sich im Innern des Landes mehr erhalten hat. (Vergl. Kap. 25.)

Medelpad ist kälter, als Helsingland, nicht blos weil es nördlicher liegt, sondern weil es höhere Berge hat. Die Thäler, zum Theil von reißenden Flüssen durchströmt, sind noch schöner als in Helsingland.

Bären sind in Medelpad nicht ganz selten, namentlich finden sie sich im Gränzwalde Arskog, doch sind sie den Menschen weniger gefährlich als den Heerden. Auch Wölfe gab es vor nicht langer Zeit im Walde Arskog, und giebt es wahrscheinlich dort noch; doch versicherte man, seit ein alter Lappe einem Wolfe begegnet und ihn behext, seyen die Wölfe gewichen. Hier und da geht solcher Aberglaube noch im Schwange. So ließ es sich mein Skjutsbonde von Gryttje, als sein dickes Pferd ermüdete, nicht ausreden, daß man in Arskogskrogen, wo ich bei den Sennhütten angehalten, es behext habe.

Achtzehntes Kapitel.

Medelpad und Angermanland.

Norrlands Ströme. — Stadt Sundswall, reizende Lage; Bergland. — Der Indals-Elf ohne Fische. Norrlands schnelle Vegetation. — Eintritt in Angermanland. Sabrå. Hernösand: Stadt, Stift, Län; der Rectoratswechsel. — Das heitere, anspruchslose Leben des Norrländers. — Die liebliche Feldbeere (återbär). — Utansjö. — Die Angermanländer. — Der Angerman-Strom. — Angermanland, ein großer Garten. — Nahrungszweige. — Kirche Arnäs. — Prämienleinwand. — Landhandel. — Ländliche Industrie. — Kirchspielshandwerker. — Landmärkte. — Orn-

sköld's Verwaltung von Westernorrland. — Der Gideå-Elf. — Der Ore-Elf. — Gränze von Westerbotten.

Am 12. Jun. Von Maj nach Sundswall 2½ Meile; von
Sundswall nach Wifsta 1¼ Meile; von Wifsta nach
Jål 1 Meile; von Jjål nach Mårt 2 Meilen. — Zu-
sammen 6½ Meile.

Höchst anmuthig ist der Weg von Maj nach Sundswall:
waldbewachsene Anhöhen mit lieblichen Aussichten wechseln mit
üppigen weiten Thälern. Den Vordergrund bildet Nolby's
hoher Felsen, links schlängelt sich in der Tiefe der Maj-Fluß.
Bald erreicht man die kleine, von Kirchstuben für die entfernteren Gemeindeglieder umgebene Kirche Njurunda, neben welcher
der breite reißende Njurundastrom, oder, wie er eigentlich *)
heißt, der Ljungan, dem Meere zustürzt; an der Mündung ist
der majestätische Strom eine Viertelmeile breit. Der Ljungan
ist der erste der großen Ströme Norrlands, die an Ungestüm,
Breite, Wassermasse, wie an Erhabenheit und Schönheit der
Ufer, die übrigen Flüsse Schwedens übertreffen; der zweite, zu
welchem man dann kommt, ist der Indals-Elf, der dritte der
Ångerman; die 5 übrigen: Umeå-Elf, Piteå-Elf, Luleå-Elf,
Calix-Elf, Torneå-Elf gehören Wester- und Norrbotten an.
Außer den genannten, giebt es noch viele andere beträchtliche
Flüsse in Norrland, ja, einige derselben stehen in den bemerkten
Bezeichnungen jenen acht großen Strömen wenig nach; doch
dürften sie ihnen nicht gleich gestellt werden können; auch ergie-
ßen sie sich zum Theil in einzelne jener acht Ströme.
Eine schöne steinerne Brücke führet bei der Kirche Njurunda
über den hier mehrere hundert Ellen breiten Ljungan. Dann

---

*) Nicht selten führen die Schwedischen Flüsse mehrere Namen,
nach den Kirchspielen, durch welche sie fließen.

läuft der Weg, eine kleine Strecke längs des Flusses, Waldhöhen hinan, in Thäler herab, und abermals am Ufer des Ljungan, unweit seiner Mündung, im Angesicht schön bebuschter Felsenthäler. Jetzt fährt man unter dem Nolby-Felsen hin. Auf dem Gipfel ist, als Wahrzeichen im Kriege, ein Holzstoß errichtet, und man genießt von da einer weiten, herrlichen Aussicht über Land und Meer; im letzten Kriege war hier ein Posten ausgestellt. Vom Dorfe Nolby aus führt ein guter Fußpfad in einer halben Stunde zum Gipfel hinan; die Seiten des Felsens sind theilweise bewaldet. Bald gelangt man zur Mündung des Ljungan, der, um eine mit Holz bewachsene Felseninsel herum, seine brausenden Fluthen in einen Meerbusen, der die Rhede von Sundswall bildet, ausschüttet. Jetzt fährt man in das liebliche Thal, in welchem die einzige Stadt Medelpads belegen ist, hinab. Die Lage von Sundswall ist eine der reizendsten, die es giebt; eine Gegend, wie man sie kaum an dem herrlichen Schweizersee Lungern, oder am vielgepriesenen Lago Maggioro findet: ein weites Thal, von hohen Bergen, die mehrere Arten von Laub- und Nadelholz in mannigfaltigen wahrhaft malerischen Mischungen bekränzen, und deren Fuß ländliche Wohnungen oder einfache Heuscheuern bedecken, umlagert; im Thale selbst fruchtbare Felder und Wiesen, und die Stadt Sundswall mit stattlicher Kirche, mit Hafen und großen Schiffen; weiterhin der Meeresbusen, mitten in demselben eine waldige unbewohnte Felseninsel, und, ihr gegenüber, die Insel Alnön mit Kirche, Dörfern und einzelnen Höfen, von Wald und Felsen umgeben. Einem kleinen Gesundbrunnen und dem hübschen, gräflich Fröhlichschen Landsitze Jacobsdal vorüber, fährt man in die Stadt ein, bis zu welcher die Straße von Maj zwei Mal neben Sennhütten hinführt.

Sundswall, unter 62° 23′ 18″ Polhöhe, ist ein freundliches Städtchen, im Jahr 1815 mit 1592 Einwohnern, mit hübschem Markte und Rathhause, gutem Gasthofe, aber ungepflasterten Gassen. Es treibt nicht unbedeutenden, auch auswärtigen

Handel, und hat zwei Schiffswerfte, das eine an Ort und Stelle, das andere, gemeinschaftlich mit Ångermanlands einziger Stadt, Hernösand, welche auch ein eigenes Werft am Orte selbst hat, — bei Wiffta, 1 Meile von Sundswall. Eine Schmiede auf jenem, Sundswall eigenthümlichen Werft veranlaßte, bei heftigem Sturm, den letzten großen Brand am 7. Sept. 1803, der einen großen Theil der Stadt in die Asche legte.

Bei Sundswall reifen zuletzt gegen Norden Aepfel. Bei Hernösand hat man zwar auch Obstbäume, aber die Früchte werden selten schmackhaft und reif.

In Sundswall machte ich die Bekanntschaft des Layman über Ångermanland und Westerbotten, Strömbom, der in Stockholm wohnt, und eben zu seinem Gerichtssprengel (lagsaga) reisete, um die beiden jährlichen Lagmansting zu Aeland bei Hernösand, und zu Piteå zu halten. Der gefällige Mann suchte mir auf alle Weise zu dienen. Als er bemerkte, daß ich mich für das Eigenthümliche des Schwedischen Volks interessire, lud er mich ein, einem Lagmansting beizuwohnen; gerne wäre ich der Einladung gefolgt, hätte es nicht meine beschränkte Zeit verboten. Als er hörte, daß ich die Kirche der Stadt zu sehen wünschte, traf er sofort die nöthigen Veranstaltungen, und gab mir seinen Begleiter, den braven Dalkarl Fahnehjelm, zum Führer mit. Die Bekanntschaft dieses biedern jungen Mannes machte mir viel Freude. Er hing mit ganzer Seele an seinem lieben Darlekarlien, und kannte die theure Heymath, wohin er mich zu seinem Vater aufs dringendste einlud, nicht reizend genug schildern. In Westerbotten begegnete ich späterhin noch ein Mal den braven Männern und verlebte mit ihnen kurze, aber schöne, Augenblicke.

Die Kirche, von einem weiten Kirchhofe umgeben, ist ein geräumiges massives Gebäude, einfach und geschmackvoll im Innern; Altar und Kanzel sind vergoldet; den Altar schmücken das schöne Bild des Erlösers am Kreuze, und ein zweites, wie ihn der Engel in Gethsemane stärkt. Minder gelungen sind ein Paar andere Bilder: „Mariä Verkündigung" und „die Taufe Jesu im Jordan." Die Orgel und ein Chor daneben sind mit Bildern der Apostel und biblischen Schriftstellen geschmückt; in der Mitte erblickt man das Bild Christi als des guten Hirten. — Vom Thurm hat man eine herrliche Aussicht auf das Thal von Sundswall, die Meerbusen und Inseln, und, im Hintergrunde, die Kirche Sillängar, deren Filiale die Stadt Sundswall und das Kirchspiel Sättna sind.

Das neue Armenhaus der Stadt war noch nicht ganz vollendet; der vollendete, bewohnte Theil zeigte große Mängel.

In früherer Zeit war Sundswall Sitz eines Landshöfding, der jetzt zu Hernösand residirt; neuerdings (im Jahr 1818) erhielt der zweite Provinzialarzt in Hernösands Län zu Sundswall seine Station.

Hinter Sundswall wird das Land immer bergiger; man fährt einen hohen Berg hinan, dessen Gipfel schöne, doch minder viele Aussichten, wie der Thurm der Kirche zu Sundswall, gewährt. Dann läuft der Weg über Waldhöhen neben fruchtbaren, wohlangebauten Thälern. Das anmuthigste dieser Thäler ist das Thal um die Kirche Stön; Blumenteppiche bedecken die Wiesen, Tausendschönchen, Feldnelken und andere liebliche Blumen umkränzen die Straße, die völlig Bergweg ist; ununterbrochen geht es bergauf und bergab, bis sich plötzlich ein Meerbusen öffnet, der die reizendste Landschaft einschließt. Auf einem Hügel am Meer liegt die prächtige Kirche Timrå, Filial von Stön. Hinter Timrå fährt man bald in das schöne Thal von Wissta ein.

Von Wissta nach Fjäl hat man viel Wald mit freundlichen Thälern; zuletzt kömmt man auf einer Fähre, über den reißenden Indals-Elf, an dessen jenseitigem Ufer Fjäl liegt. Mein Skjutsbonde war dießmal ein funfzehnjähriges Mädchen, eines der lieblichsten Gesichter, welches ich je sah, ein wahres Madonnengesicht; die einfache Walmarkleidung, eine sonore

Stimme, ein unbefangenes, mildes, schuldloses, wahrhaft Ehrfurcht gebietendes, Wesen erhöhten die Reize des Mädchens; sie war die Tochter eines Bauern, der sich im Sommer auf den Küsteninseln (skärgård), 4 Meilen von seinem Hofe entfernt, mit Strömlingsfang beschäftiget; mittlerweile mußte die Tochter dem Skjuts vorstehen. Und in der That fuhr sie mit vieler Geschicklichkeit, wie überhaupt die weiblichen Skjutsbönder, die in Norrland nicht selten sind, besser und vorsichtiger zu fahren pflegen, als die Männer.

Der Indals-Elf ist da, wo die Fähre überführt, etwa eine Viertelmeile breit. In der Mitte bildet der Fluß eine kleine Waldinsel, wo ein herrliches Echo ist; hier stehen die Fährhäuser, und hier landet man, um am jenseitigen Ufer wieder die Fähre zu besteigen. Nach der Seite von Wifsta zu war der Fluß durch die Alpenfluth, wie durch die häufigen Regengüsse dieses Sommers, übergetreten, so daß ich eine Strecke im Wasser zu Wagen fahren mußte. Der Indals-Elf kommt aus Jemteland, wo er dem See Storsjö entfließt, herab, macht während seines Laufes viele Krümmungen und kann meistens mit Flößen und Böten, nicht aber mit größeren Fahrzeugen, befahren werden. Seine Ufer sind an vielen Stellen hoch und schön, bald angebaut, bald Wiesen, von Waldbergen begränzt, bald bewaldet. Gar freundliche Uferprospekte gewährt der Gäste gifvaregård Ffäl. Man erzählt hier noch von der furchtbaren Ueberschwemmung im Jahr 1796: der Fluß stieg selbst zu den hohen Ufern hinan; zerstörte Wohnungen und fruchtbare Felder, und ganze große Erdstücke stürzten in sein Bette herab. Seit dieser Zeit wurde das Wasser so trübe und schlammig, daß die Lachse verschwanden und der früher sehr einträgliche Lachsfang völlig aufhörte. Unvorsichtigkeit, aber auch plötzliche Regengüsse und Alpenfluthen hatten die Ueberschwemmung veranlaßt, indem beim Abzapfen eines Sees unweit Ragunda in Jemteland in den Indals-Elf jener, statt allmählig abzufließen, mit Einem Male seine gesammte Wassermasse mit größter Heftigkeit in den

Fluß stürzte. Noch immer hat der Indals-Elf keine festen Ufer gewonnen, noch jährlich lösen Ufertheile sich ab, und selbst kleinere Fische haben sich verloren, nur im Frühling zeigt sich zuweilen ein Schnäpel (Salmo Lavaretus). Die Bäche umher enthalten Forellen, doch nicht in Menge. Die Fischerhäuschen, welche man bei Fjäl erblickt, werden beim Einsalzen der Strömlinge, die unterhalb Fjäl in einem Meerbusen gefangen werden, benutzt; denn Fjäl liegt fast schon an der Mündung des Indals-Elf.

Heute, am 11. Junius, sah ich mehrere Saatfelder, deren einige erst vor 8, andere vor 14 Tagen bestellt worden waren; ja, auf dem Hofe des Gästgifvaregård zu Wissta lag unter den Sägespähnen Schnee; im Mai hatte man noch Schlitten gefahren. Solche Erscheinungen sind in dieser Polhöhe nicht selten. Desto schöner und dauerhafter, obgleich kurz, ist der Sommer. Nach einem Frühling von, oft nur wenigen, Tagen, beginnt der Sommer um die Mitte des Junius; die Hitze wächset in starken Progressionen, schnell und üppig ist die Vegetation; trifft irgendwo das Sprüchwort ein: „Gras wachsen sehen,“ so ist es in Norrland, denn kaum ist der Schnee ein Paar Tage gewichen, so hat das Gras schon die Länge eines Fingers erreicht; zwischen Aussaat und Ernde verfließen oft kaum 9, höchstens 11 oder 12 Wochen. Das Heu wird zwei Mal gemähet. Der Horizont ist fast ununterbrochen heiter und klar, wie man ihn in Deutschland nicht kennt. Nicht gar häufig regnet es, selten anhaltend, doch hinreichend, da auch die aus den vielen Seen und Wasserzügen aufsteigenden Morgen- und Abendnebel das Land befeuchten. Mit dem Anfange des Septembers endet der Sommer, es folgt ein kurzer Herbst, und dann sofort der Winter in seiner ganzen Strenge. So wechseln die Jahreszeiten in Norrland, doch machen Polhöhe und Lokalitäten einen Unterschied. Der dießjährige Sommer hatte viel Regen und viel trübe Tage, also daß ich nur mit häufigen Un-

rrbrechungen die Schönheiten des Norrländischen Sommers genießen konnte.

In Fjäl verursachte der Pferdewechsel einen langen Aufenthalt, doch fuhr ich noch um 7¼ Uhr weiter. Anfangs läuft
die Straße längs des Indals-Elf, dann im Walde, bis man
das schöne Thal von Häßjö erreicht, wo auf einem Hügel
mit weiter Aussicht über einen freundlichen See sich die vor
einigen Jahren neuerbaute prächtige Kirche Häßjö erhebt.
Eiserne Gitterthüren, oben mit einer Sonne, als Symbol der
Auferstehung, führen zum Kirchhof, der aber, wie die meisten
Kirchhöfe Norrlands, für das Auge nichts Anziehendes hat, denn
fast alle Gräber sind ohne Grabzeichen, ja ohne Grabhügel, völlig platt und eben. Den Kirchhof umgeben, in einiger Entfernung, Kirchenställe für die reitenden und fahrenden Kirchgänger
der Kirchspielsstube, auch die Wohnung des Kirchenwärters. Die
Gemeinde Häßjö ist Filial von Liustorp und zählt an 1000
Seelen. — Hinter Häßjö kommt man über Waldhöhen und
durch frisch grünende Thäler, die aber weniger bewohnt und
minder schön als die Thäler um Sundswall sind. Der Weg
läuft nicht selten sehr steil von den Höhen in die tiefen Thäler
herab; oft rieseln Bäche am Wege oder stürzen über denselben
unter Brücken hin. Eben eine halbe Meile vor Märk, an einem
kleinen See, beginnt Angermanland: eine weiße Tafel mit der
Inschrift, durch ein kleines Bretterdach vor Schnee und Regen
geschützt, bezeichnet die Gränze. — Um 10¼ Uhr langte ich in
Märk an, wo ich übernachtete. Der Gasthof ist sehr geräumig
und reinlich, außer den Fremdenzimmern im unteren Stock findet
man im obern einen Saal nebst einer Suite von drei Zimmern.
Solche große Landgasthöfe sind in mehreren Schwedischen Provinzen nicht ganz selten. — Die Lage von Märk ist reizend.

Am 13. Jun. Von Märt über Säbrå nach Hernösand 1¼ Meile.

Am Frühmorgen verließ ich Märt. Ich wählte den Um= weg von einer Achtel=Meile über Säbrå, weil ich hier den Bi= schof über Hernösand's Stift, Dr. Almquist, zu treffen hoffte. Denn in Säbrå, einem der drei *) Präbendepastorate des Bischofs, hat dieser seinen Sommersitz, ja das Pfarrhaus von Säbrå war der einzige Amtssitz, oder, wie man im Schwe= bischen spricht, Residenz des Bischofs, bis derselbe im Jahr 1816 auch in der Stadt Hernösand, wo das Stiftsconsistorium, in welchem der Bischof präsidirt, seinen Sitz hat, ein Amtshaus erhielt.

Der Weg ist ganz bergig, ein tiefes Waldthal folgt dem andern, einige Thäler sind eng und von Wiesen, welche Birken und Fichten beschatten, ausgefüllt; andere sind weiter und ange= bauet, von Seen und Bächen durchschnitten, alle sehr anmuthig; das herrlichste ist das letzte, das Helgom (sprich Hälgom) Thal; hier donnert zwischen hohen Waldufern der Helgom= fluß, jetzt Wasserfälle, jetzt schön bebuschte kleine Inseln bil= dend. Im Dorfe Helgom führt, mitten über Fälle zwischen platten Felsen, eine Brücke über den Fluß, über diese Brücke geht die Straße. — Unweit Helgom erreicht man Säbrå. Da der Bischof nicht dort war, so fuhr ich ohne Aufenthalt wei= ter nach Hernösand. Der Weg ist bis zur Helgombrücke der Weg nach Märt, dann läuft er gegen Nordost, anfangs am Helgom, bald neben Bergwiesen, die ein Teppich von Tausendschönchen, Veilchen, Ranunkeln, Marien und andern schö= nen Blumen kleidet, nach Bonnsjö, wo der Landrentmeister, Assessor Rossander, ein schönes Landhaus besitzt, im Angesicht des hohen Wålkasberges, über eine Brücke zur Insel Hernö, auf welcher die Stadt Hernösand liegt. Nahe vor der Stadt kömmt man dem auf Staatskosten gebauten und durch Legate und

---

*) Säbrå, Hernösand und Nora.

Sammlungen unterhaltenen Arbeits- und Corrections-
hause vorüber, wo Vagabonden und liederliche Frauenspersonen
zur Arbeit gezwungen, auch Diebe, theils zur Strafe, theils
während der Untersuchung, gefangen gehalten werden. Im
Hause empfangen auch arme Kinder freien Unterricht. Die Zimmer sind freundlich, reinlich und wohl verwahrt. Nur Eins vermißte ich, als am Abend der Bürgermeister, Commerzienrath
Linström, die Güte hatte, mich in der Anstalt umherzuführen
— Beschäftigung der Gefangenen. Als wir in eines der
Gefangenzimmer traten, bat ein 17jähriger Jüngling, den böse
Gesellschaft zum Diebstahl verleitet hatte, aufs dringendste, daß
man ihm doch Arbeit geben möge; ein anderer, schon mehr be-
jahrter Dieb bekannte, daß Liebe zum Trunk ihm zuerst sein
Hemman (Hof) gekostet und dann ihn zum Diebe gemacht habe; er hatte Frau und Kinder und fühlte sich so verworfen, daß
er sich auf ewig für verloren hielt. Ich suchte ihn aufzurichten,
so viel ich vermochte und durfte, und konnte ihn zugleich zum
Lesen einiger zweckmäßigen kleinen Erbauungsschriften ermuntern,
die die evangelische Gesellschaft zu Stockholm im Hause
vertheilt hatte. — Gefühle anderer Art erregte ein 23jähriges
Mädchen, das schon mehrere Diebstähle begangen hatte und jetzt
die Schuld auf ihre Mutter schob. — Durch die Legate des
Lector Salberg, der im Jahr 1811, und des Rådman Nyberg, der im Jahr 1817 starb, fließen der Anstalt jährlich
nicht ganz unbedeutende Zinsen zu; letzterer hat auch für den
Unterricht der Kinder der Armen gesorgt. — Uebrigens ist das
Haus für das gesammte Län bestimmt. Das Län Westernorrland, oder Hernösand, weil die Verwaltungsbehörde
an diesem Orte ihren Sitz hat, umfaßt die Provinzen Ångermanland (22 Meilen lang und 16 Meilen breit) und Medelpad, oder 217 □Meilen, im Jahr 1819 mit 69,216 Seelen,
seit man im Jahr 1810 Jemtland davon trennte und aus dieser Provinz nebst Herjeådalen, welches bis dahin zum Län Gefleborg gehört hatte, ein neues Län (Österlands Län) bildete.

Die Residenz des Landshöfdings liegt an einer schönen Pflege, dem großen Markte; in dem stattlichen steinernen Gebäude haben auch die Lands-Canzley und das Lands-Comtoir ihr Geschäfts-Locale. Sämmtliche, obere und niedere, Provinzial-Verwaltungsbeamten des Län Hernösand errichteten im Jahr 1807 für ihre Wittwen und Kinder eine Pensionscasse.

In einem Gebäude sind zu Hernösand das Hospital und das Lazareth des Län vereinigt; ersteres nimmt nicht blos Irre auf, sondern gewährt auch alten Leuten einen ruhigen und freundlichen Aufenthalt. Die Kammern der Irren sind mit verschlossenen Gitterthüren versehen. Im Krankensaal fand ich die Venerischen nicht von andern Kranken getrennt. Aus den geräumigen und reinlichen Zimmern genießt man liebliche Aussichten auf die schöne Umgegend.

Im Jahr 1805 ward zu Hernösand, auf Veranlassung des Bürgermeisters Lagman Lind, eine Landhaushaltungs-Gesellschaft gestiftet, die für das ganze Län bestimmt ist; bisher hatte sie kleine ökonomische Schriften vertheilt, Auszüge aus ihren Protokollen drucken lassen, auch Preisfragen aufgestellt; Bischof Almquist war eben Präses der Gesellschaft.

Der Bischof, wie das Consistorium des Stifts, haben, wie oben bemerkt, zu Hernösand ihren Sitz, mithin findet man, nach der in Schweden bestehenden Einrichtung, dort auch ein Gymnasium und eine Trivialschule. — Das Stift Hernösand, bis zum Jahr 1697 Theil des Stiftes Upsala, begreift, nach den neuesten Abtretungen an Rußland, noch einen Flächeninhalt von 2062 □ Meilen; es ist etwa 150 Meilen lang und mehr denn 30 Meilen breit, umfaßt, außer Helsingland und Gestrikland, das gesammte Norrland nebst allen Schwedischen Lappmarken. Es ist das größte aller Stifte des Reiches, der Localität wegen ist die Verwaltung desselben schwieriger als die irgend eines andern Stiftes; dennoch gehört es, der bedeutenden Erhöhung des Einkommens in neuester Zeit ungeachtet, noch immer zu den minder einträglichen. Dagegen sind die Lectoren des Gymnasiums besser als alle übrigen Lectoren im Reich besoldet; eine Dompropststelle besteht noch nicht. — Zur Erleichterung der Geistlichkeit ist das Stift in zwei Synodalkreise (synodallag) getheilt, so daß die Geistlichkeit des unteren Stifts sich in Hernösand, die des obern Stifts (Wester, und Norrbotten) zu Piteä, wohin, 47¼ Meile von Hernösand, dann der Bischof reiset, zur Synode versammelt. Bei solchen Synodalreisen zahlt die Geistlichkeit dem Bischof das Fuhrgeld für 6 Pferde. — Für die Geistlichen und Schullehrer des Stifts ist durch jährliche Beiträge, die im Jahr 1806, kraft einer vom Könige bestätigten Vereinbarung, erhöhet wurden, eine Wittwenkasse gegründet; jeder Pastor (mit Ausnahme von drei kleinen Pastoraten) giebt jährlich drei Tonnen Korn, jeder Comminister und jeder Schulcollege, einige ausgenommen, 1 Tonne, und jeder Adjunct eine Vierteltonne; einige sind von der erhöhten Bewilligung frei. — Für arme Geistliche, die ohne feste Anstellung blieben, besteht eine besondere Kasse durch Beiträge der Geistlichkeit.

Ein geräumiges steinernes Gebäude, welches im Jahr 1791 fertig wurde, vereinigt das Gymnasium und die Trivialschule; auch hält in demselben das Consistorium seine Sitzungen, und findet man dort das Consistorialarchiv, wie die Gymnasienbibliothek. Letztere war im Jahr 1721, als die Russen die Stadt anzündeten, völlig zu Grunde gegangen; allmählig hatte man wieder einiges gesammelt, worauf im Jahr 1806 die in der alten Literatur reiche Bibliothek des Bischofs Hesselgren, von fast 2500 Bänden, angekauft wurde; an Manuscripten mangelt es völlig. Kleine mineralogische und physikalische, naturgeschichtliche Sammlungen sind vorhanden. Das Gymnasium hat zwei Lehrzimmer im obern Stock, deren eines auch als Betsaal dient. Die Zimmer der Trivialschule befinden sich im unteren Stock; ein eigener Festivitätssaal ist angelegt worden. — Zur Wohnung für Schüler der obern und der niedern gelehrten Schule bauete man seit 1806 das sogenannte Stifts, oder Communitätshaus;

nur einige untere Zimmer wurden vollendet und einige Jahre
benutzt; da aber die Miethpreise in der Stadt nicht hoch sind,
so wird man wohl bald das hölzerne Haus wieder abbrechen.
Versetzungen hölzerner Häuser sind nicht ungewöhnlich.

Die Kirche ist alt und von mittelmäßiger Größe; die Bil=
der Christi, der Apostel und der Propheten des A. T. an den
Thören sind vorzüglich gelungen; die geräumige Sakristey ist in
späterer Zeit angebauet worden. Der Bau einer neuen Kirche
ward schon längst beabsichtiget. Die Aussicht vom Kirchhofe ist
schön. Im Armenhause, der Kirche gegenüber, wohnen ein=
zelne Arme, die übrigen werden durch Geld und Arbeit in ihren
Privatwohnungen unterstützt.

Hernösand hat Stapelgerechtigkeit. Der meiste Handel
wird auf den Marktplätzen im Innern und nach Stockholm
getrieben; auswärtigen Handel treiben von den etwa 20 Kauf=
leuten der Stadt nur 4. Die bedeutendste Ausfuhr bilden Bret=
ter und die feineren oder Prämien=Sorten der berühmten An=
germanländischen Leinewand, die in den oberen Kirchspielen der
Provinz gefertigt werden. Den Handel mit wilden Vögeln, an
welchen Ängermanland Ueberfluß hat, treiben die Bauern selbst
über das ganze Reich, am meisten nach Stockholm; einige
führen ganze Ladungen nach Götheborg, von wo sie nach
England versandt werden. Auch hat man neuerdings angefan=
gen, die köstliche Feldbeere (åkerbär) eingemacht ins Aus=
land zu senden; nach Stockholm wird mit diesen Beeren aus
Norrland längst ein ansehnlicher Handel getrieben.

Die Fischerey der Stadt ist bedeutend. Die Hinterge=
bäude der am Hafen liegenden Häuser sind als Fischerhütten
eingerichtet und mit Brücken und Ladungsplätzen versehen; am
jenseitigen Ufer liegt das Stadtwerft. Alle Fischerey Treibenden
bilden eine eigene Gesellschaft, wie auch in den übrigen Küsten=
städten Norrlands, Sundswall ausgenommen. Am beträcht=
lichsten ist der Strömlingsfang; man bereitet auch sauern
Strömling (surströmming), indem man ihn wenig salzet, der

Luft aussetzt und in einer verschlossenen Tonne durch Gährung zur Säure bringt. Viele finden den sauren Strömling nahrhaft und wohlschmeckend; mir war er zuwider. Man verführt ihn weit, doch meistens nur innerhalb Norrland, wo ihn insbesondere der geringe Mann ißt. — Ueberhaupt ist der Fischfang Hauptnahrungszweig in Angermanland, daher diese Provinz im Wappen drei Fische führt.

Im Jahr 1815 zählte die Stadt nur 1780 Einwohner; vor dem letzten Kriege war die Einwohnerzahl größer. Die meisten Häuser sind von Holz, auch das hübsche Rathhaus am großen Markte, die Straßen, einige Nebengassen abgerechnet, gepflastert. Hernösand hat zwei Märkte. Neben den Häusern, wie außerhalb der Stadt, findet man nicht selten Gärten, und weiterhin auf der Insel Hernö Landsitze der Lectoren, Kaufleute und Anderer; an mancher dieser Stellen werden Apfelbäume gezogen, aber unter einer Polhöhe von 62° 38′ geben sie selten reife Früchte. Die Meerbusen, welche an zwei Seiten die Insel Hernö einschließen, und zwischen der Insel und dem festen Lande den trefflichen Hafen der Stadt bilden, sind Mündungen des großen Angermanflusses, der aber auch nördlicher, um die Insel Hämsö hin, sich ins Meer ergießt. Uebrigens ist Hernösand eine der älteren Städte Norrlands; sie ward schon gegen das Ende des 16ten Jahrhunderts vom König Johann III. angelegt, und schon lange vorher, ehe eine Stadt entstand, ward am Hernösunde ein berühmter Markt gehalten.

Die Buchdruckerey zu Hernösand hat das ausschließende Recht, Bücher in Lappischer Sprache zu drucken.

Die Stadt besitzt in ihrem Bezirk eine, freilich nicht sehr mineralhaltige, Heilquelle, mit geräumigem Brunnenhause von zwei Stockwerken. Ein Rasenweg führt von hier zum Stadtgarten, einer öffentlichen Promenade mit freundlichen Gängen und Alleen neben Kornfeldern.

II. D

Bisher habe ich nur von der Stadt und ihren Merkwürdigkeiten geredet. Jetzt muß ich auch einiges über ihre heiteren
und gefälligen Einwohner und die frohen Stunden meines Aufenthalts unter ihnen hinzufügen.

Herzliche Gastfreundschaft war von jeher ein Hauptzug im
Character der Ängermanländer; wie sehr sie auch den Bewohnern von Hernösand eigen ist, habe ich im reichsten Maaße
erfahren. Mit inniger Dankbarkeit werde ich stets der freundlichen und liebevollen Aufnahme gedenken, die mir in Hernösand zu theil wurde, und nie wird es mir aus dankbarem Gedächtniß entschwinden, wie gar viel ich selbst auf meiner ganzen
Reise durch das Stift der unermüdeten Dienstfertigkeit des braven Bischofs Almquist verdanke; ja durch welche mannigfaltige
Beweise herzlicher Freundschaft der würdige Bischof, die Lectoren Forsberg und Berlin und andere ehrenwerthe Männer
mich erfreuten.

Gleich nach meiner Ankunft ging ich zum Bischof; der
freundliche Mann hieß mich herzlich willkommen. Eben sollte
der jährliche Rectoratswechsel im Gymnasium Statt finden; denn
nur die Trivialschule hat einen bleibenden Rector, im Gymnasium wechselt das Rectorat jährlich unter den Lectoren; das
halbjährige Examen war vorangegangen. Der Bischof führte
mich zu dem feierlichen Akt, der im Festivitätssaal des Gymnasiums erfolgte. Nach stillem Gebet, begann der abgehende Rector mit einer Rede in lateinischer Sprache; nach freundlichem
Wunsche und nach den üblichen Anreden an Ephorus, Lehrer
und Lernende, entwickelte er in dieser Rede geschichtlich das Dog-
ma von der Erbsünde; dann forderte er seinen Nachfolger auf,
das Katheder zu besteigen, sprach, mit dargereichter Rechte, als
Zeichen der Treue und des Gehorsams, die Ernennung des neuen
Rectors aus und übergab demselben die Bibel als oberste
Richtschnur, die Schulordnung, das Album (die Schulmatrikel),
das Buch über Vermögen und Einkommen des Gymnasiums,
das Buch über Einkommen und Rechte der Lehrer, das Siegel,
die Schlüssel des Gymnasiums und die Schlüssel zum Career,

jedes einzeln von passenden Worten begleitet. Jetzt folgte die Rede des neuen Rectors, in welcher er zur Uebernahme des Amts sich willig erklärte, um den Beistand des Höchsten flehte, zweckmäßige Worte an Ephorus, Lehrer und Lernende richtete und mit Gebeten für König und Vaterland schloß, worauf, nach stillem Gebet, die Versammlung auseinander ging.

Am Mittage wohnte ich dem Mahle bei, welches der abgehende Rector gab. Alles, was Hernösand an Honoratioren besitzt, 30 bis 40 Personen, waren zugegen; denn keine Sonderung findet Statt, alles lebt friedlich und freundlich mit einander, ja, ist wie zu Einer Familie vereint. Dieses einträchtige Leben mit und für einander macht das gesellige Leben im Norden so angenehm und erhöht so sehr seine Freuden. Auch heute war dieser Geist ganz herrschend; man ward seines Beisammenseyns wahrhaft froh. Nach Landessitte wurden Gesundheiten in Menge ausgebracht, des Königs und einzelner Glieder des Königl. Hauses, des Bischofs, der Lectoren, des abgehenden und des antretenden Rectors, mehrerer aus der Gesellschaft, einzeln und im größten Ganzen; einige dieser Gesundheiten wurden vom Gesange schöner Nationallieder begleitet. Am Abende wurde wieder bei Tische gespeiset; denn das hier und da in Deutschland übliche Speisen am Spieltisch, oder stehend und gehend, kennt man im Norden nicht, man will fröhlich seyn mit einander, darum muß man auch mit und bei einander sitzen, bei Speise und Trank — Kartenspiel fand überdieß gar nicht Statt. — Um 10½ Uhr ging man aus einander. Am gestrigen Tage war Examen in der Trivialschule gewesen, und der Rector derselben hatte ein Mittagsmahl gegeben.

Am 14. Jun. Von Hernösand nach Nesland 1 Meile; von Nesland nach Weda 1½ Meilen; von Weda nach Herrskog 1½ Meilen. — Zusammen 4½ Meilen.

In Gesellschaft einiger Freunde, die, wie ich, die Mitternachtssonne auf Afvasaxa zu sehen wünschten, verließ ich um

D 2

5 Uhr Nachmittags Hernösand. Schon am Frühmorgen hatte ein dichter Nebel sich auf den Höhen gelagert, allmählig war er in die Thäler hinabgestiegen und jetzt füllte er sie also, daß man kaum einige Schritte vor sich sehen konnte. Nebel dieser Art sind an den Küsten Norrlands nicht selten. Doch bald erhob sich der Nebel, es ward wieder hell, und wir genossen ganz der schönen Gegend. Bis gegen Såbrå war unser Weg ganz der gestrige. Rechts zeigt sich ein Meerbusen, der hier einen Bergstrom aufnimmt, links erquickt das frische Grün der vom Birkengebüsch umkreuzten Wiesen, an welchen sich Höfe ausbreiten. Ueberhaupt mischt sich jetzt die freundliche Birke immer mehr unter die düsteren Fichten. In Nesland trafen wir einen Kaufmann, der zum Markte nach Hammar am Ångerman reisete. Dieser Markt, am 16. Junius, wird von Kaufleuten aus Hernösand, Sundswall und Hudikswall besucht, welche hier insbesondere Bretter und grobe Leinwand einkaufen. Bedeutender ist der Markt zu Sollefta am Ångerman (s. Kap. 24).

Das schöne Thal, welches sich vor Nesland ausbreitet, läuft noch eine Strecke auf jener Seite des Gästgifvaregård fort. Blühende Feldbeeren (åkerbär) am Wege erfüllten die Luft mit Wohlgerüchen; die Blume ist tellerförmig, anfangs hochroth, dann nimmt sie ein milderes Roth an; die Frucht hat an Farbe und Gestalt Aehnlichkeit mit der Brom= oder Himbeere und einen lieblichen aromatischen Duft und Geschmack. Man speiset die Åkerbär frisch mit Sahne, auch als crème. Man macht sie auch mit Zucker ein, auf folgende Weise: zu 1 Pfund Åkerbär nimmt man 1 Pfund Zucker, löset den Zucker auf, schäumt ihn ab und durchkocht mit demselben die vorher sorgfältig von den unteren Blättern getrennten und gereinigten Beeren; solche eingemachte Beeren halten sich mehrere Jahre. Ferner bereitet man aus den frischen Beeren, mittelst einfachen Aufgusses von Wasser, ein wohlschmeckendes Getränk, welches durch Zumischung von Zucker und Traubenwein noch verbessert wird; die hierzu schon benutzten

Beeren können mit hinzugefügten neuen Beeren noch einmal auf gleiche Weise verwandt werden, und geben sie keinen Wein mehr, so theilen sie wenigstens noch dem Branntwein einen Akerbärgeschmack mit. Die Bereitung des Akerbärweines sollte häufiger seyn, als sie ist. Getrocknete Akerbär lassen sich in verschlossenen hölzernen oder gläsernen Gefäßen Jahre lang aufbewahren.

Aus dem Thale, in welchem Nesland liegt, fährt man eine Höhe hinan und bald in ein enges Waldthal hinab. Nun folgen abermals Waldhöhen, unaufhörlich wechselnd mit den reizendsten Thälern, die bald ein Dorf, bald ein See mit üppigen Wiesenufern ausfüllt. Endlich fährt man von einem hohen Berge in ein tiefes Thal hinab, welches ein Waldstrom durchfließt, dann eine Viertelmeile auf Waldhöhen neben dem lieblichen See Skog, dessen Ufer Wiesen, Birken und Fichten bedecken. So gelangt man zu einem See, an welchem das Gut Utansjö liegt; das hübsche Wohnhaus wird von Birkengebüsch umgeben. Gegenüber, in einiger Entfernung, hinter einem Birkenhain, in einer tiefen Schlucht am Ängerman, liegt das zum Gut gehörige Bruk, welches mittelst eines Stab- und eines Nagelhammers jährlich 900 Schiffpfund Eisen ausschmiedet; auch eine Ziegeley ist angelegt worden. Utansjö gehört dem Landssecretaire Lagman Gavelius in Herndsand. Der freundliche Mann, durch sein Amt in der Stadt zurückgehalten, hatte uns so dringend gebeten, bei seiner lieben Frau vorzusprechen, daß wir nicht widerstehen konnten. Da wir nicht übernachten wollten, mußten wir uns wenigstens eine gute Mahlzeit gefallen lassen. In der Unterhaltung mit der liebenswürdigen Frau verflossen ein Paar Stunden unbemerkt; einer der schönsten Genüsse war es zu schauen, mit welcher Innigkeit die Kinder an die zärtliche Mutter sich anschmiegten und sie liebkoseten. Wie verschwindet doch alles Schein- und Flitterwesen vor Einfalt, Natur und ächter Häuslichkeit! — Frau Gavelius ist eine Ängermanländerin, Schwester des Brukspatron Classon zu Graninge an der Jemteländischen Gränze. Die Ängersmanländer sind ein kernhaftes, biederes, höchst interessantes Volk; feurig ist ihr Auge, heiter und geistvoll ihr Blick, in dem sich oft so unverkennbar die Einfalt des Herzens ausspricht; ihr Gesicht ist länglich, ihre Statur mittelmäßig und gedrungen. Sie sind wohl unterrichtet, höflich, in hohem Grade gutmüthig und gefällig, gastfrei, immer fröhlich, gesprächig und zeigen viel Leichtigkeit und Grazie in den Bewegungen des Körpers, in welcher letzteren Beziehung man sie die Franzosen des Nordens nennen könnte.

Eine Viertelmeile jenseits Utansjö, nachdem man einen hohen Berg hinter sich hat, erreicht man Weda am Ångerman. Hier theilen sich die Wege: ein Weg führt, aufwärts am Ångerman, in das Innere des Landes; hier ist die schönste Gegend der Provinz und eine der anmuthigsten in ganz Schweden; rechts läuft die Straße nach Norden über den Ångerman. Die Ueberfahrt geschieht auf großen Fährböten. Der Ångerman, Norrlands größter Strom, hat hier, unweit seiner Mündung, eine Breite von fast einer Viertelmeile; aufwärts ist er schmäler, kann aber, wie kein anderer Fluß Schwedens, von den größten Kriegsschiffen, Acht, und von Kauffahrteyschiffen, Zehn Meilen (bis Sollefta) befahren werden; dann hemmen Wasserfälle die weitere Fahrt. — Die Fähre wird von den Fährleuten unterhalten, die hier nicht, wie bei andern Fähren, Unterstützung an Korn u. dergl. m. vom Hårad empfangen, daher das Fährgeld höher, als gewöhnlich, aber noch immer sehr mäßig ist; denn für die Person bezahlt man 4, für eine Kärra 8, für einen Wagen 16 Bankschillinge. Auch auf dem entgegengesetzten Ufer steht ein Fährhaus, wie der Gästgifvaregård Hönö, für die von Norden kommenden Reisenden.

Von Hönö nach Herrskog fuhr mich ein 13jähriges Mädchen, das man im nördlichen Deutschland für ein 18jähriges gehalten haben würde; überhaupt hat es mir oft geschienen, als wenn im Allgemeinen die körperliche Ausbildung beider Geschlechter, doch vorzugsweise des weiblichen, in Nordschweden schneller fortschreite und früher vollendet werde, als in Deutschland, ohne daß die jugendliche Blüthe in gleichem Verhältnisse früher schwinde, wie solches in südlichen Ländern der Fall ist; es ist gar nichts Seltenes, in mehreren Provinzen Schwedens, insbesondere des nördlichen und nordwestlichen Schwedens, Frauen von 40 Jahren und darüber zu sehen, die noch immer Schönheiten sind. — Uebrigens bestätigte auch dieses Mädchen die Erfahrung, daß die Weiber geschickter und vorsichtiger fahren als die Männer; diese führen die Zügel mit Einer Hand, jene mit beiden Händen. Soll das Pferd schneller seyn, so zieht man die Zügel stark an oder schlägt mit denselben; denn durch den Gebrauch der Peitsche glaubt man in Angermanland und Westerbotten dem Pferde einen Schimpf anzuthun.

Der Weg bis Herrskog ist sehr schön: links hat man Wald- und Wiesenthäler, rechts Wasserzüge, die zum Theil Meerbusen sind und deren waldige Vorgebirge und Erdzungen ein recht malerisches Ansehen geben. Man fährt der Kirche Nora vorüber und im Angesichte schöner Thäler, bis man den Gästgifvaregård Herrskog, unweit der Kirche Skog, erreicht. Hier ward um 1¼ Uhr frühe Nachtlager genommen, es war noch so helle, daß man das Thal überschauen konnte, in welchem, rings von hohen Waldbergen und üppigen Wiesen umgeben, das Dörfchen recht freundlich da liegt. Der Gästgifvaregård hat hübsche und geräumige Gastzimmer.

Am 15. Jun. Von Herrskog nach Affja 1¼ Meile; von Affja nach Dockſta 1¼ Meile; von Dockſta nach Spjute 1¼ Meile; von Spjute nach Hörnäs 1¼ Meile; von Hörnäs nach Bröſta 1¼ Meile; von Bröſta nach Täfra 1¼ Meilen. — Zusammen 6¼ Meilen.

Eine herrliche Tagesreise durch den großen Garten Angermanlands. Ein steter Wechsel von reizenden Thälern, von freundlichen Waldhöhen, von Flüssen und Seen, von Hainen, in denen die Nordische Nachtigall, der Talltraſt (eine Droſſelart, Turdus iliacus, Weindroſſel), auch Nattvaka (die Nachtwachende) genannt, flötet. Schnitten nicht hier und da Meerbuſen in die ſchöne Landſchaft ein, man würde ſich nach der niedern Schweiz verſetzt glauben. Und doch ſind die Ufer des Ängerman noch ſchöner (Kap. 24). Unläugbar iſt Ängermanland die ſchönſte Provinz Schwedens. Zwar haben auch andere Provinzen reizende Gegenden, aber keine, kaum das ſchöne Blekingen ausgenommen, deſſen Umfang aber geringe iſt, kann in ihrer geſammten Ausdehnung, ſo ununterbrochen große und ſchöne Naturſcenen aufweiſen, als Ängermanland. Die, im Nordweſten an Jemteland gränzenden, Paſtorate Reſele und Ramſele ausgenommen, habe ich die ganze Provinz durchreiſet und überall, wo ſie angebaut und bewohnt iſt, die anmuthigſten Gegenden gefunden. Freilich ſind in den meiſten Kirchſpielen noch Urbarmachungen eben ſo nothwendig als ausführbar, ohne daß dadurch den beiden Hauptnahrungszweigen, der Viehzucht, die hier ganz als Schweizeriſche Bergs Sennenwirthſchaft getrieben wird, und der Fiſcherey Eintrag geſchehen würde. Die Meerfiſcherey beſchränkt ſich meiſt auf Strömlingsfang; zum Robbenfang iſt wohl Gelegenheit, aber es fehlt an den nöthigen Kenntniſſen und der erforderlichen Art von Böten. Lachsfang wird in den Flüſſen nicht ohne Gewinn getrieben. Ueberhaupt iſt der Ertrag der Fiſcherey in Flüſſen und Landſeen bedeutend. Theer wird bei weitem nicht ſo viel gebrannt, als es die Lokalität verſtattet; in dieſer Hinſicht könnte man von den Weſterbottniern lernen. Die Waldungen liefern viel Balken und Bretter; an wildem Geflügel und anderem Wild iſt Ueberfluß. Korn gewinnt man nicht hinreichend, wiewohl die Äcker einen reichen Ertrag gewähren. Die Förderung des Ackerbaues hemmt der Landhandel, den die Bauern mehr treiben, als das Bedürfniß erheiſcht; dagegen verdankt Ängermanland ſeine Wohlhabenheit größtentheils der Bereitung verſchiedener Arten von Leinewand. Wie Medelpad und Helſingland, ist Angermanland am meisten in den Thälern und an den Flüssen angebaut; die Ufer des Angerman sind die bewohntesten Theile der Provinz; hier wird auch das meiste Korn producirt.

Ich komme zur Reise zurück. Um 6½ Uhr Morgens verließen wir Herrskog. Der Weg führt anfangs neben einem großen Wasserzuge, Storsjö (großer See) genannt, welchen Erdzungen mit Birkengebüsch und kleine Inseln schmücken, dann durch abgeschiedene kleine Thäler mit Gebüschen, Heuscheuern und Höfen, und abermals an einen schönen See, in welchen mächtige Waldhöhen sich senken, deren Abhänge das lichte Grün mit Heuscheuern bedeckter Wiesen bekleidet. Jetzt fährt man aus einem lieblichen Birkenhain in enge Thäler hinab, wo kleine Seen die grünen Matten hoher Waldberge, auf welchen sich zuweilen nackte Felsen zeigen, bespült. Zu beiden Seiten des Weges duften zahllose Veilchen, Tausendschönchen und blühende Akerbär. Nun erweitern sich die Thäler, Dörfer mit stattlichen Bauerhäusern, die aber eine geringere Zahl von Nebengebäuden, als in Helsingland, umgiebt, füllen sie aus. Man fährt der kleinen Kirche Ullånger (Filial des Pastorats Nordingrå) vorüber. Es war Sonntag. Ich besuchte die Kirche, deren Inneres sehr freundlich ist. Den Altar schmücket ein hübsches vergoldetes Schnitzwerk, „Christus, wie er in Gethsemane betet." — Eine gute Strecke jenseits Ullånger's Kirche erreicht man den Gästgifvaregård Aeskja, in dessen Nähe man eine Menge Buden erblickt; hier wird zu gewissen Zeiten Markt gehalten, wo die Bauern gegen Butter und Leinewand allerlei Nothwendigkeits - und Luxuswaaren eintauschen.

Die Straße von Aeskja nach Docksta läuft an einem Theile des großen Meerbusens Ullångersfjärd; hier sieht man mitten im Wasser auf Pfählen kleine Fischerhütten, deren man sich beim Einsalzen der Strömlinge bedient. Oft fährt man an schauerlichen Abgründen hin, wo die Fahrt im Dunkeln, da es an Geländern fehlt, die man überhaupt in Norrland an den Wegen nicht findet, sehr gefährlich ist. Unweit Aeskja kommt man der auf einem Felsen gelegenen Kirche Widbygs gerå vorüber. Zwischen Dockſta und Spjute ſind die erſten beiden Drittheile des Weges minder ſchön; neben Meerbuſen, die hohe Felſen einſchließen, gelangt man an den von wenigem Gebüſch bedeckten Fuß der nackten Felſenwand Skulu, deren ſteile Höhe zu 400 Fuß angegeben wird; an der oberen Wand zeigt ſich eine anſehnliche Höhle; der Gipfel beſteht aus drei Erhöhungen, von denen die nördliche die höchſte iſt. Der Skuluwald ſcheidet Nord- und Süd-Angermanland. Längſt den ſich krümmenden Ufern des lieblichen Skuluſees erreicht man Spjute.

In Nåtra, eine halbe Meile jenſeits Spjute, kamen die Leute eben aus der Kirche; ihre Kleidung verrieth Wohlſtand und Tüchtigkeit; viele, zumal unter den Frauen und Mädchen, waren ſchön. Von Nåtra fuhren wir neben einem freundlichen See über Birkenhöhen nach Finborg, wo wir beim Lagman Lunell das Mittagsmahl einnahmen. Finborg liegt recht hübſch an einem See, den waldbewachſene Höhen und Wieſen umgeben. Um 4¼ Uhr brachen wir wieder auf. Der Weg läuft auf Höhen fort, unter welchen Seen und Wieſen ſich ausbreiten, Erdzungen mit Birkenhainen durchſchneiden die Wieſenzüge, zur Seite erheben ſich Waldberge; die Birke iſt nun vorherrſchend, und viele Kornfelder erblickt man am Wege. Von den Höhen fährt man endlich in ein weites, mit Dörfern ausgefülltes Thal herab, in welchem auch der ſtattliche Gäſtgifsvaregård Hörnäs liegt.

Höchſt maleriſch ſind die fünf Viertel Meilen von Hörnäs nach Bröſta. Am Fuße der Anhöhen, auf welchen man fährt, breiten ſich üppige Wieſen, von jungen Birken beſchattet, aus; dann und wann zieht ſich ein Meerbuſen hinein; links ſteigen hohe Felſen zu den Wolken empor. Bald erreicht man die Kirche Själawad, die, wie die meiſten Norrländiſchen Kirchen, völlig iſolirt liegt. Von hier bis Bröſta wechſeln die herrlichſten, aufs mannigfaltigſte gruppirten Thäler. Von Brößa hat man ein Sechstel Meile zu der Kirche und dem Pfarrhof Arnäs, in einem unbeschreiblich reizenden Thale, dem anmuthigsten meines ganzen gestrigen und heutigen Weges. Die steinerne Kirche, ein Oblongum mit Thurm, ist einfach und freundlich im Aeußern wie im Innern; ein Kreuz schmückt den Altar. In Arnäs sprachen wir beim Propste Deilde'n vor. Da wir nicht übernachten wollten, so mußten wir wenigstens mit einer Mahlzeit fürlieb nehmen (hälls til godo, wie der gastliche Schwede spricht), denn man würde ja Frieden und Freude stören, wenn man, ohne etwas zu genießen, wieder abreisen wollte; das ist die liebevolle Sitte der freundlichen Menschen des Nordens. Nachdem die Kirche besichtigt und ein Paar Stunden im Kreise der höchst liebenswürdigen Familie schnell und angenehm verflossen waren, setzten wir um 9¾ Uhr die Reise fort. Eben ging die Sonne unter, aber der Horizont blieb geröthet und es war fast hell wie am Tage. Abend- und Morgendämmerung sind durch keine Dunkelheit getrennt, und man kann nicht sehen, wann die eine aufhört und die andere beginnt, denn die erstere verschwindet in die letztere. — Reizend ist der Weg bis Täfra: die herrlichsten Birken- und Felsenthäler wechseln mit einander; auch über einen Waldstrom, der viele Fälle macht, führt die Straße. Unweit Arnäs kommt man dem Wege vorbei, wo das Meer zum Marktplatz von Strömsund geht: hier wird im Junius ein großer Markt gehalten, wo die Bauern ihre Leinwand und Butter gegen Waaren oder baares Geld absetzen. Um 11¾ Uhr langten wir in dem geräumigen Gästgifvaregård an, wo wir übernachteten, die Zimmer waren nett und freundlich, die Betten trefflich, Bewirthung und Bedienung ließen nichts zu wünschen übrig. Auch hier fanden wir ganz das heitere, sanfte und gutmüthige Wesen der Angermanländer, ihre Dienstfertigkeit und Behendigkeit. Alles, was sie thun, geht ihnen schnell und leicht von Statten, und ist doch tüchtig und ordentlich; ihre Höflichkeit und Gefälligkeit gegen Fremde kennt keine Gränzen, erstere ist besonders groß; von Allen, denen wir begegneten, empfingen wir Grüße; selbst im heftigsten Regen zogen die Männer ihre Hüthe ab.

Die heutige Tagesreise hat mich durch einige Kirchspiele geführt, in welchen die größte Leinwandsfabrikation Statt findet, insbesondere die meiste feinere oder Prämienleinewand verfertiget wird. Ich will daher jetzt erzählen, wie dieser sehr beträchtliche Nahrungszweig des Landes zuerst begründet, gefördert und vervollkommnet wurde, bis er endlich die Höhe erreichte, deren er sich gegenwärtig erfreuet. Zugleich werde ich Einiges über die Bereitung selbst erwähnen.

Schon zu Anfang des 16ten Jahrhunderts wurde in Angermanland ein ansehnlicher Flachsbau und eine nicht unbedeutende Weberey getrieben, doch war die gefertigte Leinwand meist gröberer Art. Der Flachs war immer von vorzüglicher Güte, und man kannte schon lange eine vorzügliche, freilich im Laufe der Zeit vervollkommte Bereitungsart desselben, die unter dem Namen der Norrländischen bekannt ist, und die eben so wie das feinere Weben, die Regierung gegenwärtig auch in den mittleren und südlichen Provinzen allgemein zu machen sucht. Die Güte des Flachses brachte einige Angermanländerinnen, um die Mitte des 18ten Jahrhunderts auf den Gedanken: der Norrländische Flachs möge sich wohl auch zur Bereitung feinerer Gespinnste eignen. Der erste Versuch wurde im Pastorat Nätra von einer Bauersfrau, Sigrid Olsdotter in Wik gemacht; der Versuch gelang ausnehmend. Ihre Tochter, die Wittwe Marta Olsdotter in Kjästad und die Frau des Gästgifvaregärd Stenslyft daselbst, Chr. Bröms, folgten nach. Spinnschulen wurden angelegt, die erste von der Pröpstin Norberg in Nätra, und Nätra wurde der Stammsitz der feinen Linnenweberey, und ist bis auf den heutigen Tag der Hauptsitz derselben geblieben, von wo sie sich aber über mehrere Kirchspiele, zumal des nördlichen Angermanland, verbreitet hat. Die Regierung ertheilte jenen ehrenwerthen Frauen Belohnungen: silberne Becher und Kannen; F. Sigrid erhielt 1756 *) die erste, nämlich eine große silberne Kanne, die mir von der verstorbenen Sigrid Tochter, der jetzigen Gästgifverska in Brösta, gezeigt wurde, nebst einer silbernen Medaille (von 1751), die an der einen Seite des Königs Adolph Friedrichs Bild, an der andern Seite das Bild eines Weibes mit einem Spinnrocken und die Inschrift trägt:

til heder för den qvinna,
som sint och snällt kan spinna.

(zur Ehre für das Weib, was fein geschickt spinnen kann).

Solche Becher, Kannen und besonders Medaillen wurden öfter vertheilt. Mehrere Predigerfrauen wirkten für die Verbreitung und Vervollkommnung dieses Nahrungszweiges auf eine sehr rühmliche Weise. Die Sache wurde Gegenstand der Berathung der Reichsstände, und so kam es dahin, daß auf die Bereitung feiner Leinwand, nach gewissen Klassen, Prämien ausgesetzt wurden, die nun schon seit mehr denn 50 Jahre aus Staatsmitteln ausgezahlt werden und viel dazu beigetragen haben, die Kunst zu dem Grade der Vollkommenheit zu steigern, auf welchem sie sich jetzt in Ångermanland befindet. (Auch für Wolle- und Baumwollengespinnst giebt die Krone Prämien, die im mittlern Schweden, insbesondere Dalekarlien, jährlich sehr bedeutend sind). Der brave Landshöfding, Pehr Abraham Örnsköld, hat während seiner Verwaltung des Läns von Westernorrland in den Jahren 1762 bis 1769 den Flachsbau, wie die Leinwandsbereit

*) Nach einer andern Angabe hatte die Mutter des berühmten Orientalisten, Norberg in Lund, Christina Wallanger, Gattin des Länsman Athats Norberg in Nätra, bereits 1752, als Prämie für feines Gespinnst und Gewebe, welches sie zuerst getrieben haben soll, eine silberne Kanne erhalten; auch wurden ihr noch ein Paar andere Silbergeschenke zu theil.

·ung ausnehmend gefördert; 1764 reisten sogar, auf Kosten des Manufacturcomtoirs, Lehrende von Dorf zu Dorf. Örnsköld's Versuche, die Kunst auch in Medelpad und Jemteland zu einem gewissen Grad der Allgemeinheit und Vollkommenheit zu bringen, blieben ohne dauernden Erfolg.

Die feinere Leinewand, für welche Prämien gegeben werden, ist in 8 Klassen getheilt. Zur ersten Klasse gehört alle Leinwand, welche im Aufzug (Ratte) von 2720 bis 2920 Enden (Fäden) hat oder im Weberkamm (väfsked) wenigstens 1600 doppelte Fäden beträgt; jede der folgenden Klassen wird mit 200 Enden (Fäden) erhöhet. So bestimmt die königl. Verordnung vom 22. Februar 1762, die die Prämien feststellte. Ferner muß alle Prämienleinewand wenigstens ⅞ Ellen breit, fest, weiß gebleicht und darf nicht zerrissen seyn. Die Güte innerhalb der Klasse selbst bestimmt das mehr oder minder ebene Gewebe, ob nämlich jeder Faden dem andern gleich ist. Die Prämie beträgt in der ersten Klasse für die Elle ⅜ Bankschillinge; die Erhöhung für jede der folgenden Klassen beträgt ¼ Schill. Banco für die Elle; die Prämien sind mithin im jetzigen Münzwerth nur unbedeutend. Die Beurtheilung und Stempelung geschieht durch eine Commission, welche im Gemeindehause drei Mal im Sommer, jedes Mal auf einen oder zwei Tage zusammentritt, der Pastor führt den Vorsitz; der Länsman und zwei Nämndemän (Bauernbeisitzer des Häradsgerichts) sind Mitglieder. Die Prämien werden in Zetteln ausgegeben, welche folgendermaßen lauten: „NN. hat gefertiget und aufgewiesen — Ellen Leinewand — ⅞ breit und von — Faden, von gehöriger Güte, wofür die Prämie von — Schill. die Elle, bewilliget worden, zusammen Werth —" (Unterschriften der Prüfungsbehörde). Diese Zettel werden statt baares Geld in Steuern angenommen und gelten auch im gemeinen Leben völlig gleich mit der übrigen curirenden Zettelmünze des Reichs. Mit der Zuerkennung der Prämie ist ferner die Stempelung verbunden: ein Zettel, der die Klasse anzeigt, zu welcher die Leinwand gehört, auch unterschrieben und besiegelt ist, wird auf jedem Stücke befestiget; nach dem Inhalt dieses Zettels geschieht der Verkauf. Ueberdieß wird von jedem Stück Prämienleinewand ein Probeläppchen abgenommen, mit dem Stempel des Stücks versehen und ans königl. Kammercollegium in Stockholm eingesandt. Im Jahr 1817 wurden 163,882 Ellen Prämienleinewand gefertiget und 3001 Rthlr. 17 Schill. 7 Rundst. Prämiengelder gezahlt; im Jahr 1818. 3181 Rthlr. 16 Schill. 8 Rundst. Banko. Den jährlichen Ertrag des Verkaufs von Prämienleinewand rechnet man zu 140,000 Bankthalern, wovon man nur 3000 Rthlr. für Zuthaten abzuziehen hat. Noch bedeutender ist der reine Ertrag der groben Leinewand. Ein Frauenzimmer kann jährlich an‧ 100 Rthlr. durch Leinewandweben verdienen.

Die meiste Prämienleinewand wird gefertiget im Kirchspiel Nätra, dann in Sidensjö, Själawad, Arnäs, Widbygerå, Nordingrå, Ullånger, Grundsunda. Die meiste ist von der 2ten, 3ten und 4ten Klasse, ziemlich viel auch aus der ersten und 5ten, aus der 6ten und 7ten sehr wenig. Leinewand der 8ten Klasse ist nur ein Mal in Nätra gewebt worden; sie war an wirklicher Güte nicht viel besser als die der 7ten Klasse; denn nicht selten muß die höhere Klasse, um der inneren Güte willen, im Verkauf einer niedrigeren Klasse nachstehen. Die Preise sind nicht jedes Jahr gleich; doch die höchsten, welche bis zum Jahr 1817 gezahlt worden, waren: für die 1ste Klasse 40 Schill. bis 1 Rthlr. 24 Schill.; für die 2te 1 Rthlr. bis 1 Rthlr. 32 Schill.; für die 3te 1 Rthlr. 8 Schill. bis 2 Rthlr.; für die 4te 1½ Rthlr. bis 2½ Rthlr.; für die 5te 2 Rthlr. 32 Schill. bis 3 Rthlr. 8 Schill.; für die 6te 3 Rthlr. bis 3 Rthlr. 8 Schill.; für die 7te 3 Rthlr. 8 Schill. bis 3 Rthlr. 16 Schill.; für die 8te 3 Rthlr. 16 Schill. Menge und Güte der jährlich verfertigten Prämienleinewand sind sehr verschieden, sie hängen von der größern oder geringeren Weichheit des Flachses ab; hat der Flachs nicht die gehörige Weichheit, so fällt das Linnen gröber aus und kommt nicht zur

Prämie. Wiewohl Angermanland viel Flachs bauet, so zieht man doch zur Bereitung feinster Leinewand den Russischen Flachs vor und verwendet den einheimischen meistens für gröbere Sorten. Diese werden in einer sehr viel größeren Quantität, als die feinen Arten, verfertigt. Das Stück Prämienleinewand enthält 80 bis 100 Ellen. Nicht immer wird die Prämienleinewand in dem Kirchspiele gestempelt, in welchem sie gefertiget worden, denn häufig wird sie vor geschehener Stempelung von Handelsbauern anderer Kirchspiele aufgekauft und nun in diesen Kirchspielen gestempelt. Dieser Aufkauf geschieht besonders von den Bauern aus Nätra, daher ist die Zahl der dort gestempelten Stücke so unverhältnißmäßig groß; doch auch abgesehen hiervon, wird in Nätra die meiste Prämienleinewand verfertiget.

Die Angermanländische Prämienleinewand übertrifft die Holländische an Festigkeit und Dauerhaftigkeit, wovon zum Theil die Ursache darin zu finden ist, daß jene nicht künstlich gebleicht wird; indeß steht sie an Weiße und Appretur, weniger an Feinheit, der vorzüglicheren ausländischen Leinewand nach.

Die Weber spinnen nur einen kleinen Theil des Garnes, welches sie gebrauchen, selbst, das übrige kaufen sie. Das meiste und schönste Garn wird in Arnäs bereitet; es ist so fein, daß es zu einer 9ten und 10ten Klasse benutzt werden könnte *). Für das Garn werden keine Prämien ertheilt.

Das Weben wird am meisten von Frauenzimmern, doch auch von Männern, aber von beiden Geschlechtern nur in den Wintermonaten, vom November oder December bis April, getrieben; die übrige Zeit des Jahres arbeiten Männer und Weiber draußen. Im Durchschnitt webt eine Familie jährlich 2 bis 3 Stücke, jedes von 80 bis 100 Ellen. Die Gesundheit leidet durch diese Beschäftigung nicht; mögen auch die Weber etwas

----

*) Hylphers in seiner Beschreibung von Angermanland S. 233 sagt, daß schon damals (im Jahr 1758) Garn in Nätra verfertiget wurde, welches in 1 Loth 4000 Ellen enthielt.

reichlicher seyn, als die übrigen Bauern, so sehen sie doch kei= nesweges bleich und kränklich aus. Die Weberey ist ein für die langen dunkeln Winter sehr wichtiger Nahrungszweig. Wie er, nach der Behauptung Einiger, dem Ackerbau Eintrag thue, ist nicht einzusehen, denn so wie man jetzt das Weben betreibt, werden die Ackerarbeiten nicht vernachlässiget. Wenn also im nördlichen Angermanland des uncultivirten und cultivirbaren Landes mehr ist, als im südlichen Theile dieser Landschaft, so ist dieses aus andern Ursachen als aus der Weberey abzuleiten.

Vor 12 Jahren sandte die Regierung 27 Dalekarlierinnen nach Nord=Angermanland, um dort das Weben zu lernen; zu gleicher Zeit kamen Dalekarlier, um sich in Verfertigung der We= berbäume, in Bereitung des Flachses und dergl. zu unterrichten. Die Pastoren, welche zum Beßten dieser Leute sehr thätig wa= ren, erhielten königliche Dank= und Belobungsschreiben. Neuer= dings hat man Angermanländische Weberinnen nach Wermeland und andern Theilen des Reichs requirirt; aber es hat schwer ge= halten, Frauenzimmer für diesen Zweck zu engagiren und manche Aufforderungen mußten unbefolgt bleiben; denn die Mädchen dieses Landes verlassen ungern ihre Heimath. Indeß sind an mehreren Orten des Reichs Lehrinstitute für Norrländische Flachs= bereitung, Spinnerey und Weberey angelegt worden; eines der ansehnlicheren besteht in Gårdsby bei Wexiö in Småland, wo Ulla Widengren aus Arnäs als Lehrerin angestellt ist und ein Gehalt von 500 Rthlr. von der Krone bezieht.

Arnäs ist das nördlichste Kirchspiel in Angermanland, wo die feinere Leinewand in Menge bearbeitet wird; in dem nörd= licher gelegenen Kirchspiel Grundsunda beschäftigen sich damit etwa 4 bis 5 Familien, wogegen dort desto mehr gröbere Haus= leinewand verfertiget wird. In den Pastoraten Nordmaling und Umeå wird nur sehr wenig zum Verkauf gewonnen, und sind bisher keine Prämien verlangt worden.

Wenn gleich in einzelnen Jahren die feine Leinewand so schlecht bezahlt worden ist, daß das Weben nicht nur keinen Ge=

II.   E winn, sondern Verlust brachte, so hat doch, wie schon oben bemerkt, im Allgemeinen durch die Bereitung der Prämienleinewand, die meist nach Hernösand und auf den Landmärkten abgesetzt wird, der Wohlstand sehr zugenommen; leider auch mit dem Wohlstand der Luxus und der Eigennutz. Indeß sind Luxus, Eigennutz und Unredlichkeit weit mehr durch den Handelsgeist der Bauern gewachsen, der freilich durch die Weberstühle neue Nahrung erhielt. Ohne Landhandel können zwar diese Kirchspiele nicht bestehen, denn die Entfernung bis zur nächsten Stadt beträgt 10 (Schwedische) Meilen; aber der Handel könnte viel beschränkter seyn, als er ist. Die meisten Handelsbauern findet man in Själawad und Näfra, dort 50, hier 30; in dem volkreichern Arnäs zählt man nur 6 bis 7, und etwa eben so viele in Sidensjö. Sie handeln mit den Producten des Landes, die sie nach Upsala, Stockholm ꝛc. führen, und wofür sie dort allerlei Waaren einkaufen. Die Bauern von Själawad kaufen auch junge Pferde in Norwegen, füttern sie auf und verkaufen sie dann wieder. Daneben durchziehen auch die handelnden Westgothen mit ihren verderblichen Luxuswaaren das wohlhabende Angermanland. — Bis auf Gustav III. war der Landhandel beschränkt. Als aber die kleinen Städte diese Beschränkung zum großen Nachtheil des Landmannes mißbrauchten, wurde letzterem verstattet, nicht blos die Erzeugnisse seines Bodens, sondern auch die von ihm oder seinen Nachbaren gefertigten Fabrikate aller Art nach einem jeden Theile des Reiches zu verkaufen. Diese Erlaubniß ist späterhin sehr gemißbraucht worden, und bringt der Landkaufmann oft mehr Waaren zusammen, als der Stadtkaufmann, ohne die Abgaben zu zahlen, die dieser zahlt. Der Landhandel ward nun allgemeiner, zumal in den Provinzen, in welchen es wenige oder gar keine Städte giebt; auch Bauernsöhne, Knechte und Dienstjungen trieben nun Handel, wozu sich nämlich letztere eine gewisse Zeit ausbedungen. Durch einen solchen übertriebenen Landhandel litt der Ackerbau, und Gewinngeist und böses Beispiel verderbten

die Sitten. Möchte bald ein strenges Gesetz diesen argen Miß-
brauch hemmen! Uebrigens dürfen die Landhändler eigentliche
Kaufmannswaaren, z. B. Tuch, Wein, Spezereien ꝛc. nicht feil
bieten; dagegen findet man bei ihnen Tabak, Salz, Papier ꝛc.
Jedes Kirchspiel hat seinen eigenen, unter Genehmigung des
Háradsgerichts angenommenen, und vom Landshöfding mit Vollmacht versehenen, Handwerker; meistens sind es aber nur Maurer,
Schuster, Schneider und Schmiede, falls nicht ein Landshöfding,
nach Maaßgabe der Localität, mit Genehmigung des Königes,
auch andere Handwerker zuläßt. Tischler- und Wagenmacher-
Arbeit kann jeder Landbewohner für sich und zum Verkauf verfertigen. Auch Schmiedearbeiten fertigt der Bauer zum Verkauf. In vielen Schwedischen Landschaften und überall in Norrland bereitet jeder Hof, was er bedarf, selbst; auch Walmar,
oder grobes Tuch, in welches der Bauer fast in ganz Schweden
sich kleidet. In allen Provinzen webt man Leinewand, baum-
wollene und wollene Zeuge; unter den ländlichen Industrie-
zweigen Schwedens ist die Weberey der bedeutendste. Ohne
die Fabrikstühle, rechnet man jetzt in Schweden 300,000 Privat-
Webestühle, die jährlich 18 Millionen Ellen liefern, zur Hälfte
Leinewand, und zur Hälfte Baumwollen- und Wollenzeug. Die
Prämien für Baumwollengespinnst betrugen in Fahlu-Län
(Dalekarlien) im Jahr 1817. 3419 Rthlr. 19 Schill. 1 Rundst.
Banko für 386,396 Strenge. Auch Gestrikland, Jemteland,
Ostgothland, Westgothland, Småland, Halland und andere Pro-
vinzen weben viel zum Verkauf *); die Wollenzeuge von Win-

*) Gefleborgs Län fertigte im Jahr 1818 1 Million 49,000,
Skaraborgs Län 500,000, Elfsborgs Län über 1 Million
206,000, Calmare Län über 908,000 Ellen; das einzige Marks-
Härad in Elfsborgs Län webte im Jahr 1817. 550,000 Ellen.
Am 3. Febr. 1819 bewilligte der König für Leinewandweben in Småland und Blekingen, späterhin auch in Wermeland, Prämien, und zwar
also, daß, wer das erste Mal gute Prämienleinewand ersten Grades
nach Norrländischer Weise selbst gesponnen und gewebt hat, 4 Bank-

E 2

gåler in Södermanland sind berühmt (Kap. 33); an mehreren
Orten werden Nanking und andere Sommerzeuge verfertigt. —
An Flachs gewann man in ganz Schweden, im Jahr 1817.
150,000 Liespfund; überdieß wird viel fremder Flachs eingeführt. Salpeter wird, insbesondere in Nordschweden, viel bereitet, im Jahr 1817. 11,000 Liespfund, im Jahr 1818. 9750
Liespfund; Salpeterhütten zählte man im Jahr 1817. 1728, die
aber nicht alle im Gange waren. Auch Leder bereitet der Lands-
mann. — Die Papierfabrication stieg im Jahr 1819 zum Werth
von 230,000 Bankthalern; viel Schwedisches Papier geht ins
Ausland. — Landjahrmärkte werden an vielen Orten gehalten.
Beim Anfang des Marktes wird der Marktfriede abgekündigt,
also daß alle Uebertretungen des Gesetzes während des Marktes
außer der gewöhnlichen noch mit einer besonderen Strafe, wegen
des Marktfriedens, belegt werden.

Ich habe oben erwähnt, daß um die Leinwandsbereitung in
Angermanland sich der Landshöfding Örnsköld besondere Verdienste erworben habe. Ich füge hinzu: die vorzüglichen Einrichtungen, deren sich die Provinzen Angermanland, Medelpad
und Jemteland erfreuen, und der Wohlstand, den man meistens
dort findet, sind großentheils Örnsköld's Werk. Während seiner Verwaltung in den Jahren 1762 bis 1769 durchreisete
Örnsköld fast jedes einzelne Kirchspiel und vollführte dort in
eigner Person, was sonst Andern übertragen zu werden pflegt,
um selbst Land und Menschen näher kennen zu lernen und auf
letztere persönlich einzuwirken; er selbst gab Anweisungen, ver-
theilte eine faßliche Druckschrift, die die Verbesserung des Ackerbaues bezweckte, indem sie auf die entdeckten Fehler sorgfältig
Rücksicht nahm, ließ durch Vermessungen den Besitz eines Jeden
genau bestimmen und vom fremden Eigenthum durch feste Gränzen sondern, veranstaltete in fast 400 Dörfern Separation der

schillinge, ist die Leinwand noch feiner, 6 Bankschillinge für die Elle als
Prämie empfangen soll.

Gemeinheiten, ließ an vielen Orten, mittelst Verabredung mit den Kirchspielen, von den Aeckern die Steine, womit sie übersäet waren, wegführen, das überflüssige Wasser von Feldern und Wiesen ableiten, Moräste austrocknen, Wälder, die man bisher als Schutzwehr gegen die Kälte betrachtet, aber deren Sümpfe und Wildnisse die häufigen Nachtfröste mit veranlaßt hatten, lichten, und brachte es auf diese Weise dahin, daß die Nachtfröste ganz ausblieben, oder doch seltener und minder verderblich wurden, und der Ertrag der Felder auf das Sechsfache stieg. Er förderte die Aussaat des Roggens, der dem Froste weniger ausgesetzt ist, wie die Gerste, und zwar als Herbstsaat, der Roggen gab das 18te, die Gerste das 20ste, und der wenige Waizen, der hier und da gebaut wurde, das 26ste Korn. Viele Urbarmachungen wurden vorgenommen, eine Menge neuer Höfe entstanden; die Population wuchs auf eine dem Staat wahrhaft nützliche Weise; denn alle fühlten sich wohl und glücklich in ihrer Lage. Der Kartoffelbau war bisher wenig gekannt, Örnsköld führte ihn allgemein ein und war anfangs oft selbst beim Legen und Aufnehmen der Kartoffeln lehrend zugegen, wo er denn auch Anweisung zur vortheilhaftesten Benutzung gab; auch in Åsele Lappmark wurde nun der Kartoffelbau von Ångermanland aus eingeführt. Jetzt werden die Kartoffeln in allen Theilen von Norrland, in allen Lappmarken, selbst über den Polarkreis hinaus, angepflanzt, und gewähren überall einen äußerst reichlichen Ertrag. Den Bottnischen Städten verschaffte Örnsköld das verlorne unbeschränkte Stapelrecht wieder. Dieser und vieler anderer Wohlthaten ungeachtet, die der einsichtsvolle und thätige Mann seiner Statthalterschaft erwies, blieb Örnsköld nicht ohne mannigfaltige Anklagen und Verfolgungen. Aber die gerechte Nachwelt hat dankbar seine Verdienste anerkannt. Im Jahre 1808 ließ die Geistlichkeit eine Denkmünze prägen, die auf der Vorderseite Örnsköld's Brustbild, mit der Unterschrift, in Schwedischer Sprache: „Freiherr Pehr Abraham Örnsköld, Landshöfding, Commandeur des Königl. Nordstern-Ordens," zeigt; auf der Rückseite lieset man in einem Kranze von Eichenlaub: „Schöpfer der Nahrungszweige (foslrare af näringarna) in Wester-Norrland;" unten: „Die Dankbarkeit der Einwohner" (inbyggarnes erkänsla). „1808." — Zugleich mit der Denkmünze ward eine kleine Druckschrift: „Nachricht über Örnsbölds Verwaltung von Westernorrland. Hernösand 1808. 31 S. 8." ausgegeben, — aus welcher ich das Mitgetheilte entlehnt habe.

Örnsböld wurde im Jahr 1769 als Landshöfding nach Södermanland versetzt; als er 3 Jahre hernach zum Commandeur des Nordstern-Ordens ernannt wurde, erkohr er sich zum Ordenswahlspruch „virtuto niti," welches der Grundsatz seines ganzen Lebens gewesen war. Er starb in Nyköping am 16. April 1791, ohne männliche Descendenten. Sanft ruhe des Biedermannes Asche!

***

Am 16. Jun. Von Täfra nach Önsla 1½ Meile; von Önsla nach Afva 2 Meilen; von Afva nach Lefvar 1½ Meile; von Lefvar nach Angersjö 1½ Meile; von Angersjö nach Sörmjöla 1½ Meile; von Sörmjöla nach Stöckssö 1½ Meilen. — Zusammen 10½ Meilen.

Zwischen Täfra und Önsla ist die erste Meile meist Wald, dann kommt man an den reißenden Gideå-Elf, über welchen, neben schönen Wasserfällen, eine Brücke führt; der Fluß strömt zwischen hohen mit Wald bewachsenen Felsenufern, und hat in seinem Bette ein Paar freundliche Inselchen; an der Brücke hat man eine Lachsfischerey errichtet. In der Nähe liegt der Gesundbrunnen Gideåbacken. Weiter aufwärts trifft man ein Eisenbruk und die vor etwa 10 Jahren gestiftete Kapelle Gideå, neben welcher ein Comminister wohnt. Zu der 2 Meilen entfernten Mutterkirche Arnäs kann man von der Kapelle nur zu Fuß oder zu Pferde gelangen. Am jenseitigen Ufer des

Gideå fährt man einen hohen Berg hinan und erreicht bald Dombäck, wo wir beim Kronvoigt Assessor Svedbom eine frohe Stunde verlebten. — Von Dombäck läuft die Straße längs des Flusses Husom, der anfangs ruhig zwischen Wiesenufern dahin fließt, dann aber Fälle bildet, die freilich weder so zahlreich noch so furchtbar sind, wie die des Gideå; eine Brücke führt über den Husom.

Eine Strecke jenseits Önska fährt man der Kirche Grundsunda vorüber. Dann hat man Wald, Felsen, enge Thäler und ein Paar schöne Meerbusen, Degerfjärd und Hämmarsundsfjärd. Mit letzterem beginnt das Pastorat Nordmaling, welches in administrativer Hinsicht schon Theil des Län Umeå oder Westerbottens ist; in juridischer Beziehung gehört aber das Pastorat noch zu Ångermanland. Die Sitten sind in Nordmaling meistens die der Westerbottnier. Ein vom Landshöfding Örnsköld 1769 errichteter Stein bezeichnet die Gränze der Län Hernösand und Umeå.

Von Asva kommt man, neben dem See, Fluß und Dorf Asp, nach Lögde, wo eine Fähre über den, gleich allen Flüssen Nord-Ångermanlands und Westerbottens, aus den Lappmarken herabkommenden Fluß Lögde führt; am jenseitigen Ufer liegt das Dorf Mo. Nach einer kleinen Strecke erreicht man einen zweiten Arm des Lögde, über diesen führt eine Brücke bei Olofsfors, einem Bruk mit 2 Stabhämmern, 4 Stabeisenheerden, einem Hochofen und einer feinblätterigen Sägemühle. Das Bruk gehört dem Kaufmann Paull in Stockholm. Jenseits Olofsfors erreicht man die Kirche Nordmaling, in deren Nähe man den weiten Meerbusen Nordmalingsfjärd überblickt; nach ¼ Meile Weges folgt der Gästgifvarestård Lefvar. Die Gegend ist jetzt schon mehr eben, aber auch weniger schön. Wiesen und niedriger Birken- und Nadelwald wechseln mit Kornfeldern. Erst vor 10 Tagen hatte man gesät und schon waren die zarten Hahne fast eine Viertelelle hoch. Asva ist der Schlußstein des großen Gartens von Ångermanland. Wester- und Norrbotten haben wohl auch manche schöne Gegend, zumal in der Nähe des Polarzirkels; aber mit Angermanland kann auch die schönste Gegend Westerbottens kaum verglichen werden.

In Nordmaling (wo im Jahr 1820 ein Pastorat errichtet wurde) sprachen wir beim Pastor Oldberg vor. Die alte, in späterer Zeit erneuerte Kirche, deren einfaches und freundliches Innere so eben durch eine von Strand in Stockholm gefertigte, 2000 Bankthaler kostende neue Orgel von 10 Registern noch verschönert worden war, ward besehen, ein gastliches Mahl eingenommen und um 5 Uhr Nachmittags die Reise fortgesetzt.

¾ Meile von der Kirche erreicht man den Fluß Öre, der aus Lycksele-Lappmark herab kommt, wo er eine mächtige Katarakte bildet (Kap. 23); hier sind seine Fälle zwischen Waldufern zwar zahlreich, aber wenig bedeutend. Ueber den Öre führt eine Brücke. Bis ans jenseitige Ufer, wo das Dorf Långed liegt, waren im letzten Finnischen Kriege die Russen vorgedrungen, als sie die Nachricht von der Landung der Schweden bei Ratam, im Rücken der Russischen Armee, vernahmen und nun plötzlich den Rückzug antraten. — Ueber einen schönen Wiesenbach durch Wald gelangt man bald zur Station Angersjö, dem letzten Dorfe im Pastorat Nordmaling. In Angersjö lag ein ganzes Russisches Corps 13 Wochen lang. Die Einwohner flüchteten zu den Bergen, aber auch dorthin folgten die Feinde und raubten ihnen das Wenige, was sie noch gerettet hatten. Aller Anforderungen ungeachtet, haben die Bewohner von Angersjö (so klagten sie) keine Unterstützung erhalten, wiewohl in Westerbotten ansehnliche Summen vertheilt worden sind. Die Bauern in Angersjö sind daher blutarm und in Schulden versunken. Im vorigen Jahre hatte das Dorf durch Mißwachs sehr gelitten; aus Finnland hatte man Korn kaufen müssen.

Von Angersjö nach Sörmjöla hat man meist bergigen Waldweg, hier und da unterbrechen kleine Wiesen den niedrigen Birkenwald; auf der Mitte des Weges fährt man, bei Hörnefors, auf einer Brücke über den Hörnefluß. Hier ließen sich im letzten Kriege die Schweden überrumpeln, vertheidigten sich hernach aber mit desto größerer Tapferkeit. Das Bruk Hörnefors hat einen Nagelhammer und eine Sägemühle; die kleine hübsche Brukskirche liegt hart am Wege. — Hier ist nun ganz Westerbotten, welches mit dem Pastorat Umeå, eine Viertelmeile hinter Angersjö, beginnt. Eine, vom Meere an bis aufwärts gegen Lappland, im Walde ausgehauene, hier und da mit Steinmauern versehene Linie, die vorhin alle 3 Jahre erneuert werden mußte, bezeichnet die alte Gränze der Provinzen Ångermanland und Westerbotten.

Um 10 Uhr fuhren wir von Sörmjöla weiter. Man hat viel Wald, einige Dörfer und Kolonistenhöfe (nybyggen); das Land ist eben und sandig. Mein Skjutsbonde war ein Mädchen, das nach Westerbottnischer Sitte, über die schlichte eigengemachte Kleidung ein mit Franzen besetztes wollenes Tuch trug. — Um 12 Uhr waren wir in Stöcksjön, wo wir, freilich nicht am besten übernachteten. Die Sonne war untergegangen, aber, des bewölkten Horizonts ungeachtet, war es hell wie am Tage. Man findet nun schon in Bauerhöfen und selbst in den kleinen Gasthöfen viele silberne Geräthe, besonders Becher und Kannen.

Neunzehntes Kapitel.

Aufreise in Westerbotten.

Stadt Umeå. — Seeweg nach Wasa. — Län Umeå. — Umeå's Gesundbrunnen; Brunnengottesdienst. — Kornbau. — Die Eisennächte im August. — Die Gefechte von Säfvar und Ratan 1809. — Bygdeå. — Reinlichkeit der Bauernhäuser. — Dorfgottesdienst ohne Kirche. — Die Leser. — Das Volk der Westbottnier. — Die Ehrennächte. — Skellefteå; prächtige Kirche; Kirchstuben. — Byske. — Län Norrbottn. — Fluß, Stadt, Pastorat Piteå. — Luleå. — Råneå. — Bettel- und Weide-Lappen. — Hvitån. — Fluß Calix. — Das Lager bei Nåsbyn; Regiment Westerbotten. — Gottesdienst in Neder-Calix.

Am 17. Jun. Von Stöckfjön nach Umeå ½ Meilen; von Umeå nach Tafle ¼ Meile; von Tafle nach Säfvar 1,¼ Meilen; von Säfvar nach Djekneboda 1⅐ Meile; von Djekneboda nach Rickleå 1¼ Meile; von Rickleå nach Gumboda 1¼ Meile; von Gumboda nach Grimmark 1¼ Meile. — Zusammen 9,₁₄ Meilen.

Je mehr man sich dem Umeå-Strom, über welchen man auf Ruderböten zur Stadt fährt, nähert, desto bewohnter wird die Gegend; die Dörfer, welche die Ufer des Umeå bedecken, sind sehr groß, z. B. Röbäck, dem man vorüber fährt, zählt 70 Bauern. Große Dörfer sind Westerbotten eigen, während in Ångermanland die einzelnen Höfe vorherrschen. Indeß findet man auch in Westerbotten die großen Dörfer nur an den großen Strömen. Um die Dörfer her breiten sich fette Wiesenflächen aus, die mit Heuscheunen wie besäet sind, deren jeder Bauerhof 9 bis 10 hat; die Wiesen sind in längliche Quadrate abgetheilt.

Am dießseitigen schönen Wiesenufer des Umeå liegt das Fährhaus, jenseits auf einem sandigen kahlen Hügelrücken die kleine Stadt Umeå, die mit ihren hölzernen Häusern einen wenig anziehenden Anblick darbietet. Der Strom ist bei der Stadt 450 Ellen breit, abwärts theilt ihn die ¼ Meile lange, bewohnte Insel Ön in zwei Arme, deren kleinerer schiffbar ist; er kann hier Fahrzeuge von 60 bis 70 Lasten tragen. Eine Meile von der Stadt abwärts bildet der Strom einen großen Busen, Umeåfjård genannt, und fällt in zwei Armen, die die Insel Obola umfließen, in das Bottnische Meer. Ueber den westlichen Busen, vestra Qvarken, wo eine Feuerbake unterhalten wird, im Süden der Insel Holmön, und über den östlichen Qvarken führt der nächste Seeweg nach Österbotten, 12 Meilen von Umeå nach Wasa *), doch findet eine regelmäßige Passage nicht Statt. Im Winter fährt man zu Eise nach Holmön; die weitere Fahrt nach Österbotten ist aber gefährlich, denn die breite östliche Quarken friert selten vor Februar zu, und auch dann ist er oft mit Gefahr zu passiren; indeß haben die Bewohner der Insel Holmön ihre Zeichen, woran sie die Sicherheit des Eises erkennen. Bei Schiffbrüchen und andern Unglücksfällen haben diese Inselbewohner sich stets sehr edel benommen und vielen Menschen das Leben gerettet **). — Im März 1809 ging ein Russisches Corps unter Barclay de Tolly von Wasa aus über den gefrornen Meerbusen nach Umeå: zwei Nächte lagerte es auf Klippen im Meer, die dritte Nacht auf dem Umeåstrom.

---

*) Der gewöhnliche und bequemere Weg ist folgender: zu Lande von Umeå nach Ostnäs 1½ Meile; von da zur See nach Holmön 1½ Meile; auf Holmön bis Hallören 1½ Meile; über Östra Qvarken nach den Wallö-Inseln 3 Meilen; nach Bjortön 2 Meilen; nach Wasa 5 Meilen. — Zusammen 14½ Meilen. — Der Landweg von Umeå nach Wasa über Torneå beträgt 94 Meilen.

**) S. Hülphers Westerbotten S. 43.

Seit 1765 hat die Stadt Umeå ununterbrochen Stapels gerechtigkeit genossen. Ihren Hafen hat sie unmittelbar neben den Häusern; die Wassertiefe beträgt gewöhnlich zehn Fuß; hier sind die Schiffsbrücken und Vorrathshäuser. Am südlichen Ufer findet man mehrere kleine Schiffswerfte, auf welchen besonders im Amerikanischen Kriege viel Schiffe gebauet wurden. — Oberhalb der Stadt ist der Strom nicht schiffbar, sondern so reißend, daß selbst das Flößen und die Lachsfischerey dort jährlich mehreren Menschen das Leben zu kosten pflegt.

Die Stadt ward im Jahr 1620 angelegt. Sie ist regelmäßig gebauet; aber nur die Hauptstraße ist, seit 1781, gepflastert, selbst der Markt ist ungepflastert. Die Einwohnerzahl betrug im Jahr 1815 nur 1080; indeß wird seit dem letzten Kriege viel gebauet; die Volkszahl der übrigen Westerbottnischen Städte ist noch geringer. Die Stadt Umeå lebt von Fischfang, Ackerbau, Handwerken und Handel. Letzterer wird hauptsächlich mit Brettern, Theer, Fellen und Federn aus Lappland, meistens zur See auf Stockholm, doch auch auf Landmärkten getrieben. Eben so ist es in den übrigen Bottnischen Städten. Bretter und Theer sind die einträglichsten Producte des Län Umeå, dessen sandiger Boden den Ackerbau hemmt. Indeß wird die Einfuhr von der Ausfuhr übertroffen, insbesondere seit man, auch in der Stadt Umeå, wo sonst viel Luxus herrschte, durch das Beispiel und die Bitten des trefflichen Landshöfding, Gustav Edelstam *), und der Geistlichkeit ermuntert, jüngst zu einem frugaleren Leben zurückgekehrt ist.

Umeå ist der Sitz des Landshöfding über Umeå-Län. Dieses Län umfaßte früherhin die gesammte Provinz Westerbotten; seit 1810 hat man, rücksichtlich der Verwaltung, diese Pro-

_____

*) Edelstam führte den Namen Jullander, bis, seit er sich im letzten Kriege als Oberst des Finnischen Bataillons Cajana sehr auszeichnete, der König ihn unter jenem Namen in den Adelstand erhob.

rinz in zwei Län: Umeå- und Norrbottens-Län, getheilt.
Das Län Umeå, auch Westerbottens Län genannt, begreift das
südliche Westerbotten (668 ☐M. mit 36,000 Einwohnern im
Jahr 1819) oder die Pastorate Nordmaling, Umeå, De-
geerfors, Bygdeå, Burträsk, Löfånger und Skellefteå nebst Piteå, Lyckseles und Åsele-Lappmark; die
nördliche Hälfte von Westerbotten nebst den übrigen Schwedischen Lappmarken faßt das Län Norrbotten, dessen Landshöfding bis zum Jahr 1819 in Luleå gamlastad, jetzt zu Piteå, seinen Sitz hat. Norrbotten enthält 751 ☐M., im Jahr
1819 mit 36,345 Seelen.

Der größere Theil des Län Umeå besteht aus Wald, Felsen und Morästen; die Lappmarken sind Alpenland. Der Ackerbau gewährt nicht den Bedarf, wenn gleich er sehr zugenommen
hat, und eine Menge Kolonistenhöfe (nybyggen) überall zerstreut
liegen. Der ansehnlichste Nahrungszweig ist die Viehzucht, die
als Sennenwirthschaft betrieben wird. Jagd, Theerbrennerey
und Fischfang liefern beträchtlichen Gewinn. Mehrere Eisenhämmer sind vorhanden, auch eine Glashütte, Strömbäck im
Pastorat Umeå. Eine Landhaushaltungsgesellschaft besteht zu
Umeå; der König bestätigte im Jahr 1814 die Statuten, Präses ist der jedesmalige Landshöfding; ein Ausschuß, der jede
Mittwoche zusammentritt, führt die Verwaltung. Die Gesellschaft versammelt sich, der entfernten Wohnorte der Mitglieder
wegen, nur zwei Mal im Jahre, am 24. Februar und am Jah-
resfeste, dem 21. August, an welchem Tage im Jahr 1810 die
Wahl eines freien Volks Carl XIV. Johann zum Schwedischen Thron berief.

Bisher bildete das ganze Län Umeå nur einen Gerichtssprengel (hårad), im Jahr 1820 ward es in zwei geschieden. —
Der Provinzialarzt des Län wohnt zu Umeå.

Die Kirche der Stadt, Filial der ½ Meile entfernten alten
Landkirche, ist eine hölzerne Kreuzkirche von mittelmäßiger Größe,
einfach und sauber im Innern; die Sacristey ist eine der freund-

lichsten und zweckmäßigsten, die ich sah. Mehrere Bilder schmük-
ten die Kirche, unter ihnen zeichnen sich drei aus: die Flucht
Joseph und Maria's mit dem Jesuskindlein nach Aegypten, —
Abraham, der den Isaak opfern will, und die Geschichte des Jonas.
— An einem der hohen Gothischen Kirchenfenster sieht man
noch die Stelle, wo im letzten Kriege, als die Russen die Stadt
besetzt hielten, eine Schwedische Kanonenkugel einschlug und das
Fenster zerschmetterte; die Kugel wird noch in der Wohnung des
Comministers aufbewahrt, soll aber neben dem Fenster einge-
mauert werden. — Meine Begleiter aus Umeå verrichteten,
als sie in die Kirche traten, ein stilles Gebet; eine Sitte, die
ich häufig in Westerbotten, so wie an manchen andern Orten
Schwedens, traf, und die mehr als Gebrauch ist.

Auf dem Kirchhofe sind mehrere Gräber mit Denksteinen
bezeichnet, unter ihnen das Grab des Obristlieutenants Joach.
Zach. Dunker, bei Savolar Jäger-Regiment, der im Gefecht
bei Hörnefors am 5. Jul. 1809 fiel; in demselben Grabe
ruhen die Gebeine des Russischen Majors, der Dunkern entge-
genstand. — An der Nordseite des Kirchhofes, wo sonst in
Schweden Missethäter begraben zu werden pflegen, hat sich ein
vor kurzem verstorbenes junges Mädchen, Anna Sophia
Nätzén, Tochter des Provinzialmedicus Dr. Nätzén, ihre,
wie sie sich ausdrückte, ungestörte Ruhestätte erwählt. Ausgezeichnet durch Geist, Sprach- und Musikkenntnisse, hatte sie
bereits einen akademischen Preis gewonnen, als sie, etwa 10
Jahre alt, starb; sie soll häufig die meteorologischen Beobachtungen, die ihrem Vater oblagen, angestellt haben und eine Meiste-
rin in der Schönschreibekunst gewesen seyn.

Seit 1810 besitzt die Stadt eine Trivialschule, nachdem bis
dahin nur ein Pädagogium bestanden hatte. Die Trivialschule
zerfällt in 5 Klassen, hat aber nur 4 Lehrer, indem der Fonds
die Anstellung eines fünften Lehrers bisher nicht gestattete. Die
drei niedern Lehrer (Collegen) sind sehr geringe besoldet, nur
das Amt des Rectors ist besser dotirt. Das Schulhaus ist von

Holz; in den freundlichen Klassenzimmern haben dankbare Schüler seidene Kränze zum Ehrengedächtniß geliebter Lehrer aufgehängt. Der Schülerzahl beträgt gewöhnlich zwischen 60 und 70. In den Trivialschulen zu Umeå und Hernösand sind bereits lateinische Disputirübungen über Theses gehalten worden; solche Uebungen sind, in der Regel, in Trivialschulen selten.

Durch die Bemühung des würdigen Comministers Häggbom ward im Jahr 1811, mittelst Beiträge der Einwohner, zu Umeå eine Armenschule gestiftet, und im Jahr 1818, am 1. December, bei der Feier des Namenstages des Kronprinzen Oskar, wo auch Arme gespeiset wurden, mit einer Sammlung zum Ankauf eines Schulhauses der Anfang gemacht. — Ueberhaupt ist das Armenwesen wohl eingerichtet. Der Comminister und ein Rathsverwandter (rådman) sind Armenvorsteher. Den Armen sind Distrikte angewiesen, aus denen sie ihren Unterhalt beziehen; auch den Eximirten, namentlich den Geistlichen, sind Arme zur Beköstigung zugetheilt. In der Stadt herrscht viel Wohlthätigkeitssinn; jedes im Herbst heimkehrende Schiff giebt, zum Danke für die glücklich vollbrachte Fahrt, ansehnliche Beiträge zur Armenpflege. Der Buchbinder und Rathsverwandte Hamren stiftete ein Armenhaus, wo in 3 freundlichen Zimmern arme Familien und einzelne Arme wohnten. Eine andere Schenkung für die Armen der Stadt machte der Landshöfding von Stenhagen.

Das Länslazareth und das Länsgefängniß liegen vor dem Westerthore, jenes nimmt auch Irren auf. Gegenüber liegt der Landwehrkirchhof. Hier ruhen die bei Umeå gebliebenen oder in Lazarethen gestorbenen Krieger, namentlich die Westerbottnische Landwehr, die fast ganz aufgerieben wurde, weniger durch den Feind, als durch Krankheiten, die eine Folge schlechter Nahrung und Bekleidung waren. Auch bei der Landkirche ist ein solcher Kirchhof angelegt worden.

Umeå hat mehrere kleine Gärten, in denen Erbsen, Gurken und mehrere andere Gartengewächse gedeihen; doch nur einer

dieser Gärten, der der Kirche gegenüber gelegene, den Landshöf=
ding Edelstam anlegte, ist mit Bäumen bepflanzt, nämlich mit
Sperber (rönn, Sorbus aucuparia) und mit schwarzen Vogel=
kirschbäumen (hägg, prunus Padus).   Weiterhin trifft man das
große, aus Piteå hieher transportirte hölzerne Wohn=
haus des Landssecretair Cygnäus, und das schöne steinerne
Kornmagazin.   In Umeå besteht eine Leihbibliothek.

Umeå hat einen Gesundbrunnen, am Ufer des Flusses.
Die Quelle ist mit einem hölzernen Gebäude überbauet, übri=
gens wenig mineralhaltig, doch wird sie benutzt.   Nach Schwe=
discher Brunnensitte, begiebt sich an jedem Morgen, nach vollen=
detem Trinken, die Gesellschaft in die Kirche (oder den Brun=
nensaal, wo keine Kirche ist), hier wird gesungen, ein Geistlicher
spricht ein Morgen= und dann das in der Liturgie verzeichnete
schöne Brunnengebet, worauf, nach einem kurzen Gesange, man
aus einander geht; dieser Gottesdienst währt eine Viertelstunde.
— Eine mehr mineralhaltige Quelle sprudelt auf der oben ge=
nannten Insel Ön, der Kirche gegenüber.

Das Korn reift in der Gegend von Umeå frühestens 10,
gewöhnlich 11 bis 12 Wochen nach der Frühlingssaat. Am 11.,
12. und 13. August (im Schwedischen Kalender tragen diese
Tage die Namen Susanna, Clara und Hippolytus) treten Nacht=
fröste ein, die indeß weniger dem Korn, das dann oft schon reif
ist, als den Gartengewächsen schaden; man nennt diese Nächte
Eisennächte (jernnätter). Dann bleibt es wieder schönes Wetter
bis Ende Septembers; es friert selten, oder der Frost thut doch
keinen Schaden. Bleiben jene drei Augusttage ohne Frost, so
pflegen die Eisennächte nach 12 oder 13 Tagen dennoch ihr
Recht zu üben. Die Polhöhe beträgt bei Umeå 63° 49' 46".

In Umeå's nettem Gästgifvaregärd hielten wir ein tüchti=
ges Frühstück. Auch geräuchertes Rennthierfleisch war aufgetra=
gen; dieses, zumal die Zunge, hat einen gar angenehmen fei=
nen Geschmack, kräftiger und pikanter als die auch minder fette
Ochsenzunge; fast wie der beste, saftigste Westphälische Schinken,

doch ziehe ich die Rennthierzunge vor. Auch das trockene Renn= thierfleisch ist mürbe und kräftig. Mit Rennthierfleisch, insbe= sondere Zungen, meistens Lappischen Producten, wird ein nicht unbedeutender Handel, vorzugsweise nach Stockholm getrieben.

Da die eigentliche Fähre verdorben war, so verstrichen ein Paar Stunden, bis man unsere Wagen übergesetzt hatte. Um 10 Uhr fuhren wir weiter, anfangs am Ufer des Umeå, wel= ches hier mit mehreren Fischerhütten für den Lachsfang besetzt ist, und wo sich auf einem Hügel der freundliche Pavillon Åbergslust erhebt, dann im niedrigen nur mit wenigen Bir= ken untermischten Nadelwalde. Bald erreicht man das weite, meist kahle Thal, in welchem das große Dorf Tafle sich aus= dehnt; der kleine Fluß Tafle, aus dem See Micheltråsk herabkommend, fällt hier ins Meer. Tafle hat, als es die Russen besetzten, durch Plünderung nicht gelitten, da die Einwoh= ner nicht geflüchtet waren.

Bis Såfvar hat man niedrigen Wald, doch mehr Birken, ein freundliches Waldthal und das Dorf Teste. Das große Dorf Såfvar liegt in einem Thale, durch welches der reißende gleichnamige Fluß dem Meere zueilt. Der Ort ist im letzten Kriege durch ein Gefecht bekannt geworden. Ein Schwedisches Corps unter General Graf Wachtmeister war am 17. Aug. 1809 bei Ratan, einem Hafen im Pastorat Bygdeå, einem der besten Häfen Norrlands, gelandet, und nach einem glück= lichen Gefecht bei Djckneboda, südwärts auf der Straße nach Umeå, wohin die Russen retirirten, vorgedrungen. Nachdem die Russen den größten Theil ihrer bei Umeå stationirten Macht an sich gezogen, kam es am 19. August bei Såfvar zum Ge= fecht; die Schweden leisteten langen und muthigen Widerstand, mußten aber zuletzt weichen. Das Treffen begann auf dem Hügel südlich von Såfvar, wo der Weg von Umeå aus dem Walde herabkommt, und seitwärts am Saume des Waldes selbst, und dehnte sich durch das ganze Dorf aus; indeß ging kein Hof in Feuer auf, nur die Brücke über den Såfvar ward

II.   F von den Russen angezündet, damit ihnen nicht das Schwedische Corps unter General Wrede im Süden des Umeå-Elf, in den Rücken falle. — Die Zahl der Todten war so groß, daß bald ein furchtbarer Gestank die Luft verpestete und wer sich nahte, erkrankte. Die Einwohner hatten alles verloren und waren, zum Theil nackt, in den Wald geflüchtet; mehrere hüllten sich, als sie nach einigen Tagen zurückkehrten, in die Kleider der noch auf dem Schlachtfelde liegenden Todten; keiner von diesen entrann, alle tödtete der mephitische Dunst ihrer Kleidung. — Die Schweden zogen sich in Ordnung und fechtend nach Djekneboda zurück. Gräber, an welchen Steine aufgerichtet sind, ja an einer Stelle noch Menschenknochen, bezeichnen noch heute den dahin führenden Waldweg. Von Djekneboda zogen sich die Schweden nach Ratan, wo man vor dem Dorfe gleich nach der Landung den Wald hatte fällen lassen. Schon am 20. August folgten die Russen nach, wurden aber von einem dichten Kugelregen aus den Schwedischen Batterien und Kanonenböten empfangen, ja, als sie sich schon des Dorfes Ratan bemächtiget hatten, noch zahlreich barniedergestrecket, zum Theil während sie eben im Begriff waren zu plündern, von Kugeln durchbohrt; ja einen Russischen Soldaten fand man in einem Bauerhause, mit der Hand in einem erbrochenen Büreau, getödtet. Dennoch drangen die Russen mit größter Unerschrockenheit an das Ufer vor und schossen ihre Gewehre auf die Böte ab. Endlich traten sie den Rückzug gegen Norden an. Am 29. August vereinigten sich nun die Corps der Schwedischen Generale Wachtmeister und Wrede bei Umeå, kehrten aber, da der Friede nahe war, am 10. September auf der Flotte nach Upland zurück.

In den für die Schweden so ehrenvollen Gefechten bei Säfvar und Ratan, in welchen die Schwedische Artillerie ihren alten Ruhm bewährte, focht auch eine Amazone, die Frau des Soldaten beim Regiment der Königin, Servenius. Sie hatte Mittel gefunden, in Mannskleidern sich am Bord der nach Ratan bestimmten Flotte einzuschiffen, um an ihres Mannes

Seite zu leben oder zu sterben. Bei Säfvar ward ihr Mann erschossen oder gefangen; mitten unter dem feindlichen Feuer sammelte sie neue Ammunition und versah damit die Soldaten, die ihre Patronen verschossen hatten. Schon hatte das heldenmüthige Weib auch dem Treffen bei Ratan beigewohnt, als ihr Geschlecht entdeckt wurde; der commandirende General ertheilte ihr die Tapferkeitsmedaille.

Die Gefechte von Säfvar und Ratan waren die letzten des blutigen Krieges, der für Westerbotten so drückend gewesen ist. Sieben Monate lang war die Provinz vom Feinde besetzt; im folgenden Jahre traf sie fast allgemeiner Mißwachs. Im Jahr 1811 ward über das ganze Reich für Westerbotten collectirt; die Stände liehen 50,000 Bankthaler auf 5 Jahre zinsfrei an, Korn und Vieh wurden auf Kosten des Königes gesandt, aus England bezog Westerbotten 8000 Bankthaler, wie denn auch andere, durch Feuer oder Mißwachs verarmte Städte und Landschaften, und die nach Stockholm geflüchteten Finnen, durch die edlen Britten unterstützt wurden.

Von Säfvar fährt man eine Strecke längs des zwischen lieblichen Wald- und Wiesenufern fließenden Säfvarflusses, und dann durch niedrigen Wald nach Djekneboda. Zahlreiche Spuren des Gefechtes bezeichnen den Weg, der auch über eine schmale Erdenge zwischen zwei Seen läuft; eine, wie es scheint, bedeutende militairische Position. — Mein kleiner Skjutsbonde von Säfvar schien dem Pferde nicht gewachsen; ich rief den zuverläßigeren Skjutsbonde des zweiten Wagens, den der Bediente fuhr, ein stark und kräftig gewachsenes 19jähriges Mädchen. Anna Kajsa, einfach in ihrer Kleidung, wie einfach und schuldlos in ihrem Wesen, war die Tochter eines Bauern in Rickleå; sie diente in einem anderen Hofe, während ihre Schwester, an der Stelle der verstorbenen Mutter, der Wirthschaft des väterlichen Hauses vorstand. Der Bauer hält hier zu Lande wenig Dienstleute, sondern er und die Kinder arbeiten

F 2

selber; so vermindert man die Wirthschaftskosten und Wohlstand ist fast überall vorherrschend.

In Djekneboda traf ich viele Soldaten des Westerbottnischen Regiments, die zum Möte giengen. — Von hier führt ein Fußsteig durch den Wald nach Ratan; auch auf diesem, wie in Djekneboda, ward gekämpft; dieser nähere Weg beträgt eine halbe Meile; der Fahrweg läuft etwa eine halbe Meile nördlich von Djekneboda, von der großen Straße aus, von Dalkarså nach Ratan.

Von Djekneboda hat man ¾ Meilen zur Kirche Bygdeå: man fährt am Waldrande neben lieblichen Wiesen und Seen, der Sägemühle des Major Turdfjäll vorüber. In Bygdeå sprachen wir im Pfarrhofe, bei Dr. Genberg, einem der ehrwürdigsten, musterhaftesten Geistlichen und einem der mildesten und liebevollsten Gemüther, die ich je kennen lernte, vor, und nur ungern verließen wir nach ein Paar glücklichen Stunden den Kreis der liebenswürdigen Familie, deren Haupt jetzt entschlummert ist. — Vor der Weiterreise mußten wir noch ein Mahl einnehmen, denn ohne Bewirthung, und zwar die beste, die Herz und Haus vermag, darf der Fremde nie aus der gastlichen Wohnung des Norrländers scheiden, und er würde den stillen Frieden stören, wenn er das mit so vieler Liebe Dargebotene verschmähen wollte; in jeder, nur einigermaßen wohlhabenden Familie ist man immer auf die Bewirthung von Fremden vorbereitet.

Die freundliche alte steinerne Kirche liegt auf einem der nackten Felsen, an denen die Gegend reich ist; zwischen den Felsen erblickt man die lieblichsten Thäler. — Auf dem Kirchhofe ist das Grab eines Russischen Generals, der bei Säfvar fiel; zur Errichtung eines Grabsteins ließ man dem Dr. Genberg 70 Rubel zurück. Wie an vielen Orten des Schwedischen und Norwegischen Norrlandes, findet man in der Nähe der Kirche eine Anzahl Kirchstuben, in welchen entfernt wohnende Kirchgänger übernachten, und Kirchställe. Ersterer waren in Bygdeå nur 10, da eine Feuersbrunst viele verzehrte; auch der Pfarrhof brannte vor einigen Jahren ab. Mitten unter diesen, an Werktagen unbewohnten Häusern, stehen die Wohnungen des Organisten und einiger Wittwen. Ein Dorf trifft man, wie gewöhnlich in dem Schwedischen Norrland, um die Kirche her nicht. Das Pastorat Bygdeå, eines der kleinern in Westerbotten, unter 64° 2′ Polhöhe, hat 5¼ Meilen in der Länge und 3 Meilen in der Breite.

Von Bygdeå an wird der Weg immer schöner; man fährt auf Waldhöhen neben Wiesen hin. Auch Rickleå hat eine hübsche Lage.

Zwischen Rickleå und Gumboda ist Hügelweg mit weiten reizenden Aussichten. Seitwärts liegt das Eisenbruk Robertsfors mit eigener Brukskirche. In der Ferne erscheint ein hoher Berg, Sudssaltsklanke von den Eingebornen genannt, mit waldigen Vorbergen. Von der Spitze dieses Berges soll man 5 Kirchen erblicken, was, bei den weitläuftigen Kirchspielen, viel sagen will, wahrscheinlich die Kirchen Löfånger, Burträsk, Bygdeå und die Lands und die Stadtkirche Umeå, oder Degerfors und Skellefteå, eine Linie von 10 Meilen. Das dem Berge zunächst liegende Dorf ist Flacke, 2 Meilen von da; doch ist der Abhang des Berges noch weiters hin mit Nybyggen besetzt. — Rechts an der Straße zeigt sich der Bottnische Meerbusen.

In Gumboda hält das Südbataillon des Regiments Westerbotten *) sein Möte; das Lager ist unfern des Dorfes. Ich nahm das in einem Bauerhause errichtete Lazareth von 8 Betten, und das kleine Magazin, in einem andern Hofe, in Augenschein und fand alles gut und zweckmäßig.

Zwischen Gumboda und Grimsmark hat man noch ansehnlichere Hügel. Der oben genannte Berg erscheint noch deutlicher. Die mannigfaltigsten, lieblichsten Aussichten wechseln.

---

*) Nur Westerbottens Städte stellen Seeleute.

Auch Sennhütten fährt man vorüber; die schwarze Vogelkirsche (hägg) blüht am Wege. Die Sonne ging eben unter, aber es blieb hell wie am Tage. Um 11¾ Uhr langten wir in Grimsmark an, wo wir in einem netten, reinlichen Zimmer übernachteten.

Reinlichkeit in den Häusern wie in der Kleidung ist eine schöne Eigenthümlichkeit der meisten Schwedischen Provinzen; doch nirgends findet man sie im höhern Grade wie in Westerbotten, zumal dem nördlichen Theil dieser Provinz. Da wird kein Sand, nur Knirk oder Granreiser, in die Zimmer gestreuet, deren man in jedem Bauerhofe zwar nicht so viele wie in Helsingland, aber doch gewöhnlich 4 bis 6 findet (auch die Zahl der Nebengebäude ist geringer, wie in Helsingland), und häufig wird gescheuert; man glaubt in ein Putzzimmer zu treten, indem man in ein Bauerhaus tritt. Im Fremdenzimmer, welches in keinem Hofe fehlt, sind allerlei Geräthe, insbesondere silberne, aufgestellt, und in den Gasthöfen werden gar oft silberne Becher statt der Gläser gereicht. In der Wohnstube, die zugleich Küche ist, sind die einfachen zinnernen, irdenen und hölzernen Hausgeräthe geschmackvoll geordnet, und Fußboden und Wände nicht minder reinlich wie in den Fremdenzimmern, die theils zur Aufnahme von Gästen, theils für den Hausgottesdienst, der in den von der Kirche entfernt liegenden Dörfern und Höfen sonntäglich gehalten wird, bereit stehen. Zu diesem Hausgottesdienst versammeln sich aus dem ganzen Dorfe oder aus einer Zahl benachbarter Höfe alle, die nicht zur Kirche gingen; es wird gebetet, gesungen, ein vom Pastor gesetzter Vorleser lieset aus einer Postille, deren jeder Hof mehrere hat, aus der Liturgie, auch wohl aus der Bibel, alles zur selbigen Stunde und auf gleiche Weise, wie in der Kirche, die Stelle der Predigt vertritt die Postille. Der Versammlungsort oder das Bethaus, wie man hier spricht, wechselt jährlich unter den Höfen. Auf einem großen Tisch liegen Erbauungsbücher geordnet. Wo die Höfe weit von einander entfernt sind, hält jede Familie ihre besondere Hausandacht.

Diese Sitte heiligt den Sonntag für die durch häusliche Geschäfte oder Kränklichkeit von dem Besuch der Kirche Zurückgehaltenen, mindert aber denselben keinesweges; vielmehr kommt auch der entfernt Wohnende, so oft als möglich zum Gotteshause. An den meisten Orten wird auch am Abend des Sonnabend eine Erbauungsstunde gehalten; gewöhnlich in jedem einzelnen Hofe, seltener versammelt sich hiezu das Dorf. Morgen- und Abendsegen hält jeder Hausvater mit den Seinigen, auch dem Gesinde, oder jeder verrichtet sein Gebet kniend für sich *).

Der sonntägliche Gottesdienst, in der Kirche wie in den Höfen, wird gewöhnlich nur Vormittags gehalten. Eine im Anfange dieses Jahrhunderts entstandene und besonders nach dem letzten Kriege verbreitete Gesellschaft, der man den Namen „Leser" beigelegt hat, feiert auch am Sonntagsnachmittage den Gottesdienst. Die Leser (läsare) halten mit großem Ernst und Strenge auf ächt-christliche Lehre und ihr gemäße Gesinnung und Handlungsweise. In dieser Hinsicht sind sie sehr ehrwürdig und haben wohlthätig auf die Gemeinden eingewirkt. Zugleich vernachlässigen sie aber das Gesetz der Liebe durch Urtheilen über den Bruder, nicht eingedenk, daß nur der Allwissende das

*) Man könnte hier anwenden die kunstlosen Worte aus Christian Donaleitis Litthauischem Gedicht: „Das Jahr, ein ländliches Epos, in gleichem Versmaaß ins Deutsche übersetzt von Dr. Rhesa." Königsberg 1818. 162 S. 8.

       Mylas — —

ist zwar nur ein Bauer, doch fromm und edel an Tugend;
wenn du sein Haus einmal gastfreundlich wolltest besuchen,
wie die Kirche geschmückt, anständig wirst du es finden;
anzusehen darin ist der Tisch als ein heiliger Altar,
worauf immer ein Buch, ein heiliges, lieget, damit er
selber oder im Kreis seiner wohlunterrichteten Kinder,
wenn sie getreu und flink sich müde gequälet in Arbeit,
gleich ergötzen sich mag an wonneseligen Liedern,
und aufheitern also vergessen die Mühen des Lebens.

Herz erforscht; sonst kann man sie freilich eines undienstfertigen, unfreundlichen, lieblosen, oder gar unbarmherzigen Wesens nicht beschuldigen. Jenes Urtheilen hat an einigen Orten einen Gegensatz gegen die Geistlichkeit erzeugt, deren Lehre man für unevangelisch hielt, ein Gegensatz, der bei einigen exaltirten Köpfen zur Vernachlässigung des öffentlichen Gottesdienstes führte und deßhalb schon Gegenstand obrigkeitlicher Untersuchungen geworden ist, auch viele Gemeindeglieder gegen die Leser eingenommen hat. Indeß schlossen sich auch solche Leser von der Theilnahme am heiligen Abendmahl nicht aus, vielmehr genossen manche dasselbe häufiger als andere Gemeindeglieder, die doch gleichfalls nicht selten das heilige Mahl feiern. — Bisher verfuhr man gegen die Leser mit weiser Schonung, eine Schonung, die um so nothwendiger war, da selbst solche Gemeindeglieder, die nicht zu ihnen gehörten, und deßhalb nicht selten von denselben verachtet wurden, nicht verkannten, wie löblich im Ganzen der äußere Wandel der Leser sey. Nur durch ein sanftes und weises Verfahren wird man am ehesten dahin gelangen, das unter den Waizen gesäete Unkraut zu tilgen, ohne zugleich den Waizen selbst auszureißen. — Die Leser halten hoch auf Luthers Schriften, und haben selbst eine neue Auflage von Luthers Postille veranstaltet. Eigenthümliche Lehren haben sie nicht. Die merkwürdige Entstehungs- und Bildungsgeschichte der Leser habe ich an einem andern Orte *) mitgetheilt.

Religiösität und Kirchlichkeit ist Hauptzug im Charakter der Westerbottnier, darum zeichnen auch Nachdenken und Sorgfalt bei Geschäften, Scharfblick, ein hoher Grad von Gewissenhaftigkeit auch in kleineren Dingen, Uneigennützigkeit, ein heiterer und liebevoller Sinn, Achtung für Obrigkeit und Gesetz, thätige Theilnahme am öffentlichen Wohl, Ordnungsliebe und Sparsamkeit neben Mildthätigkeit und herzlicher Gastfreundschaft und ächtes

*) in Stäudlin und Tzschirner Archiv für alte und neue Kirchengeschichte. Bd. 4. H. 3. Bd. 5. H. 2. Leipzig 1820. 1822.

Familienleben die Bewohner Westerbottens aus. Wo sollte man also seines Lebens froher werden können, wie hier? Wahrlich, wem es beschieden ist, unter diesen Menschen, in einer auch äußerlich glücklichen Lage, zu leben, der pflückt die schönsten Blüthen des irdischen Lebens. — Freilich hat der letzte Krieg im Ganzen auf die Sittlichkeit nicht erfreulich eingewirkt; dennoch ist auch heute jene Schilderung völlig anwendbar.

Reichthum findet man in Westerbotten nicht; aber Wohlhabenheit ist allgemein. Die hauptsächlichsten Nahrungszweige sind Viehzucht und Fischerey, zumal der Lachsfang, der in den großen Strömen sehr beträchtlich ist, indeß gegen frühere Zeiten sehr abgenommen hat. Die Viehzucht wird zum Theil als Sennenwirthschaft betrieben; die Heerden werden oft von armen Lappen geweidet. Der Ackerbau ist nicht unbedeutend; das Korn giebt den reichlichsten Ertrag, doch gedeihet kein in südlichen Provinzen gebautes Saatkorn. Daß Westerbotten jährlich Korn kaufen muß, ist der geringen Zahl der bebauten Felder zuzuschreiben; viel Land könnte noch urbar gemacht werden, und dann die Provinz weit mehr Menschen ernähren, als es jetzt der Fall ist. Die Aermeren bereiten ihr Brot aus dem schlechtesten Mehl (slöbröd) mit zugemischter Spreu (agnar). Dieses Alltagsbrot ist ganz dünne und wird viermal zusammengelegt. Einige Hüttenwerke sind vorhanden. Am schönsten ist das Land bei den großen Strömen, weniger die übrigen Theile des Landes.

Was ich Kap. 1. eine Annehmlichkeit des Reisens in Schweden nannte, die Bildung der Skjutsbönder, mit denen man sich über allerlei Gegenstände, zumal der Provinz, unterhalten könne, trifft nirgends mehr als in Westerbotten zu. Das erfuhr ich heute insbesondere auf den beiden letzten Stationen, wo biedere und wohlunterrichtete Jünglinge durch interessante Gespräche den Weg verkürzten; das habe ich hernach fast täglich erfahren, auch bei den weiblichen Skjutsbönder, die ich, nach Sitte des Landes, öfters erhielt. Feste Schulen findet man hier wenige, oft nicht einmal bei den Kirchen; ambulatorische giebt es zwar in vielen Dörfern, aber das meiste thut die treue Benutzung des kirchlichen Unterrichts und der kirchlichen Einrichtungen, und dann die Unterweisung des Vaters, oder der Mutter, oder der ältern Geschwister im häuslichen Kreise an den langen Winterabenden.

Die Westerbottnier sind von mittlerer Größe und kräftigem Körperbau; in den Gesichtszügen herrscht Lebendigkeit und heiterer Ernst. In den meisten Kirchspielen ist der größere Theil des weiblichen Geschlechts schön. Die Sprache ist sehr weich, wie im übrigen Norrland, ähnlich der Norwegischen; an einigen Orten sehr unverständlich, und fast in jedem Kirchspiel dialektisch verschieden. Die Kleidung ist sehr einfach, nur in einzelnen Kirchspielen sind in neuern Zeiten die kattunenen Kleider beim weiblichen Geschlecht häufiger geworden, namentlich ist in S t e l l e f t e å der Luxus sehr gestiegen. Im Allgemeinen ist aber Einfachheit der Kleidung wie der Sitten vorherrschend. Letztere wird durch den uralten Gebrauch der K o m m n ä c h t e, oder wie man sie mit Recht nennen könnte, der E h r e n n ä c h t e, — ein Gebrauch, der in Norrland allgemein ist, und von jeher nicht blos in Skandinavien, sondern auch in Deutschland, der Schweiz und andern Ländern gefunden wurde, freilich dort auf eine minder ziemende und schuldlose Weise, keineswegs gefährdet. So bald ein Mädchen zu den Jahren der Mannbarkeit gelangt und confirmirt ist (welches letztere auch nothwendig vorhergehen muß, indem man dann erst ihre christliche Gesinnung für befestigt hält), erhält es nächtlichen Besuch junger Männer; beide liegen gekleidet mit einander, in aller Ehrbarkeit, und nicht einmal einen Kuß darf der Jüngling auf des Mädchens Wange drücken, wenn er nicht für immer verstoßen und zwar auf eine sehr unsanfte Weise durch des kräftigen Mädchens Hand verstoßen seyn will; biederer Händedruck und freundliche Rede ist die einzige Würze dieser Stunden, die auch häufig nur mit einander verschlafen werden. Der Jüngling kommt mit Wissen der Eltern, doch will die Sitte, daß die Eltern des Mädchens seine

Ankunft nicht bemerken dürfen; auf gleiche Weise geht er wieder, doch vor Tagesanbruch, gewöhnlich nach einer kleinen Bewirthung. Nur in gewissen Nächten geschehen diese Besuche, meistens in der Nacht vom Sonnabend auf den Sonntag, doch auch in der Nacht vom Sonntag auf den Montag. So hat jeder Jüngling sein Mädchen, was er besucht; in der Regel nur Eines, was er oft mehrere Jahre hinter einander besucht, bis er für oder wider das Mädchen entschieden hat, es ehelichet oder verläßt und nun zu einem andern Mädchen sich wendet, worauf das verlassene Mädchen von andern Jünglingen besucht zu werden pflegt. Zuweilen besucht auch wohl ein Jüngling zu gleicher Zeit mehr als Ein Mädchen, doch nur so lange er noch nicht gewählt hat. Hat er gewählt, so sind die Ehrennächte häufiger und nicht mehr geheim. An vielen Orten wird es für unsittlich gehalten, wenn ein, auch nicht verlobter, Jüngling mehrere Mädchen zugleich besucht. Einem Jüngling, der einmal berauscht war, pflegt, wenigstens in einzelnen Gemeinden, von keinem Mädchen der Ehrenbesuch gestattet zu werden. Ein Mädchen, welches keinen nächtlichen Ehrenbesuch erhält, wird an manchen Orten für tadelnswürdig gehalten, und ist es auch gewöhnlich; denn kein gefallenes Mädchen wird besucht, ein junger Mann würde sich durch den Besuch eines solchen Mädchens um Achtung und Ehre bringen. — Hat ein Jüngling nach, kürzere oder längere Zeit fortgesetzten, Ehrennächten, sich mit einem Mädchen verlobt, so fehlt es zwar nicht an Beispielen, daß einzelne Verlobte sich dann factisch von ihrer gegenseitigen physischen Ehefähigkeit überzeugten; aber diese Beispiele sind noch immer nicht so gar häufig, und wird dieser unzeitige Beischlaf (otidigt sängelag) mit kirchlicher Geldbuße und ernsten Verweisen geahndet, und die Ehe noch vor der Geburt des Kindes vollzogen. Die Erfahrung, wie ich mich durch Einsicht der kirchlichen Geburtstabellen überzeugt habe, lehrt, daß die Sitte der Ehrennächte in moralischer Hinsicht nicht so verderblich einwirkt, wie man vermuthen könnte. Denn die Zahl der unehelichen Kinder ist in den Provinzen, wo jene Sitte herrscht, bei weitem nicht so groß, als in den Landschaften des mittleren und südlichen Schwedens, wo man den Gebrauch nicht kennt. Erklären läßt sich dieses freilich nur aus dem ernsten und festen Sinn des Norrländers und aus der Schande, die das Volk an den Begriff der Unzucht knüpft, ein Grundsatz, der durch die gegen Unzucht gesetzlich ausgesprochene und wirklich geübte Kirchenbuße im Herzen des Volks befestiget wird: geschwächte Mädchen sind nicht nur in Geldstrafe an die Kirche verfallen, sondern die bei allen Wöchnerinnen durch das Kirchengesetz vorgeschriebene kirchliche Einsegnung wird an ihnen auf eine minder ehrenvolle Weise und unter ernsten Verweisen und Ermahnungen vollzogen. Während die ehelichen Mütter vor Anfang des Gottesdienstes öffentlich und feierlich vor dem Altare eingesegnet werden, nun am Gottesdienste Theil nehmen, wollen Gesetz und Sitte, daß gefallene Mädchen zuvor in der Sacristey in Gegenwart weniger Zeugen, unter zu Grundlegung eines eigenen liturgischen Formulars, nach reuigem Bekenntniß ihrer Sünde, Absolution empfangen, bevor es ihnen verstattet ist, am öffentlichen Gottesdienst und am Genuß des heiligen Abendmahls Theil zu nehmen. — Den schuldlosen nächtlichen Besuch der Jünglinge nennt man gå ut på (drauf ausgehen). Nicht leicht wird eine Ehe vollzogen, die nicht durch solche Ehrennächte vorbereitet worden wäre. Als ich einmal (es war in Jemtland) einem jungen Bräutigam, der fromm und einfältig mir von seiner Liebsten erzählte, und gestand, wie er schon Jahr und Tag mit ihr die Ehrennacht vollzogen und sich nun wirklich mit ihr verlobt habe, entgegnete, daß dergleichen Ehrennächte in meiner Heimath nicht üblich wären, fragte er sehr naiv: ob denn da die Leute gar nicht heiratheten? — Auch habe ich nirgends in Norrland beim weiblichen Geschlecht jenes freie Wesen gefunden, was die sittliche Zartheit verletzt; freilich herrschen dort nicht die verschrobenen und erzwungenen Begriffe von Anstand, die oft nur dazu dienen, das Laster zu übertünchen. Auch dem fremden Manne wird öffentlich der biedere Händedruck und die freundliche Rede des unbefangenen Mädchens; nicht glaubt sie dadurch den Anstand verletzt, nur eine Pflicht der Menschlichkeit will sie erfüllen. Heil dem Lande, wo das ächt Menschliche geehrt wird! — Auch wo die Sitte der Ehrennächte herrscht, zeichnet sich das weibliche Geschlecht durch ächt weibliches Zartgefühl aus, was auch der Mann respectirt; selbst der Gatte küßt sein Weib nicht öffentlich, und ein kräftiger Händedruck ist auch die Sprache liebender Seelen.

Auch in Norwegen herrscht ganz die Sitte der Ehrennächte, die aber, wenigstens im südlichen Norwegen, höchst ausgeartet ist.

———

Am 18. Jun. Von Grimsmark nach Selet 1¼ Meile; von Selet nach Daglösten 1¼ Meile; von Daglösten nach Bureå 1¼¼ Meile; von Bureå nach Innervil 1¼¼ Meile; von Innervil nach Sunnanå 1 Meile; von Sunnanå nach Storkåged 1¼ Meile; von Storkåged nach Bysle 1¼ Meile. — Zusammen 9¼¼ Meilen.

Auf der Hälfte des Weges von Grimsmark nach Selet fährt man durch niedrigen Birken- und Fichtenwald; dann wird die Gegend mehr belebt; in den Thälern liegen oft kleine Dörfer, aber meist nackt und kahl; nahe vor Selet kommt man der kleinen Kirche Löfänger vorüber. Mein Skjutsbonde, ein 40jähriger Bauer, saß bald auf bald ab und sprang dann wie ein Reh neben dem schnell fahrenden Wagen einher; das ist die Kraft der Nordischen Menschen; doch sind die Westerbottnier nicht so leichtfüßig und behende wie die Ångermanländer. In Selet frühstückten wir; die Hausfrau säugte ihr fast dreijähriges Kind; der Junge sah dick und frisch aus, und man merkte, daß ihm die mütterliche Liebe recht wohl bekam, nebenher genoß er auch andere Speise. Auf mein Befremden über dieses lange Säugen versicherte die Frau, daß es Mütter gebe, die ihren 5 und 6jährigen Kindern noch die Brust reichten. Ob dem so ist, lasse ich dahin gestellt seyn; aber daß 2 und 3jährige Kinder noch gesäugt werden, habe ich fast überall in Westerbotten, auch unter den Finnen am Torneå, gefunden.

Von Selet nach Daglösten fährt man ganz in dem kleinen Pastorat Löfånger. Der Weg ist bergig, meist Wald, nur beim Dorfe Månbyn erblickt man Kornfelder. In Dagelösten sah ich ein munteres gesundes Kind von 6 Jahren, welches an der rechten Hand 3 Finger und 2 Zehen hatte.

Auch die beiden folgenden Stationen haben meist Wald, Birken, Tannen und Gränen, meist hohen Wuchses; man passirt mehrere kleine Flüsse auf Brücken. Am Wege außer dem Walde blühte eine Fülle von Åkerbär. Innervik ist ein großes Dorf, welches mit seinen vielen Heuscheunen (der wohlhabendste Bauer hat deren über 40, der ärmste wenigstens 10) wohl eine Viertelmeile einnimmt. Bereits von Bureå an fährt man in dem weitläuftigen Pastorat Skellefteå, dessen Länge an der Straße 8⅜ Meilen, und dessen Flächeninhalt 52 □M. beträgt; es ist eben so groß als ganz Upsala Lån; kein anderes Westerbottnisches Pastorat hat diesen Umfang und wird es von mehr Standespersonen als irgend eines der übrigen Landpastorate, bewohnt.

Zwischen Innervik und Sunnanå fährt man durch die Dörfer Kårr und Böle, die recht freundlich von Wiesen umgeben sind.

Gleich hinter Sunnanå läuft die Straße auf einer 450 Ellen langen Brücke über den breiten und reißenden Strom Skellfteå; jenseits liegt die Kirche nebst dem prächtigen Pfarrhof. Die Ufer des Stroms sind unbeschreiblich reizend. Der Fluß ist sehr fischreich, hat auch ergiebigen Lachsfang, ist aber nur bei seinem Ausflusse ins Meer von der Kirche an schiffbar; 2 Meilen oberhalb der Kirche bildet er den gewaltigen 50 Klafter hohen Bomansfors und 1 Meile weiter den noch ansehnlicheren Finnfors; er entspringt in Piteå-Lappmark. Am südlichen Ufer unweit Sunnanå liegt das schöne Gütchen des Obristlieutenant Ulfhjelm, Fredrikslund. Ueberhaupt ist die Gegend hier sehr bewohnt und angebaut; Baumfrüchte gedeihen zwar nicht mehr, aber Gartengewächse aller Art, auch Erbsen.

In Skellefteå waren wir beim dortigen Pastor Dr. Ström angemeldet, der zugleich als Contractspropst der Prop, stey Skellefteå vorsteht, zu welcher Piteå-Lappmark gehört. Eine zahlreiche Gesellschaft und ein treffliches Mahl wartteten unsrer. Nach Tische wurde die prachtvolle steinerne Kreuzkirche in Augenschein genommen; sie ist die schönste in ganz Norrland; vor etwa 10 Jahren ward sie auf Kosten der Gemeinde erbaut und faßt etwa 5000 Menschen, ist aber für die an 8000 Seelen starke Gemeinde zu klein. Die schön gewölbte Kuppel, die großen Gothischen Fenster, die Säulen vor dem Eingange, machen schon von außen einen mächtigen Eindruck; auch das Innere ist des Aeußern werth: würdig, einfach und erhaben, mit trefflicher in der Provinz selbst gefertigter Orgel, und einem kunstreichen, noch aus alten Zeiten herstammenden, Altarblatt. In der Sacristey werden die der Kirche gehörigen prächtig-gestickten Amtsgewänder aufbewahrt; das eine derselben, mehrere 100 Rthlr. an Werth, war von einer Bäuerin geschenkt worden. Unter den Bildnissen einiger Pastoren von Skelleteå findet man hier auch das Bild des geistreichen, um Lappland so verdienten Högström, dessen Neffe hier jetzt Comministter ist. Von der Gallerie des Thurms hat man eine schöne Aussicht auf den Fluß und seine Wiesenufer. Der Kirchhof wird nicht mehr benutzt; ein zweiter ist in einiger Entfernung angelegt und eingeweiht. Weiterhin liegt die Kirchstadt (kyrkostad). So heißt in Westerbotten die Anzahl der vielen hölzernen Häuser, wo die entfernt wohnenden Kirchgänger übernachten, auch ihre Sonntagskleider verwahrt haben und die früherhin, wo Sonnabendspredigten Statt fanden, noch unentbehrlicher waren. Diese Häuser sind zu Skellefteå besonders zahlreich, doch nicht so todt, wie an andern Orten; denn mitten unter denselben halten die Kaufleute von Piteå Buden, wo einige Handelsartikel zu demselbigen Preise, wie in Piteå, feil sind; auch sind dort die Wohnungen der beiden Comminister, des Adjuncten und des Küsters; desgleichen hat der Major des Süderbataillons des Westerbottnischen Regiments dort sein Boställe, und ist daselbst ein königl. Postcomtoir errichtet, welches früherhin in Sunnanå bestand; dieß ist das einzige zwischen Umeå und Piteå, oder auf einer Strecke von 23½ Meilen (33 Deutschen Meilen).

Wie bemerkt, ist in Skellefteå die Zahl der Kirchbuden besonders groß, theils wegen der volkreichen Gemeinde, die im Jahr 1815. 7855 Seelen zählte (außer der 8 Meilen entlegenen Kapelle Norrsjö — wohin jetzt ein Fahrweg angelegt wird — mit 450 Seelen), theils wegen der zweckwidrigen Sitte, daß auch nahe Dörfer ihre Kirchstuben haben. Da man in diesen zahlreichen Kirchstuben Unordnungen verspürt zu haben glaubte, so ward beim Könige auf ein bestimmtes Gesetz rücksichtlich der Kirchstuben angetragen, worauf der König im Jahr 1817 (6. Mai) verordnete, daß zwar jeder die Kirchstube, die er jetzt habe, behalten, künftig aber nur denjenigen, welche mindestens Eine Meile Kirchweg haben, der Bau oder Ankauf von Kirchstuben gestattet werden solle, worüber jedesmal zuvor die Einwilligung des Landshöfdings einzuholen sey; auch ward bestimmt, daß vom 1. October 1817 an außer den Marktzeiten keine Waaren in der Kirchstadt sollten feil gehalten werden.

In der Kirchstadt wohnen auch während des Confirmandenunterrichts die jungen Leute, welche, etwa 15 Jahre alt, eingesegnet werden und zum ersten Mal communiciren sollen.

Das Pfarrhaus, wenn gleich nur von Holz (steinerne Wohnhäuser findet man in ganz Norrland, außer etwa in Gefle, nicht), ist eines der geräumigsten, schönsten und am geschmackvollsten eingerichteten Pfarrhäuser Norrlands. Hinter dem Hause trifft man einen hübschen großen Garten, wo alle Gartengewächse herrlich gedeihen, wo Dr. Högström um 1750

auch Aepfelbäume pflanzte, die reichliche Frucht trugen, in dem
harten Winter 1763 aber meist ausgingen. Im Pastorat herrscht
viel Wohlhabenheit, freilich aber auch Luxus in einem höheren
Grade, als in irgend einem der übrigen Westerbottnischen Pastorate; die Bauern fangen hier schon an den Vornehmen nach-
zuahmen, geben sich nicht selten Zunamen, und die Mädchen
müssen zwei Vornamen haben, während nach alter Bottnischer
Sitte bisher nur Ein Vorname üblich war; auch die Kleidung
der Bewohnerinnen von Skelleftea ist zierlicher und mehr aus-
ländisch, als an andern Orten von Westerbotten. Doch kann
man nicht behaupten, daß in gleichem Verhältniß die Sittlichkeit
im Allgemeinen abgenommen habe, wenn gleich die Einfachheit
der Sitten hier minder groß ist, wie im übrigen Westerbotten:
indeß war im Jahr 1816 das 14te Kind unehelich (unter 260
Gebornen 19 Uneheliche), ein im obern Schweden ziemlich seltenes Verhältniß, welches auch in Skelleftea oft geringer ist,
(in Luleå Landgemeinde befanden sich 1815 unter 255 Gebornen nur 9 Uneheliche, also das 28ste Kind war unehelich; 1816
unter 261 Geburten 7 uneheliche, mithin nur das 37ste unehelich) *).

Um 9 Uhr Abends fuhren wir von Skelleftea ab. Der
Weg führt anfangs neben üppigen Wiesen, dann in den Wald,
bis man die weite Wiesenebene erreicht, durch welche sich der
Fluß Storkågeå schlängelt und wo das große Dorf gleiches
Namens mit seinen Heuscheunen sich ausbreitet; die Lage des
Dorfes ist reizend; das Dorf hat den besten Hafen an der gan-
zen Westerbottnischen Küste, daher auch 1666 der Plan ent-
worfen, aber nicht ausgeführt wurde, die damals eben abgebrann-

---

*) Im Jahr 1820 vereinigte sich das Pastorat Skelleftea zur
Besoldung eines eigenen Landfeldscheers, worauf das königl. Gesund-
heitscollegium die Anstellung eines promovirten Arztes beschloß. Bis
dahin hatte es in dem ganzen Län Umeå, außer Militairärzten, keine
andern Aerzte als in der Länsstadt gegeben.

II.   G

te Stadt Piteå, bei Storkågeå wieder aufzubauen. Auch einem Theerofen, der den Bauern gehört und wo eben gebrannt wurde, fährt man vorüber; Theerbrennerey wird in Westerbotten viel getrieben.

Von Storkågeå ward die Reise nach Byske 1¼ Meile fortgesetzt. Der Wald, meist Birken, wechselt mit freundlichen Wiesen; man kommt dem Dorfe Drångsmark und den kleinen Sennhütten von Östvik vorüber. Um 12½ Uhr langten wir in dem kleinen, aber reinlichen Gästgifvaregård Byske an, wo wir übernachteten, hatten also die 2½ Meilen von Skellefteå in 3½ Stunden zurückgelegt. Schnell hatte die freundliche und unverdrossene Wirthin das Nöthige in Stand gesetzt. Die Kinder schliefen schon, drei derselben, ein holdseliges Kleeblatt, kleinen Engeln gleich, neben einander in Einem Bette unter der Schaafsdecke. Unter den Fenstern donnerte der Byskefluß, doch bald hatten auch uns Morpheus Arme umfangen.

Alles war freundlich und nett in Byske. Nach eingenommenem Kaffee setzten wir um 8½ Uhr die Reise fort.

———

Am 19. Jun. Von Byske nach Åby 1¼ Meille; von Åby nach Kinbäck ½½ Meile; von Kinbäck nach Jäfre 1,¼ Meile; von Jäfre nach Piteholm 1½ Meile; von Piteholm nach Oljeby 1 Meile. — Zusammen 6,¼ Meile.

Man fährt über den Byskefluß auf einer Brücke, die wie die Brücke über den Skellefteå und viele andere größere Brücken Schwedens auf mit Holz eingefaßten Steinkisten ruhet, folgt dem Laufe des Flusses bis zur Mündung, und kommt dann in den Wald, der bis Åby nur selten durch kleine Wiesenthäler, in deren einem ein Dorf liegt, unterbrochen wird. Bei Åby führt eine Brücke über den ansehnlichen Abyfluß. Åby, wie Byske, hat einen ziemlich guten Hafen.

In dem hübschen Gästgifvaregård von Åby ward ein trefflliches Frühstück eingenommen. Dann gings weiter nach Kinbå ck ¼ Meile. Nachdem man die durch Höfe und Sägemühlen bedeckten Ufer des Åby hinter sich hat, fährt man in den dichten Wald; bei Kinbäck erblickt man das offene Meer. In Kinbäck ist eine bedeutende Theerbrennerey. Auch fand ich hier Dreschwagen, hölzerne Walzen, vor welche man Pferde spannt; solche Dreschwagen werden jetzt in Westerbotten immer häufiger.

Auch von Kinbäck bis Jäfre hat man viel Wald und nur selten den Anblick des Meeres, dem man doch sehr nahe ist. Eine kleine Viertelmeile hinter Kinbäck endigt das Pastorat Skellefteå; das Pastorat Piteå beginnt und mit ihm das neue Län Norrbotten, wo in Hinsicht des Skjuts die Einrichtung getroffen ist, daß die Bauern mehrere Tage hinter einander auf Håll liegen und während dieser Zeit ununterbrochen skjutsen, doch mit Zwischenstunden; Reisenden, die in diesen Ruhestunden eintreffen, werden Reservepferde aus einem nahen Dorfe, welches nur zur Reserve angeschlagen ist, geliefert. Diese Einrichtung ist dem Ackerbau sehr vortheilhaft, und hat unter den Bauern großen Beifall gefunden. — Ein Sennendorf, dem man im Walde vorüberfährt, ist bis auf 5 Hütten im Kriege zerstört worden. Mein Skjutsbonde war diesmal ein sanftes 14jähriges Mädchen, die Tochter des Gästgifvare in Kinbäck, des Fahrens sehr kundig, in 1 Stunde war der Weg von 1⅞ Meile zurückgelegt. — In Jäfre, welches am Meere liegt, werden zuweilen Schiffe gebauet.

Von Jäfre erreicht man in wenigen Minuten die Papiermühle und den Eisenhammer Degerfors; dann geht es fast ¾ Meile im Nadelwalde fort, bis zur Fährstelle am Piteåstrom, wo man noch die Ueberbleibsel einer Brücke trifft, die die Russen innerhalb 3 Wochen erbauet hatten. Der breite Piteåstrom, der in Lappland entspringt, ist nur von der Mündung bis zur nahen Fähre aufwärts schiffbar. Der Fluß bildet hier eine beträchtliche Insel, Piteholm, über welche die große Straße führt, und wo ein Gästgifvaregård angelegt ist; die In-

G 2

sel hängt bei der Stadt Piteå durch eine Brücke mit dem festen Lande zusammen. Die Insel ist mit Nadelwald bedeckt; nur gegen die Stadt hin hat sie freundliche Wiesen. Nachdem wir im Gästgifvaregård Pferde gewechselt, fuhren wir über die Brücke in Piteå ein. Mein Skjutsbonde von Piteholm war ein Bauer, der in seiner Schlafmütze, und mit dem Zügel, womit er nach Hause zu reiten gedachte, über der Brust, einen seltsamen Anblick gewährte und durch seine unverständliche Sprache und Antworten uns belustigte.

Während einer unserer Wagen reparirt wurde, verflossen uns zu Piteå einige frohe Stunden im Hause der Frau Burman, einer Kaufmannswittwe. Auch besuchte ich den Rector der Trivialschule, Herrn Gadd, und nahm mit Frau Burman's Schwager die Merkwürdigkeiten des Orts in Augenschein. Piteå, unter 65° 20' 40" Polhöhe, ist die kleinste der Westerbottnischen Städte, im Jahr 1815 zählte sie 625 Einwohner. Alle Häuser sind von Holz und haben meist nur Ein Stockwerk; die schönsten sind die der Frau Burman und und des Kaufmanns Degerman. Die Straßen, auch der Markt, sind ungepflastert. Die hölzerne kleine Kirche ist ohne Thurm, doch freundlich im Innern und mit einer Orgel versehen; am nahen hölzernen Glockenthurm hat man eine zwar beschränkte, aber hübsche Aussicht auf die Umgegend. Den geräumigen Kirchhof beschatten schwarze Vogelkirschbäume, die eben in Blüthe standen. Die Trivialschule zählt, in 4 Klassen, an welchen 1 Rector, 2 Collegen und 1 Apologist lehren, 50 Schüler, die, wie auf allen Schwedischen Gymnasien und mehreren Trivialauch andern öffentlichen Stadtschulen (Pädagogien) kein Schulgeld bezahlen *). Uebrigens sind die Lehrer an den Westerbottnischen Schulen besser, wie im übrigen Schweden, besoldet. Die Trivialschule besitzt eine kleine Bücher- und Instrumentensammlung. Der Bau des neuen Schulhauses war noch nicht

---

*) S. Schwedens Kirchenverfassung B. 2. S. 576.

vollendet; die Stadt gab das Bauholz, die übrigen Kosten wurden bestritten theils aus der Schulkasse, die durch zwei jährliche Collecten, wie durch Beiträge der Geistlichkeit Westerbottens, entstanden war, theils durch den Einjährigen reinen Ertrag des eben erledigten Pastorats Piteå, an welchen keine Wittwe Anspruch zu machen hatte, dieser belief sich zu 3361 Bankthalern, einer höheren Summe, als ein Pastor die Pfarre benutzen kann; aus der Schulkasse flossen 1500 Bankthaler. Da der große Brand im Jahr 1806 auch das Rathhaus in die Asche legte, so hat der Magistrat sich ausbedungen, in den ersten 15 Jahren die Sessionen in dem neuen Schulhause zu halten.

Die Stadt ist Filial der Landgemeinde Piteå, in welcher der Pastor wohnt. Der obere Theil des weitläuftigen Pastorats dieses mißt 6¾ Meilen in der Länge und 10 Meilen in der Breite (im Jahr 1815 mit 6253 Seelen), ward im Jahr 1808 zu einer besonderen Kapellgemeinde, Elfsby, abgeschieden. In Elfsby wohnt ein Comminister, so daß nun das Pastorat außer dem Pastor und dessen Adjuncten 3 Comminister (bei der Landkirche, in der Stadt und zu Elfsby) zählt.

Die erste Gründung der Stadt geschah neben der Landkirche durch Gustav II. Adolph. Nachdem die neue Anlage im Jahr 1666 durch eine Feuersbrunst verzehrt war, baute man, da die Meeresbuchten immer seichter wurden, wie denn überhaupt eine Abnahme des Bottnischen Meeres an der Küste von Westerbotten verspürt wird, die Stadt ¾ Meilen weiter seewärts, an der Stelle, wo sie noch heute steht, wieder auf; der Platz um die Landkirche und das Dorf Hijeby hieß nun Gamla staden (Altstadt). Im Jahr 1721 ward die Stadt, mit alleiniger Ausnahme der Kirche, von den Russen eingeäschert.

Die Stadt Piteå liegt auf einer Insel des Flusses Piteå, an der Mündung desselben in das Bottnische Meer, doch noch 2 Meilen vom offenen Meere entfernt. Sie ist See- und Stapelstadt, treibt indeß den meisten Handel auf Landmärkten, auch in Lappland, und zur See nach Stockholm; von den 16 Kaufleuten der Stadt beschäftigt nur 5 oder 6 ausländischer Handel, wie denn überhaupt weder der aus-, noch der inländische Handel bedeutend genannt werden kann. Hauptgegenstand des Handels ist Theer, doch handelt man auch mit Brettern, etwas Pelzwerk, besonders Hermelinfellen, Vögeln, Lachs, Strömlingen, Butter 2c. Fabriken giebt es nicht. Die Stadt besitzt 16 Schiffe und benutzt, außer diesen, theilweise fremde, besonders Stockholmer, Schiffe; man bauet auch Schiffe zum Verkauf. In den Hafen der Stadt können nur unbeladene Schiffe einlaufen; die Seeschiffe laufen daher vom Hafen Ratan (im Pastorat Bygdeå) aus. — Fischerey wird getrieben. Die der Stadt geschenkte einträgliche Lachsfischerey im Piteåfluß ist verpachtet. Die Stadt besitzt Ländereien, aber der Ackerbau ist geringe.

Die Lage am Strom, den in der Nähe und Ferne Waldberge umschließen, während an Lappland gränzende blauende Gebirgszüge den Hintergrund bilden, ist hübsch. Auch Gärten findet man, freilich ohne Fruchtbäume; doch hatte der Kaufmann Burman, mein gütiger Führer, in seinem Garten den Versuch gemacht, einen Apfelbaum zu pflanzen und Weinreben im Freien zu ziehen. Alle Gemüsekräuter gedeihen vortrefflich, kurz nach Pfingsten gelegte Zuckererbsen waren schon eine halbe Elle hoch, Radiese waren schon eßbar. Alles war grün und im vollen Treiben, wiewohl erst vor 14 Tagen der Schnee geschmolzen war, ja man ihn noch an den Abhängen der Berge erblickte; noch im Mai war man auf Schlitten gefahren. Die Erndte geschieht um Piteå wenigstens 8, spätestens 12 Wochen nach der Aussaat. Man hat bei Piteå die Mitte des Weges zwischen Umeå und Torneå, oder die Mitte von Westerbotten. Die Synode der Westerbottnischen Geistlichkeit wird daher in Piteå gehalten. Seit 1819 ist Piteå auch Sitz des Landshöfdings über Norrbotten.

Unter die Armen in Piteå wird Geld und Korn vertheilt; Waisen werden von Haus zu Haus verpflegt. Zur Armenpflege liefert die Schifffahrt ansehnliche Beiträge, denn es ist üblich, auf den Fahrten nach Stockholm bei Sturm, auch sonst, unter der Mannschaft für die Armen zu sammeln; auch werden nach glücklich vollendeter Reise die Armen bedacht. Diese Sitte herrscht an mehreren Orten.

Bei Frau Burman machte ich die Bekanntschaft ihres Bruders, des jungen Mytzell aus Sundswall, eines 20jährigen Jünglings, der 1813. 7 Monate zu Algier in der Gefangenschaft gesessen hatte, bis die Ankunft des Schwedischen Präsentschiffs ihn befreite. Mit einem eisernen Ringe am Fuß und unter Mißhandlungen hatte er auf Schiffen arbeiten müssen; noch trauriger schilderte er die Lage der Sklaven in den Plantagen. Späterhin, in Portsmouth gepreßt, hatte er der Expedition gegen Algier unter Exmouth beigewohnt, in Frankreich und Holland Schiffbruch erlitten, und von Holland aus die Rückreise ins Vaterland zu Fuße über Deutschland und Dännemark gemacht. Vor kurzem erst zurückgekehrt, sann der kräftige Jüngling schon auf neue Fahrten ins Ausland.

Nach einem fröhlichen Abendessen bei Frau Burman, fuhren wir um 10½ Uhr nach Öijeby, wo wir übernachteten. Als wir um 11¼ Uhr anlangten, war eben die Sonne untergegangen, und die Morgenröthe stand am Horizont. Öijeby hat einen netten und geräumigen Gästgifvaregård. — Der Weg von Piteå nach Öijeby oder Gamlastaden (Altstadt) führt durch Wald und neben fetten Wiesen. Auf einem Hügel hat man den vortheilhaftesten Ueberblick über die Stadt, in welcher die oben genannten beiden Wohnungen, der Frau Burman und des Herrn Degerman nebst dem Schulhause über alle übrigen Häuser hervorragen.

Bei Gamlastaden ist der Piteå sehr breit; üppige Wiesen mit freundlichen Dörfern und Landsitzen verschönern die Ufer; auf einer Halbinsel liegt, im Gebüsch versteckt, Gran, der Amtshof des Obersten von Westerbottens Regiment. Gran treibt ansehnlichen Ackerbau; das Wohnhaus ist von Holz, doch groß und schön. Die Kirche ist eine schöne steinerne Kreuzkirche, indeß nicht geräumig genug für die Volkszahl; der Altar, der Kanzel gegenüber, hübsch, aber dunkel; an seiner ehemaligen Stelle, dem Haupteingange gegenüber, muß er sich besser ausgenommen haben. An einer Wand der Kirche hängt ein Lobgedicht auf Karls XII. Siege, wie man es in mehreren Kirchen trifft. In der Sacristey erfreuen mehrere zierliche Darstellungen in Holz aus der Geschichte Jesu, von einem hiesigen Künstler, dem die Gemeinde für seine Arbeit eine jährliche Unterstützung bewilligte. In einem Schrank wird die Sammlung kirchlicher, Westerbotten betreffender, Akten aufbewahrt, die man im Jahr 1787 von der Wittwe des Propstes Solander kaufte. — Durch den massiven Glockenthurm führt einer der Eingänge zum Kirchhof, den hunderte von Kirchenstuben und Kirchenställen umgeben.

Auf einem freien Platz, der Kirche gegenüber, erhebt sich eine Pyramide von grüngesprenkeltem Marmor. Sie pflanzt das Gedächtniß der Anwesenheit des Königs Adolph Friedrich auf der Rückreise von Torneå, auf welcher er zu Gran übernachtete, fort, und trägt folgende Inschrift:

När. Wåra. Munnar. Tystna. Skall. Stenen. Denne. Tala. Om. Westerbottningars. Glädje. Dä. Svea. Konung. A D O L P H. Den. Förste. Stadd. Å. Eriksgatan. Sina. Hit. Anlände. Den. 28. Julii. 1752.

(Wann unsere Lippen schweigen, soll dieser Stein reden von der Freude der Westerbottnier, als Schwedens König, Adolph Friedrich I., auf seiner Reise durch das Reich hier eintraf am 26. Jul. 1752.)

Efterwerlden. Nyttje. Länge. Dess. Arbete. och. Berömme. Ewärdeligen. Dess. Bedrifter,

Die Nachwelt genieße lange sein Werk und preise seine Thaten immerdar.)

Auf dem viereckigen Piedestal (die Pyramide selbst ist achteckig) liest man:

Westerbottens. Prästerskap. Och. Civil-Betjento. Reste. Stenen.

(Westerbottens Geistlichkeit und Civilbeamte errichteten den Stein.)

———————

Am 20. Jun. Von Oijeby nach Portsnäs 1⅓ Meile; von Portsnäs nach Rosvik 1⅓ Meile; von Rosvik nach Ersnäs 1¼ Meile; von Ersnäs nach Gäddvik 1⅜ Meile; von Gäddvik nach Luled Gamlastad ¾ Meile; von Luled nach Pärsön 1¼ Meilen; von Pärsön nach Raneå 1⅜ Meilen. — Zusammen 9⅓ Meilen.

Um 7⅓ Uhr verließen wir Oijeby. Der Weg führt neben hohen Felsenwänden, an welchen sich malerisch Gebüsche herabsenken, dann in den Wald, der aber oft durch Wiesen unterbrochen wird. Bald kamen wir zu einer entwaldeten Stelle, wo ein scheußlicher Anblick uns überraschte: ein Richtplatz mit den unter Kleidern versteckten Ueberbleibseln zweier Missethäter aus dem nahen Dorfe Kopparsnäs, eines Bauernsohnes, der einen Schmide für 50 Bankthaler und 2 Tonnen Korn gedungen hatte, seinen Vater zu ermorden, um die Theilung des väterlichen Guts unter die Geschwister zu hintertreiben; der abscheuliche Sohn, 32 Jahre alt, hatte schon früher eine Menge Diebstähle begangen, worin ihm der Vater mit dem Beispiel vorgegangen war. Seit Menschengedenken war in diesen Gegenden keine Mordthat begangen worden. Zwei Schwestern des Bösewichts sind in Kopparsnäs verheirathet und sollen wohldenkende Leute seyn. Mit wehmüthigen Gefühlen fuhren wir durch das große Dorf; dann geht es über den Alter-Elf, dem kleinen Dorfe Kakesjö vorüber, neben Wiesen und Getraidefeldern nach Portsnäs. In einer Stunde waren die 1¼ Meilen zurückgelegt; so schnell war ich seit Hernösand fast immer gefahren; denn die Norrländischen Pferde, zwar nur von mittlerem Wuchs, sind die besten Traber, die man in Schweden findet.

In Portsnäs frühstückten wir in einem Zimmer, unter dessen Fenstern sich ein herrliches Kornfeld ausbreitete. Die Gegend ist schön und fruchtbar.

Auch zwischen Portsnäs und Rosvik hat man anfangs Wiesen, Saatfelder und Höfe; freundliche Meerbusen zeigen sich, zuletzt fährt man durch viel Wald. Indem man aus dem Walde kommt, befindet man sich auf einem Hügel, wo man an der einen Seite einen Meerbusen mit bewaldeten Inseln und Landzungen, an der andern ein weites, von Waldbergen umgebenes Thal erblickt, in welchem sich das große Dorf Rosvik ausbreitet; über die Mündung eines kleinen Flusses fuhren wir zum Gästgifvaregård, wo in dem freundlichen Innern nach Bottnischer Sitte ein Stangengerüst die Garderobe bildete. Die Hitze war drückend, wie gestern, und plagte, sammt dem Staube und den Mücken; einigen Schutz gewährte indeß die grüne Florkappe, womit ich mich versehen hatte, das nahe Meer verbreitete einige Kühlung. Die Mücken sind eine gar arge Plage, sie sind in Norrbotten und Lappland größer als im übrigen Norrland und verfinstern bei stillem Wetter die Luft. Schwaches Vieh sollen sie sogar zuweilen tödten, indem sie das Blut bis auf den letzten Tropfen aussaugen, so daß man das Fleisch ganz weiß gefunden hat.

Von Rosvik nach Ersnäs ist nichts als Waldweg, doch meist sind es lieblich duftende Birken; auch sieht man Waldwiesen und zweimal Sennhütten; bei einer derselben stieg ich ab, ließ mir Milch reichen; die Sennin war eben mit der Käsebereitung beschäftiget; die Käsekammern sind besondere kleine Gebäude oder mit den Wohnstuben verbunden, neben denen auch ein Eiskeller angelegt ist. Das eine Sennendorf gehört nach Rosvik, das andere nach Ersnäs. Die Bewohner von Ersnäs haben nur einen Theil ihrer Kuhheerde bei den Sennhütten, damit die Weide nicht zu sehr abgefressen werde; die Bewohner von Rosvik behalten blos Ziegen daheim. Bei Ersnäs bildet ein kleiner Fluß an seiner Mündung einen breiten Busen, Ersnäs Fjärder genannt.

Von Ersnäs bis Gäddvik hat man einen recht freundlichen Weg, zumal auf dem ersten Drittheil, wo üppige Wiesen, von Heuscheuern bedeckt und von Gebüschen umgeben, mit Bächen und Meeresbusen wechseln. Das in die Heuscheunen, deren jeder Bauerhof 7 bis 50 besitzt, im Sommer gesammelte Heu wird im Winter auf Schlitten zu den Höfen geführt. Durch Birken- und Fichtenwald gelangt man an das Ufer des majestätischen Luleä-Stroms, der hier 600 Faden breit ist; am Ufer ist eine Tafel errichtet, an welcher man die Fährtaxe lieset; auch erblickt man das Westerbottnische Wappen mit der Inschrift: Deo, Regi et patriae omnia (Gott, dem König und dem Vaterlande Alles), gegenüber einen hohen Steinhaufen mit steinerner Meilentafel. Die Russen bauten hier eine Brücke über den Strom, die aber nicht mehr besteht. In einer Viertelstunde fuhren wir in Böten ans jenseitige Ufer, wo Gäddvik, der größte Gasthof Norrbottens, liegt. Rechts zeigt sich in der Ferne der Kirchthurm der Stadt Luleä, wo der Strom sich ins Bottnische Meer ergießt.

Von Gäddvik bis Luleä Gamlastad, oder der Landkirche Luleä (unter 65° 50′ 20″ Polhöhe), hat man ¼ Meile nichts als Wald. Die Altstadt hat eine reizende Lage mitten zwischen fruchtbaren Kornfeldern, üppigen Wiesen und lieblichen Hainen. Die prächtige Kirche umgeben mehr denn 600 Kirchbuden. In einigen derselben wohnten eben Confirmanden, welche, nach Norrländischer Sitte, mehrere Tage vor der Confirmation sich bei der Kirche versammeln und, nachdem sie gewöhnlich bereits längere Zeit zuvor, an einzelnen Tagen, unterwiesen worden, nun täglich Vor- und Nachmittags und Abends unter-

richtet werden und deßhalb auch im Kirchorte übernachten. Sie
leben hier ganz der Vorbereitung auf den ernsten Schritt, den sie
zu thun im Begriffe stehen; und in der That äußert dieses ganz
religiöse Beisammenleben den heilsamsten Einfluß.

Nach einem kurzen Aufenthalt beim Dr. Nordmark setzten wir die Reise fort. Bis Pårsön hat man Birkenwald
mit herrlichen Wiesen und das Dorf Rutvik. Pårsön liegt
höchst anmuthig zwischen Wiesen, Kornfeldern, Gebüschen und
Wasserzügen. Eine Viertelmeile fährt man in dem weitläuftigen
Dorfe, bis man den Gåstgifvaregård erreicht; mitten im Dorfe
sind Felder und Wiesen; links bildet ein Fluß einen weiten Busen, der durch einen schmalen Lauf mit dem Meere zusammenhängt.

Hinter Pårsön hat man viel Birkenwald, den zuletzt das
Dorf Byrjeslandet unterbricht; dann fährt man über den
Larkabäck; reizend sind die Ufer dieses Flusses, Wiesen und
Birkengebüsch fassen ihn ein, kleine Inseln füllen seinen Lauf;
den Hintergrund bilden im Westen blauende Berge. Abermals
fährt man in Birkenwald, dem Dorfe Sunhom vorüber, neben
Wiesen an das Ufer des Råneå-Stroms, über welchen wir
in einem Boote fuhren; der Strom ist bei der Fähre 543 Fuß
breit. Im Flusse liegt eine schön bebuschte Insel, Anholmen,
wo mehrere Häuser stehen, ein Lieutenant sein Boställe hat, auch
Markt gehalten wird. Am jenseitigen Ufer erhebt sich die hölzerne Kirche; rings umher sind Kirchbuden, etwa 150 an der
Zahl, auch liegt hier der Pfarrhof, der Gåstgifvaregård nebst
einigen Höfen, und hart am Dorfe eine Anzahl Sennhütten,
wo ein Lappe die Heerden weidet und wohin die Mädchen des
Dorfes Morgens und Abends zum Melken gehen. — Bald
nachdem wir im Gåstgifvaregård angelangt waren, wo wir übernachteten, ging ich zum Kirchhof, und freute mich der herrlichen
Aussicht, die er gewährt, auf den Fluß und die schönen Ufer;
auch das Rauschen eines kleinen Wasserfalles vernimmt man.
Auf dem Rückwege begegnete ich 4 Lappinnen aus Gellivare-

Lappmark. Sie lagen, nach Lappischer Weise, auf der Erde; ihre Kleidung bestand in Fellen, an welchen vorne allerlei Kleinigkeiten, als: Schlüssel zu dem Kästchen, was die Baarschaft von Schillingen und Stübern enthält, Messerchen, Knöpfe und andere blendende Sachen, an Schnüren befestiget, eine Sitte, die man bei allen Lappen findet; ihre Gesichtsfarbe war wenig gelb. Nicht selten stößt man in mehreren Theilen Norrlands, insbesondere in Norrbotten, auf umherziehende Lappen, die sich durch Arbeit und Betteln ernähren; es sind die Aermeren ihres Volks, die durch Unglücksfälle ihre Heerden verloren haben; einige verdingen sich als Hirten; ein solcher Hirtenlappe, auch aus Gelliware, gesellte sich bald zu der kleinen Gesellschaft, er war mehr als die übrigen des Lesens kundig. Schwedisch verstanden diese Lappen wenig. Ich schenkte ihnen zum gemeinschaftlichen Gebrauch ein Lappisches Neues Testament, welches ich in Hernösand erhalten hatte. Ihre Statur war nicht ganz klein. Die Alten verjüngte der unerschöpfliche Frohsinn, der diese armen Leute beseelte; überhaupt sieht man die Lappen fast nie traurig.

Die Brunnen hiesiger Gegend sind so weit überbauet, daß nur der Platz frei bleibt, der zum Herunterlassen und Aufziehen des Eimers erforderlich ist; eine zweckmäßige Einrichtung, wodurch manches Unglück verhütet wird.

———

Am 21. Jun. Von Råneå nach Hviteån 1¾ Meile; von Hviteån nach Töre 1¾ Meile; von Töre nach Månsby 2¼ Meilen; von Månsby nach Grötnäs ¾ Meile. — Zusammen 6½ Meilen.

Der Weg nach Hviteån führt durch Nadel= und Birken= wald, der öfters von freundlichen kleinen Thälern unterbrochen wird. Hviteån liegt sehr hübsch an einem Meerbusen. Der Busen von Hviteån ist der nördlichste des Bottnischen Mee= res; daher auch das Dorf Hviteån, etwa eine halbe Meile nördlicher liegt als die Stadt Torneå; von Hviteån bis Torneå fährt man mehr gegen Südwest. Eine halbe Meile von Hviteån, im Walde, liegt ein ziemlich hoher Berg, Eliskörberget, von welchem man die Mitternachtssonne um Johannis freier und länger als von Nieder=Torneås Kirchthurm erblickt, wo sie bekanntlich mehrere Minuten verschwindet. Ueber= haupt sieht man um diese Zeit in den Pastoraten Råneå und Neder=Calix eben so wohl als in Neder=Torneå die ganze Nacht hindurch die Sonne. Ein besserer Standpunkt ist freilich der Berg in Ober=Torneå, 7½ Meile nordöstlich von der Stadt Torneå, so wie die im Norden von Neder=Ca= lix gelegene Kirche Ober=Calix und, in deren Nähe, der Lappberg.

In Hviteån, wo sehr reinliche und nette Fremdenzimmer sind, insbesondere im Clashof (denn der Gästgifvaregård wechselt im Dorfe), labten wir uns an trefflicher Sahne, frischer But= ter und geräuchertem Rennthierfleisch. Als wir weiter reisen wollten, kam ein Lappe, welcher bettelte, wiewohl er nicht ganz arm war; er wohnte ¾ Meilen von Hviteån im Walde in einer ächt Lappischen Hütte, und hatte eigene Kühe und Ziegen, auch einige Rennthiere. Er sang uns ein Liedchen vor und tanzte dabei. Die Farbe seines Gesichts war, wie bei vielen Lappen, schmuzig gelb. Die wenigen, in den Schwedischen Gemeinden ansäßigen Lappen leben ganz wie in Lappland.

Unweit Hviteån fährt man über den Lascarsfors=Elf, der sich zwischen Gebüschen und Wiesenufern hinschlängelt, dann kommt man durch Nadel= und Laubwald. Auch Schwendeland erblickt man, wo aber die Bäume noch halbverbrannt da standen; an einem freundlichen See erscheint ein Sennendorf. Es war ein sehr heißer Tag an 30° Celsii (24° Reaumur) und die Mücken plagten. Am Ende der Station erreicht man die Sä= gemühle und das Dorf Töresors, fährt auf einer Brücke über den Töre=Elf und gelangt gleich darauf zum Gästgifvaregård, den eine Meilentafel bezeichnet. Um Töre wird viel Korn ge=

bauet. An das Dorf lehnen sich Sennhütten, die von den Höfen aus Morgens und Abends benutzt werden, so daß die Milch nicht in den Hütten zu Käse bereitet wird.

Gleich hinter Töre erblickt man den Meerbusen Töreviken, der nur um weniges südlicher liegt als Hviteäsjärden, und dessen Lage bewaldete Landspitzen verschönern. Dann fährt man wieder in den Wald, den aber hier und da Seen und Wiesen unterbrechen. Hier — es war Sonnabend Mittag — begegneten wir vielen Kirchbesuchern zu Fuß und zu Wagen, die nach der Kirche Nieder-Calix zogen. Mein Skjutsbonde, der Sohn des Gästgifvare in Töre, beklagte sich, mit großer Innigkeit, daß sein Vater ihn seit Ostern nicht zur Kirche habe gehen lassen. Wie selten hört man bei uns solche Klagen aus dem Munde der Dienenden, denen Gleiches wiederfährt?

Aus dem Walde fährt man an das Ufer des majestätischen Calix-Elf, eines aus Lappland herabkommenden Stroms, und dann am Fuße hoher Waldberge längs desselben nach Mänsby. Da, wo man den Strom zuerst erblickt, bildet er mehrere kleine Wasserfälle. Das jenseitige Ufer ist mit Dörfern, Höfen und Heuscheunen bedeckt, die mit den Wiesen, Gebüschen und entfernten Waldbergen recht malerische Gruppen bilden. Hier liegt auch der freundliche Landsitz des Kriegsraths Petersson, Ätroten. In Mänsby begehrte ich Milch; in einem silbernen Becher, dem väterlichen Erbstück (silberne Geräthe findet man sehr häufig in den Westerbottnischen Bauerhöfen), ward sie mir gereicht; als ich fragte, was ich schuldig sey, wollte man keine Bezahlung haben *), und doch war es ein Gasthof, nur mit Mühe konnte ich dem Wirthe eine kleine Vergeltung aufbringen.

*) Als Henderson auf seiner Reise in Island die Milch bezahlen wollte, die er in einer Meierei getrunken, entgegnete ihm die Hausfrau: „nein, ich werde nichts dafür nehmen, denn wir selbst erhalten es ja umsonst von Gott." S. Henderson Island. B. 2. S. 195.

Bei Månsby ziehen sich die Berge auch am östlichen Ufer zurück; ein liebliches Wiesenthal erscheint, mit Höfen und Heuscheunen bedeckt. So fährt man an den üppigen Wiesenufern des Calix-Elf, auf welchem Dörfer und Höfe in fast ununterbrochener Reihe sich folgen, durch das Dorf Innanbäcken nach Grötnäs, wo ein hübscher und geräumiger Gästgifvaregård ist. In Grötnäs erfrischte ich mich abermals durch Milch, und hatte wiederum viele Mühe, zur Annahme einiger Bezahlung, die man nicht verlangte, zu bewegen. Grötnäs gegenüber liegt die schöne Kirche Nieder-Calix; auf einem Boote fuhren wir in Gesellschaft mehrerer Kirchgängerinnen hinüber, der Fluß ist hier, nicht gar weit von seiner Mündung, 510 Ellen breit und hat oberhalb viele Fälle; er entspringt an der Norwegischen Gränze und kommt an Breite und an reißendem Lauf dem Skellfteå und dem Piteå-Elf gleich. — Die Polhöhe bei Grötnäs beträgt 65° 50′ 20″.

Eben war ½ Meile von der Kirche, beim Dorfe Näsby das Norder-Bataillon des Westerbottnischen Regiments zu seinen jährlichen militairischen Uebungen versammelt, schon in Grötnäs hörte man die Trommeln. Die große Landstraße läuft durch Näsby; wir sprachen daher im Lager vor, wo gerade auch der Landshöfding von Norrbottens Län, Baron Koskull, anwesend war. Mit großer Artigkeit wurden wir empfangen. Als wir ankamen, ward exercirt, dann ward Chorum gehalten, d. i. der Abendsegen gesprochen, auch, mit vieler Andacht, gesungen; eben so wird an jedem Frühmorgen Betstunde, und an den Vormittagen der Sonntage feierlicher Gottesdienst gehalten; an den Sonntags-Nachmittagen werden Katechismusverhöre mit den Soldaten angestellt. — Nach dem Chorum begaben wir uns zu einem Mahl, welches der freundliche Major Lychon in Näsby veranstaltet hatte; der größere Theil des Officiercorps, so wie der Bergmeister Quensell nebst seiner aus Torneå-Stadt gebürtigen Gattin, waren zugegen. Die guten Leute wußten nicht, wie sie uns Fremden ihr herzliches Wohlwollen bezeugen sollten.

Bei Tische fiel das Gespräch unter andern auch auf die Musik
des Regiments; ich äußerte, daß ich bei einer Gelegenheit schon
die vollständige Musik des Westerbottnischen Regiments gehört
und sie mir viel Freude gemacht habe. In diesen Worten glaubte
man den Wunsch zu erkennen, auch jetzt jene Musik zu hören;
ganz in der Stille wurde sie sofort beordert, und als ich noch
im traulichen Gespräch da saß, ward ich plötzlich von den süßen
Tönen der wirklich trefflichen Regimentsmusik überrascht. Gerührt dankte ich. Unsere Gemüther waren ganz Freude, mit
Innigkeit schlossen wir uns an einander, sangen dem allgeliebten
Karl Johann ein herzliches God save tho king, und tran-
ken Gesundheiten. So ward es Mitternacht, da riß ich mich
los von den liebreichen, gastlichen Menschen und fuhr unter voller Musik durch den Wald nach Grötnäs. Still und milde
war die Luft, still und ruhig floß der herrliche Calixstrom, lieblich dufteten die Birken von den Ufern; rechts erschien eine hübsche bewaldete Insel, links die Insel Fiskeholm, von Kaufbuden bedeckt, wo der Markt von Calix gehalten wird; ringsum üppige Wiesen, die Vögel zwitscherten ihr Morgenlied; alles
erinnerte an südliche Zonen. Kirchgängerinnen belebten den
Weg, sie kamen aus fernen Höfen herbei, um bis nach vollendeter Festfeier (das Johannisfest wird in Schweden am Johannistage selbst, kirchlich begangen) in ihren Kirchstuben zu verweilen. — Um 1¼ Uhr, bei vollem Tageslicht war ich in Grötnäs; eine Viertelstunde später strahlte die Sonne am Horizont.
— Meine Gefährten setzten noch in derselbigen Nacht von Näsby aus die Reise nach Öfver-Torneå fort. Ich blieb, um
am folgenden Tage in der frommen Gemeinde Calix dem Gottesdienst beizuwohnen.

Um 9 Uhr begab ich mich in die Kirche, ein altes, steinernes, thurmloses Gebäude. Wiewohl nur etwa der dritte Theil
der Gemeinde zugegen war, so war die Kirche doch so angefüllt,
daß selbst die Thürschwellen der Stühle als Sitze benutzt wurden. Der gar sanfte, milde, und doch so kraft- und lebenvolle,

II.   H andächtige Gemeindegesang ergriff mich wunderbar, also daß ich zu Thränen gerührt ward und mit Augustinus (Confess. B. 9. K. 6) sprechen konnte: „diese Stimmen der lieblich singenden Gemeinde flossen mir in meine Ohren, und deine Wahrheit ward in mein Herz ausgegossen?" — Mit größter Aufmerksamkeit hörte alles der Predigt zu, es war ganz so, als wenn jedes Wort in das Innerste aufgenommen werde. Versah es etwa ein Zuhörer mit diesem oder jenem, wodurch ein Anderer Würde und Sitte ein wenig verletzt glaubte, so besserte jenen ein Verständigerer sofort in der Stille. Als der Gottesdienst begann, waren fast alle schon versammelt, nur wenige kamen später, und diese traten nur während des Gesanges, nicht während des Altardienstes, in die Kirche. Zuvörderst wurden einige Wöchnerinnen eingesegnet, indem über sie, während sie knieten, das in der Liturgie vorgeschriebene Gebet gesprochen wurde, worauf sie der Prediger mit einem geistlichen Glückwunsch und mit biederem Händedruck in die Gemeinde entließ. Nun nahm der eigentliche Gottesdienst seinen Anfang: erhebende Altargebete, das Sündenbekenntniß, wobei alle knieten und die jungen Leute, welche am nächsten Johannistage confirmirt werden sollten, besonders gerührt waren, die Verlesung der Epistel, das vom Geistlichen vor der stehenden Gemeinde gesprochene Glaubensbekenntniß wechseln mit Collecten und Responsorien und dem Gemeindegesange; der Predigt, die in den Schwedischen Kirchen selten über ½ Stunde dauert, folgen allgemeine und besondere Kanzelgebete. Nachdem der Prediger die Kanzel verlassen, singt die Gemeinde, worauf die Feier des heiligen Abendmahls anhebt, oder, falls dieses, wie heute, ausfällt, der Gottesdienst mit Responsorien, einem Altargebete und dem kirchlichen Segen geschlossen wird *).

---

*) Bei meiner Rückkehr von Torneå erzählte man mir von der großen Rührung, die bei der Confirmation am Johannisfeste Statt gefunden habe (an einem der nächsten Sonntage sollten die Confirmirten zum ersten Mal das heilige Abendmahl empfangen), einzelne, die nicht persönlich den Dank ihres Herzens zu bezeugen vermochten, schrieben

Nach dem Gottesdienst ging ich in die Kirchstuben, die ganz wie Wohnhäuser eingerichtet, auch mit Kaminen versehen sind. Hier lesen die aus der Kirche Kommenden im Gesang, und Evangelienbuch, bevor sie den Heimweg antreten. — In der Nähe der Kirche liegt auch das Gemeindehaus, für die gemeinsamen Berathungen, mit drei Zimmern, davon eines zur Aufbewahrung zu verauctionirender Sachen dient.

Zwanzigstes Kapitel.

Finnisches Westerbotten.

Abnahme des Bottnischen Meerbusens. — Haparanda, — Strom und Pastorate Torneå. — Hohe Kultur der Polargegenden. — Die Finnen: Pörten, Schwitzbäder. — Ueppige Vegetation. — Lachsfang im Torneå-Elf. — Gränze gegen Rußland. — Malerische Gegenden. — Ofver-Torneå. — Berg Afvasaxa. — Die Mitternachtssonne. — Die Johannisfeier. — Gottesdienst in Ofver-Torneå. — Die neuen Kirchen am Russischen Ufer des Torneå. — Neder-Torneå. — Stadt Torneå.

Am 22. Jun. Von Grönäs nach Sangis 2¾ Meile; von Sangis nach Saifvits 1¼ Meile; von Saifvits nach Nickala 1¼ Meile; von Nickala nach Haparanda 1¼ Meile; von Haparanda nach Wojakkala ¾ Meile. — Zusammen 7¾ Meilen.

einfache, kunstlose Briefe an den Lehrer, der ihnen den vorbereitenden Unterricht ertheilt hatte; ich sah einen dieser Briefe; in schlichten, herzlichen Worten war hier ausgesprochen der Dank, zu welchem sich dem treuen Lehrer der Confirmande für Zeit und Ewigkeit verpflichtet fühle, wie das Versprechen durch stilles Halten an dem gepredigten Worte ihm Freude zu bereiten. — Der Ausdruck des Briefes war richtig; die meisten Bauern und Bäuerinnen Norrlands sind des Schreibens ziemlich kundig.

H 2

Um 12 Uhr fuhr ich ab. Zu Näsby sprach ich eine kurze Weile im Lager vor, um für gestern zu danken. Bis Sangits hat man Nadel- und Laubwald; nur zuweilen erblickt man Seen und üppige Waldwiesen, von einem Bache bewässert. Lands järf ist die einzige Menschenwohnung, die man trifft; eine Glas- hütte im Walde steht unbenutzt. Der Weg ist meist eben und sehr sandig. Um Sangits, wo 19 Bauern wohnen, sieht man viele Kornfelder; das Dorf liegt in einem Thale, das der breite Sangitsfluß durchfließt.

Nach Saifvits, einem Dorfe von 8 Höfen, führt ein sandiger, hügeliger Waldweg. Von dem Hügel vor Saifvits schauet man über den schönen Meerbusen von Saifvits weit in das Bottnische Meer hinaus.

Zwischen Sangits und Saifvits beginnt das Pastorat Neder- (Nieder) Torneå, und mit demselben das Gebiet der Finnischen Sprache. Die Bewohner von Saifvits reden schon Finnisch, verstehen wenig Schwedisch und sprechen es un- gern. Nordwärts und westwärts findet man nun nur Finnen; doch wird in der Stadt Torneå, wo viele Schweden wohnen, mehr Schwedisch als Finnisch geredet; und die Sprache der Ho- noratioren ist auch auf dem Lande hier, wie in ganz Finnland, die Schwedische. Die Finnen um Torneå sind des Schwedischen mehr wie die übrigen Westerbottnischen Finnen kundig. Für Reisende, die des Finnischen nicht mächtig sind, ist in den Finni- schen Dörfern hiesiger Gegend im Gästgifvaregård gewöhnlich durch Dolmetscher gesorgt. Freilich gewinnt man durch diese Einrichtung unterweges nicht. Sind vielleicht die Finnen auch nicht ganz so unterrichtet, wie die Schwedischen Norrländer, so sind sie es in der Regel doch mehr, wie die Postillione in Deutschland, und der Reisende verliert wirklich, wenn er sich mit ihnen nicht unterhalten kann. Auch ich war des Finnischen nicht mächtig und mußte mich daher begnügen, durch auswendig ge- lernte Worte anzudeuten, so oft still gehalten oder schneller gefahren werden sollte. — Die Wohnhäuser sind meistens noch auf Schwedische Art gebauet, doch findet man auch schon Pörten. Die Gastzimmer sind klein, aber freundlich; man sieht viel Silbergeräthe, wie denn überhaupt im Finnischen Westerbotten Wohlstand herrscht.

Liebliche Wiesen und Bäche im Walde und Meerbusen verschönern den Weg von Saivits nach Nickala. An einem dieser Meerbusen, eine halbe Meile disseits Nickala, hatte im Jahr 1810 der Landshöfding Ekorn die Stelle erwählt, an welcher eine neue Stadt die abgetretene Stadt Torneå ersetzen sollte; die Lage ist aber für den Landhandel völlig ungünstig; ein guter Hafen ist vorhanden, doch zu weit vom Flusse Torneå entfernt, auf welchem die meisten Transporte beschafft werden, welcher Umstand um so größere Hindernisse bereitet, da die Böte, deren man sich auf dem Torneå bedient, zwar beim Durchfahren der vielen Strömungen und Fälle des Flusses, wenn gleich keinesweges ohne Gefahr, anwendbar, aber zum Befahren des Meeres, selbst an der Küste, durchaus nicht geeignet sind. Diese widrigen Umstände hatten das Entstehen der neuen Stadt bisher gehindert. Man wollte die neue Stadt Carl-Johans-Stad nennen; doch erging im Jahr 1821 der Befehl, daß sie Haparanda heiße. Bei Haparanda, unweit der Mündung des Torneå, wäre allerdings eine sehr günstige Stelle zur Anlage einer neuen Stadt. Auf dem Schwedischen Ufer des Torneå wohnen bereits mehrere Kaufleute, die früher in Torneå ansäßig, seit der Abtretung in der neuen Stadt das Bürgerrecht gewonnen, um auf eine vortheilhaftere Weise, als es vom Russischen Torneå aus geschehen konnte, den Handel nach Stockholm, der immer in Torneå der bedeutendste war, zu treiben; die Stadt Torneå hat durch die Auswanderung dieser Kaufleute sehr verloren. — Zur Anlegung einer Schule in der neu zu gründenden Stadt hat das Consistorium zu Hernösand schon einen beträchtlichen Fond gesammelt.

Der Wald zwischen Saivits und Nickala besteht meist aus jungen Birken; oft fährt man einzelnen Höfen, zum Theil Kolonistenhöfen (nybyggen) vorüber; blühende Äckerbär erblickt man, wie bereits auf der vorigen Station, am Wege. Fast eine halbe Meile fährt man neben den 40 zerstreuten Bauerhöfen, die das Dorf Nickala bilden, an einem Meerbusen und über denselben auf einem Damme und einer Brücke, bis man den Gästgifvaregård erreicht. Auf der Brücke erhebt sich, über einem Piedestal von Granit, eine Marmorsäule, an der einen Seite mit einer Schwedischen, an der andern Seite mit einer Finni-schen Inschrift, folgenden gleichlautenden Inhalts:

„Im zweiten Regierungsjahre Königs Gustav III. 1772, als die Grundgesetze des Reichs verbessert wurden, bauten die Gemeinden Torneå diese Brücke und errichteten dieses Denkmal."

Auf der Brücke wehte ein ziemlich kalter Wind, im Walde war die Hitze drückend; der gestrige Tag war noch heißer. Die größte Hitze, die in diesen Polargegenden ziemlich oft eintritt, ist 30° Celsi (24° Reaumur), seltener steigt sie in Norrbotten bis 34° Celsi, wo man fast keine Kleidung dulden kann; im Winter hat man zuweilen eine Kälte von 40° Celsi (32° Reaumur).

Die Busen des Bottnischen Meeres werden hier immer seichter, ja gehen in Sümpfe und Wiesen über. Im Jahr 1736 fuhren die Französischen Astronomen da in Böten, wo jetzt fast nur sumpfige Wiesen sind. Auch der Hafen der Stadt Torneå ist seichter geworden.

In Nickala war Begräbnißschmaus (graföl), eine über ganz Schweden und Finnland, insbesondere bei dem Tode Er-wachsener, mehr oder weniger übliche Sitte, die aber in neuester Zeit in immer mehreren Schwedischen Gemeinden gänzlich abge-legt worden ist. In der Regel wird ein solches Graföl nur mit Einem Mahle, oder doch mit Einer Mittags- und Einer Abendmahlzeit, gefeiert; die Finnischen Bauern hiesiger Gegend bleiben zwei Tage zusammen und thun sich gütlich mit Fischen,

Suppe, Braten, Kuchen, Wein und Punsch. Auch sind wohl Gesänge zu Ehren der Todten üblich.

Eine Viertelmeile jenseits Nickala erscheint zuerst die Stadtkirche Torneå und bald die noch schönere Landkirche Neder-Torneå; auch letztere liegt auf Russischem Gebiet. Man fährt durch Wald, der, nur weil er jung ist, nicht in Folge des Klimas, eine geringe Höhe hat, denn weiter landeinwärts, wo man die alten Bäume nicht gefällt hat, findet man gleich hohe und dicke Bäume, wie in den südlicheren Landschaften. Auch neben Wiesen führt die Straße; in einem Meeresbusen erscheint eine liebliche kleine Insel mit Gebüschen. — In dem großen Dorfe Wuonom gab ich ein Schreiben des Landshöfding an den Kronvoigt (kronobe fallningsman) Örling ab, bei dem eben Graföl war, welches bei den Honoratioren aber nur einen halben Tag dauert. Der brave Mann war sehr betrübt über den Tod seines einzigen Söhnleins; dennoch ließ er sofort durch den anwesenden Häradsschreiber mehrere Anstalten treffen, durch welche meine Reise in den Finnischen Bezirken aufs möglichste erleichtert und angenehm gemacht werden sollte; der freundliche und biedere Sinn der Einwohner überhob mich indeß der Nothwendigkeit, durch häufige Benutzung dieser Verfügungen vielleicht Beschwerde zu verursachen.

In der Ferne erblickt man die Mündung des Torneå-flusses mit vorliegenden schön bebuschten Inseln. Am Wege sieht man viel Korn, auch Winterroggen; doch wird nicht hinreichend gebauet. — Bald fährt man in das Gränzdorf Haparanda ein, wo die kleine Gränzwache postirt ist. Das Gränz-Postcomtoir Haparanda besteht gegenwärtig zu Kocklund, dem ersten Hofe der benachbarten Dorfschaft Mattila; doch dauert der Name: Haparanda Postcomtoir fort. Ueber Haparanda geht die Winterpost von Stockholm nach Åbo, sobald der kürzeste Weg über Ålands Haf nicht mehr sicher ist. Auch ward im Jahr 1822 ein Winterpostgang von Haparanda durch Lappland nach Alten im Norwegischen Finnmarken, unter 70°, und ein anderer nach Tromsoe im Norwegischen Nordland, unter 69⅔ Grad Polhöhe, eröffnet.

Von Haparanda führt ein Weg rechts ins Russische Gebiet und zur Stadt Torneå; ein anderer, links, am Schwedischen Ufer des Flusses Torneå, nordwestlich, ins Pastorat Öfver-(Ober) Torneå und durch dasselbe nach Lappland und Norwegen. Ich wählte den Weg nach Öfver-Torneå, um dort auf dem Berge Afvasaxa die volle Mitternachtssonne ununterbrochen zu schauen, für welchen Zweck sich der von vielen Reisenden als Standpunkt benutzte Glockenthurm der Stadtkirche von Torneå nicht so sehr eignet.

Die ganze Strecke von Haparanda bis zur Kirche Öfver-Torneå, mehr denn 7 Meilen Weges, ist eine der fruchtbarsten, anmuthigsten und bevölkertsten Gegenden Schwedens. Kornfelder wechseln mit lieblichen Wiesen, die die reichste Vegetation, ja ellenhohes, dicht stehendes Gras, schmückt; ein großes Dorf reihet sich an das andere, alle sind von Finnen bewohnt. Der treffliche Anbau dieser Polargegenden ist eine Folge der Einwanderungen aus dem eigentlichen Finnland, wie der Ansiedelungen der Söhne bereits ansässiger Bauern. Seit der bekannten Französischen Gradmessung, und noch mehr seit den letzten Jahrzehnten, hat die Kultur unglaubliche Fortschritte gemacht. Kein schöneres Denkmahl konnte sich die Schwedische Regierung errichten; auch in den abgetretenen Distrikten lebt ihr Andenken gesegnet fort. Der herrliche Grundsatz, das Reich im Innern zu erweitern und also im Reiche selbst neue Provinzen zu schaffen, zeichnet mehrere der gepriesensten Könige Schwedens aus; dieser Grundsatz ist es, den auch in unsern Tagen Karl XIV. Johann mit so viel Eifer und Kraft geltend macht. Man muß mit eignen Augen sehen, um sich zu überzeugen, wie mächtig jetzt Schweden in seinem Innern wächset.

Den Weg von Haparanda nach Wojakkala, fast eine Meile, begränzt eine lange Reihe von Höfen, die nur eine Viertelweile eine Zahl Heuscheuern unterbricht. Rechts fließt der breite Torneå, den mit Gebüschen bedeckte Inseln oder Landzungen schmücken. Links breitet sich eine weite Ebene aus, auf welcher liebliche Birken mit Gärten, freilich ohne Fruchtbäume, Roggen und Gerstenfelder mit den üppigsten Wiesen wechseln. Einige Wohnhäuser werden von hohen Ulmen beschattet. Einmal fährt man über einen kleinen Bach, der aus einer Waldschlucht (ein seltener Anblick in dieser weiten Ebene) hervorrieselt. Auch am jenseitigen Russischen Ufer erscheint eine Reihe von Dörfern, die oft Theile der Dörfer am Schwedischen Ufer sind, denn mehrere Dorfschaften dehnen sich an beiden Ufern aus. — Nachdem ich schon auf zwei Stationen nur in wenigen, auswendig gelernten Wörtern und durch Pantomimen hatte sprechen können, freute ich mich nicht wenig, in Wojakkala mich in Schwedischer Sprache einigermaßen verständlich machen zu können.

Alles schlief schon, als ich anlangte, nur die Wirthin war noch munter, aber sie verstand nur Finnisch. Doch flugs sprang eines der Mädchen hervor und rief den Gästgifvare, der etwas Schwedisch verstand, und dem ich nun meine Wünsche vortrug. Kaum hatte er sie vernommen, als auch schon mit Unverdrossenheit ein Mahl und ein reinliches Bette bereitet wurden.

Der Gästgifvaregård in Wojakkala besteht zur Hälfte aus Zimmern nach Schwedischer Weise, zur Hälfte aus einer Finnischen Pörte, der ersten, die ich sah, und die zugleich als Wohn- und Schlafgemach und als Küche dient. Es war ein überraschender Anblick, als ich eintrat: den ansehnlichen innern Raum umgaben dicke Balken, als Wände, mit eingehauenen Löchern, die mittelst Luken verschlossen werden konnten, statt der Fenster; die Stelle der Decke vertrat das schräggebaute Dach, mit einer Oeffnung, als Rauchfang (andere Pörten des Dorfs und mehrere Höfe in Öfver-Torneå haben wirkliche Schornsteine), dennoch hatte der Rauch Dach und Wände völlig geschwärzt. Rings an den Wänden waren die Schlafstätten des Hausherrn, der Hausfrau, der Kinder, der Knechte und Mägde, ja neben den

Kindern auch der Hunde und Katzen. Auf der Decke des einen Bettes, in welchem ein Mädchen lag, saßen einige junge Männer; fast schien es, als hielten sie in freundlichen Gesprächen und im Bewußtseyn des Beieinanderseyns die Ehrennacht; der Begriff von Verletzung des Anstandes steigt bei diesen Naturmenschen nicht auf.

Pörten giebt es viele in den Finnischen Dörfern, ja vor 50 Jahren noch in der Stadt Torneå, wo indeß schon Fenster die Stelle der Wandlöcher vertraten. Es bedarf einer festen Gesundheit, wie sie die Finnen haben, um in diesen Pörten wohnen zu können, ohne zu erkranken. Denn die Wandlöcher verursachen, selbst geschlossen, einen steten Zug. Den ganzen Vormittag, so oft der gewöhnlich in einer Ecke eingemauerte Ofen geheizt wird, sind Wandlöcher und Thüren geöffnet, um den Rauch auszulassen; der Fußboden ist selten mit Brettern belegt, sondern feuchte, unbedeckte Erde, in welche sogar oft eine mit Hobelspänen oder Kaff ausgefüllte Grube gegraben ist; in diese Grube zieht sich zwar die Feuchtigkeit des an den Wänden und auf dem Dache schmelzenden Schnees herab; aber Späne und Kaff und die die Erde berührenden Balken faulen und verbreiten einen widrigen Geruch, den indeß die Finnen nicht empfinden. Das Bett der Finnen besteht gewöhnlich aus ein wenig Stroh und Heu auf kalter Erde und einer dünnen Decke oder einem Schaaffell. Gegen dieses eiskalte Lager bildet die furchtbare Hitze in der geheizten Pörte, oft von 15 bis 20° (Celsii), während draußen eine Kälte von 20 bis 30° herrscht, einen gefährlichen Contrast. Nur die Größe der Pörte (pirtti) verbessert einigermaßen die Luft; die Länge beträgt gewöhnlich 10 bis 18, die Breite 10 bis 15, die Höhe 5 bis 9 Ellen, die Pörte enthält also an 200 □Ellen. — Im Sommer zieht man an manchen Orten die Schlafstätten in kleinen Nebengebäuden vor. — Uebrigens findet man die Pörten nicht in allen Theilen des Großherzogthums Finnland.

Die Westerbottnischen Finnen sind ein schöner und kräftiger Schlag von Menschen, mit runden vollen Gesichtern, und von starkem Knochenbau, auch das weibliche Geschlecht, das sich überdieß durch eine feine und weiße Haut auszeichnet, vielleicht eine Folge des bei den Finnen uralten Gebrauchs der Schwitzbäder. Jeder Hof hat seine Badestube, die alle Sonnabend benutzt wird. Auch in Wojakkala fand ich eine solche Badestube: ein kleines hölzernes, vom Wohnhause abgesondertes Gebäude mit einem steinernen Heerd oder Ofen, oberhalb und an den Seiten läuft ein hölzernes Gerüste, auf welchem gebadet wird. Der Ofen wird bis zum Glühen erhitzt, ja, oft, wie man behauptet, bis zu einer Temperatur von 50 bis 60° Reaumur; der Rauch wird ausgelassen, und Wasser gegen die heißen Steine gespritzt, so daß Dampf entsteht. Nun steigt man entkleidet zu den oberen Brettern hinauf, reibt sich, zur Vermehrung der Ausdünstung, mit einem Birkenquast, oder läßt sich damit durch ein Mädchen, dem solches als eine der häuslichen Verrichtungen des weiblichen Gesindes obliegt, peitschen, und sich dann, gehörig verhüllt, von dem Mädchen rein waschen, worauf man zu den unteren Brettern hinabsteigt, wo man sich völlig ankleidet. Uebrigens baden beide Geschlechter, nicht gemeinschaftlich, wie manche Reisende erzählt haben, und die Weiber werden von den Weibern bedient. Die Sitte des Bedienens der Männer durch Weiber herrschte von jeher, und man weiß kein Beispiel, daß sie von unsittlichen Folgen begleitet gewesen sey. Freilich darf man hier nicht mit dem Maaßstabe messen, der unter feinen, gebildeten Völkern gilt. Was Einfalt und Natur heiligen, kann zur Sünde werden, wo die feinere Kultur Einfalt, Natur und Unschuld verdrängt hat, und nun sündliche Gedanken auch bei solchen Veranlassungen aufsteigen, bei welchen dem Naturmenschen noch immer sein schuldloser Sinn bewahret bleibt. Dem Reinen ist alles rein. — Auch in dem von Schweden bewohnten Theile Westerbottens hat man auf ähnliche Weise, wie die Finnischen, eingerichtete Badestuben, die aber häufiger zum Dörren des Korns als zum Baden gebraucht werden.

In Wojakkala übernachtete ich recht gut; das Zimmer war klein, aber reinlich; über reinem Laken diente ein sauberes und zierlich zubereitetes Schaaffell, was in den auch im Sommer oft kalten Nächten ganz willkommen ist, als Bettdecke. Die Menschen waren so freundlich, so dienstfertig, so einfach und arglos, daß es mir unter ihnen ganz wohl ward. Als ich am Morgen bei meiner Abreise Kupfergeld einwechseln wollte, aber nicht so viel vorhanden war, als mein Zettel betrug, gab man alles Kupfergeld, was man hatte, mit der Aeußerung: wenn ich zurück käme, möge ich erstatten. In Kuckola reichte man mir, in einem ähnlichen Fall, eine Schachtel mit Kupfergeld, um daraus zu nehmen, wie viel ich wollte, ohne zu sehen, wie viel ich nahm, und ohne zu wissen, wie viel darin gewesen. In selbigem Hofe frühstückte ich Lachs, Butterbrot und Milch; man wollte keine Bezahlung haben, und als ich dennoch zahlte, sollte ich zu viel gezahlt haben. Im selbigen Hofe wußte der Skjutsbonde nicht, wie ihm geschah, als ich einige Schillinge über das Meilengeld gab; „das sey ja viel zu viel." — In der Stadt Torneå fand ich es späterhin freilich anders; Eigennutz hatte hier von manchen Herzen Besitz genommen; und auch die schönen Fährmädchen von Kemi waren davon so wenig frei, daß sie vielmehr das Trinkgeld für Bestellung der Pferde sich im Voraus bedangen. Im Allgemeinen sind die Finnen Westerbottens ein harmloses, allezeit freundliches und fröhliches Volk; auch das Sehnsucht athmende Auge der Weiber dieser Gegend (welches ich übrigens in Finnland selbst nicht bemerkte) stört jene schöne Eigenthümlichkeit wenig.

In Wojakkala schaute ich zum ersten Mal kurz nach Mitternacht die Sonne, nur etwa 18 Minuten war sie verschwunden, und bald nach 12 Uhr stand sie schon wieder am Horizont.

Am 23. Jun. Von Wojaktala nach Kuckola 1,⅓ Meile; von Kuckola nach Korpikylä 1⅓ Meile; von Korpikylä nach Päkilä 1⅓⅓ Meile; von Päkilä nach Niemis 1,⅓ Meile; von Niemis nach Matarenge (und Kirche Of-ver-Torneå) 1½ Meile. — Zusammen 6⅓⅓ Meilen.

Um 7 Uhr fuhr ich ab. Nach einem warmen Tage wehte heute ein kalter Nordwind. In der vorigen Woche war es noch so kalt gewesen, daß eine Eisrinde die Felder bedeckt hatte. Die seit zwei bis drei Wochen gestreute Saat hatte daher noch wenige Fortschritte gemacht; gewöhnlich erndtet man das Sommerkorn neun Wochen nach der Aussaat, zuweilen eine Woche früher oder später; man baut Roggen, doch meistens Gerste, die das 5te, selten das 6te Korn giebt. Das Brot ist bald ganz aus Gersten-, bald ganz aus Roggenmehl bereitet, bald aus Roggen- und Gerstenmehl gemischt.

Zwischen Wojaktala und Kuckola fährt man mit weni-gen Unterbrechungen neben Höfen hin; oft erblickt man kleine Kornfelder, Wiesen, Birken und Nadelholz, wiewohl schon vor 30 Jahren gepflanzt, noch niedrig; das Holz wächset hier lang-sam, erreicht aber allmählig dieselbe Höhe, wie in südlicheren Ge-genden. Den Weg umschließen liebliche Ackerbä. Man sieht auch viel weißes Rennthiermoos, welches schon seit Neder-Ca-lix sich häufig zeigt. — Die Wälder sind im Finnischen We-sterbotten Gemeindegut (allmänning); doch hatte die Regierung eben die Vermessung und Austheilung derselben unter die Ein-zelnen angeordnet, und eine Commission ward für diesen Zweck erwartet. Im übrigen Schweden und in Finnland haben schon früher Gemeinheitstheilungen häufig Statt gefunden.

Die Wiesen werden immer üppiger, je mehr man sich der Kirche Öfver-Torneå nähert. Die kleinen Aecker sind von Gräben umgeben, deren Ränder die schönsten Blumenteppiche bilden. Gedroschen wird mit Dreschflegeln; unter Einem Dache mit der Dreschtenne jedes Hofes befindet sich ein steinerner Backofen, durch dessen Rauch das danebon auf Stangen ausgebreitete Korn völlig getrocknet wird, nachdem bereits auf den Norrländischen Hässjor, die man auch hier, gewöhnlich neben den Wohnhäusern, findet, das erste Trocknen geschehen ist. Die Wohnhäuser haben, wo sie nicht Pörten sind, ein Winter- und ein Sommerzimmer, beide gewöhnlich geräumig. Nicht selten wird ein Hof von mehr als einem Bauern bewohnt. Der Vorraths-häuser auf Pfählen mit zwei Böden über einander giebt es viele; man steigt auf Treppen hinan. Die Dächer der Finnischen Gebäude sind theils von Brettern, theils auch mit Birken-rinde belegt.

Im Anfange des Dorfs Kuckola trat ich in eine Torpare-wohnung; sie hatte nur ein Zimmer, wo auf Stroh und weißen Rennthierhäuten unter Schaaffellen die Familie schlief und am Tage wohnte. Selten schläft ein Finne auf Betten; die Stelle des Kopfkissens vertritt, nach Lappenweise, ein mit einer kleinen Decke oder einem kleinen Kissen bedeckter Kasten; selten hat man mehrere Kopfkissen. Auch am Tage findet man die Finnen, wenn sie müssig sind, nicht selten auf ihren Fellbetten liegen. In dem Zimmer des Torpare war übrigens alles rein und nett, auch der Fußboden; ein kleines Brett bewahrte den ganzen Speisevorrath in guter Ordnung, die Fenster waren klein, aber zierlich; auf der Diele war noch ein Kämmerchen. Die Eltern waren mit hübschen und freundlichen Kindern gesegnet.

Von Kuckola ging ich an das Ufer des nahen Torneå. Auf einer weiten Strecke zwischen einer Menge von Fischerhüt-ten, die beide Ufer bedecken, bildet hier der Fluß mehrere Fälle, die zwar nicht an Höhe, wohl aber an Wassermasse beträchtlich sind und ein furchtbares Getöse verursachen; liebliches Gebüsch breitet sich an den Ufern aus. Ich trat in eine der hölzernen Hütten, Pörten der schlechtesten Gattung; ein großes Zimmer, dessen Fußboden die bloße Erde bildet; Wandlöcher, die durch hölzerne Luken verschlossen werden können, vertraten die Stelle der Fenster, ein Dachloch die Stelle des Schornsteins; rings um an den Wänden laufen Bänke, die Schlafstellen der Fischer; in der Mitte des Zimmers ist, nach Lappenweise, die Feuerstätte auf der bloßen Erde, oder auf einem erhöhten Feuerheerd. Die Fischer treiben meist Lachsfang, der im Torneå-Elf noch immer sehr bedeutend ist, wenn gleich er abgenommen hat, übrigens, wie überhaupt in Schweden, Regale ist. Der Lachsfang in Torneå-Elf ist seit 1791 auf 160 Jahre verpachtet; die Pacht fällt, nach Abtretung des nördlichen Ufers, theilweise Schweden und Rußland zu, je nach dem Antheil, den die Unterthanen der beiden Reiche daran nehmen; die übrige Fischerey erstreckt sich, nach dem am 20. Nov. 1810 zu Torneå abgeschlossenen Gränztractat nur bis zur Gränze im Torneåfluß *).

*) Die durch den Friedenstraktat von Fredrikshamn am 17. Sept. 1809 und den Gränzregulirungs-Traktat von Torneå am 20. Nov. 1810 festgesetzte Gränzlinie beginnt an der Norwegischen Gränze zwischen den Bergen Kolta Pahta und Kuolmia Pahta, oder Pailas maara, da, wo der kleine Fluß Radje jokke oder Kuolima jokke im See Koltejaur entspringt, geht längs dieses Flusses durch den See Kuokimajaur bis zum Auslauf desselben in den See Plinen Kilpisjaur, theilt diesen See, wie den See Alanen Kilpisjaur, und geht von da durch den See Parsajaur in den Köngämä, folgt dem Bette dieses Flusses durch die Seen Kjelisaur, Mukujaur, Pousujaur, Kellottijaur, bis zu der Stelle, wo der Köngämä und der Låtås Eno zusammenfließen; von da, wo der Muonio seinen Anfang nimmt, läuft die Linie längs dieses Flusses, und folgt, nachdem derselbe sich mit dem Torneå-Elf vereiniget hat, dem Bette des Torneå bis nördlich von der Halbinsel Svensarö, hier verläßt sie den Torneå und geht westlich durch den Bach Näran und die Stadtinwiek, läßt die Insel Kalfholmen rechts, geht dann wieder in den Lauf des Torneå südlich von der Stadt Torneå, und folgt dem Torneå bis zu seiner Mündung in den Bottnischen Meerbusen. Was auf der rechten Seite dieser Linie liegt, ist Schwedisch, was links liegt, Russisch. Schwedische Gränzorte sind, von Norden nach Süden: Mauno, Gunnari, Karesuande, Kuttanen, Munion-Alasta, Parkejoensu, Huuki, Lißiowaara, Uttumaodta, gehörig nach Kengis-Bruk, Lardis, Jarhois, Pello, Svanstens-Bruk, Juoxängi,

Gegenüber erblickt man auf dem Russischen Ufer eine der neuen noch im Bau begriffene Kirche; auch ist die Kirche Carl Gustav am Schwedischen Ufer sichtbar.

Marjosaari, Kuiwakanjas, Haapakylä, Matarengi nebst der Kirche Ober-Torneå, Russola, Alkula, Niemis, Urmassaari, Koiwukylä nebst der Kirche Hietaniemi, Pädilä, Witsoniemi, Potila, Korpikylä, Karungi nebst Carl-Gustav's-Kirche, Kudola, Wojaklala, Mattila, Haparanda. Russische Gränzorte sind: Naimaka, Kellotti, die Kirche Enontelis, Palajoensa, Songa Muodka, Kettesuwando, Ober-Muonista, Nieder-Muonista, Kihlangi, Kolare, Jadljalka, Pello, Mämmilä, Turtula, Juoxängi, Kauesari, Murjusari, Kauliranda, Kuiwakanjas, Närki, Alkula, Niemis Urmassari; Helsingby, Korpikylä, Karungi, Kudola, Wojaklala, Kiwiranda, die Stadt Torneå auf der Halbinsel Svensarö, die Kirche Nieder-Torneå, Hällalä und Närsari auf der Insel Björkön. Von der Mündung des Torneå an geht die Gränze durch den Bottnischen Meerbusen, mitten durch den Quarken Ålands-Haf in die Ostsee, so daß im nördlichen Theil des Meerbusens die Inseln Beckholm, Sållöu nebst dem Hafen Reutehamn und die Insel Östra Sarvenmaat, und im südlichen Theil des Meerbusens die Insel Åland und Signilskär die äußersten Russischen Besitzungen sind.

Die Inseln im Osten der größten Tiefe der oben genannten Landseen und des Flußbettes der drei Gränzflüsse Kongämä, Muonio und Torneå sind Russisch, die im Westen gelegenen Schwedisch, mit Ausnahme der Halbinsel Svensarö mit der Stadt Torneå. Eben so gehören die Inseln zunächst dem festen Lande von Finnland und Åland an Rußland; die an der Schwedischen Küste an Schweden. Nach 5 Jahren darf kein Uferbewohner auf beiden Ufern der Flüsse ansäßig seyn; die Inseln aber dürfen nach wie vor von ihren frühern Besitzern benutzt werden, mit Ausnahme der Insel Flurinsaari, Flygarinsaari, der Halbinsel Svensarö und der Insel im Süden von Svensarö. Nach Ablauf von 5 Jahren zahlen die Besitzer an die andere Regierung, der die von ihnen benützten Inseln gehören, nur ein Grundgeld von 8 Schill. Banko. Drei Jahre lang dürfen die Uferbewohner ihre frühern Kirchen besuchen; dann scheiden sie aus der bis-

Der Gästgifvaregård in Kuckola hat ein geräumiges und hübsches Gastzimmer. Der Hof heißt Frankila; jeder Finnische Bauerhof hat einen eigenen Namen, nach welchem auch die Bewohner sich nennen, z. B. Pehr Jönsson Frankila, Ebba Olofsdotter Frankila ꝛc.; Knechte, die noch keinen eigenen Hof besitzen, nennen sich nach dem Hofe, in welchem sie geboren wurden. Auf diese Weise führen alle Finnische Bauern Zunamen, welches bekanntlich bei den Schwedischen nicht der Fall ist; die Bruksarbeiter geben sich, wie dieß gewöhnlich auch unter den Schweden geschieht, Eigennamen. In einigen Theilen des eigentlichen Finnlands führen die Bauern Familiennamen. (Kap. 36.)

Kuckola ist ein großes, weitläuftig gebautes Dorf, fast ¾ Meilen lang; es liegt, wie Wojakkala, an beiden Ufern des Torneå, so daß von den 62 Bauern, die das Dorf zählt, 45 auf der Schwedischen und 17 auf der Russischen Seite wohnen. — In einem dieser Höfe, in welchen ich trat, sah ich ein Kind von 9 Wochen aus einem am Kuhhorn befestigten Beutelchen saure Milch saugen. Es ist nämlich eine uralte Sitte dieser Gegenden, daß die Kinder selten die Mutterbrust bekommen, dagegen mit Kuhmilch, zuerst süßer, dann saurer, genährt werden. Unläugbar kostet diese Sitte jährlich vielen Säuglingen das Leben, aber das Vorurtheil ist zu fest eingewurzelt, als daß es bisher hätte ausgerottet werden können. Dennoch ist der Ueberschuß der Gebornen jährlich sehr groß. Alle ernähren sich gut und man sieht wenig Arme, denn Viehzucht und Fischfang geben ansehnlichen Ertrag, und die Fruchtbarkeit der Getraidefelder ist groß; freilich wird manches Jahr der Einschnitt durch frühen

---

herigen kirchlichen Verbindung aus, und erhalten für das, was sie bisher aus ihren Mitteln auf den Bau der Kirche, des Pfarrhofes, des Kirchspielmagazins, der Kirchspielstube, des Gerichtshauses (tingshus) verwandt haben, Ersatz. Die Bewohner zahlen an den Gränzen kein Transito. Verbrecher werden von beiden Seiten ausgeliefert.

II.   9

Froſt vernichtet. Sicherer und gleichfalls ſehr lohnend iſt der Kartoffelbau, mit dem man ſeit einigen Jahren den Anfang gemacht hat. 3 Meilen aufwärts von der Kirche Öfver-Tor- neå, zu Turtola, haben der dortige Länsman und deſſen Bruder Kartoffeln in ſehr großer Quantität gebaut und zu Branntwein benutzt. Bei Svanſtein, 1 Meile unterhalb Turtola, hat man auch im Kleinen nicht ohne Erfolg Verſuche gemacht, Syrup und Zucker aus Kartoffeln zu bereiten. Noch tief in Lappland hinein gedeihen die Kartoffeln vortrefflich. In Öfver-Torneå gedeihen in den Gärten die Zuckererbſen, aber Obſtbäume ſieht man nicht.

Von Kuckola fährt man längs herrlicher Wieſen und wo- gender Roggenfelder der ſchönen Karungi oder Carl-Gu- ſtav's Kirche vorüber, durch einen kleinen Wald und neben mehreren zerſtreuten Wohnungen, die indeß nicht ſo zahlreich ſind, wie auf der vorigen Station. Mein letzter Skjutsbonde hatte Schwediſch verſtanden; er war mir, weil ich es wünſchte, von Wojakkala gefolgt, wiewohl das Pferd ihm nicht gehörte; mein Skjutsbonde von Kuckola war deſto weniger des Schwe- diſchen mächtig. — Eine Viertelmeile vom Gäſtgifvaregård wird die Gegend beſonders hübſch, eine reizende Landſchaft breitet ſich aus, die der Torneå durchſtrömt; Gebüſche und Heuſcheunen bilden maleriſche Gruppen, auch am jenſeitigen Ufer, wo die Wieſen allmählig an einen hohen Waldberg hinanſteigen.

Von Korpikylä, wo die Gaſtzimmer ſchlecht ſind und kei- ner Schwediſch ſpricht, hat man eine Viertelmeile nach dem Waſ- ſerfalle Matkikoſki, den der Torneå bildet. Er iſt nur in geringer Entfernung hörbar, aber ſchöner als der Fall von Ku- ckola. Schwarze Felſenplatten begränzen die Ufer und verlieren ſich dann in Wieſen, auf welchen man einzelne Fiſcherhütten er- blickt, den Hintergrund bilden Hügel und der erwähnte hohe Waldberg. Mitten im Fluſſe ragt ein Fels hervor, um welchen mehrere große und kleine Fälle brauſen; die kreisförmigen neh- men ſich beſonders ſchön aus. Dieſe verſchiedenen Fälle führen den gemeinschaftlichen Namen Matkikoski und streichen in einer Länge von etwa 600 Ellen fort. Hier ist ein ansehnlicher Lachsfang. Der Weg zu den Fällen führt durch Kornfelder, liebliche Wiesen und eine kleine Waldschlucht, durch welche sich malerisch ein Bach schlängelte. Auf dem Rückwege trat ich in ein Gehöft des Dorfes Korpikylä, wo eine freundliche, schöne Finnin auf einer Handmühle Gerste mahlte.

Auf dem Wege von Korpikylä nach Päckilä hat man anfangs niedrigen Birkenwald; dann erblickt man den Torneå, der hier den langen, aber wenig beträchtlichen Wuojenafall bildet. Nun beginnen die herrlichsten Gegenden; von Waldhöhen, auf denen man fährt, zeigen sich im Vordergrunde Wiesen und Felder mit der schönen Kirche Hietaniemi, und der hier sehr breite Torneå mit seinen Inseln, im Hintergrunde jenseits des Flusses ein Halbkreis blauender Berge; durch liebliche Waldthäler gelangt man zum Häll Päckilä, wo ein hübsches und geräumiges Gastzimmer ist. Wie fast in allen Finnischen Dörfern, wo Fremde eine Seltenheit sind, ward ich auch in Päckilä von einer Menge Neugieriger umringt, mit denen ich aber nur in der Gebährdensprache reden konnte.

Hinter Niemis kommt man bald der Kirche Hietaniemi vorbei, um welche sich Kornfelder und mit Gebüschen geschmückte Wiesen ausbreiten, die durch ihr hohes üppiges Gras ganz an Italien erinnerten. Man fährt am Abhange von Waldbergen und hat ununterbrochen die lieblichsten Aussichten; bald ziehen sich die Berge zurück; man kommt in ein Thal, aus welchem der Armasjocki dem Torneå zuströmt, über den eine zierliche im Jahr 1814 neu erbaute hölzerne Brücke führt; die Berge treten wieder näher, auch ein nackter Felsen zeigt sich und man fährt, eine Anhöhe hinan, in Niemis ein. Ein Wagen mit Finninnen fuhr hinter mir; auch im Gästgifvaregård traf ich mehrere Kirchgängerinnen, deren eine mit viel Anstand die Dolmetscherin machte.

J 2

Von Niemis nach Matarenge fährt man auf Waldhö-
hen, in der Tiefe zeigt sich das schöne Thal des Torneä; beide
Ufer sind mit Höfen bedeckt. Immer schöner wird die Gegend,
schon von der Kirche Hietaniemi an; am schönsten sind die Thäler
von Ruskola und Matarenge; ersteres hat eine solche Fülle
der Vegetation, daß man sich zu den Savannen Amerika's oder
den Gefilden Italiens versetzt glauben könnte; mit Wiesen und
Gebüschen wechseln Kornfelder, rings umher erblickt man einen
Kranz von Waldbergen; mitten durch die reizende Landschaft
strömt der Torneä. — Am Nachmittage war ich in Matarenge, wo ich meine Reisegefährten wiederfand und vom
Propste Wikström, an den ich empfohlen war, auf's gastfreund-
lichste empfangen wurde.

Den westlichen Schlußpunkt des großen Dorfes Matarenge bildet die Kirche Öfver-Torneä; unweit der Kirche liegt
der Pfarrhof, aber schon im Dorfe Hapakylä. Hier endet
die im Jahr 1780 angelegte fahrbare Straße, die mit den
trefflichsten Chausseen Deutschlands verglichen werden kann. Weiter westwärts und nordwärts kann man nur zu Fuß, zu Pferde
oder zu Boot fortkommen *). Auf dem Russischen Ufer des
Torneä giebt es bisher gar keine Fahrwege, auch nicht bis
Öfver-Torneä.

Das Pastorat Öfver-Torneä, mit einer Volkszahl von
8000 Seelen, besteht aus der Muttergemeinde Öfver-Torneä
und den Filialgemeinden Hietaniemi und Pajala (10 Meilen
von der Kirche Öfver-Torneä, ¼ Meile vom Hüttenwerk Kengis);
bei jeder der Filialkirchen wohnt ein Comminister. Durch die
Abtretung des linken Ufers ist ein beträchtlicher Theil des Pastorats unter Russische Hoheit gekommen, für welchen jetzt drei
neue große Kirchen von Holz, Karungi, der Carl-Gu-

*) Beim Reichstage 1823 schlug Major Montgommerie die
Fortführung des Fahrweges von der Kirche Öfver-Torneä bis zum
Bruk Kengis, auf Staatskosten, vor.

stav's Kirche gegenüber, Öfver-Torneå oder Alcala, Hieta-niemi gegenüber, und Turtola zwischen Öfver-Torneå und Pel-lo, nebst einer Kapelle Kolare, am Muonio, oberhalb Kolore erbaut werden *). Auch nach der Vollendung dieser neuen Kir-chen haben einzelne Höfe noch einen Kirchweg von 11 Meilen, wie denn auch auf dem Schwedischen Ufer die Erbauung einer neuen Kirche nothwendig ist. Denn das ungetheilte Pastorat Öfver-Torneå ist das größte der großen Pastorate Wester-bottens, von der Gränze des Pastorats Carl-Gustav bis an die Gränze von Torneå-Lappmark ist es 20 bis 30 Meilen lang, und von der Gränze Österbottens bis zur Gränze der Pastorate Öfver- und Neder-Calix 8 bis 20 Meilen breit; der Flächeninhalt be-trägt an 200 □M. Freilich ist der obere, an Lappland grän-zende Theil des Pastorats wenig angebauet, wenn gleich auch hier in den letzten Jahrzehnten der Anbau zugenommen hat. Uebrigens ist das Pastorat Öfver-Torneå viel bergiger als das Pastorat Neder-Torneå.

Seit der Abtretung des linken Ufers des Torneå soll zwischen den Bewohnern beider Ufer eine Art von Haß sich er-zeugt haben. Die Bewohner des Russischen Ufers waren bisher von Abgaben frei. Da manche Eigenthümer auf dem Schwedi-schen und Russischen Ufer Besitzungen haben, so ward zur Er-zielung einer Austauschung im Jahr 1820 eine Schwedisch-Russi-sche Commission gesandt.

Der Schwedischen Kirche Öfver-Torneå gegenüber er-hebt sich am Russischen Ufer der Berg Afvasaxa, wo An-ders Celsius († 1744) und die Französischen Astronomen Maupertuis, Clairaut, le Monnier, Camus und Ou-thier in den Jahren 1736 und 1737 die berühmte Gradmes-sung zwischen hier und Pello anstellten. Den größten Theil des Sommers brachten sie in einer Hütte auf dem Gipfel des ziemlich hohen Berges zu, von welchem aus sie die übrigen zu

---

*) Diese neuen Kirchen wurden im Sommer 1820 eingeweiht.

Observationsstellen benutzten Berge überschauen konnten. (Outhier voyage au Nord en 1736 et 1737. Amst. 1746. 8. Jordens Figur, upfunnen af Maupertuis etc. Stockholm 1738). Auch die, auf Veranlassung der Akademie der Wissenschaften zu Stockholm, in den Jahren 1801—1803 unternommenen, genaueren und über die äußersten Punkte der Französischen Gradmessung ausgedehnten Messungen des Professors Svanberg aus Upsala und der Herren Öfverbom, Holmquist und Palander fanden auf Afvasaxa Statt. Die Resultate dieser Messungen sind bekannt gemacht worden in Svanberg's, in Schwedischer Sprache erschienener Schrift: „Historischer Ueberblick über das Problem von der Gestalt der Erde, wie über die Veranlassung und die Resultate der neuen Lappischen Gradmessung." Stockholm, 1804; und in Svanberg's Abhandlung (die den Preis des Instituts der Wissenschaften zu Paris erhielt): Exposition des operations faites en Lapponio pour la détermination d'un Arc du Meridien etc. à Paris 1805. Der Maupertuissche Grad wurde um etwas über 200 Toisen zu groß befunden.

Der Berg Afvasaxa liegt völlig frei, und eignet sich daher auch ganz vorzüglich zur Beobachtung der Mitternachtssonne. Auf Afvasaxa ist die Sonne, etwa eine Woche vor und eine Woche nach Johannis, ohne die mindeste Unterbrechung sichtbar, während sie am Fuße des Berges und in Matarenge schon auf einige Minuten, und in der Stadt Torneå, welche um einen halben Grad südlicher liegt, fast eine Viertelstunde verschwindet.

Auch ich hatte daher Afvasaxa zu meinem Standpunkt in der Johannisnacht gewählt. Nach dem Abendessen bestieg ich um 8¾ Uhr ein Boot, um, in Begleitung einiger anderer Fremden, ans jenseitige Ufer zu fahren. Die Böte, deren man sich hier bedient, sind wenig sicher, und kein Jahr soll vergehen, wo sich nicht durch sie ein Unglück ereignet; sie sind lang und sehr schmal, an beiden Enden nach oben gebogen, fast halbmondför-

mig, und schlagen leicht um; die größte Gefahr ist bei den Fällen, die der Strom bildet, daher denn zur Begleitung der Böte
an den gefährlichsten Stellen Lootsen verordnet sind.

Waldberge schließen die Ufer ein, am Fuße derselben breiten
sich üppige Wiesen aus; in großer Zahl zeigen sich an beiden
Ufern Höfe und Dörfer; mitten im Fluß liegt eine bewohnte
Wieseninsel. Der Wind, der am Tage ziemlich heftig gewehet
hatte, war schwächer geworden, und wir fuhren sorglos gerade
auf den waldigen Afvasara zu, dessen einen Theil eben die
Sonne vergoldete. Bald aber bemerkten wir, daß das Boot leck
war oder ward, und sich immer mehr füllte. Wir landeten daher an einer Russischen Insel, um zu schöpfen. Dann setzten
wir die Reise fort und erreichten, zwischen schönbebuschten Inseln
hindurch, um 9¾ Uhr das jenseitige Ufer. Wolken hatten sich
am Horizont gelagert, aber noch blickte die Sonne hervor und
voll Hoffnung traten wir die Wanderschaft an. Auf mühsamem
Pfade, zwischen Birken, Tannen und hohen Gränen, und über
Felsentrümmer erstiegen wir in einer halben Stunde den platten,
kahlen Gipfel des Afvasara. Aber die Sonne war verschwunden, und ein heftiger Nordwind trübte den Horizont; doch hinderte diese Widrigkeit nicht, sich der herrlichen, durch vorstehende
Bäume nur wenig beschränkten Aussicht zu freuen, die sich nach
allen Richtungen vor den staunenden Blicken ausbreitete, wenn
gleich einzelne der weiteren Gegenstände verdunkelt waren. Im
Osten zeigt sich der Fluß Torneå mit mehreren kleinen Inseln,
deren eine ein Länsman und 4 Bauern bewohnen; am rechten
Ufer Matarenge mit der Kirche Öfver-Torneå und Hapakylä mit dem Pfarrhofe; an die Dörfer lehnt sich der Berg
Särkiwaara, dessen Gipfel eine weite und reizende Aussicht
gewährt; den Hintergrund bilden hohe Bergketten. Auch im
Norden erscheint der breite Torneå, nebst dem See Sutka-
lajervi und dem Dorfe Kuwakanjas, weiterhin der Berg
Horrilawaara, einer der Beobachtungspunkte der Französischen
Astronomen, wo eine Tafel errichtet war, die aber nicht mehr

sichtbar ist; auch auf Afvasara ist sie verschwunden. Am schön=
sten ist die Aussicht im Nordwesten: die lieblichsten Wald = und
Wiesenthäler öffnen sich; die Wiesen sind mit Heuscheunen be=
deckt, man erblickt das Dorf Tenjeli, und weiterhin die Sä=
gemühle und das Dorf Christineström am See Portimo=
jervi. Mitten durch diese schöne Landschaft schlängelt sich der
Panjelifluß, welcher die Gewässer des Portimojervis
Sees dem Torneå zuführt. Den vortheilhaftesten Standpunkt
für die nordwestliche Aussicht hat man einige hundert Schritte
unterhalb des Gipfels, wo man auch die jähen Felsenwände der
nordwestlichen Seite des Berges am besten überblickt. Im Sü=
den folgt das Auge dem Torneåstrom abwärts in seinem
Laufe zum Meer; seitwärts zeigen sich üppige Thäler, Waldber=
ge und Dörfer. Bei klarer Luft erkennt man die 7 Meilen ent=
fernte Kirche Neder=Torneå, jetzt war nicht einmal die
um einige Meilen nähere Carl=Gustavs Kirche sichtbar; desto
lieblicher zeigte sich das schöngelegene große Dorf Ruskola.

Aber nicht blos der herrlichen Natur durfte ich mich freuen,
auch einfache und fröhliche Menschen umgaben mich. Der Frem=
den, die, oft aus fernen Gegenden, zur Johannisnacht nach Af=
vasara herbeiströmen, waren diesmal nur wenige eingetroffen,
aber eine große Zahl von Bewohnern der Gegend versammelte
sich, nach Jahresgebrauch, auf Afvasara, zwar nicht wie sonst,
bei Musik und Tanz, wohl aber durch Spiele und Scherz und
fröhliche Gespräche die Johannisnacht zu feiern. Zwar nur we=
nig konnte ich mit ihnen reden, fast alle waren blos ihrer Finni=
schen Muttersprache mächtig; aber es war lustig, ihre Freude zu
schauen, und zu beachten, wie sehr sie mein Tubus interessirte
und wie sie alle daran Theil zu bekommen suchten. Ein großes
Feuer ward angezündet, wenn gleich es eben nicht empfindlich
kalt war. Um das Feuer ward ein großer Kreis gebildet, und
weidlich gescherzt und geschäkert. Die Finnischen Männer warfen
Wacholdersträuche ins Feuer, also daß den Mädchen die Funken
in die Augen sprangen und diese nun wacker kämpften, die Feuer

sprühenden Büsche wieder herauszuziehen. Die Zahl der Mädchen war besonders groß, alle waren munter und kräftig, aber
keine hübsch, die meisten häßlich, ihre Tracht war wenig von der
Schwedischen abweichend; selbstgewebt waren Mieder und Röcke,
welche eine einfache linnene Schürze bedeckte, der Kopf war mit
schwarzseidenem Tuche umwunden, und über den Rücken hing
das Haar in Flechten herab.

So saßen und harrten wir, es war helle wie am Mittag;
aber nur eine starke Röthe zeigte sich am Horizont, der Sonnen-
körper war wenig sichtbar. Etwa eine Stunde nach Mitternacht
traten wir den Rückweg an; auch die Finnen und Finninnen,
die meist nach Öfver-Torneå zur Kirche gekommen waren,
gingen mit uns. Auf der Westseite waren wir hinaufgestiegen,
auf dem nämlichen Pfade stiegen oder glitten wir über Stein-
trümmer hinab. Dieser Weg kann gewiß nicht auf Schönheit
Anspruch machen; aber vom Flusse aus, der hier die Breite eines
Sees annimmt, zeigt sich die Westseite des Berges besonders
vortheilhaft durch den lieblichen Contrast, den das frische Grün
des untern Wiesen- und Birkenabhanges gegen das Dunkel der
Gränen und Tannen des obern Berges bildet.

Auf dem Rückwege unterhielt einer aus der Gesellschaft sich
mit einem der Finnischen Mädchen, das der Schwedischen Sprache nicht ganz unkundig war. Das Mädchen glaubte sich hier-
durch geehrt, das Kind der Natur trat zu ihm, drückte ihm dankbar die Hände und sprach: „söte Herre, bossa mig“ (lieber
Herr, küsse mich). Kaum hatte es diese Worte gesprochen, als
es, beschämt, davoneilte. Jener antwortete: „ich verstehe deine
Worte nicht.“ Wirklich konnte der Sinn des corrumpirten Wortes „bossa“, auch nur aus den Reden des Mädchens, die es in
Schwedischer Sprache an andere der nahestehenden Mädchen
richtete, errathen werden. Mittlerweile hatte ein Officier, der
sich in der Gesellschaft befand, die Worte des Mädchens vernommen und wohl verstanden, und suchte aufs angelegentlichste sich
zu erwerben, was ihm nicht zugedacht war. Aber das Kind der

Natur war nicht frei, — weigerte und lief davon. Der Officier küßte nun eines der andern Mädchen. Kaum war es geküßt worden, als es, voll Schaam, sich entfernte und auf ihrer Flucht noch dazu Streiche von einem der andern Mädchen empfing.

Nachdem wir den Fuß des Berges erreicht, stiegen wir in unsern Nachen und fuhren ab. Aber der schon heftige Wind ging bald in Sturm über, das Boot zog abermals Wasser und wir mußten landen, um zu schöpfen. Dann fuhren wir längs des Ufers (legebamus litora) und schifften, als der Sturm sich etwas gelegt, quer über zum Gästgifvaregärd, wo wir ans Land stiegen. Der Gästgifvaregärd ist ein geräumiges und nettes Gebäude, mit hübschen und freundlichen Zimmern. Vom Gästgif= varegärd ging ich die kurze Strecke zum Pfarrhof, wo ich um 1¼ Uhr anlangte.

Am Vormittag wohnte ich dem Gottesdienst bei, denn in ganz Schweden wird der Johannistag auch kirchlich gefeiert. Der Gottesdienst, der in allen Gemeinden von Ofver=Tornaä nur in Finnischer Sprache gehalten wird, begann um 10 Uhr, und dau= erte, da zahlreiche Communion war, bis um 1¼ Uhr Nachmit= tags. Die Kirche ist groß und freundlich, wenn gleich nur von Holz, auch mit einer Orgel versehen, die früherhin Theil der großen Orgel der deutschen Kirche zu Stockholm war, und hier verbessert aufgestellt wurde (die andere Hälfte erhielt die Kirche Hietaniemi). Um die Orgel her haben die Honoratioren ihre Plätze; die Einsetzung des heil. Abendmahls, die Kreuzigung und ein Paar andere biblische Bilder schmücken den Altar; auch eines der Chöre ist mit biblischen Gemälden geschmückt. — Zuerst wurde ein Begräbniß verrichtet: nach dem Gesang der Gemeinde warf der Prediger zu dreien Malen Erde auf den Sarg, indem er sprach: „von Erden bist du kommen, zur Erde sollst du wieder werden. Jesus Christus, unser Erlöser, wird dich auferwecken am jüngsten Tage!" Dann folgte das in der Liturgie vorge=

schriebene Grabgebet *) worauf nach einem Gemeindegesange der eigentliche Gottesdienst mit Altargebet, Collecten ꝛc. seinen Anfang nahm; der Festgesang ward stehend gesungen. Unter der Predigt wurden in der Stille von mehreren freiwillige Opfer für Kirche und Armen in der Sacristey niedergelegt; insbesondere geschah es von solchen, die von schweren Krankheiten genesen waren, oder die sonst ihr Herz zur Bezeugung ihres Dankgefühls trieb. Sehr feierlich war die Austheilung des heiligen Abendmahls, welches knieend und mit großer Andacht unter dem sanften Gesang der Gemeinde, in mehreren Umgängen, von 250 Communicanten empfangen wurde. Während der heil. Spende, wobei über jeden Einzelnen die heiligen Worte gesprochen wurden, verbeugten sich alle, nicht blos der Empfangende, sondern auch die zur Seite und hinten Stehenden. Der Pastor war im großen Amtsschmucke, d. i. im purpurnen Meßgewande, auf dessen Vorderseite eine Sonne mit dem Namen יהוה (Jehovah), und auf dessen Rückseite das Bild des Heilandes am Kreuz gestickt ist; dieses Festgewand wird von den Geistlichen an Festen und bei der Verwaltung des heil. Abendmahls getragen. — Unter den Communicanten befanden sich auch ein Paar Lappinnen aus Juckasjärvi, Mutter und Tochter; sie waren zierlich mit erbettelten Kleidern geschmückt; doch erkannte man sie bald an ihrer spitzen schwarzen Mütze und an der schmutzig-gelben Farbe ihres Gesichts; auch ein männlicher Lappe in seiner Rennthierhaut war in der Kirche.

Die Versammlung war sehr zahlreich; von den etwa viertehalbtausend Seelen, die in die Mutterkirche Öfver-Torneå eingepfarrt sind, war fast die Hälfte anwesend. Freilich war es heute Festtag und deßhalb auch die Zahl der Communicanten so groß; aber auch an den gewöhnlichen Sonntagen ist die Kirche stark besucht; alle 3 bis 4 Wochen wird Communion gehalten. Meh-

---

*) S. über Schwedens Kirchenverfaffung und Unterrichtswesen Bd. 2. S. 158. 159.

rere hatten kein Gesangbuch; überhaupt ist der Mangel an Exemplaren der Bibel und an Erbauungsschriften in den Finnischen Gemeinden Westerbottens groß. Neuerdings hatte aber der Propst Wikström, durch Veranstaltung der Schwedischen Bibelgesellschaft in Stockholm (bis Oct. 1817) an 1000 R. T. nebst vielen kleinen von der evangelischen Gesellschaft in Stockholm herausgegebenen Erbauungsschriften im Pastorat unentgeldlich oder gegen Bezahlung vertheilt; auch war in Öfver-Torneå, eben so wie in Piteå, und andern Theilen des Bisthums Hernösand, ein Bibeldepot errichtet worden. In den meisten Pastoraten ist der Bibelmangel groß; so gab es z. B. in dem Pastorat Skellefteå, welches 8000 Einwohner zählt, nur 679 Bibeln.

Kirchstuben um die Kirche findet man in den Finnischen Gemeinden Westerbottens, der weiten Kirchwege ungeachtet, nur wenige; die Kirchgänger übernachten daher in nahen Bauerhöfen, wo sie auch ihren Sonntagsschmuck in Zimmern und auf Böden aufbewahren; Kleiderschränke kennt der gemeine Mann in Norrland und fast ganz Schweden nicht. Die meisten Gemeindeglieder haben zur Kirche Bootweg; der größere Theil wohnt nur 1 bis 5 Meilen von der Kirche entfernt; bis Svanstein, einige Meilen oberhalb der Kirche Öfver-Torneå, beträgt die weiteste Entfernung zwischen den Höfen eine halbe Meile; weiter aufwärts liegen die Höfe in größeren Entfernungen von einander.

Feste Schulen giebt es weder in Öfver-Torneå noch in einem andern Finnischen Kirchspiel Westerbottens; aber die Eltern unterrichten ihre Kinder. An Sonntagen halten die daheim gebliebenen in Dörfern und Höfen Dorfgottesdienst. Gasthöfe und Kruge duldet man nur in geringer Zahl, in der Nähe der Kirche gar nicht; doch wird über heimliches Branntweinschenken geklagt. Die Zahl der Gebornen steigt im Pastorat Öfver-Torneå jährlich an 200 (im Jahr 1816. 183, worunter 14 uneheliche, also das 13te Kind war unehelich); größer ist die Zahl der unehelichen Kinder im Pastorat Neder-Torneå, ja wohl die 8te Geburt ist eine uneheliche, insbesondere in der Stadt Torneå. Von den Gebornen stirbt in Neder-Torneå eine große Zahl, ja zuweilen die Hälfte, noch vor zurückgelegtem erstem Lebensjahr, eine Folge des Auffütterns der Kinder mit Kuhmilch ꝛc. statt des Reichens der Mutterbrust, eine Sitte, die auch in Osterbotten jährlich vielen Kindern das Leben raubt. In den Schwedischen Kirchspielen Westerbottens, namentlich Neder-Calix, findet man diese Sitte nicht, oder doch selten; dort ist aber auch die Sterblichkeit unter den Kindern viel geringer. — In Ofver-Torneå sind Diebstähle fast unerhört, in Neder-Torneå desto häufiger.

Nach dem Gottesdienst nahm ich eine der Pörten der Gegend in Augenschein. Zu Mittag war Gesellschaft beim Propst, dessen Namenstag eben fiel. Die Finnen feiern ihre Namenstage, nicht ihre Geburtstage. Der 1. Mai und der Johannistag pflegen auf den Pfarrhöfen durch Einladung der Honoratioren gefeiert zu werden. Auch der geringe Mann speiset an diesen Tagen besser, und am Johannistage findet man die Bauernhäuser nicht selten mit Blumen und Maibüschen geschmückt. Doch die rechte Feier des Johannisfestes findet man nur im südlichen Theil von Norrland und im mittlern Schweden, am meisten wohl in Dalekarlien. Da beginnt die Feier schon am 23. Abends: man richtet vor den Höfen und an den Wegen hohe schlanke, mit Blumen, Laub, Kränzen, hölzernen Vögeln, Schwerdtern und Pfeilen gezierte Bäume auf, an welche zuweilen auch geschmückte kleine Stangen befestigt sind; Musikanten erscheinen und man tanzt um den Johannisbaum bis tief in die Nacht hinein; am Abend des 24. und des 25., an einigen Orten am Abend des 24. oder 25. Junius, auch wohl am Abend des nächsten Sonntages, wird der Tanz fortgesetzt, doch dann gewöhnlich nicht im Freien, sondern in den Höfen. An einigen Orten ist das Tanzen um die Johannis- oder, wie man sie nennt, Maistange, am Vorabend des Johannistages außer Gebrauch gekommen. Auch in Städten wird auf dem Markt die Maistange errichtet. An vielen Orten bleibt die Maistange einen großen Theil des Jahres hindurch stehen, an andern Orten nur 8 Tage. Die

Vornehmern feiern das Johannisfest durch Bälle, Gastmähler und andere Vergnügungen in ihren Häusern *).

In früheren Zeiten war die Feier des Johannisfestes noch mit allerlei Aberglauben verbunden: man opferte am Johannis-Vorabend in heiligen Quellen, pflückte Blumen, die man in Sträußer band und in den Ställen aufhängte, damit das Vieh nicht behext werden könne, und hatte viel andern Aberglauben. Auch waren gewisse Höhen und Auen zum Sammlungsplatz großer Distrikte am Johannisabend bestimmt u. dergl. m. Alles dies ist seit mehreren Jahrzehnten fast geschwunden. Ueberhaupt sind die abergläubischen Sitten und Meinungen, an welchen früher der Norden so reich war, in den letzten Zeiten in Schweden sehr abgekommen. Am häufigsten ist wohl noch der Aberglaube der Walpurgisnacht, wenn gleich auch dieser mehr zum Scherze geworden ist. Ehemals bekreuzte man überall Wege und Thüren, um die in dieser Nacht nach dem Blåkulle (blauer Hügel), dem Schwedischen Blocksberg, dessen Lage keiner weiß, ziehenden Hexen von sich abzuhalten; auch dieß ist seltener geworden. Aber an vielen Orten verlebt man noch die Nacht zum 1. Mai in Lust und Freude, damit der Böse nicht unbereitet finde. Man tanzt, man schmaußt, man scherzt und spielt. Zu Leksand in Dalarne sammelt sich noch heut zu Tage die weibliche Jugend auf einem Hügel, die männliche auf einem andern, man zündet Feuer an, und Mädchen und Jünglinge belustigen sich gesondert; dann treffen sie zusammen auf einer dritten Stelle und begrüßen unter Spielen aller Art den kommenden Morgen. In Halland durchziehen in der Nacht zum 1. Mai fröhliche Jünglinge, religiöse Dank- und Loblieder singend, die Dörfer, und empfangen von den Hausvätern Bewirthung. Auch der ganze 1. Mai wird als Freudentag begangen, der sein Licht über das ganze Jahr verbreitet. In Stockholm hält man eine feierliche Lustfahrt in den

---

*) In Finnland hat man selten Maistangen (es sey denn um Weihnachten), wohl aber Freudenfeuer.

Thiergarten; Vornehme und Geringe nehmen Theil, selbst der Hof fehlt nicht.

Nachmittags machte ich Spaziergänge. Ich ging zu dem Hofe des Dorfes Hapackylä, wo der fahrbare Weg auch für Karren (kärror) völlig aufhört; der Hof liegt etwa ¼ Meile vom Pfarrhof. Nichts desto weniger trifft man noch weiter aufwärts große Dörfer, Hüttenwerke und viele einzelne Höfe. Ja, ein Besuch, den ich in dem nahen Hofe des Landmessers Grape abstattete, führte mich bald wieder mitten in das Getreibe der größern Städte zurück. Herr Grape, dessen Frau die Tochter eines Finnischen Bauern an der Lappischen Gränze ist, hat in seinem Hause seit drei Jahren ein Liebhabertheater errichtet, welches mit hübschen Decorationen versehen war; hier wird, freilich nur selten, von Dilettanten der Gegend und besonders Fremden, zuweilen zur Zeit der Märkte von 32 Personen gespielt, wobei freilich Herr Grape das Beste thut. Auf dem Rückwege trat ich in eine Finnische Soldatenwohnung, der Soldat war im Lager, aber die junge Frau mit 3 Kindern, ein herrliches Gesicht voll himmlischer Milde, war daheim. Große Reinlichkeit herrschte in dem geräumigen und freundlichen Wohnzimmer; vor dem Hause standen einige kleine Wirthschaftsgebäude und man erkannte an allem den Wohlstand und die Gemüthlichkeit der Bewohner. Nachdem wir weggegangen, sprang die Mutter mit den Kindern uns nach, um uns die Hände zu küssen und noch einmal Lebewohl zu sagen. So dankbar sind diese einfachen Menschen auch für das kleinste Gute, was man ihnen erweiset, ja für das freundliche Wort, was man zu ihnen redet.

Ofver-Torneå hat einen sehr unterrichteten Organisten, Namens Fortin, dessen treffliches Orgelspiel ich schon am Morgen bemerkt hatte. In der Nachahmung des Donners auf der Orgel besitzt dieser Mann eine große Geschicklichkeit, wie ich mich am Nachmittag in der Kirche überzeugte; viele Kirchgänger, die noch im Dorfe waren, strömten in die Kirche, die schönen Töne zu vernehmen. Herr Fortin hat auch eine stattſtiſche Beſchreibung des Paſtorats verfaßt; die aber nicht gedruckt worden iſt.

Nach dem Abendeſſen beabſichtigte ich den dem Pfarrhofe gegenüber liegenden ziemlich hohen Berg Särkiwaara, von deſſen Gipfel man zwar nicht ganz, doch faſt ſo gut, wie vom Afvaſaxa, die Mitternachtsſonne beobachten kann, zu erſteigen; aber eine Unpäßlichkeit hinderte mich den Plan auszuführen, auch fing es bald an zu regnen. Indeß beſchloß ich wenigſtens die Mitternachtsſtunde wachend im Pfarrhof zuzubringen, wenn gleich der trübe Horizont mich wenig hoffen ließ, — damit es mir nicht gehe, wie jenem Reiſenden, der nach Torneå kam, um die Mitternachtsſonne zu ſehen und — ſie verſchlief. Noch immer war es trübe, um 11¾ ward es ſogar auf Augenblicke ein wenig dunkler; plötzlich aber, gegen 12 Uhr, entwölkte ſich der Himmel, und die volle Sonnenſcheibe war in ihrer ganzen Herrlichkeit ſichtbar. Voll Freude ſchaute ich empor, als ſie ſchon wieder verſchwand; nach etwa einer halben Stunde war ſie wieder da und blieb nun, nicht gar blendend, am Horizont. So war denn mein Wachen nicht unbelohnt geblieben. Alles um mich her war in Schlaf verſunken; meine Reiſegefährten aus Hernöſand waren ſchon am Nachmittag abgereiſet, und auch ich begab mich nun zur Ruhe. — Im Pfarrhofe iſt um Johannis die Sonne bei klarem Horizont nur 15 Minuten unſichtbar. Im Winter ſind die Tage deſto kürzer; doch iſt es auch an den kürzeſten Tagen von 10 bis 2 Uhr hell *).

Am folgenden Morgen ſollte die Rückreiſe angetreten werden. Bei der Abfahrt beſichtigte ich noch das Tingshus (Gerichtshaus), wo das Landgericht des hieſigen Kreiſes (Härad) ſeine Sitzungen hält. Das Gebäude iſt von Holz, ſelbſt die inneren

---

*) Nach Hellant's Berechnung (im Kalender von 1744) geht in Nieder-Torneå im December die Sonne auf: 10 Uhr 43 Minuten, unter: 1 Uhr 17 Minuten; zur ſelbigen Zeit in Stockholm auf: 9 Uhr 3 Minuten, unter: 2 Uhr 57 Minuten.

Wände sind unbekleidet; es enthält außer der Gerichtsstube ein Nebenzimmer für die Parteien, ein Zimmer für die Richter (Häradshöfding), ein Zimmer für den Schreiber, überhaupt 6 Zimmer nebst Küche. Ein Theil des Gebäudes wird als Kirchspielsstube benutzt und darin die Kirchspielsstände gehalten. — Gegenüber stehen die Marktbuden; zwei Mal jährlich, im März und December, wann das Gericht zusammentritt, hält man Markt, den aber die Lappen nicht besuchen (die Lappen kommen zum Markt nur nach Pajala). Auf den Märkten verkaufen die Einwohner ihre Produkte an Stadt- und Landkaufleute; einige verfahren ihre Erzeugnisse selbst, ja bis nach Stockholm; dasselbige ist in Neder-Torneå der Fall. Neben den Marktbuden steht die Voigtstube (Fogdestufva), wo der königl. Voigt während der Marktzeit Upbörd hält, d. h. die Kronsteuern erhebt. In der Voigtstube ward eben von dem braven Pastors-Adjuncten Burman, einem lieben, gefälligen Mann, der durch seine Dienstfertigkeit mich sehr verpflichtet hat, etwa 50 Schülern und Schülerinnen Confirmations-Unterricht ertheilt. Im Tingshus wird ältern Personen, die in ihren jüngern Jahren vernachlässigt waren, Religionsunterricht ertheilt; ihrer waren dießmal etwa 5, welche alle noch nicht communicirt hatten, unter ihnen sogar eine 50jährige.

Weiterhin steht die Salpeterscheune des Kirchspiels: in großen Küben wird hier der Pferde- und Kuhurin aufbewahrt, und damit Walderde oder Erde, auf welcher alte Gebäude gestanden haben, angefeuchtet, diese dann dem Luftzug ausgesetzt und endlich der Salpeter ausgesotten. Die Salpeterbereitung wird seit neuerer Zeit in Schweden mit solchem Eifer betrieben, daß man schon der Zufuhr des Salpeters vom Auslande entbehren kann. Eigene Vorsteher sind von der Regierung ernannt worden, die umherreisen, das Landvolk in der besten Bereitungsart zu unterweisen, zweckmäßige kleine Schriften werden vertheilt ꝛc.

II.   K

Auch ein Gefängniß ist vorhanden; der Pfahl, an welchem Ruthenhiebe ertheilt werden, zeigt seine Bestimmung sehr faßlich durch einen hölzernen Kerl mit einer Ruthe in der Hand.

Aerzte giebt es in Ofver-Torneå nicht. Der Adjunct Mag. Burman ist indeß nicht ohne medicinische Kenntnisse und hat in seiner Wohnung eine mit dem Nothwendigsten versehene kleine Kirchspielsapotheke.

Hauptnahrungszweige des im Ganzen sehr wohlhabenden Pastorats sind Viehzucht, Fischerey und Kornbau. Letzterer, wiewohl man, im Durchschnitt, nur das 5te Korn rechnen kann, hat so zugenommen, daß in guten Jahren Ueberfluß ist, ja Ofver-Torneå-Pastorat fast jährlich ein wenig Korn verkauft. Die Kapellgemeinde Pajala, wo auf 275 geometrischen Tonnen Land 1048 Menschen wohnen, versorgt Jukkasjärvi-Lappmark, welches früher vom Bruk Kengis mit Korn versehen wurde, mit dem nöthigen Getraide und verkauft überdieß noch zuweilen nach der Küste. Freilich ist der Kornbedarf verhältnißmäßig hier nicht so groß als in südlichen Orten. Auch bei feierlicheren Gelegenheiten trinkt man kein Bier, und selten findet man Branntewein. Das gewöhnliche Getränke ist sauer gewordene Buttermilch und, in Ermangelung derselben, sauer gewordene gewöhnliche Milch. Der Genuß dieses sauern Getränkes bewahrt eben so wie der Genuß des sauern Gerstenwassers, dessen sich die Russen, unter dem Namen Qvaß, bedienen, die Einwohner vor scorbutischen Krankheiten, welche sonst gewiß Folge des langen Winteraufenthalts in den heißen Pörten seyn würden. Uebrigens ist in Pajala der Ackerbau um deßwillen vorzüglicher als im Kirchspiel Ofver-Torneå, weil daselbst nicht, wie hier, die Zerstückelung des Hemman (Hufen) üblich ist; vielmehr behält gewöhnlich der älteste Sohn das ganze Hemman, und findet die übrigen Kinder durch ein Geringes ab; diese haben nun, so lange sie wollen und es bedürfen, bei dem Besitzer ihren Unterhalt, wofür sie an den Arbeiten Theil nehmen. Der Ackerbau ist indeß noch der Erweiterung und Verbesserung fähig. Brache kennt man nicht.

Die Aecker bearbeitet man, wie früherhin fast in ganz Norrbot=
ten, mit dem Spaten. Gerste wird mehr als Roggen gebauet.
Zuweilen vernichten Nachtfröste die reiche Erndte.

Der Fischfang ist am einträglichsten im Torneå=Elf, und
zwar mehr im Kirchspiel Ober=Torneå als in Pajala, denn am
bedeutendsten ist der Lachsfang, der freilich von einer Interessent=
schaft betrieben wird.

Der ansehnlichste Nahrungszweig ist die Viehzucht, deren
Ertrag in allen Finnischen Kirchspielen unter übrigens gleichen
Verhältnissen größer ist als in den Schwedischen; denn die Fin=
ninnen verstehen sich meisterhaft auf die Behandlung des Viehs,
und haben in dieser Hinsicht gleichen Ruhm, wie in Schweden
die Dalekarlierinnen. Dieser Ruhm gilt wenigstens für die Fin=
nischen Bewohner Westerbottens und Lappland; ob aber auch
für das eigentliche Finnland? mehrere haben es geläugnet. Die
ganze Kunst besteht darin, daß man in dem Wasser, das man
den Kühen giebt, Heu und kleines Stroh kocht, und zwar Heu,
welches die Pferde verspillt haben oder nicht fressen mögen, auch
Rennthiermoos und frischen Pferdemist; daß man ferner das
Vieh sehr regelmäßig wartet, das Futter am frühen Morgen
bereitet und auf sechs bestimmte Zeiten vertheilt; daß man die
Kühe, die den ganzen Winter im Stalle bleiben, sehr reinlich
hält; daß man die Milch in Bütten mit dicken Dauben und
Boden einseihet, sie ohne die mindeste Berührung oder Erschüt=
terung eine volle Woche in den Bütten stehen läßt, bevor man
die Sahne abnimmt, und daß, wenn gebuttert werden soll, man
nicht blos die dichte Sahne, sondern auch eine dünne Scheibe
der obersten Milch ins Butterfaß thut. Nicht minder sorgt man
für die richtige Temperatur der Milchkammer, für das Gerinnen
der Milch; welches man durch einen kleinen Löffel voll geronne=
ner Milch, die man gleich beim Einseihen in jede Bütte thut,
zu befördern sucht. Bei dieser Behandlung bringt man es nicht
selten dahin, daß eine Kuh, wiewohl nur vom kleinen Schlage
und unerachtet sie nur unkräftiges Sumpfheu erhält, jährlich 5

K 2

Schwedische Liespfund (100 Pfund) Butter giebt; das wenige bessere Heu, welches man auf hochliegenden Wiesen gewinnt (hårdvallshö), bekommen die Pferde. In Gegenden, wo reicher Zugang zu kräftigem Heu ist, könnte jener Ertrag noch sehr vermehrt werden. — Zur Streu gebraucht man Stroh, auch Moos.

An Wald hat das Pastorat Öfver-Torneå keinen Mangel, wiewohl seit längerer Zeit Hüttenwerke angelegt waren. Es wird gekohlt, auch einiger Theer gewonnen. Doch ist Theerbrennerey meistens Nebenerwerb, denn der weiten Transporte wegen ist sie wenig lohnend. Die Jagd, hauptsächlich Beschäftigung der Kolonisten, gewährt einen nicht unbedeutenden Ertrag, wenn gleich minder bedeutend, wie in Lappland. — Der Grubenbau ist alt. Ein Bauer im Dorfe Junosuwando, an der Gränze der Gemeinde Pajala und der eigentlichen Torneå-Lappmark, entdeckte um 1640 die reichen Eisenlager. Der Entdecker überließ sein Recht einigen Kaufleuten in Torneå, die aber bald den vom Könige erhaltenen Privilegien wieder entsagten. Seitdem ward der Bau, theils von Einzelnen, theils von Interessentschaften, aber selten mit großem Vortheil betrieben, daher er auch oft ruhete. Im Pastorat Öfver-Torneå liegen zwei Hochöfen: 1. Junosuwando, an der Gränze von Lappland, oder eigentlich schon in Lappland, wo auch theilweise die Erzlager streichen, wenn gleich die Gruben noch im Pastorat Öfver-Torneå belegen sind; — und 2. Tornefors, 3 Meilen südlicher, am Torneå. Hier wird das Roheisen bereitet und dann auf dem Torneå 5½ Meile nach Kengis und 7 Meilen weiter nach Svanstein geführt, dort zu Stabeisen und Manufakturwaaren ausgeschmiedet und in dieser Gestalt auf dem Torneå oder, landwärts im Winter, nach dem Ladeplatz bei Haparanda transportirt. Da aber das Land bis Svanstein, zwar meistens eben, wie fast ganz Öfver-Torneå, doch wenig bebaut ist, so würde der mehr bewohnte und überdieß kürzere Weg auf dem Calix-Elf nach Törefors am Ausfluß des Calix im Pastorat Nieder-Calix, wo ein sicherer und tiefer Hafen ist, allerdings vorzuziehen seyn. Zur Untersuchung der Lappischen

Erzlager und ihrer rechten Benutzung durch Fahrbarmachung der Ströme, die mittelbar oder unmittelbar dem Bottnischen Meer zufließen, zur Auffindung der rechten Stellen für Hochöfen und zur Prüfung, inwiefern die Errichtung einer ordentlichen Bergwerks-schaft (bergslag) zu Kengis nützlich sey, ordnete der König im J. 1817 eine Commission ab, die aus dem Landshöfding von Norrbotten, Baron Koskull, dem Oberjägermeister Petersson, dem Berg-meister von Norrbotten Quensel und dem Assessor des königl. Bergcollegiums, Roman, bestand und vom 16. Jul. bis 30. Aug. 1817 ihre Untersuchungen an Ort und Stelle unternahm. Der sehr interessante von mir benutzte Bericht ward 1818 zu Stock-holm von Roman herausgegeben. Schon früher bildete Norr-botten eine eigene Bergmeisterschaft (bergmästaredvine) und es wurden Grubengerichte (bergsting) zu Kengis, Junosuwando, und mit dem Hermelinschen Distrikt zu Råneå von dem Bergmeister in Norrbotten gehalten. Im Jahr 1819 wurden die Hütten-werke Kengis und Svanstein, welche bis dahin geruht hatten, nebst Zubehör aus der Concursmasse des Kämmerer Ostermark und des Brukspatron Ekström feil geboten; die Commission schlug vor, daß die Krone sie erstehen möge.

Eine auffallende Erscheinung im Pastorat Öfver-Torneå bie-tet der Tärende-Elf dar. Er geht aus dem mächtigen Tor-neå-Strom hervor und fällt, nachdem er einige Meilen fast in gleicher Richtung mit dem Torneå geflossen, in den Calix-Elf. Der Calix-Elf ist der Ausfluß einiger Seen an der Gränze von Torneå- und Luleå-Lappmark, fließt an dieser Gränze fort, tritt in gleicher Linie, doch in einiger Entfernung von Junosu-wando, in das Pastorat Öfver-Torneå, nimmt daselbst den Tä-rende-Elf auf und fließt dann durch die Schwedisch redenden Pa-storate Ober- und Nieder-Calix ihrer ganzen Länge nach, bis er bei der Kirche Nieder-Calix sich ins Meer ergießt. Der Torneå kommt aus Seen an der Gränze von Torneå-Lappmark und Norwegen hervor, durchfließt die Torneå-Lappmark, nimmt im Pastorate die großen Flüsse Lainio und Muonio auf, bildet nun die Gränze gegen Rußland und fällt bei der Stadt Torneå ins Meer. Beide Ströme, der Caliẽ und der Torneå, bilden eine Menge Fälle, die die Bootfahrt sehr erschweren und die Schifffahrt ganz unmöglich machen. Der ansehnlichste Fall des Torneå ist bei Kengis, 100 Faden breit und in einer Länge von 150 Faden mehr denn 60 Fuß hoch. Der Torneå legt sich erst im October oder November und geht auf im Mai. Land-seen, deren einige sehr fischreich, giebt es viele.

Die Kleidung der Bewohner der Pastorate Ofver- und Ne-der-Torneå, besonders des letzteren, ist halb Schwedisch, halb Finnisch. Die Weiber tragen vorne ausgeschnittene Mützen, gleich den Schwedinnen in Neder-Caliẽ, mit Spitzen besetzt und mit Silber oder Gold gestickt oder mit Blumen ausgenäht, und Jacken von eigengemachtem Zeuge, einzelne tragen auch große Tücher, die an 24 Bankthaler kosten. Die Männer tragen Jacken, auch Chenillen mit kurzem Kragen, oder weite, Schlaf-röcken ähnliche, bis auf die Füße herabwallende, weiße oder blaue Ueberröcke ohne Knöpfe, von einem Gürtel zusammengehalten. Schwarzsammtene oder tuchene Collets und schwarze, vorne zuge-knöpfte Ueberröcke, deren Herr von Buch in seiner Reise er-wähnt, sah ich nicht; auch konnte ich nicht erfahren, daß diese Tracht irgendwo in Ofver-Torneå oder einem benachbarten Finni-schen Kirchspiel gefunden werde.

Wohnungen, Lebensweise, Sitten der Einwohner des Finni-schen Westerbottens sind ganz Finnisch. Die große Mäßigkeit, die die Finnen beobachten, zeigt sich bei ihren Hochzeiten und andern feierlichen Mahlen nicht. Zu den Hochzeiten ladet man nicht selten 2 bis 300 Gäste, die 8 Tage beisammen bleiben; selbst beim Gratuliren wird zwei Tage geschmauset. Die Ge-schenke der Gäste an Braut und Bräutigam belaufen sich oft über 600 Bankthaler und übersteigen die Kosten der Hochzeit. Zu Hochzeiten brauen die Finnen auch Bier, was man sonst nur in den Häusern der Honoratioren findet, wo dem Fremden am Abend ein Krug Bier vors Bette gestellt wird; das gewöhnliche Getränk der Bauern ist Wasser mit Milch oder die oben genannte saure Milch. Die verheiratheten Finninnen tragen, als Zeichen der Ehe, eine Kette um den Hals. Männer und Weiber der niedern Klasse rauchen aus sehr kurzen Pfeifen.

Unter den Finnischen Honoratioren herrscht, wie in Nord-schweden und in den Bergwerksdistrikten des mittleren Schwe-dens, bei freundschaftlichen Mahlen die Sitte, daß, die Damen den Herren beim Aufstehen auf die Schulter klopfen; das nennt man matklapp. Sind Fremde zugegen oder ist es eine mehr ceremonielle Tafel, so fällt die Sitte weg.

Auch Lappen wohnen im Pastorat Öfver-Torneå, aber nur einer derselben hat Rennthiere; er wohnt, drei Meilen von der Kirche Öfver-Torneå, im Walde. Die übrigen Lappen nähren sich durch Verfertigung hölzerner Geräthe, Reife aus Baumwur-zeln ꝛc. In Torneå-Lappmark verfertigen die Lappen auch höl-zerne Kasten, die, oben mit der rauhen Seite des Kalbfells über-zogen, keinen Regen durchlassen.

———

Am 25. Jun. Von Öfver-Torneå's Pfarrhof und Ma-tarenge nach Niemis 1¾ M.; von N. nach Päckild 1,¼ M.; von P. nach Korpikyld 1½ M.; von K. nach Kudola 1½ M.; von K. nach Wojakkala 1,¼ M. — Zusammen 6½ M.

Nach herzlichem, dankbaren Abschiede von der gast-freien Familie Wikström, trat ich um 9¾ Uhr Vormittags die Rückreise an. Nach großer Hitze schneite es heute ein wenig; solcher plötzlicher Wechsel ist um diese Zeit nicht sel-ten. Länsman Burman begleitete mich bis Hietaniemi, auf welcher Strecke ich einzelne Punkte näher in Augenschein zu nehmen wünschte und doch kaum hoffen durfte, Schwedischredende zu treffen. Bei Ruskola fuhren wir seitwärts zum Dorfe Alkola, dessen Höfe auf beiden Ufern des Torneå liegen. Hier besah ich eine Finnische Badestube. Dann gingen wir längs des schönen Wiesenufers nach einer, ¼ Meile entfernten, Lachsfischerey, wo man täglich 2 bis 300 Lachse fängt. Früher war der Lachsfang noch bedeutender, er hat von der Mündung des Torneå an bis weit aufwärts statt. Am reichlichsten fällt er noch im niedern Theil des Flusses aus, und ist wahrscheinlich im Torneå noch immer ergiebiger, als in irgend einem andern der Schwedischen Ströme. Ein Boot wollte eben abstoßen, wir stiegen hinein, dem Fange zuzusehen. Wir fuhren längs des vom Ufer anfangenden Zauns, an welchen sich andere kreisförmige Verzäunungen anschließen, in denen nur kleine Oeffnungen freigelassen sind, damit der Lachs eingehen könne. An der einen Seite war schon ein Netz gezogen, ein anderes Netz ward jetzt an der andern Seite aus dem zweiten Boote gezogen, um also die eingegangenen Lachse einzuschließen. Das erste Netz war leer, im zweiten fanden sich 7 Lachse, deren Werth man an 10 Rthlr. schätzte (die Fischer haben die Lachsfischerey für einige tausend Rthlr. von der Gemeinde und diese vom König gepachtet). Die gefangenen Lachse wurden im mitfolgenden dritten Boote todtgeschlagen. Diese Art des Lachsfanges ist in Torneå insbesondere üblich. Die Verzäunungen gehen von einem Ufer zum andern fort, also daß nur ein kleines Fahrwasser, oft nur von der Größe, daß ein Boot hindurch kann, übrig bleibt. Der Lachs wird von hier gesalzen in Tonnen verführt; geräucherten Lachs hat man wenig oder gar nicht, wohl aber in Luleå und Umeå, wo man auch die Kunst des Räucherns am besten versteht. Geht das Eis im Meere frühe auf, welches gewöhnlich nach schneereichen Wintern geschieht, so soll der Lachsfang am reichlichsten ausfallen; der Lachs steigt nun aus dem Meere in die Flüsse auf, um süßes Wasser zu suchen. Eben daher ist denn auch der Lachsfang in großen Strömen ergiebiger als in kleinen Flüssen, weil jene ihr süßes Wasser weiter ins Meer verbreiten und dadurch in größerer Entfernung von den Ufern der Lachs angezogen wird. Aber auch die Lage der Ströme, das Buschwerk, welches die Ufer bedeckt, was der Lachs liebt ꝛc., ist Ursache des ergiebigern und bessern Fanges. In Norrland hielt man den Indal's (worin jetzt keine mehr sind) und Luleå's Lachs lange für den besten. Auch an der

Meeresküste, wo süßes Wasser ist, wirft man Netze aus. In Strömen legt man die Lachsgerüste am liebsten neben Fällen an *). Jährlich gewinnt Wester- und Norrbotten ansehnliche Summen durch den Verkauf des gesalzenen und geräucherten Lachses nach Stockholm; auch geräucherte Lachsforellen (laxöring) und geräucherte Neunaugen, gesalzener Strömling, trockene Fische ꝛc. werden in ansehnlichen Quantitäten nach Stockholm ausgeführt.

Von den Lachsgerüsten führen wir hinüber ans Russische Ufer. Hier hat man zu Russisch-Alkala seit 1813 eine neue Kirche gebaut, die meist vollendet war: eine sehr große Kreuzkirche von Holz; über der Kuppel erhebt sich ein einfaches Kreuz, eben so über dem Eingange. Aus den Gothischen Fenstern hat man eine reizende Aussicht auf die Umgegend. Die für die Gemeinde zu große Kirche ist 78 Fuß lang und eben so breit. Wir fuhren, einer freundlichen bewohnten Wieseninsel vorüber, ans Schwedische Ufer zurück. Im Angesicht des Felsenkegels Luppio, der, an Waldberge gelagert, mitten unter üppigen Wiesen da steht, landeten wir bei Niemis. Vom Gästgifvaregård fuhren wir zum Comminsterhof Hietaniemi. Bauerhöfe, auch Kirchthüren, sind in diesen Gegenden häufig mit Rennthierhörnern geziert.

In Hietaniemi's Comministerhofe fanden wir den Vicepastor Burman nicht daheim; doch herzlich empfing uns des Würdigen treffliche Gattin. Sie wollte uns nicht weglassen, bevor wir ein Mahl eingenommen, und schnell waren mehrere Schüsseln aufgetragen; auch gekochter fetter Lachs, der durch einstündiges gleiches Kochen mit Salz, Pfeffer und Dill so mürbe und wohlschmeckend geworden war, wie ich ihn in Deutschland nirgends gegessen habe; auch Blaubeerencrème mit Kartoffelmehl. Die geschäftige Martha, eine der 10 Geschwister, wartete auf, eine

---

*) Ueber den Lachsfang in Norrland vergl. die Abhandlungen der königl. Schwed. Akademie der Wissenschaften; Jahrg. 1751. B. 12. S. 268 ff.; 1752. B. 13. S. 11 ff. S. 93 ff.

Sitte, die man faft in allen Familien der Geiftlichen und andern Honoratioren Norrlands findet. In der ¼ Meile entfernten Kirche Hietaniemi fanden wir den treuherzigen Burman im Kreiſe von 76 Confirmanden. Die Kirche hat eine gute Orgel, eine hübſche Kanzel und Altar, auch einen Thurm, wiewohl die Glocken in einem beſonderen Glockenthurm (klockſtapel) hängen. Die nahe Umgebung der Kirche iſt kahl, deſto ſchöner iſt die entfernere Landſchaft, hier bilden große Dörfer, üppige Wieſen, reiche Kornfelder, und der Strom mit ſeinen Buſen, Landſpitzen und Inſeln die reizendſten Gruppen. Alles erinnert an die Vegetation ſüdlicher Zonen. Die Gegend von Hietaniemi iſt unſtreitig eine der ſchönſten am Torneå.

Die Wohlhabenheit dieſer Gegenden iſt allgemein und groß, insbeſondere durch die treffliche Viehzucht. Eine Kuh giebt gewöhnlich 100 Pfund Butter jährlich; freilich wird von der Milch kein Käſe bereitet. Die Gebäude ſind faſt immer ſo gebaut, daß ſie oben breiter als unten ſind und unten ſpitz auslaufen; dieß hat den Vortheil, daß der Regen abſchlägt und nicht durchdringen kann.

Nach herzlichem Lebewohl, ſchied ich in Hietaniemi von meinem gütigen Begleiter und kehrte auf die große Straße zurück. Päckilä gegenüber auf dem Ruſſiſchen Ufer liegt das Dorf Helſinge, und in deſſen Nähe der Berg Hvitberi, wo weiße Lingon wachſen, die eben ſo gut ſchmecken, als die rothen. Vor Korpikylä fährt man rechts einem See vorüber, dem einzigen auf dem Wege von N. Torneå; im Innern des Landes iſt kein Mangel an Seen. Im Gaſthofe von Korpikylä war man beim Kartenſpiel um Geld ſehr laut. Es iſt nicht ſo gar lange, wo den Finnen das Kartenſpiel noch ganz unbekannt war; die Fremden haben ſie damit bekannt gemacht.

Eine Viertelmeile von Kuckola fuhr ich in einem Boot über einen kleinen Fluß zur Kirche Carl Guſtav oder Karunge. Ich ging auf den Pfarrhof, den der Landmeſſer Bergner gepachtet hat, denn der Mangel an Finniſchen Geiſtlichen iſt ſo groß, daß

das Pastorat schon eine Zeitlang nicht hatte besetzt werden können. Alles schlief; nur ein Mädchen fand ich noch wachend,
die, da ich um die Schlüssel zur Kirche bat, mich zum Küster
führte. Das Innere der großen Kreuzkirche entsprach nicht dem
Aeußeren: nackte Bretterwände, der kleine, mit einem weißen
Laken bedeckte Altar, an einer Seite der Kirche, die wenig zierliche Kanzel, machten keinen guten Eindruck. Aber reizend war
die Aussicht vom nahen Glockenthurm: man überschaut eine reizende Landschaft, die der Torneå durchströmt, und aus welcher
am Russischen Ufer der hohe Niawaara-Berg sich erhebt. Kirche,
Pfarr- und Küsterhof rc. liegen auf einer kleinen Insel, die sich
durch ihre fruchtbaren Felder und ihre schönen Blumenteppiche
auszeichnet; die blühenden Feldbeeren (Åkerbär) machten sie jetzt
besonders schön. Mittlerweile hatte das Mädchen der schlafenden Herrschaft die Ankunft eines Fremden berichtet; die guten
Leute achteten die Gastfreundschaft höher denn ihre nächtliche Ruhe. Nur wenige Minuten waren verflossen, als Herr Bergner mich aufsuchte, um zum Abendessen und Nachtquartier ein-
zuladen. Es war Mitternacht, Wolken verdunkelten die Sonne,
ich folgte dem freundlichen Manne. In der Eile war eine tüchtige Mahlzeit bereitet, Bergner und seine liebenswürdige Frau,
aus der Stadt Torneå gebürtig, baten dringend, bis zum nächsten Morgen zu bleiben. Es kostete mir wirklich Ueberwindung,
zu widerstehen; aber der Plan für den nächsten Tag schien die
Weiterreise oder doch das Uebernachten in einem Gasthofe zu
fordern, um recht frühe aus dem Quartier kommen zu können.
Nach sehr angenehmen Unterhaltungen kehrte ich daher über die
Fähre zu meinem Wagen zurück, fuhr nach dem nahen Kuckola,
und da hier kein Zimmer frei war, noch eine Station weiter
nach Wojakkala, wo ich schon bei der Aufreise übernachtet hatte.
— Das ganz von Finnen bewohnte Karunge bildet seit 1782
ein eigenes Pastorat; bis dahin war es Kapelle zu N. Torneå.

Am 26. Jun. Von Wojakkala nach Torneå 1 Meile.

Wie gestern, so fielen auch heute, als ich ausfuhr, Schnee: flocken, und die Luft blieb selbst am Tage kalt; ein Paar Tage hernach war wieder große Hitze. Eine Viertelmeile vor Hapa: randa führt der Weg links von der großen Straße ab in die Stadt Torneå. Neben einem Gränzpfeiler fährt man auf einem schrecklichen Damme über eine schöne mit Buschwerk besetzte Wiese, durch den kleinen Bach Näran, dessen Brücke das Eis weggerissen hatte, in die Stadt; hinter dem Bache steht der Ruß: sische Gränzposten. Unmittelbar vor der Stadt liegt der Zoll, wo man den Paß unterschreiben läßt, der hernach vom Bürger: meister und vom Commendanten unterschrieben wird; für Fremde bedarf es Russischer Pässe.

Die Stadt liegt auf einer kleinen etwa ¼ Meile langen Insel, an der andern Seite ist sie vom Torneå umflossen, der 1¼ Meile von der Stadt sich in den Bottnischen Meerbusen er: gießt. Die Insel, oder, wie man der Geringfügigkeit des Baches wegen, der sie nach der Seite von Haparanda zu begränzt, ehe: mals aber ein ansehnlicher Arm des Torneå war, gewöhnlich spricht, die Halbinsel, heißt Svensarö. — Die Stadt besteht aus drei neben einander fortlaufenden Hauptgassen, die, gleich den Nebengassen, ungepflastert, ja letztere sind, zumal an den Seiten, mit zum Theil hohem Grase bewachsen, eben so die Vorhöfe der Häuser; aber weder der eine noch der andere Grasplatz dient zur Weide, noch sind des Graswuchses halber einige Straßen gesperrt, wie einige Reisebeschreiber erzählen; alle Straßen dür: fen befahren werden. Alle Häuser, neben welchen oft kleine Gärten, sind von Holz, mehrere von zwei Stockwerken. Am Markt sieht man einzelne hübsche Häuser, die Straße am Fluß hat die besten. Die vielen kleinen Häuser an der östlichen Gasse sind seit mehreren Jahren von Armen angebaut worden. Die Armuth in Torneå ist groß und wächset, durch Luxus und stocken: de Erwerbsquellen, mit jedem Jahre. Wiewohl die Stadt, seit 1767, Stapelfreiheit genießt, ist der Handel jetzt doch unbedeu:

tend. Handelsgegenstände sind: Lachs, getrocknete Fische, Theer, Bretter, Butter, Hanf, eingemachte Bärbär, auch Felle und Federn aus Lappland. Aus sämischem Rennthierkalbleder bereitet man gelbgraue, feine Frauenhandschuhe, die zwar nicht dauerhaft sind, aber sich weich und angenehm tragen; auch Schächte zu Mannsstrümpfen. In den Kirchspielen umher werden Schiffe zum Verkauf gebauet. Der Hafen der Stadt ist seit längerer Zeit immer seichter geworden; nur kleine Fahrzeuge können einlaufen, größere müssen bei Reutehamn, ¼ Meile südlich von Björkön, gelöscht werden. Die Zufuhr geschah bisher, wie in den meisten Westerbottnischen Städten, größtentheils aus Stockholm. Auch nach Lappland wird Handel getrieben. Jährlich wird Markt gehalten. Handwerker aller Art findet man, aber sie sind wenig wohlhabend. Die Einwohner, etwa 600 an der Zahl, sind meist Schwedischer Abkunft, daher in der Stadtkirche Schwedisch, und nur so oft, unsichern Eises wegen, die Finnen nicht zur Finnischen Landkirche N. Torneä kommen können, auch Finnisch gepredigt wird.

Eine schreckliche Fluth erging über die Stadt Torneä (deren Lage doch, zumal im nordöstlichen Theile, nicht ganz niedrig ist) und deren nahe Umgegend am 18. Mai 1818: Während im oberen Torneäfluß das Eis am 17. Mai aufging, lag es noch in der Mündung zunächst der Stadt fest, weil es hier ohne Schnee, als reines Kerneis, gefroren war. Innerhalb einer kleinen Viertelmeile bildete nun das Wasser des Flusses eine 17 Fuß hohe Eisfluth, die auch die Stadt überschwemmte. — Im selbigen Jahre hörte in Torneä die Sommerwärme am 2. August auf; und am 11. August hatte man schon Eis von der Dicke eines halben Zolles; doch traten dann wieder wärmere Tage ein und erst am 2. Nov. ward der Torneäfluß mit Eis belegt.

Die Stadt Torneä, unter 65° 50′ 43″ Polhöhe, ward im Jahr 1621 durch König Gustav II. Adolph gegründet. Nicht lange hernach erhielt sie eine öffentliche Stadtschule (Pädagogium), deren einziger Lehrer besser als die Lehrer der übrigen

Finnischen Pädagogien besoldet war, bis er in neuester Zeit, seit der Abtretung an Rußland, diesen gleichgesetzt wurde. Die Schülerzahl hat zuweilen 50 betragen; einzelne gingen aus der Schule auf die Universität. — Das Rathhaus, am alten Markt, ist ein hübsches hölzernes Gebäude, mit Thurm, Uhrwerk, Spritzenkammer und Buden für die Russischen Waaren. Am untern Markt liegt das Wage- und Packhaus. Vor der Stadt trifft man mehrere Windmühlen. Die Lage der Stadt ist sehr gesund.

Des geringen Wohlstandes der Stadt ungeachtet, findet man in derselben zwei Keller und zwei Billards; zum Frühstück versammelt man sich auf der Apotheke, die erst seit 1787 besteht. Die gutgelohnten Russischen Beamten machen viel Aufwand und ihr Beispiel findet Nachahmung. Die Sittlichkeit der Stadt wird nicht gerühmt.

Ich beabsichtigte, von Torneå aus das, eine halbe Meile jenseits beginnende, eigentliche Finnland zu besuchen; Kemi, die erste Kirche in Osterbotten, deren Pastor der kenntnißreiche Propst Dr. Castrén ist, 2¼ Meile von Torneå, sollte der nordöstlichste Punkt meiner Reise seyn. Eine Fähre führte mich von der Stadt aus jenseitige Ufer des Torneå. Hier liegt der Gästgifvaregård, wo ich ein Pferd nach Kemi bestellte; die nach Westerbotten Reisenden erhalten Skjuts in der Stadt Torneå. Bevor ich indeß die weitere Reise nach Kemi antrat, wollte ich die Landkirche N. Torneå, zu welcher die Stadt als Filial gehört, und neben welcher der Pastor wohnt, sehen; sie liegt auf der Insel Björkö im Torneå. Ein kurzer Wiesenpfad führte mich ans Ufer, von wo ich in einem Boote zur Insel fuhr. Mit vieler Güte empfing mich hier der Pfarrer, Propst Appelgren. Ich sah die Kirche, eine vor wenigen Decennien neuerbaute, einfache steinerne Kreuzkirche mit Orgel. Aus der Kuppel genießt man eine weite Uebersicht über die flache Gegend bis Kemi, über den Torneå-Strom und dessen Mündung. Unweit der Kirche, zu welcher man durch eine Allee gelangt, liegt die Kirchspielsstube, jetzt Soldatenwohnung. An der Kirche sind ein Pastor und ein Comminiſter angeſtellt, welche auch in der nur ¼ Meile von Björkön entfernten Stadt Torneå den Gottesdienſt verrichten. Eine feſte Landkirchſpielsſchule giebt es nicht; die Eltern ſind Lehrer ihrer Kinder, die oft ſchon in ſehr frühen Jahren fertig leſen und den Catechismus auswendig wiſſen; die ſchwächeren unterrichtet der Küſter jährlich zwei Wochen. Die Landgemeinde iſt ganz Finniſch. Die Pfarre N. Torneå ſtand bisher im Rufe ſehr großer Einkünfte; doch den anſehnlichſten Ertrag gewährte der Lachszehnte, der mehrere hundert Tonnen betrug, jetzt aber durch verminderten Lachsfang ſo abgenommen hat, daß der Paſtor jährlich nicht 100 Tonnen erhebt. Uebrigens ſind die kirchlichen Einrichtungen der Finniſchen Gemeinden, auch im eigentlichen Finnland, im Weſentlichen ganz die Schwediſchen. Die Zahl der unehelichen Kinder verhält ſich im Paſtorat zu der Zahl der ehelichen leider ſchon wie 1 : 8, ja einmal ſchon wie 1 : 5; und doch zählt das Paſtorat nur 5000 Seelen. Im übrigen Weſterbotten kennt man ein ſolches Verhältniß nicht.

In älteren Zeiten war der Umfang des Paſtorats N. Torneå ſehr groß; 30 Meilen erſtreckte es ſich gegen Lappland herauf; auch O. Torneå, oder, wie es anfangs hieß, Sarkllar war darunter begriffen, bis 1618; 1782 ward auch die Kapellgemeinde Karunge oder Carl Guſtaf zu einem eigenen Paſtorat erhoben, ſo daß der Umfang des Paſtorats N. Torneå jetzt nur mäßig iſt. Es beſteht bisher aus Ruſſiſchem und Schwediſchem Gebiet; doch wird die Erbauung einer beſondern Kirche für die Schwediſchen Unterthanen beabſichtigt. Zum Paſtorat N. Torneå gehören die Fiſcherkapellen Sandſkär und Malörn, wo zuweilen im Sommer vor den daſelbſt mit dem Fange von Strömlingen und Blüten (Löja, Cyprinus alburnus) beſchäftigten Einwohnern der Stadt- und Landgemeinde gepredigt wird; die ſehr hohe Kapelle auf Malörn dient den Schiffern als Merkzeichen.

Auf Björkön liegt auch ein Dorf. Vor Erbauung der Stadt Torneå war daſelbſt ein berühmter Marktplatz, wo die älteſten Handelsleute Weſterbottens, die Birkarlar, ihren Handel trieben.

Diese Birkarlar, deren Geschichte sehr im Dunkeln liegt (selbst die Ableitung ihres Namens ist ungewiß), waren die ersten Einwohner der neuen Stadt und der übrigen Westerbottnischen Städte.

Erst nachdem ich ein tüchtiges Mahl eingenommen, durfte ich den Pfarrhof verlassen. Dadurch ward meine Rückkehr zum Gästgifvaregård verzögert. Als ich zurück kam, hatte das Pferd schon ein Paar Stunden gestanden, und überdieß wilder Natur und mit Fehlern behaftet, die es zum Zugpferde untauglich machten, sprang es, sogleich nachdem ich den Wagen bestiegen, im vollen Galopp davon und warf mich in einen Graben. Die Kopfwunde, welche ich davon trug, veranlaßte mich, die Reise nach Kemi aufzugeben und zur Stadt zurückzukehren, wo ich einen Arzt vorzufinden hoffte. Glücklicherweise war Dr. Deutsch, der, ¼ Meile von Torneå, in Raumo wohnt, anwesend. Er eilte mir einige Mittel zu verordnen, und da er die Verwundung für nicht bedeutend erklärte, so übernachtete ich nur in dem netten, aber theuern Gästgifvaregård, einem geräumigen Gebäude von zwei Stockwerken, und trat am nächsten Morgen die Rückreise an. Zuvor besuchte ich noch den Apotheker Pippo, der eine Sammlung von inländischen Käfern und Schmetterlingen besitzt; auch Deutsch hat eine entomologische Sammlung. Auch sah ich die Stadtkirche nebst dem Glockenthurm, von welchem Karl XI. und viele Reisende die Mitternachtssonne beobachteten. Man geht durch den Glockenthurm, bevor man in die hölzerne Kirche tritt. Der Glockenthurm ist über 50 Ellen hoch und ist derselbige, den Karl XI. am 14. Junius 1694 bestieg; nur hat er späterhin eine bequemere Treppe erhalten. Das Meer ist nicht sichtbar. Die Kirche, im Innern recht freundlich, ist klein, nur 50 Ellen lang und 20 Ellen breit, von Holz, liegt auf einer geringen Anhöhe, ist mit Schindeln gedeckt und hat einen hohen spitzen Thurm; sie brannte 1682 ab, ward aber schon im folgenden Jahre, 300 Ellen von der vorigen Stelle, wieder erbauet. Unter den Gedächtnißtafeln, die man hier trifft, ist diejenige die merkwürdigste, welche den eigenhändigen Bericht Karl XI. über seine Beobachtung der Mitternachtssonne in Torneå am 14. und 15. Jun. 1694 enthält:

„Im Jahr 1694 am 14. Jun. bestiegen Se. Königl. Majestät, der damalige Landshöfding Graf G. Douglas, der Staatssecretaire Piper, der Kriegsrath Joh. Hoghusen, nebst mehreren andern von der königl. Suite den Glockenthurm von Torneå. Wir sahen in dieser Nacht die Sonne bis ¾ auf 12 und 8 Minuten. Da bedeckte eine Wolke die Sonne; aber um 12 Uhr 6 Minuten nach Mitternacht, also am 15. Junius, sahen wir die Sonne mit ihren vollen Strahlen wieder. Wäre keine Wolke gekommen, so hätten wir die Sonne die ganze Nacht über gesehen; denn unter dem Horizonte war sie nicht. Wenn es nicht trübe, sondern klar ist, so kann man in Torneå die Sonne die ganze Nacht sehen." Unter diesen Worten lieset man noch eine Bemerkung, daß die Worte nach der eignen Handschrift des Königes verzeichnet worden seyen.

Der die Kirche umgebende Kirchhof hat einige Grabkreuze, theils blos mit den Namen der Gestorbenen, theils auch mit Versen; Grabkreuze sind im übrigen Westerbotten nicht üblich. Der Kirchhof wird an der einen Seite der Kirche von hohen Espen und Birken beschattet. Auf dem Kirchhof wächst eine schöne und seltene Nelkenart, Dianthus superbus Linn., die sich auch über die nahen Höhen verbreitet hat.

Nachdem ich auf diese Weise die Merkwürdigkeiten der Stadt in Augenschein genommen, fuhr ich in einem Boot über den Torneå nach Haparanda. Im Gästgifvaregård fand ich eine Einladung zum Häradshöfding über ganz Norbotten, Dahl, vor, der noch in Haparanda wohnte, aber eben nach dem nahen Dorfe Mattila ziehen wollte, wo er den schönen Hof Nickala gekauft hat; das dortige Wohnhaus gewährt, seiner hohen Lage wegen, einen guten Standpunkt zur Beobachtung der Mitternachtssonne, die indeß auch hier nicht ohne Unterbrechung geschauet wird.

II.   L

Am 27. Jun. Von Haparanda nach Nickala 1½ M.; von N. nach Saivits 1½ M.; von S. nach Sangits 1½ M. — Zusammen 3½ Meilen.

Mein Weg war heute derselbe, wie bei der Aufreise. Aber meine Unpäßlichkeit und die Hitze des Tages ließen mich diesmal wenig genießen; auch der freundlichen Einladung nach Wuonom zu Herr Örling mußte ich entsagen. Noch frühe nahm ich Nachtquartier in Sangits.

Am 28. Jun. Von Sangits nach Nåsby 1¾ Meilen.

Fast schlaflos hatte ich die Nacht zugebracht. Schon am frühen Morgen brach ich auf, um möglichst bald das Lager von Nåsby zu erreichen, wo ein Arzt anwesend war. Ein Aderlaß, den Herr Utterström sofort verordnete, entfernte die Gefahr, und nach einigen Tagen war ich so weit wieder hergestellt, daß ich wenigstens in kurzen Tagereisen, und in den kühleren Tagesstunden meinen Weg fortsetzen konnte.

Ein und zwanzigstes Kapitel.

Rückreise durch Westerbotten.

Der Ball im Lager von Nåsby. — Excursionen in die schöne Umgegend. — Große Bauernhäuser. — Biedere Menschen. — Norrlands Nachtigall. — Sommerhitze. — Karl des IX. Frühstücksgabe. — Die Pastorate Neder- und Ofver-Calix. — Töre. — Hermelin's Anlagen. — Die Mücken des hohen Nordens. — Råneå. — Melderstein. — Sundom; das Strohflechten. — Gamla Luleå: große Fruchtbarkeit der Gegend; weitläuftiges Pfarrgebiet; Gesundbrunnen; Wohlhabenheit; schöne Körperbildung; die Kirche Gamla Luleå, ihr merkwürdiges und kostbares Gemälde; weite Kirchwege; Armenhaus; Geistlichkeit des Pastorats; die Bentsteller; Fahrwege. — Hermelin's Verdienste um Norrbot-

4

ten und Lappland. — Der Sonnabend-Abend in Gamla Luleå's Kirchgaffen. — Die Stadt Luleå; Einfachheit ihrer Bewohner. — Sonntagsgottesdienst. — Luft-
fahrt nach Bälinge. — Steigender Flor von Norrbottens Län. — Bergbau. — Eigenthümlichkeiten der Bewohner. — Gäddvik; der Weidelappe. — Stadt und
Fluß Piteå. — Die Weideinfeln im Meer. — Kinbäck;
die sieben Töchter. — Die Sennhütten. — Das Abschälen der Waldbäume. — Skelleftea. — Burträsk. —
Die Ruffen in Bureå. — Kirche Löfänger: herrliche
Lage. — Das Heiligenbild von Webbomark. — Gottesdienst in Rosådra. Rickleå. Byggdeå. — Das Schlachtfeld. — Pastorat Umeå. — Hochzeitsgebräuche der
Schweden, Norweger und Finnen. — Theerbrennerey.
— Große Wälder. — Pastorat Degerfors.

Die Tage meines Aufenthalts in Näsby verfloffen durch die
Güte des Magister Almquist aus Neder-Calix und der anwesenden Officiere sehr angenehm. In einem der größern Bauerhöfe des Dorfs bewohnte ich einen hübschen Saal *) nebst ein
Paar freundlichen Nebenzimmern; die Wände waren mit biblischen Bildern geschmückt. Der Hof, Eigenthum eines Tolfman,
d. i. beisitzenden Bauern im Häradsgericht, wurde, außer der
Familie und dem Gesinde, noch von mehreren sehr biedern Menschen bewohnt, die mir auf alle Weise ihren guten Willen zu
bezeigen suchten, also daß mir in keiner Hinsicht etwas fehlte.
Wahrhaft erfreuend war der Anblick eines etwa 14jährigen Mädchens, die mit ihrer Mutter die Aufwartung besorgte; sie war
nicht schön, wie die bereits 45jährige Mutter, sondern hatte ein
kränkliches Aussehen; aber ihr Antlitz verklärte eine himmlische
Milde und Anmuth, ein Friede und eine Freudigkeit hatten sich
über daffelbe ergoffen, wie man sie an den edelsten Menschen in
den schönsten Augenblicken ihres inneren Lebens gewahrt. —
Gleich der Familie des Tolfman, lernte ich hernach mehrere ein-

_____

*) Bauerhöfe mit Sälen giebt es mehrere in Näsby.

L 2

fache gottesfürchtige Familien kennen; die herrlichsten Genüsse des Menschenlebens wurden mir zu Theil und ich dankte Gott, daß selbst ein Unfall mir hatte Gelegenheit geben müssen, mit solchen Menschen bekannt und durch sie solcher Genüsse theilhaftig zu werden.

Nur am Tage meiner Ankunft hütete ich das Zimmer, Freund Almquist leistete mir Gesellschaft. Am nächsten Morgen (es war ein Sonntag) wohnte ich dem Gottesdienst im Lager bei: Almquist hielt eine recht zweckmäßige Predigt; die Stelle der Orgel vertraten Blase-Instrumente, ohne sie freilich zu ersetzen. Große Andacht herrschte in der Versammlung, auch Bäuerinnen waren zugegen, die zum Theil ihren Männern und Verwandten Lebensmittel gebracht hatten. Als ich zurückkehrte, bemerkte ich, daß man in einem der Bauernhäuser in Erbauungsbüchern las. Die Sonntagsfeier ist hier sehr strenge; schon in der Frühe, vor Anfang der gottesdienstlichen Stunde, enthält man sich aller Arbeit und eine Wäscherin weigerte sich, auch nur eine Kleinigkeit am Frühmorgen zu waschen.

: Nach dem Gottesdienst fuhr ich zu Boot auf dem Calix zum Kirchort, wo ich bei Magister Almquist das Mittagsmahl einnahm, und am Nachmittag ans jenseitige Ufer nach Rolfs, wo ich die oben erwähnten Leser näher kennen zu lernen beabsichtigte und zu dem Zweck immer ihren Versammlungen beiwohnte. Die Ufer des Calix bilden hier eine der reizendsten Landschaften. — Von Rolfs fuhr ich zur Kirche und dann nach Näsby, um einem vom Officiercorps veranstalteten Balle beizuwohnen. Die Honoratioren der Gegend waren hier versammelt; manche Frauen und Mädchen hübsch, alle schlicht und einfach. Man war herzlich froh. Ich blieb bis 11 Uhr; der Ball dauerte bis 5 Uhr Morgens. Dergleichen Bälle hat man jährlich zwei, höchstens drei; doch geben die Officiers nicht bei jedem Möte einen Ball. Das Regimentsmöte wird gewöhnlich jährlich gehalten, das demselben vorangehende Officiersmöte, zur Uebung der Officiers und Unterofficiers, auch in Beziehung auf Rekruten, fällt nie aus. Das Regimentsmöte steht hier 16 Tage: an jedem Werktage wird, von frühe bis 9 Uhr Morgens, und von 4 bis 8 Uhr

Abends exercirt, zwei Tage wird marschirt und eine Nacht bivouaquirt. Mehrere Compagnien, z. B. Luleå und Piteå, hatten den Weg zum Lager in Böten zurückgelegt. Die Böte, deren man sich auf dem Calir-Elf bedient, sind breiter und sicherer, als die, welche man auf dem Torneå benutzt. Die Soldaten des Westerbottnischen Regiments erhalten von den Bauern weniger als in südlichen Orten; indeß hat jeder Soldat ein Wohnhaus nebst den nöthigen Wirthschaftsgebäuden, ein Ackerstück von 1 Tonne (4 Scheffel) Gerste Aussaat, und Weide für ein Paar Kühe und Schaafe; manche Bauern geben ihren Soldaten die Kühe selbst.

Am Montag Abend machte ich einen Spaziergang in die liebliche Gegend: nach einer Tageshitze von 24° Reaumur, war jetzt die Luft lau und milde, über den grünen Fluren strahlte die Sonne, die Vögel sangen; doch nicht der Tallkrast, der hier sehr häufig ist, übrigens außer Norrland nicht gefunden wird, und der sein Lied erst nach 10 Uhr Abends beginnt. Es war ein ächt Norrländischer Sommerabend, dem freilich auch die Mücken nicht fehlten. Das Ziel der Promenade war das Lager, wo ich dem schönen Zapfenstreich beiwohnte. An der Dunkelheit spürt man es nicht, daß die Stunde des Schlafes gekommen ist; in ganz Westerbotten zündet man bis in den Anfang Septembers kein Licht an; in Angermanland wird es schon vom Anfang des August an ein Paar Stunden dunkel. Die schöne Linnaea borealis wächset um Näsby, wie an vielen anderen Nordischen Orten. — Unter den Vögeln dieser Gegend sind die wilden Gänse, deren Fleisch hier besonders wohlschmeckend ist, sehr häufig.

Am Dienstag Mittag unternahm ich mit Mag. Almquist eine Bootfahrt nach dem ¼ Meile entfernten Dörfchen Breviken; die Schwester meines Wirthes war unsere Ruderin. Man kommt drei fetten Weideinseln, welche Blumenteppiche, Gebüsche und Heuscheunen schmücken, vorüber. An den Ufern bilden Dörfer, Landstellen und Amtshöfe freundliche Gruppen. Im Calir-Elf erblickt man viele Lachsgerüste; doch ist der Fang nicht so ergiebig wie im Torneå, wo man zuweilen an Einem Tage auf Einer Stelle an 2000 Lachse fangen soll. Es war ein sehr

heißer Tag. Zu Breviken, wo eben mehrere Schiffe Bretterla-
dungen einnahmen, erquickten wir uns im Hofe des Bauern
Johan Carlsson mit Speise und Trank; auch Roggenbrot war vorhanden; fast nur in den Jahren des Mißwachses
ißt man Rindenbrot, welches aber auch dann gewöhnlich nur
Speise der Armen ist: man verwendet dazu am liebsten die Birkenrinde. Bei Carlsson zeugte alles von Wohlstand, Reinlichkeit, Sauberkeit. Es war eine rechte Freude, die herzlichen, gottesfürchtigen Aeußerungen des biedern Ehepaars über Gegenstände des Lebens zu hören. Nach Norrländischer Weise bestand
Carlsson's Hof aus mehreren Wohngebäuden, in deren einem
die Wittwe des Geistlichen Grape von N. Torneå wohnte.
Die biedere Alte hatte uns zum Kaffee geladen; wir folgten.
Ein Webestuhl neben einer Bibel und einigen Erbauungsschriften, unter den Fenstern ein Gärtchen, in welchem Erbsen und
allerlei Küchengewächse gediehen, auch ein Sperberbaum blühte,
daneben eine kleine Bleiche, bezeichneten einfach und wahr das
Leben dieser glücklichen Menschen. Als ein Kleinod
verwahrte Frau Grape ein Büchlein, welches aus einzelnen
Kärtchen bestand: auf jedem Kärtchen las man einen Bibelspruch
und einen Liedervers; das sprach die gute Alte, sey zuweilen in
der Frühe ihre und ihrer Wirthin schönste Frühkost (frukost).
Sie machte uns aufmerksam auf ein ihr vor allen theures Blatt,
mit Sprüchen, die, von ihrem seligen Mann noch als Bräutigam geschrieben, ihr unaussprechlichen Trost gegeben zu einer
Zeit, wo sie bei bevorstehender Hochzeit traurig gewesen und über
die durch den Ehestand bevorstehende Veränderung in ihrem Innern geseufzet habe. Von Frau Grape gingen wir abwärts in
die Wohnung eines Schiffers, von wo wir die nahe, durch Wald-
inseln verschönte Mündung des Calix-Stroms in den Bottnischen Meerbusen überschaueten. Zu Carlsson zurückgekehrt,
wurde uns in einem silbernen Becher, die man überall bei den
Bauern findet, der Ehrentrank vorgesetzt. Wir sagten den guten
Leuten, die durchaus von keiner Bezahlung wissen wollten, ein
herzliches Lebewohl und ruderten in lieblicher Abendkühle nach
Räsby zurück. Meine Ruderin, die ich, wie es ihre Thätigkeit

und Gefälligkeit verdiente, bezahlt hatte, wußte nicht, was sie mir alles zu gut thun sollte, um sich dankbar zu beweisen; und als ich ihr kleine Verrichtungen auftrug, war sie voll Freude, daß sie nun doch Gelegenheit habe, einigermaßen ihre Dankbarkeit zu zeigen. Gleich einfache und freundliche Weise schmückte die Hausfrau. O ihr unverdorbenen Menschen, ihr erinnert mich ganz an die fernen Alpenthäler meiner lieben Schweiz und ihre durch Einfalt und Natur glücklichen Bewohner! — Auch in den Häusern der Honoratioren, nicht blos der Geistlichen, herrscht in Westerbotten noch große Einfachheit: die Häuser sind von Holz; rauhe Bretter bilden die inneren Wände der Zimmer, die Fugen sind mit Moos ausgestopft, die Stühle sind von Holz, selten sieht man ein Sopha. Töchter oder Hausfrau warten bei Tische auf; aber daneben zeugt alles von Wohlhabenheit, wohlschmeckend und reichlich sind die Speisen, und die schlicht, aber reinlich gekleideten Menschen zeigen feine Bildung in Gesprächen und Benehmen. Elegant fand ich es nur in Einem der ansehnlichen Pfarrhöfe Westerbottens, wiewohl auch dort die alte Einfachheit noch nicht ganz gewichen war.

Neder-Caliy ist eines der kleineren unter den Schwedisch redenden Pastoraten Norrbottens; 6 Meilen lang und 6 Meilen breit, zählte es im Jahr 1815. 3653 Einwohner. Seiner Berge im Norden ungeachtet, baut es ziemlich viel Korn. Viehzucht und Fischerey geben einen bedeutenden Ertrag: an den Küsten sind mehrere Fischerlagen errichtet, wo im Sommer die Kirchspielsbewohner und die Bürger der Stadt Luleå Strömlingsfang treiben; Robben und Seevögel werden erlegt, auch Schiffe gebaut. Die Pfarre ist an Einkommen eine der mittelmäßigern des Landes; früher bezog der Pastor auch die acht Tonnen Korn, welche Karl IX., als er 1602, damals noch Herzog, Westerbotten durchreisete, dem Pastor Birger Erici, für ihn und dessen Amtsnachfolger, zum Frühstück schenkte. Der muntere Pfarrherr, so erzählt man, begleitete den Herzog eine Strecke Weges; der Herzog fragte ihn, wie er heiße? Der Pfarrherr entgegnete: „Herr Börje" (Birger). „Wie," sprach der König, „Herr?" „Ja," erwiederte Birger, „die Bauern Ew. Majestät nennen mich so." Karl, dem die Antwort gefiel, fragte nun weiter: ob er um etwas zu bitten habe? Birger antwortete: er habe keine Beschwerde, als die eine, daß seine Frau ihm kein Frühstück geben wolle, — worauf Karl ihm die Versicherung ertheilte: es solle ihm künftig nicht am Frühstück gebrechen. — Einige Zeit hernach bewilligte Karl aus dem Kronzehnten 8 Tonnen Korn, die lange unter dem Namen: „Herr Börje's Frühstück" der Pfarre verblieben. Herr Börje liegt in der Kirche Neder-Calix begraben.

Zwischen dem Pastorat N. Calix und Lappland mitten inne liegt das Pastorat Ö. Calix, bis 1644 Theil des Pastorats N. Calix, seitdem eigenes Pastorat. Neun Meilen lang, wird es, seiner ganzen Länge nach, vom Calixstrom durchflossen, der außer einigen Geh- und Reitwegen, die einzige Verbindungsstraße bildet, deren Benutzung überdieß durch die vielen Wasserfälle schwierig und langwierig ist, also daß man zwei volle Tage bedarf, um die 6 Meilen zwischen den Kirchen O. und N. Calix zurückzulegen. Fahrwege nach oder in O. Calix giebt es gar nicht. Die größte Breite des Pastorats beträgt 4 Meilen. Die Zahl der Einwohner war im Jahr 1815. 1609. Man rechnet gegenwärtig 106 alte Bauerhöfe, 35 steuernde Kolonistenhöfe, von welchen 22 der Krone angehören, und 13 Frälse und als solche Eigenthum des Bruk Melderstein im Pastorat Råneå sind; ferner 89 Kron- und 3 Frälse-, noch nicht steuernde, Kolonistenhöfe (nybyggen). O. Calix ist mit Bergen ausgefüllt; auf dem der Kirche gegenüber liegenden Berge, Lappberget, genießt man einer herrlichen Aussicht. Um Johannis bietet dieser Berg einen eben so freien Standpunkt zur Beobachtung der Mitternachtssonne dar, als der Berg Afvasaxa; dagegen kann man bei der Kirche O. Calix um Weihnachten kaum zwei Stunden bei Tage lesen. Die Kirche, von Holz, liegt am südlichen Ende des Kirchspiels, im Mittelpunkt der fruchtbarsten und angebautesten Striche desselben. Die Einwohner, meistens Schweden, leben einfach und frugal, doch sind sie bei weitem nicht so wohlhabend, wie ihre Finnischen Nachbarn in Pajala. Bei dem großen Reichthum an Wäldern ist das Theerbrennen so sehr Hauptnahrungszweig, daß Ackerbau und Viehzucht darunter leiden. Brache kennt man nicht. Der Ackerbau könnte sehr verbessert und erweitert werden, und hat auch wirklich sich in den letzten Jahren gehoben; in guten Jahren wird Korn verkauft. Man schneidet mit Handsicheln, und die Weiber dreschen mit Dreschflegeln. Die Viehzucht liefert zum Verkauf nur ein wenig Butter und Kalbfelle, wiewohl die Wiesenufer der Flüsse so üppig sind, daß das Gras nicht nur sehr dick wird, sondern bisweilen eine Länge von mehr denn zwei Ellen erreicht, ohne deßhalb unschmackhaft zu seyn; man leitet diese Ueppigkeit von dem vielen Laube, Rinde, verfaultem Grase und andern Vegetabilien her, mit welchen die Frühlingsfluth die Wiesen überschwemmt, so wie von den dichten Sandschichten, die die Berg (fjäll) Fluth über die vegetabilische Lage ausbreitet; die übrigen Wiesen sind freilich mager, mit Moos bedeckt und sumpfig. Auch Jagd und Fischfang sind Erwerbsquellen der Einwohner; die Lachsfischerey im Calix-Elf ist, von der Krone verpachtet, bald mehr, bald minder lohnend. Die Einwohner besitzen im Durchführen der Böte durch die Wasserfälle eine besondere Geschicklichkeit, so daß sich selten Unglücksfälle ereignen; 3 oder 4 rudern mit möglichster Schnelligkeit, der Steuermann steht im Hintertheil des langen und schmalen Bootes, welches mit unglaublicher Geschwindigkeit die Fälle durchschneidet. — Die Zahl der Gebornen betrug im Pastorat Öfver-Calix im Jahr 1816. 62, die Zahl der Gestorbenen 27; im selbigen Jahre wurden im Pastorat Neder-Calix geboren 127, und starben 66; ein ähnliches günstiges Verhältniß findet man in ganz Westerbotten.

————

Am 2. Jul. Von Näsby nach Grötnäs ⅜ M.; von G. nach Månsby 1¼ M.; von M. nach Töre 2¼ M.; von T. nach Hoitedn 1¼ M. — Zusammen 4⅜ Meilen.

Um 10 Uhr verließ ich Näsby, nach einem herzlichen Abschiede von meinen biedern Wirthen: „bei Gott möchten wir uns wiederfinden," waren die Worte, mit denen sie mich entließen. Bevor man die Kirche N. Calix erreicht, fährt man durch Wald, in welchem abwärts am Ufer des Calix ein Gesundbrunnen liegt. In N. Calix sprach ich auf dem Propst= hofe vor und mußte zu Mittag bleiben. Propst Schmalz ist sinnesschwach; ein vom Consistorium beauftragter Geistlicher, Mag. Almquist, verwaltet das Pfarramt. Jetzt war die Krankheit gemildert. Ich saß mit dem guten Alten im hochgelegenen Gar= ten und freute mich der herrlichen Aussicht, die man von hier über den Calix=Elf und die schöne Umgegend genießt, während der Propst von seinen Thaten im Finnischen Kriege, wo er als Feldprediger einen Officier gerettet, von seinen Blumen und Fi= schen ꝛc. erzählte. Die Pröpstin ertrug ihr Leiden mit einer ächt christlichen Geduld und Ergebung. — Nach dem Mittagsessen ließ ich mich über den Calix nach Rolfs rudern, wo Magister Almquist mit seiner biedern Gattin eben anwesend war, sagte den guten Leuten, die mir so viel Freundschaft erwiesen hatten, ein herzliches und dankbares Lebewohl und fuhr dann, unter weh= müthigen Gefühlen, weiter. Der Weg, eine lange Strecke am Ufer des Calix, ist sehr anmuthig. Am schönsten ist die Gegend jenseits Mänsby. Durch Wald und neben kleinen Wiesen, welche dichten Blumenteppichen gleichen, gelangt man zum an= sehnlichen Dorfe Töre, mit trefflichem Hafen, mit Brettermüh= len und Stabhammer Törefors; die Bretter von Töre sollen besonders gut seyn. Töre verdankt dem Baron Hermelin sei= nen Wohlstand, fast durch alle Norrbottischen Kirchspiele ziehen sich an der Seite von Lappland die hundert Nybyggen, welche der Baron anlegte. — Zwischen Mänsby und Töre liegt der Berg Raggdyna, von welchem man die Mitternachtssonne beobachten kann.

Eine Viertelmeile hinter Töre erblickt man Johannisro, eine Besitzung des Bergmeisters Quensel; weiterhin, links, einige Sennhütten; auf dem übrigen Wege eine menschenleere Wassermühle, keine Menschenwohnung. Der Weg war schlecht. Nicht ohne Moräste war der dichte Wald, und Mückenschwärme verfinsterten die drückend heiße Luft; zweimal stürzte das Pferd, und erst um 10½ Uhr langte ich in Hviteän an, wo ich über= nachtete. Die Hitze dauerte fort; man stellte, die Luft abzuküh=

len, Birkensträuche ins Zimmer. Die Mücken, die in dieser Jahreszeit am schlimmsten sind, machten, daß kein Schlaf in meine Augen kam. Auch der Labetrunk fehlte, denn die ganze Heerde war bei den Sennhütten.

Am 3. Jul. Von Hvlteän nach Räneä 1$\frac{7}{11}$ M.; von R. nach Pärsön 1$\frac{1}{4}$ M.; von P. nach Luleä gamla stad 1$\frac{1}{4}$ M. — Zusammen 5$\frac{1}{11}$ Meilen.

Um 7 Uhr fuhr ich ab. Bis Räneä hat man dichten Wald, in welchem der Rauch entfernter Theeröfen und eine Wassermühle, außer kleinen Thälern, die einzige Abwechselung darbieten. Theeröfen giebt es viele in der Gegend; auch bei Hvitcän findet man mehrere. Die kleinen Wassermühlen gehören gewöhnlich mehreren Bauern gemeinschaftlich, sind aber nur zur Zeit des Mahlens bewohnt.

In Räneä sah ich die kleine, hölzerne, seit 1765 mit einer guten Orgel versehene, Kirche. Bis 1654 war Räneä Kapellgemeinde von Luleä, dann wurde es besonderes Pastorat. Das Pastorat Räneä ist zwischen Gellivare-Lappmark, woran es gränzt, und dem Meere, 7 bis 8 Meilen breit, aber der bewohnte Theil des Pastorats beträgt nur 4 bis 5 Meilen. Die Einwohnerzahl des Pastorats war im Jahr 1815. 2594. Mehrere haben Boote weg zur Kirche, durch eine Menge Fälle des Räneä. In früheren Zeiten soll die Fahrt auf dem Räneä von Degersele durch mehr denn 10 Fälle so gefährlich gewesen seyn, daß die zur Kirche Fahrenden von den Zurückbleibenden für dieses Leben Abschied nahmen, weil sie fürchten mußten, nicht lebendig zurück zu kehren; aber auch durch diese Gefahr ließen sie sich vom Besuch der Kirche nicht abhalten.

Unter den Bewohnern des Kirchspiels herrscht viel Wohlhabenheit; Kornbau, Theerbrennen und Viehzucht sind ansehnlich, die Lachsfischerey im Räneä ist weniger bedeutend. Im Pastorat Räneä liegt das Eisenhüttenwerk Melderstein, welches der Professor und Capitaine Meldercreutz im J. 1744. 1 Meile westlich von der Kirche anlegte; der Hochofen Strömsund, 1$\frac{1}{4}$

* Meile von Melderstein, an einem Meerbusen, nebst Schiffswerft, einige andere Werke und mehrere Nybyggen gehören dazu; das Erz wird aus Gellivare-Lappmark meist durch Rennthiere herbeigeführt, und bei der Verarbeitung mit Upländischem Eisen, besonders aus Utö, vermischt. Der gesammte an Meldercreutz unentgeldlich überlassene und von ihm cultivirte und benützte Landstrich zwischen den Flüssen Luleå und Calix, in den Pastoraten Råneå, Luleå, Nieder= und Ober=Calix und Gellivare=Lappmark ist an 20 Meilen lang und 8 bis 12 und mehr Meilen breit. Bei Meldercreutz Tode (1785) betrug die Zahl der von ihm angelegten Nybyggen 67, mit 349 Seelen. Die Polhöhe bei Melderstein ist 65° 56′ 50″.

Nach einem Frühstück beim Pastor Euren dem Jüngeren, wozu ich die Einladung im Gästgifvaregård vorfand, setzte ich meine Reise über den Råneå-Elf nach Pårsön fort; man kommt dem Meerbusen Möfjård, an welchem ein Dorf gleiches Namens liegt, vorüber, und erreicht bei Sundom das Pastorat Luleå. Sundom ist ein großes Dorf, das sich durch seine Strohflechterey einen Namen erworben hat. Ein armer Mann, Lundmark, wanderte vor etwa 10 Jahren aus Wermeland ein, der Bauer Nils Larsson in Sundom überließ ihm ein Häuschen. Lundmark legte sich nun mit Frau und Kindern auf das Flechten gröberer und feinerer Strohhüte, die großen Abgang fanden, und ihm bald nicht blos einen eigenen Hof, sondern noch außerdem ein nicht unbedeutendes Vermögen verschafften. Schon hat Lundmark Nachahmer in Sundom gefunden, welche aber nur für ihren eigenen Bedarf flechten. Lundmark ist auch Schulmeister und Schneider des Dorfes und beschäftigt sich außer dem Flechten, mit andern Handarbeiten; man rühmt ihn als einen offenen Kopf und einen ehrlichen, biederen Mann. Sundom liegt ein wenig abwärts vom Wege; ich fuhr hinein, um mir einen weißen Strohhut zu kaufen, denn weiße Strohhüte gewähren in heißen Sommern den besten Schutz, weniger die schwarzen. Ich ließ hernach in Luleå, weil ich in Sundom keinen auftreiben konnte, einen Strohhut anfertigen, der mir die Reise gar sehr erleichterte.

In Pårsön langte ich um 2¼ Uhr an. Die drückende Hitze von etwa 22° Reaumur bei gänzlicher Windstille, bewog mich, erst nach 4 Uhr die Reise fortzusetzen.

Zwischen Pårsön und Luleå gamla stad hat man Wald und üppige Wiesen; im Dorfe Rutvik sah ich ein steinernes Viehhaus, was man in Westerbotten nicht häufig findet. Nahe vor Luleå liegt, wie in den meisten Norrländischen Pastoraten, ein kleiner Gesundbrunnen.

In Luleå gamla stad (Altstadt) verflossen mir einige angenehme Tage im Hause und durch die Güte des Propstes, Doctor Nordmark, wie durch die Gewogenheit des Landshöfdings über Norrbotten, Baron Koskull, der eben noch in Altstadt Luleå seinen Sitz hatte.

Luleå gamla stad, wo einst die Stadt Luleå stand, bis diese näher ans Meer verlegt wurde (daher der Name), enthält jetzt die alte, vielleicht schon im 13ten Jahrhundert erbauete Landkirche Luleå, den Pfarrhof, einige wenige andere bewohnte Häuser und mehr denn ein halbes Tausend Kirchstuben, in denen man nur zur Zeit der Sonn- und Festtage Menschen findet. Die Umgegend ist eine der fruchtbarsten des ganzen Nordens; dichtes, fast zwei Ellen hohes Gras (am Torneå soll es zuweilen noch höher wachsen) bedeckt die Wiesen; der Roggen giebt, bei mittelmäßiger Bearbeitung, das 16te, bei etwas besserer, das 20ste bis 40ste, ja, auf dem sehr sorgfältig bearbeiteten Pfarracker gab, wie mich Doctor Nordmark versicherte, die Gerste das 10te und der Roggen das 64ste Korn *). Dieser große Ertrag ist die gemeinschaftliche Wirkung der Fruchtbarkeit und sorgfältigen Bearbeitung des Ackers, der Menge des Düngers bei dem großen Viehstande und achtmonatlicher Stallfütterung, der großen Wärme und des ununterbrochenen Lichtes in den Sommertagen; wobei aber dünne gesäet werden muß, indem man darauf rechnen kann, daß jedes Korn aufgeht und Aehre trägt. Der Pfarrhof Luleå und der Amtshof des Obersten vom Westerbottnischen Regiment,

*) In Norrbotten hat der Roggen, freilich selten, das 90ste Korn gegeben.

Gran bei Piteå, haben jetzt die größte Aussaat in ganz Norrbotten. Roggen wird viel weniger gesäet als Gerste, weil ersterer leichter vom Froste Schaden leidet, auch schwerer abzusetzen
ist. Das Pfarrgebiet erstreckt sich eine volle (Schwedische) halbe
Meile um die Altstadt her; mehrere Kolonisten, denen der Pastor Freijahre ertheilt hat, oder die für immer dort unentgeldlich
wohnen, haben sich auf dem Pfarrboden angesiedelt, auch hat
Doctor Nordmark viele Urbarmachungen vorgenommen und
dadurch den Ertrag des Pfarrackers von 100 auf 150 Tonnen
und mehr jährlich gebracht; überhaupt ist Luleå die einträglichste
Pfarre des Stifts Hernösand und eine der einträglicheren in
ganz Schweden. Der Pfarrhof hat einen bedeutenden Viehstand, 40 Kühe ꝛc.; doch wird nichts zum Verkauf gewonnen;
der hier bereitete Kuhkäse kommt an Fettigkeit dem besten Schweizerkäse gleich.

Im Pastorat Luleå herrscht große Wohlhabenheit; Ackerbau,
Viehzucht, Fischerey, Theerbrennen und Bretterverkauf sind bedeutend. In früherer Zeit waren auch Råneå und Piteå Theile
des Pastorats Luleå. Seit diese zu besonderen Pastoraten ausgeschieden wurden, ist das Pastorat Luleå noch 12 bis 15 Meilen
lang, 6 Meilen breit (von N. nach S.) und hat ein Areal von
50 □M. Außer der Filialgemeinde, Stadt Luleå, im J. 1815
mit 919 Einwohnern, zählte im selbigen Jahre die Landgemeinde
7460 Seelen; im J. 1749 betrug die Volkszahl 3192, im J.
1780. 4799; sie hat sich also in 35 Jahren fast verdoppelt.
Luleå hat die größten Dörfer in Norbotten, z. B. Sunderbyn mit 70 Vollbauern. Den Viehstand des Pastorats rechnet
man zu 1500 Pferden, 180 Ochsen und 5700 Kühen. Der
Kornbau ist bedeutend, doch minder bedeutend wie im Pastorat
Piteå. Ueberhaupt ist die Kornproduction in Norbotten so gestiegen, daß man jetzt nur nach zwei auf einander folgenden Mißwachsjahren Zufuhr bedarf. Nichts desto weniger giebt es noch
immer Gelegenheit zu besserer Benutzung der cultivirten Aecker
und Wiesen und zu vortheilhaften Urbarmachungen; aber es fehlt
an Menschenhänden. Das Säen, welches im übrigen Norrland
Geschäft der Männer ist, wird in ganz Westerbotten von den

Weibern verrichtet. Man sáet gewöhnlich zu Ende des Mais oder zu Anfang des Junius und erndtet im August; doch giebt es Ausnahmen: 8 bis 12 Wochen verstreichen zwischen Saat und Erndte. Am 15. Mai fuhr man in diesem Jahre (1817) noch auf dem Eise, und am 24. Mai fing man an, zu sáen. Es ist ganz gewöhnlich, innerhalb 14 Tagen Schnee und Eis, Thauwetter, frisches Gras und grünes Korn zu sehen *). Die Heuerndte dauert von der Mitte des Julius bis in den August; die Máher haben auf den Wiesen viel von den Mücken zu leiden, indem der Schweiß den Theer, womit sie das Gesicht bestreichen, bald auflöset. Die Mücken sind die wahren Plagegeister des Nordens, in Lappland sucht man durch angezündete Kohlenfeuer sie aus den Schlafzimmern zu verscheuchen; in Westerbotten spannt man an kleinen Tonnenbándern befestigte grüne Florkappen über das Gesicht, ein Mittel, welches auch ich anwandte, an mir sich aber nicht bewährte.

Gegen Lappland hin hat das Pastorat Luleå viele Berge, Wälder finden sich in allen Theilen des Pastorats; doch haben sie abgenommen, besonders durch das in Westerbotten sehr übliche Abschälen der jungen schlanken Fichten, deren Rinde als Viehsfutter benutzt wird. Das Klima ist sehr gesund, und daher ein hohes Alter nicht selten. Erderschütterungen sind, wie überhaupt in Norrland, oft hörbar. Auf den Inseln an der Küste und weiterhin im Bottnischen Meerbusen sind Fischerlagen errichtet, wo im Sommer die Kirchspielsbewohner insbesondere Strömlings- und Robbenfang treiben; auf zwei dieser Inseln sind Kapellen erbauet worden. Der Lachsfang in Luleå-Elf ist nicht sehr bedeutend. Die Abnahme des Bottnischen Meeres an der Schwedischen Küste ist auch bei Luleå merkbar; doch war diese Wasserabnahme nicht Ursache der Verlegung der Stadt Luleå.

Zuweilen treten im August Nachtfröste ein, die den Jahreswuchs vernichten; doch folgen oft viele gute Jahre auf einander. In der Regel legt sich der Luleåstrom um die Mitte Octo-

---

*) Ich aß Spinat, der um Pfingsten (Ende Mai's) gesäet und seit Johannis eßbar war.

bers und geht zu Ende Mai's wieder auf. Der Luleå, nächst dem Ångerman der breiteste der Ströme Norrlands, hat, gleich den übrigen Strömen, drei Fluthen, die erste trifft gewöhnlich im Anfang des Junius ein. In der Mitte Novembers ist oft schon festes Eis und Schlittenbahn; fast acht Monate bleibt die Erde zugefroren.

Die Bewohner des Pastorats Luleå zeichnen sich durch schöne Körperbildung, freien, heitern Blick und Einfachheit des Lebens aus; der größere Theil des weiblichen Geschlechts kann schön genannt werden. Fleißig besucht man die Kirche, und allgemein hält man Erbauungsstunden, insbesondere an Sonntagen und an den Abenden der Wochentage.

Die lichte und freundliche steinerne Kirche Gamla Luleå, die größte in Westerbotten, 81 Ellen lang und 27 Ellen breit, ist für die Gemeinde nicht geräumig. Die Kirche hat eine Orgel, prächtige Meßgewänder, viele silberne Kelche, und eine, wie man behauptet, in Italien gearbeitete stark vergoldete Altartafel, ein wahres Meisterstück der Bildhauerkunst. Die Tafel stellt, kräftig und ausdrucksvoll die gesammte Lebensgeschichte des Heilandes dar. Die heiligen Gemälde auf den die Tafel bedeckenden Thüren sind nicht bedeutend, sie wurden in neuerer Zeit von einem Westerbottnischen Maler gefertiget. Von desto höherem Werth ist das Gemälde, dessen Alter unbekannt, unter der Altartafel: es stellt Christum mit den zwölf Jüngern dar. In den Gesichtern herrscht ungemein viel Würde und Ausdruck. Unfern des Altars zeigt man eine alte Bank, Mönchsbank (Munkebänk) genannt. Man hält sie für den Ehrensitz katholischer Domherren; Luleå soll nämlich Domkirche gewesen seyn. Schon frühe war Luleå wenigstens als ein großes und wohlhabendes Kirchspiel bekannt. Die Kirche ist ohne Thurm. Zwei große Glocken hängen in einem besondern hölzernen Glockenthurm, der eine höchst reizende Aussicht über die schöne Umgegend mit ihren Wiesen und Feldern und den anmuthigen, mit Dörfern und Landsitzen bedeckten Ufern des nur ¼ Meile entfernten Flusses Luleå, der hier an Breite einem See gleicht, gewährt. Zu jenen Landsitzen gehört der freundliche Wittwenhof in Bälinge, welchen Doctor Nordmark, nach Sitte vieler Norrländischer Pfarrherren, für seine Gattin am jenseitigen Ufer des Luleå erbauet hat.

Die äußerst zweckmäßig angelegten, mit reichlichem Kleider= vorrath versehenen Kirchstuben bilden zwei Hauptstraßen und eine große Zahl von Nebengassen. In den Wochentagen sind die Kirchstuben verschlossen, desto lebhafter ist es hier am Sonnabend Abend. Einzelne Dörfer und Höfe haben sehr weite Kirchwege, z. B. das Dorf Storsand an der Lappischen Gränze liegt 11 Meilen von der Kirche entfernt. Nur wenige, von Beamten, Handwerkern ꝛc., bleibend bewohnte Häuser findet man zwischen den Kirchstuben.

In einer der Kirchgassen liegt das Armenhaus mit zwei heizbaren Zimmern, eines der reinlichsten und freundlichsten Ar= menhäuser, die ich je sah: man glaubte in die Wohnung einer vornehmen und wohlhabenden Familie zu treten. Das Haus ist zur Wohnung von 15 Armen bestimmt, die schwach und krank oder doch ohne Anverwandte und Freunde sind, die sie bei sich aufnehmen können; das ist die Bestimmung aller Schwedischen Gemeinde=Armenhäuser. Nur wenige Arme fand ich im Hause, manche ziehen es vor, in den Dörfern zu wohnen, wo sie wohl= feiler leben. Das Armengeld beträgt 12 Bankschillinge monat= lich und 1½ Tonnen Gerste jährlich.

Für das Pastorat Luleå sind außer dem Pastor zwei Com= ministri angestellt, deren einer in der Stadt wohnt. Die Kü= sterstelle ist vorzüglich dotirt. Die Eltern unterrichten ihre Kin= der selbst; doch giebt es in den Dörfern wohnende, so wie am= bulatorische Schullehrer, aber keine allgemeine Kirchspielschule. Aus Luleå sind mehrere berühmte Männer hervorgegangen, un= ter andern die um die Schwedische Kirche hochverdiente Familie der Benzelier, deren Stammvater, Erzbischof Erich Benze= lius, 1632 zu Benzeby geboren wurde; sein Vater, Henrik Jacobsson, war Bauer und Tolfman (Beisitzer des Härads= ting).

Außer der großen Nordstraße von Stockholm nach Torneå, die das Kirchspiel von Süden nach Norden durchschneidet, findet

II.   M man Fahrwege nur nach der Stadt Luleå, nach einzelnen Küstendörfern und am Luleå 3 Meilen aufwärts bis Svartbjörnsby, die sämmtlich von der Altstadt auslaufen. Weiterhin findet man nur Boot-, Reit- und Fußwege; doch ließen sich die Fahrstraßen wahrscheinlich ohne große Schwierigkeit weiter ausdehnen. Aufwärts von Svartbjörnsby und gegen Lappland hin findet man die von Baron Hermelin angelegten Kolonistenhöfe, auch Dörfer und die Eisenhütte Svartlå nebst Hochofen Edefors, jene 6¼ Meile von der Altstadt entfernt, dieser 3¼ Meilen nördlicher am Luleå, etwa 2 Meilen von der Lappischen Gränze gelegen und noch nicht vollendet, beide Eigenthum des Brukspatron Fahlrot, waren bisher nicht im Gange. Ein zweites Eisenwerk, Sehlet, Hochofen und Ankerschmiede, liegt südlicher, 1 Meile vom Luleåstrom. Svartlå und Sehlet sind Anlagen des würdigen Hermelin, der, als seine Zugänge erschöpft waren und er nicht hinlänglich unterstützt wurde, sein Bemühen, wüste Gegenden anzubauen und ihren Wohlstand durch Bergbau und Hüttenwesen zu fördern, aufgeben mußte; worauf die schon gemachten Anlagen mehreren Privatpersonen durch Kauf zufielen. Mittlerweile genießt der Staat schon Einkünfte von Gegenden, die früher nur wilden Thieren zum Aufenthalt dienten, — während die Besitzer noch heute nur sparsame Früchte erndteten. Vermehrung der Freijahre für die Kolonisten und öffentliche Unterstützung der Hüttenbesitzer sind wünschenswerth. Auch die unerschöpflichen Eisengruben von Ruotivare in Jockmocks-Lappmark und ein großer Theil der Eisengruben von Gellivare, ehemals den Herrn Meldercreutz und Hermelin gehörig, befinden sich jetzt in Herrn Fahlrot's Besitz, der ohne Zweifel der reichste Erzeigner in Europa ist. Auch eine große Anzahl Nybyggen, die dem kleineren Theile nach zu den Meldercreutzischen Anlagen gehören, dem bei weitem größten Theile nach aber von Hermelin angelegt sind, hat Herr Fahlrot angekauft. Nach einer officiellen Angabe, die mir während meines Aufenthalts in Gamlastäden durch die Güte des Landshöfding, Baron Koskull, dem ich mich in vielfacher Hinsicht verpflichtet fühle, mitgetheilt wurde, betrug, im Julius 1817, im Län Norrbotten die Hufenzahl (Hemmantal) 560⅔⅔, die Zahl der steuerpflichtigen Höfe (hemmans-rökar, gårdar) 2812, der steuerfreien Nybyggen 533. Von den steuerpflichtigen Höfen lagen 2018 in dem Theile von Norbotten, wo die Schwedische Sprache, 625 in dem Theile des Län, wo die Finnische Sprache die herrschende ist, und 169 in den Lappmarken. Von den Kolonistenhöfen kamen 371 auf die Schwedischen, 135 auf die Finnischen Kirchspiele und 27 auf Lappland. In Lappland hatte Baron Hermelin 16⅔, in den Schwedischen Kirchspielen aber, nebst Meldercreuß und Bedoir, 43⅔⅔ hemman aufgenommen, in den Finnischen Kirchspielen keine. — Den Nybyggen ist, nach Umständen, eine geringere oder größere Zahl von Freijahren (15, 30 bis 50) bewilligt. Während dieser Freijahre stellen zuweilen Kronbeamte Besichtigung an, ob die Nybyggen gut angebauet werden, widrigenfalls sie Andern übertragen werden können. Hat der Kolonist sein Nybygge in guten Stand gesetzt, so fällt es ihm, kraft einer Verordnung vom Jahr 1817, nach Ablauf der Freijahre als Eigenthum zu, wovon er nur einen jährlichen Zins an die Krone erlegt, oder, wie man spricht, sein Hof wird Skattehemman, und zwar ohne Entrichtung des sonst üblichen geringen Kaufschillings. Bis zur genannten Verordnung von 1817 wurden solche Höfe Kronohemman (Kronhusen), gingen als solche nicht zu Erbe, und konnten in gewissen Fällen dem Nutznießer entzogen werden.

Auch einen Sonnabend und Sonntag brachte ich in Luleå zu. Viel Volks versammelte sich zur Kirche. Am Sonnabend Abend machte ich einen Spaziergang zwischen den Kirchstuben, wovon die meisten offen waren. Männer und Weiber wandelten in den Straßen, einige schon im Sonntagsschmuck, Mädchen und Jünglinge gingen, einfältig und schuldlos, Hand in Hand umher; unter den Mädchen bemerkte man ausgezeichnete Schönheiten, runde, liebliche Gesichter. In einer der Kirchstuben hatte sich eine Gesellschaft versammelt, wo Weiber und Männer, jede besonders, sich vergnügten, die Männer sich auch die Flasche gefallen ließen; doch kommt es selten zu Unordnungen.

Um 6¾ Uhr fuhr ich zur Stadt Luleå, die von der Altstadt 1 Meile entfernt liegt. Der Weg führt anfangs durch

M 2

Wald, dann neben Seen, Meerbusen und üppigen Wiesen, zu:
letzt zwischen einem Meerbusen und einer Reihe niedriger Felsen
in die offene Stadt, deren hoher Kirchthurm schon in der Ferne
sichtbar ist; fast die Hälfte des Weges ist Pfarrgebiet. Die
Stadt liegt gar anmuthig auf einer Halbinsel zwischen einem
Meerbusen und der Mündung des Luleåstromes; ihr Hafen ist
der beste aller Westerbottnischen Städte. Die Kaufleute treiben
in- und ausländischen Handel; doch die Hälfte der Einwohner
lebt vom Fischfange; auch Schiffe werden zum Verkauf gebauet,
wie selbst in mehreren Dorfschaften am Luleå-Elf. Die Stadt
ward von Gustav II. Adolph zuerst an der Stelle erbauet,
wo man jetzt noch die Landkirche findet, und 1621 mit Privile:
gien versehen. Die Birkarlar, welche bis dahin den Handel in
Bottnien getrieben hatten, wurden, wie der übrigen neuen Bott:
nischen Städte, so auch Luleå's erste Einwohner. Bald aber er:
kannte man, daß der Platz zur neuen Stadt nicht gut gewählt
sey; man verlegte sie daher 1649 südöstlich von der bisherigen
Stelle, eine halbe Meile weiter ans Meer; 1657 brannte die
Stadt völlig, 1762 dem größten Theile nach ab. Die Stadt
ist auf einer sich gegen das Meer senkenden Höhe erbauet, daher
die ungepflasterten breiten Straßen bald wieder trocken werden.
Der Markt, neben der Kirche, bildet ein großes schönes Viereck.
Alle Häuser sind von Holz; das größte gehört dem Kaufmann
Ruth; es liegt an der langen Drottninggata (Königinstraße)
und ward vom Dorfe Afva, 1 Meile vom Bruk Sehlet, am Lu:
leå, wo es der Baron Hermelin sich erbaut hatte, hieher ver:
setzt. Dergleichen Häusertransporte sind im nördlichen Schwe:
den nicht selten. Mehrere Häuser haben hübsche Gärten, der
schönste gehörte dem Provinzialarzte Lange, einem lieben, freund:
lichen, eben so dienstfertigen als uneigennützigen Manne, dessen
leider seitdem erfolgten Tod eine zahlreiche Familie betrauert.
Im Hafen lagen eben zwei Dreimaster. Der hauptsächlichste
Seehandel wird nach Stockholm und Finnland getrieben; in
Finnland tauscht man Korn gegen Strömling ein; aus Stock:
holm, wohin man jährlich mehrere Reisen unternimmt, hohlt man
allerlei Bedürfnißwaaren. Die Schifffahrt beginnt gewöhnlich

im Anfange des Junius. Die Seestadt Uleåborg in Österbotten liegt Luleå fast gerade gegenüber und ist nur 24 Meilen entfernt.

Wiewohl die meisten Kaufleute zu Markt nach Calix gereist und die größere Hälfte der Einwohner, der Fischerey halber, abwesend war, so war doch der Gottesdienst ziemlich zahlreich besucht, wenn gleich minder zahlreich, wie sonst. Ueberhaupt soll viel Einfachheit und Frömmigkeit und ein hoher Grad von Sittlichkeit unter den Einwohnern, und zumal unter den Kaufleuten, herrschen. Schlicht und einfach geht der wohlhabende Bürger und der reiche, weit ins Ausland handelnde Kaufmann gekleidet; und zuweilen verstreichen mehrere Jahre, ohne daß unter den etwa 30 jährlichen Geburten sich eine uneheliche findet. In wenigen Schwedischen Städten, vielleicht in keiner, dürfte so viel Einfachheit und Unverdorbenheit gefunden werden, wie in Luleå. Die Kirche ist von Stein, und bisher die einzige in Westerbotten, die einen steinernen Thurm hat; sie wurde in den Jahren 1764 bis 1790 gebauet, hat aber schon einen so bedeutenden Riß, daß sie den Einsturz droht. Aus der geräumigen Sacristey führt eine Treppe zu einem Saal, der für die Sitzungen des Kirchenraths bestimmt ist und aus dessen Fenstern man eine schöne Aussicht hat. Aus dem 73 Ellen hohen Thurm genießt man einer reizenden Aussicht auf die Umgebungen der Stadt und mehrere Meilen weit in die See hinein. Die Glocken hängen in einem besonderen Glockenstuhl. Der die Kirche umgebende Begräbnißplatz ist ohne Mauern. Nachmittagsgottesdienst wird in den Sommermonaten, wo die Bürger die Strandfischerey treiben, nicht gehalten; diese gehen mehrere Meilen weit zu den äußersten Inseln, wo sie in einer eigenen Kapelle ihren sonntäglichen Gottesdienst feiern. Nur einmal im Sommer kommt der Comminister aus der Stadt zu diesen mitten im Meere gelegenen Inseln, wo er denn in der Kapelle Gottesdienst hält und zugleich seinen Fischzehnten einsammelt.

Die Stadt hat eine öffentliche Schule (Pädagogium), an welcher zwei geringe besoldete Lehrer angestellt sind. Die Zahl der Schüler hatte im letzten Termine 49 betragen; früher war

ren aber auch schon 70 Schüler gewesen. Das hölzerne Schulhaus ist neu, aber der obere Stock noch nicht vollendet; im unteren Stock findet man zwei kleinere Zimmer für die Lehrer und
zwei größere für die beiden Klassen. Zuweilen sind die Zimmer
zu einem Picknickball, deren zwei jährlich Statt zu finden pflegen, benutzt worden. Nach dem schönen Gasthof Gddvvik, dessen
Entfernung von der Stadt auf dem Luleå nur eine halbe Meile
beträgt, pflegen Lustpartien angestellt zu werden, eben so nach
einer an der Küste gelegenen schönen Insel, wo zwei Bauern
recht patriarchalisch wohnen.

Nach geendigtem Gottesdienst fuhr ich mit dem Mag. Eu-
renius, der als Adjunct des Pastors gepredigt hatte, nach der
Altstadt zurück. Das Volk war schon in großen Schaaren um
die Kirche herum versammelt und zog nun als zum letzten Mal,
mit allen Glocken, geläutet wurde, langsam und feierlich in die
Kirche. Dießmal konnte die Kirche, in welcher etwa 3 bis 4000
Menschen Platz finden mögen, die Menge fassen; oft, zumal an
Festtagen, müssen, aus Mangel an Raum, viele auf dem Kirchhofe zurückbleiben. Da der Adjunct auch in der Altstadt predigen sollte, so hatte der Pastor nur Beichte gehalten, und der
eigentliche Gottesdienst begann erst jetzt, nachdem zuvor eine
Leiche auf dem Kirchhofe bestattet worden war. Im Allgemeinen
herrschte Andacht und Stille, besonders feierlich und rührend
war die Austheilung des heiligen Abendmahls, welches hier sonntäglich gehalten wird; großen Eindruck machte das Agnus Dei.
Der Communicanten waren heute 340; fast nie sind ihrer unter
50, gewöhnlich zwischen 100 und 200; die höchste Zahl ist 400;
mehrere communiciren zwar nur ein Mal, aber weit mehrere
zwei Mal, ja 3, 4 und 5 Mal jährlich. Keinen der Abend-
mahlsgäste sah ich, der nicht schwarz oder weiß gekleidet war,
außer zwei Lappinnen (überhaupt war die Kleidung einfach
und selbstgefertiget, nur wenige trugen schwarz seidene und kattunene Kleider). Nach der heiligen Spende kehrte jeder in seinen Stuhl zurück und sank dort betend auf die Knie. Ein
schöngebildetes Mädchen betete so fast eine Viertelstunde lang,
und Thränen standen ihr im Auge; eine schöne Körperbildung

erscheint doch nie schöner, als wenn der Sinn dem Ernsten und Heiligen zugewandt ist. — Nach Beendigung des Gottesdienstes überstand ein gefallenes Mädchen den ganzen Grad der Kirchenbuße in der Sacristey in Gegenwart des Küsters und der Kirchenvorsteher als Zeugen, wobei der Geistliche ganz nach Vorschrift der Liturgie verfuhr. Erst nachdem eine uneheliche Mutter auf diese Weise die Absolution erhalten, darf sie an der Feier des heiligen Abendmahls Theil nehmen; der höhere Grad der Kirchenbuße wird öffentlich vor der Gemeinde vollzogen.

Sämmtliche Geistliche waren während des Gottesdienstes in der Kirche zugegen. Der Pastor war in die feierliche Amtstracht, das bereits erwähnte Meßgewand, gekleidet. Alles war würdig und feierlich, nur der Küster in seinem hellblaugestreiften Ueberrock und langen weiten Beinkleidern machte einen widrigen Eindruck; nur an Festtagen geht der Küster schwarz gekleidet. Schade, daß in Schweden, wo der Gottesdienst mit so vieler Würde und auf eine so erhebende Weise, wie kaum sonst wo gefeiert wird, den Küstern keine eigene kirchliche Tracht vorgeschrieben ist. Der schlechte Gesang des Küsters stimmte ganz mit seinem Aeußern überein, doch die Gemeinde sang sanft und langsam; auch das Orgelspiel war gut. Beim Ausgange aus der Kirche, ward, des Begräbnisses halber, geläutet.

Am Nachmittage machten wir eine Lustfahrt zum Wittwenhof in Bälinge. Mehrere Freunde nahmen Theil. Bei günstigem Winde legten unsere Böte bald die kleine halbe Meile über den Luleå, der hier, wiewohl noch ¾ Meile von der Mündung entfernt, am breitesten ist, einer bewaldeten Insel, in deren Nähe viel Lachs gefangen wird, vorüber, zurück. Die Hitze war drükkend, nur ein aufgespannter großer Schirm sicherte einigermaßen. Der Sonnenstich ist unter dieser Polhöhe oft so heftig, daß es fast unmöglich ist, ohne Schirm auszugehen; noch in Stockholm soll man um diese Zeit auch Männer mit Sonnenschirmen gehen sehen. — In Bälinge verflossen uns einige angenehme Stunden: wir spazierten zu den umliegenden schönen Wiesen (die Aecker sind, des vielen Sandes wegen, weniger fruchtbar), pflegen trauliche Gespräche und freueten uns der lieblichen weiten Aussichten aus dem oberen Stockwerk auf den Luleå und seine Ufer, aufwärts bis Sunderbyn, und abwärts bis zur Stadt Luleå. Nach dem Abendessen traten wir um 10 Uhr die Heimreise an, auch die Frau Oberstin Klingstedt, die von Sehlet gekommen war, begleitete uns zurück. Aber der Wind war uns günstig geworden, und eines unserer Boote überdieß ein schlechter Segler. Nur dem Boot, welches die Bagage führte, gelang es, das Ufer der Altstadt zu erreichen; unser zweites Boot mußte, nach mehrstündigem Kreuzen, bei Gäddvik landen, von wo aus man zu Wagen und zu Fuß heimkehrte. Von meiner bei Torneå erhaltenen Verletzung noch nicht völlig genesen, mochte ich es nicht wagen, den hölzernen Bänken einer Bauernkarre meine milden Glieder anzuvertrauen; ich übernachtete daher in Gäddvik, wohin ich meinen Wagen nachbestellte. Der Gasthof Gäddvik hat zwei Säle und mehrere Gastzimmer. Das Zimmer, in welchem ich schlief, schmückte sogar ein gemalter Fußboden; alles war gut und billig, und die Menschen milde und freundlich, dienstfertig und uneigennützig: ein Knecht, der am Morgen mein Sielengeschirr ausbesserte, war sehr verwundert, als ich mich durch eine kleine Gabe dankbar bezeigte, darauf hatte er nicht gerechnet, „dessen bedürfe es nicht.“ Im Wagen, durch denselben Schirm, der mich am Tage vorher gegen die Sonne geschützt hatte, gesichert, und durch die Sorge meiner Wirthe mit einem Pferde, das den Schirm ertragen konnte, versehen, kehrte ich am nächsten Morgen glücklich zum Pfarrhof zurück; die übrige Gesellschaft war in der Nacht angelangt, zum Theil jämmerlich auf einer Bauerkarre zerstoßen. So endete die frohe, wenn gleich abentheuerliche Fahrt, die für mich noch dadurch wichtig wurde, daß ich in Bälinge eine tüchtige Strohflechterin fand, die mir einen weißen Strohhut anmaß, der mir auf der weitern Reise beim Sonnenbrande großen Nutzen gewährte.

In Bälinge sah ich die fein und dicht aus Baumwurzeln geflochtenen Brotkörbe, die die Lappen feil bieten. Viele der im Sommer in Westerbotten umherziehenden Lappen betteln, die übrigen weiden das Vieh der Bauern; sie alle sind arm und ohne Heerden; die wohlhabenderen bleiben daheim. Heute, am Sonntag, sah ich viele Bettellappen im Pfarrhof, wo sie gespeiset wurden; sie waren kleiner Statur, aus Luleå-Lappmark gebürtig. In Bålinge suchte man in einem der Bauerhöfe die Mücken, nach Lappenweise, durch Feuer zu vertreiben.

Bevor ich erzähle, wie ich von Luleå aus meine Reise fortsetzte, will ich noch einige Nachrichten über das Län Norrbotten, dessen Verwaltungsbehörde bisher zu Gamla Luleå ihren Sitz hatte, mittheilen.

Schon oben ist bemerkt worden, daß in den letztern Jahren der Ackerbau sehr gestiegen sey. Wirklich bildet er jetzt neben der Viehzucht (zumal in den obern Kirchspielen) und dem Lachsfange den ansehnlichsten Nahrungszweig des Län; dann folgen, in Allgemeinheit und Ergiebigkeit, Theerbrennerey und Strömlingsfang *); Eisenhämmer sind vorhanden; auch die Wälder liefern einen ansehnlichen Ertrag, besonders seitdem, mittelst jährlicher Zuschüsse, die der Staat giebt, die Theilung der Gemeinwälder unter die Participienten (skogsafvittring) immer weiter fortschreitet. Die Auseinandersetzung der entfernten Gemeinweiden (utmark) wäre noch zu wünschen. Der Kartoffelbau hat in Norrbotten unglaubliche Fortschritte gemacht: die Kartoffel giebt 10mal die Aussaat wieder. Unter diesen Umständen ist das Verhältniß der Aus- und der Einfuhr für Norrbotten sehr günstig: nach den Zollregistern des Jahres 1816 betrug die Ausfuhr 324,000 Rthlr. Riksgälds.; dagegen die Einfuhr kaum 40,000 Rthlr. Rgd., und doch wird vieles ausgeführt, was bei den Zöllen nicht angegeben wird, insbesondere nach Uleåborg und Wasa

*) Man hat in Norrbotten mehrere Arten von Strömling: der im Herbst gefangene ist der beste und fetteste, aber nicht der größte. Man salzt den Strömling ein, speiset ihn frisch oder bereitet ihn zu sauerm Strömling, d. h. setzt ihn, wenig gesalzen, in offenen Tonnen, der freien Luft aus, bis er durch dieselbe gesäuert ist. Eine treffliche Naturgeschichte der verschiedenen Arten des Strömlings hat Gisler geliefert in den Handlingar der Kongl Wetenskaps-Akad. Bd. 9. für 1748. S. 107—140.

in Finnland; bei den ausgedehnten Küsten ist eine strenge Bewachung unmöglich. Die Einfuhr besteht hauptsächlich in Kaffee und Zucker; in der Ausfuhr bilden die Waldprodukte den Hauptartikel, dann folgen die Produkte der Viehzucht und der Fischerey.

Eine Landhaushaltungs-Gesellschaft (hushålls-sällskap) ward 1816 für Norrbottens Län errichtet. Mit Anstellung genauer Beobachtungen über Witterung, Saat- und Erndtezeit ꝛc. sind drei Männer in Luleå, Öfver-Torneå und Qvickjock (Luleå-Lappmark) beauftragt. Die Salpeterbereitung ist, der starken Viehzucht wegen, ansehnlich; das Län hat, wie die übrigen Läne, einen eigenen Salpetersiederey-Director.

Bergbau ward schon früherhin in den Norrbottnischen Lappmarken getrieben. Der Biedermann Hermelin erwarb auch in dieser Hinsicht sich um das Land große Verdienste. Durch seine Versuche veranlaßt, durchreisete, wie oben erwähnt, nachdem bereits im Winter 1816 und 17 der Landshöfding Baron Koskull die Lappischen Bergwerke besucht hatte, eine vom König angeordnete Commission im Jahr 1817 den größten Theil der Schwedischen Lappmarken, um über die Möglichkeit der Schiff- oder Floßbarmachung der ins Bottnische Meer fallenden Lappischen Ströme und somit die Nützlichkeit der Einrichtung eines regelmäßigen Bergbaues in Norrbottens Län Untersuchungen anzustellen. Das Resultat fiel günstig aus, und es ist Hoffnung vorhanden, daß auf diese Weise die reichen Erzgänge Lapplands künftig mehr benutzt werden, als es bisher, des kostbaren Landtransportes wegen, geschah. Mehrere der Hüttenwerke Norrbottens mußten ruhen, weil es an Gelegenheit, das Erz wohlfeil zu erhalten, gebrach. Das eigentliche Norrbotten, in sofern es nicht Lappmark ist, hat keine oder wenigstens keine bedeutende Erzlager.

Außer den Predigerhäusern, den Civil- und Militairbeamten, so wie den Officiers des Westerbottnischen Regiments giebt es in Norbotten auf dem Lande keine oder sehr wenige Honoratioren. Auch diese leben, wie das Volk, schlicht und einfach mit einander; nur ihre Töchter senden sie zuweilen auf kurze Zeit in Pension nach Stockholm; doch habe ich nicht bemerkt, daß diese dadurch der väterlichen Sitte abhold werden, wenn gleich dieſer Gebrauch im Ganzen nicht empfehlenswerth ſeyn dürfte. Auf Verwandtſchaft hält man viel, wie ſolches überhaupt vorzugsweiſe in Norrland geſchieht: jüngere nennen ihres Gleichen Vetter und Couſine, die ältern Onkel und Tante, ohne daß gerade wirklich dieſe Verwandtſchaft Statt findet; nur Verhältniſſe der Freundſchaft und Achtung werden dadurch angedeutet. Die Anrede Bror (Bruder) iſt hier, wie in ganz Schweden, ſehr üblich, zumal als Höflichkeitsbezeugung der Höhern und Aelteren gegen Geringere und Jüngere. Bei Mahlen ſtellt man zwei große ſilberne Becher mit Bier auf den Tiſch zum gemeinſchaftlichen Gebrauch, außer der Mahlzeit dient dazu ein großer hölzerner angemalter Krug; das iſt allgemeine Landesſitte. Uebrigens ſind die Sitten und Gebräuche der gebildeten Klaſſe ſich in ganz Schweden ziemlich gleich, manches Provinzielle ausgenommen. Nach Tiſche verneigt man ſich gegen Hausfrau und Töchter, und küßt ihnen dann die Hände, auch wohl fremden Damen.

Einzelne Bauern in Luleå und noch mehr in Skelleftå legen ſich jetzt nicht gar ſelten aus Eitelkeit Zunamen bei; doch verſchwinden dieſe Zunamen gewöhnlich nach einiger Zeit wieder aus der Familie.

——————

Am 9. Jul. Von Luleå nach Sädbvik ½ M.; von S. nach Eränäs 1½ M.; von E. nach Rosvik 1½ M.; von R. nach Portnäs 1⁷⁄₁₆ M.; von P. nach Dijebyn 1⁷⁄₁₆ M.; von D. nach Piteholm 1 M. — Zuſammen 6½½ M.

Mein Weg war heute und an den folgenden Tagen bis Umeå ganz der bei der Aufreiſe, denn, einige wenige Seitenwege abgerechnet, giebt es in ganz Weſter- und Norrbotten nur die Eine große Straße längs der Küſte von Süden nach Norden, und von Hvited (im Paſtorat Räneå) von Weſten nach Oſten. Auch auf der Rückreiſe bemerkte ich überall die größte Dienſtfertigkeit und Uneigennützigkeit der Weſterbottnier; man läuft, die Schlagbäume zu öffnen und auf alle Art und Weiſe

dem Fremden behülflich zu seyn, ohne an Belohnung zu denken, nirgends ist mir in Westerbotten von Skjutsbauern Trinkgeld abgefordert worden, und für jede kleine Gabe über das ge-
setzmäßige Stationsgeld war man sehr dankbar; so war es früherhin in ganz Schweden, ist es aber jetzt nicht mehr überall. In den Dörfern um Luleå herum spricht man sehr breit
und unverständlich.

In Gåddvik gab man mir dasselbe Pferd, das ich das
letzte Mal gewünscht hatte, weil es den Schirm ertragen konnte.
Jetzt hatte ich diesen Wunsch nicht geäußert, aber stillschwei-
gend suchten die guten Leute dem Wunsche zuvorzukommen.
So sind die Menschen in Norrland.

Von Gåddvik zog ich mit einem Lappen über den Luleå,
welcher hier 950 Ellen breit ist. Der Lappe war ein nöteborn,
Heerdekind, wie man hier spricht, d. h. ein Weidelappe, der
im Sommer die Rindvieh (nöt)-Heerde der Gegend hütet. Alles war Leben und Heiterkeit an dem armen Manne, der des
Schwedischen unkundig war. Er bettelte; da aber die Lappen
die erbettelten Geschenke häufig bald wieder für Branntewein
verwenden, so sandte ich eine kleine Gabe dem Hausherrn, damit dieser im Winter, wo die Weidelappen entlassen werden,
sie ihm zustelle; das konnte der Lappe schwerlich ahnden, denn
noch sprang er, als wir gelandet waren, am jenseitigen Ufer
den Schlagbaum zu öffnen und sagte ein freundliches Lebewohl.

Vom Ufer des Luleå bis Ersnäs hat man anfangs viel
Wald; erst das letzte Drittheil des Weges wird freundlicher.
Ersnäs ist der letzte Gästgifvaregård im Pastorat Luleå, Rosvik
der erste im Pastorat Piteå. In Rosvik ließ ich mir Ziegen-
milch reichen; man wollte keine Bezahlung haben und nur mit
Mühe konnte ich eine Kleinigkeit aufdrängen. Freilich sind die
Bottnischen Gästgifvare wohlhabend und der Verdienst durch Rei-
sende ist Nebensache.

Zwischen Rosvik und Portsnäs ist meist Wald, in den
sich beide Dörfer getheilt haben; ein Stein bezeichnet die Gränze.
Man fährt wohl ¼ Meile zwischen den zerstreuten Wohnungen
von Portsnäs, die von Aeckern, Wiesen und Theeröfen umge-

ben find, bis man den Gåſtgifvaregård erreicht. Mein Skjutsbonde von Rosvik beſtätigte durch ſeine Perſon, was mir von
der Schönheit der Jünglinge Piteås geſagt worden war, die daher bei den ſchönen Luleå-Mådchen mehr Beifall finden, als
die Jünglinge des eigenen Kirchſpiels. Dieſer und mein Skjutsbonde von Pertsnås nach Oijebyn waren die erſten, welche nicht abſtiegen, wenn es bergauf ging. Unter den Bauern
ſah ich mehrere mit gelben, blauen und mehrfarbigen Scherpen,
eine Tracht, die keinesweges den Finnen eigenthümlich iſt.

Um Mittag war ich in Oijebyn. In der Altſtadt Piteå
verweilte ich einige Stunden, ſah Kirche und andere Merkwürdigkeiten, und fuhr dann zur Neuſtadt, wo ich Frau Burman beſuchte und bei Rector Gadd zu Abend ſpeiſete, da die
guten Leute mich durchaus nicht ohne Mahl weglaſſen wollten.
Um 11½ Uhr reiſete ich ab und nahm das Nachtquartier in
Piteholm.

In den heute durchreiſeten Gegenden ſind die oben erwähnten Leſer ſehr häufig. Sie haben aber in manchen Dorfſchaften ſo wenig Sectirerisches, daß Leſer und Nichtleſer ſich am
Sonntage zu dem nämlichen Dorfgottesdienſte vereinigen. An
einigen Orten verſammelten ſich früherhin die Leſer auch an Wochentagen, welches aber jetzt aufgehört hat; an mehrern Orten
wird der Sonnabend Abend von 3 oder 4 Uhr an von Leſern
und Nichtleſern durch gemeinſchaftliche Erbauungsſtunden gefeiert;
Hausgottesdienſt im Kreiſe der einzelnen Familien am Sonnabend iſt in vielen Schwediſchen Landſchaften ſehr üblich.

———

Am 10. Juli. Von Piteholm nach Jäfre 1¼ M.; von J.
   nach Kinbäck 1 7/16 M.; von K. nach Åby ¾ M.; von Å.
   nach Byſke 1 7/16 M.; von B. nach Storkåges 1¼ M.;
   von St. nach Stellefteå 1½ M. — Zuſ. 7 11/16 M.

Ein dichter Wald läuft bis an das Ufer des Piteå-Stroms,
der um die Inſel Piteholm ſich ins Bottniſche Meer ergießt.
Im Walde ſieht man viel Rennthiermoos. Abwärts im Walde
haben die Bewohner von Piteholm ihre Fåbodar (Sennhütten);

ihre Pferde und Ochsen haben sie auf einer der vorliegenden Inseln, bei denen zum Theil ein sehr einträglicher Lachsfang ist; ihre Schaafe auf Södra Haraholmen. Andere Inseln sind Eigenthum der Stadt und werden nebst der von den Pitcholmern gepachteten Insel Bondön, von den Bürgern für sämmtliches Vieh benutzt, das also mitten im Meere seine Weide hat. Der Piteå ist bei der Fährstelle 604 Fuß breit. Bis zur Altstadt ist er schiffbar, an den seichtesten Stellen 7 Fuß tief. Das Fährhaus liegt am jenseitigen Ufer, in Högsböle.

Jäfre mit mehreren Sägemühlen, in einem weiten und stark bewohnten Thale am Meer, ist der letzte Gästgifvaregård im Pastorat Piteå. Zwischen Jäfre und Kinbäck beginnt das Pastorat Skellesteå und mit demselben das Län Westerbotten. Erst nachdem man abermals 5 Meilen gereiset ist, erreicht man die Kirche Skellesteå, so daß die Kirchen Piteå und Skellesteå eine volle Tagesreise (8¼ M.) von einander entfernt sind.

Eine Tochter des Gästgifvare in Kinbäck hatte mich schon bei der Aufreise gefahren; die älteste ihrer Schwestern, die 17-jährige Saara, fuhr mich dießmal. Der Gästgifvare in Kinbäck hat nämlich den ganzen Skjuts für die Bauern übernommen und läßt ihn durch die vier ältern seiner 7 Töchter verwalten. Die Mädchen fahren schnell und gut, wiewohl das 4te erst 9 Jahr alt ist, und bestätigen also aufs neue, was ich schon öfter über die Geschicklichkeit der weiblichen Skjutsbönder in Norrland erwähnte. Das Dorf Kinbäck besteht nur aus drei Bauerhöfen. Am Sonntag versammeln sich die Bewohner in dem Gästgifvaregård oder in einem der beiden andern Höfe zum Postillenlesen, zu Gesang und Gebet. So sind sie in Liebe und Frömmigkeit vereiniget und selbst der Gasthof dient nicht zur Entheiligung, sondern zur Heiligung des Feiertages. Das Vorlesen verrichtet bald der Gästgifvare, bald seine Frau, bald ein Anderer. In Jäfre hält man am Sonntage keinen gemeinschaftlichen Dorfgottesdienst, sondern wer nicht zur Kirche geht, lieset zu Hause in der Stille für sich.

Zwischen Åby und Byske fährt man dem Dorfe Jomå vorüber, welches an einem Bache im Walde eine gar freundliche

Lage hat; die 6 Bauern des Dorfes gehören alle zu den Lå= såre; ihren Dorfgottesdienst halten sie einmal am Sonnabend und zweimal am Sonntage.

Im Walde hinter Byske kommt man neben mehrern Senn= hütten hin, in denen die Bauern von Ostwick mit dem größe= ren Theile ihrer Haushaltung wohnen; in eine dieser Hütten ging ich ein: die Besitzer hatten nur 3 Kühe, das Wohnzimmer war, nach Norrländischer Weise, auch Küche, daneben ein Milch= teller, weiterhin ein Stall, alles klein und ärmlich. Im Walde sah ich viel abgeschälte Bäume, einige waren unten, andere von unten bis oben, der Rinde beraubt; die Rinde wird als Futter für die Schaafe gebraucht, und der abgeschälte Baum giebt nach drei Jahren völlig ausgetrocknetes Brennholz, was für die Theeröfen wichtig ist. — Vor Storkågeå fährt man auf Berghöhen hin, von welchen man in das schöne Thal hinab= schauet; blauende Berge und das Meer bilden den Hintergrund. Der Gästgifvaregärd hat freundliche Gastzimmer.

Vor Skellefteå, wo man aus dem Wald herabkommt, übersieht man das reizende, sich von hier aus am vortheilhafte= sten zeigende Thal, in welchem der Skellefteå fließt. Noch zu guter Zeit war ich in Skellefteå, wo ich vom Dr. Ström herz= lich empfangen wurde.

Am nächsten Mittage machte ich einen Spaziergang nach der Kirchstadt; es war Freitag und daher alles öde und stille. Nur die Kaufbuden waren geöffnet, in welchen die Kaufleute von Pi= teå allerlei Waaren für die Einwohner des Pastorats zu gleichen Preisen, wie in der Stadt, feil halten; die Verkäuferin er= hält von jedem gelöseten Thaler 5 Schill. In einer der Buden gab es auch Riechfläschchen, deren schon nicht wenige Bäuerin= nen von Skellefteå sich bedienen sollen, wahrscheinlich auf Veranlassung der Kaufleute, denn diese Sitte habe ich sonst in Norrland nicht gefunden.

In dem großen Pastorat Skellefteå bilden Viehzucht, Acker= bau, Theerbrennerey und Fischfang die Hauptnahrungszweige. Außer dem Skellefteå wird das Pastorat von 4 nicht unbedeu= tenden Flüssen Bureå, Kågeå, Byskeå und Åbyå durchströmt, über welche jetzt sämmtlich Brücken führen; überall schneiden Meerbusen ein, die mehrere gute Häfen bilden. Auf den vorliegenden Inseln wird Strömlingsfischerei getrieben; auch sind dort ein Paar Kapellen errichtet, in welchen im Sommer zuweilen geprediget wird.

Bisher gab es nur immer eine große Straße; von Skellefteå führen zwei Fahrwege nach Süden; der eine, der gewöhnlichere, nähere und minder bergige, an der Meereskäste, über Löfänger; der andere landeinwärts über Burträsk; ich wählte ersteren. Letzterer wurde im Jahre 1780; angelegt; auch giebt es nun Fahrwege von der Kirche Burträsk nach den Kirchen Löfänger und Nysätra. Das Pastorat Burträsk gränzt an die genannten Kirchsprengel im Osten und Norden; im Süden an Degerfors, im Westen an Lycksele-Lappmark; erst im 17ten Jahrhundert wurde es als eigenes Pastorat eingerichtet, und aus Theilen von Skellefteå, Löfänger, Bygdeå und Umeå gebildet. Die Ausdehnung des Pastorats beträgt von N. nach S. 3, von O. nach W. 7¼ Meilen; die Zahl der Einwohner beläuft sich auf 2500. Die Entlegenheit von der großen Straße mag dazu beigetragen haben, daß im Kirchspiel noch immer viel Einfachheit und ein hoher Grad von Unverdorbenheit herrschen; unter den 70 bis 80 jährlichen Geburten befinden sich oft nur 2, höchstens 4 bis 5 uneheliche. Viehzucht, Ackerbau und Theerbrennerey, auch Fischfang in den vielen Seen, sind die Hauptnahrungszweige.

———————

Am 11. Jul. Von Skellefteå nach Innervik 1 M.; von J. nach Bureå 1¼ M. Zus. 2¼ M.

Um 4¼ Uhr fuhr ich ab. Jenseits der langen Brücke, die über den Skellefteå führt, kommt man dem kleinen Gästgifvaregård von Sunnanå vorüber. Dichter Regen verdunkelte die schöne Gegend zwischen Sunnanå und Innervik und das Thal von Innervik. In Bureå übernachtete ich. Im letzten Kriege hatte das Dorf viel gelitten, die Russen hatten auf ihrem Rückzuge geplündert; bloß der Verlust im Gästgifvaregård betrug, selbst nach der niedrigen Taxe, 1600 Bankthaler; Ersatz wurde gar nicht. Der herbeikommende russische General Eriksson, der den Jammer der Einwohner sah, die außer dem, was die Skjutsbauern von ihrem Vorrath gaben, von aller Speise entblößt waren, theilte mit den Hungernden sein Mittagsmahl.

Am 12. Jul. Von Bureå nach Daglösten 1$\frac{1}{4}$ M.; von D. nach Löfånger's Kirche 1$\frac{1}{2}$ M.; von Löfånger nach Grimsmark 1$\frac{1}{2}$ M.; von G. nach Onnis $\frac{3}{4}$ M.; — Zus. 5$\frac{1}{4}$ M.

Schon um 6$\frac{1}{4}$ Uhr fuhr ich heute aus. Im Walde lagen eine Menge kleiner und großer umgehauener Bäume, die der Fäulniß überlassen werden, so wenig Werth hat hier das Holz. Bei Selet verließ ich die große Straße und fuhr ein Paar Hügel hinab und hinan zum hochgelegenen neuerbauten Pfarrhofe, der an Größe und Schönheit dem von Skellefteå wenig nachsteht; rings herum sind die üppigsten Wiesen. Eben so schön ist die Lage der eine kleine Strecke entfernten steinernen Kirche; den Kirchhof selbst bedeckt hohes Gras; die schöne Umgebung bilden Felsen und Wiesen, und ein Wasserzug, der zwischen romantischen Ufern sich unweit der Kirche ins Meer ergießt. Die Kirche ist klein, aber freundlich. Als der Pastor eintrat, verrichtete er zuerst ein stilles Gebet; diese Sitte, nichts weniger als bloße Gewohnheit, trifft man ziemlich allgemein in Norrland. In der Kirche findet man noch ein altes Heiligenbild, das einst bei Wedbomark im Walde stand; da verrichteten diejenigen, die aus den entfernten Höfen nicht zur Kirche kommen konnten, ihre Andacht. Noch jetzt kennt das Volk dieses Bild unter dem Namen des Gottes von Wedbomark. Noch andere Bilder aus der katholischen Zeit werden in der Kirche aufbewahrt, z. B. das Bild der heiligen Anna, mit der Jungfrau Maria auf den Knien. Die Kirche, deren Erbauung man ins 15te Jahrhundert setzt (freilich ist sie seitdem erneuert und vergrößert worden), soll der heiligen Anna gewidmet gewesen seyn. Eine Orgel ist vorhanden. Die Kirche, neben welcher ein niedriger Glockenstuhl steht,

II.   N

ist ohne Thurm. Seitwärts liegt die Kirchstadt; hier trifft man kleine Kirchenbuden, wo zuweilen auch Hochzeiten gehalten werden, beträchtliche Kaufhäuser, die nun wegfallen, das Armenhaus und die Gemeindestube.

Das Pastorat Löfänger (Laubwiek, von angur, Goth. Invick) hat nur 2½ Meilen in der Länge und 3 Meilen in der Breite; die Seelenzahl betrug im J. 1815. 2182. Die Zahl der Gebornen steigt jährlich zu 80, unter welchen sich oft nur 1 oder 2 uneheliche befinden. Viehzucht ist Hauptnahrung, auch Strömling wird gefangen; der Ackerbau ist in Löfänger und in der benachbarten, zum Pastorat Bygdeä gehörigen, Gemeinde Nyfätra sehr unsicher, weil, der Localität halber, plötzliche und frühe Nachtfröste hier häufiger sind, als in den südlichern und nördlichern Kirchspielen; viel Korn muß zugekauft werden. Größere Flüsse giebt es in Löfänger nicht, wohl aber Bäche und Seen in Menge; die Küste hat gute Häfen. Die Einwohner zeichnen sich durch einen hohen Grad von Einfalt und Sittlichkeit aus. Im Winter vergnügen sie sich mit kleinen Mahlen, aber mit Fastnacht ist alles zu Ende. Abendmahl wird alle 4 Wochen gehalten; die geringste Zahl der Communikanten ist 80, die größte 400; man communicirt gewöhnlich 2 oder 3 mal jährlich. Eine feste Kirchspielschule ist nicht vorhanden; aber die Jugend wird von Eltern und Schullehrern gut unterwiesen. Häusliche Betstunden, zumal am Sonntag und am Sonnabend Abend, sind sehr allgemein. Der Winter ist auch hier noch so hart, daß man die Leichen im Leichenhause beisetzen muß und erst im Mai begraben kann; in andern Gemeinden werden im Herbst Wintergräber geöffnet.

Nachdem ich einige Stunden bei dem braven Pastor Unaeus verweilt, setzte ich um 3 Uhr die Reise fort. Der Weg nach Grimsmark ist sehr schön, liebliche Thäler und Anhöhen wechseln. ¼ Meile hinter Grimsmark fuhr ich in das Dorf Önnis, welches an der Straße liegt, wo ich den Magister Rosenius besuchte. Meine Absicht war, im nahen Gästgifwaregård Nyby zu übernachten, da dieser unweit der Kirche Nyfätra liegt, wo ich am nächsten Tage dem Gottesdienst beizuwohnen gedachte. Aber Mag. Rosenius wollte es nicht zulassen, und ich mußte in Önnis mein Nachtquartier nehmen.

Am Sonntag Vormittag wohnte ich dem Gottesdienste in Nysätra bei. Man fährt längs des Flusses Nyby, der auf sefsigem Grunde zwischen freundlichen Wiesenufern fließt; die Kirche ist ½ Meile von Önnis entfernt. Als ich anlangte, hatte der Gottesdienst noch nicht begonnen; ich trat in eine der Kirchstuben, wo die Zahl der Versammelten sich bald mehrte; einige derselben gehörten zu den Lesern, die sich hier nur durch eine besonders herzliche Frömmigkeit in Gesinnung und Handlungsweise auszeichnen, und von denen der Prediger sagte: „sie seyen sanft und schuldlos wie die Lämmer." Ich ließ mich mit ihnen in allerlei Gespräche ein; bald bat man mich, zu ihnen ein Wort der Erbauung zu reden; aber ich fühlte mich zu schwach, und schlug einen gemeinschaftlichen Gesang vor, den man selber wählen möge; man wählte aus dem kirchlichen Gesangbuch ein herrliches Morgenlied, welches nun mit innigem Gefühl gesungen wurde. Während des Gesanges kamen immer mehrere hinzu; aber jeder sang sogleich mit. Der sanfte, andächtige Gesang bewegte mich tief. Das war eine rechte Vorbereitung auf den Gottesdienst. So bereitet man sich oft durch gemeinschaftliche Andacht vor, wenn man frühe genug in den Kirchstuben anlangt, denn die meisten Kirchgänger kommen erst am Sonntag Morgen. Nur zur Zeit der hohen Feste und der Fastenpredigten, die am Sonnabend gehalten werden, kommt man am Vortage und bleibt mehrere Tage, wo dann durch die Andachtsübungen die Kirchstuben zu Gotteshäusern werden. Tägliche Morgen- und Abendgebete in den einzelnen Familien sind, zumal im Winter, ziemlich allgemein; einzelne, die sie in ihrem Hause eingeführt haben, halten sie nicht jeden Abend, damit sie nicht zur Gewohnheit werden; an solchen Abenden, wo sie ausfallen, betet dann jeder in der Stille. Am Sonnabend hatte ich Gelegenheit, einem dieser Abendgebete, die ein Hausvater im Kreise der Seinigen hielt, beizuwohnen; man sang, dann knieten Alle, der Hausvater betete, und schloß mit dem Vater-Unser und dem Segen, worauf, nach einem kurzen stillen Gebete, mit dem Gesange ei

N 2

nes Liebes die Abendandacht endete; das Ganze dauerte kaum eine Viertelstunde.

Während des Gottesdienstes herrschte tiefe Andacht; sanft und innig war der Gesang; die Gebete des Predigers, auch einige der von ihm genannten Bibelsprüche, wurden leise nachgesprochen; dem Altardienst folgte eine wahrhaft erbauende Predigt über den Unterschied zwischen einem lebendigen und einem todten Glauben. Das heilige Abendmahl ward dießmal nicht gefeiert. Zum Schlusse des Gottesdienstes ward ein Predigtverhör (Predikoförhör) gehalten: der Prediger fragte nach Einzelnem aus der Predigt, nach den Theilen derselben, besonders nach den angeführten Bibelsprüchen, und begleitete Alles mit zweckmäßigen Ansprachen. Nach einer Schlußrede und stillem Gebete ging die Versammlung aus einander. Man begab sich in die Kirchstuben, wo man im Gesang- und Evangelienbuche las, bevor man heimkehrte. Fast jeder Hof, auch wenn er nur ¼ M. von der Kirche entfernt ist, hat eine Kirchstube oder Theil an einer solchen, denn die meisten Kirchstuben haben wenigstens zwei Besitzer. Der Kirchenbesuch ist sehr fleißig; selbst 1 Meile entfernt Wohnende kommen sonntäglich; so ist es im ganzen Pastorat Bygdeå, wo sich so viele schöne Früchte der echten Thätigkeit des trefflichen Dr. Genberg zeigen. — Die Kirche Nysätra ist von Holz, aber freundlich außen und innen; der Kirchhof ist ohne Grabzeichen. — Auch am Nachmittage sah ich in den Höfen in Postillen lesen.

Nach der Kirche kehrte ich zurück nach Önnis; den Knaben, welcher mich gefahren, konnte ich nur mit Mühe bewegen, das Fuhrgeld anzunehmen; er wollte so gerne ohne Bezahlung gedient haben.

Um 4¼ Uhr setzte ich die Reise fort. Mein Pferd hatte 5 kleine Glocken; einige Pferde tragen deren bis 7; solche klingelnde Pferde sind in dieser Gegend sehr häufig.

Am 13. Jul. Von Daufs nach Gumboda ¼ M.; von G. nach Rifleå 1¼ M.; von R. nach Bygdeå ¼ M. — Zuf. 2¼ M.

Bis Rifleå hat man meist Hügelweg; man merkt, daß man sich dem Ende Westerbottens nähert, das, je nördlicher, je ebener wird. In Gumboda war das Lager aufgehoben. In Ringsjö, zwischen Gumboda und Rifleå, riß das Sielenzeug, sogleich eilten die Bauern herbei, Hülfe zu leisten, und binnen Kurzem war Alles gebessert; einer derselben nöthigte aufs drin= gendste bei ihm einzutreten, wobei es denn auf Bewirthung ab= gesehen war, die Eile aber verbot jeden Aufenthalt; es kostete Mühe, hiervon zu überzeugen. Mein Skjutsbonde war eine Bauertochter aus Vebbomark, ein schlichtes einfaches Mädchen; mit edlem Unwillen erzählte sie, wie um Johannis, als noch das Lager bei Gumboda gestanden, die Soldaten daselbst mit den Mädchen der Gegend getanzt, allerlei Unarten verübt, geflucht und gesoffen; leider hätten sie aber auch dießmal keinen Geistli= chen bei sich gehabt; sie sei nicht zugegen gewesen; auch über andere, zumal religiöse Gegenstände, äußerte sie sich mit vieler Kenntniß und Wärme. So sind die Bäuerinnen des Nor= dens.

Von Rifleå, wo im Flusse gleiches Namens viel Lachsfang ist, hat man noch ¼ Meile bis zur Kirche Bygdeå, die ich um 9¼ Uhr erreichte. Doctor Genberg war auf einem Besuch in der Nachbarschaft abwesend. Bis zu seiner Rückkehr spazierte ich zwischen den nahen Kirchstuben; die Umgebungen sind wun= derschön.

Die Gemeinde von Bygdeå ist in Hinsicht der Sittlichkeit eine der ausgezeichnetsten Gemeinden Westerbottens. Unter den 160 jährlichen Geburten sind oft kaum 3 uneheliche Kinder; fast jede, auch ärmere, Familie hat ihre Bibel und Erbauungsschrif= ten, zumal die kleinen von der evangelischen Gesellschaft in Stockholm herausgebenen; und daß diese Lectüre Frucht schafft, zeigt das Leben dieser Leute. —

Am 14. Jul. Von Bygdeå nach Djeknebøda ½ M.; von
D. nach Såfvar 1½ M.; von S. nach Tafle 1¼ M. —
Zuf. 3¼ M.

Nach herzlichem Abschiede von der liebenswürdigen Familie
verließ ich um 1½ Uhr Bygdeå. Die Gegend war seit meiner
Hinreise frischer und schöner geworden. In Djeknebøda verursachte die Flucht meines Pferdes einigen Aufenthalt. Zwischen
Djeknebøda und Såfvar fährt man im Walde dem öden Stabhammer Johannisfors vorüber; der Krieg und Mangel an Absatz hatten ihm den Untergang gebracht; auch die Grabsteine am
Wege zeigen von dem Kampfe, der hier einst Statt fand. (Kap. 19.)
In den Wänden der Wohnung meines Skjutsbonde, am Wege,
waren noch Kugeln sichtbar.

Såfvar ist ein großes Dorf mit Sägemühle, Stab- und
Nagelhammer. Die freundlichen Gebäude des dem Kaufmann
Forssell in Umeå gehörigen Bruk schließen sich unmittelbar
an die kleinen Bauerhöfe an; zu Forssel's Wohnhause führt eine
Allee von Espen (populus tremula) und Sperberbäumen (sorbus aucuparia). Seit einigen Jahren wird in Såfvar eine
Kirche auf Kosten Forssell's und der Bauerdörfer gebauet, denn
der König hat erlaubt, daß aus Såfvar und der Umgegend, die
bisher nach Umeå eingepfarrt war, ein besonderes Pastorat gebildet werde; da indeß die neue Gemeinde zu klein und arm
seyn dürfte, um einen Pastor anständig zu lohnen, so scheint
es, daß der Bau nicht vollendet werden wird.

Um 6 Uhr langte ich in Tafle an und übernachtete daselbst. Heute und gestern bemerkte ich zuerst, daß bei trüber
Luft es um 11 Uhr ein wenig dunkel ward, so daß man nur
mit Mühe noch schreiben konnte.

Am 15. Jul. Von Tafle nach Stadt Umeå ½ M.; von U.
nach Hissjön 1½ M. von H. nach Tafvelsjön 1½ M.; von
T. nach Neder-Rödå 1 M. Zuf. 4½ M.

Um 6½ Uhr brach ich auf. Nahe vor Umeå bestieg ich die
fahle Felsenplatte am Umeåstrom, auf welcher sich ein Lusthaus

erhebt; man hat von hier eine weite Aussicht über den Umeå bis zur Mündung, und die vielen Dörfer längs der Ufer; hier feiert man die frohe Johanniszeit, und von hier sehen die Kaufleute ihre Schiffe absegeln.

Gleich nach meiner Ankunft in Umeå, wo ich, zu meiner Freude, den Lagman Strömbom nebst dem braven Dalkarl Fahnehjelm wieder vorfand, ging ich aus, den Brunnengästen am Brunnen einen Besuch abzustatten. Aber die Damen begegneten mir schon; das Trinken war für heute beendiget, und die meisten Gäste waren schon abgereiset.

Der Vormittag verging unter Besuchen und Zurüstungen zur Lappischen Reise, die jetzt von Umeå aus angetreten werden sollte. Auf Veranlassung des Bischofs, waren durch die Gefälligkeit des Doctor Genberg auf der ganzen Route nach Lycksele-Lappmark alle Veranstaltungen getroffen, welche die Reise erleichtern und meinen Wunsch, mit den Eigenthümlichkeiten des Lappischen Volks genauer, wie es gewöhnlich bei schnell Reisenden der Fall ist, bekannt zu werden, fördern konnten; auch hatte man die im Sommer gewöhnliche Versammlung der auf den Fjäll (Alpen) nomadisirenden Lappen für die Zeit meines Aufenthalts in Lycksele angesetzt. Leider war meine Ankunft durch den Unfall bei Torneå verspätet worden, und ich mußte daher nun eilen, nach Lycksele zu gelangen, welche Lappmark, als die nächste und mit den mindesten Beschwerden zu erreichende, ich als Ziel der Reise mir erwählt hatte. Auch der Landshöfding, Herr von Edelstam, an den ich einen Brief abgab, hatte die Güte, Veranstaltungen zur Förderung meiner Pläne zu treffen. Durch die Gefälligkeit des Provinalarztes Dr. Carlsten schnell mit Arzneien zur Hebung der von der Verwundung noch zurückgebliebenen Schwäche versehen, verließ ich um 1 Uhr die Stadt. Die große Straße läuft gegen Süden fort; aber auch gen Westen, nach Degerfors, geht 5¼ Meilen weit ein brauchbarer Fahrweg, dieß ist die Straße nach Lycksele. Ich wählte letztere, mein Weg führte mich zuerst durch einige Dörfer zur Landkirche Umeå, wo ich jetzt beim Dr. Hambraeus nur kurze, längere Zeit aber bei der Rückkehr, verweilte. Diese Landkirche ist die

Mutterkirche, zu welcher die eine halbe Meile entfernte Stadt als Filial gehört. Eine Menge Kirchstuben umgeben die Lands kirche. Sie ist massiv und geräumig, wenn gleich für die an 9000 Seelen starke Gemeinde nicht groß genug; sie scheint im 16ten Jahrhundert erbauet zu seyn, ist freundlich in ihrem Ins nern, hat eine gute Orgel und einen hübschen Altar; sie ist ohne Thurm; der Glockenstuhl steht auf dem geräumigen, rings mit Bäumen bepflanzten, und mit hübschen eisernen Thüren vers sehenen Kirchhofe *). Aus dem Glockenstuhl genießt man einer schönen Aussicht auf den Strom und seine hohen Walds und niedrigen Wiesenufer bis abwärts zur Stadt; der Strom macht hier auch kleine Fälle. An den schönen Ufern, wo Dörfer eine lange Kette bilden, führte der Weg zur Stadt, bis, vor einigen Jahren, der Verwüstungen des Flusses halber, die Straße obers halb durch einen Tannenwald und ein Paar Dörfer verlegt wers den mußte, wo sie nun wenig Reize hat. Außer dem weitläufs tigen Pfarrhofe, bei welchem man einen hübschen Garten ans gelegt hat, der, durch seine Lage vor Nachtfrösten geschützte, zwar ohne Fruchtbäume, doch desto reicher an Gartengewächsen (zu Ende Juli waren die Gartenerbsen schon eßbar), sich einen Hügel hinan zieht, findet man zwischen den Kirchstuben oder auf dem Backen (Hügel), wie man spricht, auch die Wohnungen der beiden Comministri der Landgemeinde und einiger anderer Familien, das Gemeindehaus, die Armenstube. Eine feste Kirchs spielschule hat die Landgemeinde nicht; die Eltern und ein tüchs tiger ambulirender Schullehrer besorgen den Unterricht; letzterer bleibt 4 bis 6 Wochen in einer Dorfschaft, wofür er, außer den Reisekosten und freiem Aufenthalt, 8 fl. wöchentlich für jedes Kind erhält; für den Unterricht armer Kinder wird mittelst der

*) Hier ruhet der im Jahr 1724 verstorbene Propst von Umeå, Nils Grubb; sein Grabstein trägt die einfache passende Inschrift: „1724 Psalm 81, 19. 21,‟ denn sein Leben war nur Ein Kampf ge gen Neider und Lästerer, aus welchem der würdige Mann freilich sehr ehrenvoll schied. Er war 1681 in Umeå geboren, ward 1707 Docent und 1710 Professor in Greifswald, und 1711 Pastor in Umeå.

Armenkasse gesorgt. — Die Geistlichkeit des Pastorats Umeå ist ziemlich zahlreich: der Pastor hält immer einen Adjuncten, der freie Station und 100 Bankthaler baar genießt, außer den vielen freiwilligen Geschenken der Gemeinde; ferner sind angestellt die genannten beiden Comministri (Capelläne) für die Landkirche, 1 Stadt-Comminister und 1 Bruks-Prediger für das Eisenwerk Hörnefors und die Glashütte Strömbäck; letzterer wohnt in Hörnefors, wo er an dem einen Sonntage predigt, am folgenden hält er Gottesdienst in Strömbäck; an dem Sonntage, wo in dem einen Bruk die Predigt ausfällt, hält der Küster Postillenlesung. Der Gehalt des Bruks-Predigers besteht nur in 20 Tonnen (80 Scheffeln) Korn und 25 Bankthalern, daneben hat er freie Wohnung und einige andere kleine Vortheile, auch Gaben aus nahe gelegenen Dörfern, die er bedient, wiewohl sie eigentlich nicht zum Sprengel seiner nur auf die Bruke beschränkten Gemeinde gehören. Die Bruksgemeinde ist Theil des Pastorats und steht somit unter Aufsicht des Pastors von Umeå, der auch in der Bruksgemeinde die Hausverhöre hält; gewöhnlich sind die Schwedischen Bruksgemeinden nur Filiale, die indeß ihre eigenen Geistlichen haben. In Strömbäck trifft man auch einige Katholiken, die aus Deutschland stammen. Mehrere Russen giebt es in der Gemeinde, die aber theils in dem evangelisch-lutherischen Bekenntniß geboren, theils zu demselben übergetreten sind. — Die Armeneinrichtungen des Pastorats sind zweckmäßig und umfassend; ein in Stockholm verstorbener Bottnier, der Kaufmann Öman, hat denselben ein nicht unbedeutendes Kapital vermacht. — Die Zahl der Gebornen in der Landgemeinde beträgt jährlich 3 bis 400, etwa das 18te Kind ist unehelich, fast das vierte Kind stirbt im ersten Lebensjahre. Diese große Sterblichkeit unter den Neugebornen schreibt man auch hier dem Auffüttern mit säuerlicher Milch zu; die Mütter entziehen sich zwar dem Stillen nicht, so oft sie aber auf Arbeit oder sonst abwesend sind, erhalten die Kleinen fette, säuerliche Milch oder Brey. Die Macht des Vorurtheils ist so groß, daß man von dieser schädlichen Sitte, aller Warnungen ungeachtet, noch nicht zurückgekommen ist.

Im Pastorat herrscht viel Wohlstand: Viehzucht, Ackerbau, Theerbrennen, Lachs- und Strömlingsfang, sind die Haupterwerbs-quellen. In den letzteren Zeiten hat der Luxus zugenommen, zumal im östlichen Theil des Kirchspiels; hier sah ich z. B. ein Mädchen im kattunenen Kleide Heu harken; doch die meisten kleiden sich noch ganz nach altväterlicher Sitte in Walmar und andere eigengemachte Zeuge. Bei Hochzeiten herrscht viel Aufwand; freilich ist es eben so in dem größeren Theile Norr-lands und in anderen Schwedischen Landschaften. Die Hoch-zeitsgebräuche sind, bis auf einzelne Abweichungen, in allen Schwedischen Provinzen, wo die Hochzeit feierlich begangen wird, und in Finnland gleich. Feierliche Verlobungen in Ge-genwart des Predigers sind in Schweden selten; wohl aber fin-den sie auf den jetzt Russischen Älandsinseln auf folgende Weise Statt: nachdem bereits früher das Jawort im Stillen erfolgt ist, begiebt sich der Prediger, in feierlicher Procession, ins Brauthaus, fordert noch einmal das Jawort der Braut und der Braut-eltern, und übergiebt, indem nun Braut und Bräutigam einander die Hände reichen, oder er die Hände derselben zusam-menlegt, der Braut, als Geschenk des Bräutigams, Gesangbuch, Ringe, seidene Tücher, Handschuhe und einige blanke Thaler, jedes einzelne von passender Anrede begleitet; worauf er mit Er-mahnungsrede und Ertheilung des Segens schließt. Ein Mit-tagsmahl folgt, wo aber nur die Braut und die Männer zuge-gen sind. Nach dem Mahl zieht sich die Braut zurück; am Abend wird sie von ihren und des Bräutigams näheren Ver-wandten beschenkt, worauf sie jedem, auch dem Prediger, ein Paar Strümpfe verehrt; jede Tochter im Hause hat nämlich ihre eigene Kleiderkammer, die sie vom zwölften Jahre an durch eigene Ar-beit füllt. Der Prediger kehrt am Abend heim, die Uebrigen bleiben bis zum nächsten Morgen. Auf ähnliche Weise, doch minder feierlich, wird im oberen Theil von Neu-Finnland und in Alt-Finnland eine feierliche Verlobung vor dem Prediger ge-feiert.

Die Trauung geschieht, wenn sie feierlich seyn soll, in der Kirche, an einem Sonn- oder Festtage. Schon am Vorabend begeben sich die Gäste ins Hochzeithaus; auch kommt wohl die Predigerfrau oder wer sonst von den angesehenern Frauen des Kirchspiels dieses Geschäft übernommen hat, um das Kleiden der Braut zu verrichten, falls nicht die Braut sich erst am nächsten Morgen im Pfarrhofe kleiden läßt. Die, oft silberne, Brautkrone, auch wohl Kranz, diese schönen Sinnbilder des Sieges über die Sinnlichkeit, gehört der Kirche, die für das Anleihen Bezahlung erhält; das Brautkleid gehört der Kleidenden, oder, häufiger, der Braut. In früheren Zeiten pflegte die Kirche gegen besondere Bezahlung auch einen Bräutigamsmantel zu halten, wozu oft der Predigersmantel benutzt wurde; jetzt ist diese Sitte meist verschwunden. — Den Sonnabends-Abend im Brauthause nennt man Mökqväll (Jungfernabend): da wird der Möqälling (Jungfernbrey, Jungferngrütze) verzehrt, auch wohl schon getanzt; beiderseitige Eltern geben das Mahl.

Am Sonntag Morgen beginnt die Procession zur Kirche, gewöhnlich vom Pfarrhofe aus: Musikanten ziehen voran; dann der Prediger mit dem Bräutigam *), die männlichen Gäste, die Braut mit der Brautkleiderin (brudframma) und den weiblichen Gästen; doch ist die Ordnung nicht überall gleich. Der Bräutigam ist schwarz gekleidet, mit weißer Weste, in Schuhen und weißen Strümpfen, an einigen Orten auch mit bunten Gehängen und Blumenkranz; die Braut ist mit allerley bunten Zierrathen auf dem Haupte und auf dem Kleide geschmückt, einer glänzenden Haarbinde, Scherpe, Halskette, Ohrgehängen, Brustnadel zc.; die Krone ruht auf einem Kissen. An manchen Orten ist auch eine feierliche Procession aus dem Brauthause zum Pfarrhofe, auf geschmückten Pferden und zu Wagen, üblich **). Unter

*) In Dalekarlien befindet sich auch der Kirchenwächter mit seinem langen Weckerstabe (spögubbe, der Alte mit dem Stabe) in der Procession.

**) In Småland sind auf dem Wege zur Kirche Schlagbäume mit Tannenzweigen verziert. Auch reiten dort die Brautdiener zur Kirche voran, melden die nahe Ankunft des Zuges, reichen allen Kirchgän-

Musik wird die Braut vor den Altar, oder auch nur bis zur Kirchthüre, worauf sofort das Orgelspiel beginnt, geführt. Jetzt wird, nach Vorschrift der Liturgie, der erste Theil der Trauung oder die eigentliche Trauung verrichtet. Dann folgt der Gottesdienst und, nach demselben, der zweite Theil der Trauung oder die Brautmesse, die hauptsächlich in einem Gebete besteht, welches der Prediger spricht, während zwei Jünglinge und zwei Mädchen aus der Zahl der nächsten Anverwandten Brautdiener (brudsvenner) und Brautmädchen (brudpigor) genannt (in Wingåker oft 20 bis 30 auf jeder Seite), den Brauthimmel (pell), eine viereckige, große, seidene Decke, über das Brautpaar halten, worauf der ganze Akt mit dem kirchlichen Segen endiget. — Aus der Kirche geht der Zug in gleicher Feierlichkeit und Ordnung, wie in die Kirche, zum Pfarrhofe zurück, wo die ganze Schaar, oder auch, wie in Wingåker, nur die, welche nicht zur Hochzeit geladen sind, bewirthet wird. Vom Pfarrhofe zieht man, in feierlicher Procession, mit Musik zum Hochzeitshause; bei der Ankunft ertönt Musik; es folgt eine kleine Bewirthung, unter freiem Himmel, oder im Hochzeitshause, und endlich der 3te oder letzte Theil der Trauung: die Einführung ins Ehegemach(sånglednng), der in einem Hochzeitsgesange und einem vom Prediger verrichteten Segensgebet besteht *). Jetzt werden die Glückwünsche abgestattet, vom Prediger im Namen Aller, oder von allen Einzelnen, während dessen, in Alt-Finnland, musicirt wird. Das Hochzeitmahl beginnt: vor und nach demselben betet ein Kind; auch stimmt, nach dem Mahle, der Prediger ein geistliches Lied an, welches die Versammlung fortsetzt; Braut und Bräutigam sitzen beisammen, an der Seite der ersteren die Pre-

gern einen Trunk, und kehren dann wieder zum Wagen der Braut zurück. — In Småland setzt sich ferner die Braut, in der Kirche, in einen schön geschmückten Stuhl; zur Seite stellen sich die Brautdiener, welche unaufhörlich mit Maienbüschen wedeln.

*) Ueber die Trau-Liturgie vergl. Schwedens Kirchenverfassung 2c. Bd. 2, S. 106—115. — Geschieht die Trauung im Hause, so werden die drei Theile verbunden; zuweilen ist dieses auch bei kirchlichen Trauungen, zumal an einigen Orten, der Fall.

digerfrau, neben dem letzteren der Prediger, dann die übrigen, nach Verwandtschaft geordnet, das weibliche und das männliche Geschlecht gesondert. Brautritter und Brautmädchen warten auf. Die Hochzeitsgerichte sind fast überall dieselben: Schinken, Rinderbrust, Ochsenzungen, Fleischwurst, Fleischsuppe, Fische, Braten, Kuchen, Kreme aus Lingon oder anderen Beeren, auch wohl Kohl; an einigen Orten auch mehrere (bis 7) Arten dünner Brote. Während man den Braten, auch wohl die übrigen Gerichte, aufträgt, wird musicirt. In einigen Gemeinden herrscht der Gebrauch, auch Schaugerichte aufzustellen. In Dalekarlien muß die Braut zuvor die Hochzeitsspeisen in der Küche gekostet haben. In Wingåker bringt jede geladene Familie einen Topf voll süßer, dicker Grütze mit, der, während des Mahles, damit jeder koste, die Runde machen muß; der Braten wird in Wingåker erst am Abend gespeiset.

In einigen Provinzen redet gewöhnlich nach dem Mahle der Prediger einige ermunternde Worte über christliche Führung des Ehestandes, auch über die rechte Hochzeitsfeier von Seiten der Gäste. Wo aber diese Ermahnungsrede nicht gebräuchlich ist, da bringt doch der Geistliche die Gesundheit der Neuvermählten aus; worauf beide einen Becher ergreifen, und jeder die Hälfte desselben austrinkt; zum Zeichen, daß von nun an sie alles mit einander theilen wollen. Dann hält der Geistliche die Brautrede *) (brudtal), in welcher er auffordert, der Bedürfnisse des neuen Ehepaars thätig zu gedenken; ein jeder tritt nun an den Tisch, an welchem der Geistliche und die jungen Eheleute sitzen, und reicht nun seine Gabe oder eine Anweisung auf dieselbe, falls sie nicht in Gelde besteht, dar; an einigen Orten macht der Bräutigam mit einer Gabe an die Braut, bestehend in einem

*) In Wingåker trinkt, nach vollendeter Brautrede, die Braut dem Bräutigam, dann dem Geistlichen, der Brautkleiderin, den Verwandten und übrigen Gästen zu, und empfängt von einem jeden die Brautgabe; welche die Hofritter (Brautdiener) sammeln; worauf die Verwandten andere Gaben verheißen, die der Geistliche aufzeichnet.

Gesangbuch und Silberzeug, den Anfang, nachdem er schon frü= herhin die Braut mit Handschuhen und Tüchern beschenkt hat (an einzelnen Orten werden die Gaben, in der Stille, beim Ab= schiede der Gäste, gegeben, in Westerbotten am zweiten Tage, oder am ersten Tage um Mitternacht beim Kronablegen; in Småland am zweiten Tage). Der Geistliche nimmt die Gaben in Empfang und dankt, gleich dem Ehepaar, mit einem Hände= druck; die Gebenden werden mit Branntewein oder Wein, Punsch oder Kaffee, bewirthet; die nächsten Verwandten treten zuerst heran; die Gaben werden vom Prediger verzeichnet und einzeln verlesen. In Dalekarlien geht die Braut, in silbernem Becher einen Trunk reichend, umher, während einer ihrer nächsten Ver= wandten einsammelt. Die Gaben steigen gewöhnlich zu mehre= ren hundert Thalern und höher; eine zweite Gabe am Montag Nachmittage, die Wiegengabe, ist nur an einigen Orten üb= lich *). Endlich wird für Arme, Kirche und Lazareth gesammelt. Kaffee wird nach dem Mahle oft nur dem Geistlichen und dessen Frau, so wie den jungen Eheleuten, gereicht.

Nach den Einsammlungen beginnt, am Abend, der Tanz, den der Prediger mit der Braut und die Predigerfrau mit dem Bräutigam, an einigen Orten der Bräutigam mit der Braut, eröff= net **), gewöhnlich führt der Prediger die Braut dem Bräutigam zu. Nun erst tanzet jeder der männlichen Gäste mit der Braut, und jeder weibliche Gast mit dem Bräutigam, jeglicher eine Po= lonaise; die Brautdiener führen die, welche tanzen sollen, zur Braut oder zum Bräutigam. In Herjeådalen sind die tanzen= den Männer, nur den Prediger ausgenommen, während des Brauttanzes, mit dem bunten Bräutigamshut bedeckt. In mehr

---

*) Im mittleren Schweden sammelt man schon beim ersten Hoch= zeitsmahle für die Braut und hernach für die Wirthschaft besonders.

**) In Finnland ist der Tanz des Predigers nicht überall üblich, überhaupt willkürlich; der Taleman (Redner) eröffnet vielmehr den Tanz mit der Braut und die Brautkleiderin den Tanz mit dem Bräuti= gam. In Småland steigen die Brautdiener, mit Lichtern in der Hand, auf Stühle, um, bei jedem Tanz der Braut, zu leuchten.

reren Provinzen wird von Allen, die mit der Braut tanzen, derselben eine kleine Gabe dargebracht, ein Knecht oder ein Mädchen gibt ½ bis 2 Rthlr., Hausväter und Hausmütter geben mehr; kleine Kinder, die die Braut auf ihren Armen tanzen läßt, reichen wenigstens einige Schillinge dar; denn der ganze Hof geht zur Hochzeit, und der nächste Nachbar muß das leere Haus mittlerweile hüten. Außer mit der Braut, tanzt der Prediger, an einigen Orten, auch mit der Mutter der Braut und mit der Mutter des Bräutigams, und eben so die Predigerfrau, außer mit dem Bräutigam, noch mit einigen Männern. Sind diese Pflichttänze vollendet, dann erst mag jeder nach Belieben tanzen. — Bald erscheinen nun die nicht geladenen Mädchen der Gegend mit Milch zum Brautreis (brudgröt), worauf zur Dankbarkeit mit jeder von ihnen die Braut wie der Bräutigam tanzen; auch speisen diese Mädchen am Abend im Hochzeitshause. — Jetzt folgt das Vesperbrot (aftonvard), und, nach abermaligem Tanze, die Abendmahlzeit, wobei nothwendig jener, ohne beigemischtes Wasser, blos mit vieler Milch dick gekochte Reis-, Gerst- oder Hafergrütze aufgetragen werden muß. Endlich folgen das Kronabtanzen und der Kampf. Die Brautkrone wird abgetanzt, indem die von allen Mädchen umtanzte Braut, eine Binde vor den Augen, die Krone auf dasjenige Mädchen setzt, das ihr nun zunächst als Braut nachfolgen soll; das mit der Krone beschenkte Mädchen wird wieder umtanzt, und setzt die Krone auf einer zweiten, und diese auf das Haupt einer dritten. Der Kampf der Verheiratheten und der Unverheiratheten beginnt; die Frauen suchen die Braut zu rauben; die Mädchen widersetzen sich; eben so stehen die verheiratheten Männer wider die Jünglinge, den Bräutigam zu rauben; nach einigen Reibungen, führen die Frauen die Braut und die Männer den Bräutigam in ihre Mitte und tanzen mit den Geraubten; auch wird die junge Frau auf einen Stuhl gesetzt, dieser vor den Mädchen in die Höhe gehoben und umtanzt, während sie einen Becher leert und auf das Haupt des Mädchens setzt, das nun zuerst Braut werden soll; eben so verfahren die Jünglinge mit dem jungen Manne: der Bräutigam trinkt den Abschiedsbecher den Jünglingen, den Ankunftsbecher den Männern zu. In Herleädalen werden, nach vollendetem Kampf, Mädchen und Jünglinge bewirthet. Nachdem alles dieses beendigt ist, entfernt sich die junge Frau, legt ihren Hochzeitsschmuck ab und kehrt gekleidet als Hausfrau, in einem schlechteren Gewande zurück, den Tanz fortzusetzen, oder geht zu Bette. Im letzteren Fall setzen die übrigen Gäste den Tanz fort oder werfen sich auf die Flatbänk (Flache Bank), auch syskonsäng (Geschwisterbett) genannt: Jünglinge und Mädchen liegen hier, auf ausgebreiteten Betten und Fellen, wie Schwestern und Brüder, neben einander; die Mädchen legen sich zuerst, die Jünglinge schleichen sich zwischen sie; man entwendet einander die Schuhe, die dann wieder ausgelöset werden müssen, man störet einander im Schlaf; einige agiren Fiskåle, indem sie, wo sie einen Jüngling neben einem Mädchen treffen, beide auf ein Bärenfell werfen und da mit einander trinken und zahlen lassen.

Am zweiten Tage machen die jungen Ehegatten die Wirthe. Gleich am Morgen, zum Dank, daß sie Gatten geworden, bewirthen sie die Hochzeitsgäste auf dem Bette mit Kaffee, Branntewein ꝛc., die junge Frau ist ganz als Hausfrau, mit schwarzer Mütze, gekleidet. Die Jugend folgt mit Musik und tanzet in jedem Hause; oder die jungen Eheleute kommen selber mit Musik, an einzelnen Orten von Marschällen und einigen Gästen begleitet. Nun stehen Alle auf: der Prediger, wenn er noch anwesend ist, hält ein Morgengebet. Man frühstückt, tanzt, stellt kleine Spiele an, schmauset, und so geht es oft bis Donnerstag oder Freitag fort; man erklettert auch eine im Hofe aufgerichtete Gräne ꝛc.; an einzelnen Orten wird an jedem dieser Tage Morgengebet gehalten. — Am nächsten Sonntag geht das junge Ehepaar schwarzgekleidet zur Kirche, unter Begleitung der sich bei der Kirche sammelnden Hochzeitsgäste. Diesen Begleitern giebt das neuvermählte Paar, nach der Rückkehr aus der Kirche, in seinem neuen Wohnsitze, einen kleinen sogenannten Heimkehrschmaus (hemkomstöl), eine Art von Nachhochzeit, die indeß an vielen Orten nicht gebräuchlich ist. Ueberhaupt sind einzelne der geschilderten Gebräuche an einzelnen Orten abgelegt worden;

Die beschriebenen Hochzeiten sind allerdings sehr kostbar, daher sie in ärmeren Gegenden sehr eingeschränkt werden, und oft nicht länger als 1 oder 2 Tage dauern. Die Geschenke geben einigen Ersatz. In Dalekarlien zehren die Gäste, den Prediger ausgenommen, während der ganzen Dauer der Hochzeit von dem Mitgebrachten. In vielen Provinzen bringen sie allerlei Lebensmittel, den sogenannten Hülfskorb (hjelpkorg), zum gemeinschaftlichen Gebrauche mit; in diesem Falle bestreiten die Eltern des Bräutigams und der Braut nur die Kosten am Sonnabend Abend und am Sonntag Morgen, die Kosten vom Sonntag Mittag an aber die Gäste; doch wird, während der ganzen Dauer der Hochzeit, von dem, der sie ausrichtet, Bier und Branntewein gegeben; in Dalekarlien halten die Gäste gemeinschaftlich das Bier.

An vielen Orten ist es üblich, daß auch solche, welche nicht zur Hochzeit geladen waren, dem jungen Ehepaar Geld schicken; diese werden nach dem Kirchgange in den Kirchstuben, oder vor dem Kirchhofe, frugal bewirthet.

Der Prediger reiset häufig noch am Hochzeitsabend nach Hause, spätestens am folgenden Tage nach dem Frühstück, wo dann bei seiner Abreise musicirt wird. Beim Schlusse der Hochzeit beschenken die Neuvermählten sämmtliche Gäste, oder die nächsten Anverwandten, mit Strumpfbändern und dergl. mehr; der Prediger aber, und die Predigerfrau, falls diese kleidete, erhält Handschuhe oder Strümpfe, oder eine Fitze Garn oder Leinewand. An einigen Orten giebt auch der Bräutigam den Gästen kleine Geschenke.

In Jemtland fand ich die Sitte, daß die Braut am Sonntage vor der Hochzeit in die Kirche geht, und, mit Blumen und silberner Halskette geschmückt, den Ehrenplatz neben der Predigerfrau einnimmt; sie heißt dann kleine Braut (lillbrud).

In Dalekarlien, wo überhaupt mehrere eigenthümliche Hochzeitsgebräuche Statt finden, und in andern Provinzen, z. B. in Westermanland und Södermanland, ziehen am Vormittage des zweiten Hochzeittages die Jünglinge in den Wald, fällen eine Tanne oder Gräne, und führen sie unter Musik zum Hofe und

II.   O in der Stille mit dem dicken Ende ins Haus; die Alten vermögen den Baum nicht heraus zu bringen und müssen die Hülfe der Jünglinge ansprechen, die sich mit Branntwein bezahlen lassen; in Westmanland reitet man auf diesem Baume und zahlt dann an die Musikanten, die öfters keine andere Bezahlung erhalten, in Småland reitet und tanzt man um den Baum, schon wenn man aus der Kirche kommt. — In Dalekarlien hebt man ferner, am zweiten Tage, den Bräutigam auf die Schultern, tanzt in dieser Stellung mit ihm herum, und läßt ihn nicht eher los, bis er mit Kreide auf den Boden geschrieben, wie viel Branntwein er geben will, denn Kreide führt der Dalkarl immer bei sich, um auf dem Schurzfell, womit er stets gekleidet ist, rechnen zu können.

In einigen Gegenden sind die Brautgaben am Hochzeitstage nicht üblich; dagegen werden dort Schmausereien bei Gelegenheit der Kündigung des Ehepaars angestellt, wo dann die Braut Gaben erhält.

In Bohuslän läßt man den Tag der Trauung ohne alle Feier verstreichen; dagegen versammelt man sich am Freitag Abend vor der ersten Kündigung; am nächsten Sonntag geht man insgesammt, doch ohne Procession, zur Kirche, kehrt in den Hof zurück und bleibt da bis Dienstag oder Mittwoch, tanzend und schmausend. Man feiert also eine Vorhochzeit, bei welcher der Prediger nicht zugegen ist. Die Gäste bringen auch hier viele Lebensmittel zum gemeinschaftlichen Gebrauche mit.

In einigen Gegenden, namentlich Ostgothlands, wird, für den Hochzeitstag, von jungen Mädchen der Eingang zum Hochzeitshause mit Grünreisern festlich geschmückt.

In Småland äußert der Hochzeitszug seine Freude auch durch Schießen, und bei der Kirche werden alle Kirchgänger und Kirchgängerinnen mit Brot und Branntwein bewirthet. Geschieht die Trauung daheim, so geht man dem Prediger mit Musik entgegen; die ganze Schaar, nur den Bräutigam ausgenommen, ist mit Pistolen versehen, die sie löset. In Småland ist auch die Bewerbung in so ferne feierlich, als, bei wohlhabenderen Bauern, der das Jawort suchende Bräutigam an einem Sonnabend, zu Pferde, in festlicher Begleitung, erscheint, doch ohne daß ein Prediger zugegen ist, und die Verlobten am folgenden Tage, mit den gegenseitigen Geschenken gekleidet, in Begleitung der Anverwandten, einen festlichen Kirchgang halten.

In Westgothland, wo die Trauung im Hause vollzogen zu werden pflegt, wird der Bräutigam durch berittene Jünglinge aus seiner Wohnung ins Hochzeitshaus geführt; es versteht sich, daß er die ankommenden Reiter anständig zu bewirthen hat; das nennt man sparöl, welches aber schon am Vortage gehalten wird. Geschieht in Westgothland die Trauung in der Kirche, so reiset der Prediger zuvörderst zum Bräutigamshause, wo er bewirthet wird, von da zu dem Hause, in welchem die Braut aufgeputzt wird, und nun erst in Procession zur Kirche, unter Musik.

Uebrigens finden die bisher beschriebenen Hochzeitsgebräuche nur auf dem Lande unter den Bauern und geringeren Grundbesitzern Statt; unter den Vornehmeren und in den Städten trifft man nur den einen oder andern dieser Gebräuche und die Hochzeiten sind von kurzer Dauer; Brautgaben sind bei Honoratioren nicht üblich. Hochzeiten der Aermeren geschehen in der Stille, mit größter Einschränkung, und sind in einem Tage geendiget, oft schon in einem halben Tage. Am vollständigsten und feierlichsten sind die Hochzeitsgebräuche in Norrland, am wenigsten feierlich werden die Hochzeiten in Schonen begangen. In Blekingen und an einzelnen Orten Schonens, auch in Halland, wo die Geistlichen bei den Hochzeiten nicht zugegen sind, hat man besondere Redner (talemán), die die nöthigen Anreden halten, so daß der Prediger nichts als den Trauungsakt zu verrichten hat; diese Redner sind auch die Anwerber. Die Zahl der Schwedischen Landgemeinden, deren Geistliche nicht mit der Braut tanzen, ist geringe; die meisten dieser Gemeinden findet man wohl in Schonen.

Die Hochzeitsgebräuche der Norweger sind denen der Schweden sehr ähnlich; die Trauungsliturgie ist verschieden. Krone und Thronhimmel sind nicht gebräuchlich. Die Trauung muß in der Kirche geschehen, während sie in Schweden auch im Hause geschehen darf. Das Kleiden der Braut verrichtete eher

O 2

mals die Predigerfrau, jetzt nicht mehr. In Procession zieht man
aus dem, der Kirche zunächst gelegenen, Hofe mit Musik zur
Kirche, und mit Musik aus derselben zum Hochzeitshause; Braut
und Bräutigam gehen Hand in Hand, ihnen voran der Ehrenmar-
schall (kjögmästare), der den Wirth macht; Brautmädchen folgen
der Braut. Der Prediger wird nicht immer zum Hochzeitsmahl
geladen. Wenn die Hochzeitschaar aus der Kirche kommt, wird
sie zuerst im Freien, ganz wie in Schweden, bewirthet, dann
folgt das feierliche Hochzeitsmahl; während des Mahls steht man
auch auf, geht, sich zu erholen, umher, oder raucht; mit Gesang
und stillem Gebet wird das Mahl begonnen und geendiget; bei
Tische werden die Brautgaben gesammelt und jede derselben vom
Kjögmästare genannt. Der Kjögmästare eröffnet auch den nach-
folgenden Tanz mit der Braut, worauf ein jeder männliche Gast
mit der Braut und jedes Frauenzimmer mit dem Bräutigam
tanzt. Der Prediger kann mittanzen, wenn er will, wie er es
auch zuweilen thut; nach beendigten Pflichttänzen, tanzt jeder
nach Belieben; bei den Polnischen Tänzen führt man seine Da-
mie also, daß man die Hand hinten in die ihrige legt. Lebensmittel bringen auch in Norwegen die Gäste mit, doch nicht hinreichend.

Viel Eigenthümliches haben die Hochzeitsgebräuche auf den
Alands-Inseln. Hochzeiten werden dort nur im Sommer
gehalten, und zwar im Hause des Bräutigams, wohin die Braut
drei Tage vor der Hochzeit auf einem großen Erndtewagen mit
ihrer ganzen Ausstattung zieht: sie selber sitzt auf dem Wagen,
hat sie einen Bruder, so fährt dieser; der Wagen ist mit Laub
und Maienbüschen geschmückt, eben so die Pferde, die so schön, als
irgend möglich, seyn müssen; zwei Violinisten reiten spielend
voran. Am Sonntag geschieht die Trauung in der Kirche, nach
dem Gottesdienst: in die Kirche zieht man in Procession, der Prediger mit dem Bräutigam, die Braut, die Brautkleiderin (brudframma), die Brautmädchen ic. Nach der Trauung begiebt man
sich, in feierlichem Zuge, zum Hochzeitshause: die Braut mit den
Brautmädchen im Wagen des Predigers, der Bräutigam auf
einem schöngeschmückten Pferde reitend, gleich den übrigen

Männern; nur der Prediger darf fahren. Die Männer eröff-
nen den Zug, dann folgen die Musikanten, der Brautwagen;
die übrigen Frauenzimmer auf Quersätteln reitend. Nachdem
man im Hofe angelangt ist, beginnt die Sängledning. Nach
dem Mittagsmahl hält der Prediger die Brautrede; man wünscht
Glück, die Brautgaben werden gesammelt, die nächsten Anverwandten geloben ein Pferd, eine Kuh, ein Schaaf ꝛc.; der Prediger eröffnet den Tanz mit der Braut ꝛc. Jene Hochzeitsfuhr
erinnert an die Schweizerische Zügelfuhr oder Trychleten
im Berner Oberlande, wo, freilich erst am Hochzeitstage, die Braut,
welche aus einem Dorf in ein anderes heirathet, mit ihrer ganzen beweglichen Habe den feierlichen Einzug in ihre künftige
Wohnung hält, begleitet von den Jünglingen ihrer Heimath, die
mit Peitschen, Kuhglocken (trychle), Hörnern, Pfeifen ꝛc. einen
gräßlichen Lärm machen, bis sie vor der Wohnung anlangen, wo
sie, unter Gesang, eine strohene Puppe an eine Stange aufstek-
ken oder in einer Wiege darbringen *). Ueberhaupt ist es merkwürdig, daß die Hochzeitsgebräuche selbst solcher Völker, die mit
einander seit langer Zeit in keiner Verbindung stehen oder nie
standen, in manchen Punkten ganz übereinstimmen. — Das Ab-
tanzen des Brautkranzes und das Scheingefecht kennt man auch
im nördlichen Deutschland; auch den Pflichttanz, den aber nur
der Brautdiener mit der Braut, den Brautmädchen und sämmtlichen Frauen und Mädchen anstellt.

Die Hochzeitsgebräuche in Finnland sind den
Schwedischen meist gleich; nur in einigen Stücken abweichend,
insbesondere wenn, wie es dort nicht selten ist, die Trauung an
einem Wochentage und im Hause vollzogen wird. Da zieht am
Vorabend der Bräutigam in das Brauthaus: voran gehen Mar-
schälle, welche im Namen eines fremden Prinzen den Hausvater
feierlich fragen: ob derselbe bei ihm Quartier bekommen könne.
Der Hausvater mit den Seinigen macht allerlei Schwierigkeiten;
endlich wird eingewilliget, der Bräutigam zieht ein, auch die Gäste kommen, und die ganze Nacht wird getanzt. Am nächsten

*) S. Wyß Reise in das Berner Oberland. Bern 1817.

Vormittage erfolgt die Trauung; beim Hochzeitsmahle sitzen Braut und Bräutigam, Sprecher und Kleiderin (taleman und brudsätta) beisammen; ersterem Ehrenamt steht der Prediger oder sonst einer der Vornehmern vor; letztere ist häufig die Predigerfrau. Beim Wegfahren vom Brauthause hält der Taleman eine Rede, und ein geistlicher Gesang wird angestimmt. Im oberen Finnland sammelt am nächsten Morgen der Prediger die Brautgaben. Mit dem Brauthimmel, Kronabtanzen, Schein-gefecht und dergleichen mehr hält man es ganz wie in Schweden. — Am Abend des zweiten Hochzeittages kehren die Gäste heim; nur die beiderseitigen Verwandten bleiben noch ein Paar Tage zurück, die des Bräutigams im Braut- oder Hochzeitshause, die der Braut im Hause des Bräutigams. Am folgenden Tage geht man zur Kirche, doch nicht in Procession.

In mehreren Theilen von Finnland wohnt der Prediger, wenn die Trauung in der Kirche geschieht, nicht dem Hochzeits-mahle bei.

In Alt-Finnland verfügen sich, nach der in der Kirche vollzogenen Trauung, Braut und Bräutigam, jedes nach seiner Wohnung; doch bald zieht der Bräutigam mit den Freiwerbern und nächsten Anverwandten zum Brauthause; hier läßt er sich anmelden, aber der Hausvater weigert den Empfang; ein Papierläppchen wird nun als Paß verlesen, und zwar von solchen, die nicht buchstabiren können; noch immer werden Einwendungen und allerlei Fragen gemacht; endlich bahnen Geschenke und Bewirthung dem Bräutigam und seinem Gefolge den Eingang; die Bewirthung wird erwiedert, und man zieht zuweilen erst am 2ten Tage zum Bräutigamshause, wo nun das eigentliche Hochzeitsmahl beginnt. Bei der Procession zur Kirche wird, so oft man durch Dörfer kommt, musicirt.— Doch ich komme, nach dieser Abschweifung über Schwedische Hochzeitfeier, zur heutigen Tagereise zurück. Der Weg von der Landkirche Umeä nach Hißsjön ist sehr sandig und steinig, und als bloßer Kirchspiels-weg nicht mehr so gut, wie die bisherige große Landstraße; in-deß ist der Weg bis Lycksele ausgemessen, wenn gleich die Meilenpföste jetzt vergangen sind. Lange fährt man im Nadelwalde,

wo ein Paar Seen, ein unbewohntes und ein bewohntes Häus=
chen mit Wassermühle die einzige Abwechselung bilden. Nach=
dem man den Wald hinter sich hat, erblickt man viel Korn
und erreicht bald das Dorf, dessen freundlicher Gästgifvaregärd
ein recht hübsches Gastzimmer hat.

Zwischen Hißsjön und Tafvelsjön hat man nichts als Wald;
aber mit Fichten und Gränen wechseln Birken, und Convalla=
rien mit schönem röthlichem Kelch duften am Wege. Zuletzt
fährt man auf Bergrücken, unter hohen bewaldeten Felsen, am
großen Tafvelsee hin zum Dorfe. Der ganze Weg von Hißsjön
ist sehr bergig, aber die Seen, denen man vorüberkommt, ma=
chen ihn schön. Höfe erblickt man nur in der Ferne, am We=
ge trifft man nichts als eine Sägemühle, ein Nybygge, Senn=
hütten und Heuscheunen. In Tafvelsjön ist ein guter Gästgif=
varegärd, ¼ Meile abwärts von der Straße, da die näher woh=
nenden Bauern sehr arm sind. Die Menschen im Gästgifvare=
gärd waren bieder und unverdorben. Desto widriger war es
mir, dort einen der Boräshändler zu finden, die die Einfachheit
und Sittlichkeit des Landmanns untergraben, indem sie ihn aller=
ley Luxuswaaren kennen lehren und mit Verlangen nach densel=
ben erfüllen. Doch handelte dieser, ein heiterer und fröhlicher
Mann, nur mit Wallmar (grobem Tuche) und wollenen Strüm=
pfen, letztere hat er in Halland gekauft; er kehrte eben von
der Lappischen Gränze zurück.

Zwischen Tafvelsjö und Röbä ist der Weg ein wenig bes=
ser, wie bisher; man hat wieder viel Wald, anfangs Fichten,
dann gemischten Wald. Wiewohl Theerbrennerey den Hauptnah=
rungszweig dieser Gegenden ausmacht, so sieht man doch eine
Menge umgefallener oder für den Zweck der Erweiterung des
Weges abgehauener Bäume, oder Tröpfe gefällten Schiffsbau=
holzes am Wege; so wenig Werth hat hier das Holz, oder viel=
mehr, so wenig herrscht sorgfältige Holzwirthschaft. Die Tonne
Theer wird mit etwa 3½ Bankthalern bezahlt; einzelne Bauern
sind durch Theerbrennerey sehr wohlhabend geworden; ein Bau=
er in Fallfors soll sich auf diese Weise ein Vermögen von 90,000
Thaler, d. i. 5000 Bankthaler erworben haben, was man hier

für einen großen Reichthum hält; doch giebt es Bauern z. B.
den Gästgifvare in Degerfors, die noch reicher sind. — Man
fährt auf Waldhöhen hin, von denen man in sehr tiefe Thäler
hinabblickt, dem Nybygge Fredrikshall vorüber, wo viel Kornbau und Theerbrennerey getrieben wird; am Wege und in der
Ferne dampfen Theeröfen, neben ein Paar hübschen Seen fährt
man hin, an den Seiten erheben sich überall sehr hohe bewaldete Felsen. So erreicht man das von wohlhabenden Bauern
bewohnte Dorf Neder-Röbä, wo ich, da es zu spät war, um
noch Degerfors zu erreichen, übernachtete. Um Röbä wird viel
Korn gebauet; besonders sah ich wogende Roggenfelder.

In Neder-Röbä war ein hübsches freundliches Gastzimmer,
und auf dem Hofe ward noch ein neues Gebäude für Fremde
aufgeführt. Die Menschen waren brav, herzlich, dienstfertig
und unverdrossen. Alles war tüchtig und ordentlich, verständig
und zweckmäßig eingerichtet. Die freundliche und geschäftige
Hausfrau gab sich alle erdenkliche Mühe, mit ihren Diensten
auch dem leisesten Wunsche zuvorzukommen. In der That, es
ist ein eigenthümlicher großer Genuß, der dem auf den großen
Straßen vielbesuchter Länder ziehenden Reisenden nicht zu Theil
wird, wenn man sich von solchen einfältigen und doch keinesweges rohen und ungebildeten Naturmenschen umgeben weiß. —
In einer Scheune befand sich eine Dreschmaschine mit 2 Rädern; die Maschine wird von einem Pferde getrieben; die
Scheune war ein regelmäßiges Viereck; üblicher sind die länglichen Scheunen.

In Röbä, welches Dorf noch nach der 4 Meilen entfernten Landkirche Umeå eingepfarrt ist, wird, wie in den übrigen
Dörfern seit Umeå, nicht bloß am Sonntag-Vormittage, sondern in den Fasten auch an den Nachmittagen des Sonnabends und Sonntags Dorfgottesdienst gehalten; tägliche Mor-
gen- und Abendbetstunde hält man in jedem Hofe.

—————

Am 16. Jul. Von Neder-Röbä nach Degerfors 1¼ M.

Um 5¼ Uhr brach ich auf; die erste halbe Meile ist sehr

bergig; man fährt auf hohen Bergrücken hin, von welchen man theils auf den breiten Windelelf, der bei Wannås mit dem Umeå zusammenfließt, theils in tiefe Waldthäler herabblickt. Man kommt über die breiten Mündungen der Flüsse Rödaå und Krokå, die sich in den Windelelf ergießen, und durch das Dorf Öfra Röbå, welches von einigen Bauern und zwei Torpare bewohnt wird; letztere bezahlen für Aecker, Wiesen, Wald und Vieh, welches alles sie als Eigenthum der Bauern benutzen, der Bauerschaft gemeinschaftlich. Hinter Öfra Röbå fährt man mehr denn 1 Meile lang durch Tannenwald, in welchem vor 10 Jahren ein Waldbrand wüthete, der sich zum Theil von selbst löschte. Am Wege sieht man abgeschälte Tannen, deren Rinde von armen Leuten hier häufig zu Brot vermahlen wird. Eine Viertelmeile von Degerfors liegt, hart am Wege, das aus mehreren Kolonistenhöfen zusammengekaufte Nybygge Rosindal, dem Schulkollegen Biroir aus Umeå gehörig, welches bedeutenden und einträglichen Ackerbau hat. Um 8¼ Uhr langte ich in Degerfors an, wo mich der ehrwürdige Probst Sädenius, ein 80jähriger heiterer Greis, nebst seiner biedern Gattin und seinem Sohn, dem Magister, der ihm im Amte als Gehülfe beigeordnet ist, mit großer Herzlichkeit willkommen hieß. Degerfors, der Kirchort des Pastorats gleiches Namens, ist (ein in Nordland seltener Fall) zugleich ein Dorf. Die ganz hölzerne Kirche ward im Jahr 1769. von 30 Bauern auf eigene Kosten erbauet, auch 30 Kolonisten (Nybyggare) gaben einige Beiträge; die Kosten beliefen sich auf ungefähr 400 Bankthaler; damals ging Lappland noch bis Granön, 2¼ Meilen von Degerfors, also 3 Meilen weiter, als jetzt. Anfangs war Degerfors eine zu Umeå gehörige Kapelle; seit 30 Jahren bildet es ein eigenes, kleines Pastorat, in welchem die Zahl der Geborenen jährlich etwa 30 beträgt; die Seelenzahl ist 1500. Eine feste Kirchspielsschule ist nicht vorhanden, doch an gutem Unterricht kein Mangel. Die Kirche ist bisher noch ohne Orgel. Dorfgottesdienst wird am Sonntage in allen, auch nahen, Dörfern gehalten; Morgen-, Abend- und Tischgebete sind allgemein. Im Sommer, wo die Eltern oft entfernt und die

Kinder allein zu Hause sind, halten diese ihre Tischgebete mit einander.

In Degerfors hatte man mich bereits eine längere Zeit erwartet; die nöthigen Anstalten waren getroffen und noch am
selbigen Tage, Mittags 1 Uhr, trat ich in Begleitung des Adjuncten Magister Sådenius die Lappische Reise an.

Zwei und zwanzigstes Kapitel.

Reise nach Lycksele-Lappmark.

Oede Fußwege. — Die furchtbare Krankheit Radesog-
ge. — Die Sennhütte — Dorf Tågsnås. — Die Fahrt
auf dem Umeå; die Strömungen, Stromkähne. —
Die Schwedischen Kolonisten, ihr einfaches, frommes Leben. — Die Kataralte Hellefors. — Ankunft in
Lycksele; Lappenschule; Kirche, Gottesdienst in Lycksele: Schwedische Kirchstuben, Lappische Kirchenhüt-
ten; Lappische Schlitten; Tracht der Lappen; anmuthige Gegend; biedere Menschen, fröhliches Leben.

Am 16. Jul. Von Degerfors nach Tågsnås 2¼ M.

Bei Degerfors endet der Fahrweg; beide Wege, die von hier
nordwestlich nach Lycksele-Lappmark führen, sind Reit-, Fuß-
und Bootwege. Der eine, der beschwerlichere, wenn gleich die
ausgemessene Landstraße, hat 3 Gästgifvaregårder Hjuken, Ekorsele und Ekorträsk: von Degerfors nach Hjuken ¾ Meile Boot-
oder ⅞ Meilen schlechter Reitweg; von Hjuken nach Ekorsele, im
Sommer 1 Meile Reitweg (im Winter nach Stryksele 1 Meile
und Ekorsele 1 Meile, wo der Weg ebener ist); von Ekorsele
nach Ekorträsk, dem ersten Dorfe in Lappmark, 1 Meile Reitweg; von Ekorträsk nach Lycksele's Kirche 1¼ Meilen, theils
Boot-, theils Gehweg; über Tandsele Nybygge (¾ Meile).
Ich wählte den zweyten, bequemeren Weg, anfangs 2 Meilen
Reitweg; dann meist Bootweg auf dem Umeå-Elf.

Von Degerfors Pfarrhofe hat man nur eine kleine Strek-

227

te an das Ufer des Windelelf. Des heftigen Stromes wegen, fuhren wir schräge hinüber; in geringer Entfernung zeigte sich der donnernde Fall des Windelelf, gleich Dorf und Kirche, Degerfors genannt. ⅛ Meile höher hinauf liegt ein noch beträchtlicherer Wasserfall; sonst hat der Windelelf lange nicht so bedeutende Fälle, wie der Umeelf. Am jenseitigen Ufer standen die wohlgerüsteten Rosse, und der mühselige Waldweg ward angetreten; auch ein armes 15jähriges Mädchen aus Åsele Lappmark schloß sich an. Die Radesyge, eine aus Norwegen, wo sie heimisch ist, eingeschleppte Krankheit, hatte sie furchtbar entstellt, so daß sie einen Erbarmen erregenden Anblick darbot; sie kam aus Umeå, wo sie im Lazareth gewesen war, und kehrte jetzt mit Kronskjuts über Lycksele nach ihrem Geburtsort, so viel möglich geheilt, zurück. Diese Krankheit hatte sich, von Åsele Lappmark aus, wohin sie aus Norwegen gebracht worden war, vor einigen Jahren auch ins Kirchspiel Degerfors verbreitet; da man aber sofort ein eigenes Kurhaus zu Granön, wo die Radesyge herrschte, errichtete und in dasselbe alle Kranken aufnahm, so gelang es, die furchtbare Seuche bald völlig zu tilgen. Die Krankheit hat in ihren Erscheinungen zwar manche Aehnlichkeit mit der venerischen Seuche, ist von derselben aber wesentlich verschieden. In Norwegen kannte man die Radesyge längst, und sie soll zuerst an den westlichen Küsten Norwegens entstanden seyn. Ueber mehrere Schwedische Provinzen verbreitete sich die Krankheit erst in neuerer Zeit, und zwar, wie es mir wenigstens rücksichtlich Norrlands erwiesen scheint, nur von Norwegen aus, doch wurde sie durch tüchtige medicinische Anstalten, namentlich eigene Kurhäuser, jedesmal bald wieder gehemmt; auch mochte in einzelnen Schwedischen Provinzen von Aerzten wohl manches mit dem Namen Radesyge belegt worden seyn, was eigentlich nur ausgeartete venerische Krankheit, und nicht die wahre Norwegische Radesyge, war. Die Radesyge gehört keineswegs zu den venerischen oder diesen ähnlichen Krankheiten, die freilich in vielen Schwedischen Provinzen nicht selten sind, keineswegs immer als Folge eigner Unsittlichkeit, sondern oft als Folge der Ansteckung durch näheres Zusammenleben, ge-

meinschaftliches Speisen aus Einer Schüssel, Benutzung gemein=
samer Kleidungen und Betten, durch Einwirkung des Schwei=
ßes beim Tanze und dergl. Wo sich in Schwedischen Provin=
zen venerische Krankheiten erzeugten, da waren es meistens ein=
zelne Seefahrer oder Vagabunden, auch wohl, zur Zeit eines
Krieges, Soldaten, die bald in Folge eigner Unsittlichkeit, bald
ohne eigene Versündigung durch Andre angesteckt, die Krankheit
einbrachten, worauf sie nun durch Unvorsichtigkeit um so leichter
sich verbreitete, da man auf dem Lande meistens weder von der
Krankheit noch von ihrer Ansteckung einige Kenntniß hatte, und
als die Krankheit sich zeigte, das tiefe Schaamgefühl nicht so=
fort zu überwinden vermochte, um sich einem verständigen Ärzte
zu entdecken. Dieß ist, mit wenigen Zügen, die Geschichte der
Verbreitung venerischer Krankheiten in Schweden. Vor allen
gilt es von den nördlichen und nordwestlichen Provinzen Schwe=
dens, daß, so oft dort venerische Krankheiten, die an einigen
Orten noch völlig unbekannt sind, herrschten, sie wohl nie der Un=
sittlichkeit der Einwohner ihren Ursprung verdankten; in diesen Ge=
genden hat das Laster noch keine Freystätte gefunden. Die Ra=
desyge ist nie Folge eigener oder Anderer Unsittlichkeit, wenn
gleich es möglich ist, daß sich in einzelnen Fällen eine veneri=
sche Krankheit mit der Radesyge vereinigte; wäre dieses, so
würde es sich leichter erklären, daß verschiedene Krankheiten mit
dem Namen Radesyge bezeichnet wurden; eine Bemerkung, die
sich selbst dem Nichtarzte bei Durchlesung der ärztlichen Be=
richte und Schriften über diesen Gegenstand aufdringt. Ich wer=
de öfter, besonders Kap. 31. auf die Radesyge zurückkommen,
und bemerke nur, daß, wie durch die venerische Seuche, so auch
durch die Radesyge ganze Familien, bis zum Kinde an der
Mutterbrust herab, angesteckt worden sind.

Das arme Mädchen aus Åsele begleitete uns die erste Meile;
dann ritt sie, während wir bei einer Sennhütte verweilten, mit
dem sie begleitenden Skjutsbonde voraus, und ich habe die Unglück=
liche hernach nicht wieder gesehen.

Der Weg vom Ufer des Windelelf bis Tågsnäs beträgt 2
Meilen. Es ist ein schmaler halsbrechender Waldweg, bald

sperren ihn gewaltige Steine, bald Baumwurzeln, bald führt er plötzlich von Höhen in bedeutende Tiefen herab, bald durch breite und steinige Bäche, bald durch Moräste oder sumpfige Waldwiesen; nur auf einem Pferde, das desselben gewohnt ist, kann man ihn furchtlos passiren. Der Versuch, ihn mit kleinen zweirädrigen Wagen (kärror) zu befahren, ist mit Lebensgefahr verbunden, und wird selten gewagt; der Vater meines 15jährigen Skjutsbonde hatte es unternommen, war aber umgeworfen. Hohe Berge durchziehen den Wald, der aus Nadel- und Laubholz besteht und in welchem man eine Menge abgerindeter Bäume erblickt, welche für die Theerbrennereyen bestimmt sind. Man setzt das Abrinden drei Jahre hinter einander fort, im ersten Jahre schält man drei Seiten ab, nur die Nordseite bleibt stehen; im 2ten Jahre rindet man etwas höher hinauf ab, und entblößt endlich im Frühlinge des dritten Jahres auch die ganze Nordseite von ihrer Rinde, worauf im Herbste desselben Jahres der Baum gefällt wird; die meisten vollenden indeß das Abrinden in zwei Jahren. — Die tiefste Stille herrschte ringsum, nicht einmal das Zwitschern eines Vogels war hörbar. Mit Freude erblickten wir die erste Menschenwohnung, eine Sennhütte des Länsman Sundelin, die bloß 3 Wochen im Jahre zur Zeit der Heuernte, bewohnt wird.

Die Sennhütte war offen, aber kein Mensch war darin zu finden. Wir riefen in den Wald, das Echo wiederholte unsern Ruf, der bald auch von den Bergen beantwortet wurde. Mittlerweile labten wir uns an der Milch, die wir verfanden. Der Senne kam, gab uns ein Pferd, dessen wir bedurften, reichte uns Brod und Butter, und — das einzige Stückchen Lachs, was er hatte; letzteres nahmen wir nicht an; mit ersterem stillten wir unsern Hunger. Bezahlung wollte man durchaus nicht annehmen. Die Sennhütte liegt in einem hübschen Wiesenthale, auf der Mitte des Weges nach Tågsnäs. Heu ist das Bette der Sennen, und einfach ihre Kost; ihr Brot ist aus Gerste und Roggen gemischt, in Form dicker, runder Kuchen, oder vierfach zusammengelegte dünne Gerstenfladen; ein Paar Kühe geben, was es sonst an Nahrungsmitteln bedarf.

Um 7 Uhr langten wir im Bauerdorfe Tågsnås an, hatten also, den Aufenthalt in der Sennhütte abgerechnet, 5 volle Stunden auf dem öden Wege zugebracht. Mein Wunsch war es, heute noch weiter zu reisen. Als ich aber durch den eben aus Lycksele kommenden Kaufmann Eriksson erfuhr, daß die Lappenversammlung zum nächsten Sonntag in Tårna, 10 Meilen oberhalb Lycksele, angesetzt sey, sah ich ein, daß es völlig unmöglich sey, zur bestimmten Zeit dort einzutreffen, um so mehr, da meine Gesundheit noch nicht so weit wiederhergestellt war, daß ich Nachtreisen unternehmen konnte. Ich beschloß daher, die Reise nach Lycksele mit mehr Gemächlichkeit fortzusetzen, und um mich von den Strapazen des heutigen Tages zu erholen, in Tågsnås zu übernachten, welches in dem Hofe des Bauern Olof Israelsson geschah, wo man uns mit vieler Freude aufnahm. Ich schlief in einem großen Zimmer, wo mehrere Gardinenbetten standen, zum Theil nach Landessitte mit Schränken versehen, in reinlichen Betten, unter einem Schaafsfell, was in der kalten Nacht sehr wohl zu ertragen war. Am Abend empfing ich noch mehrere Besuche aus dem Dorfe, die den lange erwarteten „fremden Herrn", wie sie sich ausdrückten, gerne sehen wollten. Die Unterhaltung mit den einfachen biedern Menschen machte mir viel Freude, wie auch sie erfreut waren, daß ich mit ihnen einige freundliche Worte wechselte. Ueberhaupt lebt in Tågsnås ein biedres und kräftiges Volk. Ich machte einen Spaziergang an das Ufer des Umeå-Elf, der Tågsnås bespült und hier kurze, aber donnernde Fälle bildet; und ging in den Hof des Bauern Anders Pehrsson, der uns am nächsten Tage rudern sollte; mit Herzlichkeit wurden wir willkommen geheißen, und keine größere Freude konnten wir der Hausfrau bereiten, als indem wir ihre Bitte bewilligten, uns eine Reiseprovision, in Eyern bestehend, mit auf den Weg geben zu dürfen. Bei Pehrsson fanden wir Postillen und Vorlesepulpet. Das Bethaus, wie man spricht, oder der Hof, wo das Dorf sich am Sonntag Vormittag zum Gottesdienst versammelt, war aber jetzt der Hof, in welchem ich wohnte; auf einem langen Tische lagen hier die Postillen und eine Menge Gesangbücher;

eine dicke Quartpostille lag aufgeschlagen auf einem kleinen Lese=
pult.

Die Bauerhöfe sind hier ins Viereck gebauet, und haben
in der Mitte einen freien Platz; das Haupthaus enthält zwei
große saalähnliche Zimmer mit Kammer; die Nebengebäude be=
stehen aus einem zweiten Wohngebäude mit Zimmer und Kam=
mer, auch wohl einem dritten und mehrern Wirthschaftsgebäuden,
deren einzelne außerhalb des Vierecks liegen, ganz auf Norr=
ländische Weise. — Einer der Bauern in Tägsnäs ist zugleich
Soldat im Westerbottnischen Regiment; ein Fall, der hier sel=
ten, häufig aber im benachbarten Pastorat Burträsk eintritt.

——————

Am 17. Jul. Von Tägsnäs nach Granön ½ M.; von G.
nach Lillsele 2 M.; von L. nach Tuggensele 1 M.; von
T. nach Tandsele 1 M. Zus. 4½ Meilen.

In Tägsnäs beginnt der Bootweg auf dem Umeå, und
reicht, einige Unterbrechungen ausgenommen, wo man, der schwe=
ren Forssar wegen, gehen muß, bis zur Kirche Lycksele. Da
man stromaufwärts fährt, so kommt man nur langsam fort; da=
her die heutige kleine Tagereise.

Um 6½ Uhr stiegen wir in den Kahn. Die Stromkähne,
deren man sich hier bedient, hopar genannt, sind ganz darauf
eingerichtet, mit Leichtigkeit die Wasserfälle hinan zu laufen: sie
sind sehr schmal; doch hat man auch breitere Böte, welche man
båtar nennt. Die Lappischen Böte sind noch schmäler, als die
hopar, und werden, statt der Nägel, mittelst gepichten und ge=
theerten Bindfadens zusammengehalten; doch haben die Lappen
in den letzten 80 Jahren angefangen, auch eiserne Nägel zu ge=
brauchen. Die Hopar schlagen leicht um, wenn man sich zu
sehr nach einer Seite hinlehnt: man darf nur in der Mitte und
an den Enden sitzen; an einem der beiden Enden hat der Ru=
derer seinen Platz. — Man kommt drei Theeröfen vorüber,
deren hier jeder Bauer einen hat; ein ansehnlicher Bach ergießt
sich mit einer breiten Mündung in den Umeå. Nach einer hal=
ben Meile Weges erreichten wir Granön, ein von 12 Bauern

und 2 Soldaten bewohntes Dorf, von fruchtbaren Kornfeldern umgeben, auf welchen Sommerroggen und Gerste vortrefflich standen. Ehemals soll in Granön eine Lappenkapelle gewesen seyn; jetzt wohnt nur ein Rennthierlappe in dieser Gegend. Vor einem halben Jahrhundert war das Kirchspiel Degerfors, einem großen Theile nach, noch Lappland; jetzt wohnen in Degerfors Schweden, und selbst in dem heutigen Lycksele-Lappmark werden die Lappen von den Kolonisten immer weiter gegen die Norwegische Gränze hin gedrängt. Die Bewohner von Granön stehen im Rufe der Ungefälligkeit, Störrigkeit und Trunkliebe, fast scheint es, nicht ohne Grund. — Nach einem kurzen Aufenthalt setzten wir die Fahrt längs des rechten Ufers fort. Die Ufer des Umeå sind bewaldet, nur selten erblickt man Wiesen und Felder; das Flußbette ist anfangs enge, dann erweitert es sich und liebliche Waldprospecte zeigen sich im Hintergrunde; der Fluß ist hier meist nur 10, an einigen Stellen 30 Fuß, tief; mitten im Fluß und, noch mehr, an den Ufern, wird die Fahrt oft durch große Waldbäume, die von den Ufern losgespült, oder sonst hinabgefallen und nun der Fäulniß überlassen sind, gehemmt. Bald deckt die Ufer nur dichter Wald; man kommt neben einer niedrigen Sandinsel hin, wo unser Boot auf einen, vom Wasser bedeckten, Waldbaum stieß; doch ging die Gefahr glücklich vorüber. Es war völlige Windstille, und die Sonnenhitze zwischen den Ufern drückend; aber plötzlich wehte zuweilen ein kühler Wind. Ueberhaupt ist der Wechsel der Witterung in Westerbotten und Lappland im Sommer groß: nach einem hohen Wärmegrad am Tage folgt oft am Abend und in der Nacht eine empfindliche Kälte; indeß sind die Bewohner an diesen Wechsel gewöhnt und er schadet ihrer Gesundheit nicht. — Hier und da waren die Mücken sehr arg. Nackte Felsen zeigen sich. Der Wald ist gemischt aus Gränen, Fichten (pinus sylvestris), Birken und Espen; die Fichten sind vorherrschend. ¼ Meilen von Granön werden die Ufer höher; hier wollen die Bauern von Granön ein Nybygge anlegen; bald werden die Ufer wieder flacher; eine Strecke lang, etwa ₁⁄₁₆ Meile, fährt man sogar über Wiesen, die freilich nur im Herbste trocken sind. Vom

andern Ufer erhate das Geschrei der Täucher, deren Eier, etwas
größer als Gänseeier, eßbar sind, nicht aber das Fleisch der
Vögel. Aus der Bauchhaut der Täucher bereitet man Handschuhe; 4 Vögel werden aber zu einem Paar Handschuhe erfordert; auch füttert man mit der Haut das Sielengeschirre aus.

Jetzt wird das Ufer schöner durch seine Krümmungen. Eine Weile ist zurückgelegt: man kommt an einen heftigen Strom-
zug, wo das Wasser, gleich einem Strahl, vom Ufer zurückgeworfen wird; wir landen, klimmen einen steilen Hügel hinan
und gehen längs des Ufers einher, während das Boot vom Ufer
aus gezogen wird; dann steigen wir ein, abermals zeigt sich eine
heftige Brandung, wir müssen aussteigen und das Boot wird
aufs neue gezogen. Doch bald setzen wir die Bootfahrt fort;
hohe Waldwege bilden nun die Ufer, bisweilen mit Wiesen wechselnd, wo Heuscheunen und Heustangen (hässjör) errichtet sind.
Im Hintergrunde zeigt sich ein hoher Lappischer Berg. Gebüsche, auf welchen sich wilde Enten sonnen, senken sich in den
Fluß, oder spiegeln sich gar lieblich in demselben. Der Fluß
erweitert sich bis zu 1200 Ellen; ein Bach stürzt über Steine,
donnernd, hinein. Bald kommt man einer fetten Wieseninsel
vorüber (Inseln trifft man nur wenige im Umeäfluß), die mit
Heuscheunen bedeckt ist; ein Adler kleinerer Art fliegt über den
Fluß; wir landen, dem Ruderer einige Ruhe zu gewähren, an
an einer, jetzt umflossenen, Landstrecke, wo das Dorf Grandn
eine Wiese hat, und suchen selber, vom Sonnenbrande ermattet, Erquickung im Schatten einer Darrhütte (badstuga), die
wahrscheinlich zum Trocknen der Fische zur Zeit der Heuerndte,
wo die Eigner der Wiese in der Nähe sind, bestimmt ist; jetzt
war auf den Brettern Heu ausgebreitet, die Bretter dienten also als Schlafstelle; auch ließen ein Paar Jacken in der Hütte
auf die Anwesenheit von Menschen schließen, die aber nirgends
sichtbar waren. Ruhe war freilich in der Darrhütte nicht zu
finden; denn wie bisher die Hitze geplagt hatte, so plagten
nun Tausende von Mücken. In der Mitte der Hütte war ein
steinerner Heerd errichtet, auf welchem man beim Dörren Feuer
anzündet.

II.   P

Nach einer halben Stunde ruderten wir weiter. Ein günstiger Wind hatte sich eingestellt und förderte die Fahrt; aber die Sonne brannte immer mehr zwischen den hohen Ufern. Der Fluß ist noch immer theilweise mit Bäumen ausgefüllt, die die herrlichsten Mastbäume abgeben könnten. Lachse giebt es hier nicht mehr: der gewaltige Fällfors, der sich, gleich einer Wand, einige Meilen unterhalb, erhebt, läßt sie nicht heraufkommen; aber andere Fischerei ist auch hier sehr bedeutend.

Um 3¼ Uhr landeten wir in Lillsele, hatten also auf 2⅜ Meilen Flußweg, den Aufenthalt abgerechnet, etwa 6¼ Stunden zugebracht; so schwierig ist die Fahrt auf dem Umeå, zumal stromaufwärts. Auf sele endigen sich in Westerbotten und Lappland, wie in andern Norrländischen Landschaften, viele Ortsnamen; gewöhnlich bezeichnet es sehr richtig die Localität, denn sele bedeutet „stilles Wasser zwischen Wasserfällen und Stromzügen."

In Lillsele verließ uns unser bisheriger Ruderer Anders Pehrsson, dieser herrliche Mensch, so kräftig und lebendig, und dabei so sanft, so freundlich und geduldig, wie ein Lamm. Er hatte uns weiter führen wollen; aber seine Kräfte waren so erschöpft, daß er es, bei der schwierigen Fahrt oberhalb Lillsele, wo viele Strömungen und Fälle sind, nicht länger mit uns wagen durfte. Wir nahmen daher in Lillsele einen andern Ruderer.

Lillsele ist ein einzelnes Nybygge, welches ein Kolonist aus Piteå bewohnt. Ueber den armen Mann war im letzten Frühling ein hartes Schicksal ergangen: er hatte, am Scharlachfieber, seine Frau und zwei Töchter verloren; die eine, bei der Krankenpflege angesteckt, war bald darauf, in Degerfors, wohin sie sich begeben, gestorben. Alle waren ohne Arzt gestorben; aber den Prediger hatte man holen lassen. Jeder Bewohner des Hofes war erkrankt, auch das Vieh aus Mangel an Pflege. Doch solche Drangsale hatten die guten Leute nicht verzagt gemacht. Jetzt war alles wieder frisch und gesund. Der Nybyggare, ein rüstiger 70jähriger Greis, kam herab ans Boot, in welchem ich ruhete, während meine Begleiter in den Hof gegangen waren, und lud, in seiner Armuth, zu frischen Eiern und Fischen ein. Als ich es verbat, kamen zwei Töchter mit einer Schaale Milch herbei; die eine reichte mit so viel Freund-lichkeit und Einfalt den gastlichen Trunk, daß ich nicht länger weigern konnte, ja ausstieg und in den Hof ging. Alles war nett und reinlich. Von 14 Kindern lebten noch 7; die 3 Töch-ter führten den Haushalt. — Als Nahrung für Kühe und Schaafe sah ich hier Birken- und Espenlaub trocknen, welches ich zu diesem Behufe, auch in andern Theilen Norrlands, na-mentlich in Westerbotten und in Angermannland, sammeln sah. *)

Um 5 Uhr fuhren wir, des schwierigen Weges halber, in zwei Böte vertheilt, weiter. Die Ufer sind bald Sandhügel, bald felsig. Durch zwei Stromzüge mußten wir hindurch, bei deren einem wir ausstiegen und das Boot gezogen ward. Fast eine halbe Meile fährt man längs des nach Lillsele gehörigen Waldes hin; dann beginnt das Gebiet der beiden Bauern von Tuggensele, und damit Lycksele Pastorat oder das eigentliche Lappland. Die Ufer sind auf dieser Strecke vorzüglich schön. Nachdem wir ¾ Meilen zurückgelegt, wurden die Forssar so heftig, daß das Boot wieder gezogen werden mußte. Eine Stunde lang gingen

*) Mit Gränzweigen Kühe und Ochsen zu füttern, hat man in Schweden oft vorgeschlagen, doch wenig befolgt. Die Zweige dürfen nicht zerhackt werden, weil dann der widrige Harzgeschmack hervortritt, weßhalb die Zweige alter Gränen anwendbarer sind, als die von jun-gen. Uebrigens besprengt man die Zweige mit Lohn oder Menschen-urin, damit sie feucht bleiben. Um das Vieh an dieses Futter zu ge-wöhnen, muß man anfangs eine Handvoll Gerstenmehl aufschütten, was hernach unterbleibt; gegen die Nacht muß man, wo möglich, Heu oder Heckerling reichen. Man kann auch im Winter mit entlaub-ten, weichen Erlen-, Birken- und Espenzweigen wechseln; auch Haide (Erica), Rennthier- und Isländisches Moos geben. S. Inrikes Tid-ningar 1818. No. 121. In Dalekarlien wird das Harz der Gränen gekauet, um die Zähne zu reinigen und zu stärken, auch zu Pflastern benutzt. Die Reiser haben einen balsamischen Duft und werden in Lappland gegen Kopfschmerzen gebraucht.

P 2

wir nun zu Fuß durch den Wald, auf einem ziemlich bequemen Pfade: Felsenblöcke wechselten mit Blaubeer- und Lingonfeldern und zuletzt mit Rennthiermoos. Ermattet, langten wir in Tuggenfele, dem ersten Lappischen Ort, an. Auf dem Wege sprang eine Birkhenne (orrhöna tetrao tetrix) schwarz und gelb gesprenkelt, vor uns auf. Dergl. eßbare Vögel giebt es hier in großer Menge; auch die größte Art, der Auerhahn (tidder, tetrao urogallus), der in den Morästen der dichten Fichtenwälder lebt. Er läßt sich zähmen, aber zahme Hennen bauen weder Nester, auch wenn man ihnen die Materialien hinlegt, noch brüten sie Eier aus, gleich allen der Freiheit beraubten Waldvögeln, doch paaren sie sich und legen Eier; berührt man im Walde ihre Eier mit der Hand, so verläßt die Mutter dieselben, ganz wie alle wilde Vögel; die von der Hand ausgehende feine Ausdünstung wird nämlich von der Mutter sogleich bemerkt und ist ihr widrig. Bei den Weibchen ist die Sehnsucht so groß, daß, wenn die Hähne der Gegend weggeschossen sind, sie völlig in diese Liebessehnsucht versinken, und, sonst scheu, jetzt sich mit den Händen greifen lassen.

Tuggenfele besteht aus zwei Nybyggarehöfen, in denen alles sehr freundlich und reinlich ist. Von dem einen Hofe war alles abwesend, bis auf ein etwa 30jähriges Lappenmädchen, das die Kinder wartete; die Kinder werden hier, wie in ganz Degerfors, mit süßer Kuhmilch genährt, die sie aus einem, am Kuhhorn befestigten, Säckchen von bereitetem Schaaf- oder Kuhleder saugen. Die Lappin hatte, in zarter Jugend, durch die Blattern die Nase und den freien Gebrauch ihrer Füße verloren. Auch in Westerbotten sieht man durch die Blattern furchtbar Entstellte nicht selten; jetzt wird die Vaccination immer allgemeiner. — Wir begaben uns nun in den zweiten Hof, wo der treuherzige Hausvater uns mit Speise und Trank zu erquicken eilte. Die Frau war in der nahen Sennhütte; bald kam sie mit frischer Milch zurück. Frische Aeschen (harr, Salmo Thymallus) und Forellen waren vorhanden; aus Sahne, Gerstenmehl und frischer Butter ward eine Sauce bereitet, und so entstand ein Mahl, welches auch nach geringerer Anstrengung vortrefflich geschmeckt haben würde. Das Brot bestand in dünnen, zusammengeschlagenen Gerstenfladen; nur in Mißwachsjahren ißt man Rindenbrot (von der weißen innern Rinde der Fichte (tall) oder Gräne (gran). Die Wand des geräumigen Zimmers, in welches man uns führte, bedeckten die Kleidungsstücke der Familie; ein Kammbrett mit Tellern ꝛc. war zierlich aufgestellt; Alles, auch die Bauart des Hofes, ganz nach Westerbottnischer Weise. Dieses Zimmer diente auch zu den gottesdienstlichen Versammlungen, die hier, wie auch in Granön und sonst, jeden Sonntag Vormittag gehalten werden; mehrere Postillen fanden sich im Hofe. — Johann Jansson, so hieß der Nybyggare — ist ein Schwede, wiewohl in Lappland, zu Tandsele, geboren.

In Tuggensele hatten wir unsere beiden Boote von Lillsele entlassen. In Einem Boote setzten wir, um 8 Uhr Abends, die Fahrt fort; Jansson ruderte. Kaum waren wir einige Minuten gefahren, als wir, einer schweren Strömung halber, ⅛ Meile über Land gehen mußten; nach wenigen Ruderschlägen landeten wir abermals: jetzt mußten wir einen steilen Berg hinanklimmen, bis wir, nach einer halben Stunde, zum Theil auf felsigem, schwer reitbarem Pfade, ans Ufer gelangten, und, nachdem wir auf diese Weise den schwierigen und langen Tuggenselefors vermieden hatten, das Boot bestiegen. Immer häufiger und höher werden die von dichtem Wald bedeckten Berge, deren mannigfaltige Formen den Reiz der schönen Gegend, die wir an dem schönen Abend ganz genossen, erhöheten. Still und milde war die Luft, ruhig das Wasser; der Talltrast flötete; allmählig ward es zwar kälter, aber die Luft blieb rein und angenehm: ein herrlicher Lappischer Abend, den ich nie vergessen werde. Der Boden ist in dieser Gegend wenig fruchtbar; überhaupt ist Sandboden in Lycksele-Lappmark vorherrschend; er fordert mehr Mist, als man geben kann, und lohnt die Arbeit des Nybyggare nicht. — Um 10½ Uhr trafen wir in dem Nybygge Tandsele ein, wo wir bei dem Besitzer, Anders Holmgren, übernachteten. Dieser hat das Nybygge, dessen Freijahre schon verflossen sind, nicht selbst urbar gemacht, sondern gekauft.

Holmgren und seine liebe Frau, eine Tochter des Pastors Alenius in Lyckfele, waren schon zu Bette, als wir anlangten; aber sogleich erhoben sie sich und empfingen uns mit vieler Freundlichkeit; ein Paar hübsche mückenfreie Zimmer wurden uns angewiesen.

Am nächsten Morgen nahm ich den Hof in Augenschein. Alles zeugte von Tüchtigkeit und Sorgfalt. Der Viehstall ist, wie man es neuerdings an mehreren Orten in Westerbotten einsgeführt hat, im zweiten Stockwerk eines Gebäudes angelegt: von hier rinnt die Jauche in das erste Stockwerk herab, wo ein trefflicher Dünger bereitet wird; gegenüber, im zweiten Stockwerk, ist der Heuboden angelegt, zu welchem man, wie ich es auch im Schwarzwalde fand, über einer amphitheatralisch erhöhten Wölbung aus Brettern hinauffährt. — Das Korn, um das Nybygge herum, stand gut; aber es ist dem Frost sehr ausgesetzt, mehr, wie in Abbortäsk, einem anderen Eigenthum Holmgren's. — In Tandfele erblickt man die 1 Meile entfernte Kirche Lyckfele nebst einigen der umstehenden Häuser.

Um 18. Jul. Von Tandfele nach Lyckfele 1 Meile.

Um 7½ Uhr fuhren wir ab; Holmgren und seine Frau ruderten uns auf zwei kleinen Hopar. Der Wald geht noch immer fort, der Fluß macht aber viele Buchten. Um 9 Uhr hatten wir ¾ Meilen zurückgelegt, und landeten, eine kleine Strecke unterhalb des großen Wasserfalls Hellefors, nachdem wir durch heftige Strömungen mühvoll uns durchgearbeitet hatten; es bedurfte Muth und Vertrauen, um in den, bald hoch emporgehobenen, bald tief gesenkten, Böten nicht zu verzagen. Wir gingen nun durch Wald auf nackten Felsenplatten, die zuweilen der Fluß überschwemmt. Plötzlich standen wir am Uferrande, im Angesicht des Hellefors, dessen mächtiger Donner schon lange hörbar gewesen war. Voll Staunen und Bewunderung stand ich da im Anblick der großen Naturscene, am Felsenufer, der Mitte des Falles gegenüber, wo der beste Standpunkt ist: oben erscheint eine vom Wasser bedeckte, wellenförmige Felsenkette, über welche die Spitze der Kirche Lycksele hervorragt, unten stürzt der Fluß in langen, ununterbrochenen Fällen, in der Mitte sind die vielen tiefen Fälle in einer Breite von etwa 1000 Ellen und in einer, noch um vieles beträchtlicheren, Länge; zwischen diese Fälle treten bewaldete Felseninseln, wodurch der Anblick noch malerischer wird; himmelan steigt der Staub einzelner Fälle, während andere, gleich einer Cascade, sich erheben und zurückgeworfen werden, andere sich donnernd durch einander stürzen; es ist ein Getöse, als würden Vierundzwanzigpfünder gelöset. Die Ufer deckt Wald, den Hintergrund bilden blauende Gebirge. — Eine Meile oberhalb Lycksele bildet der Umeå einen noch größeren Wasserfall.

Am Falle bewillkommte mich ein aus Lycksele angelangter Geistlicher, der leider seitdem verstorbene Magister Grönlund; weiterhin ein zweiter, der ordinirte Schullehrer Rådström und der Kronbefehlshaber (Fogde, Kronobefallningsman) in den Lappmarken, Lindahl, mich zu einem Mahle im Walde einladend. Nach Lappenweise lagerten wir uns, mit untergeschlagenen Füßen, auf platten Felsen und ließen uns geräucherte Rennthierzungen, geräuchertes Rennthierfleisch und was sonst aus Lycksele herbeigeschafft worden war, wohl schmecken. Dann stiegen wir in die aus Lycksele gesandten Böte. Neben hohen senkrechten Felsenwänden, hatten wir bald den kurzen Weg von ¼ Meile vollendet, und begaben uns ins Pfarrhaus, wo alles zu unserer Aufnahme bereitet war. Frisch und lebendig bewillkommte uns die 75jährige Pfarrerin mit Kindern und Kindeskindern; der Pastor lag krank darnieder *).

---

*) Späterhin ward Pastor Anders Xlenius so weit wiederhergestellt, daß er am 15. Januar 1819, 76 Jahre alt, mit seiner Gattin Eva Maria, Tochter des Probstes Fluur in Umeå, seinen 50sten Hochzeittag feiern konnte: am Vormittag brachte eine Anzahl Geistlicher ihren Glückwunsch; am Mittag folgte ein gesangreiches Mahl für Verwandte und Freunde; Nachmittags spielte der Greis auf der Cymbel und sang, mit reiner und kräftiger Stimme, Choräle und schwerere lyrische Stücke. Kinder und Kindeskinder (der ersteren sind 6, der letztern 36) umtanzten nach hochzeitlichem Brauch, unter Absingung

Sehr angenehm verflossen mir in Lyckfele die Tage des 18. bis 24. Julius. Wie konnte es auch anders seyn in der lieblichen Gegend und unter den freundlichen, einfachen, biederen Menschen, die auf alle Art und Weise meinen Aufenthalt zu verschönern, und selbst den leisesten Wünschen zuvorzukommen suchten. Stets werden mir diese frohen und glücklichen Tage im dankbaren Gedächtniß bleiben. Mit Ungemach und Entbehrung hatte ich wahrlich nicht zu kämpfen: ich wohnte in hübschen freundlichen Zimmern, wo es an keiner Bequemlichkeit fehlte; täglich ward wacker geschmauset, wobei die herrlichen Schnäpel *), Forellen und Rennthierzungen meine Leckerbissen waren, und, da mehrere Honoratioren bei der Kirche wohnen, so folgte das eine Fest dem andern. Herzlich und einfach, wie ich sie gern habe, waren diese Feste, Alles zeugte von Wohlhabenheit und Ueberfluß, aber Prunkliebe und vom fernen Auslande befriedigten Luxus sah man nicht; wahre und innige Freude führte überall den Vorsitz. Schmerzlich war es mir, wenn ich, um des Zwecks der Reise nicht zu verfehlen, oft die dem geselligen Frohsinn geweihten Stunden verkürzen und literarische Beschäftigungen an die Stelle treten lassen mußte.

Meine Absicht, in der Mitte der Lappen selbst ein Paar Tage zuzubringen und mit eigenen Augen sie zu beobachten, war vereitelt worden: es war ja Freitag, als ich in Lyckfele anlangte, nur bis Montag sollten die Lappen in Tärnå beisammen bleiben, und dann wieder mit ihren Heerden auf den Fjällen umherziehen dürfen, Tärnå war aber wenigstens 3 Tagereisen (30 Deutsche Meilen) von Lyckfele entfernt. Nichtsdestoweniger gelang es mir, durch die Gefälligkeit des Kronbefehlshabers Lindahl und

***

von Versen, das elterliche Brautpaar, indem sie es bekränzten, und, auf Stühle sitzend, erhöhten; und erst am Abend endete das Fest. Als äußeres Zeichen seines Dankgefühls gegen Gott schenkte der Pastor der Kirche ein Meßgewand. Alenius ward in Pited-Lappmark geboren, wo sein Vater Pastor in Arfvidsjaur war.

*) Der Schnäpel (fit) wird wie auch andere Fische, gleich dem Lachse, als Grafsift bereitet. Vergl. Kap. 16.

der Geistlichkeit, authentische und vollständige Nachrichten über die Westerbottnischen, Schweden verbliebenen, Lappmarken und die Bewohner derselben, Schweden, Finnen und Lappen, zu sammeln. Was ich daher in diesen Beziehungen mittheile, kann auf Zuverlässigkeit Anspruch machen; um so mehr, da ich ältere gedruckte Berichte, namentlich die Högströmschen, zum Grunde legte und mit dem, was ich über die gegenwärtigen Verhältnisse erfuhr, verglich, woraus viele Berichtigungen und Aenderungen hervorgingen, und da die Männer, welche ich zu Rathe zog, nicht blos des Lappischen sehr kundig, sondern auch in Lappland und unter Lappen viel gereiset waren und sich aufgehalten hatten. Späterhin besuchte ich selbst, von Jemtland aus, die nomadisirenden Lappen. Was ich unter ihnen sah und durch die Geistlichen, zu deren Gemeinden diese Lappen gehörten, in Erfahrung brachte, werde ich in der Spezialbeschreibung der südlichsten Lappmarken benutzen. Uebrigens vergl. man auch, Kap. 26, die Reise zu den Jemtländischen Lappen.

Hier werde ich zuerst von meinem Aufenthalt in Lycksele reden, dann das Schwedische Lappland und seine Bewohner im Allgemeinen und endlich sämmtliche einzelne Lappmarken beschreiben, Alles nach dem gegenwärtigen Zustande; nur bei Beschreibung des Norwegischen, des Alt= und des Neu=Russischen Lapplands bin ich größtentheils gedruckten Quellen gefolgt.

Wie die Freude selten ohne Leid ist, so ging es mir auch in Lycksele. Ich erwähnte, wie ich mit Ungemach nicht zu kämpfen gehabt; — ich hätte hinzufügen sollen: „am Tage"; denn nächtliches Ungemach bereiteten die argen Wanzen, die an meinem Blute ein besonderes Wohlgefallen zu finden schienen, und, einige Nächte, keinen Schlaf in meine Augen kommen ließen; sie nisten am liebsten in alten Holzhäusern. Alle Mittel wider sie waren, bei mir wenigstens, fruchtlos; auch der Wechsel der Zimmer half nichts, sie folgten mir überall.

Lycksele, der Hauptort von Lycksele=Lappmark, enthält die Kirche, die Lappenschule, den Pfarrhof, das Tingshus, die Küsterey, die Wohnungen des Kronobefallningsman über Lycksele=, Pitea= und Luleå=Lappmark, des, diesem untergeordneten, Läns=

man über Lyckfele-Lappmark, so wie mehrerer anderer Honoratio-ren-Familien, insbesondere der Wittwen Lappischer Geistlicher; alle Gebäude sind von Holz. Am Sonnabend Vormittag be-suchte ich die Lappenschule, am Nachmittag nahm ich die Kirche in Augenschein.

In der Lappenschule werden 6 Lappenkinder unterrichtet und erzogen, sie wohnen im Hause unter Aufsicht des Schulleh-rers (Scholämästare), und werden ganz auf öffentliche Kosten unterhalten. Nach einem kürzeren oder längeren Aufenthalt, höchstens von 2 Jahren, verlassen sie die Schule, worauf die Knaben sehr häufig als Katecheten unter ihrem Volke angestellt werden. Eine solche Lappenschule giebt es in jedem Lappenpa-storat, bei der Mutterkirche. Jede dieser Schulen hat 6 Zöglin-ge; bis 1773 hatte die Schule von Lyckfele 10; dann wurde aber auch hier die Zahl auf 6 beschränkt und der Gehalt des bisher besser besoldeten Lehrers verringert; dagegen der Etat für die Lehrer und Zöglinge der übrigen Lappenschulen, der bis dahin geringer gewesen war, erhöhet. Neben der Schule wohnt, in einem besonderen, freundlichen Gebäude, der Schullehrer. In der Schule von Lyckfele werden auch zuweilen, gegen besondere Bezahlung, außer den 6 etatsmäßigen Zöglingen, Kinder von Lappen, Schwedischen Kolonisten, ja Kinder der Geistlichen, un-terrichtet. Nach einer Verordnung von 1759 sollen 1 bis 2 Ny-byggare-Kinder das Recht der Aufnahme in die Schule von Lyck-fele haben.

Das Schulhaus ist neu; erst im Jahr 1816 ward der Bau vollendet, ja ein Zimmer zum Aufenthalt des Schullehrers in den Zwischenstunden 1c. neben der Schulstube, stand noch im Bau. Die Baukosten flossen aus dem Kirchenfond für die Lapp-marken, aus welchem überhaupt die Bedürfnisse der Lappischen Kirchen und Schulen bestritten werden. Als Lohn hat der Schul-meister 30 Tonnen Roggen, Gerste und Erbsen, Wiesen für 10 Kühe und 2 Pferde, Fischerey und 33 Rthlr. 16 ßl. Banco baar, nebst freier Wohnung; für Beköstigung der Zöglinge erhält er 14½ Tonnen Korn (vom Kronzehnten in Umeä) und 76 Bankthaler baar, wovon 9 Rthlr. 1 ßl. zur Anschaffung der All-

tagskleider für die Zöglinge und das aufwartende Mädchen verwandt werden; die Sonntagskleidung müssen sie sich selber halten.
In der Schulstube wird auch gespeiset, und im Winter auch geschlafen; im Sommer schlafen die Kinder in den Ställen auf
Heu über Rennthierfellen, die auch Bettdecke und Kopfkissen bilden. — Um 5 Uhr stehen sie auf, um 6 Uhr wird Gebet gehalten,
worauf der Unterricht mit Auswendiglernen beginnt; um 8 Uhr
wird gefrühstückt (Milchgrütze oder Brey (velling), Strömling und
Brot; Butter wird nur an Festtagen bestanden); von 9 bis 12
Uhr wird unterrichtet: Lesen, Hersagen und Erklärung des Aus-
wendiggelernten; von 12 bis 1 Uhr wird zu Mittag gespeiset
(Suppe, Kartoffeln und Rennthierfleisch mit Brot), von 1 bis 2
ist Freistunde; um 2 Uhr beginnt wieder der Unterricht und
dauert bis 5 Uhr, wo er mit einem Abendgebet geschlossen wird;
der Unterricht am Nachmittage ist ganz wie am Vormittage; von
5 bis 7 Uhr haben die Kinder Freistunden; dann wird zu Abend
gespeiset: Milchgrütze oder Brey mit Brot. An Sonntagen
wird besser gespeiset, an hohen Festen erhalten sie auch Fest-
kuchen; überhaupt sind die Speisen gut bereitet und nahrhaft.
Branntwein und Tabak erhalten die Zöglinge nicht, falls
nicht etwa Erwachsenen nach körperlicher Arbeit, die sie für
den Lehrer verrichten, ein wenig Branntwein zu Theil wird.
In Handwerken werden die Zöglinge nicht unterwiesen, kaum
dürfte es auch ihre künftige Bestimmung fordern; einige lernen
aber schreiben und rechnen. An den Mittwochs- und Sonn-
abends-Nachmittagen haben die Zöglinge frei; auch in den Hunds-
tagen sind 6 Wochen Ferien. Die Bücher, welche die Kinder
in der Schule erhalten, bleiben ihr Eigenthum. In der Schule
werden folgende Bücher gebraucht, alle in Lappischer Sprache:

1. Das Neue Testament. Hernösand 1811. (Die Correctur
besorgten Mag. Erik Grönlund und Mag. Isaac Grape).

2. A, B, C Buch, ins Lappische übersetzt von Fjällström,
nach der neuesten, von Erik Grönlund und Isaac Grape
1804 besorgten Ausgabe.

3. Högström's Katechismus. Neueste Auflage 1779.

4. Luthers kleiner Katechismus, übersetzt von Fjällström. Neueste Auflage 1807.

5. Svebilii Erklärung des kleinen Lutherschen Katechismus; übersetzt von Fjällström. Neueste Auflage 1779.

6. Das Gesang- und Evangelienbuch; übersetzt von Fjällström. Neueste Auflage 1806 *).

7. Gütner's (Deutsche) Postille, aus der Schwedischen Uebersetzung ins Lappische übersetzt von Högström. Högström schloß alles Polemische aus und fügte einige Predigten hinzu.

Der Unterricht wird in Lappischer Sprache ertheilt. Zur Erlernung der Schwedischen Sprache erhalten die Zöglinge in der Schule keine Anleitung, indeß werden sie mit dem Schwedischen zuweilen als Weidelappen, im Dienste der Schweden, bekannt.

Der, Allen gemeinsame, Unterricht besteht ausschließlich im Lesen und im Christenthum. Am Sonntag Morgen stehen sie etwas später, wie gewöhnlich, auf, und gehen, nachdem mit ihnen noch einmal das schon am Sonnabend Mittag erklärte Evangelium ist durchgegangen worden, in Begleitung des Lehrers, zur Kirche. Da hier aber gewöhnlich Schwedisch geprediget wird und Kinder diese Sprache gar nicht oder wenig verstehen, so wird mit ihnen am Sonntag Nachmittag, eine Stunde lang, die Lappische Postille gelesen. An den Abenden des Sonnabends und des Sonntags wird mit ihnen Gebet gehalten, welches mit Gesang beginnt und schließt: ein Zögling lieset das Gebet, während alle übrigen knieen. Ich wohnte dem Abendgebet am Sonnabend bei, auch die Weidelappin auf dem Hofe kam herzu und stellte sich mit den Kindern in Eine Reihe, über welche sie, wiewohl 30 Jahre alt, nicht hervorragte: die große Andacht der

_____

*) Die erste Auflage erschien 1744; die 2te 1786 ꝛc.; an den verschiedenen Auflagen haben mitgearbeitet: Högström, Holmbow, Propst und Pastor Erik Lindahl in Lycksele, Pastor Johann Lestadius in Arjeplog, Bernhard Aß, welcher 40 Jahre lang Schulmeister in Lycksele war, Pastor Pehr Edin in Arfvidsjaur, Pastor Samuel Öhrling in Jeckmod.

Lappen war unverkennbar. Nach dem letzten Gesange schieden die Lappen mit stillem Gebet und gingen, ihre Schlafstätte zu bereiten. Auch Tischgebete sind üblich, bei denen ich gleichfalls am Sonnabend zugegen war.

Jährlich, im Januar, zur Marktzeit, wird ein Schulexamen gehalten, welches mit Gesang beginnt und mit Ermahnungsrede, Segen und Gesang schließt; hier geschieht auch die Entlassung aus der Schule. Auch eine Visitation findet Statt, gewöhnlich durch den Pastor.

Die Schule hat ein Buch, in welches die Namen der Schulkinder eingezeichnet werden: bei jedem Namen wird der Befund beim Examen ıc. eingeschrieben; auch Schule und Kirche betreffende Ereignisse findet man in diesem Buche verzeichnet.

Die Tracht der Lappischen Knaben und Mädchen ist, wie überhaupt beider Lappischer Geschlechter, sehr ähnlich; die einen wie die anderen tragen gewöhnlich drei Ueberröcke über einander, die der Mädchen heißen mit Schwedischen Wörtern Kjortel, die der Knaben Kolt; sie sind völlig gleich; nur ist der Rock der Mädchen mit, der der Knaben ohne Kragen; die Röcke der Mädchen und Knaben sind ferner ganz die der Erwachsenen. Außer dem Kolt erhalten die Knaben jährlich ein Paar lange Beinkleider; auch, gleich den Mädchen, ein Paar Schuhe; statt der Strümpfe tragen Knaben und Mädchen in den Schuhen feines und weiches Alpengras (Riedgras, Carex); zur Sammlung dieses Grases haben sie 8 Tage im Herbste frei. Den Winterpelz müssen sie sich selber anschaffen. Die Mützen der Männer sind mehr rund als die der Weiber, welche spitziger sind; auch tragen die Männer an ihren Kleidern nicht so viel Schimmerndes, als die Weiber.

Die Kirche lag früherhin weiter aufwärts, auf einem Wiesenhügel an einer afva oder Bucht des Umeå, der hier aber oft so sehr überschwemmte, daß man nur auf Böten zur umflossenen Kirche gelangen konnte. An einem schönen Abend besuchte ich den alten Kirchplatz: Fluß, Wiesen, Wald und Berge bilden eine freundliche Umgebung. Wo noch vor etwa 10 Jahren die Kirche stand, trifft man jetzt nicht blos Gebüsche, sondern mannes-hohe Bäume; das alte Beinhaus bewahrte die Kanzel und einige andere Ueberbleibsel der alten Kirche; außerdem war nichts als ein Paar Kirchstuben und einige Marktbuden übrig. Die alte Kirche war auch zu klein im Verhältniß zur vermehrten Menschenzahl; eben so der Kirchhof und der Platz für die Kirchstuben. Die neue Kirche, welche in den Jahren 1796—99 erbauet wurde, ist größer, und hat eine vortheilhafte Lage auf einer Anhöhe, in beträchtlicher Entfernung vom Flusse. Sie ist ganz von Holz, Kreuzkirche, und ohne Orgel; die hübsche, mit den Gesetzestafeln und, über denselben, einem vergoldeten Kreuz, gleichsam als jene vernichtend, einfach verzierte Kanzel ist, wie gewöhnlich, zur Seite angebracht; die Hauptthüre führt gerade auf den Altar zu, welchen ein ziemlich gutgerathenes Bild: „der Erlöser am Kreuz," von einem Bruder des um Lappland viel verdienten Propstes Pehr Fjällström, schmückt. An den Wänden der Kirche hängen die Bilder des genannten Propstes und des Schullehrers Ask. Die Sakristey ist geräumig und hell, und enthält die kleine Kirchenbibliothek. Der Bau der Kirche kostet 3489 Rthlr. Riksgäld, zu welcher Summe aus dem Lappenfond nur 1000 Rthlr beigetragen wurden. Die Kirche ist licht und freundlich. Vom Kirchthurm, in welchem die Glocken hängen, hat man eine sehr schöne Aussicht: hohe Waldberge umher, deren Fuß zum Theil Getraidefelder schmücken; im Hintergrunde blauende Gebirge, doch keine Gletscher, die nicht sichtbar sind; mitten durch die schöne Landschaft schlängelt sich der Umeå Elf in vielfachen Krümmungen, und der Hellefors verbreitet ein furchtbares Getöse. In der Nähe der Kirche, im Südwest, ist der Finnenhügel (finnbacke), wo einst Finnen wohnten, jetzt aber die hübsche Wohnung des Länsman, mehrere Schwedische Kirchstuben und Lappische Kirchhütten stehen; in kleiner Entfernung findet man wiederum Kirchstuben und das Tingshaus mit den Gefängnissen; weiterhin ist der Borgareplats (Bürgerplatz) mit den Marktbuden und Lappischen Kirchhütten; dann folgt der sogenannte Hafen (hamnen), wo nichts als Kirchstuben stehen. Das eigentliche Dorf liegt im Nordost der Kirche, in geringer Entfernung von derselben; da wohnen der Pastor, der Schulmeister, der Küster, der sich auch in der Nähe der Kirchstuben am Waldsaume ein kleines Nybygge angelegt hat ꝛc. Hinter den Häusern sind hübsche kleine Küchengärten eingerichtet. Auch auf den genannten Plätzen trifft man einige Wohnhäuser; so wohnt z. B. auf dem Bürgerplatz der Kaufmann Eriksson, zwischen den Kirchstuben der Fjerdingsman (Gehülfe des Länsman zu geringeren Diensten). Die Kirchstuben sind unbewohnt, bis auf zwei, in welchen Wittwen wohnen; die meisten sind gemeinsames Eigenthum mehrerer Familien.

Am Sonntag Morgen besuchte ich den Gottesdienst in der Kirche von Lycksele. Um 8 Uhr ward zum ersten Mal geläutet; beim zweiten Läuten, um 9 Uhr, begann die Beichte, bei welcher einzelne bis zu Thränen gerührt wurden. Nach geendigter Beichte folgte ein abermaliges Läuten, worauf der eigentliche Gottesdienst, ganz nach Schwedischen Kirchengebräuchen und in Schwedischer Sprache, seinen Anfang nahm. Sanft und lieblich ward gesungen, und große Andacht herrschte; am Schluß ward das heil. Abendmahl gefeiert. Wie man es oft in Schweden findet, so waren auch hier kleine Kinder anwesend, die aber die allgemeine Stille nicht unterbrachen. Die Zahl der Communicanten war heute nur geringe; zuweilen sind derselben 200 bis 300, wiewohl die Seelenzahl nur 900 beträgt. Die weiblichen Communicanten gingen in schwarzwollenen Kleidern, einige der übrigen Frauenzimmer waren in Cattun gekleidet; an hohen Festen trägt man schwarzseidene Kleider; die Mützen waren, ganz nach Westerbottnischer Weise, gestickt, und vorne ausgeschnitten, über sie war ein Tuch gebunden. Freilich gilt dieß alles nur von den Schweden; Lappen sind gewöhnlich, außer den wenigen in Lycksele, nicht zugegen; auch heute war beim Gottesdienst die Zahl der anwesenden Lappen sehr klein.

Auch die Kirchstuben und Kirchhütten nahm ich in Augenschein. In den Kirchbuden ist alles ganz häuslich eingerichtet, wie in den Wohngebäuden; die Bettstellen sind mit Schränken versehen; die Sonn und Festtagskleider hängen an den Wänden. Zwischen den Kirchbuden sind Pferdeställe errichtet, die freilich nur im Winter gebraucht werden, weil es nur dann Fahr wege giebt, im Sommer aber selbst Reitwege selten sind; Buden für Lebensmittel, die in den Marktzeiten auch zu Waarenlagern dienen, und deren auch die Lappen haben ꝛc. Die Kirchstuben sind ziemlich zahlreich, und bilden ordentliche Gassen, an welchen man auch Brunnen findet.

Die Lappischen Kirchhütten oder Koten, die von den Lappen, wenn sie zur Kirche und zu Markte kommen, bewohnt werden, stehen in drei Abtheilungen, in kleinen Entfernungen von dem Kirchplatz. Sie sind von Schweden erbauet: die größeren weichen in einigen Stücken von den Hütten der nomadisirenden Lappen ab, indem sie zwar die cylindrische Form der ächten Lappenhütten haben, aber von Brettern erbauet sind, und die hintere und vordere Seite, anstatt aus schrägen Brettern zu bestehen, bis zum Dache gerade aufgezimmert; während die ächten Lappen-Koten auf bloßer Erde oder auf Einem aufrechtstehenden Brette ruhen, ruhen die Kirchhütten auf mehreren aufrechtstehenden Brettern, weßhalb der Eingang oft so hoch liegt, daß man sich eines Trittes bedienen muß. Andere Hütten sind mehr auf die gewöhnliche Weise eingerichtet. Alle haben, in der Spitze, ein offenes Rauchloch (die Hütten der Vornehmeren haben auch Räuchlöcher an den Seiten), das gerade auf den, von kleinen Steinen umgebenen, Feuerheerd führt, der sich in der Mitte der Hütte befindet. Ueber dem Heerd ist ein Stock befestiget, an welchen man den Kessel hängt; um den Heerd herum bis zu den Wänden der Hütte sind Reiser ausgebreitet, auf welchen die Lappen am Tage mit untergeschlagenen Beinen sitzen und in der Nacht, über Rennthierfellen, liegen; als Kopfkissen dient ein Kästchen oder Felle. In den Ecken werden die schrägen Bretter durch Stäbe zusammengehalten; die Bretter selbst sind mit Birkenrinde bekleidet, über welcher Stäbe von Fichtenholz befestiget sind. Durch kleine, mit Thüren versehene, Löcher steigt man in die durchräucherten Kegelhütten, ganz wie sonst bei Lappenkoten. In einigen Hütten sind zwischen den Brettern kleine Schränke zum Aufbewahren von allerlei Sachen angebracht, oder in der Hütte ist ein Brett zu gleichem Zweck befestiget; beides, wie die Bretterhütten selbst, sind nicht Lappisch: die Lappen bauen in der Regel nur mit Birken- oder Gränstäben. Hinter den Koten trifft man viereckige Böden zur Aufbewahrung von Lebensmitteln und Marktwaaren, sie ruhen auf 6 Stützen. Auch die Lappen auf den Fjällen haben dergleichen Vorrathsböden, die aber dort nur auf einem Pfahl in der Mitte ruhen; diese erhöhte Bauart soll den Vielfraß abhalten. — Die vornehmeren Lappen haben keine Koten, sondern ordentliche Kirchenstuben nach Schwedischer Weise mit Fenstern und Bettstellen.

In einigen Koten fand ich Lappische Achzien (kein Lappisches Wort) oder Schlitten, Kerez von den Lappen genannt. Die Schlitten sind an den Seiten rund, sehr schmal, kaum eine halbe Elle hoch; sie sind aus 6 Brettern zusammengesetzt, die die ganze Länge des Schlittens haben; auf dem Boden mit doppelten Brettern versehen; vorne lauten sie in einen spitzigen Kiel aus, im Hintertheile haben sie ein aufrechtstehendes Brett, welches zur Rücklehne des Fahrenden dient. Die Breite und Länge der Schlitten ist verschieden: die Frauenzimmerschlitten sind nur ⅓ Elle breit und 2¾ Ellen lang; die für Männer und zum Waarentransport bestimmten sind länger. Eine Achzie, welche wir in einer Kote fanden, war ¾ Ellen breit und 3¼ Ellen lang. Die Höhe der Achzien beträgt etwa eine halbe Elle. Die Stelle der Schienen (medar) vertritt ein breiter Kiel unter der Achzie.

In der, auf Schwedische Weise eingerichteten, Hütte eines Lappischen Länsman wohnte eine alte Lappin, die ihre Jahre nicht mehr zählen konnte; sie begleitete uns in eine gewöhnliche Lappenhütte, setzte sich dort, auf Lappische Art, am Heerde nieder und sang eine Lappische Weise, die freilich nichts weniger als wohlklingend war. Schon vorher hatte sie erzählt (sie sprach nämlich Schwedisch), wie sie für eine große Summe (sie nannte dieselbe) von ihrem Manne gekauft worden sey; wie sie einen Sohn geboren, von dem sie seit langen Jahren nichts gehört; bald hielt sie ihn verloren (er war wirklich ertrunken), bald hoffte sie, sie werde ihn wiedersehen; an mir glaubte sie Aehnlichkeit mit ihrem Sohne zu entdecken; das von den Blattern so furchtbar entstellte Mädchen in Tuggensele war ihre Tochter.

II.   Q

Die Lappin hatte jetzt ein Stückchen Kartoffelland bepflanzt, auch ein Kornäckerchen bebaut: das eine dieser Landstücke gehörte der unglücklichen Tochter, die eine vorzügliche Stiefelnäherin ist. Beim Weggange sandte ich der Lappin eine Plate nach, und so lange ihre Augen uns sahen, ließ sie nun Dank- und Freuden-lieder erschallen.

Bei der Kirche Lycksele findet man, außer den Schulkindern, nur einige arme Lappen, insbesondere Weidelappen. Eine der-selben, ein 19jähriges Mädchen, das früher die Schule besucht hatte und jetzt auf dem Pfarrhofe als Weidelappin diente, Chri-stina Pehrsdotter, auf den Fjällen geboren, erschien, auf meinen Wunsch, in ihrer Sonntagstracht: der grobtuchene Ober-rock, ohne Knöpfe, ist mit rothem Bande umfaßt; unter demsel-ben eine Art von Spenzer, åchzebella genannt, von blauem oder rothem Walmar, mit kleinen silbernen Schildern und anderen Zierrathen versehen, als Brustlatz; beide Gewänder können zu-gemacht werden. Dann folgt die bungalapp, die, bei Männern und Weibern, die Stelle des Hemdes vertritt. An die bunga-lapp, die nur bis zum Gürtel reicht, schließt sich, unten, ein an-deres Walmargewand, die wuallah. An den Kragen der ver-schiedenen Gewänder erblickt man allerlei silberne (bei den Aer-meren zinnene) Zierrathen. Der Gürtel besteht aus Rennthier-leder und geflochtenen Rennthiersehnen, am Gürtel hängen aller-lei zinnener Schmuck, Glaskorallen ꝛc., ferner ein Ring mit einer Scheere im Futteral, mit Fingerhut, Nadelbüchse, auch ein ledernes Beutelchen, das, selber mit kleinen Ringen geziert, einen Löffel aus Rennthierhorn enthält. Das Mädchen trug auch Strümpfe, die sonst bei den Lappen nicht üblich sind, von Wolle, und über den Strümpfen Pjeror, eine Art von Schnürstiefeln. Christina Pehrsdotter war freundlich, sanft, schön, und doch soll es noch viel schönere Lappenmädchen geben; in neuester Zeit sind die Lappen schöner wie vorher. Keinesweges ist die Gesichts-farbe der Lappen immer schmuzig gelb; oft ist sie es freilich, aber nur als Folge des Aufenthalts in den Rauchhütten; denn wenn die Lappen auf den Fjällen im Sommer umherziehen, zeigt sich an ihnen wenig von der gelben Farbe. Herr Rädſtröm, der zugegen war und das Mädchen früher unterrichtet hatte, legte ihr einige Chriſtenthumsfragen vor, die ſie eben ſo richtig, als mit Ernſt und Herzlichkeit, beantwortete.

Die Witterung begünſtigte mich ſehr während meines Aufenthalts in Lyckſele. Zwar war die Hitze am größten Theil des Tages gewöhnlich drückend; aber milde und lieblich waren der Morgen und der Abend: zahlloſe Vögel ſangen in der ſtillen Luft. Da ſpazierte ich in lieber Geſellſchaft, freute mich der ſchönen Gegend und horchte, ſtaunend, dem Donner der gewaltigen Katarakte Helleforß, deren Getöſe, wenn der Wind im Begriff iſt, ſüdweſtlich zu gehen, am ſtärkſten ſeyn ſoll; Vergißmeinnicht und andere ſchöne Blumen ſchmückten die Wieſen, und fröhlich reiften die Saaten der nahen Erndte entgegen; nur einzelne Acker- und Wieſenſtriche waren von der Sonnenhitze verſengt; und gar lieblich zeigten ſich, auf den Anhöhen, die Wieſen- und Waldufer des nahen Umeå-Elf. Wie in ſüdliche Zonen glaubt man ſich gezaubert. Die trefflichen Weiden erhöhen den Ertrag der Viehzucht gar ſehr, die Milch iſt beſonders fett, und die mancherlei Speiſen, die man hier mit Sahne bereitet, haben einen vorzüglichen Geſchmack. Die Gewäſſer enthalten eine große Mannigfaltigkeit von Fiſchen, unter welchen die Löja (Blüte Cyprinus alburnus), an Milde und Lieblichkeit des Fleiſches, ſelbſt die Forelle hinter ſich läßt. Fiſcherei wird, wie in vielen Gegenden Nordſchwedens, auch von Honoratioren, zum Vergnügen eigenhändig betrieben; jeder Haushalt fiſcht, ſo viel er bedarf, ſelbſt. — Die ſchönſten Beeren hat man im Ueberfluß; aus einigen bereitet man Wein, z. B. aus Himbeeren (hallon) eine Art von Wein, der einen pikanten, aromatiſchen Geſchmack hat, doch vom Åkerbärwein übertroffen wird. Gartengewächſe aller Art gedeihen; ſo aß ich Spinat, Salat ꝛc.; die Erbſen blühten noch. Åkerbär waren noch nicht reif. Die Wohnungen ſind recht freundlich eingerichtet und an Bequemlichkeit mangelt es nicht; die Wände ſchmücken nicht ſelten hübſche Kupferſtiche und Gemälde, unter denen mich insbeſondere die Gemälde auf Marienglas, welche Gegenſtände aus der heiligen Geſchichte darſtellen, intereſſirten.

Ω =

Abgeschieden von der Welt ist man hier keineswegs: man hat Posten nach Westerbotten und den andern Lappmarken (während meiner Anwesenheit kam die Fußpost von Arjeplog); man liefet Stockholmer Zeitungen, und hat Lesebücher aus der Leihbibliothek in Umeå: Kotzebues (ins Schwedische übersetzte) Reisen fand ich in Lyckfele. Vor ein Paar Jahren lieferte der Kronobefallningsman Lindahl, auf Verlangen der Behörde, einen Plan zur Anlegung einer Reitpost von Lyckfele nach Norwegen ein: sie sollte von Lyckfele nach Sorfele, von da auf dem Windel-Elf bis an den Fuß der Alpen und über dieselben, die auf der Höhe meist ebene Rücken bilden, bis Salten in Norwegen gehen; der Weg ist nur beim Aufsteigen zu den Alpen etwas beschwerlich; an vielen Stellen könnten, da ein großer Theil des Weges wenig bewohnt ist, Postbauern angesiedelt werden. Im J. 1822. hat man einen Postenlauf vom Torneå aus nach dem nördlichsten Norwegen eröffnet. (S. Kap. 20).

Drei und zwanzigstes Kapitel.

Lappland und seine Bewohner.

A. Schwedisches Lappland und seine Bewohner im Allgemeinen:

   a. Kirchliche Verhältnisse; Lappische Sprache.

   b. Juridische, administrative, commercielle Verhältnisse.

   c. Ausdehnung, Klima, Boden, Natur- und Kunstprodukte.

   d. Bewohner: Lappen, Schweden, Finnen.

B. Spezialbeschreibung der einzelnen Schwedischen Lappmarken.

C. Das Norwegische, das Alt-Russische und das Neu-Russische (Finnische) Lappland.

A. Schwedisches Lappland und seine Bewohner im Allgemeinen.

   a. Kirchliche Verhältnisse; Lappische Sprache.

Lange herrschte unter den Lappen die dichteste Finsterniß des Heidenthums. Außer einem höchsten guten Gott (Jub-

mel, Gott) und einem höchsten bösen Gott (Pårkel, Teu-
fel) verehrten sie eine Menge niederer Gottheiten; die Einzelnen beteten in heiligen Steinen, Bäumen, geschnitzten Bildern ꝛc. ihre Schutzgötter an, vor welchen, eben so wie auf
Bergen, man opferte, oder vor welchen man Weihgeschenke nie-
derlegte. *)

Auch nachdem das Christenthum unter den Lappen bekannt
geworden war, dauerte noch lange, neben demselben, das Heidenthum fort; selbst als schon christliche Kirchen in Lappland gegründet waren, erhielten sich heidnische Gebräuche und Meinungen. Nur sehr allmählig gelang es, diese zu tilgen. Jetzt
sind, wenigstens seit mehreren Jahrzehnten, auch die letzten Ueberbleibsel heidnischen Aberglaubens aus dem Schwedischen Lappland geschwunden, und die Lappen erfreuen sich, im Allgemeinen, einer hohen Stufe lauterer christlicher Erkenntniß und echt
christlichen Wandels; zwar pflanzen sich auch heute noch die Ue-
berlieferungen der alten Zeit fort, aber man setzt auf dieselben
wenig Werth. In den, im J. 1809 an Rußland abgetretenen,
östlichen oder Finnischen Lappmarken sind die Verhältnisse in dieser Hinsicht fast gleich, unter den Norwegischen Lappen ähnlich,
wenn gleich das Kirchenwesen dort viel zu wünschen übrig läßt.
Im Alt-Russischen Lappland giebt es noch Heiden; die dort zum Christenthum bekehrten Lappen sind dem Griechi-

---

*) Die gegenwärtige Abhandlung hat vorzugsweise die Beschreibung
Lapplands, wie es jetzt ist, zum Gegenstande. Nur diese kurzen allgemeinen Bemerkungen über das Heidenthum der Lappen durften daher
hier Platz finden. Freilich liegt vieles, was sich auf die Religion der
heidnischen Lappen bezieht, noch sehr im Dunkeln. Das Meiste und
Zuverläßigste findet man in Högström Beschreibung von Lappland;
aus dem Schwed. übers. Copenh. und Leipz. 1748. Kap. 2. §. 18 —
20. und Kap. 11. und in Knud Leem, von den Lappen in Finnmarken. Aus dem Dänischen von Gunner. Leipz. 1771. Kap. 19. — Vergl.
auch Mone Geschichte des Heidenthums im nördlichen Europa. Th. 1.
Darmst. 1822. S. 21 — 42.

schen Bekenntniß zugethan. Alle übrigen, östlichen, westlichen, südlichen, Finnischen, Schwedischen und Norwegischen Lappen bekennen die evangelisch-lutherische Religion, eben weil die Bekehrungen von Schweden und Norwegen aus geschahen. Von der Bekehrung der Norwegischen Lappen wird unter der Ueberschrift „Norwegisches Lappland" geredet werden. Hier nur von den Bekehrungen, die von Schweden aus geleitet wurden.

Bereits zu katholischen Zeiten machte man Versuche, christliches Bekenntniß und christlichen Kultus, oder das, was man damals so nannte, unter den Lappen einzuführen; es läßt sich aber nicht bestimmen, wann und mit welchem Erfolge solches geschah, vielleicht schon, als im 13ten Jahrhundert, unter König Magnus Ladulås, durch Betrieb der unter dem Namen „Birkarlar" berühmten mächtigen Nordischen Kaufleute, Lappland an Schweden kam. Es konnte wenigstens nicht fehlen, daß der Handel, den die Lappen mit Schweden und Norwegern trieben, sie allmählig auch mit dem Christenthum bekannter machte, wenn gleich man die Birkarlar beschuldigt, daß sie aus Eigennutz der Bekehrung der Lappen Hindernisse in den Weg legten. Erwiesen ist es, daß katholische Geistliche nahe gelegener Pfarreien zu gewissen Zeiten Reisen in Lappland anstellten, um die bereits Bekehrten im Christenthume zu stärken und zu befestigen und ihre Zahl zu mehren. Doch scheinen diese Bekehrten in der That mehr Heiden geblieben als Christen geworden zu seyn.

Endlich brach auch über Lappland das volle Licht des Evangeliums an. Seit in Schweden das evangelische Bekenntniß eingeführt und befestigt wurde, dachte man auch schon daran, es in Lappland zu verbreiten. Gustav I., dieser große König, sandte christliche Lehrer in die Lappmarken; Geistliche benachbarter Kirchspiele begaben sich, zu bestimmten Jahreszeiten, namentlich im Winter zur Marktzeit, wo man die Lappen versammelt fand, nach diesen öden Gegenden, um das Amt der christlichen Liebe durch Lehre und Ermunterung zu üben, mußten sich aber dabei der Dolmetscher bedienen. — Um das J. 1600 ließ König Carl IX. in Lappland Kirchen bauen. Auch Stipen= dien für studirende Lappische Jünglinge wurden zu Upsala ge= stiftet.

Anfangs waren die neuen Lappischen Kirchen Filiale der am wenigsten entlegenen Schwedischen Pastorate. Königin Christina aber stellte Geistliche an, die neben den Kirchen wohnen sollten, und richtete damit feste Lappische Pastorate ein; auch die Zahl der Kirchen ward jetzt und späterhin vermehrt. Die Geist= lichen mußten Lappisch verstehen, und ward ihnen, nach einer gewissen Zeit, Beförderung zu besseren Stellen außerhalb Lapp= land verheißen. — Von nun an wurde regelmäßiger Gottes= dienst gehalten.

Die erste Schule für Lappenkinder gründete Gustav Adolph der Große 1619, zu Piteå, von wo sie 1632 nach Lycksele ver= legt und durch des Reichsraths Johann Skytte Donation erwei= tert und verbessert wurde; Königin Christina schenkte dieser Schule Kronkorn und andere Einkünfte. Carl XI. erhöhte die Lappischen Stipendien und vermehrte, gleich anderen seiner Nach= folger, die Lappischen Pastorate. König Friedrich I. stiftete bei den meisten Mutterkirchen Schulen.

Im J. 1739 ward eine Direktion für das Kirchenwesen in Lappland (Direction för Ecclesiastique-Verket i Lapp- marken) niedergesetzt; sie verwaltete die öffentlichen Fonds, aus welchen Kirchen und Schulen unterhalten und Lehrer besoldet wurden, und leitete alle kirchlichen Angelegenheiten Lapplands. Jetzt ist diese Direction erloschen, und werden die früheren Ge= schäfte derselben von der Königl. Kanzleiverwaltung (Canzlisty- relse) besorgt. — Der Lappenfond entstand durch Einsammlun= gen vor 1739, und durch eine Hufenanlage über das ganze Reich 1738. Auch Kronkorn ist den Lappischen Kirchen und Schulen bewilligt worden. Bei der ersten Einrichtung wurden die Lappischen Eltern, welche ihre Kinder zur Schule schickten, beschenkt.

Seit die Lappischen Geistlichen sich nicht mehr der Dolmet= metscher bedienten, waren eine Lappische Bibel und andere kirchliche Bücher in Lappischer Sprache unentbehrlich. Bereits

Guſtav II. Adolph ließ für dieſen Zweck Ueberſetzungen ins Lappiſche veranſtalten. Häufiger geſchah es ſeit 1733, der Druck
ward auf öffentliche Koſten veranſtaltet. Durch Herausgabe ſol-
cher Schriften erwarben ſich im vorigen Jahrhunderte insbeſondere Pehr Fjällſtröm, zuerſt Schulmeiſter, dann Paſtor
und Probſt in Lyckſele (1739 — 1764), und Pehr Högſtröm, Paſtor in Gellivare, und dann Paſtor und Probſt in
Skellefteå († 1784) große Verdienſte. Auf dieſe Weiſe hat
man jetzt das Neue Teſtament, die kirchliche Liturgie, das kirchliche Geſang- und Evangelienbuch, Luthers kleinen Catechismus
nebſt Svebilii Erläuterung deſſelben und andern Catechismen
und A. B. C. Büchern, in Lappiſcher Sprache, wenn gleich
an Exemplaren des A. B. C. Buchs und des kleinen Lutheri-
ſchen Catechismus im J. 1816 Mangel war. Mit der Ueberſetzung des Alten Teſtaments ins Lappiſche hatte man bereits früher den Anfang gemacht. *)

———————

*) Es dürfte nicht unintereſſant ſeyn, hier mehrere in Lappi-
ſcher Sprache verfaßte kirchliche und religiöſe Schriften, ſo wie einige Schriften über (meiſt Schwediſches) Lappland und Lappiſche Sprache, ſo weit ſie beſonders dem Norden angehören, kennen zu lernen.
Ich nenne meiſt nach Schwed. Titeln:
Nicolai Andreae (Paſt. in Pileå), en liten ſångebok, huru Meſ-
ſan ſkall hållas, läſas aller ſjungas (ein kleines Singebuch, wie die
Meſſe gehalten, geleſen oder geſungen werden ſoll). Stockh. 1619.
8. (1. Meſſe. 2. Lobgeſang und Pſalmen. 3. Taufe. 4. Trauung.
5. Kirchliche Einſegnung der Wöchnerinnen. 6. Begräbniß).
Nicolai Andreae A. B. C. Bok. Stockh. 1619.
Mag. To. I. Tornaei, Paſt. et Praepos. Tornensis, Manuale Lapponicum,
continens Pſalterium Davidis, Proverbia Salomonis, Ecclesiasten,
librum Syracidis, Catechismum Lutheri, Rituale Ecclesiasticum,
Pericopas Evangeliorum et Epistolarum Dominicalium et Festivali-
um (cum praemissis Collectis et subjunctis precatiunculis), Histo-
riam Passionis Christi et vastationis urbis Hierosol., Hymnos ſa-
cros et Preces solemnes, lingua Lapponica. Stockh. 1648. 8.
A. B. C. Bok, Lappiſch und Schwediſch. Stockh. 1667. 8.
Olof Graan, Pith. Praepos. et Paſt., Lutheri Catechesis, nqli-

Das Schwediſche Lappland, zum Stifte Hernöſand gehörig, zerfällt in Paſtorate, welche Contractspröpſten in Weſterbotten, Angermanland und Jemteland untergeordnet ſind. Biſchof und Domkapitel in Hernöſand führen die unmittelbare Verwaltung

---

gen på Lappſta ſpråket uthſatt och uthtålkat, ſåſom Lappſockot för denna tiden naturligen och klarligen talar uti Pitheå och Luleå Lappmarker (in dem Lappiſchen Dialekt von Piteå und Luleå Lappmark). Stockh. 1667?) Lappiſch und Schwediſch.

Olof Graan, Korta och enfaldige ſpörsmål öfver Catechiſmum (Kurze und einfältige Catechiſmusfragen), lämpade til ungdomens förkofring i Chriſtendomen, enkannerligen ſammanfattade för Pitheå och Luleå Lappmarker, ſamt medh flijth deraß egit ſpråk bjfegat. (im Dialect von Piteå und Luleå Lappmark). Stockh. 1667. 8.

Olof Stephan Graan (Paſtor in Lyckſele) Enfaldige och kårta frågor ſampt ſvar aff Theſauro catechetico ſammanhåmtade för Lapparnes ungdom, uti Lyckſele Umeå Lappmark, på Lappeſſa tungomålet förvåndt och ſammanfattat, af — Graan, verb. div. Comminiſtro, p. t. Paedagogo (dann Paſt. in Lyckſele). Stockh. 1668. 8. (Catechiſmus für die Jugend in Lyckſele).

Ol. Steph. Graan Manuale Lapponicum minus, ubi agenda ecclesiastica et omnia quae supra in Manuali Tornaei, exceptis libris biblicis. In usum Lapponum Markiae Umensis. Stockholm. 1669.

Liber abecedarius Lapponico-Suethicus. Stockh. 1726. 8.

Catechismus minor b. Marth. Lutheri Lapponico – Suethicus. Stockh. 1726. 12.

Andr. Alenius (Paſtor in Arfvidsjaur) Gallegagie Chriſtenhwoten hiettielwaſeh je waſtezeh, nuitehwoten ankan diet diſetalletum miſſionariaſt Andr. Alenio, Angerm. Kongalagie majeſtaten Koſtademan. d. i. Einige Chriſtenthumsfragen und Antworten, zum Dienſt der Jugend herausgegeben auf Koſten des Königes, vom Miſſionar Andr. A. aus Engermanland. Stockh. 1742. 8. Dieſer Catechiſmus, den ich in Lyckſele ſah, iſt für die Lappen unlesbar, da er der nothwendigen Berückſichtigung der Dialecte ermangelt.

Pehr Fjällſtröm, Ol. Svebilii Catecheſen Fjålgeſtem Katjelwaſi ja raſtaduſi pafti d. i. Ol. Svebilii Erläuterung des kleinen Catechiſmus Luth. ohne Bibelſprüche. 1738. mit Bibelſprüchen 1775. 12. — 1779.

des Lappischen Kirchen- und Schulwesens, unter Oberaufsicht der
Königl. Kanzleiverwaltung (kantsliftyrelse) in Stockholm, an
welche das Domkapitel den Ertrag der jährlichen Collecten ein-
zusenden hat, auch von den Beschlüssen des Domkapitels appellirt werden kann.

Pehr Fjällström, A. B. C. Buch Lappisch. Stockh. 1744. 8.
Stockh. 1779. 8. von Grönlund und Grape. 1804.

Pehr Fjällström, Dr. Mart. Lutheri Urriel Catechismus (Kleiner
Catech. Luth). Stockh. 1744. 16. Upsala 1761. Hernösand 1807.

Pehr Fjällström, Psalm-Kirje ꝛc. d. i. kirchliches Gesang- und
kirchliches Evangelienbuch (Perikopen, Collecten, Gebete, Leidensgeschichte). Stockh. 1744. 8. 1786. 1806.

Pehr Fjällström, Gudt-Kirje ꝛc. d. i. Kirchenhandbuch. Stockh. 1744.
8. — Die neue Kirchenagende von 1811. ward 1812. ins Lappische
übersetzt und sofort kirchlich gebraucht.

Pehr Fjällström, Jtde Testament, same Kiäll puoktetum d. i. das
Neue Testament, auf Lappisch. Stockh. 1755. 8. Hernösand 1811.

Die Fjällströmschen Uebersetzungen sind besonders brauchbar, weil
sie in einem Mitteldialect geschrieben sind, den fast alle Lappen verstehen; sie wurden von den Pastoren der verschiedenen Lappmarken rücksichtlich der Sprache revidirt.

Pehr Högström, Catechismus, Katjelvasi ja Wastadusi pakti (Cate-
chismusfragen und Antworten.) Stockh. 1748. 8. 1779. 12.

Pehr Högström, Tat rektesjalfoles Christendom ꝛc. d. i. Gabr.
Gütner Postille (das rechtgläubige Christenthum); aus der Schwedischen Uebersetzung in einen Lappischen Auszug gebracht, und hier und
da geändert. Stockh. 1748. 4.

Zelus regum septentrionalium in convertendis Lappis. Praes. And.
Grönwall, resp. And. Svedelius Upsal. 1721.

G. Tzderi und Thom. von Westen zwei Berichte über die Bekehrung der
Lappen. Stockh. 1773. 8. mit literarischer Vorrede von Lönbom.
Vergl. Jöran Wallin, Acta literar. Sueciae. 1728. S. 474. ff.
(Verzeichniß Lappischer kirchlicher und religiöser Schriften); Porthan
historia bibliothecae Aboensis. S. 351 — 355. Alenii diss. acad.
statum politices et religionis in Lapponia Pitensi praesentem de-
lineatura. 1769. — Warmholz, bibliotheca Sueogothica. Bd. 1. S.

Das Lappiſche Kirchenweſen iſt ganz wie in Schweden eins gerichtet, ſo weit es nur irgend die Localität geſtattet; ſelbſt die wichtigen Hausverhöre werden mit den Koloniſten wie mit den Lappen an den meiſten Orten gehalten: **) man nennt ſie

---

252 — 274. Lönbom's Vorrede zu Joh. Tornaei Beſchreibung von Ternäs und Kemi Lappmarker. Stockh. 1772. 8.

Ioann. Schefferi Lapponia, seu gentis regionisque Lapponum descriptio accurata cum fig. Francof. 1673. 4.

O. Petri Njurenii descriptio Lapponiae (Mſpt. auf der Univerf. Bibl. zu Upſala).

Io. Renhorn de origine Lapponum. Mſpt.

Rhen, descriptio Lapponiae.

Damiani a Goës, Equit. Lusitani, Deploratio Lappianae gentis et Lappiae descriptio. 1500.

Olavi Rudbeckii, filii, Nora Samolad, sivo Lapponia illustrata eto. Ups. 1701. unvollendet.

I. E. Askii diſſ. de urbe Uma et adjacentibus paroeciis. Praes. F. Törner. Ups. 1731. 4.

P. Steckseuii Graan diſſ. do urbe Pitovia et adjacentibus paroeciis. Praes. F. Törner. Ups. 1731. 4.

N. Hackzell diſſ. do urbe Lula ejusque paroeciis Praes. Jo. Hermansson. Ups. 1731. 4.

C. Brunnii diſſ. do urbe Torna ejusque adjacentibus paroeciis. Praes. Er. Aestrin. Ups. 1731. 4.

I. D. Steckseuii diſſ. do Westrobottnia. Praes. F. Törner. Ups. 1734. 4.

P. N. Matthesii diſſ. do Ostrobottnia. Praes. F. Törner. Ups. 1734. 4.

C. Linnaei, Flora Lapponica. Amst. 1737.

Ehrenmalm Refa genom Weſternorrland til Åfele Lappmark. Stockh. 1743.

Högſtröm, Beſkrifning öfver de til Sveriges krona lydande Lappmarker. Stockh. 1747. 8. (Beſchreibung des Schwediſchen Lapplands). Bisher Hauptwerk, wenn gleich ein großer Theil der Nachrichten jetzt veraltet iſt.

**) In den Finniſchen Lappmarken ſind überdieß beſondere Hausverhöre mit den Kindern üblich.

Kåtaförhör, Hüttenverhör, weil der Prediger in den Lappenhütten diese Verhöre anstellt. Einzelne Abweichungen und, den
Lappmarken eigenthümliche, Einrichtungen finden Statt.

Der Gottesdienst wird sonntäglich gehalten, jedoch nur an
jedem zweiten Sonntage geprediget; an dem Zwischensonntage,
wo der Geistliche keine selbst ausgearbeitete Predigt vorträgt, lieset er, statt derselben, eine Predigt aus einer Postille vor. So
oft Lappen, die nicht hinlänglich Schwedisch verstehen, den Kirchen vorüberziehen, wird Schwedisch und Lappisch, sonst bloß

Fjällström, Kort berättelse om Lapparnes björnafånge (über den
    Bärenfang der Lappen). Stockh. 1755. 8.
Frøkell afhandling om Westerbottens och Lappmarkens u);
    barmachung); in den Akten der patriot. Gesellschaft. St. 2. Mehrere
    Abhandlungen in den Akten der Akademie der Wissenschaf-
    ten zu Stockholm.
Sköldebrand, voyage pittoresque au Cap Nord. Stockh. 1804.
    8. mit großen Kupfern.
Wahlenberg beskrifning om Kemi Lappmark. Upf. 1804. 4.
(Stael von Holstein) anmärkningar om Pited Lappmark. Stockh.
    1809. 8.
Hermelin, beskrifning öfver Lappmarken och Westerbotten. Stockh.
    1810.
Hermelin, Tabeller öfver folkmängd och näringar (Volksmenge und
    Nahrungszweige) i Lappmarken och Westerbotten. Stockh. 1810. 4.
Rowan, berättelse om Norrbotten och deß Lappmarker. Stockh.
    1818. 4.
Pehr Fjällström Grammatica Lapponica. Stockh. 1738. 8. (die
    erste, welche erschien.)
Pehr Fjällström, Dictionarium Sueco-Lapponicum. Stockh.
    1738.
Ioh. Öhrling diss. s, Observationes in Orthographiam Lapponi-
    cam. Praes. Ioh. Ihre. Ups. 1742. 4.
H. Ganandri, Grammatica Lapponica. Stockh. 1743. 8.
Er. Lindahl et Ioh. Öhrling, Lexicon Lapponicum cum inter-
    pretatione vocabulorum Sueco-Latina et indice Suecano-Lappo-
    nico; auctum grammatica Lapponica. Stockh. 1780.

Schwedisch oder Finnisch, oder in beiden, oder in allen drei Sprachen gepredigt. So lange sich die Lappen mit ihren Heerden in der Nähe der Kirche aufhalten, wird sonntäglich vollständiger Gottesdienst gehalten. Giebt es in einer Lappmark Fischerlappen mit festeren Wohnsitzen, so wird an jedem zweiten Sonntage erst Schwedisch und dann Lappisch gepredigt. Ein Sonntag, wo vollständiger Gottesdienst Statt findet, heißt Helgedag, Feiertag; ein Sonntag, wo die eigene Predigt des Geistlichen ausfällt, der übrige Theil des Gottesdienstes aber dann ganz der gewöhnliche ist, heißt bönedag, Bettag (wohl zu unterscheiden von den jährlichen großen Buß= und Bettagen). Der Helgedag wird jedesmal vorher abgekündigt; an den Bettagen wird die Kirche weniger besucht, doch kommen die näher Wohnenden jeden Sonntag zur Kirche. Das heilige Abendmahl wird in der Regel monatlich gefeiert, aber auch außerdem, so oft es verlangt wird. Die der Beichte vorangehende Anzeichnung derer, die das heilige Abendmahl begehen wollen, ist mit einer Betstunde verbunden; wie denn auch an den Vorabenden der hohen Feste Betstunden gehalten werden.

Im Schwedischen Lappland *) hält man im Sommer auf den Alpen (Fjäll), in eigends dazu erbauten Alpenkapellen, für die Hirtenlappen Gottesdienst, in den Westerbottnischen Lappmarken auf folgende Weise: Der Geistliche trifft am Freitag Abend bei der Kapelle ein; die Lappen sind schon versammelt; am nächsten Morgen ist Gesang und Gebet; die Anwesenden werden verzeichnet, ein mehrstündiges Verhör über christliche Erkenntniß und Sitten, unter zu Grundelegung des Catechismus, und nach Anleitung der Nachrichten, die der Geistliche durch die Catecheten und Sechsmänner über die Lappen einzieht, wird angestellt;

---

*) In den meisten Finnischen Lappmarken giebt es keinen Alpengottesdienst, wohl aber Kantpredigten in Dorfhütten, wobei dann auch Hausverhör und andere kirchliche Handlungen Statt finden; an einigen Orten des Finnischen Lapplands werden die Kantpredigten in besondern Predigthäusern gehalten. S. Schwedens Kirchenverfassung ꝛc. Bd. 2. S. 19 — 21. S. 433 — 435.

nach einer Ermahnungsrede, nach Gebeten und Sprechung des kirchlichen Segens folgt die Aufzeichnung derer, welche communiciren wollen. Am folgenden Tage (Sonntag) wird zuvörderst Frühgottesdienst, in welchem über den Text eines der jährlichen großen Buß- und Bettage gepredigt wird, gehalten; dann folgen, nach Verlauf einer halben Stunde, Taufe, Einsegnung der Sechswöchnerinnen, Beichte, Vormittagsgottesdienst, Communion, Trauung, Begräbniß. In mehrern Lappmarken findet jenes Verhör am Sonnabend nicht Statt, weil es, zu anderer Zeit, vom Geistlichen in den Lappenhütten gehalten wird.

Bei jeder Mutterkirche besteht eine Lappenschule, in welcher 6 Kinder unterrichtet und erzogen werden; für jede Schule wird eine Köchin gelohnt. Ueber den Unterricht selbst vergl. Kap. 22. Für die Fortbildung der Schulkinder nach ihrer Entlassung aus der Schule wird an einigen Orten gesorgt. Man hat Beispiele, daß schon der in der Schule ertheilte Unterricht höchst wohlthätig auf die gesammte Familie, zu welcher ein Schulkind gehört, einwirkte.

Den Unterricht der Lappenkinder, welche nicht in die Schule aufgenommen werden können, besorgen die Katecheten, die mit den Lappen umherziehen; diese Katecheten lesen auch, so oft die Lappen am Sonntage nicht zur Kirche kommen können, in den Hütten derselben Predigten aus einer Postille vor. In Ju-Kasjervi-Lappmark wohnt der Katechet bei der Kirche, dagegen giebt es dort Reisekatecheten, die zwischen den Wohnplätzen der Lappen, zur Ertheilung des nöthigen Unterrichts, umherreisen. In Luleå-Lappmark giebt es, außer den gewöhnlichen Katecheten und zur Beaufsichtigung dieser, Reisekatecheten. Die Katecheten genießen aus dem Lappenfond ein jährliches Gehalt von 8 bis 16 Rthlrn., werden von den Lappen beköstiget und müssen an die Pastoren, von welchen sie auch abgesetzt werden können, berichten. Für die bequemere Fortschaffung der Reisekatecheten haben die Lappen zu sorgen; die gewöhnlichen Catecheten wandern zu Fuß mit den übrigen Lappen. — Die Anstellung besonderer Schullehrer außer den Katecheten ist von der Königl. Kanzleiverwaltung vorgeschlagen worden; auch haben sich die Lappen dazu willig erklärt, sobald es ihnen möglich seyn würde, die Besoldung derselben zu bestreiten.

Jährlich wird von den Lappischen Pastoren über Pfarre, Schule und Schulkinder an die Pröpste umständlich berichtet. Die Pröpste berichten an das Domkapitel in Hernösand. Auch pflegt dieses die Pröpste oder andere Pastoren naher Schwedischer Gemeinden jährlich mit Abhaltung von Kirchen- und Schulvisitationen in den Lappmarken zu beauftragen; seltener verrichtet ein Lappischer Pastor die Visitation selbst in seiner Gemeinde. Oefter sind die Lappischen Pastoren zugleich Schulinspectoren ihres Pastorats; in diesem Falle halten sie die Schulvisitation, bei welcher auch die Schulkinder gefragt werden, ob sie mit Kost und Kleidung zufrieden sind. Selten haben Bischöfe in Lappland Visitationen angestellt. Das Domkapitel sendet die Visitationsberichte, nebst Gutachten, Vorschlägen und dem jährlichen Etat an die Königl. Kanzleiverwaltung zu Stockholm ein.

Die Einkünfte der Pastoren bestehen theils in baarem Gelde und Korn aus dem öffentlichen Fond, theils im Zehnten von Korn, Butter, Fischen, nach alter Vereinbarung, und andern Gefällen aus der Gemeinde. Von den Lappen erhalten die Pastoren: Rennthierbraten, Rennthierzungen, Rennthierkäse, Felle, Handschuhe von Rennthierleder, getrocknete Hechte; beim Begräbniß eines Lappischen Hausvaters oder einer Lappischen Hausmutter ein Rennthier (eines Schwedischen Ehegatten eine Kuh), und dergl. m.; die Quantität richtet sich nach der Größe des an die Krone zu erlegenden Lappenschatzes. Auf ähnliche Weise werden die Küster, die keine Amtswohnungen haben, von den Gemeinden besoldet, z. B. ein wohlhabender schatzpflichtiger Lappe oder Nybyggare giebt 4 Bankschillinge oder eine Rennthierbrust, ein minder wohlhabender 2 Bankschillinge oder ein kleineres Stück Rennthierfleisch. — Die Lehrer der Lappenschulen (an jeder Schule Einer) erhalten Korn und Geld aus dem öffentlichen Fond; sie sind alle ordinirte Geistliche.

Die Wittwen der Lappischen Geistlichen erhalten aus dem Lappenfond Gratiale von 16⅔ Bankthalern, und aus der Wittwenkasse des Stifts 1½ bis 3 Tonnen Gerste; wenig genug für die Wittwen von Männern, die unter den beschwerlichen Amtsverrichtungen oft frühe unterlagen. Nach 10 bis 12 Jahren Dienstzeit dürfen indeß die Lappischen Pastoren sich um Pfarren königlichen Patronats im ganzen Reiche bewerben, ohne also an das Stift gebunden zu seyn, in welchem sie geboren sind; auch werden den Lappischen Pastoren ihre Dienstjahre doppelt gerechnet. Bei Beförderung zu Lappischen Predigerstellen fällt ein großer Theil der sonst üblichen Abgaben: für die Vollmacht ꝛc. weg. Von der Mantalspenningar (Kopfsteuer), die die übrige Geistlichkeit erlegt, ist die Lappische Geistlichkeit frei.

Die Lappischen Stipendien in Upsala werden des Lappischen kundigen Studirenden ertheilt.

Außer der oben genannten ersten Begründung, wird der oft erwähnte Lappenfond theils durch Kronmittel, theils durch zwei jährliche Collecten gebildet. Diese Collecten werden in den Kirchen des ganzen Reichs gesammelt; ursprünglich sind sie auch für die Kirchen der Distrikte bestimmt, die zwar nicht jetzt, aber früherhin zu Lappland gehörten. Die jährlichen Revenüen des Lappenfonds rechnete man sonst auf 4600 Rthlr.

Jede Lappische Kirche hat, gleich den Schwedischen Kirchen, ihre besondere Kirchen- und ihre besondere Armencasse. Letztere wird gefüllt durch Einsammlungen bei Taufen, Trauungen und Begräbnissen, und durch freiwillige Gaben, erstere auf gleiche Weise und überdieß durch den Ertrag des Klingelbeutels. Die Armen werden theils aus der Armencasse, theils auf andere Weise unterstützt. Waisen pflegen von kinderlosen Gatten unentgeldlich aufgenommen zu werden. Zur Anschaffung des Kirchenweins wird Kronkorn geliefert; das Fehlende wird durch eine, 1 bis 4 Bankschillinge betragende, jährliche Gabe der nicht ganz armen Communikanten, oder falls diese Gabe nicht hinlänglich ist, gemeinschaftlich vom Kirchspiel bestritten.

Im Jahre 1816 waren die jährlichen Ausgaben des Lappenfonds folgende: Unterhalt von 12 Pastoren, 2 Comministern und 1 Kapellprediger ungefähr 300 Rthlr. banco und 426 Tonnen Gerste (eingerechnet die 12 Tonnen, welche Hede's und

Undersåker's Geistlichkeit erhält); für Schulen und Katecheten 390⅝ Tonnen Gerste und wenigstens 900 Bankthaler. Rechnet man die Tonne Gerste zu 6⅞ Rthlr., so würde das Ganze 6643½ Rthlr. Banko betragen.

Im Jahr 1816 schlug der Comminister in Skellefteå, Mag. Isaac Grape, in einem, dem Consistorium zu Hernösand eingereichten Gutachten, zur Vervollständigung der kirchlichen Anstalten in Lappland, statt der gewöhnlichen Katecheten, die Anstellung von Reisekatecheten und Missionären in jedem Lappischen Pastorat, nur Fölinge ausgenommen, vor. Letztere, ordinirte Geistliche, sollten über Lehre und Wandel der Katecheten die wachsamste Aufsicht führen; wo es nöthig scheint, bei dem Unterricht, den die Katecheten ertheilen, gegenwärtig seyn, um die Fehler in der Methode zu verbessern und die Achtung und das Vertrauen für die Katecheten zu mehren; auch sollten sie selber in den Jahreszeiten, wo Reisen zu den Lapphütten möglich sind, die Lappen unterrichten und über die Fortschritte der einzelnen Buch führen; übrigens selbst den Pastoren untergeordnet seyn und unter deren Aufsicht stehen. In den Zeiten, wo die Lappkoten nicht zugänglich sind, soll der Missionar die Kinder der Nybyggare unterweisen, falls man ihn darum bittet, wofür er nichts als Kost, falls die Eltern diese zu reichen im Stande sind, so lange er im Nybyggarehause anwesend ist, erhält. Bei Krankheit und sonstiger gesetzmäßiger Behinderung des Pastors hat er denselben unentgeldlich zu vertreten. Als Gehalt genießt er aus dem Lappenfond 10 Tonnen Gerste, und hat den Vorzug, seine Dienstjahre bei Beförderungen doppelt rechnen zu dürfen. Auch die Reisekatecheten müssen so gelohnt seyn, daß sich geschickte Männer zur Uebernahme des beschwerlichen Amtes bereit finden lassen, und sie nicht nöthig haben, die armen Lappen um Unterhalt zu bitten; der Lohn betrage daher etwa 8 Tonnen Gerste jährlich. Die Katecheten könnten bei den Lappischen Pastoren und Comministern gebildet und unterhalten werden, für etwa 100 Rthlr. jährlich. — Auf Amtsreisen haben die Lappen den Skjuts der Missionare und Katecheten zu bestreiten; für Beköstigung müssen diese selber sorgen. — Endlich, um den Eifer der Pastoren zu

II.   R unterstützen, möchten für immer Pröpste verordnet werden, denen es oblüge, jährlich die Lappischen Pastorate zu visitiren: einer für die zu Norrbotten's und einer für die zu Westerbottens Län gehörigen Lappmarken; beide müßten des Lappischen, ersterer zugleich des Finnischen kundig seyn; ferner ein General-Visitator, welcher über ganz Lappland sich verbreitende Visitationen, doch seltener, hält; in dem Jahre, wo dieser visitirt, fallen die Propstvisitationen aus. In den Jemteländischen Lappmarken kann die Visitation von den Pröpsten verrichtet werden, denen sie nach der bisherigen kirchlichen Eintheilung zusteht, da es hier der Kenntniß des Lappischen nicht bedarf. — Ueber diese wohlerwogenen Vorschläge war bei meiner Anwesenheit noch nichts entschieden worden. So viel ist gewiß, daß eine Vermehrung der Zahl der Geistlichkeit in Lappmark und eine Verbesserung des Gehalts der Katecheten, die jetzt von den Lappen sehr abhängig sind, nothwendig ist. — Bisher war es üblich, daß, wenn, wie gewöhnlich, die Visitatoren der Lappischen Sprache nicht mächtig sind, sie die, die Visitation nach dem gewöhnlichen Gottesdienst eröffnende, Altarrede auf Schwedisch hielten, und dann ins Lappische übersetzt von einem Lappischen Geistlichen verlesen ließen; in den nördlichen Lappmarken auch in Finnischer Sprache, falls dort die Rede nicht auch Finnisch gehalten wurde. Die Einrichtung der Visitationen ist überhaupt folgende:

1. Gottesdienst. 2. Altarrede über einen biblischen Spruch. 3. Christenthumsprüfung, nach dem Katechismus, zuerst mit den Aelteren und dann mit den Jüngeren, wobei auch die Lesefertigkeit erforscht wird. 4. Ermahnungen und Ermunterungen in Beziehung auf den Befund des Verhörs. 5. Kirchspielsstand (socken-stämma), nachdem Weiber und Kinder sich entfernt. Die Sechsmänner und die Dorfaufseher werden aufgefordert, sich zu erkundigen, welche Gemeindeglieder bei der Visitation, Propstgericht (prosteting) genannt, wo keiner fehlen darf, zugegen gewesen, und mit den ohne gültige Ursache Ausgebliebenen gesetzlich zu verfahren. Dann richtet der Visitator die erforderlichen Fragen an den Pastor über das kirchliche und sittliche Betragen der Gemeinde und an die Hausväter über Amtsführung und Wandel

des Paſtors, beſichtiget Kirche und Pfarrhof, unterrichtet ſich über die Bewirthſchaftung der Pfarrländereien, über die nöthige Förderung einzelner Nahrungszweige und ſonſtige Verhältniſſe und Bedürfniſſe des Paſtorats. Hat dann keiner etwas weiter vorzutragen, ſo ſchließt der Viſitator den Akt mit religiöſen Ermahnungen, mit Gebet und Ertheilung des kirchlichen Segens. — Auch wird die Kirchen- und Armenkaſſe revidirt. — Die Schulviſitation beginnt mit Gebet; die Kinder werden geprüft, und mit Sprechung des Segens und Geſang endet der religiöſe Theil des Akts; nun folgen die Unterſuchungen über die äußere Lage der Kinder, über die Schulmatrikel ꝛc., endlich Ermahnungen an Lehrer und Lernende. Die Schulviſitation wird nicht ſelten in der Kirche gehalten; auch die Geiſtlichkeit und einige Gemeindeglieder ſind zugegen.

Jedes Lappiſche Paſtorat hat, nach Schwediſcher Sitte, einen aus mehreren Mitgliedern beſtehenden Kirchenrath, zwei Kirchenvorſteher, einen Kirchenwächter, Sechsmänner für jeden Gemeindediſtrikt (rote), auch wohl Gemeindeälteſte (ålдſte). Kommen einzelne Lappen und Koloniſten an den großen Buß- und Bettagen nicht zur Kirche, oder nehmen, eine längere Zeit, am Gottesdienſt und heiligen Abendmahl nicht Theil, ſo hat die Kirchenpolizey zu unterſuchen und der Kronbeamte die verhängte Strafe zu vollziehen.

Eine Orgel giebt es bis jetzt in keiner Lappiſchen Kirche.

Die Vorbereitung der Confirmanden geſchieht gewöhnlich an den Vortagen der Predigtſonntage, und ſchließlich, eine oder zwei Wochen täglich, Vor- und Nachmittags im Pfarrhofe oder an einem andern paſſenden Orte; im erſten Falle übernachten die Kinder in den Kirchſtuben oder in der Kirche nahegelegenen Höfen; dann folgen Confirmation und Genuß des heiligen Abendmahls; in den Finniſchen Lappmarken pflegt indeß der Confirmation noch, nach Verlauf einiger Wochen, ein abermaliger, mehr prüfender, ein Paar Tage dauernder Unterricht voranzugehen.

Die gewöhnlichen Kirchſpielsſtände finden am häufigſten an Wochentagen Statt.

R 2

Häuslicher Gottesdienst an Sonn- und Festtagen, mit Gesang, Gebet und Lesung einer Predigt aus einer Postille, wird in allen Lappmarken, von denen, die nicht zur Kirche gingen, gehalten.

Kleine Erbauungsschriften hat, in neuester Zeit, die evangelische Gesellschaft in Stockholm unter Lappen und Kolonisten unentgeldlich vertheilt, auch Bibeln umsonst oder zu geringem Preise. Bibeln, Postillen, Katechismen und Gesangbücher sind, zumal in den Kolonistenhöfen, sehr allgemein; unter den Postillen findet man insbesondere: Luther's Postille, Ekmansson's Postille, Johann Arndt vom wahren Christenthum, Bälter Leben Jesu Christi, Leß Erklärung der Sonntagsevangelien rc., unter den Katechismen die von Möller, Gräberg rc.; unter den Gesangbüchern, außer dem kirchlichen, die Zions-Lieder, die Lieder Moses und des Lammes rc.

Kolonisten und Lappen beten bei ihren Mahlzeiten, selbst beim Frühstück, kurz, einfach und mit herzlicher Andacht. Die Sonntagsfeier wird aufs strengste beobachtet; nur im Nothfall erlaubt man es sich am Sonntage zu erndten, und zwar erst nach 5 Uhr Abends.

Die Lappische Sprache ist sehr weich, und hat unverkennbar große Aehnlichkeit mit der Finnischen; doch, wie Leem behauptet, nicht so viel, wie die Dänische mit der Deutschen; daß Finnen und Lappen einst Ein Volk waren, scheint unbezweifelbar. Nordin glaubte eine Aehnlichkeit des Lappischen mit dem Lateinischen entdeckt zu haben, und folgerte hieraus weiter über die früheren Wohnsitze der Lappen; allein diese Aehnlichkeit scheint eben so geringe und zufällig, als die Aehnlichkeit mit dem Griechischen und Hebräischen. Die Lappische Sprache hat mehrere Dialecte, die theils durch Veränderung einzelner Buchstaben, theils durch größere oder geringere Vermischung mit Finnischen, Schwedischen und Norwegischen Wörtern entstehen; die im Sommer in Norwegen weidenden Lappen mengen manches Norwegische ein; die Aussprache ist überall ziemlich gleich. Die Lappische Sprache ist reich an Wörtern zur Bezeichnung sinnlicher Gegenstände, die in das Leben und in die Verhältnisse der Lappen eingreifen, aber arm an Wörtern zur Bezeichnung abstrakter Begriffe. ·

b. Juridische, administrative, commercielle Verhältnisse.

In juridischer Hinsicht bilden die Schwedischen Lappmarken Distriktsgerichtsbezirke (háráder). Ein solcher Bezirk, dem ein Háradshöfding vorsteht, der einmal jährlich im Tingshause neben der Kirche zu Gerichte sitzt, umfaßt gewöhnlich nur Ein Pastorat. Da aber dem Háradshöfding nicht blos ein oder mehrere Lappische, sondern auch Westerbottnische Háráder untergeordnet sind, so wohnt er in Westerbotten und reiset nur zur Gerichtszeit in die Lappischen Distrikte. Im Gerichte sitzen, außer dem Háradshöfding, 12 Zwölfmänner, Bauern und Lappen, je nach dem Verhältniß der Lappischen und Nicht-Lappischen Einwohnerzahl des Distrikts; der Háradshöfding führt den Vorsitz. Bei den gerichtlichen Verhandlungen zieht er, mag er der Lappischen Sprache kundig seyn oder nicht, der nicht Lappischen Partheien wegen, einen beeidigten Dolmetscher zu; auch die Zwölfmänner sind beeidigt; sie werden vom Háradshöfding, unter den in Rücksicht auf Einsichten und Charakter vortheilhaft bekannten, Hausvätern erwählt. Bei den Gerichtssitzungen müssen die Zwölfmänner vollzählig seyn; sind einige derselben behindert zu erscheinen, so werden Stellvertreter ernannt und beeidigt. Betrifft eine zu verhandelnde Sache Schwedische und Norwegische Unterthanen, so werden auch Norwegische Zwölfmänner zugezogen. Der Háradshöfding wohnt im Tingshause; zu speisen pflegt er im Pfarrhause, wie es sich in diesen gastfreien Gegenden von selbst versteht, ohne Bezahlung; nur durch ein kleines Abschiedsgeschenk an die Pastorin kann er sich dankbar beweisen. Auf gleiche Weise speiset der zur Gerichtszeit anwesende Voigt im Pfarrhause; in Åsele speisen die Beamten für sich, und wird dann eine Geldsumme bestanden; überhaupt sind Natural-Abgaben (die sogenannten Nästen) an den Háradshöfding und den Voigt in Lappland üblich; doch haben diese Beamten auch Geldhebungen. Die Gerichtssitzung dauert in Åsele 5 bis 6, in den übrigen Sprengeln 8 Tage; sie wird jedesmal im Winter gehalten, im Januar und Februar, zuerst in Åsele, bald nach Neujahr, dann in Lycksele, in Arjeplog, in Arvidsjaur, in Jockmock, in Gellivare; in Torneå-Lappmark wird gleichfalls im Winter Häradsting bei der Kirche Karesuando gehalten, ferner für Juckasjervi in Wittangi, und für den dortigen Bergwerksdistrikt besonders zu Junosuando. Auf diese Weise hat Åsele-Lappmark, seiner 4, und Lycksele-Lappmark, seiner 2 Pastorate ungeachtet, nur 1, die übrigen Lappmarken aber 2, Torneå sogar 3 Ting. Auch in den östlichen Finnischen Lappmarken wird auf gleiche Weise Ting gehalten. — Neben jedem Tingshause findet man auch ein Gefängniß und einen Strafpfahl mit Halseisen.

Von dem Häradsgericht kann an das Lagmansgericht appellirt werden. Für das ganze Schwedische Lappland nebst den Provinzen Ångermanland, Wester- und Norrbotten besteht Ein gemeinsames Lagmansgericht, welches, unter Vorsitz eines Lagman, jährlich zweimal zusammentritt.

Die politische Verwaltung der Schwedischen Lappmarken führen die Landshöfdinge von Westerbottens (Umeå) und Norrbottens Län, und unter ihnen die Kronvoigte, deren gegenwärtig zwei sind. Unter den Kronvoigten *), welche Schweden sind, fungiren die Kronlänsmänner (kronlänsmän); diese werden vom Landshöfding ernannt; unter den Kronlänsmännern die Lappischen Dorf-Länsmänner, die der Voigt bestellt. Es sind nämlich die Lappen in sogenannte Dorfschaften (byalag) vertheilt, denen sie selber seit langer Zeit den Namen gegeben haben. Diese Dorfschaften sind aber nicht Dörfer im gewöhnlichen Sinne des Worts, sondern liegen viele Meilen weit auseinander; sie bestehen aus Bezirken, die von einer gewissen Anzahl Lappen als

---

*) Den Kronvoigt nennen die Lappen Sunje, d. i. Oberherr, den Kronlehnsmann Låddi, den Fiskal Piscater oder Kronseipik, d. i. Kronwolf, den Häradshöfding Lagamanni, d. i. Gesetzesmann, oder Herranshöfding, d. i. der Hauptmann des Herrn, den Landshöfding Landsherra, d. i. Landesherr. Den Voigt nennen sie auch wohl Hetransfallningsmän, d. i. Befehlshaber des Herrn, oder Fallningsman atje, d. i. Vater Befehlshaber.

Weideland oder zu Fischereyen ꝛc. benutzt werden, und wo die Hütten der einen Familie oft durch große Gebirgs- und Wasserzüge von denen der anderen gesondert sind. Eine jede Dorfschaft dieser Art hat einen Lånsman, der als oberster Vorgesetzter über Ordnung wacht, Uebertretungen des Gesetzes, Vergehungen ꝛc. dem Voigt anmeldet, darüber hält, daß alle Lappen an den großen Buß- und Bettagen dem Gottesdienst beiwohnen und bei der jährlichen Steuererhebung zugegen sind, kleine Zwiste ausgleicht, in Schuldsachen, die nicht mehr denn 4 Rthlr. betreffen, richterlich entscheidet und die Sentenz sofort in Ausführung bringt ꝛc. Dem Dorflånsman untergeordnet ist der Skickare, ein Bothe, der zu Versendungen und Ausrichtung von Befehlen aller Art vom Dorflånsman gebraucht wird; auch die Zwölfmänner müssen dem Dorflånsman gehorchen; dieser erhält Befehl vom Kronlånsman, wie vom Voigt.

Der Håradshöfding, der Voigt und der Kronlånsman sind besoldet; die Dorflånsmän und die Bothen genießen nur Freiheit von der Kronsteuer, vom Skjuts und von Gemeindelasten; die Zwölfmänner von Skjuts und Gemeindelasten.

Die Upsyningsmän (Dorfaufseher), die im eigentlichen Schweden angesetzt sind, hatte man bisher in Lappland nicht. Die oben genannten Sechsmänner sind für kirchliche Zwecke verordnet.

Bei Streitigkeiten über Grundbesitz werden zuweilen Commissionäre zur Localuntersuchung ernannt; der Voigt oder Kronlånsman leitet dann die Untersuchung; aber auch die Zwölfmänner müssen zugegen seyn.

Das Håradsgericht wird zur Marktzeit gehalten. Dann ist auch Upbörd, d. h. der Voigt erhebt die Steuern. Diese sind, vermöge der Lappmarks-Privilegien, äußerst geringe. Kraft dieser Privilegien genießen alle Bewohner der Lappmarken Freiheit vom Militairdienst jeder Art, so wie von Erlegung der ordentlichen Personensteuer (mantalspenningar) und der von den Ständen bei Reichstagen gemachten Bewilligungen (bevillning). Die Lappen entrichten eine für alle Zeiten fest bestimmte Abgabe für ihr Weide- und Fisch-Land, welches sie dann ganz als ihr Eigenthum betrachten können; für jede Lappische Dorfschaft ist nämlich eine

große Steuer angesetzt, die unter sämmtliche Theilnehmer vertheilt, und selbst, wenn die Zahl der Hausväter sich mehrt, nicht
erhöhet wird, wohl aber, wegen Armuth und Unglücksfälle, herabgesetzt werden kann. Den Kolonisten (nybyggare) wird, je nach
den Umständen, eine größere oder geringere Zahl von Freijahren,
die auch prolongirt werden können, höchstens 50, bewilliget; dann
werden sie zu einer geringen jährlichen Steuer (statt) gesetzt,
wodurch sie zu dem eigenthümlichen Besitz des ihnen zugemesse-
nen Landstriches gelangen; diese Steuer beträgt für das Mantal,
d. i. 8 Tonnen Aussaat nur 6⅔ Bankthaler. Auch an dem, eigentlich für die Lappen bestimmten Weide- und Fisch-Land (dem
sogenannten Lappland) haben sie in neuerer Zeit durch Erlegung
des Lappenschatzes Theil genommen; ein Umstand, der oft Reibungen zwischen Schweden und Lappen veranlaßt hat. Seit
etwa 40 Jahren sind, insbesondere durch Verlust der Rennthiere,
mehrere Lappen bewogen worden, Ackerbau zu treiben und dadurch in die Klasse der Nybyggare überzutreten; diese Lappen
erlegen gleichen Schatz mit den Nybyggare; indeß ist die Viehzucht bei ihnen Hauptnahrung, selbst noch mehr, als sie es schon
bei den übrigen Nybyggare ist. — Vor Vereinigung Norwegens
mit Schweden entrichteten die Norwegischen Lappen, welche in
gewissen Jahreszeiten auf Schwedischem Gebiet weideten, Weide-
geld (mulbetespenningar) an die Schwedische, und umgekehrt, im
gleichen Falle, die Schwedischen Lappen an die Norwegische Krone; diese Abgabe hat jetzt aufgehört. Dagegen dauert die Bö-
selafgift (Miethabgabe) fort; sie wird von den Schwedischen Lappen entrichtet, welche in Norwegen sich Weideland miethen; denn
zu Schatz (Jahressteuer, Grundgeld) nehmen, d. h. kaufen, darf
kein Schwedischer Lappe Norwegisches Lappland. — Die Kolonisten sind während ihrer Freijahre nicht blos von den Abgaben
an den Staat, sondern auch an die Geistlichkeit frei. Zu den
Lappmarksprivilegien durfte man bisher auch die Vergünstigung
zählen, daß in Kriegen zwischen Dänemark und Schweden die
Lappmarken unbeeinträchtiget bleiben sollen; wie denn solches
auch noch im letzten Kriege geschehen ist.

Die Schatzung wird von Kolonisten und Lappen in Papiergeld, der gewöhnlichen Münze im Verkehr, erlegt; denn die Lappen besitzen jetzt wenig oder gar kein Silbergeld, worauf sie sonst
so sehr hielten; Kaufleute und Andere wechselten es ihnen ab.
Als die Ausfuhr des Silbers verboten wurde, hatten die Lappen
es schon nicht mehr. Was sie noch an Silber besitzen, besteht
meistens in silbernen Bechern, Löffeln ꝛc.; dieses bewahren sie
in kleinen länglichen, mit Eisen beschlagenen Kästchen auf, die
sie, verschlossen, im Pfarr- oder Voigthause, oder in der Kirche
zur Aufbewahrung einsetzen.

Der jährlichen Märkte sind in jeder Westerbottnischen
Lappmark zwei, nur Piteå-Lappmark ausgenommen, wo nur einmal jährlich Markt gehalten wird; beide werden im Winter, doch
nicht an allen Orten zu bestimmten Tagen, gehalten. Der zweite
Markt ist der geringere, seine Dauer 1 oder 2 Tage, nur wenige Kaufleute kommen, es wird wenig gehandelt, meist liquidirt.
Der erste Markt steht 6 Tage; er ist der eigentliche Kaufmarkt.
Am ersten Markttage wird das Häradsting durch eine Predigt
eröffnet; der Richter nebst sämmtlichen Beamten ist zugegen;
die Predigt verbreitet sich, nach Anleitung eines freien Textes,
über die Verhältnisse des Richters zu den Partheien und der
Partheien zum Richter und zu einander. Der Gottesdienst währt
etwa 1½ Stunde (solche Gerichtspredigten sind in ganz Schweden bei Eröffnung der ordentlichen Häradsting gebräuchlich).
Nach Beendigung desselben beginnt die Gerichtssitzung mit Verlesung gewisser Verordnungen, Abkündigung des Gerichtsfriedens
(kraft dessen bei Vergehungen, die während der Gerichtszeit
Statt finden, die gewöhnliche Strafe vermehrt wird) ꝛc.; dann
wird der Markt ausgerufen, worauf dieser seinen Anfang nimmt.
Das Ting steht allemal länger als der Markt.

Am zweiten Tage ist Upbörd: die Erhebung der Abgaben
dauert mit den Kolonisten 2 Tage, mit den Lappen 1 Tag.

Auch der Zehnte für den Prediger, und der Gehalt des
Küsters wird eingefordert.

Nach Beendigung dieser Verrichtungen kehren die Kolonisten heim, die Lappen bleiben bis zur Beendigung des Marktes.

Die Lappen verkaufen ihre Waaren gegen baares Geld, und kaufen sich dann ein, was sie bedürfen; selten tauschen sie Waaren gegen Waaren. Sie nehmen jetzt Papiergeld fast eben so gerne als Silbergeld, weil ihnen letzteres von den Kaufleuten sehr hoch angerechnet wird, z. B. 1 Thaler zu 3⅞ Rthlr. Riksgåld; auch Kupfergeld nehmen sie. Früher war ihnen das Papiergeld sehr verhaßt. Beim Handel reicht der Kaufmann den Handels= sup, einen Trunk schlechten und schädlichen Brannteweins. Die Lappen schlürfen ihn mit großer Freude, ja das für sie köstliche Getränk erregt ihre Begierde in einem so hohen Grade, daß man während der Marktzeit nicht selten betrunkene Lappen sieht; freilich können sie nur wenig vertragen. Auch erbetteln sich die Lappen oft Branntewein. Der letzte Markttag heißt Walmars= tag: hier wird am meisten gekauft, auch das grobe Tuch, Wal= mar, was zu Kleidungen und zur Bedeckung der Hütten gebraucht wird. An diesem letzten Markttage darf, vermöge der königl. Resolution vom 7. Jul. 1752 auf die Beschwerden der Städte, Branntewein an die Lappen verkauft werden; doch ist das Ver= kaufen in kleinen Partien oder das Ausschenken durch das Gesetz verboten. Das Brannteweinbrennen in den Lappmarken ist im Allgemeinen verboten, und es wird, selbst zum eignen Bedarf, nur wenig gebrannt; Kaufleute und Bauern des niedern Landes führen aber freilich auch außer der Marktzeit nicht selten Brann= tewein den Lappen und Kolonisten zu, welches, sobald nur nicht geschenkt wird, eigentlich nicht verboten ist.

Während der Marktzeit ist auch der Landfiskal anwesend. Zwei Wächter gehen in den Nächten umher.

In früheren Zeiten waren die einzelnen Lappenmärkte ge= wissen Städten zum Handel überwiesen. Seit 1769 sind aber die Handelsdistrikte der Städte abgeschafft, und die Kaufleute be= suchen, nach Belieben, diesen oder jenen Markt. Indeß kommen, der großen Entfernungen wegen, gewöhnlich nur die Kaufleute der zunächst gelegenen Stadt. Die Kolonisten verkaufen ihre Waaren auch außerhalb der Lappmarken. Viele Lappen handeln sogar nach Norwegen.

An Sonn= und Festtagen darf in der Nähe der Kirchen, bei schwerer Strafe kein Branntwein geschenkt werden.

Vor der jährlichen Steuererhebung geschieht bei den Lappen eine Ausgleichung, d. h. der Voigt sucht zu erforschen, ob einige Lappen ärmer geworden sind, wie bisher, in welchem Fall man sie in der Steuer herabsetzt, und weil die Gesammtsumme immer herauskommen muß, das Fehlende unter die wohlhabend= deren vertheilt wird. Jedes dritte Jahr hält der Voigt eine Volkszählung. Jedes 5te Jahr berichtet er über den Zustand der von ihm verwalteten Lappmarken an den Landshöfding. (Königl. Verordnung vom 10. Mai 1805).

Fahrwege giebt es nur im Winter; im Sommer hat man fast nur Geh= und Boots=, wenig Reitwege. Indeß sind, zumal in den südlichen Westerbottnischen Lappmarken, öffentliche Ein= richtungen zur Fortschaffung von Reisenden getroffen, Gasthöfe an= gelegt, und die Lappmarken theils mit einander, theils mit We= sterbotten durch Posten verbunden, die an einigen Orten regel= mäßig, an andern nur, so oft Amtsbriefe eintreffen, gehen. In den südlichsten oder Jemteländischen Lappenbezirken, wo in der Regel keine oder wenige Nybyggare wohnen, giebt es weder Gast= höfe noch Posten; doch pflegt man auch dahin aus den nahen Schwedischen Dörfern Skjuts erhalten zu können. Wo Post= gang Statt findet, wird für jede bei der Expedition verzögerte Stunde 1 Bankthaler Strafe erlegt; die sonstigen Beamten sind Postmeister. Der Postillon erhält für jede Meile 8 Bankschil= linge Bothenlohn; alle 5 Jahre wird dieser Preis bestätiget oder geändert. Keine Station ist über 2 (Schwedische) Meilen; die Zeit, binnen welcher die Meile zurückgelegt werden soll, ist nicht bestimmt.

Auf einigen durch unbewohnte Gegenden führenden Tings= wegen (zum Ort, wo das Häradsgericht gehalten wird) sind, im dichten Walde und in der Nähe guter Rennthierweide, Statio= nenhäuser angelegt und mit Feuerheerd und Bettstellen versehen; Betten muß man mitbringen. Auf öden Handelsstraßen bauen die Kaufleute solche Häuser. Man findet sie indeß nur zwischen Lycksele und Arvidsjaur (2), zwischen Arvidsjaur und Arjeplog

(1), zwischen Arseplog und Jockmock (2), zwischen Jockmock und Gellivare (1).

c) Ausdehnung, Klima, Boden, Natur- und Kunstprodukte.

.Das Schwedische Lappland hat eine sehr weite Ausdehnung. Es liegt, die Jemteländische Lappmark, welche nur Theile von Jemteland und Herjeädalen bildet, abgerechnet, zwischen dem 64° und 68° Polhöhe, gränzt im Westen an Norwegen, im Osten an Westerbotten, und, einem kleinen Theile nach, an Angerman=land und Jemteland, im Süden an Angermanland, im Norden an Rußland (Russisch=Torneå=Lappmark).

Die bei weitem größere Hälfte dieses weitläuftigen Landes füllen Gewässer, Moräste und hohe Bergketten aus, deren viele, besonders an der Norwegischen Gränze, mit ewigem Schnee be=deckt sind. Das ebene Land an der östlichen Seite ist wenig zum Kornbau geschickt, sondern Wiese oder Wald; auch die Ber=ge sind treffliches Weideland für Rennthiere. Der Boden der Ebene besteht aus mehreren Erdarten: Gartenerde, Thonerde ꝛc., doch scheint Sanderde vorzuherrschen.

Das Klima ist sehr rauh; der Winter dauert fast 9 volle Monate, doch kann man auch in den kürzesten Tagen wenigstens vier Stunden ohne Licht lesen. Nach geendigtem Winter schrei=tet die Vegetation desto schneller fort, und ist desto üppiger. Früh=ling und Herbst sind sehr kurz, der Sommer dauert ein Paar Monate. Die stärkste Hitze herrscht im Julius und August *), und ist so heftig, daß man auf Mittel sinnen muß, sich gegen

---

*) In Schweden von Johannis bis in den Anfang des August, dann nimmt sie ab, aber nicht so schnell, wie sie im Junius stieg; der Junius gehört in Schweden schon zum Sommer, der September zum Herbst. Die Vegetation ist nirgends schneller und sichtbarer als in Lappland. S. Wahlenberg über die Lappische Vegetation; in den Akten der Akademie der Wissenschaften zu Stockholm, Jahrg. 1810. S. 106—114. Daselbst behauptet auch Wahlenberg, daß das Lappi=sche Gras nicht blos sehr zart (was es allerdings ist), sondern auch arm an kräftigeren Bestandtheilen sey.

die Einwirkung derselben zu sichern; die Nybyggare tragen mål-
kor, d. i. Hemden aus dünnem, weißem Walmar, der aus feiner
Schaafwolle bereitet wird und die Hitze sehr abhält, seltener
aus dünnem Rennthierleder, dessen sich die Lappen zu dem Un-
tergewande bedienen, welches bei ihnen die Stelle des Hembes
vertritt. — Die größte Kälte tritt im Januar und Februar ein;
dann beschmiert man, zur Sicherung vor Frost, Nase und Ohren
mit Rennthierfett; die Füße bedeckt man mit trockenem Heu
statt der Strümpfe, worüber die Lappen Pelzschuhe anziehen;
denn lederne Stiefeln über dem Heu, wie die Nybyggare gebrauchen, sichert noch nicht vor dem Erfrieren der Füße; das
Heu muß sehr dick gelegt werden, man nimmt dazu zerkämmtes
feines Gras. Der Winter beginnt mit dem October; der Schnee,
welcher jetzt fällt, bleibt liegen und schmilzt erst um die Mitte
des Junius. Um diese Zeit treibt man das Vieh aus; ist das
Jahr warm, so kann man schon nach 2 bis 3 Tagen grünende
Felder sehen, gewöhnlich wird es aber erst um Johannis ein
wenig, und im Anfange des Julius völlig grün. Zu Ende des
Julius fällt die Heu-, im August die Korn-Erndte; denn die
Sonne steht ununterbrochen am Horizont oder verschwindet nur
auf wenige Stunden; bis in den August kann man die ganze
Nacht hindurch lesen *); um den 10. und 14. August treten
Nachtfröste ein, dann wird die Witterung noch einmal wärmer;
erst um die Mitte Septembers kehren die Nachtfröste zurück, die
nun nicht wieder aufhören. Man kann also an drittehalb Monate Sommer rechnen. Was bisher erwähnt wurde, gilt indeß
nur vom niedern Lande; auf den Gebirgen ist das Klima noch
rauher: der Schnee schmilzt zwar oft oben so frühe, wie im untern Lande, ja, bei westlichen Winden, noch früher und schneller;
grün wird es im Anfange des Julius, die Nachtfröste treten um

---

*) Im Winter, zur Zeit der Sonnenwende, scheint die Sonne we-
nig oder gar nicht, aber die starke Dämmerung macht, daß man mehrere Stunden ohne Licht lesen kann; die Nacht wird von Nordlichtern
erhellt, und Mond und Sterne scheinen Tag und Nacht, fast 2 Monate lang.

dieselbe Zeit, wie im niedern Lande, ein; aber der erste Schnee fällt schon im August, welches im niedern Lande selten geschieht*). Kirchspielsmagazine giebt es in ganz Lappland nicht.

Die hohen Alpen bestehen theils aus nackten Felsen, theils sind sie mit Gräsern und struppigen Gewächsen bedeckt, seltener mit Rennthiermoos, und bestehen aus feiner Erde. Auf den mittleren Höhen trifft man verkrüppelte Birken, auch Gränen. Im niedern Lande erreichen die Waldbäume ihre gewöhnliche Höhe, die Rinde ist, der Kälte wegen, dicker wie gewöhnlich, aber das Holz schwächer; es giebt Birken, Gränen, Fichten, Tannen, Erlen, viele Weidenarten, Espen, Sperber und schwarze Vogelkirschbäume (Prunus padus, hägg), die Wälder sind aber oft, Moräste halber, im Sommer wenig zugänglich: Fruchtbäume gedeihen nicht. — Das Gras wächst sehr hoch und dicht. Eßbare Waldbeeren wachsen in großer Menge, am meisten Multbeeren (hjortron), Lingon (Preißelbeeren) und Blaubeeren, Himbeeren (hallon) trifft man nur auf Schwendeland; aus letzteren bereitet man Wein. — Mit den abgeschnittenen Stengeln der Angelica (Engelwurz) stillen die Lappen, auf Reisen, ihren Durst; auch kauen sie sie als Präservativ gegen die Blattern, wenn sie ins niedere Land ziehen; mit der Kuhpockeneinimpfung ist, im Allgemeinen, bisher nur ein geringer Anfang gemacht worden. Auf andere Weise benutzt man die Angelica nicht; die Rumex acetosa wird mit Milch verspeiset, ohne Milch aber als Laxativ gebraucht.

Kartoffeln und Rüben gedeihen überall vortrefflich. Erbsen sáet man nie, geschweige denn Waizen. Das Hauptkorn ist Gerste. Von der Sommersaat bis zur Erndte verstreichen wenigstens 10, oft 12 Wochen; nur in sehr seltenen Fällen sáet man um die Mitte Mai's, gewöhnlich erst nach dem Anfange des Junius.

---

*) Was man bei einigen Geographen, z. B. Djurberg, lieset, daß, nachdem es grün geworden, alles in 8 Tagen seine Höhe erreicht, nach 8 Tagen in Blüthe steht, nach 8 Tagen reif ist, und nach abermals 8 Tagen wieder der Winter eintritt, ist ungegründet.

Der erste Vogel, den man im Frühling sieht, ist der Schwan, der sich im März und April in großer Menge blicken läßt. Ueberhaupt ist an einheimischen und Zugvögeln kein Mangel; unter den Singvögeln zeichnet sich das Blaukehlchen (motacilla suecica Linn., sylvia *) cyanecula; von Meyer und Wolf, deutsche Vögelkunde Bd. 1. 1810. S. 240, blaukehliger Sänger, sylvia suecica, Nilsson) durch einen melodischen Gesang aus. An eßbaren Vögeln hat man Auerhühner, Birkhühner, Schneehühner, deren rauhe Stimme fast dem Lachen eines Menschen gleicht, und andere; die Zugvögel kommen mit dem Sommer, brüten, füttern ihre Jungen auf und verschwinden, sobald der Winter sich nähert. Seevögel hat man in Menge. Die Eulen wissen hier mit ihren, wie es scheint, nur für Dämmerung und Nacht geschaffenen Augen auch im lichten Sommer ihre Nahrung zu finden. Die Federn der Vögel werden gesammelt und verkauft. Außer dem Vogelwildprett, hat man Haasen, Bären, deren Fleisch, an Geschmack dem Schweinefleisch sehr ähnlich, den Lappen Leckerbissen ist rc. In den meisten Lappmarken findet man indeß Bären eben so wenig häufig, als Elennthiere und Biber; letztere wurden insbesondere durch das Schwenden des Waldes, um Wiesenland zu gewinnen, wodurch den Bibern das nöthige Holz geraubt wurde, vermindert; ihr Fleisch ist sehr wohlschmeckend. Wölfe, Luchse, Füchse, Vielfraße, Eichhörnchen, Ottern, Marder, Hermeline, hat man viel. Auf den Alpen giebt es im Herbste Leminge (Mus Lemmus) in großer Menge; von den Alpen wandern sie zuweilen in langen Zügen zu den niedern Gegenden herab, wo sie Graswurzeln fressen; Zobel findet man nicht. Auch wilde Rennthiere trifft man an, zahlreicher aber sind die zahmen. Adler sieht man in allen Lappmarken.

Die Bären und Wölfe erlegen die Lappen im Laufen, indem sie sie todt schlagen, freilich nur wenn Schnee gefallen ist,

---

*) Die eigentliche Nachtigall (sylvia luscinia) dürfte kaum nördlicher als Upsala zu finden seyn: im Westen steigt sie nicht zu gleicher nördlicher Höhe hinauf.

wodurch jene Thiere aufgehalten werden. Die Bären schaden den Menschen nicht, wenn sie nicht angegriffen werden; in diesem Falle tödten sie wohl Menschen, aber fressen sie nicht. Weiber können sich aber jederzeit durch Entblößung des Unterleibes retten; eine oft in den Lappmarken bestätigte Erfahrung *).

Die Gewässer in den Alpen haben sehr reines Wasser; im niedern Lande sind Flüsse und Seen gewöhnlich mit Gras und Rohr ausgefüllt.

Fische findet man reichlich und in vielen Arten; in einigen Flüssen wird auch Lachs gefangen.

An Insekten aller Art ist Lappland reich. Die größte Plage sind die Rennthierbrömsen und die Mücken, erstere fürs Vieh, letztere auch für Menschen; die Mücken verfinstern die Luft und nur durch Rauchfeuer und Beschmieren des Gesichts kann man einigermaaßen sich schützen.

Schlangen giebts viele.

---

*) Vor einigen Jahren ereigneten sich in Lycksele-Lappmark ein Paar merkwürdige Begebenheiten, welche zeigen, wie viel der Mensch durch Geistesgegenwart selbst gegen wüthende Bären auszurichten vermag. In der Brunstzeit der Bären gingen zwei Nyboggare durch einen Wald; der eine trug eine Art, der andere war unbewaffnet. Plötzlich springt ein Bär mit aufgehobenen Klauen auf die Wanderer los; aber der Unbewaffnete steckt muthig die Hand in den Rachen des Bären, während der andere mit der Art auf den Kopf des Bären einhieb und also ihn fällte, wobei aber der kühne Gefährte durch die Art seine Finger verlor. — Ein anderes Mahl umarmte ein Lappe mit Einer Hand einen Bären, der auf ihn zukam, und drückte ihn so fest an sich, daß dieser nicht beißen konnte; mit der anderen Hand lösete er seine Schlittschuhe, zog ein Messer aus der Tasche und stieß es dem Bären ins Herz; dieser wurde wie wüthend, aber der Lappe hielt ihn dennoch fest; endlich sank der Bär zusammen, worauf der Lappe in seine Kote eilte. Der Lappe mußte aber die Umarmung mit Blutsturz büßen, woran er ein halbes Jahr darnieder lag. Dann ging er zum Schlachtfeld, wo er den Bären todt fand. Dieser Vorfall hatte sich kurz vor meiner Anwesenheit zugetragen.

Biehzucht ist in allen Lappmarken der wesentlichste Nahrungszweig *): ein großer Theil der Lappen lebt einzig von Rennthieren; die übrigen Einwohner haben mehr Kühe, Schaase und Ziegen; auch Pferde und Ochsen werden gehalten; die Kühe sind von mittelmäßiger Größe und meist weiß; viele Ochsen und Kühe sind ohne Horn. Die fetten Wiesen an den Flüssen, auch Moosfelder, gewähren reichliche Nahrung, daher die Kühe im Sommer täglich 4 Pott Milch geben. An Pflanzenarten ist Lappland verhältnißmäßig arm; Linné zählte 537 Pflanzenarten; seit Linné hat man viele neue Arten entdeckt, besonders ist solches in neuern Zeiten von dem eifrigen und scharfsinnigen Botaniker, Georg Wahlenberg in Upsala, geschehen. Das Korn leidet nicht selten durch Frost; gefrornes Korn wird theils zu Grützen und zu Brey, theils, mit besserem vermischt, zu Brot verwandt; zur Saat ist es unbrauchbar.

An Eisenerz sind mehrere Theile von Lappland, insbesondere Luleå- und Torneå-Lappmark, sehr reich.

Perlenmuscheln finden sich an einigen Orten, in Lyckseli gewöhnlich ohne, in Åsele mit Perlen.

d) Bewohner: Lappen, Schweden, Finnen.

a. Lappen.

Der Ursprung des Namens: „Lappen" ist ungewiß. Die Lappen selber nennen sich Sami und ihr Land Samilanda; der Name Lappen wird ihnen von den Schweden und Finnen beigelegt, die sie aber auch Sami nennen, und ist es ihnen keineswegs zuwider, wie mehrere Geographen fälschlich behaupten, Lappen genannt zu werden. Die Schweden und Finnen, welche neben den Lappen Lappland bewohnen, heißen im niedern Lande Lappfinnen (Lappfinnar).

---

*) Heuscheunen hat man nur in Åsele und Lyckseli; Stangengeriste (håßjor) zum Trocknen des Heues und des Kornes hat man in allen Lappmarken. Wo Scheunen sind, nimmt man das Heu im August von den Håßjor ab: sonst bleibt es auch im Winter darauf.

II.   S

Die Lappen *) sind ein durchaus eigenthümliches Volk, was sich fast ganz unvermischt von seinen Nachbaren, den Schweden, Finnen, Russen und Norwegern erhalten hat; denn eine Heirath zwischen Lappen und Nicht-Lappen gehört zu den Seltenheiten. Die Lappen zerfallen, theils nach den einzelnen Lappmarken, theils nach den Dorfgebieten, in mehrere Stämme, die zwar alle das Eigenthümliche des Volks gemein haben, doch im Einzelnen von einander abweichen. Wir reden hier nur von dem Allgemeinen; von dem Einzelnen unten.

Man hat lange behauptet: „alle Lappen seyen von Natur klein und häßlich, von Farbe schmutzig gelb.“ Weder die eine, noch die andere Behauptung ist richtig. Viele Lappen sind allerdings klein, insbesondere die südlichen; aber viele, namentlich in den nördlichen Lappmarken, sind auch hoch von Wuchs, doch nicht über 3 Ellen, dieß gilt von ganzen Stämmen. Eben so wenig ist die schmutzig-gelbe Farbe allgemein, wenn gleich sehr gewöhnlich; aber sie ist Folge des Aufenthalts in den räucherigen Hütten; daher die Alpenlappen, welche die längere Zeit ihres Lebens unter freiem Himmel zubringen, wenig gelb sind; ich habe Lappinnen gesehen, die den schönsten weißen Teint hatten. Ueberhaupt sind keineswegs alle Lappen häßlich; man findet auch Schönheiten unter ihnen, unter Männern wie unter Weibern. Das Gesicht ist gewöhnlich breit, auch die Nase ist abgestumpft; das Haar schwarz oder schwärzlich; die Augen sind braun, wenig geöffnet, aber lang geschlitzt; der Mund ist klein; schwachsichtige, triefäugige oder blinde Lappen trifft man häufig, was theils durch den Aufenthalt in den Räucherhütten, theils durch die Gewohnheit, den Wiegenkindern geschliffene Glasperlen zum Spielen

---

*) Ob die Lappen jemals über ganz Scandinavien verbreitet waren und nur durch die vom Kaukasus einwandernden Asiaten weiter gegen Norden verdrängt wurden, läßt sich schwer entscheiden. Merkwürdig ist es, daß im Sommer 1820 in der Tiefe eines Torfmoors in Schonen ein Schädel gefunden wurde, der ganz die Form eines Schädels der Lappschen Menschenrace hatte. S. Nilsson Scandinarisk Fauna. Bd. 1. Lund 1820. S. 293.

vor die Augen zu hängen, veranlaßt wird. Körperstärke findet man bei den Lappen nicht; sie sind aber behende, lebendig und leicht beweglich, insbesondere Meister im Schlittschuhlaufen; auf ihren Wanderungen ertragen sie die größten Strapazen ohne alle Beschwerde, oft gehen sie in starker Kälte mit bloßer Brust; nicht selten werden sie über 70 Jahre alt. Nichts kann ihren stets fröhlichen und heiteren Sinn stören; sie lachen gern und herzlich. Redlichkeit und Treue ist unter ihnen allgemein; kindliche Liebe gegen mehr oder weniger betagte Eltern üben auch Erwachsene mit großer Herzlichkeit. Dem Schwören im gemeinen Leben sind sie sehr abhold. In Genüssen sind sie äußerst mäßig, nur der Begierde zum Branntwein können sie nicht widerstehen; doch wird im alltäglichen Leben kein Branntwein *) getrunken; ihr tägliches Getränk ist Wasser, zuweilen mit Milch vermischt. Ausschweifungen in der Liebe sind fast unbekannt.

Die Lappen begreifen leicht; die Kinder lernen das Schwedische sehr bald. In den Himmelsgegenden wissen sie sich überall schnell zu orientiren. Auf Reichthum setzen sie einen hohen Werth; sie sind sehr neugierig, von Hochmuth und Furchtsamkeit nicht frei, wohl aber von Geister- und Gespensterfurcht. Grobe Verbrechen sind unter ihnen selten, auch kleinere Diebstähle. Geschwätzigkeit ist insbesondere den älteren Lappen sehr eigen. Reinlichkeit und Ordnungsliebe findet man bei den Lappen in hohem Grade, doch verbreiten das den Körper unmittelbar bedeckende und selten gewechselte, durchräucherte, grobe Tuch (Walmar) und die Rennthierfelle, welche man zuweilen trägt, einen widrigen, den Lappen eigenthümlichen Geruch. Wöchentlich reinigt der Lappe seine Felle über dem Feuer.

In Hinsicht der Lebensart unterscheidet man Alpenlappen (fjälllappar) oder Rennthierlappen, Waldlappen, Fischerlappen, Bettellappen.

---

*) Den Branntewein nennen sie vina; den Ausdruck polemvin, wie die genaue Uebersetzung des Wortes Branntewein lauten würde, kennen sie nicht. Einen Trunk Branntewein nennen sie Jullastola, von jullet, trinken, d. h. Trunk, im vorzüglichen Sinn des Worts.

S 2

Alpenlappen leben, einige wenige ausgenommen, welche auch Fischerey treiben, ausschließlich vom Ertrage ihrer Renn-thierheerden; sie haben ihr eigenes Weideland, wofür sie an die Krone Schatz erlegen. Im Sommer ziehen sie auf den Alpen, im Winter, des Holzmangels auf den Alpen wegen, im niedern Lande der Lappmarken und der angränzenden Schwedischen Pa-storate umher; auf jeder Stelle bleiben sie, je nach Beschaffen-heit des Bodens, einige Wochen, und schlagen, für diese Zeit, ihre Hütten auf, zu denen sie die Materialien mit sich führen; in gewissen Entfernungen in den Strichen, die sie beweiden, ha-ben sie ihre Stabur, d. i. hölzerne, des Vielfraßes wegen auf einem hohen Pfahle ruhende Hütten, in welchen sie Lebensmit-tel, besonders Käse, aufbewahren (wovon unten).

Die Waldlappen haben wenigere Rennthiere, als die Alpenlappen, ziehen mit diesen Rennthieren nicht auf die Fjäll, sondern geben sie bei den Alpenlappen auf die Weide, oder treiben sie in die Wälder, wo sie sich selbst überlassen sind, — vermie-then das waldige Weideland, was sie besitzen, und treiben Fischerey.

Die Fischerlappen haben noch wenigere Rennthiere, oft gar keine, und leben, noch mehr, wie die Waldlappen, von der Fischerey, die sie, von einem See zum andern umherziehend, treiben. Ihre Rennthiere geben sie bei andern auf die Weide, oder schicken damit die Hausfrau, oder Kinder, auf die Alpen. Ihr Weideland thun sie zur Miethe aus.

Bettellappen nähren sich durch Betteley im niedern Lande Westerbottens, Ängermanlands und anderer Provinzen. Man kann zu den Bettellappen auch diejenigen rechnen, welche sich bei Schwedischen Bauern als Hirten vermiethen: solche Wei-delappen findet man in ganz Norrland, viele andere verdingen sich in Helsingland, als Kirchspielslappen (socknelappar), zu aller-lei Verrichtungen, besonders als Abdecker (s. Kap. 17). Andere nähren sich durch Verfertigung von Körben und Reifen aus Baumwurzeln, von großen und kleinen, zuweilen mit allerlei eingeschnittenen Figuren gezierten, Schachteln, von Schalen und Milchgefäßen aus Birkenrinde (was viele auch für eigenen Ge-

brauch anfertigen; überhaupt bereiten die Lappen ihre meisten
Bedürfnisse selbst) u. dergl. m. — Man könnte diese vierte
Klasse der Lappen die der armen Lappen nennen, wenn gleich
auch die 2te und 3te Klasse gewöhnlich arm ist. Größtentheils
bestehen diese drei Klassen aus verarmten Rennthierlappen. Die
Verarmung entsteht meistens durch Verlust von Rennthieren,
den Wölfe oder Unglücksfälle verursachen; seltener ist sie eine
Folge des unmäßigen Branntweingenusses. Diese immer mehr
zunehmende Verarmung der Lappen, so wie die geringe Frucht=
barkeit der Lappinnen, ist Ursache der fast jährlichen Vermin=
derung der Lappischen Volkszahl. Nach den Zählungen der letzten
8 Jahre (im Jahre 1815. 3906) beträgt sie im gegenwärtigen
Schwedischen Lappland nur an 4000 Personen, wovon die mei=
sten in Luleå=, Torneå= und Piteå=Lappmark wohnen; in Nor=
wegen wird die Zahl der Lappen auf 3900, in Alt= und Neu=
Russisch=Lappland, außer Kuolajervi, auf 2000 geschätzt; die Ge=
sammtzahl des Lappischen Volks würde also nur etwa 9000 See=
len betragen. Größer ist die Zahl der Schwedischen und Finni=
schen Kolonisten und anderer Nicht=Lappischer Bewohner: in den
zu Wester= und Norrbotten gehörigen Schwedischen Lappmarken
betrug sie im Jahr 1815 etwa 7500 *); in den, im Jahr 1809,
an Rußland abgetretenen Lappmarken, außer Kuolajervi, etwa
4200 (Sodankyla und Kusamo sind nämlich fast nur von Fin=
nen bewohnt; die für Kusamo ausgesetzte Volkszahl ist vom Jahr
1769, wogegen man in Utsjocki und Enare fast nur Lappen
findet). Ueber Kuolajervi, das Alt=Russische und das Norwegi=
sche Lappland besitze ich keine genaue und sichere Angaben.

In neueren Zeiten haben immer mehrere Lappen feste
Wohnplätze erwählt, und treiben nun Ackerbau und noch mehr
Viehzucht. Von diesen Ackerbau treibenden Lappen werde ich,
in der speciellen Beschreibung der einzelnen Lappmarken, näher
reden. Hier nur die Bemerkung, daß solche Lappische Nybyg=
gare nicht mehr in ihren nationellen Hütten, sondern in ordent=

---

*) Im Jahr 1816 zählte man in den Schwedischen Lappmarken
11,540 Einwohner (Schweden, Finnen und Lappen).

lichen, freilich sehr kleinen, Häusern wohnen: das Haus eines Lappischen Nybyggare hat nur eine Stube mit Vorzimmer (Far-stuga), das zugleich die Stelle der Diele vertritt; der Hof besteht aus einem Viehstalle, einer Heuscheune und einer Vor-rathsbude.

In Jockmock haben Lappen als Soldaten und Matrosen Dienste genommen und sich durch Tapferkeit ausgezeichnet; auch in andern Theilen von Lappland scheinen, von Zeit zu Zeit, Lappen in Kriegsdienste getreten zu seyn.

Den Rennthierlappen ist das Rennthier ihr Alles. Im Lappischen heißt das Rennthier pâtso, der Rennthierochse hirke, die Rennthierkuh vaija; übrigens haben die Lappen für die ver-schiedenen Arten der Rennthiere, nach Alter, Verschneidung ic., eine Menge Namen. Wilde Rennthiere findet man jetzt nur noch in den nördlichen Lappmarken. Aber auch die zahmen Rennthiere bleiben immer noch sehr wild, so daß man ihnen Stricke um den Hals werfen und sie anbinden muß, wenn sie gemolken werden sollen. In dem Umwerfen des Strickes besitzen die Lappen große Geschicklichkeit; doch mißlingt zuweilen der erste Versuch; dann rächt sich das Thier mit seinen Hörnern und mancher Lappe wird auf diese Weise ein Krüppel; schwache und alte Lappen treten daher erst in die Melkhürde, nachdem das Anbinden aller oder der meisten Rennthiere vollendet ist. Um ihr Eigenthum wieder zu erkennen, versehen die Lappen jedes ihrer Rennthiere, schon als Kalb, mit einem Zeichen an den Ohren.

Das Rennthier ist ein schönes Thier, von Farbe grau, nur am Halse und Schwanz weiß, an den Füßen weißlich, an meh-reren Theilen des Körpers hat es weiße Striche; der ganze Körper ist dicht behaart; die Haare erneuern sich alljährlich im Herbst; im Sommer sind sie schwarz, werden aber bald völlig grau, nur auf dem Rücken bleibt ein schwarzer Fleck *). Unter

---

*) Eine treffliche naturhistorische Beschreibung des Rennthieres hat Jonas Hollstén, in seiner Abhandlung vom Rennthiere, in den Acten der königl. Akademie der Wissenschaften zu Stockholm, 1774, S. 124—147 geliefert. Hollstén war 20 Jahre lang Pastor in Jockmock.

dem platten Horn, welches die Füße bedeckt, liegt ein kleiner Knochen, von dem Umfange eines Krebssteines, nur etwas länger; dieser erregt, so oft das Rennthier auftritt, ganz wie beim Elennthier, ein Knarren, welches man in einer Entfernung von hundert Schritten hören kann; dieses Knarren hält, bei dichtem Nebel, Heerde und Hirten beisammen, selbst die Rennthiere horchen darauf. Der Geweihe sind zwei, sie stehen gerade auf, und sind mehr denn eine Elle lang; die beiden Stämme beginnen einige Zolle von dem Hirnschädel, und theilen sich in mehrere Zweige. Im Sommer bedeckt die Geweihe eine dünne rauhe Haut, die im Herbste wieder vergeht. Wo die Weide vorzüglich ist, wachsen die Hörner am längsten. Jährlich wechseln die Rennthiere die Geweihe: sie verlieren sie im April (die Bullen im Herbst); im Mai sind schon wieder neue sichtbar, und im September völlig ausgewachsen. Die Geweihe der Ochsen sind die größesten.

Die Rennthiere, welche im Frühling, Sommer und Herbst auf den Alpen weiden, sind kleiner; die, welche im Winter und Sommer Waldweide haben, sind größer. Wilde Rennthiere sind fast doppelt so groß, wie zahme Alpenrennthiere, und sehr scheu vor Menschen und Hunden, welche letztere bei jeder zahmen Rennthierheerde zahlreich sind. Die zahmen Rennthiere sind fast von gleicher Größe, wie der Hirsch; nur die Beine sind kürzer und dicker. Die Nase ist dick und mit kurzen Haaren bewachsen, die Augen sind groß und vorstehend, die Ohren lang und oval. Die Rennthiere paaren sich um Michaelis und werfen nach 8 Monaten selten mehr als ein Kalb, welches, sobald es nur einige Tage alt ist, sein Futter selbst unter dem Schnee hervorsucht.

Die Rennthiere sind leicht zu unterhalten: im Sommer fressen sie alle Rumices, Ranunculi, besonders Ranunculus nivalis, und allerlei Grasarten, Wasser-Pflanzen, das Laub von Weiden und Birken, weniger Rennthiermoos; im Winter fressen sie Rennthiermoos (lichen rangiferinus, renmåssa), welches auf Höhen und im trockenen Nadelwalde wächset, und alle Arten der Lichenen, auch die Wickelflechte (lichen plicatus,

laſ); der Schnee dient ihnen im Winter als Trank. Moos
kratzen ſie ſelber aus dem Schnee hervor, unter welchem ſie es
ſchon in der Ferne wittern. Zuweilen bildet ſich, bevor der
Schnee fällt, aus eiſigen Schneeflocken oder beim Thauen, über
dem Mooſe eine Eiskruſte, die ſo hart wird, daß die Rennthiere
ſie nicht mit den Füßen zerſtampfen können; in dieſem Falle
müſſen die Lappen die Wickelflechte mühſam auf den Bäumen zu-
ſammenſuchen, und da dieſes Futter ſelten hinreicht, ſo kommen
viele Rennthiere um. Uebrigens riechen die Rennthiere durch 2
bis 4 Fuß hohen Schnee das Moos, bleiben ſtehen und ſtampfen
mit den Vorderfüßen. Der Lappe ſchlägt hierauf ſeine Zelte ein;
liegt der Schnee höher, ſo vermögen die jungen Thiere nicht
durchzuſtampfen. — Die Rennthiere ſind ſehr reinlich, nie findet
man Ungeziefer an ihrem Leibe; daher können denn auch die
Lappen ſich ſo rein halten. Aber die Ausdünſtungen der Rennthiere ſind ſo durchbringend, wenn gleich nicht unangenehm, daß
man, wenn man ſich auf die Erde legt, in ziemlicher Entfernung,
die Anweſenheit der Rennthiere durch den Geruch erkennen, ja,
mehrere Wochen riechen kann, wo Rennthiere weideten; am
ſtärkſten empfinden die Pferde den ihnen widrigen Geruch, und
werden wie wild, wenn ſie ſich Rennthieren nähern, doch gewöhnen ſie ſich daran. Weder Pferde noch Kühe freſſen da, wo
Rennthiere weideten oder getrieben wurden; aber auch, wo Kühe gefreſſen haben, freſſen die Rennthiere nicht. — Nie legen
die Rennthiere ſich auf einer ſchmutzigen Stelle nieder. Ihr
Geſchrei iſt eine Art Grunzen, ähnlich dem Grunzen der Schweine. Die weiblichen Rennthiere werden bis 15 Jahre alt; zuletzt
verlieren ſie die Zähne und können ſich dann nicht weiter ernähren; die männlichen leben kürzer.

In ihren Hörnern beſitzen die Rennthiere große Kraft; doch
vermögen ſie den Wölfen nicht zu widerſtehen; dieſe tödten nicht
ſelten mehrere hundert auf einmal; Bären ſchaden weniger, ihres Winterſchlafs und ihrer geringern Zahl wegen*). Im Som-

*) Auch andere Unglücksfälle vernichten zuweilen ganze Heerden;
vor einigen Jahren brach plötzlich das Eis eines Meerbuſens bei Stel-

mer haben die Rennthiere viel von den Mücken und Brömsen
zu leiden, von welchen sogar zarte und junge Thiere getödtet
werden. Die Rennthierbrömse, von der Größe einer Wespe,
schadet nur im Sonnenschein; sonst ist sie machtlos. Man unterscheidet zwei Arten: Pata Pätsko und Sarke; erstere (Östrus
Tarandi) legt ihre Eier in Löcher, die sie in den Rücken der
Rennthiere gräbt, letztere (Östrus Trompe) in das Nasenloch;
bald werden die Eier lebendig, und nur sehr allmählig vermag
das Rennthier sie abzuschütteln; die erstere Art zeigt, wenn sie
schaden will, hinten einen Stachel, die letztere nicht. — Die
Mücken hält man, besonders von Pferden, Kühen, Schaafen,
durch Rauchfeuer ab, die man rings umher auf abgedunten
Stellen anzündet; das Vieh stellt sich, von selbst, so, daß es
vom Rauch getroffen wird. Auf ähnliche Weise suchet man durch,
am Eingange der Häuser angezündete Rauchfeuer, die mit Torf
oder Moos unterhalten werden, die Mückenschwärme von den
Wohnzimmern abzuwehren; auch räuchert man oft; im Freien
führt man Flaschen mit einer Mischung von Fischfett oder Pech-
öl bei sich, womit man sich oft das Gesicht bestreicht, was in
der Sonnenhitze einen brennenden Schmerz verursacht. Die
Rennthiere kann man gegen die Mücken nicht sichern. Auch
vielen Krankheiten ist das Rennthier unterworfen, z. B. der
Randocka oder dem Zittern: das Rennthier kehrt, wenn es liegt,
die Schnauze gegen die Erde, fährt auf, und zittert, so oft es
berührt wird; zuletzt fließt Eiter aus dem Munde und den er-
weiterten Nasenlöchern; die Milz wird allmählig verzehrt und
das Thier stirbt nach einigen Monaten. — Eine andere Krankheit ist die Sluppo, die mit Geschwulst in den Fußgelenken und
zwischen den Pfoten beginnt; bald fließt Eiter aus und die Füße
faulen wie ab; eine andere, die Wuobda taud, welche die Lunge,
die Leber, und zuweilen den Hinterbauch ergreift; — eine andere die Pauka taud, wo der Magen plötzlich aufschwillt und oft

lestes, als eben über denselben ein Paar tausend Rennthiere getrieben
wurden; die ganze Heerde kam um.

nach einer halben Stunde der Tod erfolgt; — eine andere die Oive-Wicke, oder Kopfkrankheit: das Thier hält den Kopf stets nach hinten, und scheint toll zu seyn. — Andere Krankheiten sind die Tjalme-Wicke, Augenkrankheit; — Njalme-Wicke, die Mundkrankheit, wo Zunge und Kinnlade inflammirt sind; Waibmo-Wicke, Herzkrankheit, wo das Herz im Tode einige Bläue zeigt und das Fleisch so verderbt wird, daß es nicht einmal Hunde fressen; ferner die Fallsucht; — und die Schwindsucht. Alle diese Krankheiten ziehen, nach kürzerer oder längerer Zeit, gewöhnlich den Tod nach sich.

So lange die Kuh ein Kalb zu säugen hat, wird sie nur einmal, sonst zweimal täglich gemolken. Sollen die Kälber nicht saugen, so legt man ihnen eine Art von Maulkorb an. Die beste Milchzeit ist gegen das Ende des Julius, wo eine mittelmäßige Rennthierkuh $\frac{1}{16}$ Pott oder mehr bis etwa $\frac{1}{4}$ Pott täglich giebt. Man melkt von der Mitte des Junius bis um die Mitte des Oktobers, zuletzt nur einmal täglich. Die Milch ist sehr fett und nahrhaft, an Geschmack der Schaafmilch ähnlich, und so kräftig, daß aus 1 Kanne (2 Pott) Milch ein Käse von $1\frac{1}{2}$ Pfund Schwere bereitet wird; mit ein wenig Schnee vermischt, schmeckt die Milch am besten. Im Winter bewahrt man sie gefroren in Tonnen, die in die Erde vergraben werden, auf, und hauet Stücke ab, die man aussaugt oder schmelzen läßt. Der Rahm ist doppelt so dick, als der Rahm der Kuhmilch. Die Butter ist schneeweiß und schmeckt sehr weichlich, fast wie Schaafbutter: sie ist nicht so fett, wie Kuhbutter, weil sie nicht aus abgenommener Sahne, sondern aus ungerahmter Milch bereitet wird. Der Käse wird auf mancherlei Weise gegessen: am besten schmeckt er mit Zucker gebrannt; damit der Käse nicht Schimmel ansetze, räuchert man ihn. Lappen, welche nur wenige Rennthiere haben, bereiten keine Butter, aber Käse, welches sie vortheilhafter finden. Die Käseformen sind hübsch gezackt: auch der Flechtkörbe bedient man sich. Käse und Butter werden nicht aus derselben Milch gemacht, oder man gießt doch zur Buttermilch, aus welcher man noch Käse bereiten will, frische Milch. Uebrigens wird der Käse nicht durch Kochen, sondern durch Gerinnen mittelst Labs bereitet und dann geformt. — In kalten Frühlingen erfrieren leicht die Kälber, und die Kühe geben keine Milch.

Nichts ist am Rennthiere, was der Lappe nicht auf irgend eine Weise benutzt. Das Fleisch wird theils frisch verzehrt, theils geräuchert aufbewahrt; geräucherte Rennthierzunge ist ein Leckerbissen. Im October und November sind die Rennthiere am fettsten; da ist also die beste Schlachtzeit: man sticht dem Thiere in den Nacken und ins Herz, worauf es nach ein Paar Minuten todt ist; das geschlachtete Rennthier wird mit größter Sorgfalt gereinigt; das Blut benutzt man zu Wurst oder zu Suppe, doch verwenden es mehrere Lappen nur für die Hunde; aus den Sehnen macht man sehr starken Zwirn, aus den Geweihen kocht man, nachdem sie geraspelt worden, Leim oder Gelée, macht auch daraus Löffel, Messerstiele, Stockknöpfe. Magen und Gedärme werden gekocht; aus den Füßen bereitet man Sülze; aus den Knochen verfertiget man Nähnadeln, oder gewinnt daraus Mark. Die Felle dienen als Betten, oder als Pelze; zu Pelzen eignen sich am besten die Felle von 3 Monate alten Kälbern; denn die Felle solcher junger Thiere haaren erst nach langem Gebrauche sehr ab, während bei Fellen älterer Thiere diese Unannehmlichkeit leicht sofort sehr stark eintritt. Die Lappen verstehen sich vortrefflich auf die Zubereitung der Felle; doch haaren die unbereiteten, wie die bereiteten, ein wenig ab; die unbereiteten sind sehr hart. Ein Rennthierpelz ist viel leichter, als ein Wolfspelz; Wolfspelze sind aber dauerhafter, ja lassen sich wohl 3 bis 4 mal länger tragen, und sind daher jetzt in Schweden sehr gebräuchlich. Rennthierpelze werden seltener von Schweden, desto häufiger von den Lappen getragen.

Aus dem Kopf= und Fußleder nähen die Lappenweiber die sogenannten Lappenschuhe (Lappskor), die auch Handelswaare sind; sie reichen eine Handbreit über den Knöchel hinauf, und werden mit wollenen Bändern festgebunden, sind also eine Art von Schnürstiefeln; die Sohlen sind aus demselben Leder ohne Absatz. Da aber die Haare im Nassen abgehen, so eig=

nen sich jene Schuhe nur für den trockenen Winter; in der feuchsten Jahreszeit bedient man sich einer Art wasserdichter Schuhe, an denen man nur zum Oberleder Rennthierhäute, übrigens Rindleder verwendet; das Rindleder kauft man, gegärbt, von den Schweden.

Das Rennthier wird auch zum F a h r e n gebraucht, aber die Abrichtung ist sehr schwer. Man fängt damit an, das Rennsthier an Pfählen neben den Hütten festzubinden, um es an den Anblick der Menschen zu gewöhnen, dann leitet man es, legt ihm den Zaum an, läßt es am Wege gehen, spannt es endlich vor den Schlitten und setzt diese Uebung fort, bis das Thier völlig eingefahren ist. Auch zum Tragen, im Sommer, werden die Rennthiere eingeübt. Vom dritten Jahre an läßt man sie ziehen und kann so Ochsen und Kühe zehen Jahre lang benutzen. Anfangs sind junge Rennthiere gar schnell und wild, und werfen, zumal nicht sehr geübte Reiter, oft ab; ältere Rennthiere sind langsam und träge. Ein Rennthier legt im Winter 10 bis 11 Schwedische Meilen, besonders auf dem Eise, in 10 Stunden zurück, und braucht dazwischen nur ein wenig auszublasen und etwas Schnee zu nehmen. Will man recht schnell reisen, so muß man Morgens von 7 bis 9 Uhr die Rennthiere fressen lassen, und dann erst ausfahren; je mehr gegen den Abend, desto schneller laufen sie. Für Futter braucht man nicht zu sorgen, überall am Wege finden sie es. Geritten wird in Lappland fast nur im Sommer; da ist das Rennthier langsamer, und Schweden, deren Körper schwerer ist, als der des leichten und behenden Lappen, müssen das Rennthier öfters wechseln.

Die Kunst des Fahrens besteht bloß darin, daß man den innen aus Rennthiersehnen, außen aus Rennthierleder geflochtenen, einfachen, Zügel auf der rechten Seite hält, und dann und wann stark anziehe; da weiß das Thier, daß es nicht widerstehen kann; wo nicht, merkt es bald, daß der Fuhrmann nicht zu fahren versteht, und ist widerspenstig; peitschen darf man nicht oft, das Anziehen an den Zügel genügt. Das Lenken geschieht, indem man den Zügel nach der Seite wendet, wohin das Rennthier gehen soll. Ermüdet ein Rennthier, so sieht es sich um, ob die übrigen Schlitten nachfolgen, und springt vom Wege ab, waldeinwärts; zuletzt wirft es sich nieder und liegt eine Zeit lang wie todt; man läßt es ruhen, oder treibt es zum Futter. Geräth man in sehr tiefen Schnee oder in Aufwasser über dem Eise, so muß man aus dem Schlitten steigen und auf Schlittschuhen nebenher laufen. Fahren mehrere mit Waaren beladene Schlitten hinter einander, so bedarf es für 5 bis 6 nur Eines Führers; dieser fährt voran, und setzt die vor die übrigen Schlitten gespannten Rennthiere mittelst eines Strikkes mit dem Schlitten, in welchem er fährt, in Verbindung.

Gute Fahrrennthiere, welche die Straße halten, sind seltener als gute Trag- und Zugthiere.

Das Rennthier zieht mit dem Nacken, wo es seine meiste Kraft hat. Ohne anzuhalten, kann man mit einem Rennthiere 8 (Schwedische) Meilen fahren. Fährt man anfangs nicht zu schnell, so kann ein und dasselbe Rennthier mehrere Tage hinter einander 11 Meilen täglich zurücklegen. Bei Lastzügen hat man für 6 Rennthiere, die Einen Zug bilden, 1 oder 2 Reserve-Rennthiere. Rennthieren, deren man sich zum Fahren bedient, hängt man kleine Glocken um die Ohren: auch pflegt man in den Heerden einzelnen Schellen anzuhängen, damit die von der Heerde getrennten Thiere sich leichter zurück finden; noch mehr hält man Hunde, die die Heerde zusammen treiben.

Außer dem Zügel liegt über dem Nacken des Fahrrennthiers ein mit Zinn zierlich ausgenähtes Halsband, gleich dem Gürtel, von Rennthierleder, mit bunten Tuchecken und Schellen geschmückt, der Zugriemen ist aus dem dicksten Rennthierleder; die Halfter über dem Kopf ist aus Sehnen und Leder geflochten, mit aufgenähten Zinnstreifen. Der Schlitten, Achzia, von den Lappen eigentlich Kerez genannt, ist von der Größe, daß ein Mensch darin sitzen kann: er besteht aus mehrern kleinen, krummen, vorne spitz, in Gestalt des Vordertheils eines Schiffes, zusammengesetzten, Brettern; nach unten zu werden die Bretter doppelt gelegt; endlich wird unten, in der Mitte, ein breites Brett, worauf, als Kiel, statt der Schlittenbäume, der Schlitten geht, befestiget; alles ist durch hölzerne Nägel wohl verbunden, so daß keine Feuchtigkeit und kein Luftzug eindringen kann. Durch Felle und Walmar befestigt und verwahrt man sich im Schlitten. Die Lappen haben besondere Achzien für Männer und für Frauen. (Vergl. Kap. 22.); die größten Achzien sind etwa 3 Ellen lang. — Auch im Sommer bedient man sich, zum Transport von Sachen, der Rennthiere: man bindet den Rennthieren Leitern an, zwischen welche man die Waaren legt. Ein Rennthier trägt auf diese Weise 120 Pfund, zieht in der Achzie aber 360 Pfund, falls der Weg nicht sehr bergig ist.

Auf den Seen halten die Lappen Böte; die größeren kaufen sie gewöhnlich von den Schweden; die kleineren, auch größere, machen sie selbst: und zwar die kleineren ohne eiserne Nägel, bloß mit Seilen und Baumwurzeln verbunden. Die größeren Böte haben Nägel, und werden zu Kirchböten oder auf großen Seen gebraucht, die kleineren zieht man bei heftigen Strömungen und Wasserfällen ans Land und trägt sie, indem man eine offene Schachtel aus Birkenrinde, wie man ihrer zum Wasserschöpfen bedarf, auf den Kopf, und die Ruder über die Schachtel legt, und so das Boot aufhebt. Die von den Lappen gefertigten Böte sind schwach und schlagen leicht um. Jene Seile werden aus den Wurzeln der Birken und Gränen geflochten und sind sehr dicht und fest; man braucht sie zum Binden, zu Fischernetzen 2c.; arme Lappen verfertigen sie zum Verkauf; 30 Klafter dieser Seile, von der Dicke eines halben Federkiels, werden in Arvidsjaur mit 18 Schillingen Ricksgäld bezahlt.

An Netzen haben die Lappen mehrere Arten für größere und kleinere Fische; man zieht sie ans Ufer oder zieht sie von zwei Böten aus zusammen.

Die Lappen wohnen in Hütten, die sie Koten nennen. Es giebt mehrere Arten, die aber alle kegelförmig sind: die eine Art aus Holz gebauet und oben mit Birkenrinde *) gedeckt, gewöhnlich vier-, auch achteckig, oben rund, hat mit den, Kap. 22. beschriebenen, Kirchhütten einige Aehnlichkeit; ihrer

---

*) In Norwegen auch mit Erde und Rasen.

bedienen sich diejenigen Lappen, welche eine längere Zeit an einem Orte zubringen,' also die Fischerlappen. In diesen Hütten findet man auch Bänke zur Aufstellung der Speisen. Eine andere Art ist leichter gebauet: sie bestehet aus pyramidalisch neben einander gestellten Birken- oder Tannenstäben; über diese Stäbe wird, um die ganze oder halbe Hütte, dicker Walmar gehängt, wodurch der Luftzug abgehalten wird; der Walmar wird mit Büschen bedeckt; ein Stückchen Walmar hängt vor der kleinen Thüröffnung. Die Lappen kaufen in Norwegen, oder von Kolonisten, die ihn weben, den Walmar für 32 Schilling die Elle. Zur Bedeckung einer halben Hütte werden 24 Ellen erfordert. Solche Walmarhütten werden, so oft man den Weideplatz verändert, abgebrochen und auf Rennthieren transportirt. Sie fassen etwa 16 Menschen. Oft sind aber die Hütten der Alpenlappen auch ohne Walmar, in welchem Falle man die Löcher zwischen den Stäben mit Moos und Rasen verstopft und beides dick darüber anhäuft. Solche Hütten werden nicht abgebrochen, sondern bleiben an den verschiedenen Weideplätzen stehen. Neben den Hütten der Alpenlappen findet man gewöhnlich Gerüste zur Aufstellung von Geräthen und Sachen aller Art.

Der Boden der Hütte ist mit Birkenreisern bedeckt, auf welchen man, mit kreuzweise untergeschlagenen Beinen, sitzt und auf und unter Rennthierfellen schläft; Stühle und Bänke kennen die Rennthierlappen nicht. Kleine Pfähle um die Hütte herum dienen zur Stütze, eben so aufrecht gestellte Steine; ein solcher Stein ist auch Thürschwelle. — Zuweilen reißt der Schnee, wenn er schmilzt, seltener ein Sturm, eine Kote mit sich fort. Oft besitzen zwei Familien Eine Hütte gemeinschaftlich.

Auf ihren Zugstraßen haben die Rennthierlappen Stabur, erhöhte Speisebuden, etwa 3 für den Sommer und 1 für den Winter. Eine solche Bude besteht aus dicken Birkenpfählen, über welchen enge zusammengelegte Birkenzweige einen Boden bilden; andere Birkenpfähle sind als Stützen angebracht. Das Ganze ruht in der Mitte auf einem hohen Pfähle; eine Birke mit eingekerbten Stägen dient gewöhnlich als Leiter zum Eingang, welcher verflochten iſt. In ſolchen Buden bewahren die Lappen Fleiſch, Käſe, Fiſche und dergl. auf. Unter der Bude hängen ſie, ganz offen und frei, Kleider und andere Gegenſtände auf, die durch den Vielfraß und andere wilde Thiere keinen Schaden nehmen können; Diebſtahl fürchten ſie nicht. Insbeſondere bewahren die Lappen hier ihre Sommerſpeiſen, Sommergeräthe und Kleidungen auf, wann ſie im Herbſt von den Alpen aufs ebene Land herabziehen. Man findet ſolche Buden auf dem eigentlichen Alpenwege, nicht im platten Lande; auch die Fiſcherlappen errichten ſie in Entfernungen von 4 bis 6 Meilen. Die Buden ſind viereckig, 2 Ellen lang, 2 Ellen breit und 2½ Ellen hoch; oft liegen ſie auf Inſeln; zuweilen bleiben ſie unverſchloſſen.

Die Lappen ſind treffliche Schlittſchuhläufer; mit bewunderungswürdiger Schnelligkeit laufen ſie, ſelbſt durch Wälder und über Moräſte, 1 Schwediſche Meile in einer Stunde. Die Koloniſten ſind noch größere Meiſter in dieſer Kunſt; ein Schwediſcher Bauer aus Örträſk in Lyckſele-Lappmark legte einmal den Hin- und Rückweg von der Kirche Lyckſele nach Umeå, 24 Meilen, in 24 Stunden zurück; die Lappen laufen nicht ganz ſo ſchnell.

Im Winter hüllen ſich die Lappen in einen Rennthierpelz, deſſen Haare nach außen gekehrt ſind; unter dem Pelze tragen ſie ein Kolt oder langen Rock von Walmar, der von der Bruſt bis auf die Füße reicht und die Stelle des Hemdes vertritt; auch tragen ſie lange Beinkleider. Dieſe Bedeckung iſt bei Männern und Weibern völlig gleich, nur geht der Weiberrock noch tiefer herab und iſt ohne ſtehenden Kragen; bei feierlichen Gelegenheiten ſetzen aber auch die Weiber einen oder zwei, mit Silber geſtickte, Kragen auf und legen einen zierlichen Gürtel an.

Im Sommer tragen Männer und Weiber einen einfachen oder doppelten Kolt, von Walmar oder Leder, keinen Pelz; die Stelle des Halstuchs vertritt ein Bruſtlatz aus Walmar; auch tragen ſie lange Beinkleider von Walmar oder leichtem Leder ohne Haare, wie im Winter; ferner einen mit Silber- oder Zinnfäden genähten ledernen Gürtel; die Sonntagskleidung iſt auf gleiche Weise, nur hübscher und zierlicher. Am Gürtel tragen sie allerlei kleine Zierrathe, als Beutelchen, Messerchen, Löffel, messingene Ringe ꝛc., die Männer hinten, die Weiber vorne. Den Kopf deckt eine spitzige Mütze von feinerem rothen, blauen oder grünen Tuche; die Weiber tragen sie etwas platter und über dieselbe noch eine zweite, die, oben nach hinten ein wenig offen, einige Aehnlichkeit mit der Schwedischen Bischofsmütze hat; in Luleå=Lappmark sind die Mützen höher und hängen mit den Zipfeln herab. Trauernde Wittwen tragen blaue Manns= mützen. Die verheiratheten Frauen tragen an den Fingern sil= berne Ringe, aus welchen andere kleine Ringe herabhängen, die bei Bewegung der Hand ein Geräusch hervorbringen.

Zum heiligen Abendmahl gehen die Lappinnen mit überge= schlagenem Tuch und mit weißen wollenen Handschuhen, auf welche rothe, gelbe und blaue Rosen gestickt sind.

Die Schuhe sind bei Männern und Weibern völlig gleich. Die Stelle der Strümpfe vertritt Heu.

In allen Lappmarken ist die Kleidung der Lappen im Gan= zen gleich.

Am zierlichsten ist die Hochzeitskleidung, die übrigens von der gewöhnlichen nicht abweicht.

Die Hochzeitsgebräuche selbst haben viel Eigenthüm= liches. Ein Lappe, welcher heirathen will (und dieses geschieht häufig schon im 17ten und 18ten Jahre, wie solches die Königl. Verordnung vom Jahr 1745, in Wilßmann, Ecclesf. verf, S. 400., gestattet), erwählt sich einen Fürbitter, dem er sei= ne Neigung entdeckt. Der Fürbitter ladet nun das Mädchen, dessen Eltern und sonstige Verwandte in seine Hütte ein; auch der Ehelustige, mit Eltern und andern Verwandten, ist zugegen; diese sitzen auf der einen, jene auf der anderen Seite, der Jüng= ling neben dem Mädchen. Der Fürbitter, suognion=oiwe, d. i. Haupt der Freierei, macht den Wirth und läßt den Brannte= wein kreisen, dann macht er den Antrag an die Eltern des Mädchens und reicht den zu Verlobenden aus einem Becher (kußa) zu trinken. Willigen die Eltern nicht sofort ein, so be= ginnt der Fürbitter aufs neue seine Bewirthung, und so mißlingt

II.   T

selten ein Antrag. Der Bräutigam führt schon die Morgengabe
für die Braut mit sich; ein Preis oder Geschenk an die Eltern
ist nicht mehr üblich, oder sehr selten. Die Morgengabe ist
größer oder geringer, je nach den Vermögensumständen des
Bräutigams; sie besteht in blanken Thalern, in silbernen kleinen
Bechern (kuror), und 10 bis 12 Rennthieren. Ist das Ja=
wort ausgesprochen, so küssen sich Braut und Bräutigam; dieß
ist die Verlobung, während und nach welcher gesungen wird.
Die Bewirthung wird nun so lange fortgesetzt, bis alles aufge=
zehrt ist und die Anwesenden in Schlaf versunken sind. Am
nächsten Morgen begiebt sich das Brautpaar zum Prediger, um
ihm die Verlobung anzuzeigen, worauf das Aufgebot und schon
nach 3 Wochen die Trauung erfolgt. Die Kosten der Hochzeit
bestreiten die beiderseitigen Anverwandten, welche nebst Nachba=
ren die Gäste sind; einer aus der Gesellschaft macht den Wirth.
Doch noch vor dem Hochzeitsmahl, gleich nach der Trauung, be=
wirthen sich die Gäste unter einander mit Branntewein, von
welchem aber nur in sehr geringen Gaben aus der kleinen Fla=
sche eines jeden gereicht wird: Die Hochzeitstafel wird, nach
Lappenweise, auf dem Boden einer Hütte oder eines Hauses ge=
deckt; die Gerichte bestehen in fettem Rennthierfleisch, Renn=
thierkäse und einer fetten Fleischsuppe mit Mehl, die man mit
hölzernen Tassen schöpft; das Getränk ist Branntewein. Beim
Anfange des Mahls spricht ein Kind ein lautes Gebet, am
Schlusse wird ein geistlicher Gesang angestimmt; auch wird, nach
Schwedischem Gebrauche, für Arme und Lazareth gesammelt.
Man sitzt auf untergeschlagenen Füßen. Nachdem man also
mehrere frohe Stunden verlebt, begiebt man sich auf den Markt,
falls, wie sich häufig ereignet, die Hochzeit grade zur Marktzeit
gefeiert wird, und bleibt einige Tage in den hochzeitlichen Klei=
dern. Dann erfolgt die Heimführung: das junge Ehepaar
wird auf dem Zuge zur künftigen Wohnhütte von Vielen beglei=
tet, die es mit ein wenig Branntewein zu bewirthen hat; auf
Scheidewegen, wo ein Theil der Begleiter abgeht, wird ein
Trauergesang angestimmt. Nachdem der junge Mann seine Frau
in seine Hütte eingeführt hat, tritt das eheliche Verhältniß ein.

Selten wohnt das neue Paar ein Jahr bei den Eltern, die der Tochter Rennthiere, etwas Walmar zur Kote, und Hausgeräth mitgeben.

Der Fürbitter erhält vom Bräutigam, zum Dank, ein Renne thier. Auch der Arme muß mit einem Fürbitter und etwas Branntewein versehen seyn.

Die Lappinnen, insbesondere die Weiber der Alpenlappen, gebären nicht oft: die Alpenlappinnen haben meistens nur ein oder 2 Kinder, oft gar keines, selten 3 oder 4 Kinder; die Walds und Fischerlappinnen 4 bis 6, höchstens 8 Kinder; seltener sind sie kinderlos. Die Lappinnen gebären leicht und schnell, oft auf Reisen, wo wenige Stunden nach der Geburt schon die Wanderung fortgesetzt wird; nach ein Paar Tagen treiben sie wieder die gewöhnlichen Geschäfte. Die Mütter stillen selbst. Das Kind wird mit weichem, stark behaartem Leder umwunden und in einem Kont transportirt: Kont, oder Jirkum, nennt man einen kleinen Lappischen Schlitten, aus Granholz, innen mit Fellen, außen mit Leder überzogen; über den Kont wird Leder gespannt, welches mit einer kleinen Oeffnung versehen ist, die bei üblem Wetter zugezogen wird. Täglich wird das Kind in laulichtem Wasser gebadet. Die Bewirthung bei der Taufe besteht in etwas Branntewein. Die Gevattern geben ein Renns thierkalb, oder Geld für das Kind; auch die Eltern schenken dem Kinde ein Rennthierkalb; auf diese Weise bekommen die Kinder allmählig eine Heerde, denn die Rennthiere vermehren sich sehr stark *). Strenge Kinderzucht ist den Lappen eigen. — Die Kinder der Alpenlappen sterben häufiger, als die Kinder der Walds und Fischerlappen.

Auf die Mutters und Vaterfreuden des ehelichen Lebens halten die Lappen sehr hoch; außereheliche Genüsse verabscheuen sie.

Die Lappen essen wenig; ihre Hauptmahlzeit halten sie, im Sommer, gegen Mitternacht, worauf sie ein Paar Stunden

---

*) Auch die vornehmern Schweden in Lappland schenken ihren Kindern, bei der Geburt, ein Rennthier; in 47 Jahren entstand einmal durch ein solches Kindtauss-Rennthier eine Heerde von 100 Häuptern.

T 2

der Nahe pflegen; ihr Tisch ist die Erde, mit Rennthierfell oder dergl. m. bedeckt. Am Tage essen sie nichts, als ein bischen Fisch und Käse, auch wohl Beeren; getrockneter Fisch oder gedörrtes Rennthierfleisch vertritt die Stelle des Brots *). Im Winter essen die Lappen viel gedörrtes oder gefrornes Fleisch von Rennthieren, Vögeln und Bären. Salz gebrauchen sie noch immer sehr wenig, ja in den nördlichen Lappmarken, wie ehemals überall, gar nicht; dem wenigen Genuß von Salz schreibt man die Leichtigkeit und Lebendigkeit der Lappen zu, die aber doch mehr in ihrer steten Bewegung, von Jugend auf, ihren Grund hat. Bärenfleisch ist den Lappen Leckerbissen. Mehl gebrauchen die ärmeren Lappen mehr, als die reichern; diese jährlich höchstens 160 Pfund. Im Sommer schlafen die Lappen wenig, suchen es aber im Winter, wo ihnen die Heerde weniger Beschäftigung giebt, nachzuholen; im Winter verfertigen sie auch ihre Handarbeiten; die zinnernen Zierrathen auf Kragen und Gürteln machen die Weiber.

Vier bis fünf mal am Tage waschen die Lappen Hände und Angesicht. Der Taback ist schon lange ihr größtes Bedürfniß und ihr liebster Genuß. Männer und Weiber rauchen, auch schnupfen sie viel; doch wird mehr geraucht und gekauet, als geschnupft. Sie gebrauchen Virginische Blätter, die sie in Norwegen kaufen. Den Schnupftaback vermischen sie auch mit gepülverten Wachholderbeeren.

Ihre Arzenei verordnen sie sich selber; sie gebrauchen Kampher mit Branntewein, schröpfen rc. Als Präservativ gegen die Blattern kauen sie die Wurzel der Angelica; doch sind die Blattern unter den Lappen selten.

Ihr Reichthum besteht, außer Rennthieren, in silbernen Bechern und Thalern, die sie, in eisenbeschlagenen Kistchen, den Predigern, Kronbeamten oder Bauern zur Aufbewahrung über-

*) Nach Vargas Bedemar Reise in den hohen Norden Bd. 2. 1819. S. 117., genießen zuweilen die Norwegischen Lappen auch frisches Brot, das sie auf heißen Steinen backen.

geben; die Fischerlappen besitzen dergleichen nicht. Die Lappen nehmen auch Papier- und Kupfergeld; aber Silbergeld ist ihnen noch immer das liebste. Die silbernen Becher, Kuror genannt, haben, wenn sie am größten sind, eine Höhe von 2 Zoll, und 3 Zoll im Durchmesser; die meisten sind nur halb so groß. Die Löffel sind rund, mit allerlei Zierrathen versehen, und haben einen kurzen geriefelten Stiel, an welchem zuweilen kleine Ringe befestiget sind, und der in einen runden Knopf ausgeht; ein solcher Löffel wiegt 3 bis 4 Loth. Die Becher sind inwendig vergoldet und gewöhnlich mit Handgriffen versehen.

Schon oben ist von dem allezeit fröhlichen Sinne der Lappen geredet worden. Sie singen gerne und viel; aber ihr Gesang besteht in einem unverständlichen, eintönigen Lallen, welches sie lange fortsetzen. Musikalische Instrumente kennen sie nicht. Sie tanzen nie; denn ihr sogenannter Tanz bei Hochzeiten, der überdieß nur selten Statt findet, ist ein bloßes Springen ohne Takt, auch wenn Schwedische Musiker spielen. — Zuweilen statten die Lappen einander Besuche ab: da betrachten sie die Rennthiere des Wirthes, schwatzen, und schmausen das Beste, was sie haben, Fische, Milch, Käse und Fleisch. — Den Johannistag feiern sie durch Kosten der an diesem Tage zuerst gemolkenen Rennthierkühe. Sie sind sehr gastfrei. Bekommen sie Branntewein, was nicht oft geschieht, so theilen sie davon an Gesinde und Kinder, selbst an halbjährige Kinder, mit. — Ihre Grüße bestehen in Handdruck und Gegeneinanderstellen der Nasen. Nach dem Mahl drücken sich erst Wirth und Wirthin die Hände, dann folgen die Händedrücke der Gäste; bei alltäglichen Mahlzeiten ist der Handdruck nicht gebräuchlich. Im Ringen mit einander ihre Kraft zu versuchen, gewährt ihnen großes Vergnügen. Kindekarten oder anderes Kartenspiel kennen sie nicht. Ihr einziges Spiel ist das auch in Deutschland von der Jugend gekannte Wolfsspiel.

Das Kochen besorgen gewöhnlich die Männer, seltener die Weiber; diese haben sich dagegen ausschließlich mit den Kindern zu beschäftigen.

Nur die wohlhabenderen Lappen halten Dienstboten, welchen sie Kleider und Geld, so wie jährlich eine Rennthierkuh nebst Kalb, die mit der Heerde des Herrn weiden, geben. Auf solche Art sammeln sich die Dienstboten allmählig selbst eine kleine Heerde.

Alle Lappen führten 1. einen Taufnamen (z. B. Olof), 2. einen Vatersnamen (z. B. Johansson), ganz wie die Schwedischen Bauern; in Åsele zuweilen auch 3 einen Zunamen (z. B. Sandin), der aber mit dem Tode dessen, der ihn führte, erlöscht; nur von gleicher Dauer ist der Beiname, den, nach gewissen körperlichen Eigenschaften, die Luleå-Lappen einander beilegen und der die Stelle des Zunamens vertritt, doch haben die Lappen an einzelnen Orten auch bleibende Geschlechtsnamen. Nicht selten erhalten Töchter zwei Taufnamen, z. B. Anna Greta; ein Gebrauch, den man auch bei den Schwedischen Bauern findet.

Bei Leichenzügen heulen die Lappen, und setzen dieses Geheule oft lange am Grabe fort.

Die Lappen sind tüchtige Jäger, bedienen sich aber nur der Gewehre, die sie auf Märkten kaufen, nicht der Bogen. Bogen gebrauchen nur die Nybyggare in Gellivare, und zwar zur Vogel- und Eichhornjagd; diese Bogen sind aus Birkenholz und mit eiserner Feder. Die Vogeljagd gewährt den Lappen keinen geringen Theil ihres Unterhalts. Auch Jagdhunde halten sie, zur Jagd von Bären ic. Von jedem erlegten Bären erhält der Pastor das Vorderblatt. Der Hermelinfang wird wenig beachtet, weil die Felle nur zu sehr geringen Preisen veräußert werden können.

In früherer Zeit bedienten sich die Lappen der Runen-Kalender, auf dünnen Brettern, oder auf Rennthierhörnern; jetzt sind diese Kalender verschwunden; dagegen werden die gewöhnlichen Schwedischen Kalender unter die Lappen unentgeldlich durch die Prediger vertheilt. *)

---

*) Jährliche für Schweden berechnete Kalender erhielt man erst spät in diesem Reiche. Bis dahin begnügte man sich mit den Calenda-

b. Schweden und Finn'en.

Lappland hat auch Schwedische und Finnische Bewohner, einem sehr kleinen Theile nach Beamte, dem bei weitem größten Theile nach steuerpflichtige Bauern und steuerfreie Kolonisten, wirkliche Nybyggare. In welchen Bezirken die Schweden, in welchen die Finnen angesessen sind, und wo sich Lappen als Kolonisten angesiedelt haben, soll in der speziellen Ortsbeschreibung erwähnt werden.

Wann jene Anbauer sich zuerst in Lappland niederließen, ist ungewiß; daß unter Karl XII., als die Russen Finnland verheerten, mehrere Finnen ihr Vaterland verließen und nach Lappland zogen, ist sicher; diese kamen aber nicht nach den Distrikten, wo jetzt Finnen wohnen, sondern nach Lycksele, wo jetzt Schweden wohnen, sind also völlig Schweden geworden. Diese Finnen haben das Roggensäen und das Schwenden eingeführt. Die Schwedischen Kolonisten stammen aus Dalekarlien, Ungermanland und Westerbotten.

Bei ihrer Ansiedelung werden den Nybyggare Freijahre bewilligt, während welchen sie von allen Arten der Steuer frei sind. Die Zahl der Freijahre richtet sich nach der größeren oder geringern Schwierigkeit des Anbaues: 15, 20, 30 Jahre, und überdieß, wenn es die Umstände erfordern, Prolongation; auf Pfarrboden angelegten Nybyggen werden gleich Anfangs 50 Freijahre bewilliget. Nach Ablauf der Freijahre werden die Nybyggare zu Schatz gesetzt, und treten aus der Klasse der Nybyggare in die der steuerpflichtigen Bauern; doch genießen sie auch noch als solche Lappmarks-Privilegien, von denen oben geredet worden ist, und können die von ihnen bisher benutzten Ländereien, unter sehr günstigen Bedingungen, in Eigenthum verwandeln.

Bei allen Kolonisten ist Viehzucht der erste und ergiebigste Nahrungszweig. Ackerbau ist Nebenerwerb, Fischerei und Jagd

---

ria perpetuis, die sich in den meisten Breviarien fanden, oder mit Runenstäben; zuweilen gaben die Synoden Anweisungen über die beweglichen Feste heraus; auch übersetzte man Kalender aus dem Deutschen.

treiben sie mit großem Gewinn; bei letzterer gebrauchen sie, an einigen Orten, Bogen. Sie sind sehr geschickte Jäger und treffliche Schlittschuhläufer.

Arm kamen sie ins Land, jetzt sind sie im Allgemeinen wohlhabend, eine Folge ihrer Mäßigkeit und unermüdeter Arbeitsamkeit. Ihre Zahl vermehrt sich mit jedem Jahre, weniger durch neue Ankömmlinge, die nur bei großer Anstrengung ihr Fortkommen finden, als durch Theilung des väterlichen Erbgutes unter Kinder und Schwiegerkinder (hemmansklyfning), wodurch eine Menge neuer Wohnsitze und Familien entsteht. Die Weiber der Kolonisten sind sehr fruchtbar; es ist sehr gewöhnlich, 9 bis 12 Kinder in einer Familie zu finden, zuweilen 16, 20, 24, und wenige dieser Kinder sterben im zarten Alter. Ueberhaupt sind die Nybyggare durch einfache und mäßige Lebensweise und Arbeitsamkeit ein gesundes und kräftiges Volk, und werden nicht selten sehr alt. Bieder, gastfrei und gottesfürchtig, hängen sie mit ganzer Seele an Religion und Kirche.

Die meisten Nybyggare haben sich in der Nähe von Flüssen und Seen niedergelassen, theils der Fischerei, theils der bessern Wiesen halber, theils weil sie dafür halten, daß die im Herbst aus dem Wasser aufsteigenden Dünste das Land erwärmen.

Im Allgemeinen leben sie friedlich unter einander und mit den Lappen; indessen entsteht zuweilen mit den letztern Streit über Rennthierweide, für welche die Kolonisten von den Lappen Bezahlung fordern, insofern sie auf das Weideland Anspruch zu haben glauben. Zuweilen verderben die Lappischen Heerden die Schwedischen Heuhaufen, daher man diese, wo sie üblich sind, umzäunt.

Die Nybyggare besitzen viel Geschicklichkeit in Verfertigung von allerlei Handarbeiten. Jeder macht selbst, was er bedarf an Schmiede-, Tischler-, Zimmermanns-, Schneider- und Schusterarbeit. In jedem Haushalt wird zum eignen Bedarf gesponnen und gewebt; in Lycksele macht man auch Spinnrocken, hölzerne Teller, Schalen 2c. Ziegeleien hat man nicht, aber ungebrannte Mauer- und Ziegelsteine bereitet man, nach Bedarf.

Das Geschäft des Säens verrichten die Weiber. Gesinde halten die Kolonisten wenig.

Die Namen der Kolonisten sind ganz wie die der Schwedischen und Finnischen Bauern; nur wenn sie Handwerker werden, — was aber selten geschieht — legen sie sich Eigennamen bei.

In der Regel halten die Nybyggare mehr Kühe, als sie im Winter ausfüttern können, wodurch mancherley Verluste entstehen.

Die Nahrungsmittel der Nybyggare sind einfach, aber gut. Um 5 Uhr frühe wird das Frühstück eingenommen, bestehend in ungerahmter Milch und Brot; um 10 Uhr folgt die Morgenkost (morgonvard): eine dicke Suppe, gesalzener Fisch und Brot; um 3 Uhr das Mittagsessen: Fisch oder Milch und eine andere gekochte Speise; um 9 Uhr das Abendessen: eine breiartige Suppe (velling). Branntewein gebrauchen sie nur als Medicin, oder als Getränk für Fremde. Ihr Brot besteht in dünnen Gerstenfladen, denen, nur des Backens wegen, ein wenig Roggenmehl zugemischt ist. In Mißwachsjahren ißt man Rindenbrot, neueingezogene Kolonisten, bevor sie zu einigem Vermögen gelangt, auch wohl sonst. Man trocknet zu diesem Behufe das weiße Innere der Fichtenrinde in der Darrbude, bricht es in Stücke und zerstampft diese in einer Tonne; dann trocknet man wieder und fängt nun an zu mahlen. Das Rindenbrot hat einen bittern Geschmack. Einige sollen Heu zum Brote gebrauchen.

Auch die wohlhabenden Standespersonen in Lappland leben sehr einfach; Kaffee trinken sie selten, Wein nie; die Stelle des Weins vertritt gutes Bier. Das Getränk der Kolonisten ist Milch oder Milch mit Wasser, nur in Åsele Bier.

Nach guten Erndten feiern die Kolonisten einen Erndteschmaus (skördagdllscalas): Dorf und Anverwandte werden zu einem fröhlichen Mittagsessen geladen; man speiset frische Fische, Fleischsuppe mit Fleisch, Lammbraten, Vogelwildpret, Kartoffeln, Käsekuchen, hat Gersten- und weiches Roggenbrot, und zuweilen sogar ein wenig Branntewein; als Getränk dient Wasser mit Milch oder unvermischte Milch. Am Abend wird ein zweites Mahl eingenommen, worauf die jungen Leute tanzen. — Am folgenden Tage giebt ein anderer Hof den Erndteschmaus, und so geht es fort, bis alle Höfe des Dorfes an die Reihe gekommen sind; doch wird das Schmausen nicht länger als höchstens 4 Tage hintereinander fortgesetzt. — Bei den Hochzeiten ist Musik und Tanz; man tanzt, nach dem Takt, Polonaisen, Menuetten und Quadrillen. — An hohen Festen speiset jede Familie besser als gewöhnlich; am Weihnachtsabend dickgekochte Gerstgrütze und etwas frisches, als Fische, genießt auch wohl Braten und ein wenig Branntwein. Am 20sten Tag nach Weihnachten, am Knutstage (13. Januar), dem letzten der fröhlichen Weihnachtszeit, pflegt man zu tanzen, auch ein kleines Mahl anzustellen. Der Johannistag wird durch bessere Speise gefeiert; Rahm, süßen Käse, der dieser Jahrszeit' eigenthümlich ist, Vogeleyer, frische Fische und ein wenig Branntwein, falls es die Umstände erlauben. — Aber auch an den Feiertagen wird die Mäßigkeit nicht verletzt, und keine Ausschweifung findet Statt.

Im Sommer erzeugt der häufige Genuß der Milch — Wiesen fast die einzige Speise — insbesondere der süßen, häufig Obstructionen. Fremde pflegen von dem Uebel am heftigsten befallen zu werden; Wahlenberg überwand die Krankheit durch laue Bäder und inwendig gebrauchte zerlassene Butter. Nicht selten sind die Obstructionen tödlich. Wechselt man mit mehreren Speisen ab, oder genieße mehr saure Milch, so wirkt auch der häufige Milchgenuß wenig oder gar nicht schädlich.

B. Spezialbeschreibung der einzelnen Schwedischen Lappmarken.

Wie in kirchlicher Hinsicht das Schwedische Lappland Pastorate bildet, so zerfällt es in politischer Hinsicht in Lappmarker, d. i. Lappengebiete, Lappendistrikte. Das gesammte Land nennt man Lappmarker, nicht „Lappland," denn mit dem Worte „Lappland" bezeichnet man zur Weide für Rennthiere geeignetes Land, welches die Eigner, Lappen und Schweden, gegen Lappenschatz (Lappensteuer an die Krone) inne haben.

Es giebt 6 Schwedische Lappmarker, und zwar von Süden nach Norden folgende: Jämtelands=Lappmark, Åsele=Lappmark, Umeå= oder Lycksele=Lappmark, Piteå=Lappmark, Luleå=Lappmark und Torneå-Lappmark. Der *) 7te Schwedische Lappmark, Kemi-Lappmark, ward im Frieden von Fredrikshamn nebst einem Theil von Torneå-Lappmark an Rußland abgetreten.

I. Jämtelands-Lappmark,

oder richtiger, Jämtelands- und Herjeådalens-Lappmark, begreift die Alpen (Fjäll) und Thäler längs der Norwegischen Gränze, von Nord-Jämteland bis Nord-Dalarne (Dalekarlien), also Theile der Provinzen Jämteland und Herjeådalen, oder des Läns Östersund. Dieser Lappendistrikt bildet nicht, wie die übrigen Lappmarken, eigene Pastorate, sondern gehört zu den Schwedischen Pastoraten Hammardal, Fölinge und Undersåker in Jämteland, so wie Hede in Herjeådalen; man pflegt daher auch Hammardals (Ström's) Fölinge's, Undersåker's und Hede-Lappmark zu unterscheiden.

a. Ström's- und Fölinge-Lappmarker.

Hammardal's- und Fölinge-Lappmarker, oder die Lappendistrikte in den Pastoraten Hammardal und Fölinge werden vom Pastor in Fölinge, der aber keineweges blos Lappen-Pastor ist, sondern eine viel beträchtlichere Schwedische Gemeinde hat, besorgt. Die Lappen von Hammardal beweiden einen Theil der zum Pastorat Hammardal gehörigen Filialgemeinde Ström (im übrigen Pastorat giebt es nur 2 Lappen, welche betteln oder als Hirten sich verdungen haben). Im Jahre 1815 war die Zahl der Lappen von Ström und Fölinge an Erwachsenen und Kindern 294, wovon 138 männlichen und 156 weiblichen Geschlechts, nämlich 52 Ehepaare, 20 Wittwer und Wittwen, 83 Unverheirathete über 15 Jahren, 87 unter 15 Jahren. Unter diesen Lappen waren 47 Ehepaare, 2 Wittwer und 5 Wittwen im Besitz von Rennthieren; nur 4 Ehepaare, 5 Wittwer nur 3 Wittwen hatten keine Rennthiere. Der im Pastorat (meist bettelnd) umherziehenden Lappen waren 1 Ehepaar und 5 Wittwen, der dienenden Lappen 7. Unter den Lappenfamilien befanden sich 7 reiche, 27 wohlhabende, 20 dürftige, 9 ganz arme. — Uebrigens wohnten von den 294 **) Lappen, in Fölinge-Lappmark 115 (was

---

*) Mark ist im Schwedischen masculinum.
**) Im Jahr 1810 noch 311.

von 34 unter 15 Jahren) und in Ström's-Lappmark 178 (wovon 53 unter 15 Jahren). Die Lappen von Fölinge besaßen
ungefähr 4000, die von Ström 6000 Rennthiere; die wenigen
Rennthiere, welche die Schwedischen Bauern halten, werden von
den Lappen gehütet. Diese Lappen leben von dem Ertrage ihrer
Heerden; einige fischen auch, treiben aber keinen Ackerbau; nur
ein einziger Lappe ward Nybyggare. Sie sind, etwa einige Alte
ausgenommen, der Schwedischen Sprache so kundig, daß vor ihnen nur Schwedisch geprediget und von ihren Katecheten oder
reisenden Schullehrern der Unterricht in Schwedischer Sprache
ertheilt wird. Sie lesen fleißig in der Schwedischen Bibel, von
welcher, seit der neuesten Vertheilung, fast jede Familie ein Exem-
plar besitzt; sonst sprechen sie das Schwedische nur gebrochen, jedoch verständlich; unter sich reden sie Lappisch. Im Winter ziehen diese Lappen in Norwegen und in den, ihren Lappmarken
benachbarten, Gemeinden Ramsele, und Resele (in Ängermanland),
Fölinge, Stugua, Ragunda, Häggenås, Ström, Hammardal (in
Jämtland) umher, an jedem Orte bleiben sie gewöhnlich nur 8
Tage, wohnen daselbst dem Gottesdienst bei, communiciren auch
in diesen Gemeinden; doch müssen sie, um zum heil. Abendmahl
zugelassen zu werden, ein Zeugniß ihres Seelsorgers aufzeigen,
das über ihre Zulassungsfähigkeit Auskunft giebt; bei ihrer Rückkehr haben sie über jede in fremden Gemeinden gefeierte Communion ihrem Seelsorger ein Zeugniß des Geistlichen, bei welchem sie communicirten, einzuhändigen. Auch Norwegische Lappen kommen hieher und erhalten Zeugnisse, ob sie hier dem Gottesdienst beiwohnten und am heiligen Abendmahl Theil nahmen.
In der Kirche Ström hält der Pastor von Fölinge am Neu-
jahrstage und am Sonntage vor Fastnacht Gottesdienst und Communion für die Lappen, wo aber auch einige Schweden Theil
nehmen; der Comminister von Ström unterstützt den Pastor in
dieser Amtsverwaltung. Die Aufzeichnung zum heil. Abendmahl
geschieht am Vorabend, das Communionverhör (s. Schwedens
Kirchenverfassung Bd. 2. S. 59 — 61) und die Beichte am
Frühmorgen, worauf der eigentliche Gottesdienst mit Predigt und
die Communion folgen. Weingeld (Vinören zur Anschaffung des

Abendmahlweins) erlegen die Lappen nicht. Im Sommer hält der Pastor von Fölinge Lappen-Gottesdienst in den Kapellen Hotagen und Frostvik in dem an Norwegen gränzenden nordöstlichen Theile von Jemteland, an jedem Orte zweimal, Johannis und Michaelis, wo dann auch die Schwedischen Bewohner dieser Kapellgemeinden (im Jahr 1815 in Frostvik 245, in Hotagen 162, meistens Norwegischer Abkunft) Theil nehmen. Die hölzerne Kapelle Hotagen liegt 4 Meilen Boot- und ½ Meile Gehweg von der Kirche Fölinge entfernt, auf dem Wege nach Frostvik. Hotagen entstand um 1793 als eigne Gemeinde, doch ohne eigenen Prediger. Die hölzerne Kapelle Frostvik *), um 1793 erbauet, liegt noch näher der Norwegischen Gränze; der nächste Weg dahin von Fölinge aus führt durch die Norwegischen Kirchspiele Söder- und Norra-Lie und beträgt 15 Meilen; ein zweiter Weg, ganz durch Schwedisches Gebiet, 21 Meilen, nämlich von Fölinge nach Hammardal 4½ Meilen, nach Ström 3½ Meilen, nach Frostvik, Bootweg auf dem Wasdol, einem langen Zuge von Seen und Flüssen, 3 Landengen (edar) ausgenommen, wo man der Wasserfälle wegen, das Boot ziehen muß, 13 Meilen. — Nachdem mehrere Monate vorher vom Geistlichen die Tage angesetzt und bekannt gemacht worden sind, sucht derselbe seine Reise so einzurichten, daß er am Freitag oder Sonnabend eintrifft; Lappen und Schweden sind schon versammelt. Die kirchlichen Akte beginnen mit der Anzeichnung derer, die das heilige Abendmahl genießen wollen. Ist etwa einer derselben in Streitigkeiten verwickelt, so muß er sich, durch Zuthun des Geistlichen, mit seinem Gegner versöhnen, bevor er angezeichnet wird; auch werden die jungen Leute vorbereitet, welche zum ersten Mal com-

---

*) Die Kapelle ist auf Norwegische Weise gebauet: der Thurm steht auf dem Kirchdache, und vom Chor aus wird geläutet, auch sind die Fenster höher. — In früheren Zeiten ward in Håkansfot auf freiem Felde, dann zu Gäddbedet in der Scheune eines Kolonisten gepredigt; jetzt weder an dem einen, noch an dem andern Orte. Auch ist bei Brandflogsvlländet kein Begräbnißplatz mehr. Dieß zur Berichtigung von Djurberg's (svergies Geographie) neuen, aber veralteten Angaben.

municiren wollen, worauf auch der Abend des Sonntages, zuweis
len ein ganzer Tag verwandt wird. Diese Vorbereitung dauert
bei den Einzelnen aber mehrere Jahre; ein anderer Confirmans
denunterricht findet, bei der weiten Entfernung von der Mutters
kirche, nicht Statt. Um 6 Uhr Abends wird der Feiertag eins
geläutet. Am Sonntag Morgen wird in der neben der Kapelle
gelegenen Kirchspielsstube (sockenstufva), 1 Stunde lang, Coms
munionverhör gehalten (Rede, Prüfung, Lehre, Gebet, Segen
und Gesang). Dann begiebt man sich in die Kirche. Hier fols
gen Beichte, Taufe (die Kinder sind zuweilen 9 Monate alt und
haben schon die Nothtaufe erhalten; vor einiger Zeit ereignete
es sich, daß während der Prediger mit der rechten Hand den
Segen ertheilen wollte, der Knabe das Buch ergriff, das jener
in der Linken hielt), die Einsegnung der Wöchnerinnen, die
Trauung (die zweite Hälfte des Traualts — brudmessa — wird
nach dem Gottesdienst verrichtet, wo dann auch über Lappen
der Brauthimmel — pellet — gehalten wird), der eigentliche
Gottesdienst, das heil. Abendmahl; gepredigt wird über das
Sonntagsevangelium. In den übrigen Stunden des Tages, oft
bis Mitternacht, ist der Geistliche mit Abfassung der Leichenpers
sonalien, Unterricht der Confirmanden, Beantwortung von Vors
fragen und anderen Akten der speziellen Seelsorge beschäftiget. —
Am Montage hält der Geistliche Communionverhör, Beichte und
alle übrigen kirchlichen Akte, ganz wie am Sonntage; Predigts
text ist der Bettagstext, falls über diesen nicht etwa am Sonntage
gepredigt wurde. Nach geendigtem Gottesdienst eröffnet der Geists
liche den Kirchspielsstand (sockenstämma), erst mit den Schweden,
wo aber auch die Lappen zugegen sind, dann mit den Lappen, wo die
Sechsmänner rc. gewählt und andere kirchliche Angelegenheiten
abgemacht werden; so wird z. B. in der Lappischen Sockenstäms
ma bestimmt, zu welchen Lappen sich jetzt der Katechet wenden,
welche Lappenkinder in die Schule aufgenommen werden sollen,
es werden Nachrichten über die Amtsverwaltung der Katecheten
eingezogen rc. Am Schluß der Sockenstämma nimmt der Geists
liche Abschied und ertheilt den Segen.

Für den Geiſtlichen iſt neben den Kapellen ein eigenes Wohnhaus erbauet; die Nybyggare ſpeiſen ihn mit Milch, Fiſchen und Fleiſch, nach einer gewiſſen Reihenfolge. Die Lappen übernachten bei den Nybyggare, oder im Freien am Feuer, denn Hütten haben ſie hier nicht. — Neben beiden Kapellen ſind Begräbnißplätze, daher denn auch, bei Anweſenheit des Geiſtlichen, die Begräbniſſe nach Schwediſcher Liturgie verrichtet werden.

Hausverhöre werden mit den Lappen dieſer Diſtrikte nicht gehalten. Fehlen die Lappen zweimal hinter einander beim Gottesdienſt, ſo werden ſie gewöhnlich mit einer kleinen Geldbuße belegt. Ihre Andacht beim Gottesdienſt iſt rührend; gemeiniglich gehen ſie bei jedem dieſer Alpengottesdienſte auch zum heil. Abendmahl. Ihre chriſtlichen Kenntniſſe ſind richtig und umfaſſend, Religioſität und Sittlichkeit wachſen mit jedem Jahre; dem Hange zum Branntewein widerſtehen ſie immer mehr, zu Hauſe trinken ſie ihn nie. Für die Seelſorge der Lappen erhält der Paſtor von der Krone 26 Tonnen Gerſte, von ſteuerpflichtigen Lappen 1 Rennthierfell, 1 Rennthierbraten und 1 Rennthierkäſe, von Hushållslappar oder Sprintar, oder ſolchen, die nicht für eigenes Lappland ſteuern, ſondern auf ſolchem Lappland, wofür andere an die Krone ſteuern, wohnen, 1 Rennthierbraten.

Der Katecheten ſind 2, einer in jedem Lappmark. Sie reiſen im Sommer von Hütte zu Hütte und ertheilen Unterricht im Chriſtenthum. Auch im Winter folgen ſie den Lappen. An den Sonntagen halten ſie auch Poſtillenleſung und Gebet, und gehen beim Alpengottesdienſt dem Prediger mit Nachrichten über die Lappen an die Hand. Sie ſind Schweden oder Lappen. Von den Unterrichteten erhalten ſie freie Station, und aus dem Lappmarksfond einen jährlichen Gehalt von 8 Bankthalern. So lange der Paſtor mit ihnen zufrieden iſt, bleiben ſie im Amte. Jährlich erſtatten ſie an denſelben einen Bericht, in welchem ſie jedes einzelne der von ihnen unterrichteten Kinder nach Faſſungsgabe, Kenntniſſen ꝛc. ſchildern. Der Paſtor berichtet alljährlich im Junius über die geſammte Schweden- und Lappengemeinde an das Conſiſtorium, und hält für dieſen Zweck im Mai eine feierliche Visitation seiner Gemeinde. Ueber die Lappen werden besondere Mortalitäts = und Populations = Listen geführt.

Die Lappenschule für Ström's = und Fölinge = Lappmark hat bei der Kirche Fölinge ihren Sitz, sie ward im Jahr 1746 errichtet und besteht durch öffentliche Mittel. Selten werden in die Schule mehr als 6 Kinder aufgenommen, gewöhnlich 3 Knaben und 3 Mädchen. Der Unterricht wird in Schwedischer Sprache ertheilt und wohnen die Zöglinge vor ihrer Entlassung aus der Schule, auch dem Confirmandenunterricht der Schwedischen Kinder bei, werden zugleich mit ihnen confirmirt und zum ersten Genuß des heil. Abendmahls nebst andern Lappenkindern zugelassen. Der Schulunterricht besteht hauptsächlich im Lesen und in den Hauptstücken des Christenthums; nur diejenigen, welche Anlagen haben, dem Amte eines Katecheten einst mit Erfolg vorzustehen, werden auch im Schreiben und Rechnen unterwiesen. Jeden Morgen und Abend wird mit den Kindern gebetet, nach dem Abendgebet werden gewöhnlich kurze Unterredungen über das Christenthum angestellt. An den Abenden des Sonnabends und des Sonntages wohnen sie dem Gebete bei, welches der Pastor mit sämmtlichen Bewohnern des Pfarrhofes hält. Gewöhnlich bleiben die Kinder zwei Jahre in der Schule. Das Schulmeisteramt verwaltet gegenwärtig der Pastor, Johann Axel Huß, wofür er aus dem Lappenfond 33 Rthle 16 ßl. banco jährlich bezieht. Auch sorgt er für Nahrung und Kleidung der Kinder, wofür der Marktpreis von 56 Tonnen Gerste bestanden wird; Knaben und Mädchen erhalten alle 2 Jahre Koltar oder Röcke, und abwechselnd jährlich lange Beinkleider und Kamisöler. Ein eigenes Schulhaus ist nicht vorhanden, der Pastor räumt dazu ein Nebengebäude des Pfarrhofes gegen eine jährliche Miethe von 3½ Bankthalern ein; im Schulzimmer schlafen auch die Knaben; die Mädchen schlafen in einem besonderen Locale neben den Viehmädchen des Pfarrhofes.

Die Lappen von Fölinge und Ström werden mit Schwedischen Namen, ganz wie die der Schwedischen Bauern, z. B. Pehr Petersson, Sigrid Mänsdotter ꝛc., in die Kirchenbücher eingezeichnet; unter sich führen sie Lappische Zunamen. Sie ge=

hen Lappisch gekleidet. Ihre Hütten, in Kegelform, sind mit Walmar oder Rennthierleder bedeckt. Mit jedem Jahre nehmen diese Lappen an Zahl und Vermögen ab, theils der geringen Fruchtbarkeit der Lappischen Weiber, theils des Eindrangs der Schwedischen Nybyggare wegen. Letztere verfahren oft sehr ungerecht gegen die Lappen, indem sie durch Rennthiermoos ganz besonders zur Weide geeignetes Land in Besitz nehmen, für welches doch die Lappen den Schatz entrichten. Durch diesen Eindrang entstehen Haß und Streitigkeiten, ja im Jahr 1813 wurde auf diese Weise ein Mord veranlaßt. Ein Nybyggare erhielt nämlich vom Landshöfdingsamt die Erlaubniß, auf Lappenland, wofür schon ein Lappe schatzte, sich niederzulassen. Auf diesem Lande lag ein See, in welchem der Lappe zu fischen pflegte. Der Lappe fischte nach wie vor; aber der Nybyggare nahm ihm die Netze. Der Lappe, welcher einsah, daß er oder der Nybyggare verhungern müsse, drohte; ja, endlich gingen 3 Lappen zum Nybygge und erschossen den Nybyggare nebst dessen Frau. Nach einigen Monaten kamen Schweden zum Nybygge, und fanden — die Eltern erschossen und drei Kinder, nebst dem gesammten Vieh, zu Tode gehungert; die älteste, 11jährige, Tochter hatte noch zuletzt das Leiden ihrer jüngsten Schwester mildern wollen, indem sie sie durch Vorzeigung an der Wand aufgehängter Bilderchen zu beschäftigen suchte. Bald fiel der Verdacht auf 3 Lappen, welche Drohungen gegen den Nybyggare ausgestoßen hatten, insbesondere als man bei ihnen einen gesalzenen Fisch fand, den sie dem Nybyggare entwandt zu haben schienen, denn die Lappen haben hier keine gesalzene Fische, und brauchen überhaupt wenig Salz; auch hatte der Nybyggare diesen gesalzenen Fisch einem andern Schweden zugesagt. Die 3 Lappen wurden nun eingezogen, des Mordes überführt und gehängt. — Dennoch herrscht keinesweges zwischen allen Lappen und Nybyggare Haß; im Ganzen vertragen sich beide gut, wenn gleich sie nie unter einander heirathen. Man sollte wirklich den Lappen ihr Lappland lassen und streng gegen diejenigen Nybyggare verfahren, die in den rechtmäßigen Besitz der Lappen eingreifen, oder sie den Schweden, denen sie sich überdieß immer mehr nähern, ganz ein-

II.   U

verleiben, welches letztere freilich seine großen Schwierigkeiten hat. — Mehrere Lappen dienen als Knechte und Mägde bei den Schwedischen Bauern; diesen könnten ihre Hausherren den Lohn in Ackerland geben und sie dagegen verpflichtet seyn, den Bauern als Torpare zu dienen; zugleich könnten diese Lappen Rennthier, land gegen Schatz besitzen. Auf solche Weise würden die Lappen allmählig an Verbindung von Ackerbau und Viehzucht gewöhnt werden.

Lappenmärkte sind für Fölinge, und Ström's-Lappmarker gesetzlich nicht angeordnet. Doch wird, nach altem Gebrauch, jährlich ein Markt für die Lappen zu Ström gehalten. Die Anordnung bestimmter Lappenmärkte in Ström und Fölinge wäre zu wünschen, indem jetzt die Schweden mit allerlei Waaren zu den Lappenkoten reisen, welches mancherlei Nachtheile verursacht. Die Lappen verkaufen Rennthierbraten, Rennthierhäute, Reife aus Rennthiersehnen, und die sogenannten Lappenschuhe aus Rennthierleder; dagegen kaufen sie Walmar (grobes Tuch) zu Hütten und zu Kleidern, ein wenig Mehl und Tabak, denn Tabak rauchen und kauen Männer und Weiber mit größtem Wohlgeschmack, der sie zumal bei den Hochzeiten, wo sie sich am Tabak recht gütlich thun, zu freudevollen Liedern begeistert. Ihr Gesang ist häßlich; auf den Gräbern stoßen sie Klaggeschrei aus. Branntewein brauchen sie wenig, selbst bei Hochzeiten trinken ihn viele nicht, eingedenk, daß sie bald berauscht werden würden; die Lappen können von starkem Getränke nur wenig ertragen: schon drei kleine Gläser Branntewein ziehen ihnen einen Rausch zu. Uebrigens feiern sie ihre Hochzeiten noch ganz nach Lappenweise: haben Brautwerber rc.; die Freiergaben bestehen in Geld. Der alte Aberglaube ist unter ihnen fast ganz erloschen, die Zaubertrommeln sind verschwunden. Statt der Bogen bedienen sich die Lappen jetzt der Büchsen. Sie sind leicht und behende, treffliche Schlittschuhläufer und tragen ihre Böte zwischen den Seen auf den Schultern. Sie sind heiter und lebendig, aber furchtsam und argwöhnisch, mäßig und wohlthätig, doch fast nur gegen Lappen. Die Zierrathen auf ihren Kleidungen, die silbernen ausgenommen, verfertigen sie selbst. Sie schlafen wenig, im

Sommer wie im Winter; eine Folge ihrer Lebensart. Die meiſten Lappenmädchen ſind ſchön.   Die Vaccination iſt eingeführt worden.   Der Runenſtäbe ſind einige Lappen noch kundig, eben ſo einige Nybyggare bei Froſtvik; überhaupt gebrauchen die Nybyggare im ganzen Paſtorat Föling meſſingene Tabaksdoſen mit Runenalmanachen; in dieſer Doſe bewahren ſie auch die kleine thönerne Pfeife auf, deren man ſich in Jemteland allgemein bedient.

Die Lappen ſind gaſtfrei und dienſtfertig.   Dieberey giebt es unter ihnen gegenwärtig mehr als zuvor.   Die Lappiſchen Wiegen (jurkum) ſind unter ihnen noch üblich; auch hängen ſie den Kindern Glasperlen, als Spielzeug, vor die Augen.   Hebs ammen kennen ſie nicht.   Unzucht iſt unter ihnen eine große Seltenheit; geſchwängerte Mädchen werden faſt nie verheirathet.

Auf ihren Nomadenzügen führen ſie ihre geſammte Habe mit ſich, auch Silber, was ſie aber nur ſelten beſitzen, oder verwahren ſie in ihren ſtabur, d. i. den auf einem hohen Pfahl ruhenden Speiſehütten, die in den Alpen auf dem ganzen Wege, den ſie auf den Zügen mit den Heerden berühren, in gewiſſen Entfernungen von einander angelegt ſind.

Gletſcher giebt es in Föling s und Ström's s Lappmarker nicht, wohl aber hohe Alpen, die ſtets mit Schnee bedeckt ſind.

Die Schwediſchen Koloniſten, welche in dieſen Lappmarker wohnen, treiben wenig Ackerbau.   Nie reift das Korn ganz, und ſie ſind ſehr froh, wenn ſie nur das nöthigſte Brotkorn erhalten; an Saatkorn iſt nicht zu denken.   Man ſäet zu Ende Mai's und erndtet zu Ende Auguſts.   Uebrigens ſind es einfache und fromme Menſchen, deren Wandel, die oft ungerechten Verhältniſſe gegen die Lappen ausgenommen, ſtreng ſittlich iſt.   Das Brot backen ſie, zumal um Froſtvik herum, nicht in Oefen, ſondern, nach Norwegiſcher Weiſe, auf dem Feuerheerd auf eiſernen Platten (hällar).

b. Underſåker's s und Offerdal's Lappmarker.

Die Seelſorge der in den Alpen der Jemtländiſchen Paſtorate Underſåker und Offerdal nomadiſirenden Lappen iſt ſeit

U 2

etwa 40 Jahren dem Comminister in Undersäker, gegenwärtig Mag. Lars Erik Festin, anvertrauet, wofür er 6 Tonnen Gerste und 3 Banktthaler an Gehalt bezieht. Die Lappen von Undersäker werden, nach den Namen dreier zum Pastorat Undersäker gehörigen Kirchspiele, in Kall's, Åre's und Undersäker's Lappen, abgetheilt; letztere waren früherhin in kirchlicher Hinsicht dem Pastorat Hede in Herjeådalen untergeordnet.

Die Zahl der Lappen betrug im Jahr 1816

in den Alpen von Kall	. . .	68
. . . . . Åre	. . .	21
. . . . . Undersäker	.	56
. . . . . Offerdal	. .	19
		164 Seelen.

Von diesen 164 waren 25 Ehepaare, 6 Wittwer, 9 Wittwen; sie bildeten 45 Familien oder Wirthschaften (matlag), nämlich 20 in Kall, 5 in Åre, 14 in Undersäker, 6 in Offerdal; 23 dieser Matlag lebten auf den Alpen vom Ertrage ihrer Rennthierheerden, die übrigen dienten auf den Alpen oder im niedern Lande, wo sie auch bettelten.

Die eigentlichen Rennthierlappen dieser Bezirke verlassen nie ganz die Alpen, wie z. B. die Westerbottnischen Lappen, welche im Winter auch im niedern Lande mit ihren Heerden umherziehen; nur theilweise gehen sie ins Land, um zu kaufen. Im Sommer leben sie auf den entferntern, im Winter auf den, dem niederen Lande nähern, Schwedischen oder Norwegischen Alpen. Der Nybyggart giebt es in diesen Bezirken wenige, daher von ihnen die Lappen keinen Eintrag erleiden und hinreichende Weide haben, weshalb sich ihre Zahl nur durch Auswanderung nach Norwegen und Krankheiten verminderte, wie letzteres z. B. vor einigen Jahren in Kall der Fall war.

Eigentliche Fischerlappen giebt es hier nicht, wenn gleich auch die Rennthierlappen zuweilen Fische angeln; die Fischereien gehören in der Regel den Bauern. Die Kinderzahl eines Lappischen Ehepaars wird hier eben so groß als die eines Schwedischen angegeben; doch scheint mir diese Angabe weder sicher noch allgemein. Zuweilen ereignet es sich, daß Lappen, welche nur wenige Rennthiere haben, sie denen, die mehrere haben, zur Weide geben, während sie selbst im niedern Lande betteln, doch wird die Betteley nur von wirklich Bedürftigen geübt. Der reichste Lappe soll an 1000 Rennthiere besitzen, der wohlhabende 400 bis 500. Die wenigen Bauern, welche Rennthiere halten, geben sie den Lappen zur Wartung, büßen aber diese Rennthiere nicht selten ein, wobei sich die Lappen zuweilen Betrügereien zu Schulden kommen lassen sollen. Viele der hiesigen Lappen sind in Norwegen geboren und erhalten in Norwegischer Sprache ihren Unterricht, wiewohl sie auch des Schwedischen kundig seyn mögen; mehrere Norwegische Lappen halten sich im Winter auf der Schwedischen Seite auf, doch ohne dafür Schatz zu geben.

Die hiesigen Lappen wollen ungerne Lappen heißen, sondern Fjällmän (Alpenmänner) oder Finnar (Finnen), weil sie von den Finnen abzustammen glauben, nennen sich auch selber so, doch ohne den Namen Lappen zu verabscheuen. Kein einziger dieser Lappen treibt Ackerbau. Ihre Namen sind, wie die der Schwedischen Bauern; doch haben einige auch Zunamen, mit denen sie in den Kirchenbüchern aufgeführt sind. Die Lappen von Kall sind die ärmsten.

Der Lappen-Gottesdienst wird in Schwedischer Sprache, deren sie völlig mächtig sind, wenn gleich sie unter einander Lappisch sprechen, gehalten (auch Schweden nehmen Theil), — mit den Lappen von Åre und Undersåker einmal im Sommer, (im Julius) in der Kapelle des Schwedischen Dorfs Handöl, einem hölzernen, 12 Ellen langen, 10½ Ellen breiten, 4½ Ellen hohen, mit doppeltem Bretterdach und mit Thurm versehenen Gebäude, mit alter, aus Fröson geschenkten Kanzel (die Kapelle ward vor etwa 10 Jahren durch die Thätigkeit des eifrigen Festin, der die größere Hälfte der Kosten hergab, gegründet; die kleinere Hälfte bestritt die Gemeinde, Schweden und Lappen; die eine der Glocken gaben die Lappen, die zweite das Bruk; die Unterhaltung der Kapelle haben die Bauern von Handöl übernommen), und im Winter mehrere Male im Comminister-hofe Nyland oder in der Kirche Undersåker; — mit den Lappen von Kall und Offerdal, einmal im Sommer im Schwedischen

Dorfe Käläsen, Kirchspiels Kall, auf einem Hofe, und einmal im Winter in der Kirche von Offerdal.

Der Alpengottesdienst in diesen Lappmarken wird 4 Wochen vorher angekündigt. Der Prediger trifft am Freitag ein. Am Sonnabend werden die Anwesenden verzeichnet (die Fehlenden bestraft), und mit Alt und Jung, unter Gebet und Gesang, ein Katechismusverhör, mehrere Stunden lang, gehalten; auch die, welche am nächsten Tage communiciren wollen, aufgeschrieben. Am Sonntag Morgen folgt Communionverhör, Beichte ꝛc., ganz wie oben beschrieben worden ist. Nach der Predigt über das Sonntagsevangelium wird der Gränztraktat zwischen Schweden und Norwegen vom 7. Oct. 1751, nebst anderen Verordnungen, verlesen. Am Nachmittage erhebt der Prediger seinen Sommerzehnten, einen Rennthierkäse von jeder Wirthschaft, nebst 1 ßl. Weingeld von jedem Communicanten (wofür der Abendmahlswein gehalten wird), im Winter wird ein Rennthierbraten, auch wohl eine Rennthierzunge, gegeben. So oft Geschäfte es fordern, findet auch Kirchspielsstand Statt. An einem der 4 Bettage müssen die Lappen eine Schwedische Kirche besuchen, oder in Norwegen, am Norwegischen Bettage, dem Gottesdienst beiwohnen.

Im Winter wird der Lappengottesdienst auf gleiche Weise gehalten; nur daß in Nyland nicht gepredigt wird. Jeder Lappe communicirt 2 Mal jährlich. Die Lappischen Confirmanden werden mit den Schwedischen zugleich vorbereitet, drei Wochen hintereinander, Vor- und Nachmittags.

In ihren Hütten halten die Lappen sonntäglich unter einander Gottesdienst, wobei sie in Schwedischen Postillen lesen. Tischgebete sind unter diesen Lappen allgemein, Morgen- und Abendgebete der Einzelnen häufig; im Allgemeinen herrscht viel christliche Erkenntniß und Sittlichkeit; geschwängerte Mädchen trifft man höchst selten. Die Lappen von Kall und Offerdal haben weniger christliche Erkenntniß, freilich leben sie am weitesten vom Prediger entfernt. Mehrere bejahrte Lappen können nicht lesen.

Zwei Katecheten reisen im Winter umher, die Kinder der Lappen zu unterrichten, die sie an gewissen Stellen versammeln; an jeder dauert der Unterricht 6 Wochen. Das Amt des einen Katecheten versieht gegenwärtig der Prediger, der die Kinder zu sich kommen läßt. Der zweite Katechet ist ein Lappe, der auch an Sonntagen Gottesdienst mit den Lappen hält, und eben so, wie die Lappenlexmän, dem Prediger bei den Alpenreisen mit Nachrichten an die Hand geht. Dieser Lappischen Sechs-männer sind 4; sie wollen den Sechsmannseid nicht leisten, weil sie fürchten, ihn nicht ganz halten zu können, versprechen aber, nach besten Kräften dem Amte vorzustehen. Ein besonderer Lappen-Länsman ist angestellt und dem Comminister von Undersåker, als Lappenprediger, untergeordnet.

Alle kirchlichen Akte sind bei diesen Lappen, ganz wie bei den Schweden, denen sie sich, zumal in kirchlicher Beziehung, immer inniger anschließen. Hausverhöre sind nicht üblich.

Eine besondere Lappenschule giebt es nicht. Ein junger Lappe, Anders Renander, besuchte 1817 die Trivialschule zu Fröson und wollte Theologie studiren.

Besondere Lappentabellen über Volkszahl und Mortalität werden auch hier geführt. Der Jahresbericht an das Consistorium wird im Sommer abgesandt; aber eine Visitation findet nicht Statt.

Die Lappen nennen sich unter einander Du; eben so nennen sie die Fremden, auch wohl den Prediger, den sie gewöhnlich „Vater" heißen. Runenstäbe haben sie nicht mehr, wohl aber gewöhnliche Almanache, die jährlich umsonst vertheilt werden. Einen eigentlichen Lappenmarkt giebt es nicht; doch besuchen die Lappen den Markt zu Dufveby. Bauern aus Oviken, Undersåker und Åre kommen auf die Alpen, um von den Lappen gegen Branntewein, woran sie viel Geschmack finden, Rennthiere einzutauschen, deren Fleisch sie dann in Norwegen verkaufen. Ist Gelegenheit, so berauschen die Lappen sich gerne. Tabak brauchen sie viel; doch hat der Gebrauch, zumal bei Weibern, abgenommen; sie rauchen und kauen, aber schnupfen selten. Rennthierfleisch und Häute sind ihre Verkaufsartikel. Erst seit etwa

12 Jahren haben sie angefangen, ein wenig Salz zu gebrauchen. Brot haben sie selten; Käse und trockene Fische vertreten die Stelle.

Sie sind von mittlerer Statur, behende und schwach gebauet, so daß ein Jämte 3 bis 4 Lappen zu Boden werfen kann; auch ein Rennthier einen Lappen länger zu tragen vermag, als einen Schweden. Sie laufen schnell, am liebsten in die Krümme, dauern aber nicht lange aus; die meisten haben schwarzes Haar. Ein hübsches Lappenmädchen ist hier eine Seltenheit. Die Lappen dieser Gegend sind friedliebend, reinlich, dienstfertig und gastfrei; doch nicht ohne Eigennutz, Ehrgeiz und Argwohn, und nur gegen Verwandte wohlthätig; von Diebstahl hört man unter ihnen nicht.

Ihre Kleidung ist meist *) Lappisch, und wird von den Weibern verfertiget. Seit etwa 20 Jahren haben die Lappen angefangen, statt der unteren Walmarkleidung, linnene Hemder zu tragen. Bei Festlichkeiten haben sie Schwedische Schuhe und Stiefeln, die sie, nebst ihren Kleidern, den Bauern zur Verwahrung zu geben pflegen; die Weiber haben auch zum Theil kattunene Kleider und Tücher; auch Schwedische Schürzen. Lappen, welche den Schweden dienen, gehen Schwedisch gekleidet. Lappen und Schweden heirathen sich nicht; doch leben beide ruhig mit einander.

Ihre Hütten, die aus kegelförmig zusammengesetzten Stäben bestehen, sind über den Stäben mit Walmar bekleidet; oben mit Granrinde, Reisern und Nadeln, auch mit Moos und Rasen, gedeckt; bei Aermeren fehlt der Walmar.

Zaubertrommeln hatten die Lappen noch vor etwa 20 Jahren, jetzt nicht mehr; alle heidnischen Gebräuche sind verschwunden. Vor 10 Jahren versteckten sie noch ihr Silber in Felsenklüften; jetzt führen sie es mit sich, wollen aber nicht Wort haben, daß sie es besitzen.

Die Lappen dieser Distrikte halten nur zweimal am Tage, 6 Uhr Morgens und 6 Uhr Abends, Mahlzeit; sie essen weni-

---

*) Vergl. unten Reise nach Handöl. Kap. 26.

ger als die Schweden. Blinde soll es gegenwärtig (1817) nur Einen geben. Kartenspiel verstehen einige, aber üben es selten. Selbstmörder und Venerische hat es nie unter den Lappen gegeben; auch die Radesyge hat unter ihnen nicht geherrscht.

Eigentliche Gletscher giebt es auch in diesen Lappmarken nicht, wohl aber hohe Schneealpen, auf welchen aber vor Ende Augusts kein Schnee fällt.

c. Ovikens und Hede's Lappmarker.

Beide Lappmarken, erster Theil des Jämteländischen Pastorats Oviken, sind in kirchlicher Beziehung dem Pastor (Ruuth) zu Hede in Herjeådalen untergeordnet, seit 1780 der Pastor zu Oviken, Mag. Behm, die ihm zustehende Seelsorge für die Lappen seines Pastorats nach Hede übertrug, wohin nun auch der Lappzehnten (1 Braten und 1 Käse von jedem schatzpflichtigen Haushalt) fiel. Die Lappen im Bezirk des Pastorats Hede wurden bis zum Jahre 1806 vom Bruksprediger zu Ljusnedal im Pastorat Hede besorgt; dann hörte aber die Brukspredigerstelle in Ljusnedal auf, und die kirchliche Verwaltung des Lappendistrikts wurde nach der Mutterkirche Hede verpflanzt, wo nun der Pastor und der Comminister gemeinschaftlich den Geschäften vorstehen.

Im J. 1814 enthielten Ovikens und Hede's Lappmarker 10 Lappische Haushaltungen, die man zu etwa 80 Personen rechnen kann, wovon ungefähr ¼ zu Ovikens Lappmark gehört. Auch diese Lappen verstehen Schwedisch, sprechen aber unter einander Lappisch.

Im Sommer reiset der Pastor im Julius nach Storsjö-Kapell, an der Jämteländischen Gränze, wo die Lappen sich versammeln. Von Hede führt dahin ein 5 Meilen langer Reitweg, auf welchem man nur eine einzige Menschenwohnung, das Nybygge Sarfsjön, trifft. Die Kapelle ist neu, von Holz, mit Thurm und Glocken versehen, und wird daselbst jährlich zweimal Gottesdienst gehalten. Neben der Kapelle liegt das Dorf Storsjö.

Im Winter kommen die Lappen oft zur Kirche nach Tennäs, Ljusnedal und Hede. Hausverhör wird mit ihnen in der Kirche Hede gehalten, man singt, die Jugend liest, der Katechismus wird erklärt ꝛc. Kirchspielsstände sind mit den Lappen hier nicht üblich. Besondere Begräbnißplätze für Lappen giebt es nicht.

Die Lappen dieser Distrikte sind völlig Rennthierlappen, und 3 oder 4 unter ihnen besitzen 3 bis 400 Rennthiere, die meisten sind arm; Fischfang treiben sie wenig. Im Sommer ziehen sie mit ihren Heerden auf den Gebirgen und in den Thälern an der Jemteländischen und Norwegischen Gränze umher, stehen aber mit den Schwedischen Bauern in sehr gespannten Verhältnissen, weil sie zu gewissen Jahreszeiten sich den Dörfern sehr nähern, und indem sie die Rennthiere über die Dorfwiesen treiben, oder auf denselben gar weiden, diese für das Schwedische Vieh un: brauchbar machen, indem weder Kühe noch Pferde dort fressen, wo Rennthiere früher gefressen haben oder getrieben worden sind. Der Lappenschatz, der für die Alpenweide in Skärvagsdaler an den Alpen Helagsstolarne und Skarffjäll erlegt wird, ist sehr geringe. Im Winter halten die Lappen mit ihren Heerden sich im niederen Lande des Pastorats Hede auf. Ein Katechet, selbst ein Lappe, wandert .mit ihnen umher und unterrichtet im Win: ter gegen Kost und einen Lohn von 12 Bankthalern aus dem öffentlichen Fond, aus welchem der Pastor 6 Tonnen Korn und 2 Bankthaler bezieht.

Die Lappen gehen hier Lappisch gekleidet, besitzen aber auch Schwedische Kleidung. Ihre Hütten sind von Granreisern ohne Walmar.

Sie halten viel auf Frömmigkeit und sittlichen Lebenswan: del, grobe Verbrechen sind unter ihnen unerhört, kleine Diebe: reien höchst selten. Geschwängerte Mädchen trifft allgemeine, tie: fe Verachtung, weshalb Unkeuschheitssünden sehr selten sind; in 9 Jahren fand nur Eine uneheliche Schwängerung Statt: das Mädchen blieb unverheirathet. Strenge Arbeit sichert sie auch, wie überhaupt die Lappen, vor Ausschweifungen der Sinn: lichkeit.

Bettellappen, oder bei den Schweden verdungene männliche Weidelappen giebt es in ganz Herjeådalen nicht; zuweilen dienen aber auf den Schwedischen Höfen Lappinnen, die sich dann ganz in die Schwedische Tracht kleiden. Männer dienen auf diese

Weise nie. Auf Hede's Pfarrhofe fand ich eine solche dienende Lappin.

Aus dem Bisherigen erhellt, daß die Lappen von Jemteland und Herjeådalen sich, wenn gleich in ihrer Nähe nur wenige Kolonisten wohnen, den Schweden schon sehr genähert haben, und da unter ihnen die Schwedische Sprache die gottesdienstliche ist, allmählig ganz mit ihnen zusammenschmelzen werden. Auch sind die Lappmarker von Jemteland und Herjeådelen keinesweges so abgeschiedene Lappendistrikte, wie die Westerbottnischen, die in administrativer Hinsicht ganz für sich stehen. Uebrigens sind die Lappen, von denen bisher die Rede war, ihrem ursprünglichen Nomadenleben treuer geblieben als die Westerbottnischen, von denen fast täglich eine immer größere Zahl sich feste Wohnsitze erwählt und auch Ackerbau treibt.

Nach den obigen Angaben beträgt die Seelenzahl in
Fölinge und Ström . . . 294 (im J. 1815.)
Undersåker und Offerdal . 164 (im J. 1816.)
Oviken und Hede . . . 80 (im J. 1814. nur ungefähr angegeben.)
——
538

II. Westerbottens Lappmarker oder Åsele, Umeå und Piteå Lappmarker.

a. Åsele Lappmark,

auch Ångermanlands Lappmark genannt, weil es bis auf die neueste Zeit zu Ångermanland (Hernösand's Län) gehörte.

Es gränzt im Norden an Umeå-Lappmark, im Westen an Norwegen, im Osten und Süden an Ångermanland und Jemteland. Die Länge beträgt 4 bis 12 Meilen, die Breite etwa 28 Meilen; der Arealinhalt nach Hermelin's Charte 130 □M. In juridischer Hinsicht bildet das Land ein Härad; in kirchlicher Hinsicht 4 Pastorate: Åsele, Fredrika, Dorothea und Wilhelmina, welche zur Propstei von Nord-Ångermanland gehören; Åsele bildet den südwestlichen, Fredrika den südöstlichen, Dorothea den nordwestlichen, Wilhelmina den nordöstlichen Theil des Landes; Wilhelmina hat einen größern Umfang als die übrigen ; Pastorate zusammengenommen. Die Einwohner sind Lappen und Schweden, im J. 1815. 2933, wovon 1031 in Äsele, 420 in Fredrika, 477 in Dorothea und 1005 in Wilhelmina. Unter dieser Einwohnerzahl waren 5 Geistliche, 2 Schullehrer, 1 Studirender, 7 Kirchenbediente, 2 Kronbeamte, 287 eigne Bauern, 4 Pachtbauern, 3 Torpare, 14 wirkliche Kolonisten (seit 1810), 5 Einlieger, 71 arme und gebrechliche Landbauern, 171 Knechte, 138 Jungen, 1 Schuster, 2 Schneider, 1 Tischler, 1 Glasermeister, 316 Mägde, 189 dienende Mädchen unter 15 Jahren (tjenstflickor), 19 Arme, die von ihren Kindern unterhalten werden, 6 Arme, welche von der Gemeinde Armengaben genießen, 3 Arme im Armenhause. Die Zahl der Lappen betrug 110 Männer und 196 Weiber, zusammen 306, wovon 57 Männer und 81 Weiber Rennthierlappen, 37 M. und 43 W. ohne Rennthiere, 16 M. und 72 W. umherstreichende und Weidelappen. *) In ganz Äsele-Lappmark wurden im J. 1816 geboren 106, worunter 3 uneheliche; es starben 58.

Der Viehstand betrug:

	Pferde	Ochsen	Kühe	Kälber	Schaafe.
im Pastorat Äsele	125	50	739	300	1200.
Fredrika	75	25	348	120	330.
Dorothea	95	24	380	93	470.
Wilhelm.	98		300	100	350.

Der Kornertrag ward im J. 1815 ungefähr angegeben: Roggen 2 bis 3tes, Gerste 2 bis 4tes, Kartoffeln 3 bis 5tes, Korn.

Das Land ist sehr bergig und hat an der Norwegischen Gränze auch Schneeberge und Gletscher. Mehrere ansehnliche Flüsse und Seen durchschneiden es. Unter den Flüssen ist der

*) Im J. 1805 war die Gesammtzahl der Einwohner von Äsele-Lappmark 2366, worunter 244 Lappen. Am meisten hat die Volkszahl in Wilhelmina und Äsele zugenommen. Im J. 1779 betrug die Einwohnerzahl nur 1200. Die Zahl der Bauern und Kolonisten wuchs 1770 bis 1812 von 71 auf 306; die Zahl der Lappenfamilien sank von 59 auf 36 (außer den Sprintare).

bedeutendste der Angerman, dessen nördlicher Arm im Pastorat Wilhelmina aus mehrern Gränzseen entspringt. Die Ufer dieses Flusses, an welchen die Kirchen Wilhelmina und Åsele liegen, sind, gleich den Ufern der meisten Lappischen Ströme, durch ihre Fruchtbarkeit berühmt. An den Ufern des Angerman findet man auch in Lappmark nur wenige unfruchtbare Gegenden; überall wird viel Gerste, wenig Roggen gesäet. Amer giebigsten sind die Wiesen, deren große Fruchtbarkeit eine Folge der Ueberschwemmung der zweiten Fluth, der Alpenfluth (fjällflod), ist, die durch den plötzlich in den Alpen aufthauenden Schnee bewirkt wird, zwischen Johannis und der Mitte des Julius; das Ackerland wird nicht überschwemmt. Die erste Fluth (vårflod, Frühlingsfluth) überschwemmt weniger und nutzt nicht. Außer dem Angerman haben noch folgende, in den Lappmarken entspringende, Flüsse zwei Fluthen: Orån, Umeå, Windelelf, Calix und Torneå; die übrigen Lappischen Flüsse haben innerhalb der Lappmarken weniger Wiesenufer. — Der Angerman hat innerhalb Lappmark keine bedeutende Wasserfälle, wohl aber in Angermanland.

Fahrwege giebt es im Sommer weder nach, noch in Åsele-Lappmark; nur Reit-, Geh- und Bootwege. Der bequemste Weg führt nach Hernösand, über Junsele und Sollesteå (22 Meilen); nach Umeå aber über Lycksele, der nähere über Fredrika und Normaling ist Gehweg. Zwischen den Kirchen Åsele und Lycksele beträgt der Weg 10 Meilen; er ist bloß Fußweg und führt über das hohe Gebirge Stöttingfjäll, welches Åsele im Südost von Lycksele scheidet.

Das Stöttingfjäll ist mit Gränen bewachsen und im Sommer nicht mit Schnee bedeckt; es hat gute Alpenweide. Auf dem Rücken läuft die Gränze; hier, wie an den Abseiten, liegen mehrere Dörfer, die aus Schwedischen Kolonistenhöfen, höchstens 5, bestehen. Die Kolonisten leben meist von Viehzucht; auf dem steinigen Boden gedeihen nur Kartoffeln, Gerste wird wenig gebauet, selbst die Fichtenrinde zum Brote müssen die Bewohner des Fjäll kaufen, da auf dem Gebirge nur Gränen, Birken und Espen wachsen. Lappen wohnen auf dem Gebirge jetzt gar nicht; die wenigen Rennthiere, welche die Kolonisten besitzen, geben sie bei den entfernteren Lappen auf die Weide.

Von Lycksele nach Wilhelmina sind 10 Meilen über das Stöttingssjäll, Boot, und, meistens, Gehweg; aber nur auf der Seite von Lycksele einigermaaßen gehbar.

Von Åsele nach Junsele in Angermanland 6 Meilen Boot, Reit, und Gehweg; von da nach Sollefteå 4 Meilen Fahrweg.

Von Åsele nach Anundsjö in Angermanland 10 Meilen Reitweg.

Von Åsele nach Jemteland 5 Meilen, nach Dorothea, meist Geh, wenig Bootweg; von da nach Täsjö in Angermanland an Jemtlands-Gränze 2⅜ Meilen, wenig Boot, meist Gehweg.

Von Åsele nach Fredrika 5 und von Åsele nach Wilhelmina 7⅛ Meilen Geh, und Bootweg.

Von Fredrika nach Björna in Angermanland 6 Meilen Geh, und Bootweg.

Von Fredrika nach Nordmaling 8 Meilen bloß Winterweg.

Im Winter fährt man bequem auf Schlitten, die von Pferden oder Rennthieren gezogen werden.

Bis zum Jahre 1800 bildete ganz Åsele-Lappmark Ein Pastorat Åsele *), die übrigen drei Kirchen waren, zum Theil erst seit 1797 eingerichtete, Kapellen (Wilhelmina ward 1785 gebaut) nebst einer älteren, 1781 gestifteten, Kapelle Fatmematke.

1800 wurden 2 neue Pastorate Fredrika (ehemals Wiska) und Dorothea (ehemals Bergvattnet), und 1812 ein drittes, Wilhelmina (ehemals Wolgsjö), eingerichtet; nur Fatmematke blieb Kapelle unter Wilhelmina. Bis zur Erbauung der Kapelle von Fatmematke, eines hölzernen Saals ohne Kanzel und Glocken, hatten die Lappen auch im Sommer zur Kirche Åsele herabkommen müssen. Fatmematke liegt 12 Meilen westlich von Wilhelmina, an dem 7 Meilen langen Kultsee, einem Theil des Angerman; kein Geistlicher wohnt hier; der Pastor von Wilhelmina reiset dahin einmal um die Mitte des Julius und

---

*) Die Kirche Åsele ward erbauet 1648, neugebauet 1749, erweitert auf Kosten der Gemeinde 1779.

einmal am Schluſſe Septembers, um mit den, dann dort verꞏ
ſammelten, Lappen Alpengottesdienſt in Lappiſcher Sprache zu
halten, dann werden auch die Todten begraben, die mittlerweile
in die Erde gegraben oder zum Austrocknen aufgehängt wurden.
Im Winter bringen die Lappen ihre Leichen nach Wilhelmina, auch
nach Anundſjö und nach Sidenſjö in Angermanland, denn nur
vom April bis Ende Novembers ziehen ſie auf den Gränzalpen
um und hinter Fatmematke, im Winter im niedern Lande von
Åſele, ſo wie in den Angermanländiſchen Kirchſpielen Anundſjö,
Sidenſjö, Junſele, Reſele, Sollefteå, Ed, Nätra, Botheå, umher
und bringen bei ihrer Rückkehr Predigerſcheine über Beiwohnung
des Gottesdienſtes und heiligen Abendmahls, Begräbniß der
Todten ꝛc. mit.

Eine, 1732 errichtete, Lappenſchule, in welcher ein Schulmeiꞏ
ſter 6 Lappenkinder auf Lappiſch unterrichtet, und die gleich den
andern Lappenſchulen aus dem Lappenfond unterhalten wird, beꞏ
ſteht bei der Kirche Åſele; 1817 ward die Theilung derſelben
beabſichtiget, ſo daß die eine Hälfte nach Wilhelmina verlegt
werden ſollte. Zuweilen werden auf eigene Koſten auch Schweꞏ
denkinder unterwieſen.

Katecheten waren 1 in Åſele und 1 in Wilhelmina; einer
derſelben hält auf den Fjäll mit den Lappen an den Sonntagen
Betſtunde.

In den Kirchen wird, wenn Lappen auf ihren Zügen anweꞏ
ſend ſind, Lappiſch gepredigt, eben ſo da, wo es Fiſcherlappen
giebt, alle 14 Tage nach vorhergegangener Schwediſcher Predigt.

Hausverhör (Hüttenverhör, käteförhör) wird mit den Lapꞏ
pen theils in der Kirche, theils im Pfarrhofe, theils in den Dörꞏ
fern und Hüttenlagen, nach Bezirken gehalten. Auch beim Alꞏ
pengottesdienſt werden ſolche Verhöre über chriſtliche Erkenntniß
ꝛc. angeſtellt. Bei ÅſeleꞏKirche iſt ein Armenhaus, in welchem
die Aermſten Aufnahme finden, die übrigen werden auf die
Höfe vertheilt.

Die fruchtbarſten Gegenden von ÅſeleꞏLappmark trifft man
in den Kirchſpielen Åſele, Fredrika und Dorothea, welche, bei der
mäßigen und ſparſamen Lebensweiſe ihrer Bewohner, faſt ſo viel

Korn bauen, als sie brauchen. Asele bauet viel Gerste und etwas Winterroggen auf Schwendeland (svedjeråg, Schwenderoggen) und kauft nur wenig Korn; mehr müssen Fredrika und Dorothea kaufen, wo der Ackerbau geringer ist; noch mehr das arme und unfruchtbare Kirchspiel Wilhelmina, wo der Kornbau sehr unbeträchtlich ist, doch in den letzten Jahren zugenommen hat. Hauptnahrungszweig aller Kirchspiele ist Viehzucht; *) Rennthiere haben die Schweden wenig, und bildet die Haltung derselben keinen eigentlichen Nahrungszweig, wie bei den Kolonisten in Luleå-Lappmark. Rennthiere und Felle kauft man von den Lappen; auch Vogeljagd und Fischerei wird getrieben; letztere ist nur in Wolgsjö etwas ergiebig; Lachse und Brachsen fängt man nicht, wohl aber Hechte, die man getrocknet verkauft, Schnäpel, Aeschen, Barse, Plötzen (Cyprinus Rutilus, mört) Alpenlachse (Salmo alpinus, röding), Forellen. — Man spinnt und webt, auch verfertigen die Bauern, wie in allen Lappmarken, Eisengeräthe zum eigenen Bedarf. In Dorothea ist ein Schmid, der Büchsen zum Verkauf macht.

Wilhelmina ist der gebirgigere Theil von Asele-Lappmark: hier trifft man mit ewigem Schnee bedeckte Alpen in Menge, die schon vom Pfarrhofe aus überall sichtbar sind; der Wald, meist aus Gran und Birken nebst wenigen Fichten bestehend, ist niedrig, eben so in Dorothea; Fichten findet man am meisten in Asele und Fredrika. Sumpfeisen ist vorhanden, aber bisher nicht benutzt worden.

Der Boden ist sehr sandig, meist Staubsand (sandmylla). Man säet zu Ende Mai's und erndtet zu Ende des August; selten beginnt die Erndte schon 7 Wochen nach der Aussaat. Gewöhnlich gedeiht das Korn nur mittelmäßig; oft leidet es durch Frost, oder wird nicht ganz reif; bereits um die Mitte Augusts treten

---

*) Der Wiesenbau ist in neuerer Zeit sehr verbessert und vermehrt worden; man leitet Wasser aus Bächen in Sümpfe und über nasse Wiesen, läßt es 6 Jahre stehen, bis das Holz und Buschwerk verfault ist, und trägt es dann im Winter als Eis ab, worauf nach 6 Jahren die trefflichste Wiese entsteht.

Nachtfröste ein, vor Anfang Oktobers bleibt der Schnee aber nicht liegen, und Schlittenbahn hat man erst im November. Erbsen sät man wenig, Hafer gar nicht. Kartoffeln pflanzt man in Menge und sie gedeihen vortrefflich. Seit in den letzten 30 Jahren die Schwedischen Bauern ihre Ländereien zum Besten von Söhnen und Schwiegersöhnen vielfach zerstückelt haben (hemmansklyfning), sind die einzelnen Höfe kleiner geworden, und der wohlhabendste Bauer hat jetzt nicht mehr als 8 Kühe, andere haben nur 4 oder 5.

Das Waldbrennen (svedjande), welches, um Äcker, oder noch mehr, um Wiesen zu bekommen, zuweilen von den Nybyggare vorgenommen wird, hat die Lappen rücksichtlich des Weidelandes gefährdet, indem es nach einem Waldbrande ein halbes Jahrhundert bedarf, um wieder Rennthiermoos zu erzeugen, hat sie weiter an die Gränze gedrängt, und die Jagd sehr verringert; ja, man behauptet, daß hier und da, nach solchen Schwendungen, die Nachtfröste früher und schädlicher gewirkt haben. — Sägemühlen hat man nur zum eigenen Bedarf. Theer brennt man gar nicht, da der Verkauf, der Entlegenheit und des schwierigen Transports wegen, keinen Gewinn bringen würde. Das Hauptsächlichste, was die Schwedischen Bauern (denn Kolonisten, deren Freijahre geendigt sind, treten in die Klasse der schatzpflichtigen Bauern) und Kolonisten, im Lande reisende Kaufleute und Einkäufer, oder auf den Märkten, zumal dem großen Markt zu Sollefteå in Hernösand oder sonst in Ångermanland, oder in Stockholm, wohin einzelne Bauerknechte, die mit einem Paß als Hofeinkäufer versehen sind, jährlich allerlei Waaren für den Hof und was sie sonst im Auftrage der Bauern mitnehmen, führen *), ist vortreffliche Butter, getrocknete Hechte, Felle, meist von zahmen Thieren, wilde Vögel, insbesondere Haselhühner (hjerpar), auch Birk- (orrar) und Auerhühner (tjädrar), etwas Talg und ein wenig Käse. Die Lappen verkaufen Rennthierfleisch, Rennthierfelle, Lappenschuhe (den Käse verzehren sie meist selbst) an die Schwedischen Bauern, welche es weiter verfahren; Körbe

---

*) Nach Umeå- und Piteå-Lappmarker kommen fremde Hofeinkäufer.

II.   X verfertigen die Lappen von Åsele-Lappmark nicht. Die Nybyggare haben, wie in Lycksele- und Luleå-Lappmark, Sennhütten (fäbodar); die Weide ist in Åsele-Lappmark so gut, daß, statt sonst gewöhnlich nur zweimal, dort die Kühe dreimal täglich gemolken werden.

Die Lappen von Åsele-Lappmark haben nur Ein Dorf, welches aber von der Norwegischen Gränze durch den obern Theil von Wilhelmina, so wie einen kleinen Theil von Dorothea, viele Meilen hintereinander, freilich mit großen Unterbrechungen, fortläuft. Unterhalb dieses Dorfes oder Dorfbezirks beginnt das Lappland (Rennthierweideland) der Nybyggare, wofür diese den Lappenschatz entrichten. Die Rennthierlappen leben von Fleisch, Milch und Käse; nur die ärmeren treiben Jagd und Fischerei.

Seit etwa 40 Jahren sind, nachdem schon früher damit der Anfang gemacht war, immer mehrere Lappen Ackerbauer geworden, und als solche in die Klasse der Schwedischen Nybyggare getreten; sie werden deshalb von den Rennthierlappen nicht verachtet; sie nähern sich immer mehr den Schweden.

In Åsele-Lappmark werden folgende Nybyggen von Lappen bewohnt.

Im Kirchspiel Åsele: Gårdsjön, Lappe Erik Olsson.

Kirchspiel Wilhelmina:

Latikberget: 3 Höfe, bewohnt von den Söhnen des Johann Larsson.

Stensele, 1 Hof: Anders Johnsson.

Grönsjön, 1 Hof: Nils Pehrson.

Kittelfjäll, 1 Hof, bebaut durch zwei Brüder, Olof und Clemet Matsson.

Woimsjöluspen, 1 Hof: Lars Ersson.

Kirchspiel Dorothea:

Granåsen, 2 Höfe: Sjul Zacrisson und dessen Sohn Zacris Sjulsson. (Sjul ist ein Lappischer Vorname, den die Schweden nicht kennen).

Kirchspiel Fredrika:

Stensjön, 2 Höfe: Nils Olofsson und Anders Hermansson.

Lögda, 2 Höfe: die Brüder Puhl Bryngelsson, und Pehr Bryngelsson.

Stafversjaur, 1 Hof: Erik Bryngelsson.

Morrfors, 1 Hof: Pehr Bryngelsson.

Alle diese Akerbau treibenden Lappen in Åsele-Lappmark sind Schwedisch gekleidet.

Außerdem waren in Åsele-Lappmark 43 Skattlappar (für Lappland steuernde Lappische Hausväter), ohne die Sprintare, d. h. Lappen, welche von den Skattlappar Land mietheten, deren etwa 10 sind.

Der Lappenschatz für Åsele-Lappmark betrug 41 Rthlr. 40 ßl. banco: von dieser Summe erlegen die Lappen 27 Rthlr., das übrige die Schwedischen Bauern. Die Steuern der schatzpflichtigen Schwedischen Bauern betragen 330 Rthlr. 18 ßl. banco.

Die 287 steuerpflichtigen Bauern von Åsele-Lappmark waren im J. 1817 folgendermaßen vertheilt.

im Kirchspiel Åsele	100	Bauern in	38	Dorfschaften,
‚ ‚ Wilhelmina	63	‚ ‚	19	‚
‚ ‚ Dorothea	60	‚ ‚	16	‚
‚ ‚ Fredrika	64	‚ ‚	24	‚
	287	Bauern in	97 *)	Dorfschaften.

In Åsele Kirchspiel hatte das größte Dorf, Gaffele, 19 Bauern; Lomsjön 6, Nora 4, Hellan 4 zc.

In Wilhelmina K. Jersjön 9, Latikberget 7, Rästransjön 6 Bauern zc.

In Dorothea K. Anaträsk 9, Lassjön 8, Mårdsjön 6, Svanabyn 6, Ormsjön 5 Bauern zc.

In Fredrika K. Balsjö 8 Bauern (gehen zur Kirche nach der nähern Kirche Bjurholm in Ångermanland), Bredträsk 6, Stennäs 6, Tallsjön 6 zc.

Die Kronhufenzahl (mantal) betrug in Åsele 20⅝, in Wilhelmina 11⁴⁴⁄₇₆, in Dorothea 9⅝, in Fredrika 9½ mantal.

Bei Åsele's Kirche wird das jährliche Landgericht im Tings-

---

*) Im J. 1804 gab es nur 64 Dorfschaften.

X 2

hus, und zweimal jährlich Markt gehalten, zur selbigen Zeit werden auch die Steuern erhoben.

Die Schwedischen Bauern und Kolonisten stammen meist aus Angermanland, auch aus Dalekarlien und Finnland. Sie sprechen alle Schwedisch, sind indeß zum Theil auch des Lappischen kundig, wie fast alle Lappen des Schwedischen. Der Lappische Dialect in Åsele=Lappmark ist sehr gedehnt und corrumpirt.

Nach der vom verstorbenen Adjuncten Magister Rhen in Lycksele, der sich um Beförderung der seit 1807 sehr beliebten Vaccination in Lappland große Verdienste erworben hat, indem er fast allen Kindern in Åsele= und Lycksele=Lappmark die Kuhblattern einimpfte, entworfenen Grundlage hat der Länsman Holmström in Lycksele neuerlich eine Landkarte über Åsele=Lappmark angefertigt, die aber eben so wenig als die von Holmström entworfene und von Rhen illuminirte über Umeå=Lappmark bisher gestochen worden ist. Die Polhöhe bei der Kirche Åsele beträgt 64° 12′.

Im Ganzen sind die Bauern und Kolonisten von Åsele=Lappmark wohlhabend und ein frommes und biederes Volk. Durch die nach Stockholm reisenden Knechte wurde vor einiger Zeit die venerische Krankheit eingebracht, doch bald völlig wieder ausgerottet. Unkeuschheitssünden sind unter Schweden und noch mehr unter Lappen höchst selten; die Verführungskünste der nach den Lappmarken reisenden Kaufleute finden selten Eingang. In sittlicher Hinsicht werden im Allgemeinen die Lappen in Åsele=Lappmark weniger gelobt.

Eisengruben giebt es eben so wenig als in Umeå= und Piteå=Lappmark, daher, außer Korn, Hanf, Blei und Salz, auch Eisen eingeführt wird.

In Åsele= und Lycksele=Lappmark giebt es ordentliche Gästgifvaregårdar, wo man gegen das gewöhnliche Skjutsgeld, im Sommer Böte, Ruderer, Träger und Wegweiser, im Winter Pferde erhält; die Gästgifvaregårdar sind vorzüglich eingerichtet: man hat ein hübsches Gastzimmer ꝛc. Die Straßen führen innerhalb der Lappmarken, so wie nach Angermanland und Westerbotten, nicht aber nach Norwegen. Dergleichen mit Gästgif=

varegårdar versehene Straßen giebt es zwischen Åsele und Wilhelmina, zwischen Åsele und Fredrika, zwischen Åsele und Dorothea, zwischen Åsele und Anundsjö, so wie zwischen Åsele und Junsele in Angermanland, von Lycksele nach Degerfors rc. In den nördlichen Lappmarken giebt es dergleichen Einrichtungen bis jetzt nicht, und auch in den genannten Lappmarken nur seit Anfang dieses Jahrhunderts. Briefposten gehen nach Lycksele, Fredrika, Dorothea und Wilhelmina, so oft Amtsbriefe eintreffen.

Der Gehalt der Pastoren dieses Lappmark ist folgender: die Pastoren von Åsele und Wilhelmina 24½ Tonnen Gerste und 25 Bankthaler, die Pastoren von Fredrika und Dorothea 12½ Tonnen Gerste und 20 Bankthaler; desgleichen erhält der Pastor von Wilhelmina für seine Lebenszeit, zur Haltung eines Adjuncten, 33⅓ Bankthaler,

b. Umeå- oder Lycksele-Lappmark.

gränzt im Westen an Norwegen, im Osten an Westerbotten (Umeå, Degerfors und Burträsk Pastorat), im Norden an Piteå und im Süden an Åsele-Lappmark; die Ausdehnung rechnet man von O. nach W. zu 24, und von N. nach S. zu 9 Meilen. Der Arealinhalt beträgt, nach Hermelins Karte, 230 ☐M.

In politischer Hinsicht gehört es zu Westerbottens Län, in juridischer hat es ein eigenes Häradsgericht. In kirchlicher Beziehung gehört es zu Westerbottens erster Propstei, die seit 1818 ihren Sitz in Umeå hat.

Ganz Umeå-Lappmark bildet Ein Pastorat, Lycksele, mit 4 Kapellen. Die Lappenschule für 6 Kinder findet man neben der Mutterkirche *) Mit den Lappen zieht ein Katechet umher; im Winter und Sommer.

---

*) Gustav Adolph richtete diese Schule 1632 zuerst in Umeå mittelst der Skytteschen Donation ein; von da ward sie 1633 nach Lycksele verlegt. Bis 1723 war sie die einzige in den Lappmarken; da verordnete König Friedrich die Stiftung einer Lappenschule bei einer jeden Mutterkirche. Anfangs, als Lycksele noch Filial von Umeå war, war der Schulmeister zugleich Kapellan. Derselbe wird, wie der Pastor,

Kirche Lycksele, Mutterkirche. Der Pastor genießt, außer dem Zehnten von der Gemeinde, an Lohn 40 Tonnen Kronkorn und 13 Rthlr. 16 sl. banco; desgl. ad dies vitæ 50 Rthlr. banco zur Haltung eines Adjuncten. Gleiche öffentliche Unterstützung zur Besoldung von Adjuncten genießen der Commiminister in Sorsele und der Pastor in Wilhelmina (Asele-Lappmark).

Bis 1673 war Lycksele Kaplanei von Umeå Pastorat. Dann wurde es eigenes Pastorat. Erster Pastor ward nun der bisherige Comminister und Schulmeister, Olaus Stephans Gran, ein Lappe. Er schrieb ein Fragebuch zur Unterweisung der Lappen im Christenthum 1668, und ein Manuale Lapponicum 1669. Er starb 1690. Ihm folgten bisher 7 Pastoren *).

Kapelle Sorsele, ward unter Karl XI. angelegt; es wohnt daselbst ein Comminister. Erster Comminister in Sorsele ward 1691 Herr Hindvik, ein Lappe, welcher aber bereits 1692

vom Consistorium in Hernösand vorgeschlagen, von der Kanzleiverwaltung ernannt, und ist, gleich allen Lappischen Schulmeistern, ordinirt. Seit der Stiftung haben an der Schule 12 Schulmeister gelehrt: 1. Jakob Bark, Kapellan in Umeå. 2. Ol. Gran, Schulmeister und Kapellan 1657 bis 1673, wo er Pastor in Lycksele ward. 3. Sein Sohn Nils Gran, Schulmeister; Pastor 1701. 4. Erik Plantin, starb 1704. 5. N. Klingberg, Pastor in Hede 1706. 6. Dan. Rundlief, Comminister in Bygdeå 1716. 7. König Granlund, Comminister in Sorsele 1719. 8. Pehr Zjällström, Pastor in Lycksele 1739. 9. Bernhard Ust † 1777 (war früher Bataillonsprediger gewesen). 10. Carl Alenius † 1789. 11. Dessen Bruder Anders Alenius, Pastor 1801. 12. Pehr Rüdström seit 1803.

*) 1. Magnus Bäng, aus Medelpad † 1699. 2. Nils Gran, des ersten Pastors Olof Gran, Sohn † 1714. 3. Olof Gran, Sohn des Nils, ward Pastor in Neder-Calir 1739; ihm lieferten die Lappen im J. 1723 ihre Zaubertrommeln aus, und gelobten, nie dergleichen wieder zu gebrauchen. Unter Olof Gran ward die alte Kirche 1734 abgebrochen und der Grund zu einer neuen gelegt, die 1799 wiederum durch eine neue ersetzt wurde. 4. Pehr Zjällström, 1739 — 1764; er bekam ein Gratial zur Haltung eines Adjuncten. 5. Erik Lindahl, Zjällström's Schwiegersohn † 1794. 6. Sam. Öhrling † 1799. 7. Anders Alenius, seit 1801.

starb. Ihm folgten bisher 9 Comminiſtri *). Das Commini:
ſtergehalt beträgt 30 Tonnen Korn und 23 Rthlr. 16 ſl. banco
nebſt 8 Rthlrn. für die beiden Fjällreiſen, auf welchen die Ge:
meinde den Stjuts beſteht.

Die Kirche zu Sorſele, 1742 erbauet, 1791 und 92 re:
parirt, liegt auf einer Inſel des Windelelf.

Sorſele iſt 12 Meilen, meiſt Geh:, wenig Bootweg, von
Lyckſele entfernt.

Kapelle Stenſele **)

Erſt ſeit 1816 wohnt daſelbſt ein Kapellprediktant, der in
einer großen Kirchſtube predigt, die ein Bauer kurz zuvor er:
bauet hatte. Eine Kirche iſt im Bau begriffen: die Hälfte der
Baukoſten ward aus dem Lappenfond mit 666⅔ Bankthalern be:
zogen. Der Kapellangehalt beträgt 10 Bankthaler, 12½ Tonnen
Gerſte, nebſt Butter, Wolle, getrocknetem Fleiſch und einem
Vogel von jeder der 25 Haushaltungen, die die Gemeinde bil:
den; desgleichen von jedem ſteuerpflichtigen Lappen einen Renn:
thierbraten. Stenſele iſt 9 Meilen von Lyckſele entlegen, der
Weg iſt meiſt Boot:, wenig Gehweg.

Alpenkapelle Terna.

Hier wohnt kein Prediger, der Kapellprediger zu Stenſele
begiebt ſich dahin, zweimal im Sommer, gewöhnlich um die

---

*) 1. Lars Ranglus, ein Lappe, 1694 — 1709, wo er Paſtor in
Silbojecki ward; ſeine Ueberſetzung des N. T. ins Lappiſche wird auf
der Bibliothek zu Upſala im Manuſcript aufbewahrt. 2. Sjul Gran:
berg, ein Lappe, Paſtor in Arjeplog 1719. Er kam 1731, auf der Rück:
reiſe vom Alpengottesdienſt, im See Arvidsjaur um. 3. König Gran:
lund † 1745. 4. Anders Alenius, Paſtor in Arvidsje:r 1754.; er ließ
auf Koſten einiger Lappen eine Alpenkapelle zu Alesnöle bauen. 5. Erik
Lindahl Paſtor in Lyckſele 1767. 6. Mag. Tegerman aus Upland, Pa:
ſtor in Aſele 1783. 7. Pehr Rådſtröm. 8. Jonas Grönlund. 9. Olof
Augman.

**) In den Kirchſpielen Lyckſele und Stenſele wurden im J. 1814.
geboren 73, worunter ein uneheliches Kind.

Mitte des Julius und gegen das Ende des August, um vor den auf den Hochgebirgen oberhalb der Kapelle nomadisirenden Lappen Gottesdienst in Lappischer Sprache zu halten. Die Kapelle ist von Holz, ward 1763 erbauet und ist nicht eingeweihet; umher stehen hölzerne Kirchhütten für den Prediger und die Lappen. Auch ein Begräbnißplaß ist daselbst angelegt worden. Der Weg dahin von Stensele aus, meist Bootfahrt, das übrige Gehweg, beträgt etwa 11 Meilen.

Alpenkapelle Gillesnöle.

Auch hier, mitten in den Alpen, wohnt kein Prediger; der Comminister von Sorsele hält dort zweimal im Sommer, gewöhnlich am Sonntage vor der Predigt zu Terna, und um die Mitte Septembers, Gottesdienst mit den Lappen. Die gegenwärtige Kapelle ward 1796 vollendet und hat 80⅓ Rthlr. banco gekostet; die frühere ward um 1740 gebauet. Sie ist nicht eingerichtet. Der Weg dahin von Sorsele beträgt 6 Meilen Bootfahrt. Von Terna ist sie 6¼ M., meist Geh-, wenig Ruderweg, entlegen. Sorsele und Gillesnöle haben eine gemeinschaftliche Kirchenkasse. Die Alpenkapelle Alt-Umeå am Umeåträsk ist eingegangen.

Die Einwohnerzahl von Lycksele-Lappmark betrug im Jahre 1810. 2166, im J. 1815. 2375, unter welchen 4 Geistliche, 1 ordinirter Schulmeister, 4 Kirchenbediente, 257 Bauern, 11 Nybyggare, 24 Alt-Bauern (die nicht mehr auf ihren Hemman sind) und Torpare 186 Knechte, 103 Jungen; an Kronbeamten 1 Voigt und 2 Länsmänner.

Der Lappen waren:

Rennthierlappen . . . 96 Männer
Lappen ohne Rennthiere . 30 -
arme Lappen . . . . 13 -
                                   139 Männer
Lappenweiber . . . . 192 Weiber,
                                   331 Lappen.

worunter 99 Arme.

Geboren wurden in Lycksele-Lappmark im J. 1814 88, worunter 2 uneheliche. Es starben 47. Ehen wurden geschlossen: 11.

Die Aussaat ward in den Gemeinden Lycksele und Stensele aufgegeben zu 550 Tonnen Korn; der Roggen gab das 12te, die Gerste das 6te Korn. Die Hufenzahl (hemmantal) war im J. 1813 in ganz Lycksele-Lappmark 35¹¹⁄₂₄.

Der nördliche und westliche Theil von Lycksele-Lappmark ist mit hohen Gebirgen ausgefüllt, die, besonders an der Norwegischen Gränze ewiger Schnee deckt. Auch der übrige Theil des Landes ist wenig eben; die größte Ebene findet man im Süden, vor Knaften bis Örträsk, 2 Meilen, wo Korn, selbst zum Verkauf viel gebauet wird.

An Wald ist Ueberfluß; Gran und Birken findet man wenig, desto mehr Fichten (tall). In der Nähe der Flüsse würde noch mancher Strich Landes sich trefflich zum Kornbau eignen; aber man bedarf des Wiesenlandes nothwendiger.

Zwei große Ströme entspringen in diesem Lappmark, der Umeä und der Windel, beide auf den Norwegischen Gränzalpen in mehreren Armen. Beide fließen durch Umeä-Lappmark ins Paftorat Umeä herab, wo sie sich unterhalb Wennäs vereinigen und unter dem gemeinschaftlichen Namen Umeä-Elf unterhalb der Stadt Umeä sich ins Meer ergießen. Der Windelelf ist der kleinere, wiewohl sich mit ihm bei Sorfele der beträchtliche, aus Piteä-Lappmark herabkommende, Lais-Elf vereiniget, hat auch nur geringere Wasserfälle, die es dem Lachse möglich machen, hinan zu schwimmen, so daß im Windelelf der einzige Lachsfang in Lycksele-Lappmark ist. Die Aufräumung dieses bisher wenig floß- oder fahrbaren Stromes war daher nicht gar bedeutenden Schwierigkeiten unterworfen, und hat dieselbe im Jahre 1818 mit Erfolg begonnen: die Paftorate Degerfors und Umeä leisteten dabei unentgeldlich Handdienste, ein Patriotismus, den der gerechte König öffentlich anerkannte. Wird auch der Wasserfall Degerfors, unweit der gleichnamigen Kirche, unfahrbar bleiben müssen, so läßt sich doch eine Bootfahrt von 14 Meilen erzielen, die nur durch diesen Fors unterbrochen wird. Am Schlusse des Sommers 1820 waren von der Mündung des Umeä 12¼ Meilen aufwärts im Windelelf für gröbere Holzwaaren, 9¼ Meilen aber auch für Theer und Bretter oder sogenannte

veredelte Holzwaaren, floßbar. Je unerschöpflicher die Waldvor=
räthe dieser Gegenden sind, desto wichtiger ist das Unternehmen;
selbst die Hauptstadt wird künftig einen großen Theil ihres Be=
dürfnisses an Brennholz von hier beziehen können, wie denn
auch neuerdings für diesen Zweck eine besondere Societät zusam=
mentrat. Zu gleichem Zwecke sucht man gegenwärtig den Ljun=
ga=Elf in Medelpad floßbar zu machen. Der Reichstag von
18½⅞ setzte für Stromreinigungen bis zum nächsten Reichstage
eine Summe von 100,000 Bankthalern jährlich aus.

Ein beträchtlicher Fluß ist ferner der Oeän, den man, we=
der in Djurberg's Geographie, noch auf Hermelins Karte über
Westerbotten findet. Er entspringt in drei Armen, 1 — 3 Mei=
len hinter dem, um 1810 angelegten, von 2 Bauern bewohnten
Nybygge Norrbäck innerhalb Lycksele=Lappmark, am Fuße des
Stöttingsfjäll, läuft 10 Meilen innerhalb des genannten Lapp=
mark und 9 Meilen im Pastorat Norrmaling, bis er, zwischen
Ångersjö und Lefvar, in den Bottnischen Meerbusen fällt. Sei=
ne Ufer sind sehr wiesenreich und mit einer Menge von Dörfern und
Höfen bedeckt: hier liegen Björkberg (1 Hof), Winliden (drei
Höfe), Orafvan (2 Höfe, afva bezeichnet einen Busen, vik), Hög=
liden (1 Hof), Brattfors (4 Höfe), Röddingträsk (2 Höfe), Wi=
binge (1 Hof), Knaften (9 Höfe), Wänjaurbäck (4 Höfe),
Oretorp (1 Hof), Lomfors (1 Hof), Långsele (7 Höfe), Skar=
da (2 Höfe), Orträsk (19 Höfe), Oreström (1 Hof), Ström
(2 Höfe), Strömsjönäs (2 Höfe). Der Fluß bildet, außer meh=
reren kleinen Fällen, eine gewaltige, weit hörbare Kataracte, vier
Meilen unterhalb der Kirche Lycksele bei Långsele, wo er 120
Ellen schräge herabstürzt.

Die bedeutendsten Fälle im Umeå, innerhalb des Lappmark,
sind der Bölefors, der Tuggenselefors, der Hellfors, der Grundfors.

Auch große Seen findet man in diesem Lappmark: Stora
Uma, 6 Meilen lang, ¾ Meile breit, Stora=Windeln 3¼ M.
lang, ⅚ Meile breit, Umajaur, Fallträsk, der sich in den Win=
del ergießt, Orträsksjön.

Viehzucht bildet den Hauptnahrungszweig der Schweden
und Lappen; doch sind Ackerbau und Theerbrennerei nicht unbe=

trächtlich; Balken werden zugehauen und theils auf dem Öre nach der Sägemühle Högsnäs in Norrmaling, theils auf dem Windel nach der Sägemühle Bagböle bei Umeå, freilich nicht ohne Beschwerde, herabgeflößt. Auf Stangen getrocknete, auch zuweilen-gesalzene, Hechte werden verkauft, noch mehr Bären-, Eichhorn- und Biberfelle. Treffliche Butter, jährlich wenigstens 1500 Liespfund (à 20 Pf., 30,000 Pf., — in Åsele 2000 Lpf.) wird veräußert. Auch treibt man Jagd und Vogelfang. Korn verkaufen nur zwei Dörfer Örträsk und Badstuguträsk; außer Gerste und Kartoffeln, bauet man Roggen, besonders Winterroggen, der in den übrigen Lappmarken selten ist; der Winterroggen giebt das 32ste Korn, schlägt aber oft fehl; der Sommerroggen giebt das 10te, die Gerste das 4te bis 10te Korn; den Dünger vermischt man mit Granreisern, Torfrasen und Ameisenhaufen (myrstackar). Kartoffeln verkauft man nicht. In keinem Lappmark darf Branntewein gebrannt werden, selbst nicht zum Hausbedarf; nur Geistlichkeit und Kronbeamte dürfen brennen, so viel sie bedürfen. Flachs und Hanf wird zum Bedarf gewonnen. — Man hält viel Kühe und Schaafe, aber wenige Ziegen, Rennthiere haben nur wenige Schweden.

Schwedische Dörfer zählt Lycksele-Lappmark 90; das größte derselben ist Örträsk mit 19 Bauern.

Der steuerpflichtigen Nybyggare oder der wirklichen Bauern sind 225, der steuerfreien Nybyggare, deren Freiheitsjahre noch nicht abgelaufen sind, 76. Die Kronsteuer der Bauern betrug im Jahr 1816. 232 Rthlr. 29 ßl. banko.

Der Lappendörfer sind 4: Umbyn mit 5 Skattlappar und 14 Nybyggare auf Lappland, jene steuern 3 Rthlr. 8 ßl., diese 11 Rthlr. 32 ßl.; Granbyn, mit 44 Skattlappar und 5 Sprintare (23 Rthlr. 8 ßl. Schatz) und 6 Nybyggare (4 Rthlr. 20 ßl. Schatz).

Ranbyn mit 18 Skattlappar, deren herabgesetzte Steuer 10 Rthlr. 12 ßl. beträgt.

Wapstebyn mit 25 Skattlappar und 5 Sprintare; der Schatz beträgt 17 Rthlr.

Umbyn dehnt sich auf einer Strecke von 25 Meilen in der Länge und 6 Meilen in der Breite aus; nur 7 Meilen werden von den 5 Lappen bewohnt; diese sind Waldlappen (skogslappar).

Fischerlappen giebt es in Granbyn; doch findet man in Lycksele-Lappmark nur wenige Lappen, die sich ausschließlich von der Fischerey nähren, wie es deren in Piteå-, Luleå-, und insbesondere in Åsele-Lappmark, wo der Verlust von Rennthieren am größten war, viele giebt. Granbyn liegt an der nördlichen Gränze gegen Piteå-Lappmark und am Windel-Elf; es dehnt sich in einer Länge von 9, und in einer Breite von 3 Meilen im Sprengel von Sorsele aus.

Ranbyn bildet ein großes Dreieck im Norden an der Norwegischen Gränze; es mißt 5 Meilen nach allen 3 Seiten hin, nur ein Theil von Wapstebyn trennt es. Die Lappen dieser Dorfschaft sind Fjäll (Alpen)-Lappen, die von Rennthieren leben, mit welchen sie auf den Alpen umherziehen; sie haben kein Waldland, das auch als Weide dient. Einige derselben — fast die einzigen in Lycksele-Lappmark — geben auch an die Krone Norwegen Steuer.

Wapstebyn enthält blos Alpenlappen, deren Einer an Norwegen Lappenschatz entrichtet. Das Dorf ist 6½ Meile lang und 4¾ Meilen breit, und wird von Norwegen, von Åsele-Lappmark und Ranbyn begränzt.

Im Winter ziehen die Lappen mit ihren Rennthieren nach Skellefteå und Burträsk, wenigere in das Pastorat Degerfors; in Umeå finden sie, Waldbrandes halber, keine Weide mehr.

Auch in Lycksele-Lappmark treiben jetzt einige Lappenfamilien Ackerbau. Sie wohnen in Sorsele; ihre Höfe sind folgende:

Jersbäcken, bewohnt von Anders Larsson.

Kausträsk, bewohnt von Abraham Sjulsson.

Grannås, bewohnt von Enar Andersson, der zugleich Katechet ist.

Öfra Sansele, bewohnt von Anders Nilsson; die ersteren drei gehen mit ihren Familien Lappisch, der vierte Schwedisch gekleidet.

In dem Schwedischen Dorfe Orträsk brach vor einigen Jahren die ansteckende Krankheit Radesygen (oder eigentlich wohl mehr eine venerische Krankheit) aus, und zwar, wie man behauptet, durch ein von einem Kaufmann verführtes Mädchen, worauf die Krankheit durch Unvorsichtigkeit weiter fortgepflanzt wurde; mehrere starben. Da indeß ein Kurhaus zur Behandlung der Kranken errichtet wurde, so gelang es, die Seuche bald wieder auszurotten; jetzt ist sie völlig verschwunden. Dergleichen Fälle sind höchst selten. Ueberhaupt sind in ganz Lappmark uneheliche Geburten und Vermischungen der Verlobten höchst selten, und unter den Lappen fast unerhört; denn die Schwedischen Bewohner von Lycksele-Lappmark sind ein treues, biederes Volk, welches hoch auf Religion und Sittlichkeit hält und sich durch Dienstfertigkeit und Gastfreiheit auszeichnet; ihre Sonntagsfeier in der Kirche und zu Hause ist sehr strenge. Die Lappen dieses Lappmark werden zwar den von Åsele vorgezogen; doch tadelt man ihr störriges, argwöhnisches und unredliches Wesen, und nimmt nicht ohne Wahrscheinlichkeit an, daß sie durch die Schwedischen Handelsleute verdorben worden.

Am ärgsten schildert man die Lappen von Wapstebyn, unter welchen selbst grobe Verbrechen nicht selten seyn sollen.

Bei der Kirche Lycksele wird zweimal jährlich Markt gehalten, während des Markts im Januar hält auch das Häradsgericht seine Sitzungen und wird die Kronsteuer erhoben.

Für Reisende sind Gästgifvaregårdar eingerichtet; eine Briefpost (s. Åsele) geht von Lycksele nach Umeå jeden 14ten Tag; auch nach Åsele, und über Stersele und Sorsele nach Arjeplog; von da nach Arvidsjaur und Skellefteå in Westerbotten, so oft Amtsbriefe eintreffen.

Das Armenwesen ist ganz auf Schwedischen Fuße eingerichtet; doch giebt es kein Armenhaus. Die Armen, Schweden und Lappen, werden, wenn sie nicht zu schwach sind, von dem einen zum anderen Schwedischen Hofe gefahren: 1 bis 4 Wochen hinter einander bleiben sie auf jedem dieser Höfe, und werden daselbst mit allem, was sie bedürfen, versehen; die, welche nicht mehr umher reisen können, werden auf Einer Stelle einaccordirt; die Unkosten bestreitet die Armenkasse, aus welcher auch diejenigen, die noch einen Theil ihres Unterhalts selbst verdienen können, Unterstützung erhalten. Die Lappen, welche in Lycksele keinen festen Sitz haben, tragen nur zur Armenkasse bei.

Die Polhöhe beträgt bei der Kirche Lycksele 64° 34′ 40″, bei Sorsele 65° 33′.

Gegen Piteå-Lappmark hin, 1 Meile südlich von Bonnäs Fjäll, an der Norwegischen Gränze, bricht ein weißgrauer feinglimmiger Kalchstein oder Bergkalch, der so dicht ist, daß er zu Marmor geschliffen werden könnte.

c. Piteå - Lappmark

enthält zwei Pastorate, Arvidsjaur und Arjeplog *), deren jedes sein eigenes Häradsgericht hat. In politischer Hinsicht ist dieser Lappmark Theil des Läns Westerbotten, in kirchlicher, Theil der zweiten Probstey von Westerbotten, die ihren Sitz in Skelleftea hat.

Piteå-Lappmark gränzt im Norden an Luleå, im Süden an Lycksele-Lappmark, im Osten an die Westerbottnischen Pastorate Burträsk, Skellefteå (Norrsjö Kapell) und Piteå (Elfsby Kapell), im Westen an Norwegen. Die Ausdehnung von N. nach S. beträgt etwa 10, von W. nach O. 20 Meilen. Der Arealinhalt beträgt 230 ☐Meilen, wovon mehr als die Hälfte Wasser und Alpen.

Das Land, zwischen 65° und 67° Polhöhe, ist mit Alpen, zumal gegen Norwegen hin, und vielen Seen und Wasserzügen ausgefüllt: die beiden großen Ströme Norrlands, der Skellefteå, oder Sildut, wie die Lappen sprechen, und der Piteå entspringen an der Norwegischen Gränze dieses Lappmark, welchen sie, seiner ganzen Ausdehnung nach, von W. nach O. durchfließen; der Sildut ist Ausfluß der zusammenhängenden drei großen Wasserzüge Hornafvan, Udjaur und Storafvan. Auch der Lais, der bei Sorsele sich mit dem Windel vereinigt, hat hier seinen Ursprung.

*)1696 bis 1733 war Arvidsjaur Filial von Arjeplog, ward dann aber wieder besonderes Pastorat.

Das Pastorat Arvidsjaur bildet den südlichen, das Pastorat Arjeplog den nördlichen, bei weitem größeren, Theil des Landes. Die Kirche von Arvidsjaur ist alt und zu klein für die Gemeinde; die Kirche von Arjeplog ward, um 1780, zur Zeit des Pastors Örling, neu gebauet. Außer diesen beiden Mutterkirchen, welche beide an Seen liegen, giebt es nur eine dritte, die am nördlichen Ende des Hornafva - Wasserzuges gelegene, zum Pastorat Arjeplog gehörige, alte Kapelle Löwmock, 8 Meilen (bis auf ¼ Gehweg) Bootweg von der Kirche Arjeplog; der Pastor von Arjeplog reiset zweimal im Sommer dahin, um mit den, auf den umliegenden Alpen nomadisirenden, Lappen Gottesdienst zu halten; für die Reise bekommt er freie Fuhre und 5 Bankthaler. ...

Die auf Karten und in geographischen Handbüchern noch verzeichnete Kirche Sülbojock ist eingegangen; eine andere, Gräträsk, kennt man auch nicht dem Namen nach. Der Pfarrergehalt aus Kronmitteln beträgt 40 Tonnen Gerste und 13 Bankthaler; der gegenwärtige Pastor in Arjeplog, Sundelin, ist ein geborner Lappe. Hausverhöre werden auch mit den Lappen gehalten.

Die Kirchen Arvidsjaur und Arjeplog sind 9 Meilen (7 Meilen Boot- und 2 Meilen Gehweg) von einander entfernt; von Arjeplog nach Lycksele sind 18 Meilen, über Sorsele, Geh- und Bootweg. Von Arjeplog nach Lycksele geht eine Briefpost. Von Arvidsjaur nach der Stadt Piteå sind 14 Meilen, meist Reit-wenig Gehweg; nach Skellefteå 15 Meilen *) ganz Reitweg, aber schlecht; zur Kapelle Norrjö giebt es gar keinen Weg. Nach Jockmock kann man nur von Arvidsjaur aus gelangen, und zwar nur im Winter, die Entfernung beträgt 9 Meilen: auf der ganzen Strecke trifft man kein Haus, daher sie auch nur mit Rennthieren, die ihr Futter am Wege finden, befahren werden kann.

Die Einwohnerzahl in Piteå-Lappmark betrug im J. 1815. 1787, wovon 1040 in Arvidsjaur und 747 in Arjeplog.

*) Im 17ten Jahrhundert, als die Silbergruben der Nasaalpe noch bearbeitet wurden, gab es Fahrwege von da nach Piteå und Skellefteå: vom Nasafjäll nach der Stadt Piteå rechnet man 40 Meilen.

Lappen waren:

mit Rennthieren	. . . . .	194 Männer	219 Weiber
ohne Rennthiere	. . . . .	93 . .	87 . .
Bettel= und Weidelappen	. .	29 . .	67 . .
(die fremdes Vieh aller Art weiden	316 . .	373 . .

zusammen 689 Lappen.

Die Zahl der Gebornen war im Jahre 1816 in ganz Pi=
teä=Lappmark 54, worunter 1 uneheliches Kind; es starben 28,
Ehen wurden geschlossen 14.

Die Aussaat wird in der Tabelle des Jahrs 1815 angege=
ben zu 2 Tonnen Roggen, 120 Tonnen Gerste, 10 Tonnen
Mengkorn, 40 Tonnen Erbsen; der Ertrag zum 4ten Korn vom
Roggen, 3ten von der Gerste, 2ten vom Mengkorn, 10ten von
den Kartoffeln. Diese Angaben sind aber sehr allgemein und
wenig zuverlässig. Man darf Aussaat und Ertrag höher anneh=
men. Die Kron=Hufenzahl war im Jahre 1813 in Arvidsjaur
$8\frac{7}{17}$, in Arjeplog $\frac{1}{4}$ hemmantal.

Seit 1810 waren 99 Personen aus diesem Lappmark weg=
gezogen.

Die Lappenschule für 6 Kinder ist in Arjeplog. — Zwei
Katecheten sind angestellt. Markt, Steuerhebung und Häradsge=
richt wird bei den Mutterkirchen gehalten. Arvidsjaur hatte nie
eine Lappenschule, doch ward bei der Visitation, 1745, verordnet,
daß 1 Kind aus diesem Pastorate in die Schule von Arjeplog
aufgenommen werden solle.

Die Lappen sind in diesem Lappmark zahlreicher als in ir=
gend einem der übrigen Lappmarken. In Arvidsjaur giebt es
zwar nur ein einziges Lappendorf, Arvidsjaur, aber es wird von
80 Skattlappar bewohnt; sie sind arm, haben keine Rennthiere,
und leben vom Fischfang, von Handarbeiten und vom Betteln,
ihr Lappenschatz beträgt 22 Rthlr. Banko.

Auch wohnen im Pastorat Arvidsjaur 43 an die Krone
steuernde Nybyggare in 24 Dörfern, und 16, dem öden Bruk
Nasafjäll mit Tagediensten steuernde, Nybyggare auf 10 Nybyg=
gen; ferner 30 steuerfreie wirkliche Nybyggare. — Im Pastorat
Arjeplog sind 5 Lappendörfer: Locteä mit 32 Skattlappar (Steuer

17 Rthlr. banko); Norrwesterbyn mit 23 Skattlappar, worunter 3 Sprintare, die gar kein eigenes Land besitzen, denen aber
die übrigen Lappen Land gegeben haben, wofür sie nun schatzen;
der Schatz beträgt 15 Rthlr. 8 ßl.; Simisjaur, 35 Schatz-
lappen, 27 Rthlr. 8 ßl. Schatz; Sörvåsterbyn, 10 Schatz-
lappen, 8 Rthlr. 20 ßl. Schatz; Arjeplog 22 Schatzlappen,
11 Rthlr. 28 ßl. Schatz; 10 Nybyggare mit 3 Rthlr. 10 ßl.
Lappenschatz.

Ueberhaupt giebt es in Arjeplog 16 schatzfreie Nybyggare,
und einen steuernden, dessen Schatz aber nur 40 ßl. beträgt; in
Arvidsjaur beträgt dagegen der Nybyggare-Schatz 54 Rthlr. 38 ßl.
Von jenen 16 Nybyggare wohnen 8 auf Bruksland, wofür sie
dem Bruk steuern.

Die Ackerbau oder vielmehr Wiesenbau (Umschaffung der
Moräste in Wiesen) treibenden Lappen sind in Piteå-Lappmark
nicht zahlreich:

Im Pastorat Arvidsjaur: Häppejaur, bewohnt von Pehr
Hansson.

Im Pastorat Arjeplog: Jarjaur, bewohnt von Thomas
Pehrsson; Sandäs, bewohnt von Pehr Sjulsson. Alle
gehen mit ihren Familien Lappisch gekleidet.

Das Pastorat Arvidsjaur hat meist ebenes, aber mageres
Land; die vielen Moräste sind mit Steinen angefüllt. Man
hält dafür, daß mit bedeutendem Gewinn urbar zu machendes
Land nicht vorhanden sey. Einer der höchsten Berge ist Sten-
träskberget, auf welchem der Schnee erst zu Ende des Julius
schmilzt. Glömmerträsk, mit 7 Bauern, ist das größte Dorf.
Nybyggare und Lappen sind arm; erstere bauen nicht hinreichen-
des Korn und haben wenige, letztere haben zum Theil gar keine
Rennthiere und leben dann vom Fischfange. Uebrigens sind die
Rennthiere hier größer als sonst wo, weil man sie gewöhnlich
im Sommer, ohne sie zu melken, in den Wäldern gehen läßt,
so daß die Kälber vollauf zu saugen haben; sie sind auch wilder,
und lassen sich nur, wann Schnee liegt, greifen. Im Winter
ziehen diese Lappen mit ihren Rennthieren in das niedere Land,
nach Skellefteå.

II.   Y

Die Lappen verkaufen Leder, getrocknete Hechte und Bast-
reife; das Rennthierleder, welches von hier kömmt, ist das größte
und beste, das man hat. Die Nybyggare veräußern Butter,
Theer, getrocknete Hechte und Leder; Korn müssen sie kaufen,
Roggen bauen sie nie, wohl aber Gerste, Kartoffeln und Rüben;
selbst die Gerste reift nicht immer.

Das Pastorat Arjeplog hat noch unfruchtbareren Boden als
Arvidsjaur; der größte Theil des Pastorats besteht in Morästen
und Seen mit einer Menge von Inseln; einer dieser Seen soll
366 Inseln zählen. Das wenige feste Land ist steinig, selbst
die Wiesen sind schlecht; die nordwestliche Hälfte besteht aus Alpen, die, an der Gränze, mit nichts als Rennthiermoos und Alpenbirken (betula nana) bewachsen sind; 6 Meilen unterhalb der
Gränze beginnt Fichten- und Birkenwald.

Die Nybyggare leben von Viehzucht und Fischerey; erstere
befriediget nur ihren eigenen Bedarf, letztere ist sehr ergiebig:
man veräußert getrocknete Hechte und gefrorne oder frische Schnäpel; für 100 große Schnäpel erhält man eine Tonne Korn.
Die kleinen Getraideäcker bringen selten reife Frucht, auch in
guten Jahren wird das Nöthige nicht gewonnen. Viele säen
nur des Strohes halben, welches aber zu Dächern nicht gebraucht wird *).

*) Was ich bisher über die Unfruchtbarkeit von Pited-Lappmark
angeführt habe, beruht auf Aussagen von Kronbeamten und anderen
Männern, deren Beruf eine genaue Bekanntschaft mit dem Gegenstande
erforderte. Ich muß also dahin gestellt seyn lassen, was, bei Gelegenheit der Anträge des Herrn Stael von Holstein um öffentliche Unterstützung zur Anlegung von Nybyggen in Pited-Lappmark, von Einzelnen behauptet worden ist: „es sey hier noch viel Land übrig, welches
mit großem Gewinn urbar gemacht werden könne; auch die Sümpfe,
welche meist einen feinen, mit Sand vermischten Thon, einige Gries-
sand, enthielten, ließen sich anbauen." — So viel ist gewiß, daß einzelne Sümpfe bereits in gute Wiesen umgeschaffen worden sind; und
würde die Austrocknung der sumpfigen und morastigen Gegenden, die
jetzt frühe Nachtfröste erzeugen, und auch sonst durch ihre Ausdünstungen schaden, die Erndte wenigstens sicherer machen. Kartoffeln gedeihe

Die Lappen im Dorfe Arjeplog sind Fischerlappen, leben, gleich den dortigen Nybyggare, vom Fischfange und besitzen nur wenige Rennthiere, die sie im Sommer in den Wald treiben. Die Lappen der übrigen 4 Dörfer sind Alpen (Fjäll)=Lappen, die ganz von ihren Rennthieren leben. Sör= und Nortwäster= byn haben ihre Sommerweide in Norwegen und ihre Winter= weide in Schweden, daher sie in beiden Reichen Steuern erle= gen und ihr Schatz auf der Schwedischen Seite im Jahr 1811 herabgesetzt wurde. Lookteå, hart an den Schneealpen gelegen, ist das wohlhabendste dieser Lappendörfer. Im Winter ziehen die Lappen von Piteå=Lappmark gewöhnlich in die Pastorate Skellefteå und Piteå.

Im Skellefteå=Elf und in den Wasserzügen, aus welchen dieser Strom hervorgeht, fängt man auch Lachs, der sehr wohl= schmeckend und nicht abgemagert ist, denn er hat vom Meere an nicht viele bedeutende Wasserfälle hinan zu schwimmen. Der Skellefteå hat mehr Strömungen, die freilich so zahlreich, ja so wenig unterbrochen sind, daß man fast gar kein stilles Wasser (sele) findet. Viele Lachse haben im Flusse selbst ihre Geburts= stätte, daher fängt man sie auch im Winter unter andern Fischen. Die häufigsten Fischgattungen sind hier, außer dem Lachs, Schnä= pel, Hechte, Barsse, Lachsforellen, Karpfenarten (Cyprinus As= pius); überhaupt sind die hiesigen Gewässer sehr fischreich.

Was den Charakter der Bewohner von Piteå=Lappmark anbetrifft, so sind die hier wohnenden oder nomadisirenden Lap= pen ein gottesfürchtiges und sittliches Volk, wohlbewandert in christlicher Erkenntniß, voll Liebe für Kirche und häusliche An= dachtsübungen, gastfrei, dienstfertig, freundlich und heiter *).

---

vortrefflich, auch in Arjeplog. Mit dem Resultat der öffentlichen Un= tersuchung über mögliche Urbarmachungen, welche im Sommer 1807 auf Stael von Holstein's Antrag Statt fand, stimmen die von mir oben mitgetheilten Angaben überein.

*) Der fromme Pastor Pehr Edin, der nach fast 40jähriger Amtsverwaltung im Jahre 1803 zu Arvidsjaur starb, scheint für die hohe religiöse Bildung der Lappen viel gewirkt zu haben.

Y 2

Auch die Nybyggare in Arjeplog sind gastfrei und gefällig, be=
suchen sehr fleißig den öffentlichen Gottesdienst und zeichnen sich
in jeder Hinsicht durch einen ernsten und sittlichen Wandel aus.
Den Nybyggare von Arvidsjaur, die aus vielen Gegenden hier
zusammengeflossen sind, mangeln aber alle diese löblichen Eigen=
schaften, wenn gleich man sie nicht gerade lasterhaft nennen
kann.

Der Berg = und Hüttenbau, welcher früherhin im obern
Theil dieses Lappmark betrieben wurde, hat, der großen Schwie=
rigkeit des Transports wegen, und da er nicht gar lohnend war,
aufgehört. Bereits im Jahre 1635 ward das Silberbergwerk
der Nasaalpe (Nasafjäll), an der Gränze von Norwegen gegen
Lycksele=Lappmark, aufgenommen; die erste Entdeckung hatte ein
Lappe gemacht. Die Königin Christina ließ mehrere Jahre
darin arbeiten, 1637 ward eine Schmelzhütte erbauet; bald wur=
den die Gruben an die Stadt Piteå überlassen, die sie bis 1659
bearbeitete. Bei dieser Veranlassung ward das Land näher be=
kannt, und die Königin trug alle Sorge, dasselbe mit christlichen
Kirchen und Lehrern zu versehen; sie stiftete die beiden Pasto=
rate, in welche das Land noch jetzt vertheilt ist. Seit 1659,
wo die Dänen das Werk zerstörten, lagen die Gruben öde, nach=
dem in 22 Jahren, außer Bley, 4294 Mark Silber gewonnen
worden waren. Erst 1769 fing man die Arbeit wieder an;
Nybyggen wurden auf Bruksboden mit allen Rechten des Berg=
frälse (adelichen, auf Bergwerksgrundstücken haftenden, Privile=
gien) angelegt, die Kolonisten erhielten Freijahre und arbeiteten
für das Bruk, gegen Bezahlung. Eine Schmelzhütte, Adolph=
ström, ward 7 Meilen unterhalb der Nasaalpe, am Ladevi=Flusse,
der in den Lais fällt, 6 Meilen oberhalb der Kirche Arjeplog
und mehr denn 30 Meilen von den Kirchen Piteå und Skelef=
teå angelegt, und die Arbeit seit dieser Zeit, wenn gleich mit
Verlust, von einer Interessentschaft fortgesetzt; man erhielt, nach
geschehener Schmelzung, außer einigem Bley, jährlich 20 bis 50
und etwas über 100 Mark Silber; bis zum Jahre 1781 wa=
ren der angelegten Nybyggen 21. Seit 1804 machte der Ma=
jor Stael von Holstein, der sich zu Adolphström niederließ,

und für die alte Interessentschaft den Bau betrieb, sowohl beim Silberwerk, als beim Nybygge Kaster, 6 Meilen unterhalb Nasafjäll, Versuche mit Ableitung und Austrocknung von Sümpfen, worauf er bis und mit 1808 die Summe von 2253 Rthlr. 17⅓ ßl. *) verwendete. Die Arbeit wurde meist durch Dalekarlier betrieben, welche versicherten, daß sie in ihrer Heimath dergleichen Sümpfe mit Vortheil ausgetrocknet hätten. Die frühen Nachtfröste, welche bisher die Erndte vernichtet hatten, blieben aus, indeß konnte, mangelnder Fonds halber, wenn gleich einige öffentliche Unterstützung bereits früher erfolgt war, die Arbeit nicht mit Kraft fortgesetzt werden. Auch hörte im Jahre 1808 die Bearbeitung der Gruben der Nasaalpe, die bereits in den letzten Jahren wenig betrieben worden war, völlig auf, und Adolphström verfällt immer mehr. — In Adolphström gedeihen auch Küchengewächse., — Die Norwegische Gränze läuft über die Nasaalpe, doch liegen die Gruben auf Schwedischem Gebiete; man hat neuerdings dafür gehalten, daß letztere mit großem Gewinn von der Norwegischen Seite aus würden bearbeitet werden können, indem wirklich reiche Erzgänge vorhanden seyen, deren Benutzung auf der Schwedischen Seite durch physische Hindernisse erschwert werde, auch ist auf der Norwegischen Seite näherer Zugang zu Holz. — Der Gipfel der Nasaalpe bildet einen langen runden Rücken, der, dem größten Theile nach, mit ewigem Schnee bedeckt ist. Bereits 10 Meilen unterhalb der Alpe im Schwedischen Lappmark nimmt die Waldung an Dichtigkeit und Wuchs ab; 6⅓ Meilen von der Alpe stehen die letzten Fichten; bald verschwindet auch die Gräne, und nur einzelne Birken und kleine Sperberbäume oder vielmehr Sträuche findet man hier und da auf den, mit steiniger Erde und losen Steinen bedeckten, Fjäll. Dann verkrüppeln die Birken bis zu einer Höhe von 3 bis 4 Ellen, und die Zweige werden krumm und vielfach gebogen; endlich findet man nur Birkengebüsch, bis, 3 oder 4 Meilen von den Alpen, auch dieses völlig verschwindet;

*) S. Seine anmärkningar öfver Piteå-Lappmark ꝛc. Stockholm 1809. 32 S. gr. 8.

die Alpenbirke (betula nana) wird immer kleiner und kleiner; zuletzt erblickt man nichts als Schneefelder, oder von aller Vegetation entblößtes, kahles Alpenland, mit kleineren und größeren Steinen an vielen Stellen bedeckt. Doch hat man von der Höhe nach der Schwedischen Seite hin eine recht freundliche Aussicht auf das breite Thal, in welchem der Lais-Elf fließt; man erkennt das 7 Meilen entfernte Adolphström, an der südlichen Seite des Flusses läuft eine Kette hoher und steiler Alpen. An der Norwegischen Seite erblickt man nichts als hohe, mit ewigem Schnee bedeckte, Alpen, über einander gethürmt, und, gleich einem Theil der Nasaalpe, in Wolken gehüllt. Die Bergart der Nasaalpe ist Granit; unterhalb der höchsten Höhe, gegen Südost, breitet sich eine stets feuchte Masse verwitterter Felsen aus, die sich immer tiefer herabzusenken scheint. Viele Quarzgänge durchstreichen das Felsengebirge. Der Bleyglanz, welcher das Silber enthält, ist theils rein, theils mit Zinkblende und Schwefelkies gemischt, die mittelst Schlackenreinigung durch den Hammer ausgeschieden werden können, wo dann der reine Bleyglanz 50 Prozent Bley und 4 bis 5 Loth Silber im Centner giebt. Die Zinkblende findet sich in Menge; man hat, nach geschehener Röstung, daraus Galmey gewonnen, der sich auf Messinghütten recht gut zu Messing verarbeiten ließ, im Vergleich mit ausländischem aber die Kosten nicht lohnte. Die Erzlager gehen nicht tief. Versuche, an anderen Stellen der Alpenkette auf Bleyglanz, Zinkblende und Schwefelkies zu arbeiten, haben wenig Ertrag gewährt: am Berge Tsaggek, westlich vom Lais-Elf, ließ die Interessentschaft im Jahre 1773 eine Menge loser Steine mit feinglimmerigem Bleyglanz, die sich, auf einer Strecke von einigen hundert Klaftern, mit Dammerde vermischt, fanden, säubern.

Uebrigens werden die großen Alpenketten des oberen Piteå-Lappmark durch breite abhängige Thäler getrennt, und haben auf diese Weise oft Zwischenräume von 1, 2 und mehreren Meilen. Mehrere Wasserzüge sind mit einer 5 bis 6 Ellen dicken, völlig sichern Eis- und Schneedecke, auch im Sommer, bekleidet, und mehrere Alpen zeigen sich auch in der größten Sommerhitze als Eis-berge. Hunderte von Bächen und Flüssen rinnen von den Alpen herab und bilden durch ihre Vereinigung den Lais-Elf.

Die Bergart dieser Alpen ist, wie bemerkt, in der Nasaalpe Granit, übrigens gewöhnlich Glimmerschiefer; in einem Theil von Piteå-Lappmark findet man auch Kalchberge, die in den Nordischen Alpen eine seltene Erscheinung sind.

Im niedern Theil von Piteå-Lappmark, wie in ganz Lyckselse und Åsele-Lappmark, hat man bisher keine Anweisungen zu Erzgängen gefunden.

Was endlich die Sprache in Piteå-Lappmark anbetrifft, so verstehen die Lappen von Arvidsjaur das Schwedische; ihr Lappischer Dialekt ist rein, und von dem Åsele-Dialekt so verschieden, daß die Lappen von Arvidsjaur und Åsele einander nicht verstehen; von den Lyckseler werden die Åseler, wie die Arvidsjaur-Lappen verstanden. Der Dialekt der Arjeploger nähert sich dem Dialekt der Jockmock-Lappen, welcher der reinste aller Lappischen Dialekte ist, obgleich viel Finnisches mit demselben vermischt wird. Die Lappen von Arjeplog verstehen die von Arvidsjaur, sind aber des Schwedischen nicht kundig. Die Schwedischen Nybyggare in Arjeplog sprechen, wie die in Jockmock, viel Lappisch.

d. Luleå-Lappmark

wird im Westen von Norwegen, im Osten von den Westerbottnischen Pastoraten Luleå, Råneå und Öfver-Calix, im Süden von Piteå-Lappmark, im Norden von Juckasjervi-Lappmark begränzt. Die Ausdehnung von N. nach S. rechnet man zu 18, von W. nach O. zu 24, das Areal zu 324 ☐M. Die nördlichsten Berge dieses Lappmark, Ribatjock und Jokatismorka, liegen unter 68° 61' Polhöhe.

Luleå-Lappmark gehört zu Norrbottens Län, bildet 2 Gerichtssprengel, und 2 Pastorate, Jockmock, mit dem Filial Qvickjock, und Gellivare, die der dritten Westerbottnischen Propstey Luleå untergeordnet sind.

Das Pastorat Jockmock oder die südliche Hälfte dieses Lappmark, zählte im Jahr 1815. 1300 (680 in Jockmock und 620 in Qvickjock); das Pastorat Gellivare, oder die nördliche Hälfte,

1122 Seelen. Die Familienzahl dieses Lappmark betrug 504: unter ihnen 219 wohlhabende, 210 bedürftige und 75 ganz arme. Geboren wurden in Jockmock 25, in Qvickjock 11, in Gellivare 52 (zusammen 88, unter welchen 5 uneheliche); es starben, in Jockmock 25, in Qvickjock 9, in Gellivare 33. In der Gemeinde Qvickjock sind die meisten Einwohner Lappen. Die Aussaat bestand in Gerste und Kartoffeln, und in Gellivare etwas Roggen; das urbare Land betrug in Jockmock 49, in Qvickjock 7, in Gellivare 76 Tonnen.

Der Viehbestand war: Pferde, Ochsen, Kühe, Kälber, Schaafe

	Pferde	Ochsen	Kühe	Kälber	Schaafe
in Jockmock	45	30	233	75	430
in Qvickjock	16	9	56	20	160
in Gellivare	69	58	343	64	500

Im Jahre 1813 war die Zahl der Schatzlappen, also der Hausväter, in den verschiedenen Lappendörfern von Luleå-Lappmark folgende:

Pastorat Jockmock:

1. Lappendorf Turpenjaur mit 40 (im J. 1799. 35 Männer, 37 Frauen) Skattlappar und 2 Sprintare, Schatz 18 Rthlr. 8 ßl.

2. Lappendorf Sirkasluckt, 47 (1799. 51 M. 52 Fr.) Skattlappar, 30 Rthlr. Schatz. Das Dorf umfaßt etwa 10 ☐M.

3. Lappendorf Jockmock, 30 (1799. 27 M. 27 Fr.) Skattlappar, Schatz 12 Rthlr. 32 ßl.

4. Lappendorf Sjockjock, 34 (1799. 39 M. 38 Fr.) Skattlappar, Schatz 11 Rthlr. 32 ßl.

Pastorat Gellivare:

1. Lappendorf Jockmock-Sjockjock mit 9 Skattlappar, Schatz 3 Rthlr. 32 ßl. Diese Lappen gehören noch zu den Jockmocks-Lappen, aber zu Gellivare Pastorat; die Dorfschaft wird von der in Jockmock belegenen Dorfschaft Sjockjock durch den Luleå-Elf geschieden.

2. Gellivare-Sjockjock Lappendorf, liegt gleichfalls neben dem Jockmocks Lappendorf Sjockjock, es hat 33 Skattlappar nebst 1 Sprintare, der Schatz beträgt 13 Rthlr. 24 ßl.

Im Jahr 1799 zählten beide zu Gellivare Pastorat gehörigen Sjockjock 49 Hausväter und 49 Frauen.

3. Söbra und Norra Kajtumjaur, 65 Skattlappar, 2 Sprins
tare, Schaß 52 Rthlr. Im Jahr 1799 waren hier 89 Haus
väter und 90 Frauen.

Nybyggare waren in Luleå-Lappmark im Jahr 1813:
Paſtorat Jockmock:
1. Kronhöfe, 32 ſteuernde (alſo eigne Bauern) *) in 22
Dörfern, Schaß 34 Rthlr. 8 ßl. 17 ſteuerfreie Nybyggare
auf 17 Nybyggen.

2. Hermelinſche Höfe: 20 Nybyggen (16¼ mantal) am gros
ßen und kleinen Luleå-Elf.
Paſtorat Gellivare:
1. Steuernde Kron-Nybyggare 45 (Finnen) in 17 Dörfern,
Schaß 53 Rthlr. 16 ßl.; ſteuerfreie Nybyggen 4.

2. Melderſtein's Bruks, adelige Nybyggen 40 (27¼ mantal),
wovon aber 18 unbewohnt.

Sämmtliche Kronſteuern in Luleå-Lappmark betrugen 249
Rthlr. 8 ßl. banko. Die Hufenzahl (hemmantal) war in Jock
mock 8¼, in Gellivare 8¼.

Viele Lappen in Luleå-Lappmark treiben ſchon Ackerbau oder
haben doch feſte Wohnplätze erwählt; im Jahr 1813 folgende:
Paſtorat Jockmock:
Purkijaur, 1 Hof, Jacob Abrahamsſon mit Frau, Lappiſch
gekleidet.

Nautejaur, 1 Hof, Påhl Larsſon, mit Frau und Kindern
Lappiſch gekleidet.

Weikijaur, 2 Höfe, die Brüder Anders und Johann Jo
hansſon, mit ihren Familien Schwediſch gekleidet.

Kitajaur, 1 Hof, Lars Andersſon, mit Frau und Kindern
Lappiſch gekleidet. Er hat viele Rennthiere, die er auf eigenem
Lappland weidet, ohne mit ihnen auf die Fjäll zu gehen. In der
Regel haben die Lappiſchen Nybyggare keine oder wenige Rennthiere.

Kainaure, 1 Hof, Knut Larsſon Tebble, mit Frau und Kin
dern Lappiſch gekleidet; hat Rennthiere, die er auf eigenem Lapp
land weidet.

*) Im Jahr 1816 nur 30 ſchaßpflichtige Bauern.

Nedra Neckerim, 1 Hof, Anders Larsson, mit Frau und Kind Lappisch gekleidet; ist arm und ohne Rennthiere.

Nausta, 1 Hof, Lars Michelsson, mit Frau und Kind Schwedisch gekleidet; er hat Rennthiere, die er auf seinem Lappland weidet.

Lommejaur, 1 Hof, Pähl Mickelsson Tullnär, mit Familie Lappisch gekleidet. Den Beinamen: Zöllner (Tullnär) erhielt er, weil er von andern Lappen, die auf seinem Lappland weiden wollten, Zoll genommen; solche Verpachtung des eigenen Lapplandes an Andere ist bei den Nybyggare, wie bei den Fischerlappen, üblich.

Kainaure, 1 Hof, Pehr Larsson Julkus (der langbeinige), mit Frau und Kind Lappisch gekleidet.

Radnijaure, 1 Hof, Larsson Julkus, mit Frau und Kind Lappisch gekleidet.

Bredträsk, 1 Hof, Nils Larsson Lusi, mit Frau und Kind Lappisch gekleidet.

Paijerim, 1 Hof, Thomas Larsson Julkus, mit Frau und Kind Lappisch gekleidet.

Pastorat Gellivare:

Sautajervi, 2 Höfe, Hendrik Olofsson und Anders Hindriksson Stålnakke (haben Rennthiere und Kühe), beide mit ihren Familien Lappisch gekleidet. Einem Französischen Emigranten, dem Präsidenten de Vesverotte, der im Jahr 1792 das Land mit großer Pracht durchreisete und deshalb von den Lappen für einen Fürsten gehalten wurde, sich daneben aber durch allerlei Liebesabentheuer bekannt machte, gelang es, die Tochter des Stålnakke zu verführen; die Lappen, denen sonst die Unkeuschheit sehr verhaßt ist, begehrten nun das Mädchen zahlreich zur Ehe, weil sie dadurch in eine fürstliche Verwandtschaft zu treten glaubten!! Ein anderes Mädchen aus Juckasjervi, die gleichfalls den Verführungskünsten Vesverotte's unterlag, nahm dieser mit sich nach Frankreich, von wo sie ihren Eltern in Lappland zuweilen Geschenke übersandte. Sie ward späterhin an einen wohlhabenden Handwerker in Paris verheirathet; jetzt ist sie Wittwe, soll ihr Vermögen in baares Geld verwandelt und sich auf den Heimweg nach Juckasjervi begeben haben. Die Heimathsliebe der Lappen ist sehr groß.

Muskojervi, 2 Höfe, Marcus Olofsson und Michel Hindricsson, mit ihren Familien Lappisch gekleidet.

Saiwits, 1 Hof, Mats Mätsson, mit Frau und Kindern Lappisch gekleidet.

Nattaware, 6 Höfe, deren Bewohner, 2 Brüder Mats und Michel Michelson, Jacob Israelson nebst Sohn Olof Jacobsson, Michel Israelsson, Bruder von Jacob Israelsson, Jöns Larsson und Påhl Andersson, mit ihren Familien Lappisch gekleidet gehen, auch Rennthiere haben.

Sarwasoiwe, 2 Höfe, Mats Matsson und Jöns Olofsson, mit ihren Familien Lappisch gekleidet.

Risträsk, 1 Hof, Hans Ersson, mit Frau und Kind Lappisch gekleidet.

Neitiswando, 2 Höfe, Erik Hindriksson und Jöran Bengtsson, mit Familien Lappisch gekleidet.

Randaträsk, 1 Hof, John Knutson Kilka, mit Frau und Kind Lappisch gekleidet.

Das Pastorat Jockmock hat 2 Kirchen, die Mutterkirche Jockmock, welche grade unter dem Polarzirkel liegt, und die Filialkirche Qvickjock, nebst Kapelle Alkavara. Bei der Mutterkirche besteht seit 1733 eine Lappenschule mit 6 Kindern; Schulmeister ist seit 1796 der Pastor, welcher beide Löhne genießt; der Pastorgehalt beträgt 40 Tonnen Gerste und 13 Rthlr. 16 ßl. banco; derselbe genießt auch als ehemaliger Bruksprediger einen kleinen Gehalt von 25 Rthlr. banco aus Staatsmitteln. An der Filialkirche, welche 13 Meilen von Jockmock, meist Bootsweg, entlegen ist, steht ein Comminister, dessen Lohn 20 Tonnen Gerste und 25 Rthlr. aus öffentlichen Mitteln, desgl. 8 Tonnen Gerste vom Pastor, beträgt. Dieser Comminister predigt 2mal im Sommer, im Julius und September, vor den Lappen in der Alpenkapelle Alkavara, wofür er 8 Rthlr. erhält. — Hausverhöre werden auch unter den Lappen gehalten. Die Confirmation der Lappenkinder pflegt erst zwischen dem 16ten und 25sten Jahre zu geschehen.

Das Pastorat Gellivare hat nur eine Kirche, deren Pastor, außer etwas Geld, 30 Tonnen Gerste an Lohn genießt; bei der

Kirche besteht seit 1755 eine Lappenschule mit 6 Kindern und
eigenem Schulmeister. Im Sommer hält der Pastor Alpengottesdienst in der Kapelle Killingsnando an der Gränze von Torneå-
Lappmark. Auch reiset er zu den entlegenen Wohnsitzen der
Waldlappen, um dort mit ihnen Gottesdienst und Verhör zu
halten.

Wie in allen Westerbottnischen Lappenschulen, wird auch in
denen von Luleå-Lappmark der Unterricht in Lappischer Sprache
ertheilt; indeß ward bei der Visitation 1817 in Jockmock verordnet, daß, da die Schulkinder meist zu Katecheten bestimmt
seyen, denen es auch obliege, die Kinder Schwedischer Nybyggare
zu unterrichten, sie auch in der Schwedischen Sprache unterwiesen werden sollten. Schon ein altes Gesetz (Wilskman Eccle-
siastique Verk S. 399) verordnet ein Gleiches; doch ist solches,
der beschränkten Schulzeit und anderer Ursachen wegen, wenig
zur Ausführung gebracht worden. — Eigene Schulhäuser giebt
es in diesem Lappmark nicht.

Der Katecheten sind für Gellivare 2, für Jockmock 2; ferner Ein Reisekatechet gemeinschaftlich für Gellivare- und Jock-
mock-Lappmark (man theilt gewöhnlich Luleå-Lappmark in diese
beiden besonderen Lappmarker). Reisekatecheten giebt es nur in
den nördlichsten Lappmarken, sie reisen umher, um nach den Wir-
kungen des Unterrichts der Katecheten, nach den Verhältnissen der
einzelnen Familien ꝛc. zu forschen, auch selbst zu lehren.

Sowohl Jockmock als Gellivare hat sein eigenes jährlich zu-
sammentretendes Häradsgericht, nebst 2 Märkten und Steuererhebung.

Der Boden von Jockmock ist mager; der Wald besteht
meist aus Fichten, wenigen Birken. Qvickjock, unter 67¼° Polhöhe, hat ein ziemlich mildes Klima, längeren Sommer (der auf
den nahen Alpen nur 6 bis 7 Wochen währt), die üppigsten
Wiesen, die lieblichsten Bäche und Laubhaine; ja, die Lage der
Kirche und des Pfarrhauses ist entzückend schön; überall erblickt
man Schneeberge; die Aussicht von der Voralpe Vallebacken,
1 Meile um Nordwest der Kirche, auf die Laubhaine, Inseln,
Seen und Flüsse, ist unbeschreiblich reizend. 1½ Meile von

Qvickjock stürzt der zuweilen sehr wasserreiche Bach Kobtajock, vom hohen Berge Kassavare herab, in den Sagatsee. — Der 1817 verstorbene Comminister Lestadius hat in Qvickjock den Ackerbau zu einer, in diesem Klima ungewöhnlichen Höhe gebracht.

Besser als in Qvickjock, ist der Boden in Gellivare: man findet hier große Ebenen; die Wiesen sind vorzüglich, besonders durch die Ueberschwemmungen der Flüsse; im Allgemeinen sind Wiesen und Aecker fruchtbarer, als in den übrigen, oder den meisten der übrigen Lappischen Pastorate; doch reift die Gerste selten. In Gellivare sind die großen Lappischen Erzlager; außer den Erzgebirgen giebt es nur Einen Berg, den Dunduri, ½ M: von der Kirche; er hat die Gestalt eines Hufeisens und verliert nie allen Schnee; auf der Höhe findet man einen kleinen See; bei klarem Wetter sieht man auf dem Dunduri, um Johannis, mehrere Wochen lang, die Mitternachtssonne.

Ein 18 Meilen langer Weg führt von Jockmock nach Luleå, meist Bootweg auf dem Luleå, wenig Gehweg; die Wege von Jockmock nach Gellivare, 8 Meilen, und von Jockmock nach Arvidsjaur, 9 Meilen, sind bloß Winterwege; von Gellivare nach Öfver-Calir, 14 Meilen, ist Reitweg längs dem Lina-Elf, und dann 6 Meilen Bootweg auf den Flüssen Skrof, Landsjärf, Tvärä und Angesä; von Öfver-Calir bis TöreforS am Ausfluß des Töre ins Meer sind 4½ Meilen, wovon nur 1¾ Meilen Bootweg auf dem Calir; von Gellivare, über Nattivare, nach Strömsund im Pastorat Råneå, ungefähr 18 Meilen, ist ein Winterweg für Erztransporte, gar kein Bootweg; von Gellivare über Nattivare nach dem Ladeplatz und Nybygge Storbacken am Luleå-Elf 10 Meilen, oder nach Edefors am Luleå 12 Meilen Winterweg, im Sommer Gehweg; von Storbacken hat man bis zur Stadt Luleå 12½ Meilen, und von Edefors 10 Meilen Bootweg auf dem Luleå (nur von Hedenfors bis Räbäck auf Flossen oder in Stromböten).

Die Sprache der meisten Nybyggare ist, insofern sie nicht Lappen sind, Finnisch, einiger Schwedisch; die 4 Bauern von Stor-Luleåby in Jockmock verstehen nur Finnisch und Lappisch. Von den Lappen des Pastorats Jockmock verstehen nur die Sjockfjocklappen Schwedisch. Auch in Gellivare verstehen die Lappen nicht Schwedisch; ihre Sprache ist ein vermischtes Lappisch-Finnisches, auch wohl ganz das Finnische. Die Geistlichen müssen hier ihre Predigten hintereinander in den 3 Sprachen dieses Lappmark halten: sie beginnen mit dem Schwedischen, halten dann dieselbe Predigt auf Finnisch und zuletzt auf Lappisch.

Die Nybyggare in Luleå-Lappmark sind, wie in Lycksele und Arfoidsjaur, von schöner Körperbildung; in den meisten Lappmarken ist unter den Nybyggare das männliche Geschlecht schöner als das weibliche. Ihre Nahrungszweige sind in Jockmock und Gellivare ziemlich gleich: Viehzucht und Fischerey sind die Hauptnahrungszweige; überdieß in Gellivare die Erztransporte, die mit Rennthieren und Ochsen von den Erzgruben bis zum Ladeplatz Edefors beschafft werden. Die Fischerey ist besonders ergiebig; Lachse fängt man im Luleå-Elf auch zum Verkauf; ferner werden getrocknete Hechte, gesalzene Schnäpel, Häute, Käse, Fleisch und Leim aus Rennthierhorn (mehr als in andern Lappmarken) veräußert; Butter und Talg in geringeren Quantitäten. Vieles wird nach Westerbotten geführt. Die Sennenwirthschaft ist eingeführt. Theerbrennereien sind angelegt, könnten aber noch sehr vermehrt werden; der Theer wird auf den Strömen, auf Flossen ins niedere Land geführt. Ochsen, die sehr groß sind, und deren viele man verkauft, werden, ganz wie die Pferde, zum Fahren gebraucht, weshalb man der letzteren wenigere hält. Rennthiere haben die Nybyggare viele, die Lappen weiden sie; auch zum Transport von Kaufmannswaaren werden sie benutzt. Die Jagd ist nicht unbedeutend: man verkauft Bären-, Eichhorn- und Marderfelle.

Der Ackerbau ist sehr unbedeutend; nichts als Gerste wird gesäet, und diese reift in Gellivare sehr selten *), in Jockmock

---

*) Eine Hauptursache des Nichtreifens des Getreides in Lappland ist die späte Aussaat, diese aber Folge des späten Schmelzens des Schnees. In Savoyen, im Chamouni-Thal (hier und da soll es auch in Schweden geschehen), streuet man auf den Schnee, der die zur Saat bestimmten Aecker deckt, schwarze Erde aus, welche, indem sie die Sonnenstrahlen

öfter. Faſt jedes dritte Jahr fällt Mißwachs ein; geſchwendet wird nicht. Jährlich muß Korn gekauft werden. Doch leidet man keine Noth, es ſey denn etwa in Gellivare, wo die Nybyggare ärmer ſind, als in Jockmock. In beiden Paſtoraten gehen ſie Lappiſch gekleidet, nur die Kleidung der Weiber nähert ſich mehr der Schwediſchen. Ihre Lebensart iſt ſehr mäßig, ihr Brod Spreubrod (agnbröd) wie in allen Lappmarken; doch für Fremde hat man beſſeres, ſelbſt Roggenbrod. Einem Fremden Gaſtfreundſchaft zu erweiſen, iſt ihnen ein wahrer Genuß, und für keinen Preis wollen ſie Bezahlung nehmen. Die Nybyggare von Jockmock werden vorzugsweiſe als ein treues, bieders, wahrhaft frommes Volk geſchildert; weniger lobt man die von Gellivare, welche ſich gegen die Lappen oft ſehr eigennützig bezeigen ſollen: z. B. laſſen ſie ſich für die Beweidung ihrer Landſtücke durch Lappiſche Rennthierheerden bezahlen. Unter den Nybyggare von Jockmock hat der religiöſe Verein der Leſer (ſ. Kap. 19.) Eingang gefunden.

Die Importwaaren beſtehen, außer Korn, in Salz und Taback. Was man an Eiſenarbeiten u. dergl. m. bedarf, verfertiget man ſelbſt. Branntewein wird weder von Nybyggare noch von Lappen irgend eines Lappmark, außer den Marktzeiten getrunken, und faſt in keinem Hofe iſt Branntewein vorräthig, zuweilen führen ihn aber die Bauern aus Luleå, auf Handelsreiſen, heimlich ein.

Ein beträchtlicher Theil der Lappen von Luleå-Lappmark, die oben genannten Ackerbautreibenden ungerechnet, hat feſte Sitze: dies gilt von den, an Zahl und Wohlſtand ſeit etwa 15 Jahren ſehr geſunkenen, Sjockſjock Lappen in Jockmock und Gellivare. Wölfe haben ihre Heerden meiſt vernichtet; die wenigen Rennthiere, welche ſie noch beſitzen, treiben ſie nicht auf die Alpen, ſondern behalten ſie in ihrer Nähe; viele haben gar keine, andere halten Kühe,

───────────

in größeter Menge einſchluckt, das Schmelzen des Schnees fördert und die Ackerbeſtellung 2 bis 3 Wochen früher möglich macht. Die aus den Sümpfen und naſſen Wieſen ſich entwickelnde Kälte erzeugt frühe Nachtfröſte.

mit denen sie innerhalb ihres eigenen Lapplandes, also in kleinen
Kreisen, und ohne dadurch ihren festen Wohnsitz zu verlieren,
umherziehen. Andere verfertigen sehr feine Körbe, Matten, Reife, so wie aus dem schwarzen Rennthierleder, welches aus der
Beinhaut bereitet wird, die warmen und meist wasserdichten Lappenschuhe, die einen Handelsartikel bilden. Viele dienen, als
Hirten oder Erndtearbeiter bei den Nybyggare, im Lande, oder
auf Westerbottnischen Höfen. Die übrigen leben von Fischerey
auf ihrem Lappland, für welches sie an die Krone Schatz geben;
ihr sonstiges Lappland ist zur Ansiedelung von Kolonisten verwandt worden. Sie sind ein biederes und gottesfürchtiges Volk;
an jedem Sonntage halten sie unter sich Gottesdienst, falls sie
nicht die Kirche besuchen können. Sie sind sehr reinlich, von
schöner Körperbildung, insbesondere das weibliche Geschlecht, und
von hoher Statur. Sie ziehen nie auf die Alpen.

Die Turpun-, Sirkas- und Jockmocks-Lappen in Jockmocks-
Lappmark sind wohlhabende Alpenlappen: im Sommer leben sie
auf den Alpen, im Winter ziehen sie in den Pastoraten Piteå,
Luleå und Calix umher. Sie sind roh, wenig lebendig und von
kleiner Statur, die Turpun-Lappen ausgenommen, die gleich
den Sjockssockslappen lang von Wuchs sind; Lastern sind sie
nicht ergeben. Sie treiben Handel mit Norwegen und Norrbotten: in Norwegen verkaufen sie Rennthierfleisch und Rennthierfelle, kaufen Heringe, Kabeljau und besonders viel Dorsch ein, um es in
Norrbotten wieder zu verkaufen. Von ihren Handelsreisen haben sie die Radesyge mitgebracht, die nun unter diesen Lappen
forterbt, indeß nicht tödtlich ist; auch unter den Kolonisten findet sie sich. Wenn diese, wie andere Alpenlappen von Luleå-
Lappmark, im Winter ins niedere Land ziehen, müssen sie an die
dort angesiedelten Nybyggare eine Abgabe in Geld und Rennthierfleisch für das Land, welches sie auf diesen Zügen beweiden,
entrichten, da doch die Nybyggare desselben nicht bedürfen; es ist
auf Abstellung angetragen worden.

Die Kaitum-Lappen in Gellivare-Lappmark, die zum Theil
auch in Torneå-Lappmark wohnen, sind gleichfalls Alpenlappen,
die im Sommer auf den Alpen, im Winter im niedern Lande,

in den Paſtoraten Öfver= und Neder-Calix und Öfver=Torneå,
mit ihren Heerden nomadiſiren; oft halten ſie ſich auch in Nor=
wegen auf. Sie ſind hoch von Wuchs, roh und leidenſchaftlich,
ſelbſt ausſchweifend, aber ehrlich; Dieberey findet man unter
ihnen ſelten; überhaupt hat es ſich mit ihnen in den letzten Jah=
ren in ſittlicher Hinſicht gebeſſert. Wohlſtand iſt ziemlich häu=
fig. — Der Aberglaube hat auch hier, wie in allen Lappmar=
ken, aufgehört. — Der Armen nehmen ſich auch die Lappen
thätig an.

In Gellivare=Paſtorat betrug im Jahr 1815 die Zahl der
Rennthiere 10,448; der reichſte Lappe beſaß 600; in Jockmock
und Qvickjock wird die Zahl der Rennthiere zu mehr denn
10,000 geſchätzt.

Luleå=Lappmark hat hohe Alpen, die unter allen Lappiſchen
für die höchſten gehalten werden und die ein ewiger Schnee
deckt; es ſind die Norwegiſchen Gränzalpen. Eine der merk=
würdigeren derſelben iſt der Sulitelma=Gletſcher, den Baron
Hermelin, von mehreren Seiten aus, hat in Kupfer ſtechen laſ=
ſen; er erhebt ſich 2600 Fuß über die Schneegränze, und 5541
Fuß (an der öſtlichen Seite) über das Meer; die Ausſicht von
dieſer Höhe hat wenig Reizendes, weil alles Niedere in Dun=
kelheit verſchwindet. *) Der Name ſoll Feſtberg bedeuten, und

---

*) Vergl. Dr. G. Wahlenberg's in Upſala, „Reiſe auf
den Sulitelma (im J. 1807) und Beſchreibung dieſer Al=
penkette"; — in deſſen: berättelſe om mätningar och obſervationer för
at beſtämma Lappſka fjällens höjd och temperatur vid 67 graders pol=
höjd, förrättade år 1807. (Bericht über Meſſungen und Beobachtungen
zur Beſtimmung der Höhe und Temperatur der Lappiſchen Alpen unter
67° Polhöhe, im J. 1807.) Mit Karte und 3 Ausſichten 58 S. gr. 4.
gedruckt auf Koſten des Baron Hermelin, der ſammt der Akademie der
Wiſſenſchaften in Stockholm die Koſten der Reiſe beſtritt, welche durch
Luleå=Lappmark über Qvickjock längs des Kamajocki nach Norwegen
an dem Nordſeebuſen Lerfjord nach Rörſtad und Kåringön ging, von da
nach Saltensfjord, worauf, von der Norwegiſchen Seite aus, der Sulitelma
erſtiegen wurde. Der Reiſeplan (Jenaer allgemeine Literaturzeitung,
Jul. 1807. n. 54. Intelligenzblatt) konnte nicht ganz befolgt werden.

II.   3

an die Opfer erinnern, die hier einst die heidnischen Lappen dem Alpengott darbrachten. Auf den Norwegischen Gränzalpen müssen oft die Lappen mitten im Sommer auf Schlittschuhen laufen. Jenseits zeigt das schmale Land bis zur Nordsee nichts als nackte Felsenketten mit kleinen, hier und da bewohnten, grünen Thälern. Auf der Schwedischen Seite stehen die Felsen mehr einzeln, niedriger Wald und Grasland sind sichtbar, die Vegetation reicht mehr, denn 800 Fuß höher, als auf der Norwegischen Seite. Die Birke steigt am höchsten; ihr zunächst die Gräne (pinus abies), dann die Kiefer (pinus sylvestris, tall): so in Qvickjock. In den übrigen Lappmarken steigt die Kiefer höher, als die Gräne, deren hoher Stand in Qvickjock durch eine günstige Localität veranlaßt wird. Im Allgemeinen kann man annehmen, daß auf den Lappischen Gebirgen die Birke 2100, die Kiefer 1300 bis 1400, die Gräne 1000 Fuß über die Meeresfläche steigt. Die Norwegische Seite ist, weil sie zwischen Alpen und Meer mitten inne liegt, ungleich rauher, als die Schwedische, daher dort die Vegetation schon auf einer geringern Höhe aufhört. Weiter unterhalb in Luleå-Lappmark findet man keine Alpen, sondern nur einzelne Waldberge, die sich 3 bis 400 F. über den Luleåstrom erheben. Wo die Kiefer nicht wächst, reift auch kein Korn mehr, doch trifft man noch Menschenwohnungen, z. B. Naimaka im Kirchspiel Enontekis, 1600 Fuß unter der Schneegränze: man lebt hier von Viehzucht, Fischerey, Kartoffeln und Rübenbau. Bis 2000 Fuß unter der Schneegränze sieht man Birken, wo diese verschwinden, giebt es auch keine Fische mehr: am höchsten findet man salmo alpinus (rödding, Alpenlachs). Den Namen Alpen führen eigentlich nur die Berge, welche über die Birkengränze emporsteigen: anfangs trifft man noch salix glauca, betula nana, salix hastata etc. als Stauden, dann verschwinden auch diese. Die Rennthierweide läuft aber bis 800 Fuß unter der Schneegränze, höher schlagen die Lappen fast nie ihre Hütten auf. Jetzt beginnt die Schneeregion: es zeigen sich isolirte, nie schmelzende Schneefelder, durch schwache Spuren von Vegetation auf nacktem Boden geschieden; bald erweitern sich die Schneemassen: die eigentliche Schneegränze hebt an und man erblickt nun nur hier und da eine kleine, von Schnee entblößte, Bodenfläche. Freilich beginnt die Schneegränze nicht überall in gleicher Höhe: auf den Alpen von Quickjock mit 4100, an der Norwegischen Seite mit etwa 3100 Fuß über der Meeresfläche *): hier ist das Klima von Spitzbergen an der Meeresseite und von Novaja Sembla. Noch bis 500 Fuß über die Schneegränze hinaus sieht man zuweilen einen Ranunculus nivalis und ähnliche Pflanzen, bis 2000 F. lichenes umbilicati etc., in den Spalten aus dem Schnee hervorragender Felsen. Dann verschwindet alle Vegetation. Die Schneeammer (emberiza nivalis) ist auf diesen Höhen das einzige lebendige Wesen. Mit der Schneeregion beginnen die Gletscher, die, je größer sie sind, desto tiefer unter die Schneegränze herabsteigen. Aus den von Wahlenberg (a. d. a. O. S. 49. ff.) angestellten Vergleichungen erhellt, daß Schneeregion und Gletscher in Schweden höher steigen als in andern Nordischen Ländern, und daß unter allen nördlichen Ländern, in gleicher Polhöhe, Schweden die höchste Schneegränze und eben damit zugleich das mildeste Klima hat: das Klima von Kamtschatka unter 53° Polhöhe ist fast gleich kalt, wie das Klima von Finnmarken unter 71°.

Schon längst kannte man die Erzlager von Luleå-Lappmark. In Quickjock fand man im 17ten Jahrhundert in den Alpen Kedkevare und Alkevare, und in der Nähe derselben Anweisungen zu Silberadern; 5 Meilen von den Gruben, zu Quickjock, ward 1661 eine Schmelzhütte angelegt und eine Kirche gegründet. Der Grubenbau ward anfangs von der Krone, dann von Privatpersonen, abermals von der Krone und endlich von der Westerbottnischen Bergwerkssocietät (Westerbottnisla Bergslagssocieteten) betrieben, doch stets mit Verlust, worauf seit 1702

---

*) Am Riesengebirge mit 6400, auf den Schweizeralpen mit 7812, an der Italienischen Seite mit 8400, am Libanon mit 9100, in Mexiko mit 14,100 Fuß; auf dem Chimborasso findet man Städte bis zu einer Höhe von 10,950 Fuß. Westlich von Spitzbergen senkt sich die Schneelinie zum Meere hinab.

3 2

die gesammte Arbeit ruhte; nur ein Häuschen mit der Krone gehörigen Bruksgeräthschaften, wozu der Comminister von Qvick-jock den Schlüssel hat, ist noch vorhanden: 1661 gab das Erz von Kedkevare 54, im J. 1663 39 Mark Silber; 1695 gab das Erz von Alkevare 77 Schiffpfund Werkbley, woraus 155 Mark Silber gewonnen wurden, im J. 1700 55 Mark Silber und 15 Schiffpfund Bley. *) — Das Kedkevare-Fjäll liegt 6 Meilen von der Kirche Qvickjock und eben so weit von der Norwegischen Gränze; es übertrifft alle benachbarten Alpen an Höhe, und Wolken ruhen fast immer auf demselben. Das Erz geht wenig tief, es hielt 5 bis 6 Loth Silber im Zentner und 20 — 30 Prozent in reiner Stuffe oder gewaschenem Erz. — Alke-vare-Fjäll liegt 3 Meilen von Kedkevare-Fjäll, und 8 Meilen von Qvickjock; es steigt zu einer Höhe von 4750 Fuß; auch hier war der Bau nicht lohnend. Eben so wenig gaben die übrigen geringen Silberanweisungen, welche man an mehrern Stellen fand und versuchte, hinreichenden Gewinn.

Viel ergiebiger sind die Erzlager, die der Berg Routes-vare, d. i. der Eisenberg, 1½ M. nordnordwestlich von Qvick-jock's Kirche, enthält. Der Berg liegt zwischen dem Alpenfluß Mätsojock im N. O. und den lachenden Ufern des Alpenflusses Kamajock im S. W. Das Eisenerz bricht in großer Menge und Reichhaltigkeit: es giebt 56 bis 58 Prozent. Baron Her-melin hat zuerst (1797 durch den Bergrath Robsahm) diese un-erschöpflichen Gruben untersuchen und bearbeiten, auch Gebäude daselbst aufführen lassen; die Benutzung derselben würde sehr er-leichtert werden, wenn auf dem kleinen Luleäfluß zwischen Qvick-jock und Jockmock durch Wasserfälle und Strömungen hindurch eine Bootfahrt eingerichtet werden könnte, was der Baron beab-sichtigte, und wozu er bereits Nybyggen an den Ufern anlegte. Nur im niedern Lande, wo reicherer Holzvorrath ist, könnte man die Schmelzung mit Erfolg bewerkstelligen; der Wintertransport mit Rennthieren ist schwierig, weil mehrere Meilen um Qvick-

*) Baron Hermelin's försök til Mineralhistoria öfver Lappmarken och Westerbotten. S. 36.

jock herum sich keine Winterweide für diese Thiere finden soll. — Auf der Höhe des Berges trifft man 3 kleine Seen. Die Erzlager streichen in der ganzen Länge und Breite des Berges $\frac{3}{8}$ und $\frac{1}{8}$ M. Das eine lothrechte, am Tage stehende Erzlager hat 60 Ellen Höhe und 120 Ellen Breite; hier liegen viele 1000 Schiffpfund Erz, die von der Wand herabgefallen sind und nur zur Verarbeitung fortgeführt zu werden brauchen; andere Erzstücke hängen zum Sturz. Das Erz ist blaugrau, schlackendicht, glänzend und magnetisch, das Eisen guter Art.

Der Berg Routevare, d. i. Eisenberg, in Jockmock, $\frac{1}{2}$ M. im S. W. von Jockmock's Kirche ist bereits 1638 als Erzberg angegeben worden, aber die 1796 angestellte Untersuchung hat keinen Erzgehalt ergeben.

Die Oberfläche des Kassavare, $1\frac{1}{2}$ M. von Qvickjock, deckt eisenschwarzer Schiefer, aus welchem Allaun, weißgrauem Mehle ähnlich, auswittert; ein Gleiches zeigt sich auf den großen Blöcken, die vom Berge niedergestürzt sind. Das Volk sammelt diesen Allaun und benutzt ihn zum Färben. Eigentlicher Allaunschiefer ist nicht vorhanden.

Noch merkwürdiger als die Eisenlager von Qvickjock sind die Eisenlager von Gellivare. Diese streichen in 2 Bergrücken, $\frac{3}{8}$ Meile nördlich von der Kirche Gellivare. Den $\frac{3}{8}$ Meile von da südlich gelegenen Berg Dundari ausgenommen, liegt das Erzgebirge mitten im ebenen Lande, welches hier und da nur von Hügeln durchschnitten wird. Die Ebene besteht, einem großen Theile nach, aus Sümpfen, das übrige Land ist mit Rennthiermoos oder, meistens niedrigen, Gränen und Fichten bewachsen; der Graswuchs ist üppig, zumal am Lina-Elf, der, 5 Meilen im O. N. O. des Erzgebirges aus dem See Tjerkokjervi entspringend, dem östlichen Fuß des Berges in einer Entfernung von etwa 1000 Ellen vorüberfließt und 14 M. unterhalb in den Calir-Elf fällt. 3 M. südlich vom Berge fließt der Râncâ; etwa 6 M. südlich der Calir und etwas weiter im Nordosten der Luleâ, kleinere Flüsse und Bäche bewässern überdieß die Umgebungen des Berges. Die Höhe reicht über die Birkengränze hinaus, beträgt indeß nur einige hundert Ellen über die untere

Fläche; bis zur Mittelhöhe findet man niedere Erlen und Birken, dann nur Rennthiermoos und Alpengewächse. In das Erzgebirge schneidet ein Thal ein: der eine Bergrücken ist etwa 9000, der andere 5000 Ellen lang; die Breite ist an 3000 Ellen. Von einzelnen Kuppen hat man weite, fast nach allen Seiten unbeschränkte Aussichten, im N. und W. 10 bis 15 Meilen weit auf die Schneealpen, im S. und O. auf die Ebenen am Lina-Elf, bis zum Pastorat Öfver-Calix. Die Oberfläche bildet meistens eine tiefe Dammerde, aus weißem Sand und Steingraus bestehend, mit großen und kleinen, losen, Granitblöcken und Erzsteinen.

Bereits zu Anfang des 18ten Jahrhunderts kannte man den Erzberg; doch erst seit um 1730 ein Bauer aus Råneå die Aufmerksamkeit auf denselben hinlenkte, schritt man zur Untersuchung. Capitaine Tingwall, und dann Capitaine Meldercreutz in Gemeinschaft mit Brukspatron Steinholz, suchten und erhielten die Erlaubniß zur Bearbeitung: der Bau begann, und im Pastorat Råneå entstand das Bruk Melderstein. Seit dieser Zeit brach man, bis um 1790, fast jährlich; das Erz transportirten Lappen, mittelst Rennthiere, zum Hochofen Strömsund am Bottnischen Meerbusen, freilich nicht in hinreichender Menge, nur einzelne Jahre 1000 Schiffpfund. Eifriger und mit großen Opfern betrieb seit 1797 den Bergbau Baron Hermelin, der das gesammte Eigenthum vom Brukspatron Bedoir, in dessen Hände es nach Meldercreutz gekommen war, für 84,000 Bankthaler angekauft hatte. Neue Gruben wurden, auf des Barons Veranstaltung, durch Bergrath Robsahm, eröffnet; in den ersten Jahren brach man jährlich 2000 bis 3000 Schiffpfund, die man zu den Hochöfen Strömsund und Schlet führte; späterhin nahmen der Grubenbau und der Erztransport ab, und hörten, seit Hermelin seine Besitzungen verkaufte, völlig auf. Die Composition des Erzes ist, in den verschiedenen Gruben, in mechanischer und chemischer Hinsicht, sehr verschieden, doch meistens los, harte Lagen sind seltener; einzelner Eisenstein wird vom Magnet nicht angezogen. Der Gehalt ist 68 bis 72 Prozent; die Erzlager sind unerschöpflich. Eine neue Grube, Koskullskul-

lar, ward im J. 1817 durch die erwähnte Untersuchungskom=
mission auf noch undisponirtem Kronlande geöffnet. Die übrigen
Gruben liegen auf dem Gebiet dreier adelichen Nybyggen, die
Baron Hermelin zur Beförderung des Grubenbaues anlegte:
Puoitaks (Hermelins), Capitains und Robsahms Nybyggen; er=
steres mit seinem Grubenfeld, dem größeren Theil des westlichen
großen Feldes, gehört zu den Bruksanlagen des Barons im Pa=
storat Luleå, Svartlå und Schlet, die andern beiden Nybyggen,
Capitains mit dem südöstlichen, und Robsahms mit dem nordöst=
lichen Grubenfeld, gehören zum Bruk Melderstein. Capitains=
Nybygge steht öde, Robsahm's=Nybygge war noch nie bewohnt;
nur Puoitaks=Nybygge ist mit einem Bewohner versehen, der
geringen Ackerbau treibt, ohne Bruksdienste zu thun. Gelänge
es, den Lina=Fluß für Böte fahrbar zu machen, so ließe sich,
am paßlichsten von der neuen Grube Kostullskullar aus, ein
Landweg zu dem nur $\frac{1}{4}$ M. entfernten Flusse anlegen; das
Land umher giebt treffliche Weide für Rennthiere wie für
Pferde.

Bisher führen von Gellivare zum niedern Lande und zum
Meer 3, oben beschriebene, Wege, die aber nur im Winter zu
Transporten benutzt werden können, und im Sommer bloße
Gehwege sind: nach Storbacken 10, und Edefors am Luleå 12
M.; nach Strömsund's Hochofen 18 M.; nach Ober=Calix
14, und Töreforß 18½ M. Längs der Erzwege sind Moosstri=
che zur Weide für die Zugrennthiere bestimmt worden, und dür=
fen diese Striche sonst nicht beweidet werden.

Eine Meile vom Erzgebirge, auf dem Gebiet des adelichen
Nybygge Wassera, am Wasserafluß, hat Baron Hermelin zwei
Frischeisenheerde anlegen lassen, weil das Erz von Gellivare, sei=
ner großen Reinheit und Reichhaltigkeit wegen, in den Hochöfen
viel Neigung zum Zähewerden zeigte, und ohne Zusatz ärmerer
Erze, nicht zum Fluß gebracht werden konnte. Jene beiden
Heerde wurden in den Jahren 1803 und 1804, nach einer ei=
genthümlichen Construktion, errichtet: die angestellten Blaseversu=
che glückten, man erhielt z. B. aus 12 Liespfund Erz (à 20
Pfund) und 3½ Tonnen Kohlen durch 5½ stündiges Blasen ein

9 Liespfund schweres Frischstück, welches aus ziemlich gutem und geschmeidigem Eisen bestand. Indeß blieb es bei den ersten Versuchen; weder der Baron noch die späteren Eigenthümer setzten dieselben fort. Ofen und Gebläse sind noch im brauchbaren Stande, nur der Damm hat durch das Wasser gelitten *). Am Wasserstraßfluß und am Harrsee findet man Eisensand, mit 50 Prozent Gehalt.

Neuerlich hat man am Ufer des Calix-Träsk, im Pastorat Gellivare an der Gränze von Torneå-Lappmark, abermals einen sehr reichhaltigen Erzberg entdeckt, den die Bauern in Tärende Ekströmsberg nennen, weil der Brukspatron Ekström vor einigen Jahren eine Reise dahin machte **) Eine genaue Untersuchung der Erzlager dieses Berges ist noch nicht vorgenommen worden. Fast scheint es, als wenn in Luleå- und Torneå-Lappmark noch manche Entdeckungen von Erzbergen gemacht werden können.

In der Alpe Hjertavando (Herzchen) unweit der Norwegischen Gränze, westlich vom Kaitomsee, hat man 1749 Versuche auf Silber angestellt. Die Bergart ist aus Quarz, Kalchspat und insbesondere Strahlstein zusammengesetzt; man fand Bleyglanz, der aber nur 46 Prozent Bley und 2½ Loth Silber im Zentner gab. Die nicht lohnenden Versuche wurden wieder aufgegeben.

Ziemlich reines und feines Bleyerz findet man, in einem 2 Fuß breiten Gange des Röddingsberges, 6 — 7 M. südlich von Gellivare, um 1760 ward es gebrochen und scheint allerdings mit Vortheil benutzt werden zu können.

Nennen wir jetzt noch die ansehnlichsten Flüsse von Luleå-Lappmark, deren Fahrbarmachung man zum Theil vorgeschlagen hat, um die unerschöpflichen Eisengruben mehr benutzen zu können; jene ist indeß entweder unmöglich, oder zu kostbar. Die Anlegung neuer Landstraßen würde, bei dem 8 bis 9 monatli-

*) S. Roman's berättelse om Lappmarker och deß Lappmarker Stockholm 1818. 4to. S. 15.

**) Roman. S. 28.

chen Winter dieser Gegenden, unstreitig nützlicher und vielleicht viel weniger kostbar seyn.

Der beträchtlichste dieser Flüsse und einer der bedeutendsten im ganzen Reich ist der Luleå-Elf. Er wird durch 2 Arme gebildet, den großen und den kleinen Luleå-Elf, welche bei Porsiedar, unweit der Gränze von Luleå-Lappmark und Luleå Postorat, 13 Meilen oberhalb der Stadt Luleå, zusammenlaufen. Beide Arme entspringen aus großen Wasserzügen am Fuße der Gränzalpen.

Der kleine Luleå entfließt den sieben Seen, die zwischen den Kirchen Qvickjock und Jockmock eine 12 Meilen lange zusammenhängende Kette bilden; der oberste bei Qvickjock ist der Saggat, dann folgen Tjomotisjaur, Stalkajaur, Parkijaur, Randijaur, Purkijaur und Waikijaur; worauf, nach einem Laufe von etwa 4 Meilen, der kleine Luleå-Elf, wie erwähnt, bei Porsiedet in den großen Luleå fällt. Die Wassermasse des kleinen Luleå ist so ansehnlich, daß sie in der Frühlingsfluth bis zu 12 Fuß lothrechter Höhe steigen soll; die Wasserfälle und Strömungen desselben scheinen weniger bedeutend zu seyn.

Der große Luleå entspringt an der Norwegischen Gränze am Fuß der Alpe Lettnavardo, nahe an der Norwegischen Kapelle Mansfjord und fällt, nach einem Laufe von etwa 39 Meilen, in den Bottnischen Meerbusen. Auf den ersten 16 Meilen besteht der große Luleå aus einer Kette von Seen, die sich stufenweise über einander erheben und durch gewaltige Kataracten geschieden sind; dann beginnt das eigentliche Flußbette. Die eine dieser Kataracten bildet der See Kaskajaur, der sich von einer jähen Felsenwand in 3 Absätzen in den See Paijiplolijujaur hinabstürzt; der erste Sturz ist 80 Fuß hoch; beim dritten Absatze oder Sturze fällt der ansehnliche Fluß Vieleskoski mitten in den großen Wasserstrahl hinein. Rings umher sind nackte und steile Felsen. Die ganze Kataracte heißt: der große Fall oder Adna Murki Korki. — Theils Alpen, theils niedriger Wald mit Morästen ohne Zahl, umgeben diese Kette von Seen; Wüsteneien, die nur von Lappen besucht werden. Erst 15 Meilen unterhalb der Gränze da, wo der große Sjaungafluß einfällt, fand man seit 1800 eine

Menschenwohnung, einen von Baron Hermelin angelegten Koloni= stenhof, der aber jetzt öde steht. 1 Meile unterhalb dieses ehe= maligen Nybygge Sjaunga endet der letzte See mit dem etwa 80 Fuß hohen Wasserfall Luspakoski; das Strombette beginnt und geht fast in gerader Linie, 22 oder 23 Meilen, bis zur Mündung fort. Hinter Luspakoski folgen 2 fast gleich hohe Wasserfälle, Porjos und Napor, und endlich der größte im ganzen Luleå und wahrscheinlich in ganz Schweden, der Niaumelfaskas, der mehrere Meilen weit hörbar ist. Durch eine enge Felsenkluft hindurch stürzt der Strom in ein tiefes Thal; wo er sich gegen die Felsen bricht, wird der Strahl mehrere Faden hoch in die Luft zurückgeworfen. Die ganze Länge des Falles beträgt über ¼ Meile, die Höhe ohngefähr 400 Fuß. Der Name ist eigent= lich nur dem obersten Absatz des Falles von den Lappen beige= legt worden. Der Fall ist hier am heftigsten und jähesten, die unaufhörlich aufsteigenden dichten Staubwolken verwandelt die Winterkälte in Eisgewölbe, über welche man Haasen laufen sah; daher der Name Niaumelfaskas, d. i. Haasensprung.

Etwa eine Viertelmeile von Niaumelfaskas beginnt die un= geheure Felsenkette Norra Ananas, welche 8 Meilen lang am nordöstlichen Ufer bis Porsiedat und Storbacken fortläuft, und dann allmählig sich senkt und vereinzelt; von der Spitze des Norra Ananas überschauet man den größern Theil des Luleå= Lappmark; von hier dehnt sich bis an den Fuß des Dundur bei Gellivare das ebene Lappland Stora Maddus, 4 bis 5 Meilen lang und fast eben so breit, einem großen Sumpfe gleich, aus. Eine etwas niedrigere Bergkette läuft am südwestlichen Ufer, 5 Meilen lang, dem Ananas gegenüber, dann senkt sie sich, hört aber erst weiter gegen das Meer hin völlig auf. Etwa 2 Mei= len unterhalb Niaumelfaskas, ¼ Meile hinter der Mündung des Anajocksflusses, hat der Luleå ruhiges Wasser (sele); hier findet man die ersten Böte im Strombette des Luleå, seit er den Seen entfloß, und ¼ Meile vom südwestlichen Ufer des Luleå, am Anajocki das von Hermelin angelegte Nybygge Anajocki, den er= sten bewohnten Hof seit der Norwegischen Gränze. Nun folgen bis Suolovolli, ¼ Meile, heftige Strömungen; das nackte nord=

östliche Felsenufer, durch tiefe Thäler getrennt, ist oft unzugäng-
lich; das gegenüberliegende Ufer bildet eine fruchtbare Ebene:
aus schwarzer Gartenerde erhebt sich ein dichter Laub- und Nadelwald, und mehrere üppige Wiesen zeigen sich. Baron Hermelin ließ hier zwischen Anajocki und (der Bootstelle) Suolovolli
einen Fußsteig anlegen, der aber jetzt meist wieder zugewachsen
ist; der Winterweg zwischen den Kirchen Jockmock und Gellivare
durchschneidet ihn. Bei Suolovolli findet man eine kleine
Fischerhütte, wo zu gewissen Jahreszeiten Lappen, die sich von
Rennthierzucht und Fischfang nähren, fischen. Hernach folgen
einzelne Nybyggen und mehr oder minder beträchtliche Wasserfälle und Strömungen. Die Fahrbarmachung derselben würde
wenig nutzen, da jenseits Anajocki die Bootsfahrt unmöglich ist.
Die Ufer sind bald trockene Haiden, bald Felsen. Vom Nybygge
Missouri an bis zur Mündung sind noch 16 Meilen, auf welchen man aber nur 3 Wasserfälle trifft. Der eine dieser Wasserfälle, der Porsifors, mit welchem das eigentliche Flußbette beginnt, ist völlig unfahrbar, und kann auch durch Reinigung nicht
zugänglich werden, es sey denn durch Schleusen; der Fall ist
eine starke Viertelmeile lang und etwa 60 Fuß hoch. ¼ Meile
unterhalb liegt das Nybygge Storbacken, vom Baron Hermelin
angelegt; hier wohnen 2 Familien, auch ist hier ein Ladeplatz
mit Materialbuden für das Erz, welches zuweilen mit Rennthier-
fuhren von Gellivare für den Hochofen Sehlet herabgebracht
wird. Von Storbacken bis Edefors 2¼ Meile ist der Fluß fahrbar; der Edefors selbst, ein mächtiger Wasserfall von 68 Fuß
Höhe und ¼ Meile Länge, hemmt dann die Fahrt; beim Anfange und am Ende des Falles trifft man zwei Nybyggen, Öfver-
und Neder-Edefors, zwischen welchen zur Erleichterung des Erztransportes, ein Fahrweg angelegt ist. Von Edefors an wird
der Fluß breiter und ist 6¼ Meile bis zu den Hedensforssar
fahrbar. Edefors liegt schon in Luleå Pastorat. Das Land ist nun
mehr angebauet und bewohnt. Die Hedensforssar nehmen eine
Strecke von ¼ Meile ein; beim Anfange derselben ist das feinblätterige Sägewerk Petronellnaeström angelegt; ein Theil der
Forssar kann befahren werden. Würden diese Forssar mittelst

eines 3000 Klaftern langen Kanals beim Dorfe Heden umgangen, wie die Untersuchungs-Committee 1817 vorgeschlagen hat,
so würde dadurch der Luleå, 10½ Meile oberhalb der Stadt Luleå,
schiffbar. Einen Sommerfahrweg hat Baron Hermelin von Heden, den Fällen vorbei, zum Nybygge Råbäck, und dann weiter
am rechten Ufer nach dem Dorfe Afva und Bruk Sehlet anlegen lassen, um das Erz, was zu Boot von Storbacken und Eder-
fors bis Heden transportirt wird, zum Hochofen führen zu können; dieser neue Weg ist zusammen 3 Meilen lang. Die Hedensforssar sind die letzten Wasserfälle im Luleå, der nun bis
zur Mündung still und ruhig fließt. Bald erweitert er sich zu
einer Breite von 1000 bis 2000 Ellen, bildet bei Luleå gamla
stad einen mehr denn eine Viertelmeile breiten See, Sunderbyfjärden, verengt sich bei Gäddvik's Fähre bis zu 950 Ellen, bildet bald einen zweiten großen Busen, Lulefjärden, von fast gleicher Breite wie Sunderbyfjärden, umfließt die Landzunge, auf
welcher die Stadt Luleå liegt, und ergießt sich endlich ¼ Meile
südöstlich von da, bei Sandön, ins Meer.

Im Ganzen sind die Ufer des Luleå, bis zum Dorfe Ha-
rads im Pastorat Luleå, sehr unfruchtbar: der Boden besteht
aus Felsen oder Sand. Weiterhin, insbesondere jenseits Heden,
werden die Ufer fruchtbarer und angebauter; man trifft große
und wohlhabende Dörfer, aber die üppigen Wiesen am Torneå
findet man nicht, nur die nahen Umgebungen von Luleå gamla
stad ausgenommen. Die Ursache der geringeren Fruchtbarkeit scheint
vorzugsweise darin gesucht werden zu müssen, daß die wohlthätige
Alpenfluth, der hohen Lage wegen, nicht einwirken kann. Der
Eisgang tritt gewöhnlich am Schluß des Mai oder im Anfange
des Junius ein; die erste oder Frühlingsfluth beginnt:
das Wasser schwillt von 2 bis 6 Fuß. Erst mehrere Wochen
später schmilzt der Schnee in den Alpen; nun folgt, zu Ende des
Junius, die zweite oder die Alpenfluth, die den Strom bis
zu 10 und 12 Fuß, ja höher, anschwelle; die plötzliche Hitze um
Johannis, wo die Sonne den ganzen Tag hindurch wirkt, erzeugt dieses plötzliche Steigen. In 5 bis 6 Tagen hat die Fluth
ihre Höhe erreicht; das Wasser fängt an zu fallen, welches aber

so allmählig fortgeht, daß erst zu Ende des Julius der gewöhn=
liche Wasserstand wieder eintritt. Bei Regenwetter im Sommer
und Herbst schwillt überdieß das Wasser des Luleå, wie aller Lap=
pischen Flüsse, sehr an, der vielen Moräste und sumpfigen Wie=
sen halber, die das Regenwasser nicht einsaugen können. In der
Mitte oder zu Ende Octobers legt sich der Fluß, und zu Anfang
Novembers trägt das Eis.

Ein zweiter großer Strom, der in Luleå=Lappmark entspringt,
ist der Råneå. Er entfließt dem Radnejaur (Rånträsket), einem
See in Gellivare Pastorat, 3 Meilen südlich von der Kirche
Gellivare, mitten zwischen den Flüssen Luleå und Lina. Anfangs
ist er wenig bedeutend, nimmt aber bald mehrere größere und
kleinere Flüsse auf, und fällt endlich nach einem Laufe von etwa
17 Meilen in den Jämtöfjerd, einen Busen des Bottnischen
Meeres. Der ansehnlichste jener Flüsse, und fast eben so be=
trächtlich als der Råneå vor der Vereinigung, ist der Röträsk=
Elf, welcher beim Dorfe Degersele im Pastorat Råneå, 4½ Meile
von der Mündung, in den Råneå fällt. Der Råneå hat eine
Menge von Wasserfällen, deren beträchtlichster Korpforssan ist,
⅓ Meile oberhalb des Dorfes Degersele, 1/12 Meile lang und 60
Fuß hoch. Die gewaltigen Steine, die an vielen Stellen den
Fluß ausfüllen, hemmen die Fahrt, und veranlassen, daß nur bei
hohem Wasser Böte abwärts fließen, aber nie aufwärts fahren
können.

Eben so wenig eignen sich zur Fahrbarmachung, für den
Zweck des Erztransportes von Gellivare, der Seichtigkeit und der
geringen Wassermasse des Flußbettes halber (s. Bericht der
Stromreinigungs=Committe für 1819 in Inrikes tidningar. n. 40.
Apr. 1820), die Flüsse Lina und Ångeså, die dem östlichen Fuße
des Erzgebirges vorüberfließen und 14 Meilen von da bei der
Kirche Öfver=Calix in den von Torneå=Lappmark herabkommen=
den Calix=Strom fallen.

Der Lina entspringt aus dem See Tferkokjervi, 5 Meilen
nordwestlich von der Kirche Gellivare, nimmt mehrere Flüsse in
sich auf und fließt in einer Entfernung von 1000 Ellen dem
Erzgebirge vorüber. Bevor er sich mit dem Calix vereiniget,

fließt er mit dem Angesä zusammen, dessen Namen er nun annimmt, bis er seine Gewässer dem Calir zuführt. Fast ein Viertel der ganzen Länge des Lina (3¾ Meile) wird von 50 Wasserfällen eingenommen, die aber alle, bis auf zwei, Linkan und Rauta-koski, die Bootfahrt nicht hemmen; der ansehnlichste und schönste ist der 59 Fuß hohe, fast lothrechte, Linkan. Die Wasserfälle sind voll großer und kleiner Steine; durch die nicht sehr schwierige Aufräumung derselben würde aber der Fluß auch nicht fahrbar werden, weil die Wassermasse zu geringe ist. Sonst könnte man freilich die Forsböte anwenden, welche mit besonderer Rücksicht auf die Fahrt durch Wasserfälle eingerichtet sind, und deren man sich auf dem Torneä, Kemi und andern Lappischen Flüssen bei noch schwierigeren Fällen bedient. Die Finnischen Uferbewohner verstehen die Fahrt durch Wasserfälle auf jenen Böten meisterhaft. Die Böte sind sehr lang, fast ohne Kiel, und gehen nicht tief; der Vordertheil steht hoch aus. Bei Rautekoski hält man eine Schleuse für nöthig. Leere Böte könnten auch zurückgeführt werden.

Die Ufer des Lina und des Angesä sind meist eben und mit Laubwald, Gränen und Fichten besetzt; der Boden besteht aus Stauberde (mylla), die zwar oft sehr steinig ist, doch nichts destoweniger an vielen Stellen das üppigste Gras hervorbringt und sich sehr zum Korn- und Wiesenbau eignet, wozu die Frühlingsfluth viel beiträgt. Am meisten findet diese Fruchtbarkeit der Ufer von Gellivare bis Niskasuando, auf einer Strecke von 5¾ Meilen Statt; aber auch unterhalb, besonders wo die Bauern das den Graswuchs hemmende Weidengebüsch ausgerottet, wächst 2 Ellen hohes Gras. Schon jetzt findet man einzelne Nybyggen in der Nähe der Ufer.

Bei Öfver-Calix Kirche verliert sich der Angesä in den Calir. Der Calir, einer der größeren Ströme Lapplands, entspringt aus 4 oder 5 zusammenhängenden großen Seen am Fuße der Norwegischen Gränzalpen, weit im Westen der Kirche Juckasjervi, und bildet die Gränze von Gellivare und Juckasjervi-Lappmarker, bis er in das Pastorat Öfver-Torneä tritt, hier beim Derfe Tärende den Tärende-Elf, einen Arm des Torneä, der

ganz innerhalb des Paſtorats Ober-Torneå fließt, und keine unfahrbare Waſſerfälle hat, aufnimmt und dann mitten durch die
Paſtorate O. und N. Calix ſich den Weg zum Meere bahnt.
Bis Tärende läuft der Calix, 14 oder 15 Meilen lang, parallel
mit dem nur einige Meilen entfernten Torneåfluß, geht dann
10¼ Meile ganz ſüdlich zur Kirche Ober-Calix, von welcher, bis
zur Mündung ¾ Meile im Süden der Kirche Nieder-Calix, die
Entfernung nur 6¾ Meilen beträgt; die Mündung ſelbſt iſt 6
Meilen von der Mündung des Torneå entfernt.

Bis Tärende findet man längs des Calix-Elf nur 2 Nybyggen; Tärende ſelbſt iſt ein wohlhabendes Dorf mit 26 Bauern, und weiterhin, bei Ober-Calix Kirche, wohnen in einer Ausdehnung von 1½ Meilen von Angeſä und Calix 83 vermögende
Bauern. Die Ufer des Calix ſind meiſt eben und ſteinig, die
meiſten Waſſerfälle daher wenig ſteil; indeß nennt man 5, die
bisher unfahrbar waren und zum Theil ſchwerlich je fahrbar
werden können; der jäheſte iſt Jockforſſen, unterhalb des Dorfes
Jock, 22 Fuß hoch und 24 Fuß lang zwiſchen zwei hohen Klippen; kein Lachs ſchwimmt denſelben hinan.

Unterhalb der Kirche Ober-Calix trifft man 17 Forſſar, von
denen aber nur der Kamlunge-Fors, beim Auslauf des Elf aus
dem Kamlunge-See ſchwierig iſt, vor einigen Jahren ward er
zuerſt befahren. Zur Fortſetzung des Erztransports von Gelliware
bedarf man aber der Bootsfahrt durch den Kamlunge-Fors nicht.
Man fährt vielmehr von Ober-Calix-Kirche 1¾ Meilen ohne alles
Hinderniß auf dem Calix bis Räktfors, wo man den Fluß verläßt und zu Lande durch eine bewohnte Gegend, 2¾ Meilen bis
Töre geht; hier müßte freilich ein Fahrweg erſt eingerichtet werden, der für die Communication mit Ober-Calix ſchon längſt ge-
wünſcht worden iſt; der Weg wird dadurch um 2 Meilen verkürzt und jene 17 Forſſar werden vermieden. Töre hat einen
trefflichen Hafen ſelbſt für die größten Fahrzeuge.

Geringer als der Calix-Elf iſt der Lainisjock oder, wie er
hernach heißt, Strof-Elf, Landsjervs-Tvärä, der ſich 1¾ Meile
oberhalb der Kirche Ober-Calix in den Angeſä ergießt. Anfangs
ein Bach, wird er ſchon oberhalb des Dorfes Strof (noch in

Gellivare-Lappmark), durch Vereinigung mit anderen Wasserzügen, fahrbar und bleibt es bis zu seinem Ausfluß, 6 Meilen lang.
Nur ¼ Meilen, bei Sockedet, machen Wasserfälle ihn unzugäng-
lich; hier bedient man sich eines schon angelegten, ¼ Meile langen, fahrbaren Landweges. Unterhalb Sockedet gelangt man noch
einmal an einen Fors, Turredet, wo man wiederum nur zu Lande
fortkommen kann. Die Ufer sind waldreich und fruchtbar und
bieten die trefflichste Gelegenheit zu Urbarmachungen dar; schon
trifft man dort die Dörfer Skrof, Öfre- und Yttre-Landsjero
und mehrere Nybyggen. Die Beachtung dieses Flusses ist daher
bei Errichtung einer Bergwerkschaft sehr wichtig. An Wäldern
für den Bedarf der Hütten ist Gellivare und Ober-Calix reich;
ja, unerschöpfliche Waldvorräthe findet man hier, eben so wie in
den Pastoraten Luleå und Råneå.

e. Schwedisch-Torneå-Lappmark

besteht gegenwärtig aus den Pastoraten Juckasjervi und Karesuando (bis 1809 Enontekis). Es gränzt im Süden an Luleå-
Lappmark, im Norden an Russisch-Torneå-Lappmark, im Westen
an Norwegen (Finnmarken), im Osten an das Westerbottnische
Pastorat Ober-Torneå. Die Hauptflüsse sind: der Torneå,
der Lainio und die beiden Gränzflüsse: gegen Luleå-Lappmark der oben beschriebene Calir, gegen Russisch-Lappmark
der aus der Vereinigung des Köngämä, welcher oberhalb
die Gränze bildet, und des Låtås-Eno entstehende Muonio,
der, nachdem er weiterhin den Namen Kolare angenommen hat,
bei Kengis im Pastorat Ober-Torneå in den Torneå fällt. Der
Torneå entspringt aus einem der größeren Schwedischen Landseen,
dem Tornetäsk, am Fuße der Norwegischen Gränzalpen; man
schätzt die Länge des Tornetäsk auf 7 Meilen zwischen hohen
Schneealpen, die Breite zu 2 Meilen; die Entfernung von der
Nordsee 3 Meilen. Der Torneåfluß geht der Kirche Juckasjervi
vorüber, tritt hinter Junossuando in das Pastorat Ober-Torneå
und fällt endlich nach einem Laufe von 37 Meilen in den Bottnischen Meerbusen. Bei Junossuando, einem stillen Gewässer
(see, finnisch suando), fließt aus demselben der Tärende aus,

welcher sich in den Calix ergießt, bald darauf verbindet sich ein zweiter Arm des Torneå mit dem aus den nördlichen Norwegischen Gränz-alpen kommenden Lainio, bis dieser selbst, ½ Meilen unterhalb, seine gesammte Wassermasse dem Torneå zuführt. — Die Flüsse von Torneå-Lappmark haben gewöhnlich drei Fluthen: im An-fange des Frühlings beim Eisgange (Anfangs Juni), die Alpen-fluth, 2 bis 3 Wochen später, und die Herbstfluth, im August oder September. Vor Mitte Octobers legen die Flüsse zu.

Das Ufer des Torneträsk bilden nackte Alpen, auch die Ufer des Torneåflusses sind bis hinter Juckasjervi sehr bergig, allmäh-lig wird die Gegend ebener und waldiger; an der Grenze von Ober-Torneå Pastorat wird sie fruchtbar, und weiterhin erblickt man nichts als die üppigsten Wiesen und die herrlichsten Felder, deren Ertrag fast unglaublich ist. Wasserfälle hat der Fluß in Menge, aber nur einer derselben, der Fall beim Bruk Kengis in Ober-Torneå, 1000 Fuß lang und 72 Fuß hoch, ist völlig unfahrbar.

Moräste, Seen und Berge finden sich in großer Zahl. Die Berge sind an der Norwegischen Gränze mit ewigem Schnee und Eis bedeckt; andere enthalten reiche Erzlager, von welchen unten.

Den Arealinhalt des Pastorats Juckasjervi schätzt man auf 100 ☐M., wovon freilich ein großer Theil für Sümpfe, Seen, Flüsse, Berge abgerechnet werden muß. Aber auch im Verhält-niß zu dem urbaren oder urbarzumachenden Lande und den vor-handenen Waldungen ist die Einwohnerzahl sehr geringe. Nach den Tabellen gab es im Jahr 1815 im Pastorat Juckasjervi nur 34 Kolonisten- und Bauerhöfe mit 304 Personen, nebst 33 Pferden, 350 Stück Rindvieh und 475 Schaafen. Rechnet man zu der Personenzahl noch die Bewohner von Junossuando, die in kirchlicher Hinsicht zur Kapellgemeinde Pajala, Pastorats Öfver-Torneå, in politischer Hinsicht aber zu Juckasjervi gehö-ren, so darf man die Seelenzahl zu 350 annehmen, in welche die Lappen nicht mit einbegriffen sind. Die Zahl der Lappen, die von Rennthieren und Fischerey leben, war im Jahr 1815. 704, worunter 230 Kinder; nur 126 besaßen Rennthiere, zu-

II.   A a

sammen an 12,000 (der reichste 700), worunter nur 800 zum
Fahren eingelöste; denn wohlhabende Lappen suchen den Erwerb
durch Fuhren nicht, auch ist das Fett des nicht verschnittenen
Rennthiers um 50 bis 60 Procent theurer als das Fell eines
verschnittenen oder Zug-Rennthieres. Die Lappen wohnen in
4 Dorfschaften, Palaswuoma mit 4110, Rautuswuoma
mit 2780, Talma mit 3370, und Saariwuoma
mit 1490 Rennthieren; letztere Dorfschaft ist durch die Fül-
lerey ihrer Bewohner seit 10 Jahren so tief herabgesunken.
Andere haben durch Unglücksfälle ihre Rennthiere verloren.
Die arm gewordenen Lappen ziehen nach Norwegen, wo sie an
der Küste der Nordsee Fischfang treiben, oder begeben sich nach
Norrbotten, um das Vieh der Bauern zu weiden, oder zu betteln. Auf diese Weise hatte sich die Volksmenge in den Jahren
1800 bis 1815 nur mit 43 Seelen vermehrt. Im Jahr 1812
betrug die Zahl der Schatz-Lappen 75, der nicht schatzenden 72,
also zusammen die Zahl der Lappischen Familien in Juckasjervi
147. In den Jahren 1805 bis 1810 waren 52 Personen aus
Juckasjervi nach Norwegen gezogen.

Der Dialect der Lappen in ganz Torneå-Lappmark weicht
so sehr von dem Lappischen der niederen Lappmarken ab, daß
jene Lappen die im gewöhnlichen Lappischen verfaßten Lehrbücher
gar nicht verstehen. Derselbige Fall findet in Kemi-Lappmark
Statt. Wohl aber verstehen die Lappen von Torneå und Kemi
das Finnische; daher man in den dortigen Lappenschulen und
sonst sich Finnischer Bücher bedient, und da sämmtliche Nybyggare Finnen sind, der Gottesdienst in Finnischer Sprache gehalten wird. Die Lappischen Bibeln, welche 1811 in Hernösand
gedruckt wurden, waren für diese nordlichen Lappen nicht brauchbar, weshalb im Jahr 1808, auf Kosten der Brittischen und
ausländischen Bibelgesellschaft zu London, die Vertheilung Finnischer Bibeln unter die Lappen von Kemi veranstaltet wurde (s.
Bericht der Bibelgesellschaft von Åbo 1817 bis 1818). Indeß
sind nicht alle Lappen, zumal in Torneå-Lappmark, des Finnischen mächtig, wiewohl die Kenntniß desselben unter ihnen mit
jedem Jahre zunimmt.

Das Pastorat hat nur 1 Kirche zu Juckasjervi, aber einen 2ten Begräbnißplatz bei der Kupfergrube Svappewaara. Der Pastorgehalt beträgt an Kronkorn 30 Tonnen Gerste. Der großen Entlegenheit der Kirche wegen, hat man die Verlegung der Kirche nach dem Dorfe Wittangi, 5 Meilen unterhalb am Torneå, vorgeschlagen. Da der Wunsch nicht gewährt werden konnte, beschloß man, einen Saal nebst Nebenzimmer in Wittangi zu erbauen und der Pastor ward gebeten, 1mal im Sommer und 1mal im Winter, wann er das Pastorat durchreiset, um mit den Bewohnern Hausverhör zu halten, dort zu predigen. Früherhin, als die Kirche gegründet wurde, bestand die Gemeinde fast nur aus Lappen, die in der Nähe der Kirche ihre beste Weide hatten. Jetzt ist die Weide durch Brand vernichtet, und erst nach 50 Jahren darf man Erneuerung des Mooswuchses hoffen. Seitdem haben die Nybyggare im niederen Theile des Pastorats sich vermehrt. Die Lappen haben sich aber sehr vermindert, wozu zwei Ursachen mitwirkten: Wölfe, die die Rennthierheerden verringerten, und die wachsende Neigung zum Brannteweintrinken, die theils Westerbottnische Bauern, theils hiesige Nybyggare, durch den Handel, den sie mit den Lappen treiben, unaufhörlich nähren; die Finnen sind weniger dem Branntewein ergeben. Im Sommer ziehen die Lappen mit ihren Heerden auf den Alpen, im Winter im niederen Pastorat umher; beide Male ziehen sie der Kirche vorüber, und benutzen diese Gelegenheit, um zu communiciren; dann pflegt selbst täglich das heilige Abendmahl ausgetheilt zu werden. Dann hält man auch wohl Christenthumsverhör mit denjenigen Lappen, mit denen es in ihren Hütten nicht gehalten werden konnte; sonst sind die Hausverhöre mit Finnen und Lappen üblich. Viele Lappen von Juckasjervi haben nur schwache christliche Erkenntniß, besuchen auch nur selten die Kirche, eben so wie mehrere Finnen, woran freilich zum Theil die große Entfernung der Aufenthalts und der Wohnorte von der Kirche Schuld ist.

Bei der Kirche ist eine Schule angelegt, worin 3 Lappenkinder unterwiesen und erzogen werden. Der Unterricht geschieht in Finnischer Sprache. Der Pastor ist zugleich Schulmeister. —

Auch ein Katechet wohnt bei der Kirche, wo er Kinder unterrichtet, er zieht nicht mit den Lappen umher; dagegen giebt es zwei Reisekatecheten. Die Polhöhe der Kirche Juckasjervi beträgt 67° 51′ 9″.

Das Pastorat Karesuando enthält den, Schweden verbliebenen Theil des Pastorats Enontekis *). Dies ist der größere Theil, denn nur der kleinere, mit etwa 4 Lappen und 7 Nybyggare, kam an Rußland. Auf dem abgetretenen Ufer des Muonio lag aber die Kirche Enontekis, die, bisher selbst Mutterkirche, jetzt Filial der Kirche Muoniska ward, die bisher selbst nur einen Theil des Pastorats OberTorneå gebildet hatte. Die Schweden erbauten für den übrig gebliebenen Theil von Enontekis eine neue Kirche, der alten gegenüber, zu Karesuando, die am 25. Februar 1816 vom Propst Wikström aus OberTorneå eingeweihet wurde. Zum Bau waren aus dem Lappenfond 300 Bankthaler bewilliget worden. Die Hälfte der Lappenschule von Juckasjervi, die dort bisher mit 6 Kindern bestanden hatte, ward 1813 hieher verlegt, eben so einer der dortigen Reisekatecheten hierher gewiesen; der hiesige Pastor ward auch Schulmeister, der Küster wurde zugleich zum Katecheten bestellt und ein neuer Pfarrhof mit 3 hübschen Zimmern gebauet, wozu die Schulmeisterwohnung in Juckasjervi, mittelst Austausch, verwandt wurde. Unter den Lappen und Finnen des Pastorates Karesuando herrscht weniger sittliche Verdorbenheit, wie unter denen von Juckasjervi; sie kommen oft zur Kirche, und leben still und friedlich, in Unschuld dahin. Lappen, wie Nybyggare, sprechen Finnisch. Die neue Kirche ist groß und außen und innen freundlich. Im Jahr 1812 waren im Pastorat Karesuando 19 Finnische Bauern, 6 Finnische Nybyggare, und an 60 schatzpflichtige Lappen **).

——————

*) Enontekis war anfangs Filial von NederTorneå, dann von Juckasjervi, erst seit 1748 eigenes Pastorat. Bei der Kirche war früherhin keine Schule, sondern 2 Kinder aus Enontekis nahmen an der Schule von Juckasjervi Theil.

**) Um das Jahr 1800 zählte man in dem gesammten Pastorat Enontekis 890 Einwohner, worunter 566 Lappen. S. Er. J.

Háradsgericht, Steuererhebung und Markt wird im Winter, für Karesuando bei der Kirche, für Juckasjervi in Wittangi gehalten; der Bergwerksdistrikt hat sein eigenes Gericht (Bergsting) zu Junosuando. Außer der Bergwerkschaft von Torneås Lappmark giebt es in Norrbotten noch zwei Bergslag, das von Kengis und das des Hermelinschen Gruben= und Hüttendistrikts; mit letzterem wird zu Råneå, mit ersterem zu Kengis Gericht gehalten. Die Richter bedienen sich der Dolmetscher. Lappen und Finnen handeln nach Norwegen; auch Kaufleute von Torneå, wie Bauern und Bauernknechte aus Westerbotten kaufen allerlei Lappländische Produkte, auch wohl aus Norwegen bezogene Waaren.

Die Mitternachtssonne ist bei der Kirche Karesuando um Johannis sieben volle Wochen sichtbar; zur dieser Zeit kann man um Mitternacht mittelst des Sonnenglases Feuer anzünden. Dagegen ist es im Winter, der fast ⅓tel des Jahrs dauert, 2 bis 3 Wochen lang, nur 3 bis 4 Stunden Tag; überhaupt sieht man im Winter die Sonne selten; nur zuweilen um Mittag.

Schneelavinen, welche Menschen und Vieh begraben, sind nicht selten.

Fahrwege giebt es nicht; man reist im Sommer zu Fuß oder zu Boot, im Winter mit Rennthieren. Gästgifvaregårdar bestehen nicht; man findet nirgends Skjuts, sondern muß sich durch Werbung fortschaffen *).

Die Lappen, aber auch die Finnen, sind klein von Statur, meist 62 bis 65 Zoll. Augenkrankheiten sind des Rauchs der Hütten wegen sehr häufig. Venerische Krankheiten sind völlig unbekannt. Die Finnen baden sich jeden Sonnabend; sie sind träg und ernst. Rennthierdiebstahl ist nicht selten.

Grape beskrifning öfver Enontekis Pastorat; in den Nya Handlingar der Königl. Akademie der Wissenschaften in Stockholm. Bd. 24 und Bd. 25. 1803. 1804. — In 50 Jahren (1750—1800) wurden im Pastorat Enontekis nur etwa 13 uneheliche Kinder geboren, und nur 1 Selbstmord trug sich zu.

*) S. Grape a. d. a. St.

In den entlegeneren Dörfern versammeln sich die Bewohner, welche nicht zur Kirche gehen, sonntäglich zur Postillenlesung. Hausverhör wird mit Finnen und Lappen gehalten. Die meisten Kinder empfangen die Nothtaufe, und sind nicht selten 6 volle Monate alt, wenn sie die kirchliche Taufe erhalten; eine Folge der großen Entfernung von der Kirche.

Die Lappen sind leicht und lebendig, doch nicht minder kräftig, wie mancher Westerbottnier, davon zeugen ihre Bärenjagden, ihr Lasttragen ꝛc. Aber anhaltende Arbeit und Mühe ist ihnen zuwider, daher sie denn im Allgemeinen Acker= und Wiesenbau hassen. Ihr Nomadenleben geht ihnen über alles. Doch treiben sie daneben Jagd und Fischfang. Die Felle und das Fleisch der Rennthiere vertauschen sie bei den Nybyggare gegen Mehl und Tabak. Auch handeln sich letztere von den Lappen Rennthierhörner ein, woraus sie Tischlerleim bereiten, der nach Westerbotten und seewärts nach Stockholm und anderen Orten ausgeführt wird. Fischerey ist einer der hauptsächlichsten Nahrungszweige der Nybyggare. Bedeutend sind auch die Viehzucht und Jagd; man erlegt wilde Rennthiere, Bären, Wölfe; man schießet oder fängt in Sprenkeln, im Herbste, Birk=, Auer=, Schnee= und Haselhühner; so wie im Sommer Seevögel, die sich um diese Jahreszeit in unzähliger Menge hier aufhalten. Man benutzt nicht blos das Fleisch und die Eier dieser Vögel, sondern auch ihre Federn, die einen wichtigen Handelsartikel bilden, und für welche man Mehl eintauscht; der Vogelverkauf ist unbedeutend: man läßt die Vögel frieren, wo sie dann mehrere Monate liegen können, ohne zu verderben. Finnen und Lappen treiben auch Transitohandel, indem sie in Norwegen getrocknete Fische, unter welchen die berühmten Torneå=Schellfische (Gadus. Torneå=gräsidor), aufkaufen und dieselben über die Alpen nach Muoniska und von da, oft auf Böten, die 30 Schiffpfund und mehr tragen, auf dem Torneå, bei hoher Fluth über alle Wasserfälle hinweg, nach Haparanda an die Küste bringen. Bei der Ankunft hat das Boot durch erspartes Fuhrlohn sich bezahlt gemacht, und wird oft zu einem sehr geringen Preise verkauft. Manche dieser Böte sind, wegen Eisenmangel, sehr schwach ge=

bauet und werden zum Theil nur durch hölzerne Nägel zusammengehalten, so daß man sie nur als Brennholz nutzen kann.

Die Gewässer sind reich an Fischen; am meisten fängt man Hechte und Schnäpel, die man zum eigenen Bedarf und zum Verkauf trocknet; zuweilen fängt man auch Aalraupen (Gadus Lota) in Menge, die man gleichfalls trocknet, um im Nothfall sich ihrer statt des Brotes, in Ermangelung von besseren Arten gedörrter Fische zu bedienen. Auch Barse und Plötzen (Cyprinus rutilus) fängt man in ziemlicher Menge, trocknet sie aber nicht. Weniger häufig ist die Alpenforelle (Salmo alpinus), röding genannt, weil sie unter dem Bauche hochroth ist. Das Einsalzen der Fische ist nicht gar üblich, weil der Transport des Salzes, bei den weiten Entfernungen, seiner Schwere wegen, sehr schwierig ist.

Lappen und Finnen sind treffliche Jäger, ihr Schuß fehlt nicht leicht. Ihr Schießgewehr besteht in einem gezogenen Rohr mit höchst einfachem Schloß, was im südlichen Schweden zuweilen unter dem Namen Snapphane=Schloß vorkommen soll. Der Hagel oder die Kugel, deren man sich bedient, ist gewöhnlich sehr fein und klein, nie ⅓ Zoll im Umfange. Das Kaliber der Büchse ist sehr fein, um Pulver zu sparen, welches hier sehr theuer ist, auch der Lappe auf seinen Wanderungen schwer vor Nässe bewahren kann.

Der Wiesenbau wird in Torneå=Lappmark auf dreierlei Weise betrieben. Die eine Art, die gewöhnlichste und leichteste, ist die, daß man die Zwergbirken (betula nana, ripris), die hier auf fast allen, zum Graswuchs fähigen sumpfigen Stellen (myror) in Menge wächset, abhauet und dann die Wiese jährlich mähet, so daß jenes Strauchwerk nicht wieder überhand nehmen kann. Freilich ist das Heu solcher Wiesen kurz und kraftlos und steht sehr dünne. Eine zweite Art des Wiesenbaues ist das Schwenden. Man wählt hiezu solchen Boden, welcher aus rothem Staubsand oder, noch besser, aber seltener, schwarzer Dammerde besteht, was man an dem frischen Wuchs der Gränen, ihren dicken Stämmen und großen Wurzelästen erkennt; auch wachsen Sperberbäume, Espen und Birken auf solchem Lande; findet sich ein Bach in der Nähe, so daß Erlen und Weiden dort fortkommen, so ist es um so viel besser. Man hauet nun das Holz ab, bis auf eine Elle über der Wurzel, sammelt es in Haufen und zündet es an. Nach 1 oder 2 Jahren trägt das Land Gras. Ist der Boden sehr feucht, so wächset Equisetum (Kannenkraut), welches zwar die Milcherzeugung fördert, aber von den Pferden nicht gefressen wird; bei guter Behandlung des Bodens zeigt sich Equisetum mehrere Jahre hintereinander. Ist das Schwende-land weniger naß, so wächset Gras, welches auch als Pferdefutter dient. — Eine dritte Art des Wiesenbaues besteht darin, daß man das Land zu Acker verwendet, und, falls es nicht trägt, als Wiese benutzt; eine solche Wiese giebt, wenn sie oft gedüngt wird, treffliches Heu. — Viele Wiesen wurden bisher nie gemähet.

Kornbau ist Nebenerwerbszweig: Roggen wird gar nicht gebauet; selbst Gerste reift nicht, zumal bei der Kirche Juckas-servi, besser gedeiht sie 4 Meilen unterhalb beim Nybygge Wittangi. Aecker, die hohen Sandboden haben und Wasserzügen zunächst liegen, scheinen in Norrbotten und Lappland am wenigsten den Nachtfrösten ausgesetzt zu seyn; auch scheint im Frühling der Frost aus denselben früher zu weichen. Weht in einer Frost-nacht Wind, so leidet das Korn nicht; man soll daher an einigen Orten nicht ohne Erfolg versucht haben, mittelst Seilen eine künstliche Bewegung der Halme hervorzubringen. Der Sand-boden fördert die Schnelligkeit des Reifens, muß aber stark gedüngt werden und unten eine Schicht Lehm oder dergleichen haben. Gewiß kann der Ackerbau in Torneå's Lappmark vermehrt werden, aber nie sich zu einem Hauptnahrungszweige erheben. Als Saatkorn verwendet man am besten Korn, welches in Lappland selbst gewonnen wurde, denn dieses reift früher, als Korn, welches in südlichern Gegenden gebaut wurde. Diese Kraft des Schnellreifens behält das in nördlichen Gegenden gewonnene Korn, wenn es in südlichen Orten ausgesäet wird, wenigstens mehrere Jahre bei.

Der Kartoffelbau ist lohnend, da der Frost wenigstens den schon angesetzten Knollen nicht mehr schaden kann. Doch bauet

man bisher nur wenig Kartoffeln, weil das Hinaufführen der
Saat aus dem niedern Lande mit Schwierigkeiten verknüpft ist.
Der Kartoffelbau ward vor nicht langer Zeit zuerst in Jukasjervi
durch den frühern Besitzer von Kengis, Bruкspatron Ekström,
eingeführt.

Bemerkenswerth ist, daß in nördlichen Zonen reif geworde-
nes Korn das in südlichen Gegenden gereifte an Schwere übertrifft, und eben so alle Gartengewächse im Norden schmackhafter
sind. Auch in der belebten Natur tritt die Reife früher ein;
daher das Gesetz den Lappen früher zu heirathen verstattet, als
den Schweden. — Die Bäume wachsen, der langen Winter
wegen, sehr langsam.

Beträchtlicher als alle anderen Nahrungszweige könnte für Jukasjervi Pastorat der Bergbau werden; denn unerschöpfliche Erzlager breiten sich daselbst nach allen Richtungen aus; in Karesuando und Enontekis hat man bisher keine Erzanweisung getroffen. Die ansehnlichsten dieser Erzlager, so viel sie bisher entdeckt worden, sind Luossawaara, Kitunawaara, Haukiwaara,
Svappawaara, Junosuando. Alle diese Erzberge und Gruben
sind im untern Theil des Pastorats Jukasjervi belegen.

Luossawaara liegt am nördlichsten, der Weg dahin führt
von der Kirche auf dem Torneå 1½ Meilen nordwestlich nach
Kurrawaara, dem nördlichsten Nybygge des Pastorats, wo drei
Familien sich von Fischerey nähren; Korn wird wenig gebauet,
und kömmt oft nicht zur Reife. Hierher zog sich der Bruкspatron Ekström von Kengis zurück, als er, in Folge unglücklicher
Conjuncturen, das aus patriotischem Eifer für den Bergbau über-
nommene Bruк den Creditoren überlassen mußte, und lehrte seine Nachbaren in Kurrawaara und Jukasjervi Kartoffeln pflanzen und den Ackerbau verbessern.

Von Kurrawaara hat man noch 1½ M. ungebahnter Pfade,
bis man den Gipfel des etwa 1000 Fuß über den Torneåstrom
sich erhebenden Erzberges erreicht; vom Gipfel genießt man einer weiten Aussicht über die Gränzalpen und die Wildnisse umher. Bäume gedeihen nicht mehr, nur Weidenbüsche und kleine
Alpenbirken findet man; doch ist der Gipfel kahl; der Schnee

schmilzt jeden Sommer. Die Länge des Berges schätzt man auf eine halbe, die Breite auf eine Viertelmeile. Die Eisenlager durchstreichen den Berg von N. W. nach S. O.; auch lose Erzsteine finden sich in Menge. Das hier gebrochene Erz hält 64 Prozent. Die Bergart ist grober Granit-Porphyr.

Um ein Weniges niedriger ist der Eisenberg Kirunawaara, dessen Gipfel gleichwohl eine weite Aussicht gewährt. Der Berg wird vom Luossawaara durch einen kleinen See, den Luossojervi, getrennt, und liegt ⅓ M. südlicher, als dieser. Der Gipfel ist eine Viertelmeile lang und besteht aus reinem Eisenerz. Das Erz hält 61 bis 68 Prozent, und ist magnetisch und von gleicher Beschaffenheit wie das von Luossawaara. Die Lager streichen tief. — Beide Erzberge wurden entdeckt oder bekannt durch die Reise, die der Baron Gyllengrip, Landshöfding in Westerbotten, 1736 in Torneå-Lappmark unternahm. Fünf bis sechs Wochen bleibt hier die Sonne um Johannis ununterbrochen über dem Horizont.

Haukiwaara, südöstlich von Luossawaara, und nur in geringer Entfernung vom Fuße dieses Berges entlegen, ist in Höhe und Umfang viel geringer, als die bisher genannten Erzberge, fast rund, und hat kaum ⅜ M. in der Quere, besteht aber, soviel man weiß, aus nichts als Eisenerz, welches in großen losen Felsstücken vorkommt. Man hat das Erz für weniger reichhaltig als das Erz der Berge Luosso und Kiruna gehalten. Die Entdeckung und erste Bearbeitung dieses Eisenberges geschah 1759 durch den Besitzer von Kengis Bruk, Abr. Steinholtz.

Der großen Entfernung wegen ist das reiche Erz der Berge Luosso, Kiruna und Hauki bisher nur wenig benutzt worden; einiges hat man in dem 11 Meilen entlegenen Hochofen Junosuando verarbeitet; der Hochofen Tornefors ist 3, Kengis ist 8 Meilen weiter entfernt. — Die Umgebungen dieser Erzberge sind wild und schauerlich. Die Entfernung von der Stadt Torneå beträgt 34 Meilen, vom Hafen Töre im Pastorat Neder-Calix auf den Flüssen Torneå, Tärende und Calix 30 Meilen.

Svappawaara liegt 1 Meile südöstlich vom Torneåfluß, 7 Meilen nordwestlich von Junosuando Hochofen und 30 Meilen

von der Stadt Torneå. Der Berg erhebt sich nur um 132 Ellen über die nahen Sümpfe und ist von N. nach S. 6 bis 700
Ellen lang. Bereits im 17ten Jahrhundert ward hier auf Kupfer gebauet, nachdem 1654 der Lappe Olof Tolk darüber die
ersten Angaben gemacht. Die Herren Abraham und Jacob
Renstjerna begannen nun, schon 1655, den Bau; das Erz
war reich und lohnend; man bereitete, bis zum Jahr 1670,
jährlich 6 bis 800 Schiffpfund Kupfer, dann aber wurden die
Gruben zu tief und zu sehr mit Wasser angefüllt; die Arbeit
wurde immer weniger betrieben und endlich 1684 der Bau der
großen Grube völlig eingestellt. Doch setzte man das Waschen
in den alten Halden, das Pochen und Schlämmen der Schlakkenhalden bei den Hütten, so wie das Bearbeiten kleinerer Gruben noch fort; 1699 ward eine eigene Societät zur Betreibung
der Kupfer- und Eisenwerke in Torneå-Lappmark und Pastorat
gestiftet, deren Rechte 1745 Bruckspatron Steinholtz an sich
kaufte; auch wurden einzelne Gruben noch 1775 bearbeitet; aber
keine derselben war lohnend. Eine Kupferhütte ist ¼ Meile von
den Gruben am Longasjockifluß, der 1½ Meile von da in den
Torneå fällt, eingerichtet gewesen. Das reichhaltigere Erz, welches
sogleich auf 4 oder 5 Feuern gekehrröstet (vändrostad) und geschmolzen wurde, gab in 24 Stunden 3 bis 4 Schiffpf. Kupfer.
Als im 17ten Jahrhundert die Gruben Erz gaben, waren bei
Kengisfors, 14 Meilen von Svappawaara, am Torneå-Strom,
Garhütte, Kupferhammer und Münze angelegt; man münzte hier
das gewonnene Kupfer zu den damals gültigen Platen (plåtar)
mit Gepräge aus; 1717 wurden aber, im Russischen Kriege,
diese Anlagen zerstört. — In der Nähe von Svappawaara hat
man noch ein Paar andere Berge, Sårkiewaara und Kilawaara,
auch einige Meilen oberhalb, den Kurrawaara und andere Berge
bearbeitet, wo aber das Kupfererz theils bald ausging, theils in
zu geringer Quantität vorhanden war; Schiangeli Fjäll an der
Norwegischen Gränze, 49 Meilen von der Stadt Torneå, 3 Meilen von Torneträsk, dessen Erzlager 1696 ein Lappe entdeckte,
worauf sie bis 1701 die Besitzer von Svappawaara bearbeiten
ließen, gab von etwa 20 bis 50 Procent Kupfer nebst

7 bis 8 Loth Silber im Centner Erz; einiges Erz enthielt auch Gold.

Das Kupfererz von Svappawaara bestand, dem größeren Theil nach, aus Kupferglas und vielfarbigem Kupfererz oder Kupferlazur, etwas gelbem Kupfererz oder Kupferkies, zuweilen gediegenem Kupfer auf drusigem Quarz; und bei den Ablösungen der meisten Gänge Kupfergrün und Kupferblau, theils derb, theils dünnblätterig. — 1741 fand man auch in der Stockenström's Grube gediegenes Gold in Kupferlager mit Quarz.

Wichtiger ist der große Eisenerzgang, welcher, neben und zwischen den Kupfergruben, in einer Breite von 100 und einer Länge von 4 bis 500 Ellen, von Norden nach Süden streift und meist überall am Tage liegt. Erst um 1740 begann man an die Benutzung dieser reichen Vorräthe zu denken.

Das Eisenerz von Svappawaara ist ein dichtes und derbes, feinkörniges Blutsteinerz, welches im Bruche völlig dem Stahle gleicht. Man glaubt, es halte zwischen 60 und 70 Procent. Ein Theil des Erzes, welcher nahe den Kupfergruben streicht, ist spröde, das übrige völlig gut; vermischt man beide Arten, so erhält man ganz vorzügliches Roheisen, was ein treffliches und geschmeidiges Eisen giebt.

Das Eisenerz von Svappawaara ist bisher, eben so wie das von Kirunas, Luossos und Haukiwaara, auf dem kürzesten, aber schlechten, Landwege durch Lappen mit Rennthieren nach Junosuando transportirt worden.

In der Nähe von Svappawaara giebt es jetzt nur Birkenwald, der hier stets niedrig bleibt; weiterhin giebt es reichere Holzvorräthe.

Das Erzfeld von Junosuando liegt auf der Gränze des Pastorats Ober-Torneå, zwischen den Flüssen Calix und Torneå, 1 Meile von den Ufern derselben, 16⅔ Meilen von der Kirche Ober-Calix, 22⅔ Meilen von der Kirche Nieder-Calix und 21⅔ Meilen vom Hafen Thré, 24 Meilen von der Stadt Torneå. Es streicht im N. N. W. und S. S. O. dem Kompasse nach zu urtheilen, in einer Länge von mehr denn ⅓ Meile im Thale zwischen zwei Bergrücken, und folgt dann dem linken Ufer des

Flusses Rautasocki, der 1½ Meile von den Gruben in den Tärende fällt.

Junosuando wurde zuerst unter allen Erzlagern von Torneå- und Luleå-Lappmark entdeckt und bearbeitet, bereits 1644. Man hat viele Gruben geöffnet, aber, des einströmenden Wassers wegen, gewöhnlich nicht tiefer als 4 oder 5 Klafter bearbeiten können; nur die weiteste, die Kunstgrube, zunächst dem Hochofen belegen, ist mittelst einer Kunst bis zu 10 Fuß gebrochen worden. Das Erz der Magnetgrube ist in einem hohen Grade magnetisch.

Das Erz von Junosuando ist schwarzblau, magnetisch, im Bruche feinkörnig, kristallinisch und meist dicht, und hält 60 bis 70 Procent. Es schmilzt leicht, auch ohne Zusatz, und giebt, von Schwefelkies gereiniget, ein treffliches Eisen; mischt man ⅓ Svappawaara-Erz zu, so entsteht ein noch vorzüglicheres Roheisen. Die Hochöfen von Junosuando, in der Nähe der Gruben, und Tornefors (Palokorva) haben das benöthigte Erz immer aus den Gruben von Junosuando erhalten, aus entfernteren nahm man nur so viel, als zur Mischung nöthig war. Nicht alles Erz von Junosuando soll mit Schwefelkies verbunden, sondern auch viel reines Harz vorhanden seyn. Nur der bei weitem kleinste Theil des großen, mit Erde bedeckten, Erzfeldes ist bisher versucht worden.

Gegenwärtig ruht der Gruben- und Hüttenbau völlig; die Gruben sind mit Wasser ausgefüllt und liegen schon lange öde. Die vormaligen Hütten- und Grubenarbeiter nähren sich jetzt kümmerlich von geringem Ackerbau, Viehzucht und Fischfang. Der Hochofen von Junosuando liegt unter 67° Polhöhe und ist der nördlichste in Europa.

Der Transport von den Gruben nach Palokorva ist nicht gar beschwerlich. Die Entfernung beträgt nur 3 Meilen, wovon 1½ Meilen Sommer-Fahrweg bis ans Ufer des Torneå, dann Flußweg auf dem Torneå, bis zum Tornefors, ¼ Meile oberhalb des Hochofens Tornefors oder Palokorva; Zugang zu Kohlen ist zu Palokorva näher und leichter als zu Junosuando. Die Roheisenbereitung auf beiden Mengöfen hat jährlich nie 1 bis 2000 Schiffpfund überstiegen.

Außer den genannten Erzbergen giebt es vielleicht viele andere und nicht minder reiche, die aber bisher noch nicht aufgefunden oder untersucht sind; rücksichtlich einiger, die als erzhaltig angegeben wurden, hat die Untersuchung ergeben, daß der Erzgehalt zu geringe ist, um die Kosten des Baues zu ersetzen.

Silbererz hat man schon früherhin in mehreren Gegenden von Torneå-Lappmark vermuthet; aber nie konnte eine Vermuthung dieser Art zur Gewißheit gebracht werden.

Bergkristalle, theils klar mit ordentlichen Kristallen, theils unbestimmt angeschossene, haben in früheren Zeiten die Lappen gefunden und verkauft; aber keine edle Steine, wie in Büchern erzählt wird. — Schleifsteine soll man am obern Ende des Sees Nieder-Vuolusjocki, 1½ Meilen von der Kirche Juckasjervi, treffen; — Bleierz, theils rein und los, theils eingesprengt mit Kalch und Quarzkörnern, zuweilen auch etwas Schwefelkies, hat man an einigen Stellen gebrochen, und einige Tonnen nach Stockholm versandt, wo es zu Tiegeln u. dergl. m. brauchbar befunden wurde *).

C. Geographisch-statistischer Ueberblick
über das Norwegische, das Alt- und Neu-Russische (Finnische) Lappland.

a. Das Norwegische Lappland **).

Alpen- und Fischerlappen giebt es an der ganzen Norwegischen Nordwest- und Nordküste, fast von Trondhjem an

---

*) Vergl. Hermelins Mineralhistorie öfver Lappmarken och Westerbotten. Stockholm 1804. — Reman berättelse om Norbotten och deß Lappmarken. Stockholm 1818.

**) Als Quellen dienten mir theils Knut Leem Nachrichten von den Lappen in Finnmarken. Aus dem Dän. Leipzig 1771 (Leem war ziemlich lange Missionar unter den Norwegischen Lappen, und seine Nachrichten tragen ganz das Gepräge der Zuverlässigkeit). Thaarup Statistik der Dänischen Monarchie, Bd. 2. Abth. 2. (wo S. 1—5 mehrere Quellen zur Kenntniß von Finnmarken angeführt werden);

bis Wardöhuus; die Fischerlappen nähren sich von dem reichen Fischfang in der Nordsee. Man kann diese Landstrecken aber nicht Lappland nennen; denn die eigentlichen Einwohner dieser Distrikte, d. i. des obern Theils von Trondhjem's Amt und der ganzen Aemter Nordland und Finnmarken, sind, im Süden Norwegen, im Norden Finnen, Lappen findet man dort meist nur zu gewissen Jahreszeiten; doch wird ein großer Theil von Finnmarken nur von Lappen als Fischern bewohnt oder von Lappen als Hirten im Sommer beweidet; — am Meere trifft man große Handelsniederlagen.

Mit dem Namen: Norwegisch Lappland bezeichnet man gewöhnlich Finnmarken *) und das Pastorat Kautokeino (Lappisch Kondekeino). Das Pastorat Kautokeino, von Theilen Torneäs und Kemi-Lappmark's, den Pastoraten Enontekis und

---

Stöldebrand voyage au Cap Nord; Wahlenberg om Kemi-Lappmark; von Buch Reise durch Lappland; Vargas Bedemar Reise nach dem hohen Norden, durch Schweden, Norwegen und Lappland, in den Jahren 1810—1814. Frankf. am M. 2 Bde. 1819 ꝛc., theils im Schwedischen Lappland von mir selbst eingezogene Nachrichten.

*) In älteren Zeiten verstand man unter Finnmarken das gesammte, von Lappen bewohnte oder beweidete Norwegische Gebiet, nebst dem Alt-Russischen Lappland und einem Theile der heutigen Schwedischen Lappmarken. Diesen großen Landstrich bewohnte, ganz oder meist, ein, wie es scheint, Finnischer Stamm, die Quenen. Die Quenen hatten ihre eigenen kleinen Könige, die den benachbarten Norwegischen Königen zinspflichtig waren. Im 14ten Jahrhundert erlosch dieses Reich, indem es Russen, Schweden und Norweger unter sich theilten. Den Namen Lappen findet man für die alten Besitzer dieses Reichs erst um das 12te Jahrhundert, in der Schrift: Fundin Norvegar (entdecktes Norwegen), deren Verfasser man nicht kennt (herausgegeben von Börner in seinen Sagostocker). Die heutigen Finnen in Finnmarken wanderten später ein, und scheinen einem von den Lappen verschiedenen Finnischen Stamme anzugehören; Finnische Stämme verbreiteten sich über das östliche, Europäische und Asiatische, Rußland. Vergl. Reiter diss. de veteri Finmarkia. Upsaliae, 1798.

Utsjocki begränzt, ward von dem um die Lappische Kirche hoch-verdienten König Karl XI. gestiftet: Karl erbaute zu Kauto-keino eine Kirche und bestellte daselbst einen Pastor, dessen kirch-licher Sprengel sich über alle Lappen bis zur Mündung des Al-ten in die Nordsee, und an den Ufern des Tana-Elf, der östlich vom Nordkyn ins Meer fällt, also auch über das heutige Uts-jocki, ausdehnte. Zu Aviowaara, zwischen den Flüssen Alten und Tana, ward eine Kapelle erbauet. 1708 fand man es zweck-mäßiger, an der Mündung des Flusses Utsjocki in den Tana-Elf eine Kirche zu gründen, die den Namen Utsjocki erhielt und Filial des Pastorats Kautokeino wurde; Kautokeino nebst Uts-jocki rechnete man zu Torneå-Lappmark.

Mittlerweile entstanden Gränzstreitigkeiten mit den Norwe-gern, die auf den ganzen Lauf des an fetten Lachsen und Forel-len reichen Tana-Elf Anspruch machten. Diese Streitigkeiten wurden im Jahr 1751 dahin verglichen, daß Schweden das ei-gentliche Kautokeino (180 □M.) an Norwegen abtrat, wogegen Norwegen seine Ansprüche auf den Tana-Elf und das Kirchspiel Utsjocki aufgab. Utsjocki ward nun Mutterkirche, und erhielt die Kirche Enara, die bisher zum Pastorat Kusamo gehört hatte, zum Filial. Die Norweger ersetzten das Filial Utsjocki durch das Filial Mast, welches bisher Theil des Pastorats Talvig am Altenfjord gewesen war, und jetzt Filial der näher gelegenen Kir-che Kautokeino wurde; im Jahr 1799 fand Stöldebrand die Kirche Mast wüste.

Die Finnen am linken Ufer des Tana-Elf, von Karasjock bis ans Eismeer, kamen jetzt unter Norwegische Hoheit, die Fin-nen am rechten Ufer blieben Schwedische Unterthanen. Statt der Kapelle Aviowaara, die jetzt einging, ward eine neue Kapelle zu Karasjocki gegründet, diese aber im Jahr 1807 mit einer neuen und größeren Kirche vertauscht. — In der Nähe der Mündung des Tana-Elf in den Tanafjord liegt die Kapelle Tana; in der Mündung selbst trifft man die kleine Insel Guld-holm mit einem Handelsetablissement. — Auch Alpenkapellen bestehen.

Neben den Lappen wohnen in Finnmarken, wie im Pastorat
Kautokeino, Kolonisten, insbesondere Finnen, die hauptsächlich
vom Fischfange, zumal dem reichen Lachs- und Dorschfange, leben, aber auch Viehzucht und Jagd treiben; Korn und Küchengewächse gedeihen nicht, weder in Finnmarken, noch in Kautokeino
und Utsjocki. Im Sommer hat das Pastorat Kautokeino wenige
Bewohner; denn die Fischerlappen, wie die betriebsamen Finnen ziehen an den vielen Landseen, wo sie Fischerhütten errichtet
haben, und an den Ufern der Nordsee, um zu fischen, die Rennthierlappen auf den Alpen, umher; nur wenige bleiben daheim,
selbst der Pastor von Kautokeino zieht mit an die Nordsee. Im
Winter kehrt alles heim, auch die Lappen mit ihren Heerden
weilen dann in der Nähe der Kirche; viele Norwegische Lappen
ziehen aber im Winter nach Schweden, wo sie kirchliche Bedienung genießen und an die Geistlichkeit Accidentien erlegen; Rennthiermoos findet sich nämlich, der Höhe der Berge wegen, in
Norwegisch-Lappland nicht in solcher Menge, wie in den Schwedischen Lappmarken.

Das Land ist sehr bergig, doch um die Kirche Kautokeino
ziemlich eben und angebauet, man findet vortreffliche Wiesen,
aber keine Aecker. Die Finnen halten Kühe und Schaafe; die
Lappen haben viele Rennthiere, einzelne reiche sollen an 1000
besitzen. Im Winter durchziehen viele zu den Märkten reisende
Kaufleute aus Torneå und Finnmarken die Gegend. Der mächtige, gleich mehreren Flüssen des Norwegischen Lapplands, lachs-
reiche Altenstrom entspringt im Pastorat unweit der Kirche Kautokeino, welche, unter fast 69° Polhöhe, 786 Fuß über das Meer
erhöht liegt. Das Pastorat breitet sich am Fuße des Gebirges
Kölen aus, welches hier keinesweges die Gränze zwischen Schweden und Norwegen bildet; der Alten durchschneidet das Gebirge.

Leider kann der Pastor von Kautokeino zu seinen Finnischen
und Lappischen Gemeindegliedern nur mittelst des Katecheten als
Dolmetschers reden. Derselbige Fall tritt bei allen oder doch
den meisten Norwegischen Geistlichen, denen die Seelsorge der
Lappen und Finnen anvertrauet ist, ein. — Nachdem Ericus
Bredahl, Bischof über Trondhjem's Stift, nicht ohne Erfolg

II.   B b

1643 bis 1671 für die Bekehrung der Lappen durch Anstellung
von Lehrern und Unterweisung junger Lappen gewirkt hatte, 1714
für diesen Zweck eine eigene Missionsanstalt errichtet worden war,
und Thomas von Westen *), als Missionsvikar, sich um die
Befestigung und Erweiterung der Bekehrung sehr verdient gemacht hatte, indem er Kirchen erbauen ließ, Lehrer verordnete ꝛc.,
auch Missionarien umherreiseten und Schulmeister wirkten, und
endlich im Jahr 1752 zur Bildung von Lappenpredigern ein
Seminar zu Trondhjem entstanden war, welches freilich 1774
schon wieder einging; — hat es doch nie gelingen wollen, eine
hinlängliche Anzahl von Predigern, die des Lappischen und des
Finnischen kundig waren, zu gewinnen. Seit Aufhebung des
Seminars bemühte man sich, die Lappen Norwegisch zu lehren,
womit man aber bei vielen Lappen nicht zum Ziele kam, so daß
noch heute, selbst beim Alpengottesdienst, der auch in Norwegen
im Julius und August gehalten wird, die Geistlichen sich der
Dolmetscher bedienen müssen; ein Umstand, der um so verderb-
licher wirkt, da die Norwegischen Lappen in ihrem Dialecte noch
keine Bibelübersetzung besitzen. In den südlicheren Distrikten,
die an Jemteland gränzen, verstehen die Lappen mehr Norwegisch, und die Geistlichen reden zu ihnen in Norwegischer Sprache ohne Dolmetscher. — Jede Norwegische Lappengemeinde hat
einen, des Lappischen kundigen Katecheten, der zugleich Schulmeister ist, aber nicht umhergewandert, wie die Schwedischen Lappen-
katecheten. — Zur Unterhaltung des Missionswesens unter den
Norwegischen Lappen sind vom Staate gewisse Einkünfte und
Abgaben angeschlagen; doch besteht, unläugbar, die Seelsorge in
den Schwedischen Lappmarken auf einem ungleich besseren Fuße,
als im Norwegischen Lappland. — Heidnische Lappen findet man
im Norwegischen Lappland nicht.

*) Vergl. H. Hammond, den nordiske Missionshistorie i Nord-
landene, Finmarken og Trondhjems Amt til Lappers og Finners Om-
vendelse fra förste begyndelse indtil hen ut aaret 1727, da Lappernes
og Finnernes Apostel, Thomas von Westen döde. Kiöbenhavn 1787.
951 S. 8.

Den Schatz an die Krone erlegen die Norwegischen Lappen in Fellen.

Wilde Rennthiere sind, wenigstens in Finnmarken, nicht selten.

Die Zahl der Norwegischen Lappen soll kaum 3000 betragen. Sie haben viel Ehrfurcht für Christenthum und Kirche, sind sanft und friedlich und führen einen sehr sittlichen Lebenswandel: Morgen-, Abend- und Tischgebete sind unter ihnen allgemein; doch Liebe zum Trunk und Betrug im Handel findet man nicht ganz selten. — Die Fischerlappen wohnen in hemisphärisch gestalteten Hütten, gemeinsam mit Kühen und Schaafen; so bald sie einiges Vermögen erworben haben, kaufen sie sich Rennthiere und ziehen nach Schweden. Alle' auf Schwedischem Gebiet umherziehende Norwegische Lappen müssen an die Krone Schweden den Lappenschatz entrichten.

Das Klima ist sehr rauh, doch hat man bei Stetengaard angefangen, Kartoffeln zu pflanzen; auch Korn wird gesäet; man hält Ziegen, Kühe und Schaafe. Im Sommer bringt der Nordwind den sogenannten Havstaag, d. i. eine kalte Luft mit dichtem und feinem Regen.

Anleitung zu Mineralien ist vorhanden, aber die Benutzung wegen Holzmangels schwierig. Durch den Fischfang in Finnmarken werden jährlich große Summen gewonnen, die aber freilich nicht den Lappen zufallen.

Oberster Administrativbeamte in Norwegisch-Lappland ist ein Amtmann, unter dem ein Voigt steht. Für die Justizpflege sind ein Lagman, und, unter ihm, ein Sorenskrivere (Häradshöfding) bestellt; dieser hält jährlich, jener alle drei Jahre Gericht; zu gleicher Zeit soll der Propst die kirchliche Visitation halten.

In Finnmarken liegt die kleine Gränzfeste Wardoehuus, die nördlichste in Europa.

b. Das Alt-Russische Lappland.

Das Alt-Russische Lappland begreift den Kreis Kola in der Statthalterschaft Archangel; es bildet eine von dem Eismeer und

Bb 2

dem weißen Meer bespülte Halbinsel. Hier wohnen, auf weiten Räumen, Finnen und Fischerlappen, diese etwa 1000 an der Zahl; einige Lappen sind dem Bekenntniß der Russischen Kirche zugethan, die übrigen sind Heiden. — Weiter gegen Süd-osten trifft man Samojeden.

Das Alt-Russische Lappland ward im 14ten Jahrhundert den alten Bewohnern, einem wahrscheinlich Finnischen Stamm, entrissen, und ist seitdem Russisch geblieben.

Die Bemühungen der großen Russischen Bibelgesellschaft, ihre Wirksamkeit über Alt-Russisch Lappland zu verbreiten, blieben bisher, durch Schuld der dortigen Geistlichkeit, ohne Erfolg.

Zu Alt-Russisch Lappland darf man auch die Fälled's-Distrikte rechnen, an welche zwar die Krone Norwegen Ansprüche macht, die aber Rußland schon lange inne hat; indeß holt von hier die Garnison der Norwegischen Gränzfeste Wardoehuus alljährlich ihr Winterholz, ohne welches sie nicht subsistiren könnte. Jedes dritte Jahr pflegt der Dänische Voigt nach Kola zu reisen, um beim dortigen Russischen Commandanten gegen den Russischen Besitz zu protestiren; auch sollen in den Fälled's-Distrikten Norweger wohnen, die bisher keinen Schatz an Rußland erlegten, während andere an Norwegen und Rußland zugleich schatzen sollen *). Die Behörden sind Russisch. Das Land hat viel Rennthiermoos, doch trifft man nur im Winter Rennthierlappen. Die übrigen Lappen sind Fischerlappen. Diese leben von Fischen, die sie auf Kohlen rösten, von Rindenbrey, aus der zartesten Haut unter der oberen Tannen- und Fichtenrinde, von Mehl, welches sie von den Russen eintauschen, und von Milch, denn sie halten auch Schaafe. Sie sind reinlich, froh und heiter, während die Norwegischen Lappen mehr zu Trübsinn hinneigen. Einzelne haben schon Balkenhäuser mit Kamin, erhöhter Schlafbank und einem kleinen Glasfenster; die Zahl dieser Häuser mehrt sich, ja manche haben zwei solcher Häuser, eines für den Winter im Walde, und eines, zum Fischen, an den

---

*) S. Barges Bedemar Reise c. Bd. 2. S. 145.

Seen. Man macht Jagd auf Hermeline und wilde Rennthiere; letztere, wie der Fischfang, nehmen ab.

Uebrigens werden die Fälleds-Distrikte von Norwegen durch den Buggefjord und dessen Küsten getrennt und gränzen bei Mudkiefjäll und den Fischerinseln an das eigentliche Alt-Russische Lappland oder den Kreis Kola. Die Distrikte durchströmt der ansehnliche Fluß Patsjocki, der den See Enareträsk dem Pas-vigfjord zuführt. Außer den beiden genannten Meerbusen sind hier noch zu bemerken: der Meerbusen Neidenfjord und die Han-delsplätze Neiden, Pasvig und Peise, welche sämmtlich an Er-weiterungen von Flüssen liegen, nämlich dem Neutansjocki, Pats-jocki und dem Ausflusse des Sees Mämeljaur an der Gränze von Kemi-Lappmark.

c. Das Neu-Russische (Finnische) Lappland.

Das Neu-Russische Lappland besteht aus den, im Frieden zu Fredrikshamn am 16. Sept. 1809, von Schweden an Ruß-land abgetretenen Finnischen Lappmarken, nämlich einem Theil von Torneå- und ganz Kemi-Lappmark. Diese Lappmarken ge-hören zum Erzstift Åbo, und zum Län Uleåborg; ihre Verwaltung, in kirchlicher, politischer, juridischer Hinsicht, ist der Verwaltung der, Schweden verbliebenen, Lappmarken gleich.

I. Theil von Torneå-Lappmark.

Dieser Theil von Torneå-Lappmark begreift einen kleinen Theil des Pastorats Enontekis, mit der Kirche; aber nur wenigen Lappen und wenigen Finnischen Kolonisten; die Einwohnerzahl des abgetretenen Theils von Enontekis betrug im Jahr 1805 373, dagegen die des Schwedisch verbliebenen Theils 496. Die Kirche Enontekis (zu Gustavs I. Zeit in Raunula an der Nor-wegischen Gränze), unter 68° 50' 30'' Polhöhe, ist gegenwärtig Filial der 11 Meilen entfernten Kirche Muonioniska, welche, jetzt Mutterkirche, bis zur Abtretung an Rußland, Filialkirche des Pastorats Öfver-Torneå war. Im Jahr 1815 zählte die Ge-meinde Muonioniska 342, die Filialgemeinde Enontekis 216 See-len, außer den nicht schatzpflichtigen Lappen; schatzende Lappenfamillen giebt es in Enontekis 6 bis 7. Die Confirmanden bei der Gemeinden werden alljährlich im März bei der Mutterkirche Muonionista zum Unterricht versammelt; ein zweiter, mehr prüfender Unterricht und die Confirmation folgen am Ende Aprils. Die Hausverhöre werden in Muonionista im April und Mai, und besonders mit den Nichtconfirmirten im August und November gehalten. Auch im Filial Enontekis finden zwei Mal jährlich Hausverhöre Statt; Predigten werden in der Kirche Enontekis, so wie Kantpredigten *) zu Peldovuoma, wo Finnen wohnen, die sich mit Theerbrennen beschäftigen, und zu Buontisjervi gehalten; der Pastor reiset im Sommer zu Fuße oder zu Boot, im Winter in Schlitten, die von Rennthieren gezogen werden.

Außer den Gränzflüssen ist der Aunasjocki zu bemerken, der bei Rovaniemi in den Kemi fällt. — Korn reift nicht. — In der Nähe der Kirche Muonionista trifft man eine kleine Nagelschmiede, ein Erwerbsmittel des armen Pfarrers.

Auch der im Frieden von Fredrikshamn abgetretene Theil der zum Pastorat Öfver-Torneå gehörigen Filialgemeinde Pajala (mithin nicht Lappmark) gehört jetzt zum Pastorat Muonionista.

II. Ganz Kemi-Lappmark **)

Auf einem Flächenraume von 534 ☐M. (im J. 1799 mit 794 Lappen und 1618 Nybyggare, Männern und Weibern) enthält Kemi-Lappmark drei Pastorate: Utsjocki mit Enare, Sodankylä mit Kittilä (unter Schwedischem Scepter war es Theil von Westerbotten), und Kusamo nebst Kuolajervi, einem Theil des Pastorats Kemiträsk, welches schon innerhalb des eigentlichen Finnlands liegt. Kusamo und Kuolajervi waren bereits zu Schwe-

---

*) Schwedens Kirchenverfassung. Band 2. S. 19 und 20.

**) Ich folge in der Beschreibung hauptsächlich Wahlenberg bestrifning om Kemi-Lappmark i Westerbottens Höfdingedöme. Stockh. 1804, und Lagus bestrifning om Kusamo, in den Handlingar der Akad. der Wissensch. zu Stockh. 1772 1773. Bd. 33. S. 17. ff. S. 222. ff. S. 349 ff. Bd. 34. S. 76. ff.

discher Zeit Theile des Finnischen Län Uleåborg. In kirchlicher Hinsicht gehört ganz Kemi-Lappmark zur Propstey Kemi, und wird der Gottesdienst überall in Finnischer Sprache gehalten.

1. Utsjocki mit Enare.

a. Utsjocki.

Utsjocki, zwischen 69° 22′ und 70° 4′ Polhöhe, gränzt im Westen an die Kapellgemeinde Karasjocki, im Norden an die Kapellgemeinde Tana (erstere Theil des Norwegischen Pastorats Kautokeino, letztere des Norwegischen Pastorats Köllefjord), im Osten an das Kirchspiel Wadsöe, und an Neiden im Alt-Russischen Lappland, im Süden an Enare. Der Flächeninhalt beträgt 34 ☐ Meilen.

Der Tanafluß, welcher den größten Theil der Gränze gegen Norwegen bildet, entsteht zwei Meilen östlich von der Kirche Karasjocki durch Vereinigung der Flüsse Enara und Karas, und ergießt sich endlich in den Meerbusen Tanafjord, eine halbe M. nördlich vom Handelsplatz Guldholmen in Finnmarken. Viele größere und kleinere Flüsse fallen in den Tana-Elf.

Berge füllen das Land aus, doch schmilzt auf denselben im Sommer der Schnee. Im Anfange des Junius geht das Eis auf, um Johannis (drey Wochen später als in Torneå) schlägt das Laub aus, im August wird das Gras gemähet, zu Anfange Octobers friert die Erde und 14 Tage später hat sich eine feste Eisdecke über den Flüssen gebildet. Vom 20. November bis etwa 20. Januar ist die Sonne nicht sichtbar.

Neben der aus Holz 1700 erbauten Kirche Utsjocki, unter 69° 51′ 52″ Polhöhe, wohnt, seit 1747, der Pastor. Die Kirche liegt 12 (Schwedische oder 8 Finnmärkische) Meilen von der Mündung des Tana, 12 Meilen von der Kirche Karasjocki, 30 Meilen von der Kirche Kautokeino, 75 von Torneå entfernt, und wird von den Buden der Kaufleute aus Torneå, die hier mit Lappen und Norwegern Handel treiben, und dem Gerichtshause umgeben.

Die Lappen sind theils Hirten- (Alpen-), theils Fischerlappen. Jene haben Rennthiere, diese Kühe, Ziegen und Schaafe, die aber nicht mit den Menschen in demselben Raume stehen, wie man es bei den Norwegischen Fischerlappen findet. Die Hütten bestehen aus kegelförmig zusammengestellten, mit Torf und Erde bedeckten Stäben. Besitzen die Fischerlappen Rennthiere (welcher Fall selten ist), so lassen sie sie durch die Hirtenlappen weiden.

Die Einwohnerzahl von Utsjocki betrug im J. 1805. 366, im J. 1815 nur 253; alle Lappen, die Beamten ausgenommen. Die Familienzahl war im J. 1815. 40; im J. 1805 zählte man noch 55 Lappenfamilien, von welchen 32 zu den Hirten und 23 zu den Fischerlappen gehörten; jene besaßen über 7000 Rennthiere (zwei Lappen waren Eigenthümer, jeder von tausend Rennthieren); diese etwa 10 Rennthiere und 14 Kühe; überdieß besaß jeder Fischerlappe 6 bis 12 Schaafe.

Die Hirtenlappen ziehen im Sommer auf den Gränzalpen, oder an den Küsten der Nordsee umher; im Winter hat Utsjocki die beste Weide, im Sommer ist die Alpenweide kräftiger.

Mehrere Fischerlappen sind Finnischen Ursprungs, indem manche eingewanderte Finnen sich mit Lappen verheiratheten. Ueberhaupt stehen die hiesigen Fischerlappen den Finnen sehr nahe: die Männer reden beide Sprachen, die Weiber verstehen nur Lappisch. Die Lappen von Utsjocki sind träge und dem Branntewein sehr ergeben. Der Tana=Lachs ist Hauptnahrung der Fischerlappen: dieser sehr fette Lachs wird über Guldholmen ausgeführt, ist auch Handelswaare auf dem Markt von Utsjocki. Nächst dem Torneå hat der Tana unter allen Nordischen Flüssen den reichsten Lachsfang; mehr denn tausend Menschen leben in diesen Gegenden fast nur vom Tana=Lachs. Die Jagd ist unbedeutend. Korn reift nicht. Rüben gedeihen. Mit Kartoffeln hat man noch keinen Versuch gemacht. Pferde und Schweine werden nicht gehalten. In regnigen und kalten Sommern sind die Mücken eine große Plage; Wahlenberg vermuthet, daß die Mücken in diesen nördlichen Gegenden als Dünger dienen, ohne welchen der Boden noch unfruchtbarer seyn würde, als er jetzt ist.

Der gegenwärtige Pastor von Utsjocki (im J. 1815.) versteht nicht Lappisch, seine Predigten werden zuweilen von einem Dolmetscher ins Lappische übersetzt. Der Bettags-Frühtext wird hier, wie in Kusamo, in der Einleitung zur Vormittagspredigt erklärt. Fastenpredigten werden gehalten, nicht aber Katechismuspredigten, weil im Sommer die Lappen gewöhnlich in Norwegen sind; eben so wenig finden Kantpredigten Statt.

b. Enare.

Enare, zwischen 68° 25' und 69° 45' Polhöhe, wird im Westen von Norwegen und von Utsjocki, im Nordosten und Osten von Alt-Russisch Lappland, im Süden von Sodankylä, begränzt.

Das Filial Enare, mit einem Flächeninhalt von 188 □M., begreift alles Land um den Enaresee und die in diesen See fallenden Gewässer. Der Enareträsk (das Wort träsk bezeichnet in Nordschweden und Finnland einen Landsee) nimmt mehr als den achten Theil (24 □M.) des gesammten Areals ein, ist etwa 12 Meilen lang, 7 M. breit, eine unzählige Menge von Inseln füllt ihn aus. Durch den Patsjocki ergießt er sich in die Nordsee. — Das feste Land von Enare ist bergig und mit Fichten bewachsen, doch bilden üppige Wiesen die Ufer einiger Flüsse.

Das Klima ist dem von Muonioniska, unter 68° Polhöhe, ziemlich gleich; es verstattet den Kornbau, aber der unfruchtbare Boden ist nicht günstig; doch kommt bei Ivalojocki die Gerste recht gut fort.

Die Kirche Enare, unter 68° 56' 43" Polhöhe, liegt von der Kirche Utsjocki 15, von der Kirche Sodankylä 30, von Torneå 65 Meilen entfernt: Marktbuden und das Gerichtshaus umgeben sie. Der Handel, besonders mit den Norwegischen Lappen, ist hier sehr bedeutend.

Die Kirche ward zuerst 1639 als Kapelle des Pastorats Kusamo gegründet; 1747 ward sie Kapelle des Pastorats Utsjocki; 1761 ward eine neue geräumige Kreuzkirche erbaut. Um die Kirche werden, der Bären halber, die nirgends in diesen nördlichen Gegenden so zahlreich sind, wie hier, und früherhin die Kirche fast untergraben haben sollen, keine Todte bestattet;

man hat daher zu Begräbnißplätzen 2 Inseln im Enaresee, 1½ Meilen von der Kirche ausersehen; aber auch hierhin schwimmen zuweilen die Bären.

Der Pfarrhof wird nur dann und wann bewohnt *), andere bewohnte Häuser giebt es neben der Kirche nicht; bis zur nächsten Menschenwohnung hat ma n¾ Meilen. Zu Kirch- und Marktzeiten ist es desto lebhafter. Während des Vorüberziehens der Lappen wird, einige Sonntage hinter einander, Gottesdienst gehalten. — Wie in Utsjocki, so findet auch in Enare bei der Kirche Haus- (Lese-) verhör Statt, weil in den Lappkoten solches unausführbar ist; der Confirmandenunterricht währt in Utsjocki 2 Wochen, in Enare 1 Woche. Der Katecheten, welche die Kinder buchstabiren und lesen lehren, giebt es in Uts-jocki 2, in Enare 1. Der Katechetenlohn beträgt 14 Rubel 88 Kopeken Silber; eben so besteht der Pastorlohn in Geld (360 Rubel Silber), weil die Einwohner kein Korn bauen; doch hat der Pastor auch Lachszehnten von dem Fange in den Flüssen Tana und Utsjocki, und statt der Leichenkuh ein Rennthier. — An Nybyggen fand Wahlenberg 5, die Bewohner waren Fin-nen; jeder Hausvater hat 6 oder 7 Kühe und viele Schaafe, gute Wiesen, Gerste- und Rübenfelder; der Acker wird mit dem Spaten gegraben; Pferde hält man nicht. Im Jahre 1815 gab es gar keinen Nybyggare und kein Korn ward gebaut. Die Einwohner sind arme Fischerlappen, die zwischen ihren Sommer-hütten an den Seen und ihren Winterhütten in den Wäldern, wo Weide für Schaafe und Rennthiere ist, umherziehen; Kühe haben sie nicht. Ihre Hütten sind aus behauenem Holz. Sie fangen wilde Rennthiere. Die Zahl dieser Lappenfamilien be-trug, im Jahre 1803, 65; die Personenzahl im Jahre 1805. 411; im Jahre 1815. 442 in 75 Familien. Sie führen alle 3 Namen: Vornamen (z. B. Johann), Vatersnamen (z. B. Olofsson) und Geschlechtsnamen (z. B. Morotaja, Name des zahlreichsten und vornehmsten Geschlechts in Enare.

---

*) Nach Åbo Stiftsmatrikel. 1607. S. 238. soll der Pastor im Winter zu Utsjocki, im Sommer zu Enare wohnen.

Die Lappen von Enare haben gar keine Gemeinschaft mit ihren Nachbaren. Sie sprechen Lappisch und Finnisch, verstehen auch etwas Russisch. Unter einander vorfallende Streitigkeiten schlichten sie selbst, auf Versammlungen der Hausväter der Dorfschaft. Das ordentliche Gericht, das in allen, dem Schwedischen Rechte unterworfenen, Landschaften einmal oder mehrere Male jährlich, hier nur alle 2 Jahre, von dem Ortsrichter gehalten wird, hat fast nie Gegenstände der Untersuchung, denn Verbrechen sind unerhört; Diebstahl kennt man nicht: die Kaufleute lassen überall ihre Waaren unverschlossen liegen, ohne daß auch nur das geringste entwandt wird. Sonntäglich versammeln sich die Lappen an bestimmten Orten, um ihre gemeinschaftliche Andacht zu verrichten. Sie haben viel Liebe zur Obrigkeit. Des Geizes, des Hochmuths, der Eigenliebe und des Eigensinns werden sie nicht ohne Grund beschuldiget.

Frische und getrocknete Fische sind die Hauptnahrung dieser Lappen; die Brühe, in welcher Fische gekocht worden, trinken sie mit dem größten Wohlbehagen; im Winter essen sie viel dicke Rindengrütze, d. i. die getrocknete innerste Fichtenrinde, mit Wasser und Rennthiertalg zu dickem Brey gekocht.

Einige Fischerlappen haben Rennthiere, aber keiner mehr als 10. Die Rennthiere sind 4 Fuß hoch, überhaupt größer, stärker und lebendiger als in andern Lappmarken und eignen sich besonders zum Fahren. Im Herbste gehen diese Lappen auf die Jagd wilder Rennthiere. Die vielen Bären schaden nur im Frühlinge.

In allen Richtungen von Enare aus findet man, mehrere Tagereisen, keine Menschenwohnung, nur Hütten, die zur Bequemlichkeit des Voigts und der Kaufleute auf ihren Reisen erbauet sind; sie sind oben offen, und gewähren daher nur einigen Schutz gegen den Wind, nicht gegen die Kälte.

Im Norden von Enare liegt der obenerwähnte, von den Russen occupirte Fälledsdistrikt mit nackten Klippen an der Küste, Bergen, die nicht die Höhe der Schneealpen erreichen, und vielem ebenen mageren Lande, das Rennthiermoos und verkrüppelte Fichten bedecken, im Innern.

2. Paſtorat Sodankylä.

Zwiſchen 67° und 68° 27′ Polhöhe, gränzt im Norden an Enare, im Weſten an Enontekis und Muonioniſka, im Süden an die Finniſchen Paſtorate Rovaniemi und Kemiträſk, im Oſten an Knolajervi-Lappmark. Der Flächeninhalt beträgt 239 ☐M. Bis 1747 war Sodankylä Kapelle von Kuſamo.

Eine Menge großer Flüſſe durchſtrömen dieſen Lappmark und ergießen ſich in den Kemifluß (Finniſch Kemmijocki); die Seen ſind nicht zahlreich. Die meiſten Flüſſe entſtehen aus Sümpfen und ſind wenig fiſchreich.

Faſt ⅔ des ganzen Landes bilden Sümpfe, oder feuchte Wieſen, zum Theil mit Holz bewachſen; im Sommer iſt völlig unmöglich zu Pferde fortzukommen. Der feſte Boden iſt meiſt Sand, im obern Lande mit gelber Walderde vermiſcht. Die Alpen ſind ziemlich zahlreich, haben aber meiſtens eine iſolirte Lage, und verlieren um Johannis den Schnee; an den Seiten ſind ſie ganz mit Rennthiermoos bedeckt.

Die kleine Kirche liegt, unter 67° 23′ Polhöhe am Ufer des Kittinenjocki. — In der Dorfſchaft Kittilä, 9 Meilen von der Kirche Sodankylä, iſt ein Predigthaus errichtet, wo man 3 mal jährlich Gottesdienſt, und an den Tagen, wo Hausverhör iſt, auch Katechismuspredigten hält. Auch wird jährlich im niedern Theil der Dorfſchaft Sodankylä 3, in der Dorfſchaft Sompio 1 und im Dorfe Kemikylä 1 mal Kantpredigt, und zwar in Bauernhäuſern, indem es an den genannten Orten keine Predigthäuſer giebt, gehalten; in Nieder-Sodankylä finden auch Katechismuspredigten bei den 2 Hausverhören, in Sombio und Kemikylä nur 1 Hausverhör, Statt.

Das Paſtorat enthält 2 Gerichtsſprengel: Kittilä und Sodankylä, jenen mit den Dorfſchaften Kittilä und Sodankylä, dieſen mit den Dorfſchaften Sombio und Kemikylä. Jede Dorfſchaft hat ihre abgetheilten Plätze zur Jagd und zum Fiſchfange, die allen Bewohnern gemeinſchaftlich ſind; auch ihre eigenen Dorfſtände (byating); die einzelnen Höfe der Dorfſchaften liegen weit auseinander; die bedeutendſte iſt Kittilä mit 74 ☐Meilen, 89 Höfen und 823 Seelen (im J. 1802). Das Tingshaus von Kittilä steht zunächst dem Predigthause, in dessen Nähe man auch mehrere Höfe trifft. Sodankylä begreift 73 ☐Meilen, 71 Höfe und 557 Seelen (im J. 1802); hier findet man die Kirche und ¹⁄₁₆ M. von derselben den Pfarrhof. Sombio hat 61 ☐Meilen, im J. 1802 mit 35 Höfen und 296 Seelen; Kemikylä aber nur 31 ☐Meilen, im J. 1802 mit 10 Höfen und 106 Seelen. Im Jahre 1805 zählte ganz Sodankylä überhaupt 1814 Einwohner, Finnen und Lappen; im Jahre 1815 nur 1587. Der Confirmandenunterricht wird im Pfarrhofe (im Februar) und in Kittilä (im März) ertheilt.

Vor etwa 100 Jahren sollen fast nur Lappen im Lande gewohnt haben, jetzt trifft man nur Finnische Kolonisten aus Österbotten, die in ordentlichen Bauerhäusern wohnen, und die, im Jahre 1818, in den Visitationsacten, der Trunkliebe beschuldigt werden. Den Branntewein sollen ihnen die vielen Landhändler, welche aus Finnland heraufkommen, zuführen. Die Volkszahl hat sich binnen 40 Jahren verdoppelt: im J. 1755 bestand sie in 760, im J. 1802 in 1782 Seelen; also 7 Menschen, in Kittilä sogar 11 auf 1 ☐M., die stärkste Bevölkerung innerhalb des Polarzirkels.

Die vornehmste und sicherste Nahrung ist die Viehzucht, die ansehnlich ist, aber bei dem reichen Zugange zu Futter noch sehr vermehrt werden könnte; Phalaris arundinacea wächset mannshoch. Heuscheunen kennt man nicht; man trocknet das Heu zwischen aufrecht 1 Elle von einander stehenden Stäben, gegen welche, das Herabfallen des Heues zu verhindern, von beiden Seiten Strebepfeiler angebracht sind.

Die Kolonisten halten Schaafe und Kühe (10 bis 20), Pferde (1 — 3) und Rennthiere (10 — 12) zu den Winterreisen. Letztere werden von gedungenen Lappen geweidet. — Man verkauft Häute, Butter und Käse, die man auf dem Kemi, selbst nach Torneå bringt, oder durch die Bauern vom Kemi träst dort verkaufen läßt; denn im Pastorat Sodankylä wird, seit daselbst keine Lappen wohnen, kein Markt gehalten.

Der Ackerbau ist Nebensache, und lohnt wenig; oft reift das Korn nicht, am ersten noch auf Sandboden. Gerste säet man

am Ende May's und erndtet um die Mitte des August; jeder
Nybyggare fäet etwa 16 Scheffel, und erhält das 4te Korn.
Noch öfter, als die Gerste, erfriert der Roggen. Man fäet
ihn sehr dünn, zu Anfange Augusts, doch reift er nicht vor Sep=
tember des folgenden Jahres; wird er reif, so giebt er das 18te
Korn. — Vom 7ten Juni bis 5ten Juli ist die Sonne die ganze
Nacht sichtbar. Hafer und Flachs bauet man in ganz Kemi=
Lappmark nicht. Hanf wird gebauet und gedeiht.

Man mahlt auf Handmühlen; nur 1 Wassermühle besteht.
Rüben gedeihen vortrefflich. Kartoffeln hatte man bisher
nur auf dem Pfarracker gepflanzt, wo sie großen Ertrag gaben.
Auch mit Zuckererbsen hatte man dort gelungene Versuche gemacht.

Im Sommer ist man oft mit Stroh vermischtes Gersten=
brot; in den übrigen Theilen des Jahres hat man reineres und
besseres, im Herbste sogar Roggenbrot.

Fische hat man wenig, zuweilen fängt man beim Pfarrhofe
Lachs. — An Thieren erlegt man nur einige Biber.

Die Wohnungen der Kolonisten sind gute Bauernhäuser mit
vielen Nebengebäuden.

Das Kronkorn des Pastors ist seit 1809 mit 25 Tonnen
(halb Roggen, halb Gerste) vermehrt worden.

3. Pastorat Kusamo

liegt zwischen dem östlichen Finnland und dem Gouvernement
Archangel mitten inne. Die Länge von N. noch S. beträgt 35,
die Breite von O. nach W. 10 bis 15 Meilen, der Flächenin=
halt 75 □Meilen. Einen großen Theil des Landes füllen Flüsse,
Seen und Moräste aus; unter den Seen ist der Kusamo zu be=
merken, an welchem die Kirche, unter 65° 53' Polhöhe, erbauet
ist. Zu den beträchtlichsten Flüssen gehören der Oulang und
der Pisto.

Das Pastorat ist sehr bergig, einige dieser Berge sind Schnee=
alpen; der Pyhätunduri (heiliger Berg) war einst Opferstelle
der heidnischen Lappen.

Der Sommer ist sehr heiß, oft so heiß, daß man keine
Kleidung dulden kann; doch wird es auch an heißen Tagen oft
plötzlich kalt.

In der ersten Hälfte des Octobers legen die Flüsse zu, und erst zu Ende Mai's verlieren sich Schnee und Eis. Vom 1sten December bis 1sten März tröpfeln selten die Dächer, die Tage sind kurz und dunkel; doch geben die lange Morgen- und Abend-dämmerung und der Nordschein einigen Ersatz.

Lappen giebt es jetzt in Kusamo nicht mehr, alle Einwohner sind Finnen; seit längerer Zeit, vielleicht schon seit Carl IX., ent-richteten sie, um vor Russischen Ueberfällen, auch im Kriege si-cher zu seyn, an die Russische Krone eine bestimmte Abgabe, Bogensteuer (Bågeskatt) genannt; jedes Bågelag 1½ Rubel; Kusamo hat 11½ Bågelag. Auch Sodankylä und Enare erlegten zum Theil diese Steuer, die der Commandant von Kola durch einen Unterofficier einfordern läßt; dieser erhält dann auch von jedem Dorfe ein Geschenk in Pelzwerk.

Lappen sind hier schon seit langer Zeit Ackerbauer gewor-den. 1769 gab es in Kusamo nur noch 10 Lappenfamilien, wel-che, neben Ackerbau und Viehzucht, vorzugsweise Jagd trieben. Die gesammte Einwohnerzahl betrug im J. 1769. 1910 (wahr-scheinlich Kuolajervi mitgerechnet); im J. 1718 nur 655. Um das Jahr 1807 betrug die Volkszahl etwa 2940, ohne Kuola-jervi. Im Jahre 1815 zählte Kusamo, ohne Kuolajervi, nur 2536 Seelen, 207 steuerpflichtige Familien und 12 auf Freijahre sitzende Nybyggare. In der Regel beträgt die Zahl der Gestor-benen jährlich nur die Hälfte der Zahl der Geborenen.

Die Finnen sind groß und lebendig, wohlgebauet, kräftig und abgehärtet; sie baden sich oft. Man redet Finnisch, doch auch Lappisch; an der Russischen Gränze ist das Finnische mit Russischen Wörtern vermischt. Das Lappische weicht von dem Lappischen der westlichen Lappmarken sehr ab.

Die Einwohner sind fleißig, dienstfertig und ehrerbietig ge-gen Vorgesetzte. Lange war es üblich, reisenden Geistlichen und Kronbeamten jährlich die Ehrengabe zu reichen, diese bestand in Pelzwerk, ein Paar Thaler an Werth. Im Winter dienen den Finnen der große und kleine Bär und der Orion als Uhr und Kompaß.

Man lebt sehr mäßig, das gewöhnliche Getränk ist Milch und Wasser; doch hat man auch schon Branntwein kennen gelernt. Die gewöhnlichen Speisen sind Fische, Milch- und Fleischspeisen; Suppe trinkt man aus hölzernen Schaalen. Man schläft auf einer über Stroh ausgebreiteten Rennthierhaut unter einer wollenen Decke, ganz nach Finnischer Sitte.

Allerheiligen feiert man noch höher als Weihnachten. Der Gebrauch, mehrere Jahre hintereinander Gedächtnißmahle zu Ehren der Todten zu halten, hat meist aufgehört.

Der Wald besteht aus Gränen, Fichten, Birken, Espen, Erlen, Weiden, die aber alle niedrig bleiben; geschwendet hat man unmäßig. Åkerbär hat man wenig, Mültbeeren desto häufiger; letztere werden von den Russen wider den Scharbock gebraucht. Rennthiermoos giebt es viel.

Man bauet Roggen und Gerste, ersterer wird im August, letztere im Anfange des Junius gesäet; besonders hat man viel Schwendeland. Viehzucht und Fischerey sind ansehnlich; auch Rennthiere werden gehalten, außerdem Pferde, Kühe und Schaafe.

Die Bauern treiben Handel nach Rußland und Osterbotten; Korn kauft man nur in Mißwachsjahren.

Gericht und Markt wird neben der Kirche gehalten. Der Richter kommt jährlich einmal, im März; dann ist auch Markt, und der Voigt erhebt die Steuer.

Die Bekehrung der frühern Lappischen Bewohner von Kusamo geschah im 17ten Jahrhundert, auf Betrieb der Königin Christina, die in Kemiträsk und Enare Kirchen bauen ließ; namentlich durch Jac. Lapodus und Esaias Ijander, die der Bischof von Åbo, Isaac Rothoff, 1648 nach beiden Orten sandte; nach des Lapodus Tode wurden dem Ijander beide Gemeinden anvertraut; 1680 ward auch eine Kapelle in Sodankylä angelegt. Dem Ijander folgte Puderus, diesem Hans Cajanus, unter welchem eine Predigtstube nebst Predigerwohnung am Kusamosee gestiftet wurde; Kuolajervi hatte seinen eigenen Kapellan; 1694 ward die Predigtstube von Kusamo in eine Kirche verwandelt, die ¾ Meile von da gebauet wurde.

Außer dem Gottesdienste in der Kirche Kusamo wird jetzt zuweilen in den Dörfern Heikyld und Pousu, 4 Meilen von Kusamo, Gottesdienst in Bauernstuben gehalten; auch finden drei jährliche Kantpredigten im Dorfe Posso, 6 Meilen von der Kirche Kusamo, während der Hausverhöre, in Bauernhäusern Statt. Der Confirmandenunterricht wird 2 Wochen im Mai und 2 Tage vor Johannis ertheilt, worauf sogleich die Confirmation folgt.

4. Kuolajervi Lappmark,

gehört zum Pastorat Kemiträsk, von dessen Kirche dieser Lappmark 10 bis 20 Schwedische Meilen entfernt ist; er liegt nördlich von Kusamo. Die Localverhältnisse des Landes sind ziemlich denen von Kusamo gleich; doch soll es hier viele Lappen, Hirten und noch mehr Fischerlappen geben. 1800 enthielt Kuolajervi-Lappmark 48 Familien *); im Jahre 1817 zählte dieser Lappmark über 200 Communikanten. Zur Abhaltung der Hausverhöre ist Kuolajervi-Lappmark in 2 Förhörslag getheilt (der übrige Theil des Pastorats Kemiträsk in 6) und wird von der Kirche Kemiträsk aus zweimal jährlich besucht; dann hält man Verhör (Prüfung der Christenthumskenntnisse), auch Gottesdienst in Finnischer Sprache. Wer dem Verhöre nicht beiwohnt, wird das erstemal mit Geldbuße belegt, bei Wiederholung in den Fußblock (Stock), am Sonntage, während des Gottesdienstes, gespannt, endlich zur Bestrafung dem weltlichen Gerichte übergeben. Zuweilen hält der Contractspropst (Kemiträsk mit Kuolajervi gehört zum Contract, d. i. Propstei Kemi) Propstvisitationen, bei welchen oft allerlei Einrichtungen getroffen und Verordnungen erlassen werden, die sich auf Kirche, Schule, sittliches Leben beziehen, durch die Bestätigung des Consistoriums treten sie in Gesetzeskraft. Eine solche Visitation ward zuletzt 1817 vom Doctor Castrén von Kemi gehalten; in dem ans Consistorium zu Åbo eingesandten Visitationsbericht bemerkt derselbe, wie er eine große Abnahme der Sittlichkeit gespürt; es

---

*) S. Åbo Stiftsmatrikel. Åbo 1807. S. 234.

II.   C c

herrſche Kälte gegen die Religion; Morgen= und Abendgebete an
Sonntagen fänden nicht mehr Statt; uneheliche Kinder ſeyen
zwar noch ſelten, aber deſto häufiger ſey der anticipirte Beiſchlaf
(otidigt ſängelag); Kartenſpiel und Tanz an Sonntagen wären
ſehr üblich geworden. Es wurden nun Strafverordnungen gegen
das Tanzen außer den Hochzeiten und gegen Kartenſpiel erlaſſen,
auch ward die Anſtellung eines Katecheten durch die Krone vor=
geſchlagen; und allerdings iſt die Annahme eines Katecheten für
den ſo weit von der Mutterkirche entlegenen Lappmark ſehr noth=
wendig. — Die Einwohner ſind ſehr arm.

Vier und zwanzigſtes Kapitel.

Rückreiſe aus Lappland; Reiſe durch Angerman=
land.

Der Abſchied. — Drückende Hitze.— Das Rybygge Tand=
ſele; das Rudern durch Strömungen. — Tägsnäs. —
Gefährlicher Ritt. — Degerfors. — Kirche Umeå —
Dorfgottesdienſt in Männå. — Der majeſtätiſche
Waſſerfall Fällfors. — Stadt Umeå — Das Paſtorat
Norrmalling; Schulſtiftung — Weite Ausſicht vom
Berge Stofverhälla. — Der Garten von Angerman=
land beginnt — Grundſunda. — Urnås. — Anundſjö;
reiſe Åderbär — Gottesdienſt in Anundſjö; Einfach=
heit der Menſchen. — Sennenmädchen — Bergwerk;
wohlfeiler Waldkauf. — Sidenſjö. Nätra — Die ein=
zige Apotheke auf 24 Meilen.— Der Berg und die Kir=
che von Bidbyggerå. — Norbingrå; eigenthümliche Be=
ſchaffenheit des Landes; — die alte Kirche. — Kirche
Nora; Elfa; Kungsgården. — Die reizenden Thäler
am Angerman;— Kirche Styrnås;— Kirche Botßed;—
die Grabhügel. — Kirche Oforländå. — Edelhof
Holm. — Kirche und Geſundbrunnen Sänga. Kirche
Multrå. Sollefta; der große Markt; Bergsting. Die
Paſtorate Reſele, Ramſele, Ragunda; die Brut; das
Waldfeuer; der Erndtetanz; Thorsåler. — Viterlå=

näs; der Markt Hammar; der Hafen Nyland; der Abend in Gudmundrå; reizende Gegend; Kirche Hägsjö; Brut Utansjö. Kirche Säbrå. — Hernösand. Wardkas-Berg. Eintritt in Medelpad.

Am 24. Jul. Von Lycksele nach Tandsele 1 M.; von T. nach Tuggensele 1 M.; von T. nach Lillsele 1 M.; von L. nach Tågsnäs 2½ M. Zus. 5½ M.

Nach einem herzlichen Lebewohl, bestieg ich um 7½ Uhr das Boot. Es war ein wehmüthiger Abschied. Die guten Leute, deren Freundlichkeit und Liebe ich so genußreiche Stunden verdankte, unter ihnen die ehrwürdige Pröpstin, deren Antlitz die heiterste Frömmigkeit wie verklärte, begleiteten mich auf dem Wege zum Ufer. Vom Hofe des Kronvoigt aus schiffte ich, mit allerlei Lappländischen Producten beschenkt, mich ein; außer meinem Gefährten aus Degerfors waren noch der Kronvoigt, zwei Geistliche und der Rector Rådström mit in den Böten, indem sie erst an der Gränze des Pastorats von mir Abschied nehmen wollten.

Bei völliger Windstille ruderten wir ab, doch war der Betsele=Fors, der dem Hellefors an Höhe nachsteht und nur bei nordwestlichen Winden erschallt, hörbar, zum erstenmal seit meiner Anwesenheit in Lycksele; bald blies auch würklich ein günstiger Wind aus Nordwesten, doch die Hitze blieb drückend. Oberhalb des Hellefors stiegen wir ans Land; in den aufsteigenden Staubwolken bildete die Sonne einen Regenbogen. Dann umgingen wir die gewaltige, völlig unfahrbare Katarakte, und setzten unterhalb derselben, wo sie Ebbe und Fluth bildet, die Fahrt fort. Zwischen waldigen Ufern glitten wir den schönen Fluß herab; die Mücken spielten im Schatten der Bäume, die Sonne brannte. Erst um 9½ Uhr waren wir in Tandsele, nur ¼ M. von Hellefors, die Landung an einer schönen Insel hatte uns aufgehalten. In Tandsele ging ich zu der, von Wahlenberg untersuchten Quelle, deren Kälte mir indeß nicht so bedeutend schien, was in zufälligen Umständen seinen Grund haben mochte

Cc 2

te; auf dem Wege zur Quelle, wohl ½ Meile, standen reife
Beeren in Menge, auch die schönen gelben Hjortron; die Wachholderbeeren ißt man hier als durststillend. Man geht über einen ausgetrockneten Morast, doch viele Moräste sind noch unaus-
getrocknet und machen die Luft kalt, so daß Tandsele oft durch
frühe Nachtfröste leidet.

Um 11 Uhr setzten wir von Tandsele aus die Reise fort.
Der aufgespannte Regenschirm gewährte einige Erleichterung in
der drückenden Mittagshitze. Vor Tuggensele, wo wir um 1½ U.
landeten, donnerte uns der Fors entgegen, der indeß lange nicht
so bedeutend ist, wie der Hellefors. In Tuggensele fanden wir
den Hof des Nybyggare, der uns auf der Aufreise so freundlich
empfangen hatte, menschenleer, doch die Zimmer waren offen,
wir nahmen von dem größeren, mit Laub ausgestreuten, Besitz;
die Eßkober wurden ausgepackt. Mittlerweile kamen einige Kinder aus dem zweiten Hofe herbeigelaufen; wir äußerten den
Wunsch, frische Milch zu essen, ohne indeß den Kindern einen
Auftrag zu geben; nur die Frau des zweiten Hofes ließen wir
rufen. Sie kam und brachte eine große Schaale voll Milch;
nun erfuhren wir, daß Jansson, der Bewohner des Hofes, in
welchem wir uns eben befanden, zwei Tage unserer gewartet
und erst heute Morgen auf die Hegerndte gegangen sey; doch
waren, wie er es verheißen hatte, die Böte zwischen Tandsele
und Tuggensele bereit gewesen. — Um 3½ Uhr brachen wir wieder auf, zuginggen in einer Stunde zwei Forssar, warteten eine
Stunde auf eine, in Tuggensele vergessene Posttasche, deren Beförderung von Lycksele nach Umeå wir versprochen hatten. Unsere Lappischen Freunde kehrten heim und wir übrigen schifften
uns ein. Von der Einschiffungsstelle bis Lillsele sind ¾ Meilen;
gleich nach der ersten Achtelmeile, wo an beiden Ufern eine
Menge Bäche in den Umeå fallen und kleine Buchten (afva)
bilden, ist die Gränze von Lappland. Das Pastorat Degerfors
und mit demselben Westerbotten, beginnt; doch bleibt die Beschaffenheit des Landes dieselbe; der obere Theil von Degerfors
ist ganz Lappisch: wilder Wald und selten Menschenwohnungen.
Eine Viertelmeile von Lillsele landeten wir, ein Paar heftigen

Strömungen zu entgehen; unsere kräftige, 60jährige Ruderin fuhr mittlerweile am entgegengesetzten Ufer, wo das Wasser still ist, und lenkte dann, uns einen längern Gehweg zu ersparen, mitten zwischen zwei kleinen Wasserfällen hindurch, zum andern Ufer hinüber. Aber ihre Gutmüthigkeit brachte sie in große Gefahr: der untere Strudel riß das Boot fort und es war ängstlich vom Lande aus zu sehen, wie das kleine Boot, einem Theile nach, vom Wasser überdeckt, bald hoch in die Luft emporgehoben, bald in die Tiefe zurückgeschleudert wurde. Doch, einer beim Befahren von Strö= mungen und Wasserfällen bewährten Regel gemäß, hielt die Ru= derin das Ruder fest, und so floß das Boot endlich unversehrt zu den stilleren Gewässern fort. Wir stiegen ein und waren um 6¼ Uhr in Lillsele. Hier wechselten wir das Boot; statt der ju= gendlichen Alten ruderte ein schönes 19jähriges Mädchen; um 6¾ Uhr fuhren wir weiter. Es war ein herrlicher Abend: die Hitze hatte nachgelassen, die Luft war milde und lieblich; in un= nennbarer Klarheit, wie man sie in Deutschland nicht kennt, wölbte sich der Himmel über uns. Da wir mit dem Strome ruderten, so brauchten wir der Strömungen halber nicht auszu= steigen, sie förderten vielmehr unsere Fahrt; in einer Stunde ward die Meile zurückgelegt. In Granön wurden Erkundigun= gen über einen Rennthierlappen eingezogen, der in der Gegend sich aufhielt und dessen Rennthiere ich zu sehen wünschte. Durch früher ausgesandte Boten erfuhr ich auch, daß seine Hütte nur ¾ M. entfernt liege; aber der Weg dahin war nur ¼ M. Bootweg, und führte dann ½ M. durch Moräste und dichten Wald, durch welchen nicht einmal ein Fußsteig läuft. Rücksichtlich der Ungebahntheit der Wege war zwar der Lappe beordert wor= den, mit einem Rennthiere nach Granön zu kommen, aber die Thiere waren weit von seiner Hütte entfernt gewesen, er war nicht gekommen, und hatte wohl kein Rennthier greifen können. Es blieb also nur übrig, den Lappen nach Tägsnäs zu bestellen; er war aber für diesen weiten und beschwerlichen Weg zu alt und zu schwach, und das Rennthier durch einen jüngeren Schwe= den hinleiten zu lassen, war nicht möglich: Rennthiere, selbst zahme, lassen sich nur durch Lappen, die sie an ihrem eigen=

thümlichen Geruche erkennen, leiten. Nun aber war der alte
Lappe der einzige seines Volkes in der Gegend; und so mußte
ich mich denn begnügen, in Granön einen Rennthierkäse einzukaufen, und Lappland und dessen Gränze verlassen, ohne ein
Rennthier gesehen zu haben. Einige Wochen später, sah ich in
Jemtelands-Lappmark die Rennthiere in desto größerer Zahl. —
Wir waren in Granön aufgehalten worden, und erst um 11½ Uhr,
als es noch völlig hell war, landeten wir in Tågsnäs, wo wir diesmal in einem andern Bauerhofe, als bei der Aufreise, Quartier
nahmen. Der Bruder unserer Ruderin diente in dem Hofe, wo
wir übernachten wollten, sie eilte, ihn zu rufen; alles war schon
zu Bette; aber schnell war Johannes da, und half der lieben
Schwester im Auftragen der Sachen.

Alles ist jetzt auf der Heuerndte, zumal die Männer, von
denen in dem großen Dorfe Granön nur ein Paar daheim waren. Die Wiesen sind zum Theil mehrere Meilen entfernt.

In unserm Nachtquartier war alles recht nett und reinlich; nachdem ein treffliches Mahl, wobei auch buttergebackene
kleine Kuchen nicht fehlten, eingenommen war, begaben wir uns
zur Ruhe. Am nächsten Morgen luden wir unsere Wirthin,
Pehrssons mor (Pehrssons — so hieß der Mann — Mutter —
Mutter nennt man in diesen Gegenden alle verheirathete Frauen,
zumal Bäuerinnen, ohne Rücksicht, ob sie Kinder haben oder
nicht), zum Kaffee ein, was sie sehr dankbar annahm; dann mußten wir Reißsuppe, Eyer ꝛc. als Frühstück speisen, und, als nun
nicht daran zu denken war, eine Bezahlung in Geld aufzubrin-
gen, suchte ich durch ein Geschenk an Kaffee, der in diesen Gegenden selten und theuer ist, mich dankbar zu beweisen. Pehrsson, der eine Einbuße von mehr denn einem halben Tausend Bankthalern gethan, war noch immer ein sehr wohlhabender Bauer;
silberne Geräthe fand man in Menge in seinem Hause.

Am 25. Jul. Von Tågsnäs nach Degerfors 2½ Melle.

In Tågsnäs endete die Bootfahrt, der übrige Weg nach
Degerfors ward zu Pferde gemacht. Um 8½ Uhr ritten wir ab.

In Sundling's Sennhütte sprachen wir vor und ließen die Tochter von den Wiesen rufen. Bald war sie da und erquickte uns mit köstlicher Milch; ein tüchtiges Mädchen, voll Lust und Kraft zur Arbeit, und doch mit großer Feinheit im Benehmen, wie man es in einer Sennhütte nicht erwartet. Nach einer Viertelstunde ritten wir weiter. Auf den Steinfeldern, über welche nun der enge Waldpfad führt, ragen auch ziemlich hohe Felsenwände hervor, über deren niedere Absätze man hinweg muß; mein Pferd hatte eine unersättliche Begierde nach Grashalmen und jungen Birkenzweigen; ich ließ es im Gehen fressen nach Herzenslust, ahndete keine Gefahr, da es des Weges sehr kundig und gewohnt war, und achtete mehr auf die schönen Aussichten in Thäler und auf von Bächen bewässerte Gründe, als auf den Weg. Ehe ich es bemerkte, war das Pferd, von einem niederen Felsenabsatz aus, eine schroffe Felsenwand hinangeklettert, an deren glattem schmalem Rande, in der Nähe von Abgründen, es nun einherging. Mein Schrecken war nicht geringe, denn ein Stolpern hätte das Leben kosten können; aber es war nichts zu thun, als dem Pferde ganz seinen Willen zu lassen und mit Ergebung dem Ausgange entgegen zu sehen. Das edle Roß bewährte sich als ächten Berggänger; behende stieg es die glatte Höhe hinab, und das Abentheuer war glücklich überstanden. Doch ließ ich mir nun den Vorfall zur Lehre dienen und das Pferd durfte nicht mehr nach Belieben sich gegen Zweige und Halme neigen.

Am Ende einer Moorwiese, über welche eine lange Knüppelbrücke führte, sprang eine Zahl gelbgrau gesprenkelter Auerhühner aus dem Gebüsche hervor; die Thiere leben also keinesweges einsam, wie man behauptet hat. Wir waren ohne Feuergewehr, sonst hätten wir unserer Wirthin in Degerfors einige schöne Braten mitbringen können. — In der Nähe des Winsbelelf senkt sich das Land; man reitet aus dem Wald an das Ufer hinab, unter den lieblichsten Aussichten auf den breiten Fluß, seine Wasserfälle, seine Waldschluchten und das hohe jenseitige Ufer, auf welchem sich das große Dorf Degerfors mit seiner hölzernen Kreuzkirche ausbreitet. Ein Boot lag bereit;

balb waren wir am jenseitigen Ufer, klimmten in der brennend-
sten Hitze die Höhe hinan und erreichten um 2 Uhr den Pfarrhof von Degerfors.

Die Hitze war heute so groß, daß man noch am Abend
kaum Kleidung dulden konnte. Bis um 10½ Uhr blieb ich daheim; als es nun etwas kühler zu werden anfing, ging ich hinaus, die Umgebungen und das Innere der freundlichen Kirche
zu beschauen, wozu es noch immer hell genug war. Sie liegt
auf einer Höhe zwischen zwei Schluchten; die Gewölbe sollen
das Predigen erschweren. Rings umher läuft der Kirchhof, dessen Gräber aber weder Kreuze noch Steine bezeichnen. Zur
Aufnahme der Leichen im Winter gräbt man, ehe die Erde gefroren ist, Ein großes Grab, um das Graben mehrerer Gräber
in der harten Erde zu sparen.

In der Nacht ward ich von Wanzen geplagt; ich flüchtete
in ein Nebengebäude, aber auch hier fand ich keine Ruhe. Dem
Fremden spielen gewöhnlich diese bösen Thiere arg mit; sie
schwärzen sich mit dem Moose ein, welches man in den hölzernen Häusern Westerbottens zur Ausstopfung der Fugen zwischen
den Balken gebraucht, ohne diese Fugen mit Papier und dergl.
zu überkleben; ihren Wanderungen steht nun also nichts im
Wege; wo die Fugen mit Papier überklebt werden, wird man
nicht durch Wanzen belästiget. Am reichsten ist das Moos an
diesen Bewohnern, wenn es zu gewissen Jahreszeiten und unter
Wacholderbüschen gesammelt wird.

———

Am 26. Jul. Von Degerfors nach Neder-Röda 1¼¼ M.;
von R. nach Tafvelsjön 1 M.; von T. nach Hissjön 1¼ M.;
von H. nach Umeå Landkirche 1½ M.; von U. nach Brattby 1¼ M. — Zusammen 6¼¼ Meile.

Nach herzlichem Danke fuhr ich um 8 Uhr Morgens ab;
der 80jährige Propst begleitete mich bis Umeå, wo er seine verheirathete Tochter besuchen wollte. Der Weg war derselbe, auf
welchem ich gekommen war; bei Hissjö begegneten wir ter liebenswürdigen Gattin des Magister Saedenius, meines gefäl-

ligen Begleiters auf der Reise nach Lyckſele, die von Umeå's Geſundbrunnen zurückkehrte. Der alte Propſt bewies auf der Reiſe eine unerſchöpfliche Heiterkeit und Lebendigkeit; raſch und lebendig ſtieg er die ſteilſten Berge hinan, wie ein Jüngling, und zeigte große Unerſchrockenheit, als der Sturz des Pferdes gefähr= lich zu werden ſchien. Nachmittags 5½ Uhr langten wir im Pfarrhofe von Umeå an, wo der Doctor Hambraeus uns herzlich bewillkommte.

Nach eingenommenem Vesperbrot, wobei ich zum erſten Mal in dieſem Jahre auch reiſe Walderdbeeren aß, ſetzte ich um 6½ Uhr Abends die Reiſe bis Brattby fort; es war nämlich meine Abſicht am nächſten Sonntag=Morgen dem Dorfgottesdienſt in Wånnås beizuwohnen. Der Comminiſter Stenberg hatte die Gefälligkeit, mich zu begleiten. Der Weg bis Brattby beträgt nur 1½ Meile, iſt aber ſo bergig und ausgefahren, daß wir erſt um 10½ Uhr anlangten. Man erblickt viele fruchtbare Felder und üppige Wieſen. Die hohen Ufer des nicht fernen Umeåfluſſes ſind überall mit Dörfern bedeckt, welche, zum Theil eine Viertel= meile lang, liebliche Haine, Getreidefelder und Wieſen ſondern; die Lage der Dörfer auf Höhen oder in Niederungen iſt ſchön; nicht ſelten zeigen ſich maleriſche Uferſchluchten. Der Fluß bil= det faſt unaufhörlich Waſſerfälle und Strömungen, der eine dieſer Fälle unterhalb Norrfors iſt faſt eine Meile lang; lang und tief iſt auch der Fors bei Norrfors ſelbſt. Man fährt durch mehrere enge, reizende Thäler; die Heuerndte hatte begonnen und die Wieſen dufteten herrlich in der milden Abendluft. Bei Söder= fors, am jenſeitigen Ufer, erblickt man die Trümmer einer Brücke, welche im letzten Kriege zerſtört wurde. Der heftigen Strömun= gen halber, war es im Sommer unmöglich die Brücke wieder= herzuſtellen; die Ruſſen konnten hier alſo kein Geſchütz überfüh= ren, und mußten lange bauen, bis die Brücke bei Umeå, wo das Waſſer ſtiller iſt, vollendet wurde; ein Umſtand, welcher das Vordringen der Ruſſiſchen Armee ſehr erſchwerte und die niedern Provinzen Norrlands vor einer Invaſion ſicherte. — Auf dem Wege nach Brattby, wo wir in einem Bauerhofe übernachteten, beſtätigte ſich es mir, daß, wo das Land bergig und ſteinig iſt,

die Luft milder und wärmer, wo aber niedrige Wiesen und Sümpfe
sich in der Nähe befinden, die Luft empfindlich kalt ist; eine Erfahrung, die ich späterhin oft an Morgen und Abenden machte.

Am 27. Jul. Von Brattby nach Wännäs ⅓ M.; von M.
nach Ryby ⅓ M.; von M. nach Pengafors ⅓ M.; von P.
nach Fällfors ⅓ M.; von F. zurück nach Pengafors ⅓ M.;
von P. nach Wännäs ⅓ M. — Zus. 3⅓ M.

Nach Wännäs führt, seit kurzem, von Brattby aus ein Fahrweg, der aber sehr schlecht ist; auch fehlt noch eine 5te Brücke
über einen Bach, den man jetzt umfahren muß; der Weg läuft
bis ans Ufer des Windelelf, über welchem zuletzt eine Fähre
führt. Wir wählten den leichteren Flußweg, der eine halbe
Meile beträgt. Auf dem kurzen Wege aus dem Dorf zum
Boote kommt man einer Anzahl von Schuppen vorüber, in welchen die entfernter wohnenden Bauern, die ihre Kirchreisen nach
Umeå, bis Brattby zu Wasser, machen, ihre Kirchkärror stehen
haben.

Eine gar angenehme Wasserreise ist die Bootfahrt nach
Wännäs: hohe Waldberge steigen aus dem Flusse empor; den
Vordergrund füllen die üppigsten Kornfelder und Wiesen mit
Heuscheunen und Gebüschen; dazwischen Dörfer und einzelne
Höfe, die meisten in höchst malerischer Lage. Der Fluß macht
mehrere hübsche Krümmungen. Nur die Burgruinen fehlen, um
an die Ufer des Rheins und der Donau zu erinnern; auch ist
der Umeå meistens breiter als jene Ströme. Eine halbe Viertelmeile unterhalb Wännäs fällt der Windel in den Umeå, dessen
Namen er nun annimmt; beide Flüsse bilden hier einen Busen;
die Stelle hat viel Aehnlichkeit mit der Elbe bei Dessau, wo sie
die Mulde aufnimmt. Bald gelangt man auf dem Umeå
neben lieblichen Wiesen- und Buschufern nach Wännäs. Die
Lage von Wännäs ist sehr angenehm: gegenüber erheben sich ein
Paar Waldberge, an welchen Wiesen und Wohnungen hinauf-
steigen.

Nicht lange nach unserer Ankunft begann der Gottesdienst,
der in einem Bauerhofe gehalten ward; das Versammlungszim-

mer war gescheuert und mit Riedgras (Carex) ausgestreuet.
Wiewohl von den 22 Familien des Dorfs 11 gegenwärtig in
den Sennhütten wohnten, von wo aus sie die Heuerndte auf
den fernen Wiesen beschaffen, und wo sie am Sonntage sich
gleichfalls durch gemeinschaftliches Postillenlesen erbauen, auch
einige aus dem Dorfe nach Umeå zur Kirche gereiset waren, so
bestand die Versammlung doch aus etwa 25 Männern und eben
so viel Frauenzimmern; alle waren sehr einfach gekleidet, meist
in selbstgewebten Kleidern; nur eines der Mädchen, die Tochter
eines Länsman in Bygdeå, war mit seidenem Tuch und schwarz
seidenem Hut geschmückt. Viele Männer und Weiber trugen
Sträuße.' — Als ich eintrat, waren schon die meisten versammelt; man saß still und andächtig da, kein Wort ward gewechselt; die Kommenden verrichteten, ganz wie in der Kirche, ein
stilles Gebet. Die Geschlechter saßen getrennt. An der einen
Seite des Zimmers stand ein großer Tisch mit dem Vorlesepult,
mit Postillen und Gesangbüchern; denn viele lassen ihre Gesangbücher hier zurück, weil jeder Hof mehrere Exemplare besitzt;
jeder Einzelne hat ein Gesangbuch und jede Familie eine Bibel.
An dem großen Tische hatte der Vorleser seinen Platz.

Der Gottesdienst begann mit einem Gesange, den der Vorleser nannte. Nach Beendigung desselben knieten alle; der Vorleser, in seiner einfachen Bauerkleidung, las die Altargebete der
alten Liturgie (aus dem Evangelienbuch): das Morgengebet, das
Sündenbekenntniß; leise sprach man die Worte nach. Dann
erhob man sich, ein zweiter Gesang ward angestimmt, es war
ein Lob- und Danklied an die heilige Dreieinigkeit, weshalb die
Gemeinde während des Gesanges stand. Nach geendigtem Gesange setzte man sich, der Vorleser sprach ein kurzes Gebet, dann
folgten die Epistel und das Glaubensbekenntniß, während die
Gemeinde stand. Nachdem der Kanzelvers gesungen worden, begann die Vorlesung einer Predigt über das Evangelium des Tages, aus Ekmanssons Postille; während der Vorlesung des Textes erhob sich die Gemeinde. Nach der Predigt folgten ein Gebet, ein gemeinschaftlicher Gesang, die gewöhnlichen Kanzelgebete
für König und Vaterland, Kranke ꝛc., das Vaterunser; endlich

schloß der Vorleser mit Sprechung des kirchlichen Segens: der Herr segne uns 2c. Während der Gebete und des Segens kniete die Gemeinde. Nach einem abermaligen Gesange und stillem Gebete ging man auseinander. Der Gottesdienst hatte etwa 1½ Stunde gedauert; großer Ernst und Andacht herrschte.

Als man scheiden wollte, nahm der Comminister das Wort, äußerte seine Freude über das christliche Beisammenseyn und lobte den Vorleser, dessen deutliches, langsames und richtiges Lesen er den Eltern zur Nachahmung im Unterricht ihrer Kinder empfahl; mit Bescheidenheit lehnte der Vorleser das Lob ab. — Auch ein Kind bemerkte ich in der Versammlung, still saß es da. Es ist überhaupt in Schweden, zumal im nördlichen, nichts Seltenes, auch kleinere Kinder in der Kirche zu erblicken; so gewöhnt man sie schon frühe an Ehrfurcht vor dem Heiligen. — Kein einziger verließ das Versammlungszimmer, bevor der Gottesdienst völlig geendiget war. — Zwei der versammelten Männer ruderten uns am Nachmittag; ihr stilles freudiges Wesen athmete ganz den Geist einer ächten Sonntagsfeier, wie man nothwendig seyn muß, wenn man mit wahrer Andacht seinen Gottesdienst begangen hat. In den Höfen waren nur so viele zurückgeblieben, als uns umgänglich nöthig waren. Der Vorleser hatte jetzt schon seit drei Jahren sein Amt verwaltet; er wählt die Gesänge, die sonntäglich wechseln, nur der Kanzelvers ist oft derselbe. Geht der Vorleser zur Kirche, so tritt ein anderer Bauer an seine Stelle. Heute waren nur 3 oder 4 Dorfbewohner zur Kirche gereiset; im Winter besucht man die Kirche sehr oft. Früherhin versammelte man sich in Wännäs, auch am Nachmittage des Sonntages, zum Postillenlesen; aber nach dem Tode eines frommen Schulmeisters hörte solches auf.

Vor kurzem haben die Bewohner von Wännäs, aus eigenem Triebe, beschlossen, im Dorfe eine Kirche zu bauen; auch andere Dörfer hatten sie zur Theilnahme bewogen. Im Frühling 1817 war etwa in der Mitte des Dorfes der Bau begonnen worden und schon sehr fortgeschritten; die Kirche wird aus Holz gebauet, 59 Ellen lang und 21 Ellen breit.

Von Wännäs begaben wir uns zum Fällfors, einem der
merkwürdigsten Wasserfälle in ganz Schweden. Der nächste Weg
dahin führt über die nach Wännäs gehörigen Sennhütten, wo
man im Sommer das Vieh unter Aufsicht von Milchmädchen
trifft, zur Zeit der Heuernöte aber, 4 bis 5 Wochen lang, ganze
Familien wohnen; bei den Sennhütten hat man auch zwei Wassermühlen und eine feinblätterige Sägemühle angelegt. Dieser
Weg über die Sennhütten würde interessant gewesen seyn, da
er aber nur Reitweg ist, so wählte ich, der Hitze wegen, die
Bootfahrt über Nyby, wohin von Wännäs aus auch ein gleich
weiter Fahrweg führt. Die Wasserfahrt bis Nyby beträgt eine
halbe Meile, ist aber, mehrerer kleinen Strömungen halber, beschwerlich; die Ufer sind hier weniger bewohnt, nur Ein Nybygge, Trinliden (liden bezeichnet einen steinigen langen Waldberg)
zeigt sich; doch hier und da breiten sich an den Ufern bunte Wiesen-
teppiche aus, auf denen man auch Heuscheunen erblickt; den Hintergrund bilden Waldberge; aus Waldschluchten rieseln Bäche
hervor, die mit weiten Mündungen in den Umeå fallen; der
Wald ist gemischter Laub- und Nadelwald; die Ufer sind niedriger als unterhalb Wännäs; an vielen Stellen ist der Fluß mit
herabgestürzten Bäumen ausgefüllt. Das Dorf Nyby hatte im
vorigen Sommer sechs Höfe durch Brand verloren; das Feuer
soll beim Branntweinbrennen ausgekommen seyn. Als die Einwohner von der fernen Heuernöte zurückkehrten, waren sie ohne
Obdach; nur einige abwärts gelegene Höfe waren verschont geblieben. Schon war man mit dem Wiederaufbau beschäftiget,
und ziemlich weit vorgerückt; denn im Pastorat Umeå ist es üblich, daß bei Feuersbrünsten der Werth des abgebrannten Hauses
und des eingebüßten Eigenthums amtlich geschätzt und vom Kirchspiel erstattet wird; diese schon durch das Schwedische Gesetz
begründete Sitte (Byggninga Balk cap. 24) wird besonders in
Norrland strenge befolgt; entsteht der Schade durch Schuld Einzelner, so sollen diese, und falls sie unvermögend sind, die Gemeinde den Ersatz leisten.

In Nyby mietheten wir ein Pferd, welches zu Lande nach
Pengafors abgehen und vor die Kärra des dortigen Nybyggare

gespannt werden sollte; dann setzten wir die Wasserfahrt bis zum Nybygge fort, da der Landweg von Nyby nach Pengafors ein schlechter Reitweg ist, der über hohe Berge und durch tiefe Thäler führt. Die Ufer sind hoch, waldig und unbewohnt; der Bach Penga fällt in den Umeå; er giebt ohne Zweifel dem Nybygge den Namen. Der Bootweg beträgt ¼ Meile. Beim Nybygge, welches sehr hoch, von Wald und fruchtbaren Kornfeldern umgeben, da liegt, wendet sich der Fluß; sein Bette, bisher ein weiter Busen, verengt sich, und der Fluß bildet bedeutende Wasserfälle. In Pengafors endet der Bootweg, der uns heute immer längs Ufern geführt hatte, an welchen die Strömungen weniger hindernd und gefährlich sind.

Von Pengafors an hat man Wald-, doch ziemlich guten Fahrweg ⅞ Meile.

Eine Menge Bäume faulten am Wege, während schon junge neben denselben emporwuchsen. Mehrere Kolonistenhöfe liegen im Walde zerstreut. Bei Fällforsselät, einem dieser Nybyggen, machten wir Halt; der Nybyggare, Johann Nilsson, der vor nicht langer Zeit seine Frau verloren hatte, und den wir im einsamen Kämmerchen die Bibel lesen fanden, empfing uns mit Freundlichkeit; dann geleitete er uns ans Ufer des Umeå, der hier wieder nahe ist, und ruderte uns hinüber zu einem, dem Fällfors benachbarten, Ufer. Der mächtige Wasserfall, den hier der Umeå bildet, war jetzt, da der Wind abstand, kaum ¼ Meile weit hörbar; bei günstigem Winde hört man ihn in einer Entfernung von 2 bis 4 Meilen; ja noch zu Orträsk in Lappland, 5 Meilen von hier, soll er hörbar seyn. Von der Landungsstelle gingen wir durch den Wald zum Fällfors, dessen Wassermasse unter furchtbarem Krachen über nackte Felsen hinabstürzt. In der Mitte des Gesammtfalles erhebt sich eine hohe Felsenwand, über und neben welcher der Strom sich sein Bette bricht. Der ansehnlichste Fall ist der östliche: von Westen nach Norden, aus unergründlicher Tiefe wirbeln dichte Staubwolken gen Himmel; die Wassermasse ist so groß, daß ihr selbst die des Rheinfalls bei Schaffhausen nicht gleich kommt; der 2te Fall, an der westlichen Seite, von Osten nach Süden, hat weniger Wasser, fällt minder tief, sendet aber auch mächtige Staubwolken empor. Zum 3ten und letzten Fall arbeiteten wir uns mühsam durch den Wald hindurch, zum Theil mußten wir erst den Weg bahnen; er ist weniger bedeutend als der östliche Fall: eine mit Nadelholz bewachsene kleine Felseninsel gewährt einen freundlichen Anblick. — Beim Rückwege vom dritten Fall trafen wir einen Fußpfad. Noch einmal ging ich zu den beiden andern Fällen; da entdeckte ich eine Landzunge, die zur Uebersicht dieser Fälle besonders vortheilhaft gelegen schien; über Felsenstücke gelangte ich mit vieler Beschwerde dahin, ward aber herrlich belohnt, der östliche niedere Fall zeigte sich hier in seiner wahren Beschaffenheit: von einer schrägen Felsenwand stürzt die ungeheure Wassermasse in die Tiefe hinab, aus welcher sie, in dichte Staubwolken aufgelöset, wieder aufwärts steigt; mitten in diese Staubwolken hinein stürzt seitwärts aus einer Felsenecke ein anderer mächtiger Wasserstrahl, drängt sie zurück und stürzt sich mit ihnen weiter in die Länge fort.

Von der Landzunge aus erstieg ich den nahen Waldberg, und folgte dann einem Fußpfade, der am Rande desselben hinführt. Hier ist der schönste Standpunkt: man überschauet den zweiten Fall nebst dem untersten oder dritten Fall, welcher sich in zwei Fälle theilt, in einer Ausdehnung von etwa 200 Klaftern, wovon der dritte Fall etwa 130 Klaftern einnimmt. Wer hier steht, der müßte ein Herz von Stein haben, wenn ihn nicht ergreifen sollten die Gefühle der Ehrfurcht und Demuth und er nicht staunend hinsänke in den Staub, anbetend vor Dem, aus dessen Hand „der Thau der Morgenröthe, wie diese Katarakte quoll."

Am Ende des Fällfors erblickt man ein liebliches Waldufer, an welches sich eine schöne Wiese mit ein Paar Heuscheunen herabzieht. Nicht selten sind in dieser Gegend an den Abseiten der Uferberge längliche Plätze ausgehauen, diese werden als Wiesen benutzt und nehmen sich, vom Flusse aus, mitten im Walde sehr hübsch aus.

Es war 7½ Uhr, als wir nach Fällforsselet zurückkehrten. Fällforsselet, Fällforsliden und Fällforssjö, letzteres mit 4 Höfen, bilden das Dorf Fällfors, wohin auch von Dägerfors aus ein

Weg führt; dieser Weg beträgt nur 3 Meilen, aber blos die letzte Meile von Ramfele bis Fällfors ist guter Reitweg, das übrige Gehweg über Mordäste. Am zugänglichsten ist Fällfors von Umeå und Wännäs aus. Das Nybygge Nygård liegt dem Wasserfall am nächsten.

Von Fällforsselet fuhren wir wieder nach Pengafors, hielten dort unsere Abendmahlzeit und traten dann nach 10 Uhr in milder Abendluft zu Boot die Rückreise nach Wännäs an, wo wir um 11¾ Uhr anlangten und übernachteten *).

———

Am 28. Jul. Von Wännäs nach Brattby ¼ M.; von B. nach Umeå Landkirche 1¾ M. — Zus. 2 M.

Der Rückweg von Wännäs war derselbe, auf welchem wir gekommen waren; von Brattby aus fuhren wir wieder zu Lande, nahmen aber diesmal die schönen Wasserfälle des Umeå zwischen Brattby und Umeå in Augenschein, die aber freilich mit dem Fällfors nicht verglichen werden können.

Nachdem ich in Umeå's Pfarrhause ein Paar genußreiche Tage verlebt, nahm ich am 30. Morgens von den lieben Bewohnern, deren dankbares Gedächtniß mir theuer ist, Abschied und trat die Rückreise an.

Bis zur Stadt Umeå begleiteten mich der alte Propst Saebenius und der Adjunct Fall, ein von Liebe für sein Amt begeisterter junger Mann. Um 8 Uhr war ich in der Stadt, machte einige Besuche, sah Kirche, Schule und andere Merkwürdigkeiten, und wollte dann um Mittag weiter reisen. Aber der Rector Häggvist, welcher eben von einer Reise zurückgekehrt war, und seine liebe Frau, ein Fräulein Modée, auf der Insel Rügen geboren, baten so dringend, bei ihnen einen Tag zu bleiben, daß ich wenigstens um einige Stunden die Reise verschob.

———

*) Die Sprache in diesen Gegenden hat etwas Eigenthümliches: der Artikel, den der Schwede, wenn er bestimmt reden will, dem Worte anhängt, wird hier dem Worte vorangestellt, z. B. spricht man statt bonden, der Bauer, en bonde; statt flickan, das Mädchen, a flicka.

Endlich, nach einem frohen Mittagsmahle erfolgte die Abreise um 4 Uhr Nachmittags. Nach herzlichem Abschiede am Ufer des Umeå bestieg ich das Boot, in wenigen Minuten war ich jenseits, wo der Wagen schon bereit stand, und fuhr unter wehmüthigen Gefühlen, im Angesicht eines doppelten Regenbogens, immer näher und näher an die Gränze der Provinz Westerbotten, in welcher ich so viele glückliche Stunden verlebt hatte und so viele biedere Menschen meinem Herzen theuer geworden waren.

———

Am 30. Jul. Von Umeå Landkirche nach Umeå Stadt ½ M.; von U. Stadt nach Stöckfjö ½ M.; von St. nach Sörmjöle 1½ M.; von S. nach Angersjö 1½ M. — Zus. 4½ Meilen.

Mein Weg bis Angersjö war der nämliche, den ich vor 6 Wochen bei der Aufreise gemacht hatte. In Hörnefors besichtigte ich die hübsche Brukskirche, von wo bis Angersjö der Weg meist durch Birkenwald führt. Um 10½ Uhr hatte ich die fast 6½ deutschen Meilen bis Angersjö zurückgelegt, wo ich in einem netten und billigen Gasthofe übernachtete; der Gästgifvaregård wechselt hier unter den Bauern. Vor Angersjö erreicht man das Pastorat Nortmaling, welches früherhin zu Ångermanland gerechnet wurde, jetzt zu Westerbotten gehört. Angersjö, ein Dorf mit 8 Bauern und 3 Torpare, liegt auf einem kahlen niedrigen Bergrücken, dessen Fuß theils der große Angersee bespült, theils fruchtbare Felder bedecken.

———

Am 31. Jul. Von Angersjö nach Lefvar 1½ M.; von L. nach Afva 1½ M.; von A. nach Onsla 2 M.; von O. nach Täfre 1½ M. — Zus. 6½ M.

Ich fuhr Lefvar vorüber und bestellte das Pferd nach dem ½ Meile von da entlegenen Pfarrhofe von Nortmaling, wo ich einen Besuch versprochen hatte, auch die Schule besichtigen wollte. Nortmaling ist das letzte Pastorat in Westerbotten; die Einwohner, im Jahr 1815, 2508, leben hauptsächlich vom Theerbrennen, vom Brettersägen, von Fischerey und Viehzucht; letztere

II.   Dd ist sehr bedeutend, auch viele Ziegen werden gehalten. Salpeter wird mehr bereitet als im ganzen übrigen Westerbotten und in ganz Ängermanland zusammen; im Jahr 1816 waren 300 Liespfund (à 20 Pfund) Salpeter verkauft worden, und im Jahr 1817 sollte die Bereitung noch viel höher steigen; die Kunst, in Scheunen Salpeter zu gewinnen, ist von Finnland nach Schweden verpflanzt worden. Die Norrmalinger stehen zwischen den Westerbottniern und Ängermanländern mitten inne; doch nähern sie sich in Sitten mehr den ersteren.

Norrmaling hat, wie wenige Norrländische Pastorate, eine feste Kirchspielsschule. Diese wurde durch das Vermächtniß des Gürtelmachers Jonas Malmberg und dessen Ehefrau Brita Christina Wetterström von 1500 Rthlrn. im Jahr 1796 gestiftet. Im Jahr 1800 nahm die Schule ihren Anfang, im Jahr 1816 waren in derselben 32 Kinder unterwiesen worden. Die Unterrichtsgegenstände sind: Lesen (auch nach lateinischen Buchstaben), Christenthum, Schreiben und Rechnen. Das Kapital, von dessen Zinsen der Schulmeister den Gehalt bezieht, steht unter Verwaltung des Pastors und der beiden Kirchenvorsteher; zum Schulhause hat bisher der Comminister Klockhoff, der auch dem Schullehreramt vorsteht, seine Wohnung eingeräumt. 6 Stunden täglich wird unterrichtet; doch sind auch hier die großen Ferien üblich: die Unterrichtszeit dauert nur 7 Monate, vom 1. Oct. bis 14. Dec., und vom 2. Febr. bis 14. Junius. Die Zahl der schulfähigen Kinder in Norrmaling ist viel größer, als die Zahl der wirklichen Schulkinder; die übrigen werden aber, nach Norrländischer Weise, durch die Eltern und einen ambulatorischen Schullehrer zweckmäßig unterwiesen.

Das Pastorat hatte bisher zwei Kirchen; die eine, Bjurholm, im Jahr 1807 erbaut, war Kapelle; da sie aber von der Mutterkirche 5 volle Meilen entfernt lag, so ward sie im Jahr 1815 in eine Mutterkirche verwandelt und erhielt als solche einen eigenen Pastor. Noch gab es nach Bjurholm keinen Fahrweg, der aber jetzt angelegt werden sollte. Das neue Pastorat ist nur klein; die Zahl der Gebornen war im Jahr 1815 in Bjurholm 48, während sie in Norrmaling 117 betrug (unter den 117 Ge burten waren in Norrmaling im Jahr 1815. 5, im Jahr 1816 unter 116 aber nur 1 uneheliche Geburt). Das heilige Abends mahl wird in Norrmaling gewöhnlich 12 Mal im Jahre gehalten; da beträgt die Zahl der Communicanten 40 bis 500. Die Zahl der Todten ist gewöhnlich unter den Einjährigen Kindern besonders groß, weil das Auffüttern derselben sehr üblich ist; in benachbarten Ångermanländischen Gemeinden; z. B. Arnäs, wo jenes Auffüttern selten ist, vielmehr die Mütter ihren Kindern lange die Brust reichen, ist die Sterblichkeit unter 1 und 2jährigen Kindern ziemlich geringe.

Um 3½ Uhr Nachmittags verließ ich Norrmalings Pfarrhof. Bald erreicht man das Bruk Olofsfors, und über die Flüsse Lögde und Asp des Häll Afva. Die Brücken dieses Weges sind schlecht, sie bestehen, nach Sitte mehrerer Gegenden Norrlands, aus losen Brettern; auf der einen dieser Brücken ward beim ersten Tritt des Pferdes ein Brett hoch in die Höhe geworfen, und es hätte leicht ein Unglück geschehen können, wäre das Pferd scheu gewesen. Die Brücken bilden einen grellen Contrast gegen die trefflichen Wege. Afva ist der letzte Gästgivaregård in Norrmaling und Westerbotten. Unweit Afva tritt man in das Ångermanländische Pastorat Grundsunda ein. Das Land wird bergiger, aber auch schöner; der Garten Norrlands beginnt. Der Ueberblick von den Höhen auf Seen, enge Thäler, weite Wiesen, Laubhaine, oder das offene Meer ist unbeschreiblich schön. Immer reizender wird die Gegend, seit man die Ufer des Meeres erreicht hat. Man fährt einen hohen und steilen Berg, Stofverhälla, hinan, von dessen Gipfel man weit über Land und Meer hinblickt; einsam am Gestade liegt ein Fischerhäuschen, das zur Aufbewahrung der Geräthschaften benutzt wird. Dann fährt man in ein tiefes Thal hinab, welches von hohen Waldbergen umschlossen wird, und abermals bergauf und bergab und auf Bergrücken, bis ans Ende der Station; rechts steigen nackte oder mit Wald bekränzte Felsen empor, während links sich liebliche Thäler bis an den Fuß anderer Felsen ausbreiten; die Abseiten der Felsen sind mit Höfen bedeckt. Den Rand eines Bergrückens, über welchen die Straße läuft,

Dd 2

faſſen zum Theil natürliche Birkenalleen, von denen Gebüſche ſich
in das Thal ſenken, ein. Am reizendſten erſchienen mir die
Thäler von Fillinge und Gummelſta. Aus letzterem fährt man
wieder Berge hinan, und gelangt ſo zur Kirche Grundſunda, wo
ich eine gute Stunde bei dem (jetzt verſtorbenen) Prepſte Hell-
man verweilte. Die Lage der Kirche iſt herrlich, vom Kirchhof
hat man die anmuthigſten Ausſichten; die Kirche iſt ohne Thurm;
der Glockenthurm, ſo wie die Kirchenbude (kyrkoherberge) für
das Kronzehntekorn, ſteht außerhalb des Kirchhofs. Das Paſtorat hat nur Eine Kirche und zählt 1200 Einwohner.

Um 10½ Uhr verließ ich Grundſunda und langte nach einer
Viertelſtunde in Onſta, dem erſten Gäſtgifvaregård in Angermanland oder Hernöſand's Län, an. Hier beabſichtigte ich zu
übernachten. Als aber auf meinen Wunſch, daß ſogleich das
Bett bereitet werden möge, ſich die Hausfrau wenig bereitwillig
zeigte, forderte ich ein Pferd. Wiewohl noch ein Hällpferd vorhanden ſeyn mußte (man läugnete es zwar, aber das Tagebuch
erwies das Gegentheil), ließ man mich 7 Viertelſtunden warten,
bis, langſam genug, ein Pferd von den Wieſen herbeigeſchafft
war. Als ich die Lüge entdeckte, begann das Ehepaar allerlei
böſe und ſpitzige Reden. Jetzt drohte ich mit einer Klage; da
fing man an, zu ſchmeicheln und bat, daß ich doch übernachten
möge. Der betrunkene Gäſtgifvare bot, was für ihn auf Erden
das Köſtlichſte war, — Branntwein; die hübſche Ehegattin trat
zierlich gekleidet ins Zimmer, brachte Licht, und knüpfte, als ich
entgegnete, daß es des Lichtes nicht bedürfe, allerlei freundliche
Geſpräche an, ich aber blieb ernſt und feſt bei meiner Forderung,
weil mir das Lug- und Trugweſen dieſer Menſchen gleich vom
Anfang an mißfallen hatte. Als ſie nun ſahe, daß weder ihr
ſüßes Auge noch ihre ſüßen Worte Frucht ſchafften, verließ ſie
mit einer feinen Wendung das Zimmer. Jetzt kehrte man zur
Grobheit zurück; der betrunkene Gäſtgifvare, dem das Pferd gehörte, drohte, ſelber zu fahren, wenn ich ins Tagebuch eine Klage einſchreiben würde; und um eines ſolchen Fuhrmanns
überhoben zu ſeyn, unterließ ich die Klage in Onſta. Der Gäſtgifvare, der ſchon manches Reiſenden Unwillen gereizt hatte, ent-

ging aber nichts destoweniger seinem Schicksal; ich schrieb ins Tagebuch zu Tåfra den Vorfall ein, und ließ, da der Monat abgelaufen war, das Buch sofort zum Kronvoigt, Assessor Svedbom zu Dombåck, tragen. Endlich kam das Pferd; der Gästgifvare suchte sich noch weiter zu rächen, indem er dem Knechte verbot, anzuspannen; doch dieser achtete des Gebotes nicht; um 12½ Uhr fuhr ich ab. Der Weg bis Tåfra 1½ Meile ist Bergweg, und konnte, da es ziemlich dunkel war, nur langsam zurückgelegt werden. Bald nach 11 Uhr vermochte man heute nicht mehr ohne Licht zu sehen; aber schon um 2 Uhr war es wieder helle; die Thäler füllte ein dichter Nebel, aus welchem die Berggipfel unumwölkt, wie Inseln aus dem Meere, hervorragten. Mit wehmüthigen Gefühlen fuhr ich Dombåck vorüber, wo die nächtliche Zeit den guten Svedbergs für die bei der Aufreise bewiesene Güte zu danken nicht verstattete.

Um 3 Uhr Morgens war ich in Tåfra. Die freundliche Schwester der Hausfrau bettete sofort, und nach einer halben Stunde war ich im Schlaf. Fast gegen 10 Uhr stand ich auf, trank Kaffee, frühstückte, schrieb ins Tagebuch, und fuhr um 11½ Uhr nach Arnäs ab. Welchen Contrast bildeten doch die lieben Menschen in Tåfra mit denen von Ånska; in ihrer Ruhe gestört, waren sie dennoch unverdrossen und wußten nicht, was sie mir alles zu Gute thun sollten; als ich am nächsten Morgen Nachtlager, Zehrung und Beschwerde bezahlen wollte, war ihre Forderung so geringe, daß ich sie erhöhen mußte, um nur einigermaßen dankbar zu seyn. Solche Menschen, wie in Tåfra, habe ich viel in Norrland gefunden; auch habe ich, öfter als in Tåfra, die Forderung der Gastwirthe erhöhen oder selbst bestimmen müssen; solche Menschen, wie in Ånska, habe ich nirgends weiter gefunden.

———

Am 1. Aug. Von Tåfra nach Pfarrhof Arnäs 1 Meile.

Der Weg bis Arnäs ist ein höchst anmuthiger Bergweg. Unaufhörlich wechseln Berge und Thäler; die Thäler durchfließt ein Fluß, der in steinigem Bette Mühlen treibt, oder begränzt ein stiller See oder umschließen waldbewachsene Felsen, auf den Höhen oder am Abhange derselben erblickt man Höfe und Dörfer in malerischen Lagen. Schon von Täfra an zeigt sich ein Halbkreis hoher, meist runder Felsberge, hier und da mit Wald; bei Arnäs ist man ihnen nahe gekommen und sieht vom südlichen Rande derselben das Dörfchen Strand herabhängen. Um diese Felsen fährt man ins Thal von Arnäs hinein; Felsen umlagern, gleich Mauern, das Thal; am Fuße der Felsen erhebt sich die freundliche weiße, mit Thurm versehene Kirche; an der Südseite, nach Brösta hin, öffnet sich das Thal, indem es sich in die Krümme wendet. Ueberall waren heute die Leute mit der Heuernte beschäftiget und ein lieblicher Duft war über die Wege verbreitet. Um 1 Uhr langte ich in Arnäs an, wo ich von der liebenswürdigen Familie Dalden mit Herzlichkeit empfangen wurde. Ich blieb den Tag und die Nacht; erst am nächsten Vormittag setzte ich, nach wahrhaft frohen Stunden, die Reise fort.

Arnäs ist eines der volkreicheren Pastorate von Angermanland; zugleich, unter dem braven Pastor, eines der unverdorbneren, wenn gleich seit 20 Jahren sich auch hier manches geändert hat; damals war uneheliche Schwangerschaft etwas unerhörtes; jetzt giebt es fast jährlich uneheliche Geburten, wenn gleich unter 131 Geburten sich im Jahr 1816 nur 3 uneheliche befanden; und auch unter den übrigen Müttern nur 4 oder 5 die Strafe unkeuscher Bräute (otidigt sängelag) erlegten. In den letzten 30 Jahren hat sich die Volkszahl um ein Drittel vermehrt. Der Pastor von Arnäs ist gegenwärtig zugleich Propst von Nord-Angermanland; die Propstey (Contract) umfaßt die Pastorate Arnäs mit der Kapelle Gideä, Norrmaling, Bjurholm, Grundsunda, Själawad mit dem Filial Björna, Nätra, Sidensjö mit Skorped's Kapelle, und Anundsjö; ferner die vier Pastorate von Asele-Lappmark (vergl. Kap. 23); außer diesem Lappmark zählte der übrige Theil der Propstey, im Jahr 1815, 15,128 Einwohner, und, im Jahre 1816, 706 Geburten, worunter 21 uneheliche. Von der, insbesondere Nord-Angermanland eigenthümlichen feinen Leinewandsweberey habe ich oben (K. 18) geredet.

Arnås besitzt ein bedeutendes Kirchspiels-Kornmagazin, welches, durch Einschüsse der Bauern gegründet, jetzt durch sich selbst
besteht, so daß die Einschüsse schon zurückgenommen werden
konnten; aus dem Magazin wird Korn verliehen, gegen 12½
Procent Zinsen in Korn; der Pastor ist Vorsteher des Maga-
zins, als einer mit dem Armenwesen und namentlich der Vor-
beugung des Verarmens nahe zusammenhängenden Einrichtung;
mit Bewilligung der Gemeinde wird auch der Unterricht armer
Kinder durch Magazinkorn bezahlt. Ein Armenhaus besteht, neben der Kirche; es faßt etwa 8 Personen, die übrigen werden
auf den Höfen, nach einer Reihenfolge verpflegt, oder man führt
ihnen, wenn sie nicht mehr ihre Wohnung verlassen können, ihre
Bedürfnisse zu. — Kraft eines freiwilligen Vereines unterstützen
die Kirchspielsbewohner einander bei größeren Ausgaben, z. B.
bei Hochzeiten, Bauten, Feuersbrünsten ꝛc., durch Geld und andere Leistungen.

———

Um 2. Aug. Von Arnås Pfarrhof nach Brösta ¾ M.; von
B. nach Hörnås 1½ M.; von H. nach Mo 1,⅛ M.; von M.
nach Anundsjö ungefähr 1½ M. — Zus. an 3½ M.

Um 10½ Uhr fuhr ich ab. Auf dem kurzen Wege nach
Brösta überschauet man die reizende Lage des Thals von Arnås.
In Brösta ließ ich mir die große silberne Kanne zeigen, welche
die Mutter der gegenwärtigen Gästgiverska für die Bereitung
von Prämienleinewand, nebst einer Medaille mit König Adolph
Friedrichs Bilde 1756 zum Geschenk erhielt; ich habe über
diese Prämienvertheilung Kap. 18 ausführlicher geredet.

Anmuthig ist der Weg von Brösta nach Hörnås; zu dem
schönsten Stellen gehören die Gegend des Dorfes Högland, zwischen dessen Höfen ein hübscher Mühlenbach rinnt, und die Umgebungen des Dorfes Ljungänger, welches sich auf einer Höhe
an einem großen Meerbusen hinzieht; rings umher sind Waldberge. Själawads Kirche und Pfarrhof vorüber, erreicht man
Hörnås. Själawad treibt viel Weberey, aber auch viel Handel;
man zählt hier 50 Handelsbauern, welche theils mit Leder, Fel-

len, Talg, theils mit Pferden, die sie aus Norwegen holen, auf=
füttern, und dann in Stockholm 2c. verkaufen, Handel treiben;
auch in den umliegenden Kirchspielen giebt es viele Handels=
bauern, doch nirgends so viele als in Själawad; in Anundsjö
findet man nur einen einzigen.

Der Weg von Hörnås nach Mo führt rechts ab von der
großen Landstraße; er ist Kirchspielsweg nach Anundsjö, aber
ziemlich gut unterhalten und mit Gästgifvaregårdar versehen, die
freilich viel schlechter sind, als die an der großen Straße. Man
fährt längs des Wasserzuges, der von Anundsjö herabkommt und
oft einem See oder Meerbusen gleicht, endlich ein Paar Meilen
unterhalb der Kirche Själawad, nachdem er bereits früher den
Namen Meerbusen angenommen, ins Meer fällt; dieser Wasser=
zug führt von den Kirchspielen und Ortschaften, die er berührt,
mehrere Namen. Die Ufer sind sehr malerisch: Wiesen, Ge=
büsche und fruchtbare Felder wechseln mit zahlreichen Dörfern
und einzelnen Höfen. Dann verengt sich der Wasserzug, die
Ufer werden höher; auf Uferhöhen läuft nun der Weg, bis man,
nach ⅓ Meile, Mo erreicht. Zwischen Hörnås und Mo fährt
man durch eine Reihe von Dörfern.

Mo, an Wiesen und jenem Gewässer hoch und freundlich
gelegen, besteht aus einem Dorfe und dem Hofe des Oberjäger=
meister Nyberg, einer Sägemühle tief unten im Thale und
daneben dem Gästgifvaregård, einem der schlechtesten in ganz
Schweden; alles wimmelte dermaaßen von Wanzen, daß man sich
nicht einmal setzen konnte, ohne sogleich mit diesen Thieren über=
deckt zu seyn; das Tagebuch mußte ich vor die Thüre bringen
lassen, um einschreiben zu können, welches aber freilich auch nur
nach gehöriger Lüftung und Reinigung zu bewerkstelligen war;
fast wie an einem Pestorte; ein Fremdenzimmer war nicht vor=
handen. Hier mußte ich zwei volle Stunden auf ein Pferd
warten, wiewohl ich zum Hofe des Herrn Nyberg hinaufschick=
te, der eigentlich Gästgifvare ist; wahrlich kein beneidenswerther
Aufenthalt; mittlerweile besah ich die Sägemühle. Endlich kam
das Pferd, aber schon nach ⅓ Meile Weges war es völlig ermü=
det und ich mußte es in Ytterselet wechseln.

Man fährt den steilen Berg hinan, Herrn Nyberg's Hofe, welchen Gärten und Baumpflanzungen umgeben, vorüber, durch das Dorf, von wo man in ein weites, wiesenreiches Bergsthal hinabblickt, in den Wald. Im Walde läuft die Straße steile Berge auf und ab; aber zu den Seiten hat man immer die fettesten Wiesen, freundliche Gebüsche und von den Höhen schöne Bergprospecte. Man erreicht das Ufer des von Anundsjö herabkommenden Wasserzuges, der hier sehr schmal ist, entfernt sich von demselben, kehrt zurück und fährt auf einer Brücke an das jenseitige Ufer, welches mit seinen Wiesen und Gebüschen recht freundlich da liegt. Bald ist man im Dorfe Yttersele, dem ersten im Pastorat Anundsjö, wo ich schon die im Pastorat allgemein üblichen Flechtschuhe aus Birkenrinde fand, die zwar nicht wasserdicht, aber sehr warm sind; auf Wiesen trägt man in diesen Schuhen Heu. Im Walde zwischen Mo und Yttersele war ein Theil des Weges verlegt worden; da fuhr ich eine Strecke auf der neuen Straße, über welcher Moos und Blaubeerenkraut eine weiche Decke bildeten; zur Seite lagen die abgehauenen schönen Bäume, die vielleicht noch manches Jahr da liegen mögen, da der Transport mehr kostet, als das Holz selbst in diesen holzreichen Gegenden werth ist.

Auch von Yttersele bis zur Kirche Anundsjö ist der Weg sehr bergig; doch sind die Berge weniger hoch und lang, wie zwischen Mo und Yttersele. Man hat die lieblichsten und mannigfaltigsten Aussichten, besonders nachdem man den Saum des weiten und schönen Thales erreicht hat, in welchem die Kirche auf einem kleinen Hügel liegt; zu den Seiten breiten sich eine Menge von Dörfern aus. Von Yttersele an bis zur Kirche ist das Gewässer fahrbar für Böte; weiterhin, der Fälle wegen, nicht; der Lachs steigt nur bis Mo hinan, wo sein weiterer Aufgang durch das, der Sägemühle halber, eingedämmte Wasser gehemmt wird; früherhin ging er bis Anundsjö, und müssen daher die Einwohner oberhalb Mo noch Lachsfanggeld entrichten. Bei Anundsjö trifft man den Ursprung des Wasserzuges, der hier aus zwei Armen entsteht, die weiter aus dem Inneren herabkommen. Auf einer Brücke fährt man an das jenseitige Ufer zurück, und erreicht so, neben dem Dorfe Bredby hin, wo ein guter Gäst: gifvaregård ist, die Kirche und den Pfarrhof von Anundsjö, wo ich um 10½ Uhr vom Pastor S e l l i n dem Sohn freundlich bewillkommnet wurde; der Sohn verwaltet das Amt für seinen 85jährigen lebenskräftigen Vater, der noch in voller Mannskraft einhergeht. Meine Ankunft ward durch den Verlust meines Kof: fers verzögert, den ich aber bald auf dem Wege wiederfand. Unterweges hatte ich mich zum ersten Mal mit frischen reifen Åkerbär, die mir mein Sjutsbonde pflückte, gelabt; sie sind dun: kelbraun, fast wie eine Brombeere, der sie auch an Gestalt ähn: lich sind; ihr Geschmack ist etwas süß, äußerst lieblich und aro: matisch. In Anundsjö aß ich Kreme von frischer Åkerbär, der mit fetter Alpensahne köstlich schmeckte; diese Sahne gab selbst dem Salat einen vortrefflichen Geschmack, wovon ich schon in Lappland die Erfahrung gemacht hatte. Walderdbeeren hat man hier jetzt in Menge; sie sind klein, aber schon überreif, und mit der fetten Alpensahne eine wahre Götterspeise; mit der Erdbee: renzeit geht es jetzt zu Ende; sie hat drei Wochen gedauert; bei dem schönen Wetter, was man hier lange gehabt, wurden die Erdbeeren ganz vorzüglich wohlschmeckend. — Der Pfarrhof hat, nebst der Kirche, eine sehr schöne Lage am See. Vor einigen Jahren brannte der Pfarrhof ganz ab; aber nach 5 Wochen war durch die Betriebsamkeit und den Eifer der Bauern schon alles wieder aufgebauet.

Am Sonntag:Morgen wohnte ich dem Gottesdienst bei. Die Wege waren mit Kirchgängern bedeckt: als aus dem Sü: den, auf dem Anundsee, die Kirchböte angelangt (sie kommen fast sonntäglich; in jedem Hofe bleiben nur die unentbehrlichsten Per: sonen daheim) und die Geistlichen in die Kirche getreten waren, wo sie, in der Sacristey, durch ein stilles Gebet sich bereiteten, begann das letzte Läuten, und nach Beendigung desselben, die Einsegnung einer Wöchnerin und der Gottesdienst. Eine Orgel ist nicht vor' handen, aber der Gesang der Gemeinde war innig und sanft, und die herzlichste Andacht herrschte. Die Kirche ist von mittel: mäßiger Größe und einfach verziert. Links am Altar, den ein Gemälde, die Einsetzung des heil. Abendmahls, schmückte, saßen die ältesten Männer der Gemeinde. Die Kleidung beider Geschlechter war ziemlich einfach, besonders die der Männer; die Kleider der Weiber waren von eigengemachtem Zeuge oder Kattun; den Hals bedeckte ein kattunenes Tuch, das Haupt eine seidene Mütze mit Spitzen, vorne ausgeschnitten, hinten mit Schleifen; über die Mütze war ein Band oder ein Tuch gebunden; schöne Gesichtsbildung sah man weder bei Männern noch bei Weibern. Nur sehr wenige ausgenommen, waren alle Kirchgänger vom Anfang des Gottesdienstes an gegenwärtig und blieben bis nach Beendigung desselben. Nachdem der Ausgangsvers mit ergreifender Kraft und Herzlichkeit und gen Himmel gewandtem Antlitz gesungen worden war, schied man nach langem stillem Gebet; zuerst gingen die Männer, langsam und ohne Gedränge, ihnen folgte die Geistlichkeit, dann die Weiber. — Die Versammlung war zahlreich; selbst in der geschäftsvollsten Erndtezeit kommt man häufig; die nahewohnenden sonntäglich.

Nach dem Gottesdienst besuchte ich das Armenhaus, welches mit dem Kirchspielshause (sockenstuga) unter Einem Dache ist; alles war nett und reinlich und mit Laub ausgestreut. In der Nähe giebt es auch einige Kirchstuben (kirkstugor); der mit Feuerstätten eingerichteten sind nur wenige, etwa 6; in diesen wohnen auch Arme. Entferntwohnende Gemeindeglieder, welche keine Kirchstuben haben, übernachten im Winter in nahen Dörfern; für den Sommer haben sie kleine Kammern, in' welchen sie ihre Sonntagskleider aufbewahren, auch ein Bette steht; den Eingang zu diesen Kammern bildet ein Pferdestall, der aber so rein gehalten wird, daß der Fußboden ganz dem Fußboden eines Wohnzimmers gleicht; die Stelle des Fensters pflegt eine Luke zu vertreten. — Die Sonntagsfeier ist in diesem Pastorat so strenge, daß man nur im höchsten Nothfall an Sonntags-Abenden erndtet, und auch hiezu sich höchst ungerne entschließt; ein Bauer fragte den Prediger: ob es nicht Sünde sey, an Sonntags-Abenden Heu einzubringen? Die Nachmittage der Sonntage werden zum Lesen in der Bibel und in Postillen verwandt. In entfernteren Dörfern wird Vormittags Dorfgottesdienst gehalten. Am Abend tanzt zuweilen die Jugend.

Das Pastorat Anundsjö zählte im Jahr 1815. 1875 Einwohner, worunter 633 unter 15 Jahren; an Armen fand man
im ganzen Pastorat nur zwölf, wovon 8 im Armenhause
sich befanden, 3 Armengeld genossen und 1 von seinen Verwandten unterhalten wurde; jedem Armen werden Höfe angewiesen,
aus welchen er bezieht, was er bedarf, ohne daß dieses genau
im Voraus bestimmt ist. Lappen giebt es im Pastorat 5, keiner derselben hält Rennthiere. Die Zahl der Gebornen betrug
im J. 1815, 66, worunter 1, im J. 1816, 62, worunter 2
uneheliche Kinder; 1815 starben 33, 1816, 49; copulirt wurden
1815. 13, 1816. 16 Paare. Das heil. Abendmahl wird etwa
16 Mal jährlich gefeiert; da sind zuweilen an 600 Kommuni-
kanten; man geht gewöhnlich 2 oder 3 Mal jährlich zum heiligen Abendmahl.

Im Ganzen herrscht in Anundsjö viel Wohlstand, denn die
Bauern sind fleißige Ackerbauer und gute Haushalter; nur im
obern Theile oder im Alpenlande, welches an Åsele-Lappmark
gränzt, ist der Wohlstand geringer; das Getreide erfriert dort
oft, und Viehzucht ist Hauptnahrung. Im untern Lande schaden selten Nachtfröste dem Korn. Die Aussaat des Pastorats
wird auf 90 Tonnen Roggen, 800 Tonnen Gerste, 160 Tonnen Mengkorn, 30 Tonnen Erbsen, 60 Tonnen Kartoffeln geschätzt; der Roggen giebt das 6te, Gerste und Mengkorn das
5te (1816 das 7te und 8te), Erbsen das 6te, Kartoffeln das
10te Korn. Außer Pferden, Kühen und Schaafen, hält man
auch Ziegen und einige Rennthiere.

Die Bewohner von Anundsjö sind ein munteres, geistreiches
und noch unverdorbenes Volk. Während 17 Jahren ereignete
sich keine Ehescheidung, und nur zweimal entstanden ernste Un-
einigkeiten zwischen Ehegatten. Die Einwohner sind sehr hülf-
reich und liebevoll gegen einander; bei Bauten, Hochzeiten rc.
unterstützen sie sich gegenseitig, bei Feuersbrünsten wird
der gesetzliche Ersatz gegeben. Kartenspiel kennt man nicht.
Ihre Lebensweise ist mäßig und einfach; nur bei festlichen
Gelegenheiten trinkt man Kaffee; ganz anders ist es im benachbarten Pastorat Sidensjö: wo schon mehr Luxus herrscht. Die

Die Mädchen von Anundsjö tragen faſt allgemein ſilberne Hals-
bänder; ſeidene Kleider ſind ſelten.

Die Bewohner von Anundsjö verſtehen ſich trefflich auf
den Brückenbau; nirgends habe ich in Norrland beſſere Brücken
gefunden, als hier. Dieſe Brücken beſtehen aus wohlverbunde-
nen gehobelten Brettern, über die der Wagen rollt, ohne anzu-
ſtoßen; dagegen in den meiſten übrigen Theilen Norrlands die
Brücken aus wenig oder gar nicht gehobelten Balken und Bäumen, die oft ohne gehörige Verbindung ſind, zu beſtehen pflegen; das Fahren über ſolche Brücken iſt eben ſo fühlbar als oft
gefährlich. Auch in Sidensjö findet man gute Brücken.

Handelsbauern giebt es in Anundsjö nur 4 oder 5; ſie führen die Producte des Ortes nach Stockholm und bringen Zucker,
Kaffee, Tabak, Färbewaaren zurück. — Die Vaccination iſt allgemein eingeführt.

Im Winter durchziehen Lappen das Land; viele betteln, wiewohl ſie nicht ganz arm ſind.

Die Viehzucht wird im Sommer faſt ganz als Sennenwirthſchaft von Mädchen betrieben. Wenn die Sennenmädchen
zurückkehren, geben ſie außerhalb des Kirchhofes (på kyrkowallen)
eine kleine, aus Branntewein, Butter und Käſe beſtehende Bewirthung, und beſchenken ihre Gevatter mit fetten Alpenkäſen
(fjälloſtar). Der Gevatter ſind bei Bauern 3 oder 4, bei Vornehmen 7 oder 8 Paare; jeder Gevatter ſendet, einige Zeit nach
der Taufe, Einen Tag, eine anſtändige Mahlzeit ins Taufhaus.

Das weitläuftige Paſtorat hat nur Eine Kirche; das entfern-
teſte Dorf, Degersjö an der Lappländiſchen Gränze, hat 6 Meilen Kirchweg; die Anlegung einer oder zwei Kapellen wäre zu
wünſchen.

———

Am 3. Auguſt. Von Anundsjö nach Hemra 2¼ M.

Um 6¼ Uhr Abends brach ich auf. Eine ſtarke halbe M.
weſtlich fährt man im Walde noch auf Pfarrboden, der ſich gegen
Oſten etwa ¼ Meile ausdehnt; hier iſt alles Wald, aber auch
viel Acker und Wieſen gehören zur Pfarre. Einen großen Theil

des Nachmittages hatte es heftig gedonnert und geblitzt, und noch
ergoß sich der Regen, als ich abfuhr. Zuerst läuft die Straße,
einige Tausend Fuß hoch, die ziemlich steile Katzenklippe, dann
einen zweiten steilen Berg, der aber minder lang ist, hinan, in
grausenvolle Tiefe liegt Anundsjö versteckt; nach ¾ Meile Weges
fährt man über einen dritten Berg, der lang, aber nur eine
kurze Strecke sehr beschwerlich ist. Man erreicht das Dorf Gu-
lasjö, nachdem man ¾ Meile im Walde gefahren; auf der folgenden Meile, stetem Waldweg, sieht man nichts als ein einziges Nybygge, dessen Aufbau eben begonnen hatte; der Kolonist
hatte sich eine schmale, aber eine Viertelmeile lange Waldstrecke
für etwa 420 Bankthaler gekauft; so wohlfeil ist hier das Holz.
Immer geht es im Walde fort, der meist aus Laubholz besteht,
bergauf und bergab; mitten im Walde trifft man große Seen, deren
Ufer zum Theil sehr schön sind; auch Schwendeacker sieht man.
Köstliche Ackerbär erquickten am Wege. Auf einem hohen Berge erblickt man die nach Myra gehörigen Sennhütten (fäbodar).
Wildpret ist hier sehr häufig; junge Haasen sprangen am Wege;
einige Wochen alt, werden sie von den Müttern sich selbst überlassen, und suchen nun ihre Nahrung selbst; sie waren so wenig
scheu, daß mein Skjutsbonde einen derselben mit den Händen
griff, den ich aber wieder laufen ließ; auch Birkhühner zeigten
sich. Wölfe sind im Winter häufig; sie folgen den Lappen und
ihren Heerden, mit denen sie im Sommer in die Fjäll zurückkehren; Bären trifft man selten. Vor dem Dorfe Myra fährt
man einen langen jähen Berg zum Dorfe herab; hier verzweigt
sich der Weg; der eine Arm führt nach Sidensjö, der andere
nach Skorped, einer zum Pastorat Sidensjö gehörigen Kapelle,
2⅝ Meile von der Mutterkirche; sie ward 1771 angelegt; es
wohnt daselbst ein Kapellprediger, welcher sonntäglich predigt;
die Kapellgemeinde besteht aus 50 Bauern und zählte, im Jahre
1815, 474 Bewohner. Hinter Myra verschwindet der Wald;
man fährt in einem Thale, welches durch einen von Skorped
herabkommenden Fluß, der in Nätra, wo er sich erweitert, den
Namen Nätra-Än annimmt und unter diesem Namen ins
Meer fällt, bewässert wird; das Thal ist reich an Korn; längs

des kleinen Flusses läuft zwischen Laubgebüsch der reizende Weg nach Skorped. Von Myra hat man ¾ Meile bis Hämra, wo ich, des bergigen Weges halber, erst 10½ Uhr anlangte und in dem vorzüglichen Gästgifvaregärd übernachtete.

Am 4. August. Von Hämra nach Spjute 2 M.; von Sp. nach Dockfta 1½ M.; von D. nach Åftja 1 1/12 M. — Zuf. 4 11/12 M.

Um 7¾ Uhr verließ ich Hämra und fuhr nach dem nur eine Sechszehntelmeile entlegenen Pfarrhofe von Sidensjö zum Pastor Ledin. Mit Herzlichkeit, doch nicht ohne Vorwürfe, daß ich 'im Gasthofe übernachtet, ward ich empfangen. Ich besichtigte die Kirche und blieb bei den freundlichen Menschen bis 11 Uhr; erst nach eingenommenem Mahle durfte ich weiter fahren; hier aß ich frische und eingekochte Åkerbär und kostete den aromatischen Åkerbärwein, der eben bereitet wurde. Die Lage von Hämra und Sidensjö's Kirche und Pfarrhof ist sehr schön. Das Pastorat Sidensjö zählte, ohne Skorped, im J. 1815, 1473 Seelen; unter den 50 bis 60 jährlichen Geburten beider Gemeinden befinden sich zuweilen gar keine, höchstens 3 bis 4 uneheliche. Die Kirche ist alt, sie besitzt ein schönes schwarzseidenes neues Meßgewand (messhake) *); zur Anschaffung desselben, welche an 150 Bankthaler kostete, gab der Comminister Olof Sidenborg ⅔ der gesammten Kosten. — Bewohnbare Kirchstuben giebt es nur für die entferntesten Dörfer, die näher wohnenden haben nur Ställe, mit Kammern für die Sonntagskleidung. Der Luxus hat in Sidensjö sehr zugenommen; Ehescheidungen ereigneten sich seit vielen Jahren nicht.

Zwischen Sidensjö's Kirche und Spjute liegt die Kirche Nätra; der Weg dahin führt am Rande eines reizenden Thals, das neben Gebüschen und Wiesen der Nätra-Å in mannigfaltigen Krümmungen durchfließt; auf den Anhöhen liegen Dörfer, welche Felsen und Gebüsche umschließen; im Hintergrunde zeigen sich

*) Ueber Schwedens Kirchenverfassung. Band 1., S. 373. ff.

bald steile Höhen, bald Bergwiesen; es ist eine ganz Schweizerische Landschaft. Schlechte Brücken bezeichnen den Anfang des
Pastorats Nätra. Auf der letzten Viertelmeile kommt man durch
Nadelwald und das Dorf Bjästa, wo die einzige Apotheke zwischen Umeå und Hernösand, d. h. auf einer Strecke von 23⅓
(Schwedischen) Meilen angelegt ist; die kleinen Hausapotheken
ausgenommen, welche man hier und da, z. B. in Anundsjö, im
Pfarrhofe findet. In Nätra wohnt einer der beiden Provinzial-
ärzte des Län Hernösand.

In Nätra sprach ich beim Propste Narèn vor, wo ich einen Besuch zugesagt hatte. Der Pfarrhof liegt recht freundlich
auf einer Anhöhe; die Lage der Kirche ist weniger schön; überhaupt ist das Thal von Arnäs viel schöner, als das Thal von
Nätra. Die prächtige steinerne Kirche mit Thurm ward erst
1807 und 1808 gebauet. Das Orgelchor ruht auf 6 Säulen-
reihen, zwischen denen der große Eingang gerade auf den mit
einfachem Kreuze geschmückten Altar zuführt. Die Kirche ist
ganz nach den Regeln der Akustik gebauet, aber von welchem
Baumeister? einem einfachen Landmann, Geting aus Högsjö am
Angerman. Hell und lieblich schallt die Stimme des Predigers,
wie der kunstlose Gesang der Gemeinde. Die Kirchthüren sind
von Kupfer. Die Kosten des Baues trugen Kirche und Gemeinde.
Gegenüber liegt das Armenhaus mit mehrern Zimmern; der
obere Stock wird als Gemeindehaus benutzt; das Armenhaus
zeichnet sich, wie das in Sidensjö, nicht vortheilhaft aus. Auch
kleine Kirchenställe mit Kleidekammern sind vorhanden. Die Einwohnerzahl des Pastorats betrug, im Jahre 1815, 2376; außer
der Mutterkirche giebt es drei Fischerkapellen, Marviken, Ulfön
und Tresunda, wo im Sommer 1 Mal gepredigt wird; in Tresunda predigt auch die Geistlichkeit von Själawad einmal im
Jahre; in der Nähe dieser Kapellen halten sich die Fischer aus
Geste und Hernösand vom May bis September, besonders des
Strömlingsfanges halber, auf. Die Insel Ulfö hat einen guten
Hafen; sie ist der einzige Ort im Pastorat, wo Dorfgottesdienst
gehalten wird, indem die übrigen Ortschaften der Kirche so nahe
liegen, daß es dessen nicht bedarf. — Der Handelsbauern

giebt es in Nåtra eine große Zahl; es herrscht unter ihnen viel Luxus.

Von Nåtra's Kirche fuhr ich nach Svedje zum Lånsman Svedberg, einem Bruder des Assessor, um genaue Angaben der jährlichen Fabrikation von Prämienleinwand zu erhalten; hier ist auch das Postkomtoir, welches früher in Bjåsta war. Bei Svedje hat man hübsche Uebersichten über Seen, Meerbusen, Landzungen und hohe Uferfelsen. Nach ¼ Meile erreicht man den Gåstgifvaregård Spjute, wo der reiche Bauer Iwar Wallin sich ein großes zierliches Wohnhaus, wenn gleich nur von Holz, von drei Stockwerken mit Eckzimmern im dritten Stocke ge= bauet hat.

Hinter Spjute läuft der Weg neben den Krümmungen des Skulusees hin; dann wird er minder interessant, bis man hinter dem Dorfe Skulu an den Fuß des steilen Skulufelsens gelangt; nun fährt man neben Meerbusen, die ganz das Ansehen von Lands seen haben und die hohe Felsenwände umschließen, nach Docksta. Auf der Straße begegnete ich mehrern Wagen Westgothischer Han= delsbauern. Mein Skjutsbonde von Spjute nach Docksta hatte einen durchdringenden, höchst widrigen Geruch; schon öfter war mir solches in Angermanland vorgekommen; es ist Folge der Unreinlichkeit und des schlechten Tabaks, den die Bauern rau= chen, auch wohl kauen; die Angermanländer werden in der Re= gel von den Westerbottniern in Reinlichkeit sehr übertroffen.

Unweit Docksta, auf dem Wege nach Åsеja, kommt man der hochgelegenen Kirche Vibbyggerå, Filial von Nordingrå, vor= über; ich fuhr hinauf, Kirche und Glockenthurm in Augenschein zu nehmen. Die Kirche ist ein freundliches, aber uraltes, steiner= nes Gebäude ohne Orgel; eines ihrer beiden Chöre ist mit Dar= stellungen aus der biblischen Geschichte, die Kirchenstühle sind, gleich den Altarschranken, mit einfachen Landschaftsgemälden ge= schmückt; das Altarbild ist ein Holzschnitt: der betende Erlöser, dem ein Engel mit dem Becher erscheint. Die Sakristey ist ge= räumig. Eine kleine Strecke von der Kirche steht der hölzerne Glok= kenthurm, merkwürdig durch seine Glocken und die herrliche Aus= sicht, die man von hier genießt: man überblickt die schönen

II.   S e

Thäler umher, nebst dem nahen Dorfe Sätra, in welchem die Kirche liegt und wo der Küster, der Pfarrcolonus und 5 Bauern wohnen, den weiten Meerbusen, an dem die Landstraße, von hohen Felswänden ummauert, hinführt. Die beiden Glocken sind durch ihren schönen Klang berühmt; an der kleineren lieset man, in Mönchsbuchstaben, die Inschrift:

Kom, Christen, willigt i Guds Tempel,
Till Kyrkan Kallardig mitt Gud,
Men gif od akt på Herrans bud,
At hjertat ditt får Andans stämpel.
När tro från gerning ej bil stild,
Så tryckes in Guds egen bild.

(Auf deutsch:
Komm, o Christ, gerne in Gottes Tempel;
Zur Kirche rufet dich mein Klang;
Doch gieb auch Acht auf des Herren Gebote,
Damit dein Herz des Geistes Stempel empfange.
Wann der Glaube nicht getrennt ist von der That;
So wird Gottes Ebenbild eingeprägt.)

Ich fuhr den Berg hinab zur Landstraße und war um 10½ Uhr in Åstja, einem trefflichen Gasthofe, wo ich das Nachtlager nahm. Auch Ångermanlands Bauerhäuser sind ansehnlich, wenn gleich nicht ganz so groß wie die Westerbottnischen.

Am 5ten August. Von Åstja nach Nordingrå etwa 1½ M.

Meist nur Kirchspielsweg, aber an Güte der großen Straße gleich, wie es auch der Kirchspielsweg von Sidensjö nach Nätra ist. Man fährt dem Gästgifvaregård Wede und vielen Dörfern vorüber. Eine Viertelmeile von Åstja hat man auf einem Bergrücken einen herrlichen Ueberblick über ein Paar Thäler im Südosten von Åstja; hier liegt auch die Kirche Ullångar; ein Bergabhang trennt die Thäler. Dann fährt man am Meerbusen Ullångersfjärd hin und erreicht bald das Kirchspiel Nordingrå, von dessen Gränze an es unaufhörlich bergauf und bergab geht; fast jeder Berg und jedes Thal hat einen Schlagbaum. Die Gestalten der Berge und Thäler sind sehr wechselnd, die Aus-fichten aber überall beschränkt. Einigen hübschen Seen kommt man vorüber, insbesondere bei Wreta, wo zwei Seen durch eine kleine Landenge geschieden und von steilen Waldbergen begränzt werden. Um 10½ Uhr war ich in Nordingrä's Pfarrhofe, wo ich bei Doctor Renström einen frohen Tag verlebte.

Doctor Renström ist zugleich Propst über Ångermanlands östliches Contract (Propstei); bis zum J. 1803 war die östliche und westliche Propstei durch den Ångerman getrennt; dann durch eine Linie, welche queer über den Ångerman läuft, so daß nun die östliche Propstei durch die Pastorate Nordingrä, Gudmundrä und Thorsäker, die westliche, deren Sitz jetzt in Sollefta ist, durch die Pastorate Sollefta, Resele, Ramsele und Boteå *) gebildet wird; eine Zeitlang wurde die östliche Propstei vom Bischof verwaltet. Die Einwohnerzahl der östlichen Propstei betrug, im J. 1815, 12,044; die Zahl der Gebornen, im J. 1816, 371, worunter 16 Uneheliche, 1814 waren unter 360 nur 10 uneheliche Geburten.

Das Pastorat Nordingrä zählte, im J. 1815, 4164 Seelen. Es besteht aus der Muttergemeinde Nordingrä und den Filialgemeinden Ullånger und Wibbyggerä; die erstere ist die volkreichste (an 2000 Seelen). Die Zahl der Geburten im Jahre 1816 war in Nordingrä 59 (2 uneheliche), in Ullånger 31, (keine uneheliche), in Wibbyggera 33 (1 uneheliche). Unter 1 Jahr stirbt jährlich etwa das 4te oder 5te Kind; das Selbststillen ist allgemein; unkeusche Bräute gab es im J. 1810 (vom 1sten

*) Zur Berichtigung falscher geographischer Angaben will ich hier bemerken, daß man mit dem Namen Ådalen (Flußthal) in Ångermanland nur diejenigen Kirchspiele bezeichnet, welche am Ångerman liegen; hier wohnen viele Schiffer und Seeleute, aber wenige Handelsbauern. Die unverdorbensten sind die Kirchspiele am obern Ångerman, weil die Bewohner desselben am wenigsten auswärts gehen. In Medelpad heißen die Kirchspiele, welche an den Flüssen Indal und Njurunda (Tuna) liegen, gleichfalls Ådalar; diese beiden Ådalar werden durch Berge geschieden, und bilden mit diesen die ganze Provinz; in den Ådalar herrscht große Fruchtbarkeit.

Ee 2

Juny 1810 bis dahin 1815) bei 40 Ehen 8; im J. 1811 bei 34 Ehen 5, im J. 1813 bei 27 Ehen 2, im J. 1815 bei 15 Ehen keine; Ehezwiste sind selten, Ehescheidungen fast unerhört. Das heilige Abendmahl wird, in der Regel, in der Mutterkirche jeden 4ten, in den Filialkirchen jeden 5ten oder 6ten Sonntag begangen, doch nicht in der Erndte und während der strengsten Winterkälte; jeder communicirt gewöhnlich 2 Mal jährlich. Zum Pastorat gehört auch eine Fischerkapelle Norrfäls-viken beim Dorfe Mjällom; hier wird im Sommer 1 Mal vor den Fischern aus Geffe und andern Orten geprebigt.

Die Kirche Nordingrä ist ein sehr altes steinernes Gebäude; der erste Grund soll im zwölften Jahrhundert gelegt worden seyn, seitdem ist sie oft erneuert worden; jetzt verfällt sie immer mehr, so daß eine neue Kirche gebauet werden soll; schon mußte das Gewölbe abgetragen werden; im Innern ist alles nett und freundlich. Das Altarblatt stellt einen Theil der Leidensgeschichte Christi trefflich in Holz dar; das Bild wird durch ein Paar Flügelthüren bedeckt, auf deren innerer und äußerer Seite man einige schöne biblische Gemälde erblickt; einige dieser Gemälde verrathen eine Meisterhand; unter dem Schnitzwerk ist der Heiland mit den Aposteln abgemalt; dieses Bild ist weniger bedeutend. In der Kirche sieht man an den Wänden in Rahmen eingefaßte Denkschriften auf merkwürdige Ereignisse des Reichs, Karls XII. Tod, auf Siege, auf die Feier des Reformations-Jubelfestes; die Aufstellung solcher politischer Tafeln in den Kirchen ist also schon lange gebräuchlich gewesen; die Aufstellung von Reichstagsreden der Könige ist erst seit Gustav III. üblich geworden; auch diese findet man in der Kirche Nordingrä. Vor dem Altar ist das Grabmal des um die Verschönerung der Kirche sehr verdienten Propstes Bojacus (im 17ten Jahrhundert); auf dem Steine lieset man unter andern die Worte: Determinati sunt dies hominis. Hospes sum mundi, sed civis et incola coeli. Homo, memento mori!

In der Nähe der Kirche liegt das Gemeindehaus, in dem Ein Zimmer als Armenstube dient; hier wohnen vier arme Frauen; eine derselben ist Vorsteherin; am Sonntage bringt die

Gemeinde ihnen, einer Reihenfolge nach, Lebensmittel; die übrigen Armen werden von Hof zu Hof verpflegt und erhalten überdies Austheilungen aus der Armenkasse. Die Armenkasse ward im J. 1780 durch eine Schenkung der Demoiselle Ramström, Tochter des Propstes, von 500 Rthlrn. begründet, und ist seitdem, durch gute Verwaltung, schon zu 900 Bankthalern gewachsen. — In der Nähe des Gemeindehauses stehen Kirchstuben, die aber nichts als Ställe, und selbst ohne Kammern sind; doch tritt man bei bösem Wetter hinein.

Aus dem Glockenthurm neben der Kirche übersieht man die Gegend umher: ein hübscher Meerbusen, von steilen Waldfelsen umgeben; durch einen engen Hals, der aber vom Thurm aus nicht sichtbar ist, läuft der Busen ins Meer aus; ehemals war der Auslauf viel breiter, aber das Wasser hat auch an dieser Küste, wie an den Küsten von Westerbotten, abgenommen. Eine der Glocken hat einen eben so schönen Klang, als die Glocke von Widbyggerä.

Das Pastorat stellt, wie ganz Angermanland, statt Fußvolks, (42) Bootsleute; man miethet sie, wo und wie man kann; oft sind es Säuflinge; die Disciplin unter ihnen ist schlecht und sie verderben die Gemeinden. Bei der Anwerbung von Fußvolk geht man mit größerer Vorsicht zu Werke. Die Bootsleute haben, wie die Soldaten und Matrosen überhaupt, gewöhnlich Zunamen, die in dieser Gegend auch auf die Kinder überzugehen pflegen, während sie an andern Orten mit dem Tode derer, die sie annehmen, erlöschen.

Früherhin herrschte in Nordingrä große Wohlhabenheit, die aber durch den letzten Krieg und durch die zu große Zerstückelung der Ackerstücke unter Familienglieder jetzt sehr gesunken ist; doch ist man noch immer nicht unbemittelt, wenn nur der Strömlingsfang nicht fehlschlägt; dieser bildet einen ansehnlichen Nahrungszweig (das Fischen in der Nacht vom Sonnabend auf den Sonntag wird nicht geduldet); Lachs wird nicht gefangen. Grobe Leinewand wird viel verfertiget, auch Prämienlinnen; ferner schmiedet man, besonders Sensen, zum Verkauf. Viehzucht und

Ackerbau sind nicht hinreichend. Die Zahl der Handelsbauern ist gering, nur einige derselben fahren nach Stockholm.

Kirchspielschulen giebt es, wie fast in ganz Angermanland, nicht.

Am 6. Aug. Von Nordingrå bis Nora's Kirche 1¼ M.; von N. nach Herrflog (ungefähr) ½ M.; von H. nach Kungsgården 1⅛ M. — Zus 3¼ M.

Um 8 Uhr fuhr ich ab; der 1¾jährige Sohn des Doctors wollte mich begleiten; ich nahm ihn neben mir in den Wagen; noch konnte er nicht sprechen, wohl aber schon mit der Zunge schnalzen, und bis sagen, ersteres, für Pferde, das Zeichen des Schnellergehens, letzteres des Stillstehens. So ist der Norrlän-der ein geborner Fuhrmann. Mann und Weib lernt schon frühe diese Kunst und übt sie noch im spätesten Alter, der Knabe und das Mädchen, wie der Greis, mit gleicher Geschicklichkeit und Un-erschrockenheit, oft aber auch Unvorsichtigkeit. Der liebe Junge freute sich inniglich des Fahrens, schlang sich fest an mich und wollte mich nicht lassen; doch, als der Schlagbaum erreicht war, mußte es geschieden seyn; ich gab ihn dem Vater zurück, drückte dem herrlichen Manne und seinem braven Adjuncten, dem Magister Byström aus Jemtland, die Hände und fuhr davon; im Herbste ward mir die Freude, unter den Reichstagsmännern den Doctor Renström wieder zu finden.

Fast bis zum Gästgifvaregård Salten, 1 Meile lang, führt man im Kirchspiel Nordingrå, welches hier ganz seine Eigen-thümlichkeit zeigt: kleine Thäler mit Seen, kahlen Wiesen- und Waldufern, Dörfer auf den Höhen und unaufhörliche Schlagbäu-me; hier und da ein Bach, welcher Mühlen treibt. Sobald man das Kirchspiel Nora erreicht, erweitern sich die Thäler, die aber noch immer nackt und kahl sind. Bei Salten sieht man hübsche Seen. Eine Viertelmeile jenseits Salten erreicht man Nora's Pfarrhof, wo ich bis 4 Uhr Nachmittags verweilte.

Nora ist Präbende des Bischofs; der brave Vicepastor Brandell führt die Verwaltung; doch predigt auch der Bischof. Zu Nora gehören die Filialgemeinden Skog und Högsjö und die

Fischerkapellen Berghamn und Hemsö; in Hemsö wird 3 Mal, in Berghamn 1 oder 2 Mal jährlich, im Sommer, gepredigt; auch hält dort der Hafenvoigt Gebet; die Bewohner der Stadt Hernösand und mehrerer Dörfer treiben an den Küsten Strömlingsfang. — Viele Mädchen aus Dalekarlien dienen im Pastorat. Eine Armenstube ist nicht vorhanden; aber die Armen werden gut versorgt.

Die Kirche Nora ist eine der schönsten des Landes; ein großes steinernes Gebäude, ein Oblong, imponirend durch Würde und Einfachheit im Aeußern und Innern. Sie wurde vor kurzem erbauet, Baumeister ist Geting in Högsjö, derselbe, welcher Nätra's Kirche erbaute. Sie ist ganz akustisch gebaut, es predigt sich sehr leicht, wenn man langsam spricht; doch ist der Klang in Nätra's Kirche noch schöner. Das Altar schmückt ein einfaches Kreuz. An beiden Seiten des Altars führt eine Thüre in die geräumige Sacristey. Wie in Nätra, so ist auch hier das Gewölbe der Kirche von Holz. Kanzel, Altar und alles andere Schnitzwerk hat der Bildhauer Dalquist, welcher in Nora wohnte und starb, gefertiget. Ein geräumiger Kirchhof umgiebt die Kirche; hier ruhet unter einfachem Stein der letztverstorbene Bischof über Hernösand's Stift, Nordin, dessen große Sammlungen zur Geschichte des Nordischen Mittelalters jetzt, auf Veranstaltung der Regierung, durch eine in Upsala angeordnete Commission herausgegeben werden *). Der Kirchhof ist aufgemauert und erhöhet worden; ein gleiches geschah in Nätra.

Von der Kirche aus setzte ich Nachmittags die Reise fort. Bei Nora werden die Thäler allmählig schöner. Nach ¼ Meile erreicht man, die große Straße von Stockholm nach Torneå. Plötzlich ward das Pferd wie wild, stampfte mit den Füßen und schien durchgehen zu wollen; ich stieg ab und ließ dasselbe leiten. Nach einer Strecke versuchte ich es wieder, zu fahren; aber das Thier wurde noch wüthender. Jetzt rief ich ein Frauenzimmer, das sich in der Nähe fand, und bat mir

---

*) Scriptores rerum Suecicarum medii aevi. Tom. I. sect. 1 et 2. Ups. 1818. fol. 262 und 348 S.

ein anderes Pferd zu verschaffen. Sie führte mich ins Dorf auf eine Scheundiele, wo gerade ein Pferd vor der Heukarre stand; Else, die eben mit ihrer 23jährigen, seit der Geburt blinden Schwester das Heu ablud, hatte kaum meine Bitte gehört, als sie flugs das Pferd abspannte, sich kleidete, vor meinen Wagen spannete und mit gleicher Schnelligkeit als Geschicklichkeit mich bis zum nächsten Gästgifvaregård Herrskog fuhr; Else war die Tochter des Bauern Jöns Ersson. Bald waren wir in Herrskog, dessen Thal jetzt, nach vollendeter Heuerndte weniger anmuthig schien, als vor 6 Wochen. Die Heukarren haben zwei Räder in der Mitte der Karre.

Eine halbe Meile jenseits Herrskog, bei Lungviken, beginnen die schönen Thäler, welche sich mit kurzer Unterbrechung am ganzen Ångerman hinaufziehen; bei Lungviken führt eine Fähre ans jenseitige Ufer nach Gudmundrå. Vorzüglich schön ist das Thal von Lockne mit seinen Seen, die an der einen Seite mit dem Ångerman, an der andern mittelst mehrerer Wasserzüge und Seen, bei den Kirchen Skog und Nora vorüber, mit dem Meere zusammenhängen. Auch der obere Theil des Thals, wo die alte Kirche Bjerträ liegt, ist schön, die Gegend sehr fruchtbar. Eine Viertelmeile hinter Bjerträ erreicht man Kongsgården, wo ich mein Nachtlager nahm. Kungsgården, ein Dorf mit 10 Bauern, liegt an einer Bucht des Ångerman; eine Fähre führt hier über den Strom; dann findet man eine eigentliche Fähre erst wieder einige Meilen oberhalb, bei Sollefta; doch können Fußgänger auch anderwärts überkommen. Mein Skjutsbonde von Herrskog forderte eine kleine Erhöhung des Meilengeldes, schwererer Fuhr halber; eine Seltenheit in Norrland; als ich ihm sein Unrecht vorhielt, bat er bescheiden um Verzeihung.

In Kungsgården übernachtete ich vortrefflich; ein Saal und zwei Zimmer wurden mir eingeräumt, alles war tüchtig und reinlich, und die Menschen so schön, so freundlich, so liebreich und unverdrossen, daß es eine Freude war. Es wohnt in diesen Gegenden ein großer, schöner und kernhafter Schlag von Menschen.

Am 7. Aug. Von Kungsgården nach Undrom 1½ M.; von U. nach Hullsta 2¾ M. — Zus. 4¼ M.

Eine kurze Tagesreise, wiewohl ich schon um 6½ Uhr aus- fuhr und erst um 10½ Uhr Quartier nahm; und doch wäre sie in diesen reizenden Gegenden, wo fast jede Viertelmeile mehr denn Eine Merkwürdigkeit darbietet, noch kürzer geworden, hätten nicht die Schnelligkeit der Pferde und mein Eilen von allen Stellen die Fahrt so gefördert.

Unweit Kungsgården erblickte ich zuerst den Angerman, des- sen ich gestern nicht ansichtig geworden war; dann geht es am Fuße hoher Waldberge zwischen Wiesen und Gebüschen, neben dem Gute Berg hin, nach Lo, ½ Meile von Kungsgården. Lo ist eine Sägemühle und ein Herrenhof (herregård, Gut,) wie man spricht, herrlich gelegen mitten zwischen Wiesen und Gärten und an den Ufern des kleinen Flusses Lo und des gewaltigen Stromes Angerman; die Gebäude sind in Berg, wie in Lo, wenig bedeutend. Vielen Dörfern fährt man vorüber. Hinter Lo erreicht man die Kirche Styrnäs (Schörnas, spricht man hier, und so wird der Name auch in alten Urkunden geschrieben), welche eine reizende Lage auf einer Höhe am Angerman hat, welcher hier eine Krümmung macht; in der Mitte liegt eine liebliche Busch- insel; gegenüber senkt sich ein niedriger Felsrücken in den Fluß; dort zeigt sich die thurmlose Kirche Thorsåker auf einer kleinen, Ebene am Fuß von Waldbergen, mit dem Pfarrhofe.

Die Kirche von Styrnäs ist ein altes steinernes Gebäude mit zwei Thürmen, die ein schmales Dach trennt; ein besonderer Glockenthurm steht oberhalb des Kirchhofs, auf welchem sich ein hübsches, thurmähnliches Grabmal erhebt; ein Paar kleine Schil- der nennen den Namen einer Frau Liffman, und Psalm 16, 6. Psalm 27, 13. — Das Innere der Kirche ist klein und bunt. Den Altar schmückt ein offener vergoldeter Rahmen, wie oft in Angermanland, mit allerlei Emblemen und Figuren: an den Seiten erblickt man eine Figur mit dem Kreuze, und eine andere mit dem Anker der Hoffnung; oben zwei Engel mit Po- saunen, ganz in der Höhe den Erlöser, von göttlicher Glorie umgeben, auf den Wolken; unter dem Rahmen die Einsetzung des heil. Abendmahls, in Holz dargestellt. Auch die Kanzel zieren allerlei heilige Sinnbilder.

Ursprünglich war die Kirche ein Kastell; dies beweisen die Kirchfenster, wie eine noch vorhandene, nur von außen zugemauerte Schießscharte, und nahe alte Festungswälle.

Von Styrnäs fährt man etwa ¼ Meile im Angesicht des Angerman, dessen Ufer dichte Ketten von Dörfern und Höfen umgeben, doch sind nur die Thäler und Abhänge der Höhen, nicht die Höhen selbst mit Dörfern besetzt; dann erreicht man den, von Gäljö Bruk herabkommenden Wasserzug und fährt nun ¼ Meile durch Nadelwald bis zum Dorfe Undrom, wo der Gästgifvaregård ist. Ich fuhr vorüber nach dem ¼ Meile entfernten Pfarrhofe von Botheä, wo ich beim Propste Lindahl einige Stunden verweilte. Aus dem Pfarrhause und von einem Hügel neben demselben hat man hübsche Aussichten über den Angerman ab- und aufwärts.

Unweit des Pfarrhofes liegt die Kirche, zu welcher eine Allee von Sperberbäumen (rönn) führt; das Gebäude ist alt, das Innere wurde vor 8 Jahren neu ausgebauet; Altar, Kanzel, Stühle hat der schon oben erwähnte geschickte Bildhauer Dalquist aus Mora, ein Bauer, gefertiget; besonders gelungen ist der, in der Mitte offene, vergoldete Altarrahmen, welchen passende heilige Figuren und Bilder schmücken; unten schließt sich an den Rahmen ein Oelgemälde an, welches den betenden König darstellt, der Krone und Harfe niedergelegt hat, vor diesem Bilde eine Landschaft, mit einem nach Wasser schmachtenden Hirsch; Strahlen senken sich aus den Wolken auf den Beter herab, und man liest die Worte des Psalm 42, v. 2 und 3.

Den Kirchhof umgeben der Glockenthurm, einige Kirchställe und das Gemeindehaus, in welchem der Kirchenwächter wohnt; die einzige Haushaltung neben der Kirche, außer dem Pfarrhofe. Kirchenbuden giebt es nicht; nur einige Köhler der Bruksgemeinde haben eine Meile zur Brukskirche; die entferntesten der übrigen Einwohner haben eine halbe Meile Kirchweg. Das Pastorat Botheä besteht aus der Mutterkirche Botheä, den Filialen Styrnäs, Öfver-Länäs und Sånga, und der Brukskirche

Gålsjö, neben jeder dieser 5 Kirchen wohnt ein Prediger, ausgenommen Sånga, wo der Comminister in Styrnås und der Socken (Kirchspiels-) predikant in Öfver-Lånås, 36 Mal jährlich, predigen. Sämmtliche 5 Gemeinden zählen an 2000 Einwohner; Botheå, mit 80 Bauern, ist die volkreichste. Viele Bauern des Pastorats fahren als Schiffer für Hernösands Kaufleute, Bauersöhne und Knechte als Matrosen; auf ihren Seereisen treiben sie Handel; für inländische Produkte kaufen sie Tabak, Salz, Zucker, Kaffee, Kattun. Es herrscht viel Luxus.

Eine Armenstube giebt es nicht; aber die Armen werden aus der Armenkasse und durch Beköstigung auf den Dörfern versorgt.

Botheå hat viele Sennhütten auf den Fjäll zwischen Botheå und Sidensjö; hier richten die Bären oft unter den Pferden und Kühen große Verwüstung an.

Nach dem Mittagsessen verließ ich den Pfarrhof. Propst Lindahl begleitete mich ¼ Meile bis Sundby, einem von seiner Frau ererbten Gütchen. Sundby hat eine herrliche Lage hart am Ångerman; neben dem Garten erblickt man eine freundliche Waldinsel mit hohen Ufern; neben dem Hofe einen Altehög, d. i. einen Grabhügel der Altvordern, rund, oben abgeplattet, an einer Seite eingedrückt, unten mit einem Graben umgeben, von welchem man freilich jetzt nur noch einige Reste findet. Solcher Grabhügel giebt es mehrere in Ångermanland, z. B. bei Holm ꝛc.

Hinter Sundby verließ mich der Propst. Ich setzte meine Reise fort mitten zwischen Dörfern, im Angesicht des majestätischen Flusses und der jenseitigen hohen Uferberge; am diesseitigen Ufer breitet sich, seit Kungsgården, bisher eine größere Ebene aus. Nach ⅜ Meilen Weges erreichte ich die Kirche Öfver-Lånås. Sie ist vor einigen Jahren neu aufgebauet worden und kommt an Größe der Kirche Botheå ziemlich gleich. Sie ist einfach, freundlich. Den Altar schmückt ein in der Mitte ausgefüllter Rahmen, oben erblickt man die strahlende Sonne mit einem Dreieck, worauf der Name 'Jehovah mit hebräischen Buchstaben, rings umher Wolken und Engel; an den Seiten eine Figur mit dem Kreuze,

ihr gegenüber eine andere mit dem Anker; in der Mitte des
Rahmens einen Beter, gegen den ein Engel sehnend die Hände
ausstreckt. Die Kanzel ist vergoldet und mit heiligen Sinnbildern geschmückt. — Vom Kirchhofe hat man eine reizende Aussicht über die Ufer des Flusses; ein Grabgebäude gehört der Familie Nordensalk auf Holm. Neben dem Kirchhof steht der
Glockenthurm, die reinliche Kirchspielsstube und einige Kirchenställe.

Von der Kirche Öfver-Lännäs hat man ¼ Meile bis Holm,
dem einzigen adelichen Gute in Angermanland und in ganz Norrland, Gestrikland ausgenommen. Es hat eine herrliche Lage hart
am Angerman, und befindet sich gegenwärtig im Besitz der Familie Nordensalk; ein Paar Bauerndörfer und das Bruk Gálsjö
gehören mit zum Eigenthum. Um nicht für unhöflich angesehen
zu werden (denn für unhöflich hält man es in diesen nördlichen
Gegenden, wenn ein Fremder einem Gute oder größern Pfarrhofe vorüberreiset, ohne vorzusprechen), aber auch um die Bekanntschaft der interessanten Familie zu machen, fuhr ich, wiewohl
meine Zeit heute sehr beschränkt war, in Holm ein. Eine noch
jugendliche 70jährige Alte, die Wittwe des Revisionssecretaire,
der das Gut erkaufte und neue Gebäude aufführte, nebst ihrem
Sohne, empfing mich. Die lieben Menschen überhäuften mich
mit so großer Güte und baten so freundlich, zu bleiben, daß es
mir wirklich schwer wurde, nach einer Stunde zu scheiden. Vor
der Weiterreise besah ich das Haus und seine schöne Umgebungen. Das Wohnhaus hat zwei Stockwerke, aus deren oberm
man die reizendsten Aussichten hat. Die eine Seite des Hofes
begränzt ein lieblicher Birkenhain mit Ruhebänken und im Hintergrunde einem Hühnerhause in Form eines zierlichen Wohn-
hauses; an der andern Seite des Hofes liegt der Garten mit
Blumenbeeten, Gängen, Terrassen; von den letzteren überschauet
man die paradiesische Landschaft. — Bei Holm, wie bei Töndal
in Botheå und Lo in Styrnäs, wird Waizen gebauet, der aber
nicht jährlich reift.

Von Holm fährt man eine Höhe hinan, auf welcher die
Aussicht noch ausgebreiteter ist als vom Edelsitz aus. Dorf reihet

sich an Dorf, rings umher erblickt man Kornfelder, Wiesen und
Gebüsche, in der Mitte den mächtigen Strom, im Hintergrunde
Wald. Im Angesicht der malerischen Ufer fährt man fort, bald
einen steilen Berg herab; im Thale rieselt ein birkenbekränzter
Bach, der die schöngelegene Sägemühle und den Eisenstabham=
mer Björkå treibt; Bauer= und Torparehöfe liegen auf der Höhe.
Nun geht es einen steilen Berg hinan zur Kirche Sånga. Die
Kirche ist sehr alt, wie man behauptet, durch Zusammenschuß von
Pilgrimmen, die zur Wunderquelle wallfahrteten, gestiftet; doch
scheint Öfver=Lånås noch älter zu seyn, indem einige, Sånga ge=
genüber liegende Dörfer nach Öfver=Lånås eingepfarrt sind. In
der Vorhalle der Kirche findet man einige alte katholische Bilder
und eine Altartafel; die Kirche selbst enthält jetzt keine Alter=
thümer mehr. Die hübsche vergoldete Kanzel, von deren Decke
eine Taube herabhängt, ist mit biblischen Emblemen, der Altar
mit einem Rahmen geschmückt, in dessen Mitte die Anbetung
des Christuskindleins und eine Beterin, auf welche ein Engel
herabkommt, dargestellt sind; zur Seite des Rahmens erscheint
eine Figur mit dem Kreuze und der Todesfackel, oben das Lamm
mit der Siegesfahne und die Sonne mit den übrigen Emble=
men, ganz wie in der Kirche von Öfver=Lånås. In einer Ecke
stand ein langes Bambusrohr, der Ehrenstab des Spåggbbe, wel=
cher jetzt außer Gebrauch gekommen ist. Die berühmte Wun=
derquelle, zu der man einst wallfahrtete, soll in der nordwestlichen
Ecke der Sacristey gelegen haben; nach der Reformation ward
sie zugeschüttet; wirklich ist der Stein, welcher die Thürschwelle
der Sacristey bildet, im Frühlinge naß, das Wasser schmeckt
salzig; jetzt war der Stein trocken. Bis zum Jahr 1760, wo
die Kirche erneuert wurde, lagen über dem Gewölbe der Kirche
einige Krücken, die noch aus den Zeiten jener Wunderquelle her=
stammten. — In einiger Entfernung von der Kirche am Saume
eines Waldes längs des Ångerman, findet man einen Gesund=
brunnen, der insbesondere gegen Gicht dient, aber erst im 18ten
Jahrhundert aufgenommen wurde; der Brunnen ist überbauet,
daneben ein Badehaus und ein geräumiger Brunnensaal angelegt,
auch sind im Walde Gänge ausgehauen.

Unbeschreiblich schön ist die Aussicht vom Kirchhofe: man überschauet eine weite fruchtbare Ebene; den Angerman deckt ein Lusthain, an welchem der Gesundbrunnen liegt; man sieht die Kirchen Öfver-Länäs und Botheå. Sänga's Kirche ist ohne Thurm; der Glockenstuhl steht außerhalb des Kirchhofes. Eine Kirchspielsstube ist nicht vorhanden. Aber einige Bauerhöfe liegen umher. Aus einem dieser Höfe zog eben die gesammte Familie, Alt und Jung, auf die Wiesen; auch ein halbjähriges Kind führte die Hausfrau in einer kleinen Wiege mit sich; es war eine Freude zu sehen, wie die bildschöne Mutter ihr Erst- und Eingebornes herzte und pflegte, und dieses so lieblich und freundlich ihr zulächelte. Ueberhaupt giebt es in diesen Kirchspielen am Angerman unter den Frauen viele regelmäßige Schönheiten.

Von Sänga aus erreicht man bald das Dorf Para, dem, am jenseitigen Ufer, der Gästgifvaregård Äs gegenüberliegt. Der langen Station wegen, wollte mein Skjutsbonde hier das Pferd wechseln, aber alle Häuser waren verschlossen und die Bewohner auf den Wiesen; das Heu wird in die Scheunen auf den Wiesen eingebracht, auch auf Trockengerüsten ausgebreitet. Para lehnt sich an einen theils bewaldeten, theils nackten hohen Felsen.

Hinter Para fährt man durch eine fast ununterbrochene Reihe von Dörfern und Höfen; nur durch Waldschluchten hindurch wird der Fluß zuweilen sichtbar. In einige dieser Schluchten führt der Weg steil hinab und eben so steil aus denselben hinauf; Bäche fließen zwischen Gebüsch und Wiesen dem Angerman zu. Man fährt durch einen Laubhain, dann durch einen Nadelwald, und bald breitet sich wieder die ganze herrliche Landschaft offen vor dem unbeschränkten Blicke aus. Diese Mannigfaltigkeit der Scenen erhöhet den Reiz der Gegend. Malerisch gruppirt liegen oft die Bauerhöfe da, ein Kreis schlanker Birken schließt sie ein. Kein Rhein- und Neckarthal ist dem Thale des Angerman zu vergleichen, nur etwa Italiens üppige Thäler zwischen dem Lago di Como und dem Lago maggiore; denn auch das Thal am Angerman hat ganz die Fruchtbar-

keit südlicher Zonen: üppige Kornfelder und Wiesen erblickt man
überall, und Hopfenhaine, welche malerisch von sanften Anhöhen
sich herabsenken, vertreten die Stelle der Rebenhaine. — Die
Ufer des Flusses, welcher oberhalb viel schmäler ist, als da, wo
er sich seiner Mündung nähert, erheben sich hier und da zu
einer ansehnlichen Höhe und lassen dann, zumal jenseits, keine
Thalfläche übrig; da liegen dann die Dörfer zerstreut auf den
Höhen, über welche der Weg führt; aber überall sind die Abhänge dieser hohen waldigen Uferberge mit Wiesen, Gebüschen
und Kornfeldern bedeckt; starke Haiden und Sandfelder sieht
man hier nirgends. — Vor Multrå überschauet man eine weite,
schöne Landschaft, aus welcher Multrå's schön gewölbter Glockenthurm hervorsteigt.

Wir näherten uns Multrå. Durch den Glockenthurm geht
man zum Kirchhof, wo man noch einige Grabkreuze findet, die
man immer seltner errichtet. Die thurmlose Kirche ist klein und
alt, aber nett und freundlich; man findet ein Altarblatt und
mehrere katholische Bilder; ersteres hängt an der Kirchwand; den
Altar selbst schmückt eine neue schöne Altartafel, mit den gewöhnlichen Emblemen, und unten, einem Oelgemälde, welches die Einsetzung des heil. Abendmahls darstellt. Der Fußboden — nicht
blos der Kirche, sondern auch der Vorhalle und des Glockenstuhls
sind rein gescheuert. — Multrå ist Filial von Sollefta.

Vor Stedom, ½ Meile von Multrå, überblickt man einen
großen Theil des obern Ångerman, in welchen bei Sollefta ab-
gestumpfte Waldberge hineintreten, was einen ungemein schönen
Anblick gewährt; zur Seite des nahen Sollefta donnert ein Wasserfall, der erste von der Mündung aufwärts. Von Stedom
fährt man über den hier schmalen, aber reißenden Strom. Man
landet am Fuße eines hohen von Laubwald bedeckten, Berges,
fährt einige Schritte auf hohen Wiesen hin und ersteigt dann,
nicht ohne große Beschwerde, den Berg; über Anhöhen und
Thäler erreicht man den Gästgifvaregård Hullesta, wo ich um
10½ Uhr anlangte und übernachtete. Der Gasthof ist einer der
größeren Norrlands; zum Logiren wies man mir ein großes
und freundliches Zimmer im oberen Stockwerke an, zum Abend-

essen war ich in den unteren Speisesaal eingeladen; alles war trefflich bereitet, selbst Kuchen mit Äkerbär fehlten nicht; das Bett war vorzüglich; zum Kaffee wurden abermals Kuchen gebracht; und für alles dieses betrug die Rechnung noch keinen halben Bankthaler. Im Speisesaal hing eine Menge kleiner Kupferstiche, welche biblische Geschichten darstellten und nicht übel gerathen waren.

Am folgenden Morgen fuhr ich auf Sollefteå's nahen Pfarrhof zum Propste Sundberg. Der Weg führt durch die Marktbuden, die sich in großer Zahl, auf dem Wege nach Ed ausbreiten; hier wird den 25. Jan. der berühmte große (Pålsmesso) Markt von Sollefteå gehalten, der von Lappen und Bottniern, Norwegern und Stockholmern besucht wird; man verkauft Pferde, Fische, Rennthierfleisch, Butter, Talg ꝛc.; Tauschhandel ist nicht mehr üblich. Der zweite große Markt am Ångerman, zu Hammar, unterhalb Thorsåkers Kirche, am 16. Junius, ist nicht ganz so bedeutend, wie der Markt von Sollefteå, und wird nicht von Lappen besucht. In Sollefteå wird auch das jährliche Bruksting, d. i. Gericht für die Hüttendistrikte Ångermanlands gehalten; alle Berg- und Hüttenwerke haben nämlich ihre eigene Gerichtsbarkeit; übrigens kommt das Bergsting völlig einem Häradsting gleich. Es wird mit einer Predigt eröffnet, worauf die Verhandlungen ihren Anfang nehmen.

Unweit des Pfarrhofes liegt die Kirche von Sollefteå; ein großes steinernes Gebäude, welches aber im Aeußern eher einem Tanzsaal oder einem Gerichtshofe, als einer Kirche, gleicht; es ward im Jahr 1773 erbauet oder meist erneuert, und ist ohne Thurm. Das Innere der Kirche ist würdig und schön; nur eine Orgel fehlt. Die Kanzel ist vergoldet und mit passenden Sinnbildern geziert; über dem Altar erhebt sich, zwischen einem auf 4 Säulen ruhenden Portal, eine schöne Altartafel: die Kreuzigung; das Händeringen der Weiber, der Augenblick, wo der Kriegsknecht die Seite durchbohren will, ist besonders gelungen; unter diesem Bilde stellt ein zweites den betenden Erlöser dar, wie ein Engel auf Ihn herabkommt; an den Seiten erblickt man ein Paar Figuren mit dem Kreuz und mit dem Anker;

oben eine Sonne und darüber eine silbergefärbte Taube; diese ausgenommen, ist alles vergoldet.

Vom Glockenthurm hat man eine herrliche Aussicht auf die reizenden Umgebungen: an dem Ufer, wo Sollefta liegt, breitet sich eine weite fruchtbare Ebene aus, Theil des Stora Ådalen (großen Flußthals); das Bruk, in einer Uferschlucht, ist nicht sichtbar, wohl aber der Wasserfall in der Nähe desselben; dem Falle gegenüber erhebt sich ein kegelförmiger Waldberg. Etwa eine Viertelmeile oberhalb schlängelt sich der Fluß zwischen Waldbergen hindurch; dieser Theil der Aussicht ist der schönste. — Die Wasserfälle bei Ed und Ramsele sind bedeutender.

Das Bruk Sollefta enthält zwei Stabeisen- und zwei Stahlheerde; es gehört dem Brukspatron Classon auf Graninge an der Jemteländischen Gränze. Graninge, das älteste Bruk im Lande, hat 5 Stabeisenheerde, einige Manufaktureisenheerde für kleinere Eisenwaaren, als Messer ꝛc., und Nagelhammer; überdies besitzt Herr Classon noch folgende Eisenwerke: Fors in Jemteland mit 2 Stabeisenheerden und einer Sägemühle; Bidcå im Pastorat Arnäs mit Stabeisenheerden; Bollsta, Hochofen in Thorsåker's Pastorat, zur Hälfte (die andere Hälfte gehört Herrn Nordenfalk), und Torp's Hammer in Medelpad, Pastorat Torp, gleichfalls nur zur Hälfte (die zweite Hälfte ist Eigenthum der Erben des Bischofs Nordin).

Sollefta's Pastorat enthält 5 Kirchen: 1. die Mutterkirche Sollefta; 2. Filial Multrå, wo kein Prediger wohnt; 3. Filial Ed mit 1 Kirchspielsprediканten; 4. Långsele, wo 1 Comminister wohnt; 5. Brukskirche Graninge, in welcher ein eigener Bruksprediger sonntäglich predigt, die aber nur Kapelle des Filials Långsele ist; in den Filialen fällt jeden dritten Sonntag, Multrå's halber, der Gottesdienst aus. Die Einwohnerzahl des gesammten Pastorats betrug, im Jahr 1815, 2911; die Zahl der Gebornen, im Jahr 1816, 84, worunter 4 uneheliche; der Ehen 25 (2 büßten für anticipirten Beischlaf). Ehescheidungen sind fast unerhört; eben so in diesem ganzen Theil von Ångermanland. Die meisten der hiesigen Pastoren haben, wie in Westerbotten, für ihre Wittwen, kleine Wittwensitze errichtet. Wenige

II.   F f sich dem Jugendunterricht widmen können. Eine Orgel findet man nur in der Kirche Ragunda; das Pastorat Ragunda ist das einzige, wo regelmäßig Dorfgottesdienst gehalten wird. Die kleinen Erbauungsschriften der evangelischen Gesellschaft in Stockholm sind vertheilt worden; im ganzen Contract liest man sie mit großer Begierde, und es ist nach denselben viele Nachfrage.

Am 8. Aug. Von Hylista nach Ås 1¼ M.; von Ås nach Thorsåker 1¼ M. — Zus. 3 M.

Um 4½ Uhr Nachmittags brach ich von Sollefta auf. Von einer Höhe am Wege blickt man in die tiefe Uferschlucht hinab, in welcher das Bruk liegt; man überschauet auch den kleinen, aber langen Wasserfall, nebst einem bewaldeten Inselchen, und die herrlichen Ufer des obern Ångerman. Bald kommt man in den Wald. Am Ausgange desselben überrascht eine schöne Aussicht auf die liebliche, meist bergige Landschaft am untern Ångerman mit Dörfern; den Hintergrund bilden die Verzweigungen blauender Berge. Multrå's Glockenthurm ist ein vorzüglich schöner Punkt in dem schönen Ganzen. Dann fährt man größere und kleinere Hügel auf und ab, freundlich blickt der dunkelblaue Ångerman durch grüne Gebüsche hervor und eine weite Bergebene breitet sich am jenseitigen Ufer aus. Die Bergebene macht die Aussichten auf diesem Ufer, auf der ersten Meile von Sollefta, noch schöner und reicher, als die auf dem jenseitigen Ufer, wo ich gestern fuhr. In Klofsta wechselte ich das Pferd, denn dort wohnte der eben zum Reservestjuts pflichtige Bauer, indem, wie ich erfuhr, das Eine Hållpferd von Ås schon ausgegangen war. Von nun an raubt ein langer Wald meistens den Anblick des Ångerman; eine halbe Meile fährt man im Walde, in welchem Wiesen und Waldschluchten mit Bächen, die in den Ångerman rinnen, wechseln. Jetzt führt der Weg über Waldhöhen, an deren Fuße, in schwindelnder Tiefe, der Ångerman fließt, und von wo man weit und breit das jenseitige Ufer mit seinen Kirchen überschauet; jetzt über Wiesen, die freundliche Baumgruppen beschatten; jetzt durch Gebüsche und sich krümmende Thäler, eine Menge Dörfer erscheint am Wege; von Holm sieht man nur ein einzelnes Gebäude, nicht die schöne Lage.

In Ås Gästgifvaregård schrieb ich ins Tagebuch und fuhr dann Hämra's Gästgifvaregård vorüber geradezu nach Thorsåker. Beim Dorfe Löckum war ein Schwendefeuer dem Erlöschen nahe, es rauchte nur noch stark; Gesträuppe, Moos und Wurzeln waren verbrannt *), die Bäume nur verkohlt, so daß man sie noch zum Kohlen verwenden konnte. Schon am gestrigen Abend hatte der Rauch einen Theil der schönen Gegend verhüllt. Bei Hämra führt eine Fähre über den Ångerman nach Undrom unweit Botheå's Kirche; daneben liegt die schöne Waldinsel Boteholm. Hinter Hämra zeigte sich am Abhange eines Waldberges ein großes Schwendefeuer, welches erst vor Kurzem angezündet zu seyn schien. Der Weg läuft nun in einem weiten Thale zwischen hohen Uferbergen und mehr oder weniger nackten Felswänden, die zum Theil hübsche Gruppen bilden. Es war ein herrlicher Abend; warme Südostwinde fächelten. Schon dämmerte es, als ich in Thorsåkers Pfarrhofe anlangte, wo mich Propst Genberg freundlich bewillkommte. Musik schallte aus dem Gemeindehause entgegen; der Propst hatte seinen Heuarbeitern eine kleine Freude bereitet: ich ging hin: man tanzte mit vielem Anstand, selbst Takt (freilich steht der Tanz der Ångermanländer dem schönen und leichten, eben so wenig erlerntem Tanze der Warmeländer nach), und mit so herzlichem Frohsinn, daß auch der Zuschauer froh werden mußte; da zeigte sich der Tanz in seiner Reinheit und Natürlichkeit, wie man ihn so selten noch trifft; auch eine kleine Bewirthung wurde den Tanzenden gereicht.

---

*) Vergl. Bd. 1. S. 141. 142. Im Siegenschen wird auf den sogenannten Haubergen, oder Niederwald, meist aus Birken und Eichen bestehend, das Holz, nach der bei jedem Berg angeordneten Eintheilung der Haue von 16 zu 16 oder 20 Jahren, mit Ausnahme einiger Saamenbäume, auf der Wurzel abgetrieben, der Boden gehackt und gebrannt, mit Roggen oder mit Heidekorn besäet, dann 4 bis 5 Jahre gehegt, und demnächst als Viehweide benutzt, bis das Holz wieder abgetrieben werden kann. S. C. F. Scheuck, Statistik des vormaligen Fürstenthums Siegen. Siegen, 1820. 464 S. gr. 8. H.

Thorsåker liegt in einer schönen Ebene, die ein Hintergrund von Waldbergen schließt. Am Ufer, der Kirche Styrnäs gegenüber, trifft man alte Wälle, Gräben und Mauerwerk, borgen genannt; Ueberbleibsel alter Festungswerke, die einst die Dänen besetzt gehalten haben sollen, während die Schweden, jenseits, in Styrnäs Befestigungen inne hatten, von welchen aus sie die Dänen besiegten. Nach einer alten Sage, die hier gefundene alte Münzen bestätigen, wurden Botheå und Thorsåker zuerst in diesen Gegenden angebauet; daher die vielen Attehögar, die man hier erblickt. Des frühen Anbaues, insbesondere des blühenden Zustandes wegen zu Karls XI. Zeit, wo die Schatzlegung geschah, haben diese Orte einen jetzt unverhältnißmäßig großen Schatz zu entrichten; ein Theil desselben ist Lachsschatz, weil von uralten Zeiten her hier Lachsfang war, der aber jetzt nicht mehr dem Hemman folgt, das den Lachsschatz entrichtet, vielmehr muß für den Lachsfang noch ein besonderer Schatz an die Krone erlegt werden.

Die Kirche ist alt; vor zwei Jahren zerschmetterte ein Blitzstrahl das Außendach. Das Innere der Kirche ist zierlich und würdig; den Altar schmücket ein offener Rahmen, an dessen Seiten man die Sinnbilder des Glaubens und der Hoffnung erblickt; in der Höhe ist das jüngste Gericht dargestellt: der Heiland erscheint in den Wolken, umgeben von Engeln; der eine der Engel hält die Posaune, der andere ein aufgeschlagenes Buch; untern ist die Geburt Jesu in Holz abgebildet. In Thorsåkers Kirche, wie in mehreren Kirchen Ångermanlands, fand ich ausgehobene und Drathfenster, zur Reinigung der Kirchenluft. — Der Glockenthurm steht innerhalb des Kirchhofs.

Gewitter scheinen in dieser Gegend besonders verderblich zu seyn. Noch letzten Sonntag hatte in einem nahen Dörfchen der Blitz sich in einem Hause, dessen Thüre und Ofensplint offen standen, den Eingang gebahnt, und ein altes Ehepaar getroffen, welches aber wieder genesen war; ein alter Mann, der auf dem Boden lag, hatte sein Gehör eingebüßt, während ein Knabe, der in der Thüre stand, unversehrt geblieben war.

In der Nähe des hübschen, vom vorigen Propste Risen angelegten, Gartens trifft man einen Ättehög, auf welchem sich jetzt ein Rasensitz erhebt; rings umher sind Sperberbäume (rönn) gepflanzt; ein zweiter Grabhügel ist bei Anlegung des Gartens abgetragen worden; auf der andern Seite liegt ein dritter, der mit Gebüsch bewachsen ist.

Das Pastorat Thorsåker besteht aus 3 Gemeinden und der Muttergemeinde Thorsåker im J. 1815 mit 603, und den Filis algemeinden Ytterlåndå mit 1086 und Dahl mit 524 Einwohnern. Handelsbauern giebt es wenig, desto mehr handelnde Seefahrer. Bei jeder Kirche wohnt ein fest angestellter Geistlicher, seit die Gemeinde Dahl auch einen solchen annahm, um sonntäglichen Gottesdienst zu haben. Dahl's Kirche liegt ¾ M. von der Mutterkirche, in einem schönen Thale. Keine dieser Kirchen hat eine Orgel. Es herrscht viel Luxus; Kartenspiel ist wenig üblich: man spielt um Branntewein und Eier. In Ytterlåndå, wo viel handelnde Seefahrer wohnen, herrscht viel Leichtsinn und Armuth. *) Große und zierliche Häuser reichgewordener Schiffskapitaine sieht man oft im südlichen Angermanland.

Am 9. August. Von Thorsåker nach Nyland ⅞ M.; von N. nach Gudmundrå 1⅞ M. — Zus. 2 M.

In Thorsåker war ich durch die Nachricht erfreut worden, daß mein Freund, der Kanzleirath Norberg aus Lund, wie er es mir schon früher verheißen hatte, in Gudmundrå bei seinem Bruder, dem dortigen Propste, wirklich angelangt sey. Ich eilte nun dahin, Propst Genberg begleitete mich. Um 12 Uhr fuhren wir ab. Der Weg führt am Rande eines schönen Thales, dann durch Wald, in geringer Entfernung vom Flusse; von der Höhe überschaut man die beiden Ufer. Eine kurze Strecke vor

---

*) Im J. 1804 machte der Großhändler Dan. Elspelund in Stockh. für seinen Geburtsort Thorsåker eine Stiftung, aus welcher jährlich 5 Rthlr. der Kirche zufallen, 45 Rthlr. als Aufmunterung zu Urbarmachungen, und 50 Rthlr. zu Brautgaben verwandt werden sollen.

Nyland erscheinen die Marktbuden von Hammar, in einer schönen Lage auf Wiesen am Ångerman; ein Bauer hat sich mitten zwischen den Buden angesiedelt. Unweit des Gästgifvaregård Nyland liegt der Ladeplatz und Hafen gleiches Namens, wo eben 7 Schiffe, worunter sich einige Zweimaster befanden, vor Anker lagen; bei widrigen Winden sammeln sich hier oft ganze Flotten. Eine Menge Bretter, meist aus Resele, oben mit Dächern versehen, und viel Roheisen (tarkjern) lagen am Bollwerk. Es herrscht hier viel Wohlhabenheit, aber auch viel Verdorbenheit.

In Nyland traf ich den Capitain Risén, welcher mit der Reinigung des Ångerman oberhalb Sollesta, wo er aufhört schiffbar zu seyn, beauftragt war; man will die Wasserfälle wenigstens so weit aufräumen, daß sie das Holzflößen zulassen, welches für Stockholm, wohin der Holztransport aus Finnland jetzt erschwert ist, von großer Wichtigkeit ist.

Hinter Nyland fährt man einen Berg hinan, von dessen Höhe man den Lauf und die Ufer des Ångerman auf einer Strecke von 1½ M. überblicket; bald gewährt eine zweite Stelle einen noch schöneren Prospect, den schönsten am ganzen Ångerman: mehrere kleine Seen, von Wiesen, Heuscheunen und Gebüschen umgeben; der Ångerman, der hier in einen großen Busen, Ångermansfjärd, ausgeht, rings umher hohe Waldberge, — bilden ein unbeschreiblich schönes Ganzes. Auf bergigem Wege gelangt man nun zur Kirche Ytterlänäs, die auf einem Hügel anmuthig da liegt; im J. 1773 zertrümmerte ein Blitz das Dach. Die Kirche ist alt und soll neu gebauet werden; sie ist zu klein für die Volksmenge. Den Altar schmückt ein offener Rahmen mit den gewöhnlichen Sinnbildern; die Figur mit dem Kreuz führt zugleich einen Becher, und die mit dem Anker einen Palmenzweig. — Die Kirche hat einen kleinen Thurm. Unterhalb des Kirchhügels breitet sich ein liebliches Thal aus.

In Ytterlänäs ward mir folgende merkwürdige Begebenheit, die vor längerer Zeit Statt fand, erzählt: der Küster läßt den, fast 2 Pfund schweren Kirchenschlüssel, der mit Aalhaut umwunden war, auf einem Hügel liegen; als er wiederkehrt, vermißt er denselben; lange hernach wird derselbe im Walde, in ei-

nem Adlerneste gefunden; man vermuthet, daß ein Schlagad-
ler den Schlüssel entführt habe.

Der Kirche vorüber läuft die Straße nach der ⅜ Meile
entfernten Papiermühle Nyebe, im Kirchspiele Dahl, der einzigen in Ängermanland.

Von Ytterländs fährt man neben mehreren schönbebuschten
Thälern hin. Beim Hochofen Bollsta führt eine Brücke über
einen ansehnlichen Busen des Ängerman; diese Brücke gewährt
die reizendsten Aussichten, auf das Thal von Nyebe an der einen, und auf Wiesen und die Ufer und Buchten des Ängerman
an der andern Seite. Dann läuft der Weg wohl ⅜ M. bergan, bis man die Höhe eines Wal-berges erreicht hat, von welcher man Gudmundrä's anmuthige Thäler und Busen weit überschauet: eine, von Felsen durchschnittene, aus vielen Thälern bestehende Landschaft erscheint: die Thäler bilden endlich eine große
Ebene; die von Gebüsch bekränzten Felsen zeigen sich, von der
bedeutenden Höhe, niedrigen Mauern gleich; auch des breite
Flußbette des Ängerman umschließen Felsen. Nachdem man eine
Sechszehntelmeile bergab gefahren, befindet man sich schon in einem jener Thäler; dieser Weg von der Spitze abwärts ist einer der
anmuthigsten in ganz Schweden. Je tiefer man hinabfährt, in
desto mehrere Theile scheidet sich die Ebene und rechts hinter
dem Berge taucht ein Thal nach dem andern hervor. Alle diese
Thäler sind höchst reizend; man wird an die schönsten Thäler
Italiens oder der Schweiz erinnert: Dörfer und Wassermühlen
füllen die von Bächen durchschnittenen Thäler aus, oder ziehen sich
an den Abhängen der Berge hinauf; Wiesenhügel oder Felsen
mit Buschwerk trennen die einzelnen Thäler, welche hier und da
der majestätische Ängerman begränzt. Man fährt eine Strecke
an und in diesen Thälern fort, neben der Sägemühle
Kramfors hin, und erreicht bald Gudmundrä's schöne Kirche, die schon beim Herabfahren, eine Weile, sichtbar war. —
Um 6 Uhr fuhren wir in den Pfarrhof ein, wo wir von den
drei Brüdern — denn auch der dritte Bruder, Brukspatron
Norberg von Söderfors in Medelpad war angelangt — herzlich
bewillkommet wurden. Der Propst hatte eben eine schmerzhafte

Operation überstanden; doch die Freude, mit seinen Brüdern nach langer Zeit wieder vereint zu seyn, hatte ihn wie neubelebt. Die drei Brüder standen zwischen dem 69sten und 75sten Jahre ihres Alters.

Schöne Stunden verflossen mir in dem schönen Gudmunsdrå. Vor Tische ward noch die steinerne Kirche besichtiget. Sie ward im Jahre 1807 von Geting gebauet, und hat im Aeußern und Innern viele Aehnlichkeit mit den Kirchen von Nätra und Nora. Sie hat einen Thurm, aber bisher keine Orgel; das Orgelchor ist dem in Stockholms Storkyrka nachgeahmt. Unter der Sakristey ist ein dreifacher Weinkeller zur Aufbewahrung des Abendmahlsweins in Felsen ausgehauen. Die Kirche liegt auf einem Hügel; eine Allee von Sperberbäumen umgiebt an der innern Mauer den Kirchhof; auch außen an den Abseiten des Hügels zieht sich ein schöner Espenkreis um den Kirchhof, wie um die Kirchspielsstube und die Kirchenställe hin. Kirchenbuden giebt es hier nicht. Von der Höhe hat man die reizendsten Aussichten auf die fruchtbare Umgegend, welche weniger zu Kornfeldern als zu Wiesen benutzt wird; man hält überhaupt in Norrland dafür, daß eine gute Wiese einträglicher sey, als ein guter Acker.

———

Am 10. Augst. Von Gudmundrå nach Fräne ¾ M.; von F. nach Weda 1⅓ M.; von W. nach Nesland 1⅓ M.; von N. nach Hernösand 1 M. — Sus. 4¼ M.

Meine Abreise war zu 6 Uhr Morgens angesetzt, da ich in Högsjö dem Gottesdienste beiwohnen, in Utansjö verweilen und doch noch bei guter Zeit in Hernösand eintreffen wollte. Aber das von Fräne bestellte Pferd kam nicht. Des Wartens müde, fuhr ich 7½ Uhr mit Genborg's Pferde ab, bis Fräne, wo ich das bestellte Pferd endlich vorfand.

Der Weg führt am Ångerman, der hier den Busen von Gudmundrå bildet, über sanfte Anhöhen, neben vielen Dörfern und Höfen. So erreicht man Fräne. Dann fährt man neben engen Thälern, auf Waldhöhen, unter wechselnden Aussichten; am schönsten ist es auf der Höhe bei Slätta und bei Nensjö.

Bei Nenfjö überblickt man den Lauf und das Waldufer des nun
immer breiter werdenden Stromes, faſt in der Ausdehnung einer
Meile. Vorgebirge und waldige Landzungen wechſeln mit hohen
Waldinſeln. Man kommt zum großen Mårdſee, an deſſen eis
nem Ufer, neben der alten Kirche, der Pfarrhof, an deſſen ans
derem Ufer Högſjö's neue Kirche nebſt Gemeindehauſe und Kirs
chenſtällen ſich zeigt. Als ich anlangte, hatte der Gottesdienſt
ſchon angefangen; mit großer Aufmerkſamkeit hörten etwa 400
Menſchen der Predigt zu; ich blieb bis ans Ende des Gottes⸗
dienſtes; die Männer gingen zuerſt aus der Kirche, dann folgte
das weibliche Geſchlecht. Die Kirche iſt ein neues ſteinernes
Gebäude; über dem Eingange lieſet man: „Guſtav III. 16,
Regierungsjahr. 1788."

„Herr, unſer Gott, erhöre das Flehen deines Knechtes und
deines Volkes Iſrael, das ſie hier thun werden an dieſer Stäte;
und erhöre es, wo du wohneſt, im Himmel, und wann du es
hörest, ſey gnädig. 1 Kön. 8, 30."

Die Kirche ſchmückt ein Thurm. Das Innere iſt einfach
und würdig. — Früher war Högſjö Filial von Gudmundrå;
jetzt gehört es als Filialgemeinde zu Nora.

Aus der Kirche ging ich nach dem nahen Weda, und fuhr
von da nach Utanſjö, ½ M. Ein hoher Waldberg mußte übers
ſtiegen werden; ſchon fuhr ich abwärts, an der Seite furchtbarer
Abgründe, als plötzlich das Sielenzeug riß; in Furcht, das noch
jugendliche Pferd möge nicht im Zaume gehalten werden können,
ſprang ich aus dem Wagen, und trug eine Contuſion am Arme
davon, die mir lange Schmerzen verurſachte. Dem Skjutsbonde
gelang es, das Pferd zu halten.

In Utanſjö ward ich von der lieben Familie Gavelius herz⸗
lich empfangen, fand auch den braven Håradshöfding Wallgrén
vor, deſſen Bekanntſchaft mir Freude machte. Die lieben Leute
nahmen ſo viel Antheil an meinem Unfall, als hätte er ſie ſels
ber betroffen; man bat zu bleiben und wollte ſelbſt Mittel zur
Heilung anwenden; doch ich ſetzte, nachdem ich die ſchöne Lage
des Bruk am Ångerman in Augenſchein genommen, nach dem
Mittagseſſen die Reiſe fort.

Der Weg bis Nesland ist sehr bergig; man hat Waldthäler und Seen; vom Angerman entfernt man sich aber immer weiter, bis auf eine halbe Meile. Bei Nesland gelangt man an
eine Meeresbucht, die in die eine Mündung des Angerman an
dem Süderende der Insel Hemsö, einläuft.

Von Nesland aus fuhr ich über Säbrä, welches nur eine
kleine Strecke von der Landstraße entfernt liegt, um die Kirche
zu sehen. Sie ist von Stein, ihrer Grundlage nach alt, aber
1759 umgebaut, noch thurmlos, und hat im Aeußern wenig das
Ansehen einer Kirche. Schöner und würdiger ist das Innere.
Das amphitheatralisch gebaute Chor ruht auf sechs Pfeilern; eine
Orgel ist nicht vorhanden; die Sakristey ist geräumig und schön.
Als Altarbild dient ein schlechtes Oelgemälde, welches die Auf-
erstehung darstellt; daneben erblickt man ein Paar Engel von
Holz, den einen mit dem Kreuze, den andern betend; über dem
Bilde in einer Nische das Lamm mit der Fahne, und unter dem
Lamme zwei schlafende Kindlein; eine herrliche Idee, welche mu-
sterhaft ausgeführt ist. — Unweit der Kirche liegt das schöne
hölzerne Pfarrhaus, welches der Bischof zuweilen im Sommer
bewohnt. Säbrä und Hernösand mit Hernö bilden, nebst den
Pastoraten Stigsjö und Häggdänger, Angermanlands südliche
Propstei (södra Contract); alle sind Präbenden, Säbrä und
Hernösand mit Hernö Landgemeinde des Bischofs, Stigsjö und
Häggdänger der Lectoren; zu Stigsjö gehört die Kapelle Wiksjö
und die Brukskirche Wästanä; in Wiksjö wohnen, wahrscheinlich
seit Karl XI., auch Finnen aus Savolax, die aber jetzt Schwedisch sprechen und mit den Schweden verschmolzen sind; auch
in Gudmundrä ließen sich Finnen nieder, die aber jetzt völlig Schweden sind. Die Propstei ist eine der kleinsten des Reichs; die
Zahl der Gebornen betrug, im Jahr 1816, 131, worunter 6 uneheliche. — Um 9½ Uhr langte ich in Hernösand an, wo ich
beim Kellermeister Bystadt abtrat.

Am folgenden Morgen wurde der Arzt consultirt; dieser,
Assessor, Doktor Medic., Lunell, welcher zugleich als Lector
der Mathematik im Consistorium sitzt, verordnete einige Mittel,
deren Gebrauch indeß die Fortsetzung der Reise nicht hinderte.

Ich blieb nun noch ein Paar Tage in Hernösand, die, ganz nach der Weise meines ersten Aufenthalts, durch die Güte des Bischofs und der Lectoren froh und nützlich verstrichen. Literärische Nachforschungen, Besichtigungen, fröhliche Gesellschaften und Excursionen in die schöne Umgegend wechselten: einer der angenehmsten Spaziergänge war der, zu welchem, nach einem hellern Mittagsmahle beim Bischofe, dieser und der Lector Forsberg, mich einluden: unser Ziel war der, eine Stunde entfernte, Wälkas (richtiger Wårdkase,) Berg. Der Weg dahin führt dem schönen Stadtgarten, einer öffentlichen Promenade, und Stenhammar, dem freundlichen Wittwensitze der Bischöfin Nordin, der, von Ulmen umschattet, gar lieblich an dem die Insel Hernö vom festen Lande trennenden Meerbusen da liegt, vorüber. Dann geht es unter herrlichen Aussichten auf die schön gelegene Stadt, auf Meerbusen und Wiesen, aufwärts auf schwierigem Sandwege; früherhin lief der Weg mehr seitwärts, aber von den Bergen herabströmende Frühlingsfluthen, die die Stadt in Schrecken setzten, haben den bisherigen Weg in tiefe Schluchten verwandelt. Man erreicht den Wald, wo Beeren den Wanderer erquicken. Immer höher und höher windet sich der Pfad. Endlich, über bewaldete Felsen hinan, gelangt man zum Gipfel, welcher, ganz kahl, eine unendliche Aussicht gewährt. Weit und breit überschauet man Land und Meer: an der einen Seite die Insel Hernö mit der Stadt Hernösand, die nicht unbedeutenden Hügel in der Stadt und um dieselbe, deren einen ein alter Festungsthurm ziert, verschwinden von dieser Höhe aus völlig in die Ebene; rings umher zeigen sich liebliche Landsitze und Wiesen; jenseits Buchten, Vorgebirge und Inseln, nebst dem Hafen der Stadt und dem Einlaufe zum Hafen. An der entgegengesetzten Seite überschauet man die Küste zwischen Hernösand und Sundswall, bis zu der, ein Paar Meilen von Sundswall gelegenen hohen Insel Brämön (die in gerader Linie etwa 5 Meilen vom Berge entfernt seyn mag). Am Fuße des Wälkas erscheint Grönviken, der hübsche Landsitz des Herrn Svedbom, Rectors der Trivialschule in Hernösand, an einem lieblichen Landsee, der nur durch einen waldigen Bergrükken vom Meere geschieden ist, und weiterhin, am Waldsaume, ein Bauerhof. Die schönen Thäler an der Küste zwischen Hernösand und Sundswall, von denen sonst die Hernösand nahegelegenen sichtbar sind, verhüllten jetzt Regenwolken. — Auf dem Gipfel des Berges ist ein Holzstoß (vårdkase) aus pyramidalisch neben einander gestellten Stangen errichtet, der in Kriegszeiten als Signal angezündet wird; inwendig ist ein leerer Raum, zu welchem an der einen Seite ein Zugang freigelassen ist, also daß die Pyramide auch als Zufluchtsort gegen Regen und Sturm, und als Schilderhaus dienen kann. Der Berg ist auch Merkzeichen für die Seefahrer.

Eine Stunde hatten wir auf unserm Wege von der Stadt bis zum Gipfel des Berges gebraucht. Der Rückweg war bis ans Ende des Waldes derselbe, dann nahmen wir einen andern Weg, der uns nach Gärresta, dem Landsitze des Lector Berlin, führte; einige Regentropfen netzten uns, doch bald waren die träufelnden Wolken vorübergezogen, und ein schöner milder Abend erquickte uns. Um Gärresta herum hat der Lector Kolonisten angesiedelt, zwischen denen er hier ganz patriarchalisch lebt. Aus dem bescheidenen Landhause hat man eine herrliche Aussicht auf die Stadt, die sich, mit ihren Wiesen umher, von dieser Seite besonders vortheilhaft ausnimmt; neben dem Wohnhause ist ein hübscher Garten angelegt, mit bedecktem Laubgange, hübschem Lusthause, in Form eines Achteckes und herrlichen Aussichten auf die schöne Umgegend. Auch Apfelbäume findet man, deren Frucht aber nicht immer reift, vielmehr einen säuerlichen, schlechten Geschmack hat; nicht minder Doppelrosen. Da Freund Berlin sehr an Rückenschmerz litt, so blieben wir nur kurz, und kehrten in milder Abendluft, auf einem anmuthigen Wege, dem schönen Capellberg, dem auf einer Höhe gelegenen Landsitze des Kammeraths Selling vorbei, nach Hernösand zurück. Am dritten Tage nahm ich von den lieben Leuten, die mir meinen Aufenthalt so sehr verschönert hatten, Abschied, und fuhr nach einem frohen Mittagsmahle bei Lector Forsberg, noch um 6½ Uhr Abends ab, da mein Reiseplan Eile erheischte.

Am 13. August. Von Hernösand nach Mörl 1⅓ M.; von M. nach Fjäl 2 M. — Zus. 3⅓ M.

In Strömen floß der Regen; zwar sicherte mich mein Regenschirm; aber der Anblick der schönen Thäler ward mir geraubt; nur das Thal, in welchem der Helgom hinstürzt, war sichtbar. Um 10½ Uhr langte ich in Fjäl, dem ersten Gästgifvaregård in Medelpad, an, wo ich trefflich übernachtete.

Fünf und zwanzigstes Kapitel.

Reise in Medelpad.

Fjäl. Der Indals-Elf. — Hafen und Werft Wifsta. — Die Bewohner der Küsten und die Bewohner des Innern. — Gesundbrunnen Solum. — Kirche Indal; reizende Aussicht am Ufer des Indal. — Medelpads Ackerbau. — Kirche Silländer. — Der Grabschmaus. — Der Njurunda-Elf. — Wasserfall Tunafors. — Kirche und Pastorat Tuna. — Einwohnerzahl von Medelpad. — Der edle Bauer John Hinderson; das Volk von Hafrö. — Die Stiftungen in Tuna. — Die Kinderverhöre in den Dörfern. — Treffliche Armenpflege. — Fahrbarmachung des Ljunga-Elf. — Der Gottesdienst in Stöde. — Eigenthümlichkeiten des Volks von Stöde. — Medelpads Finnen. — Die Dönenfalle. — Der Gimån. — Pastorat Torp. — Die Kirchen Torp und Borgsjö; die felsige Kirchgasse; das Eleunthier. — Jämtkrogen; die einfachen Menschen; der Gränzwald.

———

Am 14. August. Von Fjäl nach Wifsta 1 M.; von W. nach Kofland 1 M.; von K. nach Indal 1½ M. — Zus. 3½ M.

Bis Wifsta fuhr ich in Gesellschaft Herrn und Frau Sonerling's aus Sundswall, die ich in Fjäl traf; Herr Sonerling ist Bergungscommissair für das Län Hernösand. Bei Fjäl setzt man über den Fluß Indal, der jetzt weniger wasserreich war; von

Ufer der Insel, über welche die Straße führt, schallte uns das Geläute der Kuhglocken entgegen. Man fährt hernach eine Strecke längs des Flusses, dessen Ufer hier Wiesen und Wald-hügel bilden. ¼ Meile vor Wissta erblickt man das Meer und Wissta's Werft. Wir fuhren hinab: zwei Schiffe lagen auf dem Stapel; im Hafen, von welchem die Schiffe beladen auslau-fen, lag ein Dreidecker. Das Werft, wo gewöhnlich nur Ein Schiff jährlich gebaut wird, gehört den Städten Hernösand und Sundswall gemeinschaftlich, seit nämlich im Jahre 1810 Sundss-wall 45 der 150 Actien an sich kaufte. Hier ist auch eine Nie-derlage für Holzwaaren aus Medelpad, die hier während des Freimarkts in Sundswall feil gehalten werden. Der Hafen hat tiefes Wasser und wird durch hohe Landzungen, wie durch vor-liegende Inseln, geschützt. — Vom Werft fuhren wir zum Gäst-gifvaregärd Wissta, wo wir auf Pferde warten mußten. In Wissta ist ein junger, selten nüchterner Gästgifvare. Die Liebe zum Trunk ist in den Küstenkirchspielen Medelpads, namentlich Hässjö, Timrä, Slön, und vor allen, in den schon mehr land-einwärts gelegenen Kirchspielen Sillänger und Sättna, sehr ver-breitet: fast in jedem Dorfe trifft man Säufer. Zugleich herr-schen Eigennutz und Ungefälligkeit in hohem Grade, und fast das dritte Wort ist ein Fluch. Ohne Rückhalt spricht man seine unverschämten Forderungen aus; kann man sie nicht sofort erlan-gen, so fängt man an zu betteln, besonders um Branntewein. Ein lebendiges Beispiel dieses Gemäldes war mein Skjutsbonde von Wissta. Als mich hernach mein Weg der Kirche Timrä vorüberführte, bat ich den Skjutsbonde, die Kirche durch den nahewohnenden Küster öffnen zu lassen: erst nachdem ich Be-zahlung verheißen, verstand er sich zu dem kurzen Gange, be-merkte aber, daß es ungewiß sey, ob der Küster meinen Wunsch gewähren werde; ich benutzte die Gelegenheit, das ungefällige Benehmen zu tadeln und mit demselben das dienstfertige Wesen der Ångermanländer und der Westerbottnier zu vergleichen; er begriff gar wohl, daß ich Recht hatte, aber er ward so wenig bewegt, daß er, ganz kalt, bekannte, wie es in diesen Stücken in Medelpad allerdings ganz anders sey. Im Innern von Wes-

delpad trifft man noch mehr Unverdorbenheit. — Uebrigens sind
die Medelpader ein kluges und geschicktes Volk: fast jeder Bauer
verfertiget seine Bedürfnisse selbst, ist Schmidt, Tischler ꝛc.; doch
gilt dies von fast ganz Norrland. Die Weiber Medelpads zeichnen sich in physischer und geistiger Hinsicht vortheilhaft vor den
Männern aus: regelmäßige Schönheiten findet man selten, desto
häufiger aber interessante und geistvolle Gesichter, zumal in Tuna
und Stöde, an der Seite von Jemteland. — Männer und
Weiber fahren gut und schnell. Schuhe aus Birkenrinde (näf-
verskor) sind auch in Medelpad üblich.

In Wissta trennte ich mich von meinen Begleitern, die
nach Sundswall zurückkehrten, während ich landeinwärts fuhr.
Bis zur Kirche Timrå, in einem der üppigsten Thäler, am
Meere, ⅜ Meile von Wissta, hat man die große Landstraße.
Dann beginnt ein schlechter Kirchspielsweg; die Gegend ist gar
anmuthig: eine Menge kleiner Thäler, die bald ein Dorf, bald
ein See ausfüllt oder aus welchen mit Gebüsch und Wiesen be-
deckte Anhöhen emporsteigen; von den Hügeln, die sie trennen,
hat man hübsche Aussichten. Auf der Hälfte des Weges, beim Dorfe
Solum, trifft man eine seit etwa 10 Jahren aufgenommene
Heilquelle, welche dem Bauer Pehr Nilsson in Solum gehört;
sie ist nicht sehr mineralhaltig, soll aber viel benützt werden.
Die Quelle ist mit einem Brunnensaal überbaut; zum Saal,
der recht freundlich auf einem schönbebuschten Hügel mit hübscher
Thalaussicht da liegt, führt eine Allee; aus der Quelle wird das
Wasser in Röhren in zwei Badehäuser geleitet; das für Stan-
despersonen bestimmte ist recht gut zu kalten Bädern eingerichtet.

Hinter Kosland ist die Gegend sehr bergig, aber wohl angebauet; durch Thäler und über Höhen erreicht man einen hohen
Uferberg, von welchem man an den Indals-Elf herabfährt; die
Aussicht, die man, im Herabfahren, auf das jenseitige Ufer genießt, ist eine der schönsten in ganz Schweden: den Hintergrund bilden hohe Waldberge, dann folgen ununterbrochene Reiten von Dörfern, von welchen sich endlich Wiesen und Kornfelder, mit Gebüschen bekränzt, die Abhänge bis an den Fluß hin-
abziehen: die Ufer des Indal, wie einige freundliche Inseln be-

II.   G g

deckt Buschwerk. In demselben Boote, in welchem ich über den Indals-Elf fuhr, befand sich auch ein Torpare, mit seiner aus Stöde gebürtigen Frau, die ein lebendiges Zeugniß für die Wahrheit dessen war, was man mir schon in Angermanland von dem Biedersinn des Volks von Stöde erzählt hatte.

Am jenseitigen Ufer fährt man lange bergauf, durch Dörfer, Felder und Wiesen, bis man ¼ Meile hinter dem Gästgifvaregård die Kirche Indal erreicht, wo ich vom Pastor Auren herzlich bewillkommet wurde. Der Kirche zunächst liegt eine seinblättrige Sägemühle, die einem Kaufmann in Sundswall gehört. In Liden *) sind deren drei. Das Pastorat Indal besteht nämlich aus der Muttergemeinde Indal, dem Filial Liden und der Kapellgemeinde Holm; bei den Kirchen, wie bei der Kapelle, wohnt ein Geistlicher, so daß in jedem Kirchspiele sonntäglich Gottesdienst gehalten wird. Die Einwohnerzahl betrug im Jahr 1815 im ganzen Pastorat 2380, die Zahl der Gebornen, im Jahr 1816, 83, worunter 4 uneheliche; etwa ⅛ dieser Kinder stirbt im ersten Lebensjahre.

Am Abend besichtigte ich noch die 1761 von Joh. Hagman aus Sundswall, der auch Säbrå's Kirche baute, neugebaute Kirche. Sie ist ein hohes steinernes Quadrat, ohne Thurm. Den Altar schmückt ein Gemälde: „die Einsetzung des heiligen Abendmahls"; ein zweites größeres stellt dar: „den Heiland am Kreuz, zu den Füßen die weinenden Weiber und Johannes"; zu der Seite zwei Figuren von Holz, die eine sich stützend auf einen Anker, die andere Auge und Hand gen Himmel gewendet; oben erscheinen Engel. Auch die Sakristey hat hübsche bildliche Darstellungen, Geschenke von Bauern. Auf dem Kirchhofe findet man eine Art von Grabkreuzen; in Westerbotten sind die Grabkreuze wahrscheinlich deshalb abgeschafft worden, weil man

---

*) In Fors und Liden herrschte vor etwa 30 Jahren die sogenannte Lidenskrankheit, die am ärgsten war, als die Einwohner, bei reichem Lachsfang, meist von Lachs, oft ohne Brot, und von Branntewein lebten; seitdem dies aufhörte, verschwand die Krankheit immer mehr. Sie scheint eine Art Radesyge gewesen zu seyn.

sie für feuersgefährlich hielt. In einiger Entfernung von der Kirche stehen die Kirchställe, meist jenseits eines Baches, Indals präftä (Predigerfluß), der, in der Nähe, an 10 Mühlen treibt. Auch eine Kirchspielsstube ist vorhanden, die aber nicht bewohnt wird, so daß der Pfarrhof die einzige Menschenwohnung um die Kirche ist. Eine Schule besteht nicht, nicht einmal der Küster wird um Unterweisung ersucht, denn alle Eltern vermögen selbst ihre Kinder zu unterrichten.

Die Lebensweise der Bewohner von Indal ist einfach und mäßig, das Klima ist gesund, so daß viele ein hohes Alter erreichen, Todesfälle vor dem 45sten Jahre aber selten sind. Handelsbauern giebt es, sie führen Leinwand, Butter, Felle ⁊c. nach Stockholm, von wo sie Seife und Tabak, auch ein wenig Kaffee und Zucker, zurückbringen.

————

Um 15. August. Von Indal nach Kofland 1½ M.; von K. nach Sundswall 1½ M.; von S. nach Tuna 2½ M. — Zus. 5½ M.

Dichter Nebel verhüllte die Gegend, als ich um 7¾ Uhr Indal verließ; dieser, den Flußthälern (ådalar) Medelpads eigenthümliche, Nebel sichert das Getreide vor Frost, daher denn auch der bei weitem größte Theil der Volkszahl Medelpads in den Flußthälern wohnt, wenn gleich diese eine noch größere Zahl von Menschen nähren könnten; die Wald- und Bergdistrikte, welche die einzelnen Flüsse und Flußthäler scheiden, sind wenig bewohnt. Der Ackerbau ist jetzt in Medelpad vorzüglich, seit der, schon oben genannte, wackere Landshöfding Örnsköld so thätig in dieser Hinsicht wirkte, selbst auf Reisen und Spaziergängen die Bauern unterwies; früher mußte Medelpad jährlich Korn kaufen, jetzt verkauft es jährlich bis 6000 Tonnen (24000 Scheffel). Dreschwalzen trifft man häufig.

Nach langem Kampfe schwand, vor den Strahlen der Sonne, der Nebel. — Mein Weg bis Kofland war ganz der gestrige. Dann fuhr ich in ein tiefes Thal hinab, welches der Bach Sättna befeuchtet; der Bach treibt die Hämmer der bei

Gg 2

den Eisenbruk Sulå und Norafors; auf einer Anhöhe liegt die Kirche Såttna, Filial von Sillånger, von Fachwerk, mit hölzernem Dache und Thurm; die Kanzel steht über dem Altare. Kirchställe, die Kronzehntbude (tyrkoherberge), die Kirchspielsstube (Gemeindehaus) und die Wohnung des Kirchwächters umgeben die Kirche; der Geistliche wohnt in einiger Entfernung. — Neben, wenig angebauten, Thälern erreicht man die auf einer freundlichen Höhe gelegene, steinerne, erst 1781 neuerbaute, Kirche Sillånger, deren Inneres einfach und würdig ist; ein Kreuz erhebt sich, vor einer Nische, über dem Altar. — Vor Sillånger trat ich in ein Bauernhaus, meinen Durst durch Milch zu stillen, und fand eine Wohnung ganz nach Helsinglscher Weise, im obern Stocke mit einem Saal und Nebenzimmern.

Anmuthig ist der Weg von Sillånger nach Sundswall, in einem üppigen Thale långs des Såttnaå, der bei Sundswall ins Meer fällt. Reparaturen am Wagen halber mußte ich in Sundswall bis 6 Uhr Abends verweilen. Dann kehrte ich zurück in das schöne Thal, welches sich bis hinter Sillånger ausdehnt: Dörfer, Wiesen, Heuscheunen, Gebüsche, Haine, fruchtbare Kornfelder bilden liebliche Gruppen, die der Såttna noch verschönert. Am reizendsten ist die Gegend um die Kirche und den Pfarrhof Sillånger: ein Birkenhain zieht sich den Hügel hinan, auf welchem das Pfarrhaus liegt; unten zeigt sich ein See, der durch einen von Tuna kommenden, sich hier in den Såttna ergießenden Bach entsteht. Ehe ich wieder die Kirche Sillånger erreichte, fuhr ich einem Hause vorüber, wo ich viele schwarzgekleidete Leute erblickte: es war Grabschmaus (graföl). Solche Grabschmäuse sind hier allgemein, doch dauern sie nur Einen Tag; bloß die Entfernteren bleiben die Nacht über; Frauen und Mädchen bringen Milch; durch solche Theilnahme will man einander die Kosten erleichtern.

Jenseits Sillånger fährt man durch das nur wenige Schritte von der Kirche entfernte Dorf Kungsgården und dann lange auf Anhöhen hin, an deren Fuße sich ein hier immer üppiger und frischer erscheinendes Thal erstreckt; am See erblickt man die Trümmer einer alten Kirche. Durch Thäler und Wälder erreicht man den Gåstgifvaregård Wattjom; die Gegend ist sehr angebauet. Von Wattjom führt ein Seitenweg nach Tuna ½ M. Ein heftiger Donner verkündet die Nähe des Tuna-Elf, der aus Jemteland herabkommt und unter dem Namen Njurunda-Elf sich bei der Kirche Njurunda ins Meer ergießt; jetzt wird der Elf, der unfern einen großen Fall, den Tunafors, bildet, sichtbar, und man gelangt am waldbewachsenen Ufer zu Tuna's Kirche und Pfarrhofe, wo mich der alte Propst Doctor Dillner und sein braver Sohn, der Hofprediger und Regimentspastor (jetzt Pfarrer in Brunflo), willkommen hießen. Die Lage des Pfarrhofes an dem sich hier zum See erweiternden Tuna-Elf ist reizend.

Tuna's schöne steinerne Kirche ward um 1770 neugebauet, über dem Altare erhebt sich, vor einer Nische, ein einfaches Kreuz, auf dessen Piedestal man die Worte lieset: „Selig, die da glauben"; über dem Kreuze erblickt man zwei Engel, die einen Kranz halten; ganz oben in einem von Strahlen umgebenen Dreiecke lieset man: „Jehovah"; diese und andere Bildhauerarbeiten sind vom Jemtischen Landmann Edeler.

Der Glockenthurm steht auf einer Höhe am Wege, der Kirche gegenüber. Man hat von hier eine weite herrliche Aussicht: rings umher zeigt sich ein Kreis von Waldbergen; einem See gleicht der nahe Tuna-Elf; im Flusse zeigt sich eine freundliche Waldinsel, auf welcher der Propst einen Wittwensitz gebauet hat. Nicht minder schön ist die Aussicht aus dem Pfarrhofe.

Die Kirche umgeben Kirchställe und die Kirchspielsstube, also daß der Pfarrhof die einzige Menschenwohnung ist.

Das Pastorat Tuna besteht aus 3 Kirchspielen, Tuna im J. 1815 mit 1189, Attmar mit 1396 und Stöde mit 1354 Einwohnern; die Muttergemeinde, Tuna, ist mithin die am wenigsten volkreiche. Bisher *) war Tuna auch Sitz einer Props-

---

*) Nach Dr. Dillner ward die frühere Eintheilung in die Nord- und Süd-Propstei erneuert.

ſtel, welche ſeit 1805 ganz Medelpad unter ſich begriff. Die
Einwohnerzahl dieſer Propſtei oder ganz Medelpads betrug, im J. 1815, 19,669. Eine der Gemeinden Medelpads,
Hafrö, an der Gränze von Helſingland und Jemteland, iſt Filial
von Ytterhogdal in Helſingland; künftig ſoll ſie ein eigenes Paſtorat bilden; ſie zählte im J. 1815 nur 542 Einwohner, die
ſich durch einen hohen Grad von Unverdorbenheit und Sittlichkeit auszeichnen. Als ein Beiſpiel der hier allgemein herrſchen-
den zarten Gewiſſenhaftigkeit kann angeführt werden, daß im
Nothjahre 1812 ein Bauer, John Henderſon, ſein Korn,
woran er Ueberfluß hatte, nicht verkaufen, ſondern nur anleihen
wollte, und im folgenden Jahre, als er es in beſſerer Beſchaf-
fenheit zurückerhielt, es durchaus nicht annahm, weil das, was
er angeliehen, ſchlechter geweſen ſey, ſondern ſich ſelbſt einen bedeutenden Abzug machte. — In ganz Medelpad wurden, im J.
1816, 615 geboren, worunter 43 uneheliche; 106 Kinder ſtar-
ben unter Einem Jahre; im J. 1815 waren unter 611 Gebornen nur 38, im J. 1814 unter 596 nur 27 uneheliche.

Kirchſpielsſchulen hat Tuna und wahrſcheinlich ganz Medelpad nicht. Zur Unterweiſung armer Kinder im Chriſtenthum
vermachte ein aus dem Paſtorat gebürtiger Bauernſohn, der
Länsman zu Skinſkatteberg in Weſtmanland wurde, 1793 durch
ein Teſtament die Summe von 555 Rthlr. Riksgäld; derſelbige
vermachte an 300 Rthlr. zu einer Orgel, über 300 Rthlr. an
die Armenkaſſe, ferner Summen zu einer ſilbernen Altarkanne,
einen ſilbernen Altarkelch, einen ſilbernen Oblatenteller, einer
Kelchdecke, einem Meßgewande, für die Schule in Sundswall,
für 6 Schüler aus Tuna, Attmar und Njurunda, welche ſtudiren
wollen, oder, falls ſolche nicht da ſind, für andere, zu einer ſilbernen Taufſchale und zu anderen Kirchenbedürfniſſen, desgleichen
100 Tonnen Korn zur Errichtung eines Kornmagazins für Arme, aus welchem, ſobald es ſich durch Zinſen in Korn mittelſt
Ausleihens zu 200 Tonnen vermehrt haben würde, an Arme,
und zwar vorzugsweiſe dem Stifter verwandte, vertheilt werden
ſolle; indeß iſt das Magazin nicht errichtet worden, da ſchon
früher ein Kornmagazin in Tuna beſtand. Dieſes ſo wohlthätige

Testament war nicht in gehöriger Form abgefaßt, indem die Unterschrift von Zeugen fehlte; es hätte also von den Verwandten zu ihrem Besten umgestoßen werden können, aber diese erklärten es für bestehend. Testamente für wohlthätige Zwecke sind in Schweden noch immer nicht selten.

Eine eigenthümliche Einrichtung des Pastorats Tuna, die vom Doctor Dillner herrührt und im Pastorat Ljustorp nachgeahmt wurde, sind die Kinderverhöre (barnförhör); der Prediger reiset zu gewissen Zeiten im Jahre in den Gemeinden umher, um die noch nicht confirmirte Jugend zu unterrichten und zu prüfen; diese Verhöre beginnen mit Gebet und es wird dabei, ganz wie in den Hausverhören, Buch geführt; jede Gemeindeabtheilung kommt auf diese Weise, einmal im Frühling und einmal im Herbst, an die Reihe. Am Abend eines solchen Tages folgen unschuldige Jugendspiele. Die Confirmation selbst ist höchst feierlich; im Jahre 1816 war bei der Confirmation die Rührung so groß, daß alles in Thränen floß, und Keiner, außer dem Küster, zu singen vermochte.

Fast in jedem hiesigen Bauerhofe findet man eine kleine Bibliothek, selbst Torpare und Handwerker haben Bibeln, Postillen, Communion- und Gebetbücher; auch andere Schriften nützlichen Inhalts, als historische, Reichstagszeitungen ꝛc.

Die Einrichtung des Armenwesens ist vorzüglich. Ganz Arme, die ohne alles Eigenthum sind und nichts verdienen können, giebt es gar nicht; Armen, die nicht mehr im Stande sind, ihre kleinen Äcker- und Gartenstücke selbst zu bearbeiten, läßt die Gemeinde die nöthige Arbeit beschaffen; solchen, die auf dem Wege der Verarmung sind, wird aus der Armenkasse aufgeholfen; arme Kinder werden in die Kost gethan und für ihren Unterricht wird gesorgt.

———

Am 16. Aug. Von Tuna nach Wattjom ½ M.; von W. nach Nedansjö 1½ M.; von N. nach Kjällsta 1½ M. — Zus. 3½ M.

Meine Absicht war, am nächsten Tage in Stöde dem Gottesdienst beizuwohnen, um, durch eigene Anschauung, dieses viel-

gepriesene Volk kennen zu lernen; unter solchen Menschen am
Gottesdienst Theil zu nehmen, konnte ich mir nur als einen
hohen Genuß denken. Ich sagte daher meinen Freunden in
Tuna ein dankbares Lebewohl und fuhr um 3 Uhr Nachmittags ab.

Bis Wattjom war mein Weg der gestrige. Bei Wattjom
erreicht man die große Jemteländische Straße, die beste und be-
suchteste, die nach Jemteland führt, aber doch so wenig bereiset,
daß die beiden Hüllpferde, welche auf jedem Gästgifvaregård stehen, oft in mehreren Tagen nicht ausgehen. Mein Skjutsbonde
von Wattjom nach Nedansjö war der erste in Norrland, welcher
Wartegeld forderte. Bis Nedansjö fährt man in geringer Entfernung vom Tuna-Elf, der aber nur selten sichtbar ist; im Fluß
hat man eine feinblätterige Sägemühle angelegt, deren Eigenthümer ein Kaufman in Gefle ist; hier führt eine hölzerne Brücke
über den Fluß. Vor Nedansjö erblickt man, am jenseitigen Ufer,
Sennhütten, die, nebst einem zweiten Sennendorf, den Bewohnern von Nedansjö, einem ansehnlichen Dorfe, gehören: jeder
Hof sendet, mit dem Vieh, ein Sennenmädchen; die Mädchen
bleiben mehrere Wochen bei den Hütten, jede derselben hat ihr
Gesangbuch mit sich. Hinter Nedansjö erweitert sich der Fluß
zu einem See, welcher den Namen Stödesee erhält; der See
ist ¼ Meile breit und friert, wie der Tunasee, selten vor Januar zu; die Bewohner des Dorfs fahren in großen Kirchböten
zur Kirche nach Stöde. Schon zwischen Wattjom und Nedansjö
hat man mehrere hübsche Thäler; aber weit schöner ist der Weg
von Nedansjö nach Kjällsta: die Thäler sind enge, aber sehr angebauet; schroffe Felsen oder steile Waldberge steigen in die Thäler herab; daher die Abhänge hier weniger bebauet sind als am
Indal und am Ångerman. Auf der ersten Meile trifft man nur
einzelne Torparewohnungen, Hüttchen, wie die der Bootsmänner
in Blekingen; auf der letzten halben Meile reihet sich Dorf an
Dorf. ⅞ Meile vor Kjällsta fährt man der Kirche Stöde vorüber; der Comminister wohnt am jenseitigen Ufer. Das ganze
jenseitige Ufer, von Nedansjö an, ist von der Beschaffenheit, daß
die Waldberge sich unmittelbar in den Fluß senken, und nur sel-

ten kleine ebene Plätze frei laſſen, wo man bald Sennhütten, bald Kornfelder und Wieſen, bald Wohnhäuſer, erblickt; die gelben Kornfelder neben den grünen Wieſen nahmen ſich ſehr hübſch aus; nach acht Tagen ſollte die Erndte beginnen.

Der Fluß, welcher eigentlich Ljungan heißt, hat zwar wenig große, aber viele kleinere Fälle und Stromzüge, ſo daß er bisher nicht fahrbar war, und, ſelbſt von der oben genannten Sägemühle an, die Bretter nur zu Lande nach Sundswall transportirt werden konnten. Im Jahr 1817 befahl der König eine Unterſuchung, in wiefern der Ljungan-Elf nebſt dem Indal und Ångerman ſchiffbar gemacht werden und dann Stockholm von hier ſeinen Holzbedarf beziehen könne. Das Reſultat war, daß die Fahrbarmachung des Ljungan bis aufwärts nach Åſarne in Jemteland den mindeſten Schwierigkeiten unterworfen, und der Holzvorrath dieſer Gegenden faſt unerſchöpflich ſey. Aehnliche Unterſuchungen geſchahen, wie oben erwähnt, mit den Weſterbottniſchen Strömen. Im Jahre 1818 begann die Aufräumung des Ljungan: eine Strecke von 3 Meilen, vom Meere bis zum See Marmen, war am Ende des Sommers 1820 bereits floß- und fahrbar. Am Ausfluß des Ljungan, zu Nolby bei Svartviken, ward ein Ladeplatz und Hafen angelegt. Auch im Indal und im Ångerman begannen die Arbeiten, und mehrere Waſſerfälle wurden floßbar gemacht. Zugleich ließ man Norrbottnier kommen, welche Strombóte (forsbåtar) nach Norrbottniſcher Weiſe erbauten und dieſe Kunſt in Medelpad und Ångermanland zu verbreiten ſuchten.

Um 9½ Uhr war ich in Kjällſta, wo ich in einem der beiden zierlichen Gaſtzimmer übernachtete. In der Nacht kam noch ein Kaufmann aus Öſterſund in Jemteland mit ſeiner Frau, die in aller Frühe ſchon weiter reiſeten; — da das ihnen angewieſene Zimmer hinter dem meinigen lag, ſo baten ſie gar freundlich um Verzeihung, daß ſie mich ſtören müßten, und trugen mir zuletzt Grüße nach Öſterſund auf, wiewohl ſie mich nicht kannten, und nur hörten, daß ich nach Jemteland reiſe.

Am folgenden Morgen, 8½ Uhr, ging ich zur Kirche. Noch kämpfte die Sonne mit den Nebeln; allmählig hatte ſie überwunden und die schönen, dicht bebaueten, Ufer enthüllten sich immer mehr. Mitten in der schönen Landschaft, auf einem Hügel am Ufer, liegt die Kirche; unterhalb breitet sich der Stödesee aus, dessen Wellenschlag sehr gefährlich seyn soll, daher die Kirchböte groß und stark bemannt sind; oberhalb verengen Landzungen den Fluß, der überhaupt gegen seinen Ursprung hin schmal, aber tief ist; gegenüber gruppiren sich aufs schönste fruchtbare Felder, Wiesenhügel, Gebüsche und Dörfer. Ich kam zu den Kirchställen, die in einiger Entfernung von der Kirche liegen. Jetzt stand ich da unter dem lieben Völkchen, dessen Biedersinn und Rechtlichkeit mir schon in fernen Landschaften verkündet worden war, und freute mich gar sehr, denn der Wunsch, das Leben und Treiben dieser Menschen an Ort und Stelle zu schauen, hatte meinen Reiseplan durch Medelpad und Jemteland bestimmt. Männer und Weiber waren hier versammelt, stille und ernst wie in der Kirche, des Anfanges des eigentlichen Gottesdienstes harrend; kein Wort ward gewechselt, Aller Sinn war nur gerichtet auf das Eine, das sie heute, am Tage des Herrn, vereinigt hatte. Ich ging weiter, und kam zur Vorhalle der Kirche; hier stand abermals eine Zahl von Menschen, die nicht hatten eintreten wollen, um, da die Beichte schon angefangen, keine Störung zu verursachen, und die nun an der Thüre zuhörten. Bald war die Beichte geendigt, die übrigen Kirchgänger traten ein und der Vormittags-Gottesdienst nahm seinen Anfang; die Kirche war gedrängt voll. Eine Orgel war nicht vorhanden, aber der Gesang der Gemeinde war sanft und herzlich, und mit ununterbrochener Aufmerksamkeit und wahrer Andacht hörte man dem Worte des Predigers zu; die Gebete wurden leise nachgesprochen, eben so bekannte Bibelsprüche; die etwa halbstündige Predigt handelte, auf eine ächt-evangelische Weise, von dem Sinn, mit welchem man das Aeußere der Religion vollbringen soll. Erhebend war die Feier des heil. Abendmahls, welches heute etwa 100 Personen begingen; eine Alte war so schwach, daß sie geleitet wurde zum Tische des Herrn. Fast Alle waren in eigengemachtes, schwarzes oder doch dunkles Zeug gekleidet; nur die Tücher und Mützen Einiger waren aus ausländischem Stoff gefertiget; wenige kattune Kleider sah man. Andacht, Einfachheit und Ordnung waren überall vorherrschend. Als der Gottesdienst geendet hatte, zog man aus der Kirche, voran die Männer nebst der Geistlichkeit und Kirchendienerschaft, dann die Frauen und Mädchen. Jetzt begaben sich die Männer zum Gemeindehause, wo der Länsman mehrere, die Gemeinde betreffende, nicht kirchliche Gegenstände, z. B. wer den Transport der aus dem großen Waisenhause zu Stockholm in die Provinzen aufs Land vertheilten Kinder hiesigen Orts beschaffen solle, wie für das Unterkommen der Wärterinnen und des Lehrers zu sorgen sey ꝛc., bekannt machte. Dann ging man zu den Kirchställen und trat von hier die Heimreise an. Eigentliche Kirchstuben trifft man nicht; nur einer der Ställe ist mit zwei Zimmern überbauet, die nach dem, ⅓ M. entfernten, Dorfe Nedansjö gehören; die übrigen entlegenen Dörfer haben ihre Kirchstuben, in welchen sie ihre Sonntagskleidung aufbewahren, auch wohl übernachten, in den nahen Dörfern, andere treten in den benachbarten Bauerhöfen ab. Die Kirche, vor etwa 70 Jahren neu gebauet, ist zu klein für die Gemeinde; sie hat eine hübsche, stark vergoldete Kanzel, an deren Außenseite passende biblische Embleme ausgehauen sind, und ein schönes Altarbild, welches die Ankunft des Herrn zum Weltgericht darstellt; und unter demselben ein zweites: „die Einsetzung des heil. Abendmahls," in Holz geschnitzt; zur Seite erblickt man Moses, mit der Gesetztafel und der Inschrift: „durch Moses ward das Gesetz gegeben;" gegenüber den Heiland mit der Weltkugel, dem Kreuze und der Inschrift: „Gnade und Wahrheit ist kommen durch Jesum Christum." — Einige alte Figuren, aus katholischer Zeit, werden noch hier und da in der Kirche, wie in einem Häuschen auf dem Kirchhofe aufbewahrt, z. B. die Himmelskönigin mit dem Jesuskinde, eine Wallfahrtsfahne, Heiligenbilder ꝛc.

Es war meine Absicht, gleich nach geendigtem Gottesdienst die Reise fortzusetzen. Aber der Länsman Jöns Norlin bat so freundlich und dringend, ihm zum Mittagsessen in seine nahe Wohnung zu folgen, daß ich endlich nachgeben mußte. Nachdem ich eine Weile unter den Leuten umhergewandert und ihrer Stille und Sittsamkeit mich gefreuet, fuhren wir ans jenseitige Ufer, wo der Lånsman wohnt. Mit großer Herzlichkeit ward ich von der braven Gattin des Lånsman, die in dem Hause, wo sie jetzt wohnt, geboren und erzogen wurde, empfangen. Der Hof faßt drei Wohngebäude, deren eines die Gastzimmer enthält; alles einfach, aber reinlich und nett; in dem einen der Zimmer war eine Wanduhr mit Flötenwerk, welches 6 Stücke spielte, in Norwegen gefertigt, aufgestellt; den Hof umgeben ein Paar Gärten mit Blumen, Obstbäumen und Küchengewächsen aller Art, die Wirthschaftsgebäude und mehrere Heuscheunen. Unter den wirthschaftlichen Einrichtungen interessirte mich besonders der Dreschwagen mit 18 kleinen eisernen Rädern, 4 vorne, 4 hinten und die übrigen an den Seiten; der Wagen wird, ohne alle Beschwerde, mit einem Pferde, auf der langen bedeckten Dreschtenne im Trabe gefahren; der Fuhrmann sitzt in der Mitte. Die Landschaft, in welcher das Gehöft liegt, ist ungemein reizend; die Kirche am jenseitigen Ufer auf ihrem Hügel nimmt sich besonders schön aus. — Zum Mittagsessen kam auch der Adjunct, der brave Magister Tanblund, den ich am Morgen hatte predigen hören, und der sich in der kurzen Zeit seiner hiesigen Anstellung schon wahre Verdienste um die Gemeinde, in welcher vorher ein anderer, nach langwierigem Projeß entfernter, Adjunct viel Unheil angerichtet, erworben hatte. Wir sprachen viel über die Eigenthümlichkeiten des Volkes von Stöde, und aus allem ging hervor, daß es ein arbeitsames, tüchtiges, sanftes und biederes Volk ist, welches sich aber auf seine Rechtlichkeit auch nicht wenig zu Gute thut und große Zuversicht zu seiner Tugend hat, also daß die Hausväter wenig Aufsicht über ihre Jugend üben, welches sie aber, bei den vielen fremden Knechten und Mägden, die der weitläuftige Ackerbau erfordert, schon oft betrogen hat. Die Söhne und Töchter von Stöde dienen nie auswärts und verlassen überhaupt nicht gern ihre Heimath; selbst zur Stadt fahren sie selten; nur 4 Handelsbauern giebt es; diese führen die Producte des Ortes nach Stockholm. Diebstahl ist noch immer selten; weder die Heuscheunen, noch die Gebäude, in welchen man das Korn trocknet, noch die Wohnhäuser werden verschlossen, nur an der großen Landstraße ist man vorsichtiger geworden. In den häuslichen und wirthschaftlichen Einrichtungen ist alles sehr tüchtig und zweckmäßig, freilich nicht fein und zierlich. Die Kinder läßt man nicht gern schreiben und rechnen lernen, weil man bemerkt hat, daß mancher, der solches gelernt hat, sich über seinen Stand erhebt, Kaufmann re. wird, und — verarmt. Man beschränkt sich auf Ackerbau, Viehzucht, die als Alpenwirthschaft getrieben wird, und Weberey zum Hausbebarf, und ist in diesen Nahrungszweigen weit fortgeschritten; Stöde hat die beste Viehzucht in ganz Medelpad. Man lebt heiter und friedlich mit einander, haßt das Prozessiren, ist dienstfertig und mildthätig. In jedem Dorfe ist ein Hof ausersehen, wo man um Johannis, Michaelis und Weihnachten bei Tanz und Festmahlen sich seines Lebens freuet oder die sogenannten Lekstugor hält; die Höfe wechseln für diesen Zweck jährlich unter einander; dagegen giebt es keine Krüge und kein heimliches Branntweinschenken. Die Kleidung ist einfach *), aber geschmackvoll; die Körperbildung, zumal des weiblichen Geschlechts, ist meistens schön. Kartenspiel findet man selten. Trunkenbolde giebt es gar nicht; im ganzen Kirchspiel trifft man nur etwa 6 bis 8 Menschen, die bei fröhlichen Mahlen sich zuweilen im Trunke übernehmen. Ehescheidungen sind völlig unbekannt.

---

*) Als Gustav III. eine Nationaltracht (blau mit rothen Schnüren) einführte, die nur für Standespersonen bestimmt war, schafften sich dieselbe auch ein Paar wohlhabende Bauernsöhne in Stöde an und thaten sich nichts darauf zu Gute. Der damalige Länsman Kärffstedt, der es für Pflicht erachtete, über die Erhaltung der Einfachheit des Volks zu wachen, und Nachahmung fürchtete, ließ auf seine Kosten einen Schinderlappen (die Kirchspielslappen werden nämlich zu dergl. Gemeindediensten gehalten) die gleiche Tracht anlegen und ihn in der Kirche sich neben jene Bauersöhne setzen und auch sonst ihnen folgen. Sofort legten die jungen Bauern jene Kleidung ab, und keiner suchte ferner dadurch sich den höhern Ständen gleich zu stellen. Kärffstedt hat während seiner Amtsführung sich große Verdienste um die Erhaltung der Sittlichkeit und Einfachheit der Bewohner von Stöde erworben und auf alle Art und Weise das Bemühen der Geistlichen unterstützt.

Aus den nahen Dörfern kommt man sonntäglich zur Kirche, oft bleibt keiner zu Hause. In den, mehrere Meilen entlegenen, Dörfern halten die, welche nicht zur Kirche reiseten, den oben beschriebenen Dorfgottesdienst. In den meisten Höfen hat man Bibeln. — Selbstmörder gab es noch nie in der Gemeinde. Fluchen und Schwören ist noch immer selten. Die Hochzeiten werden mit großen Feierlichkeiten begangen und dauern nicht selten vom Sonntage bis zum Freytage; zu den eigenthümlichen Speisen gehört hier auch der Pfannkäse (pannost), welcher aus Milch, Eiern, Saffran, Reis und Syrup bereitet wird; die Pfannkuchen, die, in viereckiger Form, eine halbe Elle lang, doppelt zusammengeschlagen werden, sind eine alltägliche Speise.

Am Nachmittage sah ich auf dem Hofe des Länsman ein Paar Finnische Mädchen, deren rundes, volles Gesicht ganz das Eigenthümliche ihres Volkes verrieth. Solche Finnen wohnen, wie in mehreren Kirchspielen Medelpads (Attmar, Tuna, Ljustorp, Liden, Torp und Borgsjö), so auch in einigen entlegenen Walddörfern von Stöde; sie sprechen meist nur Schwedisch, aber gebrochen; einige Alte sprechen Finnisch. Sie verheirathen sich häufig mit Schweden, sind aber von kleinerer Statur, haben plattere Nasen, helles Haar, helle Augenbraunen, sind heiterern Sinnes, aber auch mißtrauischer als die Schweden; übrigens in ihren Sitten sehr strenge und rein; Unkeuschheit ist unter ihnen fast unerhört; im Sommer sind sie sehr arbeitsam, im Winter lieben sie aber die Ruhe gar sehr, und sind nicht leicht aus ihren Wohnungen zu bringen. Die Finnen pflegen in Waldgegenden zu wohnen, diese nennt man Finnskog, Finnenwald.

Um 6 Uhr Abends, nach eingenommenem Vesperbrot, sagte ich meinen lieben Wirthen ein herzliches Lebewohl und fuhr zurück ans jenseitige Ufer des Ljungan; der brave Länsman, der in den 10 Jahren, in welchen er hier angestellt ist, viel zur Erhaltung des biederen und rechtlichen Wesens, was die Bewohner von Stöde auszeichnet, gewirkt hat, und der Mag. Landsund begleiteten mich bis zum Gästgifvaregärd; wir landeten an einer waldigen Landzunge, von welcher man durch einen kleinen Tannenwald nach Kjällsta gelangt. Die Landzunge bildet einen

485

Bergrücken zwischen dem Bette des Ljungan und einem Busen dieses Flusses. Hierher sollen in einem Kriege, als das benachbarte Jemteland noch Dänisch war, die Schweden von Kjällsta aus die Landstraße verlegt und also die Dänen irre geführt, überfallen und vernichtet haben. Die Sage ist nicht ganz unwahrscheinlich, denn noch heut zu Tage sieht man eine Straße auf der Landzunge, und der gewöhnliche, damals von den Schweden zugebaute Weg führt längs des Ufers über einen Bergrücken, der dem Bergrücken der Landzunge sehr ähnlich ist, so daß die Dänen leicht hintergangen werden konnten.

* * *

Am 17. Aug. Von Kjällsta nach Ålbsta 2½ M.

Gleich nach meiner Rückkehr zum Gästgifvaregård fuhr ich ab, um 6¼ Uhr, und in drittehalb Stunden waren die fast viertehalb deutschen Meilen zurückgelegt. Mein Skjutsbonde war ein Finne aus dem Fryksthale in Wermeland; seine Mutter war eine Norwegische Finnin, denn auch im südwestlichen Norwegen, an der Schwedischen Gränze, wohnen Finnen, wie an der Norwegischen Gränze Schwedens, insbesondre Wermelands. Ich unterhielt mich mit ihm über seine Landsleute in Wermeland; er erzählte, daß sie unter einander noch Finnisch sprächen und wie sehr sie sich gefreuet, als im letzten Kriege Finnische Soldaten in diesen Theil von Wermeland gekommen seyen. Die Finnen Wermelands verstehen auch Schwedisch, und verheirathen sich, eben so wie die Finnen von Medelpad, auch mit Schweden.

Der Weg führt oft auf Bergrücken hin, die an der einen Seite der Fluß, an der anderen Wiesen, Felder und Dörfer begränzen; dann und wann zeigen sich nackte Felsen, oder aus enger Schlucht stürzen sich Bäche in den Ljungan. Am schönsten ist die Gegend beim Eisenstabhammer Torpshammar, wo der Fluß eine Menge kleiner Wasserfälle um bewaldete Inselchen bildet, während in denselben, in geringer Entfernung, der breite Gimån über Felsentrümmer und in gewaltigen Stürzen sich ergießt; er kommt von Jemteland herab, und ist Ausfluß des Näffundsfees. Man fährt über den Gimån auf einer hölzernen Brücke, unter und neben welcher er seine mächtigen Fälle bildet. — Von Torpshammar hat man nur noch ¼ M. nach Albsta, wo ich in einem reinlichen und netten Gåstgifvaregård, bei biederen Menschen, übernachtete. Albsta liegt unfern der Kirche Torp.

Am folgenden Morgen fuhr ich zum Propst Huß, der in der Nähe der Kirche wohnt; ich ward aufs freundlichste empfangen und mußte, da ich nicht länger bleiben wollte, wenigstens das Mittagsessen einnehmen. Der Propst ist ein unterrichteter Mann, der durch den trefflichen Anbau des Pfarrackers seiner Gemeinde ein sehr lehrreiches Beispiel gegeben hat. Ackerbau ist Hauptnahrungszweig; und es wird, da Nachtfröste, zumal an den Ufern des Flusses, selten sind, viel Korn gebauet, auch Waizen; die Viehzucht ist ansehnlich; aber die Entlegenheit der Aecker und Wiesen verursacht, daß die Bauern viele Leute halten müssen und eben daher nicht sehr wohlhabend sind. Die Finnen, welche im Pastorat wohnen, leben meist von Milch und Fischen; überhaupt werden in Torp viele Fische gefangen. Nur zu einem der 9 Finnendörfer des Pastorats (das entlegenste hat 3 Meilen zur Kirche) kann man zu Wagen kommen; zu den übrigen nur reitend oder gehend; über dem Finnendorfe Naggen, an der Gränze von Helsingland, erhebt sich eine hohe Klippe, von welcher man eine weite Uebersicht über Helsingland, Herjeådalen, Jemteland, Medelpad, selbst Angermanland haben soll; auch der Berg unweit der Kirche Torp gewährt eine hübsche Aussicht. Die Finnen von Torp zeichnen sich aus durch Religiösität und Sittlichkeit; in einigen der Finnischen Dörfer versteht keiner Finnisch, in anderen sprechen einige Alte zuweilen Finnisch, doch die gewöhnliche Sprache ist überall die Schwedische. — Die Kirche Torp ward erst 1782 neu gebauet; sie ist ein schönes steinernes Gebäude, einfach und freundlich; den Altar schmückt ein liebliches Bild, die Kreuzabnahme darstellend. Umher stehen das Gemeindehaus mit mehreren Zimmern, wo auch der Confirmandenunterricht ertheilt wird, und die Kirchställe, deren einige auch ein zweites Stockwerk mit Wohnzimmern für entfernte Kirchgänger haben; die Kirchstuben einiger Höfe sind in nahen Dörfern, andere treten in benachbarten Bauerhöfen ab, und beweisen ihre Erkenntlichkeit für die gegebene Erlaubniß jährlich durch einige Pfund Fische, woran sie Ueberfluß haben. — Das Pastorat Torp zählte, im J. 1815, 3950 Einwohner (wovon 2543 in der Muttergemeinde Torp und 1407 in der Filialgemeinde Borgsjö) und gehört mithin zu den volkreichsten Pastoraten Medelpads. Die Zahl der Handelsbauern ist schon größer als in Stöde; es mögen ihrer etwa 10 seyn; sie handeln mit Vieh und Fellen nach Stockholm.

Am 18. Aug. von Âldsta nach Borgsjö 1¾ M.; von B. nach Jemtkrogen 1¾ M. — Zus. 3½ M.

Um 2¾ Uhr fuhr ich vom Pfarrhofe ab. Der Weg führt in dem schönen dichtbebauten Thale am Ljungan, wo sich fast Dorf an Dorf reiht, um einen spitzigen Waldberg hin; rechts erblickt man einen Kreis mit Wald bedeckter Anhöhen; am linken Ufer steigen Felder und Wiesen bis an den Gipfel der Berge auf; die Bauernhäuser sind große, hübsche Gebäude. Eine Meile von Âldsta fährt man durch Backen, einen Marktplatz, wo die Kaufleute von Sundswall handeln. Auf dem Wege begegnete ich einer Helsingländerin aus Ilsbo, einer Wittwe, die in dem Nothjahr 1816 verarmt, jetzt mit ihren 5 Kindern, deren eines taub war, Hülfe suchend, doch ohne zu betteln, umherzog; Nord-Helsingland ist ein sehr armes Land, wo, so oft einiger Mißwachs eintritt, große Noth herrscht, woran aber auch wohl die Uebervölkerung Schuld ist.

Ganz nahe dem Dorfe Borgsjö liegt die Kirche gleiches Namens, sie ist von Stein, im J. 1766 gebauet und eine der 3 Kirchen Medelpads, welche Orgeln haben. Das Innere der Kirche ist einfach und würdig; ein schönes Bild, den gekreuzigten Heiland darstellend, hängt an der Kirchwand; auch die beiden Altarbilder, die Anbetung der Weisen und die Abendmahlseinsetzung, sind nicht ganz unbedeutend, nur das prächtige Gewand der Maria, auf ersterem, ist unhistorisch. Neben der

II.   H h

Kirche ist ein hölzerner Glockenthurm aufgeführt, aus welchem man die liebliche Umgegend überschaut. Gegen den Fluß hin bilden Kirchstuben (eine sogar von 2 Stockwerken) und Kirchställe Gassen, die von Felsen unterbrochen oder begränzt werden. Der Kirchhof liegt abgesondert, doch nur in geringer Entfernung von der jetzigen Kirche, da, wo einst die alte Kirche stand. Der Eingang zum Gemeindehause von Borgsjö ist mit einem Elennshorne geziert; eine Zierde, die man auch zuweilen über den Hausthüren in Jemteland findet; dies Horn ist kurz und schaufelförmig. Medelpad und Jemteland haben noch Elennthiere, die im letzten Winter sich in großen Schaaren zeigten; in Jemteland hatte ein Offizier ein solches Elennthier gezähmt, und fuhr damit, aber fuhr es todt.

Bei Borgsjö verläßt die Jemteländische Straße den Ljungan; dieser wendet sich links zur Kirche Ofvansjö, wohin ein, 2 Meilen langer, schlechter Fahrweg führt, und dann zur Kirche Hafrö; diese Kirche liegt im Sommer völlig isolirt; von keiner Seite führt dahin ein Fahrweg, nur zu Fuß oder zu Pferde kann man dahin gelangen; von Ofvansjö ist sie 3 Meilen entfernt.

Etwa eine halbe Meile auf der Jemteländischen Straße erblickt man noch aus der Ferne den Ljungan, der sich zu einem See erweitert und dessen jenseitiges Ufer mit Dörfern bedeckt ist, besonders schön ist die Landzunge Näs mit ihren vielen Höfen; dann scheiden sich die Wege nach Ofvansjö und nach Jämt- oder Storkrogen; man fährt durch dichten Wald, den 4 Meilen langen Jämtskrogen (Jemtenwald), wo keine Menschenwohnung sich zeigt; nur ein Paar Heuscheunen erblickt man und links führt ein Weg nach einer, an einem kleinen Flusse gelegenen, nahen Sägemühle; rechts trifft man, mehrere Meilen weit, keine Menschenwohnung; nichts als Wald, in welchem nur hier und da einige Sennhütten errichtet sind. Am Wege sieht man viele umgefallene Bäume, die unbenutzt vermodern.

Um 9½ Uhr war ich in Jemtkrogen, einem einzelnen Gästgifvaregård im Walde, mit einem großen, hübschen Gastzimmer, wo ich recht gut übernachtete. Der Hof ist im Viereck gebauet,

mit einem großen freien Platze im Innern, über welchen die
Landstraße führt. Auf ähnliche Weise hat man in den Schweizeralpen nicht selten die schmale Landstraße überbauet und der
Weg führt durchs Haus, wie hier über den inneren Hof; man
fürchtet nichts, verschließt weder Haus noch Ställe. Wer möchte
wohl auf unseren großen Deutschen Landstraßen so wohnen?

In Jemtkrogen lebt ein einfältiges, biederes Volk, so dienstfertig und unverdrossen, so dankbar für Alles, für jedes freundliche Wort, was man zu ihm redet; so war auch mein Skjutsbonde von Borgsjö. Man hatte sich schon schlafen gelegt, als
ich anlangte, doch flugs war die Wirthin da, bettete und ich bestieg das bequeme Lager, zu welchem eine Stufe führte. Am
folgenden Morgen kam sie mit dem Kaffee, ein noch nicht zwei-
jähriges Kind im Arme; es sprach schon einige Worte, und wurde doch noch gesäuget; die Mütter säugen hier bis zum zweiten
Jahre. Die Frau säugte und nähte zugleich; so gehen hier Einfalt und Thätigkeit Hand in Hand; und wehe dem, der ein
Aergerniß gäbe! Die einfache, reinliche Kleidung stand dem schönen Weibe vortrefflich.

Sechs und zwanzigstes Kapitel.

Reise in Jemteland und zu den südlichen Lappen.

Eintritt in Jemteland. — Kulturfähigkeit des Landes.
— Viehzucht. — Die Jemteländer. — Der See Käf-
sund. — Sundsjö. — Die Sennhütten; Die Bären.
— Das Jägervolk. — Kirche Brunflo; alter Wart-
thurm. — Stadt Ostersund. — Reizende Insel Fröfön.
— Jemtlands Trivialschule; die Feuersbrunst. — Die
Kirchspiele Hammardal und Ström; alte Einfachheit
und Sittenreinheit; Straftracht der gefallenen Mädchen. — Der Gottesdienst in Ström. — Taufe und Pa-
thengeschenk. — Die Alpenfischerey — Der Alpenpro-
spekt bei Ström. — Die Dreschmühle. — Das liebenswürdige Brüderpaar. — Kirche Föllinge; die Lappenschule; die dankbare Gemeinde. — Mechanisches Talent der Bauern. — Die Handelsbauern. — Kirche

H h 2

Am 19. Aug. Von Jemtkrogen nach Bräcke 2 M.; von B. nach Grimnäs 1½ M.; von G. nach Fannbyn 1¼ M.; von F. nach Sundsjö ½ M. — Zus. 5¼ M.

Um 7¾ Uhr fuhr ich aus. 1/8 Meile hinter Jemtkrogen beginnt Jemteland; eine durch den Wald gehauene, gerade Linie bezeichnet, nebst einem Steinhaufen am Wege, die Gränze; die Linie, welche von den Bergen herabsteigt, nimmt sich hübsch aus; gleich hinter derselben führt eine Brücke über einen Bach, den Haltarstenbäck, den man auch als Gränze betrachten kann. Der Weg ist nun schlecht unterhalten; der dichte Wald, aus Birken und Nadelholz bestehend, läuft fort, hier und da von Seen unterbrochen; aus der Ferne schallt der Ruf der Hirten. Auf der Hälfte des Weges fährt man zwei Höfen, Wallen und Lillkrogen, vorüber, deren einer ein Bauer, der zugleich Küster in

Bråcke ist, und deren anderen ein Torpare bewohnt; gegenüber, an einem See, zeigt sich das Dörfchen Bröcklinge. Vor Wallen begegnete ich der Familie des Torpare, die mit einer Kuh auf die entfernten Wiesen zog; mehrere Tage bleibt man von Hause, und nährt sich von der Milch der Kuh. Früherhin ließ man mittlerweile das Haus unverschlossen, jetzt haben Diebereien mehr Vorsicht gelehrt; doch in den entlegeneren Gegenden Jemtelands, z. B. in Sundsjö und Stugun, herrscht noch die alte Sitte, zumal wenn man nur Einen Tag abwesend bleibt. Das Dörfchen Bråcke liegt nahe der kleinen hölzernen, inwendig schön verzierten Kirche gleiches Namens, die Filial von Råssund ist. Fast alle Jemtelåndische Dörfer sind klein; der Gåstgifvaregård wechselt unter den Bauern, Hållpferde giebt es noch nicht; die Gåstgifvare und die Reservehöfe bestreiten den Skjuts. Hanf ist Hauptprodukt, Flachs hat man nicht. Obstbäume kommen nicht fort; nur Rönn (Sperberbaum, sorbus aucuparia) und Hägg (prunus padus, schwarze Vogelkirsche) gedeihen; die Quitzenbeeren werden, bereitet, verspeiset. Der Ackerbau ist geringe, könnte aber bedeutender werden, da der Boden, im Allgemeinen, gut ist; überall findet man viel Mergel, und die Erde besteht meist aus einer, Jahrhunderte lang gesammelten, Masse verroteter Vegetabilien und aus Wurzeln lebender Gewåchse, die, nach Belieben, in die fruchtbarste Erde verwandelt werden können. Jemteland bietet mehr Gelegenheit zu den lohnendsten Urbarmachungen dar, als fast irgend eine andere Provinz; diese Bemerkung hat sich mir auf der ganzen Jemtländischen Reise, selbst am Fuße der Alpen, bestätigt. Jetzt giebt der Roggen höchstens das 12te, die Gerste das 10te, der Hafer das 6te, Erbsen das 11te Korn; Waizen wird nur wechselsweise zuweilen gesået. Die Viehzucht ist sehr beträchtlich und wird meist als Sennenwirthschaft betrieben. Seit 1804 bestehen, allmählig vermehrte, Schottische Schäfereien, seit 1820 auch Isländische. — Der Kartoffelbau hat zugenommen. Zur Förderung der Weberey hat die Krone Prämien ausgesetzt; die Produktion an Wollenzeugen ist schon so groß, daß davon eine ansehnliche Quantität für den Bedarf des Heeres und der Flotte im Jahr 1822 angekauft und die Kauf-

ſumme zur Bezahlung des von der Magazindirektion, im Mß-
jahre 1821, erhaltenen Brot- und Saatkorns verwandt werden
konnte. — Die Jemtelånder ſind ein ſchöngebildetes und noch
ſehr unverdorbenes Volk; in einigen Theilen des Landes iſt es
eine Seltenheit, eine Jemtlånderin unter 50 Jahren zu ſehen,
die nicht wenigſtens hübſch genannt werden könnte. Die Höfe
ſind meiſt im Viereck gebauet, die Dåcher mit Brettern oder
kleinen Stangen belegt; die Fußböden werden möglichſt ſauber
erhalten und daher oft geſcheuert; die Betten ſtehen aufgemacht,
der Tiſch gedeckt; Weſterbottniſche Reinlichkeit trifft man freilich
nicht; in den Gåſtgifvaregårdar findet man gewöhnlich ein großes Gaſtzimmer nebſt mehreren Kammern; die Kamine (denn
Oefen kennt man nicht) ſind im Sommer mit Gebüſch ausgefüllt; das Wohnzimmer iſt zugleich Küche, nach Norrlåndiſcher
Weiſe. — Rückſichtlich der Militairſtellung iſt Jemteland, bei
ſeiner geringen Ackerkultur, ſchwerer, als andere Provinzen, be-
laſtet, denn es ſtellt 1100 Mann. In der Långe von Norden
nach Süden erſtreckt ſich Jemteland 30, in der Breite von Weſten nach Oſten 22 Meilen; der Flåcheninhalt wird von Hylphers zu 330 ⃞M. *) angegeben. In åltern Zeiten waren
Jemteland und Herjeådalen, bald Schwediſche, bald Norwegiſche
Provinzen; ſeit dem Frieden von Brömſebro 1645 ſind beide
Provinzen Schwediſch geblieben.

In Bråcke traf ich mit dem Erſten Landmeſſer Sunding
aus Brunflo, der mit ſeiner Gattin aus Lafors bei Sundswall
zurückkehrte, zuſammen; er bat ſo freundlich und dringend,
bei ihm einzukehren, daß ich es halb zuſagen mußte. Ich
reiſete nun voraus nach Grimnås, 1¾ M. Der Weg führt
långs dem großen Råſſundſee, und iſt meiſtens eben; die Ufer
des Sees ſind bewaldet; nur wenige Wieſen, Aecker und Dörfchen erſcheinen; die Inſeln, zum Theil mit hohen Bergen, und
die Krümmungen des Sees, geben hübſche Anſichten. Man
fåhrt über den Gimån bei Ån, da, wo er durch einen Ausbruch

---

*) Hagelſtam ſchåtzt das geſammte Lån Oſterſund auf 425 ⃞M.;
im J. 1819 mit 36,769 Einwohnern.

des Räsfundsees entsteht, denselbigen Fluß, welcher bei Torps-
hammer sich in den Ljungan ergießt. — In Grimnäs hielt ich
ein kleines Mahl, dessen Bereitung ich aber zum Theil selbst
anordnen mußte, indem nur ein alter Mann daheim war; der
Alte gab, was er hatte, bot auch Surfisk oder Graffisk, d. i.
roh eingelegten Fisch, nach Art des Graflax, und zwar den
schönen, lachsähnlichen Schnäpel (sik); aber wiewohl dieser Sau-
erfisch von Vielen als Leckerbissen geachtet wird, so konnte ich
ihm doch keinen Geschmack abgewinnen; desto angenehmer waren
mir die herrliche Alpenbutter und der schöne Ziegenkäse; auch
das Brot war gut; man hat dünnes Hartbrot und Weichbrot in
runder Kuchenform.

Der Weg nach Fannbyn ist sehr bergig; man fährt noch
immer an den 3 M. langen und an einigen Stellen ½ M. breiten (mitten im See liegt eine bewohnte Insel, die eine ganze M.
lang ist) Räsfundsee, und kommt auf einer langen hölzernen
Brücke über den nordöstlichen Arm, der sich zur Kirche Sundsjö
hinaufzieht; die Ufer sind hier schon mehr angebauet, und die
Uebersichten von den Höhen oft überraschend schön. In Fannbyn trennte ich mich von Sundings, mit denen ich mittlerweile
wieder zusammengetroffen war, und fuhr über den hier von lieblichen Wald- und Wiesenufern umgebenen See, in einer halben
Stunde (etwa ½ M.), zur Kirche Sundsjö; der See heißt hier
Sundsjösee und ist sehr fischreich, aber der Täucher (Lomm, Co-
lymbus) verzehrt viele Fische. In Sundsjö mußte ich beim
Comminister Carlsson über Nacht bleiben. Die steinerne
Kirche mit hölzernem Thurm, am See, ist sehr alt; sie sollte
neu gebauet werden. Der hauptsächlichste Nahrungszweig des 23
□M. enthaltenden Pastorats Räsfund, welches aus der Muttergemeinde Räsfund, im J.1815, mit 872, und den Filialgemeinden Sundsjö, mit 569, Bräcke, mit 401, und Bätsjö, mit 381
Seelen, besteht, ist Ackerbau; selbst zum Verkauf wird gebauet,
auch für Mißjahre aufbewahrt; der Frost schadet selten; Schnee
fällt zuerst im October. Auch Jagd und Fischerey wird getrieben; schon der Knabe ist Jäger. Viele Bauern treiben Handel,
ja führen bis Stockholm Vögel, Talg, Butter und Lederwaaren;

Färbestoffe, Rauch- und Schnupftabak, ein wenig Kaffee und
Zucker bilden die Rückladung. Einwirkungen dieser Handelsreisen
hat man bisher wenig verspürt; im Ganzen herrscht viel Sittlichkeit, Einfachheit in Kleidung und Lebensweise, zumal in Räf-
sund, Stugan und besonders Borgvattnet; anders ist es freilich
in Brunflo, wo Spielen und blauer Montag im Schwange gehen. Mechanische Geschicklichkeit besitzt der behende Jemteländische Bauer hier, wie aller Orten, im hohen Grade; er ist
Schmidt, Tischler, Lederbereiter 2c. Die Bereitung des bekannten wasserdichten Leders aus Ziegen- und Schaaffellen, was zu
Oberröcken 2c. selbst nach Stockholm verkauft wird, geschieht besonders in Oviken; auch aus Elennleder bereitet man Handschuhe und Beinkleider. Auch Leinewand wird in Jemteland gefertiget.

———————

Am 20. Aug. Von Sundsjö nach Fannbyn ½ M.; von F.
nach Gärde 2¼ M.; von G. nach Brunflo ¾ M. — Suf.
2¼ M.

Um Mittag verließ ich Sundsjö; der Comminister mit seinen Söhnen und dem Adjuncten Taflin begleiteten mich zu
Boot bis Fannbyn. Dann sagte ich den guten Leuten Lebewohl
und fuhr nach Gärde. Der Weg ist ein bergiger, ausgefahrner
Waldweg; doch bilden die vielen Seen zu beiden Seiten, wie
die hier und da zerstreuten Sennhütten und Dörfchen eine freundliche Mannigfaltigkeit. Die Ufer der Seen sind meistens wild,
waldig, und schön durch vielfache Krümmungen; einige auch angebauet, z. B. die Ufer des Sees bei dem malerisch-gelegenen
Dorfe Böle. Etwa ¼ M. hinter Fannbyn fährt man im Walde
mehreren schöngelegenen Sennhütten vorüber. Ich ließ halten,
stieg ab und ging hinein. Eine freundliche Jemtin kam mir
entgegen, und reichte, auf meinen Wunsch, köstliche Alpenmilch;
ohne zu fragen, was ich schuldig sey, gab ich einiges Geld als
Bezahlung, sie aber weigerte sich, es anzunehmen, denn „nicht
mit der Absicht bezahlt zu werden, habe sie gegeben!" —
So findet man es häufig in Norrland, zumal in den entlegenen

ren Gegenden. Diese Sennhütten werden nur einen Theil des Sommers bewohnt, und zwar, da das Dorf nahe ist, von Hausfrau und Kindern. Den übrigen Theil des Sommers zieht man nach entfernteren Sennhütten, doch nicht die ganze Familie, sondern von jedem Haushalt nur ein Mädchen (kinta). In der Nacht ist das Vieh in den Ställen, die neben jeder Sennhütte errichtet sind, aus Furcht vor den wilden Thieren; noch vor wenigen Tagen hatte bei einer nach Brunflo gehörigen, wiewohl 6 M. von da entfernten, Sennhütte, 3½ M. oberhalb Sundsjö, unweit Stugun, ein Bär eine Kuh getödtet und mehrere zerfleischt. — Weiterhin am Wege lag ein zweites Sennendorf, nach dem ½ M. entfernten Haga gehörig; die Weide ist gering, daher man hier nur während der Heuerndte wohnt, wo dann die Höfe in Haga ganz verlassen sind. Haga besitzt auch noch andere, entferntere Sennhütten, wie denn überhaupt jedes Dorf mehrere weit von einander entlegene Sennhütten hat, zwischen denen man im Sommer hin und her zieht. In eine der Haga-Sennhütten trat ich ein; sie hatte ein geräumiges, hübsches Zimmer nebst Kammer; ein zweites Zimmer ward gebauet; auch Wagenscheune und Ställe waren vorhanden. — Etwa auf der Mitte des Weges fährt man, am Horstsee, einer Sägemühle vorbei, in deren Nähe sich ein Sauerbrunnen befindet. Auf der letzten Viertelmeile erblickt man zuerst die mit ewigem Schnee bedeckten Alpen; es war Ovikens Fjäll; ein herrlicher Anblick; nur an den Abseiten zeigte sich der Schnee, der im hellsten Sonnenlicht glänzte; unterhalb dehnte sich eine von niedern Bergketten durchschnittene Ebene aus, die im Südosten der schöne Locknesee mit seinen fruchtbaren Ufern und der neuen steinernen, rings von Wiesen umgebenen Kirche Lockne, begränzte; eine ächte Schweizerlandschaft! Auch die offenen und biederen Menschen erinnerten mich an meine liebe Schweiz: die Jemteländer sind ein lebendiger und kräftiger Menschenschlag, von mittlerer Größe, behende und leicht, und geborne Jäger; schon der 12jährige Knabe erlegt seinen Tjäder. Die Jemteländer haben wenig Bedürfnisse; nur dem Schnupftabak ist das männliche Geschlecht sehr ergeben, weniger dem Rauchtabak, den ſie aber auch, zumal in den Alpen, gerne kauen und rauchen; ſchon der 20jährige Jüngling hält ſich eine Doſe; die Weiber ſchnupfen ſelten.

Von Gärde aus, einem hübſchen und geräumigen Gäſtgif= varegård, wollte ich den verſprochenen Beſuch beim Landmeſſer Sunding abſtatten; aber, durch ein Verſehen, fuhr ich, ohne es zu wiſſen, dem Hofe vorüber, und war bei der Kirche Brunflo, ¼ M. von Gärde, wo nun der Propſt Backman mich zu über= nachten bat. Noch am Abend beſichtigte ich die Kirche, die eine der ſchönern in Jemteland iſt; neben derſelben ſteht der alte ſteinerne Glockenthurm, der durch einen Brand an Höhe verlo= ren hat. Den Altar ſchmücken vorzügliche Bildhauerarbeiten und ein treffliches Gemälde von eingebornen Meiſtern, zwei Bauern, dem Bildhauer Edler zu Ang in Lockne, ¼ M. von hier, und Sundin, einem ausgezeichneten Kirchenmaler, im Paſtorat Sun= ne. Das Altargemälde ſtellt die Einſetzung des heiligen Abend= mahls dar; über dem Altar erhebt ſich, zwiſchen vier Säulen, vor einer offenen Niſche, der Heiland am Kreuz (von Edler), darüber erblickt man auf Wolken die Taube und das allſehende Auge Gottes; über den Säulen ſchweben zwei Engel, die den Siegeskranz halten. Auch die ſtark vergoldete Kanzel iſt mit paſſenden Emblemen geſchmückt. Die Kirche ward 1785 neu gebauet; ſie hat eine Orgel von einem Stockholmer Meiſter. Der geräumige Kirchhof umher iſt ohne Grabkreuze. Zum Pa= ſtorat Brunflo gehören die Muttergemeinde Brunflo, im Jahre 1815 mit 1095, und die Filiale Lockne, mit 982, Näs, mit 556 Seelen, Lill Marieby und Öſterſund; Lill Marieby (mit 287 Seelen) hat eine der älteſten Steinkirchen im Lande. Hauptnahrungszweig des Paſtorats iſt Ackerbau; ſchlägt dieſer fehl, ſo herrſcht Armuth, und zwar in einem um ſo viel höhe= ren Grade, da die alte Einfachheit und Unverdorbenheit mehr als in irgend einem andern Paſtorate von Jemteland gewichen ſeyn ſoll; Lockne treibt auch Theerbrennerey; die Fiſcherey iſt unbedeutend, die Zahl der Handelsbauern klein. Für das Ar= menweſen machte der Quartiermeiſter Erik Sundsberg 1781 eine

Stiftung von 600 Bankthalern, wovon die Zinsen unter die Armen von Brunflo und Marieby vertheilt werden.

Am 21. August. Von Brunflo nach Ostersund 1½ M.; von O. nach Baden auf Frösön ½ M. — Zus. 1½ M.

Nachdem ich am Vormittage noch Sunding besuchte, fuhr ich, längs des Storsjö, der mit Recht den Namen des großen Sees führt, denn er ist nicht weniger als 7 M. lang und 3 M. breit, und 17 Kirchspiele, oder etwa die Hälfte des Landes, breiten sich an seinen Ufern aus, — durch Wald nach Ostersund, der einzigen Stadt Jemtelands. Die Ufer des Sees sind sehr angebauet, im Hintergrunde zeigt sich die ansehnliche Insel Fröson und eine Kette von Schneealpen. Zu Mittage war ich in Ostersund, wo ich einige Stunden in einer fröhlichen Gesellschaft, beim Landsecretair Ramstedt, zubrachte. Ostersund ist Sitz des Landhöfding über das, seit dem 1. August 1810 neu errichtete Län gleiches Namens, welches Jemteland und Herjeådalen begreift *); ersteres hatte bis dahin zu Hernösand's, letzteres zu Gefleborg's Län gehört. Die Errichtung eines eigenen Läns für diese Provinzen war höchst erwünscht; denn die Entfernung von den früheren Länssitzen Hernösand und Gefle war sehr groß; namentlich ist Jemteland durch seine sehr ansehnlichen Kronwaldungen (sie betragen 84 ☐M.; der mehrmals erwähnte Landhöfding Örnsköld trennte sie von den Waldungen der Privatpersonen) und durch die mannigfaltigste Gelegenheit zu einträglichen Urbarmachungen sehr wichtig; bei besserem Anbau **) könnte Jem-

*) Schon im 17ten Jahrhundert bildeten, eine Zeit lang, Jemteland und Herjeådalen ein eigenes Län. — In früherer Zeit war das Land angebauter und bewohnter als jetzt; davon zeugen die vielen Odes-Hemman oder Odes-Bölen (ödeliegende Hufen).

**) Unterm 8. Dec. 1820 verordnete der König für Jemteland Gemeinheitsabtheilungen (storskifte) an: Landmesser wurden beauftragt, und schon im J. 1821 ward der Anfang gemacht. Der König gab, für das J. 1821, 8000, für das J. 1822, 12000 Bankthaler zu den Ko-

ttland wenigstens doppelt so viele Menschen nähren, als es jetzt nährt. In den Waldungen verfaulen die herrlichsten Mastbäume: weder wird Pottasche bereitet, noch Theer gebrannt; für Abzapfung der Sümpfe ist wenig geschehen.

Die Stadt Östersund liegt an einem engen Sunde des Storsjö und hängt durch eine lange hölzerne Brücke mit der Insel Frösön zusammen. Sie ist regelmäßig gebauet, und wird immer mehr erweitert; zwischen den ungepflasterten Straßen erblickt man Kornfelder und Gärten. Am Markte, der ein regelmäßiges Viereck bildet, liegt das gemiethete Local des Landcomtoirs und der Landskanzley; auch der Landshöfding ist noch ohne Amtshaus. Das hölzerne Länsgefängniß ist reinlich und gut eingerichtet. Kirche und Rathhaus befinden sich unter Einem Dache; die Kirche besteht in einem Saal von mittelmäßiger Grösse, mit alter Kanzel, die aus der Kirche von Brunflo herstammt; den Altar schmückt ein Oelgemälde „die Kreuzigung". Vor dem Altare steht das Vorlesepult, denn nur an jedem dritten Sonntage hält Brunflo's Geistlichkeit hier Gottesdienst; an den beiden Zwischensonntagen lieset ein von den Bewohnern angenommener Vorleser aus einer Postille vor. — Ein kleines Nebenzimmer dient als Rathhaus. Der 1810 angelegte Kirchhof liegt außerhalb der Stadt, am Wege nach Lith. — Ackerbau ist Hauptnahrungszweig; die Krone hat der erst 1786 gegründeten Stadt Acker geschenkt. Die Fischerey ist unbedeutend, weil die Beschaffenheit des Bodens des Sees nur an wenigen Stellen das Fischen erlaubt. Die Zahl der Handwerker ist geringe. Ueberhaupt zählte die Stadt, im Jahre 1817, 51 Häu-

sten her. Die Gemeinheiten wurden unter die einzelnen alten Höfe vertheilt, oder es wurden daraus Grundstücke für neue Höfe ausgeschieden. Diese Maaßregel wird unfehlbar die Kultur des Landes fördern. Für diesen Zweck hat auch die neugestiftete Landhaushaltungsgesellschaft, bereits nicht ohne großen Erfolg, gewirkt; durch die Bemühungen dieser Gesellschaft haben die Urbarmachungen also zugenommen, daß, im Laufe des J. 1820, 1920 Tonnen Landes, d. i. ein Fünftheil des bis dahin urbaren Landes, zu Aeckern und Wiesen umgeschaffen worden sind.

fer mit 59 Familien, und, im Jahre 1815, 252 Einwohner. Eine im J. 1809 durch Mildthätigkeit des Pastors, der seine Hebungen aus der Stadt zum Lohn des Schulmeisters hergab, eingerichtete Freischule hatte eben aus Mangel an Besuch wieder eingehen müssen. Die Stadt hat ein Postamt, eine Apotheke*) (die einzige in Jemteland), 2 Traiteurs, und 1 Kongstelle; der Kaufleute sind 10. Jahrmarkt wird gehalten. Im Jun. 1817 ward für das Län zu Östersund die oben genannte Landhaushaltungs-Gesellschafft (hushällssällskap), die im J. 1820 bereits 44 ökono-mische Kirchspielvereine zählte, gestiftet. Der Hauptzweck bei der Anlage der Stadt, die weiten Handelsreisen der Bauern zu hemmen, ist bisher nicht erreicht worden.

Um 4½ Uhr fuhr ich über die Brücke nach Fröson, zum Skolbacke (Schulhügel), wo ich bei Rector Backman abtrat. Der Weg führt anfangs einen langen Berg hinan, von dessen Höhe man hübscher Uebersichten genießt, dann bergab, neben freundlichen Birken und Wiesen, aufwärts zu der Höhe, auf welcher Kirche und Schule liegen. Letztere ist die einzige Tri-vialschule Jemtelands. Sie ward in Folge der Verordnung Karls XI. vom 2. April 1674 gegründet, nachdem bis dahin nur ein Pädagogium bestanden hatte; sie hat 5 Klassen mit 1 Rector und 3 Kollegen; auch eine Apologistclasse ist vorhanden. Der Rector, jetzt der gelehrte Gunnar Backmann, durch seinen Homerus comparans (die Gleichnisse Homers. Hernösand 1806), seine Epitaphien auf Birger Jarl und Thorkel Knuts-son **) vortheilhaft bekannt, ist vorzüglich besoldet. Die Schü-ler, im J. 1816, 75, wohnen in mehreren alten und neuen Gebäuden, und speisen bisher nicht gemeinschaftlich. Das Schul-haus hat 4 Klassenzimmer, die ich, noch seit dem letzten feyerli-

---

*) Zur Ausrottung venerischer und venerischartiger Krankheiten, Radesyge und dergl., die sich hier und da im Län finden, wurde im J. 1817 zu Östersund ein Kurhaus eingerichtet.

**) S. Kongl. Vitterhets-, Historiae- och Antiquitets-Academiens Handlingar. Bd. 8. 1808. S. 371 — 375.

chen Examen mit Granlaub geschmückt fand; im oberen Stocke sind mehrere Zimmer unvollendet geblieben, da der ursprüngliche Plan, sie für Lappenkinder zu bestimmen, nicht zur Ausführung kam. Die Bibliothek der Schule war bis jetzt sehr gering; im J. 1816 schenkte aber hieher der Professor der Medicin in Upsala, Dr. Carl Zetterström, ein geborner Jemtländer, seine an 4000 Bände starke Bibliothek, unter der Bedingung, daß zur Aufstellung derselben ein besonderes steinernes Gebäude aufgeführt werde, wozu auch der König die Einkünfte des ersten in Jemteland ledig werdenden Pastorats, bei welchem kein Gnadenjahr Statt findet, bewilligt hat; zur Einrichtung der Bibliothek sollte der künftige Nachlaß des Professors verwandt werden. — Neben dem Schulhause steht ein hölzerner Glockenthurm, aus welchem das Zeichen zum Anfang der Schulstunden gegeben wird. Aus den Fenstern des Schulhauses hat man herrliche Aussichten auf die Alpen. — Unfern der Schule liegt die alte steinerne Kirche, neben welcher sich ein hölzerner Glockenthurm erhebt. Die Altarbilder sind uralt, ein Schnitzwerk, welches die Geburt des Erlösers, und ein anderes, das den Heiland mit der Dornenkrone, zu den Seiten Engel, darstellt. Frösön, wo ein Comminister wohnt, bildet nebst einigen Dörfern am Ufer des Sees ein Filial von Sunne. Die Insel, 1 M. lang und ½ M. breit, enthält 8 meistens kleine Dörfer und 13 bis 14 Torparehöfe; die Einwohnerzahl betrug, im J. 1815, 837.

Noch am Nachmittage machte ich mit dem Rector eine Spazierfahrt auf der Insel; zuerst gegen Südwesten, zu der Stelle, wo eine 1816 abgetragene Schanze lag; einige dazu gehörige Gebäude sind noch stehen geblieben. Von hier bis Östersund ist 1 M. Gegenüber dehnt sich eine weite Ebene aus, wo Jemtelands Infanterie-Regiment, nebst dem Jägercorps zu Pferde, seine jährlichen Uebungen hält; Gewehrschuppen, Offiziershütten, ein großer Laubsaal mit Nebenzimmern, eine Schanze mit Gruben und Wällen ꝛc. bezeichnen den Mötesplatz. Aufs lieblichste zeigt sich hier die schöne Landschaft um die Kirche Rödön am jenseitigen Ufer des Sees. — Dann fuhren wir südlich nach Kungsgården, dem Boställe des Obersten; Kungsgården liegt gar an-

muthig am Ufer des Sees; an den Hof lehnt sich ein Espen-
hain, gegenüber erscheint eine waldige Landzunge, und, im Hintergrunde, Sunne's alte Kirche. Von Kungsgården wandten wir
uns zurück zum Schulberge. Bald wurden wir nicht wenig er-
schreckt, als wir nahe vor uns ein großes Feuer aufgehen sahen.
Der Rector fürchtete, seine Wohnung brenne; als wir näher
kamen, zeigte es sich, daß das benachbarte Haus eines Schulkollegen in Flammen stehe. Glücklicherweise hatte bisher nur
das halb vergangene Bretterdach Feuer gefaßt, und so gelang es
bald, das Feuer zu löschen. Da die Leute aber nicht zu bewegen waren, die Birkenrinden, die den Brettern zur Unterlage
dienten und leicht Feuer verbergen konnten, aufzureißen, so
schien es rathsam, für die Nacht, falls das Feuer noch wieder
aufging, die nöthigen Vorsichtsmaaßregeln zu treffen, welches
denn auch ins Werk gerichtet wurde. Ein Funke, der aus dem
Schornsteine auf das alte Bretterdach gefallen war, hatte den
Brand veranlaßt. Glücklicherweise blieben meine Besorgnisse
unerfüllt; das Feuer brach nicht wieder aus. Die Kälte war
heute Abend empfindlich; die hohe Lage von Fröfön mag daran
Schuld seyn. — Auf Fröfön und bei Östersund sah ich zwei
kleine Windmühlen, sonst hat man allgemein Wassermühlen.

Am 22. August. Von Baden nach Östersund ½ M.; von
D. nach Rösta ¾ M.; von R. nach Hölje 1½ M.; von H.
nach Svedje 1½ M. — Zus. 4½ M.

Nachdem ich meinen biedern Wirthen ein herzliches Lebewohl gesagt, kehrte ich zur Stadt zurück, und setzte von da nach
ganz kurzem Aufenthalte meine Reise in den Osten von Jemteland fort. Der Weg führt dem Begräbnißplatze der Stadt
vorüber, auf welchem man ein Leichenhaus errichtet hat, um
dort im Winter, wenn die Erde zu hart ist, um graben werden zu können, die Leichen beizusetzen. Eine Strecke fährt man
nun am Ufer des Storsjö, dann durch Wald nach Rösta. Nahe dem Gästgifvaregård liegt die Kirche Ås (Filial von Rödön),
die ich in Augenschein nahm: sie ist sehr alt; gleich in der Vor-

halle trifft man einige katholische Heiligenbilder und eine alte Wallfahrtsfahne; die innere Kirchthüre ist mit einer vergoldeten Sonne und einem Engelsköpfe geschmückt; Altar, Kanzel, Chöre sind mit alten Bildhauerarbeiten und Holzgemälden geziert. — Die Gemeinde Äs treibt ansehnliche Viehzucht; die Sennhütten liegen 9 Meilen entfernt in den Alpen oberhalb Offerdal, hier weiden Kühe und Ziegen von Johannis bis Michaelis; jedes Mädchen hat etwa 15 Kühe zu besorgen; nur einmal im Sommer zieht man aus den Dörfern hinauf, um Butter und Käse zu holen.

Bei Åsta verläßt man die große Norwegische Straße und fährt landeinwärts auf Kirchspielswegen, die noch weniger erhalten sind, als die große Straße. Bis Hölje hat man nun nichts als Birken- und Nadelwald; nur selten sieht man Dörfer und Höfe. Hölje, ein Dorf mit 3 Bauern und einigen Torpare, hat ein hübsches Gastzimmer. Es giebt von hier einen nähern Weg nach Östersund, der nur 1⅜ M. beträgt, aber sehr steinig ist, und ganze Viertelmeilen, über schlechte Brücken, durch Moräste führt, daher er nicht mehr als Landstraße benutzt wird. Von Hölje zur Kirche Föllinge nordwärts ist nur Ein Häll von 4⅞ M. Ich wählte den östlichen, hügeligen und sehr schlechten Weg über den vom Storsjö auslaufenden, und oberhalb Lith durch den Långaßluß verstärkten Ragunda-Elf, der bald auch den Horka aufnimmt und nachdem er sich mit dem Amra vereinigt, in Medelpad den Namen Indalself erhält, nach Svedje oder Österåsen. Bis zum Ragunda-Elf hat man etwa ⅜ M.; der Elf ist hier sehr wasserreich und breit; auf einer guten Fähre setzt man über; am jenseitigen Ufer seitwärts liegt Lith's schöne Kirche, der ich diesmal nur vorüberfuhr. Die Ufer sind wunderschön: Gebüsche, üppige Wiesen, fruchtbare Felder, eine Menge von Dörfern und Höfen, und die steinerne Kirche Lith, ein länglichches Viereck mit Thurm, bilden eine höchst anmuthige Landschaft; den Hintergrund bedeckt Wald, über welchen die hochliegende Kirche Häggenäs (Filial von Lith) emporragt. Man fährt nun in den Wald und erreicht bald den aus Norwegen herabkommenden wilden Horkafluß, über welchen eine halb verfaulte

Brücke führt. Eine gefährliche Fahrt; unten donnert ein Waſ
ſerfall zwiſchen ſchwarzgrauen Granitplatten, eine Menge gefällter Bäume umher zeugen, daß der Brückenbau wenigſtens ſchon
beabſichtigt war; der tiefe Schnee im Frühling hatte die Ausführung gehindert. Man fährt abermals in den Wald, wo
mehr und minder ſumpfige Stellen eine empfindliche Kälte erzeugen. Bei Kogſta hatte man bereits Gerſte gemähet, zu deren Reife wenigſtens noch drei Wochen erforderlich geweſen wären; denn in der letzten Nacht hatte es ſchon gefroren. Hinter
Kogſta erreicht man bald die alte ſteinerne Kirche Häggenäs, deren hohe Lage auf drei Seiten weite Waldausſichten gewährt;
an der vierten Seite hemmt ein noch höherer Waldrücken, auf welchem ſich das, von 24 Bauern bewohnte Dorf Oſteräſen ausdehnt, den Blick. Man fährt den Waldrücken hinan und am
Rande deſſelben, unter wechſelnden Ausſichten auf Wald, Wie
ſen und die Kirche Häggenäs, und erreicht ſo, auf engen Pfaden, den Gäſtgifvaregård Svedje, der einen Theil des Dorfes
Oſteräſen ausmacht. Es war erſt 8 Uhr, als ich anlangte; aber
die halsbrechenden Wege, die ſich überdieß zuweilen in Wieſen
und Wäldern wie verlieren, verboten das Reiſen in Dämmerung
und Dunkelheit, und ich übernachtete; was ich denn auch nicht
zu bereuen hatte, denn einer der ſchwierigſten Wege, welche ich
je befuhr, führte vom Gäſtgifvaregård weiter gen Oſten, und
das Nachtquartier war ſehr gut. Zwar war der Hausvater mit
Kindern und Geſinde auf die fernen Wieſen gezogen; aber die
verſtändige Hausfrau, die freundliche, unverdroſſene Karin Göransdotter (Catherina Georgs Tochter), war daheim geblieben,
und gar lieblich zu ſchauen war die unermüdete Thätigkeit und
das einfältige, ſchuldloſe Weſen der Frau, die, wiewohl 36 J.
alt und ſchon 17 Jahre verheirathet, doch noch ſchön und ganz
Kind der Natur war. — Bald loderte das Feuer im Kamin
und verſcheuchte das Gefühl der Abendkälte; ein tüchtiges Mahl
ward aufgetragen: Forellen, fette Alpenbutter, und was ſonſt
Ort und Jahreszeit gaben. Nachdem ich Hunger und Durſt ge
ſtillt, und mich der geiſtvollen, treffenden Urtheile meiner Wir

II.   Ji

thin gefreuet, bereiteten die Strapazen des Tages im reinlichen Bette bald einen sanften und erquickenden Schlummer.

Am 23. Aug. Von Svedje nach Löräs 2 M.; von L. nach Mo 1¼ M.; von M. nach Hallen 1½ M.; von H. nach Tulingsås 1¼ M. — Zus. 6⅓ M.

Mit Tagesanbruch erhob ich mich vom Lager, denn eine weite und beschwerliche Tagesreise stand bevor; aber das Pferd zögerte, und erst um 5 Uhr konnte ich, nachdem ich die geringe Forderung der Wirthin, die ihr fast noch zu hoch dünkte, bezahlt, aufbrechen. Es war ein herrlicher Morgen: nach einer kalten Nacht, von welcher noch das scheibendicke Eis im Wege und ein starker Reif zeugten, schien, mild und freundlich, die Sonne, die aber erst 4 bis 5 Stunden nach ihrem Aufgang die durchbringend kalte, wenn gleich von keinem Winde, bewegte Luft zu erwärmen vermochte; rings umher herrschte tiefe Stille, die nur das Wiehern des Zugpferdes und des begleitenden Füllens unterbrach. Der Wald geht, mit geringer Unterbrechung durch Waldwiesen, Bäche und Flüsse, ein Paar Bauerhöfe, Krogen, und eine Anzahl Sennhütten, bis Löräs fort. Der Weg ist auf der ersten Meile bis Krogen halsbrechend, dann ein wenig besser. Mit Löräs beginnt das Pastorat Hammardal; man hat nun guten Fahrweg.

Auch von Löräs bis Mo ist meist Waldweg; doch hat man mehr Dörfer und Hügel; letztere gewähren schöne Ueberstchten über fruchtbare Thäler und den sich bei der Kirche Hammardal zum See erweiternden Amra-Elf mit seinen buschigen Ufern; seitwärts dehnt sich eine ungeheure Waldstrecke aus, über welche die zum Theil mit ewigem Schnee bedeckten Gränzalpen ihre Häupter erheben. In Mo mußte ich 4 volle Stunden warten, bis ein Pferd herbeigeschafft war; ich benutzte diese Muße, da der Pastor Ångman krank war, mit dem Adjuncten und dem Länsman, die nahe Kirche Hammardal in Augenschein zu nehmen und mich über Ausdehnung, Nahrungszweige, Sitten und Gebräuche des weitläuftigen Pastorats zu unterrichten. Die steinerne Kirche, 1781 neu erbauet, hat eine freundliche Lage;

doch liegt das Pfarrhaus, unmittelbar am Strome, noch schöner.

Das Pastorat Hammardal begreift die Mutterkirche Hammardal, die Filialkirche Ström, und die Kapellen Borgvattnet und Alanäs. Wiewohl das Pastorat 84 QM. enthält, und an Umfang also dem Smäländischen Län Kronoberg (Wexiö) gleich kommt, so zählte es im J. 1815 doch nur 2866 Einw. (im J. 1810. 2602), wovon auf Alanäs (am Fläsjö, an der Gränze von Ängermanland) 243 und auf Borgvattnet (südlich von Hammardal) 165 kommen; denn einen großen Theil des Flächeninhalts nehmen Seen und Moräste und undurchdringliche Waldungen ein; letztere werden von vielen Bären bewohnt, die häufig in ausgelegten Eisen gefangen werden und deren Fleisch man ißt. Der Kornbau ist indeß nicht unbedeutend und in guten Jahren kann Korn verkauft werden; aber der Absatz ist schwierig. Zu Urbarmachungen ist noch viel Gelegenheit; das Hauptkorn ist Gerste, doch wird auch ziemlich viel Roggen gebauet. Der Kronzehnte betrug im J. 1816 für Hammardal's Kirchspiel nebst Borgvattnet's Kapellgemeinde 5 Tonnen (à 4 Scheffel) Roggen und 84 Tonnen Gerste, für Ström und Alanäs 38 Tonnen Gerste. Im ganzen Pastorat herrscht viel Wohlhabenheit, und giebt es nur etwa 12 Arme. Die alte Mäßigkeit, Frugalität und Einfachheit ist noch nicht gewichen; viele Jünglinge trinken nie Branntwein; Kaffee wird nur bei Hochzeiten gebraucht und auch hier nur den Vornehmeren gereicht. Das Volk ist sehr arbeitsam, gastfrei, wohlwollend und sittlich, zumal in Ström und in den Kapellgemeinden. Unter den 80 bis 90 jährlich Gebornen sind oft gar keine, oft nur 1 oder 2 uneheliche (im J. 1815 betrug die Zahl der Gebornen 84, worunter nur 2; im J. 1816. 88, worunter keine uneheliche; Kinder unter 1 Jahre starben 1815. 14.; 1816. 7.), und dennoch ist die Sitte der Ehrennächte der Jünglinge und Mädchen (s. Kap. 19.) hier, wie in fast ganz Jemteland, allgemein; aber Unkeuschheit ist zugleich aufs tiefste verachtet; ein geschwängertes Mädchen wird für unehrlich gehalten, darf nicht die rosenfarbene Mütze der Mädchen, sondern nur eine dunkelrothe,

Ji 2

tragen, und wird von den Männern so wenig beachtet, daß man kaum ein Wort mit ihr wechselt, geschweige denn sie je verheirathet wird. Das ist die uralte Jemtische Sitte, die aber in manchen Gemeinden nicht mehr strenge befolgt wird; wenigstens legen an einigen Orten, z. B. in Lith, die Mädchen nach einigen Jahren die Straftracht eigenmächtig ab, was in Hammardal nicht verstattet ist. Andere üble Folgen für Sittlichkeit, deren Befürchtung in manchen Ländern die schonende Behandlung unglücklicher und strafwürdiger Mädchen — welche aber weit mehr der Sittlichkeit schadete, — veranlaßt haben, finden nicht Statt: Kindermord und ähnliche Verbrechen sind unerhört. Freilich kann es also nur unter einem Volke seyn, dem Religion und Kirche die höchsten Güter des Lebens sind und bei dem eine falsch geleitete Cultur edle Einfalt und reine Natur noch nicht verdrängt hat. — Ehescheidungen kennt man nicht, Fluchen und Schwören ist selten.

Den Unterricht der Kinder besorgen die Eltern; denn christliche Erkenntniß ist das Hauptziel; doch giebt es auch von Dorfschaft zu Dorfschaft wandernde Schulmeister.

Vor einigen Jahren war in Hammardal Kartenspiel üblich gewesen; aber ein verabschiedeter Gardist, welcher Spielen und Saufen lehrte, ward aus dem Pastorat verwiesen, und das eine wie das andre verschwand. In einigen wenigen Jemtischen Gemeinden richtet das Knotenspiel des gemeinen Mannes viel Unheil an; in Brunflo sollen einzelne Haus und Hof verspielt haben. Die Sitte des Montagsstreichens (blauer Montag) kennt man in Hammardal nicht; in andern Jemtischen Gemeinden fand sie Statt und mußte 1817 durch den Landshöfding ernstlich verboten werden.

Einige Bauern fahren nach Stockholm, wohin sie Vögel, Butter, Talg und Lederwaaren führen, und von wo sie Tabak, Färbewaaren, seidene Halstücher, Zucker und Kaffee zurückbringen; die meisten dieser Landhändler sind Hausväter, einige haben das Bürgerrecht in Ostersund gewonnen; diese heißen Contingentsbönder. Hauptnahrungszweig ist Viehzucht, auch Pferdezucht;

die Pferde sind besonders groß und schön und werden nach Ängers
manland, Westerbotten und den südlichen Provinzen verkauft.

An drei Orten im Pastorat giebt es Gesundbrunnen, näm
lich zu Fyrås, Hårkås und Ede; Brunnenhäuser sind nicht erbauet.

Das Innere der Kirche von Hammardal ist einfach und
würdig; die Kanzel vergoldet, mit eingehauenen passenden Em
blemen; der Altar mit ein Paar alten guten Gemälden, die die
Einsetzung des heiligen Abendmahls und die Kreuzigung dar
stellen und die Hauptmann Hofverberg fertigte, geschmückt. Ein
hölzerner Thurm ward eben angebauet. Umher stehen Kirch
ställe, ein Gemeindehaus, eine Kirchenherberge (für das Zehnt
korn) und, am See, ein Kirchspielsmagazin; Kirchstuben giebt
es nicht; die entfernten Kirchgänger übernachten in nahen Dör
fern. Die Geistlichkeit des Pastorats besteht aus einem Pastor,
der einen Adjuncten hält, einem Comminister zu Ström, und
einem Kapellprediger zu Alands; Borgvattnet hat keinen eigenen
Geistlichen, sondern der Prediger zu Stugun, einer zum Pa
storat Ragunda gehörigen, 4 M. Geh, Reit und Bootweg
von Borgvattnet entlegenen, Kirche, hält dort, jeden dritten
Sonntag, Gottesdienst; doch besicht man auch an den Zwischen
sonntagen, an welchen kein Geistlicher predigt, die Kirche, um
dem Postillenlesen zuzuhören. In Dörfern, die von den Kir
chen sehr entfernt sind, versammeln sich am Sonntags-Morgen
die, welche nicht zur Kirche gingen, zur gemeinschaftlichen Bet
stunde.

Um 5½ Uhr verließ ich Hammardal. Nachdem ich eine
kleine Strecke gefahren, hatte ich die Fähre erreicht: mein Skjuts
bonde, der Gästgifvare von Mo, ein 16jähriger Knabe und die
Fährfrau, eine, noch sehr rüstige, 90jährige Alte, aus Me
delpad gebürtig, die bereits 40 Jahre dem Dienste vorgestanden,
ruderten, und bald war ich am jenseitigen Ufer des Amra. Bis
Hallen, einem ansehnlichen Bauerdorf, hat man meist Wald,
doch auch ein Paar Dörfer, wo unreife Gerste schon geschnitten *)

*) In Jemteland schneidet man Roggen und Gerste mit der Hand
sichel; mit der Sense mähet man Erbsen, zuweilen auch Hafer.

wurde, denn sie hatte schon an einigen Orten durch Frost gelitten, die Kartoffeln nicht, wiewohl das Kraut welk und schwarz
geworden; das geschnittene Korn wird an eine aufrechtstehende
Stange festgebunden, so daß es fast cylinderförmig gestaltet wird.
Die Luft war warm und angenehm; nur die Moräste im
Walde verbreiteten eine widrige Kälte. Der Weg war gut;
desto schlechter aber der Wiesen- und Waldweg zwischen Hallen
und Tulingsås, der erst vor ein Paar Jahren aus schmalem
Karrenweg (kärrväg) in breiteren Landweg umgeschaffen ward,
wo nun aber die zu hoch gelegten Brücken gewaltige Stöße geben. Erst um 1 Uhr Nachts war ich in Tulingsås, da ich,
um nicht in Hallen zu warten, die 3 Meilen von Mo mit demselbigen Pferde zurücklegte. In Tulingsås, einem Bauerndorfe,
wo kein Gästgifvaregård ist, trat ich bei dem Kyrkovård (Kirchenvorsteher) ab, der mich, auch in später Nacht, herzlich willkommen hieß. Bald war ein gutes Abendessen bereitet, aus
Ziegenkäse und trefflichem Rör (tör ist ein Alpenfisch, von der
Größe der Forelle; er hat gelbliches Fleisch und einen feinen,
lieblichen Geschmack, wie der fetteste und mildeste Lachs) bestehend, und froh, daß ich das Ziel der angestrengten Reise erreicht, am nächsten Morgen in einer der entlegensten Gegenden
Jemtelands dem Gottesdienst beiwohnen und das Volk in seiner
Eigenthümlichkeit sehen zu können, begab ich mich, in einem
freundlichen Zimmer, zur Ruhe.

Am Frühmorgen ordnete die Wirthin das Gevattergeschenk,
das sie, nach uralter Sitte, dem Vater des Kindes, bei welchem
sie vor Kurzem eine Pathenstelle vertreten, bei der Kirche über-
reichen wollte. Ein solches Geschenk besteht aus dünnen Brot-
kuchen und dickgekochtem Grütze (gryngröt); es wird nur von den
verheiratheten männlichen und weiblichen Pathen gegeben; der
Empfänger reicht dafür einen Trunk Branntewein. Dann begaben wir uns zur Kirche; vom Gotteshause bleibt in jedem
Hofe nur Einer zurück. Es war ein schöner windstiller Morgen, heiter und klar der Himmel. In einer Viertelstunde hatten wir das Ufer des Seenzuges erreicht, der von der Norwegischen Gränze herabkommt, und unterhalb Ström, an der

Gränze von Angermanland, die ansehnlichen Flüsse Ångel und Fare bildet; beide ergießen sich in den Angerman-Strom, ersterer bei Liden, nachdem er den, an Åsele Lappmarks Gränze entspringenden, Sarän aufgenommen, letzterer unterhalb der Kirche Ed. Der Seenzug heißt Wesdol, hat aber an den verschiedenen Stellen auch andere Namen; unterhalb Ström heißt er Russjälen. Am jenseitigen Ufer liegt die massive Kirche (daneben ein Glockenthurm), rings von einem weiten Kreise von Dörfern umgeben. Unfern der Kirche trifft man den Comministerhof, die Kirchbuden und Kirchställe. Die Kirchbuden sind theils nur fürs Umkleiden bestimmt, theils ganz wie Wohnhäuser eingerichtet; auch Brunnen sind angelegt. Bei den Ställen werden hölzerne Schlösser gebraucht, die nicht minder sicher sind, wie die eisernen, und in Jemteland vor Ställen und Vorrathsbuden benutzt werden. Auch Zehntbuden der Krone und der Pfarre, Kirchspielsstuben, Kirchspielsmagazine und einige Terparewohnungen findet man in geringerer oder größerer Entfernung von der Kirche.

Schon im Boot hatten wir den feierlichen Glockenschall vernommen; es war das zweite Läuten; bald folgte das dritte, und der Gottesdienst begann. Zuvörderst ward eine Taufe verrichtet; das Kind war etwa 10 Tage alt; die ungefähr 45jährige Mutter war mit dem Kinde 8 (12 deutsche) Meilen weit zur Kirche gekommen; da sie aber noch nicht ihren feierlichen Kirchgang gehalten und die kirchliche Einsegnung empfangen, so saß sie während des Gottesdienstes in der Vorhalle. Nach der Taufe nahm der eigentliche Gottesdienst seinen Anfang. Die Kirche war gedrängt voll, wiewohl nur etwas mehr als ein Drittheil der Gemeinde anwesend seyn mochte. Das Innere der Kirche ist einfach geschmückt; am Altar erblickt man in Holz geschnitzte, hübsche biblische Darstellungen: „die Einsetzung des heiligen Abendmahls, den Heiland am Kreuze, das Gericht ꝛc.". Die gespannteste Aufmerksamkeit und die herzlichste Andacht herrschte; eine Orgel ist zwar nicht vorhanden, aber der Gesang war sanft und wahrhaft ergreifend. Nach beendigtem Gottesdienst, der drittehalb Stunden gedauert hatte, verließ der Prediger zuerst die Kirche, worauf das männliche und dann das weibliche Geschlecht folgten. Jetzt kehrte man in die Kirchbuden zurück; Andere standen noch lange außerhalb des Kirchhofes, und redeten mit einander, so heiter und freudig, sanft und geräuschlos, als wären sie noch an heiliger Stätte. Ich trat unter sie; sofort boten sie mir die Rechte zur Bewillkommung, und drückten, Männer und Weiber, treuherzig meine Hand. Es ist ein biederer, herrlicher Schlag von Menschen, von hohem Wuchs und kräftigem und gedrungenem Körperbau; noch 50jährige Weiber sind schön; Sanftmuth, Würde und Freundlichkeit, Klarheit, Offenheit und Herzlichkeit, Kraft und Lebendigkeit sprechen sich in ihren geistreichen Blicken aus. Es ward mir unendlich wohl unter den biederen Menschen. Ihre Kleidung ist einfach, aber geschmackvoll. Die Männer sind in Walmar gekleidet; die Weiber in eigengemachten Camelot; nur Schürze, Halstuch und Mütze sind von feinerem Zeuge, d. i. von Seide oder von Kattun. Die fast einem Bonnet gleichende, aber dicht anschließende rosenfarbene, vorne und an den Seiten ein wenig ausgeschnittene, oben von einem breiten, rothen oder sonst hellfarbigen Bande umschlungene, seidene Mütze der Mädchen steht besonders gut; die Frauen tragen schwarzseidene Mützen mit schwarzen Bändern; auch die Bänder der Mädchen sind schwarz, wenn sie zum heiligen Abendmahle gehen. Die Zähne der jüngeren wie der älteren Männer und Weiber sind weiß, wie Elfenbein; das Gesicht ist stark und länglich, die Stirne breit, die Nase länglich, der Mund rund; die großen rollenden Augen sind blau. Unter Frauen und Mädchen sah ich wenige, die nicht überall für Schönheiten gelten würden.

Im Kirchspiel Ström herrscht viel Wohlhabenheit; unter den 747 Schwedischen Einwohnern, welche Ström im J. 1815 zählte, befanden sich nur 4 wirkliche Arme. Selbstmord, Ehescheidungen, Kartenspiel sind völlig unbekannt; Völlerey ist selten, eben so das Fluchen. Unter den etwa 30 jährlich Gebornen befindet sich oft mehrere Jahre hinter einander keine uneheliche Geburt; venerische Krankheiten hat man noch nie gekannt. In entfernten Dörfern wird Sonntags Dorfgottesdienst gehalten auf Norrländische Weise (die entferntesten Höfe, Svaningen — :

Kolonisten — haben 6 Meilen zur Kirche); zieht man auf die fernen Waldwiesen, zu den Sennhütten oder zu den Alpenfische-reyen, so nimmt man Gesangbücher, auch wohl Postillen, mit; nie wird am Sonntage gefischt; überhaupt ist die Sonntagsfeier sehr strenge. Am Sonnabend-Abend und Sonntag-Morgen halten die Hausväter Gebet im Kreise der Ihrigen; am Sonntag-Nach-mittag liest man in der Bibel, in Predigtbüchern 2c.; alle Ge-bete werden knieend verrichtet.

Ackerbau, Viehzucht, Fisch- und Vogelfang sind die haupt-sächlichsten Nahrungszweige in Ström; zuweilen wird Korn zum Ueberfluß gebauet; die Viehzucht wird als Sennenwirthschaft betrieben, jeder Bauer hat 1 oder 2 Sennhütten, die bis 2 Meilen weit entlegen sind; die einträglichsten Fischereyen hat man hier, wie in einem Theil von Hammardal und einem Theil von Alands, in den Fjäll (Alpen), 4 bis 12 Meilen von den Woh-nungen entlegen; man fährt dahin nach vollbrachter Kornerndte, und fischet Rör und Laxöring (Forellen), meist nur zum Haus-bedarf. Zwei und mehrere Bauern haben Eine Fjällfischerey (Fjällfiske) gemeinschaftlich, wofür sie eine geringe Abgabe an die Krone und Boställen (Amtshöfe), welchen das Land ange-schlagen ist, erlegen. Ein Paar Bauern unternehmen theils mit eignen, theils mit aufgekauften, theils mit von Anderen ih-nen anvertrauten Producten des Orts Handelsreisen nach Stock-holm. Einen nicht ganz unbedeutenden Erwerbszweig bildet ferner die Verfertigung hölzerner Kannen, Löffel 2c., die sie mit einem trefflichen Firniß, dessen Mischung Geheimniß ist, über-streichen und nach Ångermanland und Medelpad absetzen; dieser Erwerbszweig ist seit alten Zeiten Ström eigenthümlich. Die Kolonisten zwischen der Kirche Ström und der Norwegischen Gränze, auf welchem weiten Landstrich im Sommer auch Lap-pen (die sogenannten Hammardals-Lappen) mit ihren Rennthie-ren umherziehen (Kap. 23), bauen wenig oder gar kein Korn; sie leben meistens ohne Brot, bloß von Fleisch, Fischen, Butter und Käse; Butterbrot (smörgås) nennen sie Käse mit Butter belegt; dabei sind sie kräftig und gesund. Ueberhaupt sind die Menschen stark, tüchtig und abgehärtet; sie laufen anhaltend und mit unglaublicher Schnelligkeit, zumal auf Schlittschuhen, ohne auch nur die mindeste Brustbeschwerde zu empfinden. Die umgebende Natur fordert diese Anstrengung und Abhärtung des Körpers; selbst die Geistlichen sehen sich zuweilen im Winter bei ihren Krankenbesuchen und andern Amtsverrichtungen genöthiget, auf Schlittschuhen die Reise zu machen, weil auf keine andere Weise gut fortzukommen ist, und müssen sie, auf ähnlichen Reisen, im Sommer oft zu Fuße gehen. Nach Hammardal giebt es einen Fahrweg, der aber erst seit wenigen Jahren einigermaaßen brauchbar ist; sonst giebt es nur Boot-, Reit- und Gehwege; nach dem benachbarten Angermanland hat man nur Boot und Gehwege, letztere oft über Moräste und durch dichten Urwald; auf solchen Wegen hat man 5 Meilen zur Kirche Tåsjö, wovon die Hälfte indeß Bootweg ist; zur Kirche Fjällsjö 5 M. Gehweg; zur Kirche Ramsele 7 M. (wovon 2¼ M. bis Táran Bootweg). Mittelst des langen Seenzuges, der von der Norwegischen Gränze herabkommt, kann man von Ström aus nach Norwegen zu Boote kommen, nur 3 Landengen (edar oder eben) ausgenommen, wo man, der Wasserfälle wegen, auf am Lande gelegten Stäben, ¹⁄₁₆ bis ¼ M. lang, das Boot zieht, nämlich Gäddbedet, den größten Fall, 10 M. Bågacdet, 6 M. und Ögel strömmen (Name des Falles, nicht des Flusses, wie fälschlich auf Karten und in Geographien angegeben ist) 4 M. von der Kirche Ström, ¾ M. von Gårdnäs; ein kleinerer Fall, der mit Böten befahren werden kann, ist ¼ M. unterhalb der Kirche. Zuweilen gehen hier Ausreißer nach Norwegen durch, die sich auch wohl Diebstähle erlauben. Wilde Rennthiere giebt es im nördlichen Jemteland nicht, doch soll man sie im südlichen und westlichen finden. Bei der Kirche Ström wird einmal jährlich Lappenmarkt gehalten.

Bei Ström's Kirche sah ich einige erfrorene Gerste, die weich wie Brey ist und nur zu Branntwein gebraucht wird; man trocknet sie erst auf Stangengerüsten und dann in Dörrstuben. In Mißwachsjahren ißt man Rindenbrot, welches aus Fichtenrinde, den Spitzen der Gerstenähren (grannen, agnar) und ein wenig Gerstenmehl bereitet wird; man speiset dann auch

Rindengrütze, mit Zusatz von Mehl und Milch; ein bitteres Gericht, das der Hunger würzen muß.

Bis Abend verweilte ich, der freundlichen Einladung folgend, beim Comminister Huß, und kehrte dann, da ich nicht zu Nacht bleiben wollte, nach Tulingsås zurück. An dem sonnenhellen Nachmittage machte ich einen Spazierritt auf den, vom Comministerhofe etwa ¼ M. entfernten, Bergrücken, um von da der herrlichen Alpenaussicht zu genießen. Ich ritt durch ein großes Dorf, in welchem fast jeder Hof, wie in Österåsen, seinen besondern Namen hat. Man überblickt den Rusfjälen mit seinen Inseln und seinen zum Theil angebauten waldigen Ufern, weiter gegen Südosten den Fängsjö und die von ihm in Ångermanland auslaufenden Flüsse Wängel und Faxe, rings von Wald umgeben; im Norden, Nordwesten und Nordosten überschaut man ungeheure Waldstrecken, durch welche sich die oberen Züge des Wesdol von Norwegen herabsenken, und die Alpenketten von Åsele-Lappmark an, längs der Norwegischen Gränze (Amt Norder-Trondhjem), bis zur einzeln liegenden Åresfuta, d. h. vom Fisfafjäll bis zu den Klump- und Stacksfällen und endlich bis zur Åresfuta, eine Linie von etwa 20 (Schwed.) Meilen; in blauenden Dunst gehüllt, strahlten die Alpen im schönsten Sonnenlicht, in langen Ketten und getrennt; einige schienen ganz nahe zu seyn, und waren doch 10, 20 Meilen und weiter entfernt. Die Bauern zeigten mir sehr genau die Lage der einzelnen Alpen und Alpenketten an, eine Lokalkenntniß, die sie sich auf ihren Alpenfischereyen erworben haben mochten.

Am 25. Aug. Von Tulingsås nach Hallen 1½ M.; von H. nach Mo 1½ M.; von M. nach Lörås 1½ M.; von L. nach Svedje 2 M. — Zus. 6½ M.

Mein heutiger Weg war ganz der gestrige. Um 6¾ Uhr verließ ich Tulingsås. Auf der Höhe war es warm, abwärts im Walde empfindlich kalt. Die Brücken sind auf dem neuen Wege so hoch gelegt, daß ich, um die auf der Hinreise empfundenen gewaltigen Stöße zu vermeiden und den Wagen zu schonen, die Brückenenden durch angelegte Holzstücke mit der Straße in nähere Verbindung setzen ließ. Noch immer ist der Weg schlecht, aber wie viel schlechter er ehemals gewesen, davon zeugen die großen Steinmassen, welche jetzt am Wege liegen, und einst im Wege lagen. Zwischen Tulingsås und Hallen begegnete ich zwei Heerden Kühen und Ziegen, die aus einem Sennendorfe kamen, und jetzt in ein anderes zogen, wo man sie noch drei Wochen zu lassen gedachte; denn um Michaelis fällt hier gewöhnlich schon Schnee, und noch im October ist Schlittenbahn; der Herr der einen Heerde, ein ehemaliger Fahnjunker, zog, mit einer Bürde auf dem Rücken, hinterdrein. Bei Hallen überblickt man den großen Wald bis Ström, den man im Zirkel durchreiset ist; jenseits erscheinen die Gewässer bei Ström und links die Fjällen. Zwischen Hallen und Mo fährt man, bevor man den Amra-Elf erreicht, bei Fagerdal über einen andern beträchtlichen Fluß, den Öjan, der in den Amra fällt. Ich begegnete einem Bauer aus Fynäs, der von einem Besuche bei seinen Verwandten in Ström zurückkehrte, und noch in der Nacht vom Sonnabend auf den Sonntag die 4 Meilen geritten war, um in Ström dem Gottesdienste beiwohnen zu können. In Mo besichtigte ich in dem Hofe des verstorbenen Bauern, Hans Ohlsson, eine vom Wind getriebene Dreschmaschine, die er selber erfunden: Mühlenflügel über einem Scheunendach treiben einen Baum, an welchem hölzerne Walzen mit Zacken befestigt sind, die das untergelegte Korn zerschlagen; der Tod überraschte Hans Ohlsson, bevor das Werk vollendet wurde; gewöhnlich drischt man hier mit Dreschflegeln.

Im Pfarrhofe von Hammardal verweilte ich einige Zeit beim Pastor Ångman; auch hielt mich ein Riß am Sielenzeuge eine Stunde im Torp Böle auf, so daß ich erst um 10½ Uhr in meinem alten guten Nachtquartier Svedje anlangte, wohin der letzte steinige Weg in der Dunkelheit nur mit Hülfe einer Laterne, die ich glücklicher Weise bei mir führte, zurückgelegt werden konnte; denn Steinblöcke, die gar leicht den Wagen hätten zertrümmern können, lagen im Wege. Böle's Torp ist gut gebauet, hat mehrere Zimmer und gehört zu der Art von Torp, deren Bewohner ihr Land von den Bauern gekauft haben; solcher Torpare giebt es mehrere in Hammardals Pastorat; sie sind nicht minder wohlhabend, wie die Bauern, vor denen sie noch den Vorzug haben, daß sie von Skjuts und andern Lasten der Bauern frei sind. Eine andere Art von Torpare, die gewöhnliche in Schweden, entrichten für das Land, welches sie benutzen, jährliche Abgaben an die Bauern. Nach Böle flüchtete sich vor dem Regen auch die Frau eines ambulatorischen Schulmeisters; sie kam von Hammardal's Pfarrhof, wo sie wegen einer ihrem Kinde zugestoßenen Krankheit den Rath der Pfarrerin hatte einholen wollen; sie war aus Föllinge gebürtig, und hatte ganz das einfache, freundliche Wesen der Naturmenschen. — Am Wege vor Svedje bivouacquirte ein Transport Kühe, die ein alter Bauer aus Sunne aufgekauft hatte, um sie nach Stockholm zu treiben.

Am 26. August. Von Svedje nach Huså 3 M.; von H. nach Krogen 1½ M. — Zus. 4½ M.

Wie ich jetzt die entlegeneren Kirchspiele des nordöstlichen Jemtelands bereiset hatte, so wollte ich nun auch das entlegenste Pastorat von Nord-Jemteland, Föllinge, besuchen, um auch hier die Eigenthümlichkeiten des Landes und Volks, und die einzige Lappenschule Jemtelands; welche sich bei der Kirche Föllinge befindet, kennen zu lernen. Von Svedje oder Österåsen führen drei Wege nach Föllinge: der nähere 3 M., über Norråsen und Krogen, welcher aber 1½ M. bis Krogen nur Reitweg durch Wald ist; ein anderer über Huse und der wilde Horka nach Husås (1½ M.) und von da weiter über Krogen, der zwar sonst einigermaaßen fahrbar ist, jetzt aber, da es noch am vorigen Tage heftig geregnet hatte, nicht befahren werden konnte, und wo es überdieß unmöglich ist, den Wagen über die Horka zu bringen; endlich ein dritter, der weitere, über Lith, Husås und Krogen, auf welchem man ganz zu Wagen fortkommen kann. Da ich meinen Wagen nicht zurücklassen wollte, so mußte ich letzteren wählen, und fuhr, nachdem ich meiner braven Wirthin

nur mit Mühe einige Bezahlung hatte aufdringen können, um
8 Uhr ab. Der Weg bis zur Kirche Lith, 1½ M., ist fast
ganz derselbe, den ich schon auf der Aufreise passirt hatte; die
Kirche liegt sehr malerisch am Abhange eines Waldbergs, am Ufer
des Ragunda- oder Indals-Elf; an den Kirchhof schließen sich
buschbekränzte Wiesen, während an der andern Seite sich ein
schönes Mühlenthal herabsenkt. Eine Viertelmeile fährt man
nun den hohen Bergrücken hinan, und dann meist am waldbewachsenen Rande desselben fort. So erreicht man, einigen jetzt
unbewohnten Sennhütten vorüber, das hochgelegene Dorf Byn,
aus welchem man weite Wald- und Alpenprospekte hat; am Fuße
des Berges wogt der große Byser. Nachdem ich dem Dorfe
Ringsta vorübergefahren, gelangte ich durch Waldthäler zum er-
sehnten Ombyte Husås, denn mein Pferd war ermüdet, und
fast hatte ich verzweifelt, noch Husås zu erreichen, welches auch
nicht vor 2¾ Uhr geschah. Hinter Husås begegnete ich einer
Bauerfrau aus Krogen, welche verkauftes Vieh nach Husås gebracht hatte und jetzt heimkehrte; ich bot ihr an, sich hinten
auf den Wagen zu setzen, was sie dankbar annahm; bald brach
der Wagenriemen, die Bäuerin wußte ihn sofort wieder in
brauchbaren Stand zu setzen, und ein hinzukommender Bauer
ersetzte ihn völlig durch Birkenzweige; so weiß man im hohen
Norden in allerlei Noth sich zu helfen und selbst mancherlei
Handwerke entbehrlich zu machen; im Dorfe Tonds bei Föllinge fand ich einen Bauer, der ein tüchtiger Sattler war und
den Riemen völlig wieder herstellte; einen vollen halben Tag arbeitete er daran, und verlangte doch nur eine höchst geringe
Bezahlung. — Der Weg führt durch den Wald bergauf und
bergab, über Waldwiesen und am Ufer des Horka; also daß sich
auch hier bestätigte, was einer meiner heutigen Skjutsbauern
sehr naiv bemerkt hatte: Jemteland oder Jamteland, wie der
gemeine Mann spricht, führe seinen Namen (ebenes Land)
mit Unrecht, denn es sey keinesweges eben (jämnt), sondern
uneben (ojämnt, oder, wie man hier ausspricht, ojamnt). Als
ich in Krogen anlangte, war es 7½ Uhr, und zu spät, um am
Abend noch Föllinge zu erreichen. Ich übernachtete daher in

Krogen, wie die gute Frau bat, um sich für die ihr erwiesene
kleine Gefälligkeit gerne dankbar zeigen zu können.

Krogen besteht aus zwei Bauerhöfen, die mitten im Walde
liegen. Sie werden von zwei Brüdern bewohnt, die Alles wie
gemeinschaftlich haben; der eine hat eine Schwester und einen
Schwager, der andere seinen alten Vater bei sich, welcher letz=
tere dieses Nybygge angelegt hat; ganz arm hatte er angefangen
und alles war recht eigentlich durch den Fleiß seiner Hände er=
worben. Der eine Bruder war sogar des Uhrmachens kundig,
das er ganz von selbst erlernet hatte. Auch ein Torpare hatte
sich angesiedelt. Alles war hier tüchtig, reinlich und gefällig.
Ein Kaminfeuer verbreitete eine behagliche Wärme; bald war
ein stärkendes Abendessen bereitet und verzehrt, und ein sanfter
Schlaf nahm mich in seine Arme.

Am Abend äußerte ich noch den Wunsch, eine kleine Kiste,
die zu dem Wagen passe, zu erhalten; sogleich machte sich der
eine Bruder an die Arbeit, die er die ganze Nacht fortsetzte,
ohne daß ich darum gebeten hatte; denn er glaubte, wiewohl ich
des Weges zurückkehren würde, möge es mir doch lieber seyn,
schon jetzt zu sehen, ob die Arbeit nach Wunsch ausgefallen sey.
Wo findet man solche lautere Dienstfertigkeit!

Am 27. August. Von Krogen nach Föllinge 1¾ M.

Als ich die Zeche bezahlen wollte, glaubte die dankbare
Brita noch immer für die ihr gestern bewiesene Gefälligkeit mir
verpflichtet zu seyn, und weigerte sich, Bezahlung anzunehmen;
nur mit Mühe gelang es, sie ihr aufzudringen. — Der Weg
ist schmal, steinig und bergig, 1¾ M. fährt man durch dichten
Wald, keine Menschenwohnung ist sichtbar, nur einige Seen
und die breite Hårka mit ihren bewaldeten Inseln gewähren ei=
nige Abwechselung; da wo eine nach Krogen gehörige Wassermühle an=
gelegt ist, bildet der breite Strom Hunderte von kleinen Wasser=
fällen, die sich gar lieblich ausnehmen; ¼ M. vor Föllinge er=
reicht man das Dorf Tonds, und fährt nun, an einem See,
zur Kirche und zum Pfarrhofe von Föllinge. Die Kirche liegt

auf einem Hügel am See; in der wilden Wald- und Sumpf-
gegend macht sie einen wunderbaren Eindruck; ringsumher beschränken Waldberge die Aussicht. Ich trat im Pfarrhofe ab,
wo mich der Pastor Huß, ein ehrwürdiger Greis, mit Herzlichkeit empfing. Noch vor Tische ward die Kirche besichtiget. Sie
ist von Holz und ward erst vor Kurzem (1811 — 1815) neu
gebauet. Die von dem oben genannten Bauer Edeler schon
1795 gefertigte Altartafel macht großen Effect, wenn man in
die Kirchthüre tritt, von welcher aus der große Gang gerade
auf den Altar zuführt: in der Mitte erhebt sich ein Kreuz mit
der Dornenkrone, zur Seite erblickt man ein Paar Figuren,
„die Hoffnung, mit dem Anker, Glaube, mit dem Kreuze", daneben auf dem Altartisch zwei Rauchfässer mit lodernder Flamme,
in Form von Vasen; über dem Kreuz in der Mitte, welches wie
in einer Nische sich zeigt, schweben zwei beflügelte Engel auf
Wolken, über ihnen auf einem Dreiecke Jehovah, von zwei
Engeln umgeben; dahinter ein Tempelvorhang, der von Engels-
schaaren gehoben wird; letzterer ist auf der Wand so täuschend
gemalt, daß, wiewohl die Wand vom Altar durch einen etwa
6 Fuß breiten Gang gesondert wird, Wand und Altar Eins zu seyn
scheinen. Die Malerey ist vom Jemteländischen Bauer Anders
Ersson zu Nordanelfven im Kirchspiel Näsjkott. Uebrigens ist
das Innere der Kirche sehr einfach; Chöre findet man nicht;
den einen der beiden Kronleuchter schenkte eine Landwehr-Com-
pagnie aus Ångermanland, die im letzten Kriege hieher auf einige Monate detaschirt ward; ein Glockengießer in Sundswall,
Namens Lindeberg, verfertigte die Gabe für einen sehr geringen
Preis, um den guten Zweck zu fördern. Durch den Glockenthurm, der an die Kirche angebauet ist, führt der Eingang zur
Kirche; über der inneren Thüre liest man die Inschrift: Prediger Salom. 4, 17. bewahre deinen Fuß, wann du
zum Hause Gottes gehest, und komme, daß du hörest;
über der äußern die Nachricht, daß ohne öffentliche Unterstützung
der Bau der Kirche im J. 1815 vollendet worden sey, und
Psalm 5, 8. Große Gothische Fenster geben dem schönen
länglichen Gebäude eine alterthümliche Form. Den Bau lei-

tete der damalige Adjunct in Föllinge, Ångman, jetzt Pastor in Hammardal. — Der Kirchhof hat Grabkreuze und platte Steine mit Namen und Inschriften, und wird von einem hübschen Gitterwerk umgeben. Umher liegen die Kirchspielsstube, der Pfarrhof, die Zehntbude (tyrkoherberge), Kirchstuben, die zum Theil mehrere Besitzer haben (wer 1½ M. von der Kirche entfernt wohnt, hat schon eine Kirchstube); an die Kirchstuben schließen sich ein Paar Dörfer an; ein Kirchspielsmagazin giebt es nicht, da das Korn selten reift. Der erste Gottesdienst in der neuen Kirche ward am 18. September 1814 gehalten.

Föllinge war bis 1744 Filial von Lith; seit dieser Zeit bildet es ein besonderes Pastorat; der Pastor von Lith ward für die dadurch verminderten Einkünfte von der Krone entschädiget. Seit etwa 20 Jahren gehören zu Föllinge zwei Kapellen: Hotagen, 4½, und Frostvik, 15 M. von der Mutterkirche entfernt; in den Kapellen wird von Föllinge aus, zweimal jährlich, und zwar für Schweden und Lappen gemeinschaftlich, Gottesdienst gehalten; dem Pastor von Föllinge ist nämlich die Seelsorge der Lappen in Föllinge und Ströms-Lappmarker anvertrauet; neben der Kirche Föllinge besteht eine Lappenschule; über welches alles, so wie rücksichtlich der Eigenthümlichkeiten der hierher gehörigen Lappen ich auf Kap. 23. verweise. Wiewohl Föllinge kein eigentliches Lappenpastorat ist, so genießt es doch seit alten Zeiten das Vorrecht der Lappengemeinden, keine Soldaten stellen zu dürfen.

Die Einwohnerzahl des gesammten Pastorats Föllinge, welches 18 ◻M. enthält, betrug, im J. 1815, 1130, wovon 162 in Hotagen, und 245 in Frostvik; im J. 1810 war die Seelenzahl 1069, im J. 1805, 930, im J. 1757 nur 203. Die Lappen sind in die gegenwärtige Volkszahl nicht mit begriffen. Die Schwedischen Einwohner der Kapellgemeinden sind Nybyggare, meist Norwegischer Abkunft. Hauptnahrungszweig in ganz Föllinge ist Viehzucht; die Viehställe sind mit Oefen versehen, theils der Viehmägde wegen, die auf dem Boden schlafen, theils um fürs Vieh leicht warmes Wasser erhalten zu können. Die Schaafställe hat man über den Kuhställen angelegt, so daß die

II.   Kk

Schaafe Treppen steigen müssen; die von unten aufsteigende Wärme ist ihnen vortheilhaft. Einige Bauern halten auch Rennthiere, die von Lappen geweidet werden. Auch Fischerey und Jagd wird getrieben, das Vogelfleisch wird getrocknet und ist dann besonders wohlschmeckend. Korn reist in den Kapellgemeinden fast nie, und auch in der Muttergemeinde erfriert es oft; die frühe Kälte erzeugen die vielen Moräste; selbst unfern der Kirche ist ein solcher Sumpf, der durch seine kalten Ausdünstungen die Hoffnung des Landmanns vernichtet. Urbarmachungen würden das Klima mildern und mehr Wohlhabenheit über das Land verbreiten. Roggenbrod wird mit Blut vermischt. Zum Dreschen bedient man sich mit Zacken versehener hölzerner Walzen, die ein Pferd zieht. Der Winter ist sehr strenge; der kürzeste Tag ist 4 Stunden lang (10½ bis 2½ Uhr). Die Einwohner leben einfach und sittlich; unter den 33 Gebornen des Pastorats im J. 1816, befand sich kein einziges uneheliches Kind (in den J. 1800 bis 1811 wurden nur 6 uneheliche Kinder geboren, und zwar in 6 Jahren keines, in jedem der übrigen 6 Jahre eins); der jährliche Ueberschuß der Gebornen ist sehr groß; die Zahl der Gestorbenen beträgt gewöhnlich nur ein Drittheil, ja nur ein Viertheil der Gebornen (in den J. 1800 bis und mit 1816, wurden geboren 507, worunter 11 uneheliche; es starben 195). Die Leute sind kräftig und gesund, groß und, besonders die Männer, wohlgebildet; venerische Krankheiten kennt man nicht. Anticipirter Beischlaf (otidigt fängeslag) der Verlobten kommt in manchem Jahre gar nicht vor, wenn gleich er jetzt häufiger ist, als sonst. Die Ehrennacht der Jünglinge und Mädchen ist allgemein, aber in aller Keuschheit. Diebstahl ist selten; wo er verübt wird, bestraft man ihn unter einander in der Stille; auch warnt der Pastor. Schwören und Fluchen hört man selten; wer es thut, wird verachtet; der blaue Montag ist unbekannt. Früherhin spielte man Karten, jetzt ist aber auch dieses abgelegt, seit man auf dem Kirchspielsstande sich vereinigte, daß, wer selber Karten spiele, oder in seinem Hause Kartenspiel zulasse, in eine Geldbuße von 5 Bankthalern an die Kirche verfallen seyn solle. Völlerei findet wenig Statt. Hauptvergnügen des Volks ist Tanz; jeden 2ten Sonntags Abend wird in den Dörfern getanzt, von 8 bis 12 Uhr, wobei es aber sehr ordentlich zugeht; Bewirthung wird gar nicht gereicht; im übrigen ist die Sonntagsfeier strenge; an den Sonnabends Abenden wird in den einzelnen Häusern Gebet gehalten; am Sonntage geht man fleissig zur Kirche; die Zurückbleibenden versammeln sich am Vormittage zum Dorfgottesdienst, und am Nachmittage lesen die Einzelnen in der Bibel und in Postillen ꝛc. Ehescheidungen und Trennungen der Verlöbnisse sind unerhört, selbst Ehezwiste selten. Gegen Arme, deren es aber nur wenige giebt, ist man sehr wohlthätig. Ueberhaupt ist die Gemeinde sehr gastfrei, dienstfertig und ehrbar, und, des geringen Ackerbaues ungeachtet, bei Mäßigkeit, wohlhabend. Die Kleidung ist sehr einfach; Männer und Weiber gehen in selbstgefertigtem Walmar; nach Lappenweise tragen die Weiber (auch in Hammardal) auf der Brust kleine zinnerne Ringe mit kleinen Blättchen; Halstücher und Mützen der Frauen und Mädchen sind von Seide, die Schürzen von Kattun; solche Kostbarkeiten sind Bräutigamsgaben, um den Kopf trägt man Tücher; die Mützen der Frauen sind schwarz, die der Mädchen rosenroth; Geschwängerte dürfen nur rothbraune Mützen tragen, werden auch wohl zuweilen verheirathet, aber nie kehrt die verscherzte Achtung zurück. Von dem dankbaren, liebevollen Sinn der Gemeinde zeugt ein etwa 2 Pfund schwerer silberner Krug, den sie ihrem Pastor, einiger Gefälligkeiten halber, die er ihr erwiesen, vor kurzem verehrt hatte; der Krug trägt die Inschrift:

„Aus Liebe, Dankbarkeit und Ehrfurcht verehrten dieses Föllinge's und Hotagen's Gemeinden dem Herrn Pastor, Joh. Ar. Huß, im Jahr 1811. Der Himmel verlängere unser gegenseitiges Wohl!"

— Die Kirche erhält oft freiwillige Gaben. Die Leute haben große Vorliebe für die Heimath; nur selten dient ein Mädchen außerhalb der Gemeinde. Im ganzen Pastorat giebt es nur 3 Handelsbauern; sie fahren nach Stockholm.

Kk 2

Am 28. Aug. Von Föllinge nach Krogen 1½ M.; von K. nach Hufås 1½ M.; von H. nach Söre 1½ M. — Zuf. 4½ M.

Um ıı Uhr fuhr ich aus. Das Pferd war des Ziehens noch nicht recht gewohnt, denn eben war es von den Alpenweiden wiedergekehrt, wohin man im Sommer die Pferde mager treibt und von wo man sie fett zurückbringt; auf der Anhöhe blieb es stehen: doch allmählig ging es besser, und nach 3 Stunden hatte ich Krogen erreicht; auf dem Wege sieht man viele Spuren von Waldbrand. Kaum war ich angelangt, als die dankbare Brita schon allerlei Speisen auftrug, von denen sie es gemerkt hatte, daß ich sie gerne möchte. Auch die Kiste und ein bestellter stählerner Uhrschlüssel wurden gebracht; und das Alles sollte wieder umsonst seyn, und als ich dennoch bezahlte, ließ man sich nur mit Mühe bewegen, es anzunehmen. Die Lauterkeit und Freudigkeit dieser Menschen, die gewiß nichts weniger als im Ueberfluß lebten, war so erhebend und stärkend, daß es mir recht schwer wurde, mich von ihnen zu trennen. Gleich einfach und schuldlos war mein Skjutsbonde, ein 26jähriger Jüngling, auf dessen Antlitz eine himmlische Milde ruhte; ganz durchnäßt auf seinem Sitze, war er still und geduldig, wie ein Lamm, weder Murren noch Klage ging aus seinem Munde. Eben so war das aufwartende Mädchen in Föllinge: als ich iht einiges Biergeld gab, hielt sie es für zu viel, da sie so geringe Dienste geleistet! So leben hier die Menschen glücklich in Einfalt und Unschuld.

Mein Weg war bis Lith's Kirche ganz der vorgestrige. Als ich bei Lith anlangte, war es schon zu spät geworden, um über die Fähre zu ziehen. Mein Skjutsbonde schlug vor, bei dem reichen Bauern Anders Andersson in Söre, wo auch seine Schwester diente, zu übernachten; ich fuhr dahin und ward aufs freundlichste bewillkommnet; zu meiner großen Freude fand ich dort auch den braven Sunding aus Brunflo; das Nachtlager war vorzüglich. Am folgenden Morgen nahm ich Wohnung und wirthschaftliche Einrichtungen in Augenschein. Das Haus ist erst vor wenigen Jahren neu erbauet worden; es hat in 2 Stockwerken einen Saal und 6 Zimmer, und lie auf einer Anhöhe

die eine entzückende Aussicht auf den Indalself, seine Waldin-
seln und fruchtbaren Ufer gewährt; in den zum Theil ausgemal-
ten, und mit kleinen Kupferstichen, wie häufig die Schwedischen
Bauerstuben, geschmückten Zimmern war auch eine kleine Bibliothek aufgestellt, in welcher ich Erbauungsbücher, geographische,
statistische ꝛc. Schriften, auch Svea Rikes Lag (das Schwedische
Gesetzbuch) fand. Abwärts vom Wohnhause lagen Wirthschaftsgebäude aller Art, bis zur Schmiede herab, Scheunen mit hölzernen Dreschwalzen, Viehställe mit Boden für Mägde und
Schaafe, und mit einem Ofen zum Kochen des Wassers, welches,
da es sonst zu kalt seyn würde, im Winter erwärmt mit dem
Heu vermischt wird; eine Nordschwedische Sitte, die aber, ihrer
Nützlichkeit halber, auch schon ins mittlere und südliche Schweden
verpflanzt worden ist. Alles zeugte von Tüchtigkeit und Wohlstand. Anders hatte sich sein nicht ganz unbedeutendes Vermögen durch Handel nach Stockholm und Hedemora erworben; andere Bauern waren durch diesen Handel noch reicher geworden.
Da Anders, wiewohl verheirathet, doch kinderlos ist, so hatte
er in den Nothjahren ein Paar fremde Kinder angenommen;
das eine war die Schwester meines Skjutsbonde aus Stamgärde
in Undersäker; auch er selber hatte mehrere Jahre bei Anders
gedient, bis er sich mit einem Mädchen aus Husäs verlobte, und
nun nach Husäs zog, um, da seine Verlobte die einzige Erbin
war, nach dem Tode des Vaters der Wirthschaft vorzustehen.
Das letzte Mißjahr hatte bisher die Feier der Hochzeit verhin-
dert, diesen Herbst sollte sie nun Statt finden, und schon hatte
der Jüngling seinen armen Eltern in Stamgärde geschrieben,
daß sie zu ihm ziehen möchten, damit er an ihnen die Pflicht
kindlicher Dankbarkeit erfülle. Es war ein herrlicher Mensch,
schuldlos und offen, treuherzig und bieder. Eben so sprach sich
in Anders Andersson ungemein viel Edles aus; er war ein ächt
Schwedischer Bauer, voll Gefühl seiner Freiheit und Selbststän-
digkeit, verrieth aber dabei viel Feinheit im Benehmen, die er
sich auf seinen Reisen erworben hatte, und zeigte eine so genaue
Kenntniß der Verhältnisse, selbst der kirchlichen, seines Pastorats
und seines Volks, wie man sie bei einem Bauer nicht erwartet.

Nach eingenommenem vorzüglichem Frühstück, wobei sogar zweierlei Art Kuchen vorgesetzt wurden, wie auch die Bauern für Fremde sie stets bereit halten, und nach herzlichem Danke an meinen biederen Wirth (denn an Bezahlung war nicht zu denken), fuhr ich zum Pfarrhof, um die schöne Kirche zu sehen.

Die Kirche von Lith, ein steinernes Gebäude mit Thurm, wurde auf Kosten der Kirchenkasse und der Gemeinde vom Ångermanländer Geting, der mehrere Nordländische Kirchen gebauet hat, aufgeführt und 1796 vollendet. Ausgezeichnet schön ist der Altar; in der Mitte desselben erblickt man, zwischen zwei Säulen, in einer Nische, ein Kreuz, welches ein Dornenkranz umwindet und von welchem das weiße Gewand des Auferstandenen herabwallt; zur Seite eine Figur, die das Kreuz umfaßt, während neben ihr, auf einem Felsen ein Anker ruht; hinter der Nische ist an der Wand ein Tempel gemalt; über der Nische erblickt man Wolken mit dem Dreiecke und dem Namen Jehovah's, von Strahlen und Engeln umgeben, und über das Ganze halten andere Engel den Vorhang eines Tempels. Eben so ist hinter der mit passenden Emblemen gezierten, vergoldeten Kanzel an der Wand ein Tempelvorhang gemalt. In der Sacristey wird eine der Fahnen des Regiments Jemteland aufbewahrt. Die Kirche umgiebt der Begräbnißplatz. Hier liegt auch ein Torpare begraben, welcher vor kurzem starb und 200 Rthlr. Banko zur Anschaffung eines Kirchthurms vermachte. Kirchstuben findet man nicht, wohl aber Kirchspielsstuben, Zehntbude und Kirchspielsmagazin.

Das Pastorat Lith besteht aus drei Gemeinden, der Muttergemeinde Lith, im Jahr 1815 mit 1211, den Filialgemeinden Häggenäs, mit 778, und Kyrkäs, mit 241 Seelen; in Kyrkäs hält der Comminister von Häggenäs jeden dritten Sonntag Gottesdienst. Die Zahl der Gebornen betrug im J. 1815 im gesammten Pastorat 68, worunter 2 Uneheliche (in Häggenäs war die Zahl der Geburten 24, in Kyrkäs 5). Nahrungszweige sind Viehzucht, Ackerbau (Pastor Gerdlund hat durch Hülfe Dalekarlischer Arbeiter ansehnliche Urbarmachungen unternommen), Jagd und Fischerey, aber auch Handel; vier Bauern bringen

Butter, Talg, Vögel, Lederwaaren und Norwegische Pferde nach Stockholm und auf den Markt von Hedemora und führen Rauch= und Schnupftabak, Waizenmehl, Sensen und ein wenig Kaffee und Zucker zurück; andere kaufen für diese Reisehändler auf und verkaufen für sie; mehrere Bauern führen Butter, Eisenwaaren, Hopfen, Felle, besonders von Ziegen und Eichhörnern, nach Nor= wegen und kaufen dort getrocknete Fische, Heringe und Pferde ein; die Felle verkaufen die Norweger wieder nach England, von wo sie als Saffian zurückkommen.

Am 29. August. Von Söre nach Hölje ½ M.; von H. nach Rösta 1¼ M.; von R. nach Faxelfven 2¼ M. — Zus. 4 M.

Bis Hölje fuhr mich mein Skjutsbonde von Husås. Zwi= schen Hölje und Rösta sieht man mehrere Dörfer im Walde, auch Halläsen: hier wohnt ein Bauer, Erik Erikson, der durch Handelsreisen sich ein Vermögen von 16,000 Bankthalern er= worben haben soll. Bei Hölje erblickt man zuerst die west= lichen Alpen.

Rösta ist der erste Gästgifvaregård im Pastorat Röddn, wel= ches aus den Gemeinden Röddn, Ås, Aspås und Näskott besteht. Nur noch an einigen Orten von Röddn ist die alte Einfachheit erhalten. Fast alle Bauern treiben Handel. Nach beendigter Kornernte fährt man Holz und begiebt sich dann auf Handels= reisen, zuerst nach Norwegen, insbesondere nach Levanger, 30, und Drontheim 40 M. von Östersund; hier kauft man Pferde, getrocknete Fische und Heringe, die man meist in den Seestäd= ten Ångermanlands und Medelpads wieder absetzt; dann zieht man nach Stockholm oder auf die Märkte von Hedemora und Falun (in Dalekarlien), besucht auch den großen Markt zu Sol= lefta (in Ångermanland), wohin man Talg, Butter, Vögel, Le= derwaaren und Norwegische Pferde zu Kauf bringt. Durch die= sen Handel haben manche sich ansehnliches Vermögen erworben.

Röddn ist berühmt durch seine malerischen Gegenden. Die= ser Ruhm bestätigte sich mir auch auf der Fahrt nach Faxelfven. Bald hinter Rösta, nachdem man der Kirche Ås vorübergesah=

ren, überblickt man die Insel Frösön in ihrer ganzen Ausdehnung, den ganzen langen Storsjö von Brunflo bis Mattmar
nebst Ostersund; dann fährt man durch eine reizende Landschaft
zwischen Dörfern, Wiesen und Gebüschen längs des Busens,
mittelst dessen der Storsjö dem Indalself seinen Ursprung giebt:
auf der gegenüberliegenden fruchtbaren Halbinsel von Röbön re-
hen sich Höfe an Höfe. Bei Säter, dem aus zwei gekauften
Bauerhöfen erwachsenen Gütchen des Majors Tideman, fährt
man auf einer langen Brücke über diesen Ausfluß des Storsjö;
eine Ehrenpforte aus Maienbüschen, die die Jugend auf der
Brücke errichtet, zeugte noch von der fröhlichen Feier des letzten
Johannisabends. So gelangt man zwischen Wiesen, Laub- und
Nadelwald, zur Kirche Näskott, die, so klein sie ist, doch eine
Orgel und einen hübschen Altar hat; vom Kirchhofe genießt
man einer herrlichen Aussicht über die schöne Umgegend und auf
die fernen Alpen. Bei der Kirche begegnete ich einer Anzahl
Sennenmädchen, die mit einer Heerde von Kühen und Ziegen und
den Produkten derselben aus den Fjällen zurückkehrten. Bauern
und Bäuerinnen waren entgegengezogen, den Transport zu erleichtern; heiter und fröhlich waren alle. Das Vieh gehörte
mehreren Dörfern; in Näskott trennte man sich, die einen zogen
gen Westen, die anderen gen Osten ꝛc. Jetzt ist die Zeit, wo
man die Sennhütten in den Alpen verläßt, denn im Anfange
Septembers pflegt dort Schnee zu fallen. Gewöhnlich ziehen
dann auch Männer aus den Dörfern hinauf, um die vielen
Pferde, welche im Sommer auf den Fjällen weiden, heimzuführen. Man begiebt sich nun nach Hause oder nach Sennhütten
im niederen Lande. Vor Faxelfven passirt man auf einer Brücke
einen Fluß, den Naplan, der einen von Offerdal herabkommenden See dem Storsjö zuführt; auch diese Brücke war, noch
vom Johannisabend her, mit Laubbogen geschmückt. In Faxelfven, denn es war spät geworden, durch die schlechten Wege und
wohl auch die Schwere meines herkulisch-gebauten 20jährigen
Skjutsbonde, der seine vollen 200 Pfund und darüber wog,
übernachtete ich. In Faxelfven liegt auch der Hof des Major
Orbom, der durch seine persönlichen Bemühungen und nament-

lich durch gerichtliche Anzeige der einzelnen Uebertreter, die Jugend von Råftott, welche dem Spielen und Trinken sich ergeben hatte, auf beſſere Wege zurückgeführt hat.

Am 30. Aug. Von Jarelfven nach Offerdal 2¼ M.; von O. nach Alſen 1⅛ M.; von A. nach Eggen (Mörſill) 1⅞ M. — Zuf. 6 M.

Um 7 Uhr fuhr ich aus. Der Weg führt durch niedrigen Laub- und Nadelwald, über welchen die hohen Schneeberge leuchten; beim Dorfe Wallarne kommt man durch eine Ehrenpforte, die die Jugend zum Johannisfeſt errichtete. Lange fährt man Angeſichts der Åreſkuta, die wolkenlos mit ihren himmelanſtrebenden Gipfeln und ihrem ewigen Schnee auf der Höhe und an den Seiten da liegt; links breitet ſich der ſchöne See von Alſen aus, den die Kirche Alſen im Nordoſten begränzt. Nachdem man alſo ¼ M. auf einem trefflichen, völlig ebenen Wege, dem beſten, welchen ich in Jämteland fand, gefahren, biegt man rechts, einen hohen Wieſenberg mit Birkengebüſch hinan, auf deſſen Höhe herrliche Alpenproſpekte erfreuen, und gelangt durch Wald, neben Dörfern, auf einem nicht minder vorzüglichen Wege, zur Kirche Offerdal; im Südoſten liegt der hohe Bergrücken Hellberget.

Um 10⅔ Uhr war ich in Offerdal. Aber der alte Propſt Nordenſtröm war zur Einhebung des Butterzehnten nach Mattmar gereiſet; nur eine Tochter, die Frau des Vicepaſtors, und ein Sergeant, der auf dem Hofe die Stelle des Voigtes vertrat, waren daheim. Man bat mich, zu bleiben; aber mein Reiſeplan erlaubte keine Zögerung; ich trat daher, nachdem ich mich von den Merkwürdigkeiten des Orts unterrichtet, nach dem Mittagseſſen die Rückreiſe an. Das Innere der alten, aber erneuerten ſteinernen Kirche iſt ſchön und würdig; über dem Altar, deſſen Bildhauerarbeit von dem ſchon öfters genannten Edling iſt, erblickt man, zwiſchen vier Säulen, ein größeres und ein kleineres Gemälde, dieſes, die Anbetung der drei Könige, jenes, das bei weitem vorzüglichere, die Abnahme Chriſti vom

Kreuz, auf welchem der Ausdruck des tiefen Schmerzes und der stillen Bewunderung der Umstehenden treffend dargestellt ist, auch die Wahl und Haltung der Gewänder alles Lob verdient; über dem größeren Gemälde erscheint eine Wolke mit Strahlen und eine Taube, rings um Engel; hinten an der Wand rollt der Vorhang eines Tempels herab; an den Seiten der Säulen stehen ein Paar vergoldete weibliche Figuren, die eine mit dem Kreuz, die andere mit dem Anker. Die stark vergoldete Kanzel ist mit passenden biblischen Emblemen geschmückt. An den Kirchs wänden hängen einige alte gute Gemälde, theils biblische, theils Prediger mit ihren Frauen. Die Kirche hat auch eine kleine Orgel und einen Thurm. Die Kirchbuden stehen in einiger Entfernung von der Kirche. Eine zweite Merkwürdigkeit bietet der Pfarrhof dar: eine bemalte hölzerne, 14 Kannen haltende, Schaale, die vor langer Zeit hieher geschenkt wurde, und in welcher jetzt den Bauern, die den Zehnten bringen, Bier gereicht wird. Eine ähnliche Schaale, Sven genannt, fand man vor mehreren Jahren auf dem Obersten-Boställe Kungsgården auf Frösön, wo sie jetzt nicht mehr vorhanden ist; auf die Schaale Sven beziehen sich die lustigen Reimereien, auf der Schaale Gertrud zu Offerdal, die rings umher unter dem Namen Offerdals-Bulla (Bulla bezeichnet eine ausgehöhlte hölzerne Schaale) bekannt ist. Die Inschrift nennt letztere Gertrud; auch liest man die Worte: „Gastschaale für den Bauern in Offerdal am Ehrentage seines Pastors und Propstes Mag. Ahr. L. Burman und dessen Gattin Elisabeth Zachariastochter Plantin, 24. Febr. 1690.“

Zu dem 22 □M. fassenden Pastorat Offerdal gehören die Gemeinden Offerdal, im Jahr 1815 mit 1329, Alsen mit 1036 und Mattmar mit 543 Seelen. Offerdal war bisher Sitz einer Propstey, die die Pastorate Offerdal, Rödön, Undersåker, Ragunda, Lith, Hämmardal und Föllinge umfaßt, und in welcher die Zahl der Gebornen, im J. 1815, 558 (worunter 30 uneheliche), die Zahl der Gestorbenen aber nur 236 (worunter 62 unter 1 Jahr) betrug. Der Ueberschuß der Gebornen ist überall in Jemteland sehr groß; im J. 1814 wurden in dieser Propstey geboren 489, worunter 14, im J. 1813, 329, worunter 12 uneheliche; im Pastorat Offerdal war die Zahl der Geburten, im J. 1816, 100, worunter 1 uneheliche; überhaupt wurden in der Gemeinde Offerdal in den Jahren 1802 bis 1815 zusammen 8 uneheliche Kinder geboren; in Alsen im selbigen Zeitraum 13; in Mattmar 3. Anticipirter Beischlaf war weit häufiger, z. B. in Alsen im J. 1816 unter 11 Ehen 8. Ehescheidungen waren in mehreren Decennien nicht vorgefallen. Fluchen hört man selten; Völlerei herrscht wenig, wiewohl man den Johannisabend und die Weihnachtszeit sehr fröhlich begeht; am Johannisabend sammelt man sich auf den Wiesen und bleibt dort spielend, singend und tanzend, mehrere Stunden lang; Ehrenpforten werden errichtet, Kränze gewunden ꝛc. Hauptnahrungszweige sind Ackerbau und Viehzucht, letztere als Sennenwirthschaft betrieben; jeder Hof hat zwei Sennenhütten, die eine für den Sommer, mitten in den Alpen, bis 5 Meilen vom Dorfe entlegen, die andre für den Herbst (vom Ende August bis Michaelis); diese liegt näher dem Dorfe. Bevor die Mädchen um Johannis auf die Alpen ziehen, gehen sie insgesammt, und gewöhnlich gesondert von der übrigen Gemeinde, zum heiligen Abendmahl. Es giebt auch Handelsbauern, deren einige die Märkte von Dalekarlien besuchen, die meisten aber auf Norwegen ihre Handelsreisen beschränken.

Der Weg von Offerdal nach Alsen war die ersten ¼ M. ganz derselbe, den ich am Vormittag gefahren war; dann hat man ½ M. bis zum Gästgifvaregård Åberg, wo ich Skjuts bestellte und ¼ Meile am reizenden Ufer des Alsen-Sees, zu Alsen's Kirche und Comministerhofe. Auf dem hölzernen Glockenthurme überschauet man die malerische Landschaft, die den See umgiebt; im Hintergrunde zeigen sich Alpenketten, die hier überall sichtbar sind; nur das südliche Ufer des Sees ist wenig angebaut. Die alte Kirche ist von Stein, der neue Altar ganz auf ähnliche Weise, wie der Altar in der Kirche von Offerdal, geschmückt; nur in der Höhe erhebt sich, über Strahlen ꝛc., ein einfaches blaues Kreuz, welches großen Effect macht; die Altargemälde stellen den Heiland am Kreuz und die Einsetzung des hei-

ligen Abendmahls dar. Mancherlei andere heilige Darstellungen
erblickt man an dem amphitheatralisch gebauten Chor und an der
Decke der Kirche; an den eisernen Kreuzen der Gräber auf dem
Kirchhofe lieset man die einfachen Inschriften: „hier ruhet unser
christlicher Bruder, unsere christliche Schwester" (vär Christendoms
Broder, Syster) N. N. —

Noch am Spätabend reisete ich weiter, wiewohl der Comminister Hasselgre'n dringend bat, zu übernachten; denn ich
hatte mir vorgesetzt, am nächsten Tage im Pastorat Undersåker
zu seyn, um das dortige Volk in seinem Gotteshause und in seiner Sonntagstracht zu sehen. Um 9½ Uhr brach ich auf, und
ehe ich es bemerkte, war ich in Eggen; mein Skjutsbonde hatte,
da er sah, daß ich müde war, so vorsichtig gefahren, daß ich geschlafen und kein Stein mich geweckt hatte. Auch der Alte,
den die Volkssage hier auf einem Waldberge hausen läßt, hatte
mich nicht beunruhiget. Unweit Eggen fährt man über den Fluß
Simla, an welchem eine, 1752 angelegte, Garhütte liegt.

Am 31. Aug. Von Eggen nach Nyland 1¼ M.

Am folgenden Morgen ging ich zur nahen Kirche Mörsill, Filial von Undersåker. Die Gegend um die Kirche her, an
dem von Kall sich in den Storsjö herabsenkenden Wasserzuge ist
sehr schön: freundliche Anhöhen wechseln mit fruchtbaren Äckern
und üppigen Wiesen. Die alte kleine steinerne Kirche war gedrängt voll. Zuerst ward eine Taufe verrichtet; die Kleidung
des Kindes war goldverbrämt und mit vielen bunten Bändern
geschmückt; nach der Taufe hielten die Gevattern um den Altar
den Opfergang. Nun begann der Gottesdienst; der Gesang war
ungemein sanft und herzlich; unermüdete Aufmerksamkeit und
innige Andacht sprach sich, bis zum Schluß, auf den Gesichtern,
deren einige wie verklärt waren, aus; Gebete, Perikopen, Glau-
bekenntniß rc. wurden mit Andacht halblaut nachgesprochen.
Männer und Weiber sind von hohem Wuchs und kräftigem Körperbau; Frauen, selbst bejahrte Frauen und Mädchen waren
fast alle hübsch, viele regelmäßige Schönheiten. Beide Geschlech-

ter sind in eigengemachte Zeuge gekleidet, nur die seidenen Tücher und die seidenen Mützen (bei den Frauen schwarz, bei den
Mädchen farbig) der Weiber ausgenommen; der Hauptstaat wird
mit den Mützenbändern getrieben, von denen jedes Mädchen
einen großen Vorrath in vielen Farben und Schattirungen zu
besitzen pflegt. Eine Orgel hat die Kirche nicht.

Nach dem Gottesdienst ward der von der Hebung des vorigen Tages noch restirende Butterzehnte von der Pröpstin ein-
gehoben, wobei eine kleine Bewirthung nicht fehlen durfte; auch
die Communikantenpfennige wurden entrichtet. Hier hatte ich
wieder Gelegenheit die Schönheit und Einfalt, die kindliche Un-
befangenheit und Freudigkeit der Menschen zu beobachten. Auch
mehrere der Weiber waren von herkulischem Wuchs; die eine
hatte alle ihre Kinder zur Kirche mitgebracht, auch das kleinste
von 6 Monaten, wie ich denn überhaupt in der Kirche viele
zarte Kinder sah. So will es die Sitte dieser Gegenden, theils
damit die Mutter nicht gehindert werde am Kirchenbesuch, theils
der Kinder wegen, fährt man diese schon frühe ins Gotteshaus.

Nachmittags setzte ich die Reise fort. Die vielen Kupfer-
fuhren, die die Erzeugnisse der Hütten von Kall nach Mattmar
zum Storsjö bringen, haben den Weg halsbrechend gemacht,
sonst ist er einer der anmuthigsten Wege in ganz Schweden.
Links hat man den See von Mörsill mit seinen Inseln und
Landzungen; an dem dißseitigen Ufer des Sees bilden Dörfer,
Wiesen und Felder, Gebüsche und Hügelketten eine malerische
Landschaft, während Waldberge das jenseitige Ufer bilden; über
sie erheben Ovikens Fjäll ihre schneebedeckten Häupter in die
Wolken, weiterhin steigen die Ottsjönsfjäll nebst mehreren Alpen
und Alpenketten empor. Nachdem man eine Strecke durch Wald
gefahren, tritt plötzlich die jetzt nur ein Paar Meilen entfernte
Åreskuta prachtvoll hervor. Bei Hjerpe-Skans fährt man zu
Boot über den Fluß, der den Anfang des Mörsill-Sees bildet. Es sind zwei Schanzen, die eine hart am Flusse, die andern in einiger Entfernung von da; sie wurden in den beiden
Feldzügen der Jahre 1808 und 1809 von den Norwegern zerstört, aber theilweise von den Schweden wiederhergestellt. In

der einen findet man noch Ruinen eines hohen Blockhauses, das zugleich als Commandantenwohnung diente; die unglaubliche Festigkeit des Mauerwerks zeugt von dem Alter des Gebäudes. Beide Schanzen, durch unterirdische Gänge verbunden, beherrschen die beiden einzigen Fahrwege, welche es hier giebt, nach Kall und nach Undersåker, und mithin die Straße, welche durch Jemteland nach Norwegen führt. Das Betragen der Norweger beim Einmarsche und beim Rückzuge wird sehr gelobt; selbst die Weide der Pferde bezahlten sie und gaben mehr, als gefordert wurde. Während der Heuernte, wo der ganze Haushalt nach den fernen Alpenwiesen zieht, ließ man die Häuser offen und setzte Speise auf den Tisch; die Norweger kamen, aßen und ließen Bezahlung zurück. In Kall stehen noch oft die Häuser unverschlossen, während die Bewohner abwesend sind; überhaupt ist die Gastfreiheit so groß, daß, sobald ein Fremder kommt, man sofort Speise aufträgt und durchaus nicht zugiebt, daß er bezahlet. Eine Viertelmeile oberhalb der Schanze liegt das Dorf Hjerpe. Die Gegend um Hjerpe-Strants und am jenseitigen Ufer des Wasserzuges, der von Kall kommt, ist erhaben und schön zugleich; lieblich spiegelte sich im Wasser das Blau der Berge und Wälder, an letzteren zogen tief gesenkte gesonderte Wölkchen auf und ab, während zwischen den Bergen das Grün mehr oder weniger angebauter Wiesenthäler einen angenehmen Contrast machte; hoch über das Waldland steigen die Felsenmassen mit ewigem Schnee empor. Nachdem man die Fähre passirt, wo der Undersåkers Elf seine Gewässer mit dem Seenzuge von Kall vermischt, fährt man, längs des ersteren Elf, bergauf und bergab, dem Pfarrhof und der Kirche Undersåker vorüber. Mein Skjutsbonde sang das Kriegslied der Schweden auf dem letzten Feldzuge in Deutschland, und das Lied auf den letzten Rückzug der Norweger aus Jemteland. Noch immer war ich auf der Norwegischen Straße, jetzt aber verließ ich dieselbe, und arbeitete mich einen hohen Wiesenberg nach Nyland hinauf, wo der Vicepastor Festin, dem die Seelsorge über die Lappen des Pastorats Undersåker anvertraut ist, wohnt, und wo ich mit Herzlichkeit empfangen wurde. Nyland ist der Amtshof des Comministers von Undersäker, welche Stelle der ehrwürdige Greis bekleidet. Dieser Amtshof ist Geschenk König Karls IX., welchem, als er einst des Weges zog, der damalige Comminister entgegenging; der König knüpfte ein Gespräch an und fragte: wohin geht Ihr?

Kaplan: zu frühstücken.

König. Aber hier giebt's wohl kein Wirthshaus?

Kaplan. Dort in der Quelle ist mein Frühstück.

König. Ein mager Frühstück.

Kaplan. Ja, es ist auch ein mager Land; selten reift das Korn.

König. Wo wohnt Ihr?

Kaplan. Auf Ew. Majestät Hof, hier oben.

König. Nehmt ihn an als Euer Frühstück.

Kaplan. Für mich und meine Kinder?

König. Auch für Eure Nachfolger.

So ward Nyland Boställe des Kaplan von Undersäker; dieser ist der einzige Comminister in ganz Jemteland, welcher Boställe hat. Festin hat zu Nyland einen Wittwensitz für seine Wittwe und die Wittwen seiner Nachfolger gebauet. Die Lage des Kaplanhofes ist sehr schön; den Berg zieht sich ein von Festin angelegter Garten herab, in welchem man Vogelkirsch- und Quitzenbäume, Himbeerhecken und mehrere Beete mit seltneren Gewächsen findet; vom Garten, wie vom Berge aus, hat man weite und herrliche Aussichten auf die liebliche Umgegend bis zu den Alpenketten hin; durch die schöne Landschaft windet sich der Undersäker-Elf, der unterhalb Nyland drei mächtige, donnernde Wasserfälle bildet, deren einer sehr beträchtlich ist und hohe senkrechte Fälle bildet, aus deren Tiefe das in Staub aufgelöste Wasser gleich einer Wolkensäule emporsteigt. Dies ist der Helgefors, oder, wie er nach einem nahen Dorfe auch genannt wird, Ristafors; die Fels- und Waldpartien umher machen ihn zu einem der schöneren Wasserfälle Schwedens; am vortheilhaftesten nimmt er sich vor dem Berge aus, auf welchem Nyland liegt. Die hohe Lage von Nyland macht es möglich, früher zu säen und das nöthige Saatkorn zu gewinnen.

Das Pastorat Undersåker, welches 68 ◻M. oder das ganze nordwestliche Jemteland in sich begreift, also daß es im Norden und Westen an Norwegen, im Süden an Herjeådalen und nur im Osten an das mittlere Jemteland, oder die Pastorate Offerdal und Sunne gränzt, besteht aus 4 Kirchspielen: Undersåker, Mörsill, Kall und Åre; in jedem derselben wird aber nur alle 14 Tage Gottesdienst gehalten; denn nur ein Pastor und ein Kaplan sind angestellt, die sich indeß auf eigne Kosten Adjuncten halten; die Kirche Åre ist 2, die Kirche Kall 2⅖ M. von der Kirche Undersåker entfernt. An Umfang kommt das Pastorat dem ganzen Stockholms Län gleich. Das Kirchspiel Undersåker zählte, im J. 1815, 659; Mörsill 308, Kall 1073 und Åre 816 Einwohner. Die Zahl der Gebornen im gesammten Pastorat betrug, im J. 1815, 88, worunter 6 uneheliche und 5 todtgeborne, die Zahl der Gestorbenen 39, der eingegangenen Ehen 20; im J. 1814 war die Zahl der Geborenen 73, worunter 4 uneheliche, der Gestorbenen 39; im J. 1813 waren geboren 62, worunter 1 uneheliches Kind, gestorben 63; im im J. 1812 geboren 76, worunter 3 uneheliche; gestorben 36; im J. 1811 geboren 60, worunter keine uneheliche; gestorben 33. Ueberhaupt betrug die Zahl der unehelichen Kinder im gesammten Pastorate, in den J. 1801 bis 1815, also in einem Zeitraume von 15 Jahren, 31, der todtgebornen 27, die Zahl der gebornen ehelichen Kinder 1128 (566 Knaben, 562 Mädchen), der gestorbenen überhaupt 659 (328 männlichen, und 331 weiblichen Geschlechts), der geschlossenen Ehen 293. Im Ganzen lebt das Volk noch in aller Einfachheit und Unschuld; nur der letzte Krieg und fremde Handelsleute haben in sittlicher Hinsicht übel eingewirkt, so daß sich Radesyge und venerische Krankheiten, welche lange ganz unbekannt waren, seitdem besonders in Undersåker und Åre, namentlich in den Fjällstugor, den auf der Norwegischen Straße, auf den hohen Gränzalpen gelegenen Posthöfen gezeigt haben. Noch immer trifft aber unkeusche Mädchen allgemeine tiefe Verachtung, und selten wird ein solches Mädchen verheirathet, selbst den Ehrenbesuch der Jünglinge empfängt sie nicht mehr.

Im Pastorat giebt es wenige Arme und wenige Reiche; die meisten erfreuen sich eines mittelmäßigen Wohlstandes; die wohlhabendsten sind es geworden durch Handel. Handelsbauern im Großen giebt es nur einen in jedem Kirchspiel, aber viele kleinere Landhändler, die besonders mit Norwegischen Pferden Handel treiben. Bis Drontheim hat man jetzt meist Fahrweg, nur zwischen Sul und Medstuge ist mit Wagen noch schwer fortzukommen; von Nyland nach Drontheim sind 19 M. Hauptnahrungszweig ist Viehzucht; man hat entferntere und nähere Sennhütten, jene weit in den Alpen. Der Ackerbau ist nur schwach; selten reift das Getreide; reift es, so ist es vorzüglich. Das beste Kornland findet man in Kall, das die wohlhabendsten Bauern hat, und in Mörsill. Auch Erbsen werden gesäet, können aber oft nur als Viehfutter gebraucht werden. Die Butter ist überall vortrefflich und wird auswärts sehr gesucht. Fischerey und Jagd wird getrieben. Ein nicht unbeträchtlicher Erwerbszweig ist Bergbau; insbesondere wird auf Kupfer gebauet, wiewohl die Berge auch an Eisen reich seyn sollen. Die einzige, jetzt bearbeitete, Kupfergrube ist die Bjelke's Grube am nördlichen Fuße der Skuta; die Arbeiter wohnen zu Husä, wo 1½ M. von der Kirche Åre, *) 1 Schmelzhütte ist; eine zweite zu Slagå in Undersåkers Kirchspiel; ein Garofen, Simmeläsin Mörsill. In Huß ist ein Grubenarzt angestellt, welchem Amte der Pastor Festin lange vorstand. Zu Handöl in Åre wird Topfstein (Tålgsten, steatites ollaris) gebrochen; die Grube gehört der Dorfschaft Handöl und zwei Bauern im Dorfe Wiken neben Åre's Kirche; hier arbeiten vom November bis März 20 bis 30 Männer aus Åre, die dann in der Kapelle Handöl ihren Gottesdienst halten; der Topfstein wird nach Schweden und Norwegen geführt und zu Ofenkacheln, Leichensteinen, Pfannen, die auch nach mehrjährigem Gebrauche nicht schwarz werden und der Speise keinen Beigeschmack geben, wie es eiserne Pfannen thun, u. dergl. m. verarbeitet.

Die Bergwerke von Jemteland haben mit denen von Medelpad und Angermanland Einen gemeinschaftlichen Bergmeister

---

*) Die Gustafs- och Carlbergs-Grufva, ⅓ M. von Åre's Kirche, ist seit mehreren Jahren aufgegeben worden.

II.   L l

(Wester-Norrlands Bergmästaredöme), welcher in jeder dieser Provinzen Bergsting hält.

Im Pastorat giebt es ferner zwei Gesundbrunnen: beim Pfarrhof von Undersåker (diese Quelle war schon in uralten Zeiten bekannt), und beim Dorfe Sunne in Kall. Doch auch ohne Gesundbrunnen ist man gesund und kräftig; die Luft ist sehr gesund, weder Strapazen noch Beschwerden der Witterung können die kernhafte Gesundheit vernichten; viele erreichen ein hohes Alter, 80jährige Greise findet man häufig.

Um Weihnachten vernimmt man oft ein heftiges Geräusch in der Luft (luftdön), ohne Erderschütterung; einen ebenen hohlen dumpfigen Schall (bullrande), nicht donnerähnlich, aber zuweilen mit Blitzen oder Wetterleuchten (ljungande) verbunden; am stärksten hört man es unten in den Gruben; die Bauern halten es für einen Vorboten der Veränderung des Wetters.

Die Kleidung ist noch die alte Jemteländische, Jacken und Röcke von Walmar; nur die Mützen der Weiber sind von Seide, die Tücher von Seide oder Baumwolle, die Schürzen von Kattun oder Kambrik; die wohlhabenderen Männer tragen blaue Chenillen mit Kragen. Einzelne Mädchen dienen in Norwegen.

In Mißjahren speiset man Rindenbrot und Rindengrütze; ersteres wird hier auf folgende Weise bereitet: die harte Oberfläche wird abgeschält, das übrige auf Stangengerüsten und dann in Dörrstuben getrocknet, ferner zerdroschen und zu feinem Mehl gemahlen, welches endlich, damit es zusammenhalte, mit ein wenig Roggen- oder Gerstenmehl vermischt wird. Zur Bereitung von Rindengrütze hobelt man von der getrockneten Rinde kleine Späne ab, und kocht diese in Milch zu einem Brei. Aus Noth hatte auch in diesem Jahre ein Bauer in Nyland von der eben eingeerndteten Gerste Brot gebacken, welches einen sehr widrigen Geschmack hatte. In Norwegen sollen im Jahre 1812 selbst Vornehme der Rindenspeisen sich haben bedienen müssen und unter der ärmeren Klasse mehrere des Hungertodes gestorben seyn.

Oft passiren durch das Pastorat Ausreißer nach Norwegen.

In Mörsill wachsen Åkerbär, eine Frucht, die sonst in Jemteland nur im Pastorat Ragunda, welches an Ångermanland gränzt, gefunden werden soll.

Das Pastorat hat zwei feste Schulen: die Bruksschule zu Husö, und die Schule im Dorfe Hjerpe. In letzterer, die 1815 eröffnet wurde, genießen arme Kinder freien Unterricht und freie Wohnung, müssen sich aber die Kost selber verdienen, daher denn auch nur im Winter unterrichtet wird. Die Schule entstand nicht sowohl durch das Legat eines Bauersohnes aus Ottsjön, Södergren, der sich vom Bruksbuchhalter zum Brukspatron in Ljusnedal emporarbeitete und zu Gehalten von Schullehrern 12 Rthlr. banko jährlich in Undersåker, 6 Rthlr. in Kall, und 6 Rthlr. in Åre vermachte (dies Legat ward 1817 noch nicht benutzt), als vielmehr durch das Legat (13000 Rthlr.) eines Artilleristensohnes aus Hjerpe-Skans, Olof Hansen Racklöv, der mit Nadeln zu handeln anfing und als ein reicher Kaufmann zu Drontheim 1802 starb, und mehrere Stiftungen auch in Norwegen machte. Die Zinsen werden zum Gehalt des Lehrers verwandt, das Capital darf nur zum Bau verwandt werden. Von den Zinsen der ersten 5 Jahre ward ein Ackerstück gekauft und darauf ein Schulhaus gebauet. Der Lehrer (ein Sohn des Pastors Festin) benutzt das Grundstück, ohne aber bisher Besoldung zu erhalten. Das Capital war nämlich in Norwegen angelegt, und eingetretene Mißverhältnisse hinderten, daß es gegenwärtig für seinen Zweck angewandt werden konnte.

Am 2. September. Von Nyland nach Stamgärde ½ M.; von St. nach Åreborsta 1 M. — Zus. 1½ M.

Am 1. September war Ruhetag. Am folgenden Frühmorgen trat ich die Reise zu den Undersåker's Lappen an. Meine Chaise ließ ich zurück, um rücksichtlich der Wahl der Wege weniger beschränkt zu seyn. Bis Stamgärde hatte ich Pferd und Kärra des Pastors. Bis zum Helgefors begleitete mich der Sohn und Gehülfe des alten Festin, welcher der Schule zu Hjerpe vorsteht. Der Weg ist nun die Norwegische Straße;

Ll 2

man fährt rechts am Bergrücken von Nyland hin, Angesichts eines herrlichen Waldthals, waldbewachsener Bergketten, des Vällustfjäll und des dieser Alpe nahe liegenden, hohen Skarberg, worüber der Weg zum Dorfe Ottsjön führt, bei Romo (nicht Roma, wie man auf der Charte lieset) hin zum Gästgifvaregärd Stamgärde, welcher kleine, aber freundliche Gaststimmer hat. Von hier bis Åreborsta, der Wohnung des Länsmans, hat man noch 1 Meile. Der Bergrücken rechts läuft fort, links hat man den Undersåkers-Elf; die Ufer des Flusses sind Wiesen und Wald; hier und da, wie am Abhange des Bergrückens, rinnt ein Bach, oder liegt ein Dörfchen, ein Hof, eine Sägemühle ꝛc.; aus dieser Landschaft steigen Schneealpen empor, nackte Felsen, die an den Abseiten mit Schnee bedeckt sind, Sellsjöfjäll, Anahögen, Wawrefjäll; bald erscheint, über alle Nebenalpen emporragend, die Åresfuta (auch schlechtweg Skuta genannt), in reiner klarer Luft; nur eine Viertelmeile schien sie entfernt, und doch hatte man zu ihr noch ein Paar Meilen. Im Flusse spiegeln sich die Alpen mit den grünen Matten an den Abhängen. Reizend ist die Gegend um Åreborsta, welches auf der Höhe liegt; der Fluß macht hier mehrere hübsche Krümmungen und bildet Landspitzen. Der Weg ist von Nyland an recht gut.

Åreborsta liegt am Fuß der isolirten Åresfuta, die von hier aus am bequemsten erstiegen wird. Unmöglich konnte ich diese Alpe, deren Spitze vielleicht die weiteste und schönste Aussicht in ganz Schweden gewährt, unbesucht lassen, und brach dahin in Begleitung zweier Wegweiser, unter welchen sich der durch die gefälligen Vorkehrungen des Landshöfdings-Amts von Östersund, so wie des Lappenpredigers, beauftragte Lappen-Länsman befand, um 11¼ Uhr auf. Gleich hinter Åreborsta kommt man in Gran- und Birkenwald; anfangs hat man noch einen Fußsteig, bald aber verschwindet dieser gänzlich, und man muß sich selber den Weg bahnen. Im Walde hat man mehrere sumpfige Wiesen (myror) zu passiren, über deren einige, um mich vor dem Durchnässen zu schützen, meine Begleiter in der Eile Brücken warfen. Um 1 Uhr waren wir bei den, nach dem Dorfe Wiken gehörigen Heuscheunen angelangt, und stiegen nun höher und höher durch den immer niedriger werdenden Wald; auf einer der Waldwiesen fanden wir, in Ermangelung einer Scheune, einen, gegen wilde und zahme Thiere mit Stangen umgebenen, Heuhaufen, und Spuren eines Nachtquartiers der Heuerndter, unter einer Gräne, wo in den kalten Nächten nur eine Nordische Natur ausdauern mag. Der Wald ward nun immer niedriger und weniger dicht; um 2 Uhr hatten wir die letzten Bäume oder vielmehr Stauden hinter uns; nachdem die Gräne (Fichte) schon geschwunden ist, findet man noch Birken *), Wachholderbeer- und Weidenbüsche oder Pflänzchen. Nun herrscht völlig die Alpenregion. Man arbeitet sich den Fels hinan, der nur kärglich mit Rennthier- und anderm Moose, mehreren Grasarten, und hier und da mit einem Weidenpflänzchen bedeckt ist. Jetzt beginnen die ewigen Schneefelder, die zum Theil Eis decken; sie sind fest, wie Stein. Nachdem wir auch diese passirt hatten, stiegen wir mühsam den steilen Felsen zum Gipfel hinan; auf diesem Wege sieht man weder Moos noch Gras, nur Felsenschutt und Erde ohne alle Vegetation; ganz oben findet man auch keine Erde mehr; nur Flechten und trockenes Moos decken den harten Fels; mehrere Bäche fließen herab, die sich zum Theil den Weg unter den Schneefeldern hinweg bahnen; ein Haase und ein Schneehuhn (tetrao Lagopus, in Norwegen eine beliebte Speise), war das einzige Lebendige, was wir auf der Höhe erblickten.

Unterweges waren wir auf Spuren von Rennthieren gestoßen, denn den Lappen, die im Winter die mittlern Höhen der

*) Die Birke vertritt im Norden, rücksichtlich der Vegetationsgränze, die Stelle der Fichte in der Schweiz, die im Norden ungleich tiefer erscheint; in Lappland sah ich am Fuße der Schneealpen die lieblichsten Birkenhaine. Man findet über diesen Gegenstand treffende Bemerkungen in Wahlenberg's Schrift de vegetatione et climate in Helvetia septentrionali inter flumina Rhenum et Arolam observatis, et cum summi septentrionis comparatis. Turici Helvet. 1813.; indeß sind die Angaben über die Schweiz nicht so zuverlässig, wie die über den Norden, indem der Verf. sich nur einen Sommer dort aufhielt und die höchsten Gebirgsgegenden gar nicht besuchte.

Skuta besuchen, waren einige Rennthiere entlaufen, die hier zurückblieben. Die öde Gustavs= und Karlbergs=Grube hatten wir aus der Ferne gesehen. Während des Aufsteigens hatte dann und wann ein dichter Nebel die Spitze umhüllt; aber als wir um 4¼ Uhr, also nach 5stündigem Steigen, den höchsten Gipfel, wo ein Steinhaufen aufgerichtet ist, erreichten, waren die Nebel gesunken, oder zogen in horizontaler Richtung hin, so daß zwischen den einzelnen Nebelmassen die von der Sonne beschienenen Landschaften sichtbar waren, oder über den Nebeln die weißen Häupter der Alpen glänzten. Schon während des Aufsteigens zum Gipfel hatte die Sonne bald die südliche, bald die westliche, bald die östliche Landschaft erleuchtet, und man hatte diese verschiedenen Partien einzeln beschauen können: hohe Berge ohne Zahl, von hier aus wie Hügel sich darstellend, die Abhänge von Wald, Wiesen und Höfen bedeckt, die Thäler von Flüssen und Seen durchschnitten, bildeten den Vordergrund; im Hintergrunde zeigten sich die westlichen und östlichen Alpen, unter denen zwei nach der Seite von Asele=Lappmark hin, und das hohe Handölsfjäll den erhabensten Anblick gewährten; südlich zeigten sich die Kirchen von Mattmar, Rödön, Brunflo, die Stadt Östersund, der Storsjö in seiner ganzen Ausdehnung, mit der Insel Frösön, auf welcher der Schulhügel (Stolbacke) genau erkannt werden konnte; am nordöstlichen Fuße der Skuta die Kirche Kall nebst einer Menge von Dörfern und weiterhin einer unendlichen Fülle von Seen in den Pastoraten Föllinge und Offerdal, auch wohl den Kirchspielen Ström und Hammardal. Als wir oben kamen, enthüllte sich die nördliche Gegend völlig unsern Blicken: wir sahen in einer Ausdehnung von 11 Meilen den herrlichen Seenzug, der von der Norwegischen Gränze unter verschiedenen Namen, Kall's See ꝛc. sich herabzieht, an den Ufern die Dörfer Hamburg, Kallström ꝛc., ja überblickten seine Vereinigung mit dem Storsjö, also eine Länge von etwa 18 Meilen; tief im Norden thürmten sich die hohen Norwegischen Gränzalpen, und auch an der westlichen Seite des oberen Kallsees steigt eine mit Schnee bedeckte Alpe empor. Oben sahen wir auch noch deutlicher die östliche Seite, die gro=

ßen Seen, die sich hier nach Handöl ausdehnen, nebst Thälern, Ebenen und Dörfern, als Dufve ꝛc., überblickten die Norwegische Straße nebst den hohen Gränzalpen von Skalstuga; ja, ein wunderbarer Anblick, sahen mit unbewaffnetem Auge ganz deutlich den 2⅜ M. (3⅜ Deutsche M.), entfernten Wasserfall Tenneforßen, selbst die einzelnen Strahlen, die sich im Tubus noch schöner darstellten, und hörten nicht minder deutlich seinen Donner. So hatte ich ¼ Stunden auf dem Gipfel zugebracht und dort in windstiller Luft mein Mittagsmahl gehalten, und eben wollte ich den Rückweg antreten, als plötzlich auf allen Seiten die Nebel schwanden, und, was ich bisher nur im Einzelnen geschauet, jetzt vereint vor meinen staunenden Blicken da lag; nur ein großer Theil der Fjällen war verhüllt; aber alles niedere Land, ein Umkreis von etwa 40 (60 Deutschen) Meilen lag klar und offen da. Wer kann solche Unendlichkeit schauen, ohne zu staunen und anzubeten! Nur auf Rigi hatte ich einst einen ähnlichen Anblick gehabt; aber doch kam er diesem nicht gleich; wie Bandstreifen erschienen die Flüsse und Seen, und wie Hügelchen die hohen Berge. Noch eine halbe Stunde blieb ich oben, wiewohl es schon empfindlich kalt geworden war, und begab mich dann um 5¾ Uhr auf den Rückweg, der nach 3 Stunden vollendet war; in 2¼ Stunde war die Region der Gebüsche, und bald die Waldregion erreicht, nach abermals 1 Stunde die Heuscheunen, und um 8¾ Uhr waren wir in Areborsta. Es war schon ziemlich dunkel geworden, denn der Schein des Mondes konnte in den dichten Wald nicht eindringen; eine halbe Stunde später, und wir hätten im Walde unser Nachtquartier nehmen müssen, denn in der Finsterniß ist auf dem abschüssigen, sumpfigen und durch umgefallene Bäume oft versperrten Wege nicht fortzukommen. Mit Recht waren die lieben Leute daher schon unruhig geworden über unser langes Ausbleiben. Desto freudiger und herzlicher war nun der Empfang. Freundliche Sorge, ein warmes Zimmer, ein stärkendes Mahl und bald ein erquickender Schlaf verscheuchten gänzlich das anfangs sehr lebendige Gefühl der Strapazen des Tages.

Die Höhe der Areskuta über der Meeresfläche beträgt, nach

Wahlenberg, nicht über 4850 Pariser Fuß; sie erreicht also nicht die eigentliche Schneegränze *), wohl aber die Gränze der ewigen isolirten Schneemassen; die Polhöhe beträgt 63° 25'; der Birkenwald steigt bis zu 3100 Fuß. Ein Beweis, daß die Vegetation auf den Nordischen Bergen bedeutend höher steigt, als auf den südlichen. Die Vegetationsverhältnisse der Åreskuta sind denen des höhern Nordens völlig gleich; manche hochgelegenen Theile von Jemteland haben im Winter völlig gleiche Kälte mit Torneå. Am Fuße der Alpen pflegt das Eis im Anfange des Mai's aufzugehen; die schwarze Krähe ist in Jemteland Zugvogel und zeigt den Frühling an. **)

Am 3. September. Von Åreborsta nach Mörvik ¼ M.; von M. nach Sta 1¾ M.; von St. nach Tennforssen etwa ¼ M.; von T. nach Renberget etwa 1¾ M. — Zus. 4¼ M.

Um 8¾ Uhr verließ ich Åreborsta und fuhr, am Fuße der Vorberge der Skuta, zur Kirche Åre, ¾ M. von da; die Kirche ist ein altes steinernes Gebäude, mit Gemeindehaus, Zehntbude und Kirchställen, der Wohnung des Colonus (Landbonde) und einem Hause für die Geistlichkeit, wenn sie zur Kirche kommt, umher; Kirchstuben giebt es hier nicht, da die entfernten Kirch-

---

*) Eben so wenig erreicht die 4887 Fuß hohe Riesenkoppe die Schneegränze, und hat doch die Schneegruben an den Abseiten.

**) Joh. Törnsten, in seiner Abhandlung om Norrste Fjällryggens höjd öfver hafvet, in den Akten der Königl. Akademie der Wissenschaften, für 1787. S. 226 — 234. giebt die Höhe des Storsjö über das Meer zu ungefähr 614 Schwed. Ellen (à 2 Fuß), der Åreskuta über den Storsjö zu 2040 Ellen, mithin über das Meer zu 2654 Ellen oder 5308 Fuß an, und nimmt an, daß die eigentliche Alpenregion, wo kein Wald mehr gedeiht, auf der Åreskuta 940 Ellen betrage, indem der Wald nicht höher, als etwa 1100 Ellen über den Storsjö reiche. Holphers in seiner Beschreibung von Jemteland, S. 141. berichtet: die Höhe der Skuta betrage von Åre's Kirche an ¾ (Schwed.) Meile.

gänger in den nahen Dörfern übernachten. Eine kleine Strecke von der Kirche liegt das Dorf Mörvik, wo man Pferde wechselt. Eigentliche Gåstgifvaregårdar, wo die Leute zur Bereithaltung von Kost und Gastzimmern verpflichtet sind, giebt es auf dieser Straße seit Stamgårde nicht; doch hat man auf den meisten dieser sogenannten Ombytesställen ziemlich gutes Nachtquartier. Von Mörvik, wo es an einer Kärra mangelte, fuhr ich ⅔ M. nach Lund, wo eine Kärra zu finden seyn sollte; vor Lund führt ein näherer Weg als von Åreborste, zur Skuta. Von Lund bis Tegom hat man eine freundliche Landschaft zwischen den Undersåkerself, Waldbergen und Alpen, ⅔ M.; in Tegom oder eigentlich in Forssa war abermals Pferdewechsel. Forssa ist die letzte Stelle, wo man gesetzlich Skjuts fordern kann; hernach muß man sich auf beiden Norwegischen Wegen, über die Fjäll stugor und über Wallarnes Skjuts bedingen. Neben Tegom liegt das Zollamt Dufve, und ¼ M. weiter das Dorf Dufve, wo jährlich ein, auch von Lappen besuchter, Markt gehalten wird, mit einer Schanze; nach einer kleinen Strecke Weges führt man nun über den Dufvesund, einen Theil des Undersåkerself. Die Fährfrau rauchte, wie es in den Dörfern des Jemtischen Bergs und Alpenlandes viele solche rauchende Weiber geben soll; auch in Herjeådalen rauchen viele alte Weiber. Von dem Volke an dieser Straße scheint die alte Einfachheit und Lauterkeit gewichen zu seyn; störrige und eigennützige Charaktere fand ich nicht gar selten. Die alte Dufveschanze am Elf bei der Fähre ist zerstört; eine andere auf der Höhe ward im letzten Kriege von den Schweden aufgeworfen, von den Norwegern zerstört, aber von den Schweden erneuert. Der Zoll ist jetzt wenig einträglich, indem seit der Vereinigung Norwegens mit Schweden alle Waaren Norwegischen Ursprungs zollfrei eingeführt und nur die Kolonialwaaren verzollt werden; dagegen muß bisher (1817) für alles, was aus Schweden in Norwegen eingeführt wird, Zoll erlegt werden. Außer dem Zoll von Dufve bestehen in Jemteland noch zwei andere Gränzzölle gegen Norwegen: bei Kall und Föllinge; in Herjeådalen aber bei Funnesdalen und Tennäs.

...

Auf der Fähre nahm ich einen Wegweiser zum Tennforssen und setzte von nun an die Reise zu Pferde fort. Bis Sta hat man noch Fahrweg, längs des Undersåkers-Elf. Sta besteht aus einem Bauerhof, den jetzt ein Colonus (landbonde) bewohnt, da der Besitz zwei unmündigen Kindern zugefallen ist, und einer Häuslerwohnung; den Bauer nennt man schlechtweg Staman (dem Mann von Sta), wie solches bei den isolirten Höfen dieser Gegend üblich ist, z. B. Renbergsman ⁊c. Bei Sta hört der Fahrweg auf; es beginnt nun die neue Straße nach Norwegen, an welcher seit der Vereinigung Norwegens mit Schweden gearbeitet wird; bis Skalstuga, 3¾ Meile von Sta, also fast bis zur Gränze, war sie meist vollendet, aber noch nicht fahrbar; denn es fehlten noch einige Brücken, wie die Ueberschüttung mit Steingras; in diesem Jahre wurd nicht gearbeitet *). Die alte Straße war nur Reitweg und ging sehr krumm; die neue Straße ist möglichst gerade angelegt; die eine, wie die andere, die meist dieselbe ist, führt über das Sewe-Gebirge, welches hier etwas niedriger ist als im Norden und im Süden. Von Sta bis zur Gränze findet man nun kaum andere Menschenwohnungen, als die sogenannten Fjällstugor (Alpenstuben), um welche herum kein Korn mehr gedeiht, denn sie liegen auf dem hohen Sewe-Gebirge, daher die Bewohner mit Korn für die Reisenden vom niederen Lande versorgt werden; desto vorzüglicher ist die Weide, und dies ist die Ursache, weshalb die Bevölkerung so gestiegen ist, daß, anstatt jede der drei Stuben früher nur von einer Familie bewohnt ward, gegenwärtig Stalltjernsstuga 4, Medstuga 6 und Skalstuga 4 Familien zählt. Die Reisenden erhalten hier Pferde, Wohnung und Kost. Leider herrscht in den drei Alpenstuben, wie schon einmal vor 20 Jahren, seit 1810 die venerische Seuche. Man behauptet, die Krankheit habe sich durch einen aus Drontheim zurückkehrenden Reisehändler, den Sohn eines Bauern in Stalltjern, und eine durch ihn angesteckte in Stalltjern dienende Norwegische Magd verbreitet.

*) 1822 sollte, wo möglich, die Straße von Levanger bis Sta vollendet seyn.

Nachdem ich etwa ⅓ M. auf der neuen Straße geritten, an welcher man noch Laubhütten sieht, in denen die arbeitenden Soldaten wohnten, lenkte ich rechts abwärts in den Wald ein; bis zu einer nach Sta gehörigen Sennhütte konnte ich einem Fußsteige folgen. Die Sennhütte hatte eine Kammer zur Aufbewahrung der Milch und des Käses, und eine Küche, in welcher, nach Lappenweise, neben einander gelegte Steine den Heerd bildeten, und über diesem Heerd eine Stange befestiget war, an welcher der Kessel hängt; an der Seite dienten einige Bretter zur Schlafstätte der Sennenmädchen. Außer der Hütte war ein zweiter Heerd unter einem Laubdache errichtet. Einen Viehstall, wie ein solcher sonst üblich ist, gab es nicht; vielmehr wird das Vieh am Abend in eine Umzäunung getrieben; bei heftigem Regen sucht es seine Zuflucht unter den weitabstehenden Zweigen einer nahen Gräne. Alle Sommersennhütten in Undersäker sollen auf gleiche Weise eingerichtet seyn; die Sennhütten, welche für den Spätsommer (bis Michaelis) bestimmt sind, haben Viehställe. — Der Wald, welcher aus Gränen und wenigen Birken besteht, läuft fort, aber hinter der Sennhütte hört der Fußpfad auf; ein Land, wo vielleicht noch nie, oder wenigstens nicht seit Jahren, ein menschlicher Fuß gewandelt, beginnt: dichter Urwald; der Boden ist meistens Sumpf oder mit tiefem, oft ellentiefem, Moos bedeckt, unter welchem oft umgestürzte Bäume verborgen liegen; die Zweige der Bäume sind dicht verschlungen. Nicht ohne Gefahr arbeitete ich mich, durch Hülfe meines treuen Begleiters, durch; das Pferd überstand Alles; nur dem Schalle des Wasserfalles konnten wir folgen. Endlich langten wir an: zwischen senkrechten bewaldeten Felsen stürzt eine ungeheure Wassermasse sich, in Einem etwa 10 Ellen breiten Absatz etwa 50 bis 60 Ellen tief herab. Rings umher ist Wald und Fels. Nur am jenseitigen Ufer auf dem Abhange eines hohen Bergrückens erblickt man ein Dorf, Nordhallen. Ich kletterte durch das Moos die Felsenwände herab, und hatte den schönsten Standpunkt zum Ueberblick dieser majestätischen Scene, die die Mühen und Gefahren des Weges mehr als lohnte, gewonnen. Die durch den gewaltigen Sturz in Staub aufgelösete Wassermasse verursacht am Ufer einen immerwährenden feinen Regen. Der Tennfors gehört zu den am wenigsten bekannten, ja völlig unbekannten, aber schönsten Wasserfällen Schwebens, und dürfte nur vom Fällfors im Umfelf noch übertroffen werden.

Vom Tennforssen kehrte ich auf dem mühseligen Wege zur Sennhütte zurück, folgte dann dem Sennensteige zur Landstraße, und ritt über denselben abermals in dichten Wald hinein; auch hier waren ungebahnte Pfade, über Moräste und sumpfige Wiesen, durch Dickigte (die Behausungen der in diesen Gegenden häufigen Bären); immer nur auf die Himmelsgegend zusteuernd, in welcher der zum Nachtquartier ausersehene Hof lag, arbeiteten wir uns, neben ein Paar Heuscheunen hin, zwei ganze Stunden lang, durch, und erreichten endlich, ohne gefahrvolles Abentheuer, den Hof Renberget, wohin von Sta aus ein guter Fahrweg führt, zu dem wir auch, kurz vor dem Hofe, gelangten. Der Hof besteht aus zwei Bauerwohnungen; er liegt an der Straße über Wallarne nach Norwegen, die freilich schon seit längerer Zeit auch befahren wird, aber zu Wagen nur mit großer Gefahr zu passiren ist; denn von Renberget an verschwindet aller brauchbare Fahrweg. Diese Norwegische Straße führt durch Stödalsporten, einen thorähnlichen Gränzfelsen, durch das Kirchspiel Merager, nach Drontheim und ist kürzer, als die, freilich bessere Straße über die Alpenstuben, über Suul und Levanger nach Drontheim. Alle Dörfer dieser Gegenden sind sehr klein; das größte Dorf hat 6 Bauern, die aber nicht selten, wie z. B. in Dufveby, einen Wald von 3 M. Länge und 2½ M. Breite besitzen.

In Renberget übernachtete ich; alles war mittelmäßig und sehr theuer; aber der Bauer hatte auch viel Reischandel getrieben, der nicht selten ein eigennütziges Wesen erzeugt.

Am 4. Sept. Von Renberget nach Tängböle 1 M.; von T. nach Wallarne ½ M.; von W. nach Handöl 1½ M. — Zus. 3 M.

Eine kurze, aber beschwerliche Tagesreise, theils zu Pferde, theils zu Fuß, theils zu Boot, die den ganzen Tag erforderte.

Um 7½ Uhr ritt ich von Renberget ab; die Luft war milde und rein; der Weg führt durch Wald, zweimal in einiger Entfernung Sennhütten vorbei, die man hier Bua, d. i. bobar, fábobar, Viehbuden (der allgemeine Name für Sennhütten in ganz Schweden) zu nennen pflegt, an den See Tängböle; nach einer halben Meile Weges um den See herum, zum Theil über mit Steinen ausgefüllten Morastboden, erreichte ich den schmalen Sund, welcher die Seen Tängböle und Änn verbindet, und an dessen jenseitigem Ufer das Dorf Tängböle liegt; man rudert in einem Boote über. Tängböle besteht aus zwei Bauerhöfen; im Süderhofe nahm ich ein treffliches Frühstück, aus zwei Arten von Alpenforellen bestehend, ein. Kurz bevor man den Sund erreicht, erscheint zuerst die südwestlich gelegene hohe Alpe Snasahöjd, die weit über alle benachbarten Alpen emporragt; von Schnee bedeckt und von der Sonne erleuchtet, gewährte sie in wolkenloser klarer Luft einen herrlichen Anblick.

Von Tängböle nach Wallarne hat man meist ebenen Waldweg, der fast überall fahrbar ist; ich legte die ¾ M. zu Pferde in ¾ Stunde zurück. Wie aber der Weg von Renberget nach Tängböle zu Wagen passirt werden kann, davon habe ich keinen Begriff, wenigstens an vielen Stellen muß man nothwendig zu Fuße neben-her gehen.

In Wallarne, einem aus zwei Bauerhöfen bestehenden Dorfe, waren keine Menschen daheim. Thüren und Schränke waren unverschlossen; aber Speise und Getränk war nirgends zu finden, selbst meinen Durst konnte ich nicht stillen. Mein Skjutsbonde lief umher, von Haus zu Haus, von Hügel zu Hügel, ob er nicht irgendwo einen Menschen erspähen sollte. Endlich fand er eine alte Frau, welche berichtete, daß alles Volk sich in weiter Ferne im Walde befinde. Woher sollte man nun Hülfe erwarten, da, um nach Handöl zu kommen, der Ännsjö überschifft werden mußte. In dieser Noth bot sich mein 15jähriger Begleiter an, mich nach Handöl, oder bis sich etwa unterwegs ein kräftigerer Ruderer finden würde, zu rudern. Wir machten uns auf den Weg. Zwischen dem Dorfe und dem See lag eine beträchtliche sumpfige Wiese. Den besseren Weg zum Strande zu erkunden, gingen wir zur Alten, einer 70jährigen Frau, die aber noch das Ansehen einer 50jährigen hatte; sie gab uns die 12 jährige Kjerstin zur Wegweiserin mit; Kjerstin war wohl mit Brettern versehen, und so gelang es mit Hülfe eines Pferdes, die etwa ½ Meile lange Sumpfwiese glücklich zu passiren. Nils und Kjerstin waren die lieblichsten Gesichter, welche ich mich erinnere, je gesehen zu haben: jugendliche Blüthe und Kraft, Anmuth, Geist und fromme Unschuld schufen hier wahre Christus- und Madonnengesichter.

Um 3½ Uhr stießen wir ab; Kjerstin leitete das Pferd nach Wallarne zurück und Nils ergriff die Ruder. Die Fahrt auf dem breiten Ännsjö ist bei starkem Winde gefährlich; jetzt bewegte sich kein Lüftchen, nur für eine kurze Weile erhob sich der Wind, und die Fahrt ging glücklich von Statten. Der See hat mehrere hübsche bewaldete Inseln und Landzungen. Er ist schon ganz Alpensee; denn die Snasahöjd mit ihren niederen Alpenschwestern, alle mit ewigen Schneefeldern bedeckt, bilden um den See einen Halbkreis, und das Wasser hat ganz die Natur des Schnee- und Gletscherwassers und führt Alpenfische; die vielfach gestalteten Gipfel der Alpen gewährten einen hübschen Anblick. Im Hintergrund erhob sich, am wolkenlosen Himmel, die Äreskuta. Nur bis Klockan, einem Bauerhofe auf einer Anhöhe am Ufer, war Nils des Weges kundig; ich ließ daher landen, um einen neuen Ruderer zu bekommen; aber auch in Klockan war keiner daheim, und Nils mußte nun, nachdem er seinen Hunger durch eine Rübe, und ich meinen Durst mit hartem Seewasser gestillt, das Rudern weiter fortsetzen. Bei Klockan zeigte sich der gegenüberliegende Handöl-Wasserfall mit seinen getrennten Absätzen sehr malerisch und diente jetzt als Wegweiser. Die Alpen hatten sich in einen leichten bläulichen Dunst gekleidet und waren mit ihren schneebedeckten Häuptern und einem Vordergrunde von Gebüschen und Wiesen unendlich schön; über alle leuchtete die Snasaalpe hin; gar lieblich spiegelten sich die Alpen im See. Eine Weile ging die Fahrt gut, dann aber kamen wir auf seichte Stellen und Nils mußte aussteigen und das Boot ziehen; das Boot war leck, und damit es durch verborgene Klip-

pen nicht etwa ganz zerschellt werden möge, mußte sorgfältig
vorher der Bootweg untersucht werden. Ueberdieß theilte sich
der See in mehrere Arme, und wir waren ungewiß, welcher
Arm nach Handöl führe; das Dorf Handöl war nicht zu sehen;
meine Landkarte war in Wallarne zurückgeblieben; ich konnte
daher nur nach dem, was ich mir über die Lage des Dorfes und
des Flusses, der vom Dorfe in den See führt, eingeprägt hatte,
und nach dem Wasserfall, den ich seitwärts erblickte, und von
dem ich wußte, daß er nicht gar weit vom Dorfe entfernt sey,
unter den verschiedenen Armen wählen. So kamen wir endlich
zu einer Stelle, an welcher ein Boot lag; sofort stiegen wir ans
Land, und waren glücklich genug, einen Fußpfad zu finden, dem
wir folgten und der uns nach ¼ Meile Weges zum Dorfe Handöl
brachte, freilich über Mordste und Gräben, von denen der eine
nur mittelst einer von uns erbauten Nothbrücke, der andere mittelst eines Bootes, das wir in der Nähe fanden, passirt werden
konnte. So langten wir endlich, noch vor einbrechender Dunkelheit, um 8 Uhr, in Handöl an. Auch in Handöl waren nur
wenige Menschen daheim; die meisten waren auf die Alpenfischerey gezogen; ganze Höfe standen menschenleer; auch der Sechs-
man Anders Matsson, der mir hatte als Wegweiser zu den
Lappen dienen sollen, war in den Alpen. Indeß fand ich, durch
eine freundliche Bäuerin, in einem der verlassenen Bauerhöfe ein
gutes Nachtquartier und eine gute Abendmahlzeit; und ein Bauer
erbot sich, an Anders Stelle, am folgenden Morgen mein Wegweiser zu seyn. In Handöl hatte man allerlei Geräthe aus
dem in der Nachbarschaft gebrochenen Topfstein: Pfannen, Heerd-
platten, ja ganze Oefen waren aus Topfsteinkacheln aufgeführt.
Die Zimmer waren mit den Eyern wilder Enten und anderer
Vögel und den Schwänzen der Auer- und Birkhühner, wie ich
es schon in Wallarne gefunden hatte, geschmückt. Auf den Dächern, die zum Theil mit Moos und Erde über Birkenrinde und
Brettern bedeckt sind, erblickt man oft eine ganze Flora.

Schon von Klockan an, und noch mehr in der Nähe von
Handöl plagte mich heute die große Mückenart, welche unter

dem Namen der Handöls-Mücken bekannt ist; sie sticht selbst durch die dichtesten Kleider.

———

Am 5. Sept. Ritt zu den Lappen am Fuß des Sylfjäll.

Am Frühmorgen besah ich die kleine Kapelle, die, vor etwa 20 Jahren, meist auf Kosten des Pastor Festin gebauet wurde, und in welcher zuweilen vor Schweden und Lappen Gottesdienst gehalten wird, und trat dann um 7¾ Uhr den Weg zu den Lappen an. Nur ungefähr hatte man in Handöl die Gegend angeben können, in welcher die Lappen gegenwärtig anzutreffen seyn möchten, doch ließ es sich auf 1 oder 2 Meilen nicht bestimmen. Es war daher sehr ungewiß, ob und wie bald ich die Lappen treffen würde, und durfte ich, da es, bevor ich zu einer Lappenhütte kam, keine Uebernachtungsstelle gab, unterweges nicht zögern. Ich bestieg daher auch nicht die Alpe Snasahöjd, wiewohl ich ihr bald auf eine halbe Meile nahe kam. Gleich hinter Handöl hat man schöne Alpenprospekte; auch übersieht man den Ånnsee mit seinen Inseln und Landzungen. Eine halbe Viertelmeile hinter Handöl kam ich an den oberen Wasserfall des Handölself, dessen Höhe, in zwei Absätzen, etwa 80 Ellen beträgt; die Wassermasse war jetzt sehr geringe, ein wenig weiter ist ein kleinerer Fall; der bedeutendste Fall ist beim Dorfe selbst; der obere Fall ist von Wiesen und dichten Moosbetten, Blaubeerfeldern, verkrüppelten Gränen und niedrigen Birken umgeben. Von da ward die Reise fortgesetzt, theils am Handölself, wo wir eine lange Strecke die ziemlich frischen Fußspuren eines Bären verfolgten, theils an Bächen, theils in lieblichem Laubwalde, wo die Schmetterlinge schwirrten und die Vögel ihr Morgenlied sangen. In der Nähe hielten Bewohner des Dorfes Gunnarviken Heuerndte; mein Wegweiser Anders Olsson rief sie, um sich weiter nach dem gegenwärtigen Stande der nächsten Lappenhütte zu erkundigen; sie antworteten und kamen näher, wußten aber gleichfalls nicht mehr als Anders selbst. Man hört noch immer den Handölself, der auf felsigem Bette eine Menge kleiner Fälle bildet. Nicht lange, und wir waren am Schlusse des Gebiets von Handöl und betraten das Land der Lappen. Ein hohes üppiges Wiesenthal, wo das Gras zum Theil ⅞ Ellen lang war, zwischen der Snasahsid und der Kjaltjasen-Alpe beginnt. Anfangs zeigten sich noch Bärenspuren; als wir aber höher kamen, verschwanden diese; denn der Bär weilt nicht gerne zwischen den hohen Alpen, sondern im dichten Walde, insbesondere im Dickigt der Gränen. Man kommt über viele Bäche und kleine Flüsse, über die es natürlich keine Brücken giebt, behält aber immer den Handöl zur Seite, wenn man gleich oft seiner nicht ansichtig wird; bald treten Sümpfe, welche man durchwaten muß, in den Weg. Der niedrige Wald (nur Birken gedeihen hier noch; die Raupe hatte die Blätter verzehrt) läuft fort. Oft erblickt man im Walde Umzäunungen, in welchen die Lappen ihre Heerden zum Melken eintreiben; sie bestehen aus Birken, die mit Zweigen verflochten sind; auch trafen wir alte Lappenhütten. Bald entdeckten wir Spuren von Rennthieren, und der den Lappen eigenthümliche Geruch ließ sich vernehmen. Schon hofften wir, einer Rennthierheerde nahe zu seyn; wir folgten den Spuren, aber statt einer lebendigen Heerde, fanden wir 2 Umzäunungen oder sogenannte Wälle (vallar), von denen, wie es das frischere Grün der anderen verrieth, nur die eine in diesem Sommer benutzt worden war; in der Nähe stand eine Lappenhütte aus pyramidalisch in einander gestellten Birken und Birkenzweigen, bedeckt mit Moos und Rasen; Pfosten und, am Boden, Steine dienen dem Ganzen zu Stützen; in der Spitze ist zwischen den Zweigen eine Oeffnung, die als Rauchloch dient. Die Thüröffnung war so schmal, daß ich Mühe hatte durchzuschlüpfen, ein Stein bildet die Schwelle; im Innern der Hütten bedecken Birkenreiser den Fußboden. In der Nähe der Hütte trafen wir ein ansehnliches Schneefeld. Wir setzten nun unsern Marsch fort im Angesicht des Sylfjäll, d. i. Säulenalpe, denn sie bildet hohe, mit Schnee bedeckte Säulen, die bisher nur Lappen zu erklimmen vermochten, indem sie scheugewordene Rennthiere verfolgten. Das Sylfjäll ist Gränzalpe; aller Versuche ungeachtet hat noch kein Schwede oder Norweger sie erstiegen. „Die Lappen klimmen, sagte Anders, wie die Hunde.“ —

II.   M m

Bald stießen wir auf ein Bur, d. i. Speisebauer der Lappen, wie sie deren mehrere auf ihren Sommer- und Winter-Straßen haben: eine auf einer Birke oder einem hohen Pfahl ruhende Hütte aus dicht zusammengelegten belaubten Birkenzweigen, an den Seiten durch horizontal gestellte dicke Birkenstäbe gestützt; der Eingang ist verflochten; als Leiter dient eine mit eingekerbtem Steigholz versehene Birke; in der Hütte lag eine Menge großer Rennthierkäse. Unter dem Boden der Hütte wurden, ganz im Freien, Felle, Pelze, alte Kleider, Säcke mit Rennthierhaaren, lederne Beutel, Käseschachteln, in welchen man die Käse transportirt, aufbewahrt.

Noch immer war weder Lappe noch Rennthier zu sehen. Endlich vernahmen wir einen Laut, zogen ihm nach und erblickten — eine Rennthierheerde, die eben von der Weide heimgetrieben wurde. Man kann sich vorstellen, wie groß meine Freude war, denn fast hatte ich alle Hoffnung, auf Lappen zu stoßen, aufgegeben. Ein kleines Lappenmädchen kam gesprungen und wies uns den Weg zur Hütte. Als wir uns aber den Rennthieren näherten, ward mein Pferd scheu, denn die Pferde ertragen nicht die Nähe der Rennthiere; ich mußte absteigen und es leiten lassen; die kleine 8jährige Marie, ein wahres Naturkind, ängstigte sich vor dem Pferde (noch nie hatte sie ein Pferd gesehn) und verdoppelte ihre Schritte; ich mußte, um ihre Flucht zu hemmen, ihr die Hand reichen, welche sie treuherzig ergriff, und so gingen wir zu den Hütten, zu denen uns die etwa ein Paar hundert Häupter starke Heerde voranzog. Die Hütten liegen 1 Meile von der Norwegischen Gränze entfernt, in einem Thale, unweit eines Flusses. Der Lappische Hausvater, Anders Olsson, hieß mich aufs herzlichste willkommen. Ich ging nun in den umzäunten Birkenhain, in welchem die Heerde gemolken wurde. 'Rings umher thronten schneebedeckte Alpen; den schönsten Anblick gewährte die hohe, spitzige, etwa 1 Meile entfernte Gränzalpe Syltoppen, die westwärts weit im Meere gesehen werden kann; nach Törnstén, erhebt sich die Spitze 2712 Ellen über den Storsjö, mithin 3326 Ellen über das

Meer *); in noch geringerer Entfernung stiegen die Alpen Bun:
nerfiäll, Kjerlingfiäll und Gestifiäll zur Seite des Birkenhains
empor. — Nachdem die Heerde eingetrieben worden, nähern
sich die rüstigsten Lappen und Lappinnen und werfen einen aus
Rennthiersehnen gefertigten Strick mit bewundernswürdiger Schnel:
ligkeit um des Rennthiers Leib, Hörner ꝛc. Nicht selten reißt
sich das schlanke und kräftige Thier wieder los, springt mit dem,
der es fesseln wollte, umher, oder geht auf ihn los; und man:
cher Lappe ward schon auf diese Weise verwundet oder verstüm:
melt, ja des Augenlichts beraubt. Mißlingt der Wurf ganz, so
ergreift man das Thier beim Fuß und sucht desselben auf diese
Weise mächtig zu werden. Bekommt man schon durch den er:
sten Wurf das Rennthier in seine Gewalt, so befestigt man den
Reif an den Hörnern, und bindet das Thier an eine Birke
fest. Nun erst nähern sich auch die schwächeren, selbst die er:
blindeten, Lappen, um zu melken; das Rennthier giebt etwa
eine Viertelbouteille Milch. Ich kostete die frisch gemolkene
Milch, die man mir anfangs nur durchgeseiht reichen wollte,
„weil solches die Höflichkeit fordere;" an Geschmack
fand ich sie gleich der Schaafmilch, aber dünner und milder.
Gleich nach geschehenem Melken seiht man die Milch durch
Riedgras (starrgräs, Carex), wodurch auch der Geschmack sich
verbessert; am besten schmeckt sie ein wenig gekocht, wo sie dann
sehr dick ist. — An Größe kommt das Rennthier dem Rehe
gleich, an Hals und Schwanz ist es weiß, an den Füßen weiß:

---

*) Nordwärts vom Sylfjäll läuft der kleine Alpenpfad von Handöl
nach Tydalen in Norwegen. Hier war es, wo im Winter 1719 die
Schwedische Armee, auf ihrem Rückzuge aus Norwegen, vom See Oj:
sand aus, nachdem der Wegweiser erfroren, am Södra-Enebogen, der
sich in den Norra-Enebogen, und dann den nach Handöl führenden
Ene-Elf ergießt, des Weges verfehlte, und statt nordwärts zu mar:
schiren, sich südwärts zum Sylfjäll wandte und viele Menschen durch
Hunger und Frost verlor. Man hauete nun das Eis des Södra-Ene:
bogen auf, und — erkannte den Irrthum. Man kehrte um und ge:
langte, indem man dem Laufe des Wassers folgte, endlich nach Handöl.
Die nächtlichen Campements in den Alpen namentlich hatten Vielen
das Leben gekostet.

M m 2

lich; am übrigen Körper grau, nicht gestreift, aber mit längeren weißen Strichen. Das hirschartige Geweihe ist behaart, beim männlichen, wie beim weiblichen Thier; das Geweihe des Ochsen ist größer. Gegen Michaelis verlieren die Rennthiere die Haare, dann sind die Geweihe blutig, wie ich schon jetzt blutige Geweihe fand. — Sollen die Kälber nicht saugen, so legt man ihnen einen hölzernen Maulkorb an. Die Rennthiere bekämpfen einander zuweilen mit den Füßen. Auf alle Weise ist das Melken der Rennthiere ein wahrer Krieg zu nennen. Während ich im Wall war, kam noch eine andere Heerde; auf den ersten Ruf der Treiber sprang alles, die Umzäunung an der einen Seite aufzureißen, worauf die Heerde eingetrieben und die Oeffnung wieder verzäunt wurde. Zu jeder Heerde gehörten mehrere Hirten und Hunde. Auch Nachts sind die Heerden in den Alpen. Das Melken geschieht zweimal täglich, Morgens und Abends. Eine blinde Lappin ließ sich zur Kuh leiten und melkte. Die gesammte Heerde mochte etwa 400 Häupter betragen; die meisten gehörten meinem Wirthe, dem reichen Lappen Anders Olsson.

Nachdem ich eine längere Zeit dem Melken zugesehen, ging ich mit Anders Larsson, dem Besitzer der zweiten Hütte, diese in Augenschein zu nehmen. Nur zwei Hütten befanden sich an diesem Platze; sie wurden aber von mehreren Familien gemeinschaftlich benutzt. Jede der Hütten war etwa 8 Ellen lang und 6 Ellen breit; in jeder konnten 9 Menschen schlafen. Auf dem Boden der Hütte waren Birkenreiser ausgebreitet; nur die Stelle für den Heerd, in der Mitte der Hütte, war frei; über dem Heerde hing, an einer eisernen Kette, der Kessel. Ueber den Reisern lagen lederne Beutel mit Rennthierhaaren, hölzerne Kästchen ꝛc., die in der Nacht als Kopfkissen dienen. Stühle giebt es nicht; man sitzt mit untergeschlagenen Beinen. Neben dem Kessel hingen, an Stäben, Rennthierfleisch, Kessel mit zubereitetem Leder ꝛc.; außen um die Hütte herum auf und an Bäumen aber Felle, Kleider, Säcke ꝛc.; eben so unter der erhöhten Vorrathskammer. Anders Larsson baute eine Walmarhütte auf, um mir zu zeigen, wie man sie einzurichten pflege.

Als ich zurückkam, ward die gemolkene Heerde ausgetrieben. Meine Lappen hatten mittlerweile ihren Sonntagsstaat angelegt, um ihre Freude über den Gast auszudrücken, „der auch sie habe sehen wollen." Die Hausfrau, eine 50jährige, die aber noch rüstig, wie eine 20jährige, war, hatte ihre silberne Litze und ihre Staatsschürze auf Schwedische Weise angelegt, übrigens aber ihren Lappischen Kont beibehalten; die Tochter ging in kattunenem Kleide und mit kattunenem Halstuch, und trug nur die Lappische Mütze; die Finger zierten ein silberner und ein messingener Ring. Auch mehrere der Männer waren geputzt. Sonst tragen die Weiber Jacken von Walmar, Röcke von Leder nebst langen Beinkleidern; die Männer tragen Felle. Die Schuhe sind wasserdicht, gewöhnlich, der größeren Festigkeit halber, von Ochsenleder und der Wärme wegen immer mit Riedgras ausgelegt; Weiber tragen vorne, Männer hinten, Ringe, Messerscheiden, Beutelchen mit Zunder ꝛc. — Eine gute Mahlzeit ward zubereitet; Lappische Speisen aller Art wurden vorgesetzt, gekochte Rennthiermilch mit eingeschnittenem Rennthierkäse war die Hauptspeise, die wie ein guter Milchbrei schmeckte; ferner gebratener Käse, der aber sehr zähe war; frischer harter Käse, so mager, daß ich ihn statt des Brotes gebrauchte; er wird aus Buttermilch bereitet, zu welcher man frische Milch gießt; mit Zucker bestreuet, schmeckt er am besten; frische ungesalzene Rennthierbutter, die fast wie aufgelöstes Schaastalg schmeckte; feste, gesalzene Butter, die einen sehr angenehmen Geschmack hatte, fast wie Schaasbutter; Rennthierbraten, der im Geschmack viel Aehnlichkeit mit Rehbraten hat; der Braten wird an einem hölzernen Bratspieß oder Stabe bereitet und mit harter Butter gegessen; endlich Buttermilch. Als durststillendes Getränk diente Rennthiermilch mit Wasser vermischt. — Männer, wie Weiber, kochen.

Nach eingenommener Mahlzeit räumte man, aus Artigkeit, mir die ganze Hütte ein und schlief selbst draußen, unter freiem Himmel, auf Fellen, mit Walmar bedeckt; noch gegen Mitternacht kam man ein, das Feuer in der Mitte zu unterhalten. Nachdem der heftige Luftzug durch die Oeffnungen zwischen den

Wandstäben mittelst vorgehängter Felle gehemmt worden war, schlief ich ziemlich sanft; mein Unterbette war eine Rennthier= haut; eine andere, nebst meiner Chenille, diente als Oberdecke; Säcke, Gras und Packete als Kopfkissen.

Mein Wirth war einer der reichern Lappen; dennoch war es in seiner Hütte um nichts besser, als in der Hütte ärmerer Lappen; die Thüre der Hütte bestand, wie gewöhnlich, aus zusammengenähten Lumpen. Branntwein war nicht vorhanden, aber Anders Olsson's Frau wünschte ihn von mir zu erhalten; auch nach Zucker und Kaffee hatte man Verlangen. Die Be= zahlung ward mir am nächsten Morgen völlig anheimgestellt; aber ein altes Reif aus Rennthiersehnen mußte ich theuer be= zahlen. Von Argwohn waren diese Lappen keinesweges frei; sie hielten mich für einen Landshöfding, welcher reise, um ihre Ver= hältnisse näher kennen zu lernen und ihnen dann höhere Schatz= ung aufzulegen. Sie haben Silber, was sie mit sich führen, wollen aber nicht gestehen, daß sie es besitzen. Auf Reinlichkeit halten sie sehr; wöchentlich reinigen sie die Felle über dem Feuer, und keine Spur von Ungeziefer findet sich in ihren Hütten. Schöne Körperbildung sah ich bei den Weibern nicht, wohl aber bei den Männern. Männer und Weiber waren von mittlerer Statur, behende, aber kräftig. Der Schwedischen Sprache sind sie kundig, sprechen aber unter einander Lappisch; diese Sprache klingt ungleich rauher, als die Schwedische. Jedermann nennen sie Du, auch Fremde. Ihre Kinder behandeln sie mit großer Strenge, ja wohl Härte und Heftigkeit. Säuglinge transporti= ren sie in einer Art von Körben aus Granholz, inwendig mit rauhen Rennthierfellen, auswendig mit bereitetem Rennthierleder überzogen; solche Wiegen heißen Gurkum. In der Nähe der Hütte zeigte mir Olsson's Frau eine Milchgrube; hier bewahren sie in mit Eisen beschlagenen Tonnen im Winter die Milch auf. Die Norweger hielten solche Gruben im letzten Kriege für Grä= ber, weil Stäbe in Kreuzesform darüber aufgerichtet gewesen wa= ren. Meines Schirmes und meines Fernrohres freuten sich die Lappen sehr, konnten sich aber keinen rechten Begriff darüber fassen. — Die hölzernen Formen, deren sie sich beim Käsema=

chen bedienen, waren hübsch gezackt; sie benutzen für diesen Zweck auch grobgeflochtene Körbe. Zuweilen angeln sie auch Fische *).

———————

Am 6. Septbr. Von den Lappenhütten unter dem Sylfjäll nach Handöl — Von H. nach Wallarne 1¼ M.; von W. nach Tängböle ¼ M.

Um 6 Uhr früh trat ich die Rückreise an. Mit treuherzigem Händedruck entließen mich die Lappen und baten, alle, welche ich träfe, zu grüßen; solche Züge reiner Menschlichkeit sind diesen Naturkindern eigen. Auf dem Rückwege bestieg ich einen der benachbarten hohen Felsen, um, wo möglich, eine Aussicht nach Norwegen zu gewinnen; aber höhere Felsen hinderten. Indeß zeigten sich schon im Thale die Gränzalpen. Am schönsten war die Aussicht auf der letzten Viertelmeile; sie erstreckte sich nicht blos über den Ännsee, die Äreskuta, die Alpen von Nordhallen, sondern auch oberhalb des Ene-Elf über die Störsdalsport. Die letzte halbe Meile vor Handöl ist die beschwerlichste, und fast halsbrechend durch Steine, Moräste ꝛc. Heute traf ich ich auch, im Anfange des den Bauern von Handöl gehörigen Landes, Lappenhütten, indem man den Lappen erlaubt, diese Striche mit ihren Rennthieren zu beweiden. Auf der letzten Viertelmeile stieg ich von dem hier nahen, aber vom Dorfe Handöl ¼ M. entfernten, schönen, unteren Falle des Handöls-Elf herab: der Fall ist horizontal, etwa 300 Ellen lang, zwischen bewaldeten Felsen. Unweit dieses unteren Falles trifft man die eine Tälgsteinsgrube; die andere liegt neben dem oberen Falle; schon frühe ward hier auf Tälgstein gearbeitet.

Um 3 Uhr war ich in Handöl, wo der Handöls-Elf in den See Änn fällt. Nach eingenommenem Mittagsmahl setzte ich um 4 Uhr die Reise über den Änn-See, bis zu welchem man 1/16 M. Fußweg hat, fort; der See wogte stark bei mäßigem

—————————

*) Ausführlichere Nachrichten über Lappland und Lappen findet man Kap. 23.

Winde. Um 6 Uhr landete ich und gelangte auf einem trocknern Fußsteige, als bei der Anreise, nach Wallarne (1½ M.).

Jetzt fand ich in Wallarne Menschen. Es waren freundliche, liebe Menschen, so dienstfertig und ohne Eigennutz, so empfänglich für alles Gute. Die Familien des Dorfs leben friedlich und liebevoll mit einander und halten nicht blos ihren gewöhnlichen Dorfgottesdienst am Sonntage für die, welche nicht zur Kirche gingen, sondern versammeln sich auch am Sonnabend-Abend zu einer gemeinschaftlichen Betstunde. Gerne hätte ich bei diesen biederen Menschen länger verweilt, wenigstens übernachtet; aber die Eile, da ich am Abend noch Tångböle erreichen konnte, verbot es. Um 7½ Uhr ritt ich ab und war um 9 Uhr in Tångböle, wo ich, dießmal im Norderhofe, Quartier nahm. In Tångböle traf ich eine Rindviehheerde, die nach Norwegen getrieben wurde; man treibt viel Hornvieh nach Norwegen und bringt Pferde zurück; die meisten Pferde dieser Gegend sind Norwegischer Race, auch Norwegische Schaafe mit langer Wolle hat man schon an einigen Orten in Jemteland. Ochsen braucht man in ganz Jemteland selten zum Ziehen.

———

Am 7. Septbr. Von Tångböle nach Sta 1½ M.; von S. nach Tegom ¾ M.; von T. nach Stamgärde 2½ M.; von St. nach Noland ¾ M. — Zus. 4½ M.

Um 8 Uhr brach ich auf. Es war Sonntags-Morgen; die Sonntagsfeier ist hier so strenge, daß die Tochter des Hauses selbst Bedenken trug, zu nähen, was eben nothwendig war. Der Dorfgottesdienst beginnt hier erst um 12 und dauert bis 3 Uhr. Dann speiset man zu Mittag. Die Bewohner dieser Gegenden halten überhaupt vier Mahlzeiten am Tage; die erste, frühe, dann um 12 Uhr Frühstück; um 3 Uhr Mittagsessen; und um 8, 9 oder 10 Uhr, je nachdem es die Geschäfte erlauben, Abendbrot, worauf man, wie fast überall in Schweden, gleich nach dem Abendessen zu Bette geht; Standespersonen hiesigen Ortes halten ihr Mittagsmahl spätestens um 2 Uhr.

Mein Wirth war auch mein Skjutsbonde. Da der Wind das Ueberfahren über den See verhinderte, wodurch der Weg verkürzt wird, so fuhr ich zu Boot nur über den schmalen Sund und ritt um den See in 3 Stunden nach Renberget, und von da weiter die Viertelmeile nach Sta. In Sta, wo ein schönes und braves Volk wohnt, wechselte ich das Pferd, und setzte dann den Ritt fort. In Sta liegen die Viehställe in einiger Entfernung vom Hofe; im Frühling und Herbst, wo das Vieh nicht mehr auf Sennenweide ist, sondern auf nahe Wiesen und Aecker getrieben wird, dienen sie als Melkställe, damit es einer Viehtrift zum Hofe nicht bedürfe, also Acker und Wiese nicht geschadet und die Unreinlichkeit auf dem Hofe selbst vermieden werde. Diese Einrichtung findet man an vielen Orten, vielleicht überall, in Jemteland.

Bei Dufveby besah ich die neue Schanze; sie liegt auf einem ziemlich hohen Berge und beherrscht den Fluß und die Straße; doch möchte sie, jenseits des waldigen Berges, umgangen werden können. Die Aussicht von hier auf Thäler, Fluß, Waldberge und Alpen ist schön. — Der Skjuts von Forsa stand auch diesmal in Tegom, wo schöne und dienstwillige Menschen wohnen. Ohne daß ich darum gebeten, ward sofort Speise aufgetragen, und ich mußte, wenn ich nicht kränken wollte, wenigstens kosten. Von Tegom aus reisete ich in einer Kärra. Etwa eine halbe Meile hinter Tegom liegen Sennhütten auf einer Höhe. Ich ging hinein; ein einziges Sennenmädchen war anwesend, unbefangen zeigte sie mir die Einrichtung und bot treffliche Alpenmilch zum Gasttrunke. Bei Åre hielt ich an, die steinerne Kirche zu sehen, in welcher heute kein Gottesdienst gehalten wurde. Altar, Kanzel und Chöre sind mit Gemälden und Schnitzwerken geschmückt. An der Wand bemerkte ich das hölzerne Bild des heiligen Olof. Nur auf dem nördlichen Ufer des Flusses liegen Höfe und Dörfer. In Areborsta sprach ich eine Weile bei der braven Länsmansfamilie vor. Zwischen Brattland und Stamgärde beschaute ich ein Paar am Wege liegende mächtige Felsenplatten, während aus einer Torparewohnung auf der Waldhöhe die liebliche Jemtische Hirtenflöte erschallte, die, wenn sie stark geblasen wird, im Ton dem Waldhorn sehr ähnlich ist. Um 8¼ Uhr war ich in Nyland.

Am 8. September. Von Nyland nach Eggen 1¼ M.; von E. nach Mellbyn 1¾ M. — Zuſ. 3 M.

Um 9¾ Uhr verließ ich Nyland. Der heitere, liebenswürdige Greis und ſeine Schwiegertochter, die zum Dorfe Hjerpe zurückkehrte, begleiteten mich bis zur Schanze. In Undersåker ward bei der Pröpſtin Söderberg vorgeſprochen und die Kirche beſehen. Die Kirche iſt von Stein und ſehr alt; das Innere iſt würdig verziert. An der Kirchwand hängen, wie in vielen Schwediſchen Kirchen, Degen hier verſtorbener Offiziers; jetzt iſt die Sitte abgekommen. In der Sakriſtey befindet ſich noch ein altes katholiſches Rauchfaß. Am Altar erblickt man ein altes Schnitzwerk, die Kreuzigung, und ein anderes einen Schädel darſtellend, der von einer Schlange umſchlungen wird. — Am jenſeitigen Ufer wurden die beiden Schanzen in Augenſchein genommen. Ich fuhr nun nach Eggen; unterweges verweilte ich einige Augenblicke beim Vicepaſtor Söderberg, Sohn der Pröpſtin. Von Eggen oder Mörſill hat man meiſt Waldweg bis Mellbyn oder Mattmar; im Walde kommt man ein Paar Sennhütten vorüber. Die letzte Viertelmeile führt durch fruchtbare Felder und, wohl eine Viertelmeile lang, durch eine Kette kleiner Dörfer. Durch den mehrmaligen Aufenthalt zwiſchen Nyland und Eggen war es Abend geworden, und ich übernachtete in Mellbyn bei dem Kyrkovård Hendrik Petersson, der zugleich Gäſtgifvare iſt, in dem vorzüglichſten Gäſtgifvaregård, den ich bisher in Jemtteland gefunden hatte. Alles war nett, reinlich und tüchtig und die Menſchen gar lieb und freundlich, offen und bieder.

Am 9. September. Von Mellbyn nach Marſund 1 M.; von M. nach Trappnäs 1½ M. von T. nach Sunne. —

Um 6 Uhr brach ich auf. Es war ein ſchöner Morgen; heiter und klar lagen die Alpen da, während über den Seen ein dichter Nebel ruhte. Ich fuhr eine kleine Strecke vom Wege ab, um Mattmar's Kirche zu ſehen. Sie iſt ein altes ſteinernes Gebäude; die Chöre ſind amphitheatraliſch angelegt, das eine für Mädchen, das andere für Jünglinge; die Verheiratheten sitzen unten. Der Altar ist mit hübschem Schnitzwerke würdig verziert. — Von der Kirche kehrte ich auf den Landweg zurück, der nun einen langen Bergrücken hinab, zwischen Feldern, Wiesen, Wald und Dörfern an den Sund führt, den der von Kall herabkommende Wasserzug bei seinem Einfluß in den Storsjö bildet. Man fährt neben vielen urbar gemachten Aeckern und Wiesen hin, wie denn überhaupt seit etwa 30 Jahren in Mattmar viele Urbarmachungen vorgenommen worden sind, vielleicht mehr als in irgend einem Jemtekändischen Kirchspiele; aber es giebt in Mattmar auch keine eigentliche Handelsbauern, nur einzelne fahren zuweilen nach Norwegen, weniger zum Verkauf, als für eigenen und ihrer Freunde Bedarf Heringe einzukaufen. Mein Skjutsbonde, der Gästgifvare von Mellbyn, der selbst ansehnliche Landstrecken urbar gemacht hatte, äußerte sehr treffend: „er begreife nicht, wie man ein tüchtiger Landmann seyn und doch zugleich Handel treiben könne; nothwendig müsse der Ackerbau dabei leiden." Und wirklich bestätiget es sich bei genauer Untersuchung, mögen auch die anfänglichen Angaben noch so verschieden lauten, überall, daß der Landhandel verderblich auf die Kultur des Bodens einwirkt, und überdieß an den meisten Orten die Sitten verschlimmert; in den eigentlichen Handelskirchspielen ist die Sitteneinheit fast immer geschwunden. Mattmar zeichnet sich durch Einfachheit, Sittlichkeit und Wohlstand aus.

Von Mattmar führt der zum Kupfertransport benutzte Weg seitwärts nach Offne an den Storsjö. Die Landstraße wird nun besser. Uns begegnete ein Bauer, dem ein Bär im Walde sein Pferd zerrissen; Bären richten in diesen Gegenden oft Verwüstungen unter dem Vieh an; Wölfe lassen sich leichter durch Geräusch und Mannschaft verscheuchen, die Bären sind weniger scheu.

Der Nebel war so stark, daß die Fährleute, die auf dem jenseitigen Ufer wohnen, uns nicht sehen konnten, und da sie auch unser Rufen nicht hörten, so ruderte mein Skjutsbonde in einem kleinen Boote, welches sich vorfand, herüber, um die Fähre zu holen. Der Sund heißt von einem nahen Dorfe Sundbackesfärje fund. Ein Kahn, hinter welchem Bäume angebunden waren, floß vorüber; eine leichtere Art, Bauholz zu transportiren, als das gewöhnliche Flößen, besonders stromaufwärts. Bald verzog sich der Nebel, und die Sonne leuchtete über die anmuthige Landschaft; Wald, Wiesen, Dörfer und Inseln wechselten, hoch über dem Walde thronten die Alpen, unter welchen die Areskuta mit ihrem Schnee den schönsten Anblick gewährte.

Der Frost um die Mitte Augusts hatte auch hier der Erndte geschadet; vieles Korn war erfroren; anderes hatte man halb reif geschnitten.

Eine Viertelmeile hinter dem breiten Sunde erreicht man Marsund, ein, an einem Busen des Storsjö, bey der Wasserzug von Kall bildet und der hier Hallen's See heißt, freundlich gelegenes Dorf.

Von Marsund bis zur Kirche Hallen fährt man im Walde, doch bald erblickt man den See Hallen und den weiten Storsjö; aus dem Storsjö erhebt sich Frösön; gegenüber erscheint die schöne Kirche Rödön mit Thurm. In Hallen sah ich die steinerne Kirche, die ein Paar schöne Gemälde des Jemtischen Bauern Sundin des Aelteren, „die Einsetzung des heiligen Abendmahls“, und „die Abnahme Christi vom Kreuz“, schmücken; beide sind mit großem Fleiße gearbeitet und haben viel Ausdruck. Auch die Bildhauerarbeit an Altar und Kanzel ist wohl gerathen. Die Kirchendecke ist mit Gemälden bedeckt. Um Hallen wird viel Kornbau getrieben; der See sichert vor Frost. Der Weg von Hallen nach Trappnäs ist gar anmuthig; er beträgt fast eine Meile und führt, längs des Storsjö, durch Birkengebüsch und neben Wiesen.

Von Trappnäs läuft die Straße weiter am See ½ M. nach Oviken. Ich wollte aber zuvor noch nach Sunne, auf einer Landzunge des Storsjö, und folgte daher der Straße nur bis Marieby, wohin man bald durch Wiesen und Gebüsche gelangt. Auch Marieby hat eine Kirche, die ich in Augenschein nahm; sie ist Filial von Sunne. Ein Häusler, der sie mir öffnete, sank, gleich nachdem er eingetreten, in stiller Inbrunst betend auf die Knie. Ueberall findet man hier fromme und biedere Menschen, ohne alle Ansprüche, und so freundlich und ge fällig ohne Eigennutz. Die Kirche ist alt und von Stein; den Altar schmücken ein Paar gute Gemälde: die Kreuzigung und das Opfer Isaaks. Am See hat der Pastor von Sunne 1798 einen Gesundbrunnen angelegt, der mit Nutzen gebraucht wird. Mein Skjutsbonde, der Gästgifvare von Trappnäs, ein heiterer, herrlicher Greis, der in seinen früheren Jahren viele Kriege mitgemacht, hatte es übernommen, mich von Marieby zu Boot nach Sunne überzuführen; indeß nahm ich, ihm zur Hülfe, noch einen Ruderer, der sofort ging, ohne zu fragen, was ihm an Bezahlung werden solle. Wir ruderten längs eines lieblichen Birkenufers, dann neben der Insel Norderö, die mit ihrer Kirche, ihren Dörfern, Laubgebüschen, Feldern und Wiesen einen freundlichen Anblick darbietet; erst nach 1½ Stunde erreichten wir das jenseitige Ufer, welches schon aus der Ferne mit seinen schwellenden Hügeln einen nicht minder schönen Prospect, wie Norderö, gewährte; die Wellen gingen hoch und warfen das Boot hin und her. Von der Landungsstelle hatten wir noch eine Strecke zu Fuße zurückzulegen, bis wir den Pfarrhof erreichten. Unweit des Pfarrhofs liegt die Kirche; sie ist sehr alt, vielleicht die älteste in Jemteland, ward indeß in späterer Zeit erweitert. Jetzt sollte aber, da sie noch immer zu enge ist, eine neue geräumige Kirche erbauet werden, wozu schon der Platz abgesteckt war. Drei Gemälde auf Holz schmücken den Altar: das eine stellt die Einsetzung des heiligen Abendmahls; das andere die göttliche Offenbarung dar, welche den Evangelisten zu Theil wird; das dritte die Bildnisse des Wiclef, des Huß, des Hieronymus von Prag, des Zwingli, Luther, Oecolampadius, Bucer, Calvinus, Picard, Melanchthon, Petrus Martyr, Johann Knor, Matth. Flacius, Heinr. Bullinger, Hieronymus Zanchius, Theodor Beza, Wilhelm Perkins; alle diese Männer sitzen an einem Tische, auf welchem die Bibel liegt, von der herab ein Licht seine Strahlen verbreitet. — Auf dem Kirchhofe steht ein alter steinerner Thurm, in welchem die Glocken hängen; ehemals führte eine, jetzt vernichtete, Wendeltreppe hinauf; Ursprung und erste Bestimmung des Thurms kennt man nicht; Alter und Blitz haben ihn gespalten. Der Thurm erreicht nicht völlig die Höhe des Glockenthurms von Brunflo. Zur Seite des Pfarrhofes sind zwei gerade Linien durch den Wald gehauen; durch eine derselben erblickt man die Kirche Marieby; die andere sollte die Kirche Oviken zeigen, aber die rechte Richtung ward verfehlt.

Nach Besichtigung der alten merkwürdigen Kirche wollte ich zurückkehren; allein der schon überdieß durch die plötzlichen und heftigen Alpenwinde gefährliche Storsjö wogte jetzt so gewaltig, daß die Fährleute erklärten, es sey unmöglich, zurück zu rudern. Bald ward es zwar etwas stiller, aber der See war noch immer gerade auf Marieby hin nicht zu passiren; die Fährleute wählten nun einen andern Rückweg, indem sie auf einer schmaleren Stelle den See überfuhren und eine halbe Meile durch sumpfige Wiesen und Wald zurücklegten. Ich entschloß mich, der Bitte des Propstes Grundahl nachgebend, erst am folgenden Morgen die Reise zu Lande nach Oviken fortzusetzen. Ein angenehmer Abend verfloß mir in der liebenswürdigen Familie. Meinen Wagen, der in Marieby zurückgeblieben war, ließ ich von dort durch Skjuts geradezu nach Oviken fahren.

Das Pastorat Sunne besteht aus 5 Gemeinden, der Muttergemeinde Sunne mit 764, und den Filialgemeinden Fröfön mit 837, Hallen mit 786, Norderön mit 238 und Marieby mit 260 Seelen (im J. 1815). In der Kirche Norderön wird nur an jedem dritten Sonntage gepredigt; in Marieby fällt jeden dritten Sonntag der Gottesdienst aus. Viele der hiesigen Bauern sind Handelsbauern. Norderö hat eine Kalchbrennerey, die einzige in Jemteland, wiewohl dieses Land eben so viel Kalch hat, als Gottland.

———

Am 10. September. Von Sunne nach Oviken 2¼ M.; von O. nach Hofvermo 1¼ M. — Zus. 3¼ M.

Frühe brach ich auf. Das Pferd war aus dem nahen Gästgifvaregärd Orrviken. Der Weg führt über Wiesen, durch Birkengebüsch und Nadelwald, bis man das Fährdorf Kärgäl erreicht. Hier wird das wasserdichte Leder von Oviken bereitet; die Bereitung wird für ein Geheimniß gehalten, doch versieht man sie in mehrern Dörfern. Der Wasserzug, über welchen die Fähre führt, ist ein Arm des Storsiö. Wiewohl kaum eine Viertelmeile breit, brauchten wir doch fast eine Stunde, um herüber zu kommen; denn ein heftiger Sturm, fürchterliche Wogen erregend, schleuderte das Boot bald in die Höhe, bald in die Tiefe, und eine Frau, die im Bote war, fürchtete schon: wir würden untergehen. Doch glücklich erreichten wir das jenseitige Ufer, und bald war ich in Oviken, wo ich meinen Wagen mit allem Zubehör unversehrt vorfand; der Gästgifvare von Trappnäs hatte ihn von Marieby dahin gefahren, und wiewohl er nun einen vollen Tag von mir beschäftiget worden war, verlangte er doch nur das gewöhnliche Skjutsgeld, und als ich ihm drüber gab, wollte er es kaum annehmen.

In Oviken verweilte ich einige Stunden bei dem heiteren Greise, dem Propste Bohm. Er litt sehr an einer Beinrose und meinte: sie werde ihn wohl ins Grab bringen (wie er denn auch im Novbr. 1818, 82 Jahre alt, starb), ließ sich aber sein fröhliches Gemüth nicht rauben. Lange hatte er Portraits berühmter Schwedischer Geistlichen und einiger deutschen Theologen gesammelt; jetzt besaß er etwa 160 Stück, so wie einige Büsten. Während meiner Anwesenheit erhielt er die Nachricht, daß seinem Sohne, dem Häradshösding, der zu Eltnäs, nicht ferne von Ovikens Kirche wohnt, der 7te Sohn geboren worden. Oviken's Kirche verdiente näher in Augenschein genommen zu werden. Sie ist ein neues, schönes, steinernes Gebäude ohne Thurm, um 1770 erbauet durch Pehr Olsson, Bauer aus Dillne in Oviken, welcher 18 Kirchen gebauet hat. Die geschmackvoll geformte Orgel hat ein Bauer, der Helsingländer Hammerdal aus Arbra gefertiget; liebliche Bilder, welche untergesetzte biblische Sprüche sinnbildlich darstellen, schmücken sie. Auch am Altar findet man ein Paar schöne Gemälde: „der Heiland am Kreuz", und „die Ausgießung des heiligen Geistes am ersten christlichen Pfingstfeste", neben trefflicher Bildhauerarbeit. Aus der Sakristey führt eine Treppe zur schönen, stark vergoldeten Kanzel. Auf dem Kirchhofe ruht der Erbauer der Kirche.

Das Pastorat Oviken (16 □M.) besteht aus, drei Gemeinden: der Muttergemeinde Oviken, im J. 1815 mit 1300, und den Filialgemeinden Myssjö mit 726 und Hackås mit 688 Seelen; das Filial Hackås liegt mitten inne zwischen der sich neben Oviken und Myssjö herabsenkenden Bucht des Storsjö und dem mehrere Meilen langen See Näckten, der sich bis zu den Klössjö-Alpen erstreckt. Bisher war Oviken Sitz der Propstey von Süd-Jemteland, die außer 5 Jemteländischen Pastoraten (Oviken, Sunne, Räffsund, Brunflo und Berg), mit 13006 Seelen, die Provinz Herjeådalen mit 4328 Seelen umfaßt; in den 5 Jemteländischen Pastoraten wurden, im J. 1815, 414 geboren, worunter 18 uneheliche; 116 Ehen geschlossen; es starben 182; in Herjeådalen geboren 131, worunter 2 uneheliche.

Die Sonntagsfeier ist sehr strenge; auch in der Ernte arbeitet keiner für sich, wohl aber hilft man nach 6 Uhr Abends den Nachbaren. Diebstahl ist höchst selten. In 40 Jahren gab es nur Eine Ehescheidung. Viehzucht ist der Hauptnahrungszweig des Pastorats, in welchem noch viel Einfachheit der Sitten, neben Wohlhabenheit, herrscht. Oviken hat, wie mehrere Jemtische Gemeinden, nebst Myssjö, seine eigenthümliche Tracht: graue Walmarröcke mit blauen Kragen; man trägt auch lederne Kleidung. Mehrere Bauern treiben Handel. Ein Kirchspielsmagazin ist vorhanden, welches schon aus 500 Tonnen besteht. Das Pastorat hat zwei ordentliche Geistliche, nämlich einen Pastor, der zu Oviken, und einen Comminister, der zu Hackås wohnt; letzterer predigt an einem Sonntage in Hackås und am andern in Myssjö. Bei der letzten Visitation im J. 1816 baten die Bewohner der Filialgemeinden, daß in ihren Kirchen öfter geprediget werden möge, welches sich aber nicht ins Werk richten ließ. Oviken's Pastorat hat zwei Gesundbrunnen: Eltnäset, eine Quelle, die viel Eisen neben Kalch und Kohlensäure hält, und die sehr schwefelhaltige Quelle Wattjom. — Bevor die Trivialschule auf Fröjön eingerichtet ward, hatte Oviken eine größere Schule.

Um 4½ Uhr verließ ich Oviken, von da, oder eigentlich vom Gästgifvaregård Bugård, der der Kirche ganz nahe liegt, hat man bis Hofvermo 1½ M. Mein Skjutsbonde war dieß mal ein sanftes 17jähriges Mädchen, dessen ganzes Wesen die holdeste Unschuld verkündete. Der Vater geleitete sie, bis der schwerste Weg, eine steile Anhöhe, überstanden war. Bald erreicht man am Wege einen Hügel, der die ganze Gegend beherrscht. Ich ließ halten, um mich an der herrlichen Aussicht zu laben. Man überblickt den Storsiö mit Frösön, eine große, nur von Hügeln unterbrochene Ebene, nebst Ovikens-Fjäll und den Alpen von Herjeådalen (Hede-Fjäll). Der Weg führt neben Gebüschen und Wiesen und durch Wald längs des mit dem Storsiö zusammenhängenden Myssö-Sees, dessen grünende Ufer Höfe und Dörfer bedecken, nach Hofvermo, einem sehr mittelmäßigen Gasthofe, wo ich, da es schon 7½ Uhr war, als ich anlängte, übernachtete.

Am 11. September. Von Hofvermo nach Bergsby ¼ M. von B. nach Oster-Äsarna 2¼ M. — Zus. 3¼ M.

Frühe fuhr ich aus, nachdem ich meine Wirthe hatte wecken müssen. Man hat noch immer zur Linken den See von Myssö, der hier aber schon in den Storsiö tritt und den See von Berg bildet; die Ufer sind fruchtbar und stark bewohnt. Bergsby ist ein Dorf zunächst der Kirche Berg. Die Kirche ist von Stein und ward um 1796 durch einen Helsingländer, Namens Loell, erbauet; die Vergoldungen und Malereyen sind von Pehr Sundin zu Orviken in Sunne, die Bildhauerarbeit von Edeler in Lockße; die Orgel von Hammerdal aus Arbrä 1814 erbauet. Die Kirche ist die schönste Landkirche, welche ich bisher in Schweden, wo es der schönen Kirchen so viele giebt, sah, in einem großen und erhabenen Styl. Der Altar wird von vier Säulen getragen, über welche sich ein Bogen wölbt, der eine Wolke mit dem Dreiecke und den Strahlen der Gottheit trägt; zur Seite vergoldete Vasen; den Hintergrund bildet ein an der Wand gemalter Tempelvorhang, den Engel halten. Eben so ist, zwischen den vier Säulen, in einer viereckigen Nische der Eingang zu einem Tempel gemalt; darüber erhebt sich, in erha-

II.   N n

unter Arbeit, auf einem, mit dem Kelch, der Bibel und anderen heiligen Emblemen geschmückten Piedestal, das Lamm mit der Kreuzesfahne; nach außen lehnen sich an die Säulen zwei große weibliche Figuren, der Glaube und die Hoffnung, diese mit dem Anker, jene mit unaussprechlicher Ergebung betend; Alles vergoldet, und treffliche Produkte der Bildhauerey. Auf den Altarschranken liest man die Inschrift 1 Johannis 4, 16: „wir haben erkannt und geglaubet die Liebe, die Gott zu uns hat."

Die weite Kanzel entspricht dem großen und erhabenen Maaßstabe des Ganzen. Sie ist stark vergoldet, und auf der äußeren Seite mit den Gesetzestafeln, dem Kreuz und dem Kelche geschmückt; von der Decke der Kanzel hängt eine vergoldete Taube, das Symbol des heil. Geistes (wie gewöhnlich in den Schwedischen Kirchen) herab.

Das Piedestal, auf welches die Taufschaale gestellt wird, deckt eine Bibel; hier erblickt man eine Figur, welche Johannes den Täufer darstellt, wie er mit der einen Hand auf die Bibel zeigt und mit der andern ein Kreuz umfaßt.

Die Orgel von 8 Registern, welche 800 Bankthaler kostet, zieren allerlei biblische Gemälde und die Inschrift: „Lobsinget dem Herrn! Halleluiah!" Neben der Orgel findet man die Chöre für die Jünglinge und die Soldaten. Die verheirateten Männer und Frauen sitzen unten; eben so die Mädchen, hinter den Frauen.

Das Gewölbe der Kirche ist von Gyps; aus Holz erbauet würde es zweckmäßiger seyn; denn jetzt ist das Echo so stark, daß der Prediger schwer verstanden wird.

Das Pastorat Berg (21 □M.) besteht aus 4 Gemeinden: der Muttergemeinde Berg, im J. 1815 mit 894, den Filialgemeinden Klößjö mit 469 und Rätan mit 573, so wie der Kapellgemeinde Åsarna mit 328 Seelen. Der Ackerbau giebt meistens das nothwendige Korn; doch weit beträchtlicher ist die Viehzucht; auch gewinnt man Kohlen und Theer, und bei Åsarna wird Mooreisen bereitet. Einiger Handel wird getrieben. Im Ganzen herrscht wenig Wohlhabenheit. Einfachheit und Sitten reinheit haben sich, insbesondere in Rätan und Åsarna, in einem hohen Grade erhalten, zum Theil auch in Klöffjö. In Åsarna giebt es noch jetzt nicht ein einziges geschwängertes Mädchen, in Rätan wenige; in den J. 1749 bis 1773, also in einer Reihe von 24 Jahren, und auch in spätern Jahren, z. B. 1806 bis 1816 wurde in Rätan kein uneheliches Kind geboren; in dem Zeitraume von 1749 bis 1773 gab es auch in Klöffjö keine, und in Berg's Kirchspiel nur 2 uneheliche Kinder. In den Jahren 1800, 1803, 1807, 1808, 1809, 1810, 1813 und 1814 wurden im ganzen Pastorat keine uneheliche Kinder geboren. Freilich wird aber auch Unkeuschheit allgemein und tief verachtet, und während ehrliche Mädchen mit rosenrothen und andern hell farbigen Mützen gehen, dürfen unkeusche Mädchen in der Kirche, nur mit dunkelbraunen oder dunkelblauen Mützen erscheinen, und auch im alltäglichen Leben sich nur wie Frauen kleiden, d. i. ihren ganzen Kopf mit Tüchern umwinden, während die Mädchen den obersten Theil des Kopfes unumwunden tragen. Antecipirter Beischlaf findet im Pastorat, unter den jährlichen 20 bis 30 Ehen, etwa bei 3 Statt. Der nächtliche Ehrenbesuch ist allgemein. Zur Kirche geht man sehr fleißig und der Sonntag wird ernst und würdig gefeiert. Im ganzen Pastorat giebt es nur zwei ordentliche Geistliche, einen Pastor zu Berg, welcher 7mal im Jahre in der Kapelle Åsarna predigt, und 1 Comminister zu Rätan, welcher an dem einen Sonntag in Rätan, an dem andern in Klöffjö den Gottesdienst verrichtet. Dem Comminister kauften vor einigen Jahrzehnten die Gemeinden Rätan und Klöffjö einen eigenen Amtshof, bis dahin hatte nur der Pastor ein Vorstelle. Auch an den Sonntagen, wo keine Predigt ist, versammelt sich, im Sommer, die Gemeinde von Åsarna zum Gesang, Gebet und Postillenlesen in ihrer uralten Kapelle, wozu zweimal geläutet wird; im Winter treten die Höfe zum Dorfgottesdienst zusammen. Am Sonnabend-Abend hält jeder Hausvater mit den Seinigen Gebet, wobei auch gesungen wird, nachdem von 4 Uhr Nachmittags an alle Arbeit ruhet und der Sabbat, wie man hier spricht, begonnen hat. Am Sonntag-Nachmittag wird in jedem einzelnen Hofe in Predigtbüchern gelesen. — Nach-geendigter Heu- und Kornerndte, wie in der Winterzeit, hält man einfache frohe Mahle mit Tanz; aber Völlerey ist selten und Kartenspiel unbekannt.

Von Berg aus bestieg ich, in Begleitung des dermaligen Pastoratsverwalters im Gnadenjahre (nadatspredikant) und bisherigen Adjuncten Zetterberg (Sohn des vormaligen Propstes Doctor Zetterberg in Brunflo), des Lieutenants Challiere und eines Wegweisers, den in den geographischen Handbüchern seiner weiten Aussicht wegen, die sich über 18 Kirchen ausdehnen soll, vielgepriesenen nahen bewaldeten Hofverberg. Von einem Torp am Wege aus erreichten wir, nach halbstündigem Steigen, auf steilem, mit losen Steintrümmern bedecktem Pfade, den Gipfel des Berges, welchen ein Holzstoß (vardkase) aus pyramidalisch gestellten Stangen bezeichnet; die Aussicht ist allerdings sehr schön, wiewohl Höhenrauch die meisten Alpen dem Anblick entzog; der Storsjö mit seinen verschiedenen Busen breitet sich unter seinen Füßen aus, und mehrere Kirchen sind sichtbar; aber 18 Kirchen konnte ich nicht zählen. Ueberhaupt rauben Bäume nach mehrern Punkten hin die Aussicht.

Nachdem ich im Gästgifvaregård eine kleine Mahlzeit gehalten, holte ich vom Pfarrhofe die Wittwe des Brukspatron Wittlund von Ljusnedal in Herjeådalen, welche in meiner Gesellschaft die bevorstehende beschwerliche Bergreise nach Herjeådalen zu machen wünschte, ab und trat dann um 3 Uhr die Reise nach Asarna an. Gleich anfangs ist der Weg sehr bergig, insbesondere waren zwei steile Berge schwer zu passiren. Von den Bergrücken hat man ost schöne und weite Aussichten über die untenliegende Gebirgsebene. Oft verlieren sich die Anhöhen in tiefe, schauerliche Abgründe. Der Wald ist gemischt. Man kommt mehreren militairischen Boställen, einem Sennendorf und dem Dorfe Tosteråsen vorüber. Tosteråsen liegt am Abhange eines Berges. Auf der Höhe ist die Aussicht auf das Dorf, ein liebliches grünes Waldthal und seitwärts auf die Alpen von Oviken besonders schön. Hinter Tosteråsen fährt man über niedere Berge auf und ab im Walde, bis man die Kapelle Asarna erreicht, welche östlich und westlich vom Dorfe gleiches Namens umgeben wird; der Gåstgifvaregård liegt im östlichen Dorfe, dort nahm meine Begleiterin Quartier; ich aber übernachtete beim Kyrkovård im westlichen Dorfe, nahe der kleinen hölzernen Kapelle, deren Altar ein hübsches Gemälde schmücket: die Engel, in den Lüften die Geburt des Herrn feiernd, und die Könige des Morgenlandes, Ihm ihre Gaben bringend. An der Kanzel erblickt man in Holz und vergoldet die Bildnisse der Evangelisten mit den Sinnbildern eines Löwen, Adlers ꝛc.

Beim Kirchenvorsteher hatte ich es recht gut; alles war nett, reinlich und freundlich und die Kost gut. Am Abend wartete die Schwiegertochter auf; als ich sie am folgenden Morgen bei der Abreise vermißte, ließ ich sie grüßen. Da berichtete der alte Mann: der liebe Gott habe sie in der Nacht mit einem Söhnlein erfreuet. Ich eilte, ihr noch persönlich meinen Glückwunsch zu bringen. Ich fand sie in ein Schaaffell (man schläft auch unter Ziegenfellen, die besonders weich und zweckmäßig sind) gehüllt, kräftig und heiter, wie am Abend zuvor; sie erklärte, sie befinde sich recht wohl, und doch war sie nur vor einer Stunde entbunden worden. Innige Freude und Ergebung sprach ihr schönes Antlitz aus; neben ihrem Bette ruhte das Knäblein, an einem Beutelchen mit Zucker und Brot saugend, auf der Bank ruhte der über den Erstgebornen hocherfreute Vater.

Am 12. Septembr. Von Åsarna nach Klöffjö 2 M.

Um 6½ Uhr brach ich auf; aber mein Skjutsbonde schien des Fahrens wenig kundig; denn er fuhr gegen einen Schlagbaum; ich ließ daher erst einen andern an seine Stelle treten, holte die gute Alte vom Gåstgifvaregård ab, und so erfolgte endlich um 7¾ Uhr die Abreise. Hinter Åsarna fährt man über den Ljungan. Die Gegend ist wild und schauerlich, nichts als Wald und Berge, die zum Theil schon den Namen Klöffjö-Fjäll führen, von deren Höhe man hübsche Waldaussichten hat. Die höchsten dieser Berge sind: der Skarberg, wo man ¼ M. bergauf zu fahren hat, und zwar zur Hälfte sehr steil; hier ist es unmöglich, auf dem Wagen zu bleiben; — und Brandhinga, gleich hoch, aber minder steil. Am Fuße des Starberges liegen Sennhütten, die einzigen Menschenwohnungen auf dem ganzen Wege bis Klössö. In einer dieser Hütten sprach ich vor und ließ mir von der Sennin Milch reichen; als ich bezahlen wollte, weigerte sich das Mädchen, Bezahlung anzunehmen. Die Wohnstube ist zugleich Küche; an den Wänden laufen Bretter, die als Schlafstätte dienen, in der Mitte der Stube wird Käse gekocht. Den Mädchen der übrigen Hütten begegneten wir, die Kühe weidend, am Wege. Alle waren von schöner und kräftiger Körperbildung; nur die, der Witterung Trotz bietende Kleidung entstellte. Um 12½ Uhr waren wir im Gästgifvaregård des Dorfes Klössö. Die Hausfrau kam, von frischen und kräftigen Kindern umgeben, uns mit biederem Händedruck entgegen. Einen dreijährigen Knaben stillte sie noch, denn, wie in andern Norrländischen Provinzen, so saugen auch in Jemtland nicht blos drei-, nein 5 und 6jährige Kinder; in Herjeådalen stillt man zwei bis dritthalb Jahre. Die Jemtländischen Wiegen (auch in Medelpad fand ich sie) sind sehr eigenthümlich: an Schnuren von Balken herabhängende Wagschaalen, in welchen die Kinder sich schaukeln.

In Klössö lebt ein biederer Schlag von Menschen; so freundlich und gefällig und so dankbar auch für das Geringste. Sie sind groß von Statur und fast alle schön gestaltet, ihre Zähne sind weiß wie Elfenbein.

Die Kirche liegt ¼ M. vom Dorfe entfernt, in einem schönen Thale am See Foting, der mit dem Ljungan oder dem nach Medelpad herabgehenden Zuge von Seen und Flüssen zusammenhängt. Sie ist von Holz, und ward vor etwa 20 Jahren erbauet; ihr Inneres ist freundlich und würdig.

Sieben und zwanzigstes Kapitel.

Reise in Herjeådalen.

Reise zu Wagen über die Klössö-Alpe: nächtliches Bivouac. — Die erste Sennhütte in Herjeådalen.

Wemdalen. — Der Kirchenmaler Sandin. — Die kunstliebende Bauernfamilie. — Hohe Unschuld der Menschen. — Kirche Hede. — Gottesdienst der Herjedaler. — Die Landschaft Herjedalen und ihre Bewohner. — Pastorat Hede. — Armuth und Frömmigkeit. — Mildthätigkeit der armen Einwohner. — Ackerbau; frühe Nachtfröste. — Viehzucht; der Kronkäse. — Jagd; die Bogensteuer. — Die hohen Gränzalpen. — Wege nach Norwegen. — Flüsse Ljusnan und Ljungan. — Eisenbruk Ljusnedal. — Ljusnedals Marmor. — Herjedalens Lappen. — Markt in Herjedalen. Kein Postamt, keine Apotheke, kein Arzt. — Der Mützenraub. — Moos- und Rindenbrot. — Oder Weg. — Die Bäuerin aus Longäs und der Norwegische Bauer. — Kirche Lindsäll; wilde Rennthiere. — Das Lillsthal. — Ollseberg. — Fluß und Thal Herjeå. — Kirche Lill-Herdal. — Kirche Sveg; altes Gemälde. — Pastorat Sveg. — Die Außenhöfe (bolanden). — Die Finnendörfer. — Gesundbrunnen. — Ein Bauer als Arzt. — Der Krieg von 1788. — Der Landsturm; die lodernden Holzstöße auf den Bergen; die Sammelplätze. — Die Mühlen an der Säbkna. — Brot aus Rinde und Aehrenspitzen. — Kirche und Dorf Elfros. — Fähre über den Ljusnan. — Kälsätt. — Eintritt in Helsingland.

———————

Am 12. und 13. Sept. Von Klöfsjö nach Wemdalen 2 M.; von W. nach Hede 2 M.

Klöfsjö ist der letzte Gästgifvaregärd in Jemtland und Gränzkirchspiel gegen Herjedalen. Furchtbare Alpenketten, die eigentlichen Klöfsjö-Fjäll, höher als die gleichbenannten Alpen zwischen Åsarna und Klöfsjö, trennen beide Landschaften, die im Sommer nur mittelst eines Reitweges, der indeß zur Noth auch mit zweirädrigem, von gehöriger Mannschaft begleitetem, Fuhrwerk befahren werden kann, Communication haben: wer mit vierrädrigem Fuhrwerk versehen ist, oder seine Kärra nicht der Gefahr der Zertrümmerung und sich selbst der Unannehmlichkeit einer höchst langsamen Reise aussetzen will, muß einen Umweg von 10 bis 25 Meilen machen, je nachdem er ins niedere,

mittlere oder obere Herjeådalen, von Jemteland aus, reiset, und
selbst dieser Umweg führt ihn auf beschwerliche Pfade; wer ge-
mächlich reisen will, fährt durch Medelpad und Helsingland, und
hat dann einen Umweg von mehr denn 40 Meilen. Diese Unannehmlichkeit zu vermeiden, und beide Provinzen durch eine
zu allen Jahreszeiten fahrbare Straße zu verbinden, wird gegenwärtig an einem neuen Wege zwischen Jemteland und Herjeådalen gearbeitet *), der von Berg bis Weimdalen 6 Meilen
fortlaufen und die hohen Berge vermeiden soll, was auch nicht
schwierig ist, da meistens Thäler in der Nähe sind, welche benutzt werden können.

Ich hatte beschlossen, auf dem kürzesten Wege Herjeådalen
zu erreichen, und ließ sofort nach meiner Ankunft in Klössjö alles in Bereitschaft setzen, was zur beschwerlichen Alpenreise erforderlich war. Die Kärra mußte völlig entladen werden, um,
wo es nöthig seyn sollte, von der begleitenden Mannschaft über
die Felsenstücke, die das Rad hemmen, gehoben oder selbst eine
Strecke getragen werden zu können; mittlerweile konnte ich denn
im leeren Wagen meinen Platz finden, die Sachen aber wurden
auf ein Pferd gepackt, und zwar in Körben, die zu beiden Seiten des Pferdes herabhingen. Alle diese Vorrichtungen füllten
mehrere Stunden aus, so daß wir erst um 4½ Uhr Klössjö verließen; Frau Wiklund ritt; ich aber fuhr oder ging zu Fuße,
je nach den Umständen. Nachdem wir noch keine Viertelmeile
zurückgelegt, begann der Bergweg; fast eine Viertelmeile fuhr
ich bergan, zuweilen beinahe senkrecht, unter lieblichen Rückblik-
ken auf das schöne Klössjöthal; der Weg war mit Steinen wie
besäet; manche Steine waren bis 1½ Ellen hoch. Und doch war
dies schon ein neuer Weg; der alte, der in der Nähe läuft und
noch vor wenigen Jahren benutzt wurde, ist noch steiler, hat
ordentliche Stufen und ist völlig unfahrbar; man begreift selbst
nicht, wie er bergab geritten werden konnte. Nach einer Stunde
hatten wir die Höhe erreicht: der Pfad wird nun ebener: man

*) Dieser neue Weg ward im J. 1821 vollendet; die Arbeit war
von den Einwohnern für 8000 Bankthaler verrichtet worden.

fährt auf dem Klöffjö-Fjäll hin, das meist schon zu Herjeädalen gehört, kleinere Höhen auf und ab, — über dichten Felsenschutt, über Bäche und Sümpfe ohne Brücken, und oft ist
der Weg so schmal, daß nur mit Mühe die Räder zwischen den
Felsen durchgezogen wurden. In 5¼ Stunden hatten wir noch
nicht völlig die erste Meile zurückgelegt, und machten, da die
Dunkelheit einbrach, an dem erhöheten Wiesenufer eines Baches,
der gewöhnlichen Ruhestelle der Reisenden, Halt. Ein Feuer
ward angezündet, gespeiset, und dann von 11 bis 4 Uhr Morgens geschlafen, Frau Wiklund ruhte in ihrem Reitstuhl, ich in
der Kärra, die Skjutsbauern auf bloßer Erde; die milde Som-
mernacht begünstigte das nächtliche Bivouac; gegen den starken Thau schützte die Kleidung.—Um 4¾ Uhr ward die Reise
fortgesetzt; bald trafen wir die ersten Meilenpfosten. Der Weg
läuft meist sanft bergab, nur einmal eine lange Strecke, wenig steil, bergan; aber schwierige, schmale Brücken konnten nicht
ohne Gefahr passirt werden. Jetzt erblickt man wieder Holz,
welches dichter und häufiger wird, je näher man Wemdalen
kommt. Wie freuten wir uns, als wir nun zuerst wieder Menschen sahen. Sie wunderten sich, eine Kärra vom Fjäll kommen zu sehen, um so mehr da sie unzertrümmert war. Auf
der letzten halben Meile führt der Weg einer Sennhütte vorüber, in welcher ich mich mit kräftiger Alpenmilch labte. Dieß
war die einzige Menschenwohnung auf dem ganzen Wege seit
Klöffjö. Nebel raubten die Ansicht des Thales, in welchem Wems-
dalen liegt, wo wir um 8¾ Uhr anlangten und also auf 2 M.
9¼ Stunden gebraucht hatten. Die Bezahlung war nicht be-
dungen worden; ich glaubte daher einen jeden bezahlen zu müssen, je nachdem er thätig und behülflich gewesen war; der eine
hatte sich die Sache weniger angelegen seyn lassen, hatte schon
unterweges Verweise erhalten und empfing nun die geringere,
aber genügende Bezahlung, womit er nicht nur völlig zufrieden
war, sondern, damit ich nicht unwillig bliebe, kam er noch späterhin zu mir und drückte mir herzlich die Hand. Einem anderen, der eine vorzügliche Sorgfalt und Thätigkeit bewiesen, be-
zeugte ich meine besondere Zufriedenheit, und äußerte, daß er

mehr verdient habe und empfangen solle, als sein Kamerad (zwei
andere waren schon früher, als die schwierigsten Stellen überstanden waren, wieder umgekehrt). Edelmüthig entgegnete er
aber: er habe nichts mehr gethan, als der andere, und wisse
daher auch nicht, wodurch er sich Anspruch auf meine vorzügliche Dankbarkeit erworben habe. Schon unterwegs hatte ich
bemerkt, wie der eine dem andern auch da, wo er selbst ent-
behrte, mitgetheilt. Natürlich empfingen nun beide reichlich.

In Wemdalen verweilte ich ein Paar Stunden in der
schlichten biederen Familie des Länsmans Svensson, der zugleich
Gästgifware ist; nachdem ich Hunger und Durst gestillet, brach
ich um 10½ Uhr auf, zuerst zur Kirche; Svensson begleitete
mich; die Kirche ist ein einfaches Gebäude mit Thurm; aus dem
Thurm überschauet man das fruchtbare Thal, in welchem sich
das große, von 52 Bauern bewohnte, Dorf ausbreitet. In der
Kirche fand ich den schon oft genannten Maler Pehr Sundin,
aus Orrviken in Sunne, beschäftigt, die Kirche mit Malerey
und Vergoldung zu schmücken; ein einfacher Bauersmann, bescheiden und anspruchlos, und doch der größte jetzt lebende Kirchenmaler, der dem verstorbenen Hörberg mit Recht an die Seite
gesetzt werden kann. Schon sein Vater war Maler, hat auch
einige Kirchen mit Gemälden geziert; doch brachte er es nicht
sehr weit in der Kunst. Aber die Neigung des Vaters weckte
die Neigung des Sohnes, der indeß, was er geworden ist, meist
durch sich selber ward. Er fing damit an, Gebüsche und Vögel zu
malen; bald brachte er es dahin, daß er biblische Gemälde, und,
noch häufiger, Kupferstiche copirte; diese trefflichen Copieen schmück-
ten viele Kirchen, insbesondere Jemtelands und Herjeådalens;
als eine seiner vorzüglichsten Arbeiten nennt man die „Abnahme
Christi vom Kreuz" in der Jemteländischen Kirche Röbön. In
späteren Jahren kam er nach Stockholm, lernte eine kurze Zeit
bei einem dortigen Maler, wohnte, freilich nur 16 Stunden,
dem Unterricht in der Akademie der freien Künste bei, und gewann eine Medaille der Akademie. In seiner Mappe sah ich
ein Paar wohlgelungene Bilder von Lappen, die nicht Copie,
sondern ganz eigene Arbeit waren. Er ist auch ein tüchtiger

Baumeister und überhaupt geschickt in allerlei Künsten und Handarbeiten. Einer seiner Söhne, Göran, scheint in des Vat-
ters Fußtapfen zu treten; erst 10 Jahre alt, hat er schon einige wohlgelungene Zeichnungen gefertiget, die in Stockholm großen Beifall fanden und ihm die Unterstützung des damaligen
Kronprinzen, jetzigen Königs, erwarben; im nächsten Winter
wollte ihn der Vater nach Stockholm bringen.

Der Weg nach Hede führt bis Wiken, wo nur, wenn man
von Hede nach Ransjö fährt, Pferdewechsel ist, — anfangs durch
Laub-, dann durch Nadelwald über den südlichen Arm des Wer-
man. Bei Wiken kommt man an den Ljusnan, der hier einen
See bildet, und fährt nun im Nadelwalde längs des Flusses,
doch ohne ihn oft ansichtig zu werden; den Boden deckt Lingon
und dürres Rennthiermoos. Mein Skjutsbonde war ein holder
18jähriger Jüngling mit blonden Haaren, voll Unschuld in seinen
Blicken, voll Ernst und Würde in seinem ganzen Wesen. In
Wemdalen herrscht noch ein hoher Grad von Sitteneinfalt und
Sittenreinheit; alles ist so herzlich, freundlich und liebevoll; der
Handdruck dieser offenen biederen Menschen, die in allen Menschen nur Brüder und Schwestern sehen, schüttert durch Mark
und Bein; man ist bei ihnen gleich wie unter alten Bekannten,
und fühlt es tief, was der Mensch dem Menschen auch ohne
äußere Glücksgüter zu seyn vermag! Solche Empfindungen
waren schon oft in mir, auf meiner Reise durch den Norden,
erwacht, doch nie stärker wie in Herjeådalen!

Eine halbe Meile vor Hede begegnete ich dem Pfarrherrn
des Orts, Runith, und seinem Adjuncten Edlund, die von einem
Hemman zurückkehrten, das der Pastor für seine Wittwe gekauft
hatte. Ich mußte mich nun anschließen, schickte meinen Wagen
auf der Landstraße zum Pfarrhofe, und begab mich selbst dahin
auf einem kürzeren Wege über den Ljusnan und am jenseitigen
Ufer dieses Flusses. Frau Wiklund folgte nach.

Fast 2 volle Tage blieb ich in Hede; denn der folgende
Tag war Sonntag, und ich wollte dem Gottesdienst unter den
Herjeådalern beiwohnen.

Hede ist eines der beiden Pastorate, in welche Herjeådalen

in kirchlicher Hinsicht zerfällt, umfaßt den oberen Theil des Landes und enthält, außer der Mutterkirche Hede, die Filialkirche Wemdalen und die Kapellen Storsjö, Ljusnedal und Tennäs. Diese 5 Kirchen haben nur zwei festangestellte Geistliche, daher denn nur in Hede, mit Ausnahme von zwei Sonntagen, sonntäglich, in Wemdalen aber nur einen Sonntag um den andern, in Tennäs nur 12 Mal, in Ljusnedal 4 Mal, und in Storsjö gar nur 2 Mal jährlich Gottesdienst gehalten wird; und doch zählte im J. 1815 Hede 512, Wemdalen 527, Tennäs 398, Ljusnedal 235, Storsjö 170, das ganze Pastorat also 1842 Einwohner; die Zahl der Geistlichen ist also offenbar viel zu geringe, auch die Kirchen liegen zu weit von einander; denn jede der Kapellen ist 5 Meilen von der Mutterkirche entfernt; meist Reitweg, nach Storsjö über Reitweg, ohne alle Menschenwohnungen, bis auf ein einziges Nybygge, Serfsjön. Aber dem Uebel ist schwer abzuhelfen, denn die Gemeinden sind zu arm, um mehrere Geistliche unterhalten zu können; wurde indeß ein Kapellprediger für Tennäs und Ljusnedal, welche Kapellen nur 1¾ M. von einander entfernt sind, angestellt; so wäre wenigstens einigermaaßen geholfen. — An den Sonntagen, wo der Gottesdienst ausfällt, halten die Küster in den Kirchen Postillenlesung, wofür sie von den Bauern besonders remunerirt zu werden pflegen.

Am folgenden Morgen war Gottesdienst in der Kirche Hede. Kurz vor dem letzten oder dem Zusammen-Läuten (Läuten mit allen Glocken) ging ich zur Kirche. Auf dem Kirchhofe waren die Leute schon versammelt; in dem Augenblick, wo nun das letzte Läuten begann, entblößten in stiller Andacht die Männer ihr Haupt: man flehte um Segen für die Stunde, deren Anfang eben verkündet wurde; die gleiche Sitte soll auch in Jemteländischen Gemeinden sich finden. Alles begab sich nun zur Kirche und der Gottesdienst hob an. Langsam und mit großer Innigkeit ward gesungen, und während des ganzen Gottesdienstes herrschte die tiefste Stille, die gespannteste Aufmerksamkeit und die herzlichste Andacht, mit sehnsuchtsvoller Begierde hörte man auf das Wort des Geistlichen; ein Schwerhörender trat sogar beim Anfang der Predigt hinter den Prediger auf die Kanzel, damit ihm nichts entgehe, und blieb dort, bis die Predigt geendigt war und die Kirchengebete begannen, die er auswendig wußte. Vor der ersten Verlesung des Sündenbekenntnisses, die nach der Liturgie der Schwedischen Kirche, bald nach dem Anfange des Gottesdienstes erfolgt, wurden die Kirchthüren geschlossen und erst nach Beendigung des Gottesdienstes wieder geöffnet. Nachdem die Gemeinde zum Schlusse, kniend, den Segen empfangen, begab sie sich, unter Vortritt des Predigers, erst das männliche, dann das weibliche Geschlecht, aus der Kirche. Einige blieben noch auf dem Kirchhofe stehen; aber keine laute Rede vernahm man; alles zeugte von der Ehrfurcht, die der heiligen Zeit und dem heiligen Orte gebührt.

Die Kleidung der Leute ist sehr einfach: Männer und Weiber sind in Walmar gekleidet, die Männer haben meist graue oder dunkele lange Röcke, zum Theil mit grünen Scherfen; die Frauen und Mädchen gehen in weißen Hemdsärmeln, und mit schwarzseidenen oder kattunenen Schürzen; die Frauen tragen schwarzseidene Mützen, mit schmalen Spitzen und mit einer, vorne auf die Stirne herabfallenden, zungenförmigen Spitze; die Mädchen flechten Bänder in dem Haaren, von bunter Wolle oder Seide, oder Tücher um den Kopf gewunden, doch auch im Winter farbige Mützen; Frauen und Mädchen flechten das Haar; die Mädchen tragen Schuhschnallen und Halsketten mit Medaillen ꝛc. Die Halstücher sind von Kattun oder Seidenzeug. Früherhin trugen alle Frauenzimmer scharlachrothe Strümpfe; jetzt haben mehrere diese alte Sitte abgelegt. Bei ihren Arbeiten tragen die Mädchen lederne Schürzen. Beide Geschlechter sind von gedrungenem Körperbau und mittlerer Statur, frisch und kräftig; aber selbst unter den Mädchen sieht man wenige schöne Gesichter; in Wendalen sind sie desto häufiger; in ihrem ganzen Wesen spricht sich hohe Unschuld, Ernst mit Milde gepaart, und Innigkeit aus; selbst bei der Jugend herrscht jener Ernst, doch ohne alle Trübseligkeit.

Die Kirche ist ein freundliches, steinernes Gebäude, ohne Thurm. Den Altar schmückt ein Gemälde Sundin's des Vaters, eine der ersten Arbeiten dieses Künstlers: „ein Kreuz von

einer Schlange umwunden; über dem Kreuze Wolken mit En=
geln, ganz oben eine Sonne mit dem Dreieck und dem Auge
Gottes; unter dem Kreuze ein Kelch." —— Der Altar ist stark
vergoldet und mit mehreren passenden biblischen Emblemen ge=
ziert. Auch an dem hölzernen Gewölbe der Kirche erblickt man
biblische Gemälde, die sich auf Tod und Gericht beziehen: schwarze
Wolken mit der Sichel und dem Stundenglase, das Auge Got=
tes, den Erlöser in den Wolken mit den Schaaren der Engel,
einen verklärten Beter. —— Auf dem Kirchhof steht ein hölzerner
Glockenthurm, aus welchem man eine hübsche Aussicht auf das
Thal des Ljusnan hat; das aus 26 Bauern bestehende Dorf
Hede breitet sich unfern der Kirche im Thale aus; die Felder
und Wiesen und das vielfarbige herbstliche Laub der Gebüsche
bildeten ein gar liebliches Ganze; rechts zeigte sich im Süden
das nahe Sühnfjäll mit seinen schroffen Felsenwänden, auf
einige Ueberbleibsel von Schnee waren sichtbar; sonst sind die
Schneefelder auf der Alpe gewöhnlich noch bedeutender. Die
übrigen nahen Berge steigen nicht zur Höhe der Alpen hinan;
zwischen ihnen laufen Thäler, die von Flüssen bewässert werden,
das Gerithal (Sersdalen) und das Ljusthal (Ljusdalen); die
Bäche, wie die Luna, ergießen sich bei Hede in den Ljusnan=Elf.
—— Ueberhaupt besteht ganz Herjeådalen, in einer Länge von
24 und einer Breite von 12 Meilen, aus Alpen, niederen Ber=
gen und Flußthälern; weite Ebenen findet man gar nicht, desto
mehr Flüsse und Seen, welche letztere aber nur einen geringen
Umfang haben. Die Flußthäler sind meistens enge und haben
mageren Boden, daher der Kornbau eben so wenig bedeutend
werden kann, als Herjeådalen reich an malerischen Thälern ist.
Man säet zwar Roggen und Gerste; aber oft erfriert das Korn,
oder muß unreif gemähet werden; daher man selten das nöthige
Brodkorn, und fast nie Saatkorn, gewinnt; den Mangel des er=
steren ersetzt man, vorzugsweise in Mißwachsjahren, durch Rin=
denbrot, das letztere muß angekauft werden, und wenn gleich die
Allgemeine Magazin=Direction des Reichs in dieser Hinsicht den
armen Bewohnern von Herjeådalen schon sehr nützlich geworden
ist, indem sie ihnen Korn anlieh, so sind doch diese durch den

Ankauf von Saatkorn, ihrer mäßigen Lebensweise ungeachtet, so tief in Schulden gerathen, daß vielen die Wiederbezahlung unmöglich ist. Indeß lassen sich, an mehreren Orten, noch vortheilhafte Urbarmachungen vornehmen, falls die nöthigen Summen außerhalb der Provinz vorgeschossen würden; im Ganzen ist freilich die Gelegenheit zu Urbarmachungen in Herjeådalen geringer als in irgend einer andern Provinz; denn der Boden besteht fast überall nur aus Sand, daher, ein Paar Stellen ausgenommen, nicht geschwendet wird. In guten Jahren erndtet man wohl das 7te Korn vom Roggen, der aber nur wenig, und zwar als Winterroggen, gesäet wird, und das 6te von der Gerste; Hafer wird sehr wenig gesäet. Neuerdings hat man eine dem Sandhafer (Elymus arenarius) gleichende Grasart aufgefunden, die ein besseres und nahrhafteres Brot geben dürfte, als das Rindenbrot; in Island wird der Sandhafer zu Mehl und Grütze gebraucht. Die Viehzucht ist zwar sehr bedeutend, doch außer dem eigenen Bedarf, giebt sie nur so viel, als zu dem Kronsteuern erfordert wird, und es ist nicht abzusehen, wie das, durch mehrere harte Mißjahre so furchtbar gesteigerte, Elend der Bewohner von Herjeådalen soll gehoben werden können, wenn nicht eine Erlassung der freilich nicht sehr beträchtlichen (denn in der Regel wird hier nur die Hälfte dessen, was in andern Provinzen erlegt wird, bezahlt), aber doch unter den gegenwärtigen Umständen drückenden Kronsteuern eintritt. Fischerey und Jagd gewähren kaum mehr als den eigenen Bedarf; die Fischerey in den Flüssen ist sehr unbedeutend; bedeutender ist die Alpenfischerey in den Alpenseen, in welchen mehrere Forellenarten, Schnäpel, Aschen u. gefangen werden. Preißelbeeren (lingon), Blaubeeren, Multbeeren, wachsen überall in Menge, Erdbeeren wenig; Feldbeeren (Åkerbär) nur in Sveg. Einige Bauern treiben, für sich und für Andere, Handel, fahren mit ihren Produkten nach Norwegischen, und, noch häufiger, nach Schwedischen Orten; aus Norwegen bringen sie Pferde, die sie wieder verkaufen, Heringe und getrocknete Fische; aus Schweden Korn, Färbewaaren, Salz, Strömlinge, Rauch- und Schnupftabak u. zurück; Schnupftabak ist das erste Luxusbedürfniß der Bewohner von Herjeådalen. Nach Norwegen führt man auch Flachs und Leinewand aus Helsingland, Kupfer von Fahlun, Sensen aus Hedemora, und Lima-Bruk in Dalarne, die Butter wird meist nach Fahlun und Gefle verkauft; einige fahren mit Butter und Vögeln nach Stockholm. Auch Ochsen und Kühe werden nach Gefle verkauft.

Die meisten Dörfer in Herjeådalen, zumal in Hede, sind sehr groß; man kann aber auch Meilen reisen, ohne ein Dorf zu finden; einzelne Höfe giebts, verhältnißmäßig, wenige; am bebautesten sind die Ufer Ljusnan-Elf; die übrigen Thäler sind weniger angebauet. Aus den Waldungen ist kein Gewinn zu ziehen, da die Flüsse nicht stoßbar sind; der Wald besteht meist aus Nadel-, wenig aus Laubholz. Kohlen bereitet man nur zum eigenen Bedarf. Durch Salpeterzubereitung ist in den letzten Jahren einiges gewonnen worden. Kartoffeln gedeihen. — Eine Stadt findet man nicht, würde auch schwerlich in dem armen Lande bestehen können.

In allen äußern Leiden verzagt der Herjeådaler nie; er ist fest überzeugt, daß seine Armuth eine Schickung Gottes sey, die ihm zum Heile gereiche, und er harret, in stiller Ergebung und mit unerschütterlichem Vertrauen auf Gott, der besseren Zukunft. Kein Murren, keine Klage vernimmt man aus seinem Munde; seine heitere Frömmigkeit begleitet ihn bis zum Grabe. Bei schmaler und schlechter Kost ist er kräftig und gesund durch Arbeit, Mäßigkeit und Sittlichkeit, und möchte um keinen Preis seine Heimath mit einem andern Lande vertauschen.

Die alte Einfachheit, Treue und Sittenreinheit hat sich fast überall in Herjeådalen erhalten; nur einige Gränz-distrikte gegen Norwegen hin dürften eine Ausnahme machen. — In ihrer Armuth haben die Herjeådaler doch immer für Noth-leidende übrig; die armen Einwohner von Särna in Dalekarlien kommen bettelnd auch hieher und man läßt sie nicht unbeschenkt gehen.

In ganz Herjeådalen, welches, wie oben bemerkt, im Jahre 1815, 4514 Einwohner zählte, werden, in manchem Jahre, gar keine uneheliche Kinder geboren; in den Jahren 1800 bis 1815 betrug die Zahl der Geburten 1667, worunter 31 uneheliche; also war ungefähr das 54ste Kind unehelich; in der Gemeinde Lill-Herdal (zu Sveg gehörig) wurden in 14 Jahren keine uneheliche Kinder geboren; gefallene Mädchen haben eine auszeichnende dunkle Trauer-Tracht. Die Ehrennächte sind allgemein. Anticipirter Beischlaf ist selten. Ehescheidungen sind unbekannt, Ehezwiste selten, Fluchen und Schwören wird wenig gehört. Der Sonntag wird mit Ernst und Strenge, aus wahrem, innern Bedürfniß gefeiert; Dorfgottesdienst wird für die, welche nicht zur Kirche gingen, allgemein gehalten, auch in den Sennhütten; am Sonntage frühe und am Sonnabend-Abend hält jeder Hausvater Gebete. Die Sprache der Herjeådaler ist rein und wohlklingend, aber mit Norwegischen Wörtern vermischt.

Die Temperatur der Luft ist sehr veränderlich: während meines Aufenthalts in Hede war die Luft warm; plötzlich wehte ein kalter Alpenwind, und es ward empfindlich kalt, aber nach einigen Minuten war es auch schon wieder windstille und warm. Diese häufigen und plötzlichen kalten Alpenwinde lassen die wohlthätigen Nebel der Seen und Flüsse nicht aufkommen, und sind eben dadurch die Ursachen der häufigen und frühen Nachtfröste, die das Korn verderben; auch die den Feldern benachbarten vielen Moräste tragen zur Erzeugung der Nachtfröste bei. Der erste Schnee fällt um Michaelis, und tritt oft schon dann Schlittenbahn ein; erst um die Mitte Mai's weichen Schnee und Eis und kann gesäet werden; zu Ende Augusts oder im Anfange Septembers wird geerndtet, falls nicht die gefährlichen Tage des 21. 22. und 23. August, an welchen die Nachtfröste einzutreten pflegen, die Erndte vernichtet haben.

Die Häuser sind von Holz und niedrig; mit Brettern, oder wo Mangel an Sägemühlen ist, mit gespaltenem Holze gedeckt. Zum Dreschen bedient man sich zweier verbundener hölzerner Walzen, die von einem Pferde gezogen werden; den Umgang hält das Pferd aber nur 10 Minuten aus; dann muß geruhet oder gewechselt werden.

Die Alpenweide ist noch vorzüglicher, als in Jemteland; daher Milch und Käse äußerst fett und wohlschmeckend sind.

II.   O o

Der berühmte Kronkäse (kronost), der aus Herjeädalen kommt, wird aus der eintägigen Milch der ganzen Heerde eines Bauernhofes bereitet, und zwar ohne daß von der Milch die Sahne abgenommen worden. Einen solchen Käse muß jeder Bauer, der ein Hemmanstheil besitzt (die Hemmanstheile sind, seit Alters, hier sehr klein), jährlich an die Krone geben; daher der Name. Diese Käse werden vom Kronvoigt erhoben, und so vertheilt, daß ein Drittheil den beiden Pastoren und ein Drittheil den Kirchen zufällt, und nur ein Drittheil der Krone verbleibt; die Kirchen theilen ihr Drittheil mit dem Contractspropst, welcher von jeder Kirche 2 Liespfund (à 20 Pfund), statt der Propsttonne, erhält; die Krone giebt von ihrem Drittheil 24 Liespfund dem Obersten von Jemtelands Regiment als pars salarii, auch anderen Kronbeamten, und verkauft den Rest. Der Käse ist sehr fett und äußerst wohlschmeckend; frisch, ist er fast fließend, wie der Schweizerkäse aus Uri; nach einem Jahre wird er fest.

Die Viehzucht wird als Sennenwirthschaft getrieben; jeder Bauer hat 2 bis 3 Sennenweiden und Sennhütten, zwischen denen er in den Sommermonaten mit den Heerden umherzieht. Die meisten Flüsse treten über ihre Ufer und erhöhen dadurch die Fruchtbarkeit der anliegenden Wiesen. Auch Ziegen hält man, deren Milch zur Käsebereitung aber mit Kuhmilch vermischt wird. Im Winter wird viel Moos gefüttert.

Wie sehr von jeher die Bewohner von Herjeädalen der Jagd kundig waren, beweiset die sogenannte Bogensteuer, die, nach altem Gesetze, jeder, welcher das 15te Jahr zurückgelegt hat und als solcher muß den Bogen spannen können, erlegen soll, und die noch jetzt mit 4 Schillingen erlegt wird; wogegen aber die Mantalspenningar der Bauern wegfallen. In den Alpen, insbesondere auf dem Klöfsjöfjäll bei Wembalen, und auf dem Sähnfjäll, unweit Hede, bei Lindsäll und Lill-Herdal giebt es viele wilde Rennthiere, auf welche man auch Jagd macht. Elennthiere und Biber sind nur noch wenig zahlreich, Hermeline trifft man gar nicht.

Von Stellung rotirter Soldaten ist die Provinz frei, wogegen sie ein Aequivalent an Gelde entrichtet.

Knechte und Mägde bedingen sich zuweilen ein Paar Wintermonate aus, die sie in Helsingland und Medelpad zubringen, um sich durch Arbeit einiges Geld zu verdienen; auch vermiethen sie sich wohl auf ein Paar Jahre in Helsingland, kehren aber stets in ihre liebe Heimath zurück.

Das Pastorat Hede nimmt einen größern Flächenraum ein, als das Pastorat Sveg, und ist dennoch das minder bevölkerte; es hat nämlich eine viel größere Zahl von Alpen und einen noch unwirthbareren Boden als Sveg. Einige dieser Alpen erreichen, zumal an der Norwegischen Gränze, eine furchtbare Höhe; aber auch die niederen Alpen sind mit ewigem Schnee bedeckt. Diese Alpen sind Theile jener Kette von Schneebergen, die fast bis zum Nordkap hinaufreicht, ununterbrochen die Gränze Schwedens und Norwegens bildet, in den Lappmarken, wie im eigentlichen Schweden, — bei Herjeådalen aber sich in zwei Aeste spaltet, davon einer, das Dovrefjeed, südwestlich, durch Norwegen bis Flekkefjord in Christiansands Stift an der Südküste Norwegens, fortläuft, der andere aber an der Gränze durch Dalekarlien bis Nord-Wermeland fortstreicht. Die Kirchspiele Tennäs und noch mehr Ljusnedal bestehen fast nur aus Alpen. Hier wird fast gar kein Korn gebauet, sondern nur Viehzucht getrieben; Brot ißt man hier sehr wenig. Kartoffeln werden gebauet; sie erfrieren selten. Das Dorf Funnesdalen, unweit der Kirche Ljusnedal, aus 26 Bauern bestehend, ist durch Handel mit Norwegen, der aber wohl nicht immer auf rechtlichem Grunde ruhen mag, sehr wohlhabend geworden; die Einwohner sind aber rauhe und störrische Menschen; seit langen Zeiten, und noch vor Kurzem, hat man sie sogar, an Reisenden in den Fjällen verübten, Mordes beschuldigt, doch ohne daß die Beschuldigung hätte erwiesen werden können; sonst sind sie freilich keinem offenbaren Laster, auch nicht dem Trunke, ergeben. Die übrigen Einwohner von Ljusnedal und die von Tennäs sind vorzüglich gute Menschen.

Unweit Funnesdalen besteht, von Alters her, ein Gränz-
zollamt; neuerdings ist ein zweites zu Tennäs errichtet worden.
Auf Funnesdalsberget, einem Berge in der Nähe des Dorfes,
hat man weite Aussichten auf die Gränzalpen. — Im Sommer
giebt es aus Herjeådalen nur einen Fahrweg nach Norwegen:
von Ljusnedal, nämlich das Thal am Ljusnan-Elf aufwärts
nach dem Norwegischen Dorfe Stuedal, am Fuße des Skarsfjäll;
nach Ljusnedal giebt es aber nur Reitweg, denn der Fahrweg
reicht nur bis zum Dorfe und zur Schanze Longäs, 1½ Meile
oberhalb Hede; von Longäs hat man dann bis Ljusnedal noch
⅝ M. Reitweg, welcher aber, da der Boden trocken ist, ohne
große Beschwerde, in einen Fahrweg verwandelt werden könnte.
Der Winterweg nach Norwegen führt über Funnesdalen, ⅜ M.
von Ljusnedal, über das Flotta- und das Rutefjäll, eine der
Gränzalpen, nach Bröcken und nach den Kupfergruben von Rö-
raas. Von Tennäs, 1½ M. südlich von Ljusnedal, giebt es
gar keinen Weg nach Norwegen. Ein anderer Weg nach Norwegen, doch kein Fahrweg, läuft von der Kapelle Storsjö am
Ljungan-Elf, und über denselben unweit seines Ursprungs, über
den Mittå- und Nia-Elf, und das Skarsfjäll nach Stuedal. —
Im Feldzuge von 1808 kamen die Norweger über die Gränze
bis Ljusnedal, bezahlten aber alles baar und benahmen sich mu-
sterhaft gegen die Einwohner; noch heute rühmt man diese, auch
als Menschen ehrwürdigen Krieger. — Bevor Norwegen mit
Schweden vereiniget ward, zogen häufig Ausreißer durch Herjeådalen nach Norwegen, und aus Norwegen nach Schweden; jetzt
geschieht es seltener; sie verübten zuweilen Diebstähle.

Die beiden Hauptflüsse des Landes, der Ljusnan und Ljungan, entspringen im nördlichen Theile des Pastorats Hede; dieser an der nordwestlichen Gränze von Herjeådalen und Jemteland, oberhalb des Berges Grönddrren; jener an der Norwegischen Gränze, oberhalb Ljusnedal, am Fuße der Skarsalpen,
aus dem Ljusnesee. Der Ljusnan nimmt innerhalb Herjeådalen
die meisten dortigen größeren und kleineren Flüsse und Seen
auf, und fällt, nach einem langen Laufe durch Helsingland, unterhalb der Stadt Söderhamn im Helsingischen Kirchspiele Ska-

derala in den Bottnischen Meerbusen; der Ljungan fließt durch
einen kleinen Theil des nördlichen Herjeådalen, wo einige weni=
ge Flüsse ihm ihr Wasser zuführen, bei der Kapelle und dem
Dorfe Storsjö vorüber, tritt, durch den Flåsjö, in das südliche
Jemteland ein, wo er den Kirchen Åsarna und Råtan vorüber=
fließt, tritt oberhalb der Kirche Hafrö in Medelpad, durchströmt
diese Provinz, in ihrer ganzen Breite, von Westen nach Osten,
und ergießt sich, unfern der Kirche Njurunda, in den Bottni=
schen Meerbusen.

Ljusnedal ist ein ansehnliches Eisenbruk; hier sind Eisengru=
ben, ein Hochofen, ein Zainhammer ꝛc.; das Privileginm des
Bruks lautet auf 400 Schiffpfund jährlich; auf Kupfer wird
nicht mehr gebauet. Die Kapelle Ljusnedal war bis 1806 Bruks=
kirche; seit dieser Zeit ist kein besonderer Brukeprediger ange=
stellt. — Vor etwa 20 Jahren ward vom Bruksinspector in
Ljusnedal, Fjerrstedt, bei Funnesdal und Ljusnedal Marmor auf=
gefunden; dieser Marmor ist sehr dicht, schneeweiß, mit blauen
oder grauen Streifen, und klarer, als der Marmor Dalekar=
liens.

Auf den Alpen, längs der Gränze, weiden im Sommer
die Lappen von Herjeådalen; im Winter halten sie sich mit ih=
ren Heerden im niederen Lande des Pastorats Hede auf. Die
Seelsorge dieser Lappen und der Lappen von Oviken ist gegen=
wärtig dem Pastor und dem Comminister von Hede anvertraut;
bis 1780 ward sie vom Pastor zu Oviken verwaltet. Die Lap=
pen Herjeådalens sind Rennthierlappen, wenig zahlreich und
meist arm; vergl. Kapitel 13. Im Sommer versammeln sie sich
zum Gottesdienst in der Kapelle Storsjö.

In ganz Herjeådalen wird nur einmal im Jahre Markt ge=
halten, und zwar innerhalb des Pastorats Hede, zu Wemdalen,
wo am 2. September ein kleiner Viehmarkt Statt findet.

Auch Distriktsgericht (Ting) pflegt bei den Kirchen Hede
und Wemdalen gehalten zu werden.

Ein eigenes Postcomtoir besaß bisher Herjeådalen nicht;
die Briefe wurden nach der Kirche Sveg geschickt, wo sie der
dortige Kronvoigt entgegennahm und alle 14 Tage mit Post nach

dem nächsten Postamt in Helsingland, Delsbo (15¼ Meilen von Sveg), beförderte; auf gleiche Weise wurden die nach Herjeådalen bestimmten Briefe nach Sveg gesandt. Nur der Kronvoigt correspondirte nach Östersund über das Klössjöfjäll mittelst Gåstgifvare-Skjuts, also mittelst einer Amtspost, wie sie überall in Schweden zwischen den Kronbeamten auf dem Lande eingeführt ist. Der allgemeine Postengang war aber auf diese Weise sehr langsam, so daß nicht selten die Verordnungen, des Consistoriums z. B., zu spät anlangten, und der erste jährliche Bettag, weil das Plakat noch nicht angekommen war, bloß nach Anzeige des Kalenders, also nach selbstgewähltem Texte gefeiert werden mußte. Im Jahre 1817 war die Errichtung eines Postamts im Dorfe Wiken, 1 M. unterhalb der Kirche Hede, wo die Wege von Norwegen, Jemteland und Helsingland zusammenstoßen, und wo auch künftig der Sitz des einzigen Kronvoigts über Herjeådalen seyn soll, verheißen worden. Unter dem Kronvoigt stehen 4 Länsmänner zu Sveg, Lill-Herdal, Wemdalen und Öfver-Hogdal; sie sind gewöhnlich Bauern; ihr geringer Gehalt besteht in etwas Korn und Kronkäse und schwachen Sporteln.

Einen studierten Arzt giebt es in ganz Herjeådalen nicht; eben so wenig eine Apotheke; die nächsten Apotheken, zu Hudiksvall und Söderhamn in Helsingland, sind 17 bis 20 Meilen von der Gränze entfernt.

Ein eigenthümlicher Gebrauch in Herjeådalen, der sich indeß auch im übrigen Norrland findet, hat nach der Geburt eines Kindes Statt: wer während der Zeit, wo die Wöchnerin noch bettlägerig ist, ins Elternhaus tritt, dem nimmt man die Mütze, unter dem Vorwande: das Kind sey nackt, man habe daher demselben Kleidung zu schaffen; und er muß sie durch Geld wieder auslösen. Allgemeine Vornamen sind Engelbrecht, Knut, Rolf, Thor, Kjäl, altnordische Namen, die aber im übrigen Schweden nicht so häufig, wie in Herjeådalen, oder gar nicht gefunden werden.

Eine eigenthümliche, aber sehr zweckmäßige Art des Fuhrwerks sind die Kårror, hinten mit verschlossenem Kasten; sie sind bequemer und geräumiger, als die gewöhnlichen Schwedischen Kårror.

Die Herjeådaler arbeiten viel und tüchtig, aber langsam und mit Gemächlichkeit; bei den öfteren Mahlzeiten, ähnlich, wie in Jemteland, speist man erstes und zweites Frühstück, Mittagsbrot, Vesperbrot und Abendbrot. Fleisch essen die Herjeådaler wenig. Nur die Frühlings- und Herbstbutter wird verspeist; die frische Sommerbutter wird verkauft.

Am 15. Septbr. Von Hede nach Wiken 1 M.; von W. nach Ransjö 2½ M.; von R. nach Gliseberg 1½ M. — Zus. 5½ M.

Um 7½ Uhr verließ ich Hede. Man fährt auf einer Brücke über den Ljusnan; die Brücken sind hier ungewöhnlich hoch, besonders in der Mitte, des starken Eisganges wegen, hoch gewölbt; in Wiken kochte man gerade Isländisches Moos, oder wie man es hier nennt, Brotmoos, zu Brot; das Moos wird dreimal gekocht, und dann mit Mehl aus Fichtenrinde vermischt *); zum Rindenmehl wird nur die zarte Rinde gebraucht; auch thut man die Spitzen der Fruchtähren (agnar) hinzu, bäckt auch aus diesen allein Brot; in Sveg benutzt man selten das Moos. In Hede ist Moosbrot nun schon Jahre lang das einzige Brot vieler Bauern; denn seit 1812 war in jedem Jahre, nur das J. 1813 ausgenommen, die Ernte durch Frost vernichtet worden; auch in diesem Sommer war das Korn erfroren, und das neue Brot schmeckte bitter und schlecht. Daneben sind die Hemman so klein, daß schon an und für sich die Aussaat zu geringe ist. So sind denn jetzt die meisten kleinen Hemman verschuldet, und außerdem hat die Magazindirection noch für Korn viel zu fordern.

Auf dem langen Häll zwischen Wiken und Ransjö sieht man keine einzige Menschenwohnung; auch in der Nähe giebt es keine; nichts als Fichtenwald und niedrige Birken; den Boden decken Rennthier- und Isländisches Moos, Preißel- und Blaubeeren; durch den Wald wird oft der klare Ljusnan, bald als Fluß,

*) Beim Bier könnte das Isländische Moos wenigstens die Hälfte des Malzes und einen beträchtlichen Theil des Hopfens ersetzen; dazu verwendet man es aber in Herjeådalen nicht.

bald zum See erweitert, sichtbar; jenseits erheben sich bewaldete Berge; am Wege erblickt man kleine Schuppen zur Bergung des Laubes, welches als Viehfutter benutzt wird, nebst zerfalle= nen Korn= und Sägemühlen. In dieser Öde berichtete mein Skjutsbonde von dem großen Elend, das gegenwärtig in Hede herrscht, und daß sein Schwager ihm noch gestern bei der Kir= che gestanden, wie er, der überdieß kränklich sey, nicht wisse, wie er sich dieses Jahr durchbringen solle. Aber den Muth lassen in allem diesem Elende die Herjeådaler nicht sinken, ihr Ver= trauen auf Gott wankt nicht.

In Ransjö, dem ersten Dorfe in Sveg, wo man, wie überhaupt in Sveg, besser und mehr Korn hat, blieb ich ein Paar Stunden, um eine nothwendige Ausbesserung an den Wa= genrädern vornehmen zu lassen. Der Rånda=Elf fließt hier durch das Rånthal (Råndalen) in den Ljusnan.

Schon in Wiken hatte eine nach Helsingland reisende Bäu= erin aus Longås, die ein Pferd mit sich führte, mich gebeten, sie zum Skjutsbonde anzunehmen, damit sie sich einiges Geld verdienen könne. Ich hatte Bedenken getragen, theils des lan= gen Håll's wegen, theils da die Räder nach der Alpenreise nicht ganz sicher schienen. Jetzt waren letztere reparirt; das Håll nach Gliseberg kleiner, und es schon so spät, daß Sveg nicht mehr zu erreichen war, und so ließ ich denn zu, daß sie von Ransjö an vorspannen dürfe. — Der Skjutsbonde, der schon vorgespannt und längere Zeit gewartet hatte (für jede Station ist in Herjeådalen täglich ein Hållpferd angeschlagen; da aber oft in einer ganzen Woche kein Reisender kommt, so läßt man die Pferde auf den Höfen stehn), war doch gleich bereit, der armen Frau ohne alle Entschädigung, ihren Wunsch zu gewäh= ren, ja lieh ihr auf mehrere Wochen eine Pferdedecke. Gerade war ein Norweger da, der nach Lindsåll fuhr, wo er diente, wie mehrere Norweger in Herjeådalen; er war aus Sundalen bei Drontheim gebürtig, und noch ganz Norwegisch gekleidet, in ei= nem vorne weggeschnittenen Rocke von grauem Walmar, mit blanken Knöpfen; es war ein biederer und treuherziger Mensch, der alle, auch mich zuweilen, Du nannte, wie solches auch in

Herjeådalen üblich ist, selbst wenn man sich vorher nie gesehen
hat; so nannte mich auch die Bäuerin von Longås. Da es der
Norweger zufrieden war, so ließ ich ihn bis Lindsäll fahren und
die Herjeådalerin nachfolgen. In Lindsäll wollte letztere ihn für
die Beschwerde, mich gefahren zu haben, belohnen; ein edler
Wettstreit entstand; er weigerte; die Frau bat wiederholt, endlich
nahm er das Dargebotene; ich hieß es ihm zurückgeben, und
belohnte ihn selber; wie herzlich dankbar waren nun beyde. Lau-
ter edle, brave Menschen rings umher; ich begegnete ihnen
freundlich, wie sie mir; bald war ihr ganzes Vertrauen gewonnen;
sie wurden so herzlich, fragten: ob sie mich wohl je wiedersehen
würden, und entließen mich mit dem Wunsche, daß wir uns
einst vor Gottes Throne wieder finden möchten!

In Lindsäll, welches Dorf zu beiden Seiten des Ljusnan
liegt, besah ich die einfache hölzerne Kapelle; sie hat einen Thurm;
den Altar schmückt ein Gemälde: die Anbetung der Weisen aus
Morgenland. Nur viermal im Jahre verrichtet hier die Geistlichkeit
von Sveg den Gottesdienst. An den übrigen Sonntagen hält
der Küster oder ein Bauer Postillenlesung.

Am jenseitigen Ufer des Ljungan erhebt sich hier die Bergkette Lindsällsvålarne, wo es, wie oben bemerkt, noch wilde Rennthiere giebt. Am südwestlichen Fuße dieser isolirten Bergkette
läuft das Läffsthal; im Nordosten das Ränthal. Das Läffsthal
dehnt sich mehrere Meilen erst süd- und dann nordöstlich fast
bis zum Pastorat Hede und zur Gränze des Dalekarlischen Kirchspiels Särna aus, wird vom Läffsä, der am Fuße des Kjälfjäll
entspringt, durchflossen, und im Südwesten vom Läffsfjäll begränzt.
Nach einer alten Sage sollen die Helsingländer einst auf ihren
Wallfahrtszügen nach Norwegen das Läffsfjäll passirt haben, und
bei ihrer Rückkehr, für die glücklich vollendete Alpenreise, in jenem Thale, beim Dorfe gleiches Namens, feierliche Lobgesänge
angestellt haben; nach einer andern Angabe soll hier ein Kreuz
errichtet gewesen seyn, an welchem die Wallfahrer ihre Andacht
hielten. Diese Begebenheit soll dem Orte den Namen gegeben
haben, eine Vermuthung, die aber in dem Worte selbst nicht
ihre Bestätigung findet.

Von Lindsäll an fuhr mich also meine Bäuerin aus Longås; sie wollte ihren Bruder in Glisberg auf einer von ihm be-
absichtigten Geschäftsreise nach Järfsö in Helsingland begleiten,
um dem Silbererze nachzuspüren, was sie vor 10 Jahren dort
in der Erde gesehen zu haben glaubte, um also ihre durch Vieh-
sterben und Korntheurung entstandenen traurigen Umstände zu
verbessern!—Der Weg führt ununterbrochen durch Fichtenwald;

II. P*

den Boden deckt Moos, besonders Rennthiermoos, welches man hier den Kühen reicht; umgestürzte Bäume liegen im Walde und sind schon mit Moos überwachsen. Nur in der Ferne erblickt man an einem See zwei Bauerhöfe,

Es war 8 Uhr, als ich in Gliseberg anlangte; die Leute wollten eben zu Bette gehen, denn um 8 Uhr spätestens geht der Helsingländer in herbstlicher oder winterlicher Zeit zu Bette, und erst um 4 Uhr steht er wieder auf; man holt nach, was man im Sommer versäumte, wo man nur von 9 oder 10 bis 11 Uhr Morgens ruht. Die Hausmutter war seit Johannis in der Sennhütte; ein verlobtes Paar wartete auf, das Mädchen trug um den Hals schwarze Korallen, und auf der Brust ein silbernes Herzchen, mit herabhängenden Silberblättchen. Die Kost war sehr geringe, und gewährte, da mir das gesalzene Fleisch nicht behagte, nicht einmal Sättigung; frische Milch war nicht vorhanden. Desto sanfter war der Schlaf. Zum Frühstück gab ich selber den Kaffee her, denn Kaffee wird nie von den Bauern Herjeådalens getrunken, ja ist manchen völlig unbekannt. — Auch hier müssen Aermere oft Rindenbrot essen.

Am 16. September. Von Gliseberg nach Sveg 2 M.

Um 6½ Uhr fuhr ich ab. Man kommt über den von Wemdalen nordwestlich herabkommenden breiten Weman Eff, unweit seines Einflusses in den Ljusnan, den man erst bei Sveg wieder zu Gesichte bekommt. Ein wenig oberhalb der Mündung des Weman ergießt sich, am jenseitigen Ufer, in den Ljusnan die Herjeå, die dem Lande seinen Namen gab. Längs den Ufern der Herjeå breitet sich das Herjeåthal aus, in welchem, 3 M. von Sveg's Kirche, die zu Sveg gehörige Filialkirche Lill-Herdal liegt. Bei den Gewohnern von Lill-Herdal hat sich in einem noch höhern Grade als sonst in Herjeådalen Sittenreinheit, Einfalt, Aufrichtigkeit und Treuherzigkeit erhalten. In vielen Stücken sind sie ihren Nachbaren, den Dalekarliern (Dalekarlier heißt hier Stora Dalarne, oder Süjans Dalarne) gleich; aber sie sind nicht so eigensinnig, wie diese. Von Sveg zur Kirche Lill-Herdal, der ältesten des Landes, die aber 1773 erneuert wurde, ist Fahrweg.

Von Sveg wünschte ich noch heute die Reise fortzusetzen; allein der Pastor Foralöf hat so freundlich, zu bleiben, daß ich den Reiseplan für heute nun aufgeben mußte.

Unweit des Pfarrhofes liegt die Kirche Sveg, ein altes steinernes Gebäude, in welchem insbesondere die alte, etwa 2 Ele len hohe Gemäldetafel neben der Kanzel merkwürdig ist. Diese Tafel ist mit Thüren oder Klappen versehen, deren äußere und innere Seite besondere Gemälde schmücken: auf der innern Tafel erblickt man die Weiber, welche den Herrn, als er schon im Grabe liegt, salben wollen; auf den innern Klappen sind vier Darstellungen, die sich auf die Geiselung, das Kreuztragen und die Kreuzigung Christi beziehen; die äußeren Klappen zeigen vier andere Bilder, die, wie es scheint, Heilige darstellen; das eine dieser Bilder, wahrscheinlich, eine heilige Magdalena, ist vorzugsweise schön und ausdrucksvoll. Neben der Kirche erhebt sich der Glockenthurm, aus welchem man das hier von Dörfern bedeckte Flußthal des Ljusnan und im Hintergrunde Waldberge überschaut; Alpen sieht man nicht. — Um die Kirche herum findet man die Kirchspielsstuben, und ein halbes Hundert Kirchenbuden, deren einzelne mehrere Besitzer haben.

Das Pastorat Sveg, das volkreichste der beiden Pastorate Herjeådalens, im J. 1815, mit 2486 Einwohnern, besteht aus der Muttergemeinde Sveg (mit 995), dem Filial Lill-Herdal (mit 789), den Kapellen Elfros (mit 263) und Lindsäll (mit 186 Seelen); früherhin gehörte zum Pastorat auch noch die Gemeinde Ofver-Hogdal (mit 186 Seelen), die aber im J. 1814 mit dem näher gelegenen Ytter-Hogdal in kirchlicher Hinsicht vereinigt wurde; die Bewohner von Ofver-Hogdal sind aus Herjeådalen, Helsingern und Jemten gemischt; doch kommen sie in den meisten Stücken den Herjeådalen gleich; daher man das Kirchspiel noch mit zu Herjeådalen rechnen kann; in die oben angegebene Einwohnerzahl von Herjeådalen ist Ofver-Hogdal nicht mit begriffen. — Die ordentliche Geistlichkeit des Pastorats besteht aus einem Pastor zu Sveg und einem Comminister zu Lill-Herdal, daher nicht sonntäglich in allen Kirchen Gottesdienst gehalten werden kann; wo der Gottesdienst ausfällt, lesen gemeiniglich die Küster aus Postillen vor; nur in Sveg, wo bloß 4 Sonntage jährlich der Gottesdienst ausfällt, findet solches nicht Statt. In Lindsäll's Kapelle wird nur 4mal jährlich gepredigt; in Lill-Herdal und Elfros einen Sonntag um den andern, und überdieß noch in Lill-Herdal alle, in Elfros, einige Festtage.

Wenn gleich das Pastorat Sveg südlicher liegt, als Hede, und der Boden besseres Kornland ist, so reift doch auch hier oft das Korn nicht, und es herrscht eben so wenig Wohlstand; Viehzucht ist der hauptsächlichste Nahrungszweig. Indeß wird hier doch mehr und besseres Korn gebauet, als in Hede. Die Dörfer sind hier nicht so groß wie in Sveg, bestehen aber nicht leicht aus weniger als 6 Bauern; Ytterberg hat 30 Bauern.

Viele der einzelnen Höfe haben Eigennamen. Fischfang und Jagd wird getrieben; daher auch ein Theil der Pfarreinkünfte in Jagdgefällen besteht, z. B. soll der Pastor von jedem erlegten Renn- oder Elennthier das Schulterblatt erhalten; ferner muß jede erwachsene Person ein Eichhornsfell entrichten; die übrigen Einkünfte bestehen in Korn ($\frac{1}{17}$ Tonne von jedem Erwachsenen), welches auch in Frostjahren gut geliefert werden soll, in dem oben erwähnten Kronkäse, in einem Bock für jede Kündigung.

Im Pastorat findet man sogenannte Bolanden, die es in Hede nicht giebt, d. i. vom eigentlichen Wohnhofe entfernte, in weniger wirthbaren Gegenden erbaute, vollständig eingerichtete Höfe, von welchen aus die umher gelegenen Ländereien bewirthschaftet werden; auf solchen Bolanden ruht kein Kronschatz. Hier bringt man einen Theil des Jahres mit dem ganzen Haushalt zu, und zehrt von den, dort gewonnenen, Producten. In Helsingland giebt es viele solcher Bolanden (Wohnlande); in Sveg's Pastorat findet man sie im Kirchspiel Elfros und im Dorfe Remmen. Dagegen trifft man in Sveg nicht, wie in Hede, Nybyggen.

Zu Sveg gehören auch ein Paar Finnendörfer, die eigentlich schon in Dalekarlien liegen, aber, in kirchlicher Hinsicht, der Geistlichkeit von Sveg überwiesen sind, da sie den Kirchen von Sveg näher wohnen, als den Kirchen von Dalekarlien, zu deren eigentlichem Sprengel sie gehören. Diese Dörfer sind Fogelsjö, im Pastorat Mora, 12 M. von der Kirche Mora, aber nur 3½ M. von Sveg, mit 8 Bauerhöfen oder 55 Seelen, und Tanssjö im Pastorat Orsa, 4½ M. von Sveg, mit 7 Bauerhöfen oder 30 Seelen. Das Eigenthümliche ihres Volks hat sich bei ihnen meist verloren; einige verstehen etwas Finnisch, doch sprechen sie unter einander Schwedisch, rein und nach Regeln, ohne die Norwegischen Wörter der Herjeådalen, aber sehr langsam und gedehnt. Sie verheirathen sich auch mit Schweden, doch gewöhnlich unter einander. Sie sind still, ernst und sinnig, offen und ungekünstelt, lieben sehr die Reinlichkeit und haben viel Sinn für Musik. Pehr Martensson in Fogelsjö z. B. hatte sich selber Klavier- und Orgelspielen gelehrt und es darin zu großer Vollkommenheit gebracht. Im Ganzen haben sie ganz die Sitten und Eigenthümlichkeiten der Herjeådalen. Sie sind von mittelmäßiger Größe. Korn bauen sie wenig; denn nicht selten treten Nachtfröste ein, aber sie pflanzen viel Kartoffeln; das nöthige Korn kaufen sie in Mora oder Fahlun. Auch treiben sie Fischerey und Jagd; besonders erlegen sie viele wilde

Rennthiere. Ihr Lebenswandel ist streng-sittlich; Unkeuschheits-sünden sind bei ihnen unerhört. Ihre Frömmigkeit ist ausgezeichnet; an den Sonntagen wird vor denen, die nicht zur Kirche gingen, regelmäßig Betstunde gehalten.

Am 17. Septbr. Von Sveg nach Nilswallen ¼ M.; von N. nach Kälsätt 2 M.; von K. nach Kärböle 3¼ M. — Zus. 5¼ M.

Um 6½ Uhr früh verließ ich Sveg's Pfarrhof. — In Nilswallen ist nur ein Gästgifvare (auf den übrigen Stationen in Sveg wechselt der Gästgifvaregärd unter mehreren Bauern); seit mehreren Wochen war kein Skjuts gefordert worden. ¼ M. von Nilswallen ist ein Gesundbrunnen, der aber wenig gebraucht wird, da es hier zu Lande wenig Kranke giebt. Mein Skjuts-bonde war Nils Wallin, der einzige leibliche Arzt Herjeädalens, ein schlichter, einfacher Bauer, dienstfertig, treuherzig und anspruchslos; er hatte seine Kunst von einem ähnlichen, un-studirten Doctor in Fahlun erlernt, und beschäftigte sich nur mit der Heilung der Wassersucht und allerlei, wie er sich bescheiden ausdrückte, geringer Krankheiten; aus der Apotheke von Gefle bezieht er jährlich für mehr denn 30 Bankthaler Arzneimittel; seine Patienten behandelt er sehr billig; denn sein Honorar, so oft seine Hülfe gefordert wird, beträgt nur 8 Bankschillinge, außer dem gewöhnlichen Meilengeld (12 ßl. für die Meile), falls man ihm kein Pferd sendet. Daneben ist er ein tüchtiger Tischler, Schmidt, Maler ꝛc., kurz, ein Allerwelts-Künstler, ein wahres Genie; seine Geschicklichkeit als Schmidt bewährte er in Kälsätt an meinem Wagen; seine Frau ist die Tochter eines Geistlichen. Er erzählte mir, wie er im Jahre 1788, als die Norweger ei-nen Einfall drohten, an der Stelle eines Länsmans, eine eilige Reise nach Gefle habe machen müssen, um Pulver und Ku-geln zu holen; dieses sey dann unter die Bauern, welche damals noch häufiger als jetzt, Büchsen besaßen, vertheilt worden, und alsbald habe sich das Gerücht verbreitet: in ganz Herjeädalen sey hinter jedem Busch und in jedem Dickigt ein Bauer mit ei-ner Büchse versteckt, und lauere auf die heranrückenden Nor-weger. Kaum hatten sie das Gerücht vernommen, als sie von Funnesdalen, bis wohin sie schon vorgedrungen waren, sofort wieder ihren Rückzug antraten. Bei dieser Gelegenheit seyen auch die Holzstöße auf den Bergen erneuert, aber nicht gebraucht worden. Seit alten Zeiten hat man eine lange Reihe solcher Holzstöße von der Norwegischen Gränze an errichtet; sie werden,

bei Annäherung des Feindes, angezündet, und haben die Dörfer, da das Land ohne Militair ist, ihre bestimmten Sammelplätze. Einen solchen Holzstoß sah ich noch auf einem Berge
bei Elfros. In früheren Zeiten, insbesondere 1611, hat das
Land in den Kriegen mit Norwegen sehr gelitten: in Hede ward
alles niedergebrannt; im Sommer wohnten nun die Leute in
den Wäldern und zogen im Winter nach Thdalen in Norwegen;
diese, nach dem Norwegischen Heerführer Balzar Beck benannte
Balzar-Fehde hatte lange eine so traurige Merkwürdigkeit,
daß die Bewohner von Jemteland und Herjeadalen nach derselben ihre Jahre und Begebenheiten rechneten.

Wiewohl der Weg nicht schlecht war, ging es doch nur
langsam fort, denn die Pferde werden hier, da so wenig gereiset
wird, meist nur zum Lastziehen gebraucht und sind daher des
schnelleren Trabens nicht gewohnt. Bis Elfros fährt man im
dichten Walde, meist Fichtenwalde. An einigen Stellen ward
Laub fürs Vieh gesammelt; man häuft es zwischen Stangengit-
tern auf. Unweit Nilsvallen kommt man, auf einer Brücke,
über den, zwischen Wiesenufern dem Ljusnan zueilenden, kleinen
Sählna-Fluß; hier sah ich einige mit Dach und Schornstein
versehne Wassermühlen; in eine derselben trat ich ein und fand
Bett und Feuerheerd; die Leute bringen hier oft eine längere
Zeit zu und machen es sich dann so bequem sie können. Windmühlen habe ich in Herjeadalen nirgends gesehen. Im Walde ward
eben Fichtenrinde getrocknet, die zum Brotbacken bestimmt ist.
In Elfros kaufte ich solches Rindenbrot, dünne Kuchen, die etwas bitter, aber nicht widrig, schmecken; man thut auch Aehrenspitzen hinein; ich kostete auch agnarbröd, d. i. aus Aehrenspitzen
und ein wenig Gerstenmehl bereitetes Brot, welches einen schlechteren Geschmack hatte, als jenes Rindenbrot. — Von Elfros
fährt man auf einer Brücke über den schlechtweg sogenannten
Elf (Fluß), welcher von Jemtelands Gränze, von Rätan herabkommt und sich hier in den Ljusnan ergießt.

Elfros ist ein großes Dorf, welches sich wohl eine Viertelmeile längs des Ljusnan ausdehnt. Die Kirche, von Holz, ward
vor etwa 20 Jahren erneuert und ist eine der freundlichsten
kleinen hölzernen Kirchen, die ich sah; Kanzel und Altar sind
vergoldet; neben der Kanzel ist ein Gemälde aufgestellt, welches
die Taufe Jesu darstellt; den Altar schmückt das Bild des Gekreuzigten. An den Chören sieht man die Bilder der Evangelisten. Neben der mit einem kleinen Thurm versehenen Kirche
steht ein Glockenthurm, aus welchem man einer recht hübschen
Aussicht auf die Wiesen- und Buschufer des Ljungan und die

nahen Waldberge genießt. Eine Kirchspielsstube ist aufgeführt; aber keine Kirchbuden trifft man, indem ja das Dorf nahe ist. Man fährt nun durch das Dorf, und dann z. M. neben mit Gebüsch geschmückten Wiesen am Ljusnan; nur eine kleine Strecke hat man Fichtenwald; links liegt das kleine Dorf Rismyra, von welchem ein Reitweg nach der Kirche Ytter-Hogdal, wie von Elfros zur Kirche Ofver-Hogdal, führt. Vor Kalfätt zieht man auf einer Fähre über den Ljusnan; ein 15jähriger Jüngling, auf dessen Antlitz hohe Unschuld und Schönheit sich paarten, und mein treuer Wallin leiteten die Fähre. In Kalfätt traf ich bei dem 70jährigen Erik Svensson, der noch rüstig war, wie ein 50jähriger, einen guten und reinlichen Gasthof. Kalfätt hat eine schöne Lage, an den Wiesenufern des hier breiten Ljusnan. In Kalfätt, wie in Elfros, fand ich große Einfachheit und Unverdorbenheit der Menschen. Mein Skjutsbonde von Kalfätt nannte mich nur Du.

Nach vollzogener Reparatur des Wagens und eingenommenem Mittagsmahl, verließ ich um 2 Uhr Kalfätt. Auf der ersten Viertelmeile erreicht man die Gränze von Helsingland, die aber jetzt nicht bezeichnet ist, denn der Gränzstein ist umgefallen, und die, im Walde ausgehauene, gerade Linie ist zugewachsen. Das lange Häll bis Kärböle hat fast nur Wald, anfangs Fichten und niedrige Birken, dann Gränen. Der Weg ist so steinig und so voll Löcher, daß man nicht anders als Schritt vor Schritt fahren kann und dennoch gewaltig zerstoßen wird; an einigen Stellen ist er um nichts besser, als der Alpenweg von Klössjö nach Wemdalen; wiewohl wir uns unterweges nicht aufhielten, erreichten wir doch erst nach neunthalbstündiger Fahrt Kärböle. — Bald nach dem Eintritt in Helsingland, kommt man zu dem Fahrwege, der zu der, ½ Meile von hier entlegenen, Kapelle Angersjö führt; sie gehört zu Ytter-Hogdal, dessen Geistlichkeit dort dreimal jährlich predigt; zur Gemeinde Angersjö gehören die Finnenhöfe Djupsjöberg, Ostsjö und Rullbo, mit 1 und 2 Bauern, 1¼ bis 1¾ Meilen von der Kapelle entfernt. — Auf der Hälfte des Weges unterbricht den Wald das Dorf Wänsjö, an einem See gleiches Namens, mit Wiesen und Feldern umher, die aber dem Froste ausgesetzt sind. Dann fährt man wieder im Walde, erst über ein Paar lange, aber nicht sehr breite, Bergrücken, den Fager- und den Kärberg, und nun, etwa eine halbe Meile, sanft bergab an den Kärsee. Zwischen dem Fager- und dem Kärberg kommt man Sennhütten vorüber, die aber nur zu Anfange des Sommers benutzt werden. Am Kärsee, an welchem man, fast bis zum Kärböle, hinfährt, trifft der Weg mit der von Ytter-Hogdal herabkommenden Straße zusammen. Bei Kårböle erblickt man wieder den Ljusnan, der bei Kälsätt eine große Krümmung gegen Nordwesten macht, von Kårböle an aber wieder südwestlich fließt.

In Kårböle lag schon alles in tiefem Schlafe. Dennoch ward auch der Ruhestörer freundlich empfangen. Die Hausfrau, eine geborne Herjedalerin, ein geistreiches Weib, schon 40 Jahre alt, aber noch schön und jugendlich, wie ein 16jähriges Mädchen, gab zur Abendmahlzeit das Kärgliche, was sie hatte, Butter und Brot (denn das Vieh war auf der Sennenweide), und bereitete schnell, in einem hübschen Zimmer, ein reinliches und bequemes Lager, auf welchem mich bald ein sanfter Schlaf in seine Arme nahm.

Die Mitternachtssonne auf Afraasara.